THE DEED OF PAKSENARRION
IS THE TRUE HEIR
TO MIDDLE EARTH

"This is the first work of high heroic fantasy I've seen that has taken the work of Tolkien, assimilated it totally and deeply and absolutely, and produced something altogether new and yet incontestably based on the master. . . . This is the Fourth Age as it has to have been. This is the real thing. World-building in the grand tradition, background thought out to the last detail, by someone who knows whereof she speaks. Her military knowledge is impressive, her picture of life in a mercenary company most convincing. I'm deeply impressed. . . .

"After so many half-baked clones of Tolkien, and so much generic medieval fantasy, I can't go on enough about how delighted I am to find something of this quality.

"Brava!"

—Judith Tarr

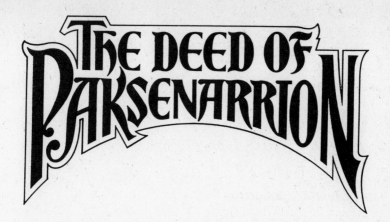

ELIZABETH MOON

THE DEED OF PAKSENARRION

This is a work of fiction. All the characters and events portrayed in this book are fictional, and any resemblance to real people or incidents is purely coincidental.

A Baen Books Original

Baen Publishing Enterprises
P.O. Box 1403
Riverdale, NY 10471

ISBN: 0-671-72104-6

Cover art by Keith Parkinson

First Printing, February 1992

Printed in the United States of America

Distributed by Simon & Schuster
1230 Avenue of the Americas
New York, NY 10020

ACKNOWLEDGMENTS
The Deed of Paksenarrion has been published in parts in slightly different form as *Sheepfarmer's Daughter*, copyright © 1988, *Divided Allegiance*, copyright © 1988, and *Oath of Gold*, copyright © 1989.

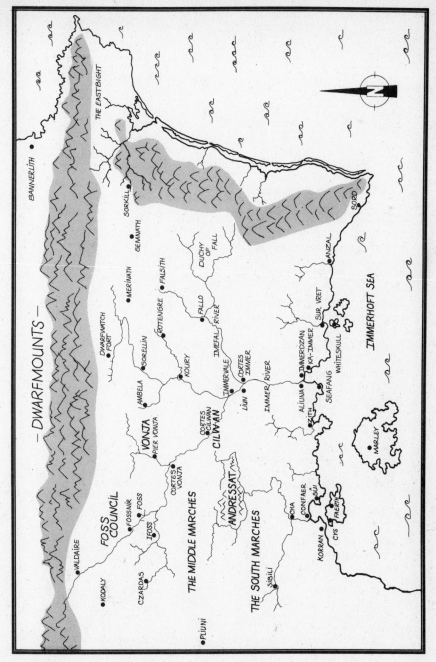

Prologue

In a sheepfarmer's low stone house, high in the hills above Three Firs, two swords hang now above the mantelpiece. One is very old and slightly bent, a sword more iron than steel, dark as a pot: forged, so the tale runs, by the smith in Rocky Ford — yet it is a sword, for all that, and belonged to Kanas once, and tasted orcs' blood and robbers' blood in its time. The other is a very different matter: long and straight, keen-edged, of the finest sword-steel, silvery and glinting blue even in yellow firelight. The pommel's knot design is centered with the deeply graven seal of St. Gird; the cross-hilts are gracefully shaped and chased in gold.

The children of that place look at both swords with awe, and on some long winter nights old Dorthan, grandfather of fathers and graybeard now, takes from its carved chest the scroll that came with the sword and reads aloud to his family. But first he reminds them of the day a stranger rode up, robed and mantled in white, an old man with thin silver hair, and handed down the box and the sword, naked as it hangs now.

"Keep these," the stranger said, "in memory of your daughter Paksenarrion. She wishes you to have them and has no need of them." And though he accepted water from their well, he would say no more of Paksenarrion, whether she lived or lay buried far away, whether she would return or no.

The scroll Dorthan reads is headed *The Deed of Paksenarrion Dorthansdotter of Three Firs*, and many are the tales of courage and adventure written therein. Time and again the family has thrilled to the description of Paksenarrion in battle — the littlest ones pressing close around Dorthan's knees, and watching her sword on the wall. They are sure it glows slightly when those tales are read.

And always they ask, the little ones who never knew her, what she was like. Just like that in the scroll? Always so tall, so brave? And Dorthan remembers her face the night she left, and is silent. One brother thinks of a long-legged girl running down errant sheep; the youngest remembers being carried on her shoulders, and the smell of her hair. Besides this, legend is all they have. "She's dead," say some. "She must be, or they wouldn't have sent her sword."

"No," say others. "She is not dead. She is gone where she doesn't need *this* sword."

And Dorthan turns to the end of the scroll, which solves nothing . . . for the *Deed* is unfinished, ending abruptly in the middle of a stanza.

And one of those children, the little ones, has climbed from stool to table, and from table to mantelpiece, and touched with a daring hand the hilt of each sword . . . and then climbed down, to dream of songs and battles.

Sheepfarmer's Daughter

Chapter One

"And I say you will!" bellowed the burly sheepfarmer, Dorthan Kanasson. He lunged across the table, but his daughter Paksenarrion sidestepped his powerful arm and darted down the passage to the sleeping rooms. "Pakse!" he yelled, slipping his broad leather belt from its loops. "Pakse, you come here now!" His wife Rahel and three smaller children cowered against the wall. Silence from the sleeping rooms. "Pakse, you come or it will be the worse for you. Will you go to your wedding with welts on your back?"

"I'll not go at all!" came the angry response.

"The dower's been given. You wed Fersin Amboisson next restday. Now come out before I come in."

Suddenly she stood in the mouth of the passage, as tall as he but slender, long blonde hair braided tightly. She had changed to her older brother's clothes, a leather tunic over her own shirt, and his homespun trousers. "I told you not to give dower. I told you I wouldn't wed Fersin or anyone else. And I won't. I'm leaving."

Dorthan glared at her as he wrapped the belt around his right hand. "The only place you're going, you arrogant hussy, is Fersin's bed."

"Dorthan, please —" began Rahel.

"Quiet! She's your fault as much as anyone's. She should have been spinning at home, not running out on the moors hunting with the boys."

Paksenarrion's gray eyes glinted. "It's all right, Mother; don't worry. He'll remember someday that he's the one who sent me out with the flocks so often. Father, I'm leaving. Let me pass."

"Over my dead body," he grunted.

"If need be —" Paksenarrion leaped for the old sword, Kanas's sword, over the fireplace. As she lifted it from the rack, the belt caught her shoulders with its first stroke. Then she was facing Dorthan, sword in hand, with the firelight behind her. The sword felt easy in her grip. Startled, Dorthan jumped back, swinging the belt wildly in her direction. Paksenarrion took her chance and ran for the door, jerked it open, and was gone. Behind her came his furious bellow, and questioning calls from her brothers still working in the barns, but Paksenarrion did not slow or turn until she came to the boundary stone of her father's land. There she thrust her grandfather's sword into the soil.

1

"I won't have him saying I stole it," she muttered to herself. She turned for a last look at her home. Against the dark bulk of the hill, she could see light at the open front door, and dark figures crossing and recrossing the light. She could hear voices calling her name, then a deep bellow from Dorthan, and all the shapes went in at the door and shut the light in. She was alone, outside the house, and she knew, as well as if she'd seen him do it, that Dorthan had barred the door against her. She shook herself. "It's what I wanted," she said aloud. "So now I'd better go on with it."

The rest of that night she jogged and walked down the well-worn track from her father's farm to Three Firs, warmed by the thought of the coming adventure. She went over her cousin's instructions time after time, trying to remember everything he'd said about recruiting sergeants and mercenary companies and training and drill. In the first light of dawn she walked into Three Firs. Only in the baker's house did she see a gleam of light behind closed shutters, and a plume of smoke out the chimney. She smelled no baking bread. She could not wait until the first baking came out unless the recruiters were still in Three Firs. She walked on to the marketplace. Empty. Of course, they might not be up yet. She looked in the public barn that served as an inn. Empty. They had left. She drew water from the village well, drank deeply, and started off again, this time on the wider track that led to Rocky Ford — or so her cousin had said; she'd never been beyond Three Firs.

As daylight came, she was able to make better time, but it was nearly noon when she came to the outskirts of Rocky Ford. The rich smells of cooking food from the inns and houses nearly made her sick. She pressed on, through what seemed to her like crowds, to the market square in the town's center. There she saw the booth that Jornoth had told her to look for, draped in maroon and white silk, with spears for cornerposts. She paused to catch her breath and look at it. On either side, a man-at-arms with breastplate, helmet, and sword stood guard. Inside was a narrow table, with one stool before it, and a man seated behind. Paksenarrion took a deep breath and walked forward.

As she reached the booth, she realized that she was taller than either of the men-at-arms. She waited for them to say something, but they ignored her. She looked inside. Now she could see that the man behind the table had gray hair, cropped short, and a neatly trimmed mustache. When he looked up at her, his eyes were a warm golden brown.

"This is a recruiting station for Duke Phelan's Company," he said as he met her gaze. "Were you looking for someone?"

"No. I mean, yes. I mean, I was looking for you — for a recruiting station, I mean." Paksenarrion reddened with embarrassment.

"You?" The man stared a moment, then looked down briefly. "You mean you wanted to join the Company?"

"Yes. My — my cousin said such companies accepted women."

"We do, though not so many want to join. Look — mmm — let's get a few things straight before we start. To join us you must be eighteen winters

2

old, healthy, with no deformities, strong, tall enough — you have no problem there — and not too stupid. If you're a drunkard, liar, thief, or devil-worshipper, we'll throw you out the worse for wear. You agree to serve for two years beyond your basic training, which takes four to six months. You get no pay as a recruit, but you do get room, board, and gear as well as training. Your pay as a private in the Company is low, but you'll share any plunder. Is that clear?"

"Aye," said Paksenarrion. "Clear enough. I'm over eighteen, and I'm never sick. I've been working on the moors, with sheep — I can lift as much as my brother Sedlin, and he's a year older."

"Mmm. What do your parents think of your joining an army?"

"Oh." Paksenarrion blushed again. "Well, to be honest, my father doesn't know that's where I am. I — I ran away."

"He wanted you to wed." The man's eyes had a humorous twinkle.

"Yes. A pig farmer — "

"And you wanted someone else."

"Oh no! I didn't — I don't want to marry at all. I want to be a warrior like my cousin Jornoth. I've always liked hunting and wrestling and being outdoors."

"I see. Here, have a seat on the stool." While she sat down, he fished under the table and came up with a leather-bound book which he laid on top. "Let me see your hands — I have to be sure you don't have any prison brands. Fine. Now — you like wrestling, you say. You've arm wrestled?"

"Surely. With my family, and once at market."

"Good. Give me a try; I want to test your strength." They clasped right hands, and on the count began to push against each other's resistance. After several minutes, with neither moving much, the man said "Fine, that's enough. Now let's go left-handed." This time he had the greater strength, and slowly pushed her arm to the table. "That's good enough," he said. "Now — was this decision to join a sudden one?"

"No. Ever since Jornoth left home — and especially after he came back that time — I've wanted to. But he said I had to be eighteen, and then I waited until the recruiting season was almost over, so my father couldn't trace me and cause trouble."

"You said you'd been on the moors — how far from town do you live?"

"From here? Well, we're a half day's sheep drive from Three Firs — "

"Three Firs! You came here from Three Firs today?"

"We live up the other side of Three Firs," said Paksenarrion. "I came through there before dawn, just at first light."

"But that's — that's twenty miles from Three Firs to here, at least. When did you start from home?"

"Late last night, after supper." At the word, her stomach rumbled loudly.

"You must have gone . . . thirty miles, I don't doubt. Did you eat in Three Firs?"

"No, it was too early. Besides I was afraid I'd miss you here."

"And if you had?"

3

"I've a few coppers. I'd have gotten some food here and followed you."

"I'll bet you would have, too," the man said. He grinned at her. "Give us your name, then, and let's get you on the books so we can feed you. Any girl who'll go thirty miles or more on foot without stopping to eat ought to make a soldier."

She grinned back. "I'm Paksenarrion Dorthansdotter."

"Pakse-which?"

"Paksenarrion," she said slowly, and paused until he had that down. "Dorthansdotter. Of Three Firs."

"Got it." He raised his voice slightly. "Corporal Bosk."

"Sir." One of the men-at-arms turned to look into the tent.

"I'll need the judicar and a couple of witnesses."

"Sir." The corporal stalked off across the square.

"We have to have it all official," the man explained. "This isn't our Duke's domain; we must prove that we didn't take advantage of you, or force you, or forge your signature . . . you *can* sign your name, can't you?"

"Yes."

"Good. The Duke encourages all his troops to learn to read and write. Now —" He broke off as a man in a long maroon gown and two women arrived at the booth.

"Got another one before the deadline, eh, Stammel?" said the man. The women, one in cheesemaker's apron and cap, and the other with flour dusting her hands and arms, looked at Paksenarrion curiously.

"This young lady wishes to join," said Stammel shortly. The man winked at him and took out a stone cylinder with carving on one end. "Now," Stammel continued, "if you'll repeat after me in the presence of the judicar and these witnesses: I, Paksenarrion Dorthansdotter, do desire to join Duke Phelan's Company as a recruit and agree to serve two years in this company after recruit training without leave, and do further agree to obey all rules, regulations, and commands which I may be given in that time, fighting whomever and however my commander directs."

Paksenarrion repeated all this in a firm voice, and signed where she was directed, in the leather-bound book. The two women signed beside her name, and the judicar dripped wax underneath and pressed the stone seal in firmly. The cheesemaker patted Paksenarrion on the shoulder as she turned away, and the judicar gave Stammel a final wink and leer.

"Now then," said Stammel. "I'm Sergeant Stammel, as you may have gathered. We usually leave a town at noon; all the rest of the recruits are at *The Golden Pig* and have eaten. But you need something in your stomach, and a rest before we march. So we'll wait a bit. From here on, you're a recruit, remember. That means you say 'yes, sir' and 'no, sir' to any of us but other recruits, and you do what you're told with no arguing. Clear?"

"Yes, sir," said Paksenarrion

An hour later, seated by a window, Paksenarrion looked curiously at the other recruits lounging in the courtyard of *The Golden Pig*. Only two were taller than she: a husky youth with tousled yellow hair, and a skinny black-

4

bearded man whose left arm had a tattooed design on it. The shortest was a wiry redheaded boy with an impudent nose and a stained green velvet shirt. She spotted two other women, sitting together on the steps. None had weapons except a dagger for eating, but the black-bearded man wore a sword-belt. Mostly the recruits looked like farm boys and prentices, with a few puffy-faced men beyond her experience. Only the men-at-arms and the recruiting sergeant were in uniform. The others wore the clothes in which they'd joined. She finished the sandwich in her hand and started another; Stammel had told her to eat hearty and take her time. She had downed four sandwiches when Stammel came in again.

"You look better," he remarked. "Is there a short form of that name of yours?"

Paksenarrion had been thinking about that. She never wanted to hear her father's *Pakse* again. Her great-aunt, for whom she was named, had been called Enarra, but she didn't like that, either. She had finally decided on a form she thought she could live with.

"Yes, sir," she said. "Just call me Paks, if you wish."

"All right, Paks — ready to march?"

"Yes, sir."

"Come on, then." Stammel led the way to the inn courtyard. The other recruits stared as she came down the steps. "This is Paks," he said. "She'll march in Coben's file today, Corporal Bosk."

"Very good, sir. All right, recruits: form up." The other recruits shuffled into four lines of five persons each, except that the first file was one short. "Paks, you march here." Bosk pointed to the last place in the short file. "Now remember, at the command you all start off on the left foot, march in step, keep even with the rank on your right, and don't crowd the man ahead." Bosk walked around and through the group, shifting one or another an inch this way or that. Paksenarrion watched him curiously until he bawled suddenly, "Eyes front, recruits!" At last he was through fussing (as she thought to herself) and stepped back.

"Good enough, Bosk," said Stammel. "March 'em out."

For the first time in her life, Paksenarrion heard that most evocative of military commands as Bosk drew in a lungful of air and shouted: "Recruits. Forward . . . MARCH!"

The afternoon's march was only four hours, with two short rest-breaks, but when they halted, Paksenarrion was more tired than she had ever been. Besides the recruits, there were six regulars (Stammel, Bosk, and four privates) and four mules that carried the booth and supplies. In the course of the afternoon, they reviewed (and Paks learned) the correct way to form up, begin marching, and turn in column. She now knew her file number and who her file leader was, and had learned to keep an even distance behind the man in front. Tired as she was, she was in better shape than one of the puffy-faced men. He groaned and complained all afternoon, and finally fell in a faint at the last rest-break. When cold water failed to rouse him, two privates hoisted him over one mule's pack and lashed

5

him there, face down. When he came to, he begged to walk, but Stammel left him there, groaning piteously, until they made camp.

Paksenarrion and the next newest recruit were set to dig the jacks trench at the camp. This was the tall yellow-haired boy; he told her his name was Saben. He had dug the night before, too, and knew how long to make the trench. As they walked back into camp, the tattooed man sneered, "Here come the ditchdiggers — look like a real pair, don't they?"

The man who'd fainted snickered appreciatively. "It took 'em long enough. I'd say they weren't just digging ditches."

Paksenarrion felt her ears steam, but before she got her mouth open, she saw Stammel, behind the others, shake his head at her. Then her file leader, a chunky dark youth named Coben, spoke up.

"At least neither of them sneaked ale and collapsed like a town bravo, Jens. And as for being ditchdiggers, Korryn, it's better than graverobbing — "

The black-bearded man jumped up and his hand reached for the sword he no longer wore. "Just what d'you mean by that, Coben?"

Coben shrugged. "Take it as it fits. Digging jacks is something any of us might be assigned — I was, and you will be. It's nothing to sneer about."

"Young puppy," muttered Korryn.

"Enough chatter," said Bosk. "Fall in for rations."

Paksenarrion was glad to find that after supper they were each issued a blanket and expected to sleep. She had no problem. She woke early and stiff, and had made her way to the jacks and to the river to bathe before a bellow from Corporal Bosk brought the others out of their blankets. The regulars, she noticed, were already in uniform: did they sleep that way? She folded her blanket as the others did, and turned it in to the privates to load on a mule. This morning she stirred porridge in one of the cookpots; three others were supervised by Saben, Jens, and the red-haired boy in velvet.

A bowl of porridge, hunk of brown bread, and slab of dried beef made an ample breakfast, and Paksenarrion felt no ill effects from the previous day's journey. She was, in fact, happier than she'd been for years: she was a soldier at last, and safe from her father's plans. When she found that Jens and Korryn had been told to fill in the trench, her mood soared even higher.

"I don't mind digging them, if they'll fill them," she whispered to Saben.

"Nor I. That Korryn's nasty, isn't he? Jens is just a drunk, but Korryn could be trouble."

"Recruits. Fall in!" yelled Bosk, and the day's work really began.

In the next few weeks, as they traveled toward the Duke's stronghold where their training would take place, Paksenarrion and the others became more and more proficient at marching and camp chores. They picked up new recruits in most of the towns they passed, until their group numbered thirty-eight. Already friendships had begun among some of them, and Paksenarrion had heard her shortened name enough to feel comfortable with it. Despite having little time to talk, she knew that Saben, Arñe, Vik, Jorti, and Coben were going to be her friends — and that Korryn and Jens would never be anything but enemies.

Stammel changed the marching order every few days, so that they all had a chance to lead a file as well as follow. Marching in front, where she could not see the motley clothing of the rest, Paksenarrion imagined herself already through training and headed for a battle. She could almost feel a sword swinging at her side. Around that corner, she thought, or over the rise — the enemy is waiting. She pictured grim-faced troops in black armor — or maybe orcs, like those her grandfather had fought. Bits of the old songs and tales ran through her mind: magic swords, heroes who fought and won against the powers of darkness, enchanted horses . . . When she marched in back, however, the visions failed, and she wondered how many more days they would be on the road.

At last Stammel told them that the stronghold was less than a day's march away. They halted early, beside the river, and spent the rest of the daylight getting as clean as possible. Paksenarrion did not mind the cold water, but others who tried to make do with a casual swipe at face and hands were ordered back in to do the job properly.

Next day Stammel put Paksenarrion, Saben, Korryn, and Seliast at the head of the first squad files: the tallest recruits. They marched without effort now, and almost without thought, rhythm even and arms swinging. As they came over the last rise, to see the blunt stone walls of the stronghold rise from a narrow plain, squads on the parade fields were shifted out of their way.

Paksenarrion, marching across that space in front of a whole army (as it seemed to her) suddenly felt she couldn't get any air. Only the habit of days on the road kept her from bolting from so many eyes. She blushed a fiery red and kept marching.

Chapter Two

"All your personal belongings you turn in to the quartermaster; he'll put 'em in a bag with your name on it and store them in the treasury. We'll issue your training uniforms today, and if you want to keep your old clothes, they'll be stored too." Stammel turned to greet a gnarled older man whose arms were full of burlap sacks. "Ah, Quartermaster . . . good to see you."

The man glared at the recruits. "Hmmph. Another bunch of beginners. And how much sentimental trash have they brought to take up space in storage?"

"Not so much; we've been on the road eight days since the last pickup."

"Good. I'll need a clerk."

"Bosk'll do it." Stammel gestured to Bosk, who came forward and took a handful of tags from the quartermaster. "File one, step up one at a time, give your name, and hand over your gear."

Paksenarrion stepped forward, unbuckling the belt on which her sheathed dagger hung. Bosk had already written out her tag, and handed it to the quartermaster, who fastened it to a sack and waited for her contribution. She held out belt, dagger, and the kerchief with her savings — eighteen coppers — in it.

"Are you going to keep those clothes?" he asked, eyeing her brother's trousers, which had slipped down her hips without the belt.

"Y-yes, sir."

"Amazing. Well, go get your uniform, and bring your clothes back here. Quickly, now."

Paksenarrion looked around to see where she should go; Stammel waved her toward a doorway on the left. There a man and woman presided behind tables heaped with brown clothing. Paks strode quickly across the courtyard, hoping her trousers would stay up. Behind her she heard Korryn's nasty chuckle and whispered comment.

When she reached the tables, she saw stacks of plain brown tunics, socks, and low boots. The woman beckoned her, and grinned. "You're a tall one, right enough. Let's see — " and she began measuring Paks with a length of knotted string: neck to waist, waist to knee, shoulder to elbow to wrist. "Here — " she held out a tunic, after rummaging in the pile. "This should do well enough for now. Change."

Paksenarrion took the tunic, stripped off her shirt and trousers, and

8

pulled the tunic over her head. The cloth was not as scratchy as the wool she was used to. The sleeves fell just short of her elbows, and the hem almost reached her knees. It felt more like a dress cut short than anything else.

"Try these boots," said the woman. Paks put on a pair of the heavy brown socks and eased her feet into the boots. They were short. The woman offered a larger pair. These fit well enough. "Here's a belt for you, and a sheath. You'll be issued the dagger later." The belt, like everything else, was plain brown; the buckle was iron. Paksenarrion took her old clothes back to the quartermaster, feeling silly with the tunic rippling around her bare thighs.

"Ooh, look at the pretty white legs she has." She was sure that mocking whisper was Korryn or Jens, and hated herself for blushing as she handed the clothes to be sacked away. But Stammel heard the whisper too.

"Korryn," he said. "Who told you to talk in ranks?"

Paks, returning to her place, dared not look at Korryn's face as he replied: "No one, Sergeant."

"Perhaps you need reminding that you are to do what you're told and nothing else?"

"No, sir." Korryn did not sound as confident as usual. "But, sir, such a pretty sight — "

"If a pair of legs can make you forget your duty, Korryn, you'll have to be better taught. I don't care if the Marshal-General of Gird's Hall in Fin Panir walks through the lines stark naked and tweaks your beard — you pay attention to me, and not to her. Is that clear?"

"Yes, sir." Korryn sounded sullen. "But — "

"No buts!" growled Stammel.

In less than an hour, Stammel's group of recruits was outfitted in the recruit uniform. They moved into one of the big barracks rooms, with Bosk and Devlin, another corporal, assigning bunks.

"File leaders will rotate from week to week for the first month or so," said Devlin. He was taller and thinner than Bosk, and looked as if he would smile more easily. Right now he was not smiling at all. "File leaders bunk here, by the door," he went on. "File seconds here, then thirds, fourths, and so on. You'll change your bunk as you change your place in the files. Now: each bunk has the same bedding, and this is how you'll make it up." The corporals demonstrated, then pulled the bedding apart. "Your turn; get busy." As the recruits struggled with the bedding, they walked from place to place, explaining and criticizing. The long, straw-stuffed pallet had to be patted into an even rectangle, muslin sheet stretched tightly over it, and the brown wool blanket folded in one certain way at the foot. Paksenarrion finally achieved an acceptable bunk, and stood beside it waiting for the others to finish. Her legs still felt chilly and exposed, and she was hungry. Most of the others looked as uncomfortable as she felt.

At last they were all done. Corporal Devlin went to fetch Stammel, and

Bosk moved around the room, positioning recruits beside each bunk, ready for inspection.

Stammel came to the door.

"Ready?"

"Ready for inspection, sir," answered Bosk.

Stammel began with the file leaders, checking the bunks first. Then he looked at his recruits, twitching a sleeve into place, here, asking about the fit of the boots, there. When he had made his way all around the room, he returned to the doorway.

"You'll present like this for inspection every morning before breakfast," he said. "And at any other time it's ordered. You'll receive your file positions here, when that's changed, so that you'll go directly to your file position in formation in the yard. Immediately after an inspection, you'll parade in the yard, and you'll march everywhere in formation — to eat, to drill, to work. You'll have a quarterglass after morning call to visit the jacks, dress and make your bunks; I'll expect every one of you to be in place when I come in." He beckoned to Bosk and Devlin, and left the room. Most of the group stood still, but a few left their places and started for the door. Bosk returned, and the rash ones halted.

"And who told you that you were dismissed?"

They stared at their feet.

"Those of you out of position, stay there. The rest of you are dismissed."

Paksenarrion gave silent thanks that she had not moved, and went quickly out to the yard. There she found the other recruit units drawn up in formation, and Stammel waiting. She aligned herself on the others, wondering what was happening to the unfortunates who had been held back. Beside and behind her the ranks filled. At last they were all in position. The corporals reported to Stammel, and after a moment he glanced at the other sergeants.

"Go ahead, Stammel," called someone from far down the row. "Take yours in first."

They were marched across the courtyard to a building with windows opening on the yard. Paks could smell cooked meat and bread. There Stammel sent them in, one file at a time. Once inside, she was urged along by a private who directed her to the serving line. There she found a stack of bowls, another of trays, and a bin of blunted knives. She took a tray, bowl, spoon, and knife, and moved toward the impatient cooks. A dipper of some kind of stew went into the bowl, and a half-loaf of bread, hunk of cheese, slab of salt beef, and an apple went on the tray. As she came off the serving line, another private directed her to a table in one corner. Soon her file was seated along the bench, and the tables were filling in strict order. A cook brought over a large jug of water and a cup to their table. Paks took a tentative bite of stew. To her surprise, it was tasty, savory with onions and vegetables. It had looked like a lot on her tray, but she found herself polishing the bowl with the last of her bread before she knew it.

"Well," said Stammel from behind her. "How do you like army food?"

10

"Seems good enough to me, sir," said Saben, from the next table.

"You'll eat a lot of it." Stammel moved away.

That first night in barracks, after so many nights on the road, was horrible. It was stuffy. It smelled. Paksenarrion jerked awake several times in alarm, only to find that she was safe in her bunk: someone had walked past the doorway. It was neither as light nor as dark as the roadside, for the dark was thicker, an indoor darkness, and the light was clearly of human origin. Several people snored, and their snores echoed off the stone walls. She missed the comfort of the old shirt she usually slept in. The new nightshift she'd been issued was scratchy. ("We're civilized," Stammel had said to those who protested against wearing a nightshift. "Besides, it'll be cold soon.") Paks had scarcely fallen asleep after her last alarm when a terrible clangor broke out: Corporal Devlin with the triangle that announced morning call.

Paks rolled out of her bunk and made for the jacks down the corridor. Then back to the room, to struggle with her bunk. She peeled off the nightshift, hoping that Korryn's eyes were occupied elsewhere. No one said anything. Everyone around her was as busy as she was. She unbraided her hair, combed it with the bone comb she wore looped into it, and rebraided it smoothly, wrapping the tip with a thread from her tunic. She didn't know what to do with the nightshift. Bosk came to the door; Paks caught his eye and he came forward.

"What do we do with these?"

"See that ledge? Fold it neatly and put it there." Bosk went around the room to tell the others. Paks tied her bootlaces, straightened her belt and empty sheath, and smoothed the sheet on her bunk one last time.

Devlin came to the door. "Ready?" he asked Bosk.

"As they will be."

"Recruits, prepare for inspection!" yelled Devlin. Paksenarrion stood where she thought she should be and stared straight ahead. Stammel entered the room, and began on the other side. He found something wrong with each person: blanket folded wrong, sheet crooked, pallet misshapen, boots laced unevenly, hair uncombed, tunic crooked, nightshift folded wrong, dirty fingernails (Paks felt a stab of panic and almost looked at her hands), untrimmed beard, messy bunk (he was only two bunks away, and Paks was sure she could not stand the suspense), nightshift *under* the bed weren't you *listening*, recruit? And then it was her turn. She felt herself begin to blush before he said a word. She heard — she did not look — him thump the bunk. He looked at her from all sides, grunted, and finally said, "Tunic's wrinkled in back," and walked out.

"Dismissed," said Bosk, and Paksenarrion headed for the yard, beginning to wonder why she'd gotten into this.

She wondered even more in the next weeks. She enjoyed the marching drill, which kept them moving about the wide fields in intricate patterns for several hours every morning and evening. It wasn't fighting, but it was sol-

11

dierly, and expected. What she didn't enjoy was the other work. Bedmaking, cleaning, and dishwashing were among the things she'd left home to avoid. If she'd wanted to be a carpenter or a mason, she grumbled to herself one day while working on repairs to the stable wall, she'd have apprenticed herself to one.

Others felt the same way.

"We haven't even seen a sword yet," complained Effa. "I signed on to be a fighter, not drag rocks around all day."

"Well — surely we'll get into that," said Saben, as he hoisted one of the despised rocks into place. "I mean, the place isn't full of workers, so they must have become fighters and gone to war."

Korryn gave a sneering laugh. "Fine reasoner you are! No, they'll keep us as laborers as long as they can, and then try to skimp on our training. As long as they can count on fools like you to join every year, they don't care how many die."

Paksenarrion snorted. "If we're fools for joining, what about you?" The others laughed, and Korryn scowled, slamming a rock into wet mortar so it splattered them all.

"I," he said, "already know how to use a sword. I don't have to worry."

"You will if you don't get busy," said Bosk. They all wondered how long he had been listening.

The closest they came to anything that Paksenarrion recognized as weapons training was hauk drill. Every day they spent two hours with the hauks, weighted wooden cylinders that looked somewhat like maces.

"I know what you want," said Armsmaster Siger, as he supervised the drill. "You want swords, you think, and spears. Huh. You couldn't wield a sword for a quarter-glass yet, none of you. Get that up, recruit — higher, that's right. Thought you were strong, didn't you? And you're all as weak as newborn lambs — look at you sweat." Siger was a gnarly, dried-up old man who looked old enough to be anyone's grandfather.

Paks had began to doubt they would ever get to real weapons — week after week, they swung the hauks: over, under, sideways. And then one day they arrived to find practice swords laid out: wooden, and blunted, but swords. Siger stood behind the row of swords like a potter behind his wares.

"Today," he said, "we find out who's making a warrior. File one, come forward." Paks led her file out of formation. "All right, file leader, are you ready to face a sword today?"

Paks took a deep breath of excitement. "Yes, Armsmaster."

Siger glared at her. "Ha! Eager, are you? You innocents are all too willing to shed your blood. Very well — pick up the first one in line — yes — that one."

Paks could not help grinning: a sword in her hand at last. She waggled it from side to side.

"No!" roared Siger. "Don't play with it, fool! It's not a toy to show off with. A sword is to kill people with, nothing less."

Paksenarrion blushed scarlet.

12

"Now — hold it just like the hauk in position one. Yes." Siger scooped up one of the other practice blades. "This is an infantry sword, short enough not to get in the way in formation. It's used to stab and slash. Now, file leader — the motions are the same as for hauk drill. Proceed."

Paks was puzzled but willing, and began to move the sword through the remembered sequences. As she did so, Siger's blade met hers, tapping it first lightly, then harder. Paks began to watch his blade, thinking back to Jornoth's sketchy lessons, and forgot all about the sequence of hauk-drill. Excitement rose in her, and she began to swing the blade harder, trying to force Siger's blade aside. Suddenly his sword was not there to be tapped; instead it rapped her sharply on the ribs.

"Ouch!" She was startled, and having lost her rhythm was whacked twice more before she regained it. Uncertain, and a bit angry, she glared at Siger, who gave her a mocking smile.

"That was the flat of the blade," he said cheerfully. "Next time it'll be the edge; keep to the drill, recruit."

Paks bit her lip, but returned to the drill pattern, meeting Siger's blade with a crisp smack. He increased the pace, and she struggled to keep up, irritated by his smile and by the snide remarks of Korryn behind her. Again Siger rapped her ribs, sore now from the earlier blows, and Paks erupted furiously into wild strokes that hit nothing — until a sharp blow in the midsection knocked the wind out of her, and she dropped the sword and sprawled painfully on the ground. Korryn laughed.

"Always a mistake to get angry," said Siger, over her head. "You've a lot to learn before trading killing blows. Catch your breath, now." His voice chilled. "As for you, recruit, that thinks it's funny, we'll have you next, if you please." Paks gasped a moment or two, and clambered up.

"Still want to learn swordplay?" Siger asked.

"Yes, sir. It's — it's harder than it looks, though."

Siger grinned. "It always is, recruit; it always is. Now you've been blooded, I want you to put on a banda next time." He jerked his head toward a pile of white objects like cushions. "Not you — " he added as Korryn moved toward the pile. "I want to see if you think it's funny when I whack *your* ribs."

Korryn glared at him and snatched up a sword with practiced ease.

"Ah-h. An expert, is it? You've handled a blade before?" Korryn nodded. "We'll see, then. You need not confine yourself to the hauk drill if you think you can do more." But Korryn began with the standard movements, holding his sword easily. "I'd say you were used to a longer blade, recruit," commented Siger.

Abruptly Korryn changed from the drill pattern, and a complicated rattle of blade-on-blade resulted; Paks could not see just what had happened. Korryn tried a quick thrust, but the short sword did not reach Siger, and Siger's blade rapped Korryn's shoulder. Korryn scowled and pressed his attack again, using his height and longer reach, but he could not touch the Armsmaster, who kept up a running commentary.

"Taught by a fencing master, weren't you? You like a thrust better than a slash. You handle that blade like you did most of your fighting in alleys. It won't do for us — you might as well forget it, recruit, and start learning it right." And with that Siger began a furious attack that forced Korryn back, and back, and back around the practice ring, taking blow after blow, until Korryn lost his grip and the sword flew out of his hand. Effa caught it in midair.

"Now," said Siger, the point of his sword at Korryn's waist. "Is it quite as funny when it happens to you? Let's hear you laugh."

Korryn was white with rage, breathless and sweaty.

"Sir," he said finally. Siger gave him a slight smile and nodded.

"Novices, that have never handled a sword, them I expect to get drunk on the excitement and do something stupid — and I thump them well for it. But those who claim to know something . . . Go wait for your turn again, recruit."

Each of them went a round with Siger without protection, and each received a complement of bruises. Then he showed them how to fasten the bandas, the quilted canvas surcoat worn for weapons practice.

"Your turn again," Siger said to Paks. "Ready? Are you sore enough?"

Paks grinned. "I'm sore, sir, but I'm ready. I hope."

"You'd better be. Now start with the drill."

This time Paks handled the sword with more assurance, and kept the cadence as even as she could. "Better," admitted Siger. "Painfully slow, but better. Speed it up, now, just a little. Keep the rhythm." The blades clacked together. Again, again, again. "Now a bit harder — not too much at once." The shock of contact was making Paks's hand tingle; her arm began to tire. Siger shifted around her, and she had to turn and strike at the same time. The ache spread up her arm. Whack. Whack. Sweat trickled down her face, stinging in her eyes. Siger moved the other way, and Paks turned with him, but she lost the rhythm. Quick as a snake's tongue his blade tapped her ribs. "Enough," he said. "You're slowing down again. Give the blade to someone else, and go work with the hauks awhile."

Once they began drilling with wooden blades, they also began to learn other weapons. By the time they marched south, Siger said, they would have a certain minimum proficiency with short-sword, dagger, bow, and spear.

The spear offered the most difficulty. As usual, it had seemed simple, just thinking about it. A long pole with a sharp end, to be poked at the enemy. No fancy strokes — simple. Effective. Surely it was easier than a sword; if nothing else you could hang onto the thing with both hands.

"We don't use polearms often," said Stammel. "We're a fast-moving, flexible infantry, and swords are better for that. But we do train with 'em and we use them sometimes. So. First you'll learn to carry something that long without getting all tangled up in it. Remember those reeds we gathered last week you were so curious about? Well, they've been drying in the storelofts, and you'll each take one."

Soon they were back in formation, each with a twelve-foot reed in hand. Stammel had shown them how to hold the mock spears upright; now he gave the command to move forward. Five of the reeds tipped backwards. The butt on one tripped the recruit in front of the careless carrier. When he stumbled, his reed swung out of control and hit the file leader on the head.

"Pick 'em up—don't stop, come on! You've got to hold them firmly—don't let 'em waver. Keep in formation, there. Stay in step or you'll trip each other."

The reeds dipped and wavered as if in a windstorm as Stammel led the unit to the far side of the parade grounds. By the time he called a halt, most faces were red.

"Now you see what I meant. The only easy thing about spear work is how easy it is to mess up the whole formation. If you ever see one of the heavy polearm companies, like Count Vladi's, you'll see how it should be done. Now — you've got to learn how to shift those things about. Together, or you'll all be tangled together. So just holding them upright, we'll practice turning in place." He called for a right face. Two recruits let their reeds lag behind the turn, and the tips bumped neighboring reeds. "No! Hold them absolutely steady when you turn. Keep 'em straight. Try it again."

After a dizzying few minutes of facing left, right, and about, the unit could turn in place without any wavering of the reeds. Stammel wiped his face and glanced at the corporals. They were trying not to grin. Far across the parade grounds, he could see another unit practicing. It looked worse than his, he thought.

"Next step is the slope," he said. "Don't move anything until I've explained. First, you'll put the butt a handspan behind the right foot of the man in front of you; file leaders, that's an armspan in front of you. Then slowly tilt the reed back over your shoulder — you have to be careful not to let the butt slip forward. Then your left hand grips two spans below the right, and you lift it onto your shoulder. That gives enough clearance in front for marching. Don't let it swing free; use your grip to hold the butt end down. Bosk, show them how to do it."

Bosk came forward and took Paksenarrion's reed from her hands. He held it upright, and demonstrated the facing movements they had practiced: the end of the reed, far over his head, scarcely quivered when he turned. Then he loosened his grip and let the butt end slide toward the ground, tilting the reed as it slid so that it grounded an armspan in front of him. While his right hand steadied the shaft, his left hand reached below and lifted; the reed rose, keeping the same steep slant. When his left hand reached his right, he shifted the right quickly to the lower grip.

"That's the position you want," said Stammel. "Now, show 'em how to move with it."

Bosk strode forward, the reed steady on his shoulder, not waving or dipping with his stride. When he turned, they could hear the whirr as the end of the reed sliced the air. He made a square, then returned the reed to an upright position and handed it back to Paks.

"Ready — " said Stammel. "Ground the butts — " Paksenarrion felt the length of reed quivering as she tried to let it slide slowly through her hands, aiming the butt somewhat ahead of her right foot. It bumped the ground.

"It's too close to you," said Bosk. "Slide it out further." Paks slid the butt along the ground until Bosk nodded.

"Now tilt 'em back along your shoulders," said Stammel. Paks let the top of the reed fall back slowly. The butt came off the ground, but she pushed it back before anyone said anything. Some were not so lucky. Stammel and the corporals were yelling at those who let the reeds get out of control. At last all were in the correct position.

"Left hands down," said Stammel. "And lift, but keep it under control. NO!" he roared. Paks heard a smack and a yelp of pain as someone's reed landed on someone's head. Her own wavered as she tried to shift the grip of her left hand. "Steady!" Paks let her eyes slide sideways to see how others in the front rank were doing. Everyone seemed to be in the right position. "Now — bring them back vertical again. That's right. Now slope 'em back — no — No! Control it, don't let it get away from you."

They repeated this exercise again and again until the whole unit could shift the reeds from vertical to sloped position without getting out of position. Paksenarrion's arms ached, and her palms tingled unpleasantly where the reed slid back and forth.

"We're going to march back with them at slope," said Stammel. "And you'd best not look as foolish as the other units, either. Anyone who drops a reed — " he scowled at them.

They managed to make it back to the courtyard before the others, without dropping anything but sweat. By the time the other units were in and halted, their own reeds were safely on the ground.

Gradually their weapons skills improved. They took fewer — but never no — thumps from Siger, and the spears seemed more manageable. After Paks took the skin off the inside of her left arm during archery practice, she learned to keep her elbow braced correctly. They all suffered a variety of lumps, cuts and scrapes, but the only serious injury in Paks's unit was Mikel Falsson, who fell from the wall while working on repairs and broke both legs. He recovered, but with a bad limp, and eventually went to work in the armory.

"He was lucky not to lose either leg," said Devlin. "That was as nasty a break as I've seen." Paks shuddered, remembering the white ends of bone sticking out.

"If there'd been a Marshal here — " began Effa. Devlin interrupted.

"No. Don't say that. Not here. Not in this Company."

Effa looked puzzled. "But I thought Phelan's Company recruited mostly Girdsmen — doesn't it?"

"Once it did, but not now."

"But when I joined, and said I was a yeoman, Stammel said it was good."

"Sergeant Stammel, to you. Oh yes, we're glad to get Girdsmen — the more the better. But there'll be no Marshals here, and no grange or barton."

16

"But why — ?"

"Effa, leave be." Arñe tapped her arm. "It's not our concern."

It was not in Effa's nature to leave be. She worried the question any time the corporals and Stammel were not around, wondering why and why not, and trying to convert those (such as Paksenarrion, Saben and Arñe) who seemed to her virtuous but unenlightened. Paks found these attempts at conversion annoying.

"I've got my own gods," she said finally. "And that's enough for me. My family has followed the same gods for generations, and I won't change. Besides, however good a fighter Gird was, he can't have turned into a god. That's not where gods come from." And she turned her back on Effa and walked off.

Meanwhile, she and Saben and Vik discussed religions in a very different way, fascinated by each other's background.

"Now my family," said Saben. "We were horse nomads once — my father's father's grandfather. Now we raise cattle, but we still carry a bit of hoof with us, and dance under the forelock and tail at weddings and funerals."

"Do you worship — uh — horses?" asked Vik.

"No, of course not. We worship Thunder-of-horses, the north wind, and the dark-eyed Mare of Plenty, though my father says that's really the same as Alyanya, the Lady of Peace. Then my uncle's family — I've seen them dance to Guthlac — "

"The Hunter?"

"Yes. My father always goes home then. He doesn't approve."

"I should think not." Vik shivered.

"City boy," teased Paks. "We gather the sheep in from the wild hunt, but we know Guthlac has great power."

"I know that. It's *what* power — brrr. Now in my family, we worship the High Lord, Alyanya, and Sertig and Adyan — "

"Who are they?" asked Paks.

"Sertig's the Maker, surely you know that. Craftsmen follow him. Adyan is the Namer — *true*-Namer — of all things. My father's a harper, and harpers deal much with names."

"You're a harper's son?" asked Saben. Vik nodded. "But you've no voice at all!"

"True enough," said Vik, shrugging. "And no skill with a harp either, though I had one in my hands as soon as I could pluck a string. My father tried to make a scribe of me, and I wrote as badly as I played. And got into trouble, liking to fight. So — " he looked at his hands. "So it became — wise — for me to move away, and make use of the skill I did have."

"Which is?" asked Saben slyly.

In an instant Vik had turned, gotten his hold, and flipped Saben onto his back. "Throwing down great lummoxes of cattle farmers, for one." Saben laughed and rolled back up to a sitting position.

"I see your point," he said cheerfully. "But will it work against a

17

thousand southern spearmen?"

"It won't have to. You and Paks will be up front, you lucky tall ones, and you can protect me."

After several weeks of switching places in formation, they received their permanent assignments. "Permanent until you do something stupid," Bosk said. Paks, to her delight, was made file leader. She still had problems with Korryn, who teased and pestered her whenever the corporals weren't around, but aside from that she had returned to her earlier pleasure in being in an army. She did wish that brawling were not forbidden. She was sure she could flatten Korryn, and ached for a chance. But after the formal punishment of three recruits from Kefer's unit who had livened a dull rainy afternoon by starting a fight, she was determined to keep her temper. She did not want to lose her new position.

One afternoon a troop of soldiers in the Duke's colors rode up from the southeast, and were passed by the gate guards into the courtyard. The fifteen men, under command of a yellow-haired corporal, were immensely impressive to the recruits. And they knew it, and swaggered accordingly.

"Get the quartermaster," the corporal ordered a recruit from another unit, and the recruit scurried away. Paksenarrion, taking her turn at cut-and-thrust practice with Siger, was tempted to turn and look, but the Armsmaster brought her attention back with a thump in the ribs.

"When you're fighting, fight," he said grumpily. "You be gazing around at everything on earth and heaven, and you'll be buzzard-bait soon enough."

Paks concentrated on trying to slash past his defenses, but the old man was more than a match for her, and talked on without a break as she grew more and more breathless. "Eh, now, that's too wide a backswing — what'd I tell you? See, you left your side open again. Somebody'll plant a blade in there when you're careless. Quicker, lass, quicker! You ought to be quicker nor an old man like me. Look now, I gave you an opening wide as a barn door for a thrust, and you used that same wide cut. Stop now —"

Paks lowered her wooden blade, gasping for breath.

"You're strong enough," Siger said. "But strong's not the whole game. You've got to be quick, and you've got to think as fast as you move. Now let's break the thrust stroke down into its parts again." He demonstrated, then had Paks go through the motions several times. "Let's try that again. Don't stand flat-footed: you need to move."

This time practice seemed to go more smoothly, and at last Paks's blade slipped past his to touch his side. "Ah-h," he said. "That's it." Twice more that afternoon she got a touch on him, and was rewarded with one of his rare smiles. "But you still must be quicker!" was his parting comment.

Chapter Three

It seemed to Paksenarrion that events had moved with blinding speed. Only that afternoon she had been a file leader, and Siger had praised her. Now she was shivering on the stone sleeping bench of an underground cell, out of sight and sound of everyone, cold, hungry, frightened, and in more trouble that she'd dreamed possible. Even with cold stone under her, and the painful drag of chains on her wrists and ankles, she could hardly believe it had really happened. How could she be in such trouble for something someone else had done? Her head throbbed, and her ears still rang from the fight. Every separate muscle and bone had a distinctive and private pain to add.

It was so quiet that she could clearly hear the blood rushing through her head, and the clink of the chains when she shifted on the bench rang loudly. And the dark! She'd never been afraid of the dark, but this was a different dark: a shut-in, thick, breathless dark. How would she know when dawn came? Her breath quickened, rasping in the silence, as she tried to fight down panic. Surely they wouldn't leave her down here to die? She clamped her teeth against a cry that fought its way up from her chest. It came out as a soft groan. She could not — could *not* — stand this place any longer. Another wave of nausea overcame her, and she felt hastily for the bucket between her feet. She had nothing left to heave into it, but felt better knowing it was there. When the spasm passed, she wiped her mouth on her tattered sleeve.

Her breathing had just begun to ease again, when she thought she heard a sound. She froze. What now? The sound grew louder, but still so muffled by stone walls and thick door that she could not define it. Rhythmic — was it steps? Was the long night already over? She saw a gleam of light above the heavy door; it brightened. Something clinked against the door; it grated open, letting in a flood of yellow torchlight. Paks blinked against it, as the torchbearer set his light in a holder just inside the cell door. Then he pulled the door closed, and turned to face her, leaning on the wall under the torch. It was Stammel: but a Stammel so forbidding that Paks dared not say a word, but stared at him in silence. After a long pause, during which he looked her up and down, he sighed and shook his head.

"I thought you had more sense, Paks," he said heavily. "Whatever he said, you shouldn't have hit him. Surely you —"

"It wasn't what he said, sir — it was what he *did* —"

19

"The story is that he asked you to bed him, and teased you when you wouldn't. And then you jumped him, and — "

"No, sir! That's not — "

"Paksenarrion, this is serious. You'll be lucky if you aren't turned out *tinisi turin* — you know what *that* is, sheepfarmer's daughter — " Paks nodded, remembering the old term for a clean-shorn lamb, also used for running off undesirables shaved and naked. "Lies won't help."

"But, sir — "

"Let me finish. If what he says is true, the best you can hope for — the very best — is three months with the quarriers, and one more chance with a new recruit unit, since *I* haven't taught you what you should know. If you say he's lying, you'll have to convince us that a veteran of five campaign seasons, a man with a good reputation in the Company, would be so stupid in the first place, and lie about it in the second. Why should we believe you? I've known you — what? Nine weeks? Ten? I've known him nearly six years. Now if your story is true, and if you can prove it some way, tell me. I'll tell the captain tomorrow, and we'll see. If not, just be quiet, and pray the captain will count your bruises into your punishment."

"Yes, sir." Paks glanced up at Stammel's stern face. It was even worse than she'd thought, if Stammel thought she could be lying.

"Well? Which is it to be?"

Paks looked down at her bruised hands. "Sir, he asked me to come to the back of the room — he didn't say why, but he was a corporal, so I went. And then he took my arm — " she faltered and her right arm quivered. "And tried to get me to bed him. And I said no, and he wouldn't let go, but went on — " She glanced at Stammel again. His expression did not change; her eyes dropped. "He said he was sure I wasn't a virgin, not with my looks, and that I must've bedded — someone — to be a file leader — "

"Say that again! He said what?"

"That I must have — earned that position — on my back, he said."

"Did he say with whom?" asked Stammel, his voice grimmer than before.

"No, sir."

Stammel grunted. "Go on, then."

"I — I was angry — about that — "

"So you hit him."

"No, sir." Paks shook her head for emphasis, but the nausea took her again, and she heaved repeatedly into the bucket. Finally she looked up, trembling with the aftermath. "I didn't hit him, but I did get angry because that's not how I got it, and I started to — to say bad things — " She heaved again. " — that I learned from my cousin," she finished.

"Drink this," said Stammel, handing her a flask. "If you're going to heave so much, you need something down, ban or no."

Paks swallowed the cold water gratefully. "Then, sir, he was angry for what I said — "

"It couldn't have been *that* bad — what did you say?"

"Pargsli spakin i tokko — "

20

"D'you know what that means, girl?"

"No — my cousin said it was bad."

A flicker of amusement relaxed Stammel's face for a moment. "It is. I suggest you learn what curses mean before you say them. Then what?"

"He clapped a hand over my mouth, and tried to push me down on the bunk." She took another swallow of water.

"Yes?"

"So I bit his hand, to make him let go, and he did and I got free. But he was between me and the door, and he took off his belt — "

"Did he say anything?"

"Yes, sir. He threatened to beat me, to tame me, and then he swung the belt, and I ran at him, trying to get away. I thought I could push past him, maybe, the way I did with my father. But he grabbed my throat — " her hand rose, unconsciously, " — and hit my face, and — and I couldn't breathe. I thought be would kill me, and I *had* to fight. I had to breathe — "

"Hmmph. That sounds more like the recruit I thought I had. Tell the rest of it."

"I — it's hard to remember. I broke the throat hold, but I couldn't get away, he was so fast and strong. We were on the floor, mostly, and he was yelling at me — hitting — I remember feeling weaker, and then someone was holding my arms, and someone was hitting me. I suppose that was after you came, though wasn't it?"

Stammel's face wore a puzzled frown. "No one hit you after I got there. When I came in Korryn was hanging onto you, Stephi was lying on the floor, and Korryn said he'd just then been able to pull you off. Captain Sejek wanted to hit you, all right, but he didn't." Stammel sighed. "If you're telling the truth, girl, I can see why you fought. But Korryn was there, or says he was, and his story is against yours, as well as Stephi."

"He was there, at the beginning, but he just laughed. I — I am telling the truth, sir, really I am." Paks swallowed noisily. "But I can see why you wouldn't believe me, if you've known him — Stephi? — so long. Only, that's what really happened, sir, no matter what Korryn says."

"If it were only your word against Korryn's — " Stammel paused and stretched, then shifted his weight to the other leg. "Paks have you bedded anyone here?"

"No, sir."

"You've been asked, surely?"

"Yes, sir, but I haven't. I don't want to. And I asked Maia — "

"Maia?"

"The quartermaster's assistant. I asked her if I had to, and she said no, but not to make a fuss about being asked, like I might at home."

"Has Korryn bothered you about it?" Paks began to tremble, remembering Korryn's constant teasing, taunting attempts to force her into bed with him. "He's asked me," she whispered.

"Paks, look at me." She looked up. "Has he done more than ask?"

"He — he has sometimes."

21

"Why didn't you say something to me or Bosk?"

Paks shook her head. "I thought I wasn't supposed to — to make a fuss. I thought I was supposed to take care of it — "

"You aren't supposed to act like a new wench in an alehouse, no. But no fighter should have to put up with that sort of thing from a companion. When you refuse, they're supposed to drop it; there's plenty enough that are willing. I wish I'd known; we'd have put a stop to that." He paused briefly. "Are you a sisli?"

"I — I don't know what that is. He — the corporal — asked me that too."

"Like Barranyi and Natzlin in Kefer's unit. A woman who beds women. Are you?"

"No, sir. Not that I know of. Does it matter?"

"Not really." Stammel shifted his weight again and sighed. "Paks, I want to believe you. You've been a good recruit so far. But I just don't know — and even if I believe you, there's the captain. Sejek is — umph. You're in more trouble than most people find in a whole enlistment."

Paks felt tears sting her eyes. It was hopeless. If Stammel still thought she could be lying, no one else would believe her. She thought briefly of Saben, who had left before the fight broke out — why hadn't he stayed? Her belly turned again, and she heaved the water she'd drunk into the bucket. She hurt all over, and tomorrow could only be worse. A sob shook her body, then another one. She tried to choke them back.

"Wishing you were back on the farm, Paks?" Stammel's voice was almost gentle.

Her head came up in surprise. "No, sir. I just wish — I wish it hadn't happened, or that you'd been there to see it all."

"Still want to be a soldier, even after this?"

"Of course! It's what I've always wanted, but — but if everyone thinks I'm lying — I'll never have the chance." She retched again.

"Paks, is all this heaving from being in trouble, or what?"

"I — I think it's from being hit, here — " She gestured at her midriff. "It hurts there."

"I thought you just had a black eye and a bloody nose — let's see, can you sit up straighter?" Stammel moved away from the light to her side. "No, keep looking toward the light. Hmm — that whole side of your face is swollen. I can't even see your eyelashes. Your nose is broken, certainly." He touched the swelling very gently. Paks winced. "That *could* be from more than one blow. Do your ears ring?"

"Yes, sir — but it comes and goes."

"What's this gash on your shoulder? He didn't have a blade, did he?"

"No. I think that was the belt buckle. My father's used to do that."

"I wish this torchlight was brighter and steadier," grumbled Stammel. "Lift your chin. Looks like your throat is bruised, too. Does it hurt to breathe?"

"Just a little."

"Well, where else are you hurt?"

22

"In — in front. It all hurts. And my legs."

"Stand up, then. I'll want a look at the damage."

Paksenarrion tried to stand, but her legs had stiffened after hours of sitting on the cold stone. At first she could not move at all, but when Stammel gave her an arm to pull up on, she staggered up, still unable to straighten. She could not repress a short cry of pain.

"Here — lean against the wall if you aren't steady." Stammel swung her around and braced her against the wall opposite the torch. "Tir's bones, I don't see how you could have half-killed him in the shape you're in." Then he paused, glancing down at his arm and then at the stone bench. "It *is* blood. What did they — "

Paks felt herself slipping down the wall; she could not seem to hold herself up.

"Here, now — don't fall," said Stammel. The warning came too late. Paks lay curled on her side, heaving helplessly.

"I'm — I'm sorry — " she gasped finally.

"Lie still then. Let me look — " Stammel raised her tunic. Even in the flickering torchlight he could see the welts and dried blood on her thighs. Her tunic was ripped in several places. Stammel swore suddenly, words Paks had heard from her cousin. Then his voice softened. "Paks, I'm going to talk to the captain. We'll get this straightened out somehow. You can't be faking these injuries, and their story doesn't hold up when you're too weak to stand." He put a hand on her shoulder. "Now, let's get you back on the bench. I'll try to get the captain to let me have Maia see you, but don't count on it." He half-lifted her. "Come on — help me. You're too big for me to lift alone."

Paks struggled up and finally made it onto the bench with Stammel's help.

"I'll be back to check again tonight, and of course in the morning. You'll be all right, though miserable. Try not to move around — that may help the heaves — and don't panic. We won't forget you." With that Stammel took down the torch, opened the door, and left, taking the light with him. Paks lay in the darkness, not quite sure whether she felt better or worse about her prospects.

Stammel came up from the cells looking, had he known it, as angry as he felt. Bosk waited near the head of the stairs. When he caught sight of Stammel's face, his own seemed to freeze for an instant. Stammel, his mind whirling with what he must do, and quickly, before the captain went to bed, stopped at the head of the stairs and beckoned. "Corporal Bosk," he said, and his voice surprised himself.

"Yes, sir." Bosk was looking at something below his face — at his sleeve, Stammel realized. He felt unreasonably irritated.

"I didn't do it, Bosk; you know better!"

"Yes, sir." Bosk's eyes came back to his.

"We have a problem, Bosk, and little time to solve it. I want you to isolate Korryn, at once. I want to speak to everyone who was in that room from the

23

time Stephi came in until we got there — no matter who, or how long they stayed — everyone. Separately — I'll use the duty room for that. And before I talk to them, I want to know what they've been doing, and what you and Devlin think. But quickly."

"Yes, sir. Do you want me to move Korryn first? And where?"

"Yes. Use that storage chamber down the way, and put a guard with him. He's not to talk to anyone. Is Dev in the duty room?"

"Yes, sir."

"Good. I'll be there. You take care of Korryn and come to me when it's done."

"Yes, sir." Bosk left the recruit barracks to find a guard, and Stammel walked to the duty room down the hall. Inside, Devlin was writing up the log of his watch, frowning. Stammel stepped into the room and Devlin looked up.

"Are they quiet?" asked Stammel.

"About what you'd expect. I thought we were going to have more trouble for a bit: Korryn and Saben. But I made 'em shut up."

Stammel realized that Devlin, too, was looking at his blood-stained sleeve. "Dev, I haven't been beating her — someone else did that."

"Sir. I wouldn't have thought she'd brawl like that."

"I don't think she did, Dev." Stammel paused to listen to feet in the passage behind him. Bosk must have found a guard. Devlin looked confused.

"But, sir, they both said the same thing. And Stephi was down."

"Yes. That'll bear thinking on." Stammel heard voices in the barracks; he and Devlin both listened. Korryn, sounding aggrieved; Bosk, sounding grim and certain. Then three sets of footsteps in the passage, going away. Stammel resumed. "Devlin, if I'd asked you this morning whose word to take on something, Korryn's or hers, what would you have said?"

"Well — Paks's, of course. But now — "

"No buts. If it's just Paks against Korryn, we *know* Paks is more trustworthy. She's never done one underhanded thing yet."

"Yes, but what about Stephi? He's not like Korryn, that I've heard."

"No, that's true, and I've known him as long as you have. But I've seen him in fights — to be as dazed as he was, with no more marks on him — that's not like him. I wish I knew how badly he's hurt."

Bosk edged in the door. "Korryn's safe, sir. And Saben wants to talk to you."

"I'll get to him. You need to hear this too, Bosk. Stephi's story is that Paks jumped him when he hadn't done more than proposition her, right? And that she halfway killed him, except that Korryn dragged her off just before we got there."

The corporals nodded. "He said — or was it Korryn? — that he'd only hit her a couple of times since the fight started, she was so wild," added Devlin.

"Then how is it," asked Stammel, "that Paks is lying down there too weak to stand, covered with bruises and welts?"

24

"Welts?"

"Yes. Stephi's belt, according to her, and Korryn still had his on, as I recall." Stammel moved restlessly about the little room. "I can't explain Stephi's part in this, but it needs explaining. He's not known as a liar, but — "

"Come to think of it," Devlin interrupted, "most of that story came from Korryn, remember? Stephi hardly said a word — nodded when Korryn said 'isn't that right' — muttered a little, but that's all."

"Still — I've got to come up with answers before the captain goes to bed. We can't spring all this in the morning. Now: Devlin, I'll be using this room to talk to those who were in the room at any time while Stephi was there. I want you to find out, as quietly as possible, whether anyone saw Stephi acting strangely at any time this afternoon or evening. Bosk, you find Maia, Siger, and the afternoon watch commander, and have them meet me in — half a glass. If I'm not through here, come along and I'll step out to meet them in the yard. Got that?"

"Yes, sir."

"I'll speak to Saben first. And remember — keep this quiet."

"Yes, sir." Bosk and Devlin left the room, and Stammel seated himself behind the desk. Almost at once Saben appeared in the doorway.

"Come in, Saben." The tall boy was obviously worried.

"Please, sir," Saben began even before he was all the way in. "No matter what they say, Paks couldn't have done anything that bad. You ought to know that. She never even hit Korryn, and he pestered her all the time — "

"Just a minute now," Stammel interrupted. "You're the one who came to find us, right?"

"Yes, sir."

"I want to know when you first saw Corporal Stephi, and how he acted, and everything you yourself saw him do, or Paks do, until you left the room."

"Yes, sir. Well, this afternoon our unit was having weapons practice with Siger, and that's when he — I mean Corporal Stephi — rode in with the others. My file was waiting turns, and I'd been watching Paks and Siger, but then I started watching the newcomers."

"How did they look?"

Saben pursed his lips. "Very — impressive, sir. Coben and I were saying we hoped we'd look like that. Anyway, Corporal Stephi sent some recruit for the quartermaster, and looked around until he came. He looked at Paks then, sir, but I didn't think anything of it. She is good to look at, and she actually got a touch on Siger." He paused, as if waiting for a comment from Stammel.

"Go on."

"When the quartermaster came out, they talked, and he and all his men took off their swords. I had hoped they'd do a demonstration for us. Then one of the men led all the horses off to the stables, and the corporal went off with the quartermaster. We were through with practice and just cleaning up for supper when I saw him speak to the guard and go through the Duke's Gate. I don't know why — "

"To arrange lodging for his captain, most likely."

"Anyway, I didn't see him again until after supper, in the barracks. Only a few of us were in there; most weren't through with their chores. Paks and I had finished ours before supper. She'd promised to show me how to do a round braid in leather; Siger had told us to start planning the wrappings for our sword hilts. And Korryn was there; he nearly always is. And two or three more. I'd just fastened some thongs together, and was showing Paks, when the corporal came in. He looked around, and saw us, and told Paks he wanted to talk to her."

"Did he seem the same as before?"

"I don't know. A little flushed, maybe, and determined. He gestured Paks to the back of the room, and he had hold of her arm. He sort of pushed her against the bunk in the corner, so she sat down, and he sat down with her, and started talking. Telling her she should bed him, she should be flattered, all that stuff. I could tell she was upset; she got very pink and then pale, and she looked around — but what could we do? He was a corporal. He kept talking louder, and then he said —" Saben stopped abruptly and blushed.

"Yes? What?"

"He said she must have bedded someone, to be a file leader. It was terrible, sir, Paks of all people, and she was really angry. I didn't think he should be acting like that, so I left to find you. Only I couldn't find you or our corporals, for the longest time — I didn't want to yell it out to the whole courtyard — and when I finally asked a guard, he said you were in the Duke's court with the captain. The guard at the gate wouldn't let me in, and at first he didn't want to take a message. I shouldn't have left, I guess, but I didn't know they'd beat her up."

"You couldn't tell. Next time there's trouble, though, go to one of the guards at once to find me. Now, do you remember who else was in the room when Stephi came, and who left before you?"

"Korryn and Jens, Lurtli, Pinnwa, and Vik, I think. Vik left just as the corporal came in; I don't know about the others. I was watching Paks."

"Saben, have you ever asked Paks to bed you?"

"No. I've wanted to, though. But she has enough trouble with Korryn bothering her; I didn't want to be that kind of worry. If she wants it, she'll let me know. We're friends, anyway."

"All right, Saben; you can go."

"Sir, you won't let them hurt her any more, will you?"

"I'm doing what I can."

But, sir — "

"Enough, Saben. Go on, now."

A full glass later, after talking to everyone he'd summoned, Stammel faced his corporals and sighed.

"I'm convinced," he said. "And you are. But I wish it were any captain but Sejek."

"He's a hard man," said Devlin, nodding.

"And stubborn. If he's still in the same mood, evidence won't mean a thing to him. Once he's made up his mind —"

26

"You can insist that Valichi preside," said Bosk suddenly.

"By Tir, I can! How did I forget that? It's not as if Valichi yielded command to Sejek; he was just away. And since she's a recruit — of course her commander has jurisdiction." He rose. "Sejek's going to be furious, I don't doubt, but with what we've found, he'll have to agree. I hope." With a wave of his hand, he left the recruit barracks for the Duke's Court.

At the gate, he spoke to the guard. "I need to speak to the captain."

"He's gone up," said the guard. "Are you sure you want to disturb him?"

"He's not asleep," said Stammel, cocking his head at a lighted window across the court. "I need to see him before he goes to bed."

"About — ?"

"Just announce me. He'll see me."

"On your head, Stammel."

"It already is." Together they walked across the court and the guard spoke to the door sentry.

"Very well, sir. Down this passage, up the stairs, second door on the right. Not carrying any weapons, are you?" Stammel sighed and handed over his dagger. "Thank you, Sergeant."

Stammel took a deep breath, checked the hang of his cloak, and strode down the passage, up the stairs, to pause in the second doorway on the right. Inside the room, a roomy study, the captain sat writing in the light of a double oil lamp. The captain finished his line and glanced at the door.

"Come in, Sergeant Stammel. Did you check on your recruit?" Captain Sejek's broad, rather flat face rarely showed much expression, and didn't now.

"Yes, sir." Stammel stood stiffly halfway between the door and the desk.

"Well?"

"Sir, I'm not — easy about this."

"Tir's bones, man, no one expects you to be happy about one of your recruits going crazy — it just happens sometimes. Has she calmed down at all yet?"

"Sir, according to the guards who took her down, she made no resistance; she is not violent now."

"Well, she was violent enough. Of course she's big, but I never thought a recruit could mix it with Stephi and come off on top. That man's known to be a tough unarmed fighter. Still, I suppose the surprise — " The captain leaned back in his chair and let the pause lengthen. Finally Stammel broke it, his voice as neutral as he could make it.

"Sir, I don't think that's the whole story."

"Well, Stammel, she'd have some sort of story cooked up."

"No, sir. It's not that."

"Well, what is it? You won't make me like it better by being coy."

"Captain, I wish you'd go and look at her — just look — or send someone you trust — "

The captain raised his eyebrows. A danger signal. "What — has she been drugged?"

"No, sir. Beaten."

27

"Beaten? You're sure? All I saw was a royal black eye and a bloody nose — maybe broken — but that's nothing."

"No, sir. More than that — a lot more."

"Well, maybe the guards gave her a few licks going to the cells."

"They say they didn't; they say she was quiet." Stammel sighed. "Sir, what she looks like now, I don't see how she could have hurt Stephi much. How bad is he, really?"

"He's in the infirmary; they say he'll live. Has two broken fingers, fingerprints on his throat — I don't know what else. He seemed dazed, couldn't really talk to me, and the surgeon said to let him sleep. But really, Stammel, that doesn't get you anywhere. She attacked a corporal. If she got beaten up, she deserved it."

"I wish you'd look, sir," said Stammel doggedly.

"I'll see her in the morning: not before. You realize there's no doubt she's guilty, don't you? An eyewitness out of your own unit, plus Stephi — don't you?"

Stammel stood perfectly still, expressionless. "No, sir. I think there is a doubt."

"Stammel, what kind of ridiculous story had she come up with?"

"It's not her story, sir; it's looking at her, and realizing that Korryn, the other recruit, must have been lying about one thing at least. She could not, absolutely could *not* have been winning over Stephi in her condition. She can't even stand up — "

"She's faking."

"No, sir. Sir, I know that recruit, one of the best we've had, and she is not faking. That Korryn, he's been walking on the edge since he joined, and if he's lying about having to pull her off, he could be lying about the whole thing."

"What about Stephi?" asked the captain coldly.

"I don't know." Stammel sighed. "I know him too, Captain, and he's always had a good reputation. But — something's wrong here, sir, and I don't think we know all the facts yet."

"Have you found out anything?"

"Yes — not enough for a full defense yet, but — "

"Stammel, are you trying to hold out for a formal trial, or something like that?"

"Yes, sir, I am."

"Oh, for — ! Stammel, how many days till Captain Valichi gets back?"

"Three or four, sir."

"All your precious physical evidence will be gone by then."

"Not Paksenarrion's. Besides, you could take evidence tomorrow."

Sejek was scowling as he considered this. "Both of us are a bit partisan on this case," he said finally.

"Yes, sir. I wouldn't ask you to accept my assessment. But what about calling witnesses from Duke's East, say, who could come, examine, and present their findings to Captain Valichi?"

The captain thought a moment. "I suppose that could be done, though it

28

seems a waste of time." He glanced up at Stammel. "You realize Val may be just as summary as I would be — "

"Yes, sir, but — "

"But Valichi is the recruit captain, and has jurisdiction. All right, I won't argue on that; you have the right to ask a trial if you think it's justified. Now, who were you thinking of as witnesses?"

Stammel frowned. "I was thinking through the Council members, sir, for those with military background and experience in court. I don't like Mayor Fontaine myself, as you probably know, but he's honest and no fool."

The captain nodded. "He's said much the same about you, Stammel. I never did know what your row was about."

"Least said, soonest mended, sir, and I don't expect he'd say different to that, either."

"Very well. Heribert Fontaine for one. D'you want two or three?"

"As few as may be; I still think something very odd is going on. I thought of Kolya Ministiera for the second. She was a corporal in Padug's cohort at the siege of Cortes Cilwan."

"I don't remember her."

"Fairly tall, dark — graying now, of course — she lost an arm that campaign, or she'd have made sergeant the next year. She has an orchard."

"I suppose I'd better write a summons. Blast you, Stammel, you might have thought of all this a little earlier."

"Sir."

"Your recruit had better look the worse for wear in the morning. Come to that, if you go back to check on her — you were planning to, weren't you?" Stammel nodded. "Well then, I want you to take a guard along — just to keep the chain of evidence quite clear." The captain went on writing. Stammel stood quietly, seething over the implication of that remark. "Here — " said the captain when he had finished. "Send these over to Duke's East tonight. We'll see the evidence — and her testimony, if you want — before breakfast. Have troops paraded by sunrise, and we'll get everything cleared up early on, I should think."

"Yes, sir. I have recruit Korryn, sir, in custody; I'd like him to be examined too."

"Very well; anything else?"

"Yes, sir, there is. I'd like to ask the captain's permission for the quartermaster's assistant, Maia, to check on Paksenarrion for the rest of the night. She has some knowledge of healing."

"Do you really think it's necessary? No — never mind: you wouldn't be putting yourself into this position if you didn't. Do what you think necessary. Just remember that she is a prisoner, not an honored guest. No one is to enter the cell alone, and the only mitigations to the ban must be lifesaving. I may not have the right to try her, but I can ban her."

"Yes, sir. Thank you, sir."

"Now take those summonses, and let me get some sleep. Dismissed."

"Yes, sir." Stammel took a deep breath as soon as he was out of the door, loosening the knot in his shoulders. He had achieved the concessions he'd come for, more than he'd expected to get. At the foot of the stairs, he almost collided with the Duke's steward, Venneristimon, whose dark robes blended into the shadowy hall.

"In a hurry so late, Sergeant Stammel?" asked Venneristimon.

"The captain's request," answered Stammel shortly. He never knew quite where he stood with Venner.

"Ah, well — then I won't keep you. I was but going to inquire about the well-being of your recruit, the one in trouble."

"Pretty well beaten up. But excuse me, Venner; I must go."

"Certainly. Is it far?"

"Not so far. Sentry — my dagger, please."

"Yes, Sergeant. Here 'tis."

Stammel could feel Venner's eyes following him as he clattered down the steps into the courtyard and headed for the Duke's Gate. The guard let him out without comment, and he broke into a jog across the main court. Maia, Devlin, and Bosk were waiting for him in the duty room. He gave them a grim smile.

"We're a little forwarder," he began. "First of all, he's agreed to a trial when Captain Valichi comes back: he wasn't happy about it, but he did agree. I have summonses for Fontaine and Ministiera, as witnesses tomorrow morning. Dev, I'll want you to ride over to Duke's East in a few minutes with them. Maia, he's given permission for you to check on Paks tonight, and even mitigate the ban if necessary — but don't push it. You'll have a guard with you, including in the cell. I'd like to know what you think of her injuries — can you tell if she was raped as well as beaten, for a start. Bosk, he wants the troops assembled before sunrise; I'm about to inform the other sergeants, but you see to it for our unit. Paks and Korryn won't be in formation. Jens will, but be ready to take him out."

"Do you have any idea yet what happened to Stephi?" asked Devlin.

"No. Neither does Sejek, if it comes to that. He can't see how a recruit — any recruit — could knock Stephi about enough that he couldn't explain himself. I still don't know how badly Stephi is hurt."

"Are you going to talk to Korryn?"

"Tonight? No. I couldn't keep my hands off him."

"Hmmph. I'll be back in about a glass, barring accidents." Devlin picked up the summonses and turned.

"Don't have any tonight. Want an escort?"

"No, sir. I'll just take the fastest horse I can find." Devlin ducked out of the room.

"Shall I go down now?" asked Maia.

"Yes. She didn't look too good when I was there an hour or so ago. Take some water. I gave her some, ban or no: she'd been heaving and was too dry."

"I'll do that. Do you need to speak to the guards for me?"

"Maybe I should." Stammel led the way from the duty room toward the

30

prison stairs. "Should be someone around here — ah, there you are. Forli, the captain has given permission for Maia to check the prisoner's injuries during the night, but she's to have someone with her in the cell. Can you see to it?"

"Certainly, sir, but I'll have to confirm those orders with the captain in the morning — "

"That's fine. I know it's unusual, but it's one of the things I went to ask him about. Do you want me to call over one of the reliefs?"

"No, Sergeant, I'll take care of that." The guard led Maia down the stairs toward the cells. Stammel walked out into the yard toward the other barracks.

Chapter Four

This time the noise of boots in the hall was much louder. Paksenarrion struggled to sit up as they came closer. It must be morning. Her heart began to pound. Maia had said that Stammel believed her, but Stammel's belief was not enough, she realized. She still didn't know if they would even listen to her side of it. The door opened. Two guards carried torches, and two came into the cell.

"Come on, now," said the darker one. "It's time."

Paks made it to her feet, unsteadily, then stumbled over the bucket. The guards caught her arms to steady her. She was even stiffer than she had been the night before, and her head swam. The guards urged her out of the cell, holding her upright. With every step, the bronze chain rattled on the stone flags and dragged at her ankles. She had never imagined how hard it would be to walk with chains on. She peered toward the stairs — a long way. The guards pushed her forward. She clenched her teeth, determined not to faint. As she walked, her tunic began to pull free from her legs; she could feel blood trickling down as one of the scabs tore loose.

At the foot of the stairs, Paks swayed as she tried to look up. Her right foot would not lift enough to clear the first step. She tried the left, and made it. With the guards' help, she hauled herself from one step to the next, but at the landing she could go no further. She broke into a cold sweat and her vision blurred.

"No sense in this," she heard one of the guards say. "Let's get her on up." She was hoisted between them and carried to the top of the stairs, and then to the barracks entrance.

Although the sun had not cleared the wall, there was ample light to see the precise formations drawn up facing the messhall and infirmary. An open space larger than usual had been left in front of them. The guards turned Paks to the left, and began moving her along the left flank of the assembly. Paks tried to hold herself upright and walk properly, but she could hardly hobble along. Not an eye slid sideways to look at her; she stared straight at the mess hall windows ahead. If only this weren't in front of everyone — everyone would see her battered face and ripped tunic. She shivered.

"Just a bit more," muttered the fair guard, holding her up as she tripped over the chain yet again. At last they came to the corner, turned right, and

32

approached the center of the open area. Now Paks could see the bearded man in chain mail — the captain — and the corporal with a mouse under one eye and a bandaged hand, and Korryn. She had caught a glimpse of Stammel, but he was now behind her, at the head of his unit. She was placed in a line with Stephi and Korryn, facing the captain. Behind him were two strangers, a gray-bearded man in a plum-colored robe, and a one-armed woman in brown. Paks shivered again at the bite of chill morning air on her cuts and bruises. The captain stepped back to confer with the two strangers; Paks could not hear what they said. Then he came forward to address the assembly.

"We are met, this morning," he said, "to consider evidence pertaining to an assault or apparent assault yesterday evening by a recruit on a corporal of the regular Company. Evidence is taken at open assembly, so that none can doubt what was seen and heard. This evidence will be presented to Captain Valichi, who has presumptive jurisdiction, on his return. Two witnesses, having nothing to do with any of those being examined, will assess the physical condition of those implicated and hear their testimony. The witnesses are Mayor Heribert Fontaine of Duke's East, and Kolya Ministiera, on the Council of Duke's East. You may proceed."

The two witnesses went first to Stephi, walked around him, and then approached Korryn. After looking him over, they came to Paksenarrion. She tried not to look at them. The woman reached out to touch Paks's swollen face; her touch was gentle, but Paks winced. One of them felt of her tunic in back, where it was stiff with dried blood. They walked back to the captain, and spoke softly. He nodded.

"Guards, strip them," he ordered. Paks was suddenly terrified; she began trembling violently.

"Take it easy, now," muttered the dark guard. "They just want to look at all the damage. Be still." Meanwhile the other guard had run a dagger along the shoulder seams of her tunic from neck to sleeve-cuff, freeing it from the chains to fall around her feet. She glanced sideways. Stephi was taking off his own uniform; the guards pulled Korryn's tunic off over his head. Again the witnesses approached them in the same order. Paks waited, trying not to show her fear.

At last they were back to her. Again they walked around her — but this time they spoke to her and each other.

"Tilt your head up," said the woman. "Look, Mayor, that's a bruise, isn't it?"

"Surely — one hand only, I think. Stand up a bit straighter, there — " Paks tried to straighten, but her belly was too sore. "Bruises there, too, and she can't straighten. Can't tell what instrument — could have been fist, foot, elbow — "

"Those welts are clearly from a strap of some sort — "

The witnesses walked back to the captain, leaving Paks shaky and sick. This time they spoke loudly enough to be heard by all.

"That man," the mayor nodded toward Stephi, "has a bruise on the left cheekbone, probably from a fist blow. Two fingers of his right hand are

33

broken. The knuckles of his left hand are skinned and bruised; he also has a bruise on his right shin. We find no other injuries.

"The male recruit has skinned knuckles on both hands, and a skinned knee. We find no other injuries."

The mayor paused to clear his throat. "The female recruit," he said, "has more extensive injuries. A cut two fingersbreadth wide above the left eye, another such cut above the right eye, much bruising of the right cheek and jaw, the right eye swollen shut, broken nose, possible broken jaw, bruised throat, bruises on both upper arms and both forearms, bruised and skinned knuckles on both hands — "

Paks, listening to the list of her injuries, felt the descriptions as an echo of the blows that caused them. She was determined not to faint in front of everyone, but her knees loosened and her head drooped. The dark guard shook her arm. "Don't listen to that," he muttered. "Look up; count the mess hall windows. You can make it." Paks stared at the windows, trying to shut out the mayor's voice.

" — two welts across her shoulders," the mayor was saying, "and a gash that could be from a blade or some stiff instrument on a whip. Similar welts on buttocks and thighs, including several more gashes. Bruises on ribs and belly — from hard blows, but with what is uncertain. Bruises on thighs, especially intense on upper inner thighs. Some sign of internal bleeding. The external evidence, Captain, is consistent with rape. Additional examination would be necessary to confirm that, if it is at issue."

Paks noticed that the captain was looking at her for the first time; she could not tell if he was still angry with her.

"Have you any additional comments, Councilor Ministiera?" asked the captain.

"Captain Sejek, when one finds a woman beaten up like this, and two men only lightly marked, the usual interpretation is that the men assaulted the woman." The dark woman's voice was brusque, with an edge of sarcasm. "But she is in chains, so I suppose she's charged with assaulting them. On the evidence, without testimony, that's absurd. Even if she started the fight, she didn't do much damage — and she's been well punished. Furthermore, chains are clearly unnecessary. She can hardly stand up, let alone escape. She should be in the infirmary if you want her in shape to stand trial."

The captain nodded. "Sergeant Stammel," he called.

"Sir."

"Convey your recruit to the infirmary; the witnesses will take her testimony later. Guards, you may strike the chains."

"Hold up, now, till we get them off," said the fair guard softly. "Seb'll have to go for a chisel and stone — not long."

Stammel slipped an arm under hers on the other side. "You'll be all right, Paks. Take it easy."

The dark guard came back with his implements, and chiseled off the bent spikes that fastened wrist and ankle cuffs. "There you go. Need any help, Sergeant?"

34

"We'll make it. Keep an eye on Bosk; he may need you."

The guard grinned. "Aha!" He picked up the fallen chains and moved to the side of the courtyard.

With Stammel's support, Paks was able to manage the few yards to the door of the infirmary. Once inside, she slumped against him, shaking and sick again. He swung her into the nearest bunk, and pulled a linen sheet over her. Maia was ready with a bowl of poultices and a jug of numbwine.

As Stammel came back out, he looked square at Korryn's face. Korryn ducked his head and turned even paler than before. Stammel walked back to the head of his unit, impassive.

"Are you ready to take testimony?" asked the captain. The witnesses nodded. "Very well. I'll begin. After supper last night, I was chatting with the recruit sergeants and corporals in the Duke's Court, when one of the guards brought word that a recruit sought Sergeant Stammel because of trouble in the barracks. The recruit stated that Corporal Stephi was involved. Stammel and I and Stammel's two corporals went directly to the barracks. As I came to the door, I saw that recruit — " he pointed at Korryn, "holding the woman. Stephi was lying on the floor with blood all over his face and tunic, and fingermarks on his throat. The woman appeared to have a black eye and bloody nose; she didn't look nearly as bad as she did this morning, nor did she complain of any injury. The recruit holding her stated that he had restrained her from killing Stephi, that he had just then gained control of her. Stephi seemed dazed and was unable to give a coherent story, but did say that he had asked the woman to bed him. The recruit said that Stephi had teased her when she refused, but nothing more, and that she had attacked him. On the evidence, Stephi appeared to be injured, perhaps seriously. I had the woman secured under ban, and set a summary trial for this morning. Sergeant Stammel requested permission to question the woman about her actions, which I granted, and several hours later he appeared with a request for a formal trial, and evidence to be taken today by witnesses."

"Did the woman say anything yesterday? Did you question her then?"

"No. The other recruit did all the talking. She didn't argue. It seemed obvious."

The mayor turned to Stammel. "Is this the way you remember it?"

"Yes, Mr. Mayor. May I amplify?"

"Go ahead."

"When I visited Paksenarrion in the cell, I realized that she had taken more damage than was at first apparent. It seemed to me that her injuries made the story told by Korryn — the other recruit — inconsistent or even impossible. Her story made more sense." Stammel repeated what Paksenarrion had told him, and then reviewed his own reasoning. "This story fit her injuries better than Korryn's. Paksenarrion has been, until this, an outstanding recruit, honest and hardworking. Korryn has a grudge against her; she has refused to bed him."

"What is her background, Sergeant?"

35

"She's a sheepfarmer's daughter, from the northwest. She ran away from home to join us."

"And this — uh — Korryn?"

"He joined us in White Creek; claimed to have been in Count Serlin's guard, but wanted more — action, I believe he said."

"And his record?"

Stammel frowned. "He has not done anything that would require his expulsion." The unsaid "yet" trembled in the air. "However, he has been the subject of complaint by Corporals Bosk and Devlin, and Armsmaster Siger."

"That's not fair!" Korryn's face twisted in anger. "You favor her; you always have! A pretty face — I'll warrant one of you has bedded her — "

Bosk and Devlin each took an involuntary step forward; Stammel was rigid and white with fury. Before he could say anything, Kolya Ministiera stepped toward Korryn and looked him up and down.

"Hmmph!" she snorted. "A fine — man — you are." She spat at his feet, and turned back to the captain with a swirl of her brown robe. "I suppose we must hear his testimony, just to keep things straight."

"He's out, whatever he says now," growled Stammel.

"Nonetheless," said the captain. "He must speak. And keep to the truth — " he said to Korryn, " — if you can, recruit."

Korryn's eyes slid from side to side. "It is the truth — what I said. She went crazy, and started hitting this corporal, and I thought he could take care of her, and I guess he did hit her a few times. Then she got a grip on his throat, and I decided to help him out and pull her off. He'll tell you — " Korryn gestured at Stephi. "I — I thought it was just a bit of fun at first, and then — I did what I thought was right," he said, pulling himself erect. "Maybe I made a mistake — but you can't punish a man for doing what he thinks is right."

The captain and witnesses received this in tight-lipped silence. "Is there," the captain asked Stammel after a pause, "any other witness to all this?"

"That recruit we met coming out of the door — the one who said he was going for help — he should have seen something."

"Where is he?"

"Corporal Bosk," said Stammel. "Escort Jens to the front, please."

"No!" came a squeal from behind Stammel. "I — I don't know anything — I didn't see — I — I just came out — "

"He's a friend of Korryn's," said Stammel, as Bosk half-dragged Jens out of formation to the front.

The captain beckoned to two of the guards. They took Jens's arms and forced him upright. "Now then — what's his name, Stammel?"

"Jens, sir."

"Jens. I expect you to tell us the truth, right now. Did you see a fight involving Paksenarrion, Korryn, and Stephi, or any two of them?"

"I — " Jens looked frantically from side to side; when he met Korryn's fierce gaze he flinched. "I — I saw a little tussle, sir — sort of — "

36

"A little tussle? Be specific now: did you see it start?"

"N-no — I was — was — uh — cleaning my boots. Sir."

"Did you see any blows struck at all?"

"Well — I saw — I saw Paks and that man rolling on the floor, and then Korryn said — said go look at the door — " Jens was staring at his feet.

"At the *door*?"

"Yes, sir. He — uh — said I should — should look for the sergeant, sir."

"Oh? And did you?"

"Yes. I looked, but I couldn't see him — I mean, until you came."

"And just what did he tell you to do if you saw the sergeant, eh?" asked Kolya. She moved to his side and jerked his head up. "Look at me! What did he tell you?"

Jens began to tremble. "He said — he said to tell him."

"Tell who, the sergeant?"

"No. Tell him — Korryn — "

"If you saw the sergeant. I see." Kolya backed away. "I don't know about your Corporal Stephi, Captain, but that recruit — " she jerked a shoulder at Korryn, "is lying in his teeth."

"Agreed," said the captain.

"And the other one isn't much better," she said with distaste, looking at Jens.

"They'd both better go under guard," said Sejek. "Captain Valichi won't be back for several days, so they can't be confined under ban the whole time, but until tomorrow morning — "

"But — but ask him!" interrupted Korryn. "Ask the corporal! He'll tell you I'm not lying."

The witnesses turned toward Corporal Stephi, who had stood silent through everything. But the captain intervened.

"Before you question him, I want to tell you what happened this morning."

"Very well, Captain," said the mayor.

"This morning when I woke, I had a message from the surgeon. Stephi woke last night, and wanted to see me, but they did not call me because it was so late. This morning I went to see how he was, and found that he had no memory of the events last evening. None at all. I did not want to suggest things to him, so I told him only that he would be examined by witnesses about some trouble. The surgeon could find no physical cause for his loss of memory, and as you can see, the blood I saw on him yesterday was not his own. I must say that since he's been in my cohort, he has always been a competent, sober soldier and a good corporal, with no faults against him. I cannot imagine what caused his behavior, but I can swear that it is not typical."

"Is it likely that he would pretend a loss of memory, if he had done wrong?" asked the mayor.

"I think not," replied Sejek. "He has always been honest, in my experience."

"Hmm." The mayor turned to Corporal Stephi. "You have seen the evidence of the injuries suffered by you and others, and you have heard what testimony has been given. What is your understanding of what happened?"

"Sir, I have no memory from just after supper last night until I woke in the infirmary. When I woke I felt strange — dizzy — and of course my hand and the bruises hurt. I asked the surgeon what had happened, but when he found I had no memory, he would not say anything, only that I had been found hurt. I — when I heard this morning — and saw that girl — Sir, I've never beaten a woman so. I've never forced one to bed. I don't understand how I could have — but I saw her injuries. Someone hurt her, and if it was — if I did such a thing — I know what you must do — " His voice trailed away.

"Why did you ask to see the captain last night?"

"Because I was frightened. I wanted to know what had happened — I thought the captain would tell me. And — and I couldn't *remember*."

"But, Stephi," said the captain, "you must remember something — maybe just the beginning — you must be able to say whether this recruit is lying." The witnesses stirred but said nothing. Stephi looked at Korryn with distaste.

"Sir — Captain — I cannot remember anything. But I'll tell you, sir, he must be lying. What we've seen and heard — "

"You say that even if it condemns you?"

"Yes. Sir, it's obvious. That girl didn't beat *me* up — and honestly, sir, there's no way she could have." Stephi conveyed all the confidence of a senior veteran, sure of his own fighting ability.

"But you can remember nothing?" prompted the mayor.

Stephi shook his head. "No, sir, I don't. But I don't expect you to believe that. You'll want to test me, I'm sure."

"You *must* remember," yelled Korryn suddenly. "You must — I told you yesterday — " He paled as they all looked at him, and he realized what he had said.

"You told him, eh?" said Kolya softly. "You told him *what*?"

Korryn drove a vicious elbow into the midriff of the guard on his left, and as the man slumped forward he snatched at his sword. The other guard drew his own weapon and darted forward, but Korryn was free with sword in hand, dancing sideways and looking for a way out.

"Take him!" roared the captain, drawing his own sword. Stammel charged, unarmed as he was, with Bosk and Devlin behind him. Korryn swung at Stammel, cursing; Stammel barely evaded the blow. Korryn backed, edging toward the unarmed witnesses as guards converged from around the courtyard. Suddenly Kolya slipped behind him and wrapped a powerful arm around his neck. Korryn fell backwards, gasping. She held him until the guards had jerked the sword out of his hands and grabbed his arms.

"If it were my decision, he'd be in chains," she said calmly, dusting her hand on her robe.

"At once," said Sejek. The guards grinned as they dragged Korryn away. "Now, Stammel — "

"Sir," said Stammel, "I'd like permission to dismiss the formation now. They've seen as much as they can learn from."

"I think you're right. Go ahead, but I'll want you for the rest of this."

"Yes, sir." Stammel turned away. The captain, frowning, spoke to the witnesses.

"Mayor Fontaine, Councilor Ministiera, I appreciate your efforts. You will want to take more testimony from both Paksenarrion and Stephi, I presume."

"Indeed yes," said the mayor. "You have quite a complicated problem here, Captain."

"You'll remand Stephi to the Duke's Court, I assume," said Kolya.

"Yes. I must. Corporal Stephi — " he gestured to the corporal.

"Yes, sir."

"This must be investigated further. You must consider yourself under arrest from this time. I'll have to see whether Stammel will trust your parole; he's within his rights to refuse it until Captain Valichi returns."

"I understand, sir. I wish I did know what happened."

While they were talking, Stammel had spoken to the other recruit sergeants and the formation had dispersed. He had told his own corporals to take the unit outside to drill. "And keep 'em busy," he said, "until I come out and relieve you. We have a lot to work off. I'll be there as soon as I find out how Paks is, and what the captain is going to do."

So it was in a nearly empty courtyard that the captain turned to Stammel and said, "Well, Sergeant, you were right. I wouldn't have thought it, but — "

"Sir, I was sure Paksenarrion was not to blame — but I'm not sure your corporal is. If Korryn gave him something, a drug or something like that — "

"I hadn't thought of that. Something strange has happened — "

"I agree," said Kolya. "And I think this should be discussed in somewhat more privacy."

The mayor nodded. "I'd suggest the Duke's Court, Captain Sejek."

"A good idea. Stephi, get dressed and come with us. Guard, you'd best come too." The captain turned away and headed for the Duke's Gate. Stammel and the witnesses followed him; Stephi pulled on his tunic and came after them, trailed by the guard.

Chapter Five

In the Duke's Court, the little group clustered near the fountain. The witnesses sat on its stone rim; the others stood.

"Tell us first, Stephi, everything that happened yesterday after you left me in Duke's East," said the captain.

"Yes, sir. Well, I came directly here with the men; we didn't stop at all in Duke's East. When we arrived, I asked a recruit to call the quartermaster for me — I don't know what his name was, a stocky brown-haired boy — and had the men put up their horses and turn in their swords. Then I talked to the quartermaster, and gave him your letter, sir, and we went into the storerooms and started marking what we were to take back. Suddenly I realized that it was getting late, and I hadn't told anyone you were coming yet, so I left the quartermaster and went through the Duke's Gate to speak to the steward."

"Had you had anything to eat or drink, Stephi?"

"No, sir, nothing but water. We got here after lunch. But when I'd spoken to the Duke's steward, he asked if I'd like some ale. Tell you the truth, sir, that's one reason I didn't stop in the village. When I came up here six months ago with a message, the steward gave me some ale while I waited for the reply, and — and I was hoping, sir, he might again. Not that I'd have asked, of course, it being the Duke's own ale. But, sir, you know how tasty it is."

"Indeed I do. So you drank ale, then? How much?"

"Well, the steward brought out a ewer and a tankard, and the ewer was full. I poured out a tankard of it, and he left to go back inside and give orders to the servants. It was as good as I remembered, or better. I finished that tankard, sir, and thought of pouring out another. But I thought how strong the ale was, and I didn't want to be drunk — but he'd said to drink hearty, and it was already out of the cask — he wouldn't pour it back in —" Stephi's tanned face was flushed with embarrassment. "So I — well — sir, I poured it into the flask I was carrying, after pouring the rest of my water out. There was maybe a swallow left in the ewer, and I drank that. Then the steward came back, and asked how I liked the ale, and I said fine, and he asked if I wanted more, or something to eat, and I said no, I'd eat with the men at mess, and thanked him."

"Where is that flask now, Stephi?" asked Kolya.

"With my things, I suppose; I took it back to the barn and put it in my saddlebags."

"Go on, then."

"After that, after I put the flask up, it was nearly time for supper. I saw you ride in, sir, and go on through the Duke's Gate, and then I collected the men and we went to eat."

"What did you eat?"

"The usual, sir. Bread, cheese, stew. The men ate the same. I remember feeling a little — annoyed — at the noise. It seemed louder, all that banging and clattering. I wondered if I shouldn't have had that last swallow of ale, but nobody else seemed to notice anything about me, and I was steady on my feet. But then, sir — it's as if I was — was thinking about something else. You know how you can do something routine, but you aren't thinking about it, and a little later you can't remember if you've done it? I know I left the mess hall, but it's hazy after that. I think I walked out into the court, but I'm not sure even of that. Then — nothing, until I woke in the infirmary." Stephi looked around at the puzzled faces.

"How long would you say it lasted?" asked Kolya of the captain.

"The violent phase — only a quarterglass or a little longer; the loss of memory seems to be about six hours."

"It's consistent with a potion or spell," said the mayor.

"A potion, I'd say. We don't have a mage in range for this," said the captain.

"I think we need to check the Duke's ale. If someone has tampered with it — " The mayor's long face scowled at them.

"I'll get the steward." Sejek disappeared into the arched doorway of the Duke's Hall. It was some little time before he came out; he had a large flask of tawny liquid, and the steward carried a ewer and tankard on a tray. Venneristimon looked concerned, and was talking as he came.

"I'm quite sure, Captain Sejek," he was saying, "that nothing is wrong with the Duke's ale. It's true that this cask has been tapped some time, but I fail to see how anything could have adulterated it. Perhaps I simply should not have given the poor fellow quite so much. I mean, he *seemed* responsible."

"We'll have to check it, Venner, and make sure. The Duke has enemies enough who might wish to poison his stores." The captain put the flask he was carrying down in front of the witnesses. "I drew this off, myself," he said. "It smelled all right. I had Venner bring out the same ewer and tankard he served Stephi with. Do you recognize 'em, Stephi?"

Stephi reached for the utensils and Venner released them. He turned the tankard around in his hands. "Yes, sir, it's the same. There's a dent here on the rim, see? And the ewer matched the pattern, same as this one does."

"I was telling the captain," Venner put in, "that of course these things were washed up at once. If there was anything, it would be gone."

The witnesses all examined the ewer and tankard. "It looks innocent enough," said the mayor. "But it could have held anything."

"Let's test the ale," said Kolya.

"Go ahead," said the captain, nodding toward the flask. Kolya picked it up and sniffed.

"Smells like good ale. But I wonder if we could smell a potion, or would the ale cover it?"

Stammel shrugged. "I don't know — I've heard that some potions have

41

a strong smell, but who's to say?"

"Try a single drop," suggested the mayor. "See what happens."

"If I go wild," said Kolya, "don't break my arm; I've got apple harvest coming soon." She sipped the ale. "Tastes good. This is what he serves at the high feasts, isn't it, Venner?"

"Yes, it is."

"Tastes just as it did last year, if I'm any judge. No aftertaste."

"I think the corporal just drank too much," Venner said again. "It is strong ale, and I should not have brought a full ewer."

"It can't be that, Venner; he didn't drink it all," said the captain. "He drank only one tankard — and one tankard of anything wouldn't make Stephi drunk. He poured the rest into his water flask."

"Stephi," said Stammel. "Do you have any sort of potion at all — anything you might have added to that ale later, and forgotten?"

Stephi thought a moment. "Well — " he looked embarrassed. "I do have a — sort of a — a love potion. I got it from an old granny down the other side of Vérella. But — there's not much to it, sir, really, and besides, I didn't take it."

Kolya looked at him. "A *love* potion?"

"It's — it's something my girl and I enjoy — we share it — "

The captain shook his head. "The things I never knew about you, Stephi."

"But it's harmless, sir, really. It's just like a bit of wine, only more so. Just makes the night more fun, is all."

"Still, we'd better check it. It might not be as harmless as you think. Did you get it from the same person this time as before?"

"Well, no, sir, I didn't. But it's a simple sort of thing — lots of the grannies sell it. I usually get it from one of the forest-folk tribes in Aarenis, but we were on the road here, and this little old lady asked did I want anything. I'm sure it's all right, sir, and even if it's not, I never took it."

"Where is it?"

"With the rest of my things, in the saddlebags."

"We'll take a look." The captain turned. "Now where has Venner gotten off to? Stephi, who knows where your things are?"

"Any of the men that came with me would know, or I could show you."

"Stammel, why don't you find them for us?"

"Yes, sir. Would you want one of the witnesses to come along?"

Sejek shook his head. "Not unless they want to."

Stammel left the Duke's Court and angled across the main courtyard to the stable. Stephi's squad was hanging around the stable entrance, looking wary. He nodded to them.

"We need Stephi's saddlebags," he said. They looked sideways at each other.

"Sergeant — what're they going to do? Stephi's a good corporal — "

"I can't say. We don't know enough yet, and anyway it's the Duke's decision. Now — where are his things?"

A lanky private led the way into the smaller tack room. "That's Stephi's," he said. "The first on that row." Stammel lifted the saddlebags from their peg and turned toward the door.

42

"Come along," he said, "and tell me who's handled these things."

"Nobody, sir; Stephi came in before supper from the Duke's Court, and put his flask in with the rest, and nobody's been at his things since that I know of."

As Stammel came across the Duke's Court toward the others, he saw Venner coming down the steps from the Hall. He wondered briefly where Venner had been, but dropped the thought as he handed the saddlebags to the captain.

"These are yours, Stephi?" asked the captain.

"Yes, sir. The flask will be in the right one, in a holder, and the potion bottle is in the left one, wrapped in my spare socks."

They all watched as the captain opened the flaps of the saddlebags and took out the contents. He found the flask and set it aside, unopened for the moment. "It has liquid in it," he said. "I can't tell how much." He began rummaging in the other saddlebags, removing a neatly rolled cloak and a comb, then a single sock, then another one, and finally a small cloudy-glass bottle with a glass stopper. "It wasn't in the socks, Stephi," he said as he slid out the stopper. "Phew! What a smell!" He looked up. "It's empty." He passed the bottle to the mayor, who sniffed, wrinkled his nose, and passed it to Kolya. She did the same before handing it to Stammel.

"Is this the same bottle?" he asked as he sniffed cautiously at the opening.

"Yes, sir. It looks like it. But it didn't have a bad smell before. May I smell it now?"

"Go ahead," said the captain. "But you wouldn't have smelled it — looks like it had a wax seal around the stopper."

Stephi sniffed the bottle. "It's strange — but it reminds me of something. Just a little. Who could have emptied it?"

"One of your men says no one touched your things, but you, when you came out of the Duke's Court yesterday," said Stammel.

"But all I did was put the flask back. I didn't open this bottle."

"Let's examine the flask," said the captain. He opened it and looked in. "It's not even half full, and the smell's here, too."

Again the witnesses checked for themselves. "If what made Corporal Stephi act unlike himself and forget what happened was in what he drank, then the evidence is that it came from this potion bottle," said the mayor.

"But I didn't open it," Stephi repeated.

"You don't remember opening it," said Kolya. "If it was strong enough magic, you wouldn't remember."

"But I remember going in to supper after putting the flask away."

"Stephi, are you sure you didn't have a few more swallows of ale — after supper, maybe?" Captain Sejek sounded more tired than angry.

"Sir, I — I thought I was sure I'd never do anything like I must have done. I don't *think* I drank any more — or opened the potion. But — how can I be sure? How can I be sure of anything?"

"Stephi — I don't know." Sejek sighed. "I believe that whatever you did was under some kind of outside influence. Right now that potion seems the likeliest to me — it wasn't what you thought. The witnesses will have their own opinions — " He glanced at them.

"We still need the woman's testimony — Paksenarrion's," said Kolya.

"From what Stammel said, I doubt it will help; but go ahead, of course."

"I wonder if we can find out what the potion is," said the mayor. "And I still have a concern for the Duke's ale. Are we sure it is not contaminated? The smell in this bottle is suggestive, but — "

"We could seal it and hope it keeps until the Duke's Court; he'll have his mage there."

"I've marked and sealed the cask," Venner said. As they looked at him in surprise, he pursed his thin lips. "That's why I went back inside. The entire cask will be available for examination at the trial."

"All right, then," said Sejek. "If you, Councilor Ministiera, will take Paksenarrion's testimony, and gather such evidence as might be needed, the rest of us can get back to our business. Stammel — about Stephi's parole — " Stammel sighed. "Sir, I've known Stephi as long as you — and I trust him. But the recruits — especially my unit — won't understand if you leave him free. They know that Paks was chained under ban last night. Korryn's under ban now — "

"Sir, he's right," said Stephi. "I can't believe that I went — crazy or something — and did *that* to anyone, but the evidence is against me. The troops won't like it; they won't understand it, if I'm not under guard."

"I don't say put him under ban," said Stammel. "He's cooperated, we think someone may have magicked him — so don't ban him. But — "

"I see your point," said Sejek, frowning. "Very well. Stephi, I'm sorry, but you'll have to spend your time in the cell. I'll be down to check on you, and you're not under ban."

"That's all right, sir. I understand. I would like — if it's possible — to know how the girl is, and if she's well enough later, I'd like to — to apologize — "

"We'll see, Stephi." Sejek nodded to the guard, and they watched as Stephi was led back to the main court. The captain sighed heavily. "I'd like to get my hands on that granny, whoever she is. Tir's gut, but that's a fine soldier to be dumped in such trouble. Stammel, you'll need to see to your unit, but I'd like to talk to you later."

"Yes, sir. Any particular time?"

"Not until after lunch, at least. It'll take me that long to settle my men and make some kind of written report of this. When you've time, check with me. I may have to put you off an hour or so, but I'll try to be ready."

"Yes, sir." Stammel bowed slightly, and headed for the infirmary, tailing Kolya who was disappearing through the door.

Paksenarrion lay quietly as Maia cleaned and poulticed her thighs; a large cool poultice already covered the swollen half of her face. She'd been given a mug of beef broth and a half-mug of numbwine, and felt as if she were floating a handspan above the bed. She heard the door open, and saw Maia glance up.

"Well, Kolya; do you need to see her again?"

"If she's able. What did the surgeon say?"

"She'll mend. Her eye's all right. She's had numbwine; she'll be drowsy and drifting a bit. Eh — Paks. Come on, Paks, wake up."

Paks swallowed and tried to speak. Not much sound came out. She tried to look at Kolya, but found she couldn't turn her head. Kolya suddenly appeared beside the bed. Paks blinked her good eye. She had not really looked at the witness before. Now she noticed black hair streaked with gray, black eyes, dark brows angled across a tan, weathered face. She blinked again, her eyes dropping to Kolya's broad shoulders, her arm — the sleeve of her robe covered the stump of her left arm.

"She's awake," said Kolya. "So — they call you Paks, eh? I'm Kolya Ministiera, one of the witnesses. We need to take your testimony on this. Can you speak?"

Paks tried again and managed a hoarse croak.

"Water might help." Kolya turned away and reappeared with a mug. "Can you hold the mug? Good. Now drink and try again."

Paks took a swallow or two of water, gingerly felt the inside of her mouth with her tongue, and managed to say, "I can speak now, Lady."

Kolya snorted. "I'm no 'lady,' child: just a pensioned-off old soldier."

"But — didn't he say — you are on the Council?" Paks stumbled over the words. Even after numbwine, it hurt to move her mouth.

"That's nothing but the Duke knowing I'm the Duke's man still. No, I farm now, and raise apples. I'm no fine lady."

"I — I didn't know you were a soldier," said Paks slowly, trying not to look for the missing arm.

"Yes — I was a corporal, same as Stephi, when I lost my arm. Don't look so solemn, child. That was just bad luck — or good luck, if you like, that I lived. And the Duke's treated me well: a grant of land, and a seat on the Council."

Paksenarrion thought briefly of being as Kolya was, beyond warfare, pensioned off to a farm. She shivered. "But — what do I call you, if not lady?"

"Well, if you want to be formal, you could say Councilor Ministiera, but with you full of numbwine I doubt you'd get your tongue around that. Kolya's fine. I won't bite."

"Yes — Kolya."

"Now, Sergeant Stammel gave me the outline of your story, but I still have some questions for you. Had Corporal Stephi spoken to you at any time before he entered your barracks?"

"No — in fact, I didn't really see him before. Only out of the corner of my eye as they rode in, and then Armsmaster Siger thumped me for not paying attention."

Kolya chuckled. "With good cause. Take it from me, you never look aside when fighting. But you didn't see him at supper?"

"No — I was talking to Saben."

"I see. I understand that he showed up in your barracks and said he wanted to speak to you. Then he tried to get you to bed him, and tried to force you when you refused. Is that right?"

"Yes. He tried to push me down. Then when I said some things my cousin taught me, he put his hand over my mouth and I bit him. And that's when he got very angry — "

"He hit you first with his belt, Stammel said — "

"And I tried to get past him and away. I really did, Kolya. I wasn't trying to hurt him, or fight, just get away."

"All right, calm down. He'd be too much for you, I imagine."

Paks began to tremble again. "I — I couldn't get free — and he was hitting me, again and again. I couldn't get my breath, and someone was holding me, so I couldn't hit back or get away, and — it hurt so much — " Tears ran down her face. "I — I'm sorry — I don't mean to cry — "

"That's all right. A hard beating takes it out of you." Even in her misery, Paks noticed that Kolya spoke as someone who knew. "You'll be all right in a few days. Paksenarrion, have you ever bedded anyone here?"

"No." Paks fought against the sobs.

"Have you ever bedded anyone?"

"No — I never wanted to."

Kolya sighed. "Paks, we need to know if you were raped as well as beaten — do you know?"

Paks shook her head. "I — I don't know what it would be like. I know it hurts, but I don't know what kind of hurt."

"Well, then, we'll have to take a look. Maia will help me, and I think another swallow of numbwine won't hurt at all. If you sleep all day, so much the better." Kolya fetched the flask of numbwine and poured some into the mug Paks held. "Drink all of that." Paks swallowed, almost choking on the heavy, sweet wine. In a few minutes she felt a soft wave of sleep roll up around her, and drifted away, unknowing.

A few minutes later, Kolya left the infirmary, and almost fell over Stammel who was waiting at the door. "Well?" he asked harshly.

"No," said Kolya. "She wasn't. They put enough bruises on her, and if they'd had another two minutes — but as it is, she wasn't raped. That may save Stephi's hide — or some of it."

"It won't save Korryn's," said Stammel grimly. "That was a neat catch you made, Kolya."

"Thanks. Some things I can still do. I agree you're well rid of that one. I wonder if we'll ever know which of them actually did what — probably not. I presume Korryn's will be a public event."

"Very. That — " Stammel growled and spat. "I can't think of a word. Filth. I should have run him out weeks ago."

Kolya tapped his arm. "Now, Matthis Stammel, you know you aren't that kind. You had to have a good reason. I'd better go on and report to the others. Cheer up — she'll be all right in a few days."

"I hope so. She's a good one, Kolya — almost as good as who she looks like — Tamarrion — if nothing goes wrong."

Kolya looked thoughtful. "Does she? I couldn't tell, with all those bruises. You know you can't protect the good ones, Stammel; it ruins them in the long run."

"I know. But this kind of thing — "

"If she's that good it won't stop her. Nothing stopped Tamarrion. Wait and see — I'd best go."

Chapter Six

By the time Captain Valichi returned, Paksenarrion was up, though her right eye was still swollen shut. She had not returned to her unit; Stammel wanted to report to Valichi, and give him the chance to talk to her if he wished, before she talked to her friends. Instead, Valichi made his decisions on the basis of the witnesses' reports, conferences with Sejek, Stammel, and Stephi, and an interview with Korryn, the last for form's sake only. So early one morning Maia helped Paks back into her recruit uniform, now cleaned and mended, and sent her to join the others in formation to witness Valichi's decisions.

Paks had scarcely time to find her place before they were called to attention. A heavy timbered framework on a low platform was centered before them; on the right stood the witnesses, and on the left was a quartet of guards near a smoking brazier, one holding a straight razor, and one a whip. Paks recognized the dark guard who had held her. She looked at the razor and whip, and shivered.

She heard the noise of boots and chains as Korryn and Jens were brought out of the building into the courtyard. Memory of her own ordeal made her choke. She thought hard about Korryn, about all the things he'd done, to keep from feeling sympathy she wasn't supposed to feel. After all, she'd wanted to beat him herself, in the past.

The prisoners passed in front of the formation. Jens hung back, having to be prodded, half-carried. She could hear his soft fearful moans. It was disgusting. Korryn had new bruises on his face. She wondered who had hit him, and why. Probably the guards, she thought. They halted in front of the platform. Captain Valichi, shorter than Captain Sejek, looking almost square in his armor, moved toward them, facing the assembly.

"You are here to witness the punishment of two former recruits of this Company," he began. "For their crimes they have been expelled from the Company; after their punishment, they will be taken beyond the bounds of the Duke's domains. Should they ever return, they will be liable to additional punishment, as the Duke may direct. Should any of you see them within this domain, you are required to report it to your officers. Their crimes are known to most of you, but I proclaim them. Korryn Maherit was charged with assisting in an assault on another recruit—"

"It's not fair!" yelled Korryn. "It wasn't my fault!" Even before Valichi's command, one of the guards holding him had slugged him.

"— with conspiracy with Jens Hanokensson to prevent detection of this assault," the captain went on, "and with lying to the witnesses called to take testimony in the case. All the evidence and testimony so far indicates that Korryn Maherit did assault and injure Paksenarrion Dorthansdotter, and did instruct Jens Hanokensson to warn him of the approach of any authority, and did attempt to instruct Corporal Stephi of Dorrin's cohort, a veteran member of the Company, in a lie explaining the assault, while Corporal Stephi was temporarily unaware of his own actions, probably through the action of some drug or potion. We have no proof that Korryn Maherit supplied this drug or potion. Jens Hanokensson stands charged with conspiracy with Korryn Maherit to prevent detection of Korryn Maherit's crimes. Both of these men have a bad record in the recruit cohort. The following sentences are imposed by me, as Duke Phelan's lawful representative and cohort commander of recruits. For Jens Hanokensson: five strokes" — Jens moaned again; the guards holding him shook him — "a shaved head, and expulsion. For Korryn Maherit, the Duke's brand on the forehead, forty strokes well-marked, and expulsion *tinisi turin*." Korryn writhed, trying to break free from his guards. "Strip them," said Valichi. Two of the guards by the platform came forward and ripped the recruit tunics from neck to hem, then turned the prisoners to face the formation. The guards forced Jens to his knees, and the one with the razor stepped up behind him. When he felt the first tug at his cinnamon-brown hair, he yelped and flinched.

"Hold still, ye fool," said the guard. "If ye jerk around, I'll cut ye." Tufts of hair fell; Jens had shut his eyes and was rigidly still. The barber worked quickly and roughly; soon nothing was left of the thick hair and mustache. A few shallow grazes oozed blood on his scalp, which was pale above his tanned face. The guards hauled him up the platform to the posts and crossbar, and bound him to it, feet dangling. Then the guard with the whip mounted the platform behind him.

"One," said Captain Valichi. The whip smacked against his back; Paks saw his face twist in pain. "Two." Another smack. He gave a strangled cry. "Three. Four." The captain paused. "Sergeant Stammel — do you want the parting blow?"

"No, sir. Not for this one."

"Five." The last blow fell. Jens's screams softened into sobs as the guards untied his arms and dragged him from the platform. Paks could see the welts standing out on his back; only one was bleeding. The guards moved him away from the platform and held him facing the assembly.

It took four of the guards to hold Korryn as one of them took the brand from the brazier where it had been heating. Paks looked down. She didn't want to see this. She could hear Korryn's muttered curses, the scuffling feet, the hiss and sizzle as the brand etched his forehead. He gave a short cry, followed by gasping sobs. She glanced up for a moment. The guard with the razor was taking off his hair; Korryn's face was white under its tan.

The brand showed stark, a stylized foxhead. Without his hair and beard, his face looked different; he hardly had a chin. His eyes met hers; he snarled a curse at her, and the guards cuffed him. Paks stared over his head; she didn't want him to think she could not watch.

The guards dragged him up the platform — still struggling to break free — and bound his wrists to the crossbar after removing his chains. Then they bound his ankles to bolts Paks had not noticed, and the guard with the razor stepped up to him. Korryn paled even more.

"What are you — ?"

"*Tinisi turin* means shaved — all over — " said the guard, grinning. "Like a shorn lamb, remember?" And shortly the hair on chest, belly, and groin made a heap on the platform. When that guard was through, he stepped back, and the one carrying the whip came forward.

By the tenth stroke, Paks no longer cared what Korryn thought; she stared straight at the mess hall windows. No one had reminded her that she might have been on that platform, but she remembered well enough what Stammel had said when he first came to her cell. She loathed Korryn — would be glad to see him gone — but she could not watch. The blows went on — and on — each counted out by the captain's calm voice. They sounded different now. Korryn sounded different too. She tried not to hear that, and lost the count. Suddenly it was very quiet. She looked up. Korryn hung from his bonds, head drooping; she could see the blood streaking his legs and staining the platform below.

"Well, Sergeant Stammel?" asked the captain.

"Yes, sir, with pleasure." Stammel left his place and mounted the platform. The guard handed him the whip, now glistening along its length. Paks watched, fascinated and horrified, as he braced himself and gave Korryn five powerful blows. Korryn's body jerked, and he gave a last scream and fainted. Stammel ran his hand down Korryn's back and returned to his unit, holding his bloody hand out. He faced Paks, and touched it to her forehead as her eyes widened in shock.

"By this blood your injury is avenged," he said, and took up his position again. Meanwhile one of the guards had taken a pot of blue dye, and was daubing it on Korryn's back. Then he was untied, and lowered to the ground. His back and legs were covered with welts and blood; the blue stain looked ghastly mixed with blood. A guard checked his pulse.

"He'll do," he reported. "Cold water, sir?" The captain nodded. After several minutes, and a bucket of water, Korryn stirred and groaned. When his eyes opened, Captain Valichi nodded, and the guards pulled him to his feet and bound his hands in front of him. Jens, meanwhile, had been dressed in a nightshift, with a rope noose around his neck; his guards looked to the captain.

"Go ahead; take him out."

"West, sir?" The captain nodded in answer, and the guards led Jens away. Korryn now had a rope around his neck too, and at the captain's second nod, his guards tugged, forcing him forward. He could barely keep

49

his feet. Paks looked away, stomach churning. She heard horses' hooves behind the formation, near the gate, muttered voices. Then the hoofbeats moved away, through the gate, and the courtyard was left in silence.

Captain Valichi looked at them for a long moment. "Some of you," he said with a grim smile, "seem impressed by what you saw — I hope you all are. The Duke will not tolerate anything that jeopardizes the strength of the Company. In a few months you will be depending on each other in battle. Each of you must be worthy of your companions' trust, both on and off the field. If you aren't, we'll get rid of you. If you injure a companion, you'll be punished. It may be that some of you don't have the stomach for army life; if so, speak to your sergeant. We don't want cowards. Sergeant Stammel, assign a detail from your unit to clean up this mess, and I'll want to speak with Paksenarrion. The formation is dismissed."

In the unit's duty room, a few minutes later, Paks tried to act calm. "Sit down, Paksenarrion," said Captain Valichi. She sat across the desk from him. Her stomach was a solid knot of apprehension. "Have you talked to any of your friends since this happened?"

"No, sir."

"Good. Paksenarrion, you have a good record, so far. This is the first trouble you've been in, and from the evidence none of it was your fault. Stammel did say that he thought you should confine your use of strong language to terms you knew the meaning of — though calling someone a jacks-hole full of soured witches milk — " Paks gasped and felt herself reddening; the captain smiled and went on, " — is not an excuse for an attack, it can cause trouble. Did you even know that was Pargunese? No? Well, stick to Common or whatever your native language is. Anyway, you're blameless of the brawl itself. Now — you've been injured in the Company, though not, we think, permanently. If you wish to leave, you may. We will give you a recommendation, based on your record, and a pass through the Duke's domain, and a small sum to tide you over until you reach home or find other employment. I can suggest several private guard companies that might hire you with our recommendation. You'll be on light duty until you can see out of that eye again: you may have that long to make your decision — unless you are already determined to leave. Are you?"

"No, sir. I don't want to leave at all." Paks had had a lingering fear that she might be thrown out.

"You're sure?" Paks nodded. "Well, if you change your mind before you're back to full duty, let me know. I'm glad you want to stay in; I think you'll do well — if you stay out of fights like this. Tell me — do you think Korryn was sufficiently punished?"

"Yes, sir." Paks could hear the distaste in her own voice.

"Ah. It bothered you, eh? I see it did. Well, it's supposed to, and if you stay in, you'll see that again — though we all hope not to. Now — about Corporal Stephi. I've agreed, with Sejek, to let him go south for his trial by the Duke. We've kept the scribes busy, and have the witnesses' testimony and the rest written down. We think this will be sufficient, and the Duke won't need to see any of you. We hope. Anyway, Stephi has been quite concerned about you — did Stammel mention it?" Paks nodded; Stammel had told her a lot about Stephi. "He's asked how you were, and he wanted to see you and apologize. He's a good man, really. We're sure that some outside influence — probably magical — affected him that night. But — it's up to you — will you see him before he goes south?"

"Sir, I — I don't know. Should I?"

The captain frowned slightly, lacing his hands together. "It would be kind, I think. He can't hurt you now, you know, even if he wanted to. It won't make any difference to his trial, but it would reassure him, to see you up. You don't have to, of course."

Paks did not want to see Stephi ever again, but as she thought about it, she realized that she would have to, next year in the south. They might be in the same cohort; he might be her corporal. Best get it over, she decided, and looked up to meet the captain's gaze. "I'll see him, sir. But — I don't know what to say."

Valichi smiled. "You needn't say much. It'll be short. Wait here." He rose from behind the desk, and went out, shutting the door. Paks felt her stomach churn. She swallowed once, then again. It seemed a long time before the door opened again. Paks rose as the two captains, Valichi and Sejek, and Stephi came in together, crowding the little room. The mouse under Stephi's eye had faded to a sickly green.

"I'm very sorry, Paksenarrion, for the trouble I caused you," said Stephi. Paks could not find her voice, and merely nodded. "I want you to know that — that I don't do things like that — not usually. I never have before." His voice shook a little. "I — I hope you won't leave the Company, because of it — "

"I won't," said Paks. "I'm staying in."

"Good. I'm glad. I hope you're feeling better."

"Yes." Suddenly Paks found herself wanting to reassure this man, even though he had hurt her. She liked his honest face. "I'm doing well — in a week I'll be fine." He relaxed a bit and seemed to have nothing more to say.

Captain Sejek opened the door and Stephi went out; Paks saw the guard waiting for him in the passage.

"Thank you, Paksenarrion, for seeing him," said Sejek a moment later. "I, too, regret your injuries and the trouble you've had. Stephi will be punished, of course — "

"But, sir, everyone's told me it wasn't really his fault," said Paks, before she remembered that Sejek was a captain. She bit her lip.

Sejek frowned and sighed. "Maybe it wasn't, but even so, he injured you. That doesn't change. We punish drunks for their misdeeds, and for being drunk. He'll be punished."

Paks thought of Korryn's punishment and shuddered. "But he's not as bad as Korryn," she persisted.

"No. He's not. But he's supposed to be better — much better — than any recruit. He's a corporal of the regular Company, a veteran. This is not an offense to regard lightly. But that's not your concern — don't worry about

51

it. I, too, am glad to hear that you're staying in the Company; I'll see you in the south next spring." Sejek went out, leaving Paks with Valichi.

Valichi's mustache twitched. "Now that's as close to an apology as I've ever heard Sejek come."

"Apology?"

Well — he's wishing he'd taken a better look at you before he banned you that night. But Sejek doesn't like to admit he could be wrong — I'll warn you of that. Don't even hint that he made a mistake on this, or he'll be down on you for years. Right now — well, he's convinced that you're acceptable. It helped that you defended Stephi — was that why you did it?"

Paks was confused. "Sir, I — "

"No. You're not the type. Go find Stammel — he's out drilling, I think, on the east grounds — and he'll keep you busy."

Paks walked out, still confused, but happy to be returning to her friends. She joined in marching drill, but Siger barred her from weapons practice. "You can't fight with both eyes open, yet," he said. "It'll be a long time before you're ready to fight with just one." Barracks chores were well within her capacity; when she thought about the cell, or the infirmary, she was glad enough to have them to do.

At first no one said anything about the fight or its aftermath. Saben explained that he had tried to find Stammel, that by the time he had returned, she was already hurt. The others simply avoided the subject. Even Effa forbore to give a lecture on the protection of Gird. This suited Paks very well; she had no desire to talk about the little she could remember. But in the other units, curiosity overcame tact, and as soon as she was back in weapons drill, the questions began. Barranyi, the tall black-haired woman in Vossik's unit, often matched against Paks in drill, went farther than most. She was well-known for her strength of arm and sharp tongue.

"You should have poked an eye out," she began one afternoon, as they walked back to the main stronghold with a load of firewood. Paks shook her head.

"I was trying to get away."

"That's stupid. Anyone can get mauled trying to get away. Attack on your own. If you'd gotten an eye — "

"I'd have been in worse trouble, Barra." Paks checked the mule she was leading, and shoved one length of wood back into place. But Barra had not gone on; she halted her own mule and went on with her lecture.

"No, you wouldn't. He started it; he was wrong. They'd have had to admit that. As it is, they owe you — "

"No, they don't. Besides, they only found out it was his fault because I was beat up worse."

"That's not right." Barra scowled and strode along silent for some distance. "If it's not your fault, they should — "

"Barra — " Natzlin, a slender, pleasant girl with warm brown eyes who had been coupled with Barra before they joined, laid a hand on her arm. "Paks came out well — and if she's satisfied — "

"No. She came out beaten half-dead, and — "

52

Paks laughed. "By the gods, Barra, I'm not that easy to kill."

"You looked it that morning. A real mess, I tell you — I was ashamed — "

Paks felt a flicker of anger. "You — and why *you*? I was the one out there in front of everyone — "

"You'd always been a strong one, Siger's pet, and there you were, looking like something that'd come from a lockup — "

Paks grinned in spite of herself. "Well — I had — "

"Blast it! You know what I mean! You looked — "

"Gods above, Barra! She doesn't want to think about that now!" Vik shoved his way between them, and winked at Paks. "Don't worry — even bruises and chains can't make you ugly, Paks."

She felt herself go red. "Vik — "

"Like a song," he went on, unmoved. "Did you ever hear 'Falk's Oath of Gold,' Paks? When Falk was taken in the city of fear, and locked away all those years?"

"No. I thought Falk was a sort of saint, like Gird."

"Saints!" snorted Barra from Vik's other side.

"He is," said Vik seriously. "And Barra — I wouldn't scoff at them. Maybe they're far above us — but they have power."

"The gods have power," said Barra. "I'm not like Effa — I don't believe that men become gods when they die. And I'd rather be alive anyway."

"But tell me about Falk," said Paks. "Isn't he the one that wears rubies and silver?"

"I don't know what he wears *now*," began Vik. "He was a knight, a ruler's son, who kept his sworn oath and saved his kin by it, even though it meant years of slavery for him."

"Ugh. Why didn't he just kill his enemies?" asked Barra. "I heard that he spent a year cleaning the jacks of some city — "

"That and more," said Vik. "It's in the song, but you know I can't sing it. My father did, and I know most of the story. You'd like it, Paks — it's full of magic and kings and things like that."

"A magic sword?"

"Oh, yes. More than one. Someday when we've made enough money, we can hire a harper to sing it for us." Vik kept the conversation going until they reached the stronghold, where they broke up into their separate units. Barra shook her head, but stayed away from the topic the next time they drilled together. But others wanted to know what the underground cells were like, and what Stammel had said, and what the corporal had said. Paks fended off these questions as best she could: the cells were cold and miserable, and she wouldn't repeat any of the talks she'd had. Eventually they let her alone.

Meanwhile, Stammel had taken the unit in to help Kolya with her apple harvest. This was their first time to see Duke's East, since they had arrived from the west. Children playing in the streets waved and yelled at them; the adults smiled and spoke to Stammel. They passed an inn, the Red Fox, and a cobbled square surrounded with taller stone houses, and came to a stone bridge over the little river. Upstream Paks could see a weir and a millpond, and a waterwheel slowly turning. Kolya's land lay south of the river, beyond a water meadow where cattle grazed.

Kolya's orchard had more trees than Paks could count; she had never seen such a thing. Her aunt had been famed for five apple trees and two plums, but Kolya had rows of apples, plums, and pears. Only the apples remained so late, scenting the air with their rich, exciting fragrance. Soon Paks was high on a ladder, picking the apples at the top of her assigned tree. It was cool and sunny, perfect weather for the job. Below, in the aisles between the trees, Stammel and Kolya strolled together, directing the pickers and talking.

Paks caught a few snatches of that conversation, between orders to the workers. It seemed to be far removed from apple harvest, something about someone named Tamarrion, who had once been in the Company.

" — wouldn't have happened like that at all," she heard Stammel say. "She would have made sure first, before she called for a ban."

Kolya snorted. "In *her* day, you'd never have brought back someone like Korryn at all, would you?"

"No — you're right about that. But things are different." Paks saw his head shake, far below, then he peered up to see that she was working. She wondered if the mysterious Tamarrion had been a sergeant — even a captain — but something in their tone kept her from asking.

As fall turned to winter, the recruits honed their weapons skills, now learning to use a shield with their swords. They began drilling in groups, one line against another, learning to work together with their weapons. They were allowed to stand guard, first with the regulars, then alone. On guard duty on the wall, with her sword hanging heavy at her side, Paks felt very much the professional. One gray, sleety day, she was on duty when a traveler came up the road from Duke's West, and called the challenge herself. She thought he did not notice that her tunic was recruit brown instead of maroon.

Along with all this, they were introduced to tactics. Paks had thought that after mastering the intricacies of drill, nothing remained to learn about engaging the enemy. She was wrong.

"But I thought we just ran at them and started fighting," said Vik, echoing her thought.

"No. That's the way to get killed, and quickly. None of you will make these decisions now, but you all need to know something of tactics. You can do your job better if you know what you're trying to accomplish." They were gathered around Stammel in the mess hall between meals; he began to set out apples on the table. "Now suppose this — here — is the Duke's Company. And this over here is the enemy. Look at the length of lines."

"Theirs is longer," said Saben, stating the obvious. "But we — "

"Listen. Now suppose we engage just as we are. What happens on each end of our line, on the flanks?"

"They can hit the side, too," said Vik.

"If they have enough, they can go all around," Paks put in.

"Yes. That looks bad, doesn't it? But it depends on why their line is so long, and what they're fighting with." He added more apples to the array. "Suppose they've only as many men as we have, so their line is long and thin. We form the square, and we engage one-on-one all the way around. With our depth, we actually have them outnumbered *at each position*. If they're fighting with swords, they won't have a chance. We have concentrated our strength on their weakness — or rather, they have stupidly chosen to make themselves weak all over."

Effa frowned at the table. "So it's better to make the square?"

"Not always. We can't move fast or far in the square — you remember — " They nodded. "Mobility is important, too. So is terrain — where is the good ground?" Quickly he showed them how slope, water, and such hazards as swamp and loose rock could change the choice of tactics. "It's the commander's responsibility to choose the best ground — for our side, of course. The Duke's famous for it. But you need to know how it's done, so you'll know what to watch out for, and which way to move — "

"But we're under orders, aren't we? We just do what we're told — "

"Yes. But sergeants and corporals get killed — even captains. In battle, there's no time to send questions to the Duke. If the regulars don't know what to do and why, the cohort will fall apart. Be captured at best. That's what Kolya Ministiera did — took over her cohort, kept 'em moving together, the right way. That's why she made corporal so young. If she hadn't lost an arm at Cortes Cilwan, she'd have been the youngest sergeant in the Company, I don't doubt. But when she went down, someone else took over — that's what we train for."

They looked at each other, wondering. Paks hoped she would do as well — without losing an arm. The only thing that frightened her was the thought of ending her career as a young cripple, with nothing left to do.

Soon the lessons in tactics had gone beyond table demonstrations to live practice fields. Each recruit unit made a mock cohort, and they practiced engagements, disengagements, squaring, flanking, and other maneuvers: first without weapons, and then with wooden swords and shields. In smaller groups they learned to fight in confined areas: stairs, passages, stables. They made ladders and scaled the walls of the stronghold in mock assaults, then learned to hold the wall against assaults. And since the Duke sometimes hired mounts when he wanted to move his troops rapidly, they learned to ride.

"This is a mule," said Corporal Bosk. Paks thought that was unnecessary. The mule flicked one long ear. On the ground beside it were saddle, saddlecloth, and bridle. "A mule is not a horse," he went on. That also was obvious. Long ears, mealy muzzle, heavy head, small hooves. Paks suppressed a yawn. Maybe some of the city people didn't know the difference. She glanced around for Vik. "How many of you," Bosk was asking, "have ever worked with mules?" Several hands went up. "You — " he said, pointing. "What's the big difference between mules and horses?"

55

"Mules can kick anyways," said Jorti, "and they're fussier about their ears, and they're smarter than horses." Jorti's father, Paks remembered, had something to do with caravans.

"Right," said Bosk. "All of that. Those of you that've never worked either will have less trouble than you horse-folk. They are *different*. Mules are more ear-shy than any horse, and if you drag a bridle over their ears, they'll plant a hoof on you. A back hoof. When you're standing in front of 'em." Paks looked at the mule, surprised. It didn't look like it could kick forward. "And they're smart," Bosk went on. "Really smart. A good one'll go farther on worse ground with less fuss — but a mule looks out for itself above all." He picked up the bridle and showed them how to put it on.

The mule assigned to Paks flicked its ears nervously as she eased the crownpiece over the top of its head. She talked to it as if it were her father's plow pony, but kept a respectful eye on the near hind leg. The mule that kicked Sif had made a believer out of her. She laid the saddlecloth on its back, and, after another look at Bosk's demonstration, set the saddle in place.

"That's right," he said, as he walked along the line. "Now fasten the girth." For that she had to bend down, reaching under its belly. The mule stood as if its feet were bolted to the ground. Paks caught the end of the girth and drew it up. The mule swelled visibly. Paks tugged the girth tight, and pulled again. The mule gave her an inscrutable look out of one amber eye, and shifted its weight minutely. Paks glanced back, and saw the tip of the near hind hoof resting lightly on the ground. Its ears flopped out sideways, swung lazily back and forth. She tugged again at the girth. The mule sighed, without losing an inch of its circumference, and the ears were still. Paks glared at it.

"Dumb mule," she said.

"That won't do," said Bosk behind her. "Mule knows you're nervous. Like this — " He grabbed the mule's reins, gave a short jerk, and yelled "Hai!" into one drooping ear. The mule threw up its head with a snort, ears forward. Bosk thumped it hard in the ribs, and jerked the girth four inches tighter with one smooth motion. "Like that," he said. The mule was back on all four legs, tail swinging gently. "Don't hurt 'em," he went on. "They won't forget being beaten, say, but you've got to get their attention and be firm. Can't bluff 'em, like you can horses."

Eventually they all learned to bridle and saddle the mules, and after hours of painful practice they all learned to ride without damaging the mules or themselves. Paks even grew to enjoy it, trying to see herself on a prancing warhorse instead of a mule. She asked Bosk once if it were the same; his face creased in a grin. "Thinking of that, are you? And you not yet a soldier! Well, Paks, it's about as much like riding one of these old pack mules as playing soldier with a stick-sword is like real warfare. You've a long way to go, girl, if that's where you're going." Paks blushed and kept her dreams to herself after that.

As that cold winter wore on, they began to feel that they were ready to go

— ready to face any army anywhere. Some from each unit had left — those frightened or shocked by Korryn's punishment, those injured too badly to continue, and a few more who decided, as the training came closer and closer to actual combat, that they didn't want to be soldiers after all. Some of the recruits — Paks and Barra among them — were surprised that these dropouts were let go with so little dispute. Why had they had to sign an agreement to stay two years, if anyone could leave at any time?

"Think about it," said Stammel when Paks asked. "Your life will depend on the skill and courage of those beside you. Look at Talis: she was warned along with the rest of you, and she got pregnant anyway. Anyone too selfish or stupid to take birthbane when it's right there on the table at meals isn't going to make a good soldier. As for courage, do you want to chance your life on someone whose only thought is getting away?"

"No, but — "

"No. And they did not know, until they tried the training, that they would fail, or be so frightened. Neither do you. That's why no one's promoted from recruit until *after* we've seen them in battle."

Paks thought about that, and looked at her companions with new intent. Vik — always joking, but quick as a ferret with his blade. Arñe, pleasant and hardworking, never flustered. Saben, good-natured and strong, quick on his feet. Effa, bossy and nosy, but totally honest and fearless. Barra, her nearest rival among the women for size and strength, and Natzlin, her gentler shadow. Quiet Sim, Jorti with his caravan tales, quick-tempered Seli, chill Harbin. Those swords would ward her, or not. Her sword would ward them — or not.

But time to think was short, with the rush of training, and soon the year turned toward spring. The first brief thaw made mush out of the snow on the drill fields; the ground below was still frozen. And then the hints began.

Chapter Seven

The Duke is coming. The Duke will be here next week — no, two weeks — no, three days. Rumors swarmed over the stronghold like hornets, stinging all the recruits with excitement and curiosity. Every square foot of the stronghold was scrubbed, and what the working parties thought clean enough was scrubbed again — and again. They cleaned the stables, oiled every scrap of leather, polished every bit of metal on all the tack. The pits that served the jacks were dug out and limed, and the stinking refuse hauled away in carts to be spread on the hayfields of Duke's West. Along the road from Duke's East, fifty recruits filled holes and ruts and cleaned out the side-ditches. They rolled the surface with a heavy stone cylinder drawn by oxen, using strings and a notched stick to make sure the crown had an even camber. Siger had a group busy oiling the wooden practice blades and scouring all metal weapons; he would not tolerate so much as a fingerprint.

None of the recruits were allowed in the Duke's Court, but from all the bustling in and out it was obvious that the same rigorous preparation was going on there as well. Messengers jogged back and forth between the two villages and the stronghold, staying off the newly worked road to avoid the curses of the road crew.

It had been raining several days, a cold thin drizzle that penetrated without cleansing, but after a shift of wind in the night, the sky cleared. Paks, on duty as recruit guard in the night watch, had spent several miserable hours pacing back and forth on the battlements before the rain quit. She and Coben had complained every time they met at the southeast corner of the wall. The windshift brought drier and colder air; they agreed the exchange was for the better. Now, as the Necklace of Torre, the winter watch-stars, sank to the west, the eastern sky began to glow. Paks looked toward the mess hall chimneys — yes, a thin column of smoke, thickening as she watched, oozed from one of them. She thought of the asar, the hot sweet drink the night guards were given as soon as it could be brewed, and blew on her cold hands, looking outward again.

The land around was still a dark featureless blur, but she could see the ridge to the northeast, black against a sky now showing deep blue. It seemed much colder; she stamped as she walked back and forth from the gate tower to the corner. Light seeped into the sky, moment by moment.

She could see the planks she walked on, and the remaining puddles, now frozen hard. She could see the paler blur of the road to Duke's East trailing away from the gate. She glanced back at the courtyard, at the mess hall chimneys, both smoking now, the smoke torn away in tatters from the tops of the stacks. She looked eastward. A white band showed beneath the broadening blue; only Silba, the dawn star, still shone in the lightening sky. She dropped her eyes to the land, emerging slowly to sight as if it rose from under dark water: the ridge to the east, and the mountains beyond it — the broad reach of the drill fields, sodden with rainwater that reflected the brightening sky. Southward, the road stood out more clearly, swerving to avoid a marshy area, lifting over a hummock of ground between the stronghold and Duke's East.

Sometimes, she remembered, you could see the smoke from Duke's East: the low buildings were out of sight in trees, behind the hummock, but she knew which clumps of trees to watch. It was still too dark. Her legs felt brittle with cold; she did a little jig at the corner, waiting for Coben to finish his circuit so they could talk.

"Gah — it's cold!" he gasped, shivering, as he came close enough.

Paks nodded, dancing from foot to foot, both of them numb. "N-not long," she said. "Did — did you see the smoke? Soon."

Coben grinned. "B-better be soon. Better go on; it's colder to stop."

Paks turned away. It was light enough to see colors now, muted though they were. There was the dark blur of trees along the river — the larger blur of the trees near and beyond Duke's East. When she got to the gate tower, the guard sergeant opened the tower door and beckoned her in.

"Here's something to warm you," he said. "Just came up from the kitchens."

Paks nodded gratefully, too cold to speak, and took the mug he offered. Even in the tower it was cold; steam rose from both mug and pitcher on the table. She sipped the scalding liquid; it burned her tongue. Her hands around the mug began to ache with cold, then warmed enough to tingle. She felt a warm glow inside, and drained her mug. "Shall I take some to Coben?"

"Let him come in, out of the wind," said the sergeant. "You walk both segments for a few minutes, then come for a second dose."

"Yes, sir." Paks rubbed her arms hard a moment, then opened the door and went back out on the wall. It was just as cold. A red streak fanned across the east. Coben was waiting at the corner; Paks waved him in. He jogged past her with a stiff grin. She walked on, looking east at the nearby slopes, and turned north at the corner to take Coben's place. North of the stronghold she could see more ridges through a gap in the nearest. Orcs laired there, someone had said. West were great rounded folds of moorland that the villages used for sheep pasture. She thought back to the moors above her father's farm. It had been cold there, too, but you could stay in with the sheep at night. Her nose wrinkled, remembering the smell. She grinned to herself. She did not want to be back there, even for a warm place at night. She turned and started south along the wall.

A chip of liquid fire lifted above the eastern horizon, south of the ridge: the sun, a fat red-gold disk. Crisp blue shadows sprang across the walk from the stones of the battlements. The early light gave the fields below a rosy glow. Evergreens along the river were clearly green, and bare branches on other trees glinted as they swayed in the wind. She looked again for Duke's East. Yes — smoke, now gold-white against a pale blue sky. She looked along the road, idly, then stiffened. She had caught a glimpse of sunlight on something — something that glittered.

She strained her eyes, squinting against the cold. Whatever it was lay between the hummock and Duke's East, where the road itself was out of sight. Another glitter, a vague sense of movement. Paks let out a yell. The guard on the other side of the tower, who had been heading for the west corner, turned and looked at her. She yelled again, and pointed toward Duke's East, then jogged to the tower. The door opened.

"What is it?" asked Coben. "Was I too long?" Behind him, Paks could see the sergeant.

"No — something on the road. On the road to Duke's East." Coben erupted from the doorway just ahead of the sergeant. "Where?" asked both of them at once. Paks pointed.

"Beyond the hummock — I saw something in the light, something moving."

"I can't see anything," said the other guard, a recruit from Kefer's unit, who had come through the tower. "What were you yelling for?"

"It may be the Duke," said the sergeant. "If she saw anything — we'll know soon enough. Get back to your posts; I'll rouse the others. If it is the Duke," he said to Paks, "I'll thank you for the extra warning. He won't catch us unprepared — not that we were."

Coben went back to the east wall, but kept looking over his shoulder to the south. Paks could not take her eyes off the road, where it came back into view over the hummock. Behind her in the courtyard she heard a sudden commotion, but she was not even tempted to turn around. The tower door opened, and half the complement of regular guards poured out, all armed, to space themselves along the wall. Paks saw two trumpeters waiting in the doorway. The other half of the guards, she realized, had gone out the far side of the tower. The sergeant reappeared.

"Paks, you and Coben come down and parade with your unit."

Paks tore her eyes from the road; the sergeant eyed her kindly. "Go on, now. I know you want to stay and see it, but the Duke likes everything done regularly. All the recruits should be together." Paks nodded, and slipped down the tower stairs to the courtyard. The recruit units were already forming. Stammel was watching for Paks and Coben with another jug of asar.

"Here — you two look half-frozen. Drink this quickly, go use the jacks and straighten yourselves up, and get back here as fast as you can." They took the jug into the barracks. Paks took down her windblown hair and rebraided it quickly, then downed a mug of asar. She ran to the jacks, rubbing her arms and stamping her feet. It seemed much warmer down off the

60

wall. When they came out, Stammel took the jug and sent them into formation. Corporal Bosk moved out of her place and into his own.

Just as Paks stepped into her position, the trumpets rang out from the tower. She wished she was up there to see. After a breathless pause, the trumpets sounded again; this time she could hear a faint answering call from outside. Captain Valichi strode around the courtyard, checking each recruit unit in turn. Across the court, Paks could see his horse waiting. The trumpets sounded again. Captain Valichi mounted and rode to the gate. A bellow from the guard sergeant, high overhead. A rumble from outside. The sergeant yelled down into the court: "Captain, it's my lord Duke."

"Open the gates!" ordered the captain. Paks could hear the grinding of the portcullis mechanism, and the great brown leaves on the main gates folded inward. For a moment nothing happened. Then the clatter of horses' hooves on stone, and a figure in glittering mail under a long maroon cloak rode through the gates. Valichi bowed in the saddle.

"Welcome, my lord Duke," he said. The cloaked figure pushed back the fur-edged hood, revealing rumpled red hair above a bearded face.

"Early for breakfast, I'd have thought," said the Duke. "What sharp eyes spotted us this time?"

"A recruit, my lord," said Valichi.

The Duke scanned each of the recruit units; Paks felt his gaze like a dagger blade, cold and keen. Then he grinned at Valichi. "Well," he said, "let's keep *that* one. Good work, Captain." He dropped his reins and stretched. "Tir's bones, Val, I'm ready for breakfast if no one else is. It's cold out there, man. Let's get to a fire." He lifted his reins and rode through the wide aisle of the formations to the Duke's Gate. Behind him came two youths, also in chain mail, a tall man in flowing robes and a peaked hat, two richly dressed men in velvet tunics edged with fur, and a troop of men-at-arms. One of these carried a pennant on a long staff. Paks wondered if its polished tip had caught the light, and that's what she'd seen.

Grooms ran out to take the horses; the men-at-arms dismounted as the Duke went through into his court, and led their own mounts to the stables. Horses, Paks noticed, and not mules. The guard sergeant came out of the tower with all but the dayshift guards; he caught Stammel's eye and made a lifting gesture with his hand. Paks could not yet read the hand signals the veterans used, but Stammel grinned. He turned to Paks. "Good eyes. The Duke tries to take us by surprise, and he likes to fail — at that, if nothing else. Where did you see him?"

"I saw something — but I wasn't sure what — between that high ground and the village. It must have stuck up fairly high; could it have been that pennant?"

"Could have been, or a squire's helmet. The sun must have caught it just right — and then you were looking in the right place. Well done, Paks."

Duke Phelan might have traveled half the night to arrive at his stronghold at dawn, but that did not mean he planned to sleep the day away. Shortly after

61

breakfast, he appeared in the courtyard to watch Kefer's unit at weaponsdrill, and by noon he had observed every recruit unit in its work. He said little that any of the recruits could hear, but his sharp glance seemed everywhere at once. In the afternoon the recruits lost sight of him; they were doing two-on-one engagements in the mud, with Stammel's unit the one, and trying to maneuver in the square. None of them had a glance to spare for the wall, or the cloaked figure atop it, watching. The sergeants saw, but said nothing.

In the next week, while the sergeants muttered and fussed over the recruits like hens with too many chicks, the Duke managed to see everything. He appeared in one barracks when the recruits were just getting up, and in another while they were sanding the floor. He walked through the mess hall during meals, and even ate there twice. The recruits could hardly choke down their food. He ate as if he liked it, and talked easily to his squires. They all knew by then that the young men in mail were his squires, and one of them a nephew of Count Vladiorhynsich of Kostandan. He was there when Vona's unit made a brilliant reverse in square and threw Kefer's unit off balance, and still there when Stammel's unit managed the same thing, not quite so well, against both the others.

"I wonder if he ever sleeps," muttered Arñe to Paks in the jacks, the one place they were almost sure he wouldn't be.

"I don't know. He was on the wall last night when we came on. Gave the watchword, just like Captain Valichi, but I nearly fell off the parapet."

"And this morning he was waiting in the courtyard when we came out. I wish I knew what he was thinking — "

"I don't." Paks had, in fact, been wondering what the Duke had done to Stephi, but she was afraid to ask anyone. Surely Stammel knew, from the men who had come, but — "If I knew," she said in answer to Arñe's quizzical look, "I'd be even more frightened of him."

"It's not like he's *done* anything to anyone," mused Arñe. "But I have the feeling he would. I'd like to be first on the road," she added, bringing up the unspoken thought of all of them. One recruit unit would be chosen to lead the march south to join the Company. The best unit, of course. They all knew who the best unit was — but a little coolness came into the friendships that had formed between recruits in different units.

"Barra and Natzlin think they're getting it," said Paks. Arñe snorted.

"After the way Vona's pulled them off two days ago? They'll have to do something big to make that up."

"Ours wasn't so sharp," Paks reminded her.

"Against both of 'em. Kefer's was only one-on-one. I hope — "

"We'll make it," said Paks, suddenly full of confidence. "We're much better with spears, and we've got four of the best swords — "

That week was, in fact, one long round of contests. Those few dimwitted enough not to catch on to that by themselves were forcibly enlightened by their companions. Mock combat the last day was hardly mock: collarbones and fingers, one or more in each unit, snapped under the blows of wooden swords. When the entire recruit cohort gathered in formation in the courtyard, there were no smiles. For the first time, they were being addressed by the Duke himself, formally.

Paks, in her usual position at the front of the formation, ignored the bruise that had three of her fingers swelled up like blue sausages. It had definitely been worth risking them broken to break the front line of Vona's square. Especially since they weren't broken; the surgeon said they'd bend in a few days. She watched for the Duke. One of his squires came through the Duke's Gate and nodded to Captain Valichi. The trumpeters blew a fanfare; Paks's skin rose up in chillbumps. The Duke strode briskly through the gate, cloak swirling. He spoke to Valichi, nodded, then moved to Vona's unit, on the far side of the courtyard. Paks suppressed a groan. Had they lost to Vona's? But the Duke made no announcement. Perhaps he was just inspecting, as he had twice before. She dared not glance over to see. Her hand began to throb more insistently; the pain edged up her arm. She listened to the rasp of the Duke's boots across the court. It seemed a very long time before the sound came closer. Now he was at Kefer's unit. She could hear that he was, indeed, passing along the ranks. She could even hear the rumble of his voice as he spoke to this recruit or that.

Then he was in front of them, greeting Stammel, and giving a quick glance along the front rank. Paks wondered if he would speak to each of them. She reminded herself of Stammel's instructions: "Say 'yes, my lord,' or 'no, my lord,' instead of just 'sir' as you would for the captain." The Duke came closer, with Stammel now a pace behind him. Paks could feel her neck getting hot. She tried to stare through him to the mess hall windows, but he was tall; it was hard to avoid meeting those gray eyes.

"Fingers broken?" he asked her.

"No, sir — my lord," said Paks, stumbling over the honorific and blushing even more.

"Good." The Duke moved on, and Paks heard nothing for some time but the blood drumming in her ears. After Stammel had told them, and she had reminded herself, she'd still said it wrong. When she could hear again, the Duke was already on his way to the front of the formation.

"When you were recruited," he said to them all, "you agreed to stay with this Company for two years beyond your training, and to fight at the orders of your commander. Back then you didn't know your commander. Now you do. All of you have qualified to join my Company, and that means you follow me — obey *my* orders, fight when I tell you to, march when I tell you to. Your sergeants will tell you — have told you, I expect — that I'm hard. That's so. I expect a lot of my soldiers. Skill, courage — and loyalty. To me, personally, as well as to the Company. Now if there's anyone who, after seeing me, can't swear fealty — now's the time to leave." There was a long breathless silence. The Duke nodded. "Very well. Then give me your oath."

Captain Valichi stepped forward to lead them in the oath of service. "We swear to you our hands, our blades, our blood, our breath — the service of the hands, and the service of the heart. May the gods witness our oath of loyalty and be swift to punish the oathbreaker."

"And I to you," said the Duke, "pledge hands and blade and blood and breath. My honor is your honor, before all enemies and trials, in all dangers high and low. The gods witness my oath to you, and yours to me." He looked back and forth at the recruits, and nodded.

"Well, now, companions — " Paks stiffened, surprised by the change in his voice and address. "You'll soon be on your way to battle. As always, one unit must be first on the road. 'Tis no easy chore to choose among you. Tir knows what I'll do if the Company grows to four cohorts. But the choice is made, and that's for Stammel's unit — " Paks suddenly felt that she could soar high in the air on the breath she drew. She locked her jaw on a yell of triumph. Someone behind her was less careful. To her surprise the Duke grinned. "One yell won't hurt," he said. "Cheer your sergeant, if you will."

And "Stammel!" they yelled, and the walls rang with it.

The Duke rode out the next morning, with a late snowstorm behind him. He had hardly disappeared into the swirling veils before the recruits were hard at work again — this time in preparation for the march south. First they were measured for their uniforms, having changed shape since they arrived. With the maroon tunics went taller boots and longer socks, a long maroon cloak with a hood, and — most exciting — armor. Instead of bandas, they would wear boiled-leather corselets ("Until you can buy something better, if you want it," remarked Devlin.) There were greaves for their legs, and wide bands to protect their wrists. And bronze helmets on top of all.

"Make up your minds," said Stammel, "how you're going to wear your hair. If it's long, I'd say keep it inside the helmet, hot as it is, or some enemy will grab it and throw you. It'll make a cushion." Paks found a way of winding her braid that was comfortable and secure. But the helmet was heavier than she'd expected. So was everything else.

"You'll get used to it," said Stammel. "After you've marched all the way to Valdaire in it, you won't even notice."

It seemed hardly any time at all since the Duke's visit when two of the captains arrived from the south to escort them. A last few days for inspection and packing the mule train that would carry their necessary supplies — and then it was the last night in the barracks. Paks found it almost as hard to sleep as she had the first one.

Chapter Eight

As Paks passed under the gate tower and out into the cold gray light of a late-winter dawn, she felt how changed she was from the girl who had left home those months before. She had not told anyone when her nineteenth birthday came, but she felt the extra year like a wall between her and the past. No one would take her for a farmer's daughter, not with the sword at her side and the skill to use it, not in the uniform of Duke Phelan's Company. Beside and behind her, eighty pairs of almost-new boots beat the same crisp rhythm on the hard-frozen road to Duke's East. Going to the war, the rhythm sang in her head. Going to the war.

By the time they reached the rise between the stronghold and Duke's East, the sun was rising, a brief red glare between the clouds. This was the last bit of known road: the curve into the village past the Red Fox, the square, the bridge. Smoke rolled out of chimneys. As their boots rang on the cobbles of the square, faces appeared at windows and doors. Mayor Fontaine opened his door to wave, along with the row of children that appeared at his back. Several children ran from houses to march alongside, singing and yelling, until they were called back. Beyond the bridge was Kolya's farm and orchard; Kolya was leaning on the gate, grinning.

"Good luck," she called. "Fight well." Paks glanced at her, and Kolya winked. Then they were past, and after another fifty paces the road swung left again, leaving the village behind to curve through a wooded swamp, now frozen. After that it climbed, and the trees fell away. A stone wall bordered the road on the west, and beyond it Paks saw a herd of shaggy cattle, guarded by several men in leather capes. All the cattle stared at them, ears wide, as they marched by. Most of them were heavy in calf, and looked as wide as they were long in their winter coats.

They were seven days on the road to Vérella, marching at first through forested ridges that gentled into farmland sprinkled with villages. The people were shorter here, and looked heavier; the women wore their headscarves knotted high, with a peak to one side. Each night they stopped by a large stone-walled barn with a fox-head design chiseled into the stone. Stammel explained that the Duke had built these barns for the farmers to use, provided they let his troops shelter there while traveling.

The column settled quickly into the habits of a long march. Recruits took guard duty in rotation with the regulars, and hardly thought of them-

65

selves as recruits. They knew the captains now: Pont, junior to Cracolnya, and Ferrault, junior to Arcolin. As they passed through the villages, they saw themselves as they were seen: mercenaries. The Duke's Company. They began to pick up the news of the road as they neared Vérella.

"Eh, Captain," shouted one graybeard. "You're late this year. They Sobanai is already come by here."

"Seen anything of Vladi's?" called Pont.

"Nay, and I hope not. They don't come this way but once in a while, and I'm glad for it."

"Why, grandfather?"

"Eh, well — he's too hard for us, that one. Better he go east."

The captain laughed and rode on. Paks wondered who the "Sobanai" were. She watched as two children, screeching to get the soldiers' attention, struck at each other with wooden swords. An older voice called them, angry, and they dropped the swords and ran off.

Then they came to Vérella — the first city Paks had ever seen, Vérella of the Bells, the seat of the Kings of Tsaia. From a distance its great stone walls and towers seemed to sail the river meadows, already tinged with spring green. They had passed slower carts and wagons all that morning, and as they neared the city, they met more traffic: trains of mules, ox-drawn wagons, foot travelers, and horsemen.

The guards at the city gates wore rose and gray, and carried pikes. They marched under the gate tower. It seemed immense to Paks, its opening wide enough for two wagons at once to pass. The way was paved with square cobbles of pale gray stone, and was even wider than the gate. Paks tried not to gawk, but she was distracted by the buildings, tall and many-windowed, and crowded wall to wall, and by the incredible noise and bustle. Against the tall stone walls lay a flotsam of bright canvas awnings over shop windows and street peddlers, merchandise of all sorts piled in alluring heaps — it seemed that only the constant current of traffic kept it from taking over the road itself. She had never imagined such a variety of people and things. Men in long gowns with fur-edged sleeves. A stack of intricately patterned carpets next to a pile of polished copper pots of all sizes. Four men carrying a sort of box on poles, with curtains swaying on the box. A woman in green velvet, on a mule, strumming a hand-harp. A fat child, broad as he was tall, with an axe at his belt — as they passed, Paks was startled to see a waist-length red beard on the child. She gasped.

"Don't gawk about," muttered Bosk. "It's just a dwarf."

She had not realized that dwarves were real. She tried to keep her eyes ahead, but it was impossible. They passed a man in red and blue motley carrying a strange skinny black animal with a long tail that wrapped his arm. Two children dashed by, balancing loaves of bread an armspan long. She heard a confused roar from the right, and Stammel yelled a halt. From a side street rode six figures in gleaming armor on chargers bigger than the Duke's; the street shook to the pounding hooves. Paks felt breathless. She watched Stammel peer down the side street before leading them on. She had never seen horses so big. Were there more?

After another few minutes of marching, the street made a sharp turn left and then right. Here were fewer sidewalk stalls, but a fascinating blend of smells: roast meats, fresh bread, ale, wine, spices. Paks heard her belly rumble in response. The buildings had benches in front of them, and a row of watching eyes followed them down the street. She saw another dwarf, and then two more, on one of the benches.

At a crossing, Stammel turned right into a narrower street the column almost filled. Ahead loomed a high stone wall, and beyond it the turret of some building. When they reached the foot of the wall, Paks saw that a wide paved area lay before it; Stammel turned left again, and they marched beside the wall for a space. Paks saw no gate, and no guards on the wall. At last it swung away to the right, and they went on, again on a wide street between buildings. Here were fewer stalls, and no peddlers. Paks saw a string of mules being led through a gate; she glanced sideways as they passed it. Inside, stables surrounded a courtyard; she saw another of the great horses, this one led by a boy.

They entered a square with a fountain in the center and trees around the fountain. Here once more the canvas awnings of shops and sidewalk stalls edged the street. A barefooted woman in a short dress struggled with a large jar of water from the fountain. A plump child in a fur-lined hood trotted behind a large fluffy white dog. Two cloaked men in tall boots strolled near the fountain, hands near the hilts of their weapons. A tall slender figure in gray trotted briskly past the column on a horse bridled in green and gold. It was past before Paks realized that its face was not human.

Past that square they marched down a quiet street with trees planted in the center. Ahead was another gate. The captains, who had ridden ahead, sat chatting with the guards as they marched up. "Everyone still with us?" asked Pont.

"Certainly, sir."

"Very good. I've arranged for a meal outside the gates — you remember *The Golden Goose*? They call it *The Winking Tomcat* now; old Penston's nephew inherited it this winter. We're called to meet with the vice-regent; wait for us there."

"Yes, sir. Do you think you'll be long enough to unload the mules?"

"No. Give 'em a feed though. We'll march through to Littlebridge today."

"Yes, sir." Stammel led them through the gates, this time onto a wide stone bridge with a waist-high stone parapet. They were far above the water. Paks looked upstream and saw a dark still surface; she could not tell how fast the water was moving. Another bridge spanned the river upstream; a wall rose from the far bank. Ahead of them, their own bridge pierced the wall at a tower, and again they passed through gates.

Here the buildings were lower, many of them wood and not stone. Paks could see over them to yet another wall. These streets were crowded, but they saw few velvets and furs, and more bare feet. Some people wore wooden clogs

67

that clattered loudly on the cobbles. A pack of lean dogs worried something in a gutter. They passed a row of taverns, reeking of stale beer; only one man huddled on the benches outside. A fat woman in gaudy clothes danced sideways beside the column, showing a trayful of glittering jewelry. Paks heard one of the corporals swear at her; she flung back an oath in return.

At the last wall, the guards waved them through the tall gates, and they came out to see loosely spaced buildings and fallow fields beyond. They passed a tanner's stinking yard, a pen of cattle on one side of the road and a pen of hogs on the other, a field fenced with split rails (which Paks had never seen) holding a dozen horses and a few mules, another field with wagons parked in rows. Ahead on the left was a large stone enclosure with a two-story building in front. On the sign hanging before it was a yellow cat with a ferocious leer. Stammel halted them, and entered the inn. Paks looked around. Across from the inn an open slope of bare ground eased up to a stand of trees. Ahead, down the road, was another building that might be an inn, then a row of cottages.

Stammel came out. "The court's too full," he said to Bosk. "We'll eat over here — " he nodded at the open space. "I'll take the file leaders in for food."

Paks followed Stammel into the inn, excited and curious. It was much larger than the inn at Rocky Ford, larger than any she'd seen. They entered a long low room filled with tables and benches and noise. The landlord, a tall heavy young man with a pale mustache, led them to the kitchen behind, where the cook's helpers were heaping platters with roast meat, bread, cheese, and dried fruit. Paks took a platter and carried it back through the dining room and across the road. The food was good, spiced with strange flavors, and Paks devoured her share. The second rank took the platters back, and they settled down to wait until the captains returned.

"How do you like cities?" Saben asked Paks.

"I don't know — it's not what I thought it would be."

"Did you see that dwarf?"

Paks nodded. "I didn't know they were real, any more. Do you know what was on that horse with the fancy bridle?"

"No. I missed that. We can ask Stammel or Bosk."

Bosk chuckled at their question. "You mean you don't know? It's a good thing you didn't point. That was an elf, from Lyonya or the Ladysforest, a messenger to the Council."

"Elf — " Paks and Saben looked at each other. "Will we see more of elves and dwarves and things like that?" asked Paks.

Bosk spat. "I hope not. Uncanny, they are, and unfriendly, too. We don't have much to do with them, and the less the better, I say."

"Now Bosk," said Devlin, who had walked up on the conversation. "Elves are good fighters, you have to say that."

"If it's fighting alone, give me dwarves — not that I want them, but they're hard as stone, and tireless. Elves — they'll sing as soon as fight, or go off after some fool idea. And they think they know everything, and have to tell you about it — without answering any question you want answered, either."

"I don't know — " Devlin looked thoughtful. "I've met a few elves — five years ago, that year you stayed north, Bosk, I talked to one. She was uncanny, but beautiful. Sometimes she'd sing in Common, about the Beginnings, and where the elves came from, and battles long ago. It was strange, but very powerful. I liked it."

"Your choice," said Bosk shortly. "And you can't say some elves haven't gone bad — "

"The kuaknom? That may be, but they're all dead."

Bosk snorted. Another recruit broke in. "But won't we go past dwarf lands in a few days?"

"South of here, yes. But we go around the mountains rather than through them. We'll see dwarves on the road between here and Valdaire, but we won't see their caves."

"Are gnomes just another name for dwarves?" asked Saben.

"Gird's arm, no! And remember that, if we see any. The Aldonfulk princedom comes near the road for a day's travel. They're not like dwarves at all, save their love of stone and living underground. You saw that dwarf — wide as he was tall, and so they all are. Gnomes are slenderer, but still short. Good fighters; they're lawful folk, knowing the value of discipline and training. They don't say much, but what they do say you can trust with your life."

"You like them, don't you?" asked Paks.

"Of the elder races, yes. Trustworthy, brave, well-organized. Some of them are Girdsmen." Paks had not realized before that Bosk was Girdish; she looked at him curiously.

The sunlight had dimmed behind thicker clouds as they ate, and now a fine drizzle sifted over the landscape. Paks stamped her feet, feeling the chill.

"I hope we start marching soon."

"We'll have to wait for the captains. I hope they don't linger over their meal."

"Where are they?"

"Probably with the vice-regent. They usually eat at the palace on these journeys; the regents always have some message for the Duke."

Paks wondered what the palace looked like. "Did we pass the palace?" she asked.

"Do you remember that wall we marched beside, before we came to the square with the fountain? That was the palace wall. You can't see the palace itself from outside."

"Have you seen it?"

Bosk shook his head. "No. But Stammel did once, I think. It's just a palace, though, like any other. I've seen the King's Hall in Rostvok."

"That's in Pargun, isn't it?" asked Vik. Bosk nodded, and Vik went on. "I heard it had a room lined in gold, polished like mirrors, and all the guards wore jewelled helmets and a ruby in one ear."

"I never saw a golden room," said Bosk. "But they do wear jewels in their ears, and not just the guards, either. I couldn't say if they were rubies. As for helmets, the ones I saw were good polished bronze, nothing more. Tell you what they did have, though: in the King's Hall itself, where the King sits and receives ambassadors and such, they had a hanging framework that held — oh — a hundred candles, I suppose. Much like what the Duke's got, so far, only bigger. But all over it, and hanging from it, were little chips that looked like clear ice — much too big for diamonds — and they glittered in the candlelight, and made sparkles of all colors that danced over the whole hall. One of their men told me it was a kind of glass, but I never saw glass anything like that. It was something to see, I'll tell you — all lit up and a hundred colors. Like the sun coming out after rain, or an ice storm, only more so."

Paks tried to imagine such a thing and failed; she had never seen even the Duke's dining hall. She shivered as the drizzle thickened. When she glanced back up the road toward the city, she saw nothing but a cloaked man on foot, trudging doggedly toward the gates. Just as Stammel spoke of moving them into the inn courtyard, they heard a shout.

"Good," said Stammel. "Here's the captains, and we can go on. What I heard of the roads, it'll be a long march."

"What about cloaks?" asked Devlin. "If this gets worse — "

"We'll need them dry for tonight," said Stammel. "If a caravan's stuck in Littlebridge, we may not have shelter for everyone."

The captains rode up. "Sorry we were held up," said Pont. "The vice-regent insisted that we witness the seal on a letter for the Duke. Ferrault will go on, and I'll stay with the column. We'd better march."

Quickly Stammel reformed the unit, and they moved out. Ferrault's bay horse trotted ahead, quickly moving out of sight. The last large building was indeed another inn, this one with a picture of a mounted fighter on its signboard. As they passed, a small group of men lounged out its wide door to stare at them.

"The carrion crows are moving, I see," said one in green, with gray boots.

"Whose are those?" asked another. He had a delicately curled mustache.

"Some northern warlord. Duke something-or-other, I forget. They all ape the nobility, that sort." Paks heard him hawk and spit. "Better they go south to Aarenis and die than cause trouble here, I say."

The others laughed. Paks noticed that Stammel's neck was redder than usual. He said nothing. She wondered if the captain had heard. They marched on, up a rise in a gentle S-curve. The road ran between low walls and hedges, with farmland on either side. Under the drizzle the plowed fields looked soft and black. Most of the cattle were dun, with white markings on their faces. Cottages near the road were stone below and white-washed wood above; the roofs were slate cut thinner than Paks had seen before. Each cottage had a block of fruit trees behind it.

The next two days taught Paks more than she wanted to learn about bad weather marching. First the hard-frozen road went from greasy to soft mud under the drizzle. As the afternoon and rain went on, the mud deepened, until they were all ankle-deep in thin slop. Paks felt the wet creep into her boots: first the toes, then the sides of her feet, and finally the whole foot, squelch, squelch, squelch with every step. Her socks pulled the dampness up her legs. Drizzle soaked her tunic at the shoulders, until little trickles of rain began to run down her back and sides. She worried about her sword in its scabbard. That was better than thinking about her cold feet. When the road lifted over low hills, the road firmed, but in the hollows mud was deep enough to slow them. Paks, in the front rank, could see how it had been churned already by heavy caravan wagons.

As the light faded, Paks began to wonder where they would spend the night. Usually by this time they had already camped. She glanced around. Thick leafless woods on either side of the road, as they toiled up yet another rise. Mud dragged at her feet. Several had stumbled in holes hidden by the mud; some had fallen. At the top, the road followed the ridge, swerving east. The drizzle thickened to a steady light rain, blown by a northeast wind. As it got darker, it was harder to see the road surface. Paks lurched as she missed her footing in the ruts and holes. The road swung right; she felt the change in grade as it dipped. Paks heard the captain coming up, the sucking of his horse's hooves in the mud. He rode past her, his horse mud to the knees, and called to Stammel.

"It's going to be black dark before we make Littlebridge in this muck, and that bad hole's still to come. We're starting to break up in the rear. There's a place to camp along on the right; it'll be out of the wind if it stays as it is."

"Yes, sir. Do you mean that old wanderer campground?"

"That's it. There's a spring straight downhill." The captain wheeled his horse and rode back past the column. Paks noticed that he looked as wet as she felt. She was glad they were stopping soon. The next two hundred paces seemed to take forever. She watched Stammel search the edge of the woods.

"See this path?" he asked. Paks could barely see a dim gap between the trees. "We follow this; it'll open out on a firm slope. Stay on the path; we don't want the tribe angry with us." He led the way, and Paks followed. File by file they slipped into the woods. After a few twists and turns, they came to a large clearing, dim now in the dusk, but easily large enough for all. Paks followed Stammel to the right, and they settled down under a row of cedars to rest. Stammel went back to direct the others. It seemed to take a long time. Paks began to stiffen in the cold, and her belly cramped and growled as if she'd never eaten lunch. She looked back through the trees and saw a flickering light — torches — someone had gotten torches from the pack mules.

The light roused her, and she stood, swinging her arms back and forth. If they were camping, Stammel would want a fire. And the captain had said something about a spring, and they'd need a ditch — she looked around for her file, and called them over. The other file leaders of her unit looked up, listening.

"As soon as we can get a torch," she began, "we can see to set up. Same assignments as night before last, except I don't know if we'll be cooking. I'll find out. Wood gatherers, try to find something dry — at least not soaked. Everybody up and get working, or we won't sleep dry." She was sure they would have a miserable night.

It seemed to take a long time to get organized. Torches sizzled in the rain, giving barely enough light to see, until the main campfire finally caught. The clearing was a slightly irregular oblong, edged all around with thick cedar trees, and sloping just enough to shed water. Off to one side was a smaller clearing where Stammel told them to dig their trench. The tribe, he explained, always used it so. Paks and Malek went with Bosk to find the spring, down slippery wet rocks until they heard a frog splash into open water. By the time they came back, the fire was burning well, and Stammel had them fill several kettles. Steam rolled up from their wet tunics. Bosk took the packet of ground roots and herbs for making sib, and poured it into the kettles.

"It'll be stronger this way, and bitter, but we need it strong."

Paks stirred the brew with a wooden spoon, enjoying the fire's warmth. More and more of them were clustering near the fire to eat their ration of trail bread and salt beef. Bosk assigned someone to stir the other kettles.

"Here, Paks." Her file-second handed her a share of bread and meat, and squatted beside her. "I don't think I've ever been so wet, and had to sleep out."

Paks grunted around the hunk of meat in her mouth.

"You should see Kefer's unit," he went on. "Mud to the waist, it looks like. I wonder how much more of this there is."

Paks finished chewing the beef into submission, and washed it down with a swig of water. "I guess it depends on how long it rains. Lucky for us we were in front today. If they change the marching order — "

Keri looked startled. "They wouldn't. The Duke himself said we were the first."

"As an honor, yes. But in this — whoever marches last has the worst of it. It slows us all down, and it's not fair."

"Maybe it will dry off tomorrow."

"Maybe." Paks stirred the brew again, and took a bite of bread. Her right side, near the fire, felt dry and hot; she shifted to the other side of the kettle and decided to take off boots and socks. She could dry her socks on the firepit rocks. She struggled with her boots, and had one off and the other half-off when she saw Stammel approaching. She tried to stand, but he waved her down.

"Don't get up. How's the sib coming?" It had begun to smell good. He dipped the spoon in and took a sip. "Another half-hour, I expect. Don't scorch your boots. I wanted to talk to you about the order of march tomorrow."

Her head came up. "You're changing it? I wondered if you would."

Stammel looked surprised. "I didn't think you'd expect it, but yes. It's nothing to do with the honor, you know; it's the mud. The last unit has the hardest time, and slows us."

Paks nodded. "I thought so. How will you change it?"

"We'll change places every two hours — the change will keep any one unit from wearing down, I hope. The mules will go first; with those narrow hooves they have a bad time in soft ground anyway. You'll be the last unit when we start, then move to second and first in rotation."

"Why can't we walk in the fields, when the road's so bad?"

Stammel shook his head. "No. We don't trample fields. It's one of the Duke's rules, and one of the reasons we can travel without trouble. The farmers don't fear to see us coming."

"How far do we need to go?"

"Tomorrow?" Paks nodded. "We're almost an hour's dry walk from Littlebridge, and the next good stop beyond that is Fiveway — a nice day's march in good weather, and I don't know if we can make it in the rain. Depends."

Paks turned her socks over; they were almost dry. "Is it usually like this?"

"Sometimes. There's a lot of rain south of Vérella, all the way to the foothills of the Dwarfmounts. Then it's usually drier, going west and over the pass — not bad at all once we're in the south itself. By then it's summer anyway. But this stretch of road — three to six days depending — is always bad if it rains. You'd think the Council in Vérella would do something, with all the trade coming this way, but they haven't since the old king died. They leave it to the local landholders. And they just leave it."

Paks thought back to the city she'd seen that morning: a very different world from the wet dark clearing. "Sergeant Stammel, why did that man call us carrion crows?"

Stammel grunted. "You heard that, did you? You don't want to listen to that sort. Well — crows follow a battle, I suppose you wouldn't know that — they come to feast on the carnage. And some folks call mercenaries that, as if we were bloodseekers."

Paks thought that over a moment. "But who were they? They had rich clothes. And why did they say that about the Duke? He really is a duke, isn't he?"

"Them? Town bravos is what they looked like. They'd like to be thought lords' sons by their dress and jewels. As for our Duke — I haven't heard anyone dispute his title — any time lately, at least. He's Duke enough for me, and more worth following than some pedigreed princeling that can't sit his horse without a tutor, or draw blade without six servants to protect him." Stammel stopped short, and stirred the fire for a moment. Paks asked nothing more, but turned her socks again. They were dry, and she brushed the dried mud from them. Stammel tasted the sib again and shook his head.

When the sib was finally ready, Stammel dipped a large spoonful of honey into each kettle. After a mugful of that stout drink, Paks felt warm to her toes. Her unit, being least tired, had the first watch. For the first hour or so the drizzling mist lightened, and Paks hoped it might stop entirely. But heavier rain returned, hissing and spitting in the fire. Stammel brought a length of waxed canvas to lay over their store of wood.

When the watch changed, Paks took her dry cloak from the protected pack with a feeling of futility. Everything was wet. She found a space under

73

a cedar where the tree's thick foliage kept the rain from falling directly on her, but she was sure she would not sleep.

Stammel's call took her by surprise. She had slept the night through, despite the damp. She unrolled her cloak and crept out. A wet mass of cedar foliage smacked her in the face. Paks shivered. Around her the camp came slowly to life. She stretched the kinks out of her back, then looked distastefully at her sodden boots, and walked barefoot to the firepit.

The last watch had put porridge on the fire as well as sib. Paks checked to see that her file was up and moving, then took her place in line. Her wet cloak dragged at her shoulders. She wondered if they would pack the wet cloaks or wear them. When she could get near the fire, she turned her back to it, hoping to dry the cloak. The hot food warmed her; she wondered if she could march barefoot, and save her boots. But Stammel explained the dangers of this, and she resigned herself to the discomfort.

Soon they were ready to leave; yesterday's last unit grinned slyly as they filed away through the trees. Only the captain on his horse stayed behind. When they came out on the road, Paks started after the rest. The road surface was churned into uneven mush, like half-eaten porridge gone cold. Their boots sank in several inches at once. Downhill the mud deepened. Rainwater on the surface splashed high up their legs. The next unit was already far ahead, but when Paks tried to pick up the pace, several of them slipped in the mud and almost went down.

She had to slow again; she and the other file leaders began a marching song to keep everyone in step, and that seemed to help. When some ran out of breath, or stumbled, others took it up. The downhill grade eased, but the mud was deeper still. It dragged at their boots; Paks felt her thighs begin to ache from jerking against that pull with every step. Around another turn of road, Paks saw that they'd gained half the distance to the unit in front of them. Then she saw why: it was floundering in a section of road that seemed to have no bottom.

"Tir's brass boots!" growled Captain Pont. "I told them that the next time I mired a troop in this place, I'd fix it myself, then and there." She looked up at him; he was scowling. "Very well — Paks — "

"Yes, sir."

"We're going to put some stepping stones in that mess. See those walls?" He pointed to the drystone walls that bordered the road. Paks nodded. "Get your unit off the road; when they get to the bad spot, take those stones and pile 'em in until you can walk across. Those Tir-damned farmers have made enough pulling wagons out of this hole — we all pay toll on this road anyway, and some of it is supposed to go for repairs."

The edge of the bad patch was obvious: the gaping hole where a mule had gone in belly deep. Already the mired unit was beginning to tear up the wall for stones. The first stones sank at once, but eventually they began to fill the hole. Finally Paks had her unit lay the flat topping stones from the wall over all, and they walked across without sinking.

Beyond that hole, they were back in ankle-deep mud, but the change of pace had rested them. Now they slogged on together, all three units chanting one song after another. "Cedars of the Valley" gave way to "The Herdsman's Daughter" after many verses. On the left, trees thinned to pasture, and across the fields Paks could see a river as gray as the sky. The road edged toward it. Soon she could see a cluster of cottages huddled near the road. As they neared them, the road firmed. Paks could feel gravel through her sodden boots. They came to a paved square, streaming in the rain. Around it were larger buildings: an inn, a tall building with wide doors painted blue and red, several large houses. Stammel halted the column. Paks shifted her shoulders under her wet cloak and wondered if they would get anything from the inn. She looked around. The square was empty but for them; their mules were caked in mud to the belly, and the other units looked as muddy as she was. Her legs ached. She tried to see out the other side of the square, where the road humped itself up — a bridge, she thought. This must be Littlebridge.

A short time later, they marched out, having seen the inside of the inn very briefly, while downing fresh rolls and mugs of hot soup. That interval of warmth and dryness helped, but all too soon Paks was back out in the rain, lining up behind Vona's unit, with Kefer's behind her.

They started briskly across the square and over the narrow humped bridge beyond it. On the other side were more houses, some large, and craftshops. Then the houses dwindled to cottages flanked by gardens, and the gravelled road softened to mud.

The rest of that day was a matter of endurance. At times the rain slackened, but mostly they marched before a chill, wind-driven rain. Mud was always with them: now thicker, and clinging to their boots with every step, now thinner and splashing like water. They passed sodden little villages, too small for an inn, and wet farms that seemed half-melted into the ground. Every two hours they halted for a brief rest and change of position. By midafternoon, they were numb with fatigue, stumbling along the road like drunks. Paks ached from head to heel. She no longer worried about her sword rusting, or where they would sleep. She put one foot ahead of the other with dogged intensity. As the light faded, her unit shifted again from last to middle, this time with no pause for rest.

"We've got to get them to Fiveway," she heard Stammel say, but she did not look up to see who else was nearby. They started again, lurching in the mud. Soon it was too dark to see anything but the nearest ranks and the road beneath. Then that faded. They marched on in the darkness more by feel than sight. The last singers lost heart and the marching songs died away. Paks could not have said how long they'd marched — it seemed like half the night — when a line of dim orange lights broke the darkness ahead. She could not tell how far away they were, nor how big — they were merely blurs that brightened step by step. After awhile, she realized that they were square: windows, she thought suddenly, with lights behind them. At once she felt even colder and stiffer than before.

Soon she could see light reflected on the wet road outside the windows.

The road firmed under her feet: gravel again. She heard the crisp hoof-beats of the captain's horse passing on the right. Torches flared ahead, wavering in the wind. By their light she could see wet pavement, the fronts of buildings, the gleam of steel. An abrupt challenge rang out before them. Stammel called a halt. She heard voices, but could not distinguish the words. She shivered. The torches came nearer; now she could see the men holding them, and the armed men behind. She slid a hand to her sword hilt. Stammel appeared, carrying a torch now. In its dancing light his face was strange; she could not read its expression.

"We've got shelter near here," he said. "Vona's unit will pick up food at the inn. Paks, yours will unpack the mules. Follow Devlin; he knows where to go."

Paks did not think she could follow anyone anywhere, but when Devlin came with a torch, she found she could still pick up her feet. They turned down a lane beside a high stone wall, and came out in a field, onto short wet grass. Not far away Paks sensed a large structure looming against the sky. Devlin led them to it: a barn, stone below and wood above, easily large enough for all of them. The mules were already tied along one end, and the skinner had lighted other torches; a warm glow spilled out to meet them.

Once inside, the relief of being out of the wind and rain was enormous. The barn was almost empty, but for hay in one corner. Paks wanted to fall headlong in that hay and sleep, but Devlin prodded her to come unload the mules. She and the others stumbled over and pulled off the packs. Kefer's unit, meanwhile, began placing torches high in wall brackets away from the hay. Then they laid out sleeping areas. Their final chore was setting up lines for drying their wet clothes; the barn had hooks built in, and Devlin handed out rolls of thin cord. By this time, Vona's unit had brought the food, plentiful and hot despite the trek from the inn.

Long loaves of bread that steamed when they were broken — crocks of butter — kettles of savory stew — Paks ate at first hardly noticing what she put in her mouth, but as she warmed up she realized how good it was. Mug after mug of a strange hot drink not so bitter as sib. Bowl after bowl of stew. Suddenly she was nearly asleep, nodding as she sat. She glanced around. Devlin and Bosk were gathering empty platters and pots; she wondered if they would make the trip back tonight to the inn. She met Stammel's eye and braced herself for the order to go back — but he smiled and told her to get some sleep. When she tried to get up, she found she had stiffened from that brief rest. She barely made it to a heap of hay and an empty blanket, falling into a deep sleep before she could review any part of the day.

Chapter Nine

The next morning rain still fell in curtains. Captain Pont decided to delay at least a day, and the barn filled with drying clothes. Everyone felt stiff and grumpy at first, but by noon they were all awake enough to be restless. Paks even welcomed a walk through the rain to the inn for food. A caravan bound for Vérella had come in; great wagons blocked the streets, and the inn was full of wet and disgruntled merchants.

"Camped!" she heard one exclaim to the landlord, as she led her file toward the kitchen. "By Simyits, we weren't camped. We were stuck — flat stuck! Gods blast your count or whatever you've got down here! I pay toll on this passage every year, and he hasn't set stone on the road since my father died." Paks glanced at the speaker, a tall, powerful man in mud-stained leather with a gold chain around his neck and a ring in each ear. The landlord, shorter and plumper, had a fixed smile on his face. "You can tell him for me," the big man went on, "that the Guild League can find another way north, if it comes to that." Then Paks was in the kitchen, dodging a squad of agitated cooks to the table where their food was laid ready. She noticed on her way back out that the landlord had escaped from the tall man, and was leading a party of velvet-clad ladies up the stairs.

When she mentioned the incident to Stammel, he laughed. "That'd be the wagonmaster," he said. "Let's see — it might be the Manin family caravan, or maybe Foss Council. Did you notice what they carried?"

"No, sir. What's the Guild League he mentioned?"

"Guild League cities, that is. Those on the north caravan route, not the Immer route." Paks felt that this explained nothing. Stammel noticed her blank look. "Don't you know anything about the south, about Aarenis?"

"It's where some spice comes from, and fancy embroidery," said Paks.

"Umm. That's not enough. We have time for better. Have you heard of the Immerhoft Sea, that lies south of the land?" Paks nodded. Jornoth had mentioned it. "Across the Immerhoft was Aare, the old kingdom. Those people settled islands in the Immerhoft, then sailed on to find a great land they called Aarenis, the daughter of Aare. They settled it, and spread, and the land was divided among great lords and their children. In time they spread to the Dwarfmounts, driving the elves ahead of them, and found passes to the north. That's what we call the south — Aarenis is what it's called when you're in the south — from the Immerhoft to the

77

Dwarfmounts. These same folk settled the western kingdoms of the north."

Paks frowned. "I thought the Eight Kingdoms were settled by seafolk and nomads from the north. My grandfather — "

"Was probably a horse nomad. In part, they were. But all these groups met in the Honnorgat valley. The eastern kingdoms, those below the great falls, have more seafolk. Tsaia and Fintha have more nomads. And Lyonya and Prealith have elves. But most of the folk in Tsaia and Fintha came from Aarenis long ago." Paks nodded, and Stammel went on. "There's a great trade between Aarenis and the Eight Kingdoms and most of it comes through the pass we'll use, up the Vale of Valdaire. Long ago it came by water, up the Immer and its tributaries. Southbound trade sailed from Immer ports to Aare itself. But Aare is a wasteland now, and the sea trade goes to other lands — I don't know where myself, and the tales are strange enough. Anyhow, for one reason and another, a group of cities agreed to build a new trade route, a land route. Some say the river trade was taxed too heavily by the lords and cities along it, and some that river pirates made it too dangerous. I think myself that these cities traded more with the north, and for that a land route was needed anyway. So their merchant guilds joined in the Guild League, and they built the road and maintain it, and they send their caravans north each year, and we send ours south. The wars in Aarenis come partly from rivalry between the Guild League cities and the river cities and old lords."

"Which side are we on?" Effa had come near to listen, with several others.

"Whoever hires us," said Bosk, leaning on the wall nearby.

Stammel nodded. "He's right. The Duke makes a contract with some-one — a city or a lord, whoever will pay his price — and that's who we fight for."

Effa looked shocked. "But — surely the Duke wouldn't make a contract with just anyone."

"Well — no. We're a northern company, after all: an honorable com-pany. He has his standards. But we've fought for one city against another, and for a lord against a city, and the reverse. It doesn't matter."

"What do you mean, we're an honorable company?" asked Barra. "Aren't all companies much alike?"

"Tir, no! I wish they were. The good ones — mostly northern — agree on some things — we won't harbor each other's criminals or traitors, we won't torture prisoners, we treat prisoners fairly, and so forth. We don't steal supplies from peasants, or destroy crops if we can avoid it. We com-pete, but we know there's wars enough to keep us all employed; we don't try to kill each other off, except in battle. And that's our business. But there are some others — " Stammel paused, and looked around the group; more recruits had come to listen to him, and Captain Pont lounged nearby. "Cap-tain Pont will bear me out — "

Pont nodded, his long face splitting in a grin. "Surely. The south is full of so-called mercenaries. Most of 'em are robbers that blackmail some poor town into hiring them to keep order. Some are fairly honest hired blades in summer, and robbers in winter. A few are fairly well-organized and independent, but downright nasty — "

"The Wolf Prince — " muttered Stammel.

"Yes — the Wolf Prince. He's definitely a bad one. Uses poison, assassins, and anything else he can think of. Tortures prisoners and sells 'em to the searovers. Takes ransom only in coins or hard jewels, and only within three days. We broke into his stockade one year — were you there, Stammel?"

"Yes, sir." Stammel picked up the tale. "He'd captured a patrol of the Sier of Westland's light cavalry, and chained them all in the open, without food or water. Three were alive when we broke in, and only one lived to make it back to Westland, with all we could do."

"But didn't you kill him?" Effa broke in.

"No. He'd gotten away a few days before; we never did know how he got through the lines." Stammel paused, his face grim. "Then there's the Honeycat. Calls himself Count of the South Marches, I think it is, and runs four companies or so along the coast and up the Immer valleys. There's a bad one. We'll probably come against him again this campaign. He's not exactly a mercenary, in the usual sense. He stirs up wars; they say he has factions in every city, and has even bought out some of the guilds. He hates the northern companies, because he can't scare us or bribe us."

"Why is he called Honeycat?"

"It's what he's like, they say — sweet words, soft voice, and then claws in your belly."

"I've heard of him," said Barra suddenly. "Isn't he the one that hung the witwards of Pliuni upside down from the city gates?"

"Yes, but it wasn't the witwards. It was the priests of Sertig's Anvil and the Lord's Hall. That's why five priesthoods have banned him — not that he cares; he believes in none of them. Some say he worships the Tangler or the Master of Torments, and others say he follows the Thieves' Creed. Whichever, he's bad clear through. His captains are as bad as he is."

"Is that why we're going to fight him?" asked Effa. Stammel glared.

"Haven't you been listening at all? We're a mercenary company; we fight for pay. If we do fight the Honeycat, it'll be because some enemy of his hires us. We have nothing to do with good and bad — not that way, I mean."

Paks was still thinking about something Stammel had said earlier. "You said the honorable companies treat prisoners well — "

"Yes. Why?"

"Well — how do we — I mean, isn't it dishonorable to surrender? And for the others? I thought we just fought until — "

"No, no," Stammel interrupted. "We're hired fighters, not fanatic hotheads. We fight hard when we're fighting, but if our Duke or captains tell us to quit, we quit. Right then. You remember that, or you won't make it back to wherever — Three Firs. There's no sense in losing the whole Company out of pride."

"But don't we owe it to whoever hired us?" asked Saben.

"No. The Duke hired *you* — remember your oath to him?" He looked around until they all nodded. "You agreed to obey the Duke, and his captains — no one else. That's where your honor lies. Somebody who has a contract with the Duke, that's between the Duke and him. Our honor is between the Duke and us."

"It — it doesn't happen often, does it? Being surrendered, I mean, and captured?" Paks still could not imagine it.

"No. Not to us; the Duke's careful. He won't take a contract where we don't have a chance. But it has, and it may again." Paks sat frowning at her bare feet as the talk went on around her. It had never occurred to her that they might surrender; she did not like that idea at all. Effa was still arguing, talking about St. Gird and the honor of a warrior, and Arñe, as usual, was trying to shut Effa up.

"Effa," said Pont finally, "if you wanted to be that sort of warrior — a paladin or something like that — you should have talked to your Marshal about joining a fighting order —"

"He said I should get experience," said Effa, red-faced.

"You'll get that here," said Pont. "And even Marshals and paladins, Effa, must follow orders —"

"But they don't surrender! They fight to the death —"

"Not always," said Bosk. "I've known them to retreat: any good warrior must learn when to withdraw."

"You've seen that?"

"Yes. Think of the legends; Gird himself retreated once, at Blackhedge, remember? If you finish your service with us, and join a fighting order, you'll see — fighting's fighting, Effa — war doesn't change. If Girdsmen never backed out of a fight, they'd all be dead." Effa looked unconvinced, but subsided.

Late that afternoon the rain stopped. By next morning, the clouds had cleared. They were on the road early. When they fetched breakfast from the inn, well before dawn, they learned that another caravan had come in the night before, from the east.

"You might's well go across the fields," the landlord told Captain Pont. "We've wagons wall to wall in town, and stuck on all the roads in. You'll not harm plowed or planted ground if you swing east a bit and then south: that's fallow this year.

So they made good time on the turf for some distance. They climbed a long gentle slope. The view opened around them: pastureland nearby, and blocks of woodland in the distance. Something along the woods edge was in bloom; puffs of white that looked like plum blossom. As they topped the rise, Paks noticed an irregular cloud bank to the south and east.

"There they are," said Stammel cheerfully.

"What?" Paks could not see anything cheerful about more clouds.

"The mountains — that's the Dwarfmounts."

"They're not very big," she said doubtfully. "I thought they were big mountains."

80

Stammel laughed. "They are. We're a long way from them. Keep watching."

Day by day the mountains crawled above the horizon, showing themselves taller and taller. Eastward the highest peaks were snow-covered from tip to foothills below — but even the western end of the range was higher than anything Paks had seen. The tales went round the fires at night: those dun-colored hills were home to gnomes, the princedoms of Gnarrinfulk and Aldonfulk. The mountains themselves sheltered tribe after tribe of dwarves: Goldenaxe, Axemaster, Ironhand. Rich dwarves, immensely rich with the gold and silver and gemstones they delved from the mountains' roots.

Now the road swung west, along the line of the range, and west again, as they climbed higher into the hills. The mountains seemed to dive into the earth just west of their path. "That's the pass," explained Stammel. "And just beyond is the Vale of Valdaire." Here the road was busy. They passed caravans headed north, great wagons pulled by powerful mules, each with its armed guard atop, and a squad or so of men-at-arms marching before and behind the train. They saw more dwarves, traveling in troops, heavily armed, peering up at the humans suspiciously from under their bushy brows. Elves here and there — single travelers, mostly, but once a small band of elven knights, who hailed the captain in silvery ringing voices that thrilled the ear like harpstrings lightly plucked.

As the road rose higher over every hill, Paks could see behind them the great tumbled rug of forest and field that sloped from the mountains to the Honnorgat. Far away north was Vérella of the Bells, and upriver from that Fin Panir that she had never seen. And somewhere very far north and west, beyond the Honnorgat and at the springing of one of its minor branches, were the moors above Three Firs and the low stone house where she'd been born. The miles to the Duke's stronghold had seemed no barrier to return, nor the crossing of the great river, nor the miles since. But when she looked up at the mountains' snowy wall, she felt that crossing them would be to leave the land of her home.

As she mused, someone noticed the blue shadow to the west. Still many miles away, it hung a blue curtain on the sky — the arm of a great mass of mountains that bordered Aarenis on the west. The pass south lay between the two ranges.

The pass itself was easier than it looked. For hundreds of years that road had been worked and reworked; it wound between hills and around them, taking the easiest way up, and only at the last did it lift itself from beside a streambed and crawl over one rocky knob. At once, having crossed, it returned to the easy path, winding along as it must, among hills now green with spring.

For it was full spring in the south, a lush spring. The Vale of Valdaire lay lovely and green before them, a vast bowl with snowy mountains in the background, green pastures on the uplands, and darker green forests below. From the top of the pass, it took two days to reach the city, but every step of the way was pleasant.

81

Valdaire, as they saw it gleaming beside the laughing waters of its little rivers, looked far more welcoming than Vérella. Its walls seemed more apt to hold up the backs of shops than to form a defense. As they neared it, great inns lined the road, each with a huge walled court for the caravan wagons and draft animals. Across the river from the road, on rising ground not far from the city, they saw what looked like a small stone village. Bosk pointed it out.

"That's Halveric Company's winter quarters," he said. Someone bolder than Paks asked what "Halveric Company" was. "Mercenaries, like us. They usually contract with the Sier of Westland, these last few years. A good company, all things considered."

"Where's ours?" someone asked.

"East of the city. We'll go through, just to show you. Now keep it sharp."

Valdaire swarmed with people, and not only merchants and craftsmen, as in Vérella: it swarmed with troops of all sorts. They had been told it was the truce city, but they had not expected so many different colors and badges. Green tunics much like their own, red tunics over black or gray trousers, green leather over brown wool, brown tunics over red — it was bewildering. Riders in chain mail on slender, quick-stepping horses, riders in plate on massive chargers, crossbowmen on mules. Now and again one of them spoke to Captain Pont or Stammel, commenting freely on the recruits' appearance. Paks noticed the strange accents, and the gods they swore by — she had no idea who or what Ashto and Senneth were.

At last they were through the city. On the right was a last inn, *The White Dragon*. A row of men in leather armor lounged outside it, and stared as the column went by.

"Phelan's new recruits," she heard one of them say.

"Wish they were ours," said another. "That load of blockheads we got this year — "

"Think these are better?"

"They march better, that's something. By Tir, I hope we don't close that contract with — "

"Hssh!" Then the column was past, and she heard no more.

They turned from the road into a lane. Ahead clustered whitewashed stone buildings, most long and low but three of them two-storied. Paks took a deep breath. This had to be the Duke's winter quarters — in a few minutes they would see the veterans for the first time, would find their places in the full Company. They marched closer. She could see people walking around between buildings. No one seemed to pay them any attention. Paks tried not to let her eyes wander as they came between the buildings. The veterans looked incredibly tough. They came to an open space, and Stammel halted them. Almost at once, a voice she did not know bellowed a command, and the Company formed so fast it seemed the bodies snapped into place. Instead of men and women casually walking about or standing in doorways, now there was a compact, precise formation of hard-eyed soldiers. Paks blinked; several behind her gasped. She could feel the veterans' eyes scanning the column. It made her uneasy, like an itch. Then the Duke rode out, and greeted Captain Pont, and within moments the column was dispersing to the three cohorts of the Company.

All in Stammel's unit went into Arcolin's cohort. He was a tall, stern-faced man with dark hair and bright gray eyes. Arcolin's junior captain was Ferrault, who had ridden with them as far as Vérella: sandy-haired, bearded, both shorter and slighter than Arcolin. Barra and Natzlin and the rest of Kefer's unit were assigned to Dorrin's cohort. Paks was startled to find that Dorrin was a woman. Sejek was her junior captain — and Stephi, then, was in another cohort. Paks was relieved.

The next few hours were even more chaotic than her first as a new recruit. Each novice was assigned to a veteran, and the veterans made it clear that they would have to prove themselves all over again — if they could. Donag, a heavy-set file leader with dour dark brows, gave Paks an unfriendly look.

"Are you the one that got Stephi in such trouble?" Paks froze; she had relaxed too soon. Donag interpreted her silence to suit himself. "I thought so. You ought to be ashamed enough to keep quiet. A good friend he's been to me, Stephi — cause more trouble, and you won't see the north again." He glowered at her a moment longer. "They say you can fight; it had best be true." He led her to her assigned bunk without another word. Paks felt a smoldering anger. She had not gotten Stephi in trouble; it had been his fault. She glared at Donag's back.

The next several days were uncomfortable. They drilled every day, marching and weapons, and it was obvious how much they had yet to learn. Paks had been coasting, as one of the best recruits. Despite Siger's nagging about speed, she had thought she was as fast as she needed to be. The slower veterans were faster. The best — and Donag was one of these — seemed inhumanly fast. She acquired a lot of new bruises, and the only time Donag smiled at her was when he dealt them.

"He's down on you, isn't he?" asked Saben one evening on the way back from supper. Paks nodded. She didn't want to talk about it. She had heard, through the grapevine, what had happened to Stephi, and had decided Donag would just have to wear out his resentment. Barra, of course, had noticed and urged Paks to complain. "It's not your fault," Saben went on. "He shouldn't be like that." Paks shrugged.

"I can't stop him."

"No, but Stammel could. Or the captain." That was what Barra had said, too.

"No. It wouldn't work. Just — don't say any more, Saben, please."

"All right. But I'm on your side, remember." He looked worried, and Paks managed a smile, her first in several days, to reassure him.

Later that evening, Stephi showed up in their barracks. Donag smiled at him, and gave Paks a warning glare. She went on with her work, polishing her helmet. To her surprise, Stephi greeted her first.

"Paks — how do you like the south?"

She looked up, startled. "It's very different. It's so hot already."

Stephi smiled. "That surprised me, my first year south. Wait until full summer; you'll think you're melting into your armor. Are you settling in all right?"

Her eyes flicked toward Donag and back. "Yes, very well."

"Good. I expect, though, you've found it a change from being a top recruit — it's usually a shock."

Paks found herself relaxing a bit. Stephi did not sound angry with her, not nearly as hostile as Donag. "It is a change — you're all so much faster."

"If we weren't, we wouldn't be here to teach you," said Donag gruffly. He had walked over while they were talking, and now turned to Stephi. "Have you heard about the contract yet?"

Stephi shook his head. "No. We were out all day in the hills. Have you?"

Donag looked at Paks.

"Don't mind her," said Stephi. "They have to learn about contracts sometime."

Donag frowned, but went on. "I saw Foss Council messengers today, and two of them rode out just after lunch with a squad of guards. And in the city they're saying that Foss Council and Czardas are squabbling over boundaries."

"Huh," grunted Stephi. "Czardas. Let's see — that's a count, isn't it? All he's got is local militia, unless he hires someone — or if Andressat joins him."

"I don't really know yet," said Donag, but he was grinning.

Stephi grinned too. "But it was one of your — umm — good sources?"

Donag just grinned, shaking his head. Paks watched him in surprise. When he wasn't scowling, he had a pleasant face: rough and weathered, but humorous. He caught her look, made a wry face, and went back to his grin. "I'm not always a grouch, no — if that's what you were thinking. And perhaps you're not as bad as I thought — if you behave."

"I'm going down to the *Dragon*," said Stephi. "Why don't you come, Donag? I'd like to see what other rumors you can pick up."

"Well — I'm on late watch. But if we don't stay long — " He looked at Paks, then back at Stephi. "I'll come. But you, Paks, don't be blabbing all I told Stephi, and be sure you're ready for watch on time."

"Yes, sir." Paks watched the two men leave with mingled relief and astonishment.

From that time on, she had little trouble with Donag, though he still thumped her during drill until she found speed she had never thought to reach. In those weeks, a few of the younger veterans made cautious overtures of friendship. Paks was glad to spend time with Canna Arendts, whose tales of her first year's battles were much more exciting than Donag's dry instruction. Canna's best friend had died, and she enjoyed having someone to tell her stories to, someone who would listen by the hour. Saben liked her too, and Vik said he liked having a woman around who was not taller than he was — which made them all laugh wildly, the last night in Valdaire, as he craned his neck pretending that Paks and Arñe were seven feet tall. Canna laughed too, dark eyes dancing. She was lean and quick, and Paks felt clumsy and huge beside her.

On the road again, marching south, Paks could think only of the fighting to come. She had thought herself close to fighting before, but this time she was. This was real, marching with battle-scarred veterans around her, and soon the fighting would be real. No more drills, no more instruction. In the back of her head the vision rose of herself with a great sword, leading a charge. She knew it was nonsense, yet — this was a long way from Three Firs. Anything could happen. Almost anything. She was marching as file second to Donag — that had been a surprise. Most of the recruits were slotted further back in the column.

After several days of marching, they came to the fields where the first battle would be fought. Across a wide space was a dark mass: the enemy army.

"Militia," muttered Donag contemptuously. "We won't have much trouble with them, unless they've a surprise for us." Paks did not dare ask how he knew. She said nothing at all. "Just remember that even militia can kill you if you're stupid," he told her. "Stay in formation — remember the strokes — and listen for orders."

To her surprise, they set up camp that afternoon as if it were any other day on the road — except for the surgeons' area. Paks eyed the rows of straw pallets and the neatly arranged tents with distaste. She had heard stories about the surgeons, too. The recruits got another lecture, from the captains, and then a final one from their own sergeants.

"And after that they expect us to sleep?" asked Arñe. "I can't keep my eyes shut an instant, I know."

"The followers of Gird — " began Effa. Arñe interrupted.

"Effa, you Girdsmen may be all you say — brave, wise, and everything else — but I'm not one of you. If you can sleep, fine. Do it. As for me, if the gods guide my strokes tomorrow, and bring me safe through, then I'll sleep — "

"And I." Saben's face was more serious than usual. "I find I'm thinking how peaceful it is in the cowbyres, on a summer's evening."

Paks thought of sheep, fanned wide on a slope and coming together at the foot. The quick light clatter of their hooves, the anxious baaing, and the wide silence over all.

The next morning they were wakened before dawn, and barely managed to choke down breakfast.

"Eat, fools," said Donag, scowling again. "You can't fight empty. You'll wear out. And be sure your flasks are full, and drink so you slosh. Hurry now."

And before the sun cleared the low hills east of them, they were standing in formation, swords drawn, waiting.

Chapter Ten

As the sun rose higher, Paks felt sweat crawling through her hair under her helmet. The dust cloud ahead came closer as the Czardians advanced. Somewhere off on the right wing, a confused clamor began: crashing, metallic, and a deep roar that seemed to shake the earth. Her heart pounded; her sword grip felt slippery. She opened her mouth for air. Surely Stammel would tell them if they were supposed to do anything. She watched his unhurried stroll back and forth in front of their ranks. Behind him the mass of enemy came closer and closer. Someone in the ranks let out a sobbing groan.

"Take it easy, now," came Stammel's rough growl. "Remember your drill. I'll tell you when to worry, recruits. And you veterans, stop acting up to scare the new ones. I'll dock you a day's pay, if anyone else tries to unsettle 'em." Paks took a deep breath and tried to relax, flexing her hand on the sword. The noise and the dust came closer. One of the captains trotted along the front of their line and paused to speak to Stammel. Paks saw him nod. Stammel swung round to face them; Paks felt him capture and release her gaze before giving the expected order. At his command they began to march forward, the corporals chanting a ritual encouragement and reminder.

"Stay in formation now, file two; keep your swords up; keep your shields up and ready; steady march, slow march, count y'r cadence, slow march; file three, pick it up; steady march; no crowding there, third and four! Remember your shields, up and out — " And then the front rank was engaged with the enemy, and the noise of battle drowned out their voices. Paks suddenly found enemy swords thrust at her as the first rank moved into the enemy formation.

She blocked one with her shield, and hacked awkwardly at another with her sword. Only her longer reach kept her alive as her more dexterous opponent disengaged and thrust again. She remembered the correct move, this time, and slashed his sword away. The attacker on her left was now fully engaged with her shield partner, so she could use her own shield for protection against the man in front. She blocked another thrust, and tried an overhand swing. Her opponent's shield caught her blade; for a terrifying instant she could not wrench it free. She was wide open to his sweeping stroke; though she deflected it with her shield, the blade slid down and sliced into her leg through the greaves.

Paks staggered as the blade bit in, and that jerk freed her own sword. She lunged straight ahead, thrusting at the man's belly. Her longer reach worked; her sword slid into him. Before she could follow up her thrust, someone ran into her from behind, and knocked her off balance. She fell among the stamping feet and swinging blades, confused by dust and noise. The man she'd stabbed was also down — she saw his face, barely a foot from her own, and the dagger in his hand. She dropped her sword and grappled with his knife hand, trying to free her left arm from the shield so she could draw her own.

Suddenly his arm went limp; she saw another blade deep in his body. She could not see who had done it. She could not see anything but shadowy legs in the dust. She groped about for her own sword, found it, and tried to get to her feet. Bodies shoved at her from all directions. Her eyes were clogged with sweat and dirt; she blinked furiously, then realized she was surrounded by fighters in the Duke's colors. She tried to pick out where she was in formation — or anyone she knew — but nothing looked familiar. Out of the whirling dust came more fighters in blue and yellow; around her rose screams and bellows of rage. She found as she thrust at one of the enemy that her own throat was raw with yelling — and still she yelled. Her shield arm ached. Her sword weighed as much as a full-grown sheep. Her left leg was on fire. She kept thrusting, countering with shield, thrusting — her head splitting with the noise and dust. She took in great gulps of air, but found herself choking on dust, coughing, sobbing against the coughs. She nearly went down again, slipping on something underfoot, but someone grabbed her arm and kept her upright.

"Go on! Forward!" yelled someone in her ear, and she went on, squinting through the dust for yellow and blue to strike at, her sword and shield work now mechanical, as in drill.

At last there seemed to be less dust in front of her, and no blue and yellow. Someone grabbed her arm; she raised her sword to strike, but Stammel's voice penetrated the din. "Paks. Stop! Paks!" Her sword arm fell as if someone had cut the tendons. She stood, half-blinded by dust, gasping for breath, shaking — at last she could see Stammel, and met his eyes. "All right, Paks," he said, more quietly. "You're wounded; go to the rear." She could not move. The light failed, as if clouds had come over the sun. She heard Stammel's voice, now urgent, but could not follow what he said.

Someone's shoulder was under her arm, supporting her; someone's hands fumbled at the buckles of her shield. She tried to stop them, but could not seem to move well. Voices talked back and forth across her hearing. Nothing made sense. Suddenly someone shoved what felt like a length of wood into the wound on her leg; she tried to push them away from her, all of them, but found herself lying flat on the ground with no memory of how she'd gotten there. One of the veterans held her shoulders down; sweat dripped off his nose onto her face. When he saw her watching him, he said "Sorry," but kept his weight on her. Someone else was holding her legs. Her injured leg throbbed fiercely. A surgeon in his dark robes bent over it. A hand appeared out of nowhere, with a kerchief dripping water.

87

"Here," said a voice. "Chew on this." She opened her mouth, and he stuffed the wet rag in. At once something — she thought the same length of wood — bored into her leg. She twisted against the hands that held her, to no avail. The pain went on, and when it finally stopped was replaced by a bath of liquid fire. Paks closed her eyes, grinding the rag with her teeth. Something tugged at her leg — would tear it off, she thought — but ceased before it came loose. She opened her eyes. Tears blurred her vision until she blinked them away. Her leg still throbbed, but farther away — a spear-length or so, maybe. The veteran released her shoulders; the surgeon was already walking away. She gagged on the wet lump of cloth in her mouth, and a hand came to pull it out.

"There," said the voice. "That's over." Paks tried to twist her head to find the speaker, but it was too much effort. "You need some wine," the voice went on. "That will ease the pain." She tried to speak up, to refuse, but a strong arm heaved her head and shoulders up, and a wineskin pressed against her lips. When she opened her mouth to protest, a squirt of wine filled her mouth; she had to swallow. The wineskin was tooled in gold, she noticed, as another squirt of wine filled her mouth — then another. The pain receded farther, and a dark haze spread across her vision.

Paks woke to darkness and the sounds of pain. Far away to her left was a bobbing yellow glow. She felt light and crisp except for her injured leg, a cold weight dragging at her. The glow came closer, paused, came closer. She realized it was a lantern — in someone's hand — someone coming near. She felt very clever — she knew what was happening, someone was visiting the wounded. Then she realized she could not find her dagger. Had she been captured? She tried to think as the lantern came nearer. Her leg began to throb, but it didn't bother her. She had just decided that it wasn't really attached at all when the lantern paused beside her. She squinted up, trying to see past the light to the person who held it. "Hmm," said a voice she thought she should remember. "Looks a bit feverish, this one."

"How do you feel?" another voice asked.

Paks worked her tongue around in her dry mouth until she could speak. "I'm — all right."

"Do you feel hot?" asked the second voice.

At the question Paks realized that she was cold, cold from the bones out. She started to answer, but a violent chill racked her body; her teeth rattled like stones in a sack. A broad hand touched her forehead.

"Fever, all right," said the first voice. "Best dose her now, and be sure she's checked on. We'll use what we have to on this one."

"She needs to drink," said the second voice. "She's dry. Here, now — " he said to Paks. "We'll lift you up, then I want you to drink all of this."

One of them lifted her shoulders and steadied her head; a jug came to her lips. Paks sipped; it was water. Despite the shaking chill and rattling teeth, she managed to empty the jug.

"Now then," said the voice. "Swallow this." Paks had half-drained the cup before the taste reached her; she gagged and tried to spit it out, but hands restrained her. "Finish it!" said the voice, and she choked down the rest of that bitter brew. "Now a swallow of numbwine." Paks swallowed that, and the arm behind her eased her back to the straw.

"Sleep well, warrior," said the first voice. Paks felt a hand grip her shoulder, and the lantern moved away to her right; three shadowy forms moved with it.

When next she woke, a lantern was on the ground beside her, and someone was peeling off her sweat-sodden clothes. She grumbled a weak protest, but the person went on, drying her with a rough towel and then easing her into a long linen shirt. "It's fever sweat," a woman's voice said. "You need dry things so you won't chill again." A warm dry blanket covered her, then the woman held a flask to her lips. "Go on — drink this." Paks gulped it down and was asleep almost before her head hit the straw.

A hand on her shoulder and a voice calling her name roused her to sunlight dappling through green leaves. She felt solid to herself, aches and all. Stammel squatted beside her. "Come on," he said. "You've slept long enough."

Paks found her mouth too dry for speech. He offered a jug of water, and helped her raise her head to drink. She tried again; her voice was thinner than usual. "I — forgot the right strokes."

Stammel grinned. "I was going to mention that. Tir's bones, girl, a battle is no place to show off. Why do you think we teach you what strokes work?"

"I'm sorry — " she began.

"Never mind; more weapons drill for you, until you can't forget it. We don't want to lose a good private — "

"What!"

"Well, you did it in a backwards, idiotic way, but you hardly fit the 'recruit' category any more. I hope you realize you very nearly got yourself killed — and why didn't you get that wound bound up before you nearly bled out?"

"I — I didn't know it was that bad."

"Hmm. You don't come of berserker blood, do you? No? Probably just first battle fever. Vanza, by the way, is sorry he told you to advance when you were already wounded. He says he didn't see it."

"That's all right," said Paks.

"Not with me, it isn't. It's his job to keep track of you novices and get you back if you're hurt. Do you remember how many you killed?"

"I killed? No — " Paks thought a long moment. "No. There's — a lot I don't remember. It's all confused."

"Likely enough. You did well, Paks, wrong strokes and all. Now — you'll be going back with the other wounded to Valdaire in a day or so. The Duke expects we'll take out the rest of the Czardians tomorrow or the next day; they've gotten in among those hills southwest of here. Vanza will stay to help with our wounded — "

"Do I have to go back to Valdaire? Couldn't I stay here — "

Stammel shook his head. "No. The surgeons say you won't be up to a route march for several weeks. You lost a lot of blood, and the fever might come back. Don't worry, though — you'll be with us again soon." He gave her a reassuring grin as he stood up. "I'll see you again before you go. Do what they tell you, and heal fast."

Paks had hoped to prove the surgeons wrong, but she could barely hobble a few steps to the wagons when they loaded. She settled into the second of five wagons, bedded deep in straw and braced into a corner against the jolting ride. Four others shared the wagon: Callexon, a recruit in Dorrin's cohort, with his broken leg bound in splints, a veteran with a huge lump on his head who never woke up, a woman named Varne, from Cracolnya's cohort, who had been burned by flaming oil, and Effa, who had been trampled by a warhorse and would never walk. Callexon and Paks helped Vanza care for the rest at halts. Paks learned how to feed and clean a helpless person, and how to help with bandaging.

The little caravan had been winding between tall trees, shade cool on the canvas-topped wagons. Paks looked out to see whether it was a road they'd marched over, but she couldn't tell. The wagon rolled smoothly; she closed her eyes and dozed off.

She was wakened by a scream and a jolt that wrenched her leg. She opened her eyes to see Vanza hurtling out the back of their wagon, sword in hand. Out the front she could see strange horses and masked riders with black wolf's heads on their red jerkins. Something blocked her view to the right; their wagon's driver was slumped against the iron bow that held the canvas. Two arrows poked through her tunic. The mules had their ears laid flat. As Paks grabbed for the reins, heaving herself over the front of the box, the lead pair surged forward.

She heard a whirr and a thunk, and saw an arrow stand quivering in the wagon box beside her — but she had the reins. She tried to haul the driver inside with one arm; she couldn't get any leverage. The wagon lurched as the mules veered from the track. Another arm appeared beside her: the burned woman.

"I'll get her — you drive!"

"I'm trying!" Paks had driven her father's pair of plow ponies, but nothing like a hitch of four frightened mules. She had a tangle of reins, all too long, and the mules were picking up speed. Suddenly one of the red-clothed riders swerved beside the lead pair and made a grab for their reins. Paks pulled some of her handful, and the mules veered.

"Now I know what those are," she muttered, and reached to shorten the others. The rider glanced up and saw her. He wheeled his horse and came at the wagon, sword raised. Paks jerked the other pair of reins as he neared it; the mules swerved back and the wagon slammed into his horse. His sword hit the iron frame and shattered. Paks hardly noticed. The mules had broken into a panicky run. She couldn't brace herself well enough to pull them in. And her best attempts at steering had the wagon veering wildly from side to side. There were trees everywhere she looked. All around came wild screeches, yells, the whinnying of horses and braying of mules. An arrow struck one of the leaders. It screamed, and lurched ahead faster. Ahead Paks saw a gap in the trees; the mules galloped toward it, flat out. Too late, Paks saw the dip that steepened into a bank of eroded stone over a stream. The wagon bounced from stone to stone, collapsing with a broken axle in the shallow streambed; the mules were jerked to their knees by the shock. Paks, already leaning over the front of the box, flew forward. Her injured leg slammed against the back of the box, all that kept her from going headlong on top of the wheel pair. She banged her chin on the footboard, and hung there dazed.

"Quick!" said a voice. Someone pulled at her. "Help with these reins. Don't let 'em take off again."

"Mmph." Paks shortened the reins and blinked heavily. Varne held the reins she'd dropped.

"I've got the nearside reins," the woman went on. "We've got to get them up. Where's the whip?"

Paks looked around and found the whip still in its socket. She slithered over and managed to reach it. She glanced back into the wagon. Most of the hay had bounced forward in their final crash. Callexon still clung to the rear board, bow in hand, his splinted leg apparently straight. He waved at Paks.

"I've got two, so far," he said. "If you can smooth the ride a little — "

Effa and the unconscious man lay tangled in the hay. Paks turned back to the mules. All but one were standing already, quietly enough; she flicked the whip at the arrow-struck mule, and it finally struggled up, not too tangled in harness. Paks looked at Varne. "Do you want me to take those reins?"

The woman gave a wry grin that creased the salve on her blistered face. "Depends — nothing like a little excitement to clear out a dose of numbwine. Maybe I should take all the reins and let you check on the others."

Paks handed over the reins, and slid back into the hay. She found the driver first; she was dead. The veteran with the head injury snored heavily, but Effa was also dead, her stubborn face wiped clean of all expression. Paks tried to straighten the injured man on top of the hay. Her leg hurt a lot; when she looked at it, the bandages were soaked with blood. She burrowed into the hay for the medical supplies, and wrapped more bandages around it. She felt nauseated and faint, and broke into a sweat trying to pull herself back to the driver's seat.

"I see someone," called Callexon.

"We aren't going anywhere," muttered Varne. "Blast! Not even a sword among us."

Paks took out her dagger. "Calle's got the bow, and I have a dagger — "

"With those, it's not enough. I wonder how many — "

"It's ours!" yelled Callexon. "Hey — Arvid!"

Paks looked back. A limping figure in maroon and white stood at the top of the bank. "Any more alive?" he called.

"Yes — but the wagon's broken."

"So I see." The man limped down the bank, chest heaving.

"What about them?" asked Callexon.

"Driven off for now. Tir's gut, I never thought even the outlaw companies would attack a sick train." He clambered up to peer in the wagon. "Hmmph. We'll have to clear you out before we can mend this. Can any of you walk?"

"I can," said Varne. Callexon shook his head.

"Let's see." Arvid climbed in and worked his way forward, checking the bodies first, then Paks's leg. "We'd best deal with that." He tore off another length of bandage and tied it tighter than Paks had managed. "Now you," he said to Varne.

"I'm no worse than I was."

"No? Let me have the reins, and see your hands." He tied the reins to the wagon frame, and looked her over. "You'll do — after a dose of numbwine. Now — " he climbed down. " — to get these mules unhitched."

Paks sank back in the hay and her eyes fluttered shut. She roused to find Vanza beside her, calling her name.

"Yes — what — "

"Paks, we have to move you out of this wagon. We're going to carry you in a blanket — don't struggle."

She felt the blanket tighten around her, then a swooping sensation that made her want to fight her way to her feet. Instead she lay still. Above her were voices, Vanza's among them.

"We'd better send word to the Duke — "

" — that's the fastest. And isn't there a Baron Kodaly or something near here?"

"Yes — off east a bit; he claims this forest. Don't forget — "

" — wheelwright, and a smith, and supplies — "

" — never heard of anything like this in all the years — "

" — Marshals or priests or something, if you can — "

" — what they thought they'd get out of it — "

" — and coffinwood — "

" — forward to Valdaire, too, but we can't spare another — "

Paks sank into unconsciousness.

Her next waking was a confused struggle through dark corridors with shadowy opponents who faded away as she came near. Far ahead was a blur of light and a clamor of sound; she came to it in bursts of random motion. Finally her vision cleared. She was lying on the ground under a tree. The surgeon knelt by her injured leg, shaking his head.

" — don't think I can do more, my lord," he was saying. "Too much blood loss, and this additional bruising — "

Paks felt a cold twinge of fear. Was that *her* leg about which he had no hope?

"Very well," said a voice from above and behind her. "We'll try a healing. Master Vetrifuge?"

"At once, my lord." A gray-bearded man in black and green robes stooped beside the surgeon and laid his hands on Paks's leg. A warming tingle ran from his touch through the wound; it did not hurt. The surgeon bent to look.

"That's better." He looked at her face and found her watching. "She's awake, my lord. We might try the potion."

"Go ahead," said the voice behind her. The surgeon took a small flask from his robes and brought it to Paks. He slipped an arm behind her shoulders and lifted her head until she could drink.

The lip of the flask was icy cold, and the two swallows of liquid in it burned her throat, but gave her the same warming tingle as Vetrifuge's hands. Her leg did not hurt any more, nor the bruises where she'd hit the footboard. Her nausea had gone too. The surgeon's face, watching her, was clear in every line; she could see the dust on his eyelashes. He turned to look at her leg.

"Ah — that's more like it. Rest and food will be enough now. Thank you, Master Vetrifuge."

"My pleasure, Master Simmitt," said Vetrifuge, with a mocking smile. "Glad to know there are yet a few things in which wizardry can aid the science of surgery." The surgeon reddened, and seemed to swell in the neck.

"Others need your skills," said the third voice, with enough bite that both men froze an instant.

"Yes, my lord; right away."

As Paks watched them stand and walk off, a mail-clad figure moved to her side and sat. When she looked back, she was face to face with the Duke himself. Paks gulped. This close she could see a few silver hairs in his fox-red beard; his nose was sunburnt and peeling; his eyes were the gray of sword-steel, just barely blue. Her eyes dropped. His cloak was fastened with a silver medallion; it was dusty. His gloves were gray kid, sweat-stained.

"First," said the Duke, "you need to drink this, and eat a little; then I want to know what happened. What *you* saw." Paks dragged her eyes back up and saw once more the gold-tooled wineskin she'd seen the night of the battle. "Try to sit up." Paks found she was weak, but able to rise on one elbow. She took the wineskin. "It's watered," said the Duke. "It shouldn't knock you out. Here — have some bread." He bit the end off a loaf and handed her the rest. Paks tore off a hunk and took a swallow of wine. She wondered how long she'd slept, and when the Duke had arrived, but under his eye she ate as he directed.

"Now," said the Duke, when she had choked down most of the bread. "Take your time, but tell it all, from the beginning. I want to know everything you can remember about the attack."

Paks blushed. "Well — sir — my lord — I was asleep. Then someone screamed, and the wagon bumped. I saw Vanza jumping out the back, and out the front were riders in red, with a black wolf's head on the front — "

"On the back as well?"

Paks thought a moment. "No — I don't think so. Just the front. Then I saw our driver'd been shot, so I tried to get the reins. The mules were scared. Varne helped me pull the driver into the wagon. One of the attackers tried to grab the lead mules' reins, but they swerved away — "

"Were you driving, or — "

"Yes, sir, I was — but I wasn't sure which reins were which. It seemed like a lot — I jerked the ones that were tightest, and the mules veered — "

"Go on."

"Then the rider turned and came at the wagon, so I pulled the other reins, and the wagon ran into his horse — "

"What did he look like?"

"The rider? He had a mask on."

"A mask? Not a — wait — have you seen anything but open helmets? Have you seen a knight's helmet, with the visor down?"

"Yes, sir. Sergeant Stammel showed us that in training. This was different. He had an open helmet over chain mail, but a mask over his face — it was some kind of cloth; I saw it ripple."

"Aha!" The Duke slammed his fist onto his thigh. "Very good. Go on — what else?"

"He seemed heavy — broad in the shoulders. Taller than Sergeant Stammel, I think. He had something on the shoulder of his tunic that glittered. The horse had no barding, but it was a war saddle, and the blanket was black with a red stripe.

"What color was the horse?"

"Light brown, dappled, with a pale mane and tail. All the others were dark, but for the spotted one."

"Spotted?"

"Yes, sir. One was black and white spotted. Now that I think of it, that one was smaller — we went by it in the trees."

"What sort of rider on the spotted one?"

Paks shook her head. "I'm sorry — I don't remember — "

"But you're sure of the horses?"

"Yes, sir — though I don't know that I saw all of them. We were moving too fast, and I was trying to steer around things, but I didn't see the stream until we were almost into it. So I broke the wagon — " Paks faltered, remembering Stammel's lectures on damaged equipment.

"Hmm." The Duke's eyes crinkled. "Are you an experienced teamster?"

Paks looked down. "No, sir — my lord."

"That's all right then. Not your equipment." Paks looked up, still worried. "Tir's bones, girl, that wagon's the least of my concerns. I've lost fighters here. A wagon's nothing — you did well. But I want to know who — " he bounced his fist on his thigh for emphasis, " — and why and how anyone would attack a caravan of wounded. No treasure — no ranking prisoners to ransom — and they must know this'll bring my Company down on them. It's costing me now, but it'll cost them — " his voice trailed off, and Paks almost flinched at the look in his eyes. He glanced back at her and half-smiled. "You were just promoted, right? Paks, isn't it?"

94

"Yes, my lord."

"Well, Paks, you've had the most expensive healing I hope you'll ever need, and you should be ready to fight in a day or so. The next time you see those red tunics, you'll have a weapon in hand. I'll expect you to fight as well as you did in your first battle." The Duke stood. "No — don't try to get up yet. The surgeon will clear you for that." Paks watched as he strode away, cloak swirling around his tall boots.

Paks looked at her leg, no longer wound in bandages. A red scar showed the line of the wound, but it looked nothing like the deep gash it had been. She wondered what they had done — how it had healed so fast — and why they hadn't healed it that way in the first place. She looked around. The makeshift camp was bigger than she'd supposed. Smoke rose from a fire near the stream crossing; loud clangs revealed a smith at work. Across the clearing, the Duke was talking to a short man in plate armor. They headed for a tent, maroon and white striped. A man in green livery led a big warhorse still lathered in sweat. Another led three lighter mounts. On the track away from the stream, the remains of the caravan clogged the way. Two burnt-out wagons, one unburned, but missing a wheel, dead mules. As she watched, a group of soldiers dragged a mule into the forest. She wondered what had happened to the other wounded; she didn't see any of them. Had they all died? Callexon hadn't looked that bad — She saw the surgeon and Vanza approaching.

"How do you feel?" asked the surgeon.

"Fine," said Paks. "Can I get up?"

"Yes — you'll be weaker than you think; you lost a lot of blood." Vanza reached down an arm, and Paks pulled herself up. She felt dizzy at first, but it passed quickly. "Try walking," said the surgeon. She took a step, then another. She felt no pain, but she was shaky. "That's expected," the surgeon reassured her. "Don't push yourself for the next day or so — rest when you're tired. Eat and drink as much as you can." He turned away. Paks looked at Vanza.

"Where are the others? Were they all — "

"No. Not all." He sighed. "We lost more than we should, though. I still can't believe it. No one does this — I knew the Wolf Prince was bad, but even he — "

"Is that who it was?"

"It must have been. You saw the wolf's head, didn't you?"

"Yes. But I'm confused — "

"We all are. Now — all you wounded are being healed, as you were, by the Duke's command. For today, stay close. You can help with food, and that sort of thing, but don't try to do too much — no hauling mules around."

"But — what did that Master Vetrifuge do? And why not do it all the time, if it works so well?"

Vanza stopped short and gave her a startled look. "You mean you don't know about magical healing?"

"No. Effa said something about St. Gird, but — "

"That's different. Or somewhat different. Let me see — first of all,

Master Vetrifuge is a mage. Wizard, they're called in the north. Surely you've heard of them?"

"Yes, but —"

"Just listen. Some mages specialize in one sort of magic; healing magic is one particular kind of magic. I don't know how it works — I'm no mage. It's great learning, I've been told, and great power — but whether of a god, or the mage himself, I don't know. But healing mages can heal wounds, if they aren't too bad. Too old, say, or full of fever. Sometimes they can heal diseases, though not so well. But it takes a lot of money. Mages don't work for nothing."

"What about potions?"

"You had that too? Mages make potions, to speed healing. Those are even more expensive; don't ask me why. Our surgeons always have a few of these, but of course they don't use them most of the time."

Paks frowned. "Why not? If wounds could be healed so fast —"

"Because of the cost. Paks, the Duke will have spent the whole contract's profit, I don't doubt, just healing the few of you here. No one could afford to have every wound magically healed. It's cheaper to train and hire new fighters. Our Duke is one of the few I've heard of who will use such healing at all for his common soldiers."

"Oh." Paks thought about it. She had no way of valuing things, but it seemed strange that a tiny vial of liquid, however rare, could be more costly than a person. "But what did Effa mean, then?"

"About St. Gird?" Paks nodded. "Well, the gods can heal, if they will. Those who serve them — Marshals of Gird, or Captains of Falk, or whatever — have the power to ask healing of the gods and have it granted. Before my time, the Duke was friendly with Girdsmen — I even heard he was one himself — and had a Marshal with the Company for healing. I've seen men who say they were healed that way."

"Does that cost so much?"

"Well — I can't say. They usually heal their own, and no one else: Marshals heal Girdsman, and Captains heal Falkians. I'd think it would cost, though maybe not in gold. Why should a god give healing for nothing?"

"The gods give rain and wind for nothing, and sunlight."

"For nothing? Surely your people gave back, wherever you're from —" Vanza stared at her. Paks remembered the little shrines by the well and the corners of her father's fields; the tufts of barley and oats, and the lamb's blood they left there. For an instant she felt cold as she realized how close she had come to impiety.

"You're right," she said quickly. "But the gods have the power to give as they choose, whatever gifts we give. That's what I meant, that we give gifts, we do not compel." She hoped that was what she'd meant.

He nodded. "True, no one can compel — but they are honorable, or the good ones are, and generous." He nodded to her and went away. Paks stared after him, thoughtfully. Wizards . . . magical healing . . . somehow when she'd heard of magic potions in songs, she'd never thought of the cost in gold. Or lives.

Chapter Eleven

The next day Cracolnya's cohort marched in. Pont, his junior captain, escorted the survivors back to the Company's camp while the Duke, Cracolnya, and most of that cohort went on to Valdaire.

"I thought the Czardians were defeated," said Callexon. "What happened?"

Erial, the junior sergeant in Cracolnya's cohort, chuckled. "They were. But they'd hired a mercenary band to help them, only it was late. Then the Duke pulled us out — so when their hirelings finally arrived, they quit talking to Foss Council again and decided to fight for it." She paused to wipe the sweat from her face. "Won't do them any good. As long as Foss Council still has three cohorts in the field, and we have two — "

"Who'd they hire?" Varne's face still looked patchy and pink, but she was otherwise healthy.

"Some southern company. We don't have to worry; they won't be any better than the Czardian militia."

"Unless they've got the Free Pikes," said Vanza.

Erial looked startled. "I never thought of that — they hardly ever hire out."

"Who are the Free Pikes?" asked Paks.

"The only decent southern company," said Erial. "They're from the high mountains in the southwest — I think they call it Horngard."

"That's right," said Vanza. "They don't hire out much — they fight in defense, or if their land needs money. But when they fight — !" He shook his head.

But the Czardians did not have the Free Pikes; they had hired, Stammel explained, a renegade baron of the Sier of Westland and his so-called knights. They were best known for their woodswork — sneaking into enemy lines at night to kill sleeping men, or steal supplies, or start fires — but could put up a respectable fight on the field, as well.

Paks had hardly realized, in the excitement of her first battle, that the Duke's Company was not fighting alone. Now she had a look at the Foss Council militia. They wore short gray tunics over trousers of bright red (from Foss) or green (from Ifoss); they carried short straight swords and light throwing javelins. Foss Council held the right wing of their position; their camp, like the Duke's, was in the forest. Trees ended on a gentle slope, opening on a wide expanse of grass and sedge that faced another tree-

97

shaded ridge some distance away. To the left, the trees made an arc connecting the two ridges; to the right, the grassy meadow grew wetter, finally producing a stream that trickled away to the north.

When the next battle came, two days later, Paks was more than ready for it. Someone had made it through the lines; Arñe was in the surgeon's care with a knife wound, and Kir of Dorrin's cohort was dead. Even so, her breath came short as the two lines closed. For an instant she was even more frightened than the first time — she could feel the sickening blow that had opened her leg. She thrust the thought away angrily as the remembered noise and confusion swept over her. This time she was able to keep her head, battering at the enemy stroke after stroke. She was aware of the man beside her, able to adjust her strokes to his so that they fought as a unit. It seemed to last forever: dust, noise, confusion, the rising and falling blades. Then the ground softened under her feet. She realized that they had advanced to the center of the field, where mud churned up instead of water.

Some time after midday, both sides withdrew a space. Paks drained her water flask and wiped sweat from her face. She had come through uninjured. Her stomach growled — a long time since breakfast. They stood quiet in formation: across the way the enemy lines shifted, milling.

"Pass your flask back," said Donag, handing her his. "They'll send water forward." Soon the dripping flasks returned, and they drank. Slabs of bread came forward, then more water. Paks ate hungrily. When she looked again, the enemy seemed a little further away. She nudged Kiri beside her.

"They're giving back," he said. "Don't look at 'em, and maybe they'll go all the way."

"But what does it mean?"

"Means they don't want to fight the rest of the day. Fine with me — it's too blazin' hot anyway."

And in fact the enemy were soon back in their own camp, and to Paks's surprise they were not sent in pursuit. In the next week, before the Duke returned, they fought several such inconclusive engagements.

"Why don't they want to fight and win?" she asked one night.

"Don't complain," said Donag. "If they wanted to win — I suppose you mean Foss Council? — it'd be our blood on the ground, and not their militia's. Think about it. They want to win, but what they want to win is whatever it is they're fighting about: where a border is, or a caravan tariff, or something like that. If they can convince Czardas to yield on that, without us having to cut our way through the entire Czardian army, so much the better."

"But — " began Arñe, now back from the surgeons.

"No buts," interrupted Donag. "Tir's guts, you idiots! You'll get all the fighting you've stomach for by the time you make corporal — if you live that long. Don't look for trouble. It's your profession — it'll come to you."

When the Duke returned, everything changed again. With Cracolnya's archers, he decided to change ground. Under cover of darkness they slipped far to the left of their previous position. This left a gap between the

Duke's Company and Foss Council's troops, and confused the novices almost as much as the enemy. Paks worried about the militia, and even more about what they might think.

"Don't be silly," said Canna. She had seen this before. "They're moving too. It's a trap, if it works, and a good move even if it doesn't."

They made it to the Duke's chosen field without interference, and Stammel explained how it was better for their purposes than the other one.

"He wants to use our archers. So far the Czardians haven't shown us any, so we don't have to worry. But look — the mixed cohort will be up there — " he pointed. "They can't get to 'em on foot or horse, but they'll be in range to feel it when Cracolnya opens up. Just watch it come."

As Stammel predicted, the Czardian forces gave way once the Duke's archers opened on them. Paks, watching the enemy ranks melt away, was glad the Czardians could not counterattack in kind. The Duke ordered a pursuit, and they began several weeks of constant movement and fighting. Although they never fought the Czardians to a finish, each time they met it was on ground of the Duke's choosing, and each time the Czardians slipped away, losing ground, back toward their city. When its walls came in sight, the Duke sent two cohorts around to the south, to stop traffic on the southern caravan route, while the other cohort and the Foss Council militia harried the Czardians. A few days after that, the campaign was over. Incoming caravans paid their tolls directly to the Foss Council commander, and he had a treaty to take back to their Table of Councilors.

"You had a good campaign for your first one," Stammel told the new privates in his cohort. "Some set battles — good moving engagements — enough fighting, but nothing really hard. And we'll be doing garrison work or caravan work the rest of the season, so you'll have a chance to learn that."

"What?" Arñe sounded as surprised as Paks felt.

"Yes. Any year a campaign doesn't last the season — which is most years — we're hired as caravan guards or garrison troops for the rest of it. Foss Council wants us to garrison the border forts between them and Czardas, for instance — "

"But — when do we get to go to a city — ?"

"He means, when do we get paid?" Vik interrupted Malek.

Stammel laughed. "Ah — thinking like real mercenaries! I expect when Foss Council pays the Duke — which shouldn't be long — it'll trickle down to you. And if we're close enough to a city or town, you might have a little time to waste your pay."

The Duke's scribe sat behind a table as the captains and sergeants set out stacks of coins. The Company lined up in order of seniority, which meant that the new privates, in the back, caught only glimpses of the glinting piles before veterans blocked their view. Paks wondered if any of them had dared ask how much they would be paid. She had no idea what to expect. For that matter, she wasn't sure how many coppers made a silver, or what a silver would buy. She had agreed, with the others, to pay into the Company's death fund. Stammel explained that this paid for having the personal effects and any salary owed sent to the heirs of those killed. But she did not know what that would leave.

The line snaked forward, slowly. When Paks could see the table again, the piles were much smaller. Suddenly she thought of her "expensive healing" — did that come out of her pay? The scribe called her name at last, and she stepped forward.

"Hmm." Captain Arcolin picked up the roll and glanced at it, then looked at Paks. "You were promoted on the first day of the campaign. You've got a small bonus for your actions when the sick train was attacked. Less the contribution to the fund — did Stammel explain the currency?" Paks nodded. He'd explained, but she didn't really understand. The Guild League cities coined under their own marks at agreed weights, with the gold nata, or father, being the coin of greatest value, followed by the gold nas, or son, silver niti (mother), silver nis (daughter), and two sizes of coppers, the page and serf. "Well, then," said Arcolin, "it will be thirty-six nitis for you." He pushed a pile forward.

"I'd advise you not to draw it all," said Stammel. "As long as we're in town, you can draw your pay once a day; you're less likely to lose it to thieves and such."

Paks had never seen so much money; it was hard not to take it all. "How much, then, sir?"

"Take ten, why don't you? That should be enough to make you feel rich. Take two of it in mixed coppers." Paks nodded to the scribe, and he marked the sum she drew beside her name. Stammel counted the coins into her hand. They were heavy; when she dropped them in her belt pouch, it dragged at her belt. She thought of all she could buy, and how soon she could save up the amount of her dowry to repay her father.

"I've never had so much money," said Saben, coming up beside her.

"Nor I," said Paks. "And to think we'll get more next month, and the next — "

"What are you going to buy?"

Paks thought through her list. She didn't know what they had, yet. "I was wondering if there was a place to buy spicebread — "

Saben laughed. "You and I are truly countryborn. I was thinking about clotted cream — that's what they had at fairs near home. I never had but a bit of it, and I could eat it by the bucket. And something for my sisters — ribbons, or something like that. Stammel said it could go north with the Duke's next courier, if it was small and light."

Paks had not thought about presents; she felt guilty. "I'm — saving to send my dowry to my father," she said.

"Dowry?" Saben looked surprised. "I thought you didn't want — "

"To repay it," she corrected. "He'd already given it, when I ran away." She had never told anyone but Stammel the circumstances of her leaving home.

100

"Oh. I see. But you hadn't agreed, had you?"

"No. I told him I wouldn't wed Fersin, but he thought he could make me, so he gave dower."

"But if you didn't agree, it's not your fault." Barra pushed in beside her.

Paks wished she'd never mentioned it. "No — I suppose not. But I'd feel better if I paid it back. There's my brothers and sisters to think of."

Barra snorted, and Saben asked quickly, "Do you know how much it is?"

"Not exactly." In fact she didn't know anything but rumor: her oldest brother had said it was as much as Amboi dowered his eldest to the wool merchant's son in Rocky Ford, and she thought she remembered what the baker's wife in Three Firs had said about that. Saben looked impressed, and asked no more questions.

When they asked Stammel for permission to leave camp and go into the city, he told them to wait. Shortly before midday, he gathered some of his novices.

"All right," he said. "You've got your pay — come along and let me show you how not to spend it."

Vik shook his pouch, listening to the jingle of the coins. "But, sir — I already know how not to spend it. And I have plans — "

"Sure you do. And I can't stop you from losing your last copper, if you're taken that way. But I can show you the safer places to drink, and maybe keep you from being robbed and beaten in some alley."

"Is Foss so dangerous?" asked Saben.

"And who'd attack us? We're armed," said Paks.

"It's exactly that attitude," said Stammel severely, "that loses good fighters every year. With the Company, you're good. But alone, in an alley with thieves — no. If you're lucky you wake up in the morning with a lump on your head and no money. Unlucky, you find yourself in a slaver's wagon with a sack over your head and a brand — or maybe just dead. You youngsters don't know the first thing about cities — well, maybe Vik and Jorti do — and that's why you'll come with me this time."

A half hour later, Stammel led a dozen of them into the wide public room of *The Dancing Cockerel*. A tall, powerful-looking man in a green apron came forward to greet them.

"Hai! Matthis, old friend — I thought we'd see you this summer. Bringing the new ones in, eh?" The man looked at them keenly. "Duke Phelan's soldiers are welcome here — what will you have?"

"Bring us your good ale, Bolner, and plenty of it. We're in time for lunch, I trust."

"Certainly. Be seated here — unless you wish a private room?"

Stammel laughed. "Not for lunch — are you thinking the Duke's raised our pay?"

"I'd trust you for it, after these years. Besides, what I heard about the Duke's contract, you're getting paid in gold for copper."

"So? You can hear anything, if you listen to all. Besides, what have contracts to do with us — poor soldiers that we are, and dying of thirst in the

101

middle of your floor." A roar of laughter from a table near the wall greeted this, and the tall landlord turned away. "Have a seat here," said Stammel more quietly, and Paks and the others sat down to a long table near the center of the room.

"How much is the ale?" asked Saben, fingering his belt pouch.

"Last time I was here, it was three pages a mug, and a niti a jug. Local coinage. Dearer than some, cheaper than others, but Bolner doesn't water his ale, and he won't take a bribe to drug it, as some taverners will. This is a good tavern, as taverns go. Just remember that any landlord loves gossip, and can no more keep a secret than a pig can weave. Anyone who talks about the Company's business will be explaining it to the captain."

"Hey — Sergeant Stammel!" They turned to see a fat redhead at the table by the wall. "Still taking your recruits about in leading strings?" His companions laughed again.

Paks looked quickly at Stammel. He was smiling, but his eyes were grim. "My dear Lochlinn, if they were recruits I might, but these are all seasoned fighters — merely friends. And how is the Baroness these days?"

The fat man jogged one of his companions with an elbow. "Seasoned? Half seasoned, I should think, close as they cling to you like chicks to a hen. Haw! They're big enough, especially that yellow-headed wench, but — "

Paks flushed and took a quick breath. Stammel's hand beneath the table dug into her elbow. "Now, Lochlinn, we realize it's been so long since you fought you can't tell the fighters from the spectators. But come to our next, and let us show you. And mind you keep civil — this 'wench' as you would say — " Stammel released Paks's elbow and thumped her shoulder lightly with his fist, " — could part you from crown to cod with one stroke. I trained her."

Paks gazed across the room at the fat man's pink face, now a shade paler than it had been. He looked from Stammel to her and made a face, lifting his brows.

"Well, pardon me for plain speaking to an old comrade." Stammel snorted. "What a fierce look she has, too. I had no wish, wolf-maiden, to anger you and risk a blow from that strong arm your sergeant boasts of." He rose from his table and made an elaborate bow. "There — will that content you, or must I attempt some other satisfaction?"

Paks looked down at the table, scarred by many diners. She would gladly have leaped on the man, and killed him then and there. Saben, sitting on her other side, nudged her with his knee.

"We would be content," said Stammel mildly, "to take our ale in peace — and silence."

"You can't order me off!" cried the fat man.

Paks suddenly realized that he was both drunk and frightened. "You don't have any right to order me around now, Sergeant — I've got soldiers of my own!"

"Tsst! Lochlinn!" said one of his companions. "Let it be, man. Don't start — "

102

Paks jumped as a tall pitcher and several mugs were dumped in front of her. Two serving wenches, as well as Bolner, were at the table, distributing the ale. Stammel turned away from the fat man to grin at Bolner. "What's the menu today, eh?"

"The usual. Common lunch is slices off the joint, bread, redroots, cheese — we've the kind you like from Sterry, no extra charge to this party. Or special — roast fowl, and we've three in the oven. Pastries. Cella's tarts, plum, peach, and strawberry, but not enough of the last for everyone. Fish — but I don't recommend it; it's river trash this time of year. Leg of mutton — it won't be done for several hours. Soup — there's always soup; comes with the common lunch or the special, or a mug of soup with bread is five pages."

"How much for the common lunch?"

"For this group — if you all take it — well, I'll take off a bit. Say a niti each, ale included."

Stammel looked around at them. "It's good food here. What about it?"

They nodded, and Stammel gave a thumb's up sign to the host, who left the table, calling orders to the kitchen. Paks looked for the fat man, but he had gone, and his friends with him.

"Who was that?" she asked Stammel.

"Who? Oh, him — the fat one?" She nodded. "His name's Lochlinn. Used to be one of ours, years back; he left the Company. Now he's in some local baron's guard. And bed, they say, when the baron's traveling."

"I'd like to —" began Paks, but Stammel interrupted.

"No, you wouldn't." She looked at him, surprised. "Don't get into fights. Remember that. The rule is the same as inside the Company — there's no good reason short of being assaulted. You get us a reputation for brawling, and we'll all lose by it."

"But what he said about Paks!" Saben scowled. "Why should we let him get away with that?"

"Because we want to come here and eat — or shop in the market — and not be prey to every cutpurse and ruffian, and have the citizens cheering them on when you and you and you — " he pointed around the table, " — are bleeding in the street. Or being hauled off to the lockup by militia. We don't want trouble. We aren't paid to fight over nothing. Tir's bones — we know any one of us could split that fat leech — what difference does it make what he says?"

Paks reached for the pitcher and poured several mugs full. She pushed one toward Stammel and took one herself. She sniffed at it; it smelled much like the ale sold at market in Three Firs.

"Paks, have you had ale before?"

She blushed. "No, sir, not really. Just a few swallows." She took a cautious sip.

"Don't drink much, then. It makes some people quick tempered; you don't need that. Vik, I don't have to ask you." Vik had drained his mug at one swallow.

"No, sir — and how I've missed good ale these long months."

Stammel grinned. "You can spend your pay quickly on ale, if that's your choice. Just keep in mind — "

"Oh, aye — no fighting, no talking — but what about wenching and dicing?"

"Well, if you must, you must. I'd recommend *Silverthorn Inn* for the one, and here for the other. Whatever you do, stay away from River Lane, across the market, and don't go to Aula's. They'll recommend it at *Silverthorn*, but don't. All the dice are magicked, and the dwarf will slit your gizzard in a second if you show you notice."

"Yes, sir — perhaps I'll wait for another day."

Arñe laughed. "Adding up the cost, Vik? Homebrew's the cheapest, they say."

"It's not so much my silver I care for as my fair white skin — you know how I dread being ill-marked." The rest laughed. Between sunburn, freckles, and healing battle scars, not much fair white skin was displayed.

"That's all right, Vik," called Coben from down the table. "You can teach me that dicing game — what is it?"

"Don't play the innocent, Cob," said the redhead. "I heard about you with that girl from Dorrin's cohort — was it five silvers, or six, you won from her while she taught you dicing?"

"More than that, my lad, more than that," said Coben, and drained his mug. "I'm a slow learner, I am. Especially when I'm winning."

"Here you are," said Bolner from behind them. He and each of the serving girls carried a platter of sliced roast meat to set out on the table. By the time they had finished stuffing themselves with meat, rounds of dark yellow cheese, redroots, bread and soup, the rest of the room was empty.

"Now," said Stammel. "A last reminder. Don't wander about alone — stay in pairs, at least. Keep alert; Foss has as many thieves and cutpurses as any city. The slavers won't bother you if you stay together. Don't brawl. Keep your mouths shut about the Company and its business, but be polite otherwise. If one of you gets drunk, the others bring 'em home. You're all to be back before supper, so the others can go. Clear?" They all nodded.

In the main market square, they scattered into clumps of three or four. Arñe and Coben stayed with Paks and Saben, poking into every stall and shop along one side of the square. One sold lace, its white tracery displayed against dark velvet. Another sold strips of silk, patterned with exquisite embroidery. Paks found a spicebread stall, and managed to stuff down a square of it despite the lunch she'd eaten. They found a shoemaker's shop, displaying pointed-toed shoes in scarlet and green and yellow, and a bootmaker's with riding boots, laced boots, and one pair made of three different leathers. Paks stared, and the man came to the door.

"You like those, fair warrior? 'Tis mulloch's hide, and goatskin, and the skin of a great snake from across the sea, south of Aare — only a nas, for you."

"No, thank you," said Paks, stunned more by the price than the boots. He smiled and turned away.

Coben stopped to look at a jeweler's display; the jeweler's guards dropped their hands to the hilts of their weapons. Paks looked over his shoulder, eyes wide. A tray of rings, gold, silver, some with bright stones set to them. Most were finger rings, but some were clearly earrings. Another tray held bracelets, and a single necklace of blue stones and pearls set in silver.

"Look at that," breathed Coben, pointing to one of the rings. "It's like a braided rope." Paks saw another that looked like tiny leaves linked together. She wondered what else was in the shop — far too expensive, whatever it was.

One shop displayed clothing; they could see the tailors inside, sitting cross-legged on their platform. Bolts of cloth were piled up behind them. Another shop was hung with musical instruments: two lap-harps, a lute, something twice the size of a lute with more strings, and many more that none of them recognized. In a litter of woodshavings the maker was working on a part, and smiled at them as they peeked in the door. He reached a hand to pluck one of the harps and show its tone. Paks was entranced. She had heard a harp only twice, when musicians came to the fair.

"Can — can you play, as well as make, them?"

His bushy eyebrows rose. "Of course, girl — how else would I know if I'd made them well? Listen — " He unfolded himself from the workbench, lifted the harp, and ran his hands along the strings. Paks had never heard that music before, but shivers ran up her spine.

"Do you know 'Torre's Ride'?" asked Arñe, nudging Paks forward.

"Certainly — three versions. Where are you from?"

"From the north — from Tsaia."

"Hmm." He paused to adjust a tuning peg. Then the thrilling sound rang out, one of the few songs Paks had learned before leaving home. She found herself humming along; Arñe was murmuring the words, as was Coben. The instrument maker finished a verse with a flourish. "There you are. But are any of you players?"

Paks could have listened all afternoon. She shook her head, and Arñe said "No, sir," and he went back to his bench, shaping a little piece of wood with a small chisel. Paks wondered which instrument it was for, and where it would fit, but was too shy to ask. They left that shop and moved on.

She found the surprise for Saben several shops down. Here were trays of religious symbols, carved of the appropriate stone or metal. Most she did not know. The crescent and cudgel of Gird were familiar, and the Holy Circle, and the wheatsheaf of the Lady of Peace. The sword of Tir was there, both plain and cleverly set with a tiny jewel in the pommel. But whose was the leaping fish, or the tree, or the arch of tiny stars? She looked at tiny golden apples, at green leaves, at anvils, hammers, spears, fox or wolf heads, little human figures clothed in flowers (swirling hair made the loop for hanging). Here was the antlered figure of Guthlac, and the double-faced head of Simyits, a harp for Garin, the patron of harpers, and shears for Dort, the patron of sheepshearers and all in the wool trade. Then she saw the little red stone horse, and remembered Saben's words that day in the stronghold. She looked up and found the shopkeeper watching her. She glanced around; Saben was in the next shop, pricing combs for his sisters.

"How much?" she asked. And, "Will it break easily?"

He shook his head. "Not these symbols, lady. And they have all been blessed, by the cleric for each one. They'll bring luck and blessings to those who wear them." Paks doubted this, but didn't argue.

"How much?" she asked again.

"The little horse? The symbol of Senneth, the horse-lord, and Arvoni the patron of horsemen?" Paks nodded. "Five nitis." She was startled and her face must have shown it. He said smoothly, "But for you, lady — you will need luck — for you, I will say four nitis, and two serfs." Paks had never bargained herself, though she had heard her mother and father.

"I cannot spare so much," she said, and looked away, shifting her feet. She sighed. She wanted that horse for Saben, but four nitis — that was four meals like lunch. And she wanted other things, too.

"Three nitis, two nis," he said. "I can't do more than that — " Abruptly Paks decided to buy it. She fumbled in her pouch for the silver.

When she came out, with the horse safely stowed in her pouch, Saben was still looking at combs; Arñe and Coben were rummaging through a pile of copper pots on the pavement. She ducked into the shop with Saben.

"I can't decide," he said, turning to her. "Suli likes flowers, so that's easy — this one — " The comb had a wreath of flowers along the spine. "But for Rahel and Maia, do you think the birds, or the fish, or the fern?" Paks thought the fern was the prettiest, and liked the leaping fish better than an angry-looking bird. He paid for the combs and they walked out. They saw fruit stalls beyond the piles of pots. Early berries, early peaches — they squandered coppers on the fruit, and walked on with sticky fingers. Coben cocked an eye at the sky.

"We'd better be going," he reminded them. They turned back across the square. Paks went to the spicebread stall again, and bought a stack it took both hands to carry. They munched spicebread most of the way back to camp.

As they were going to their posts for duty, Paks gave Saben the little horse. "I remembered you lost your bit of hoof," she said. "I couldn't find a hoof, but maybe the whole horse will do."

He flushed. "It's — it will do well, Paks. Thank you. Was it from the shop next to the comb place?"

"Yes."

"I looked at it, but didn't buy it — you shouldn't have spent so much — "

"Well — " This time Paks blushed. "I didn't — I mean I — umm — "

Saben laughed. "You, too? I bargained myself, but I couldn't get him to go lower than three nitis."

"Three!" Paks gasped and began to laugh helplessly.

"What? What did you get it for?" She shook her head, laughing even harder. A veteran walking by stared at her. Finally she stopped, sides aching. Saben was still watching her, puzzled.

"You should have — " she began, and started laughing again. "Oh, I can't! It hurts — you should have got it yourself — you're the better bargainer — "

"You mean you paid more than that?"

"Not much," she said, still laughing. "As — as a fighter I may be good, but at market — "

"Well, the man tried to tell me it was bad luck to bargain over a holy symbol, so maybe it will be better luck this way." Saben grinned. "Tell you what, Paks — the next time you want something, I'll bargain for you."

"Thanks," she said.

"And by the way," he went on, taking a comb from his pouch. "This one's really for you — the ferny one."

Chapter Twelve

Two months later, as Paks leaned against the wall of the courtyard in a border fort south of Kodaly, she felt well content with her position.

"I agree," said Saben, who was mending a tear in his cloak while she sharpened her weapons, "that it's easier than farming. I've no desire to go back to mucking out barns. But don't forget your first battle just because it's gone so well since."

"I know. That could have ended it — like Effa. But that's the chance we take, as fighters. I wish we could see other good companies too. See how they do things, how they fight. We never can see anything but what's in front of us. It's hard to keep the idea of what we're doing — I mean as a whole — in all that confusion."

Saben shrugged. "I just go for what's in front of me. It makes sense when Stammel shows us with sticks and things, but I can't see it with real people. You can't tell what they'll do. All we can do is follow commands."

"But those who give the commands have to know what they're doing," said Paks.

"We're a long way from that," said Saben drily. "Or are you planning to leave and start your own company?"

Paks stopped a moment, and squinted up at the sky. "No. Or — I don't know. I can't say. No, I suppose not — it's a silly thought. I just — just keep thinking about it. I can't stop. Why the captains put us there, or why their commander never used his archers on the flank, like the Duke did. That was stupid, Saben, that last time. They had the archers, but they held them back where they couldn't see. If they'd been in that wood on the right — "

"I'm glad their commander didn't think of it." Saben looked at his mending and tugged the cloth to test it. "Ah. One more chore done. Are you nearly finished?"

"Sword's done. I notched the dagger yesterday."

"I told you you'd honed it too fine. We're on in less than a glass."

"I haven't forgotten. I just want to smooth this — one — spot. No, I'll tell you, Saben, what I'd like. I'd like to make sergeant someday. Years away, I know, and only six in the Company, but — I'd like that."

"Well, if you don't lose an arm or leg somewhere, or get killed outright, you ought to do it. You don't get drunk, or lose things, or brawl, or cause any sort of trouble. And you fight well. Now me —"

"Saben, you're as good as I am. Better, even —"

He shook his head. "No, and you know it. *I* wasn't practicing all morning. I do what I'm told, but I don't care enough to learn every weapon in sight and practice every spare minute. You do."

"You don't need much practice; you're already quicker." Paks took a last stroke with her whetstone, wiped the dagger blade carefully with a scrap of soft hareskin, and sheathed it.

"Maybe. I used to be faster than you — but you've gotten better. The thing is, I've got what I want. A life I like, good friends, enough pay for the extras I want. The only other thing would be —" he slid a glance at Paks. When she met his eyes, she reddened and looked down.

"Saben, you know I —"

"You don't want it. I know. Not from me or anyone. Well, I'm not asking: just if you did ever change. If it was just Korryn, I mean."

Paks ducked her head lower and stared at the ground. "No. Even before. I just don't feel that way."

He sighed. "I'm glad it wasn't Korryn. Don't worry; I won't bother you."

She looked up. "You never have."

"Good. I still want to be friends. Besides that, you are — Paks if you ever did have a company, you would be a good commander. I would follow you. I don't think you'll stop at sergeant, if you want more."

Paks blushed, then grinned sheepishly. "Even a warhorse?"

Saben nodded. "Lady Paksenarrion, in shining armor on a great war-horse, with a magic sword — don't laugh at me, companion! Here I'm giving you a good-luck prophecy and you laugh at me. Ha! See if I ever warn you about overhoning your blades again."

"No, but really, Saben — a sheepfarmer's daughter? That's ridiculous!" But her eyes danced to think of it.

"So laugh. Would you rather a bad-luck prophecy? Let's see —"

"No! Don't ill-wish! Let's go; I've got to get ready for guard."

The fort's wall, high above the village, was quiet in the late afternoon. Paks and Saben reported to the sergeant, an Ifoss militiaman, and took their station. West of the fort lay the hay meadows, striped with light and dark green as the second cutting dried in swathes. They walked back and forth, watching the road and tracks that converged on the fort, and looking along the rooftops and lanes below. The sun dropped, touching the woodland beyond the hay meadows.

"Good weather — it's nice up here when it's dry," said Paks.

"Better this watch than the day, though. It's been hot. I wonder how long we'll be here."

"I hadn't thought. Do you think the Duke will get another contract this year?"

"Mmm. While you were working out this morning —"

"Go on, Saben."

"A courier came in — from the northwest. Could be Valdaire. Anyway, he went straight to the captain's chambers, Cully said."

"Wonder what that's about. Valdaire."

"Or anything in between. Maybe one of the others has found where that wolf whatever is."

"There's a fight I'd like to be in."

"And I."

They turned at the corner tower and headed south again along the wall. A cool breeze had come with the falling sun; it brought the scent of hay. Paks stretched. "Umph. I've got a kink in my shoulder."

"What from, this morning?"

"Yes. Hofrin had us working on unarmed combat, and I thought he'd tear my arm loose at the shoulder. Somehow I can't get the hang of it. Either I don't turn the right way, or not fast enough — but I keep ending up on the ground."

"Best stick to sword fighting, then."

"I'd rather, really. But Hofrin says — "

"I know what Hofrin says. Everyone should learn every conceivable weapon and unarmed combat, in case you lose your axe, sword, dagger, pike, spear, mace, bow, crossbow — "

Paks chuckled. "It's not that bad. And I enjoy it — or will, when I'm not spending all my time in the air or on the ground."

"I think," said Saben tentatively, " — what I saw when I watched you for awhile, is that you are too direct. You go straight in, just charging ahead, and then — "

"Land in the dust again. You're right; that's what he says, too. I keep telling myself, but when I get excited — bam, there I go. Today, at least, I made it through a few minutes of practice without doing that. Maybe I'll learn."

"I expect so. When — " Saben broke off as they heard a shout from the north wall. By the time the other guards had manned the walls, a trumpet call rang out. Duke Phelan had come; but even at watch-change, later that night, no one knew why. More than a day later Bosk finally explained.

"Ours wasn't the only bunch of wounded hit," he said. "Reim Company — they're small — lost a wagonful, and the guards for it. A trade caravan was hit, in spite of heavy guard. Golden Company lost some, and they even struck at the Halverics's camp — stupid of them, whoever they are. Anyway, several mercenary companies have each pledged a unit to go hunting, and — "

"We're going!" cried Coben.

"No. We're not." Over the general groan, he said, "The Duke wanted archers. He's taking Cracolnya's cohort, and some of Dorrin's. The rest of us will spread thinner to cover these forts. Half of us will move to the next, where Dorrin's half has been."

Paks, to her disgust, was one of those staying. "Nothing's happened here so far," she grumbled to Saben. "And I'll bet nothing happens now. We'll stay and walk back and forth on the walls while nothing happens, and they get to go find the Wolf Prince or whoever he is, and do some fighting."

He nodded. "At least Coben and those get to go to another fort, and see something new. But I doubt they'll see any fighting there, either."

Both were wrong. In the weeks that they held the line of forts, brigands

110

tried to strike at the villages they guarded and rob the harvest. Every garrison had at least one good fight, and most had more. When the cohort reunited, before the march back to Valdaire and winter quarters, Paks learned that two more of her recruit unit had been killed: Coben, who had been a friend since her first day as a recruit, and Suli, a cheerful brown-haired girl who was Arñe's friend. Eight of them, altogether, had died in their first year of fighting.

"If we lose this many every year," said Paks solemnly, "we'll all be gone in a few years."

"The — the veterans don't lose so many," said Arñe. Her face was still marked with tears.

"We aren't as good," commented Vik. "We've all made mistakes this year. If we live, we'll learn better."

"But it's not the worst ones who get killed. Not all of them. Coben was good — and so was Effa, and Suli." Paks felt a restless anger, and forgot how annoying Effa had been. "It's not fair."

"No," said Stammel behind them. "It's not fair. There's luck in it too. You have to accept that, to stay a soldier. Skill and courage go just so far, and then there's luck."

"Or the gods' will," said Saben.

Stammel shrugged. "You can call it that — it may be that. From what I've seen it could be either."

Paks was still dissatisfied. "But it still seems to me that the better ones should have more chance — "

"Paks, think. The better ones do have more chance — but no guarantee. Look how close you came to being killed. Three of those we lost were among the least skilled. Ilvin stood up on the wall even after Bosk yelled a warning about crossbows: that was stupid. Coben — I know he was your friend, and he was a good, honest, middling fighter — but he never learned to handle himself against a left-handed opponent, and a left-handed man knocked his shield aside and spitted him. Suli, too, was not as skillful as any of you four — just not fast enough."

"But she was as fast as I am."

"She was back north. Paks, you've been training hard; you've improved. You hadn't gone against her lately because Hofrin knew it wouldn't be any work for you. I know it's hard losing friends. It always hurts. If you stay in, you'll have that hurt every year — I have. D'you think I like seeing youngsters I trained get hurt and die? I won't try to tell you how to take it; you'll have to figure out your own way. The Company mourning, when we get back to Valdaire, will help. But wishing it were fair is no help at all." Stammel walked away, and left them to their thoughts.

For a long time they were silent.

There was more to come. The other two cohorts met them two days out of Valdaire, and they heard the tale of the campaign against the Wolf Prince.

"It was bad enough," said Barranyi, with a toss of her black hair. "We

111

marched for days through the woods west of here, up into the foothills, before we came to his stronghold."

"Don't forget what happened in the woods that night, Barra," added Natzlin. She had a bandage around her left arm, and a healing gash on her forehead.

"Oh — yes. One night — I think it was the second — during the first watch, we heard a wild screeching and flights of arrows started falling in the camp. Red Jori — you don't know him; he's a seven-year veteran in our cohort — he was hit in the leg. Others were hit too. We couldn't see anyone, and we were rushing around, with the sergeants bellowing and swearing — and then the Duke himself yelled something I didn't understand. A voice answered him from the trees, and they talked back and forth a bit — still in words I didn't know — and then the Duke told us that it was all over. And I still don't know what that was about, and no one will say!" Barranyi shook her head, glowering.

"Never mind, Barra; tell them the rest of it." Natzlin, as usual, could soothe Barra out of her sulks.

"And how many others were with you?" asked Paks. "We heard other companies were sending troops — "

Barra nodded briskly. "Yes, they did. And that was exciting, meeting those others. Let me think. Reim Company sent about twenty — they're small, Dorrin says. Halveric Company sent a whole cohort of foot, and twenty horse. Golden Company sent — what was it, Natz?"

"Near a cohort, I think."

"And we had some boundsmen from Valdaire; the city's angry that its neutrality was breached, or that's what I heard. Anyway, when we got near the Wolf Prince, we were attacked by horsemen, again and again. If we hadn't had horsemen with us, we'd have been in worse trouble. And Paks, I did see a black and white spotted horse off to one side; I'd bet that was one of his captains."

Paks nodded. "Could have been. Was it smaller than the others?"

"Yes. Then we got to the stronghold itself. Much better designed than those forts we'd been holding. If the Wolf Prince had pulled all his men inside, I don't think we could have broken the place."

"Never regret the stupidity of enemies," said Vik, who had been polishing his helmet as he listened. "There's no gift to compare with it."

Barra glared at him. "I wasn't suggesting that — "

"Please tell us the rest, Barra," said Arñe quickly, "before we die of curiosity."

Barra shrugged, gave Vik a last hard look, and went on. "We had a battle outside the walls, that's all. Fought most of the day. It was hard fighting, but finally they broke and ran for the gate. We got most of 'em outside, but enough were left to make the assault a real fight too. Black Sim, of Cracolnya's, was trying to set a ladder when he was crushed by a rock they dropped. Oh — and Paks, Corporal Stephi was killed too. It was on the wall, after we'd gotten up. Two of our men were down, and he was trying to protect them from a rush; he got a spear through the body." Barranyi looked closely at Paks, who felt a strange mixture of relief and regret.

"And then," said Natzlin, picking up the tale, "we fairly took the place apart. It was ugly. Ringbolts set into the courtyard and on the walls — with that spacing we didn't have to guess what for. Dungeons: nasty, stinking, wet holes — like a nightmare. Bones — human bones. And the servants — " Her voice faded away as her eyes clouded.

Barra nodded soberly. "They were pitiful. Not one without old scars and new welts. So we killed 'em all — "

"The servants?" asked Arñe, startled.

"No, of course not. The Wolf Prince and his men. And the Duke searched his rooms for a reason why he'd attack our caravan and the others — I hear he found nothing. And then we came back, and that's all." She stood abruptly and stretched. Natzlin rose more slowly, tucking back a strand of brown hair. "We'd better go back," said Barra. "We're on watch tonight." The two walked toward their own cohort.

"By all the gods, that one's prickly," said Vik. No one had to ask what he meant.

"She's a good fighter," said Paks, temporizing.

Vik snorted. "Paks, sometimes I think you'd forgive the Webmistress herself if she was a good fighter. That's not all that matters."

Paks felt her face growing hot. "I know that, Vik. But being touchy isn't all that matters, either — Barra's good at heart."

Vik gave her a long green stare, one of the few serious looks she'd had from him. "Paks, for once let a city-born runt give you a bit of advice. It's possible to like bad people, but liking them doesn't make them good." Paks opened her mouth, but he held up his hand and went on. "I'm not saying Barra's bad, exactly, but I am saying you think she's good at heart because you like her and want her to be good at heart. It doesn't work that way. If you don't learn to see people as they are, you'll get hurt someday."

Paks felt confused and angry. "I don't understand. It certainly sounds like you're saying Barra's bad, and she's not."

"No. I'm not really talking about Barra, but about you. Paks, my father was a harper. Harpers have to learn about people, or they can't sing with power. Even though I can't harp or sing, I learned a lot about people from him. They're complicated — being good at one thing doesn't make them good at something else: a good fighter can be treacherous, or cruel, or a liar. Do you see that?"

"Yes, but Barra — "

"I'm not talking about Barra. Listen to me. You've told us you always wanted to be a fighter, a fighter for good, right?" He waited for her nod before going on. "Well, you're so intent on that — you don't see other things. You see people as good or bad, not in between; as fighters or not, and not in between. And since you're basically a good person, you see most people as good — but most people, Paks, are in between — both as fighters, and as good or bad. And they're different. If you don't learn to see them straight — just as you'd look at a sword, knowing all swords aren't alike —

113

you'll depend on them for what they don't have."

Paks nodded slowly. "I think I see. But what about Barra?"

Vik threw back his head and laughed. "Oh, Paks! Barra's all right; she's just prickly, as I said." Arñe and Saben were both chuckling, and Paks finally grinned, still unsure of the joke.

Their winter quarters in Valdaire felt like home now. Familiar buildings, familiar people. No longer novices, after their first campaign year, the newest members of the Company found themselves accepted by the veterans. Among these friends, the Company mourning ceremony honoring all who had died that year brought more comfort than Paks expected. Canna was now an "old veteran," being past her required two years of service, but, like most such, she elected to stay in.

Their winter routine was much like training: drill, weapons practice, barracks chores. Paks spent hours in the smithy and armory, fetching and carrying, and doing what the unskilled could do. Some work always awaited them. Paks took the opportunity to begin learning longsword, and collected a whole new set of cuts and bruises.

With free time in Valdaire, they found that the salary which seemed so large at first disappeared amazingly fast.

"It's not that things are so expensive," said Arñe thoughtfully one evening in *The White Dragon*, the Company's favorite inn. "It's that there are so many things, and all we have to do is buy — "

"I know." Paks frowned at her linked hands. "I was going to save most of mine to repay my father, but I keep spending it. But except for coming here with you, I've needed what I've bought — or most of it — "

"We've gotten used to spending," said Saben. "That new dagger I bought — I could have used the Company one. But — I bought it."

"We might as well enjoy it," said Vik. "We're going to spend it one way or another. No use fretting about it."

Paks snorted. "There speaks a man who dices his way to twice his salary."

"Not always." Vik was unruffled. "And if I do, I spend it all. I'll teach you, if you like. I'll even let you start with pebbles."

"No, thank you. I just can't see taking a chance on losing it."

"You take chances when you fight — that trick you pulled on Canna today — "

"That's different." She blushed when Vik laughed. "No, it is. I know what chances I'm taking, in fighting. But with money — "

"You're still a country girl, Paks. That's exactly the difference between city and country — "

"I'm the same way," said Saben mildly. "I can't see throwing money away — or anything else, for that matter." Vik laughed, shaking his red head.

The Duke left, to ride north; they realized that he was going to inspect another group of recruits. Paks was distressed to find that Stammel was going with him.

"What did you expect?" he asked. "It's my year to recruit and train; I saw you through your first year. I'll be back a year from now." His brown eyes twinkled. "And you'd better be here to lick my recruits into shape, you and the rest. Take care — I want to hear good things of you."

"Is Bosk going too?" Paks felt like crying.

"No. He's staying down another year. Devlin wanted to stay north; his wife's had another baby."

Paks had never thought of any of them being married; she eyed Stammel but lacked the nerve to ask him.

While waiting for the new recruits to come down, they had more time off. Paks met a corporal in the Valdaire city militia who had grown up near Rocky Ford — the first person she'd met in the south who knew where Three Firs was. A bowman from Golden Company bought them all ale one night — he was celebrating his retirement, he said — he'd saved enough to buy a farm. Spring came earlier and quicker in the Vale of Valdaire than in the north. As the fields greened, grass ran like green flame up the slopes toward retreating snow. Rivers boiled with snowmelt, roaring and tumbling the rocks in their beds. Tiny yellow and white flowers starred the grass. New lambs scampered among the flocks, flipping their ridiculous tails. Paks was almost homesick when she saw the lambs. Buds swelled on the trees; wild plums flowered by every rivulet. The first caravans clogged the city with wagons and pack beasts, waiting for the pass to open.

Paks had not realized, the year before, that someone left the recruit column to warn the Company camp while the column went through the city. This year, when the courier came, the older veterans explained what to do.

"Just hang about as if you didn't know they were coming," said Donag, grinning. "Keep close to the yard. When the captain yells, throw yourself into position, fast. Whoever's closest, go for the front; never mind your usual position. What counts is speed. They don't know where we're supposed to be, and they'll be too scared to notice. Be sure to keep a straight face — they'll be funny, but don't laugh."

Paks saw the column coming up the lane; she strolled back to the yard, her heart hammering. What would the new recruits be like? Were they as frightened as she had been? And what about the sergeant who would replace Stammel? She watched as they came into the yard and halted, and tensed, waiting for the captain's shout. When it came, she was moving before it ended. Donag, still quicker, made his usual position before anyone else had a chance at it. It was all over in a moment. They stood silent and motionless, and the recruits' eyes widened.

Stammel's replacement was a black-haired, green-eyed woman named Dzerdya; Paks thought she looked forbidding. The other cohorts each had a new sergeant, and Bond, senior corporal in Cracolnya's cohort, was replaced by Jori. They had twenty-nine new recruits in Arcolin's cohort alone. Paks was glad to find that she was not assigned a recruit; she wouldn't know what to say to the bright-eyed youngsters who filled the empty bunks.

In the next few days, Paks found Dzerdya nothing like Stammel or easygoing Coben, their junior sergeant. She seemed to have a mind as quick as

115

her bladework, and she demanded instant attention and obedience. Paks was surprised to find that her recruits actually liked her.

"She was my sergeant," said Canna. "Isn't she amazing?"

That had not been Paks's first thought. Terrifying, quick-tempered, hasty, impossible — but not amazing. But Canna went on, not noticing her reaction.

"Wait until you see her in battle. She's so fast you can hardly see her blade. You ought to drill with her sometime."

"She seems kind of — kind of — angry a lot," said Paks lamely.

"Oh, that. She's quick to bite, true, but she doesn't brood on things. Don't worry about it. I don't think she knows, sometimes, when she's scared someone half to death."

In another week, Paks had begun to agree. Dzerdya was strict, and had a tongue like a handful of razors, but she was fair. She obviously cared a great deal for her troops.

This year's contract was very different. "It's a siege," explained Donag, who had used his own mysterious contacts to find out. "The Guild League cities are joining to siege and assault another city, halfway across Aarenis. They're hiring several companies as well as their own militia. I think our contract's with Sorellin, but the others are supporting it."

"What city?" asked Canna.

"Rotengre. Have you heard of it?"

"I think so. Wasn't there a caravan raid near there, last year?"

"Yes. The Guild League thinks that Rotengre harbors brigands — in fact, they suspect the city lives by preying on the northern caravan route between Merinath and Sorellin. Three or four years ago — before your time, Canna — five caravans were totally destroyed. That was the worst, so far as I know, but for the past ten or twelve years the loss has been enormous. Almost as bad as what Alured's done to the Immer River shipping."

"But why do they think it's Rotengre?" asked Paks. "Do the caravans go through there?"

"Look." Donag began to scratch a rough map on the table with the burnt end of a stick. "Here's Valdaire, in the northwest. Now here's the river. It's like a tree, sprouting from the Immerhoft Sea in the south, with branches northwest, north, and northeast. Downstream from Valdaire you come to Foss, Fossnir, Cortes Vonja, Cortes Cilwan, and Immervale, where the branches meet. On the north branch, up from Immervale, you've got Koury, Ambela, and Sorellin. The other branch, to the east, has Rotengre. Then off in the far northeast, Merinath and Semnath. And the Copper Hills — "

"Have you been to all those places?" asked Paks, awed.

"Most of 'em. The Copper Hills, now, that's where caravans come north from the coast — "

"Why don't they come up the Immer?" asked Vik. "That other's a long way out of their way, isn't it?"

"You haven't heard yet of Alured the Black?" asked Donag, brows rising. They shook their heads. "Well — that's a tale in itself. Used to be a searover

116

he did — a pirate — and somehow decided to come ashore. He controls a belt of forest near the coast, and he's pirated so much of the river trade that there isn't any. It's cheaper to go the long way around than pay his tolls." Donag rubbed his face with one meaty hand, then went on. "Like I was saying, the caravan route is north along the Copper Hills, then west: Semnath, Merinath, Sorellin, Ambela, Pler Vonja, then Fossnir and Foss and upriver to Valdaire. The road they've built is something to see.

"The stretch between Merinath and Sorellin is long — comes fairly close to Rotengre — and that's just where the caravans have been attacked. A lot of that's forest, so it's easy enough for brigands to throw off pursuit, and for Rotengre to claim they live in the forest. But they trade somewhere, and Rotengre is the obvious place. Besides, what else can the city live on? It never was part of the river trade — that branch is too shallow. No good farmland, no mines."

They nodded, staring at the blurred smears of black on the table. Paks wondered what the country looked like.

"What is a siege like?" asked Vik.

"Boring," said Donag. "Unless the first assault works, and we take the city at once, we camp outside and keep anyone from going in or out. It takes months, and it's nothing but standing watch and camp work and drill. A long wait until they get hungry, that's all."

"That sounds easy enough," muttered Saben.

Donag shot him a hard glance. "It's not. They'll have archers on the walls, and stone-throwers. You can get killed walking too close, but if you're too far away they have time to climb down the walls and get out. And it's hard to keep the camp like the Duke wants it for that long. If you don't, you have camp fever taking out half your troops. It's better than a fight every day, but it's not easy."

Canna had been looking thoughtful, tracing the smeared lines with one brown finger. "Does Rotengre have any allies?"

"Ah. That's a question." Donag frowned and rubbed his nose. "Probably yes; somebody must be buying the stolen goods. My guess is they ship it downriver. Koury, for example: it isn't a Guild League city, but it's gotten rich in the past few years — how else? Or cities passed by on the old river route: Immervale, Cortes Cilwan. Or if you want to reach far enough, there's always the Honeycat. Siniava. He wants to rule all Aarenis, they say; it takes money to hire the troops for that. If all this flows back to him —"

"Well, what if they attack us while we're sieging?" Vik looked almost eager.

"Then we'll have a fight. That's why the siege force is so large — just in case. But their allies may not want to come out of cover."

It all seemed very complicated to Paks. The only thing clear was the route they would travel. She thought of lands and cities she had never seen.

Chapter Thirteen

It was a long three days' march to Fossnir, down the river from Valdaire, with a baggage train much larger than the year before. Peach and apricot orchards were still pink, though the plum blossom had passed. Paks missed the more delicate pink and white of apples, and the white plumes of pear. When she mentioned this to a veteran, he said that apples were grown only in the foothills of the Dwarfmounts, or far to the west. Pears did not grow in Aarenis at all.

The road they marched on was wide and hard: great stone slabs laid with a careful camber for drainage into ditches on either side. To one side was a soft road, for use in good weather when the road was crowded. Northbound caravans passed them, one made up of pack animals instead of wagons. They had a nod and smile from the caravaners. The last guard on one of them looked back and yelled, "I hope you get those bastards!"

"How did he know?" asked Donag, startled, then answered himself. "It'll be those militia talking, I suppose. Can't keep any quieter than a landlord."

The next day after Fossnir, they made Foss, oldest city in Foss Council. Here they left the river, following the Guild League caravan road to Pler Vonja. Villages were spaced a few hours apart along the way, and great walled courtyards for caravans to use were never more than a day's easy journey apart. Wheelwrights, harnessmakers, and blacksmiths had their places at each caravan halt; the villages offered fresh food and local crafts.

As they crossed the Foss Council border, they found a large unit of militia ready to go with them. Paks was happy to find that the militia would march behind; she liked her forward view.

Pler Vonja, next in line, was stone-walled, but most of its buildings were wood above the first story: a great forest bordered the city on the north. It had fortified bridges across its little river. The city militia wore orange and black, and carried pikes. Paks noticed a nasal twang in the local accent that made some words hard to understand. The march from Pler Vonja to Ambela took six days; rain and a crowded road slowed them down.

Ambela was built, like Pler Vonja, across a small branch of the Immer, but it had a different look. Its gray stone walls were livened by the red and white banners that stirred above every tower and gate. Some low flower made a bright gold carpet along the water meadows. Farm cottages were whitewashed, brilliant in the green fields. The two hundred foot and fifty horse of Ambela militia that joined the column all wore bright red and white.

Four days later, they came to Sorellin. Much larger than Ambela, it had double walls, the inner one defining the old city. They marched through the west gate, under a white banner with great yellow shears centered on it. The guards wore yellow surcoats. Paks thought it looked as clean and prosperous as the best parts of Vérella and Valdaire; she wondered if it had a poor quarter. Below the bridge she saw two flatboats, loaded with plump sacks, being hauled upstream by mules. Outside the city again, on the southeast, they found a large contingent of Sorellin militia waiting for them.

After two days in a camp outside the city, they marched again on a very different road. It had never been part of the Guild League system; narrow, rough, and partly overgrown, it had to be practically rebuilt to allow the wagons to pass. Six days later they came out on the gentler slopes that lay around Rotengre and its branch of the Immer.

Even from a distance, Rotengre looked more formidable than the other cities, more like an overgrown fort: high, steep walls, massive towers, all out of proportion to the breadth. It was shaped somewhat like a rectangle with the corners bitten off; its long axis ran north and south, with the only two gates on the short ends. Paks decided that the tales must be true — it was a city built for trouble, not for honest trade.

As the head of their column cleared the forest and started across a wide belt of pasture toward the walls, trumpets blared from the city. A troop of men-at-arms in dark uniforms, their helmets winking in the sun, came out the north gate. The Duke's Company marched on, angling left toward the gate. The Rotengrens halted, and began to withdraw, as more and more of the attacking column snaked from the forest. Ahead, to the northeast, another column came into sight. These wore black, and carried spears in a bristling mass. Paks caught her breath and started to reach for her sword.

"That's Vladi's Company — don't worry about them," called Dzerdya. "We're on the same side."

"I hope so," muttered Donag, just loud enough for Paks to hear.

The compact mass of spearmen kept pouring from the forest, cohort by cohort — five in all, with a smaller body of horse. They turned south, to march along the east side of the city. After them came a troop of cavalry whose rose and white colors were bright even at that distance. Most of the horses were gray; a few were white. Paks thought they looked more like figures from a song than real fighters, but she had heard of Clart Company.

The Rotengren troops had withdrawn completely, and they heard the portcullis crash down long before they could have reached the gate. A small party of riders galloped away downstream, pursued by a squad of Foss Council cavalry, but they were clearly drawing away.

Setting up and maintaining a siege camp was every bit as hard and boring as Donag had said it would be. The Duke's Company had a position west of Sorellin's militia, just west of the north gate, and around the angle of

119

wall to the west. On their right flank the Ambela militia covered the west wall. Vonja militia had the south wall and gate, and Vladi's Company and the Foss Council troops divided the west wall. Clart Company patrolled between the siege lines and the forest.

The Duke and his surgeons had definite and inconvenient ideas about siting the camp's necessities, from the bank and palisade between Rotengre's wall and their camp, to the placement of jacks trenchs. All that work — dull and unnecessary as it seemed to Paks and the others — was better than the boring routine of the siege itself, when nothing happened day after day. Spring warmed into summer, and the summer grew steamy. Rotengre troops threw filth off the walls; its stench pervaded the camp. When it rained, a warm unrefreshing rain, dirty brown water overflowed the ditch under the walls and spread the stinking filth closer. No one complained about hauling wood or water, or cutting hay in distant meadows: any break in routine was welcome. Tempers frayed. Barra and Natzlin got in a fight with two militiamen from Vonja, and even Paks agreed it was Barra's fault. Rumor swept the camps that two cohorts of Vonja militia were down with fever from swimming in the river. Paks's captain, Arcolin, rode off to Valdaire on some errand for the Duke, leaving Ferrault in command. The cohort found that Ferrault was as strict as Arcolin had been, where camp discipline was concerned. The Duke's surgeons frowned constantly, and swept through the camp inspecting everything.

Muggy midsummer faded to the blinding heat and cloudless days that ripened grain for harvest. Paks thought longingly of the cool north. Food began to taste odd; she thought it was the terrible smell from the ditch under the wall. Dzerdya's orders to get ready for a long march were more than welcome.

"Where?" asked Paks.

Dzerdya glared at her, then answered. "North. Sorellin Council wants us to garrison a frontier fort, and let the militia up there come home for harvest. They've had a big crop this year. It's up in the foothills." She smiled, then, at Paks. "Hurry; we march tomorrow."

"Is everyone going?"

"No; it doesn't take the whole company to garrison one little fort. We could probably do it with half of you — it's only a matter of taking tolls if anyone crosses Dwarfwatch — but no one will, this late."

They started before dawn the next day, taking a road that led directly north, rather than northwest to Sorellin. After a day's march through the forest near Rotengre, they entered a rolling land of farms and woodlots, checkered with hedges. They crossed a small river on a stone bridge, and then the main caravan route, the same broad stone way they had been on before. Ferrault, reverting to his usual cheerful demeanor, pointed out the carved stone sign for Sorellin, shears in a circle on top of a pillar. The road they followed swung a little right. With every day, the ground rose in gentle waves. They saw more forest and less farmland. They crossed another road, not so well-made: the north route to Merinath, Ferrault said. The hills ahead were higher, blocking their view of the mountains they'd hoped to see. From that last crossroad to the fort was just under a day's march, a day pleasantly cool after lowland heat, through thick forest and over low ridges.

Just south of the fort they cleared the forest and saw mountains looming north, much higher than near Valdaire. Snow streaked their peaks. Dwarfwatch itself was a well-built stone keep with comfortable quarters around the inner court, and roomy stable in the outer. Its only fault was its lack of water; a rapid mountain stream rushed nearby, but inside the walls was neither spring nor well. Beyond the fort, a high and difficult track crossed the mountains, but as they had been told, no one used it. All the traffic they saw was grain wagons rolling up the road from Sorellin to collect harvest from the foothill farms, and rolling south again. Paks found it a delightful interlude: cool air, clean water, fresh food from nearby farmers happy to get hard cash for their produce. South of the river, backed up on the forest, Paks discovered an enormous tangle of brambles, loaded with berries just turning color. She kept a close watch on them.

One hazy afternoon, she and Saben were taking in the washing they'd spread on rocks near the river. She heard a yell from the wall behind them, then the staccato horn signal of alarm. They snatched their clothes and scrambled up the rocky bank, racing for the gate around the corner. Paks saw others running too. She slowed for a moment to look back to the road. The front rank of a column marched out of the forest.

"Paks! Come on!" As Paks darted under the gate tower, Dzerdya caught her arm and swung her around. "Don't *ever* slow like that! D'you want us to drop the portcullis and leave you outside? Go on — hurry and get armed."

The barracks was noisy chaos as all the off-duty people scrambled to arm. Still fumbling at the buckles of her corselet, Paks ran back out and puffed up the stairs to the wall. Whatever and whoever the approaching force was, it clearly outnumbered them. She counted three units of foot, each the size of their own cohort, and a troop of cavalry. And —

"What's that?" she asked a veteran.

He grimaced. "Siege engines. Now we're in for it."

"But — who'd be sieging us?" He didn't answer, and Paks moved along the wall to her assigned position near the gate tower. The foremost troops were almost at the river; they wore dark green tunics. It reminded her of some she'd seen in Valdaire during the winter.

"Halverics," breathed Donag beside her. "Now what'd they be doing up here? Could the Duke have sent — no, surely not." Paks glanced at him; he seemed more puzzled than worried. She relaxed, then jumped as the portcullis clanged the last few inches into the stone. Donag gave her a wry grin. "We're in a pickle now. I won't hide it," he said. "If Halveric Company wants this fort, they'll get it in the end. Might be better if the captain decides to yield."

Paks stared at him, open-mouthed. "But we can't. It's — "

Donag nodded at the siege engines rolling down the slope toward the bridge. "We will sooner or later. We can hold it a week, maybe, if we've water enough. But we'd take heavy losses, and they'd break through in the end. Tir's guts, I wasn't looking forward to being a captive again."

Paks choked down what she wanted to say, and peered over the wall. A rider in green waved a truce flag, she saw Captain Ferrault's helmet slip from the postern beside the main gate, then his foreshortened form moving forward to meet the rider. She could not hear what they said. She could not have heard it if they'd been beside her; blood pounded in her ears. She watched as they walked back. Her stomach churned. She was sure they could hold — but when she tried to think how long, she thought of the water barrels. How long would it take the Duke to come north, and how could they send word? Her mouth felt dry already.

Even so, she was not resigned when Bosk brought his word. Nor was she the only one who cried, "But we can't quit — just quit. We can't."

"Oh yes, you can." His face looked more wrinkled than before. "We follow orders, remember? When the captain tells us to lay down our arms, we do it. And I don't want any nonsense, either, from any of you."

"Arcolin wouldn't have — " began someone.

"Enough! Arcolin's not here; Ferrault is. And for my money, Arcolin would have done the same."

"But — what will happen?" Vik sounded as worried as Paks felt.

"They'll collect our weapons, and assign us an area. Usually it takes a day or so to list all the equipment and men, and then they'll send a ransom request to the Duke. Then a few weeks to settle terms and collect the ransom, and we'll be released. Usually less than a month, altogether."

"But what do we *do*?" Paks imagined a month in the cells under the fort.

"What we're told — that's what prisoners always do. Halveric Company is one of the best; we've fought beside them, now and again. They won't make it hard if we don't. I expect they'll pass their commands down through Captain Ferrault; it'll be much as usual. No drill, of course, and no weapons practice. We may work the harvest, or some such."

"I'm no farmer," said Canna, tossing her head. "I'm a fighter."

Bosk glared at her. "You're about to be a prisoner. Unless you want me on your back as well as those — " he nodded at the wall, "you'll do what you're told. You worked on the road during training."

"Aye, but — "

"No buts. There's rules for this, the same as for everything else. We agree to behave until we're ransomed; if there's any trouble, it's handled by the officers. Don't talk about the Company to them — mostly they won't ask; it's bad manners. And don't ask about theirs. No one's to run off, or anything of that sort. No brawling, of course. No bedding with them; it lacks dignity. I expect this will be the usual terms, which means they won't confiscate your belongings except weapons, but I'd keep any jewels out of sight just in case."

Paks could tell that most of the cohort was as miserable as she was, coming out the gate onto the fields by the river. They had been allowed to march out wearing their swords, but the familiar weight at her side did not make up for the knowledge that she would draw it only to give it up. She stared straight ahead, trying to ignore the green-clad troops lining the road. At last they halted between two cohorts. She let her gaze wander to Captain Ferrault, who was met by a dark bearded man in plate mail. After a few words, the captain turned to them, his usually cheerful face expressionless.

"Sergeant Dzerdya. Disarm the troops."

"Sir." Dzerdya turned. Paks was glad it was not Stammel; she could not believe Stammel would do it. "Draw your swords and drop them." Paks felt tears sting her eyes as she reached for the hilt of her sword. She blinked them back. The sword slid as easily as ever from its scabbard; she could hear the rustle of all the others. It was impossible that they should drop them. Surely —

"No!" bellowed Coben from behind, breaking into her musing. "No nonsense. Drop them!" Even now, Paks could not drop a sword to its hurt; she knelt to lay hers gently on the ground. She did not know who had prompted Coben's rebuke, but she was glad of it. At least the Halverics would know they were not afraid.

Around them now the Halveric cohorts stood with drawn swords, waiting. Ferrault was talking to the Halveric commander again, who shook his head: once, then again, more emphatically. Ferrault turned back to them. "It seems," he said in a hard light voice, "that our reputation has preceded us. We should take it as an honor that we are required to yield daggers as well as swords. Sergeant, see to it."

Before Dzerdya could say anything, the Halveric commander grinned and spoke; his voice was deep, and his accent made a musical complement to his speech. "It is indeed an honor. For so long as we have respected your noble Duke, so long have we known his soldiers to be spirited as well as brave and skilled. We would not have lives and blood lost where no need is: your men or ours, captain. These will be returned, when each has given parole." He bowed to the captain, and more slightly to the cohort itself.

"All right now," said Dzerdya. Her voice was flat. "Daggers the same; drop them."

As Paks slipped her dagger from its sheath, she felt a heavy cold weight dragging at her. She was not even tempted to use the dagger. It seemed that nothing could ever be right again. To stand unarmed in the midst of armed troops, defeated without a fight, was the worst thing she could imagine. But with the others she marched back, under guard, to await events.

Several days later, Paks had admitted that Bosk was right. Though they slept in the stables instead of the barracks, the change brought no hardship: they ate the same food, obeyed the same sergeants, and suffered only from the boredom of confinement. That would change when they had all given

123

their paroles. Bosk explained that, too: each one would come before Aliam Halveric, the commander, and agree to abide by the rules for captives — or risk being put under guard while the others went free within bounds.

Now Paks was waiting her turn. She felt her heart speeding up, and tried to breathe slowly. Only one man between her and the door. Her hands were sweaty. Vanza came out and winked at her; she was face to face with the door. She stared at the grain of the wood, finding pictures in its twists and curves. Should she give her parole? This wasn't anything like the old songs, where heroes always fought to the death if they did not win, and captivity and defiance went together like sword and scabbard. The door opened. Rauf came out, and the guard beckoned. She took a deep breath and walked in.

Behind a wide desk sat the dark bearded man who had accepted their surrender. Without his helmet and mail he seemed smaller: almost bald, with a fringe of graying dark hair, a round weathered face, broad muscular hands. He gave her a long look from dark eyes.

"Ah, yes," he said. "I noticed you — you didn't want to chance damaging your blade, did you?"

Paks blushed. "No — sir."

"Sign of a good warrior," he said briskly. "Name, please?" He held a pen, poised over the desk.

Bosk had said they should give their names. "Paks, sir."

He ran his finger down the parchment roll on the desk. "Ah — there. You're a first-term, I see." He looked back up at her. "It's harder, the first time you're captured. I daresay it's bothered you."

Paks relaxed a bit. "Yes, sir."

"You signed on to be a warrior, not to surrender," he went on. "Still, it does happen, and it's no shame to know when you're overmatched. We don't think worse of your captain for seeing the obvious. To be honest, we're glad not to have to fight it out, knowing what we know of your Company." He paused; a slight smile moved his lips. "I imagine you've been wondering whether it's honorable to give your parole — " Paks nodded. His smile broadened, not mocking, but friendly. "I thought so. Well, I won't argue against your conscience. I've given mine on occasion — if that matters. It's only until you're ransomed. You may match swords against us another season at the command of your Duke, or quarrel with my men in Valdaire next winter. They haven't been teasing you, have they?"

"No, sir. They haven't bothered us at all."

"That's good. They know, you see, that it might be the other way next time. Now — " he went on more briskly. "I'll need your answer. Can you swear to remain a prisoner under command of my company until ransomed, without rebellion or escape so long as you're honorably treated?"

Paks paused a moment, but she trusted him in spite of herself. "Yes, sir, I agree."

"Very well." His voice held more warmth. "And I and my commanders give our word that you and your companions will be honorably treated,

124

well fed and housed, and be subject to the authority of your captain, under my designated representative only. Now what that means," he continued, less formally, "is that we won't suddenly sell you to slavers, or turn you over to another company of mercenaries. We agree to be fully responsible for your welfare, just as your Duke would be."

"Yes, sir," said Paks. She found this confusing. It seemed like an extra trouble to both sides.

"I'm telling you this because you youngsters need to understand how we northern mercenaries deal with one another under the compact. We are often rivals, and sometimes hired enemies, but we have our own code, which we will not change for any employer. Your Duke and I and Aesil M'dierra started it years ago, and now most good companies abide by it. The others — well, they can be paid to do anything. If we are to stay honorable, the newest members of our companies must understand — and that means you, in your first term. Do you understand that?"

"Yes, sir," said Paks. She met his eyes and surprised a puzzled look on his face.

"You need not answer if you prefer," he said slowly, "but would you tell me where you're from?"

"Three Firs," said Paks promptly.

He looked blank. "Where is that?"

"It's — well — all I really know is it's a day's journey from Rocky Ford, and west of Duke Phelan's stronghold." Now she was puzzled by his interest.

"Oh. The reason I asked is that you reminded me of someone I once knew; I wondered if you were related. But she came, if I remember, from Blackbone Hill or something like that."

Paks shook her head. "I never heard of that place, sir. It wasn't near Three Firs."

"Well, then — you may go."

Paks nodded, and turned away, surprised at how much better she felt. That evening their daggers were returned to them — with plenty of warnings about misuse. With her dagger once more at her side, Paks felt much more secure. She found her hand returning to it again and again.

Two days later, Aliam Halveric rode away with two of his cohorts marching behind; the siege engines went with them. His captain allowed the prisoners to practice marching drill in small units, and troops of both companies went out on work details for wood, water, and food. The Halverics hardly seemed to be guarding them, as they worked just as hard as the Phelani. They all bathed in the river, and washed clothes along its banks. At first Paks was very stiff with them, but as she saw her sergeants and corporals chatting with their Halveric colleagues, she began to listen. She knew nothing about Lyonya, where most of the Halverics came from. They spoke of elves as if they'd all seen them and worked with them.

As the days wore on, the Phelani were allowed even more freedom of movement inside the bounds Ferrault received from the Halveric captain.

125

Paks saw Ferrault and the Halveric, who seemed even younger than Ferrault, playing some board game in a sunny part of the court one morning. They were laughing together; the Halveric captain shaking his head.

To Paks's delight, small groups could go to the river or the bramble patches without an escort. The berries were now ripe, and she enjoyed the hours she spent picking them. Vik didn't like it — too hot, too prickly, too tedious — but she, Saben, and Canna gathered pail after pail of dark-red berries that both Halverics and Phelani were glad to eat.

Chapter Fourteen

They were deep in the brambles one afternoon, grousing at thorns as they stuffed themselves with ripe berries, when they heard a signal from the Halverics' bugler. They stopped to listen.

"Not for us, whatever it is," said Canna. The signal for their return was four long notes, three rising and the fourth the same as the first.

"Could be a messenger from the Duke," suggested Saben, standing to peer through the tops of the brambles. They were south of the fort, even with the southeast corner of the wall; they could see only a short stretch of the road leading west from the gate.

"I think it's too soon," said Canna.

"What can you see?" asked Paks. She was pouring berries from her pail into a sack they'd brought along.

"Not much. But — wait — do you hear that?"

They did not so much hear it as feel it, a growing rumbling along the road to the south. They could see nothing, because of the angle of the woods, but as Paks stood, she could see sentries moving on the fort walls. Other work details, nearer the fort, were turning to look back down the road. The sound began to separate into rhythmic components that sounded like horses and marching feet. A deep-toned horn called from somewhere on the road. The Halverics' bugle rang out again. A horseman came in sight around the angle of wall, riding out from the fort; Paks could see something glittering on his shoulders, and his green cloak. She thought it was the captain's horse, and told Canna.

"Maybe we should go back," said Canna. She bounced up and down on tiptoe, trying to see over the brambles. Paks and Saben could just see through the upper thorny branches.

"Let's wait," said Paks. "Whatever it is — it's odd. And they haven't called us. Look, Saben; isn't that — "

"Troops. Yes. Lots." Out of the trees came a column of men-at-arms behind twenty or so horsemen. "Not the Duke," added Saben. "Whose colors are those, I wonder?"

"What colors?" demanded Canna.

"Just a second; the wind's wrong. Yellow field — something on it in black, but I can't tell what it is. The horsemen — some in chain — one in plate — yellow surcoats. Tir's bones, those men are carrying pikes!"

"Pikes? No one around here uses pikes," said Canna. "Yellow and black, and uses pikes — I can't think of anyone within range — "

"He's right, though," said Paks. "It is pikes; I can see the heads glinting in the sun."

"What are they doing?" Canna had given up the attempt to see for herself.

"Marching — no, they're halting. Whoever it was that came from the fort is riding up to the head of the column — I'm sure it's the captain. Let's see — " For a few moments, Paks fell silent as she watched. Nothing moved. "I guess he's talking to someone — passing something across or taking — Now he's backing up. I wonder what — No!" She turned to Saben. "He's down. He fell off his horse. Saben, look!"

"I see," said Saben grimly. "I don't like this."

"Tell me," said Canna, "before I — "

"I think they shot him; they're carrying crossbows. They're moving off the road — going after the work details — "

"But they're unarmed!"

"But they are — and look at the rest — they're marching on the fort. It must be an enemy — "

"But whose?" Canna's face wrinkled in a puzzled frown.

"I don't know. Halveric's, I suppose, but — Oh, no! They're — the devils! The murdering devils — " Paks started to thrash forward through the brambles.

"Paks, get down!" Saben wrestled Paks to the ground. "Be quiet, you fool! It won't help for us to go out there."

"What happened? What is it?" Canna tried again to see.

"Some of our men tried to run. They're down — arrows, I'd guess."

"By St. Gird! We have to — "

"Not you too! Think, Canna! Paks, listen. Be still. What can we do with three daggers? We don't have any armor — they'd shoot us down before we could kill one of them."

"You're right," said Paks reluctantly. "Let me up, Saben; I won't do anything. But we can't just — just run away and let them be killed."

"What about the fort?" asked Canna quietly. "Surely the Halverics will come out — "

"Not if they're smart," said Paks. "That's a big force; I don't think we've seen all of it yet. They'll be lucky if they can hold against assault, let alone mount a sally." Even as she spoke, they heard the bugler again, and the crash of the portcullis rang across the river meadows.

"We can't get back in now," said Saben. "Even supposing we wanted to."

Paks started to look toward the fort, to see how it was manned, but drew back sharply. "They're closer," she said softly. "On this side of the river." They all flattened under the brambles as best they could. They could hear the squeak and rattle of harness as armed men came nearer, but they could see nothing. Paks hoped this was true for the men outside as well.

"Ho, there!" cried a harsh voice. "We see you. Come out or be shot!" They did not move. Paks heard a rustling crackle as an arrow went into the bramble some yards away. "Come on out, cowards!" cried another voice. Another arrow and another, closer. Suddenly an arrow pinned Canna's shoulder. She made no sound. The rattle of arrows passed on, was farther away with each shot. "By the Master, I told you nothing was up here," said the second voice, complaining.

"Take it up with the lord, then: it was his orders," growled the other.

"Nay — I'll do what he says — only those prisoners are more to my liking — did you see that redheaded girl?" The voices, still bickering, moved away to their right. Still they lay unmoving, without a sound. Paks met Saben's eyes; his face was white with anger. She looked over at Canna. Canna blinked back tears; her jaw was clenched. They waited. A blue fly buzzed around the spilled berries, then settled on Canna's shoulder. They heard shouts from the fort, from the men below. A scream. More shouts. Paks glanced at Saben again, and raised an eyebrow. He nodded.

With great care they both moved to Canna's side. The arrow did not seem to be in very deep. "Hope it's no worse than it looks," murmured Saben. Paks offered Canna a wad of her cloak to bite, then steadied the shaft as Saben cut her tunic away from it. The long barbs of the head were still outside her skin; the head itself seemed to be lodged in the big muscle between neck and shoulder. When Paks pulled, the head slid out easily, followed by a rush of blood. It was both longer and wider than those used by their own Company. Saben clapped his hand over the wound, squeezing it shut. Paks emptied the berries from the sack, and looked doubtfully at the coarse fabric.

Canna spat out the wad of cloth in her mouth. "Go ahead — it'll do."

"Not too rough?"

"No. Go on."

"Wait a bit," murmured Saben. "Let the bleeding slow. We can't move now anyway." Paks folded the sack into a thick pad after cutting a strip for a tie with her dagger. They heard more confusion of noise from the fort, but nothing closer. Paks wondered how long they should wait before moving. The attackers might send scouts through the woods to pick up stragglers. She spent the time packing her belt pouch with fallen berries. Finally Saben let up the pressure he'd kept on Canna's shoulder. The wound gaped, but the bleeding had nearly stopped.

"Stopped it," he said. "Let's have that pad, Paks."

"It'll start when I move," said Canna ruefully. "By St. Gird, it was plain bad luck being hit at all, when they couldn't see." She winced as Paks pressed the folded sack onto her shoulder. "Eh — how are you — "

"Like this," said Paks softly. "Keep pressure on it, and help her sit, Saben." With Saben's help, Canna rolled to her side and sat up. Her face was pale. "Now," said Paks. "Under this arm, and up and around — and again here. There. Don't move that arm if you can help it."

"Good job. Thanks."

"Now what will we do?" asked Saben.

"We've got to get away from here before they make a proper search," said Canna. "And then we've got to get to the Duke."

Paks nodded. "I agree. But Rotengre's a long way — do you know how to find it?"

"I think so," said Canna. "As long as I'm with you — but what about you?"

Saben shook his head. "Not me. I know it's south somewhere, that's all. You, Paks?"

Paks ignored the question at first. "Canna — you aren't leaving us, are you?"

"No. But if this wound goes bad, or we have trouble on the way and I'm killed, I wanted to know if you could find the Duke yourself."

"Oh. I — I think so. At least, I'll recognize the roads when we get there, the crossroads and such."

"Good." Canna shifted, looking around the tiny space in which they lay. "Saben, can you tell what they're doing, and if it's safe to start moving? And Paks, let's get the rest of those berries packed up."

"It sounds like they may too occupied to worry about us," said Saben. He rose cautiously and peered out the upper level of the brambles. "There's a force on the walls — maroon and green both — the Halverics must have armed our men too. Wise of them. And a lot of troops below the walls, and horses. I think we can go, but we'd better stay down. Canna, can you crawl with that arrow wound?"

"As opposed to lying here to be captured by those barbarians, certainly. It's a good thing our tunics are dark. But let's eat what we can of these berries before we go." They stuffed handfuls of juicy berries into their mouths, gaining strength from the sweet juice. In a few minutes, Canna started them moving toward the trees. She sent Saben ahead, and Paks followed her, bringing one pail full of berries. They had buried the other under fallen leaves, in hopes that searchers would not find evidence of their presence.

Paks could see that Canna was having a hard time crawling; several times she stopped, swaying, but she never fell. Luckily their explorations during the berry harvest had left little trails running here and there almost to the forest edge; they did not have to force a new path. Canna managed to keep moving, and at last they fought free of the thorns. It was growing dusky; they could see fires twinkling on the meadow below.

They pushed through the hazels that fringed the woods and moved on into the darker shelter of the trees, now walking upright. When they found a sheltered hollow, they settled in to make further plans. Even in that dimness, Paks could tell that Canna was paler than usual.

"At least we've got full waterflasks," she said quietly. "And we've got some berries. I have a lump of cheese. What about you?" Saben had a hunk of dried meat, but Canna had only the berries she'd put in her belt pouch. "We can cook in the berrying pail," Paks went on.

"If we have anything to cook," said Saben. It was almost too dark to see. "Canna, how are you doing?"

"Could be worse — " Her voice was shaky.

"You'd better have the cheese and meat," said Paks. "That's what they told me when I lost a lot of blood: eat to make it up." Canna protested, but

Paks was firm. "No — you need it. Saben and I can eat berries. You're the one who will slow us down if you don't recover." She handed over her cheese, and Saben gave Canna the meat. They ate in silence; Paks and Saben, already full of berries, ate little.

"I wonder what they'll be up to tonight," said Saben at last.

"Not much, I hope. I suppose it depends on how far they've marched today — and how the assault goes." Paks suddenly found herself yawning, though she was not at all sleepy. She pushed thoughts of her other friends aside. "How glad I am, Canna, that you said we should bring our cloaks to lay over the thorns. It's going to be cold out here." It was already hard to believe how they had sweated under the brambles.

"Shouldn't we try to get farther away?" asked Saben.

"No — we'd just blunder around and make noise in the dark, and we might get lost. What do you think, Canna?" Paks remembered that Canna was senior to them.

"I think you're right. It's too dark. Though I wish we could find out what they *are* doing, to tell the Duke. And who they are." She sighed. "But that's even more dangerous. We don't know these woods well enough, and we can't risk capture." She paused, then went on in a different tone. "I know neither of you are Girdsmen, but — I wish you would join me in prayer. At least for the confusion of our enemies."

"That I'll go along with," said Saben. "But won't Gird be angry if non-Girdsmen pray in his name?"

"No," replied Canna. "He welcomes all honorable warriors." She reached into her tunic, the cloth rustling as she moved, and pulled out her holy symbol. Paks heard the faint chinking of the links of the chain. "Holy Gird, patron of warriors, protector of the weak, strengthen our arms and warm our hearts for the coming battles. Courage to our friends, and confusion to our enemies."

"Courage to our friends, and confusion to our enemies," repeated Paks and Saben. Paks felt strange, calling on one she did not follow, but surely such a simple request could not be misunderstood. She heard the chain jingle as Canna replaced the medallion, and reached to help Canna wrap her cloak around her injured shoulder. She added her own.

"I'll take the first watch," she told Saben. "You sleep."

He rolled up in his own cloak and lay next to Canna. Paks sat with her back against a tree, listening to the noises from the fort, and trying to imagine what they meant. She wondered which of her friends had been killed, and which were in the fort — and who had been captured. And who was the enemy — and why here, at the end of a road? Ferrault had said that the worst they could expect was brigands robbing the grain wagons — yet first the Halverics, and then this army, had marched up to take the fort as if it were important. Why?

She slipped her knife from its sheath and tested the edge. It had dulled on the cloth, as she'd feared. She felt for her whetstone, then paused. The sound would be distinctive if anyone heard it. Still, a dull knife — she decided to take the chance. She moved the blade lightly across the stone. Not too loud: good. It would take longer, but she had time.

When her blade was sharp, she put the stone back in her pouch and the dagger back in its sheath. She looked for stars overhead, but the leaves were too thick. No way to tell how time passed. She heard no noises from the fort, now, and only wind in the trees. She stretched first one arm, then the other. It was colder. She rubbed her arms, hard, then took down her hair and rebraided it by feel. The wind picked up; it smelled like rain. She thought she heard a drum in the distance, and wondered again who the attackers were. An owl called, a long wavering hooo — hooo — hoo hoo. She stretched one leg at a time, and wished she had not wrapped Canna in both cloaks. It seemed much colder. Saben began to snore. Paks reached out and touched his shoulder.

"Don't snore," she said when he jerked awake.

"Umph," he said, and rolled over. She stood and swung her arms vigorously to warm up. Better. The wind dropped, and she squatted down against the tree again, hoping it would not rain, hoping the wind would die away altogether. It didn't. Just when she thought she would be warm enough after all, a chill current of air flowed into the hollow and she started shivering. She rubbed her arms again, but it didn't help. Her teeth chattered.

"Paks," said a voice out of the dark; she nearly yelped. But it was Canna's voice. Paks scooted around to her side.

"What is it?"

"I woke up and heard your teeth — take this cloak; I don't need it."

"I don't want you to get chilled."

"I'm warm enough. Don't be silly; take the cloak." Canna heaved up and began unwrapping herself from the second cloak. Saben woke up.

"What's going on?"

"Paks is freezing, and I'm giving her back her cloak."

"It's time for me to take a turn watching anyway. Warm up, Paks; I'll wake you later."

"Th-thanks." Paks rolled into the warm cloak, and lay beside Canna, shivering for awhile. She fell asleep as soon as she was warm. She woke in a panic, with Saben's hand firmly over her mouth. Before she could move away from his hand, she heard the reason for it: horses somewhere nearby. She touched his wrist, and he moved his hand away. She looked at Canna. Canna looked back without moving. She had heard the horses too. A heavy wet fog lay between the trees; their cloaks were furred with moisture.

The horses came nearer. She could hear the jingling bits, the squeak of leather. And voices. "There won't be stragglers out here — we'd have found 'em holed up in that woodcutter's hut in this weather."

"Or else they're already far away."

"No — we hit late enough, they'll have been close in. The only thing is those brambles, the big ones, but Palleck's squad went over that yesterday."

"Shot arrows into it, you mean. Those lazy scum wouldn't pick through thorns. But I agree, that should have flushed anyone out. Still, if *he* wants us out here, here we'll be."

"Right enough. I won't argue. I wonder though — I thought we were going to lift the siege at Rotengre. What's he want to come up here and take a bunch of mercenary prisoners for?"

"I don't know. One of his schemes, I suppose. You know how he hates 'em. I don't doubt this Duke Whoever, the Red Duke, will be angry enough at the green ones when he finds his men where they'll be. And Tollen told me the Red Duke's at the siege."

"Is he? That's a bit clearer. My lord Siniava will be up to his usual tricks, no doubt." The voices had moved past, and now faded into foggy silence.

The three in the hollow looked long at each other. "They're taking the prisoners somewhere," said Saben softly. "I wonder where?"

"But what about the fort?" asked Paks.

"Siniava — Siniava. I should know that name. Yellow and black — and Siniava. Oh!" said Canna.

"What is it?"

"We can hope I'm wrong, but I think I know who that is: Siniava. I think it's the Honeycat. You've heard — ?"

Paks shivered. "Yes. Too much. Now what are we going to do?"

"Tell the Duke. Now more than ever. I wish I knew *where* they were taking the prisoners. He'll want to know."

"And if they're trying to break the fort to get more," said Saben.

"Yes. There's a lot we need to know — where they're going, and when, and by what road — "

"We — I — could try to get close to them and find out," suggested Paks.

"First we need to get Canna outside their skirmish lines," said Saben. "She can't travel as fast. But this fog's a big help; they can't see us."

"Do you know which way is which?" asked Canna.

Saben's face fell. "No. I didn't think of that."

"I do," said Paks. "At least I'm fairly sure. Let's go south a bit more, and then cut west to the road."

She helped Canna stand; the dark woman was steadier than Paks had expected. Then she led the way from tree to tree, with a pause behind each to look and listen. The woods were silent, except for the drip-drip of fog from every twig. They went on. It could have been hours; the light grew only slightly, and the fog was just as thick. At one pause, Saben asked, "How do you know this is south?"

"Remember the view from the wall — beyond the biggest brambles, and running south, was a belt of fir trees. I remember wondering if it had been planted there for some reason."

"Fir trees. How do you know fir trees from pines or anything else?"

"I'm from Three Firs, remember? Fir trees I know."

"Hunh. And I thought you were smart or something." Saben gave her a quick grin before going on.

They had come up a long slope, and now they felt an open quality to the silence that meant a ridgetop. When they started down the far side, the firs disappeared.

"Now what?" asked Saben.

"Now we stop for a bit," said Paks, eyeing Canna, whose face was pinched with pain or cold. She found a spot below a rock ledge, and they settled their backs against it. "We can have those berries now. Do you have a tinderbox, Saben?"

"No, worse luck. But we couldn't start a fire here, could we? So close?"

"No, but later. I don't have anything. Canna?"

"I don't know. I can't remember. There was no reason to bring it out, but I'll look in my pouch. Yes. There it is."

Paks grinned at the other two. "We're in good shape, really. We've got something to make a fire, and something to cook in — "

"And nothing to cook," Saben reminded her.

"Don't ill-wish," she retorted. "We could be dead, or prisoners, and we're not. If only Canna hadn't been hit — "

"*If* never filled the pot," said Canna. "I'm doing well — it hurts when I move that arm, just what you'd expect." Despite her words, Paks noticed that she sagged against the rock.

"Well, I need a rest, if you don't," said Paks.

"Now I know how you knew which way was south," said Saben. "But how are you going to find west? I don't remember any convenient belts of trees in that direction."

"This ridge runs west, more or less," said Paks, who had finally thought of that only a few minutes before, when she too wondered how she'd find west without the sun.

"Umm. You're right again. But I don't think following it will be as easy."

"No. I don't either. It would be nice to find someone's path going the right way."

"If we can find a path, so can their men."

"Yes. I should have thought of that. Well, we'll just have to try. If we do get lost, the sun will come out someday."

"Let's go on and share out the berries," said Canna. The berries seemed to have shrunk overnight, and did little to fill their empty bellies.

"The next time we do this sort of thing," said Saben, "let's be sure to carry three days' rations in our pouches, and tinderboxes, and bandages, and — let's see — how about mules and saddles, too."

Paks and Canna both chuckled. "In a pouch — of course," said Canna. "To be honest, I don't plan to do this again, if I can help it."

"Come now," said Saben. "We're going to be heroes in this tale. Escaping the villain, bringing word to our Duke, rescuing our friends — " Paks nodded; she had already imagined them freeing the prisoners on the road, and returning to the Duke in triumph. Of course, it wouldn't be easy, but —

"If we come out of this heroes," Canna said soberly, "we'll earn it. Every step of the way. You two — you've done well, so far, but you don't understand. There are too many things that can go wrong, too many miles. This

134

is no fireside tale, no adventure for a hero out of songs: this is real. We aren't likely to make it as far as the Duke, though we'll try — "

"I know that," Saben broke in. "We aren't veteran scouts. But still — it's easier to think about if we think of it as an adventure — at least I think so. The bad will come soon enough without looking for it — beyond being careful, of course."

"As long as you don't think we'll go dancing down the road and find the Duke as easy as finding those berries — " Canna sounded doubtful.

Paks shook her head. "We know, Canna. A lot can go wrong; we need you to keep us from making stupid mistakes that will get us all killed. One of us has to get through." She still thought they could do it; Canna was just worried because of her wound. She took a drink from her flask, then shook it. "I wonder how far downslope water is. Canna, how's your water?"

"About half. We probably should look for more."

"You stay here," said Saben. "I can't get lost if I go down and back up. I'll hoot like that owl last night when I think I'm near again." He took their flasks and disappeared into the fog.

"If they are marching to Rotengre," said Paks, "do you think they'll go through Sorellin, or around it?"

"Not through, even if they control the city — it'd be risky. I expect they'd take the fork we came up by."

"I hope so. That will be — a week on the march, at least, and more likely eight or nine days with that crowd. We'll have to get food somewhere. We can march two days on water alone, but not a week. D'you think we could buy food somewhere? I've got a silver — a nis — and some coppers — "

"It depends. If we're seen, we can be talked about. If we're far enough behind to be safe, we could lose them. Probably we'd best stick to what we can find — or steal."

"Steal!" said Paks. "But we're not supposed to — "

"I know. But it's better than capture. We can tell the Duke, when we get to Rotengre, and he'll make it good."

Paks sighed. It was beginning to seem more complicated. "If we stay close enough to know where they are, we'll be close enough for their scouts to find, won't we?"

"Yes. If we knew their route, we could go ahead of them — that would be best — but we don't." They sat in silence awhile. Canna shifted her back against the rock. Paks looked at her.

"Do you want to lie down?"

"Better not. Let me think — if they march like others I've seen, they'll have two waves of forward scouts, mounted, and a patrol on each flank. The flankers usually stay in sight of the column; the forward scouts may not. And a rearguard. The first day will be hardest, until we find out their order of march."

"I don't know whether to hope for rain, to slow them down, or dry weather to make it easy for us."

"Either way we'll have our problems; so will they. Best be ready to take what comes. One thing, Paks — "

135

"Yes?"

"We need to agree on who's in command."

Paks stared. "Why — you are, surely. You're senior."

"Yes — but I'm not even a file leader. And I'm injured; I couldn't *make* you obey, unless you — "

"*Hooo — hooo — hoo hoo.*"

"Saben's coming. *Hooo — hooo.*" Paks tried to hit the same pitch. They saw a human shape loom out of the fog.

"There's a good spring not far down," said Saben. "And I found these growing around it." He dumped out a pouchful of small shiny red berries and a few hazelnuts. "I don't know what those berries are, but they taste good."

Paks tried one. It was tart and juicy, very different from the luscious sweet bramble-berries. She and Canna ate while Saben cracked the hazelnut husks and piled the meats.

"I can take the pail down there," said Saben, "and gather more."

"I don't think so," said Canna. "Look at the fog." A light wind had come up, and the fog was beginning to blow through the trees in streamers. "We should be heading for the road. Saben, I was telling Paks that we need to agree on who's in command — "

"You're senior, Canna. Whatever you say — "

"All right. Paks agreed too. But if I'm disabled, one of you will have to take over, and — "

"Oh. Paks, of course — don't you think?" He popped a hazelnut into his mouth.

"That's what I thought." Canna sounded relieved. "I wanted to be sure you'd agree, though. I'm not a corporal or anything."

"That's all right. It's no time to worry about *that*."

"Good. Let me tell you what I think is next; if I miss anything, bring it up." They both nodded, and she went on. "We need to be close enough to know where they're going, without getting caught. That means staying out of their sight. If they head for Rotengre, we can stay together; if they don't, we'll have to separate: one goes straight to the Duke, and the others follow Siniava."

"But Canna," said Paks, "can't we do something about the prisoners? To free them, or something?"

Canna shook her head. "No — I don't think we can. The most important thing is to tell the Duke what's happened. If we try to free them and fail — and think, Paks: just the three of us, with daggers; we would fail — then we'd be caught or killed, and the Duke still wouldn't know. I don't like it either, but we won't help that way." She waited, looking from one to another. Paks finally gave a reluctant nod. Saben grunted. Canna went on. "Another thing — if one of us is caught, or killed, or — or whatever — the others must go on. Someone has to get to the Duke, no matter what, or the whole thing is wasted. Clear?"

Paks had found the other hard enough to accept; this was impossible. She and Saben spoke together. "No! We can't — " Saben stopped and Paks continued. "Canna, you're hurt now — we can't leave you. What if they

136

found you? We're — we're friends; we've fought together, and — "

"We're warriors first," said Canna firmly. "That's what we're here for. If you accept my command, you must accept this. We're warriors, and our duty is to our Duke. He's the only one who can help the rest, anyway. I'd leave you — I wouldn't want to, but I would. And you'll leave me, if it comes to that, rather than let the whole cohort be lost, and the Company after it."

"Well — all right. But I hope it doesn't." Paks stood up and stretched.

"So do I," said Canna. Saben gave her a hand up. "Now — remember to use hand signals as much as you can; sound carries, as we heard." They nodded. "Paks, if you think you can find the way west, lead off. Whatever you do, don't veer north."

"I'll be careful." Paks looked around. The fog had thinned; she could see a short way through the trees. At the top of the ridge she followed the crest of it west — or what she hoped was west. In the dampness the leaves underfoot made little noise. They could hear nothing nearby, but from time to time they heard a distant drum.

Chapter Fifteen

Paks tried to think where they were as they walked. They'd been south of the southeast corner of the fort — then they'd gone south, and a little east, with the firs. Now she hoped they were walking west; the road lay west of the fort. But how far west — she remembered several turns before it got to the bridge — where were the turns?

This was going to be trickier than she'd thought. Where the trees were open — on the ridge — she could see better, but so could any enemy. She heard a horn call off to the right, and froze. It came again. She looked at Saben and Canna behind her. Canna shrugged. Paks gestured to the thicker growth downslope, and Canna nodded. They eased their way into it, and rested for a few minutes. Paks explained her concern — noisy progress through the thick growth, or visible progress through the thinner woods. After some discussion, they decided to stay in the heavier downslope woods, moving more slowly for silence.

It was harder going, but Paks felt safer. They stopped at intervals to listen, and kept a nervous eye on the rise above them. A patrol could come very close before they saw it. Suddenly she stopped. She thought she saw a lighter area ahead — a clearing, perhaps, or the road. She gestured, and the others lay down. When she looked back at them, their white faces showed clear against the dark wet leaves. She dug into the leaf-mold with her fingers and smeared it on her face, then looked back again and pointed to show what she'd done. They nodded, and began doing the same. Paks gestured again, for them to stay in place, and began to creep forward, keeping to such cover as she could find. From her position, she could see very little. After a few damp, tiring yards of creeping, she was tempted to stand and look. But when she glanced back to see how far she'd come, Canna's hand signal was emphatic: down. Stay down. Paks nodded and went on.

She was sure she was near the opening, whatever it was, when she heard the beat of many horses coming rapidly. She started to leap up and run, but controlled herself. They were on the road, by the sound: it must be the road. They wouldn't see her unless she moved. She told herself that again and again, forcing herself to stare at the layers of leaves on the ground lest her eyes be visible. The horses came from her right: at least ten, she thought. She would have sworn that they trotted right over her. The hoof-beats passed and died away. Paks breathed again, and lifted her head. She could see a gap, and trees beyond it. She crept forward until she could see the road itself, scarred with hoofmarks and fresh wheelruts. If the enemy had wagons, that would slow them. She looked along the road as far as she could without getting out in the open. Nothing.

It was much harder creeping back to Saben and Canna with her back to the road. She was sure that someone was there, watching her, perhaps drawing a bow to shoot. She wanted to jump up and run forward. Her shoulders ached. The wet leafmold tickled her nose; she wanted to sneeze. She kept crawling, muttering silently in her head, and almost bumped into Canna.

"The road," she said unnecessarily, in Canna's ear.

Canna was pale. "I was afraid you'd jump up and bolt. Those horses — "

"I almost did," said Paks. "Let's move farther back — "

They crawled back, then turned downslope again and went deeper in the hollow, squatting under a clump of cedar. "I didn't see any sentries," said Paks. "I looked both ways. I don't know where the horsemen were going."

"Did you get a good look at them?" asked Canna.

"No. I was afraid they'd see my face, so I stared at the ground. It sounded like ten or more."

"I thought about a dozen," said Canna. "They might have been going to that farm, the one where we got the ox that time."

"I suppose so. I was hoping they were going south and wouldn't be back."

"Unlikely, unless they're messengers. I expect they were after supplies, or information."

"Now that we've found the road, shouldn't one of us try to find out what's happening at the fort?" asked Saben. "At least we can find out how big the Honeycat's force is."

Canna shook her head. "No — I'd agree if we had a few more. But as it is, we can't take the chance of losing even one."

"But if they take the prisoners away by a different route — "

"How can they?" asked Paks. "North is only that track over the mountains — why would they go there? This is the only road south; they'll have to use it."

"Unless they go across country."

"With wagons? I saw fresh wheelruts, deep ones. They'll have to stay on a road."

"How far is the crossroads?" asked Saben.

Paks looked at Canna. "Do you remember? I think it was a day's march — we got here at midafternoon, and the fork was where we halted the day before, wasn't it?"

"Yes. That's the road that goes to Merinath, east of us, and to Valdaire if you go far enough west. But they won't turn there for Rotengre. They'd stay on this road through two crossings — no — southeast at the second. The way we came, anyway. But they could go through Sorellin, or even around it to the west, for some reason."

139

Paks had been sketching in the dirt with a stick. "So — a crossroad here, where they could turn, and another here? Right. And then Sorellin, and then — how far is Rotengre? It's east as well as south, isn't it?"

Canna peered at the furrowed dirt. "Yes. Let me think. We're about two days from Sorellin, I think, and it's — oh, call it four days *this* way — " she pointed at the route east of the city, " — from that village we stopped at, coming up. I think it's about as far from us as Sorellin, but I'm not sure."

"Six or seven days altogether — about what I remembered. But we could go ahead of them this far," said Paks, pointing to the first crossroad. "They have to take this road that far, and they might not expect us to be ahead of them."

"But we don't know how long they're going to stay here," said Saben. "We could wait a month for them, and the Duke none the wiser."

Canna shook her head. "No. Siniava has a name for moving fast. I think he won't try the fort more than a day or so; if they don't break, he'll leave someone behind and take the rest of his force south. I can't see him tying up his whole army for one little fort."

"And I thought," said Paks, "that if we got ahead of them, we could get some food, too, before they came along to buy it up."

"Yes, but then we've been seen. They'll ask questions. If they find out that someone in Duke Phelan's colors has been buying food, they'll come looking for us."

Paks frowned. She was very conscious of her empty belly. A few berries and hazelnuts were not going to be enough — and they wouldn't have time to gather many.

"Well, Canna," said Saben, "do we have to stay in the Duke's colors?"

"Yes — or be taken for bandits or spies. With our scars, we can't pass as farmers. But Paks has a good idea: we can move south along this road to the first crossing, and wait a day or so. If they don't come, we can decide then who will go straight to the Duke, and who will keep watch."

"Let's go, then." Paks rose with the others. Although the fog had cleared, the light was already waning under an overcast sky. She led them downslope again, across a narrow trail, and up the next gentle rise. She tried to stay just close enough to the road to be aware of the gap in the trees. They saw no one, and heard nothing on the road.

Paks had just begun to wonder if they were nearing the farm when she smelled woodsmoke, and saw more light off to the right. She recalled the four or five huts and a barn, a rail-fenced enclosure for stock, and long narrow strips of plowed and fallow ground. Her mouth watered at the smell of the woodsmoke. She looked at Canna and Saben; they looked as hungry as she felt.

"I might be able to steal something," she said.

Saben nodded, but Canna shook her head. "No. Remember the horsemen." Paks had forgotten, in her hunger. "It would help, though, to find out if that's where they are. We haven't heard them on the road: I hope they aren't sweeping the woods."

"I hadn't thought of that," said Paks.

"I didn't think you had. We're not out of the net yet; we need to think of everything — because they will. Saben, why don't you slip up to the road this time. Just like Paks — stay down, no matter what."

"Right away. Oh — is my face dirty enough?"

"Not quite." Paks smeared leafmold across his cheek. "There."

"And I'll do as much for you next time," he said, grinning. Paks and Canna sat down to watch as he crept toward the road.

"That's hard on the arms," said Paks as she watched.

"Yes. I don't think we should talk." Canna's face was grim. Paks shot her a glance and went back to watching Saben. He looked very slow, but she knew how hard it was. She thought about the chance of a mounted sweep in the woods and shivered. No fog to hide them — not enough underbrush here. We ought to be farther apart, she thought. Then they might find only one — or that might make them look harder for more. Her belly growled loudly. Canna looked at her, and Paks shrugged. No way to stop that without food.

Saben was out of sight now, among the bushes by the road. Paks slipped her knife out and looked at it. If she hadn't given her parole, she would not have a knife — would not have been out berrying, most likely. She would have been in the fort, maybe in a cell. But then, she'd have a sword by now, because the Halverics had armed the Phelani. But besieged by such a force — she shook her head, and returned to thoughts of the route south. A day to the crossroads and wait. They could do that, even without food. Her belly growled again, louder. Except for Canna, she thought. Canna's been hurt; she has to have food. And if I can find food for one, I can find it for three. She cheered up a bit. There was Saben, creeping back toward them. The smell of smoke came stronger as the wind veered a moment. Saben came nearer. When she met his eyes, he signalled them to move farther away from the road. Saben followed them. When they stopped in a thicket, Paks saw that his face was pale under the leafmold.

"What is it?" asked Canna.

"They're there," he said in a strange choked voice. "I counted twelve horses tethered along that fence — you remember. They've — they've killed the farmers — and their families. The — the bodies are just — lying around. Like — like old rags, or — " His voice broke, and he stopped, choking back sobs. Paks had a sudden vision of an army in Three Firs. She had never thought of that, of armed men coming onto her father's farm — her brothers and sisters —

"Saben!" Canna shook his arm. "Saben, stop it. You've seen dead before. It's terrible, yes, but we don't want to be next — "

He looked up, eyes wet. "But we're fighters, Canna — that's what we're for. Those weren't soldiers; they didn't have a chance."

"Saben, it's only your second year — and we don't do things like that — but surely you know that some armies do."

"If only we'd come faster, we might have stopped them," he said.

"Three of us? With daggers? Remember what you said last night, Saben."

141

"But our people," said Paks. "What about our people? If they'd kill farmers like that, what will they do to soldiers?"

"Paks, don't think about it. All we can do is get help: tell the Duke. Whatever can be done, he'll do. You know that." Canna turned back to Saben. "Do they look like they'll be there long?"

Saben took a shaky breath, then another. "Yes. They — they were cooking. One of the cattle, I think. They're all around the fire."

"Then we can slip past, probably, and we'd better — " She broke off as a rattle of hooves rang out on the road.

"One horse," said Paks. "Messenger?"

"Could be."

"Let me look," said Saben. "I won't do anything."

"Well — "

"I'm all right, Canna. We do need to know what they're doing."

"All right. We'll stay here. Don't get caught."

"No." Saben turned away, toward the road, and disappeared. Paks found she'd slipped her dagger out again. Canna shook her head and pointed at the sheath. She slipped it back in. They waited. They heard a shout from the distance. Another shout. Paks felt her heart give a great leap in her chest.

"Saben?" she gasped.

"I hope not," said Canna. "Holy Gird defend him. If that was a messenger, maybe they're shouting at each other." Her face was paler than before.

They listened. No more shouts. Paks imagined Saben full of arrows, his body dragged to the fire, or taken alive for questioning. She shuddered. Canna touched her hand. "Don't think about it. We don't know — imagining things will make you weaker." Paks nodded without speaking, and tried to force her thoughts elsewhere. Again the noise of hooves, this time many of them, on the road. Was the whole troop leaving? They waited in a silence scarcely broken by the rustle of leaves in a slight wind. Paks gave up looking in the direction Saben had gone, and stared at the ground. She jumped when Canna nudged her.

Saben was coming toward them, walking almost upright. He was grinning. Paks felt a rush of relief that made her unsteady on her feet as she rose. "I thought you'd — "

"I know," he said. "When they yelled it scared me, and I could see what was happening. Canna, the troop's gone, ordered back to the fort, and they left a whole cow on the fire. The messenger, that single horse, told them not to wait, because they were starting south in the morning. If we hurry, we can have meat, and plenty of it." At once Paks's hunger returned.

"What about sentries?" asked Canna. "Surely — "

"No — all the horses are gone, and every horse had a rider; I made sure of that. Please, Canna — it's our best chance."

"It's risky — but you're right. It's our chance."

"We could pass the farm," said Paks. "Saben or I'll double back if it's clear. How's that?"

"Good idea. I hope they've cut that meat; I don't want to leave any obvious signs."

"I never thought of that," said Saben. "They were poking at it; I saw that the first time I looked. But I don't know about cut — "

"We'll see. Even if it hasn't, we ought to be able to find other food there — and they may think one of theirs took it."

They moved on, carefully. The farm clearing lay across the road; when they had passed it, they moved to the road edge and looked both ways. "Maybe only one of us should cross," said Paks. "If anything happens, maybe they'll look on that side — "

"I don't know if that matters," said Canna. "Still, any precaution might help. Saben, you've seen the worst already — can you go?"

"Yes, Canna." Behind the leafmold, his face was composed, his blue eyes steady.

"Good. If the meat isn't marked up, haggle a corner off; don't leave clean knife cuts. Maybe they'll think a stray dog got it. See what else you can find, but don't leave anything so stripped that it's obvious."

"Get some cloth for bandages, if you can," said Paks. She thought Canna looked worse than she had that morning.

"Yes, and another tinderbox, if you see one," added Canna.

"I'll see what I can find." After another careful look both ways, Saben darted across the road into the trees on the far side. Paks could see him skirting the clearing, coming in behind one of the huts. He disappeared. After a long wait, she saw him come back toward the trees, then turn back to the huts again. This time he was gone even longer. Then she could see him again, edging along the clearing toward the road, with a pack slung over one shoulder and a bundle in his arms.

Once across the road, he handed the bundle to Paks and urged them back into the trees. "Wait until you see what I found."

"Hush," said Canna. "We're too close." They walked on until the road was completely hidden, then sat down.

Paks unrolled the bundle, Saben's cloak wrapped around a number of things: three round loaves of brown bread, half a small cheese, six apples, a small padded sack of lumpy objects — "Careful," said Saben. "Those are eggs." — onions, a few redroots, several strips of pale linen, a small stoneware crock with a pungent smell, and a short-bladed knife.

Saben was pulling other finds from the worn leather pack he'd found: strips of half-roasted beef, another cheese, and a roll of cord. "They'd hacked the cow up with their swords," he said. "Some was bones with meat on, and some just strips of meat, so I took these. We could get more without it being noticed, I think, but I couldn't carry more, and didn't want to take too long. It must have been baking day; bread was rolling all over the hut floors. I took what had rolled under things. There was a barrel of apples; we can get more easily. Not so many cheeses, unless they're stored somewhere else. I didn't look in the barn. The eggs were under a bed; I felt them when I reached for bread."

143

Canna smiled. "Saben, you found a treasure. I don't know about going back — but now we'll eat. Let's see — we'll share a half-loaf of bread, and one of those big strips of meat, and have an apple each. More than that, and we'll be slow and sleepy."

Paks and Saben sighed at that, but by the time they'd eaten what Canna allowed, Paks felt much better. Not satisfied, but better.

"Let's see your shoulder," she said, when she had swallowed the last bit of bread. "These strips will be softer than that old sack. And I think this stuff in the crock is for wounds, isn't it?"

Canna sniffed at it. "It smells like what the surgeons use, yes." Paks unwound her hasty bandage of the day before, and Canna slipped off her tunic, wincing. The folded sack, blood-stained, was firmly stuck to the wound. Paks poured some of her water over it.

"Brr. That's cold," said Canna.

"I thought that would loosen it."

"It may, but it's cold." Paks worked as gently as she could, and finally got the sack off. Underneath, Canna's shoulder was swollen, red, and warm to touch. "It's — tender," said Canna, as Paks probed it. "Is it going bad?"

"I can't tell. It's red, and it feels different. Maybe just swollen. Here — I'm going to try this stuff." Paks smeared some of the gray-green sticky gunk in the crock over the wound. "How's that?"

"It stings a little. Not bad."

"Maybe I should have washed it first. If we had hot water — "

"No, that's all right. Just tie it up, and we'll hope for the best."

Paks folded the soft linen into a pad, then bound it on as she had before, this time with the softer linen strips. "Now you can put your tunic over it," she said. "Maybe that will be more comfortable."

"I wouldn't mind," said Canna. She was pale and sweating.

"What about another trip to the farm, Canna?" asked Saben. "This won't last long, and we may not have such a good chance again."

"We've got to travel light — "

"I know, but a week's march — "

"Let's see what we've got now. Enough bread for a couple of days, with this meat. Cut it in hunks like this, Saben — " Canna showed the size. "I don't know how that cheese will travel, but we can wrap it. Those redroots will have to be cooked, but they'll keep. You're right — we could use more. But it's getting late — "

"Less likely to be seen, then. I'll be careful."

Canna looked uncertain. "I — wish I knew — "

Paks felt a vague uneasiness. "I think we should get farther away."

"You'll think differently when we're hungry the day after tomorrow," said Saben.

Canna looked from one to another. "I — I say no, Saben. We'll go on. We shouldn't take chances we don't have to; the ones we must take are bad enough."

Saben shrugged. "Whatever you say; you're the commander. Here —

144

let me see what I can fit in this pack." The bread, cheese, onions, and redroots disappeared into the pack. They stuffed their pouches with the pieces of meat, and Paks tucked the eggs inside her tunic. Saben took the crock of ointment, and Canna stuck the knife in her boot. They filled their flasks at the little creek that flowed eastward from the farm into the woods.

"We should go as far as we can while we have light," said Canna. "I think it will be safe enough to stay near the road, but if you see anything — even a woodcutter or herder — drop and get out of sight. And be as quiet as possible."

At first Paks led the way, but Canna was clearly tiring. After the third time Paks found herself far ahead, she suggested that Canna lead. The dark woman nodded without speaking. Paks and Saben moved out to flank her, and they went on in the growing dusk.

145

Chapter Sixteen

The ground was gently rolling, each low ridge less steep than the one before it, as the land subsided from the mountains to the north. Darkness seemed to flow up out of the hollows as light faded from the gray sky. They had no idea how far they had come. Paks was thinking of nothing in particular when she realized that she had lost Canna in the gloom. She stopped and peered into the woods. An owl called from somewhere behind her. She shivered, listening for any sound of her friends. The owl called again, the last hoot sounding odd. It must be Saben, she thought, and hooted in reply. A short hoot answered her; she moved toward the sound quickly. She missed them in a thicket. Saben's voice nearly startled her into a scream.

"What happened?" she asked when she got her voice back.

"It's your long legs," said Saben. "You distanced us again, and Canna fell, trying to hurry."

"I'm all right," said Canna. Her voice was strained. "But it's too dark to walk safely in these trees."

"Nothing's on the road," said Paks. "Nobody travels this late — couldn't we use it for a few miles?" Out of the dark a hand squeezed her arm as Saben spoke.

"I'm legweary," he said. "We'll do better for a rest."

"Paks, I — don't think I can go farther tonight," said Canna. "Even on the road."

"Let's see if we can find a good place to sleep, then." Paks peered around, but could hardly see two trees away for the gloom.

"This will do," said Saben. The hand on her arm tightened and released. "You didn't see us."

"Mmm. You're right. Hope it doesn't rain, though." Canna, Paks saw, had already slumped to the ground. She herself, though still hungry, was too keyed up to feel tired.

"You had first watch last night, Paks," said Saben. "I'll take it; I'm sore but not sleepy."

Paks felt the same but did not argue. "Canna, are you warm enough?"

"I — can't get this cloak — wrapped, somehow."

"Let me help." Paks helped Canna sit up and untangle the cloak. "What did you hurt when you fell?"

"Nothing. It jarred me. I'm all right."

146

"We'll hope so." Paks doubted it, but there wasn't anything to do. "Would you rather have a back rest or front rest? I want to keep warm."

"Back, if you're giving choices."

Paks rolled herself into her cloak and lay behind Canna. "Don't eat all the bread while we sleep," she told Saben, who chuckled.

"Ha. And here I thought you'd forgotten it." She heard a rustle and saw a shape moving in the darkness as Saben took a position between them and the road. She thought she was not sleepy, but Saben's hand on her arm woke her much later to a cold night, not so damp as the one before.

"I can't keep my eyes open," he murmured. "No trouble so far." Paks stretched and unrolled herself while Saben lay down in the warm spot she'd made.

She rubbed her face hard with her hands to wake up, and took a swallow of water from her flask. No trouble so far. How long would that last? She felt her stomach clench on nothing, and thought about the meat in her pouch. No. She drank again. Canna was right about that — they had to space the food out. She thought of her father's tale about the famine when he was a boy, the year the wolves came. We tried to eat the grass, he'd said. Her stomach growled. Don't think about food. We have food, but not for now. She looked up to see if the stars were out, but could see only blackness. In that cold, hungry darkness, for the first time she doubted that they would reach the Duke. She forced herself to think. Tomorrow — tomorrow we'll get to the crossroad. Unless Canna — no, surely she's all right. I wish we could go on ahead. They must take the short way, if they're going to Rotengre. We could stay safely ahead if we knew.

She hardly noticed when the light began to grow. All at once, it seemed, she could see her hands and arms, and the two dark shapes stretched out below. She yawned and stretched, wondering if she'd dozed awhile. The light gave no color yet. She nudged Saben with her toe; he gave a sort of gasping snort and sat up.

"What?"

"Dawn. We should be going soon." Canna had not wakened. They both looked at her. "Do you think she'll be all right?" asked Paks softly.

Saben frowned. "Not all right. But it wasn't a deep wound — I think —"

"We need her."

"Yes, but we're no surgeons."

"I wonder if that — Effa said St. Gird healed people. Canna's a Girdsman. Maybe he'll heal her."

"*If* he does. But if he can, why not just do it? Already?"

"I don't know. I never heard of Gird back home — "

"What about Gird?" Canna had wakened. She grimaced as she moved, then forced a smile. "Don't look so worried; I'm fine."

"We wondered if Gird would heal you," said Paks.

Canna looked surprised. "How did you know — you aren't a Girdsman! It takes a Marshal or a paladin to heal, though."

Saben looked stubborn. "If it takes a Marshal or a paladin, what has it got to do with Gird?"

"Saben, you drink water, but when you carry it from the river, you have to have a bucket to put it in. I don't know what kind of power it is that Gird wields, but it must come through a Marshal or paladin."

"So a prayer wouldn't work?" asked Paks.

"No. A prayer for courage, or strength in battle — and it can't hurt to pray for good fortune — but not healing."

"We could try," said Paks. Canna stared at her.

"What are you, a paladin in disguise? You aren't even a Girdsman."

"No, that's true. But we need you to be well and strong."

"I'm — oh, all right. If you want to. It can't do any harm."

"But I don't know how," said Paks. "You'll have to tell me what to say."

"Paks, I don't know. I'm no Marshal, and Gird knows I'm no paladin, either." She paused for breath. "Here — " She fumbled at her neck for the chain that held her medallion. "You'll need this. Hold it. Then say what you want, in the name of St. Gird."

Paks took the metal crescent and held it a moment, thinking. Then she laid it on Canna's shoulder, over the bandaged wound. She looked at Saben, who looked back, quirking an eyebrow.

"St. Gird," she began. "Please heal this wound. This is Canna, who is your follower, and she was hurt by an arrow. We are trying to escape to tell our Duke of the Honeycat's treachery, and we need Canna's help. In — in the name of Gird — I mean, St. Gird."

"Ouch!" said Canna. "What did you poke it for?"

"I didn't," said Paks. "I just laid your symbol on it; I didn't push. What happened?"

"It must have been a cramp, then. That hurt. It's easing now. It seems — I can breathe a little easier."

"But it still hurts?"

"Yes, but the sharp pain is gone — whatever it was. Don't worry, Paks. I didn't expect a cure."

"I suppose not." She handed back the medallion and turned to the pack. "What can we have for breakfast?"

"Bread. We'll try that half-cheese, too." They divided the small cheese and each took a slice of bread from the half a loaf left the night before. That took the edge off their hunger, though Paks felt she could have eaten much more. Saben managed to fit the eggs into the pack this time. "Let's go," said Canna abruptly. Paks and Saben looked at her, surprised, but rose at once.

The morning was still and gray, with a murkiness between the trees that was not quite fog. They stayed close to the road, but Canna would not let them walk in it, fearing a forward patrol. They walked in silence, three dark shadows among the black tree-trunks. Canna set a better pace than the evening before. When she finally called a halt, they moved away from the road and stretched out under a large cedar.

Saben wiggled his shoulders. "Ugh. That pack — the straps are too short. He must have been a skinny man."

"I'll take it next," offered Paks.

"You're not a skinny man."

"No, but it'll get the cramps out of your shoulders."

"I wish I'd found a weapon," he grumbled. "A bow, or a sword — "

"We're better without it," said Canna.

"How so?"

"If you'd found one, you'd be tempted to fight, wouldn't you? You'd want to kill one of their scouts to get still more weapons — then free the prisoners — " Saben was blushing, now, and Canna nodded before going on. "There's not a weapon in the world, Saben, that would let you take on that force single-handed and survive. Our job is to get word to the Duke. For that we need wit, not blades."

"Yes, Canna. But think how much fun — "

"If we get to the Duke," said Canna grimly, "we can have all the fun we want — with weapons he'll give us." Saben subsided. Paks wondered again if it was as bad as Canna seemed to think.

"When the column does come," she asked, "how are we going to move with it without being seen? The woods don't last all the way to Rotengre."

"You would ask that. I've been trying to remember what the country is like. We can use any trees — hedges — and if it's dry, they'll raise a cloud; we can stay far off and still be sure where they are. But it's going to be hard."

"I was thinking — surely they'll take the short way, east of Sorellin. Why can't we just go straight for the Duke?"

"We can't be sure. Siniava has a name for being indirect."

"You mean he might go around in a circle, or something — ?"

"Yes. Find a weak spot in the siege lines, and try to break it there."

"But then what does he want prisoners for? They'll only get in the way."

"I don't know. Some wickedness." Canna took a swallow of water. "I wish I knew how close we were to the crossroad."

"Why?" asked Paks. "We'll find it if we stay near the road."

"If I were the Honeycat," said Canna slowly, "I'd have someone posted at the crossroads."

"But we're well ahead of the forward patrols," said Saben.

"That's exactly what I'd want stragglers to think," replied Canna. "If someone got through the sweeps and patrols, they'd think they were safe, and they'd be careless. Besides, suppose the Duke sent a courier for some reason — Siniava would have to stop that. So I think we can expect trouble — at every crossroad, and every place a messenger or straggler would be tempted to use the road. Probably disguised as traders, or brigands, or something, to keep the peasants from gossiping too much."

"How do we get around them, then?" asked Paks.

Canna shrugged. "They don't *know* that anyone's coming. We do. And we expect them. We'll move very quietly, and watch very carefully, and not set foot on the road."

After a scant ration of bread, they set off again. Canna forbade any talking until they cleared the crossroad, and they moved as quietly as they

149

could. The road wound back and forth around low rounded hummocks; Paks found it hard to keep an even distance from it.

From far behind came a long low horn call. They stopped and looked at each other. In such cold air, a horn would carry a great distance. Three short blasts of a higher-pitched horn came from the road ahead. This sounded closer than the other, but distance was impossible to judge. Canna nodded at the other two and grinned. She gestured them still farther from the road, and forward. Paks felt her heart begin to pound, drumming in her ears so that she could hardly hear. This would be the real test, getting past the guard at the crossroad. She looked at Canna, who was still moving strongly, and stumbled over a briar. Calm down, she told herself. Saben and Canna gave her a warning glance and went on.

As the road began a curve right, Canna signalled a halt. She beckoned them close, then murmured in their ears. "I think they're on top of the rise ahead — see how open the woods look up there? They could see the road and the woods both. We'll swing around the far side of the hill. Be careful. No stumbling about." Paks blushed.

They turned left along the slope, climbing no higher. As they moved away from the road, the woods thickened, and undergrowth screened them. They could not see more than a few yards uphill. More evergreens cloaked the northern slope. It was easy to walk quietly on the fallen needles, and they moved faster. Still, several hours of tense and tedious work brought them only to the eastern end of that hill, and a low saddle between it and the next rise to the east. As they came up the saddle, the trees thinned again.

Canna waved them down, then peered upslope. Paks looked too, and saw nothing. Trees masked the higher slope and crown. For a second time, they heard the long horn call. This time it seemed closer, hardly north of the hill. At once two short blasts rang out upslope. Clearly Canna had been right about the location of the watch. They crept through the trees, keeping every possible leaf between them and the upper slope as they cleared the saddle. Now they could see, at the foot of a gentle slope, a broad rutted road running east and west. It disappeared behind a south-jutting face of the hill between them and the crossroad.

When they reached the road, Canna stopped them. "I'll cross first," she said. "If anything happens, go east another hill, then head south. Don't come back for me; go to the Duke. If nothing happens, count twenty, then Paks comes. Then twenty again, and Saben. No noise, and get to cover fast on the other side. May Gird be with us." Canna turned away, crept to the very edge of the road, and looked. Nothing. Still bent low, she scurried across and dived into bushes on the far side. Paks counted on her fingers to be sure not to skip any; when she had counted twice over, she checked the road and ran across. Once in cover, she turned to watch for Saben. He crossed the road safely, and the three of them moved to deeper cover under the trees.

Canna swung right, back toward the south road, cutting the corner. They had covered what Paks guessed to be half that distance when they

150

began to hear shouts, the clatter of horses, and the rumble of wagons from their right. Suddenly a thrashing and crackling of undergrowth broke out behind. They dropped where they were. Thudding hooves pounded nearer; Paks could hear the jingle and creak of tack and armor. This time the mounted men were silent. They were spaced in easy sight of one another, passing on either side of the fugitives. Paks saw the hooves of one horse churning the leaves scarcely a length from her face. As the horse cantered on, she saw that the rider had a chain-mail shirt under a yellow surcoat, and a flat helmet with a brim. He had a sword at his side, and a short-thonged whip thrust into his belt behind.

When the hoofbeats died away, Canna urged them up and led them back east. "We know how far out he sends the sweeps, now," she said. "But without seeing the column, we don't know if these were the forward or the flank."

"At least we know he's going south," said Paks.

"How about one of us going in for a closer look?" asked Saben.

Canna frowned. "It'll be dangerous. I think we can do better. We'll climb the next hill on our side, and take a look from a distance. As long as we stay outside the sweeps — " They walked on, more quickly, in case another patrol was riding behind. The ground rose under their feet; again they were in the evergreens of a north slope. They toiled upward, panting. Paks felt the pack of food dragging at her shoulder, and wished they could stop and eat. They heard more noise from the road. A mounting excitement seized all three of them; they began to hurry up the slope, eager to see the enemy column at last.

Paks, shouldering her way through thick pines and cedars, thought only of how they hid her. When she broke into the cleared space on the hilltop, a pace or so ahead of Canna and Saben, she found herself face to face with one of the mounted men. He had turned toward the noise she'd made; as she came in sight he grinned and lifted his reins.

"So there is something here besides rabbits, eh?" He turned in the saddle, taking a breath. Paks shrugged the pack off her shoulder and threw it at him. His horse shied, and he nearly fell. "Why, you — " he began, drawing his sword. Paks had her dagger out and charged the horse, which snorted and backed. He jerked the reins and spurred. She dodged to his unarmed side and jumped to grab his arm. The horse jumped sideways as he overbalanced, and he slid out of the saddle on top of her, swordarm flailing. Paks was stunned by the fall under him. With a snort, the horse clattered off into the trees. Paks struggled to catch her breath and squirm free. Canna and Saben appeared and jerked him aside; Canna had a knife in his throat before he could make a sound.

"Now we're in trouble!" Canna gave Paks a hand up. "Get that pack, Saben. Come on!" She led them down the east side of the hill as fast as they could go, slipping in the leaves. Paks was so shaken that she had trouble keeping her balance. At the foot of the hill, Canna would not let them rest, but set off southward at a brisk pace. "I should have thought," she said

151

sometime later. "They'll have a lookout on every hill. Especially now."

"Surely they've — found him — by now," said Paks. She couldn't seem to get her breath.

"I hope not. It depends how they set it up. If they were stationed at intervals, to wait for the column to pass, they won't know until it does — or until his horse wanders back to the road."

"It won't," said Saben.

"What — "

You didn't see. I was behind you — I caught the reins, and tied it."

Paks looked at him. "That was quick thinking."

"Very good, Saben," said Canna. "I didn't think of the horse until afterwards. You were lucky not to be trampled."

"We were all lucky," he said soberly. "Paks stopped him calling an alarm — "

"Yes. When I saw you throw that pack," said Canna, "I thought we were lost."

"You're right that we must stick together, Canna. One alone couldn't have made it through that."

They walked on in silence for a space, keeping to the low ground and swinging east of the low hills they met. Some time in the afternoon, they heard several horn signals far behind, but they did not know what it meant. They only knew they had to keep going. As light began to wane behind the clouds, Paks asked, "Do you think they'll camp for the night, or march through?"

"I think they'll camp. I wish I knew the road better. Somewhere between here and the next crossroad we come out of the trees." Canna sighed. She had slowed the pace; they were all legweary.

"I'm worried about keeping up," said Paks. "We should be faster, just the three of us, but we're having to cover more ground. Once it's open, it'll be worse. What if they distance us and take a turn we don't see?"

"We'll ask someone. I don't think they will, though."

They went on until the light was almost gone, and they were stumbling with weariness. When they finally stopped in a hazel thicket, they were all exhausted and hungry. Paks had been struggling with a sharp pain in her side where she'd fallen on rocks under the horseman. Now it was worse.

"I wish we could have a fire," she said. "Those eggs — "

"We'll eat them raw," said Canna. "We can't risk a fire." She dug into the pack. Two eggs had broken, but five remained.

"You can have my share," said Paks. The thought of raw eggs revolted her.

"They're good. Don't waste 'em."

"I'm not. You eat them." Paks took a scrap of meat from her pouch. Canna looked at her.

"Paks, I should have asked — were you hurt?"

"Just bruised, I think, from the rocks. It catches when I take a deep breath. How's your shoulder?"

152

"It hurts a little, but not like yesterday. I should have remembered that the day after is worse than the day something happens. Here's some bread."

Paks took a slice. "We ought to change the bandages, and put on more ointment —"

"It's too dark," said Saben. "We can't see what we're eating."

"In the morning," said Canna. "We'll look at your bruises, too."

They settled into uneasy sleep. Saben took the first watch. When Paks woke in the early dawn, she found that Canna had taken the second. She started to sit up and bit back a groan. She was stiff from head to heel, and her right side throbbed. Canna insisted on seeing the damage.

"I thought so," she said. "A fine lot of bruises and a bad scrape — hand me that pot, Saben — and maybe a broken rib or two." Paks winced as Canna spread the ointment. It stung like nettles. "Don't move — you'll have your turn next," said Canna. But Canna's wound was clearly healing: no longer an angry red. Canna twisted her head to look. "That's much better," she said. "It's just a little sore this morning." She gave Paks a long look. "Maybe you did do something with that prayer."

Paks ducked her head. "It's not healed completely, Canna. And we put ointment on it."

Canna looked at their food. "We'll eat the cheese — and some bread. That leaves — umm. We'll be out again by day after tomorrow. Well, no help for it." After that scant meal, they were ready. Paks needed Saben's help to stand, and found walking difficult.

She was wondering how they would know if the column was still going south when they heard horsemen to their right: they could see nothing. All that morning, as a weak sun struggled through clouds, they moved with hardly a pause. Paks found it harder and harder to keep up. Near noon they reached the southern edge of the unbroken woods, and Canna waved them to a sheltered hollow.

Paks slumped onto the leaves and wished she didn't have to move. She closed her eyes for a moment and opened them to see Canna and Saben watching her. She forced a grin. "I'm just sore. It's not as bad as yours, Canna; I'll be better tomorrow."

"Let's have an apple," said Canna. Saben opened the pack and passed them around. "Paks, we need you. We need all of us. We'll slow if we have to —"

Paks shook her head. "No. You said getting to the Duke was more important than anything. I'll keep up, or you'll go on. After all, once they've passed I'll be safe enough."

"I've changed my mind," said Canna. "After yesterday — if we can possibly stay together, we should. At least for now. The column's not ahead of us."

"Speaking of the column," said Saben. "I think I'll crawl up there —" he nodded at the treeline, " — and have a look. Maybe I can spot them."

Canna nodded, and he moved away. Beyond the trees was rough pas-

153

ture; they could see his head outlined against the tawny grass. Presently he came back.

"They're there," he said. "The column and sweeps both. Very impressive. They were still coming in sight when I came back. Want to take a look?"

"I will. Paks, you stay here and rest." Paks wanted to protest, but felt more like lying still. She fell into a doze while they were gone, and woke with Canna's hand on her arm.

"Paks. Wake up. They're moving south, and the prisoners are with them. We think at least sixty prisoners, both ours and Halverics. I'm not sure how many troops, but there are ten wagons and several score horse."

"Did the whole column pass?"

"Yes. They may be trying to reach the second crossroad by nightfall. I wish I knew how far that was."

"Then we'd better go. I feel better."

"Good. Saben and I think we've found enough cover for the next stretch." Canna helped her up. Paks tried to convince herself that she would feel better moving, and they started again.

Out from under the trees, with the sun's disk showing through the clouds, it was easy to keep their heading. Luckily the fields were edged with strips of woodland or hedge, and all through the afternoon they were able to keep up with the column while staying well hidden. The mounted sweeps never came as close as they had; Canna worried more about being spotted by a herder or farmer who might tell the tale.

By late afternoon the column reached the second crossroad, where the road from Dwarfwatch crossed the great Guild League road. The three fugitives had gained on it, now even with its middle. They could see the head of the column swing left, onto the direct route for Rotengre. They could also see the mounted patrols that moved out along all the roads to screen its passage. They dared not risk moving forward before dark.

"It's not lost time, exactly," said Saben. "Now we know how many of them, and what equipment—"

"Too many," said Canna. "Over three hundred foot and a hundred horse. If the whole Company was here, it wouldn't be an easy fight."

"At least he's obvious," said Paks. "A force that size will be seen — someone's bound to tell the Duke even if we fail."

"Don't forget those farmers — he may be killing everyone he sees."

"Come on, Canna; he can't kill everyone on the road between here and Rotengre. Traders come this way, and —"

"Saben, from what I've heard of him, he'll kill anyone who stands in his way."

They had turned east across the fields, and come to the caravan road well beyond the patrol's position. Besides, they had seen the riders turn back. Even so, they took no chances. Canna scouted the road, and they crossed one by one, as before. The night was cold and clearer than the day had been; the stars gave just enough light for them to walk on open ground. They went on until they saw the fires of the encamped column.

"Here," said Canna, stopping them in a little triangular wood. "This will do. Paks, how's your side?"

Paks leaned against a tree. She felt that if she sat down she would never make it back up. "Stiff," she said finally. "A night's rest will help."

Canna handed around a meager measure of the remaining meat and bread. They had eaten it almost before they tasted it. "It has to last," said Canna. "I don't know where we can get any more — we'll do better spacing it out — " She did not sound convinced. Paks clenched her jaw to keep from asking for more. She knew Canna was right, but her belly disagreed. Saben gave a gusty sigh out of the darkness.

"My old grandmother used to tell me, when I wouldn't stop begging for sweets on market day, that someday I'd want 'em worse than I did then, and because I'd begged I wouldn't have any. What I don't understand is how the food would be here now if I hadn't begged then. Do you suppose there's some magic — ?"

Paks found herself chuckling. "Only if learning not to ask meant learning not to want. It's an idea, though: things you want and don't ask for coming when you need them."

"I don't think it works like that," said Saben. "So much the worse. Canna, if we wait until the column has passed that village, can we go and buy food?"

"No. I expect Siniava will have spies there."

"What a suspicious old crow," grumbled Saben.

"If he weren't, he wouldn't be that powerful. I'll take first watch tonight, Saben; you and Paks get to sleep."

Paks was tired, but her side hurt so that she found it hard to get comfortable. She would have sworn the ground was covered with cobbles, yet Saben was snoring lightly in minutes. She tried rolling onto her back. Her legs stuck out into the cold. Her stomach growled loudly, and she found herself thinking of stew, and hot bread, and roast mutton — I'm as bad as Saben at the market, she thought. She turned on her left side. At last she fell asleep, to be wakened by Saben on a clear frosty dawn.

As they chewed their scant breakfast, trying to make it last, they watched the distant fields. The sun rose and glinted on the enemy helmets as they assembled. Thin streams of smoke from their fires rose straight into an unclouded sky, to bend southward above the trees. The column began to move. Suddenly a puff of blacker smoke billowed up, then another and another. In a minute they could see the red leaping flames.

"They're torching the village," said Canna. "I daresay they've killed the villagers, or taken them prisoner." They watched as yet another billow of smoke stained the sky. Paks thought of the friendly folk who had waved at them on their way north.

"Why burn it?" she asked.

Canna shrugged and sighed. "I don't know. To hide the murders as wildfire? Who can imagine what that filth would be thinking."

155

As the tail of the column disappeared, they set off across the fields, angling toward the burning village. They could see the dry grass near the huts burning, flames spreading toward stubbled fields and woods beyond. A light breeze came with the morning, moving the fire south, a pall of smoke with it. Soon they were up with the smoke, paralleling the fire. The smoke set them coughing. Paks felt a stabbing pain when she coughed. She was uneasily aware of the flames creeping along the ground or rising in crackling leaps when they found more fuel than stubble. But the wind never strengthened nor shifted direction, and soon they had passed the fire by.

All that day they dodged and darted from hedge to hedge to thicket, keeping the column in distant view. As the day wore on, they worried more about farmers. They feared that Siniava had offered a rich reward for reports of stragglers. Paks moved more easily, despite continuing pain; by late afternoon what really mattered was the gnawing hole in her belly. They had scarcely spoken to each other all day, but she could see the same hunger on the others' drawn faces.

Despite the clear sky, it was still colder; Paks dreaded the night to come. The column halted; the smoke of their watchfires stained the evening sky. Canna kept moving, and they edged past at a respectful distance. Paks wondered why, but she was too breathless to ask. At last Canna stopped, well beyond the head of the column, and explained her reasoning.

"We're sure now where they're going, and by what road," she said. "Now's the time to separate. We've found no food; if one takes all we have, that's enough to make the Duke's camp — I think three days' travel. They'll take at least five, with those wagons. But without food, all three of us can't make it. The Duke must know —"

"But Canna, you said yesterday we should stay together," said Saben. "One person could be stopped by anything. And what about food for the two left behind?"

"We'd find something," said Canna.

Saben snorted. "You with an arrow wound, and Paks with a broken rib? I suppose you meant me to go?" Canna nodded, and Saben shook his head. "No. I won't leave two wounded companions and take all the food — not if there's any other way."

"Why don't we stay ahead tomorrow?" suggested Paks. "Maybe we'll find something to eat — and if there's a chance to stay together —"

"I suppose so," said Canna, sighing. "I wish we dared have a fire; those redroots would be good."

Paks felt her mouth water. "You ate raw eggs; why not raw redroots?"

"Tastes awful," said Saben. "But it might fill the holes."

They gnawed on the raw roots, bitter and dry, and ate a slice of bread each. Paks offered to take first watch, but the other two insisted that she sleep. By morning the ground was frozen, white hoarfrost over the stubble.

Chapter Seventeen

About midmorning, they were striding through a small wood when they startled a sounder of swine; the boar swung to face them with a wheezing snort. Paks froze. Beside her Canna and Saben were as still. The boar's little eyes, set in wrinkled skin, were golden hazel; the bristles up its back were rusty brown. Paks watched as the pink nose twitched in their direction. One of the sows squealed. Two others minced away on nimble hooves. The boar whuffled, and swung its head to watch the rest of the pigs. Now they were all moving, drifting along a thread of path.

"Roast pig?" said Saben plaintively. The boar looked at him and grunted.

"Not with daggers," said Paks, remembering the butchering at Amboi's farm. The boar grunted again, backed a few steps, and swung to follow the others. Paks relaxed and took a deep breath. "I hope we don't meet more of those," she said.

"Right," said Canna. "We'd have a — " she stopped abruptly as a boy dressed in rough shirt and trousers jogged into their view and stopped short. His eyes widened.

"Soldiers," he breathed. He backed up a step, fumbling for his dagger.

"We won't hurt you," said Paks. "Don't be afraid."

He was poised to run. "Ye — ye're a girl, an't ye?"

Paks and Canna both grinned. Paks answered. "I am. Were those your swine?"

His eyes narrowed. "Why'd ye ask — ye'll not take 'em, will ye?"

"No," said Paks. "I just wondered."

"Wheer ye be goin'?" he asked. Paks judged he was about fifteen or so, a short muscular redhead with pale eyes in a heavily freckled face. She thought of Vik with a pang, and wondered where he was now.

Paks winked at the boy. "We're just — taking a little trip, lad, you might say. Know where we could find some good ale?"

He relaxed a bit and grinned. "Is it ale ye're wantin'? Ye look more like robbers, I was thinkin', but if ye've got the coppers I know wheer ye can get ale."

"Robbers!" Paks tried to sound shocked. "Nay — we're but travel-worn and thirsty. As for coppers — " she jingled the coins in her pouch.

"Weel, then," he said, "ye might do worse than my uncle's place, over on the river down yon — " he pointed south. "'Tis not what ye'd rightly call an

157

inn, not bein' on th' road. But serves the farmers round, ye see, with my uncle's brew and no tax to pay like that *Silver Pheasant* out on the road. And I'm thinkin'," he added shrewdly, "ye may not be robbers, but ye look like ye won't have to do wi' roads, eh?"

Paks grinned. "As to that, lad, if you should happen to see a sergeant, you might not remember you saw us — would you?" She had a copper ready for the hand he held out.

The boy snickered. "All I seen in these woods is swine — that's all." He turned to the path they'd taken and followed it.

"I wonder how many fugitives that lad's 'not seen,' " said Canna.

"Or turned in," said Paks. "I know it was risky, Canna, but I couldn't see killing him — "

"Of course not. We're not the Honeycat. I daresay he thinks better of us for being irregular. He won't turn us in unless the price is right."

"If we're lucky, they'll try to bully him first," said Saben. "That one won't bully easily. Do you think we can stop at uncle's for anything?"

"No — " Canna began; Paks interrupted.

"It's our one chance to get food, Canna. He may not tell on us if we go, but he'll surely gossip if we don't. And we can go straight on from there, with a good start on the column."

Canna frowned. After a minute or so she said, "Well, it's worth trying, I suppose. If it works, we'll be much better off. But — they don't need to know how many of us there are. Only one will go — "

"Me!" said Paks and Saben together.

"No. Saben will. Paks, you and I stay under cover. If there's trouble, Saben, yell out how many. If we can, we'll take them. Don't hesitate to walk out if you sense anything wrong."

They could see a line of trees ahead, and the gleam of water beyond. A thin stream of smoke bespoke a chimney. Canna and Paks melted into the hedge along one side of the hay meadow they were crossing, and Saben walked openly beside it to the cluster of shanties on the riverbank.

The largest building had two chimneys, one smoking, and two children playing in a wattle-fenced dooryard. As Saben neared the fence, the children looked up and yelled.

"Ma! Ma! A man!" The door to the shanty opened, and a tall fat woman peered out.

"Good day, mother," called Saben. Paks could not hear if she answered. "A lad I met in the wood said I might find somewhat to eat here, a deal cheaper than the *Silver Pheasant*, he said." The fat woman's head moved, as if she spoke, but again Paks could not hear. Canna nudged her and pointed; Paks saw a lean figure dart from one of the huts behind the larger one. Paks slipped her knife from its sheath.

"I'll watch Saben," said Canna in her ear. "You keep an eye out for more lurkers." For several minutes Paks saw nothing. She stole a glance at Saben, now lounging against the gate of the wattle fence. She looked back at the other huts. A flicker of movement: she'd missed seeing what or how many.

Beyond the buildings, a narrow trail led westward into trees; it must go to the distant road. She glanced around the margin of the clearing, and caught a movement not ten yards to their left. A tall man in rough leathers, with a heavy bow, crept to the edge of the trees; he was watching Saben intently, his mouth agape. Paks nudged Canna, whose eyes widened. With infinite care she eased back, leaving Paks on guard, and made her way behind the bowman. Paks did not shift even her eyes, lest it call attention away from Saben.

"Ye might come in whilst ye're waitin'" called the woman from the shanty door.

"Thank you, mother, but no," said Saben casually. "I'm not fit to enter anyone's home. Another time, if it please you."

"Please yerself. We're not fine folk here," answered the woman. "The bread'll be out directly." Paks's mouth watered at that. "Ye'll be havin' a hard journey all alone," the woman went on.

"No one's lonely, going home," said Saben.

"Oh? Weel, wheer's yer home, if I may be s'bold?"

"Far away, mother, and worse that I have to dodge all around, going as many ways as a cock picking straws — why, the woods be full of sergeants, and at this rate it'll be Little-eve before I see my sweetheart again." Paks had never suspected Saben of so much imagination.

"I only wondered, ye see, because ye wanted so much — more than fer one fellow, even such a big 'un as ye be."

"Why, mother, wait till your little lads grow taller — my own family always said I ate more than any two grown men. They were glad enough to see me leave, for all I work as well as I eat."

"And will they welcome ye?"

"Aye. I told 'em the time, ye see, and she said she'd wait so long and no longer. So when they told me I must serve more months, well — I'm no deserter, mind, nor traitor — but I've served my years, as I count 'em, and I'll not lose my sweetling for any sergeant."

The woman cackled. This time her voice was warmer. "Ye're a fine one, I can tell. And ye've been savin' yer honey all this time, eh?"

"Well — " Saben sounded doubtful. "Depends what you mean. I've sweets for my sweetling, if you mean so."

"I'll say ye have." She cackled again and withdrew inside. Paks saw two figures leave the back door of her shanty. One flattened against the wall facing her; he had a naked sword in hand. The other disappeared around the far side. Nothing moved for several minutes. Paks wondered where Canna was, and if the bowman had drawn his bow. Then the shanty door slammed open, and the far woman emerged with a steaming sack.

"Here ye are, lad — hot bread, a bit of cheese, and I threw in a leg or two of fowl — ah, thank ye, lad — " as Saben dropped coins into her hand. She passed the sack over the fence. Paks saw that the man on her side had bent double and moved along the wattle fence to the corner, where he crouched in readiness. "Now, lad," said the woman. "Give us a kiss for luck, and I'll be

159

hopin' yer girl waits fer ye." She leaned over the fence, reaching out a huge red hand to Saben's face.

Saben had stepped back, out of reach. "No, mother," he said. "'Twould not be respectful, and me so dirty as I am, but thank you all the same for your good wish." He backed farther from the fence, and turned toward the trees.

"Dirty thief!" screeched the woman. "Robber! Liar! Help!!" Saben swung around to face the two men who rushed him from either side of the dooryard.

"Now, mother, that was unkindly said," he called, swinging the sack to hold them off as he drew his dagger. Paks hurtled out of the trees, heedless, as a thrashing commotion broke out where the bowman had been. She hoped Canna could handle it. The swordsman nearest her spoiled his stroke at Saben as she surprised him. With an oath he turned on her; she faced a notched but broad-bladed longsword. The other man had a curved blade; neither had shields.

Paks jumped back out of range of a sweeping blow, then darted forward. The backstroke nearly caught her, but she ducked it. Again her opponent lifted the sword for a two-handed swipe. This time she waited until the stroke was committed, then pivoted in to grab his elbow and throw him sideways, stabbing under the armpit. He yelled and went to his knees. Paks jerked the sword out of his hand as he slumped to the ground, and spun to help Saben. He was backing slowly toward the river, parrying the strokes of the curved blade with his dagger. Paks hesitated a moment, but the fat woman waddled forward with a hefty slab of wood. Paks aimed a powerful slash at the man's back. He screamed and dropped his sword. Saben scooped it up as Paks turned to face the woman.

"Murderers!" she yelled. "Bandits! Robbers! I'll teach ye — " She broke off with a screech as Saben poked her back with his newly acquired weapon.

"Now, mother," he said politely. "Calm down and be quiet. We didn't start this, but I'm not loath to finish it, if you'll have it so." The fat woman stood like a stump, chest heaving.

"Drop that," said Paks. The woman glared, but dropped her stick.

Saben grinned at Paks over the woman's shoulder. "Well met, messmate. Perhaps I do want someone to travel with. Now, mother, you'll be wise to stand still, while this lady makes sure you have no more unpleasant surprises." Paks thought the woman might explode, she was so red in the face, but she said nothing. Paks backed away and looked around the clearing. Nothing that she could see. She ran her eye along the trees and caught a quick hand-signal. She said nothing, and brought her gaze slowly back to the shanty in front of them, then to the woman's face.

"Think I'll take a look inside," she said. The woman's face lighted, then twisted in a grimace of fear.

"No! Please — my babies — don't go in there. Ye've killed my man; don't hurt my babies — "

"Your babies won't be hurt if they don't hurt us. I daresay you've a houseful of stolen bits and pieces taken from honest travelers." Again Paks

160

surprised a fleeting look of cunning and hope on the woman's face, followed by exaggerated fear. Saben quirked an eyebrow at Paks over the woman's shoulder, and Paks, moving toward the shanty, gave the hand signal for danger. She ducked behind the wattle fence, slid around the windowless end of the building, and came to the back door before the woman realized her intent. She shot another glance at Canna, who had moved to a position covering the back door. Paks took a deep breath and slammed the door open.

As she had hoped, the remaining defenders were in the front of the shanty, one to either side of the front door. She had entered the kitchen. Grabbing a poker from the fireplace, she met the faster of her opponents in the narrow opening between the two rooms. This was a gawky youth with a club. Paks caught his hand with the glowing tip of the poker and he screamed and dropped the club, stumbling back into a heavy older man armed with two daggers. He kicked the boy aside and came at Paks through the opening. With her long arms and weapons, Paks held him off easily, until he reversed one of the daggers and threw it. Pain seared her left arm; she dropped the tip of the poker. At once he rushed her, forcing her back against the heavy table, and aiming a thrust at her face. Paks rolled away and slashed at his legs with the sword. He hopped out of reach, swearing, and turned to the fire for a weapon of his own. Paks surged forward, and thrust the long blade between his ribs before he could turn. He gave a gurgling groan and sank to the floor.

Silence. Paks stood breathless, sides heaving and sweat running down her face. She felt weak and shaky. The cut on her left arm hurt more than she expected. She wondered about the boy, and looked into the front room. A crude ladder led to a loft, and she heard rustling from above. Quickly she stepped to the back door and caught Canna's glance; she signalled and looked back into the kitchen. Flitches of bacon, hams, strings of onions, fowl tied by the legs — all hung from a beam. On a shelf by the fireplace were at least a dozen loaves of dark bread. Paks stepped onto the table and cut down a small ham, then took six loaves of bread and wrapped her cloak around the lot. Then she returned to Saben.

The fat woman was as pale now as she'd been red before. Paks shot her a hard glance before opening the sack Saben had dropped. Three soggy loaves, dipped in boiling water to make them steam, a cheese that stank when she opened the sack, a string of onions. Paks held up the onions. "Fine drumsticks your fowl have," she said. The woman did not answer. Paks turned the bag inside out, filled it with the food she'd taken, and looped the string closure. "I'm thinking you should be quiet at home this day," she said. "All that yelling might have given someone the wrong idea." Paks flipped the woman's headscarf off her head and folded it. She looked at Saben. "That bit of cord?"

"Good idea," he said. "My pouch." Paks held the woman at sword point while Saben extracted the roll of cord and bound her hands behind her. Then they pushed her over to the shanty wall, forced her down, and tied

161

her ankles as well. Paks gagged her with the headscarf.

"Her babies will free her soon enough," Paks murmured, "but we'll have a short lead."

"Time to head for home, I think," said Saben, with a last look around. They re-entered the trees and worked their way to the river. There they found a convenient rock and waited for Canna. Saben had taken a cut on the knuckles of his dagger hand, and sucked at the wound. When Canna came up beside them, she was carrying the big bow.

"Nice friendly folks, uncle's family," said Saben. "I'm keeping this blade, in case we meet more cousins."

Canna nodded. "At least we got food. But now we go straight in; it's our only chance."

"I'm sorry, Canna," said Paks. She remembered that she should have waited for a command before rushing out.

Canna shrugged. "It worked — worked well, but for leaving such a trail. What was in the house besides food?"

"Two," said Paks. "Boy with a club, and a man with two daggers. He threw one."

Canna looked at the cut. "We ought to wrap that; it's still bleeding." Paks had not noticed the blood still dripping off her elbow. "We'll take off mine; we don't want to leave a blood trail."

"We forgot to change yours yesterday," said Saben. "How is it?"

"Fine. It's healing fast. Hurry; we need to cross this river and be gone." When they got the bandage off Canna's shoulder, her wound was dry and pink. Canna wound a linen strip around Paks's arm and helped her up.

They had crossed this river before on an arched stone bridge, but that bridge was on the road. Now they looked at the cold gray water and shivered. Canna sighed. "No help for it. At least it's not wide." She led the way to the bank and they took another look. Upstream, to the left, it seemed it might be shallower. An overgrown but rutted opening into the trees on either side revealed a disused ford. They took off boots and socks, and waded out into the water. It was icy; Paks's feet began to ache almost at once. The water tugged at their ankles, then their knees. They were half-way across — two thirds — and at last they were climbing the far bank, shivering. They replaced their footgear, and Canna led them away from the river into the trees before she let them stop to eat.

They started by finishing the stale bread and meat Saben had found the first day, then ate a loaf from uncle's. Paks felt strength flowing back into her; she noticed that Canna and Saben looked less pinched.

"Now," said Canna, as they finished, washing down the last crumbs, "straight south as fast as we can. If that woman sets the Honeycat on us, he'll send horses. We stay away from everyone, fill the flasks at every stream, and move."

For the rest of that day they walked steadily southward, taking care not to cross open fields where they could be seen from a distance. They drank as they marched, and stopped only once before nightfall to eat generous wedges of ham and bread. Although they crossed several narrow lanes, they saw no one but distant farmers. They could not tell if they had been seen.

By nightfall they were far south of the slower moving column, Canna was sure. They had not seen anything of a mounted pursuit, and she told them she thought they might be clear. They sheltered in a thicket for a hearty meal.

"I think we may make it," said Canna, looking truly cheerful for the first time. "But we must go on. We can see to walk in the starlight, and the more ground between us and them, the better. We might make Rotengre by the day after tomorrow, if we're lucky." Paks was stiff and sore, but able to manage another hour or so of travel. The next day they were up at first light. Again Canna served out a husky portion of food, and they set off at a brisk walk. Paks kept a nervous eye over her shoulder for the first hour or so, but saw nothing.

In early afternoon, they saw ahead of them a large forested rise, and remembered the forest near Rotengre. They pushed on as fast as they could, hoping to be well into the trees by nightfall; these last few hours the land behind them had been open, with scanty hedges. Again and again they had to cross open ground, all too visible if the wrong eyes were looking.

Thicker than the little woodlots they'd been in for the past few days, here the trees were tall, with leaves just falling from elm and oak and hornbeam. Scattered clumps of evergreens made gloomy shadows within the forest shade. The ground was more broken, with outcrops of pitted gray rock as they climbed away from the farmland. Canna took a long look at the angle of the sun before they lost sight of it. It would be hard to keep a straight course in the forest.

It was also, they found, impossible to keep going as late. Trees dimmed the starlight; they stumbled into rocks and hollows. Finally they stopped in a clump of cedar. They ate another loaf of bread, and thick slices of ham. If they reached the Duke the next day, or even the one after, they need not worry about food. Paks took first watch, a silent space of darkness in which nothing happened, and went to sleep feeling sure that the next night would see them safely warm around the campfire of the Company.

She woke to a thin cold rain falling out of thick clouds. Canna looked gloomier than the weather. "We can't find our way in this," she said. "We need the sun for directions. Unless you have another trick, Paks — "

Paks shook her head. "No. All I know about this forest is that it's big, and the farmers near Rotengre said it was full of brigands."

"That's all we need," said Saben. "Brigands. Brrr, it's cold. And wet. We can't sit here and do nothing, Canna. We'll have to find our directions somehow."

Canna spread her hands. "And if we get lost? We could get farther from Rotengre than we are now, if we wander around."

They ate an ample but damp breakfast, huddling under their cloaks. Paks looked back the way they'd come, seeing nothing but rain-wet trees.

Any brigands, she thought, would be holed up in a dry cave or fort. She shifted restlessly and a trickle of icy water ran down her back. She looked at the others. Saben, for the first time, looked sulky. Canna was staring glumly at the ground.

"Could we — " she began slowly. Canna looked up. "Could we try to find the road again and follow that? We must be far ahead of the column, and the wagons will slow in this wet. Or if you think we can't find the road by cutting through the forest, we could backtrack to the edge and go that way."

Saben smiled at her. "Good idea. Canna, we can do that, can't we?"

"I suppose. I still worry about getting lost, and if we backtrack, we'll be closer to Siniava."

"If we stay here, he's coming closer to us. At least that gives us a chance — and they can't see far in the rain."

"True. I'd be glad to be moving, myself — the Duke needs to know." Canna looked around. "Let me think. The road was off to our right, and we were headed that way — I remember that holly tree. I think we should go this way — " she pointed. "Do you agree, Paks?"

"Yes." Paks rose, and the others followed her.

Sopping undergrowth slapped against their legs; they were soon much wetter, though warmer for the walking. Rain fell out of the sky with quiet intensity: never hard enough to force a halt, but never stopping. Paks thought of her first long march, the wet days on the road south of Vérella. She glanced at Saben, wondering if he remembered; his face was thoughtful and remote.

After some time, they saw that the ground was rising in a rocky hummock. They paused to consider which way to take. Paks was not tempted to suggest a trip to the top of it.

"If we bear right," said Canna, "we'll come to the road sooner, but closer to the column. If we bear left, we could swing too far from the road."

"Let's toss," said Saben. He pulled a copper from his pouch.

Canna took the coin and tossed it. "St. Gird, guide our way," she said as it spun over and over. Paks caught it and slapped it on her arm.

"Shears, we go right," said Saben. She uncovered it, and the shears of Sorellin were uppermost.

"Right it is," she said.

Circling the hill led them back sharply right at first, but after awhile Paks felt they were back to their original heading. She wondered how close the road was; her stomach clenched in anticipation. What if the column was already there? She looked at Canna. Canna's face was set and grim. At last they came to a gap in the trees. This time Canna moved forward while the others waited. When she came back, she was grinning.

"It's the road. And it's muddy, so they'll be slowed down."

"Are you sure it's the right road?" asked Paks.

"Yes — that's the best part. Remember that place where a pine on the bank had been struck by lightning, and a bush was growing out of the dead limb? There couldn't be two such, just alike. This must be the right road.

164

We've a long march in this weather, but at least we can't get lost. I think — I really think we're going to make it. By Holy Gird, I think we are. Let's go."

It was now nearly noon; they ate as they marched, moving back from the road, but keeping it in sight. They stretched their legs, making the best time possible. Canna was smiling, and Saben hummed softly, his stolen blade bouncing slightly where he'd tied it atop the pack. With every stride Paks felt safer from the menace behind; she let herself think of hot food, a dry bed, clean clothes. The hill they had circled fell away behind them; other hummocks rose ahead. Still they kept the rhythm of their strides, not stumbling now or weary, with their goal so close.

Chapter Eighteen

They missed the armed band until they were face to face. Eight heavily armed brigands in scale and chain mail, with good swords at their sides, seemed to spring from the trees to surround them. Two had shields. Paks clawed for the blade slung over her shoulder. Canna had no time to string the bow; she was grabbed from behind and wrestled to the ground. Paks found herself facing three men, who circled to get behind her. Her longsword gave her a better chance than Saben's curved one, but not much. She backed a step, glancing around. Canna was heaving and pitching under two of the men, and Saben fenced frantically with three opponents. She parried thrusts of two blades at once, and dodged the third. One man tried to get behind her again; she backed quickly, unable even to look behind.

Paks heard a hoarse cry from Saben, then Canna: "By St. Gird!" Again she retreated, and again. Canna yelled, "Paks! Run! Run for it!" just as Paks backed another step and the ground gave way beneath her. She tucked her head and tried to roll as she tumbled down a high bank of earth and leaves into a shallow stream. Above her was a roar of laughter, voices, and the squelch of wet leaves as someone started to follow her down. She forced herself up, stumbling on a loose stone, and fell again. But her vision had cleared, and she saw the single pursuer, picking his way carefully down the slope. He was only halfway, and testing his footholds.

Paks gathered her legs under her, then realized she had dropped the sword in her fall. No wonder he wasn't in a hurry. Then she remembered Canna's words. She looked around; above her, the ruffian chuckled at her evident fright. That way, she decided, upstream. Taking two quick breaths, she hurled herself into a run along the creek bed. The brigand shouted and threw his sword at her; it missed by a foot, but she did not stop to grab it. Behind her came other shouts. She ran as fast as she could, watching her footing. After fifty yards or so, the creek banks were not so steep, and she scrambled up the south bank and set off through the woods. She heard arrows thunking into the trees around her, but none touched her.

After the first frantic spurt, she settled into a steady run, wondering if the brigands had horses. She was not sure of her direction. Darkness closed in around her. She slowed to a jog after several falls, but kept going. She could not stop. She swung right, back toward the road. When she could not run any more, she slowed to a walk, gulping for air. Wet ferns whipped her legs;

vines tripped her. Somewhere she lost her cloak, and she was wet through. Keep moving, she thought. Keep going.

When she came to the road at last, it surprised her. For a moment she could not think what it was, or why she had wanted to find it. The rain had stopped; the road was just visible against the solid dark of the trees. Paks turned and walked beside it, just out of the mud. She got her breath back, and began running again. Canna's cry rang in her head. And Saben. What had happened to Saben? She found herself running faster, and sobbing as she ran.

After some time she realized she was no longer running beside trees: the forest was behind her. She stumbled into a brimming ditch beside the road, and scrambled out on the wrong side. It didn't matter; she settled back to a jog and went on. The fields were soft with rain; she staggered when she hit the deeper mud of plowland. Her thighs ached. She slowed to a walk; the night grew lighter. She hoped for dawn, but looked up to see the clouds blowing away and stars shining between them.

At last she saw the twinkling watchfires ahead. She forced herself into a run again, terrified that something, even now, would come upon her before she reached the Duke. By the time she hit the outer guard perimeter, she was staggering with weariness.

"Halt!" came a shout from before her. Paks stopped and stood, swaying slightly as she gasped for breath. She heard the squelch of footsteps approaching. "Who's there?" demanded the guard. "Give the password."

She could not recall what the password had been weeks ago when they left for Dwarfwatch; surely it had changed by now. Besides, she had no breath for speech. A hard hand gripped her arm and shook her.

"Speak up, there. Who are you?"

"Duke Phelan's Company," she managed. "Must see the Duke."

"At this time of night? Sober up, soldier — what'd you do, go off on a tear and get lost?" Someone brought a torch near; she could see the polished armor of the guard who held her. "Tir's gut, you're a disgrace," he said disgustedly. "Duke Phelan's Company — I don't believe that. His people don't wallow in filth."

"Is that a bandage, Sim, on the left arm?" asked another voice.

"Who can tell?" grumbled the first. "Are you hurt?" he bawled at Paks.

"Just a cut," she said. Her voice shook. "Please — I must get to the Duke now — it's important."

"You've missed roll call, if that's what you mean," said the first guard. "That was hours ago. They won't thank you for showing up now."

"Well, but Sim — we don't want this mess in our area, either. Let the Phelani take care of it, if it's theirs."

"I don't know what it is — d'you think that was ever his uniform?"

"It might have been. We'll be in trouble if it is, and we don't — "

"All right, all right. You take it — her — over then, if it concerns you so. Tir's bones, I hate to be seen near such a ragbag. If it is the Duke's, I don't know what he's coming to."

"Please," said Paks. Her legs were trembling under her, and she was afraid she might faint. "Please, we must hurry. It is important, and the Duke must know — "

The second guard grabbed her arm and swung her ahead of him. "Don't tell me what I 'must,' not when I don't know who in thunder you are. We'll go, but at my pace."

Paks found even that hard to sustain as they threaded their way between tents toward the Duke's perimeter. At last they were challenged by a voice she knew. She started forward, but the guard pulled her back. "Not so fast," he said. He raised his voice. "It's me, Arvor of the Sorellin militia, with someone who claims to be one of yours. Came in on our north perimeter, dirty as a miner and no good tale to tell."

"Let's see, then." It was Barranyi holding a torch. "Who are you?"

"P-Paks," she stammered. "Barra, I've got to see the Duke. Now."

Barranyi held the torch closer. "Paks? Tir's bones, it is you! But you were with — " she flicked a glance at the Sorellin guard.

"Well now," he said. "Seeing as you know her, I suppose it's all right — "

"Yes, Arvor — thanks — " said Barranyi in a rush. "Paks. Come on. What happened?"

Paks heard the guard leave, and tried to muster her thoughts. "C-call the sergeant, Barra. I must see the Duke tonight. I — I can't explain to anyone but the Duke."

"This late? He's long abed; you can't see him now. Why do you — you're wet through!" She took Paks by the arm; Paks winced. "What's this — a wound?" Paks nodded, suddenly too tired to speak. "You might trust *me*," said Barranyi, her voice sharpening. "We trained together, after all." She paused but Paks said nothing. "Very well, then; I'll take you, but — "

"Sorry," murmured Paks. "Can — can I sit down?"

"Wait. Malek!" she called back toward camp.

"Yo."

"Mal, take over here; I have to take someone to the sergeant."

"Sure thing."

"Come on, Paks. Sergeant Vossik is by the fire; you need to warm up, I'll warrant." Paks followed Barra's stiff back to a fire some yards away. She was shivering hard now, and stumbled repeatedly. She barely heard what Barra said about her. Vossik's voice seemed to come from a great distance, and she had to puzzle out the meaning of his words before she could answer.

"But did you break your parole?" he insisted.

"She must have come all that way afoot," said another voice.

"But why? Paks, tell us — "

"The Duke — " she said again. She felt herself sagging, heard a gasp from Barra, then a grunt as Barra caught her and eased her down. Her eyes closed in spite of herself. "The Duke," she repeated. "Must see the Duke."

"She's wet through and cold," said Vossik. "Not making sense. Get warm blankets, Barra. Seli, fetch a pot of sib."

Paks tried to struggle up again; Vossik held her shoulders. "Please," she

168

said. "Please, sir — take me to the Duke. He has to know — right away."

"Know what? And we'll get you warm and dry before we — "

Paks shook her head and tried to free herself. "No — sir — must know *now*." She felt tears burn her eyes.

"Know *what*? If it's important, tell me — "

"Honeycat," said Paks. "Tell the Duke — "

"What!" Vossik lowered his voice after the first bellow. "What about the Honeycat? Is that your message? Have you seen — ?"

"Tell the Duke," repeated Paks. She felt herself hauled to her feet.

"All right," said Vossik grimly. "For that you'll see the Duke. If this is some game, Paks — "

"No, sir. Im-important." She shivered violently as Vossik supported her. He wrapped his dry cloak around her and called someone to help as he took her to the Duke's tent.

The sentries there were reluctant, but Vossik overrode them. "Either you call him now, or I'll raise a shout that'll have half the camp up." One of them ducked inside. The other stared curiously at Paks. A light flared inside the tent; dark shapes moved against the lighted walls. The sentry reappeared at the door and took up his post. One of the Duke's servants peered out the opening. "He says come in," said the man softly. Vossik pushed Paks forward into the tent's main room. Another servant was lighting oil lamps around the room, but there was already enough light to see the Duke standing by his work table with a fur-lined robe thrown about his shoulders. His hair was rumpled, and his eyes were cold.

"This had better be important, Vossik. Have you a good reason not to go through your captain?"

"Yes, my lord, I believe so." Vossik cleared his throat. "This is Paks, my lord, of Ferrault's cohort. She insisted she had to speak to you at once — and, sir, she mentioned the Honeycat."

The Duke crossed the room in two strides to stare closely at Paks. "Honeycat! What do you know about the Honeycat? Why did you leave the fort? What's happened?"

Paks tried to focus on his face. "Sir — my lord Duke — he's coming. On the road. He has — he has a large force, sir, and — "

"Did Ferrault send you?" asked the Duke abruptly.

"No, sir. He — he's been taken, I think."

"Taken! Who? Not the Honeycat; the Halverics wouldn't turn prisoners over to him."

"Sir, they took — took the — we think they took the fort. They killed the Halverics, and took prisoners, and — "

"The Honeycat? How do you know? Did you see it? Did you escape?" Paks tried to nod, but felt herself starting to fall.

"Sir, we — we weren't taken — we saw — " She could not get the words out. Her legs were limp. Vossik let her down gently on the carpets that overlay the tent floor. She heard the voices above her, but could not muster the energy to answer.

169

"Is she wounded?" asked the Duke.

"I don't know, my lord. I know she's wet and cold and filthy, but when she said Honeycat, I brought her straight to you."

"Very well. Vossik, I want you to send the captains here at once."

"Yes, my lord."

"And alert the perimeter, but don't say why. And send the surgeon, and tell the cooks I want something hot at once."

"Yes, my lord."

"You may go."

Paks was hardly aware of it when the Duke's servants stripped off her wet and filthy tunic and wrapped her in warm furs. She roused, coughing, only when the surgeon spooned a bit of fiery liquid into her mouth.

"I hate to do this," the Duke was saying, "but we must know what message she brings. Can you tell how badly she's hurt?"

Paks opened her eyes and tried to focus on the surgeon. He pressed a mug to her lips and she swallowed. Whatever it was, it sent warm currents through her cold arms and legs, and cleared the fog from her head.

"Exhaustion, mostly," said the surgeon. "Maybe a broken rib or two, and this cut — sword or knife wound, but not bad. Bruises and scrapes; I'd say she's fallen many times in the last day or so. She needs sleep, my lord, as soon as may be." He met Paks's eyes. "Better now? Drink the rest."

Paks swallowed again, and then again. He took the mug away and offered another, of steaming sib. When she had drunk half of that, she turned her head to see the room around her. The Duke was dressed in his usual mail, as were the captains with him.

"There, my lord," said the surgeon. "She'll be able to talk with you a short while; I hope it's enough."

"If not, we'll dose her again."

"My lord, that would be most unwise. She will need to sleep — "

"You may go," said the Duke. "And leave that stuff here."

"But my lord — "

"I've no more wish than you to harm a good soldier, Master Visanior, but I must know her message. You may go."

Paks felt the surface under her shift as the surgeon stood, and realized that she lay in a bed. The Duke's face replaced the surgeon's.

"Now, Paks," he began. "You were in the fort when the Halverics came. Your name is on the roll I received for ransom. What happened: did you break your parole?"

Paks shook her head. When she tried to speak, the words came easily. "No, my lord. We were waiting to be ransomed — most of the Halverics had left, and they let us go outside a lot. We were gathering berries one day when strange troops came up the road — many of them — and the Halveric captain rode out to meet them. Then he fell from his horse, and they started chasing those outside the walls — "

"Except you?"

"As far as I know, my lord. We — "

170

"Who — how many?"

"Three of us, sir. Saben and Canna and I. We were in tall brambles, and they didn't see us. We made it into the woods, and — "

"What about the fort?"

"They attacked it, sir, but the Halverics dropped the portcullis — we heard that — and we saw our men on the wall as well as theirs. So we started south to tell you — "

"You came all the way from the fort?" Paks nodded. "On foot?"

"Yes, my lord."

"How long were you? When did the attack happen?"

Paks tried to count back. "Sir, we were — seven days, coming. It was the afternoon before we started that they came."

"Were you on the road all the way?"

"No, sir; we weren't on the road at all. They had patrols, and we were nearly caught the first day, so Canna said to stay off the road, as far as we could and not get lost."

"Where is the Honeycat now?"

"I — don't know, sir. They were on the road — we watched them past the crossroads to be sure, and then we came ahead. We had — had trouble." Paks shivered at the memory of uncle's place.

"I daresay." The Duke sighed, and looked up. "Well, captains, we have trouble ahead of us, too. If he's come to relieve the siege, he'll hit the lines somewhere, and we'd best find out where." He turned back to Paks. "Where are the others, Paks? Were they killed?"

Paks had forgotten Canna and Saben in her anxiety to see the Duke. Now the memory of their last encounter returned full force. Her eyes widened. "Sir! The brigands! They attacked us in the forest, and — and Saben and Canna — I don't know what happened. Canna said to run — I had to leave them. I had to get to you, my lord, but I didn't mean to leave them to — "

"Shh. That's all right. We don't think that of you. You did well."

"But, sir, you must find them — they need help — " Paks felt her strength and awareness slipping away again. She wanted to get up and find Saben and Canna, she wanted to chase the Honeycat, she wanted — she fell into sleep as dreamless as a cave.

She woke again in broad daylight, hearing voices from the next room. For awhile she lay with her eyes closed, listening idly.

"I don't want guesses, Jori; I want facts." That was the Duke, and he sounded angry.

"No, sir. But the scouts haven't found anything else."

"They'd better. Jori, go back to the Sorellin — no, wait. Take this to Vladi — "

"Sir, the Count?"

"Yes. Don't look like that, just do it. It's around the far side; take a fast horse. Wait for an answer. I'll go to the Sorellin commander myself. Go on, now."

A much younger voice. "If only they hadn't been so careless in the forest."

The Duke snorted. "What is it, Jostin, did you expect me to scold her for that?"

"Well, my lord, you've always said to us — "

"Lad, some mistakes carry their own punishment. And consider what they did — I doubt any of you squires could make such a journey. After all that, you don't scold like an old granny for things they couldn't help."

"But they should have been watching — "

The Duke's voice hardened. "When you've done as much, squire, you may offer criticisms. For now, you may ready my mount. Go."

Paks opened her eyes. She was in the tent, in a small curtained room, wrapped in soft furs on a bed. Slumped on a stool nearby was a servant, who jumped up when he met her eyes.

"Are you awake? Can you speak?"

Paks yawned, swallowed, and managed to say yes.

"My lord Duke," called the servant, "she's awake." He offered Paks a mug of sib. She was warm and comfortable as long as she held still, but when she tried to shift her legs, she ached in every muscle. The Duke pushed through the curtains between the rooms.

"Paks, I know you need more sleep, but I need more information. Sim will bring you something to eat, while you answer my questions.

Paks tried to push herself up in the bed, but failed. "Yes, my lord."

"Good. Now, this force you reported — the colors were black and yellow, you said. Any other reason for thinking it was the Honeycat?"

"Yes, my lord. That first day we overheard one of the mounted men; he called his commander Lord Siniava. Canna said that was the same."

"Yes. It is. You said he took prisoners — do you know where they are?"

"With the column, sir. I don't know about the fort, but the ones outside are with the column."

"Just our men?"

"No, sir. Some Halverics, too. But he killed those who tried to run or fight."

"Just a moment; I want someone else to hear this." The Duke stepped to the curtain and returned with a man in dark green that looked like the Halveric uniform. "Cal, you'll need to hear this for yourself. Go on, Paks."

Paks looked curiously at the man before turning back to the Duke. She was not sure what he wanted to hear.

"Tell us again what happened when the Honeycat's force reached the fort: what did the Halverics do, and what did our men do?"

"Yes, sir. I think almost half our men and the Halverics were outside the gates. When the column was sighted, the Halverics's horn blew. Then a man rode out of the fort — we thought it was the Halveric captain. He seemed to be talking to someone at the head of the column — "

"Had it halted?"

"Yes, my lord. Then he backed his horse a length or so, and raised his arm, and fell from his horse. We thought he'd been shot; they had bowmen."

The man in green stood abruptly, face pale. "Seli! No!"

Duke Phelan shot him a glance. "Who — ?"

172

"My lord, he — my brother Seliam — you wouldn't remember him. Seli dead, and by treachery!"

"Cal, I'm sorry. I do remember — a little lad of six or so, perched on your father's saddle."

The other man turned his head aside. His voice shook. "My lord, it — it was his first command." Suddenly he was at the bedside, hand fisted in the sleeping furs at Paks's throat. "Are you sure it was Seliam? How do you — ?"

Duke Phelan reached out and removed the hand. "Let be, Cal. 'Tis not her fault." The younger man turned away, shoulders hunched. "You thought it was the captain, Paks. Why?"

Paks was frightened. "He — he wore a cloak with gold at the shoulders, my lord; it glittered. And he rode a dapple gray with a black tail."

"It must be so," whispered the other man. "Sir, I must go at once. By your leave — "

"Wait. You may need to know more of this."

"I know enough. Seli dead, my men prisoners, others sieged — "

"No. Stay and hear. Not for long, Cal." The Duke and the other matched gazes; the young man's eyes fell first.

"Very well, my lord Duke, since you insist."

"Go on, Paks. After the captain fell, what then?"

"Then the Honeycat's men moved in squads, rounding up those who were outside. Some of the Halverics fought, and tried to get back to the fort or protect our men, but they were outnumbered. Some of ours tried to escape, but we saw them fall. Then we heard the portcullis go down, and after a bit we saw ours on the walls along with the Halverics."

"Where was Captain Ferrault?"

Paks thought back. "I think, my lord — he was inside."

The Duke grunted. "And you don't know how big a force the Honeycat left at the fort?"

"No, sir. We thought of trying to sneak back and find out, but Canna had been hit. She said we should shadow the main column and come to you."

"Canna was hurt? I thought you said you weren't seen."

"We weren't, my lord, not then. But their first sweep around the fort, they shot into the brambles to scare anyone out. It was bad luck she was hit; they couldn't see us."

"I see. Now — you're sure that some of the prisoners were taken with the column?"

"Yes, sir. We couldn't see it often, because of the sweeps, but on — it must have been the third day — Canna and Saben got a clear look. They said sixty or more prisoners, both ours and the Halverics."

"And how many enemy?"

"Something over three hundred foot, and a hundred horse, and ten wagons." The Duke turned to look at the man in green. Paks watched their faces, trying to understand why the man looked so familiar — had he been at Dwarfwatch with the Halverics?

Suddenly she realized that, though taller and not bald, he looked like

173

Aliam Halveric. She looked more closely. His well-worn sword belt was tooled in a floral pattern; his cloak was fastened with an ornate silver pin. If he was a Halveric son, and the captain killed at Dwarfwatch his brother — she shivered.

"Now," said the Duke, "What time yesterday did you meet the brigands?"

"Afternoon, sir, and starting to get dark."

"And when did you last see the Honeycat's column?"

Paks thought, counting the days. "The — the fourth day, sir. They had passed the Guild League road; there's a village just south, and they burned it. Then we passed the column, the next day, and that was the fourth after we started."

"How fast were they traveling?"

"Sir, I — I don't know. Canna said when we were three days from here that it would take them five — but that was before the rain."

"Yes. With rain — those wagons should be slowed — Cal, tell your father this. I'm leaving today, with the Company, to see if I can catch them on the road. After that, I'll go north. I'll do what I can to save his men; I'll expect to meet him soon. I can't offer you much escort — "

"Sir, I'll be fine."

"Cal, the Honeycat is infinitely devious. Let me send my youngest squire, at least: he's brave, if pigheaded."

"Sir, I thank you, but my own escort will suffice."

"Be careful, then. And Cal — be fast."

"I'll kill every horse I own, if I must. May I go?"

"Yes. Luck go with you." The young Halveric bowed and withdrew. The Duke looked at Paks; she was drinking a mug of soup the servant had brought in. She started to put it down when she saw him looking. "No," he said kindly. "Go on and finish it; you need that. Paks, the first scouts I sent out last night have come back; they found no trace of your friends or the brigands. I'm not sure they went far enough; I had told them to be back an hour after sunrise. We'll keep searching, you may be sure. As for you — " he sighed, and sipped from the mug the servant had handed him. "You heard me tell Cal I'm leading the Company out. If we're lucky, we'll catch him on the road, unprepared. You're not fit for this — " Paks opened her mouth to protest, and he waved her to silence. "No. Don't argue. You'll stay here. One of my scribes will take down everything you recall — no matter how unimportant — about your journey and the Honeycat. You will not talk to anyone else about it until I give you leave. Not even the surgeon. Is that clear?"

Paks nodded. "Yes, my lord. But sir, I could — "

"No. You've had less than half the sleep you need; I'm not risking my only source of information. When the surgeon passes you as fit for duty, there'll be plenty for you to do." The Duke's sudden smile held no humor; Paks shivered. "Now. What can you tell me about their order of march, and the scouts?"

Paks explained the forward and flank sweeps as well as she could. The Duke nodded, and stood. "Very well. Remember that if anyone other than my scribe Arric tries to ask questions, you'll have a lapse of memory."

"Yes, my lord." Paks felt a wave of sleepiness rise over her. She hardly knew when the Duke left, and she slept heavily several hours. The tent was very quiet when she woke, and she fell asleep again quickly. The next time she woke, the lamps were lit, and the surgeon was beside the bed, calling her name.

"It's partly the stimulant you were given," he explained when Paks asked why she was so sleepy. "That and the exhaustion from your journey. If you didn't sleep now — well, you must. Try to eat all Sim brings, and sleep again."

Paks had trouble working her way through the large bowl of stew and half-loaf of bread. Even swallowing was an effort. She sat up briefly, but sleep overwhelmed her again. She woke in early morning feeling much better. When she asked for clothes to put on, Sim told her she was to stay in bed.

"You'll be getting clothes when the surgeon says you can get up and not before. That's the Duke's orders, so it's no good looking at me." He left her to her meal, and Paks looked around the room. It had not registered before that she was in the Duke's tent — she noticed a carved chest bound with polished metal, a three-legged stool with a tooled leather seat, the rich sleeping furs she lay under — in the Duke's own chamber. She finished breakfast. When Sim came to take the dishes, Arric the scribe arrived, a slender man of medium height whom Paks had often seen in the quartermaster's tents.

When he had readied his writing materials, she began to tell her story again. Arric was accustomed to the halting accounts of inexperienced soldiers, and prompted her with pointed questions when she faltered. Paks was surprised when Sim arrived with lunch for them both. After lunch they began again. Paks was beginning to tire when the surgeon came to check on her. He drove Arric off, and Paks slept for several hours. She woke with a huge appetite, ate everything Sim brought, and greeted the surgeon with a demand to be let out of bed.

"Being hungry's a good sign," he told her. "You'll come back fast now. I'll have Sim bring more food in an hour. Work with Arric a few hours tonight, and you may be able to get up tomorrow. I'll check on you before breakfast."

Paks devoured her second supper eagerly, and answered Arric's questions as fast as she could. She dared not ask if they had had word from the Duke; she thought she heard more noises in camp, and was determined to be ready if he called. She was sure she would not sleep, when Arric finally left, and thought of trying to sneak out of bed and find clothes. The bed was warm, though — and the surgeon woke her as he came in the next morning.

He had brought a bundle of clothes, as if certain she would be well

175

enough. Everything was new, from boots to cloak. She said nothing while he looked her over. He sighed.

"It's too early, really, but you'll be well enough if you don't exhaust yourself again. Eat more than usual for several weeks, and rest when you can. Your wounds are healing cleanly, no trouble there. Dress and come out front."

When she came through the curtain, the Duke was standing in the tent entrance, talking to someone outside. The surgeon stood frowning by the work table.

"Ah, Paks," said the Duke, as he turned and saw her. "You're better, I see. Ready to ride?" The surgeon grunted, but Paks grinned.

"Yes, my lord. When?"

"At once. We ride north, to the fort; I expect to meet the Halverics there." He moved toward the table, and sat, looking up at Paks. "We hit the Honeycat on the road, with Vladi's spears and Clart Cavalry to help. He and his captains escaped, but the rest didn't."

"And our men, my lord? The prisoners?"

The Duke frowned. "Most of 'em had been killed. We saved some — by Tir, that devil-worshipper has earned a beating — I've heard how the others died." He looked so stern that Paks dared not ask who lived. "Get some food for yourself, and a sword; we'll have to catch up with the rest on the road."

Paks left the tent to find the camp almost deserted. She got sword and scabbard from the quartermaster, and filled saddlebags with food at the cooktent. Rassamir, one of the Duke's senior squires, beckoned her from the horse lines.

"Here — I've saddled for you, and you'll lead a spare. Are you ready?"

"Yes, sir." Paks slung the saddlebags over and fastened them.

"Fine. Mount and wait here." He swung himself onto a rangy bay, and took up the leadline of one of the Duke's chargers. Paks mounted, wincing at her painful ribs. One of the horseboys handed up the lead rope for a horse much like her own sturdy mount. In a few minutes the Duke and Rassamir rode up beside her; each took another horse to lead.

"If you start feeling bad, Paks," said the Duke seriously, "I want you to drop back with the wounded that'll be coming in from yesterday's battle. You won't help us any if you can't fight when we reach Dwarfwatch. The surgeon thinks you shouldn't go, but — "

"I'm fine, my lord. I'll be all right."

He smiled. "I thought you'd say that. Just remember: you've already served me and the Company well; I won't think less of you if you can't ride and fight so soon." Paks nodded, but she was determined to find out what had happened to her friends. She knew she would make it to the fort, surgeon or no surgeon.

The surgeon, in fact, was riding north too. "Arbola's coming back with the wounded," he said. "He won't be able to catch up. You'll have plenty of work for Simmitt and me both." The Duke merely nodded and they set off.

176

Chapter Nineteen

Their return to the north was swift and direct. Mounted, with no pack train, they made the northern crossroad in two days. A fast unit of Clart Cavalry had rounded up the "huntsmen" camped on the hill over the crossroad; they thought no warning had been passed on. The Duke, Paks knew, hoped the Halverics were coming from the east, but they might be a day or so away. She wondered if he would wait for them.

That night she woke to the clatter of a single galloping horse, and slept again when no alarm sounded. They moved at dawn. Paks and the others who had been north before were assigned the forward and flank sweeps. Now it was her turn to ride through the cold woods, looking for enemy strays. For the first hour, they moved at a brisk trot. Paks found herself reaching for her sword again and again. Not yet, she told herself. After that, they slowed to a walk. Paks looked for the farmers' clearing. When it finally opened on her left, she felt a cold thrill down her back. Close. She waved the forward group to a halt, and looked over the clearing. The Duke rode up to them.

"Trouble?"

"No, my lord," said Paks. "But we're close now, and I know they came out this far. Do you want us to leave the road here?"

"No. Riders off the road mean trouble. Let them think we're friendly — or at least neutral — if they hear the horses. With the north wind, they shouldn't. How far to the last cover?"

Paks thought a moment. "I'm not sure, my lord, but there's a ridge just before the trees end, and a double curve in the road."

"If they've gotten sloppy, we might make the edge before they notice. I'll ride with you, Paks, and you point out that ridge." He turned to his captains. "I want the Clarts ready to split into two columns, just as we did before; I expect a force near the gate. Archers next; they've got crossbows. I want the swords and spears dismounted this time, and in the usual formation. If our friends are alive, and can make a sally, so much the better. After the first shock, unless things change, Clarts hit cavalry first, then sweep up and harry stragglers. There's a small chance still that we could meet them on the road — remember our plans, if we do." They nodded. "Very well. Let's go." He wheeled his horse and started up the road. Paks legged her horse up beside him, and the column followed.

That last stretch seemed the longest. Paks felt her heart hammering in her chest. A sour taste came into her mouth. Her horse began to jig and toss its head. She thought about what they might find. Perhaps the Honeycat's men had already taken the fort — killed the defenders — gone away. Or they held the fort — or the defenders had killed them at last — Ahead the road swung left to climb a steeper ridge. Paks recognized it, and waved to the Duke. At his signal, the rest halted while he, Paks, his squires, and two others rode ahead. They reached the ridgetop; Paks reached for her sword, but the Duke gestured: no.

Here the road swung right; through the wind-torn foliage they could see the open meadows below. The Duke sent one man back to bring up the column. A cold wind out of the northwest roared through the trees; Paks felt her skin stiffen under it, and never heard the column come up behind her. The Clart riders had lances in hand, tossing and twirling them; the leaders grinned as they rode up. Behind them, the Duke's men were grim-faced. Paks could see nothing of Vladi's spears but the tips bristling above the riders between.

The captains came forward, and all shook hands with the Duke and each other. The Duke gestured to the standard bearers, and they unrolled the banners: his own maroon and white, with the crest of Tsaia and the fox mask; Clart Company's white horse on rose, under a spear; Vladi's black and silver, a mailed fist over the eastern rune for ice. The Duke beckoned to Paks, and she moved her horse near him.

"When we break cover," he said, "shift left at once, and let the Clarts through. Then drop back to Dorrin's cohort."

"Yes, sir." Paks found it hard to speak; her throat was tight.

"Let's go." He lifted his reins and his horse moved forward. Paks saw his hand rise to his forehead; his visor dropped in place. Without checking his horse, he drew his sword. Paks glanced at his squires; they rode on either side, swords ready, grim-faced. She looked at the road ahead. Somewhere they must have sentries. A horn cry rang out to one side of the road. There, she thought. She heard a faint shout from somewhere ahead.

"Now!" yelled the Duke, and spurred to a gallop. Behind her, the Clart riders began their shrill battle cry, and the road erupted in a thunder of hooves. Paks leaned forward, her horse fighting for its head with the excitement of running horses before and behind. She edged to the left of the road. She was sure the Clarts were riding up her backbone. She could see the end of the trees, the open slope down to the river, the river itself. They were out. She yanked her horse to the left, and a stream of rose-clad riders poured past. She fought her mount to a bouncing trot, waiting for the archers to pass. Scattered small groups of black and yellow dotted the meadow; a larger cluster lay against the gate of the fort. The fort itself — she squinted to see the banners flying from the tower. Green and gold, the Halverics, and below, the Duke's maroon and white. From the walls came a high, musical bugling. She looked back at the column for Dorrin or Sejek, and swung her horse into formation as they plunged down the road to the bridge.

178

There were bodies now along the way, one and two together, some with lance wounds, others sprouting arrows. Ahead the battle clamored, as the Clarts ran headlong into the Honeycat's massed force by the gate. Horses and men screamed. Dorrin yelled a halt. They dismounted, the left file taking the horses, and formed again, shields and swords ready. Around the southwest corner of the fort came a cavalry unit in black and yellow; it charged, swerving away when Vladi's spearmen, still mounted, rode between. A section of Clart riders, still shrilling, broke from the melee in front of the gates and rode at the cavalry.

"Forward!" yelled Dorrin; Paks stepped forward with the rest. Directly ahead was a milling mass of horses: their own archers, shooting into the enemy. Dorrin and Sejek rode ahead, swearing at them. A path opened. Now Paks could see the pikemen, trying to form in their direction and move out from the wall. She heard the wicked thin flick of a crossbow bolt, and the man next to her stumbled. His shield partner moved over and closed in.

Now she could see the faces under the strange helmets: pale or dark, they looked the same to her with their teeth gleaming. She heard above the roar another bugle call from the gate tower, and shrill voices from the wall. She saw stones fall, aimed at the enemy. Then they were too close to see anything but the faces and weapons and bodies in front of them.

"Remember your strokes!" yelled Sergeant Vossik. "Shieldwork! Shieldwork. Get under those pikes." Paks watched the pikemen thrust and jab; the chopping stroke that made the broad blade so effective against horsemen was no good once you were inside it. They couldn't jab and chop at the same time.

She thought of Canna and Saben, and felt a wash of anger erase the last nervousness. I'm going to kill you, she thought as her rank reached the pikes. She ducked under a pike to slash at the enemy. One in the second rank chopped at her; she dodged without thinking and darted between the front pikes while he was still off balance. Her sword almost took his head off. She felt without looking that her companions followed her example, felt the first quiver of yielding as the pikemen realized that these swordsmen were not held off by the bitter tips of their weapons.

A terrible crashing and booming from the gate, and a roar of "Halveric! Halveric! The Duke! The Duke!" The defenders had come out. Paks could not see them, but she could feel, as if it were her own body, the shudder that ran through the enemy ranks. The swordsmen pressed forward in response. Suddenly the enemy stiffened again, and began to fight harder. Paks felt a give, a weakening, on her own left flank. Something had happened there; she could not see what. She fought on; it didn't matter, she was going to kill these scum until she died. She felt the pressure shifting her to the right, foot by foot, cramming the leftward files against her, and her against those to her right. Again. Another bellow added to the din. She could just distinguish the deep chant of Vladi's spears, somewhere to the left. The pressure against her eased; again she was able to drive forward.

179

The pikemen began to look aside. Through their ranks she could see Halveric green near the gate.

"Now!" bellowed Vossik. "Now! They're breaking. Hit them!" With an answering roar, Paks and the others found they could move faster, swing harder. The pikes began to melt away. Some were dropped. A few of the soldiers turned to flee. Paks drove forward. Now more dropped their pikes; they were in among the crossbowmen, who had no time to reload and shoot. Many of these had drawn short curved swords, but they were no match for the angry swordsmen of the Duke. Those who did not break and run were killed.

They were through. The little group of Halverics and Phelani in front of the gate met Paks and the others with hugs as they broke through the last of the pikes. Paks looked anxiously for her friends, but Vossik and Kalek were yelling at them.

"No talking now, you fools! Reform! Come on, there's still a battle going on!" Paks tore her eyes away from the few Phelani and finally obeyed the sergeants.

The fleeing enemy had turned south, away from Vladi's spears. Now the Clarts had cut them off. Vossik called his cohort away from that easy bait to a block of pikes still intact, near the northwest corner of the fort. These had engaged Vladi's spears on one side, but were holding together. They fought desperately, seeing they would receive no quarter. Paks was breathless and aching all over when the last ones fell. She looked around. Nothing remained of the enemy but crumpled bodies piled in rows, and scattered across the open ground between the fort and the river. The Clarts, reunited, were riding around the perimeter of the open ground — almost to the brambles, Paks noticed.

Paks wiped her sword on the dry grass of the meadow, but the blood on it had hardened. She started toward the river, limping slightly and noticing the limp before the pain that caused it. When she thought, she could recall a pike-butt slamming into her leg. Her ribs hurt, too. She pulled a handful of grass before stepping down the rocks to the water's edge to dip it in the icy flow and scour her sword. She cupped a handful and drank. When she stood, the others were already stripping the enemy bodies and hauling them to a pile. Paks sheathed her sword and walked toward the gate. She could see the Duke's horse just inside. Vossik yelled something at her, but she shook her head and pointed inside. She didn't want to be part of that, not this time.

Inside the fort, no one had much to say. Vik was alive, hobbling toward her on bandaged legs. When they met, he hugged her fiercely.

"Was it you?" he asked.

"Yes." Paks found her eyes filling with tears. She knew his next question.

"Saben? Canna?" She shook her head, tasting salt, unable to answer. She could not say she had left them, that no one knew where they were, if they were alive. Vik hugged her again. "At least you made it — I don't know how. By all the gods, Paks, it did me good to look down and see you marching up

180

from the bridge. We were sure you'd been killed in the woods. Pernoth — he's one of the Halverics — thought he'd seen you three in the brambles just when the trouble started, but nothing after that. You'll have some tales to tell, when we get the chance. But you'll want to see who's left, and the Duke told us to gather in the main courtyard."

Together they limped across the outer court. Vik told her how many had been inside, and how many were left; about the two abortive attempts to break the siege and send word south. The Halverics, he said, had accepted Ferrault as commander after their captain was killed. Within minutes, the Phelani were armed, and together they withstood the shock of the Honeycat's assault.

"It's a good thing he had only scaling ladders, though," said Vik. "They outnumbered us, but couldn't get enough of them up the walls at once."

"What about water?"

"It rained the day after they came. That helped; it got slippery down below. And it made his fire-arrows useless. And the next day — that's when he pulled out. We were collecting it in everything we could find. Then several days later it rained again for a day and a half."

As they came into the main court, Paks saw that almost everyone there was from her own cohort — perhaps twenty. She glanced at Vik. He nodded. As they came to speak to her, she realized that every one was bandaged somewhere.

"I hear you're the hero of this tale," said Rauf, a twenty-year veteran.

Paks blushed. "Not me. Canna and Saben — I'd never have made it without them." He didn't ask about them, but went on.

"But you did. Heh, you'll be working up to sergeant at this rate. We'll be calling you 'Lucky Paks,' or 'Paks Longlegs.'" Rauf displayed his wide, gap-toothed grin. Paks could think of nothing to answer; she felt a great desire to fall down and sleep somewhere warm. Hands patted her back and shoulders as they all came together for a few moments.

"Paks!" It was the youngest squire's shrill call. She looked and saw him beckon from the door to the keep. "The Duke wants you." She pushed herself away from her friends, and limped stiffly toward the door. "Are you hurt?" asked the squire, frowning.

She shook her head. "No. Not bad, anyway. Just stiff." The squire was younger than she had been when she left home. But he, if he survived his time, would be an officer — maybe a knight. She flicked an appraising glance at his thin face, still with the unformed curves of a boy despite its leanness. She felt much older than that. The squire reddened under that brief look; she wondered if he had expected her to answer with sir. Not for you, yet, she thought. Not for you yet awhile.

The room he led her to overlooked the courtyard; two narrow windows let in the cold afternoon light. Inside were the Duke, one of the surgeons, and a man on a narrow bed. Paks wrinkled her nose at the smell. The Duke looked up.

"Paks. Good. Come on in." She stepped into the room. "Captain Fer-

181

rault would like to speak with you," said the Duke formally. Paks had not recognized the captain. He was pale, his face gaunt, his usually mobile mouth fixed in a grimace. The Duke, Paks saw, held one slack hand. The surgeon bent over him, gently removing bandages with a pot of sharp-smelling liquid. Paks came to the head of the bed.

"Yes, sir," she said to the Duke. She had seen enough to know that Ferrault was dying. She knelt beside the bed. "Captain — ? It's Paks, sir."

For a moment he seemed to stare through her, then his eyes focussed. "Paks. You — did — well. To go. I told — the Duke."

"Thank you, sir. I'm sorry we weren't faster, sir, for the rest of you."

His head rolled in a slow shake. "No matter. Did enough. I hoped — " He broke off with a gasp. Paks saw his knuckles whiten on the Duke's hand. She heard a curse from both the surgeon and the Duke.

"Sorry, my lord," said the surgeon. "Sorry, captain. Just — one more — layer. There." Paks saw sweat film the captain's face. "Umm," said the surgeon. Paks glanced down Ferrault's body to the wound now exposed. No doubt where the stench came from; she swallowed hard to keep from retching. Ferrault's face was grayer now, and wet.

"You — can't do — anything," whispered Ferrault. It was not a question.

The surgeon sighed. "Not to cure it, no. Not so late, with that — a pike, they said? Yes. It's gone bad, but you knew that, with the fever. But I can — " He turned to rummage in his bag. "I can make you more comfortable. If you drink much, you'll vomit, so — " He rose and came to the head of the bed. Paks moved back.

"Will it be — ?"

"Long? No, Captain. And this should make it easier. No wine; it'll taste bad, but drink it all." The surgeon held a tiny flask to Ferrault's lips as he swallowed. Then he stepped back and returned to the pile of bandages. He took a clean one, dipped it in the pot, and laid it gently over Ferrault's wound, then gathered up the soiled bandages with his bag. "My lord, that dose should ease him for some hours. I'll be back in time to give him another, or if you have need of me I'll be with the others."

"Very well, Master Simmitt, and thank you." The surgeon left the room; the Duke turned back to Ferrault. "Captain — "

"My lord. Did I tell you — the seals — "

"Yes. You broke them."

"I'm sorry — "

"Don't be. You did the right thing. Don't worry."

"But — my lord — I lost the cohort — and then the seals — and — "

"Shh. Ferrault, it's all right. It's not your fault. You did well — you've always done well. Your patron Gird will be pleased with you, when you come to him. I don't know many captains who could have held off so many with a tiny mixed force."

"But our losses — what will you do?"

"Do?" The Duke stared at the wall a moment, then smiled at Ferrault. "Ferrault, when I'm done with him, neither Siniava nor his friends nor his followers will have a hut to live in or a stone to mark where they died. I'm going to destroy him, Ferrault, for what he did to you and the Company. We've already destroyed the army he brought north this year, and that's only the beginning."

"Can you — do all that — my lord?"

"With help. Clart Company rode with us. Vladi sent a cohort of spears. I expect Aliam Halveric to arrive any day to avenge his son. So you take your rest, Ferrault, and tell Gird we'd be glad of a little assistance."

Ferrault smiled faintly. His eyelids sagged as he whispered, "Yes, my lord."

The Duke looked up at Paks, now leaning against the wall. "And you, Paks, know nothing of my plans, is that clear?"

"Yes, my lord."

"You may go. Send my captains to me, please, and see if you can find the Halveric sergeant; I want to speak to him."

"Yes, my lord." Paks tried not to limp as she left the room, but her leg had stiffened again.

"Are you hurt?" came the Duke's voice behind her. She turned.

"No, sir, just bruised."

"Well, see the surgeon after you've given my messages. Don't forget."

"No, sir, I won't." The same squire was standing outside the room; he scowled at her and went to the door as she started for the stairs. Paks ignored him. In the courtyard she asked Vik where the Halveric sergeant might be, and he jerked his head at a group of Halveric soldiers in one corner. Paks knew a few of the faces, but was not sure of the sergeant until he stepped forward.

"I'm Sunnot," he said. "The sergeant. Were you looking for someone?"

"Yes," said Paks. "The Duke asked me to find you; he'd like to speak to you."

Sunnot grimaced. "I'll bet he would. What a mess. Where is he?"

"Up those stairs, third room on the left."

"Oh. He's with the captain, then. How is he?" Paks shook her head. Sunnot sighed. "I thought maybe your surgeons could do something. Well — I hope your Duke's not too angry — "

"He is, but not with you."

"Umm. You're the one who got through, aren't you?"

"Yes." Paks turned away. "I've got to find the captains; go on up."

"I will."

Paks limped into the outer yard, looking for the captains, and found them busy. Pont was in the barracks where the wounded had been moved. Cracolnya was preparing the pyre of enemy bodies, and Dorrin was in the enemy camp, supervising the looting. Sejek was dead, of a crossbow bolt through one eye. When Paks had finally delivered her messages, she struggled back to the fort. Erial, one of Cracolnya's sergeants, was waiting for her at the gate.

"You need to see the surgeon," she said gruffly. "The Duke's called assembly after we eat, and we want all you walking wounded there." Paks did not argue. Between her leg and her ribs, she was not sure she was still walking wounded.

Master Visanior looked up as she came into the barracks. "You again. Though I told you to stay out of trouble." Paks said nothing. How could she fight and stay out of trouble? "Hmmph," the surgeon went on. "Stubborn as a fighter always is. Well, let's see the damage." She fumbled at the thongs fastening her greaves, and he helped draw them off, and the boot beneath. A large, hard, dark-blue swelling throbbed insistently. The surgeon poked it; Paks clenched her jaw. "Not broken, I don't think, but it's taken damage. What was it?"

"Pike butt."

"And you've that broken rib, too. Anything else?"

"No — nothing like that, anyway."

"Good. If this hasn't damaged the bone, it'll hurt for ten days or so, but it'll heal. Try not to hit it again. Stay off it as much as you can — keep your leg up. I'll tell the sergeants. Have you eaten yet?"

"No, sir." Paks had not even thought of food, or mealtimes; now she wondered how late it was.

"Then you'll stay her until you do. Just lie down over there — " he pointed. "Someone will bring you food."

Paks thought of trying to leave, but the surgeon's sharp eye was on her until she stretched out on a pallet. Her leg throbbed. She closed her eyes for a moment. Someone touched her shoulder and she jerked awake. Surely she hadn't been asleep — but it was almost dark. Torches burned in the yard; lamps, in the stable itself. A private in black and white held a steaming bowl and mug toward her. She tried to gather her wits as she reached for them; he grinned and turned away.

The stew was hot and savory. Paks ate hungrily. As she finished, she saw the surgeon making his rounds of the wounded. She had not realized before how many there were. He came to her at last.

"You're to stay down. I told the sergeants."

"But the Duke — "

"Not until morning. He's staying with Captain Ferrault for now. I'll have someone help you clean up; then sleep. We don't want a relapse."

Paks thought she should argue to be allowed up, but she truly did not want to move. She was asleep within the hour.

When the Duke's summons came the next morning, all who could walk or be moved assembled in the inner court. They formed into the original three cohorts, not near filling the space they would have crowded two weeks before. In Paks's cohort, only twenty-two were left; all had been wounded. The other two cohorts mustered one hundred forty survivors of the two hundred eight they had had. Three of the six sergeants and four of the six corporals were dead or dying: all in Paks's cohort, Juris and Kalek of Dorrin's, and Saer of Cracolnya's. And two captains were dead: Ferrault and Sejek. Paks slid her eyes from side to side, meeting other worried glances. How could the Duke go on after such a loss? His words to Ferrault

184

seemed sheer bravado.

The Duke came out, trailed by his squires. He was bareheaded, the chill breeze ruffling his hair and lifting his cloak away from his mail. The captains greeted him. He smiled and nodded, then paced along the ranks, looking at each soldier as if it were any other inspection. At last he walked back to the front of the Company, and turned to face them. The silence had a life of its own.

"Sergeant Vossik."

"Yes, my lord."

"Close the gates, please. We don't want to be disturbed for awhile."

"Yes, my lord." Vossik beckoned to his remaining corporal, and they closed the courtyard gates, then stood in front of them.

The Duke raked the Company with his gaze. "You have all," he began softly, so softly that Paks had to listen closely, "you have all won such glory in these few days that I have no words for it: you still alive, and our friends we have lost. You have defeated an army more than twice your size — not with clever tactics, but with hard and determined fighting. Each one of you has won this victory. I knew, companions, that you were the best company in Aarenis, but even I never knew, until now, how good you were." His gesture evoked the two battles, the fort held against Siniava's men, Paks's journey. He nodded to them, and his voice warmed.

"Now you look from side to side and think how many friends are lost forever. Your ranks are thin. You know that no plunder can repay the losses we have taken. You want to avenge the treachery and the murders and the torture — and you wonder how." A long pause.

"I'll tell you," he went on. "You and I are going to destroy the Honeycat, and his cities, and his allies, and everything else he claims. When we are through, his name will be spoken — not in fear or hatred, as now, but in contempt and ridicule. He thought he could gut this Company. He thought he could scare *us*, chase *us* away — " a low growl from the Company interrupted for a moment. The Duke raised his hand, and silence returned. "No. I know he was wrong. You know it. Nothing scares you, my friends; no southern scum can chase you away. And he has not come close to destroying us — but, companions, we are going to destroy *him*." The Duke rocked back on his heels and surveyed each face again.

"Yes," he said firmly. "We can do that, and we will. You already know other companies are with us: the Clarts, the Halverics, Vladi's spears. More will join us. I pledge you, sword-brethren, that until this vengeance is complete, I will consider no other contract, and all I have will support this campaign." The Duke drew his sword and raised it in salute to the Company. "To their memory," he said. "To vengeance." And the Company growled in response: vengeance.

When he sheathed the sword, he motioned to Dorrin. She came near. He seemed more relaxed. "You are all worthy of praise," he began. "And we will raise the mound both here and on the battlefield near Rotengre for our fallen companions. Still, there are a few who deserve praise before the

185

Company, for deeds uncommon even in this uncommon campaign. Captain — ?"

Dorrin began. "My lord Duke, I have four soldiers to recognize. Simisi Kanasson, who held off three guards from the prisoners, though his horse had been cut down. Sim was wounded then, and again today when fighting the pikes. Kirwania Fastonsdotter, who led her file against the pikes both north of Rotengre and here, and accounted for eight dead by her own sword. Teriam Selfit, who rallied his squad after Kalek was killed, and prevented a breakout. Jostin Semmeth, who accounted for two of the mounted guard, was hit by a crossbow bolt, and went on to slay three bowmen and a pikeman before falling himself."

"Come forward, then," said the Duke. As they stepped out of line, he took from a casket held by one of the squires a ring for each of them. As they went back to their places, the Duke gestured to Cracolnya. He too had several soldiers to honor, and the ceremony proceeded. When the last of Cracolnya's men had stepped back, the Duke turned to Paks's cohort.

"You have no captain to speak for you," he said. "Nor sergeants, nor corporals. Yet your deeds speak aloud without their aid. I cannot pick and choose among you; I will have made for each of you, from these spoils, a ring to commemorate your deeds. But those to whom you owe your lives, who brought me word of your peril: even among such honor, they deserve honor. Three started: Canna Arendts, Saben Kanasson, and Paksenarrion Dorthansdotter. When they were attacked by brigands near Rotengre, only Paks was able to win free. We do not know the fate of the others; be assured that the search will continue until we know. But now — Paksenarrion, come forward."

Paks felt herself blushing, and could hardly tear her eyes from the ground. She limped forward.

"Here is a ring," he said, "that I think best represents your deed. Three strands, for the three who started together, braided into one: the one who succeeded, the message, for returning to the place you began. And imperishable gold, for loyalty." Paks took the gold ring he held out, and stammered her thanks. This was not the way she had dreamed of winning glory, when she was still herding sheep. It felt indecent to be praised so, when her friends were captive or dead.

When the blood quit roaring in her ears, the Duke was still speaking to her cohort. "I want you to stay together," he said. "You are still Arcolin's cohort; you'll remain so. When I bring the recruits down, you'll be brought up to strength. In the meantime, until Valdaire, you'll form a squad in Dorrin's cohort. She will recommend temporary corporals. We will stay here until we raise the mound for our friends, when the Halveric arrives." He turned to the captains. "You may dismiss your cohorts when you're ready."

"My lord." The captains bowed. The Duke gave them all a last grim smile and returned to the keep. In a few minutes, the muster was over, and Paks had limped back to the stables with Vik. She spent the day doing such chores as she could manage without standing. Someone brought a pile of swords for her to

186

clean and sharpen; she found her own, now notched, as she worked.

Sometime in the afternoon, they were startled by a horn cry from the gate tower. Paks stiffened, her hand clenched on the hilt of the sword she was cleaning. The fort erupted into action and noise. A squad of Clarts came boiling out of the inner court, their horses striking sparks off the stone paving. Through the open gate Paks could hear shouts from outside. These ceased, and she heard the drumming of a single galloping horse coming nearer. She glanced around the stableyard, then toward the inner gate. The Duke, armed and mounted, sat his horse in the space between the walls, his squires behind him.

The hoofbeats outside slowed, then halted. The Duke raised his hand. Into Paks's view rode a mailed figure in Halveric green on a lathered chestnut horse. He pushed up his visor; Paks thought she recognized Aliam Halveric. He rode forward until his horse was beside the Duke's and they were face to face. They clasped arms.

"I have much to say to you," said the Duke.

"And I to you," replied the Halveric.

"I fear we are crowded within," said the Duke. "Though I would welcome you and your captains to the keep, we have many wounded and I have brought them all inside the walls."

"We came prepared to camp," said the Halveric. "For a long time, if need be. I am only sorry we missed the battle. I would be glad, however, to accept your generous offer of a roof for myself and my captains. Where would you prefer I place my company?"

Paks thought she saw a smile flicker across the Duke's face. "Old friend," he said, and the Halveric relaxed visibly. "I will answer what you are too courteous to ask. Your men within these walls are at your disposition, to stay or go as you direct. Between us now there can be no question of captives. Your men acted in all ways honorably and bravely. I would suggest you leave the wounded inside the walls. Now — will you see them first, or come with me?"

The Halveric spoke in a softer voice, and Paks could not hear. The Duke nodded, and beckoned a squire forward. The Halveric spoke to him, and he rode out the gate. The other squires dismounted, one taking all the horses, and the other holding the reins for the Duke and the Halveric to dismount. The two men stood talking while the horses were led away. In a short time Sunnot, the Halveric sergeant, came from the inner court and went down on one knee before the Halveric, who raised him up at once. Some command was given; Sunnot bowed slightly and turned away, leading the Halveric toward the barracks with the worst wounded. He was smiling, clearly relieved to have his own commander there at last.

When the great burial mound was finished, all the companies assembled there for a final leave-taking. The names of the fallen were called aloud one last time. Vladi's spearmen sang "The Dance of Frostbreath" and tossed their spears over the mound. The Clarts performed a wild dance mimicking combat on horseback; the thunder of hooves, one of them had explained to Paks, would carry their fallen comrades to the endless fields of the afterworld, where horses never tire, nor riders fall. Aliam Halveric and his captains sang to his harper's playing, the old "Fair Were the Towers Whose Stones Lie Scattered" that Paks had heard even in Three Firs — but instead of the name of the Prince and his nobles, they sang the names of the Halveric dead. Then the Duke signalled his piper, and a tune Paks had never heard before seemed to drag all the sorrow and anger out of her heart with its own bitterness. It was the "Ar hi Tammarion," the lament written for the death of the Duke's lady by the half-elven harper at the Court of Tsaia, and not since then played openly. Paks did not know the history of the song, but felt its power, as the rough wind dried tears she had shed without knowing it.

Their journey back to Rotengre passed quickly and uneventfully; five days after leaving the north they were back in position. The horses they had ridden had to be returned; most had been borrowed from one or another militia. Paks led half a dozen back to the horselines of Sorellin. Coming back, she was hailed by a burly sergeant. His voice was vaguely familiar.

"Hey! Duke's sword! Aren't you the one who came across the lines that night?"

Paks looked at him, not sure of his face. "Yes. Why?"

"By the sword, you look so much better I'd not have known you but for your size and yellow hair. Why? Because we've heard about you — and I'm sorry we gave you such trouble that night."

Paks thought back to that black wet night and shivered, though it was daylight. "That's all right."

He sucked a tooth for a moment. "Well — I came close enough to tossing you in our guard cell. It was a lesson to me. Anyway, I'm glad you survived it all. I'm Sim, by the way — Sim Plarrist — and I'd be glad to stand you a tankard of ale — "

Paks shook her head. "Not until the city yields. May it be short — but until then we're to stay strictly with our Company. But thank you."

"No hard feelings, then?"

"No." He waved her on, and Paks threaded her way to her own lines in the fading light. There, in another echo of the earlier event, was Barra on guard.

"Paks, the Duke wants to see you."

"Do you know what about?" Her stomach clenched, expecting bad news.

"I think he's heard about Saben and Canna."

"Bad?"

Barra shrugged. "I don't know anything. When I asked, I was told to mind my own business and see you got the Duke's message. But if it was good news, I think we'd know."

"I suppose." Tears stung her eyes, and Barra's face seemed to waver

188

before her. Barra squeezed her arm, and Paks went on to the Duke's tent.

The lamps inside were already lit, and a brazier warmed the room. The Duke moved to his work table; Paks glanced at it, and saw on its uncluttered surface a little red stone horse strung on a thong, and a Girdish medallion on a chain. She knew them at once, and felt the blood drain from her face.

"You recognize them." Paks looked up to meet the Duke's steady gaze. She nodded. "Paks, I'm sorry. I had hoped they would be found sooner. The surgeon says Saben had taken a hard blow to the head, and probably never woke up. He died soon after they were found. Canna was not badly wounded in the fight, but when the brigands realized their hideout had been found, they tried to kill all their prisoners before they fled. Though she was still alive when the militia got in, she died several days later, here in camp. She knew you had made it, and that we'd defeated Siniava's army on the road and gone on north. The surgeon said she wanted you to have her medallion, and wanted you to know you did the right thing. She was glad you made it through; he said she died satisfied." The Duke paused. Paks was trying to blink back tears, but she could feel them trickling down her face. "Paks, are you a Girdsman?"

"No, sir."

"Hmm. Girdsmen usually want their holy symbol returned to their home grange, with an account of their deeds. I wonder why Canna wanted you to have it, if you aren't Girdish."

Paks shook her head, unable to think why or answer. She had hoped so that they would be found alive, unlikely as it had been. Even now she could scarcely believe she would never see Saben again.

"Paks — you were Saben's closest friend, as far as I know. Did he ever say what he wanted done with his things?"

Paks tried to remember. "No — sir. He had family, that he sent things to. But he — he — "

"He didn't make plans. I see. We'll be sending them word, and his pay, of course, and — do you think they'll want his sword, or were they against his choice?"

"No, my lord; they favored it. He had five brothers at home, and six sisters. They were proud of him, he said; they'd be glad of the sword."

"And this pendant — was that from his family?"

"No — my lord. It was — was — my gift, sir. It — it was a joke between us."

"Then you should take it, for his memory, as well as Canna's medallion." The Duke scooped them up from his table and held them out. Paks stared at him helplessly.

"Sir, I — I cannot — "

"You must take Canna's, at least; she wanted it so. And I think your friend Saben would be happy to know you have the other."

Paks took them from his hand, and as her hand closed around them the reality of her loss stabbed her like a sword. She fumbled at the flap of her belt-pouch and pushed them in.

"Here," said the Duke; when she looked up, he was offering a cup of wine. "Drink this. When you are calmer, you may go; I am joining the Halveric for dinner." Paks took the cup, and the Duke caught up a fur-edged cloak from its hook and went out. The wine was sweet, and eased the roughness of her throat, but she could not finish it. After wiping her face on her sleeve, she returned to her own cohort. Vik knew already, she saw, and he told her that the Duke had released word as soon as he had told her himself.

"We miss them too," said Vik fiercely, hugging her again. "But you, Paks — "

"We were so close," she whispered, as tears ran down her face. "Only a few more miles, and they — " She could not go on. Arñe got up and put an arm around her shoulders; they all sat together a long time in silence.

Chapter Twenty

The next day the regular siegework began again. The Halverics moved in beside Duke Phelan's Company, slightly narrowing the Sorellin front. This suited Sorellin, but drew catcalls from the battlements; these ceased after four men fell to the Phelani bowmen. Weapons and armor taken from the Honeycat's force were divided among the different companies; Paks had the chance to try a crossbow (at which she nearly cut off her thumb) and a short curved blade much like the one Saben had taken.

Day by day she grew to realize how much she had leaned on Canna and Saben — Saben especially. She found herself looking for his cheerful face in the meal lines, waiting for his comment when she came off watch — missing, increasingly, that steady pressure of goodwill she had always felt at her side. They had been together from the beginning. When she went to the jacks, she remembered the trench they had dug together her first night as a recruit — and cried again, knowing it was silly and ridiculous, but helpless to hold back the tears. It was impossible that he was gone, and gone forever. She had thought of her own death, but never of his — now she could think of nothing else.

She could not talk about it to anyone. She knew that Vik and Arñe watched her, and almost hated them for it. She heard a Halveric ask Barra if she and Saben had been lovers, and did not know which was worse, the question or Barra's scornful negative. She and Saben had shared everything but that: the early hopes and fears, the hours of work, the laughter, that final week of danger. Everything but love and death. For the first time, she wondered what it would have been like to bed him. It was something he had always wanted, and now there was no chance. But if she had — if it hurt more, to lose a lover — she shook her head, and went doggedly on with work she hardly noticed. Better not. She had never wanted to, and surely it would be worse to lose a lover. It was bad enough now.

For awhile she felt cool and remote, as if she were watching herself from a hilltop. Never care, came a whisper in her mind. Never care, never fear. But in the firelight that night, the concern in Vik's eyes and Arñe's roused a sudden rush of caring for them. With it came the pain again, but she felt it as a good pain: as wrenching as the surgeon scouring a wound, but necessary. Fear came, too: fear for them. She looked at her own hands, broad and strong, skilled — she could still protect, with those hands. She said nothing,

191

and the tears came again, but somewhere inside a tightness eased.

The city had been silent now for more than a week. No more taunts over the wall, no pots of hot oil, no stones. Heads showed above the battlements occasionally, and the gates were barred, but the enthusiasm of the defenders had gone. Paks wondered if they were going to surrender.

Late one afternoon, a trio of Sorellin militia rode into the siege lines from the north; in minutes messengers came to the Duke. Soon everyone knew that they had found a tunnel from the brigands' hideout, where Canna and Saben had been found, into Rotengre. A small group of Rotengren soldiers had come out in their midst; now Sorellin controlled the forest end of the passage.

"That must be how the Honeycat meant to relieve the siege," said Vik.

"And why he wanted live prisoners," said Paks. "Once he had them in the city — "

"Yes. Ugh. I wonder where the Rotengre end is. If only we could use it."

"With an attack on the walls at the same time. Yes — or if they're all trying to escape that way, we could just sit there and take them as they come."

"I'd rather go in," Arñe looked eager.

Paks grinned. "So would I. I never heard of a tunnel that long; I wonder who dug it and when."

"The reputation this city's got," said Vik, "it may have been there since the walls were built. It would explain a lot of things about Rotengre."

As dusk fell, the entire camp bubbled with speculation. They mustered after supper, and the Duke explained their plans. The Phelani would assault the wall, while the Halverics tried their ram on the north gate. Vladi had taken a couple of spear cohorts and joined the Sorellin militia for an assault through the tunnel. The remaining Sorellin militia would attack with their catapult and ladder teams. Cracolnya's cohort would lead the Phelani assault, followed by Dorrin's. These instructions were followed by a breathless wait in the dark.

Suddenly the Halveric's ram battered at the north gate, and an outcry came from the gate tower above. Torches flared along the walls. As heads showed, the Duke's bowmen let fly. Returning flights came out of the darkness to bristle in rampart and tent. Paks heard not only the regular crash of the battering ram, but the occasional stunning crack of the Sorellin catapult's stone balls slamming into the wall itself. Horn calls and shouts from inside the city redoubled, loudest from the gate tower. Then Paks heard more distant signals, from the south side. She realized that the south gate, too, must be under attack.

Now, with others of Dorrin's cohort, she stood at the base of the ladders as the specialists of the mixed cohort led the climbing teams up. These made it to the top before being seen, and secured the ladders as the first fighting teams came up. Paks, below, heard the scream of the Rotengre guard who first saw them, then a body slammed into the ground nearby. Those on the ladder surged upward. As soon as they could get footspace on the rungs, others followed.

"Keep your shields *up*," yelled Captain Pont. "Cover your heads until you're up."

Paks found the ladder harder than she remembered, as she tried to balance with her shield arched over her. By the time she reached the top, the Duke's men formed two lines across the wall, protecting access for those still climbing. She was surprised to see green-clad Halverics coming off the ladders behind her companions, but had no time to think about it. She jogged up to join the line moving toward the gate tower.

Facing them were two lines of Rotengre guards in blue, and more ran from the direction of the gate tower. The Phelani advanced; the Rotengre lines retreated, even before making contact. When they pursued and engaged, the enemy still retreated, though their swordwork was excellent.

"Keep pressing 'em!" yelled Vossik. "They'll break. Keep at 'em." Even as he spoke, those on the inside of the wall tried to slip down a stair to the city below. Bowstrings twanged behind Paks; at least two fell from the stairs. Vossik told a party to hold the stairs against any assault.

Now they were close to the gate tower; the rear ranks of defenders turned and raced for the tower doors as a heavy fire of arrows struck the Duke's men from an upper level. Several fell. Paks and the others threw up their shields and charged, trying to make the tower door before it was slammed against them. The remaining defenders went down under the charge; Paks raced through a gap to hit the closing door with all her strength. Instantly several of her companions were there to help, and together they forced the door open, battling past the defenders. More of the Duke's men poured into the opening.

They had entered a small chamber that ran along the west side of the gate tower; two doors opened into a larger room where Paks caught a glimpse of the gate machinery before the doors slammed.

"We'll need to get those doors down," said Vossik. He had come limping in after the others, having taken a crossbow bolt in the leg. "And those plaguey bowmen are somewhere overhead, too." They looked around, but saw no access to the upper level. They could feel the concussion when the Halveric ram hit the gates.

"How about that door we just took?" asked Vik.

"Good," said Vossik. "Take it apart and see if it won't make us some rams." With four stout lengths of oak from the first door, they began smashing at the inner doors, a squad for each. All at once one of them splintered between the bars that held it, and they smashed the rest of the wood free and poured through. The expected line of crossbowmen met them; the first flight bristled in their shields. Before the bowmen could reload, the Duke's men were on them, and they fell in a welter of blood that made the floor slippery. The remaining defenders, some two score, had no chance. As they darted toward the stair that led to ground level, the attackers cut them down. Vossik stopped them from following the few survivors downstairs.

"Wait. We need to get these gates open."

"Here, sir." It was a mixed-cohort man. "Just let me get to those pulleys."

"Need any help?"

"Just a moment. Yes — here. Two of you do this — " he demonstrated. "And two over here, on this one." They pushed on the windlass spokes; chains tightened and slid through great pulleys above and below. Beneath them, the heavy gate creaked open; they heard wild cheers from the Halverics. Meanwhile someone had identified the portcullis mechanism, and several were at work to raise the massive grate. Paks looked out the window that looked into the city. She could see torches in the street below and gleams of steel.

"Paks." It was Artfiel, one of the new corporals Dorrin had named. She turned. "Take a squad and make sure the gate tower is secure on the east. I expect they've all fled into the city, but I'd hate to be surprised."

Paks collected a tensquad and found a long narrow room on the east side: twin to the one they'd broken into on the west, except that here a narrow ladder led through a hole in the ceiling to the higher level. One of the bowmen scampered up this, to report no enemy above, and no one visible on the wall. Paks went back to Artfiel and he assigned a squad of archers to keep watch from the upper level; she took her own squad out onto the east wall.

From the streets below rose a confused clamor, and the deep chant of the Halveric foot. Paks found a stair going down, and positioned her squad to guard it. They could see very little, but she was not tempted to light a torch. They peered into darkness, with its confusing patches of wavering torchlight, and tried to interpret the noise.

Coming out from under the gate tower now were mounted troops, the horses' hooves ringing on stone, and behind that the Sorellin foot. Far across the city Paks saw a bright blur of flame atop a tower. Now they heard shrieks from below, and again the clash and clang of weapons. Paks yearned to go down the stair and be part of it, but she knew Artfiel was right: a desperate or cunning enemy might try to climb the wall and retake the gate tower — or escape.

Gradually the noise receded toward the center of the city. There it intensified, a harsh uneven roar punctuated by occasional high-pitched outbursts. It was cold on the wall. Paks huddled into her cloak, cursing the orders that kept her idle and cold when a good fight raged. The tower door opened. Paks glanced toward it to see a tall figure stepping out on the wall. She stood, stamping her feet, as the Duke came up.

"Any trouble?"

"No, my lord."

"Good. Foss Council militia are going to take over the wall. Bring your squad — I daresay you'd like to be in at the finish."

"Yes, my lord."

"Very well. We'll go back through the tower." The Duke led them, nodding at the Foss Council captain as they passed into the tower. At the foot of the stairs, a squire held the Duke's charger; the others who had been in the tower bunched nearby. He mounted and rode slowly up the wide street toward the battle. Paks and her squad marched on his left; two squires rode in front with torches. The street was ominously silent. Paks feared that hidden archers might shoot the Duke, but nothing happened.

As they came to the center of the city, they could see more torchlight and fires set against the walls of the old keep. This keep, the Duke had said, formed an interior defense completely separate from the outer walls. The Halveric ram battered this inner gate. Defenders crowded the wall. Fire arrows flew in both directions. Something inside the keep was burning; heavy smoke blew away on the north wind.

They had just reached the rear of the attacking lines when shrill screams broke out inside, and the men on the wall turned to look. At once the attackers flung up ladders and swarmed up the wall. Paks, waiting beside the Duke, found herself dancing from foot to foot. The gates opened, and the ram crew surged forward, followed by everyone who could cram into that narrow space. The Duke rode on, forcing a passage with his horse; Paks shoved her way alongside.

Within the gates all was confusion. Several small buildings were on fire, lighting the court with dancing yellow that glinted off weapons and armor. It was hard to tell defenders from attackers, Rotengre blue from Halveric green or Foss Council gray. Paks started yelling the Phelani battle-cry after nearly being spitted by one of Vladi's spearmen.

The fight raged until every defender lay dead in the court or passages of the keep. Even then the noise and confusion continued, for the attackers turned to plunder. Paks had never seen anything like this, or imagined it. She expected the captains to call them all to order, but instead they urged on their troops or ignored them.

Fights broke out between militia and mercenaries over bales of silk, caskets of jewels, kegs of wine and ale — only then did the officers step in to restore peace. At first, Paks stayed out of the way, carrying water to some of the Duke's wounded until wagons came to take them back to camp. But when Vossik found her standing in an angle of the inner wall, he took her arm and led her upstairs.

"This is where we make our stakes," he said laughing. "Don't worry — the Duke said we could sack the keep. Try not to get in fights, is all. Look — here's a good place to start." He shoved open the door of a small room that had been a study. Scrolls littered the floor around an overturned desk, its drawers scattered. "These things always have secret compartments," said Vossik. "And militia are hasty. Watch — " He wrenched a leg off a chair and smashed the desk apart. A handful of loose jewels bounced across the floor. "That's what I meant," he said. "Go on. Take 'em."

Paks scooped up the little chips of blue, red, and yellow: the first jewels she had ever held. Vossik looked at them critically.

"I'll take this — " he picked out a red one and a blue one, "as my share for showing you how. Get busy now, or these damned lazy militia will get all the good loot." He left Paks alone in the room. She put the stones in her

195

pouch, and looked at the smashed desk. Was there another compartment? She picked up the chair leg.

By dawn, Paks had prowled through most of the rooms in the keep. Her pouch bulged with coins and jewels. She had a strip of embroidered silk wrapped around her neck, and a jewel-hilted dagger thrust into one boot. She could not bring herself to destroy furniture, so most of her finds were bits and pieces that had rolled out of sight of earlier plunderers. Now she headed downstairs, hoping to find something to eat. Along the way she passed drunken, sleeping fighters snoring beside the dead. Paks wrinkled her nose at the stench of blood, sour wine, vomit, and smoke. In the court-yard, a circle of soldiers were cooking over the remnants of a burning shed. Every one seemed to be draped in stolen finery: velvet and fur cloaks, bits of lace and silk that might have been shawls, gold and silver chains and bracelets. Paks looked around for someone she knew. These were all militiamen from Sorellin and Vonja.

"Where's Duke Phelan's Company?" she asked one of them.

His mouth was full of sausage, but he pointed toward the keep gates. Paks made her way out into the streets.

"There you are," said Vik. He had a green velvet cap with a feather atop his helmet. "Have you had breakfast yet?"

"No." Paks yawned. "Have you? I wish I could sleep."

"Here — " Vik handed her a roll and a hunk of cheese. "I tried some of the food from their kitchen, but this is better. What'd you find in there — anything good?"

Paks nodded, her mouth full of bread.

"We're supposed to clear the northwest quadrant today, but what we find goes to the common store, worse luck." Vic shook his head, then grinned. "Though I've as much as I can carry now."

Paks swallowed noisily. "I've got some jewels, and money, and this — " She indicated the strip of silk. "Did you see those militia?"

"Furs and things? Yes — well, they have baggage wagons to go home in. How do you like my new hat?"

"Ummm." Paks thought it was as silly as a lace shawl, but didn't want to say so.

"It'll travel well, rolled up," he said seriously. "Except for the feather, and any barnyard cock will give me a new one."

"Yes — well — it's nice, Vik." Paks yawned again and ate the cheese. She emptied her water flask. A haze of smoke hung over the city; the wind had dropped. "When do we start — ?"

"When the captain gets back. Gah — I'm sleepy too." Vik settled against the wall and put his head on his knees. After a moment Paks squatted beside him. She looked around. Maybe a third of the Company was visible along this stretch of wall; most slumped against it or each other, and looked asleep. Some were chatting quietly. Bundles wrapped in a variety of unlikely things — cur-tains, bed linens — lay among them. Paks had not thought of that.

She did not realize she'd fallen asleep until Captain Dorrin's voice woke

196

her. She yawned again as she pushed herself up. She was stiff and cold; others looked worse than she felt. She was glad she hadn't been drinking all that ale and wine.

Unlike the chaos of the night before, the day's sack was systematic and careful. Paks worked with a squad of ten, assigned to go through buildings along one street. They began with a house, smashing its locked door, and opening every door of every room from cellar to garret. When they knew what it contained, they reported to a sergeant, who told them what to load in which order.

Paks carried out one armful after another. Bed linens, cook pots, clothes from clothes presses, a roll of fine wool from a room with a loom in it. Her companions brought the loom, a sackful of scrolls, dishes and spoons, shoes and boots and hats, a patterned carpet, a trunkful of uncut velvet — everything they could move. As the rooms emptied, they thumped the walls, listening for any sign of a secret hideaway. Paks felt strange, rummaging around in someone else's clothespress, carrying away a stranger's empty garments.

In a small room under the eaves, Paks found a string of tiny bells under the short bed; when she shook them, they gave a faint musical chime. A child's toy. She looked out the window, across the street, and saw a bolt of blue cloth unwinding as it fell. Erial shouted from below, angry. Paks turned away. She felt a vague pain in her head, and wondered if it came from the smoke still hazing the city.

Down in the cellar someone found a hollow-sounding panel and smashed it. Behind was a row of wine-casks, and a little iron-bound coffer. With much grunting and heaving they got these up the stairs. Erial ducked into the house to check it and came out nodding. They passed to the next building, and the next. Not all were as rich as the first, but by midday they had piled two wagons full of loot. Other companies were clearing their assigned sections, and wagons were lined up coming and going from the different camps.

All afternoon the work went on. Houses, shops, and warehouses, with a few craftshops. Paks found a secret passage in one shop, following it to a vault full of fancy leathers and fabrics. In the next house along, Paks heard a thin wail behind a wall on the third floor. For a moment she thought of saying nothing about it, but her squad leader had heard it too. Behind the false wall a thin girl of perhaps fourteen clung to an infant less than two months old; she wore only a rough shift, and an iron ring circled her neck. Her eyes were blank with fear.

"Just a slave," said Aris, the squad leader, in disgust. "Come on out, we won't hurt you." The girl shivered, but did not move. "Come on." He reached for her arm, and the girl threw herself at Paks, holding up the baby, who began to cry. Aris gave Paks a wry grin. "Your problem now, Paks. Take her to the captain." He turned away. Paks reached gingerly toward the baby, and the girl let go so fast that Paks almost dropped the child. It screamed louder, and the girl cried out in a strange language and fell to her knees.

"It's all right," said Paks, convinced that it wasn't. "I won't hurt your baby. Here, you take — " she tried to hand the baby back, but the girl was kneeling, and would not look up until Paks touched her shoulder. Even then, she would not stand, and Paks had to fold the girl's arms around the child before she would take it. "Now come," said Paks softly, and tugged her shoulder; the girl started crying. "Look," said Paks, "I won't hurt you or your baby, but you must come." The girl kept crying, and made no move to reply. Paks straightened to ease a cramp in her back, and glanced around. By just so much the crossbow bolt missed her as it passed over the kneeling slave to stick quivering in the wall. A crack showed in the back of the recess. Paks stared a split second as it widened, then yelled as she swept out her sword and charged.

Behind her she heard the girl shriek, and the clatter of boots as her squad came to her aid. Her sword smashed the half-open panel, and she grabbed the crossbow lefthanded, jerking it away from the dark-robed man who stood in a second recess. She freed her sword from the shattered panel as he reached to his belt for his dagger. Huddled beside him was a woman in a silk gown, and behind were a youth and a girl, both richly dressed.

"Come out of there," said Paks grimly. The man shook his head, and said something she could not make out. He had the dagger out, and held it as if he knew how to fight. Paks did not like the cramped space; she started to step back. The man spoke again, and a blow from behind knocked her off balance as a thin arm crooked around her neck. At once the man struck. Paks deflected the blow with her sword, feeling a sting on her knuckles, as the four of them rushed her. She heard a shout from behind, then a scream. The weight fell from her back; the arm no longer choked her. She half stumbled backwards; two of her squad were beside her, swords drawn.

"What happened?" asked Aris.

"Crossbow, from a concealed panel behind the first recess," said Paks, gasping a little. She did not take her eyes from the man in front of her. "Just missed me, while I was trying to get that slave to move. I saw the opening, and found those behind it. She jumped me from behind — I think he told her to, but I don't know the language — and they all tried to spit me."

"Damned northern war crows!" the man burst out. "May you all die strung from the walls like the carrion you are."

"Come out, or I'll call pikes," said Aris calmly. The man muttered in the unknown tongue. "Now," said Aris. The man stood still, as if considering, and the girl behind him began to cry. For some reason this made Paks angry.

"Stop that noise," she said roughly, and the girl looked at her and was still, tears still running down her face. The man glared at Paks.

"I should have killed you. Two times, you great cow, and you still live." He spat at Paks, but it fell short. She felt her companions stiffen, and Aris's voice roughened.

"Drop that knife and come out, or we'll kill you all."

The man looked at the knife in his hand, then reversed it and threw it spinning at Paks's chest. She jerked her shoulder aside, and it bounced off her corselet, but again the four rushed forward. She thrust her sword into the man's robe. His weight bore her back; when she tried to step back, she tripped over the slave's body. The silk-clad woman had pulled out a dagger to slash at the soldier before her; she too was cut down. The youth had a short sword, which he had held hidden behind the man, and fought the soldier on Paks's left with surprising skill. The girl, no longer crying, had a slim stiletto with which she attacked the soldier fighting the boy. Paks grabbed her arm, and the girl struck at her face. Almost in reflex, Paks thrust in her sword, and the girl folded over with a cry. At the same time, the soldier got past the youth's guard and sank his sword into him. The boy's weapon fell with a clatter. Paks took a breath and looked around. Aris met her eyes.

"That was a new one. Sorry, Paks; I didn't know — "

Paks shook her head. "I shouldn't have gone between them, not after the crossbow. Is the slave — ?"

"Dead. Sim stuck her when she was choking you."

"It wasn't her fault." Paks looked for the baby, but it too was dead, having caught a stray bladestroke. No one knew whose, and no one cared to guess. They wiped their blades on the man's robes, and examined the inner recess, but found nothing more.

"They'll have something somewhere," said Aris. "Let's check 'em over." The man was dead, but the woman and the two younger ones were still barely alive. At Aris's nod, the other soldiers gave each the death-stroke, and began to search the bodies. Paks, suddenly shaky about the knees, leaned on the wall. She could not get out of her mind the frightened face of the slave, kneeling at her feet. Her knuckles burned; she looked at the shallow cut — from the man's dagger, she supposed. She glanced at the window. Nearly dark, now — no, that can't be right — we couldn't see in here — She realized she was sliding down the wall.

"Paks. Paks, what's wrong?" Aris had her arm. She felt very strange.

"I think this dagger's poisoned," said someone from a distance, and someone else added, "So's this sword, if the stain on the blade means anything."

"Paks — did that dagger cut you?" Aris seemed to be yelling very softly. She held up her hand, and felt it taken and turned. Someone cursed; boots clattered over the floor and into the passage. Paks opened her eyes again, and found that everything seemed a strange shade of green. She blinked, tasting something vile, and tried to think what had happened. Someone pushed the edge of a flask against her lips and said, "Swallow." She did. For an instant or so she thought a whirling wind was loose inside her, and then her vision cleared. Sim held the daggers, stiletto, and sword; Captain Dorrin peered at their blades.

"This sticky orange stuff is almost certainly some kind of poison — either weak or slow-acting, to judge by its effect on Paks. Put these aside, carefully, and we'll let the surgeons see them." Dorrin glanced at Paks. "You better?" When Paks nodded, her face relaxed, and she offered a hand up. "You keep pushing your luck, Paks, and you won't have any left."

"Sorry — Captain." Paks still felt remote, but that sensation cleared quickly. The others had found several small pouches in the dead family's clothes, and the man's belt had a long packet sewn in, which bulged suggestively. Under his outer robes he wore a massive silver chain with a curious medallion. As Kir slid it out, the captain swore. Paks peered at it, wondering what was wrong. As big as a man's palm, it looked like a silver spider, legs outstretched on a web.

"Drop that," said Dorrin harshly, as Kir started to touch the medallion itself. Startled, he obeyed. The captain drew her sword and slipped it beneath the chain. The chain and medallion let off a pale green glow and slithered away from the sword point, which was also glowing. "By all the gods and Falk's oath," said Dorrin. "It's a real one."

"Isn't that the — the Webmistress's sign?" asked Sim nervously.

"Yes. Don't any of you touch it. It's the right size for one of her priest's symbols, and they're dangerous." Dorrin touched the point of her sword to the medallion. Green light flared upward, and a rotten stench filled the room. The sword's glow was clearly visible now, blue and steady against the pulsing green. Dorrin pulled the sword back, and both glows faded. "Well, that's that. We can hardly leave it there. We need a cleric to counter it. Paks —" Paks jerked her eyes away from the medallion: was it moving slowly? The captain nodded when their eyes met. "Go find the Duke, and tell him we need a cleric. Don't tell anyone else. Wait — do you have Canna's Girdish medallion?"

"Yes, Captain."

"You're wearing it?"

"Yes, Captain. Isn't that all right — ?"

Dorrin gave her a long look. "Seeing it probably saved your life, I would say it's all right. It's well known St. Gird has no love for Achrya Webmistress. But let's see — take it out."

Paks fished the medallion out of her tunic. Dorrin took it and let the chain slip through her fingers until it hung above the silver spider on the floor. Again the green glow rose from the spider, but the crescent above did not change. Dorrin handed it back to Paks.

"Yours is the weaker one, or at least it doesn't reveal any power. Still, you're alive and he isn't." She nudged the dead man with her boot. "Go on — find the Duke. And the rest of you search these bodies carefully. We might find more mischief."

Paks tucked Canna's medallion back into her tunic as she jogged down the stairs. By the time she had found the Duke, and carried his message to a tall man in black armor in Vladi's camp, a Blademaster of Tir, it was dark. She was both eager and afraid to see what he would do, but Dorrin met her on the stairs and sent her back to camp.

"It's priestwork now, and none of ours," she said firmly. "We've much to do tomorrow, and much to guard tonight. You're on second watch; get some food into you and rest before you're called."

The next day brought no such excitements, but more work, as they cleared the rest of their sector. Paks could not begin to guess how many bales of cloth, rolls of carpet, boxes, bags, and trunks of moveable treasure, copper, bronze, and iron pots, dresses, gowns, robes, tunics, shirts, shoes, boots, buckles, combs, scrolls, daggers, swords, shields, bows, bowstrings, arrows, war hammers and wood hammers, battle axes and felling axes, reels of yarn and fine thread, needles, knives, forks, spoons of wood and pewter and silver and gold, figurines carved of wood and ivory and stone, harps and horns and pipes of all sizes they had taken and packed in wagons. The very thought of all those things made her tired. What could people use it all for? A well-stocked larder or armory made sense, but not all the rest. In one house she had seen shelves of little carvings: horses, men, women, fish, leaves of different shapes, birds — what could anyone do with those but look at them? No one worshipped that many gods. She had run her hands over fine silks and velvets, furs of all colors, and handled lace so fine she feared it would tear in her fingers. And these were beautiful. But — Paks thought again of the militia around the bonfire in their stolen finery — they weren't for her. Not now.

More to her mind was the captain's sword and its blue glow. She wanted to ask about it, but she was with a different squad, and she did not know Dorrin's people that well anyway. Had she imagined it? Could it be a magical weapon, like those of old tales and songs? Paks remembered Dorrin's scars — those any soldier her age might carry — and thought not. Yet she worried the question, in the back of her mind. She had heard of the Web-mistress, Achrya, though around Three Firs they called her Dark Tangler, or the Dark One. But she had never seen any evidence that Achrya was real until that spider medallion reacted to Dorrin's sword. She had thought of Achrya as another name out of old stories — something in her grandfather's time, perhaps, when orcs attacked Three Firs — not a present danger. Now she had the uneasy feeling that she might not know as much as she'd thought. She pushed that aside and asked her new squad leader about the plunder they were packing.

"What do we — what does the Duke — do with chairs and tables and old clothes? The gold I can understand, but — "

"He sells 'em; either down here, or back north. There's a good market for good things — even partly worn things. You'll see."

They built another mound north of the city, and with the Halverics held another memorial celebration to honor those who had died as Siniava's prisoners or in taking Rotengre. The Guild League cities each sent a representative, but their militias stayed away; Paks was glad. After that, the heavily laden wagons of plunder followed the Company north and west to Valdaire along the Guild League route. It was later than usual, already winter, as Aarenis knew winter: cold and unpleasant enough. Their elation at breaking Rotengre drained away the closer they came to their winter quarters, for every day on the road they marched with the ghosts of the slain.

201

Chapter Twenty-one

When they reached Valdaire, Arcolin took the remnant of his cohort and assigned them the same quarters as the year before. Paks almost wished he had left them with the others; alone in a barracks meant for a hundred or more, they were achingly aware of their losses. Even the winter routine of training and work could not distract them. Every night Paks faced the rows of empty bunks, and looked aside to meet eyes as unhappy as her own. They had been told the Duke would replace the missing — he had already ridden north — but this was no comfort. Who could replace Donag? Or Bosk? She would not let herself think of Saben and Canna. Day by day she and the others grew even more silent and grim.

Then Arcolin announced a feast for them at *The White Dragon*. This was no ordinary dinner; though they came unwillingly, the splendor Arcolin had ordered had its effect. The table was loaded with roast stuffed fowl, a great crown roast with candied fruit for jewels on the crown, roast suckling pig in a nest of mushrooms, a pastry construction of the city of Rotengre, with little figures assaulting the walls and gate, and colored sugar flames rising from the roofs. Dishes Paks had never seen before: steamed grain with bits of mushroom, nuts, and spices in it, vegetables stuffed with cheese or meat or another vegetable or nuts. Thick soups and thin soups, sliced cheeses in every shade from white to deep orange, sweet cakes and pies of every kind. They ate until they were full, and over full, washing it down with their choice of wines and ales. Paks drank more than she ever had, and felt, for the first time since seeing Siniava's army come out of the trees, truly relaxed.

At the end of the meal, when the food was cleared away, and the servants had left, Arcolin passed around the rings which the Duke had made for them. Paks looked at hers before slipping it on her finger: a plain gold band with a tiny foxhead stamped on the outer surface, and the word "Dwarfwatch" and a rune that Arcolin told them stood for loyalty engraved on the inside. She ran her thumb lightly over the foxhead, and glanced aside to see Arñe doing the same thing.

Arcolin waited for them all to look up before speaking. "I wish," he said quietly, "that I had been with you, to fight beside you. Not that you could have done better. Tir knows what I — what everyone — thinks of your fighting. But you have shared something now, bitter as it is, that will bind you heart to heart for the rest of your lives." He stopped and looked around, gathering every eye that had dropped, before going on. "Very shortly," he said, "the new recruits will be down; we'll be back to size, or near it. You know, and I know, that they cannot take the place of those we have lost — but they can help avenge our friends. The Duke has sworn vengeance on Siniava. So has the Halveric. Let us, then, swear our own oath, for the memory of our friends and the destruction of our enemies." He read out again the names of those who had died; they gave a great shout after each. Paks was crying; she saw tears glisten on most faces. Hand felt for hand around the table. Then Arcolin said, "Death to the Honeycat!" and the responsive roar shook the room. Paks felt a surge of rage, felt the anger in the others that made them one. She wished they could march at once.

But some weeks passed before the new recruits arrived. After the banquet, Paks felt more at ease; she and the others began looking forward to the new campaign almost as much as backward to the past one. They drilled with every weapon they had or had captured. Paks spent more time with the longsword. She enjoyed the great advantage her height and reach gave her with the longer weapon. But not all her time was spent in practice.

That winter the Vale of Valdaire seemed even fuller than usual of wintering troops. Paks met more of the Golden Company, commanded by Aesil M'dierra, a dark hawk-faced woman from the west. She saw Kalek Minderisnir, a scarfaced, bandy-legged little man who commanded the Blue Riders, and Sobanai Company, whose dapper commander looked, to Paks, too dressy to be a good fighter. The talk was of war: battles and encounters, siege and assault, tactics for polearms and blades. It was not long before they all knew of Paks's journey. The Guild League militia had the tale from Sorellin, and the Halverics had not failed to spread it either. She found she was accepted by graying veterans as well as by eager young warriors her own age. And ever and ever again the talk turned to the Honeycat, and what could be done against him. Golden Company had fought him more than once; they argued fiercely with the Halverics about strategy. Paks listened carefully, trying to picture the coastal cities fair on their cliffs, and the grim forest where Alured the Black took toll of every passerby.

At last a runner brought them warning, and in an hour or so they saw a column approaching, with the Duke's banner flying ahead. Paks watched the marchers critically. Had it been only two years since she had come that way? Had she looked so young? She saw the whites of the recruits' eyes as they glanced from side to side. They were hardly more than children, she thought — then spotted a gray-headed man, and another, in the midst. Stammel led the second unit, and Devlin was behind him. The column halted. Paks tensed, waiting.

When Arcolin yelled, the Company formed, falling into place with the startling speed that never failed to impress the newcomers. Paks suppressed a grin, remembering her own reaction and seeing its mirror on the recruits' faces. The Duke rode forward and looked them over. He turned to Arcolin.

"Well, they look fit enough. Are they ready?"

"They'd march today, my lord," said Arcolin.

The Duke smiled. "Not quite today, Captains. Captain Valichi will break the column for you."

"Yes, my lord." The Duke rode away, and Valichi dismounted, coming to stand by Arcolin. Paks wondered why he had come. Who would captain the year's recruits?

"Well, Val, what'd you bring us?" asked Dorrin.

"About the usual, plus veterans the Duke asked back in. He's hired a captain, too, but he'll tell you about that — should be here within the week. Arcolin, you'll have Stammel and Kefer for sergeants, and Devlin and Seli for corporals. The Duke suggested that you take most of the veterans for your cohort, since it was worst hit; you'll also have almost half the recruits."

Arcolin stretched, shaking his head. "Well, then, we'd best settle the troops. Go ahead, Val."

Valichi sent two files from Kefer's unit and all of Stammel's unit to Arcolin's cohort, where they moved up behind the survivors. The rest of Kefer's unit and two files of Vona's went to Dorrin; the remainder to Cracolnya. The sergeants relocated themselves; Stammel gave the cohort a long, appraising look. When he met Paks's eyes, one eyelid drooped in the merest suggestion of a wink.

Two hours later, the newcomers had distributed their gear in the barracks, and the bustle of sixty-two additional members gave the feeling of a full cohort again. Paks had been assigned four recruits to introduce to their new life, three men and one woman. As she told them where to store things, and where they would eat and sleep, she was reminded of her first night with the regular Company. But then there had been many more veterans than recruits.

She could tell they were full of questions, but she kept them busy. She didn't want to talk about it yet with these people she did not know. Stammel came around to check, before supper, and gave her a grin.

"Well, Paks, I heard about you — you've had quite a year."

Paks nodded. "It's been — difficult."

"Sounds like it. I've heard the Duke's version; I'd like to hear yours. How about a mug at *The White Dragon* after supper?"

Paks frowned. "I've got second watch tonight — "

"That was before we came. Arcolin said to work in the recruits at once; they'll start tonight. What about it?"

"Yes, sir; I'd like that."

"Good. We're not eating in formation; just make sure your group gets over there and back. I'll be around somewhere." Stammel moved on, and Paks surprised an expression on the recruits' faces that made her uncomfortable.

"Come along," she said brusquely. "Time to eat." She led them to the serving lines, then to a table. Vik was there with three recruits. He rolled his eyes at her. Paks grinned.

"Paks, these are Mikel, Suri, and — and Saben." Paks felt her face freeze. The recruit flinched; she realized she must be glaring. She swallowed and nodded at them, trying to smile. "This is Paks," said Vik to them. The new

204

Saben was thin and dark, with green eyes. Paks looked away, swallowed again, and introduced her own recruits, pointing a finger at each in turn.

"Volya, Keri, Jenits, and Sim; and this is Vik. Don't dice with him; he'll win."

"If you're going to tell tales, Paks, I'll start on you," threatened Vik.

"Huh. There's nought to tell."

"Is there not? Well, I'll let them find out for themselves. Did you hear that Stammel's changed the watch lists?"

Paks nodded, her mouth full of food.

"We're off for two days, all the old ones. Want to come in to Valdaire with us tonight?"

Paks shook her head, spat out a piece of gristle, and said, "Not tonight. Stammel wanted to talk."

"About — ?" Vik jerked his head to the northeast.

"I expect so." Paks went on eating, aware of the recruits' interest.

Rauf sat down across the table from Paks with an older man and two recruits. "Paks, Vik — this is Hama, and Jursi, and Piter, who thought he'd retired." Piter laughed at this; he had none of the recruits' nervousness. He grinned at Paks.

"Are you the Paks that went seven days across country to bring the Duke word?" he asked.

"That's right," said Vik before Paks could answer. "Paks Longlegs — " Paks put an elbow in his ribs and he broke off.

"I'm impressed," said Piter. "What did you do for supplies?"

"The first day we scavenged some food from a farm near the fort; the farmers had been killed. We tried to space it out — but we were short until — I think it was the fifth day. We tried to buy food at a little settlement, and they tried to rob us, and — we came away with enough to finish the trip."

Piter nodded as he ate his stew. Then he frowned. "You say 'we' — I heard it was you alone that brought the message."

"Three of us started. Two died." Paks looked away, avoiding the recruits' eyes.

"Umph. I remember trying to shadow a column once, just for a day and night, and that was in summer. I could see their dust. Even so, I lost them twice and was nearly taken."

"I remember that," said Rauf. "It was my second — no, third — year, and you were in — was it Simintha's cohort?"

"No, that was the year Sim had that bad fall; Follyn had just taken it. That was Graifel Company I was following, you remember; they disbanded some ten years ago, but they had a very good light foot."

Paks listened to their remembrances, well pleased to have the conversation turned. She finished her meal, and saw that her recruits were finished too. Vik turned to her as he climbed over the bench. "Paks, I'll see you at weapons drill tomorrow, if you're not up when we get back."

"If you're coming back that late, all you'll see at drill is the ground or sky." The recruits looked shocked. Paks and Vik grinned at each other, and Paks climbed up too.

205

"Glad to have met you, Paks," said Piter, saluting her with a hunk of bread.

"And you," she said. Her group was up, and waiting for orders. "Let's get back," she told them, and led the way out.

"Paks — " It was Volya, the single woman of her group.

"Yes?"

"Will you tell us, someday, about what you did?"

Paks shrugged. "There's not much to tell."

"But surely — " began Jenits. Paks cut him off.

"Not now. Some other time, maybe, if you haven't heard enough from the others." She led them to the barracks at a fast pace.

Captain Arcolin was standing with Stammel just inside the door; the recruits shied around them. Stammel beckoned to Paks, and she came to stand nearby.

" — and that's all I know," said Arcolin. "We've two months training to make up in as many weeks. The veterans — " he nodded at Paks, "will all be instructors. I understand you've put the recruits on guard duty — "

"Yes, sir. For a few nights anyway."

"Good. Oh — by the way — the Duke was talking of taking a section for drill himself."

Stammel grunted. "It won't be the first time, sir, but thank you for the warning."

Arcolin glanced at Paks again. "You're going in to Valdaire?"

The White Dragon," answered Stammel. "I'll be back by second watch."

"No problem. I'll be checking the guard posts as usual. Take care." Arcolin went out. Stammel looked after him a moment, then turned to Paks and smiled.

"I've already told Kefer I'm going; are you ready?" Paks nodded. "Good." He started out the door. "Have you done much drilling with polearms?"

"Some. We drilled with Vladi's spears before the siege ended, but not so much since we've come back."

"Hmm. The Duke wants us to be able to use 'em. I was hoping some of you could help teach — "

"I think we could use them. I don't like 'em nearly as well as swords; they're too clumsy in close."

"We'll have to try." They were in the lane that led to *The White Dragon*; in the light spilling from open doors and windows Paks saw that Stammel was watching her from the corner of his eye. "Paks — these recruits, they're greener than you were: they've had two months less training. You heard the captain. We have to work them into the Company in a hurry. I don't know when the Duke plans to march, but I doubt he'll wait until summer. Now, the Duke's told them some of what's happened, and what you did. They're all excited — I thought you should know what he'd said, so when they ask — "

"Do I have to talk about it?"

Stammel took a great breath and blew it out, a pale frosty plume against the

206

sky. "No. No, you don't. Not even to me, if you don't want to. But you may find it hard: they'll be asking, you see. I know what you mean. Some things you don't want to make light of, by too much talk. But they'll be looking to you, Paks, whether you tell them or not. I thought you should know."

"I wish they wouldn't," muttered Paks. She could feel her ears glowing.

"You would have yourself," said Stammel reasonably. "I remember you with Kolya, and Canna: it's natural. The youngsters always want to hear the stories and dream. And it will help get them ready fast, for them to think of all you veterans as heroes: song fodder." Paks was glad they still had a distance to go; she knew she was red. "We have some old veterans back, too," Stammel went on. "They'll have their own problems — may be a bit touchy at first. Don't pay any mind if they go on about how things have changed. Once we're fighting, they'll be a big help."

"I met one tonight," said Paks. "Piter — ?"

"Yes, old Piter. He's a good man. We started together, but he took a bad wound and fever, one year, and decided to retire. He joined one of his brothers running barges on the Honnorgat. Claims he's kept his sword skill against river pirates: I don't know about that, but he's kept it. He's good with a curved blade, too; knows every trick. How did you get along?"

"Fine. He wanted to know — but it was more like one of us. He asked what we'd done about food — it seemed natural, talking to him."

"Good. Oh! I nearly forgot. Kolya sent you her greetings and a bag of apples. It's somewhere in the baggage; I'll find it tomorrow."

"That was nice of her." And a surprise; she heard it in her own voice.

"She had a good harvest this year. She wanted to come, but the Duke had other plans."

"Is it true the Duke left the stronghold empty?"

"How did you know that?"

"I heard the captains say something — "

"Well, don't you say anything. Gods above! I hope no one else mentions it. It's true — except for those in the villages — and I hope the Regency Council doesn't hear about it."

"But what if something breaks out in the north?"

"We'll just hope it doesn't. Nothing's happened for years." Stammel sighed and changed the subject. "What did you get from the sack of Rotengre? Wasn't that your first?"

"Yes," said Paks slowly. "It was."

"Didn't like it, eh? What about it?"

"It was — everyone shoving and yelling and breaking things. I — I can't see breaking up good furniture for the fun of it, and tearing things and spilling wine all over."

Stammel chuckled. "No — I suppose you wouldn't. But surely you found something for yourself."

"Oh, yes. Some unset jewels, coins, a jeweled dagger, and a length of embroidered silk. I'm keeping that for my mother. I was thinking of keeping the dagger, but it looks silly with these clothes."

207

"Couldn't you have found some finery to go with it?"

Paks snorted, then laughed, remembering the militia primped up in velvets and laces. "Well, sir — I looked at some of the others — and it just looked silly. And besides, where would I keep the things?"

"It's not impossible. You're a veteran now; you're entitled to some space in the Company wagons and stores."

"I suppose. I didn't think of that then." They were nearly at the inn, and Stammel led the way to the door. Once inside they found the usual assortment of customers: mercenaries of half-a-dozen companies, a scattering of merchants, and a few professional gamblers (or thieves) who tossed their ivory dice whenever conversation and business lagged. Stammel looked at the crowded common room and crooked his finger at the landlord.

"Yes?" Rumor said the landlord was a veteran of Sobanai Company.

"A quiet corner anywhere?" asked Stammel.

"Sergeant Stammel, isn't it? Yes, I think we can find you a quiet spot. Just follow me." He led the way down a passage to a tiny room which had a bench built against either wall and a table close between them; it might have been possible to squeeze in four people. Two fat candles in a wall sconce gave bright unsteady light. Stammel took the bench on one side, and Paks took the other.

"Bring us some ale," said Stammel, and the landlord withdrew. Paks threw her cloak back and pushed up her sleeves. Stammel looked at her critically.

"You've been keeping fit, I can see that. You may have strengthened that left arm even since last year. How's your unarmed combat coming?"

"Better. At least, when I needed it on the way, it worked."

"Ah. Now that's what I'd like to — " The door opened, and the landlord put a jug and two mugs on the table, then waited while Stammel fished out some coins. When he was gone, Stammel poured a mug of ale before speaking. "Go on," he said to Paks. "I won't drink all of this myself. Now — if you don't mind telling me about it, I'd like to hear it from you."

Paks sipped the ale before replying. "I don't mind telling you, sir. In fact, I wished you were there, right after, to talk to. But — but it still — " her voice faltered.

"You still feel it when you tell it," said Stammel. "No wonder."

Paks nodded, staring at the scarred tabletop. When she began to speak again, the story came out in fits and starts. Stammel did not interrupt, and asked few questions. By the time she came to the incident with the mounted sentry, the story seemed to be rolling out of her, almost as if she were telling a tale that had happened to someone else. Then she came to that last afternoon, and the memory bit deep. She stopped, drained her mug, and started to pour another; her hands shook.

Stammel took the jug and poured for her. "Take it easy," he said. "Do you want something to eat?" Paks shook her head. "It's amazing you made it so far without losing someone," he went on. "You took more precautions than I would have, I think. I'm not sure I would have thought of a sentry at the first crossroad. With food so short — I might have tried a village;

208

hunger's hard to ignore. You knew that place was risky; you got out of it with the food you needed. And on the last day, so close to the Duke, so far ahead of the enemy — I'd have felt fairly safe myself."

Paks wrapped her hands around the mug and stared into it. "I heard one of the squires talking to the Duke. He said we should have been more careful."

"The Duke?"

"No — the squire."

Stammel snorted. "As if he'd ever done anything like that! I'll warrant the Duke didn't back him up."

"Well — no. He didn't. But — "

"Then don't fret about a squire's opinion. Which was it, anyway?"

"The youngest one. Jostin, I think his name was. I haven't seen him today."

"You won't. The Duke sent him home. He's got Selfer, Jori, and Kessim now."

"What about Rassamir?"

"Oh, he went back to Vladi. He's a nephew, or something like that. Well, then: what happened in the forest?"

Paks had relaxed; now she hunched her shoulders again. "We were moving fast; the light was fading . . . " She told it as it lived in her mind: the brigands suddenly around them, Canna down before she could string the bow, Saben fending off three, her own fall into the stream, the grinning man who ran down after her, sword in hand. "So — so I turned and — and ran." Paks was trembling as she finished.

"Best thing you could have done," said Stammel firmly. "Did they come after you?"

Paks nodded. "For awhile. They had bows — they shot. But the trees were thick, and it was getting dark — " There wasn't much to tell about that long wet run in the dark, no way to describe what she'd felt, leaving her friends behind. "It took a long time, with the mud and all," she said. "The sentry didn't believe I was in the Duke's Company at first. No wonder, really, dirty as I was. But Canna and Saben — " Paks could not go on.

"If you'd stayed," said Stammel, "there'd have been three dead right there, besides all the prisoners, and those in Dwarfwatch as well. You didn't kill them, Paks; the brigands did. Save your anger for them." He leaned back against the wall and gave her a long look. "Do you really think their shades are angry with you? Canna left you her Girdish medallion, didn't she?"

"How did you know that?"

"The Duke, of course. He was curious about that — asked me about you two. But think, Paks — if she'd been angry, she wouldn't have left it for you."

"I — I suppose not."

"Of course not." Stammel reached across the table and laid his hand on hers. "Paks, the Duke thinks you did well — and by Tir, he should! So did Canna. So does everyone I've heard speak of it. It was a hard choice; you chose well. Sometimes there's no way — "

"I know that!" interrupted Paks, fighting tears. "But — "

Stammel sighed. "They were your best friends — and after that — Paks, you may hate me for this, but — did you ever bed Saben?"

Paks shook her head, unable to speak.

"That's part of it, then." He held up a hand as she looked up, angry. "No, hear me out. I'm not arguing about whether you did or didn't: that's your choice. But you two were closer than friends; it's natural in friends to want to have given everything. I'd wager part of your sorrow now is that you didn't give him that, when he wanted it. Isn't it?"

Paks nodded, staring at the table. "Yes," she whispered. "And yet, I — "

"You truly don't want to — that's obvious. You know, Paks, you really have chosen the most difficult way — or it's chosen you, I'm not sure which. Remember, though, that Saben respected your choice. I know, because he told me that back when you were a recruit, in that trouble with Korryn."

Paks felt herself blushing. She had never imagined Saben and Stammel discussing her that way.

Stammel chuckled. "Maybe I shouldn't have told you. Anyway, if it's not your nature — and I think it's not — you have nothing to reproach yourself for. Saben liked you, and respected you, and even loved you. Grieve for him, of course — but don't hamper yourself with guilt."

Paks shook her head. She felt hollow inside, as if she had cried for a long time; yet she felt eased, too. She realized how silly it was to think of Saben's shade hanging around unsatisfied because of her. Such a man, after such a death, would surely have gone straight to the Afterfields, to ride one of the Windsteed's foals forever. She let a last few tears leak past her eyelids, took a long breath, and sipped her ale.

"Better?" asked Stammel. She nodded. "Good. Now," he said briskly, "I'm still curious about that Girdish medallion. You never listened to Effa — had Canna been talking to you? Had you handled it?"

Paks leaned back, staring at her mug. "Well — I did handle it, once."

"Well?" prompted Stammel.

"It was — well, I don't know. It was strange."

"So you didn't tell the Duke's scribe about it?" suggested Stammel.

"No. No, I didn't. It wasn't anything that concerned the Company, like the rest of it. And I don't know what happened. If anything happened."

"Were you thinking of becoming a Girdsman?"

"No. Nothing like that. I suppose it started the first night, when Canna asked us to pray with her. She knew we weren't Girdsmen, but said it would be all right. The next day we could tell that she was having a lot of trouble with her wound. It was swollen and hot, very red. When Saben and I woke up the next morning, I remembered hearing that St. Gird healed warriors sometimes. Canna was a Girdsman; I thought he might heal her." Paks paused for a sip of ale. Stammel watched her, brows furrowed.

"I asked her; she said it had to be a Marshal or paladin. But I thought if we could pray to Gird to help our friends, why not for healing?" Stammel made a noncommittal sound, and Paks hurried on. "Canna said to hold the medallion, and then ask for what I wanted. I put it on her shoulder, where the wound was, and asked for it to be healed."

"Then?"

"It didn't work. It just hurt her; she said it felt like a cramp. It didn't get worse, and she could walk fast all that day, and from then on. But we found that pot of ointment, too. I don't know —"

Stammel heaved a gusty sigh. "That's — quite a story, Paks. Have you told anyone else?"

"No, sir. I don't truly think I did anything. But it might be why Canna left the medallion to me. Maybe she hoped I'd become a Girdsman."

"Maybe. They encourage converts. But that healing, now —"

"But it didn't work," said Paks. "Not like that magical healing, my first year. Some the mage touched, and some got a potion, but it didn't hurt, and the wounds were healed right away."

"Yes, but that was a wizard, someone whose job it was. You aren't a Marshal or paladin; I wouldn't have expected anything at all to happen. Or if it angered Gird, or the High Lord, it should have hurt you, not Canna. Did you feel anything?"

"No. Nothing."

"And she did get better, well enough to draw a bow only five days later."

"That might have been the ointment," said Paks.

"Yes. It could have been. Or else — Tir's bones, Paks, this makes my hair crawl. If you did do something — maybe you ought to find a Gird's Marshal, and tell him about it." Paks shook her head, and Stammel sighed again. "Well. Has anything strange happened since you've been wearing it? You are wearing it, aren't you?"

"Yes. And nothing's happened — really."

"No mysterious cramps that healed anyone, or saved lives?"

"No. Well — it's not the same thing at all, but — it was a cramp in my back that saved me from a crossbow bolt in Rotengre."

"What!"

"But it's nothing to do with the medallion, Stammel. I'm sure of it. We'd been loading plunder all day; we were all tired. I was stooping over this slave we'd found, trying to talk her into getting up and coming along — she was so frightened, I didn't want to drag her — and I got a kind of cramp in my back, and had to straighten up."

"Yes?"

"And the crossbow bolt went where I'd been. There was a second concealed room behind the niche where we'd found the slave, and Captain Dorrin said the man in it was a priest of the Webmistress, Achrya."

Stammel made a warding sign Paks knew. "One of *her* priests! And you — you just happened to get a cramp. What did Dorrin say?"

"That I was pushing my luck."

"She would. Well, Paks, I can see why you haven't talked about this. I think you're right, unless you decide to find a Marshal. Just in case something is going on, you might like to find out what."

Paks frowned. "But I don't think anything is going on. And I'm not a Girdsman."

"Whatever you say. You're either damned lucky or gods-gifted, or you

211

wouldn't be here today. What a year you've had!" Stammel stretched, arching his back. "Well, it's getting on toward second watch —" He took a final swallow of ale, and nodded for Paks to finish hers. "Now these recruits, Paks, have had their basic training in swords, and they can go through the pair exercises without spitting each other. But they need weapons drill in formation, and a lot of two and three on one. Their shieldwork is as bad as yours was — or worse. Tomorrow I want you to take your four and work on the basics. Be tough with 'em, but try not to scare them so they can't work. All right?"

Paks relaxed, draining her mug. "Yes, sir."

"You heard the captain say the Duke might join us. If he does — he'd rather take a fall than have one of us do something stupid."

"Yes, sir. I'll remember."

"Come on, then." They unfolded themselves from either side of the table, passed through the noisy common room, and went out into the frosty night.

Chapter Twenty-two

Siger, the Duke's old armsmaster, had come south since, as he said, the Duke had left him nothing to do at home.

"You must be some quicker," he greeted Paks. "Or by what I hear you wouldn't be alive. Here — take these bandas for your recruits. Who've you got?" Paks told him. "Volya's quick, but not strong enough yet," he said. "Her shieldwork's wretched. Keri forgets things. Keep after him. Jenits is the best of those — just needs practice and seasoning. Sim's very strong, but slow. Not clumsy, exactly — just slow. I'll check on you later."

Paks collected her little group in one corner of a yard that grew more crowded every minute. With swords alone, they looked fairly good. Sim hung a fractional beat behind the count, but it hardly showed. She had them pick up shields. Now the drill grew ragged. Sim slowed more, and Keri kept shoving his shield too far to one side. Volya couldn't seem to get hers high enough. Paks had them pair off, still working on the counted drill. With this stimulus, Volya improved her shieldwork, but Sim stayed slow. Keri made touches he should not have, and Sim failed to take advantage of Keri's bad shieldwork. Jenits still looked good. Paks moved around them, watching carefully at every stroke, and talking herself hoarse. Finally she stopped them for a water break.

"I suppose," she said, after a drink had restored her voice, "that Siger told you, Sim, that you are too slow?" He nodded. "And Volya — if your shield is down around your ankles, it won't do any good, right?" Volya blushed. "And you, Jenits," she went on. "You may be the best of this group, but you have a long way to go."

"Siger said I was coming well," said Jenits. Paks grinned. She'd hoped for a challenge; it would be a welcome change from talking.

"Well, let's see. Maybe I was fooled by watching you with another recruit. The rest of you: don't sit; you'll stiffen in the cold." Paks drew her sword, took Volya's shield, and faced Jenits. He did not look as confident as the moment before. "Come on," said Paks. "Get that shield up where it'll do you some good. Now start at the beginning."

Jenits began the drill cautiously, as if he thought his sword would break on contact. She countered the strokes easily, without any flourishes, murmuring the numbers as a reminder. He put more bite in the strokes, and Paks responded by stepping up the pace, and strengthening her own. She did not deviate from the drill, but in a few minutes Jenits was sweating and puffing, and she had tapped his banda half a dozen times. She stopped him.

"Jenits, you have the chance to be very good. But right now you're about half as fast as you should be — and half as fit. Your speed will come with practice; the way we're going to drill will take care of the fitness, too. Now walk around and catch your breath while I try the others." Paks was pleased to see that Jenits no longer looked sulky, just thoughtful. She beckoned to Volya, handed back her shield, and took another. Volya was very quick, and her strokes were firm, but she could not keep her shield high enough.

"Is that arm just weak, or did something happen to it?"

"It was broken once, by a cow. I've tried to strengthen it."

"You'll have to do better. If you can't keep that shield up, you won't survive your first battle. What have you tried?"

"Siger suggested some exercises. I do those — when I remember them."

"You'll remember them," said Paks grimly, "unless you like the idea of dying very young. Right now, while you're resting, raise and lower your shield fifty times — and go this high — " She pushed the shield until it was as high as she wanted it. "Go on, now. Sim, come here."

Sim, a ruddy young boy with a husky build, moved flat-footed. Paks pointed this out, and he tried to stand on his toes instead, moving even more stiffly and slowly. "No, Sim. Not standing on your toes. Just lift your heels a little. Did you ever skip?" She knew as she asked that he had never skipped in his life, and he shook his round head. "Let's try again, then." Sim had a powerful stroke, but so slow that Paks could easily hit twice for each of his. Nothing she said or did made him faster, and she gave up in a few minutes. At least he was strong and tireless.

Keri was the last, and his main problems were sloppy shieldwork and a very short memory. At least, he kept getting the sequence of drill wrong. Several times Paks had to pull her stroke to keep from hurting him badly; he moved exactly the wrong way. She led him through the tricky parts again and again, then turned him over to Jenits. "No variations," she said. "He's got to do this right first." Paks returned to Volya and Sim, and had them pair up without shields. When they started, she began her own exercises while watching them. All around her she heard the clatter of blades and shields, the busy voices of instructors.

"What do you think of them, Paks?" It was Siger, buckling on a sword belt. "Planning to take my job?"

Paks grinned. "I didn't know it was so hard to teach — my voice gave out. But they're about what you said. Sim's impossibly slow; he's dead if he doesn't improve."

"True. Want to go a round?"

"Gladly," said Paks. "Swords only, or shields?"

"Both. Clear your group and give us room." Paks told her recruits to break, and they stepped away.

"Ready?" asked Siger.

Paks nodded. They began with the same drill the recruits knew, but they picked up the tempo smoothly, until it was much faster. Siger began hitting harder; Paks followed suit. Then Siger left the drill sequence, skipping in for a thrust, but Paks countered it, and drove him back. Paks circled, looking for an opening. She tried to force Siger's shield, and took a smart blow on the shoulder. In the next exchange, she tapped his chest. They circled and reversed like a pair of dancers.

"You are quicker," said Siger. "You're doing well. But do you know *this* — " and with a peculiar stroke Paks had never seen he trapped her blade and flicked it away. Someone laughed. Their encounter had attracted more watchers than her recruits. Paks glared at Siger, who was bouncing toward her again. She had her dagger out now, and the watchers were very quiet. With good shieldwork and her long reach, she kept him from touching her, but she couldn't reach him. She thought hard, catching stroke after stroke on her shield until she remembered something she'd seen a Blue Rider do. Suddenly she pivotted to his shield side, jammed the edge of her shield behind his, and threw her weight toward him. Siger staggered to the side, and her dagger stroke was square in the back of his banda.

"Ha!" he cried. "Enough! And where did you learn that little trick?"

Paks grinned at him. "Here and there, you might say." She was breathless and glad for the rest.

"Here's your sword, Paks," said Rauf. She looked at the respectful faces around them and took the sword, checking it for damage. Siger drove the others away and came back, patting her arm.

"That was good. Very good. Show me slowly, please." He stood in front of her, and Paks demonstrated the pivot again. She did not explain that she had seen it used on horseback, and had coaxed the Blue Rider to show her on foot.

"It works best if you have the reach of your opponent," she said. "You have to get your shield up above his shoulder, and then as the pivot continues, you've got it here — " she locked the shields together, " — and your right hand is free for the backstroke. And it's hard for him to strike over the shields."

"Is there a counter?"

"Yes — it's easy. Just step back; don't follow the pivot. Thing is, it works best against someone who thinks he's got more weapon. The start of the turn looks like a retreat; if he follows it, you've got him. But if he stays back, you can't lock shields."

"Very good. Very good. Come this afternoon and I'll show you that little twist that cost you your blade. A favor for a favor."

"Thank you," said Paks. She turned to her recruits as Siger moved away. They looked at her with more awe than before.

"Do we have to be that fast?" asked Jenits.

"It helps," said Paks. "Suppose your opponent is. You need every scrap of speed and strength you can build. I'm faster than I was, and I hope I'll keep improving."

"I'll never do it," said Sim. "I'm strong. I know I'm strong, and I thought that would be enough. I could beat up anyone in my village. But I never was fast."

"You'll get faster," said Paks firmly. "When I was a recruit, Siger thumped my ribs and yelled 'faster, faster' at me every day — and finally I got faster. You will too, unless your ribs are tougher than mine were." They laughed, a little nervously.

From across the yard came a shout: "Hey — Saben. Come here." Paks stiffened, her head swinging automatically to look before she caught herself. She felt tears sting her eyes, and blinked fiercely. Saben was a common enough name; she'd have to get used to it.

"Paks?" They all looked concerned. Volya went on. "Did you know him before? Saben, I mean?"

Paks shook her head, and took a deep steadying breath. "No. A different Saben — a good friend. We'd been together since we came in, and he was with me on — on the trip you heard about. But he died."

"Oh."

"Well, it happens. We're soldiers, after all. It's just — there wasn't another Saben in the Company, so when I hear the name, I think — I'll get used to it. I suppose. Now, let's get back to work. Sim, you and Jenits this time, and Keri and Volya." They started again and Paks kept after them until time for the midday meal.

Within a week, Paks lost Sim to Cracolnya's cohort. She was glad; a slow archer might live longer than a slow swordsman. Less welcome was the change in cohort position resulting from the number of recruits. Normally, recruits were kept to the rear, except for a few who had showed promise. But Arcolin decided that they should be close to their veteran instructors, which meant that Paks ended up as file sixth. She understood the reasons, but didn't like it even so.

There were other changes. Horse-faced Pont was now Arcolin's junior captain, and Valichi took Pont's place with Cracolnya. The Duke had hired a captain to replace Sejek: Peska, a dark, dour man who had been a watch captain at court in Pargun. He spoke Common with a curious accent that Paks had never heard; she was glad her cohort had Pont instead, though Barra had no complaints about him.

This year Paks could not ask Donag for advance information — and no one in the cohort seemed to know what the Duke planned, except trouble for Siniava. When they marched out of Valdaire on the southern road, the one to Czardas that Paks remembered, she expected to see Halverics — but instead they met the Golden Company a few miles from the city. Aesil M'dierra, mounted on a chestnut horse and armored in gold-washed mail, rode beside the Duke; her company fell in behind. Paks eyed her: the only woman in Aarenis to command her own mercenary company. What would that be like? What could she be like?

But the next day they turned aside, through Baron Kodaly's lands, and Golden Company stayed on the road south. Through a steady rain they marched easily, guided by a wiry dark man who had come with the Baron. Paks thought he looked like a juggler, but Stammel laughed when she said it.

"Juggler! Tir, no. I'll admit the jugglers you see in Valdaire are his subjects, more than likely. That's one of the woods tribes — their king, or prince, or whatever."

"But why — ?"

Stammel shrugged. "I don't know. They have a lot of power in the forests of Aarenis, I've heard. The Duke's always made friends with them. Maybe he wants safe passage through some forest."

Whatever he was, he led them by ways that avoided all hazards of bog and mud. Three days later he was gone, but they marched easily beside a larger stream with a village in sight.

They were met, in the fields above the village, by an old man in a long robe and a fat man in helmet and breastplate commanding ten unarmored youths with scythes and pikes. Paks could not hear what the Duke said to them, but the youths suddenly trailed their weapons in the mud and turned away. The village had a cobbled square, and a group of taller buildings around it. Paks looked for an inn, hoping for ale. She saw a battered sign with a picture of a tower by a river; the sign read *Inzing Paksnor*. The inn yard was large, but part of the building had been torn down to build a stable. They marched through, to camp on the far side where one stream joined another.

Across the stream was a rising slope of farmland, and on the southern horizon a long stony escarpment running roughly west to east. It reminded Paks of the high moors behind Three Firs, and looked like nothing else she had seen in the south.

"That's the Middle Marches," said Devlin to a curious recruit. "Once you're up on those heights, it's sheepfarming land. And downstream maybe a day's march from here is Ifoss."

"Who claims the Middle Marches?" asked someone else.

"Whoever can." Devlin turned to look at the fire. "There's petty barons enough, near the river — like Kodaly. Ifoss claims some of it. More barons downstream until Vonja. Up on the high ground it's hard to say. There was a Count Somebody, when I first came south, but he died. I heard he left no heir of the body — a nephew or something in Pliuni. The Honeycat tries to claim it, as he claims everything else. I think — I think when he took Pliuni, he captured the nephew, or married him to a daughter or niece. Or maybe that was another place."

"What's beyond it?" asked Paks.

"Straight south?" She nodded. "Well, Andressat. That's ruled by a count, if I remember. An old family, anyway, and very powerful. I think the Duke hired to Andressat once, before I joined. They've got only one city: Cortes Andres. They say its inner fortifications have never been broken."

"Does the Honeycat control Andressat?"

"Tir, no! The count — Jeddrin, I think his name is — he hates him. Then south of Andressat are the South Marches. The Honeycat claims

217

that, and for all I know he may have a right to it. He also claims the cities along the Chaloquay, and the Horn Bay ports on the Immerhoft. That's Sibili and Cha, on the river, and Confaer, Korran, and Sul, on the coast."

"How did he ever claim Pliuni?" asked Paks.

"Just took it. Waited until the Sier of Westland was fighting up in the western mountains, and marched up and took it. Pliuni was a free city, but had always looked to the Sier for protection."

"What about the rest of the port cities?" asked Arñe.

"I don't know. I've heard the names, but I don't know exactly where they are or who controls them. Seafang, that's a pirate city, and Immerdzan, at the mouth of the Immer. Let's see: Zith, Aliuna, Sur-vret, Anzal, and Immer-something. No, Ka-Immer. Some are pirate cities, and some are legitimate traders — so they say."

Ifoss, when they came to it the next day, seemed small and dingy after Valdaire. A walled city of no more than eight or nine thousand, surrounded by plowland and orchards, it was bleak in winter. They camped outside the city on a long field sloping to the river, and wagons rolled out with provisions. With the wagons came Guildmasters to confer with the Duke; recruits and veterans alike gaped at their distinctive dress, the short-pointed, fur-edged hats, long pointed sleeves, and oddly cut jackets trimmed in elaborate braid.

They stayed at Ifoss several days. On the second night, Paks took advantage of her seniority to enter the city. Stammel had told them of a good new inn near the east gate, *The Laughing Fox*, so they ignored *The Falcon*, *The Golden Ladder*, and *The Juggler* to work their way across town to Stammel's choice.

It was new, clean, and the landlord seemed friendly. The ale was good, too, and not expensive. Paks ordered a fried fruit pie, and Vik decided on a slab of spicebread; soon they were enjoying an impromptu party. When Paks decided to leave, two of the group weren't ready to come and stayed behind — "just to finish the jug," they said.

"Don't come back too late," teased Vik, "and expect us to take your slot on guard, because I'm going to get my beauty sleep."

"Beauty sleep, or sleep with a beauty?" asked a townsman at the next table, emboldened by his flask of wine as he eyed Paks.

"Sleep," replied Vik cheerfully. "She's on guard before I am." Which was not true, but made a good exit. Paks had already turned away, trusting Vik to find a good answer. He always did, with everyone. They got back to camp shortly before the watch change; Stammel was not pleased to find that two had stayed behind.

"Do you think they'll be back on time, or had I better go roust 'em out?"

"Sif's not on until late watch," said Paks. "He's got a strong head, and I don't think he'll be late. I don't know Tam that well — he's Dorrin's — but surely Sif will keep an eye on him."

"I hope. It seems a clean enough place, but it is on the far side of town. If they're not back by midwatch, let me know; I'll want to find 'em."

The guard assignment had Paks partnered with Jenits; they had a short stretch on the east side of camp, from the horse lines to the entrance. It was nearly midwatch when she heard a wavering song from the lane that led to Ifoss. As the noise came closer, she could hear two voices. The guards at the camp entrance snickered. Paks hoped it was Sif and Tam, but they did sound drunk.

"Like the bee-e-e, so swift to anger . . . but her honey's . . . rich and swee-eet — " one of the two stopped to cough, then picked up the song again. "I don't fe-ear her painful stinger . . . but the honey-y. . . . I will — "

"Quiet, there!" Dorrin, the watch captain, had heard the noise. Paks heard a hiccup and indistinct mutters from the pair. "Come up to the light," said Dorrin, "and give the password." Paks saw two shadowy figures approach the torches at the camp entrance, and heard them stumble over the password.

"You're a disgrace," snapped Dorrin. "Veterans who don't know their limit — why do you think we didn't let the others into town, eh? This is no campaign for getting drunk and blabbing in taverns. And what happened to your cloak, Tam?" Paks could not hear the answer, if he made any. Dorrin cleared her throat and spat. "Your sergeants will see to you," she said. "Wait here." She strode off.

"Is it that bad to get drunk?" asked Jenits softly. "I used to — "

"It depends," said Paks. They turned back toward the horse lines. "Anything you say in a tavern will travel — if you get drunk and talk about the Company, where we're marching, or when — that's bad."

"I see," said Jenits.

"And then if you're drunk," said Paks, "you're more likely to be taken by slavers, or attacked by thieves. Or if it makes you mean, you might brawl, and that makes trouble for the Company. Of course if it's a cohort or Company banquet, that's different."

Next day Paks saw Sif grooming mules under the sarcastic guidance of the muleskinner. She was sure that Dorrin's sergeant had found something equally unpleasant for Tam.

When they left Ifoss, they angled across pastures toward the Middle Marches. By nightfall they were camped under the ridge. Sheep trails led up it. The next day they spent climbing, winding back and forth along the face of the slope. To the north their view broadened: they could see Ifoss with its wall, and downstream another wall and tower that Stammel said was Foss Fort. A cold wind scoured the height. They passed outcrops of gray stone splashed with orange and brown lichens. The outcrops grew rougher, formed into long lines like low walls. They passed through a gap in one, shoulder high on either side; it ran along the slope as far as Paks could see. Above it, the rocks disappeared once more under thick turf, still winter-tawny. The slope eased. They camped that night near that natural stone wall.

They reached the broad top of the ridge in less than an hour of marching the next morning. Paks looked at the vast and empty land to the south.

The great ridge seemed to fall slightly to the southwest, cleft here and there by steep watercourses furred with trees. The sky arched blue and nearly cloudless; they could see for miles — could see, for instance, a galloping horseman far ahead. None of the officers seemed concerned, so Paks thought it must be one of their own messengers.

Although they crossed many winding sheep trails, they saw neither sheep nor shepherds. Paks realized that they were more visible than a flock of stone-gray sheep — of course any shepherd would move out of their path. That afternoon they camped where a pool had formed below several springs; a small clear stream ran away from the low end of the pool and dropped into a narrow cleft in the rock.

It was just after lunch on the next day when Paks heard horns blowing in the south; the sound trembled in the still air. She peered south, trying to see something. Far down the slope was a knot of horsemen, but the horn calls had come from farther away than that. The thunder of hooves began to shake the ground. Stammel called them into fighting formation; other sergeants were yelling. They unslung shields, and drew their swords. Paks watched her recruits. Volya looked pale, but eager. Keri was frowning, and waggling his blade a little as if reminding himself of the drill. The back of Jenits's neck had reddened. She eased her own shoulders and took a deep breath as the riders neared. They wore brown and gray tunics, oddly loose and flapping, and carried lances with no decoration.

The leading horses slowed, and the foremost rider hailed the Duke. Arcolin rode forward with him. Once more, Paks could not hear what was said. She looked at her recruits again; they were too stiff.

"Easy," she said. "Breathe slowly." Keri's eyes slid toward hers, and he drew a shaky breath. Arcolin turned to the column and signalled the sergeants.

"Sheathe your blades," said Stammel; Paks eased her sword back in place. Some of the recruits were so tense it took them two tries. They waited. Paks glanced down and saw a fresh green blade poking up through the mat of frost-burned turf. Ahead, almost under Jenits's left foot, was a flat rosette of leaves with two tiny white flowers on top. Almost spring, thought Paks. She looked around for other flowers, but saw none. The riders were turning their horses away. The captains came back to their commands, but the Duke and his squires moved up beside the leading rider.

"We've a fast march to make," said Arcolin, "with a fight at the end of it. Take a drink now, and re-sling your shields but be ready to shift position at any time." No one had much to say as they started south again at a faster pace. An arc of riders went before them, and others rode on their flanks. Paks looked hard at the drab tunics; when one rider bent to untwist a rein, she caught a glimpse of rose through the loose sleeve. So. They were Clarts after all.

As they went they heard horns again: deep and high, long note and sharp staccato signals. It was hard to keep the pace even; the horns and the steepening downhill slope pulled them forward, ever faster. Paks could see, now, that they were coming to a broad saddle between the high ground behind them and a similar rise ahead. To left and right the land fell steeply into deep gorges. Beyond the saddle, shining in the late afternoon sun, rose a tower; around it writhed a dark mass that Paks realized must be an army. They marched on; Paks wondered if they would make that distance by dark. And whose side were they on?

As they started across the saddle, more drab-clad riders came up from the broken ground to either side. The slope rose under their feet toward the tower. Paks could not see, now, for the riders ahead, but the crash and roar of battle came clearly. Rising excitement swamped the fatigue of the day's march. The riders pulled their baggy tunics over their heads, and Clart Cavalry rose and white glowed in the slanting sun.

Arcolin leaned to speak to Stammel. He nodded, turning to the cohort. "Shields," he said; Paks took her own shield, and made sure her recruits had theirs secure. They drew swords. As they advanced, shifting from marching column to battle order, Cracolnya's cohort moved off to their right flank.

"Slow advance — keep in line, there!" yelled Stammel. Paks heard the Clarts yipping as they spurred to the attack. Dust rose in clouds. A great yell from before them; more horn signals. The Duke appeared out of the dust to ride beside them. His squires clustered around him; Paks wondered if they could see any better from the saddle.

The Duke pointed ahead; one of the squires took off at a gallop. Arcolin jogged up from the rear of the cohort, and rode beside the Duke. Paks could hear nothing but battle sounds. Arcolin dropped back, and in a few moments Dorrin's cohort came alongside on their left. Paks saw the Duke's head turn. She looked ahead. Through the swirling dust she could see struggling figures — even the colors. Green, there — black and yellow — and more green. The tower loomed higher as they neared, its parapet above the dust, and Paks saw blue-clad archers.

The Duke put a light hunting horn to his lips and blew a rapid five-note signal. At once it was answered by a call that Paks recognized as Halveric; the battle surged toward them as the green-clad soldiers retreated. Their opponents roared in triumph — a sound that stopped abruptly as they saw behind the fleeing Halverics the solid ranks of Phelani. Another horn-call, and the Halverics slipped left. The enemy fighters crashed into the Phelan's lines. Arcolin's cohort, nearly in the center of the arc formed by Clarts, Phelani, and Halverics, took the brunt of that charge. Paks had no time for a last encouraging word to her recruits; she was tightly engaged.

Despite the hours of practice, Paks found the curved blade strokes of the enemy hard to counter. She took several minor cuts before killing her first opponent, and was just in time to help Keri with the one who had shattered his shield. She fought on, trying to keep an eye on her recruits when she could. The cohort had nearly halted under the enemy rush, but they had not faltered, and the front ranks still held a good line.

"Arcolin's cohort! Drive 'em!" It was the Duke's voice, from behind them; the cohort surged forward, flattening the arc as they came. The enemy softened, rolling left away from their pressure. Still the fighting raged; Paks had no time to wonder how the battle was going. Jenits went down in front of her; she lunged across him to strike the enemy who was about to kill him. Jenits screamed as she stepped on his arm; she shifted a pace and hoped someone would get him away safely. His attacker fought wildly; she finally dropped him with a thrust to the neck. She spared a glance for Jenits and didn't see him. Good, she thought, and thrust at the oncoming soldiers.

The enemy in front melted away, though by the noise the left flank was busy enough. Paks looked around and spotted Volya and Keri. Volya was bleeding from a bad slash to her right arm; Keri's shield had fallen apart, though he still clutched the grip.

"Keri! Pick up a good shield — drop that — " He looked at her in surprise, then at his arm; she watched until he stripped off the broken one and picked up an enemy shield nearby. "Volya, get that wound tied up — drop back — one of the sergeants will tell you where to go." Other wounded were shifting to the rear, and those still sound drew together.

Paks looked for Arcolin or the Duke; she spotted Arcolin on their left front. Stammel was with him. Arcolin waved a signal to Cracolnya, who sent his cohort forward. The Clarts, having rearmed, rode up on the far right, and the right wing wheeled, compressing the enemy against Dorrin's cohort and the Halverics. Paks still could not tell how many they faced. They fought on; the enemy lines, though wavering, hardly seemed to diminish. The sun edged down; as light faded out of the sky, the enemy made one more frantic attempt to breathe through. Favored by the downward slope, they penetrated between the Halverics and Dorrin's cohort, pouring away downhill in the darkness. Paks heard curses from the Clarts, who spurred after them recklessly. Paks hoped the Duke would not command a foot pursuit. She was suddenly almost too tired to move.

Arcolin rode back to them, talking to a Clart captain. Then he turned to Stammel. "Take them to the enemy camp; the Clarts hold it. Set up a strong perimeter. I think Dorrin's cohort is pursuing, but some of them may circle back. I'll be near the tower entrance if you need me." He rode toward the tower; light spilled from its narrow windows. Paks wondered who held it.

The enemy camp was full of supplies. The Clarts had overridden some of the tents, but most were still standing. Cattle roasted over a long trenchfire. Paks's mouth watered. She and the other veterans stood guard while uninjured recruits helped the surgeons and set up camp. She wished she knew how her recruits were, and her friends. She had seen Vik and Arñe only at a distance.

It seemed long before Stammel returned to the perimeter. Paks cleaned her sword and sheathed it, then slipped off her shield and stretched. Her shoulders were stiff where the pack straps had dug in; she hadn't fought in a pack except in drill. Reluctantly she picked up the shield, yawning. Now she could feel every cut and bruise. The wind blew the smell of roasting meat past her nose, and her stomach knotted. At last a recruit came, grease still streaking his chin, to relieve her post. Stammel met her as she turned away.

"Here." He handed her a slab of beef on a split loaf. "I meant to get to you earlier. You'll want to see Jenits; his arm's broken. Volya needed stitching, but she's up and around. Keri's fine; hardly scratched." Paks mumbled her thanks past a mouthful of food.

"Whose tower?" she asked, after swallowing a huge lump of beef.

"Andressat's. Their colors are blue and gold. You'll see tomorrow."

"Why didn't they come out? I thought they hated Siniava."

"They do. But they've only got forty or fifty in there. They don't want to lose the tower to anyone: not even us."

Paks nodded as she ate, and walked on to the surgeons' tent. It had evidently belonged to an enemy officer; it was large and divided by yellow hanging panels into several rooms. Jenits lay on a straw pallet with his shoulders propped up on a frame, his left arm bound in splints. Volya sat beside him with a flask; they both looked pale, but well enough.

"Have you had any food yet?" asked Paks. They both nodded. "Good. I'll finish my supper." She squatted beside Jenits. "Did they give you numbwine?"

"Yes — they did." His voice was slightly blurred.

"I'm sorry I stepped on you," said Paks. "But that — "

"That's all right. It was — broken already. That's why — I fell."

"It's a good thing it was your shield arm," said Paks. "You won't be fighting for weeks, but it won't be as hard to retrain. You did well, Jenits. I suppose Stammel told you that — "

"Yes. But I — I forgot which strokes, after awhile — and it was so fast —"

"I forgot too, in my first battle; that's when I got the big scar on my leg. As Stammel said to me, we'll just drill you more until you can't forget." Jenits managed a shaky grin. Paks turned to Volya. "Volya, you did well too. What I could see of your shieldwork was much better. Now — did the surgeons tell you to stay with Jenits?"

"Yes. They said give him more numbwine if he needed it."

"I can do that, and let you get some sleep. We'll all be pulling watch tonight, and fighting again tomorrow, I expect."

"Oh, I couldn't sleep. I'm still too excited." Volya's eyes were very bright.

Paks sighed. "Volya, you're tired, whether you know it or not. Go roll up in your cloak, and if you aren't asleep in a half glass, you can come back and take over for me." Volya got up reluctantly, and handed Paks the flask of numbwine. "And don't start talking to anyone; that *will* keep you awake." Volya nodded and went out. The surgeon came through from another part of the tent and looked at Paks.

"Is that your blood, or theirs?"

Paks looked at her arm. "Both, I think. Nothing serious, though."

"But you've been on guard, and haven't had time to clean them. I know the story. Let me see." With painful thoroughness the surgeon scrubbed

223

the various cuts she'd taken, grumbling the while. "If I could just convince you heroes that cleaning these things out does as much good — no, *more* good — than a healing spell. It's cheap. It's easy. They don't fester and give you fever if they're *clean* — "

"Ouch!" said Paks, as the cleaning solution stung in a slice across her hand.

"Hold still. I have to see if that got into the joint — no — lucky. Maybe we need thicker gloves."

"I didn't have mine on," muttered Paks. The surgeon snorted and went on.

"Are you sure you aren't hiding something else?" he asked when he had finished wrapping bandages around her hand.

"Nothing else." She looked down and found that Jenits had followed the whole proceeding with interest. So had others in the room.

"Are you staying with him?" asked the surgeon.

"Do you need me to? I can."

"Yes. Please. We've got Clart and Halveric wounded coming in, and there'll be more later. You can give him enough numbwine to make him sleep. Three or four swallows more should do it. Same for the others — call if anything goes wrong." The surgeon passed on to the next room, and Paks lifted Jenits's head so he could drink more easily. In a few minutes, he was snoring. She glanced around at the others; they all seemed to be dozing. Paks propped the flask nearby and took off her pack to get her cloak. She wrapped it around her shoulders. From the other end of the tent came a sudden flurry that subsided after a few minutes.

When she opened her eyes next, she was stiff as a board and the surgeon was laughing at her in the lamplight. "Some watcher," he said. "If you were going to sleep, you should have found a pallet and stretched out."

Paks yawned and tried to focus her eyes. "I didn't know I was going to sleep. Sorry." She looked at Jenits, but he slept peacefully.

"No sign of fever," said the surgeon. "This time get comfortable before you go back to sleep."

Paks pushed herself up, shaking her head. "I won't sleep. What watch is it, anyway?"

"Don't worry. Stammel came by to tell you he wouldn't need you — "

"And found me asleep." Paks blushed.

"Well," said the surgeon, "he didn't wake you, and told me to let you sleep till dawn. That's another four hours."

Paks yawned again. "It's tempting — " The surgeon turned away. Three years' experience told her to take sleep when she could find it — but now she was awake, and curiosity kept her so. With a last look at Jenits, she left the tent and headed for the area assigned to her cohort.

Kefer was snoring by the watchfire, but roused when she spoke to the sentry. He confirmed what the surgeon had said, and told her to get what sleep she could.

"We'll march tomorrow, and if we catch them, we'll fight." Kefer yawned. "Clarts got many of 'em, but six hundred or so are loose."

224

Paks held her hands to the fire; the night was cold after the surgeons' tent. "Stammel said our losses weren't bad — ?"

"No — not in our cohort. Three returned veterans. One recruit. Dorrin's was harder hit — but still not bad, considering. Go on, Paks, get some sleep." He pointed to a nearby tent; Paks edged in, found an empty space, and slept until day.

Despite Kefer's prediction, they did not march the next day; instead they dismantled the enemy camp. Several squads went to the battlefield, returning with salvageable weapons and armor. Others cleared the camp itself of supplies: bags of grain and beans, great jars of wine and barrels of ale. One tent held all the gear for a smith's shop: anvils, hammers, tongs, bellows, and bars and disks of rough iron.

Most of this they carried into the storage cellars of the tower, each load tallied by a scribe from each company. Siger and Hofrin chose weapons to replace those damaged, and reserve supplies to take along. The enemy's mules were distributed to each company too, along with the feed for them.

From the talk she heard while working, Paks gathered that Siniava's army had come from the west. Before reaching this tower, they had taken those along the western border, and these were now garrisoned by Siniava's troops. But a survivor had escaped to warn the commander of the north watch, the Count of Andressat's son-in-law; when the enemy force arrived, it found the tower sealed and well defended. Clart scouts, riding ahead of the Halverics, had discovered the siege in progress, and the Halverics attacked the besiegers. Though heavily outnumbered, they had held the enemy close under the tower walls, where the Andressat archery could do its worst, until the rest of the Clarts and the Phelani arrived in force.

"They should have got out of here," said a Halveric corporal as he and Paks dragged sacks of grain across the tower court. "Only they thought they could break us and get rid of us — the fools — and we kept 'em busy enough they didn't think of anyone else."

"You had a rough time, then," said Paks.

"Oh — we fight close order, same as you. We just drew in and let 'em pound. We knew you was comin'. And we had some Clarts, to mess 'em about on the flanks."

"It's too bad they broke loose," muttered a Halveric private. "After what they did last year — "

"Too many of 'em," said the corporal. "We mauled 'em enough, they'll be wary of us awhile. Besides, let 'em go tell their master they were beat again. Enough times running away like that, and they won't be good for anything — nor the ones they tell the story to, neither."

By that night, the enemy camp was dismantled. Everything else was piled and burned, a great fire that leapt into the dark and told everyone for miles around that the enemy's camp was gone. Paks had a share marked to her in the account books. Her recruits were recruits no longer; they had all been promoted.

When they marched the next morning, Paks found herself moved up in the column; she was sorry about those whose death and injuries gave her the place, but she liked seeing ahead. All along the way she saw evidence of the enemy's flight: broken weapons, blood-stained clothing and armor, and bodies. Not all had been killed by Clarts or Halverics, as the wounds showed.

By midafternoon they reached the next tower to the west. A black and yellow banner flew from its peak, and a hail of arrows met them when they ventured closer. Their assault failed, and the two companies camped around the walls. The Clarts had ridden afar ahead, to scout the tower beyond, and returned with the news that it too was held by an enemy force.

At dawn the next day, Paks saw about fifty black-clad fighters come over the wall, barely visible in the dim light. She yelled an alarm and darted forward; an arrow glanced off her helmet. The archers were awake in the tower. She threw up her shield and plunged on with the rest of the sentries, as the camp came awake behind her. For a few desperate minutes, the sentries were outnumbered and hard pressed.

Simultaneously, enemy troops tried a sally from the south entrance, where the Halverics were just taking their positions for an assault. In minutes a howling mass of fighters swayed back and forth in front of the gate. More and more of Siniava's troops poured out, as Paks heard later from one of the Halveric soldiers.

"We had to give back; they had us outnumbered, but then your Duke brought two of your cohorts around, and it was stand and stick. That went on all morning, near enough. They couldn't break out, and we couldn't get in. Then they backed in a step at a time, and got that portcullis down — I'll say this for Andressat: they know how to build a fort."

Paks had been on the fringe of that battle, as one of the sentry ring on the other side. She met Barranyi in the cook tent.

"I'll tell you what, Paks," said Barra. "He's no fool, their captain. They came near breaking through more than once, and if they pick the right time, they might yet."

Paks mopped up the last of her beans with a crust of bread. "Not with the Halveric and the Duke. He won't surprise them. What I wonder about is how many more there are — at the next tower, and the next. We can hold these — but more?"

"Andressat has troops somewhere — "

"What — sixty or so in the first tower, and maybe as many in the next one or two? And they won't leave the towers unguarded."

"No, more than that. I heard Dorrin say something to Val about it this morning. Troops on the way, she said, and could be here this afternoon or tomorrow."

"I'll believe that, Barra, when I see it. Did you hear whether the Honeycat was in there?" she cocked her head at the tower.

"No. They all say not. And I haven't seen the banner his bodyguard carried last fall."

"I hope we don't waste too much time here, then. I wonder where that scum is."

"And what troops he has. All we can do is hope the Clarts don't miss anything."

"If he's clear off east — back toward Sorellin or those other cities — we could wander around here all season and never catch him."

Barra shrugged. "That's the Duke's business. Not yours." Paks stood up, and Barra eyed her. "Are you upset about anything in particular? More than Canna and Saben?"

"That, and — Barra, you know what he did to some of the prisoners last year — ?" Barra nodded. "We found a set of tools in one of the tents. I just want to be sure we do kill him."

"But his army'd still be — "

Paks shook her head. "No, I don't think they'll be the same, even if there's much army left. I think it's his doing."

"Maybe." Barra turned to greet Natzlin, coming from the serving line, and Paks waved and went back to her station.

The rest of that day the two forces did not change their positions. The Andressat troops arrived midmorning the next day. Paks thought they looked much more professional than the city militia she'd seen. They numbered just over a thousand, organized into four cohorts, each with two hundred foot and fifty horse. Paks watched as the Duke and the Halveric rode out to meet them. The Andressat troops moved into siege positions, and the mercenaries withdrew a space.

"I heard we march in the morning," said Vik, as he and Paks lugged tent poles from one camp to another.

"I hope so," said Paks. "That group can handle the tower without us."

"They do look good," conceded Vik. "But why d'you suppose they make their cohorts so big? They can't be as flexible."

"Huh. If we had that many men, we might find four units easier to move than — " Paks wrinkled her brows, trying to think how many it would be.

"Ten," said Vik smugly. "I wish we had — then nobody could stand against us."

"Nobody's going to." Paks grunted as they heaved the poles up in their new holes. "I hope we don't have to raise all the tents for only one night."

"I don't think so." Vik rubbed his sunburnt nose. "I'd like to know how many troops Siniava has — altogether."

"Not enough to stop us," said Paks grimly.

"I hope not. But look, Paks — if he could send eight hundred or a thousand up here — and he's not with them — he must have another army someplace. And his cities garrisoned. He could have a much bigger army than the Duke's put together."

"That's true." Paks frowned. "Well — if it is — "

"We'll do like the man with the barrel of ale," said Vik with a grin.

"What's that?"

"Don't tell me you never heard that! It's old, Paks."

"I never did. Tell me."

"Well, there was a man famous for what he could down at one swallow.

At a market fair, he won lots of free ale by betting that he could drink this jug or that, or a skin of wine, at one draught. Soon he was famous for miles around, and no one would bet. Then he went on a journey with a brother of his, and they stopped at an inn. His brother started bragging on what he could do, and the long and short of it is that the innkeeper asked him to wager. Well, he looked around the room, and saw no pot or jug he couldn't drain. He agreed to take but one swallow to empty any alepot in the room, or give up all his silver.

"But the innkeeper had his own tricks, and pulled aside a curtain by the bar, and there was a barrel half full of ale. Of course the man said it was no pot, but the others around said it was, and there were more of them, and they were armed.

"The man knew he was trapped, and he was angry besides. So he walked over and tried to lift it, and of course it was too heavy. The innkeeper told him to kneel down and drink from the bunghole — actually he said worse than that — laughing all the while, and the man was so angry he could nearly fly. So: No, he said, and I drink my ale standing, as any man may, he said, and he rammed a hole in the bottom and let the ale run out until he could lift it and drink the rest — in one swallow. His brother held the innkeeper off in the meantime with a sword off the wall. And when he had finished, he said: A pot's what you can lift in your hand, innkeeper, and any fool who can't tell a pot from a barrel might sell a barrel of ale for the price of a pot. Then the townsmen laughed, and not just because of his strong arm, and made the innkeeper pay up. And he and his brother made their way on the road alive and no poorer. So now, where I grew up, if anyone takes on too much, we say he must be like the man with the barrel of ale: cut the trouble down to his size before swallowing it."

Paks nodded, laughing, and Vik went on. "This is letting some of the ale out of Siniava's barrel — he lost more than six hundred men last fall, and he'll lose these, and the rest in Andressat — say eight hundred or more. You can't pull that many well-trained troops out of a hat, you know. However many he's got, this will hurt."

"I hope so," said Paks.

Chapter Twenty-three

For the next three days, the Halverics and the Duke's Company marched south to Cortes Andres. Rain and rugged country slowed them; the road zigzagged into steep valleys and back up to the sheep pastures. Paks saw carefully terraced slopes set with precise rows of dark sticks.

"Are those young fruit trees?" she asked Stammel.

"Tir, no! Those are grapevines. This is wine country, Paks."

"Oh. They don't look like any grapevines I've seen." Paks thought of the little black grapes of the north sprawling over bushes and walls in an untidy tangle.

"They are. Expensive ones, too. If we break off a single twig, the Count'd have our hides."

They passed through villages nestled in the sides of valleys: stone houses built so close together that the roof of one made the first story of another. Down in the narrow valleys, little plots of spring grain showed green, and a few fruit trees were just starting to bloom. Streams ran clean and clear in rocky beds. Paks saw no cattle, and noticed that the sheep and goats were often spotted in bold patterns of brown and black and white.

The rain which had slowed them covered their approach to Cortes Andres. Clart Cavalry slipped between Siniava's pickets and the city, and the retreating enemy ran straight into the front of the Duke's column.

Seen from the high ground on the northern road, Cortes Andres gave Paks an impression of great strength and stubbornness. Its outer walls were built of immense blocks of gray stone, while above the wall all the towers and battlements gleamed white. Two inner walls circled the city as well. The innermost, like the citadel which rose inside it, was built of pale gold stone. Of the buildings within the walls nothing could be seen but red-tiled roofs, which gave color to the stone around them. Paks could well believe that this citadel had never been taken by assault. She could not see anything of the rivers that came together just south of the city wall; she had been told they formed a deep gorge, and cliffs protected the city on that side.

They marched nearer. The rain stopped, and the sky lightened. Aliam Halveric rode up beside the Duke; both had their standard bearers display their colors. As they neared the gates, a blue and gold banner rose above it. Arcolin halted the column. After a short wait, a man rode from a narrow postern to meet the Halveric and the Duke. The Duke turned and waved; Arcolin started them moving again. They marched nearer. Paks noticed that the portcullis did not rise, nor the gates open. She glanced up. Bowmen edged the wall. The column had marched past the commanders in conference, but now the man from Cortes Andres rode forward and shouted up to the gate tower windows. Arcolin halted them again. Paks squinted up at the arrowslits and caught a glint of light. She felt sweat spring out on her neck, and fought the desire to swing her shield up. Suppose these were not Andressat's men, but Siniava's? The Duke rode up beside them. With a terrible screech the portcullis lifted from its bed. It moved more slowly than any Paks had seen, crawling up its tracks. Then the gates folded inward.

The gatehouse tower was uncommonly deep; Paks saw the tracks of three portcullises. Between them, when she looked up, were convenient holes for bowmen, and she thought she saw eyes gleaming behind each hole. They came out of the tower into a stone paved area between the first and second walls, bare of cover and easily commanded by either. Part of this had been fenced off for sheep pens, but all of it, Paks realized, would make a fine trap for an army that managed to take the outer gate.

The second wall loomed higher than the first, and its gate was offset to the west. They threaded their way between pens of sheep to halt outside the second gate tower. These gates too were closed, but a cluster of figures in blue and gold waited for them. Paks, marching in the first cohort, could see the deference with which the Duke and Aliam Halveric dismounted and walked up to the gray-haired man in the middle. It startled her to hear them addressed as "Aliam" and "young Phelan." She expected the Duke to object, but he answered courteously, calling the man "my lord Count." The captains were introduced, and after more conversation the Count strolled down their column. Paks wished they were not rain-wet and muddy. As he returned, he was chatting with the Duke about border towers and the condition of the vineyards. Paks could not see how they were related.

"Well, then," he said. "We haven't enough stabling within the inner walls for all those cavalry — your mount, of course, Phelan, and Aliam's, and your captains', will be in the citadel. Your troops can have barracks space in the second ring. Fersin, my aide, will direct them." One of his retinue bowed. "You'll dine with me in the citadel, and your captains as well. I expect they'll want to be housed with their cohorts, yes?" The Duke nodded. "I've arranged a suite for you and Aliam, convenient to my quarters; we have much to confer about." The Count glanced at the column again. "Do you — do you need separate barracks space for the women?"

"No, my lord Count."

"I see." He sounded doubtful. "We don't — meaning no disparagement to your troops, Phelan, but we have not seen so many women active in warfare. A paladin here or there, and occasional knight — but — well, no matter."

"I assure you, my lord, that they are quite capable." The Duke's voice was dry, and Paks suppressed a grin.

"Oh, quite — quite, I'm sure. Meant no disparagement. But one thing, Phelan, your troops can't wander about armed in the city — "

"Certainly not, my lord. They will stack their arms in barracks, and I had not planned to permit any wandering anyway."

"I didn't mean to sound inhospitable — "

"Not at all. No one wants strange troops straying loose. These won't."

"No harm if they go to the fountains — or if you need more supplies — but it might be better if they stayed close."

"Certainly."

"Very well, then. Fersin will direct my quartermaster to stand ready with any assistance. I know you brought your own surgeons, but if your wounded need special care, you have only to ask. Hobben — " He spoke to one of the gate guards. "Open this thing and let our guests through. Come along, Phelan, and tell me what you found." He turned away; the Duke and Aliam Halveric followed him through the opening gate.

The column followed Fersin, who turned left inside the gate and led them beside the wall to two-story stone barracks built against it.

"This and the next are empty," he told Arcolin. "If you need more bedding, just tell me. The baths — " he glanced back at the column, "are in the far end of this one, and the near end of the next; there's a kitchen in each cellar. By the Count's order, water's been heating since noon, for your convenience. If you need food, we can supply it, but it will take a little time, since I must speak to the quartermaster. I'd appreciate a squad of your men — uh, troops — helping me bring it — "

"We're well supplied," said Arcolin. "We have what we took from Siniava's army. But we appreciate the offer. Where shall we take the baggage mules?"

"I'll have stable boys come help you. Just a moment — " He looked up and caught the eye of one of the soldiers on the wall, then whistled a complicated phrase. The man saluted and turned away.

"We'll take the far building," said Arcolin. "The Halverics are behind us, and the Clarts behind them; we don't want any more confusion than necessary. Now, where are the fountains?"

"Just down that street," said Fersin, pointing. "There are full waterbutts in each barracks, but if you need more, feel free to get some."

"Thank you, Fersin. Stammel, two squads for the mules; send the rest in. I'll check back."

The Count's barracks were much like the Duke's: long clean rooms with wooden bunks. Each room would hold two cohorts if some slept on the floor, and there were plenty of pallets to make that comfortable. Soon the upper room was organized for the night. Paks caught Stammel's eye when he came upstairs to look.

"Why didn't that man call the Duke by his title?"

"The Count?" Paks nodded. Stammel shook his head. "Oh, he's what they call an aristocrat — one of the old kind."

"So?"

231

"Well, he doesn't think the Duke is really a Duke — from what I hear, the only duke he thinks *is* real is the Duke of Fall, over near the Copper Hills."

Paks frowned. "Is he like those bravos, then that you told me about my first year?"

"Tir, no! Nothing like. He really is a count, the sixteenth in his line, I think."

"But you told me nobody disputed the Duke's title."

"The Count doesn't dispute it; the Duke doesn't ask him to acknowledge it. That's different. Courtesy among allies. And if it doesn't bother the Duke, why should it bother you?"

"I don't understand." Paks felt that it ought to bother the Duke.

Stammel shrugged. "Remember what I told you about Aare — the old country across the sea?" Paks nodded. "Well, these southern nobles trace their titles back to it. They hardly allow that the throne of Tsaia has a king — or a crown prince, as he is — and they don't recognize Pargun and Kostandan and Dzordanya at all. You can see if they don't recognize the crown of Tsaia, they wouldn't acknowledge titles granted by it."

"I see." Paks laid out another blanket. "Well, is the Honeycat one of their kind of nobles, or our kind, or just made up?"

"I don't know. If anyone does, it'll be this count. They say he's so proud of his family that he can recite his fathers and mothers and aunts and cousins all the way back to the beginnings, and say who married whom two hundred years ago."

Paks thought about that, shaking her head. In her own family — she mused over it, coming up blank past grandparents, aunts, uncles, and near cousins. How could the count keep up with more? When she looked up, Stammel had gone on to something else.

Paks drew first shift for a bath, and came to the basement dining hall dry, warm, and comfortable. It would be strange to sleep indoors again. She wondered what it would be like to live in those barracks all the time — then remembered the count's comments on women, and chuckled to herself. Southerners had strange ideas. She wondered if southern women who wanted to be warriors went north.

The next morning they marched at first light, carrying only their weapons, to attack the besieging force that held the south road. They made they way around the city between the outer and second walls. On the south, the city seemed to tip itself over the edge of high cliffs. Before Paks could see what lay below, they dove into an echoing torchlit passage, steeply pitched, and came out on one landing of a zigzag stair winding down from wall to wall, and ending in a huge gatehouse still some way above the rivers. Here they were joined by some five hundred Andressat troops who had come by a different way. As the gates opened, Paks could see nothing at first but distant slopes, dim in the early light.

Once through the gates, the road ran steeply down to a platform above the confluence of the two branches of the Chaloquay: a wild, tossing whirlpool at this season. Upstream, on the right, a narrow road led down to a high arched stone bridge, guarded by towers at either end. The enemy held both towers.

With the roaring rivers close below, it was hard to hear the captains' commands, but their gestures were clear enough. Paks yawned, clearing her ears, and shifted her shield a bit as she marched forward with the others. Spray from the rivers drifted up, cold on her legs. As they dropped to the level of the bridge approaches, arrows skipped along the stones in front of them to shatter on the wall to their right. Archers from the bridge towers: Paks knew how bad that could be as they came closer. But a flight of arrows passed over them from the wall of Cortes Andres. Paks saw several enemy bowmen throw up their arms and fall from the nearer tower. Fewer and fewer archers cared to expose themselves to Andressat's accurate aim; the arrows stopped. Then as the road made an abrupt left turn to the bridge, Paks caught a glimpse of fleeing men on the road south. She hoped that meant the bridge was not defended. A battle was one thing, but she didn't like the thought of fighting over water, or being swept away in the Chaloquay's fierce currents.

The bridge gates, a lattice of heavy timbers rather like a folding portcullis, were closed; their own bowmen sent a volley of shafts through the lattice onto the bridge itself. The enemy retreated to the far tower. Doubling shields, the front rank of archers made it to the gates and unhooked the bar that held them closed. Another rank stepped forward to pull the gates open; soon they gaped wide. Their own archers ran for the tower stairs. Paks's cohort went forward onto the bridge. Nothing barred their way at the far tower; against the light that came through from the open air beyond she could see a dark mass: the enemy.

As they charged, Paks heard the whirr of a few arrows, but saw no one fall. The enemy fell back before them; the rear ranks were already turning to run. By the time the first two ranks were engaged, Siniava's men had retreated from the bridge approach, giving them room to spread out. Paks found herself an opponent. She pressed forward, fending off his blade easily until he left an opening, then she plunged her sword into his body. Another, and another, and the enemy was fleeing, breaking away from the fight in ones and twos and clumps to run gasping up the road away from the bridge. Paks and her cohort pursued, trying to keep their formation while pressing the attack. As they moved farther from the river, Paks could hear Arcolin shouting, urging them on.

Suddenly a thunder of hooves rose from behind them, and a company of cavalry in Andressat blue and gold rolled by, lances poised. Paks had a stitch in her side, and slowed her stride. With cavalry after them, they wouldn't get far. She looked around for her recruits. Keri and Volya were both grinning — she grinned back and took a deep breath as the stitch eased. Not as hard as she'd expected, not at all. Arcolin called them to a halt, and Stammel and Kefer checked the lines. No one seemed to be hurt badly. Paks could hear other troops coming up behind them. The Duke rode past, and the Count, and Aliam Halveric and his captains. They were all talking and laughing. A cohort of Clarts trotted by, yipping and tossing their lances. Paks looked up the slope. Sunlight gilded the top of it, and she watched as it crept toward them, lighting on the way the lance-tips of the horsemen.

After awhile the Clarts rode back at a walk; their leader laid his hand edgewise on his throat. Arcolin grinned. The commanders returned. The Duke reined in beside Arcolin, glancing over the Company with a broad smile before speaking a few words to his captain and riding on. Arcolin turned in his saddle, looking back down the slope.

"We march south today," he said. "My cohort will stay here. The others will go back to pick up all the gear. You did the fighting; no reason for you to climb all those stairs again." Paks grinned to herself, thinking of Barra and Natzlin having to go back. "Stammel," said Arcolin, breaking into her thoughts. "Take 'em to the head of that slope, and keep a guard posted in case the cavalry missed a few of those southerners." He turned his horse and rode back toward the bridge.

The road from the bridge angled toward the main stream of the Chaloquay before turning south in the river's gorge. Instead of this, Stammel led them upslope, until they were well above both road and river. Here an ambush would be impossible. From this vantage point, Paks could see how Cortes Andres had been built on and into a natural cliff. From the rough gray native stone at the river to the pale golden towers of the inner citadel, the city's southern face offered no weakness to an attacker. Paks could not see how anyone could hope to break such a wall: too high to scale, no cover for sappers, the foundation stones three or four times the length of a man, and man-high. If this was how cities were built in the far south, they would have trouble.

Andressat troops — five hundred foot and a hundred horse — marched on the lower road, while the mercenary companies traveled across the rough pasture of the upper slopes. It was pleasant weather, Paks thought, and the spring turf was a welcome change from a muddy road. The next day the valley along the river widened; Paks looked down gentler slopes to see plowland and the pink and white of fruit trees in bloom. It was almost too warm for cloaks. About midday, they moved down to join the Andressat troops on the road. That afternoon they passed through several little villages. Peasants fled, scrambling over the low field walls, and dragging away sheep, goats, and even a pig from its sty. Paks noticed that the Count permitted no straggling or looting. When she looked back, she saw the villagers sneaking back toward their homes. By nightfall, she could see that the slope west of them curved around to the south, blocking their way. She wondered if the river entered another gorge.

The next morning a rumor ran through the camp that a courier had come in with news of Golden Company.

"I don't know anything about it," Stammel kept saying. "A rider came from Andressat. It could just as likely have been word from the Viscount. More likely." But when they were ready to march, the Duke rode up, smiling.

"Just to make sure you get it straight," he said, "Pliuni rebelled against

Siniava's regents and yielded to the Golden Company — " He paused while a delighted roar went up. "Aesil M'dierra is on her way south, with Pliuni and Westland troops as well as her own. If the Honeycat is in his own cities, we'll have him in a few days. If not — well, he won't have a warm hearth to come home to."

Ahead of them, the Chaloquay swung sharply away to their left. The Duke led them away from the road, up across the rising ground ahead. As they climbed, they could see banks of cloud coming up from the south. Soon a thin steady rain began. Paks was glad to be walking on turf. She could not see far, through the curtains of rain, but by late afternoon they were moving downslope again, along a sheep track. Ahead she could see a river.

"It's the same," Stammel said. "We cut across a loop of it. Now we follow it west to Cha." That night they camped within sight of the river, and the next day they marched beside it again. Here were low terraced hills planted to grapevines and a scrubby tree Paks had never seen before. Near the river all was cultivated, in little stone-walled plots: early grain, now a hand tall, fruit trees, neat rows of vegetables. The villages were built of stone, with tile roofs on most houses and walled yards beside the larger ones. They passed a small inn, its windows crowded with staring faces. At the edge of that village, the Clarts were holding a prisoner, a man who had tried to escape west on horseback.

"And too good a horse, my lord," one of the riders was explaining to the Duke as Paks marched by. "He'll be an agent of Siniava's." Paks caught a glimpse of the man's white, frightened face, and his stout brown horse. She never saw him again.

The rain stopped in late afternoon. The next day was cloudy but rainless, and they marched through a widening belt of rich farmland. Beyond one village, the road was paved with great stone slabs, amply wide for the column. In the ditches on either side Paks saw the purple and yellow stars of early flowers. They looked like nothing she had ever seen. She saw more orchards of the scrubby trees. At one of the rest halts, she found an older veteran who knew what they were.

"Oilberry," he said. "That's what makes the best lampfuel, unless you believe the seafolk — they say some kind of sea monster's gizzard, but I never saw any. Down here they eat the berries, or press them for oil — cook with it, and all. They ship some of it north, but it's for rich folks there."

"But why don't we grow it in the north, if it's so good?"

He shrugged. "Why don't they grow apples down here? I don't know — maybe they just won't grow."

The river curved south again. Paks wondered how far away Cha could be seen. All she knew of it was that it lay north of the river; no one in the Company had been there. About midafternoon, she heard an alarm from the Clart forward scouts. Several riders galloped back to confer with the commanders. The column armed. Paks hoped the Andressat troops would fight as well as they looked. They marched on. Suddenly Paks spotted the

235

enemy: a small force forming a line behind an improvised palisade at the edge of a village.

Paks's cohort had been marching left of the road. Now they wheeled and shifted farther left, allowing Andressat troops to take the middle, between the Phelani and the Halverics. Arrows flew from behind the palisade, answered by archers on both flanks. Paks heard cries from behind the piled brush and stakes. Cracolnya's cohort sent a flight of fire arrows; most flickered out. Two seemed to catch, and wisps of smoke rose, thickening.

They closed in. Paks could see bobbing helmets behind the barricade. No more arrows. She wondered why not. Arrows from their own men whirred overhead and came down behind the brush. More yells from the enemy. Only a few yards more. She could see the helmets in retreat. The front ranks broke into a run, eager to fight. Stammel bellowed at them to halt, but several had already hit the brush and tumbled forward.

The barricade rolled into the pit behind it, and Paks could see the sharpened stakes set into the bottom just as three people fell in. Stammel cursed explosively. The rest of the front rank managed to balance on the brink. Riders leaped the pit to harry the retreating army while they lifted out the wounded. Paks was furious. Jori, the only casualty in their cohort, was lucky; he'd live, though he wouldn't be fighting for some days. But the thought of the trap made her stomach roil. She wished the enemy had not run. She ached to hit someone.

None of them slept well that night. The camp simmered, a low rolling murmur of anger and anticipation. The next day they marched warily, eager for a confrontation, but the villages they passed seemed deserted, and they arrived before the walls of Cha without any more contact with the enemy. Paks eyed the walls with professional interest. They were nothing like Cortes Andres, for this city stood on a wide plain beside the river, just above its confluence with the Chaloqueel. Sapping would work here, she thought.

Chapter Twenty-four

Their first test of the city gates proved them to be well-defended; the army pulled back to encircle the city and organize a siege. By the next afternoon, they had constructed portable shelters to protect the sapping teams, and had them in place. Several sapping crews began work, spaced around the wall. Paks spent her time helping to set up the Duke's camp. Like the other experienced veterans, she had been assigned a night guard slot.

Just before sunset, a rider galloped toward them from the west. Clart Cavalry intercepted, then escorted the rider to the Duke's tent. Paks recognized a Golden Company courier. With several friends she edged close to the Duke's tent to pick up what news she could. The rider's horse was lathered; one of the Clarts walked it out. Suddenly the Duke looked out of his tent and glanced around at the loiterers.

"Ah — Paks."

"Yes, my lord."

"Find Arcolin and Cracolnya, and send them here. Then take this — " he handed her a scroll, " — to Aliam Halveric."

"Yes, my lord." Paks was glad to run his errands, but wished the Duke had not found her idling; she had heard his opinion of nosy soldiers before. She knew where Arcolin was, looking over wood for a catapult with one of the Halveric's sons, but she had to ask Arcolin where to find Cracolnya.

"He's around the city, with that other sapping crew. You'd best take a horse." He looked around, and waved to someone leading two horses. "Take my spare; he's not been ridden today."

"Thank you, sir," said Paks. "And where would I find the — the Halveric?" She was not sure this was the correct form to use to his son.

"My father?" asked the young Halveric.

"Yes, sir. The Duke gave me a message for him." She thought the younger man might offer to take it himself, but he simply nodded.

"He's to the south, about a quarter of the way around; the sentries will guide you to the tent."

"Thank you, sir." The boy leading the horses had come near, and Arcolin took the reins of the black and handed them over. Paks mounted, finding the captain's saddle very different from the ones she'd ridden before. But the horse answered heel and rein easily, and she made good time to the opposite

237

side of the city. By the time she had given her message there and ridden on to the Halverics's camp, it was full dark; she was careful to call her name and unit clearly when challenged. Aliam Halveric was eating supper in his tent, along with his eldest son. Paks recalled them clearly from the previous season. The Halveric smiled as she handed over the scroll.

"Ah — I remember you. I was afraid you weren't going to give your parole, and then you made that remarkable journey — yes. Sit down; I may want to send a reply."

Paks sat where she was bidden, on a low stool, while the Halveric read the scroll and handed it to his son. While his son read, he finished the dish of stew before him. He cocked his head at the younger man when he finished.

"Well, Cal? I think I'd best go myself, don't you?"

"Certainly, sir. Have you any orders in the meantime?"

"No — I expect to be back in a few hours, or I'll send word. Get me a horse, please." The younger man nodded and withdrew. The Halveric looked at Paks. "Well — what was your name again? My memory has failed me — "

"Paksenarrion, sir, but I'm called Paks."

"That's right. Paks. Do you have a horse?"

"Yes, sir."

"Good. Then I won't need another escort." Paks flushed at the implied compliment. The younger man returned, and the Halveric stood, reaching for his helmet. Paks rose and held the tent flap aside as he walked out. She mounted and took the torch a guard offered. All around the city was a circle of watchfires and torches; she scarcely needed the one in her hand. At the Duke's tent, one of his squires, Kessim, was waiting to take the Halveric's. He raised an eyebrow at Paks when he recognized Arcolin's horse, but refrained from comment. She grinned at him as she rode off to the horse lines.

The next three days were simple siegework in support of the sapping teams. No one knew what the Golden Company courier had brought. The captains discouraged questions. For Paks, it was an alternation of camp chores and stretches of guard duty — a routine that dulled very quickly. But her recruits thought it was exciting. They asked her dozens of questions about the techniques of sieges, sapping, siege engines — the same questions she had asked the year before. She told them what she knew, then sent them to older veterans.

On the night of the third day, Paks had just gone off-watch and was enjoying a hot drink by one of the watchfires before going to bed when an excited Volya appeared at her elbow.

"Paks — come here!" Paks rose reluctantly and stepped away from the fire. Volya was dancing with impatience.

"What is it?"

"Paks, someone came over the wall, and wanted to talk to the Count. Someone from inside the city — what does that mean?"

Paks thought a moment before answering. "It could mean they want to surrender — or some of them do. Or maybe the Count has an agent in the city, a spy, and he came out to report. I don't think you should be talking about it — "

Volya nodded. "I know. That's what Sergeant Kefer told me, and I won't. I just — "

"You mean the sergeant told you to keep shut about it, and you came straight to me to tell?" Paks was suddenly angry; Volya flinched.

"But Paks, he wouldn't mind about you. You wouldn't tell anyone else, and — "

Paks glared at her. "Volya, an order's an order. When you're told to keep quiet, you do — you don't tell anyone, friend, lover, or whoever. I didn't get the reputation I've got by blabbing off to people or hanging around loose tongues. You say you trust me — fine, but how d'you know there's not someone else near enough to hear, eh?"

Volya sounded near tears. "Paks, I'm sorry — I won't do it again. I — I thought it was all right to tell *you* anything."

"Well, now you know it's not," said Paks shortly. Then she sighed. "Volya, there's more to being a mercenary than fighting and camp work. This thing of talking — you haven't been to a city yet, so Stammel hasn't given you his speech on it. But we don't talk to anyone about Company business, or anything that could be Company business. Even in an ordinary year, every tavern is full of spies. If someone knows who hired us, and what road we're marching on, and when — d'you see?" Volya nodded. "And this year — we can't afford any loose talk. We're almost certainly outnumbered. Our Duke will be trying to move us to the best field for battle without alerting Siniava."

"Yes, Paks. But — the Company is safe, isn't it? We're all loyal to the Duke — aren't we?"

"I hope so. Yes. But even so — you never know who might be listening. And some can't keep shut if they've been drinking. Loyal as a stone when they're sober, but everyone's friend when they've got a load of ale or wine. So when you're told to keep something quiet, you do. From everyone. Clear?"

"Yes, Paks. Should I tell the sergeant — ?"

"No. You've had your scolding. Just remember." Volya nodded, and Paks waved her away. She was no longer sleepy, however, and spent the rest of that night wondering about the man who had come over the wall.

The next morning it became clear that something was happening inside the city. They could see fights on the walls, and bodies thrown over. Sentries close to the walls heard shouts and the clash of arms inside. Older veterans reminded the younger that most sieges fell by treachery and dissension. Late in the afternoon, a small party offered to parley with the Count of Andressat. Paks watched as they filed out the postern: two men in long gowns and three in armor. The Count and all three mercenary captains went to meet them. They talked for some time, then bowed and separated.

As the party started back to the city, the two men in gowns fell with crossbow bolts bristling from their bodies. The armored men spun around and ran for the besiegers' lines, while a great cry rose from the walls.

Just as that disturbance quieted, a column of smoke rose from across the city, followed by more outcry.

"The sappers," said Stammel. "They've fired their supports, and in a little we'll find out whether they breached the wall."

"Will we go in?"

"Not around there. Halveric troops are over there; they'll go." They listened closely until Arcolin called them into formation. Paks noticed that her recruits did not look nervous any more. She herself felt an anxiety she did her best to conceal. This was one of the Honeycat's own cities — what sort of traps and powers might be here? But no word came for an attack; as the red glare of sunset faded from the walls, they were dismissed again. Assault in the morning, the rumors ran.

With morning came riders of the Golden Company, and Aesil M'dierra's senior captain. He had not finished talking to the Duke when the word ran through camp: M'dierra was at Sibili, already in position with Golden Company and the Pliuni volunteers. Westland troops were at Sibili as well. Paks felt a rising excitement. She did not doubt Cha would fall, and after it the Honeycat's home city, Sibili. Paks thought of him looking from his palace windows to see the banners of his enemies.

She squinted against the early sun and saw the city wall crowded with men. Smoke rolled up from the sapper's work near the northwest corner of the city. Paks saw archers lean to shoot into the roofed shelter; their own archers replied. An outcry rose from the main gate tower: Siniava's black and yellow banner sagged from its pole, slipped back toward the wall. Someone up there waved a smaller flag; Paks could not see the colors. The Count's herald blew a long blast. It was answered from the tower, and followed by even more noise from within the walls.

By the time they entered the city, Paks had heard that a faction favoring Andressat had opened the gates. Siniava's men still fought, but they were hampered by the factions opposing them. Despite the warning, Paks had not imagined how chaotic this could be. She soon found out. Just as they came to the first side street, a body of armed men rushed out to form a line across it. These were Siniava's, armed with pikes. They had scarcely engaged the enemy when another band — bowmen in plain leather with a twist of blue and gold on their helmets — charged out of a building behind the enemy line and fired into the back of the pikemen. Fifteen or so fell at once, hit squarely in the back at close range. One arrow hit Paks's shield with enough force to drive the head through; another struck someone behind her. She heard the yell, half pain, half fury. The enemy fighters whirled to meet this attack, and the front ranks of Paks's cohort charged, trying to run them over before the archers made another dangerous shot.

Several more fights interrupted their progress to the city's center. Twice they fought their way out of attempted ambushes. Bodies littered the streets: men, women, children, animals, caught in the street fighting and left behind when the flood of violence passed. At last, beyond a mass of frightened people crammed into a large square, Paks caught sight of the Halveric banner.

As her cohort spread around its side of the square, a small boy broke away and darted toward the street they had left. Rauf made a grab at him and missed; Paks swung her shield across his path. He ran into it headlong, and slipped to the ground, crying. Paks sheathed her sword and reached down to help him up. She heard a cry from the crowd as the terrified boy tried to twist away from her.

"Here now, I won't hurt you," she said. The boy screamed, flailing at her with pudgy fists. "Stop that," she added. He froze in her grip, staring at her with wide eyes. "Now — what did you run for? Don't you know you should have stayed with — your sister, was it?"

"I'll take 'im, Paks," said Rauf. "His sis is all upset — " But as Rauf reached out, the child started fighting again.

"I'd better — " said Paks. "Now, lad — be quiet — you're not hurt, and you won't be." He calmed again, and Paks glanced around for the girl. She was standing only a few yards away, held there by a serious-faced Keri. "Let's go back to her now, lad — and you stay with her, you hear?"

"But — but my puppy!" He choked on the words and started to cry.

"Your puppy? You lost your dog?" His accent was thick, but Paks thought she understood.

He nodded. "He was mine — my very own — and he's not here. He got lost."

Paks thought of the dogs she'd seen, dead in the gutters. "Lad — you stay with your sister. Find your puppy later — not now."

"But he's got lost. He — he'll be frightened without me." Paks thought it was the other way around, but knew it would do no good to argue.

"Even so — What's your name?"

"Seri. Seriast, really."

"Well, Seri, even though your puppy may be frightened, you stay with your sister. She'll help you find your puppy later. Now promise you'll stay with her — " The boy nodded finally. Paks thought he was the same age as her youngest brother, the year she'd left home. She put a hand on his shoulder and steered him toward the girl. "Come along now." The girl grabbed him and held him close.

"I tried to tell her, Paks, that you wouldn't hurt him," said Keri, sounding worried. "I don't know why she thought — " Paks waved him to silence. The girl looked up, her eyes blurred by tears.

"I think he'll stay with you now," said Paks. "But keep a close grip on him for a few hours." The girl nodded, tightening her grasp until the boy squealed.

"Please don't take 'im," she begged. "Please don't — he won't harm ye none."

"We won't take him. What would we want with a child that size?" But the panic on the girl's face made Paks uneasy for days. What were these people

241

used to, that they feared intentional harm to so small a child?

The next day, as Halveric Company rode away to Sibili, Paks found herself hard at work in a warehouse, cataloging plunder for the Duke's Company. This time, at least, she did not have to drag it out, but counting sacks of wool and goat hair, and barrels of wine, beer, oilberries in brine and oil was a hot, dusty, boring job. They finished this chore in one day; the next was spent loading supplies for Sibili and repairing damaged equipment. Paks got a new shield, as did Keri, and Volya had snapped a sword tip against a wall. Jenits came up while Paks was helping Volya wrap the grip of her sword; he had a lumpy bundle of shiny yellow silk.

"Wait until you see this," he said, dropping in on the ground. It clinked. He worked at the knot one-handed. Keri reached to help. "Thanks. There: look at that." They looked at a miscellaneous collection of bracelets, rings, coins, and little carved disks of ivory or shell. Jenits grinned. "That's what I get for being one-armed right now — not strong enough for the heavy stuff. Kefer had me working through the goldsmithies and jewelers' shops with him, and he said to take this much — and to share it with my friends, if I wanted to keep any. I knew that you, Paks, were stuck in those warehouses, and Keri and Volya hadn't found anything better than a stray silver, so here I am. Take your pick."

"Is it really gold?" asked Volya doubtfully.

"I think so. It's soft, like gold, and it doesn't look like copper. It's heavy."

Keri reached over and picked up a ring with a pale green stone. "I wonder what this is."

"I don't know. But let's split it up, before I lose my generous impulses. Paks, you choose first; you're the veteran."

Paks looked over the small pile. "I could take this bracelet for my sister," she said tentatively. It was made in a pattern of linked leaves, with tiny blue stones between them. "We'll take turns," she went on.

"Go on, then. Keri?"

"I'll take this ring."

"I like this," said Volya. She had found a little gold fish, arched as if it were leaping, with a loop formed by the dorsal fin to hold a chain.

Jenits held out his left hand, with a heavy gold ring set with onyx on the first finger. "I cheated," he said. "I took my favorite out first." They laughed and went on choosing. When they'd finished, Jenits folded the square of silk and tucked it into his tunic. "I feel much safer how," he said. "I was afraid I'd have a greedy fit, and you've done all the fighting. By the way, Paks — "

"Hmm?"

"My arm doesn't hurt any more — when can I come back to regular duty?"

"What did the surgeons tell you?"

"Oh — well — six weeks altogether. But it's been three, and it doesn't hurt. I don't want to miss Sibili, and I feel well enough. I thought you could say something to the sergeants."

Paks looked up from Volya's sword and shook her head. "Jenits, it's up to the surgeons. You won't do us any good if you try to fight and it's not healed. Likely it'd come apart at the first stroke, and you'd be worse off than ever. You can ask the surgeon — "

Jenits scowled. "The last time I asked him, he said to quit pestering. Bones heal at their speed, he said, and not for wishing."

"That sounds like Master Simmitt. He's the sharp-tongued one. You won't miss Sibili anyway. We're all marching — "

"But I'll miss the fighting. And if Siniava's there — "

"You wouldn't have a chance at him anyway. You'll see enough fighting, if you stay whole."

"I hope so. To break an arm, my very first — " Jenits broke off as Stammel came up; he squatted beside them with a sigh.

"Well, Jenits, is your arm holding up?"

"Yes, sir. I was just wondering — "

"No, you can't fight with us at Sibili. Not unless we're longer taking that city than I expect. Paks, the Duke's enrolled a few men from Cha — Andressat's faction, of course — and we'll have six of 'em in our cohort. You've gotten these well broken in. I'd like you to take on one of the new men."

Paks thought of several questions, but when she met Stammel's brown eyes she was guided by their wary expression. "Yes, sir. When?"

"Now." Paks rose when he did, and left the rest where they were. When they were out of earshot, Stammel had more to say. "This is new, Paks, taking new men during a campaign. The captain said it's because he wants us at full strength. I suppose that means he'll be recruiting all season. These men, now — the Count vouched for them, and they look like fighters, but of course we don't know anything about them. If you start having doubts, let me know at once." He shot her a hard glance, and waited until she nodded. "Another thing — down here they don't have many women fighters. You heard what the Count said. Well, I thought if we take these men, they'll have to get used to our ways. That's one reason I wanted you to help. Clear enough?"

Paks nodded, though she still felt confused. It was hard to imagine strangers — outsiders — *southerners* as part of the Company. But she could see that Stammel had no answers, and possibly even more questions, so she asked nothing. He sighed again and led her to a group of about twenty men standing with the captains. Three of them had mail shirts, and four had bronze breastplates. The rest wore leather armor. They were all muscular and looked fit enough. Several of Paks's friends stood nearby: Barra, Vik, and Arñe. Vik raised his expressive eyebrow but said nothing. Stammel turned away, and came back in a few minutes with three more of Paks's cohort. He spoke to Arcolin, who pointed out six of the strangers. They followed Stammel.

"Paks, this is Halek," Stammel said. Halek was a several fingers shorter than Paks, with sandy hair and mustache, and pale eyes. Stammel went on. "Halek, she'll show you where to eat and sleep, and what you're expected to do—"

"She?" Halek's tone was derisive. Paks felt a prickle of anger. "What do you think I am, some little boy to take orders from a nursemaid?" Paks clamped her jaw shut. Stammel gave the man a cold stare.

"Either you follow orders, Halek, or you go explain to the captain that you don't want to join us — and why." The man opened his mouth, but Stammel gave him no chance to speak. "No argument. Obey, or leave."

Halek glanced sideways at Paks and flushed. "Yes — sir."

"Come along," said Paks, and walked off without looking at him. She felt his resistance, then a slackening as he gave in and followed her. She was glad she was taller. When they had walked some strides she spoke over her shoulder.

"Our cohort — Arcolin's our captain — is loading today. When did you eat last?"

"This morning. Early." He sounded grumpy.

"Then we'll eat now." Paks angled toward the cooks' tent. "What weapons do you use?"

"Sword," he said. "Not like yours — longer, and not so wide. Or the curved blade Siniava's men carry."

"Are you used to formation fighting? Can you use polearms?"

"No. Where would I learn that? The only organized units around here are Siniava's, and I wouldn't fight for that." The man spat, then lengthened his stride to come up with her. "Listen — are you really a soldier, not a cook or something?"

Paks glared down at him and he reddened. "Yes, I'm a soldier — as you'll find out soon enough. More of one than you, I daresay, if all you've done is play around with a dueller's weapon. I hope you can learn formation fighting, or you won't be any use to us at all."

"Your tongue's sharp, anyway," he said.

"You can test my blade later," said Paks. She led Halek through the serving line, then to a loading crew. He was strong and willing to work; Paks tried to think better of him. By midafternoon the loading was done; they went in search of the armsmasters. Siger was already working with two of the other newcomers, these assigned to Dorrin's cohort. A number of the Duke's men stood around watching. It was always a treat to see the wizened little armsmaster drive a much bigger opponent around the practice ring. Finally he called a halt, and the two men, puffing and sweating, moved out of the ring.

"Not enough marching," grumbled Siger to their backs. "More wind's what you want, and then an old man like me couldn't make you lose breath." He turned to the circle of watchers. "Enjoying yourselves, eh? Well, you all need a workout. Suppose you, there — and you — " he pointed, "get busy with swords, and you four with pikes — " The crowds melted away. Paks and the others with new men stayed. "Ah yes," said Siger when he saw them. "What have we here? Let's see your paces." He beckoned to Halek, who stepped into the ring. "Sword?" asked Siger. "Polearms?"

244

"Sword," said Halek. "But not that short one. I've used a longer one, or the curved — "

Siger grinned at him. "You'll learn. That's what I'm for, and Paks will teach you a lot." He handed Halek a blade. "Now — are you used to a shield?"

"I've used one."

"We'll start without. Go slowly until you get used to the length." They crossed blades and Siger began his usual commentary. "Hmm. I see you've done more fencing than military — that stroke won't work with this blade. You don't have the length. No, and you can't dance about like that in formation, either." He tapped Halek's ribs when an opening came. "When you don't have a shield, your blade must do its work. A little faster now — yes." The clatter of blades speeded up. "No, you're still jigging around too much. Stop now — " As Halek lowered his blade, Siger looked around and motioned to Paks and several others. "Form a line with him," he said. "Paks, come over here and take my shield side. Now — what's your name?"

"Halek."

"Halek, good. Now you'll see what I mean about staying in formation — these on either side will protect your flanks, as you protect theirs. If you stay in line with them, you'll be fine. Clear?"

"Yes. But there's three of us, and only two of you — "

Siger glanced at Paks and smiled slightly. "That's no problem to *us*. Paks, put a banda on; we don't want you stiff at Sibili." Paks stepped to the pile of bandas and returned to Siger's side. Facing her was Sif, of Dorrin's cohort, with Halek in the middle and Vik on the far end. She found she could hold her own against him easily, with strokes to spare for Halek. Siger, despite Vik's aggressive attack, had breath and arm to spare, as usual. He continued his commentary on Halek's swordsmanship and found time to correct the rest of them.

Halek kept trying to shift to one side or the other, but found himself locked between his companions and his opponents' swords. Finally he seemed to get the idea, and began working with Vik and Sif. Sif, now that Halek was doing better, pressed harder. Paks was acutely aware of her unprotected shield arm. She found herself countering strokes rather than pressing her own attack. Halek almost made a touch on her. He grinned. That, thought Paks, is a mistake. She slipped the leash on her anger, forcing a startled Sif back, and back again, and giving Halek two good thumps with her blade. Siger moved with her, stroke for stroke, and they pushed the others to the edge of the ring.

"Hold," said Siger. As they lowered their blades, he said, "Halek, you'll need to practice this way every day. Your bladework is fair, considering your experience, but your cross-body strokes are weak; that's why you shift so. Come back here in a half-glass with a shield, and we'll start again." He turned to Paks. "Tell Stammel that Halek needs the time with me, and see if they'll release you, too." Paks nodded.

245

"Come on, Halek," she said. "We'll get you a shield from the quartermaster."

"What about a sword?"

"Not until I say you're ready," said Siger.

Paks and Halek walked back toward the quartermaster's wagon. Halek was silent for a few yards, then said gruffly. "You're — you're good with a sword."

"I ought to be," said Paks cheerfully. "Siger spent enough yelling and putting bruises on me." She felt good.

"Mmph. Well — I didn't think you would be. I've never seen women fighters before."

"Siniava doesn't use them at all?"

"Oh, I hear he's got a few girls — they duel, and that, at banquets and the like. And of course there's women with his army, but not for fighting." He chuckled. Paks felt herself getting hot again.

"Things are different in this Company," she said firmly.

"I can see that." He walked on a few paces in silence. "But — I don't see how — why — a woman would want to be a fighter. It's hard work — dirty — you can get killed —" He sounded genuinely puzzled.

Paks found herself suppressing a laugh. "Hard work? Were you ever on a farm? Working? No, I thought not. This is no harder than farmwork I was doing at home, and it's no dirtier than butchering sheep. As for getting killed — women die having babies, if it comes to that." She glanced at him to see his reaction; his face was furrowed in a frown. "Besides," she went on, "I like fighting. I'm good at it, and I enjoy it, and I get paid for it. I'd make a very bad farmer's wife."

"Well, but — aren't you going to marry someday?"

Paks shook her head. "No. Some do, but not me. I never wanted to."

"I just can't — are there many women like you in the north?"

Paks shrugged. "I don't know. Some. You saw Captain Dorrin, and Arñe at lunch. Maybe a fourth of us in this Company are women."

"I see." He still looked puzzled.

Chapter Twenty-five

Early the next morning they set out for Sibili, marching along the north bank of the Chaloqueel on a wide stone road. Those three days came back to Paks later as a kind of dream — the rich valley farmlands, with fruit trees in full bloom, clouds of pale pink flowers that strewed their petals on every gust of wind, leaving the hollows of the road drifted with delicate color. On the slopes, grapevines had sprouted tufts of furry greenish-white leaflets. Rows of vegetables, plots of grain like green velvet — but all empty and quiet.

The sun had just set on the third day when they saw Sibili's walls dark against the glowing western sky. Rain began again that night; the next day they picked up what news they could while settling into camp and readying for the assault. Sapping teams had already started work; Cracolnya's cohort joined a small group of men in rust-colored tunics who supervised the construction of more siege towers and catapults.

"Who's that?" asked Keri, of the rust-uniformed men. Paks shrugged. "I don't know. I never saw them before." She stopped Devlin and asked him.

"That's Plas Group — Marki Plas. They're a special company — all they do is siege machines. A section of them came down with Aesil M'dierra."

Despite heavier rain the following day, the assault began, with Andressat and Westland troops in two siege towers. Mercenary archers scoured the wall. The Phelani and Halverics stayed back as reserves; Paks could not see much through the rain, but watched Plas Group specialists operating the two catapults, winding down the arm, loading stones into the cup. She noticed that they adjusted the ropes with each shot, to compensate for dampness. But neither the catapults nor the assault succeeded, and the attackers straggled back that evening in no mood to explain what had gone wrong.

During the night the rain stopped. The Phelani and Halverics struggled to move a third siege tower to the walls under cover of darkness. With the others, Paks cursed angrily as its wheels sank into the mud again and again; by dawn they were still some distance from the walls, in easy range of enemy bowmen. The Duke ordered them back; Paks was glad to leave the unwieldy tower where it had stuck fast. Once out of bowshot, she finally had a chance to see what Sibili looked like. Built on a hump of ground near the river, its inner citadel stood higher than the rest; the walls were well built of buff colored stone. Although the city did not look as formidable as Cortes Andres, Paks though it would be harder to take than Cha. Overall it reminded her of a larger Rotengre, long and narrow, with heavy gates pinched between massive towers.

During that day, both sides used fire weapons. The defenders poured oil on one of the siege towers and lit it, with a cohort of Pliuni on the way up inside. The Pliuni fled, not without casualties. Plas Group lobbed stones smeared with burning pitch over the walls. The defenders fired the second tower; Andressat and Phelani troops rushed to drag it away from the walls and managed to keep the fire from burning the lower framework, but it was too damaged to use until rebuilt.

That night Paks helped drag the remaining siege tower into place while the sappers fired their tunnels. She heard a deep rumble off to her right, and shrill cries from the wall. Had the wall come down?

"Don't stop!" said Captain Pont. "Move this thing!" Over the pounding blood in her ears, Paks heard horn signals and the clamor of combat. At last the tower reached the wall. A body of men they could not see — supposedly the Halverics — jingled past and started up the tower stairs.

"Get armed and ready," said Devlin. Paks wiped the sweat from her face and stretched before slipping her arm into her shield grip. They crowded into the base of the tower, blind in that sheltered darkness.

Suddenly a crash from the top of the tower and a cry from the wall signalled the start of their own assault. The troops on the stairs surged upward. Pont held them back until the first group was halfway to the next level, then sent them on. In the blackness, Paks fell up the first two steps; someone else stumbled into her, cursing. She found her balance and went on. As she neared the top, dim light filtered in. She saw torches on the wall, and fires in the city itself. As she crossed the bridge to the wall, she tried not to think of the many feet of empty air below.

"There!" Vossik of Dorrin's cohort waved an arm to the right; Paks came up behind a line of Halverics slowly pushing enemy pikemen away from the bridge. Where were the rest of them? she wondered. She had no time to think about it; the enemy pressed hard, and the man in front of her fell. She leaped forward over him, taking his place in the Halveric line. She could feel behind her the growing pressure of her own comrades. Slowly, step by step, they forced their way along the wall.

In the dancing torchlight she found it hard to see the enemy's thrusts; she hoped they had the same problem. Paks ducked under one pike and slashed at a man in their front line. She got a hit, then another, then something — what she didn't know — hit her helmet and almost knocked her down. The enemy yelled, as she staggered, and Halverics closed around her. Then she was up, and fighting again. Someone yelled in her ear, and she shook her head, trying to understand. What did they mean, "almost there"?

Suddenly a horrible howling stunned her, followed by a blinding blue flash that lit up the entire city. For just an instant, Paks could see the breach in the wall, just behind the enemy she faced. Then came blackness, utter and thick. Screams and bellows filled the air. The lines crashed together; Paks was crushed in a welter of bodies, all struggling. Something raked her sword arm. She could not get free for a swing, but drove the tip of her sword into what she hoped was an enemy. Someone fell into her. She lost her balance and fell sprawling under a pile of men and weapons, the stink of blood and sweat strong in her nostrils.

All at once light returned: not torchlight, but a mellow golden light over the city itself. In an instant the pile of fighters separated into warring factions, struggling to kill and get free. Paks felt a stabbing pain in her leg, as she wrenched her shield free of a wounded man's shoulder and parried an enemy thrust. She made it to one knee. Someone grabbed her shield arm and pulled. She tried to pivot, but a man on the wall thrust up at her; she had to counter that. The pull steadied her; she got her legs under her again, and whoever had grabbed her let go. She was in a ragged line with several Halverics and some from her own cohort. Most of the enemy were down, some crawling away. They waded into the rest, and cleared the wall as far as the breach before the golden light faded. Paks looked for the source, but could not see it.

"Are you all right?" It was a Halveric private beside her.

Paks nodded; pain shot through her head. "Yes — just winded, I think."

"Your arm's bleeding a lot. Sorry I grabbed you like that — "

"Was that you? It helped. I thought you were one of them, at first."

"I know. You seemed dazed, and those scum were moving — "

"Paks." Devlin had come along the wall. "What besides this arm?"

Paks shifted her weight as Devlin took her arm, and the pain in her leg reminded her. "Left leg — something, I haven't looked. And something hit my head hard; it feels like the helmet's too tight."

"You'd better go back — "

"No, I'm fine. Now that I've got my breath — "

"Go back. This isn't over yet. Get that arm tied up, at least. We'll need you later." He shoved her toward the rear.

As Paks edged her way past those who had just come up, she felt the day's fatigue like a smothering sack of wool. One of the surgeons stationed near the bridge from the siege tower waved her down next to a group of wounded. Paks sank down and tried to ease her helmet off. It wouldn't come; she felt a dint in the front.

"Wait," said the surgeon. "Just sit there — " he turned to one of the others. "We'll need more torches here." The man nodded and moved off, and the surgeon tightened the bandage he was applying. "There. Yes. Now let me see that helmet — yes. Quite a dint. Do you know what hit you?" Paks shook her head. "Did you fall down?"

"Not then."

"Let me get it off." He pulled it off and touched her head. Paks winced. "Tender, eh? I'm not surprised, with that lump." Several men came up with torches. "Good," he told them. "Hold one here. Now look at it," he told

249

Paks. She squinted at the bright glare. "Not too bad. Let's see that arm — anything else?"

"Something stuck my leg." Paks moved her left leg a little. Someone — not the surgeon — took off her boot. It hurt. She tried to see what it looked like.

"Hold still," scolded the surgeon. "This arm needs work; I'll see the leg in a moment." Paks smelled the pungent cleansing solution and braced herself. It felt cold, then burned. Her head throbbed, and she closed her eyes. She felt the surgeon start probing the wound in her leg. She heard him mutter to someone else, and hands steadied her leg as the pain sharpened. She wanted to argue with him, but it was too late. She thought he must be sewing up the hole, whatever it was, but it felt much worse. She wanted to throw up.

"It's the head, mostly," said the surgeon; Paks opened her eyes. Kefer was there, staring at her, and Arcolin stood by the tent flap. Tent?

"I thought we were on the wall," she said. The surgeon turned to her.

"You were. You'd been hit on the head, and you passed out while I was working on your leg."

"Oh." She couldn't remember anything of that, just being on the wall, and fighting, and strange lights.

"Was there a blue light?" she asked doubtfully. "And a yellow one later?"

"Yes." Arcolin stepped nearer. He was scowling. "That was clerics — theirs first, then ours."

"Clerics?" Paks felt even more confused. She had never seen any priest or Marshal make strange lights.

"Never mind that now." He turned to the surgeon. "How long?"

The surgeon shrugged. "A good night's sleep, I expect. Maybe a day." He brought Paks a mug. As her vision blurred with numbwine, she saw the surgeon follow Arcolin and Kefer from the tent.

She woke to broad daylight. The surgeon, busy with others, saw her test the tender lump on her head.

"How is it?"

"Fine."

"Try moving around." Paks sat up and winced as her bandaged arm and leg twinged. But these were minor pains; she could move easily. "Go on and stand." She had no trouble with that, either, and he sent her out. "Get a new helmet — size or so too large, and use extra padding for a day or so. If you get dizzy, or your eyes blur, come back at once. And eat before you go back on duty."

Outside, their camp was in turmoil. Paks could see more troops — Westland men — marching into Sibili through the breached wall. She wondered why they weren't using the gates. Smoke rose over the city walls. As she headed for the quartermaster, she saw Dorrin's cohort returning from the city, faces black with soot and grime.

Her new helmet felt unwieldy, even after she wrapped a cloth around her head. She tried again. Still odd-feeling. When she got to the cooks' tent, she found Barra and Natzlin.

"We heard you were hurt," said Barra, dishing up stew.

"Something hit my head."

"Are you going back in?" Paks wondered if she imagined the edge in that tone.

"Of course. Where's Arcolin — or Pont?"

"They're inside. It's a mess in there, too."

"What about it?"

"They've got some kind of wizard or priest and just when you think you've got a group on the run, there'll be a stinking black cloud all around; you can blunder into anything. Walls, a fire, their fighters — you can't see your own nose."

"And look out for the ones that don't look armed," added Natzlin. "They dress like rich folk, but they carry throwing knives." She gestured to a cut on her cheekbone. "They're good with them, too. You could lose an eye."

"Who've we lost?" asked Paks.

"In Arcolin's? I heard that Suri fell from the tower last night, and someone — who was it, Natz? — took a crossbow bolt in the eye."

"Gan, that was — Gannarrion. And Halek — "

"Halek? What happened to him?"

"Sword thrust in the gut, on the wall."

Paks finished her stew in silence. She had not liked Halek, not at all. But she wished she knew it had not been her sword, there in the darkness. She found her cohort; by the end of that day, the gate tower had fallen, and the attacking troops moved freely through the twisting streets of the lower city. Paks hardly noticed; she marched with the others back to camp, aware only of great weariness.

She woke early, just at daybreak, and was startled to find Volya beside her.

"You were acting strange, yesterday," said Volya. "We thought someone should keep an eye on you."

"I was?" Paks had only the haziest memory of the previous day. There'd been fighting on a wall or a gate or something like that. "I'm fine, now."

"That's what you told Barra yesterday." Volya looked stubborn.

"It's true now, anyway." Paks combed her hair and rebraided it; the lump still hurt when she ran the comb over it. She was very hungry and wondered if she'd eaten the night before.

Although the outer part of the city had fallen, the inner citadel still resisted. Sapping teams were busy at those walls, now. Plas Group had repaired the damaged siege tower; Paks found herself once more hauling on a rope with others, and cursing the ungainly monster that lurched from stone to stone. Suddenly a shout made her look up. A black cloud rolled over the citadel wall and flowed down toward the sapper's shelter. A man in glittering mail spurred his horse toward that part of the wall, raising a mailed fist over his head. Light streaked from his fist to form a web between the cloud and the sappers. When the blackness reached it, green flames sprang up and the cloud disappeared.

Vik nudged her in the ribs. "I heard that's a paladin of Gird."

Paks stared. "That?" She had never believed she would see one.

"Yes. There's a High Marshal here too, and two Swordmasters of Tir, and more — I don't know what — from Pliuni and Westland."

Paks felt ignorant again; she didn't know what a High Marshal was. "What have they got inside?"

"I heard it's a temple to the Master of Torments — some southern god, I suppose. But their priest or whatever they call him has power enough. That's what that blue flash and darkness was, the night we broke the wall. And these black clouds."

Paks watched as the mailed figure rode away from the wall. Paladin or not, she had never seen such a warrior. Every bit of metal glittered like polished jewels, and the horse — it moved lightly as wind-blown down, yet gave the impression of strength and power. For an instant she pictured herself in that mail — on that horse — but that was ridiculous. She leaned her weight on the rope.

By the next afternoon, they were fighting their way through the citadel streets, upward and inward toward Siniava's palace. At last Paks could see an open space behind the defenders. Foot by foot they pushed Siniava's men back toward a broad paved court or square. Directly across from them, enemy troops poured from a high arched doorway in a tall building ornamented with balconies and turrets. Paks assumed it was Siniava's palace. To the left she could just see a massive edifice with a pillared porch above the wide flight of steps.

Then their own reserves managed to force themselves to the front, and Paks and the others in front edged back. She leaned on a wall and caught her breath, watching. More reserves passed her. With them were two Swordmasters of Tir, in their black armor, and a High Marshal of Gird in chainmail under a blue mantle. Beside the Marshal strode a man in glittering chainmail under a flaming red surcoat embroidered with the crescent of Gird. The paladin, thought Paks. She had not seen him so close before. Without thinking, she pushed herself away from the wall to follow him.

By this time, the attackers had forced the enemy most of the way across the square, where they battled fiercely before the palace doors. Paks and the clerics had almost reached the rear of that melee when an ill-armed rabble poured out of the pillared porch on their left to take the attackers on the flank. Quickly the unengaged rear ranks swung to meet them; Paks thought the newcomers looked too scared to be really dangerous, having lost surprise. Behind them, she saw a small group of mailed figures poised at the top of the steps. Even as she parried the unskilled blows, and killed the first of those attacking, a strange sound shook the air, and sent a tremor through her. The sunlight dimmed. Someone beside her shrieked and dropped his sword, scrambling backwards. The attackers screamed too, flailing ahead with even less skill.

From behind her a loud voice shouted a word Paks had never heard and could not afterwards remember. A crackling bolt of light shot past her ear

252

toward the group on the porch. She gaped, a cold chill rippling down her spine, and nearly fell when someone slammed into her leg. She looked back at the attackers barely in time to dodge a sword thrust at her neck. Light flickered over her in blues and yellows, but she paid it no mind. The frantic crowd in front of her demanded all her attention.

Then they were gone — dead, wounded, or runaway — and she looked around. A knot of struggling fighters still contended in front of the palace. Some of her own cohort stood near, watching her. She realized they were waiting for her to tell them where to go next; she had no idea what to tell them. The Swordmasters, High Marshal, and paladin stood just behind the battle; they seemed intent on the group on the stairs, but Paks could not tell what they were doing. She glanced again at the enemy on the stairs, and stopped, fascinated.

The tallest one wore a blood-red surcoat over dead-black mail. On its head was a horned and spiked helmet; the visor was beaked. It carried an immense curved jagged blade with one hand, and a many-thonged whip in the other. A length of black chain clasped its red cloak, and chain belted the surcoat and scabbard. The others also wore black armor, and tunics of red and black plaid. All their weapons were spiked or jagged. Paks shivered. She wondered if she should offer to guard the clerics. Did they know what they faced?

Suddenly the black-armored figures moved, racing down the steps and screaming strange words. Something stung Paks's chest; she thought at once of Canna's medallion. The light dimmed; the enemy fighters brought a cloud of darkness with them. One of the clerics spoke: golden light lay over them all, bright enough for Paks to see the glitter of eyes within the visored helmets. Then the two groups crashed together. Eerie howls, blasts of wind both hot and cold, sizzlings, cracklings, flashing lights — she fought to keep her attention on the fight.

At first both sides ignored her, and they were so closely engaged that she could not find a good opening. Then she saw that the paladin was fending off two: one with both sword and whip, and the other with an axe. The spikes on the whip were catching in the paladin's mail, little jerks that might catch him off balance. Just as Paks reached the paladin's side, the whip fouled his shield-arm, and the axeman aimed a sweeping stroke at it. Paks threw herself forward, trying to block it with her sword.

When the blades met, a flare of blinding light sprang up, and her blade shattered. The hilts burned through her glove before she could drop the broken blade. She staggered into the axeman, seeing nothing but spots from the flash. Pain shot up her arm. She couldn't seem to draw her dagger. She blinked furiously to clear her vision, and felt herself being hoisted by shoulder and hip. She kicked out strongly, and hit something. Then she fell, hard, onto the stone, and had just time to see a black-booted foot swing back before the kick landed.

She woke to the muted light in the surgeons' tent. She had no idea why she was there until she tried to move her right arm. Her hand and wrist throbbed. When she looked, a bulky bandage swathed her arm to the elbow. She was thirsty. She looked around, and saw only other wounded on pallets. A low murmur of voices came from the next room. The curtain between the rooms billowed and the surgeon came through, a man in Girdish blue behind him.

"Ah — Paks," said the surgeon softly, coming to her. "You did wake up finally. How do you feel?"

"Thirsty," she said.

"No wonder." He poured a mug from the tall jug in the corner, and offered it. Paks reached, but when she lifted her head to drink pain stabbed her head and darkened her vision. The surgeon moved quickly to help her. "Blast it. I hoped you would be over that. Go on, now — drink as much as you can." She managed five or six swallows. "Is it just your head?"

"Yes — that is, my sword hand hurts some. What happened?"

"You don't remember?"

"No. The last I remember is — is pulling a siege tower. And there was a cloud coming over the wall, and someone stopped it."

"Hmm. You've lost some time. You got a knock on your head some days ago, and then another one that left you flat out. And you've got a burned hand, though it will heal. You can thank High Marshal Kereth that it's no worse."

Paks looked at the Girdsman, now squatting on his heels beside her pallet. She had never been so close to any cleric. He had thick dark hair cropped below his ears, and the short-trimmed beard of one who fought in a visored helmet. Even out of armor and relaxed, he conveyed power and authority.

"They tell me," he began, "that you are not a follower of St. Gird. Is that so?"

Paks started to nod, but the pain lanced through her head again. "Yes, sir; it's true."

"But you wear his holy symbol. It was given to you, I understand, by a Girdsman?"

"Yes, sir. A friend — Canna."

"Ah. Did she tell you why she gave it to you? Had she been trying to convert you?"

"No, sir. I — I wasn't there when she died. The Duke told me she had left it to me. He — he said it would be right to keep it."

The High Marshal pursed his lips. "It's unusual. Most Girdsmen, if they die in battle or from wounds, want their symbols returned to the barton or grange where they joined. A friend might be asked to take it there, to tell the story of a brave death. Sometimes it's left to a family member. But to give it to a non-believer, out of the Fellowship of Gird — that's not common at all."

"Should I give it to you, then? To give to the — the barton?"

"Now, you mean?" His brows raised; he sounded surprised at the offer. Paks wondered why.

"Yes, sir."

"No." His head shake was emphatic, certain. "I don't think so. A dying

254

friend's wish deserves respect; if she said you were to keep it, I think you should. But tell me, what do you know about St. Gird and his followers?"

Paks thought a long moment. "Well — Canna and Effa both said that Gird was a fighter. So good a fighter that he turned into a god or something, and now fighters can pray to him for courage and victory. And his clerics — Marshals — can heal wounds. Girdsmen are supposed to be honest and brave and never refuse to fight — but not cruel or unfair."

"Hmm." The High Marshal's mouth twitched in a brief smile. "And this doesn't appeal to you?"

"Well — sir — " Paks tried to think how to say it politely. "I don't quite see how a fighter could become a god."

She thought he might explain, but he said merely, "Anything else?"

"When I was a recruit, Effa tried to convert all of us. She told us about Gird's power and protection and all. But it seemed to me that if Gird favored fighting, he wouldn't be protecting much. Then Effa got a broken back in her first battle, and died a week later. Gird didn't heal her." Paks paused and looked at the High Marshal, but he said nothing, only nodded for her to go on. "And Canna — nobody could have been braver than Canna; if Gird cared about his followers at all, he should have saved her. She — she said it takes a Marshal to heal wounds, but if Gird is so powerful, I don't see why he can't go on and do it, without any fuss." Paks found she was glaring at the High Marshal, furious. Her head pounded.

The High Marshal's expression was serious, but held no rancor. "Let me explain what we know about Gird. He was a farmer — the sort of big, powerful farmer you see all over Fintha and Tsaia. Tall, strong, hot-headed — " Paks thought of her father. "The rulers in his day were cruel and unjust; Gird found himself leading a rebellion after they harrassed his village. Now these were just ordinary farmers — they had no weapons. They made clubs of firewood, and took scythes and plowhandles, and trained in the walled bartons of the village. And with these weapons, and these rough farmers, Gird managed to defeat the rulers with their fine army and its swords and spears." Paks thought that almost as unlikely as Effa's version — farmers winning against real soldiers? — but she kept her mouth shut. The High Marshal continued. "That's why we call our meeting places bartons, and the larger ones granges — that's where Gird's followers met and trained, in farmyard and barn."

Paks nodded, when the Marshal seemed to be waiting for her reaction, and he went on. "His friends wanted him to be their king, but Gird refused. Instead, he used his military command to change the army into something new — the protector of the helpless and innocent, rather than the tool of the rich. He insisted that his followers be honest, fair, and that they care for the poor. We have records, in our archives, of the peaceful years when Gird was chief among guardians." Again the Marshal glanced at her before going on.

"Then came a new threat. Powers of evil, exactly what we don't know. Many feared them too much to resist, and fled far away. But Gird went out to face them with his old cudgel. No one saw that battle, but the dark powers fled the land for many years, and Gird was not seen on earth again. Gird's best friend, who had been away on a journey, had a dream in which he saw Gird ascending to the Court of the High Lord — saw him honored there, and given a cudgel of light to wield. It was after that, when he told his dream, that the priests of the High Lord recognized Gird as a saint. We don't claim Gird is a god. We say he is a favored servant of the High Lord; he has been given powers to aid his followers and the cause of right."

Paks nodded slowly. Except for the bit about farmers winning battles against trained troops, this made more sense than Effa's explanation. And it had been long ago — maybe the rulers had had no real army, or Gird had had the gods' help. That much she could believe. "He sounds like a good man — and a good fighter."

"So are you, from what I saw yesterday," said the High Marshal. "Your friend who gave you her symbol must have thought well of you. If you ever do become a Girdsman, you'd be a good one."

Paks could not think what to say to this. She wished she could remember just what she'd done the day before, and she had no desire to become a follower of Gird.

"You don't remember yesterday at all?" he asked, with a quick sideways glance.

"No, sir."

He sighed. "I wish you did. I'd like to know why it didn't kill you."

"What?"

"You crossed blades with a priest of Liart, child. That should have been the death of you. It shattered your blade, burned your hand — Fenith could scarcely believe it when he saw you kick at the priest after that. It was bravely done, but foolish, to take on such a foe — and amazing that you survived it."

As he spoke, Paks saw a shadowy version of these things in her mind — not yet a memory, but the stirrings of what might become one. "Was there — someone in a red and black tunic, and a helmet with spikes — ?"

"Yes. Are you remembering?"

"Not exactly. It's not clear at all. Why should their blades burn my hand?"

"Because his weapon was no ordinary axe."

"You mean magical?" She thought of Dorrin's sword.

"If you call a curse magic." The High Marshal frowned. "Do you know whose priests those were?"

"No . . . I'd never seen anything like them."

"I should hope not. The Master of Torments, or Liart, is an evil deity not worshipped openly in lands where the Fellowship of Gird has any influence. His priests carry weapons of great power. Evil power. No ordinary weapon can turn their strokes; unless a warrior has uncommon aid or protection he dies. Liart desires the fear of those he controls. He delights in causing strife, in murders and massacres, in bloodlust and torture. His weapons cause pain as well as death, and slavery thrives in his dominion." He smiled at her for a moment. "So you see why I am so interested in your

256

symbol of Gird. I would not expect such a symbol alone to protect an ordinary wearer — even a Girdsman — from certain death. But I cannot think what else saved you — and something surely did. Are you under another deity's protection?"

"No, sir. Not that I know of. I — we — where I grew up, we followed the High Lord — the old gods. I'd never heard of Gird until I joined the Company."

"I see. Was that in the north?"

"Yes, sir. Far north — a village called Three Firs."

"Which kingdom is it in?"

"I don't know, exactly — it's some way north and west of the Duke's stronghold."

"Fintha, or the borders of it. If you never heard of Gird, you heard heroes' tales enough, I'll warrant."

"Yes, sir. Many of them: Torre's Ride, and the Song of Seliast, and the Deed of Cullen Long-arm."

"Ah, yes. Was it those songs made you decide to be a warrior?"

Paks blushed and looked away. "Well — in a way — when I was very small. I — I did dream about it, the magic swords and winged horses, and all. But then my cousin became a soldier. When he came back he had tales to tell, and he told me the best way would be to join the mercenaries, the good ones. He told me what to look for — not to join any wild band, but an honorable company. The others, he said, were full of thieves and bullies, and cared only for gold."

"And that mattered to you? That your companions should be honest and fair?"

"Of course." Paks stared at him in surprise.

"And have you found them so, in this company?" He was looking down at his hands, not at her.

"Yes, sir. It wasn't exactly what I expected, but — surely no one could ask better companions. And it is an honorable company; the Duke keeps it so."

"How was it not what you expected?"

"Oh — " Paks grinned sheepishly. "I hadn't known about the camp work — cooking, cleaning, digging, all that. Jornoth left that out. Then I had thought I'd be fighting robbers and evil things — even orcs, maybe — as in the tales. But most of our fighting is against other mercenaries or militia — whoever we're hired to fight. This year's different, of course."

The Marshal nodded. "And would you feel better if you were fighting for such a purpose all the time?"

Paks thought about it. "I don't know. I like to fight — the Duke is very good, and fair. I'm glad to serve him. It's hard to imagine anything else. And this year, we're fighting a great evil. I like that. Siniava killed my friends last year, and tortured, too."

"Yes, this campaign is clearly one of good against evil, and that suits you. But ordinarily — ?"

She frowned, choosing her words. "Sir, I — I serve our Duke. That was my oath, when I joined. He is worthy of my service; he has never asked any dishonorable thing. I have no right to question — judge — the contracts he takes."

The High Marshal looked at her thoughtfully. "I see. Yes, your Duke is a good man; I won't argue that. And you are loyal, which is good. But something is moving you, which I do not understand, and I think you hardly realize. You may be called to leave your Duke, at least for a time. If so, I hope you will understand the need. Now I can see that you are tiring, and need your rest. Would you like anything to eat, or just more water?"

Paks was puzzling her way through what the High Marshal said; his final question caught her by surprise. "No sir," she said. "Just — just water, if it's near."

He chuckled. "Your surgeon left a bottle here. Can you manage?" He passed it, and this time nothing happened when she lifted her head to drink. The water was cold; she shivered as she drank. The Marshal rose and brought another blanket from the pile. "Rest now," he said. "I would like to speak to you again, if you don't mind — " She shook her head. "Good. May Gird's care be with you." He moved away; Paks stared, still confused.

Chapter Twenty-six

When the sentry ushered the High Marshal into the tent, Duke Phelan and his senior captains were seated around his map table in conference. They looked up. Dorrin smiled, but the rest looked wary.

"I wanted to thank you, my lord, for permission to talk with Paksenarrion."

"Have a seat," offered the Duke. "Did you find out what you wanted?"

The High Marshal gathered his robes and sat down. "Not precisely, my lord. She is still dazed, and does not remember anything of the fighting. I did not wish to tire her. But what I learned confirmed my opinion that something is happening to her — and now I am reassured that it is more likely good than evil."

"Evil!" Arcolin straightened and looked angry. "Were you thinking that Paks was evil? Why, she's the best — "

"Enough." The Duke's voice was calm, but his eyes were flinty. "The High Marshal will no doubt explain himself."

"Gladly. I had no wish to anger you, Captain, or to insult your soldier. All I had heard of Paksenarrion before I saw her was good. But one reason why a blow from such a weapon of evil might not kill is that the person hit is a servant of that same deity. If — "

"Not Paksenarrion!" interrupted Arcolin.

"No. I agree. But I had to be sure; I had to see her myself. Even with what you and others had said of her service last year. There have been a few cases of Gird's symbol being worn as a mockery by those who hate him. And there are more cases of evil pretending to be good, for a long purpose."

"I'd have thought," said the Duke, pouring another mug of wine, and passing it to the High Marshal, "that you could have told that yesterday, when you found the medallion. Or — what's his name? Fenith? — the paladin. Don't paladins claim to know good from evil?"

"Yes, my lord, but only if the being is aware, which she was not." He took a sip of wine and sighed. "And I'll say again — we did not think it likely that she served evil knowingly, not in this Company, not when a Girdsman had left her the medallion. But we had to know. That leaves us, however, with the same puzzle. If she were Girdish, and his symbol saved her life, it would mean she had received special aid from Gird. We would consider that such a one might have a call from Gird himself — should go to Fin Panir, say, and train as a Marshal or paladin. But she is not Girdish; she has never considered becoming Girdish." He paused, and a smile moved his face. "In fact, she had quite — primitive, I suppose I'd say — ideas about Gird. The recruit she met — Effa, I think she said — who told her about Gird, seems to have been highly enthusiastic and quite ignorant."

Arcolin glanced at him. "Effa — yes. She was. She was crippled in her first battle, and died soon after."

"So Paksenarrion said. She considers that reason enough for doubting either Gird's power or his interest, I'm not sure which. But back to my point: since Paksenarrion is not Girdish, it's hard to see why — or even how — the symbol could have saved her. I asked her about other deities, but as far as she's aware, she's under no special protection."

"Did you consider Falk or Camwyn?" asked Dorrin. The High Marshal smiled and nodded.

"Indeed yes, captain. But she's from the northwest — Fintha or its borders — and had never heard of Gird before she joined your Company. Falk and Camwyn are better known to the south and east." He shook his head. "I cannot say who or what saved Paksenarrion, but something most assuredly did." He took a sip of wine; the others nodded slowly. "My lord Duke," he began again. "I know you have no love for the Fellowship of Gird, but you are known to be a fair and just leader. Paksenarrion has told me that she cannot imagine following anyone else. But consider, my lord: some force is moving in her life, something which may call her away from this Company. Not me," he added quickly, to the scowls around him. "I did not even suggest to her that she should join our granges or leave you. I would not dare, not knowing what the High Lord may have planned for her — "

"What do you think?" asked the Duke abruptly.

"Think?" The High Marshal leaned back in his chair. "I think you have as fine a young warrior as I've seen. That's what I hear, as well, from all who have mentioned her. Too impulsive, perhaps, like most young fighters, but that comes as much from generosity as anything else. I think she'll go beyond a hired fighter in the ranks, if nothing breaks that will or that honesty." He sipped again at his mug. Arcolin frowned at his hands locked together on the table. Dorrin fiddled with a link of the fine chain that clasped her cloak. Cracolnya, head cocked on one side, traced a river on the map. Only the Duke locked eyes with the High Marshal.

"You think this Company would do that — would harm her?"

"No, my lord. If she is what she may be, she could not have found a better training ground than your Company. But she may grow beyond it, and if she does, her loyalty may hold her anyway. She will grow cramped, my lord, like a hawk always caged."

"All companies are cages," said the Duke.

"True. I wish, though — I hope that if she seems to be — if she needs freeing, that you will free her."

"I'm no slavemaster!" growled the Duke. "By — by Tir, you know me better than that! She's served her first enlistment; she can go when she will.

But I'll not, High Marshal of Gird, toss her out for no good reason except that you worthy people and interpreters of the gods' will think she's trapped here. You'll not get what you want that way!"

"What we want?"

"Aye, what you always want. Every good fighter should be Girdish, to fight at your Marshal-General's command. Ha! You'll find, High Marshal, that there are worthy battles never sanctioned by your fellowship — helpless victims you never see that depend on others for rescue — fighters just as honest and kind and brave as your paladins who don't get the glory of it — " The Duke paused, breathing hard, his face pale. The High Marshal did not move, and the two men stared at each other in silence. At last the High Marshal set his mug on the table.

"My lord, you know we have never claimed that only in our service is a warrior warring well. There are other saints than Gird, and gods above saints. And you know I did not lie to you: I would be glad to see that girl a Girdsman, but I did not and will not try to talk her into it."

"She could surprise you and end up a loyal servant of Tir," said Arcolin.

"That may be. As long as she serves good — and not my good, my lord, or yours — I wish her all joy. We are not quite so narrow as you think us, Duke Phelan."

"Perhaps." The Duke shifted in his seat. "I hope not. And, after all, in this campaign we are allies once more." He poured more wine in his own mug and offered the jug to the High Marshal, who refused it. "I told the captains to let the Girdsmen in their cohorts know you'd be in camp this afternoon — have you seen them?"

"Yes, my lord; most of them I've seen, and all the wounded. I appreciate the chance to meet with them."

"I," said the Duke brusquely, "don't try to influence my troops."

"No? I'd have thought you influenced them daily with your example of courage and fairness."

"Don't flatter me, High Marshal, if you want something."

"I'm not flattering. You command a fine, well-disciplined body of troops; everyone knows it. You don't get that without the other. Look at Siniava's, for example — or Sofi Ganarrion's, though the cause is different." The High Marshal shifted his weight and set his hands on his knees. "My lord, it's late, and you have much to do. I will not trespass further on your time. But if you would allow me to speak to Paksenarrion again, when her memory has returned, I would like it."

The Duke gave him a long look. "It's not my decision to prevent you — but we march in the morning."

"Can she?"

"I leave no wounded behind for that scum or his agents to capture, High Marshal. Those who can't march will ride in the wagons. If you're going our way, you can talk to her again."

"Do you expect to have need of clerical aid, where you're going?"

The Duke laughed. "Delicately phrased, High Marshal. I appreciate your delicacy. No, I think not. This city, and perhaps others on the coast, were the strongholds of those deities who cannot be fought by sword alone. I expect hard battles, but straightforward ones. Your aid in healing would be welcome, but, after all, there are other sources of healing."

"I would like to be there when you take Siniava," mused the Marshal. "But my own command lies elsewhere. We might meet again this season, should our ways to the same end cross. I must go to Vonja, among others."

The Duke's eyes twinkled. "We might be near Vonja ourselves, though I cannot say how soon. If you would ride with us, you may."

"It's a thought—"

"But if you start with us, High Marshal, you must stay. Whatever I think of your fellowship as a whole, I trust its clerics' discretion. But Siniava has agents all over the south, and torture—as you saw, in there—is one of his pastimes. I will not risk my Company."

"No, I understand. If I decide to go with you, I will tell you in the morning, early." The High Marshal stood. "I thank you, my lord, for your courtesy. And, if you'll allow, I'll pray Gird's blessing on your ventures."

The Duke had also risen. "Blessings, High Marshal, we always accept, with thanks." The High Marshal bowed slightly and withdrew. The Duke stood, looking after him with a faint frown, before turning back to his captains.

"Well. What do you think of that?" He looked around at them.

Arcolin snorted. "Anyone stupid enough to even consider that Paks could be evil, after what she's done—" He didn't finish.

"I wonder—" began Dorrin. "I don't know if I mentioned it, my lord, but there was an incident in Rotengre last fall—"

The Duke threw himself into his seat again. "No. I don't recall. About Paks?"

"Yes, my lord. Remember that we found a priest of Achrya?"

"Oh—yes, I do. Was she involved in that?"

Dorrin nodded. "I wondered at the time if Canna's medallion had saved her. She came near being hit by a crossbow, and then the priest cut her with a poisoned dagger. Luckily I was nearby . . ."

"But you're wondering if it was all luck," suggested Arcolin.

"Yes. Perhaps I look at it differently, as a Falkian." Dorrin gave each of them a long look. "But I must agree with the High Marshal that far: something has protected her, and now more than once."

"She takes wounds like anyone else," said Arcolin.

"Yes—it's not that kind of protection, obviously. But when you think of it, as much as she's in the front ranks, she has fewer scars than most."

"And she's a better fighter." The Duke shifted in his seat. "So, then— you think something protects her, at least from some kinds of injury. Do you see her leaving the Company?"

Dorrin frowned, and paused before answering. "My lord, I don't know. Once, I would have said no. But the Company has changed. If she's being guided by—by something, perhaps she will need to leave."

"She could grow in the Company," offered the Duke. "She needn't stay in the ranks, if it comes to that. Sergeant — even captain someday." They all thought that over. "I know it's unusual," the Duke went on. "But so is she — and if she's got the potential you and the High Marshal think she has, I would be open to the suggestion later."

Dorrin smiled. "I'd rather her than Peska, to tell the truth, my lord."

The Duke laughed. "Dorrin, I promise you he'll be gone after this campaign. And you must admit he's a good field commander."

Dorrin grimaced. "In a way. If you like that sort."

"I agree," said Arcolin, with a sideways look at Dorrin. "He's not what we want to keep in the Company, my lord. But about Paks — I'd thought she would make a good sergeant, when she's had more experience. I hadn't thought of more."

"We don't have to," said the Duke, "until later. And I can't see encouraging her to leave the Company any time soon. She hasn't the experience yet to be a free-lance. But I'll do this, Dorrin — with Arcolin's agreement — I'll see the armsmasters encourage her to pick up solo skills. And if anything else happens with her and that blasted medallion, be sure to let me know. All right?" Dorrin nodded, and Arcolin, and they returned to the maps.

Chapter Twenty-seven

For some days of the journey away from Sibili, Paks rode in the wagons, unable to stand without help. Between the pain in her head, the rain, and the swaying and lurching of the wagons, she was miserable enough not to regret having missed the sack of Sibili. From Volya, who came every evening to check on her, she learned some of what she'd forgotten: which night they'd assaulted the wall, which day the paladin had repelled a black cloud near them, which day the citadel had been taken. Volya's tale was incredible — it didn't seem possible that she could have forgotten such fighting, just from a knock on the head. She worried at her mind, trying to force the memories to return, but nothing worked. She had fought beside a paladin — he had come later and tried to heal her — and she could not remember.

Volya's reports of the city's sack were almost as strange, but not as disturbing; it bothered Paks less to have missed something completely than to have been there and forgotten. Volya told of rich treasure in the palace:

"Gold," she said. "I never imagined so much. Even a gold mirror. And most of the rooms had pictures on the floor, made of little bits of rock laid in patterns: all colors. And in one room, the walls and floor were all white stone, carved in patterns of vines and leaves. When the light came in the window, it glowed. We just stood and stared; it was wonderful. But underneath —" Volya paused, and went on to describe the horrors that Sibili had concealed. Both Siniava's palace and the temple of Liart overlay dungeons and torture chambers. They had found victims still alive, but hopelessly crippled, and on the high altar in Liart's temple a child's body, still warm. Paks thought at once of the girl in Cha who had feared for her little brother — was that what she'd expected?

"How many days did I miss?" Paks finally asked, when Volya had run down.

"You were out for more than a day — but from what you say, you don't remember much from the day or so before that."

"Huh. Not doing the Company much good."

"No, the fighting was almost over when you went down. Oh, and Paks — you should have seen the servants in the palace — "

"Why?"

"They all had marks on their faces — tattoos," Stammel said. "Seems Siniava marks all his own household — his personal bodyguard, too: blue or black tattoos all over the face. It should make them easy to recognize."

Paks nodded. "It should indeed. Makes it hard for them to run away, too."

Volya grinned. "I hadn't thought of that." After she left Paks realized that she'd have to quit thinking of Volya as a recruit: she and the others had come a long way since the winter. Already they had more combat experience than Paks had had in her entire first year.

By the time they passed Cha again, retracing their earlier route, Paks was walking part of the day, and had started exercising her burned hand, under the surgeons' directions. She knew that the Halverics and Clarts were traveling with them, that Golden Company had taken a contract with Andressat to govern and control Sibili and Cha; the Count of Andressat had laid claim to the South Marches and those cities.

"That's why he was so angry with the Westland and Pliuni troops for destroying the orchards and vineyards." Jenits, eating lunch with Paks and Volya, took a pull at his flask. "They made a mess — hacking down trees for cooking fires —"

"They cut down orchards?" Paks was shocked. Jenits and Volya nodded. "But we don't do things like that. What about the crops?"

"Those troops from Pliuni," said Jenits, "want to destroy everything the Honeycat ever owned. We've got some of 'em marching with us now." He made a sour face. "Huh — it's all the Duke and the Halveric can do to keep them from torching everything we pass."

"Then why are they with us?"

"Well — they can fight. They want to fight Siniava. That's it, I suppose. We've had losses — if they'll fight, that's what the Duke wants. But they're not much like us, I can tell you that."

"Are they spread through the Company, or what?" Paks glanced around, trying to distinguish them.

"No. They're in their own formation, under their own captain." Jenits craned his neck to look. "You can't see them from here; they wear green and purple."

After marching east from Cha, along the river, they took the same short-cut across the loop, this time moving northeast. But when they rejoined the river, they forded it instead of turning toward Cortes Andres. Atop the rising ground to the east was a thick forest. Paks had heard of this — the haunt of Alured the Black, the sea pirate turned brigand.

As they neared the trees she felt grumpy and nervous at once. She was still unarmed, for the skin of her hand was not tough enough to hold a weapon, the surgeons insisted. She hated marching in back with the other wounded. Once in that cool shade, undergrowth screened the view to either side; the sunlight almost seemed green. Paks had relaxed a little when the horn call for danger rang out ahead. She felt her heart thudding; her hand dropped automatically to the sword that wasn't there. Halveric fighters moved up from the rear to screen the wounded. Once they were in place, it was quiet but for the rustling leaves overhead. Paks looked at the broad back of the Halveric nearest her. He looked strong, but she still wanted her own sword.

Her first sight of Alured the Black came as the Duke and the other captains escorted him along the column, introducing him to the troops. He looked nothing like the pirate or brigand she had pictured in her mind. He had long black hair in a braid, and a black beard; his face was darkly tanned. Strong bones, strong arched eyebrows, snapping black eyes. He sat his black horse easily, his broad shoulders square and erect, his hands quiet on the reins. As he and the others rode on down the column, she saw that his glossy black braid was bound with green leather and decorated with several bright-colored feathers. Paks thought this looked a little silly, but his longbow and sword were workmanlike enough.

They spent almost four days crossing the forest, camping each night in clearings Alured designated, and closely watched by his men. These wore mottled, drab clothing well-suited for forest work, with a badge on the left breast: a gray tower on a green field. Paks wondered what it meant. Alured's men provided fresh meat each night: rabbits and other small game, for they would not hunt the red deer in spring.

On the afternoon of the fourth day, they reached the forest edge. On their left, the land dropped steeply to a river they could see but not hear — the eastern branch of the Chaloquay. Ahead were the pastures and fields of Cilwan — three days ahead was Cortes Cilwan, the city. Scattered groves and patches of forest extended some distance from Alured's domain; they marched to one of these before camping for the night. Paks thought of the band of men she had seen watching the column as it left the forest. She wished she knew what they were thinking.

By this time Jenits's arm was out of splints; he carried a shield as he marched to strengthen it. Paks had been cleared to return to her cohort. The lump on her head was much smaller, and her hand healed with little scarring. She had to rub and stretch the scars with oil every day, and wear a glove all the time, but she had a sword at her side again.

Cilwan was much lusher country than Andressat or the South Marches. Never a stone showed in the dark soil; flowers edged the garden plots on the farms they passed. Most buildings were well-kept, shutters and doors brightly painted. But the people shunned them, hiding in the fields until the column had passed.

Near noon a day or so later, they passed through a small village. Paks was shocked to see the Pliuni troops in front of her slip from the column to enter houses, emerging with arms full of food and clothing. Hooves pounded up from behind. Arcolin yelled at the Pliunis. They shambled to a halt. Paks could see the resentment in their hunched shoulders as Arcolin argued with their captain. A loose shutter creaked in the breeze.

"No raiding!" Arcolin was still shouting. "These aren't enemies — we aren't robbers; we're soldiers. You have enough food. You don't need to do this."

The Pliuni captain had pale red hair; his skin flushed to the same color. "This is silly. Siniava robbed us often enough — these are only peasants —"

"They aren't even Siniava's peasants! No. No raiding. You wanted to come with the Duke, and you agreed to obey him —"

"The Duke, yes," growled the Pliuni captain. "Not a bunch of damned nursemaids!" Paks heard a mutter of agreement from the Pliuni troops near her. Her hand slipped toward her sword; she saw Arcolin's hand move toward his. The Pliunis seemed to draw together. Paks looked for the sergeants. They both nodded slightly as they moved, one on either side of the column, to the head of the cohort. From the rear came another clatter of hooves. Pont and Dorrin rode up beside Arcolin.

"Problems?" asked Dorrin.

"They were raiding," said Arcolin, with a nod toward the Pliunis.

The Pliuni captain's face was now beet-red. "And we will raid, Duke's man, when I say so. Your Duke isn't paying us anything for our help, after all." Again a mutter of agreement from the Pliuni troops. Dorrin frowned.

"If you march with us, you follow our rules," said Arcolin.

"Not *yours*," sneered the Pliuni. "Your Duke's maybe — if it suits us."

Arcolin was white with rage. Dorrin spoke before he could say anything. "Are you not aware of the Duke's policy on raiding?"

The captain glowered at her. "Oh, he says there's to be none — and that keeps the peasants quiet — but of course he knows we must do *some*."

"Perhaps you'd like to hear the Duke's opinion in person?" Arcolin's voice was cold.

"Perhaps I'd like you to mind your own business!" The Pliuni captain glanced back at his men. "You think you're so special, Captain — just because you mercenaries fight for money instead of honor — " At the word, Arcolin's hand signal passed to the sergeants. Every blade in the cohort slipped from its sheath. Paks saw the Pliuni captain's eyes slide sideways to see what had happened. Arcolin's eyes never moved.

"Captain Pont, ask the Duke to attend us, please," said Arcolin. Pont nodded, and legged his horse to a hand gallop toward the front of the column. Paks grinned as she saw the Pliuni captain's shoulders twitch. Men in the rear Pliuni ranks glanced back at Arcolin's cohort, paling as they saw the naked blades. Their own hands twitched; those who had taken bundles from the houses dropped them.

"You can't attack us," began the Pliuni captain. "We're your allies. You shouldn't draw sword against us — "

"Against you?" asked Dorrin. "The captain has not moved his troops an inch — are you afraid to see swords inspected?"

"Inspected! It's not — he was — "

"You," said Arcolin firmly, "were insulting us. I saw a dozen hands on sword among your troops. So I thought we'd best be sure ours were clean — ready for any — difficulty." He looked at Stammel. "They are, aren't they?"

Stammel grinned broadly. "Certainly, Captain. Any time."

The Pliuni captain turned even paler. "It's — it's treason — a trap — you're looking for some excuse to kill us all." His men shifted in their ranks, murmuring.

"Tir's gut, Captain, if we'd wanted to kill you, you'd be dead by now. Don't be ridiculous." Dorrin's scornful voice caught all their attention. "We — and you, I hope — want to kill the Honeycat. That's why we're here. That's why you asked to march with us. Isn't that right — that you hate Siniava?"

"Yes." Most of the Pliuni troops were looking at her now.

"Then concentrate on that, and not on making trouble. Plunder Siniava's camp, not some poor peasants who hardly have a spare tunic."

The Pliuni captain was still disgruntled, and looked ready to argue, but they heard the beat of many galloping hooves. Duke Phelan, Aliam Halveric, Captain Pont, and the senior Halveric captain halted beside Arcolin and Dorrin.

"Do I understand, Captain, that you have a problem?" Duke Phelan was angry, his voice icy. The Pliuni captain looked around but found no support.

"My lord Duke, we — we were but — "

"Plundering," said the Duke. "*Stealing*. And from peasants we hope are still loyal to their count, who is our ally."

"No one's paying *us*," said the Pliuni, unwisely. "We have to have something — "

"No one's paying me, either," said the Duke. "I have no contract to defeat Siniava, only the vow I made to our dead. If you want plunder, Captain, you can wait until you take it from Siniava — or you can march alone. I won't have thieves under my protection." The captain flushed again, but the Duke went on before he could speak. "Either you control your men, and obey my commands as given through my captains, or you march away, right now, and stay clear. And if you leave, you'd best not use my name, or that of my allies: we'll consider you as any other band of brigands. Is that clear?"

The man turned to the Halverics, but both of them gave him a tight-lipped stare that promised no softening of the Duke's position. His shoulders sagged.

"Yes — it's clear."

"Well, then?"

"Well — " He looked around at his men. "We'll march with you."

"And obey? That means at once, without question."

"Yes — my lord."

"Good." The Duke swept his eyes over the Pliuni contingent. "Have your men return whatever they took to the correct houses, at once." The captain turned to his sergeants and gave the orders. Those who had taken bundles picked them up and moved reluctantly toward the houses. "Hurry up!" called the Duke sharply. "We've wasted enough time on this nonsense."

In a few minutes the men were back in formation and the march resumed. Paks wondered how good the Pliuni troops would be in a fight — and how loyal.

The next morning they met Vladi's Company in a narrow wood. They were grim and weathered-looking; soon the stories of their campaign spread through the troops. Vladi's men had reached Cortes Cilwan before Siniava, but had found the city divided in allegiance. The city militia, so the tavern gossip ran, was half for Siniava already. The Count of Cilwan would not risk rebellion on the eve of war, and refused to arrest even known

268

traitors — some said because his dead wife's brother was chief among them. Although it had been planned otherwise, the Vonja militia had not joined Vladi's men, wanting to be sure which way trouble was coming before moving. So although messages were sent as soon as Siniava's presence in the Immer valley was certain, the Vonja troops were several days' march away.

"And that left us," said the burly sergeant talking to Stammel. "We marched out to meet his whole army. Just us. Those damned militia wouldn't leave the city walls, and Vladi refused to take the Count's Guard — said they were loyal, and he had too few who were." He hawked and spat. "You can imagine — outnumbered about five to one — all we could do was slow 'em."

"Did you get the Count out?" asked Stammel, as he offered the other man a skin of wine.

"Mmm. That's good; we haven't had anything but water these last weeks. No, their fool Count wouldn't come. He said he was Count of Cilwan, and he was staying where he belonged." He swallowed again. "They killed him when they broke in, a couple of days later. Hung his corpse on the gate, and that. He did let us get his heir out. Boy of eleven or so. Nice lad. I suppose now, with the news you brought about the south, they'll send him to Andressat. The old Count's daughter married the Viscount of Andressat; he'll be safe enough there."

"I imagine so. We don't need a child with us on this campaign." Stammel shook his head. "Well, did they pursue you when you came here?"

"Pursue! Ha! We tried to attack their rear, before they broke the citadel, and they drove us back — pretty bad, that time; we lost too many. Then we moved south, toward Immervale, and harried their supply line. We kept hoping those Vonja militia would show up in time to save the citadel. Finally Vladi took us around north of the city. We finally found the militia, a day's march out, *after* the citadel fell. We were all well chewed up by this time, and Vladi gave their captains a few choice words. About took the bark off the trees, he did, and so they said they'd get Siniava themselves if we'd guard the Andressat approaches. That's when we moved over this way and tried to get back in shape. But you can imagine what they did."

"No, what?"

"Well, our spies said Siniava had garrisoned Cortes Cilwan and was moving toward Koury. We thought even Vonja should be able to trap him there, with Ambela and Sorellin coming down from the north. But that fell apart because Siniava's factions in Cortes Vonja and Pler Vonja revolted, and as soon as the militia heard, they hared off home to join in the fight. Sorellin never moved, so Koury fell easily, and Siniava had fresh troops. He went for Ambela next, and held off the Sorellin militia long enough to breach the wall and loot. In fact, I hear he routed both the Sorellin militia and a group from Pler Vonja. The last I heard, he was actually marching on Pler Vonja, and Foss Council had finally decided to send someone like they promised. Of course, they're on the road somewhere, and Tir knows if they'll come up in time to fight. Or if they'll fight. Militia!"

Stammel nodded his agreement. "Has it been quiet over here, then?"

"Not really. You'll find out. He must have a small army of agents in Cilwan; they can take out sentries without a sound. You'll lose a man or so every night if you don't double your guardposts. And all you ever get back is pieces — hands and feet lying in the trail, or an arm tacked up on a barn."

"And you've never caught them at it?"

"No, not since we left the city. We lost three men in Cortes Cilwan, but we caught those bastards who did it in the same house with the bodies. Out here, no."

A shout from the captains ended this conversation, and the army was soon marching again, enlarged by Vladi's Company. The rest of that day and the next they marched north and west, angling toward Cortes Vonja. By nightfall the first day, they had reached the south bank of the Immerest, the great western arm of the Immer River. They passed no bridges, and the river was too deep to ford, so the commanders decided to march upstream another day rather than risk a boat crossing. The Halverics thought they remembered a ford somewhere south of Cortes Vonja.

It was on this day, in broad daylight, that Siniava's agents struck at the column. The first Paks knew about it was in forming up again after a rest break at midmorning. Three people were missing; a search of the riverbank and woods along it yielded nothing. The Pliuni smirked, and Paks heard one mutter something about "typical mercenaries — deserters." After a half-glass spent searching and calling, the column moved on. Paks knew that old Harek, a veteran, would never have deserted.

Perhaps an hour later, Aliam Halveric rode up beside her cohort and asked Stammel if he'd seen the senior Halveric captain. When Stammel said no, he rode on up the column. Stammel looked worried. Paks wondered if the Halveric captain had disappeared. She felt a cramp of cold fear. Could he have been captured? In daylight? When the column halted at midday, orders were given that no one move out of sight of the column. Paks saw the Duke and Aliam Halveric ride down the column together, talking quietly. She had never seen the Halveric like that, gray-faced and drawn; it must be that the Halveric captain — his oldest living son, she'd heard — was gone. She thought of what might be happening to him, and felt cold again.

Shortly after dark that night, Stammel told Paks to report to the Duke's tent. When she had found her way across the darkened camp to his tent, she found the Duke and the captains and several other soldiers. She had just greeted them when three more soldiers came in.

"That should do it," said the Duke. "Now — I have a very dangerous and difficult mission for you. If any of you are not fit — if you think you're coming down with a fever, or a wound's bothering you — or if you don't want to risk yourself away from the Company — tell me now, and I'll release you. You've all been recommended by your captains, both for bravery and woodcraft. But this is no ordinary soldiering I'm asking of you; I want only those who are willing." Paks thought of what he might want them to do. Sneak into Siniava's camp and kill him? One of the others

270

sneezed explosively. "Now that," said the Duke, "is what we can't have — you may be excused."

"But my lord," said the man. "This just come on since we ate — I can pinch my nose. I wouldn't make that noise, my lord; I know I wouldn't."

The Duke smiled. "I know you'd try not to — but you can't pinch your nose if you're carrying something. This is too important to chance it. Go on, now. I don't think the worse of you." The man looked at his captain, Dorrin, who nodded toward the entrance. He shuffled out, shamefaced. The Duke glanced around. "I take it the rest of you are willing?" They nodded. "Good. Some of you may have guessed that the Halveric's eldest son has disappeared. We are fairly sure he was captured. I think they will not kill him at once; he's too valuable as a prisoner." Paks felt a thrill; the Duke must be planning to get him out. She could not imagine how they could get into Siniava's camp, find the Halveric, and escape, but it was a worthy endeavor.

"You will not be going into Siniava's camp yourselves," said the Duke, breaking into her thoughts. "We have agents who can move there openly. You don't need to know about that, but they are trying to find and free Cal — the captain — and move him out of camp. If he's already dead, they'll bring his body out. You'll meet them beside the river, on the far side, and bring him back; they cannot be seen near us. Now — several of you can handle a boat, right?"

"Yes, my lord." Tam and Amisi from Cracolnya's cohort, and Piter from Arcolin's stepped forward.

"Good. The rest of you, listen to these three when it comes to crossing the river. Come and look at this map." They all gathered around the map table. "Here we are," said the Duke. "Take this lane, west of camp, then look for a big stone barn. Cut across here — there's an orchard and two fields — and you'll come to the river. There's a big willow with a limb hanging out over the water — the only tree that size for a half-mile along here, so you should find it even in the dark. There'll be a boat there, big enough for you and Cal. Across the river is a stone ledge, three men high. Upstream of that is where you'll wait for them to bring him. Remember that sound carries more over water than on land. Whatever you do, don't separate. They'll cut you up if you do, and you're more likely to be captured. The password on the far side, to the men who'll be bringing Cal, is a question: Where lies Havensford? Their answer is: Across the mountains. Anyone else will tell you it's four days march upstream. Siniava's watchword is a challenge of apricot, and the answer is brambles. Don't confuse them." No one asked how the Duke knew the enemy watchwords. With the rest, Paks repeated them several times. The Duke nodded finally.

"Good. You'll go armed, but without shields. Make sure you don't show anything shiny. You should be back by dawn or a little after. If you have trouble on this side of the river, make as much noise as you can. I don't want to move troops around tonight, or his agents might figure out what we're doing, but I'll have them ready to move fast if you call. If they do get Cal to

271

you alive, don't let him be captured again — whatever you have to do. Give him the death-stroke before you're disabled, if it comes to that. Are you ready?"

Paks's throat felt like dust. She hardly heard the boat specialists giving them a few advance instructions: sit still, don't move around, don't stand up, don't trail your hands in the water, don't talk or spit. In a few minutes they were clear of the camp, walking quickly down the lane the Duke had shown them on the map. After some minutes of walking, Paks could hear something besides the blood pounding in her ears. In the clear night, brilliant stars gave some shape to the land and trees. A vast dark shape loomed up before them: the stone barn. They turned aside. Starlight glimmered on the blossoms left on the fruit trees in the orchard; their scent was stronger in the damp night air. The first field beyond was plowed, and their boots rasped on rough furrows and clods. The next was in grass; once more they moved quietly, slipping along the margin of the field by a hedge as fragrant as a flower garden.

Trees loomed before them, and starlight danced on the river. They slowed, looking for the willow tree they were to find. Suddenly Paks felt a hand-grip signal passed back: there. She edged forward, alert for stones that could roll beneath her feet, or sticks that could crack. Once in the willow's shadow it was even harder to see. Paks stumbled on a rock, lurching forward and biting her tongue against any sound. Someone grabbed her arm and steadied her. She did the same for another who stumbled into her a moment later. They found the limb, wide enough to walk on, and then the boat.

The boat experts urged everyone into a huddle, then loaded the boat, guiding them with nudges and handgrips. It had looked a large dark shape to Paks when she saw it empty, but once aboard it felt too small. Not crowded — but the sides were too low, and she felt too close to the water. And the boat tipped and shifted with every motion of its passengers. She tried to keep from moving in response, fearing to tip the whole thing over.

With a rower at each end, and one in the middle, they moved quietly across the current. Paks did not know how the rowers could tell where they were going. When they landed on the far side, just where they had been told to wait, she was glad to crawl from the boat to solid ground again. She crouched silently in the dark, waiting for someone to arrive. It seemed a long time.

They heard the hoofbeats coming from upstream for some time before the riders were close enough to challenge. Amisi, in a southern accent, asked, "Where lies Havensford?"

"Across the mountains," came the soft reply. The horses had stopped, and Paks could just see two cloaked and hooded shapes swing off their mounts and move to help a third.

"You've got him alive?" asked Amisi.

"Aye." Paks and the others moved toward the voice, and helped to steady the man they were supporting.

Chapter Twenty-eight

"How careless of you, Captain, to be riding alone so far from your troops." The voice was soft and gentle. The bonds on his arms and legs were not. Cal Halveric said nothing. "You might have met with some fatal accident, you know. It is fortunate for you that my servants are not quick to kill. We do not entertain guests of your distinguished rank often, Captain." Cal could see nothing through the hood that covered his head but the glint of light between dark threads. Captain they could have guessed from his clothes and his horse; he hoped very much that they did not know *which* captain. "I hope," the voice went on, sharpening a little, "that you are attending to me — "

Something, it could have been a boot or pike-butt, prodded his ribs. When he said nothing, a much harder blow slammed into the same spot. He felt one rib crack, and caught his breath in a gasp of pain.

Before he could recover, rough hands dragged him up from the ground and tightened the hood around his neck until he could barely draw a breath. A hand felt over his face, applied pressure to the eyeballs, the angle of his jaw. When he tried to twist away, the cloth around his throat tightened. He tried not to react, but at last breathlessness overcame his control and he choked, fighting the halter and the merciless hands. Instead of release, he got hard blows to the belly. When he was reeling, the tightness eased slightly, and he gasped for breath, unaware of anything else. When he could hear again, the soft voice was speaking.

"You see, Captain, I must be sure I have your attention for our very important conference — do I?" When Cal did not answer, the cloth at his throat tightened again, slowly. His throat moved convulsively and he choked. "Was that a 'yes,' Captain?" the voice went on. "You must speak clearly, so that we do not mistake one another." Cal fought back a desire to speak all too clearly to this scum, and thought instead of Seliam, dead in his first command. This time the choking continued until he passed out completely.

Someone was calling his name. "Cal — Cal — " the voice went on. A soft voice. He couldn't think who it was. "Cal — wake up." He stirred and took a long breath. Pain stabbed his ribs; his throat was sore — it was dark. He started to reach for his dagger, as always when he woke, and realized that his arms were bound. And his legs. He was flat on his back, and cold. He shifted his head, trying to remember, to think.

273

"Caliam Halveric," the voice mused. "Oldest living son of Aliam Halveric — his second in command — his heir, I understand. Cal, they call you, don't they?" A hand brushed his body and he realized he was naked — then remembered the hood — and what had come before. The hand traced some of his old scars, slowly. He shivered, telling himself it was from the cold. The voice began again, brisker. "Caliam Halveric. What are you worth to your father — " the hand touched his manhood, " — whole? What would he give for you? Anything? Or — would you fetch a better price elsewhere? As a gelding, perhaps. Or perhaps his enemies would pay for you — " the hand touched here and there, " — piecemeal, so to speak. Eh?"

Cal smiled grimly under the hood. He knew his worth to his father well enough, and the price someone would pay for his death. "I have sired sons enough," he said, answering that oblique threat.

"Ah yes." The voice carried amusement. "You are married, are you not, to — now what is her name?" Cal did not answer. "Five sons and three — no, four — daughters, as I recall. But Cal — what makes you think I have no agents over the mountains. Are five sons enough, if you cannot get more?"

He had not thought of that. Surely they were safe, so far away — young Aliam, only fifteen but furious at being left behind, Berrol the stubborn twelve year old, Malek and Kieri and baby Seli, born just a month after his uncle's death. And the girls: tall Tamar, wild as Aliam, and Zuli, and Volya and Amis. Surely they were safe. But his breath came quicker. How did they know this? Were some of his own men traitors?

After a long pause, the voice went on. "Your father, Cal — he has made a very unfortunate alliance with that crazy dukeling, Phelan." Cal suppressed a snort. Phelan was as crazy as his nickname of fox. "But perhaps, if he values you, he might be persuaded to — to forget that alliance, at least for awhile."

"He will not be likely to forgive your murdering one of his sons because of your threats to another," said Cal calmly.

"Murder? You aren't even harmed — yet — barring a rib you might have bruised falling off your horse."

"You mean your spy system does not extend to knowing all his captains? How incompetent."

"But when did — oh. Was that your brother, last fall? I had been told a hireling captained that troop. Then is that why — ?" Cal was silent, willing enough to let him think his brother's death was the only reason for the Halveric-Phelan alliance. That reason might be public knowledge; the rest were secrets he did not care to have probed. The voice went on.

"The loss of one son should not harden a man to the loss of others, surely? You must be even more dear to him — or your sons must be. We must convince him, Cal, that his desire for vengeance will condemn you, too. And to no such quick death as your brother. I do wish I'd known who he was. Even so, he would be alive had he released his prisoners to me, as any sensible person would have done. That nonsense you mercenaries spout

274

about honor — ridiculous!" With no warning, scalding liquid splashed Cal's chest. "Oh — " the voice said archly. "How clumsy of me!"

Cal was suddenly disgusted by the tone as much as the pain, so angry that it swamped his fear. "South coast scum," he began. "You're not just clumsy, you're stupid and incompetent as well. You couldn't captain a mercenary company, because the only way you can get fighters to follow you is to threaten their families — coward as you are. And you don't have the guts to stay and fight with 'em, when you lead 'em into a mess — " The blows began soon after his words, but he kept on until he passed out once more. "Stupid — cowardly — scum — that's what you are, and furthermore — "

This time pain woke him. He was wedged into a space so small that he could move nothing but his head, and that only slightly. His arms had been rebound behind him, tightly; he could not feel his hands at all. His bruised cheek rested on his knees. Everything ached and throbbed, and he had a cramp in one shoulder. With every breath his broken ribs grated and stabbed. He had had bruises and broken ribs often enough before — but not the other pain, a growing fire that gnawed between his thighs, leaving him no doubt about one irreplaceable loss. Perhaps, he thought grimly, I will bleed to death from this. If only I had been able to taunt him longer, he might have killed me at once. He felt contempt for his captor, who could so easily be moved by a rough tongue. But Halverics are not bred to despair or suicide, and his mind returned to his children. If he died, they would avenge him: but he was not dead, not yet. His mind wandered to his own childhood, when Kieri Phelan was his father's squire, and he had seen Kieri's scars. "Don't ever ask," his father had said, "and never complain, Cal, until you've borne the like."

He woke, not knowing he had dozed, at the touch of a hand on his leg. A voice — not the soft voice, but one with a northern flavor — whispered nearby. "Are you th' Halveric, are ye?" He froze, afraid to answer. It must be a trap. The hand, hard and horny, slid along his thigh to his buttocks. A whispered curse, then a comment: "Holy Falk, he's been — " Another whisper, silencing the first. He worked his tongue around in his mouth, as the hand found his ankles and a cold thin thing — blade? — slipped under the thongs that bound them. He heard the thongs snap. The blade slid up and cut the thongs at his knees. He tried to whisper, but it came out as a grunt, unintelligible even to him. "Quiet," the voice commanded, itself very soft. "Are you the Halveric?" He nodded, then realized it was dark and managed a shaky yes. "Don't make a noise," the voice said. "We'll pull — don't fight us."

A hard hand grasped his feet and pulled them to one side. The wrench of pain that followed almost drew a sound from him, but he clamped his jaws on it. He felt his legs scrape past an edge of some sort, and smelled fresher air, cold air. The hand reached up past his thighs to his body, felt around toward his arms. Again the blade, slicing the bonds at elbow and wrist. His elbows rolled out, catching on the sides of whatever held him

275

with a little thump. Again a muffled curse. The hand reached and pulled first one arm forward, then the other. Something soft bound his forearms loosely together. He leaned now against the side of the container, trying to yield to the hands without making any sound. One set grasped his legs below the knees, and the other reached in and lifted his hips slightly. He choked back a scream at that, and tried to arch his back against the surface behind him. They pulled, and his body eased out, his head sliding down the wall. He tipped his head forward so it would not thump on the floor of the container. He could feel hot blood seeping from reopened wounds. At last, inch by careful inch, the unknown hands drew him free of his prison, and he lay at full length on a flat surface.

"Be very quiet," a voice murmured in his ear. "Not out yet. Talk later." Meanwhile the hands were busy, running along his arms and legs feeling for broken bones. His hands began to come to life again, with the throbbing pain of returning circulation. He flexed them, glad to have control over something. "Need cloth," murmured the voice. "Blood trail if we don't."

"Here," said the other voice. He was lifted and a pad of cloth wrapped against his back — then he could feel them dragging a tunic over his head. A flask pressed against his lips and he swallowed. While he was dreaming, he thought, he might as well dream numbwine — but it was water, cold and clean. He realized that his mouth was full of some foul taste, blood or vomit, and swallowed again. Very quickly they had him ready to move, with loose trousers drawn up to his waist, and stockings pulled over his feet. "Will hurt," said the voice in his ear. "No sound." A hand lay along his face for a moment, and he nodded.

He felt himself slung over a shoulder, but in the pain of that jolting movement, he passed out again. He came to with a hand hard across his mouth. "Quiet," the voice said. He nodded, and the hand released its pressure. It was dark, but now he could see. Yellow blurs in the distance — torches, he thought — and a vague sense of darker nearby shapes looming over him. "Horse lines," murmured the voice. "Got to ride — too far on foot." Cal shuddered at the thought of straddling a horse.

"C-can't," he croaked.

"Quiet. You must. That or the deathstroke. You've no bones broke but ribs — we'll help you." Cal was shaking now, shaking too hard to help as they urged him up.

"By St. Falk, we'll never — " The second voice sounded scared.

"We will. The numbwine, Jori." Cal felt a flask against his lips again. This time it *was* numbwine, strong and bitter with the pain-killing herb. He swallowed twice, three times, before the flask was taken away. "No more," said the voice. "You must be awake for the sentry." In a few moments the pain eased, though the thought of mounting terrified him. The hands pulled at him, lifted. He could just stand, half-supported by one of his rescuers while the other shoved a horse over to him; he smelled the pungent sweaty hide. "Stirrup's low," murmured his supporter. "You can reach it — I'll help. Jori's on the other side."

276

Cal raised his foot, surprised that he could, and slid it into the stirrup he felt. He leaned into the horse as the man behind him shoved him up; his right leg swung to clear the saddle out of habit. He stood, leaning forward on the beast's neck, while Jori fitted his foot into the off stirrup. Then the man on the near side vaulted up behind him, and he heard Jori mount another horse. "Lean on me," said the man behind him. He sank back. The pain was impossible; sweat sprang cold on his whole body — but he did not faint. The horse began to move.

"When we reach the sentry lines," the man said in his ear, "you'll have to ride alone — maybe fifty yards — no more. Jori's got a horse for me to go through the lines with." He was fitting a hooded cloak around Cal as he spoke. "We're Vonja militia, remember that. Going back to Vonja. I'm a sergeant; you're just a private. Don't say anything. If they ask your name, say Sim. They won't ask unless their sergeant is there — if they stay bought. At worst we'll see to you. You won't be caught again. Now — when I slide off, sit up straight. Just a few yards, remember?"

"Yes — I will." Cal spoke softly. "Who are you?"

"Right now, I'm a sergeant of Vonja militia, a turncoat. We'll talk later. Almost there — I've got to change horses before we get to the torches. All right?" Cal nodded. As the man behind him slid from the horse, Cal sagged and almost fell. He managed to pull himself upright, and tried to tuck the cloak snugly around himself. The horses hardly paused before moving on. He could see, against the torches ahead, the third horse now in the lead.

A sentry hailed them. He heard the voice ahead, bantering now in a southern accent. He looked forward. It was hard to follow the conversation. Laughter. A face upturned to his, whites of eyes glinting in the light. The horses moved on, into darkness. Cal concentrated on his balance. He dared not look back to see how far they had come. It seemed forever before the voices spoke to him again. "Can you ride alone?" one asked. "We can make better time if you can — we need to get to the river."

"I — think — so," Can managed to say. "But not — not trotting — "

"No. Of course not."

"Should we tie him to the saddle?" asked the other. "If he falls — "

"If you think you can't make it," said the first voice, "tell us. Don't fall."

"No," said Cal. "I won't fall." He began to believe it might be real. They rode on. Just when he was sure he would faint, strong arms lifted him from the saddle. There were more voices now. Again he thought of a trap, and tried to sit up, but firm hands pressed his shoulders down.

"Take it easy, sir," said one of the new voices. "We've got to get you across the river. Just lie still as you can."

"But who — " His voice was harsh and unsteady; he swallowed and tried again. "Who are you? Who got me out?"

"No real names this side of the river, sir," came the reply. Cal felt the grip of many hands as he was lifted, then laid on a hard surface that seemed to dip and sway. A hand touched his face, gently.

"Good luck to you, sir," came the voice he'd heard first. "We hope to see you someday, me and Jori."

"But — aren't you coming?"

"Nay — we've to get back to Vonja and act our part."

"Tir's gut!" exclaimed someone else. "That's a dangerous game — what if you're caught?"

"We won't be," said Jori. "We've daggers and the wit to use them. And by Holy Falk and Gird, we'll meet you all in a tavern not too long from now."

"I wish," Cal interrupted. "I wish I had something for you — after all this."

"You gave us your silence," said the first voice. "That was gift enough, considering. Don't worry, Captain — Jori and me are weasels for cunning." Cal heard the horses moving away. He felt the surface he lay on tip sharply, and the muffled thuds of other bodies settling onto boards. Of course, he thought: river, a boat. He closed his eyes as the boat moved out onto the river. It fetched up on the far back with a bump that jounced him into pain again. He was lifted from the boat to the bank, and given another swallow of numbwine and as much water as he could drink. Then he was carried, on a blanket slung between poles, for a long distance: or long it seemed, when every footfall waked another twinge in his battered body.

For the most part he kept his eyes closed, but once when he opened them he noticed the sky above was paling. It must be nearly dawn. The soldiers carrying him were no longer dark blurs against the sky; he could see the shape of their helmets, and the faces beneath. The light grew. He could not distinguish color yet; their tunics were dark, and could have been any dark color. But the helmet shape — the cut — he thought it must be — One of them looked at him.

"Nearly there, Captain. You're safe now."

"You're — "

"The Duke's men, sir. We're nearly back to camp. Sorry it's taken so long."

Cal felt a ridiculous desire to laugh. He was hardly likely to complain about how far they'd had to carry him. "My father?" he asked. "Does he know?"

The man shook his head. "Don't know, Captain. The Duke will have told him, I'd think, or maybe he's waiting until you come in." Cal let his eyes sag shut. He had no idea how long he'd been in the enemy camp, and he didn't really care to know. Not yet. Enough to know he was out, and safe. As safe in Phelan's camp as in his own. He heard the challenge of sentries, and his escort's reply. A voice he knew, one of the Duke's captains, he thought, said: "Duke's tent." He thought he should open his eyes again, but it was too much trouble.

At last all motion ceased. He lay on something soft, and smelled the pungent reek of surgeons' gear. Feet stirred on the floor nearby; something rustled. He struggled to open his eyes. Sunlight bled through the tent walls. The Duke stood by the bed he lay in, staring at the floor. Cal swallowed and tried to speak. The Duke glanced at his face with the first sound.

278

"Cal. You're safe now. Your father will be here soon. My surgeons are ready — ".

"My lord — I — thank you."

The Duke made an impatient gesture. "None needed. I'm glad you're no worse."

"It was Siniava's camp, wasn't it?" The Duke nodded, and sat abruptly on a stool beside the bed. Cal rolled his head sideways, and felt his hand lifted and held. A surgeon moved to the bed. Cal swallowed. "Sir — my lord — "

"Yes, Cal?"

"Please — don't stay. Go — wait for my father."

"What? Cal, I've seen wounds before; I won't faint."

Cal shook his head. "Please — don't stay — "

"Cal — what is it?" He could not answer. The Duke met his eyes in a long silent look, and suddenly he saw the sense of what he could not say looking back at him. He saw tears fill the Duke's eyes, saw them blinked back, saw the rage he had seen last fall return. When the Duke spoke, his voice held nothing of that, nothing but calm. "As you wish, Cal. If you want me, I'll be in the front room." He sighed, and released Cal's hand; sighed again, and stood.

"My lord — "

"Yes?"

"If I could bear anyone — it would be you — "

The Duke nodded and withdrew. The surgeons unwrapped the cloak around him and set to work. Numbwine masked the physical pain for the next hour, but not the mental. Now that he was safe, now that he might have thought all was well — he told himself he should be glad of the children he already had, the campaigns he had already fought, the rank he had already won. But what he had lost intruded. How could he command a company, once it was known? He knew too well the ways of rumor to doubt that it would be known, and known widely.

He was still thinking this, gloomily, when his father arrived, bursting past the Duke with hardly a word and into the bedchamber. He saw at once that his father knew. The dark eyes were snapping, the beard bristling in all directions. Cal stared back at him.

"Well," said his father gruffly. "Thank the gods they took the only thing you *don't* need to be a commander — or my heir." Cal wondered if he'd heard rightly; he knew his face must show his shock. A grim smile parted his father's beard. "Hadn't thought of it that way, had you? Arms and legs, Cal: brains, eyes, ears — oh, and a strong voice — that's what you need. That you've got. Ask Aesil M'dierra if she ever needed balls to run a company — ask with a mile's head start, and the fastest horse in my stable — you might make it home." He sat down on the stool by the bed. "And thank the gods we didn't give in to young Ali about coming this year. That would have been a real mess." His face softened. "How much numbwine have you had?"

"Enough, sir." Cal still felt faintly affronted.

"Good. Cal, I'm not ignoring your loss. I know — I *do* know — what it means. But I know what it doesn't mean. You've got heirs of the body — more than our friend Kieri has. You've got everything else I need. I'm not going to lose a son, Cal, because you lost a few lumps of flesh — even those lumps."

"I — I thought you would mind — "

"Mind! Of course I mind; I'll serve you that bastard's balls on toast, if you don't get 'em first. But you're a Halveric. My son. My commander and heir. You still have everything else, and it's enough."

"Yes, sir." Cal felt better. A little better. "He — he said, sir, that he had agents north of the mountains. He said five sons might not be enough."

Aliam Halveric snorted. "You must have been dazed, Cal, to worry about that. Didn't you think I'd take precautions? And better, told your mother about it." He chuckled, and Cal relaxed enough to smile. "I'd like to see anyone sneak past your mother — your wife, now, she's a handful too, but Estil — " Cal thought of his tall mother, still hunting at her age with a bow many men could not bend. "Now. Did the surgeons say how long you'd be down?"

"No — not yet."

"Hmmph. I need you up, and you need to be up. Did they try a potion?"

"No — I don't think so. But — "

"Then I'll ask. Cal, think of his face when he hears you're back in command again. He'll get no joy of his doings then! I'll be back." He rose.

"Sir?"

"What?"

"How did you — who told you?" His father grimaced.

"Oh, that. Well, that scum sent them. With the badge off your cloak, incidentally. Good gold, that. It's as well he did, Cal: he has nothing to do magicks with, except some blood, and you've spilled blood all over the south. Now rest, and I'll see what the surgeons say." His father left; Cal found himself smiling.

From the front room came a murmur of voices. The surgeons would have no chance, Cal realized. Soon enough they came trooping back in, along with his father, a Captain of Falk, and the Duke's mage.

"I don't care," his father was saying, "which of you does what, or in what order — but I want him up this day."

"But, my lord — "

"Impossible. If he — "

"I can't be expected to — "

"Silence!" That roar was the Duke, just inside the chamber. "Aliam, my surgeons are at your command. My mage has some constraints I don't understand — but, Master Vetrifuge, I expect you'll do what you can. I do suggest, Aliam, that as he got no sleep last night, you might let him rest today."

"Kieri, he'll sleep better when he's healed — "

"Very well, then. As you will." The Duke withdrew. The surgeons looked at each other and at the mage and cleric. The mage stared at the floor, and the cleric looked at his father.

"Get on with it," snapped Aliam Halveric.

He woke, hungry and rested, in the long spring evening. His father sat beside him, and the Duke was sprawled in a seat at the end of the bed. They were talking strategy, low-voiced, until the Duke noticed his open eyes, and nodded to Aliam. Cal gave them a smile.

"I'm hungry."

"Good. They said you would be." The Duke sent his servant for food.

"I've got your clothes," said his father. He gestured to them, hanging over a rack. "I brought mail, too — your old set. Come out when you're dressed."

"You ought to tell him," said the Duke, "that while he slept the day away, we moved camp." He grinned at Cal. "We loaded you in one of Vladi's wagons, and you didn't even murmur. The teamster said you didn't rouse all day. We'd begun to wonder just how much numbwine you'd had." He turned and went through the curtain into the front room.

"Come on," said his father. "Don't take forever." And he, too, left Cal to stand and dress alone.

Chapter Twenty-nine

Paks snatched a few hours of sleep before they set off again, upstream along the river. She was still tired and sleepy, and concentrated on putting one foot in front of the other. No one asked her any questions. They came to a shallow stony ford just as the Clart scouts discovered an enemy party guarding it, but the skirmish ended quickly.

"Well," said Piter generally, "now we know we're going the right way—"

"If those lights we saw last night were Siniava's fires, we'll have to turn back east," said Vik.

"I'd like to find the Vonja militia," said Devlin. "At least to know which side they're on." But they found nothing that day.

The next morning they found traces of a large camp. While looking for a clue to which army had used it, they found a refuse pit half-full of bodies. Here were the missing men: young Juris, and Sim, of Dorrin's cohort, and old Harek. Harek was still alive, missing both hands, now, and with a festering wound in his belly. The other bodies bore evidence of the same bitter torment. Paks helped dig the graves; as they buried Sim and Juris, she glanced over at the Pliunis, massed across the clearing. They had said no more about deserters. Nothing could be done for Harek, but numbwine to ease his pain and a friend's hand for comfort. When he died, they laid him in the grave they'd dug. Paks heard from Piter about his family.

"It was his last year," he said. "He got his little bit of land two years ago, and he was going to retire last year, only this came up. It's a shame—" Piter spat. "His oldest boy is old enough to farm that land, but he's always been wild to join the Company. Effa, that's his wife, is a hard-working woman. Those scum—one more year, and he'd have been home, working his own bit of land."

Paks felt a pang of guilt—they had come so close, to help Cal Halveric, and had done nothing for their own companions. The rest of that day she marched with deepening anger, anger reflected in the eyes around her.

The next day they found the Vonja and Foss Council militia at last, drawn up facing Siniava's lines. In the hours of daylight that remained, Paks looked over their allies. Units from all three Foss Council cities were there, distinguished by the color of their trousers and the trim on their gray tunics: red for Foss, green for Ifoss, and yellow for Fossnir. Like the Vonjans, they wore trousers tucked into soft-topped boots in the field, though at home they went bare-legged. Vonjan militia wore russet-orange tunics over black trousers. Those from Cortes Vonja had orange helmet-plumes as well, and a leaping cat in black on their tunics. In comparison, those who had come with the Duke looked shabby and travel-worn — but, Paks noted, equally ready to fight.

Across a shallow valley, Siniava's camp was set on rising ground. In the late slanting sunlight, Paks could see troops in the familiar black and yellow, and other colors: light green, blue, and many in rough brown leather. She wondered if they would attack that afternoon; her heart leaped to think how soon Siniava might be dead, and the war over.

But overnight Siniava slipped away eastward, eluding the militia scouts who should have alerted them. The Duke came back from the council of commanders in tight-lipped fury; the militia commanders were arguing about the order of march. It was some hours before the army moved at all. They finally caught up with Siniava again at nightfall. His position was even stronger than before: rising ground sheltered from flank assaults by hummocks of broken rock.

"He'll have bowmen in there, I don't doubt," said Stammel, frowning. "We can't see 'em, and they'll have a lovely view of us. Sun behind 'em, too. Blast those militia! Why wouldn't they *move?*"

"For that matter, why didn't they notice when he moved in the night? They said they had their scouts out and didn't need ours." Kefer glared across the space as if his gaze could strike a blow.

"Militia — " began Paks and stopped short. What she knew of some Vonja militia was not to be talked about.

"Well — " Stammel stretched and sighed. "The Duke won't let 'em slip away again. We'll have a day's work tomorrow. Paks, make sure everyone in your file has rechecked their weapons. Vik, the same for you. And tell the other file leaders. We don't want any more surprises than *he* gives us."

By first light they stood arrayed in battle formation, watching the sky lighten behind the slope Siniava held. Paks flexed her hand on the shield grip, tested one more time the balance of her sword. She glanced down the line. At the far end, barely visible in the dimness, were the Pliunis and two cohorts of Vladi's spears. Next a solid block of Foss Council militia — a thousand pikemen — then the Vonja militia, half pikes and half swords. The right flank was Arcolin's and Dorrin's cohorts, and beyond them two cohorts of Halverics. Vonja archers stood behind the left flank, and Cracolnya's cohort and Halveric archers behind the right. Clart Cavalry, the rest of Vladi's spears, and some five hundred mixed militia waited in reserve.

When their advance began, Paks wanted to run, wanted to charge into the enemy lines like an arrow in flight.

"Steady now!" bellowed Stammel. "Keep the lines, Tir blast you! You'll need that strength later." Paks forced herself to slow, shortening stride slightly and keeping the drum cadence. She willed the strength she saved to flow into her sword arm. She could feel Canna's medallion and Saben's stone horse on her chest. Soon, she told them. Soon. They were halfway to the enemy lines where lowered pikes awaited them. She heard the whirr of a crossbow bolt. Someone yelped, behind her. Directly ahead, the enemy wore dark blue tunics bordered in scarlet. Paks wondered where they were from. Then she heard screams from the rocks to her right, and a roar of sound as Siniava sent his army forward. The men in blue charged, keeping no formation; the lines crashed together into chaos. Paks thrust her sword into the first blue-clad body, blocked another's slash with her shield, and drove forward.

The rest of that day the armies struggled on, hour after hour, unable to win or withdraw. The lines swayed back and forth, dissolved, reformed squad by squad. Dust choked the fighters and hid the action from their commanders — and the noise drowned out their commands. At times allies who could hardly see each other for the dust fought desperately for some minutes before they realized the error. Paks fought pikemen in blue, pikemen in black and yellow, swordsmen in brown — and nearly found herself battling a squad of green-clad swordsmen until they cried "Halverics!" She fought until she could hardly lift her sword, and still fought on, with the memory of Harek and Canna and Saben filling her mind.

At last both armies faltered. Fighters stepped back when they could, and quit driving forward. A gap opened between them; the dust settled slowly. When Paks looked up, she saw it was long past noon. She was thirsty and hungry and ached in every bone. She tried to gather her wits and help reform the cohort, but she could not see them at first. She heard the Duke's horn call and looked around — there. Still alert and wary, she picked her way across the battlefield, littered as it was with dead and wounded fighters, to join them. Stammel was checking over her cohort as she came up. Their faces were gray with dust, sweat-streaked, with eyes like dark pits of exhaustion.

"There you are," said Stammel, as she found her place. "Seli's with the surgeons; he'll be out some time. Take over for him, junior to Devlin."

"Yes, sir." Paks was too tired to feel any elation at the promotion.

"Take whoever you need — we'll need water up here, and bandages — food if you can find it."

"Yes, sir." In the next hour, she had supplied the cohort with water and food. Other companies began to regroup; the Halverics looked almost ready to fight again. But militia wandered around in apparent confusion. She could not see the Pliunis at all, and wondered if they'd deserted. Across the field, the enemy army slowly condensed into formation. Paks's bones ached as she thought about another battle. But it was late afternoon before the field was cleared, and neither army moved from its position. As the sun slipped westward, Paks began to feel chilled in her sweat-damp tunic. Her nose itched; she rubbed it on the rim of her shield. She saw Arcolin ride to meet and speak with a messenger in Foss Council gray, then he rode back. The trees behind them threw long shadows that crept across the field; their own shadows loomed tall as giants. Still nothing happened, and it was dusk.

284

That night Paks wondered if corporals and sergeants ever slept; she was busy until her turn on guard with things she had never noticed corporals doing. Checking on the wounded, counting weapons retrieved from the field, issuing new weapons or clothes to those who'd lost theirs in battle . . . an endless list of chores awaited her. That night, too, assassins slipped through the lines, trying to kill both the Duke and the Halveric. They succeeded with the captain-general of the Foss Council militia. Paks and Jenits captured an enemy trying to sneak through the lines in the confusion of the assassins' attack; she turned him over to the watch captain, and never heard what happened to him.

Morning dawned cloudy and damp. A thin rain began just as the army formed. Battle that day was even more confused and exhausting than the day before, as the hazards of mud compounded those of battle. When heavier rain fell in curtains after some hours of fighting, Siniava's troops gave back slowly. The Phelani and Halverics pushed forward, but the militia in the center could not advance. Paks slogged on through the slippery mud, rain beating in her face, but she could not keep up with the retreating army, which vanished into the woods. At last the Duke halted them. As far as Paks could tell, Siniava's army was in full retreat.

Back in camp, rumors flew that Siniava was on the run and his army dissolving. Paks had her doubts. Siniava had regrouped before. She splashed through the rain, checking on the wounded, bringing food to those who could eat, and making sure that no one was missing. When she went back to the cooks' tent at last for her own meal, Stammel, Kefer, and Haben of Dorrin's cohort were inside talking.

"You can't blame the Clarts," Kefer was saying. "They've taken losses all along, and this heavy rain is hard on 'em."

"Aye — but those Blue Riders needn't have been larking about with Sorellin's militia. Not that they could have done it alone — Vonja and Foss Council just wouldn't move." Stammel turned to Paks and grinned. "Got 'em taken care of? Good. Eat hearty; we'll be marching early."

"And late," added Haben. He was Dorrin's senior sergeant. "By Zudthyi's Spear, I hope they don't slip us and get away somewhere to regroup."

"What I heard is the Blue Riders are keeping contact."

"But can we keep contact with the Blue Riders?" Haben took his bowl back for another helping. "And even if we can, would you wager those militia could?" He gulped down several mouthfuls. "I tell you, Stammel, if they set foot out of camp by noon tomorrow, I'll buy you a jug of *The White Dragon*'s best ale."

"No bet," said Stammel gloomily. "They won't. I've heard that a good third of the Vonjans are actually Siniava's anyway."

"After today?" asked Kefer, grinning.

"Maybe not, after today. Tir's bones, I'm tired. Paks, you're watch-second to Kefer tonight. If you need me before the change, Kef, I'll be asleep near the middle post." Stammel yawned, waved, and went out. Paks finished her meal while Kefer waited. When they left the tent, Haben turned toward Dorrin's area, and Paks and Kefer walked the perimeter posts together. This was her first experience as watch second; she was very aware of her responsibility as she went from post to post during the watch.

Morning looked no better; rain had continued all night. The mercenary companies were soon ready to march, but as Haben had predicted the militia were only then struggling out of their tents to look around. When the march finally began, about noon, the mercenaries went alone, though the militia were pulling down their tents.

The Clarts had found a village, mostly burned but with several large barns intact, along the line Siniava had taken. They reached this village by nightfall; all the wounded, and most of the others, slept in shelter. Paks tried to ignore the stains where the villagers' bodies had been dragged away for burial by the Clarts. Rain continued all that night, slow and steady. In the morning light, the wreck of the village was even uglier. Paks found a body the Clarts had missed: a young girl or woman who had been trapped in a burning sheepfold. She stared at it for a time before she called someone to help carry it away for burial.

For three wet days they marched on in the mud, along crooked lanes that led from village to village. Paks heard from Stammel that the militia was finally on the move behind them. But they could not catch Siniava's army, and one day the Blue Riders reported that it had split. They were not sure which part of it Siniava was with. Finally the Duke turned them south, toward Cortes Cilwan.

"He thinks Siniava might have kept troops in reserve there," said Kefer. "The Blue Riders are still trying to find out which remnant he's with, but if the Duke is right, we could cut him off."

Several days later they came in sight of the high walls of Cortes Cilwan, the inner keep standing far above the main city. They marched closer, in battle order. Paks could see sentries on the walls, and hear horns cry the alarm.

"Hmmph. I don't see his standard," said Arcolin. "I wonder if they've changed sides already."

The Duke had ridden to the front of the column with Vladi and Aliam Halveric. "They'll wish they had, if they haven't," he said. "But I expect they're waiting to see who we are before they decide who they're for. Let 'em see our colors, Arcolin, and we'll find out." Arcolin signalled the standard bearers, who unfurled the Duke's banner to the light breeze.

"Nothing yet," said the Halveric. "Coy, aren't they?"

"Merchanters," growled Vladi. "No courage, no honor — bah! Tir take all such to the black realms!" Paks glanced cautiously at him; she'd never been so close to him before. He looked like someone who would be called the Cold Count: a pale narrow face with cold blue eyes and a pointed gray beard.

The Duke lifted his reins and rode a little forward; the others went with him. A bellow came from the walls. Paks could not understand the words, and the Duke made no reply, advancing farther. He was close under the walls when he stopped. After a few minutes, someone came from a postern gate to speak with him. The discussion went on some time. Paks counted the sentries on the wall, and tried to see if there were archers up there too. It was hotter; standing in the sun she felt sweat trickling through her hair under the helmet. It itched. She resisted the urge to scratch her nose. Sun glared on the city walls. She looked past the city to the river. A bath in the river — Stammel cleared his throat and she jerked her attention back to the Duke. He and the others were riding back.

"Siniava isn't here," he told them. "They're having riots inside, it sounds like, but they all swear Siniava isn't here, and hasn't been since he marched for Koury and Ambela. They won't open the gates to us, and I won't waste time taking the city when Siniava isn't there. We'll stay here until our scouts can tell us where he is."

Paks had her bath in the river, as refreshing as she'd hoped; the camp was festooned with drying socks and tunics. By the time the couriers came in, rest, hot food, and baths had revived enthusiasm for the chase — among the mercenaries. They heard without surprise that the Vonja and Foss Council militia would not go farther east.

"I suppose we can't complain," said Devlin. "With all these bandits running loose in the confusion, and their own cities and lands at risk, I can see they'd want to stay closer to home."

"I heard the trouble with Foss Council is that they're still arguing about who's in command since their captain-general was killed," said Paks.

"Probably. With those units from different cities, their chain of command is tangled as briars. I wish the Sorellin militia would show up. Just because they were beaten once is no reason to hang back now. Siniava's lost a lot, and not just on the battlefield."

Seli limped heavily to their fire and eased himself down.

"Are you supposed to be here?" asked Devlin.

Seli grinned. "The surgeon said to try walking a few steps." Devlin looked at the distance from the surgeons' tents and shook his head. Seli ignored him. "Well, Paks," he said. "How do you like being corporal?"

Paks blushed. "I'm not, really. Just until you're well."

"You're doing the work. You're as much of one as I am. If you weren't doing it right, Kef and Stammel would have replaced you by now. Or so they told me, when I was worrying about it a few weeks after my promotion. I remember I was scared stiff. Did you feel like that, Devlin? I thought my friends would think I'd gotten conceited, and wondered if anyone would obey my orders."

Devlin nodded. "Yes — I think everyone feels like that at first. I'd been bedding a woman in Cracolnya's cohort, and she kept teasing me about it. So I quit, and she said my new rank had made me proud. And we had a big old fellow in this cohort then — as tall as you, Paks, and immensely strong. He wasn't too bright, but he had years on me. He'd grumbled before when someone a year junior to him made corporal, and I was sure he'd cause me trouble." Devlin paused to drink.

"Well? Did he?"

"He started to. He complained — claimed I'd done gods know what all for my promotion — things like that. I was young and brash in those days —" Seli laughed, and Devlin grinned. "Brasher, then. And a quick tongue, that I've always had. So I went to him, and we had a little talk — I asked him how he thought a little runt as ugly as I was — for that's what he'd called me — could sell his favors to anyone. And then I suggested that since he was bigger, stronger and smarter — which he claimed to be — that if I'd been chosen, it must have been with divine guidance. That was in the days when no one in this company would have considered evil influence. He hadn't thought of that, he said, and had I any proof. The proof, I said, was in the promotion — surely he knew the captains and the Duke could recognize the gods' will — but if he wanted proof, to wait until nightfall."

"What did you do?" asked Seli. "Coat yourself with one of those glowing mushrooms?"

"No. Better than that, I thought. We'd had a rich haul of treasure from the last campaign, and I'd noticed something — or thought I had. The quartermaster then was a friend of mine, and as corporal I could go through the stuff. I told him what I wanted, and he laughed and agreed, as long as I brought it back by morning. I'd told my troublemaker to meet me at midwatch of the second. This was late summer, and what would be rising?"

"Torre's Necklace — by all the gods, Dev, what did you do?"

"Don't be hasty, Seli; it's not good for your wound. Well, he was there, and I was, and I'd told the watch to leave us be. I think they thought that if we wanted to fight on the walls they'd rather not know. I told the old boy that my proof was this: as I saluted the Necklace of Torre, her grace would give light to my blade — only briefly, of course, unless he was one of the evil ones."

"It's a wonder you weren't blasted out of the sky."

"The gods love the brave." Devlin stretched and went on. "When the whole Necklace was above the hills and clear to see, I drew the blade I'd borrowed, and made some kind of invocation. Sure enough, it flared as blue as could be, and my — friend — nearly fell onto his knees. I sheathed it quickly, before the glow died, and had a time keeping quiet. The thing stung my hand when it lit up, and left blisters that lasted two weeks."

"I thought something would happen," said Seli. "The gods may love the brave, but some of them wouldn't like your wit. I assume the man gave you no more trouble?"

"Right, he didn't. But there was trouble nonetheless — one of the captains was up for some reason, and saw the flash. Next thing I knew I was explaining it to her —"

"Dorrin's sword!" exclaimed Paks.

"Yes. It wasn't hers at the time; she took it in the captain's draw a few days later. She did about chew my hide off for mocking the gods. When I showed her my hand, though, she said they'd taken their revenge, and all she wanted was the sword."

"It is a magic sword, then?" asked Paks. "I thought I saw it glowing last year in Rotengre, when we'd killed the webspinner's cleric."

"Yes, it's magic. Good magic, too. She doesn't show it off — swords like that attract thieves like honey brings bees."

"Why doesn't it glow all the time?"

Devlin shrugged. "I don't know — I suppose it was made that way."

Chapter Thirty

Early the next morning they were marching again. All around the rich farmland showed scars of war: fields unsown, orchards hacked and burned, bloated corpses of cattle and sheep. Now and again they saw little bands of ragged peasants who fled into the woods and hedges at their approach. On the third day of the march, the Duke turned sharp south, and told them why.

"Our scouts report that Siniava's holed up in a ruined city between Koury and Immervale on the river. They've seen his personal banner and troops in his colors. The Sorellin militia should be coming south to meet us. I'm telling them to come ahead. We'll assault if we can, or siege until they arrive — but I don't want to let him get loose again."

By afternoon of the next day, they could see the old city. From a distance it looked more like a low hill of broken stone than a fortification, but as they drew closer, they saw that the city wall still held its shape around most of the mound. Where it had been breached, fresh piles of earth and brush blocked entry. Above the highest half-crumbled tower Siniava's banner waved in the afternoon sun. Paks could not see any sentries; she had an uneasy feeling about the whole thing.

While the commanders positioned their companies on the north and west of the ruins, archers tried to ignite the brush with fire arrows, but it was still too green. No arrows returned, and nothing showed on the walls.

"They want us to charge up there carelessly," said Vik. Paks paused beside him for a moment.

"Yes — I think so too. The Duke's smarter than that."

"I hope Siniava doesn't have something like that priest at Sibili. Or a wizard."

"If he had something that powerful, surely he'd have used it before now."

"Yes — unless it was here. Something lurking in the ruins that he knew about."

Paks shivered. "Don't say that, Vik. It's enough to spook anyone."

"Surely not you?"

"Huh. I don't think I'll answer that." Paks waved and went on. Nothing happened that night, and in the morning they prepared to assault the walls. Halveric Company would try the southern wall; Vladi's spears, the west;

290

and the Duke's Company, a breach in the northwest angle of the wall. East of Phelan's forces, the old ruins ran apparently unbroken to the river, some distance away.

After several attempts at climbing the earthworks filling the broken wall, they gave up; the outer face was slippery and sticky. An assault force could not climb that unstable slope while being pelted with stones and harried with arrows. While the main attack group stayed visible at the foot of the slope, Paks and Dorrin's junior corporal, Malek, each took a squad and found a climbable place on the walls out of sight, around a square jutting corner.

This was easier than it might have been. Over the years stones had shifted, giving hand and foot holds; bushes had grown in the gaps. At the top of the wall, Paks peeked over cautiously. She saw the backs of a small group at the edge of the earthworks, some yards to her left, and nothing else. She passed a hand signal to those following, and eased up onto the wall. She heard the rasp and scrape of others coming over the rim as she drew her sword. Another quick glance showed few enemy soldiers anywhere: some on the far side of the earthworks, but equally intent on the action below. As soon as her squad was on the wall, Paks gave a last look to Vossik, below with reserves, and waved. He returned the gesture. She headed toward the enemy, counting on surprise to make up for numbers.

One of the soldiers across the earthwork gap saw them just before she reached the rear of those on her side and yelled a warning. As the first soldiers turned, Paks drove her sword into the back of the rearmost. They had not had their swords out; she killed another before facing a useful weapon. Across the gap an archer let fly. Paks heard a yelp and a curse behind her. She drove on; in minutes they had killed those on their side of the gap. Paks looked down and across. Crude steps had been cut into the fill, leading to a walkway a few feet below the rim; similar steps led up to the wall on the far side.

"Let's get across that," she said to Malek. He glanced back; Vossik was on the wall with their reserves.

"Good idea."

Paks waved to her squad and started down the steps as fast as she could. She heard bowstrings twang both before and behind as Vossik's archers tried to drive the enemy away, and the enemy tried to shoot her. An arrow sank into wet clay near her foot. Another. She held her shield before her face as she ran across the walkway. She could hear her squad coming close behind. At the foot of the steps, she took a deep breath and surged upward, yelling encouragement to those following.

When she topped the steps, no one was there. Four crumpled bodies sprawled on the wall; the rest of the enemy were many strides away, running as fast as they could. She started to pursue, then looked back at Vossik. His hand signal was emphatic: wait. She looked back at her squad. Only Arñe was missing; she had taken an arrow in her arm, and Vossik had held her back. Paks looked down the outer face of the wall. Some were already climbing the wall, and others followed Volya, who was cutting steps in the clay earthwork.

No enemy soldiers showed on the wall, now. Paks explored eastward, finding a narrow break with a worn footpath climbing tumbled stones from inside the wall, then winding down the slope of broken rock below the gap on the outside. Stammel posted a guard here, and another at the river end of the wall. Then they moved into the ruins themselves.

It was hard to tell what the ruins had been. Both walls and buildings had crumbled into mounds of stone that angled into other mounds. Grass, bushes, and even twisted trees grew over all. Old streets made ravines, partly blocked by fallen stone and tangles of vines and brambles; they could not see more than a few yards. They found no direct route to the tower where Siniava's banner still flew. As the afternoon drew on toward evening, the intricate maze became even more confusing. Paks hated the thought of prowling there in the dark. Despite herself, she could not forget Vik's remarks about demons or wizards.

Before dark, the mercenaries linked into a protected perimeter. Although the guard posts were closely set, the brooding ruins and Siniava's presence nearby made everyone edgy. And the night had its troubles: poisoned arrows killed two in Vladi's Company, rocks heaved out of darkness bruised several sentries.

As dawnlight spread through the ruins, the companies began to move, drawing their ring tighter about the central tower. Paks looked for Siniava's banner. She could not see it. Almost at once others noticed that it was gone, and a shout rose. Then they heard the staccato alarm call from the northern wall.

As quickly as they could, they made for the north wall, boots clattering through the twisting, cluttered streets. Paks could hear the noise of other companies behind them. More horn signals ahead. She dodged blocks of stone, and crashed through bushes, went over a place she remembered as a direct line to another street. The wall should be close. She caught a glimpse of black and yellow darting through a gap ahead of her, and yelled. Something hit her helmet hard, and she staggered. Vik grabbed her arm and steadied her. She shook her head to clear it. A shower of rocks came from the gap. Paks looked back and saw a squad of Cracolnya's archers moving into position behind her. They poured arrows into the gap; all heard the sharp cry from within. Paks jogged forward and stuck her head cautiously around the corner. Then she led her squad past a body bristling with arrows.

Now only an open space lay between them and the outer wall. A little to one side was the narrow breach where Stammel had posted a guard. The guards were gone. Clearly some force had come this way and overwhelmed them. Paks could not understand how they'd gotten through the closely guarded perimeter. She clambered up the steep path over the broken stone until she could see out. There they were — marching rapidly away along the river toward the forest that lay a few miles upstream. She turned to call Stammel or Kefer, and saw the Duke himself climbing the path, his squires behind him.

292

"Do you see them?" he called.

"Yes, my lord. They're retreating to the forest."

"I wish I knew how in blazes they got through our lines," he said. "Not that it'll help them. We'll harry them now — they don't have a chance." He squinted at the retreating force. "Hmm. Looks like no more than five hundred or so. What do you think, Selfer?"

"The same, my lord. Do you think the rest of his army has just fallen apart?"

The Duke grunted. "I don't know. I wish I did. But we'll be after them. Kessim!"

"Yes, my lord." The Duke's junior squire, lean and dark, seemed afire with eagerness.

"Get back to the outer camp. Make sure the quartermaster gets everyone moving in a hurry, and knows where to go. He's to stay far enough back that the wounded are safe, but not out of touch. And Jori — "

"Yes, my lord."

"Bring all the horses we'll need — Kessim can help — for the captains, too."

Kessim and Jori scrambled down the outer face of the breach and jogged toward the camp. Paks could see mounted men approaching; the Duke smiled.

"That's a smart man," he commented. "He saw something going on, and knew I'd need mounts. Paks, tell the captains I want them to form the cohorts below the wall, and wait for me."

"Yes, my lord." The Duke turned and started down the path, followed by Selfer. Paks watched them go. Then she saw a flicker of movement, of yellow, among the tumbled rocks to one side of the path. She yelled just as a man rose from the rocks and leaped toward the Duke. Selfer dove between them, clawing at his sword. Paks charged recklessly down the path. Another enemy, this one in black, leaped from cover on the opposite side of the path to strike at the Duke, who had his sword out by this time, and was fencing with the first attacker. Selfer was down, but struggling to rise.

The Duke parried the strokes of both attackers for a moment. Then Paks was beside him, thrusting at the man in black. When he turned to meet her attack, she saw a face dark with tattoos. He had a long, narrow sword and a long dagger; the tips of both were stained brown. Paks took a slash of the dagger on her shield. She could not reach him with her short blade, but she could make sure he didn't touch the Duke. She heard yells from above, and the clatter of many boots on stone. Beside her was the almost musical jingling of the Duke's mail, and the clang of blades. Her own opponent kept trying to force her to one side, exposing the Duke, but she kept her place despite the attack of both blades. She heard a yelp from the Duke's opponent, then a grunt as the Duke lunged.

Suddenly the man in black dropped his dagger, leaped forward, and grabbed her shield with one hand, fending off her thrust with his other blade. As his weight jerked forward on the shield, Paks staggered and fell.

She saw his sword dart past her, and tried desperately to deflect it with her own. The blades scraped together. She heard him gasp, then he rolled onto her, and she felt hard hands gripping her throat. She couldn't free her shield arm.

"You — you northern bitch — " he growled, then his hands went slack, and many arms pulled his heavy body off her. Stammel, grim-faced, offered a hand, and Paks pulled herself up. Volya helped her reset her shield. The Duke stood cleaning his sword. Selfer lay propped against Arcolin, his shoulder soaked in blood. Both attackers were dead.

"My lord — " Stammel held out the blades Paks had faced.

"Yes?" The Duke glanced at the weapons; his face froze. "Poison!"

"I thought so, my lord. Did these touch you, my lord, or your squire?"

"No. That one — " The Duke pointed to the sword dropped by the first attacker, and Arcolin reached out to examine it. "But Paks — is she — "

"I'm not hurt, my lord," she said quickly.

Stammel looked closely at her. "Are you sure? The least scratch — "

Paks shook her head. "No, sir. He came close, but he didn't touch. I couldn't disarm him — "

The Duke snorted. "You did well enough to hold him off with that short sword. Arcolin, what about that one?"

"I don't think so, my lord. Selfer, how is it?"

"It — hurts." Selfer was breathing in short gasps. "But — it feels — much like any wound."

The Duke knelt beside him. "Selfer, that was well done; without you, I'd have had no chance. Let's see now — " He drew his dagger and widened the slit in Selfer's tunic. "Ahh — you'll need stitching, and some quiet days with the surgeons, but it's not as bad as I'd feared. Any other injury?"

"I think not, my lord."

"Good. The surgeons are coming." The Duke opened a pouch at his belt and wadded up the length of cloth in it to press against the wound. "Arcolin, stay with him until he's settled. I must speak to the Count and Aliam."

"Yes, my lord."

"Dorrin, get everyone in marching order below the wall."

"Yes, my lord."

"Paksenarrion." He turned to look at her.

"My lord?"

"My thanks for your warning and assistance. You have a quick eye; I hope it will be as quick to find Siniava." He grinned at her, suddenly relaxing. "You're better than a shield; I wasn't even worried."

Paks felt herself blushing. "Thank you, my lord." As the Duke turned away, Paks looked to the north. The fight seemed to have taken a long time, but she could still see the dust of the retreating force.

All that day they trailed Siniava's army, first along across the plain and then in thick forest. Little air moved under the trees. Their scouts reported that they were gaining, but they had not closed the gap by night. Very early the next day they went on again. It was even hotter, a heavy breathless heat, but Paks had no desire to slow down. The scouts had reported the enemy to be close ahead, and moving slowly.

After a brief stop for food, they moved on, swords drawn. A scout rode to meet them. "They're set up across the road, around the next turn and on a little rise." The Duke, riding just in front of Paks, nodded and turned to the Company. Every eye was on him. Paks noticed that the air had become very still; it seemed darker. Almost as she thought, a mutter of thunder troubled the air. She felt the hairs rise on her skin. Canna's medallion hung heavy as stone around her neck. They marched faster; she heard the horses' hooves crashing in the leaves on either side of the track. She glanced sideways to see them, then beyond.

The gleam of weapons in the underbrush beyond the Clart riders shocked her so she nearly stumbled. She could not say anything, for a horrified instant, then blurted "Trap! Left flank!"

"What!" Stammel swung left and peered past the riders. "Halt!" he bellowed. From the corner of her eye, Paks saw the Duke jerk his horse to a halt and turn. "Company square!" Arcolin was yelling. The Clarts slowed, looking first at the column and then at their own flanks. The Duke spun his horse on its hocks. "Both sides!" he called. "Dorrin! Square 'em!" Now the Clarts had found the enemy, and spun to face them, lances lowered. The enemy charged, roaring.

"Get in the square!" Stammel yelled at Paks. She realized she'd been standing frozen. She'd never been in square as a corporal. She backed into the lines. "On the corner," said Stammel. "Right — there, yes. Tighten it up!" he yelled to the cohort as a whole. "Link with Dorrin's and tighten it."

As the enemy charged, the Clarts spurred toward them. They slowed, but could not stop, the onslaught. Horses and men went down, screaming. The enemy pikemen slammed into the square, hacking over the first rank and the second, while their second rank jabbed at the first. Paks, on the corner, could have used four arms. She could barely fend off the enemy pikes; she had no chance to dart under the shafts. Surrounded as they were, their only chance was the tight formation. She had no time even to wonder where the Duke was, or whether the other companies had been trapped as well.

A flash of nearby lightning lit the scene with a blue glare as the storm broke over their heads. Rain blasted down on them; wind lashed the trees overhead. Paks squinted, blinking rain out of her eyes. The enemy pikemen were not withdrawing, but they pressed a little less. Between reverberations of thunder that trembled in the ground, Paks heard the Duke shouting, then Arcolin. She could not distinguish the words. Then Stammel, close behind her.

"Left flank — right by half — slow — march." With the others Paks shifted a pace forward and right, as the second rank came up into the gaps, lengthening their line. The pike in front of her wavered; she took a chance, ducking under it for one quick thrust at the pikeman. He fell, clutching his belly. "Don't charge yet," admonished Stammel. "Steady." Another long roll of thunder and gust of rain. Paks could hardly see the soldiers a pike-length away. A ripping sound, like cloth tearing overhead, and a blinding blue-white flash, followed by thunder that jarred the teeth in her head — she fought the desire to flatten herself on the ground. When a gust of wind lifted the rain like a curtain, she saw the enemy: a dark wavering mass, just out of reach. The rain came back, blinding. The enemy force wasn't attacking, but it wasn't running, either.

So the situation stayed until dark and after. In the confusion of the storm, the mercenaries could do no better than hold their formation. The enemy, though clearly outnumbering them, was curiously unwilling to press the attack. Paks, like the others, was wet, chilled, and tired. It was going to be a long night. The only good news came after dark, when word was passed that the Halverics, escorting supplies and wounded, were outside the enemy ring and still intact.

Morning dawned bleak. It had rained — though less heavily — all night. All were wet; even though the worst wounded had been covered with cloaks, in the protected center of the square, they were damp and miserable. The last of their rations had gone the previous day; they were all hungry. Paks, stamping her feet to warm up, glared through the last drizzle at the enemy lines. She could see they stretched all around the Company in the woods.

Despite this, morale was higher than Paks expected. She heard someone wonder whether they would move forward, toward Sorellin, or back, to link with the Halverics. No one answered. In the center of the square, the Duke conferred with his captains and Vladi. She turned to face the enemy. Those lines stirred, as men in mail, with long cloaks, went up and down. She heard a bowstring twang, and one of them staggered. Good. Cracolnya's archers had kept their strings dry. A ragged yell came from the enemy, and a section of their line moved forward.

"Steady," said Stammel. "Wait — " The enemy advance wavered to a halt. Paks opened her mouth to lead a derisive yell, and decided to save her breath. She'd have a chance later.

In a few moments, a ragged flight of crossbow bolts thudded into the soft ground between the lines. Paks heard Stammel laugh, behind her. "Rain's a lot harder on those than on longbows," he said. "They'll have to come closer to do damage, and I don't see any eagerness — "

"Good," said Arcolin. "It was a neat trap; I'm as glad they haven't the stomach to profit by it. In fact, I wouldn't mind if they decided to back out of here when we advance."

Stammel grunted. "I could stand to know where the Sorellin militia is."

"Keeping warm and dry somewhere," said Kefer. "Like all militia."

Arcolin laughed shortly. "Probably. Now: we're going to advance west, away from the river. We think that'll pull those on the river side after us, and the Vladi's spears will hit their flank. Vladi says they've weakened the ones between them and the river."

"What about our rear?"

"Dorrin and Cracolnya will shift when we do. We'll have to string it a bit more open while the shift is going on — listen for me."

"Yes, Captain."

"Pont'll be directing the archers on this flank. If I fall, Stammel, take over until Dorrin can."

"Yes, sir."

As they moved, Paks was glad to be on the forward side of the square. Stammel moved them slowly, so the right flank could stay together. Paks saw the pikes lower ahead of her. The enemy started yelling, a raucous blast of noise. Horns blared behind their lines. The enemy lines moved as slowly as their own. Mist lay along the ground; they all seemed to be wading. Paks stumbled over something she could not see, and cursed as she caught her balance. Foot by slow foot they went on. Part of the enemy lines to her left broke toward them; Paks heard the crash of weapons. Directly in front of her, the foremost rank of pikemen suddenly lifted their pikes and heaved them like lances. Paks yelled and threw up her shield. The pikes were ill-balanced for throwing; most fell short. Those soldiers drew curved blades and ran forward.

Shieldless, the enemy swordsmen could not stand against the Duke's men, who cut their way forward. Paks heard shouts and cries from behind but spared no glance for that. The troops in front gave back slowly. The third rank still had their pikes, and showed no inclination to throw these effective weapons away. A deeper roar from the rear: the cry of Vladi's spearmen charging the enemy flank. Paks found herself grinning. Despite the numbers facing her, she began to think they'd get out of this mess alive.

Suddenly the ground trembled. Another storm? Paks spared an instant's look at the sky, but saw nothing. The noise grew, was joined by high-pitched trumpet calls. Now she could hear the rolling rhythm of hoofbeats. If Siniava had cavalry — she set her jaw and lunged at the man before her, catching him in the throat.

Horsemen erupted into sight on the right: in blue, in red and black — the Blue Riders and Sobanai Company. They were in the enemy rear, busy with lance and sword, before the enemy realized who and what they were. The lines wavered.

"Now!" yelled Arcolin. "Forward on the left!"

"Go on!" bellowed Stammel and Kefer almost together. Paks was already yelling joyously, leaping at the enemy lines. She could feel the others with her. The enemy stiffened a moment, as the first impetus of the cavalry charge dissipated, but fell back before the Phelani charge. Then Paks heard, on the right, the battle cry of the Sorellin militia, as they came around the bend and ran forward. The enemy lines disintegrated, turning almost in an instant into clumps and individuals in headlong flight. She could see horses and riders twisting among the trees, foot soldiers dodging, fallen men and horses on the ground. She pursued, fighting fiercely for a short time, until she and her friends found themselves grinning at each other over a pile of bodies.

But that was the end of fighting for them. Vik was pale and unsteady on his feet; he fainted as she watched. When Paks turned back to find help, she found it an effort to walk; her legs felt like they had an extra joint. Kefer was not as worried about poisoned blades as she had been.

"It's fighting without food," he said. "That and cold. They'll be all right." And some hours later, fed and rested, they were. Arñe was ready to return to the cohort, and Seli was already back.

"I'm not limping," he said. "And if I can fight beside the wagons — which I was — then I can fight here."

"What did the surgeons say?" asked Arcolin.

"Turned up their noses like they do. By Tir, Captain, you can leave Paks as corporal, but I'm staying here." But Paks was more than willing to return to her place as file leader. What she wanted more than anything else was sleep.

They heard from the Sorellin militia — disgustingly smug at having rescued mercenaries — that the remnants of Siniava's army had fled south, and were trying to cross the Immer at a ford. Fewer than a thousand were left to him.

"So they say," said Arñe sourly. "I thought he was supposed to be down to five hundred two days ago."

"True." Paks yawned. "How I could sleep! But they've scoured the woods, Arñe — no more of them there. And surely he'd have used all he had in that trap."

"I hope so. We were afraid you'd all be cut to pieces up here."

Paks yawned again. "We could have been. It was near enough."

That night the talk around the camp was how the Sobanai Company horse had linked with Sorellin's foot to reach them in time. A long, lanky Sobanai hirstar was more than willing to explain.

"We'd been in the Eastmarches," he said. "Keeping an eye on the trouble in Semnath and Falsith — just in case you wondered why Siniava got no reinforcements from the east. Then Sorellin came to Sir Seti, and asked for cavalry aid: they were marching to meet you, and the Blue Riders were out of touch. Sir Seti spared a cohort to come, and when we met with Sorellin's troops, above Koury, we heard such that we thought haste wise. Only Sorellin was on foot and slow. We kept after them, and wouldn't let them stop to celebrate their restday, or whatever it was. Then we met the Blue Riders, but came on anyway. Yesterday, came a big storm after midday; they wanted to halt. So did we — the horses were jumpy. But after the worst had passed, we saw riders ahead — Clarts. So then we heard of the trap, and they led us here, a hard march. We stopped last night only when no one could see, and moved again at first light."

Paks realized she'd hardly seen a Clart rider all day. "How many of the Clarts got through?"

"I don't know myself. Not many, I think. They were hit hard, they said, and those who could stayed to harry the rear of Siniava's lines."

"What's going on in the east?" asked Stammel. "Does Siniava have guild support as in Cilwan?"

"Some. Cloth merchants, and such. He had strong factions in the east, even in Falsith. Probably a thousand to fifteen hundred left the East-marches to fight with him. There aren't that many left, of course." He grinned around the circle of listeners.

"And where's Sofi Gannarrion in all this?" asked Kefer. "I thought he was supposed to help."

The Sobanai rider laughed. "Surely you know — ? No? He's in Fallo, with the Duke. The Duke of Fall's second son, Amade, is betrothed to Ganarrion's eldest daughter. He's not about to stir out of there and risk his bride-gift being damaged."

"Well, I'll be — "

"Besides, he wants the Duke's support when he makes his bid for the throne."

"Sofi? He's serious about that?"

"So I hear. You know he's always claimed to be a prince. Allied with the Duke of Fall, he's planning to take his throne back."

"Huh. I'd always thought it was just talk. He's no use to us then — "

"Unless Siniava tried to march in Fallo. I daresay old Sofi will come out of the keep then."

"I hope so. What's it like over there? And what about crossing the Immer?"

"Rich land, good open farmland. Hardly any forest: Siniava can't hide that way. Mud's your main concern. The roads are soup when it rains. As for crossing the Immer, the nearest bridge is Koury; otherwise, ford it."

Chapter Thirty-one

The next day they crossed the Immer at the same ford Siniava had used. The Duke's column spent two days crossing, but started the pursuit well-fed and rested. Siniava's trace was clear, bearing almost due east: discarded equipment and dying men littered the way. For three days they followed the trampled trail, but saw no enemy. The Sobanai riders returned to the northeast; the Clarts and a half-cohort of Blue Riders stayed with them.

On the fourth day, they sighted a large mass of troops moving slowly northeast, and followed them for several days until they found what they'd begun to suspect: these were the Falsith and Semnath reinforcements, already headed home. The Duke turned them south, toward Fallo. The next day they intercepted a courier; within an hour the news ran through the column. Fallo had closed its gates to the Honeycat, and Ganarrion was chasing him down the Imefal. He had fewer than seven hundred men left, and those were lean and travelworn.

"He'll cut through the forest," said Vik, "and head for the coast. What else can he do?"

"Try to get to the Immer and go downriver; that might work."

"Does he have any troops left at Immervale?" asked Paks.

"He won't have any troops anywhere after they hear about the last few weeks."

They were marching as they talked, angling south and west to block any move to Immervale.

"But what if he crosses the Imefal and gets into the forest?" Paks did not want to trail Siniava into another forest trap.

Arcolin, riding beside them, grinned down. "He won't."

"But — "

"You remember Alured?" said Arcolin. Heads nodded. "He's why Siniava can't cut through the forest. He'd need Alured's permission and guidance. And Alured — well, he's finding it profitable to oppose Siniava."

"But, sir, he's a pirate," objected Rauf. "He could be playing both sides."

"He could. But he's smart. He can see that Siniava's beaten — he'll choose the winning side, I expect. Especially since our Duke offered something he wants."

"What's that, sir?"

Arcolin laughed. "I can't tell you that now. But it's what he left the sea

300

for, and he thinks we have it to give. Perhaps we do."

Day after day they marched toward Immervale as their couriers kept contact with Ganarrion's horsemen. Two days running rain slowed them — the Sobanai hirstar had been right about the roads — and finally they gave up and traveled the fields and pastures. Paks felt she had a permanent crick in her neck from staring off to the south all the time.

Paks had lost track of the days they'd marched when they came over a rise to see a small, straggling body of troops off to their left. And ahead, on top of a low ridge in front of them, were the banners of Vonja and Foss Council. They were squarely between the enemy and Immervale. The enemy army turned sharp south, and drew together.

"Now where's he going?" asked Paks.

"The river. There's nothing down there, but — " Stammel stopped and looked thoughtful.

"What?"

"I'll ask the captain — I thought I remembered something."

By nightfall it was obvious what Siniava had been making for: an old and partly ruined citadel reminiscent of Cortes Andres, built high on a rock bluff where the Imefal met the Immer. A great stone bridge spanned the Imefal below the citadel walls. Siniava had posted a rear guard here, but as the combined mercenary and militia forces came nearer, they withdrew before the archers were in range. Arcolin led his cohort across the bridge first, and swung right around the citadel, up a slope of broken rock to the forest that lay beyond its massive walls on the south side.

There they found their advance scouts talking to a company of archers in russet leather. Alured the Black, teeth flashing in his dark face as he grinned at Arcolin, waved the captain over.

"So — he's well in the trap, eh? Where's your Duke?"

"Coming," said Arcolin. "How has it gone here?"

"Easily. He wanted nothing but to put a wall between himself and trouble."

"You could not keep him out?"

"Out? But, Captain, your Duke wants him alive. I'd have had to kill him to hold him — if I could."

"I see." Arcolin looked up at the walls. "Well, he's caught now, and if we have a stiff fight to get in, still — "

"It is about that, Captain, that I must speak to your Duke."

Paks heard no more before Stammel moved them farther around the citadel, to meet the troops coming the other way. Soon a solid line circled the walls, and camps were laid out at a little distance.

Paks was waiting in line to eat when she caught sight of a tall man in Marshal's robes coming along the lines from the Vonja position. With him was another in bright red over shining mail — the paladin, thought Paks. They were chatting with different soldiers as they moved along. Paks didn't know if she wanted to talk with them or not. What little she remembered about her conversation with the High Marshal was unsettling. She saw Stammel smile as they spoke to him and looked away.

"Ah — Paksenarrion." They were in front of her. It would be rude to ignore them. Paks met the High Marshal's eyes.

"Yes, sir."

"Sir Fenith, here wanted to meet you — awake, that is. He is the paladin you fought beside in Sibili."

Fenith had dark hair and wide brown eyes. He grinned at Paks. "I've been wanting to thank you. Your help came at the right time."

Paks felt herself blushing. She wished she could remember what had happened. Without the memory, she could not *feel* she had done anything.

"But tell us," Fenith went on, "how has the fighting been, where you were?"

They listened closely, and encouraged her to continue when she faltered, as she told about the weeks of pursuit and fighting. Not until then, telling it, did Paks realize how short the time had been. She felt they'd been marching forever, yet the spring green of the trees was just darkening. She had seen newborn calves even this past week. Paks wondered where the High Marshal and paladin had been. She did not dare to ask.

"I'll be glad to see the end of this," said Fenith, when she had finished. "It was necessary, but these realms will suffer for it."

"Yes." The High Marshal's face settled into grim lines. "Evil has been wakened that will take much work to lay. And not only by Siniava." Paks felt a threat she did not understand. He looked at her, and smiled. "Does it seem strange to you that a High Marshal of Gird and a paladin should be regretting a war?"

"A little — yes — "

"Remember what I told you, in Sibili. Gird fought as a protector, to ward his people against evil, both natural and supernatural. Not for plunder or pay — " Paks felt a flicker of anger. "No, I'm not insulting your Duke or you; I know his cause in this. But you've seen the ruined farms and homeless wandering folk. That will take long years to heal, that and the breach of law and trust that lets brigands roam as they will. That's what we want to see an end of." Paks slid her gaze to the paladin; he smiled at her.

"High Marshal, Paksenarrion is our ally — not a novice yeoman in the barton. She fights for honor in this — as do we." Paks relaxed a little. The paladin, she thought, was much friendlier than the High Marshal. "Tell me," he asked, "have you had any help from the medallion you carry? Do you still wear it?"

"Yes, sir, I do wear it. I'm uncertain what the help would be like. I remember the High Marshal telling me it saved my life, but I don't remember that day at all."

"Do you ever feel anything — warmth, or cold, or such?"

Paks considered telling him about the first time she'd handled it, when Canna was wounded, but decided against it. Not in front of the High Marshal. Nothing had happened recently. She forced down the memory of that

302

weight on her chest before the ambush — she'd been very tired. She shook her head.

"If it does — if anything strange happens, if you feel anything — you'd be wise to let one of us know. It could be important, to you and to all of us." With a casual wave, the paladin turned away, and the High Marshal followed. Paks stared after them, her appetite gone.

"What was that about?" asked Jenits.

Paks shook her head. "I'm — not sure."

Jenits stared after the paladin with open admiration. "I'd like to have mail like that. I wonder how he keeps it so shiny. It makes even the Duke's look dull. Do you suppose I'll end up a paladin, Paks?" He grinned at his own joke, and thumped her arm. Paks laughed, easing her tension.

"About as soon as I will."

Shortly after dark, all those in Arcolin's cohort who wore the Dwarfwatch ring were called to his tent. There they found the mercenary commanders, Alured the Black, and a group of Halveric soldiers that Paks recognized from Dwarfwatch.

"I have a special mission for you," the Duke began. "You have known the treachery of the Honeycat longest; I assume you want him dead the most." A murmur of anger and assent followed. "Good. Our ally Alured tells me there's a secret passage between the citadel and the outside. He knows where it begins, in the dungeons under the inner keep, and where it comes out, in the forest." Paks felt a surge of excitement. She imagined them breaking in, finding Siniava in his chamber —

"He'll know of it, surely," Alured said, his rough accent breaking into her fantasy. "I sent a man to his army, when your Duke said, and he'll have told them the secret, as if he found it himself. I've used the passage a few times myself. It's narrow, but sound. You can wait at the outer end, for him to try an escape, or you can go in. If he's barred the opening, on the inside, you'd have trouble breaking in. And if he's got a wizard, you'd need a wizard to break the lock."

"Has he a wizard, Alured?" asked the Duke. Alured was silent a moment before answering.

"He's got someone in a long fancy gown. Might be a merchant or banker — a high guildsman. Or it could be a wizard. I don't know."

"Mmm. We'll wait, and let his well-known selfishness lead him out the bolthole." The Duke looked around at the soldiers. "I want you to keep watch over the forest end of the passage. *You* will not leave it unguarded, even for an instant. If he has a wizard — a mage — he may come out in disguise, even shapechanged. And he will certainly come out with his bodyguard and as much wealth as they can carry. Remember: their weapons may be poisoned, and the bodyguard is marked, dark tattoos all over the face. Siniava himself, if not in disguise, is a little taller than Aliam, here, and dark-haired. Harek told us, before he died, that Siniava has a small tattoo himself, between the eyebrows: the horned chain of Liart. I doubt you'll see it; he'll be in armor, most likely. But I want to be sure nothing escapes that way. Nothing. And when he comes, I want him alive. Can I trust you for this?"

"Yes, my lord!" came the response. The Duke smiled at them.

"I thought so. Now — you must go by night, so his sentries on the wall see nothing. You'll have to camp there — but no fires; they'll see light or smoke. One of us or our squires will be always near, within hail. When someone comes out, try to be sure they're all out before you attack. Set up your watch schedules so that some from both companies are always on. Paksenarrion — "

"Yes, my lord."

"I heard good things of you when you took over from Seli. You'll command our unit and work with the Halveric — sergeant, is it, Aliam?"

"Sergeant Sunnot." The Halveric looked at her. "You should remember him from last fall."

"Yes, my lord." Paks caught Sunnot's eye; he smiled.

Not long after, they faced the black-in-black maw of the passage, an irregular hole in a rocky outcrop south of the citadel. Paks would not have noticed it, in the darkness, if Alured had not pointed it out. The next morning Paks and Sunnot examined the situation more closely.

The passage entrance faced south; above it a steep rockface, thickly forested on top, blocked their view of the citadel a half-hour's walk to the north. Below, a gentle slope dipped more west than south, to the Immer; a small clearing gave them a good view of the passage and its surroundings. Paks poked cautiously into the near end of the passage. It crooked sharply left, then right, its rough walls looking like a natural fissure in the stone, but beyond the second turn Paks found smoothly hewn walls and floor, with torch brackets set into the walls. The passage ran straight from there, dipping gently. She backed out and told Sunnot what she'd seen. They decided to pile dry leaves just inside the entrance to give warning of Siniava's approach. Then they rearranged the guardposts, and decided on the signals to use when something happened.

That evening the Duke came to inspect their arrangements. "How long do you think he'll wait?" asked Paks.

"He can see us cutting timber for siege towers. I think he'll go soon, before his own men decide to turn on him. Tonight — tomorrow — tomorrow night. I doubt he'll wait much longer than that. And I'd say at night — it's how he's left every other position this campaign."

"Yes, my lord."

"But don't count on it. If he realizes his pattern, he'll change it. And remember, Paks: take him alive."

"Yes, my lord."

Paks and Sunnot walked the posts that night, but nothing happened. No sounds came to them from the citadel. In the dark Paks had time to think back over the campaign. It seemed that nothing could go wrong this time:

Siniava was well in the trap. But they had thought the same before, only to face another long march and battle. She sighed, louder than she'd meant to, and Arñe spoke her name softly.

"Paks? What's wrong?"

Paks moved to Arñe's post and leaned on a tree. "Nothing — it seems strange not to be marching somewhere, that's all. I keep thinking we've got him, but I thought that before."

"I know. For awhile it seemed we'd been marching a year, and would go on forever, but — "

"It hasn't been that long. We did start early — "

Now Arñe sighed. "We did indeed. I tell you, Paks, I don't feel the same. It's only our third year, but I feel older — I feel there's been more than a year between this campaign and last spring. Do you remember when we came to Rotengre?"

"Yes. I know what you mean. We were so glad to be second-years — but we knew we weren't really veterans. And then Dwarfwatch — "

"Yes. Dwarfwatch. Then Rotengre. Then this." Arñe sighed again.

Paks pushed herself away from the tree. "Well — it'll be over soon. We'll feel different when he's dead, and when we've had some rest."

"I hope so," said Arñe soberly. Paks walked on, still thinking.

The next day was as quiet as the first. No one grumbled about missing the action at the citadel, but Paks knew many shared her fears: what if he doesn't come this way? What if others make the capture? By nightfall they were edgy and watchful. Paks and Sunnot had both slept during the day, so they'd be on together.

Night chill made Paks shiver suddenly between guardposts. She looked at the tunnel mouth and saw nothing. She felt distinctly colder; she wondered if a weather change was coming. She pulled her cloak closer around her, and leaned into a tree trunk. She felt a breath of cold air drift down the slope, chilling her face. Her cloak was warm. She yawned, suddenly sleepy despite the cold. Her mind wandered.

All at once a sharp prick, like a thorn, stung her chest. She jerked her eyes open, realizing in that instant that she'd been almost asleep. She looked quickly around and saw nothing. She started to relax, and realized that she should have seen at least one guard, even in the gloom. She pushed herself up. The nearest guard had slumped to the ground. Paks felt a trickle of fear, like icewater, down her spine. The hairs rose on her arms. She shook the guard — a Halveric, she remembered — and the woman grunted.

Paks pinched her arm and muttered, "Wake up! Trouble." The woman stiffened, grabbed Paks's arm, and started to rise.

"What happened?"

"Magic, I think." Paks drew her sword as she spoke. "Pray we're not too late. Draw your blade."

"The others?"

"Wait — we'll have to wake them, but — " She peered toward the tunnel mouth again. A dark shadow seemed to flow out of it. "There — see?"

"Falk's oath in gold! But what do we — ?"

"Wake the others on this side; I'll go across. If they think we're all asleep, maybe they'll be careless. Watch — don't sit down — be sure the torchlighters are ready."

A glimmer of starlight lit the rockface, as Paks edged around in the trees to find the other guards. She could see another shadow, and another, emerge from the tunnel. She found a pair of guards and woke them, then another pair. Where was Sunnot? More shadows emerged, to cluster a few yards from the entrance. Paks had most of the guards awake; she could only hope they would stay so. She wished she knew which of those shadows was the wizard, and which the Honeycat.

The shadows took up a blunt arrowhead formation, and Paks tensed. Which way would they move? Her left hand fumbled for Canna's medallion without her thought, and it seemed to twitch left. She moved from the trees along the rockface, where she could cut off a retreat to the tunnel.

A last cloaked figure emerged, and the entire group moved slowly westward toward the trees. Paks took a deep breath and yelled, a wordless cry of mingled anger and triumph. Torches flared around the perimeter; guards stepped forward. She spared a thought of relief, that the guards had stayed awake, as she charged the group of fugitives. They turned, forming a hollow ring, blades whistling in the air as they drew them.

These were the Honeycat's bodyguard: faces tattooed in garish patterns, bladetips dark with poison even in dancing torchlight. In seconds the woods rang with the clash of swords, and the cries of the fighters. Paks swept her blade in joyful strokes across the enemy blades, exultant. Trick *me*, will you, she thought. Ha! She glanced past her opponents to those sheltered by the ring. One was a man with a narrow dark beard — surely a wizard. The other must be Siniava. Except — Paks nearly missed a parry — except that it was a woman. Very obviously a woman, in a thin silk gown. Shapechange, thought Paks, astonished, and pressed her attack.

The fighter in front of her went down: one of the guards had gotten a lateral stroke. More were down. The mercenaries surged forward, overrunning the rest, to grapple with the two in the center. They went down in a heap of bodies, each eager to grab hold. Paks, an instant too late, stood panting beside them. She rubbed her corselet absently; her chest itched. A tingle ran down her left arm, as if someone had jabbed her elbow. She whirled, searching the shadows, and stiffened as she caught a movement along the base of the rockface. She relaxed: only an animal. An instant later she charged, sword high. What animal would be out in the open with all that noise and light?

As her sword came down toward a furry back, the animal shape rippled, and she faced a man in black armor inlaid with gold. The first blow of his broadsword snapped the tip of her blade. Paks yelled a warning to the others, yanking her dagger from its sheath, as she tried to parry another of his strokes. This time her sword shattered in her hand.

306

"Phelan's bitch!" snarled the man. "This time you've gone too far — touch *me* with a blade, will you!" He lunged; Paks jerked aside. The thrust barely missed her. She tried to stab with her dagger, but it was too short. His blade sliced into her corselet; the force of the blow staggered her, though she felt no cut. He whirled and ran for the trees. Paks launched herself after him and managed to grapple his legs. They fell sprawling together. Before she could get loose, she felt him heave up and start to swing his sword.

The next instant he gave a loud screech, and writhed away.

"Hang onto him!" said a brisk voice. Paks clung to the kicking, squirming legs, and tried to see who had spoken. Against the light of the torches, her helper was only a dark shape. She heard boots running toward them. In moments, six or eight soldiers were holding the black-armored man down. Paks pushed herself up, panting. Her elbows hurt, where she'd fallen, and she had a stitch in her side.

The Duke strode into the light. "Got him, have we?"

"I think so, my lord." Now Paks recognized the paladin's voice. "We'll get his helmet off — "

"Allow me." The Duke knelt beside the man and slipped the tip of his dagger into the visor to lift it. Paks stared. The face inside was pale and angry. Dark eyes, a lock of dark hair showing, and a small tattoo between thick eyebrows.

"Well," said the Duke cheerfully. "What a surprise, Lord Siniava, to find the commander of a besieged citadel wandering the woods at night." Paks could not hear what Siniava said in answer, but the Duke's shoulders stiffened. The paladin growled. Paks looked around, suddenly remembering the other man and woman. What had they been, and who were they? She saw a circle of mercenaries, and walked over to see two captives, bound hand and foot.

"Kieri!" No mistaking that call; the Halverics had arrived, both bareheaded.

"It's Siniava," said the Duke. "We'll have to get his armor off before you can have what you're looking for."

"We can manage that, can't we, Cal?" The Halveric looked eager.

Cal was grinning too. "How badly is he hurt?"

"Nothing much," said Fenith. "Paksenarrion caught him, and I disarmed him. He's got a slashed wrist; that's all." He paused a moment. "What are you planning?"

"Don't be silly," snapped the Duke. "We're going to kill him."

"I know that," said the paladin, equally shortly. "Go on and do it."

The Duke gave him a long stare. Paks felt her belly clench. "Do you know," he asked softly, "what he did to my men? And to Aliam's sons?" Fenith nodded. "Then don't ask mercy for him," the Duke growled.

"You're a warrior," said Fenith implacably. "A warrior, not a torturer. Don't cheapen yourself."

"*Cheapen* myself?" Paks had never seen the Duke so angry, not even the day he'd held Ferrault's dying hand. "Sir paladin, you're the one with divine guidance. You're the one who can walk away when the battle's over. I do the dirty work, paladin, and I would more than cheapen myself, I would *beggar* myself for the honor of my men." All around the clearing the Duke's soldiers were frozen, listening; the Halverics hardly knew where to look. Paks felt choked with horror. The Duke's face was strange, utterly unlike himself. She was more frightened than she'd been facing the Honeycat with a broken sword.

She hardly knew it when she moved. The Duke's head swung to her. She could feel the stares of the paladin and the Halverics.

"Ask her, paladin," the Duke said more quietly. "Ask her, if she has forgotten her dead friends and how they died. Ask her if Siniava deserves a clean and easy death."

"And then?" asked the paladin, equally quietly.

The Duke shrugged. "She captured him, you say. I'll abide by her word on it." The Halverics stirred, but said nothing.

Paks felt a wave of horror and panic even before the paladin asked, "Well, Paksenarrion — how should this man die?" She met the Duke's angry gaze, and that of the Halverics: Aliam's dark, enigmatic; his son's bleak with remembered pain. The shades of her friends seemed to crowd the air — Saben, Canna — Tears choked her throat; she fought for speech.

"My lord, I have not — I cannot — forget those friends. And he had them killed, and hurt — I want him dead, my lord — " The Duke nodded, looking more like the Duke she knew, and she gathered courage. "But we don't — we are not like him, my lord. That's why we fought. Afterwards — but if it were me, my lord, I'd kill him now. But I have no right to say." The Duke gave her a look she could not read.

"Sobeit. Aliam?"

The Halveric sighed. "She's probably right, Kieri, gods blast it. I'll abide. But I was looking forward to it."

"It was my agreement. You can give the stroke." The Duke heaved himself up from beside Siniava.

"My thanks." Aliam Halveric drew his sword. "Cal, take that helmet off." Cal wrestled the helmet from Siniava's head, and tossed it aside. With a quick powerful stroke the Halveric buried his sword in Siniava's neck. The watching soldiers cheered, and in a few minutes the armor and body were hacked into many pieces. Paks watched silently, thinking of the many bodies she'd seen in the past year.

It had happened so fast at the end. She could scarcely believe it was over, and turned away, still frightened and sick. She did not realize she had fallen until a hand touched her shoulder. She flinched, fighting nausea.

"Paks?" Vik sounded worried. She nodded, unable to speak. "What's wrong? Were you hurt? Let me see." Approaching torchlight glared through her closed eyelids. She felt his hands touching her, heard the hiss when he found the gash in her armor. Other hands were about her now, supporting her. Voices. Someone swearing as he worked at the fastenings of her corselet. She forced her eyes open, squinting against the torchlight. She saw someone walking away with Siniava's head on a pole. Then the paladin's face filled her vision.

"Paksenarrion. We think it is poison. Be still." She felt an emptiness as others moved away. The paladin's hands on her were hard. A glow seemed to rise around them. She felt a streak of pain across her chest, then a wave of comfort, palpable as a handful of clover. She took a breath and it came easy. Her vision cleared.

"My apologies," said Fenith. "You moved so well I did not think to be sure you weren't hurt. How is it now?"

Paks had not felt so well for days — even months, she thought. "I'm fine, sir; thank you." She started to sit up. Around them was a circle of her friends, looking worried.

"Here," said Vik. "Have a cloak."

"I'm fine." Paks took the cloak anyway. The paladin helped her stand. She felt steady and secure.

"Paksenarrion." That was Aliam Halveric, watching her with a puzzled frown.

"Yes, my lord."

"Do you know where Sunnot is? Did he go to bring us word?"

Memory of the mysterious cold and sleep came back to her. "No, my lord. I think he must have been overcome by the sleep — "

"Sleep! What was he — ?"

A clamor of voices broke out, explaining.

"We were all asleep — "

"Magic or something — "

" — and Paks woke me up, and they — "

"Silence!" Paks had not noticed the Duke still standing nearby. "Vik, look for him. Paks, tell us about this sleep — how were you awake?"

"My lord, I don't know. Sunnot and I had doubled the guards; we had just met and parted over there — " Paks pointed " — when it seemed cold suddenly. I remember a cold breeze, and wrapping my cloak. Then I woke, and I was on the ground, beside a tree — "

"What woke you?" asked the paladin. The Duke shot him a look.

"I don't know exactly — it felt like a thorn pricking my chest — "

"Where your holy symbol rests?" Paks nodded. "May I see it again, please?" Paks slipped the chain over her head and handed it to him. As he took it, it flared to a blue glow, instantly extinguished. He held the surface to the torchlight, examining it minutely.

"Then what?" asked the Duke gruffly. Paks looked at him warily, remembering his rage.

"Well, my lord, I looked around, but saw nothing. Then I found the next guard asleep, and thought of magic. I woke her; we saw the first of them coming out. She woke the guards on this side, and I went to the other. I didn't see Sunnot, but I was going by feel, to the posts we'd set. I could have missed — " A shout from Vik interrupted her. In a moment he reappeared, leading a bewildered Sunnot, who went down on one knee to the Halveric.

"My lord, I — I don't know what happened — " The Halveric smiled and gestured him up.

"You were magicked, Sunnot; not your fault. I'm sorry you missed it — "

"Did he escape, sir?" Sunnot looked ready to cry.

"No. He's dead. It's over." Sunnot looked around, still worried. Vik spoke softly to him, and he shook his head.

"Go on, Paks," said the Duke.

She was so glad to see Sunnot alive and well that she'd lost the thread of her story.

"You woke the guards," the Duke prompted.

"Yes, my lord. More of them had come out by then. When the last one came out I yelled and we attacked."

"Where was Siniava then?"

"I don't know. The bodyguard had made a ring, with two inside it — " Paks pointed to the bound prisoners. She explained how she had thought the two were a shapechanged Siniava and a wizard, how she'd noticed what seemed to be an animal moving along the rockface, and the animal's transformation into Siniava. "When he turned to run," she said, "I jumped and caught his legs — "

"I saw her jump," said the paladin. "He was turning to strike at her, and I was just in time to stop him. The rest you know. Here, Paksenarrion, take back your medallion."

The Duke shook his head thoughtfully. "I hardly feel I know anything. What woke her up? Was it the medallion — when she's not a Girdsman?"

"What else would you suggest? I know it's unusual — but what else?"

The Duke shook his head again. "I don't know." He sighed. "More mysteries, when I thought we'd be rid of them. Paksenarrion — "

"Yes, my lord?"

"Post a guard on this end of the passage, and come back to camp. How many wounded have we?" Paks looked around.

"My men took them back," said the Halveric. "With my wounded. Things seemed — busy — around here."

"My lord, if any are poisoned, I'd be glad to try a healing."

"Thank you, sir paladin," said Aliam before the Duke could answer. "You know the way to my surgeons' tents?"

"Certainly, my lord." The paladin turned and was gone.

Paks had organized the remaining soldiers and told them to keep close watch until they were relieved.

"Can we have a fire?" asked Rauf. She looked at the Duke.

"Certainly," he said. "As big as you like. We'll send a relief down when we get back, and then you can sleep. You've earned it. Come along, Paks." He turned to go, and Paks followed, pausing to pick up the shards of her sword. She could hear the quartermaster now: sword and corselet both.

The Duke and Aliam Halveric walked side by side back to camp, the Duke's squires before them, and Paks bringing up the rear. They said nothing to her, and she could not hear what they were saying. She didn't try. She had too much to think about. She rubbed her thumb across the medallion she held — she had not put it back on. She did not understand — did not want to understand. The Duke was angry enough; she did not want him more angry with her than he was already. She thought of Canna and Saben — would they have wanted it this way? Siniava dead so easily? Saben would have — she turned away from his memory to something else. Canna had never told her the medallion had such powers. Was that its function, to warn? And if so, why hadn't it warned Canna of the brigands?

When they reached the camp, the Duke turned to Paks. "I think you should be the one to tell your cohort that Siniava is dead, and how he died." His voice was neutral; Paks could not tell if he was still angry.

"Yes, my lord."

"You have my thanks for a duty faithfully — even more than faithfully — performed."

"And our thanks also," said Aliam Halveric. His smile was as open as ever, the corners of his eyes crinkled. "Whatever power enabled you to resist the spell, it is clear that without you that scum might have escaped." He looked at the Duke. "That power, too, must have our thanks and praise."

The Duke's shoulders shifted. "We can speak of that later. As for now, Aliam, you and I must arrange the taking of that citadel. Paksenarrion has more immediate duties, as well."

The Halveric was no longer smiling. "Later, perhaps, Kieri — but after this night's work, we can no longer ignore it."

The Duke sighed. "No, I suppose not. Go on, Paks, and tell the rest. And get some sleep. If it comes to fighting, we'll want your blade as well."

If Stammel had not been awake by one of the watchfires, Paks might have fallen asleep without telling her news. But in telling him, the excitement woke her again, and soon she was the center of a breathless crowd.

"And you're sure he's dead," said someone into the silence that followed her recital.

"They brought his head back on a pole," said Paks. "I didn't see it as we came — it must be in the Halveric camp now."

"But *you* caught him," said another voice. "It should be our trophy."

"The Halveric killed him. And the paladin — Sir Fenith — helped catch him. I didn't do it alone — "

"Still — " Paks recognized Barranyi's voice, this time.

"Hush, Barra," said Natzlin. "It doesn't bother Paks, and she did it."

"How did they kill him?" asked Vossik, who had not heard the first of the story. Paks tensed.

"The Halveric killed him," she said again. "With a sword."

"Huh. Slowly, I'll bet, after what he did to his sons."

"No." Paks wished she were far away, as she felt the pressure of surprise and curiosity. She stared into the fire. "One stroke," she said finally. "In the neck."

Stammel whistled. "That's — something. To show mercy like that — "

311

He was clearly impressed. Some of the others were frowning, but Paks saw many of the older veterans relax, as if they had feared worse. Barranyi's voice broke a brief silence.

"But why? After all he'd done — I'd think the Duke would do something! It's not right, that he should die so easy." Paks felt almost sick at the venom in Barra's voice. Before she could gather her words, Vossik interrupted Barra.

"No! That's what makes us different. Such leaders as that — that you can trust to do the right thing even under pressure. By — " he paused and looked at Stammel. "By Gird and Falk and the High Lord himself, I'm proud we've got such men to lead our companies." Vossik turned to Paks, grinning. "I daresay *you* weren't eager for torture, were you now?"

Paks felt herself blushing. "No," she muttered. She hoped no one would ask what the Duke had actually said.

"I thought not." Vossik sounded relaxed and happy. "This is an honorable company, and always has been, and always will be. Remember that, Barra." She made no answer.

Stammel was smiling too. "Well now. Just let us get this citadel taken care of, and we'll be back to normal. And a lot richer, I don't doubt. You, too, Paks — you'll have a bonus for this night's work." He stretched. "Now I can sleep. I'd been so worried he'd have some magic and escape again." He stood, reaching a hand to Paks. "Come on, warrior. Even you need sleep before the assault." Paks clambered up, meeting the admiring glances of her friends as she moved away. What she had left unsaid cluttered her throat.

No one woke her in the morning; the sun was high when she finally opened her eyes. The tent was almost empty; two others slept at the far end. Paks stretched and yawned. She didn't want to move. She heard voices outside and got up reluctantly. Outside, the day was fair and warm; it would be hot by noon. She headed for the cooks' tent.

"There you are." Stammel came up behind her. "You'll be glad to know that the troops in the citadel want to surrender."

Paks pulled her mind back to the present. "Oh. Good."

"They're afraid to open the gates, they say. I don't blame them. They would expect the worst from us." He waited to say more until no one was near. "Paks — the others are back now. I spoke to Arñe and Vik. There's a lot you didn't say last night."

Paks blushed. She was afraid of his next question. Instead of asking, he went on.

"I'm glad you didn't. The Duke's a good man; you know that. I've known him a long time; I know why he might lose his temper. But you were right, Paks, however angry he was, or may be still: he's not the kind to torture. Only he wasn't himself for a bit." He went on more briskly. "I don't think the others will talk about it — I had to pull the truth out of Vik with a rope, nearly. He feared I'd be angry with you."

Paks found herself grinning at Stammel's tone. When she looked up, his brown eyes were twinkling.

"You'd best watch yourself, though," he said. "If things keep happening around you, and you keep siding with paladins, it'll rub off, and we'll only see you from far away, as you ride past on your fancy charger." His tone was only half joking.

For an instant the thought made Paks's heart leap, but she forced the image away. "No," she said firmly. "I'm staying here, in the Company, with my friends. If the Duke isn't too angry — " For she remembered the icy glare he'd given her.

"He's fair; he won't hold it against you. But Paks, it's not that bad an idea," said Stammel more earnestly. "If you have the chance, I'd say take it. You've got the fighting skills, and you care about the right and wrong of things. You'd make friends elsewhere — " Paks shook her head. Stammel sighed. "Have you thought," he asked, "that your two years is up these many months? You're due a leave — you could go north and see your family — look around — "

Paks was startled. She had forgotten all about the "two years beyond training" in her first contract. "I hadn't thought," she said. As she mused on it, the sights and smells of Three Firs came back to her. The baker's shop, the well, the striped awnings that hung out on market day. And beyond the town the great rolling lift of the moors, and the first sight of the dark slate roof of her father's house. Tears stung her eyes. "I could — I could take my dowry back — " she said.

"So you could. Your share this campaign should do it. Think about it. The Duke will be granting us all leave unless he takes us back north."

"And I wouldn't be leaving the Company."

"No. Not unless you wanted to."

"I'll think about it," she said, and Stammel nodded and left her.

Siniava's troops surrendered that day, but not to the Duke: to the combined city militia. Paks did not even see the prisoners; she heard that they'd been taken away toward Vonja. The Duke's Company entered the citadel only for plunder; they found the only treasure at the inside opening of the secret passage. Several chests of gold, Stammel said, would pay for the entire campaign, leaving aside their share of Cha and Sibili. Paks heard from Arñe that Siniava's bodyguards had all been carrying jewels and gold. "That's what slowed them down in the fight," she joked.

"Did you find out who the others were?"

"Yes. The man's some high rank in the moneylender's guild. He's got a bad wound; he may not live. The woman's his sister or niece or something." Arñe stopped and looked at Paks. "*Do* you know what happened with Canna's medallion? Was it really St. Gird who woke you?"

"I don't know. I don't understand." Paks could hardly convey her confusion. "Something happened, I know that. But — I keep wondering and wondering about it, and nothing comes clear."

Three days later, as she watched the city militias march north from the bridge, she was still wondering. The High Marshal had talked to her again, and the paladin; the Duke had apparently talked to both of them. Dorrin had told of the incident in Rotengre, and Paks finally admitted that she'd tried to use the medallion to heal Canna. She could have had, if she'd wanted it, hours of instruction about Gird. She didn't want it.

"I want to stay with you," she'd told the Duke, while the High Marshal listened. "I joined your company; I gave you my oath. And my friends are here."

The Duke nodded. "You may stay, Paksenarrion, as long as you're willing. But I must agree with the High Marshal in this: some force — we need not agree on what — is moving you as well. The time may come when you should leave. I will not hold you to your oath then."

"My lord — " the paladin had begun, but the Duke interrupted.

"Don't bully her. If she's to leave, she'll leave, in her own time. You've seen she's no fool."

"That's not what I meant, my lord."

"No. I'm sorry." The Duke had sighed, looking tired. "Paks, think about it. I know it's not easy — but think. Talk to Arcolin or Dorrin, if you'd like; talk to Stammel. This company is not the only place you can be a fighter."

But she had been determined. From a sheepfarmer's daughter in Three Firs to a respected veteran in the Duke's Company, with friends who would die for her, or she for them — that was enough. Those childhood dreams were only dreams: this place, these friends, were real. It was all she wanted, and all she ever would.

She waved, nonetheless, to Sir Fenith the paladin, as he rode out. Canna's medallion was safe in her belt-pouch now. She would let it stay there. No more of those strange warnings to deal with, no more mysteries. And if she died, for lack of its warning — she grinned, not worried. Saben's red horse would bear her to the Afterfields.

End Book I

Divided Allegiance

Chapter One

When all Siniava's troops had surrendered, Kieri Phelan's troops assumed they'd be going back to Valdaire — even, perhaps, to the north again. Some already had plans for spending their share of the loot. Others looked forward to time to rest and recover from wounds. Instead, a few days later they found themselves marching south along the Immer in company with Alured's men, the Halverics, and several cohorts of the Duke of Fall's army. These last looked fresh as new paint, hardly having fought at all, except to turn Siniava away from Fallo.

"I don't understand it," muttered Keri to Paks as they marched. "I thought we were through. Siniava's dead. What more?"

Paks shook her head. "Maybe the Duke has a contract; he's spent a lot on this campaign."

"Contract! Tir's bones, it'll take us the rest of the season just to get back to Valdaire. Why do we need a contract?"

That was a first-year's innocence. Paks grinned at him. "Money," she said. "Or were you going to forget about pay?"

Seli winked at Paks, a veteran's knowing wink, and said, "Have you ever seen the sea?"

"No — why?" Keri looked stubborn; sweat dripped off his nose.

"Well, that's reason enough to go south. I've seen it — you'll be impressed."

"What's it like?" asked Paks when Keri's expression didn't change.

"I don't think anyone can tell you. You have to see it."

Word soon trickled down from the captains that Alured was claiming the title of Duke of Immer. This meant nothing to Paks or the younger soldiers, but Stammel knew that the title had been extinct since the fall of the old kingdom of Aare across the sea.

"I'm surprised that the Duke of Fall and the other nobles are accepting it," he said.

"That was the price of his help this year," said Vossik. All the sergeants had gathered around one fire for an hour or so. "I heard talk in Fallo's cohorts about it. If Fallo, Andressat, and Cilwan would uphold his claim — and our Duke, of course — then he'd turn on Siniava."

"But why would they, even so?"

"It's an odd story," said Vossik, obviously ready to tell it.

317

"Go on, Voss, don't make us beg," growled Stammel.

"Well, it's only what I heard, after all. I don't know whether those Fallo troops know the truth, or if they're telling it, but here it is. It seems that Alured used to be a pirate on the Immerhoft — "

"We knew that — "

"Yes, but that's the beginning. He'd captured another ship, and was about to throw the prisoners over, the way pirates do — "

"Into the water?" asked Paks.

Someone laughed. Vossik turned to her. "Pirates don't want a mess on their ships — so they throw prisoners overboard — "

"But don't they swim or wade to shore?" asked Natzlin.

"They can't. It's too far, and the water is deep."

"I can swim a long way — " said Barra. Paks grinned to herself. Barra always thought she could do more than anyone else.

"Not that far. Tir's gut, Barra, you haven't seen the sea yet. It could be a day's march from shore, the ship, when they toss someone out." Vossik took a long swallow of sib, and went on. "Anyway, one of the prisoners said he was a mage. He cried out that Alured should be a prince, and he — the mage — could help him."

"I'd have thought Alured wouldn't listen to prisoners' yells," said Stammel. "He doesn't look the type."

"No," agreed Vossik. "He doesn't. But it seems he'd had some sort of tale from his father — about being born of good blood, or whatever. So he listened, and the mage told him he was really heir to a vast kingdom, wasting his time as a pirate."

"He believed that?" Haben snorted and reached his own mug into the sib. "I'd heard pirates were superstitious, but — "

"Well, the man offered proof. Said he'd seen scrolls in old Aare that proved it. Offered to take Alured there, and prove his right to the kingdom."

"To Aare? That heap of sand?"

"How do you know, Devlin? You haven't been there."

"No, but I've heard. Nothing's left but scattered ruins and sand. It's in the songs." He hummed a phrase of "Fair Were the Towers."

Vossik shrugged. "Alured didn't ask *you*. The mage told Alured that he'd seen proof of Alured's ancestry."

"It seems to me," said Erial, "that it's extra trouble to hunt up ancestors like that. What difference does it make? Our Duke got his steading without dragging in hundreds of fathers and fathers' fathers."

"Or mothers," muttered Barra. No one followed that up.

"You know they're different here in Aarenis," said Stammel. "Think of Andressat."

"That stuffed owl," said Barra. Paks had almost begun to understand what Vik meant about Barra's prickliness. She could not let anything alone.

"No — don't be that way, Barra. He's a good fighter, and a damn good count for Andressat. Most other men would have lost Andressat to Siniava

318

years ago. He's proud of his ancestors, true enough, but they could be proud of him."

"But go on about Alured, Voss," said Stammel. "What happened?"

"Well, he already believed he came of noble blood, so he sailed back to old Aare with this fellow. Then — now remember, I got this from the Fallo troops; I don't say it's true — then the mage showed him proof — an old scroll, showing the marriages, and such, and proving that he was in direct descent from that Duke of Immer who was called back to Aare in the troubles."

"But Vossik, any mage could fake something like that!" Erial looked around at the others; some of them nodded.

"I didn't say *I* believed it, Erial. But Alured did. It fitted what he wanted, let's say. If Aare had been worth anything, it would have meant the throne of Aare. It certainly meant the lands of Immer."

"And so he left the sea, and settled into the forest to be a land pirate? How was that being a prince or duke or whatever?" Erial sounded scornful.

"Well — again — this is hearsay. Seems he came to the Immer ports first, and tried to get them to swear allegiance — "

"But he'd been a *pirate*!" Paks agreed with that emphasis.

"Yes, I know. He wasn't thinking clearly, perhaps. Then he hired a lot of local toughs, dressed them in the old colors of Immer, and tried to parley with the Duke of Fall."

"Huh. And came out with a whole skin?"

"He wasn't stupid enough to put it in jeopardy — they talked on the borders of Fallo. The Duke reacted as you might expect, but — well — he didn't much care what happened in the southern forest, as long as it didn't bother him. And, his men say, he's longsighted — won't make an enemy unnecessarily."

"But what about Siniava?" For Paks, this was the meat of it: whose side had Alured been on from the beginning?

"Well, at first they had one thing in common: none of the old nobility would accept their claim to titles. Siniava promised Alured the dukedom if he'd break up the Immer River shipping, and protect Siniava's movements in the area. Alured cooperated. That's why no one could trace Siniava after Rotengre."

"Yes, but — " This time Paks spoke up; Vossik interrupted firmly.

"*But* two points: Andressat and our own Duke's cleverness. Andressat had been polite to Alured, promised him he'd accept the claim if the Duke of Fall did. So Alured wouldn't move on Andressat when Siniava demanded it. After all, he believed himself a duke — above the command of a count. As for our Duke — you remember the wood-wanderers we met in Kodaly?" Stammel nodded. "Alured had befriended them when he moved into that forest, so they were on his side. Our Duke had made his own pacts with them years ago in the north. So our Duke knew what Alured wanted. And he knew what Fallo wanted — connection by marriage with a northern kingdom. And he knew that Sofi Ganarrion had a marriageable child — "

"But Sofi's not a king — " said someone out of the darkness.

"*Yet*. Remember what he's always said. And with Fallo behind him — " Vossik let that trail off. Several were quick to catch on.

"Gods above! You mean — "

"Somehow our Duke and the Halveric convinced the Duke of Fall that Alured's help in this campaign was worth that much to him. So the Duke of Fall agreed to back Alured's claim, Alured switched sides, and we got passage through the forest and Siniava didn't."

Paks shivered. She had never thought of the maneuvering that occurred off the battlefield. "But is Alured really the Duke of Immer?"

Vossik shrugged. "He has the title. He has the power. What else?"

"But if he's not really — by blood, I mean — "

"I don't see that it matters. He'll be better as a duke than a pirate: he'll have to govern, expand trade, stop robbing — "

"Will he?" Haben looked around the whole group before going on. "I wouldn't think, myself, that a pirate-turned-brigand would make a very good duke. What's the difference between taxes and robbery, if it comes to that?"

"He's not stupid, Haben." Vossik looked worried. "It will have to be better than Siniava — "

"That's my point. Siniava claimed a title — claimed to be governing his lands — but we all saw what that meant in Cha and Sibili. He didn't cut off trade entirely, as Alured has done on the Immer, no — but would any of us want to live under someone like him? I remember the faces in those cities, if you don't."

"But he fought Siniava — "

"Yes — at the end. For a good reward, too. I'm not saying he's all bad, Vossik; I don't know. But so far he's gone where the gold is. How will he govern? A man who thinks he's nobly born, and has been cheated of his birthright — what will he do when we reach the Immer ports?"

They found out at Immerdzan, where the Immer widened abruptly into a bay, longer than it was wide. The port required no formal assault. It had never been fortified on the land side, beyond a simple wall hardly more than man-high with the simplest of gates. The army marched in without meeting any resistance. The crowded, dirty streets stank of things Paks had never smelled before. She got her first look at the bay, here roiled and murky from the Immer's muddy flow. The shore was cluttered with piers and wharves, with half-rotted pilings, the skeletons of boats, boats sinking, boats floating, new boats, spars, shreds of sail, nets hung from every available pole, and festooned on the houses. She saw small naked children, skinny as goats, diving and swimming around the boats. Most of them wore their hair in a single short braid, tied with bright bits of cloth.

Beyond the near-shore clutter, the bay lay wide and nearly empty under the hot afternoon sun, its surface streaked with blues and greens she had never seen before. A few boats glided before the wind, their great triangular sails curved like wings. Paks stared at them, fascinated. One changed direction as she watched, the dark line of its hull shortening and lengthening again. Far in the distance she could see the high ground beyond the bay, and southward the water turned a different green, then deep blue, as the Immer's water merged with the open sea.

Around the Duke's troops, a noisy crowd had gathered — squabbling, it seemed to Paks, in a language high-pitched and irritable. Children dashed back and forth, some still sleek and wet from the water, others grimy. Barefoot men in short trousers, their hair in a longer single braid, clustered around the boats; women in bright short skirts and striped stockings hung out of windows and crowded the doorways. One of Alured's captains called in the local language, and a sudden silence fell. Paks heard the water behind her, sucking and mumbling at the pilings, slurping. She shivered, wondering if the sea had a spirit. Did it hunger?

Alured's captain began reading from a scroll in his hand. Paks looked for Arcolin and watched his face; surely he knew what was going on. He had no expression she could read. When Alured's captain finished reading, he spoke to the Duke, saluted, and mounted to ride away. The crowd was silent. When he rounded the corner, a low murmur passed through them. One man shouted, hoarsely. Paks looked for him, and saw two younger men shoving a graybearded one back. Another man near them called in accented Common:

"Who of you speaks to us?"

"I do." The Duke's voice was calm as ever.

"You — you are pirates?"

"No. What do you mean?"

"That — that man — he says is now our duke — he is a pirate. You are his men — you are pirates."

"No." The Duke shook his head. Paks saw Arcolin give the others a hand signal, saw the signal passed from captains to sergeants. Not that they needed any warning; they were all alert anyway. "We are his allies, not his men. He fought with us upriver — against Siniava."

"That filth!" The man spat. "Who are you, then, if you fight against Siniava but befriend pirates?"

"Duke Phelan, of Tsaia."

"Tsaia? That's over the Dwarfmounts, all the way north! What do you here?" Confusion and anger both in that voice; his eyes raked the troops.

"I have a mercenary company, that fights in Aarenis. Siniava — " The Duke's voice thinned, but he did not go on. "We fought Siniava," he said finally. "He is dead. Alured of the forest has been granted the Duchy of Immer, and as he aided us, so I am now aiding him."

"He is no duke!" yelled the man. "I don't know you — I heard something maybe, but I don't know you. But that Alured — he is nothing but pirate, and pirate he will always be. Siniava was bad, Barrandowea knows that — but *Alured*! He killed my uncle, years back, out there in the bay, him and his filthy ship!"

321

"No matter," said the Duke. "He is the Duke of Immer now, and I am here to keep order until his own officers take over."

The man spat again, and turned away. The Duke said nothing more to the crowd, but set the cohorts on guard along the waterfront, and had patrols in the streets leading to and from their area. All stayed quiet enough, that first day. Paks felt herself lucky to be stationed on the seawall. She could look down at the boats, swaying on the waves, and catch a breath of the light wind that blew off the water. Strange birds, gray and white with black-capped heads, and large red bills, hovered over the water, diving and lifting again.

It was the next day that the executions began. Paks heard the yells from the other side of the city, but before they could get excited, the captains explained what was going on.

"The Duke of Fall and the Duke of Immer are executing Siniava's agents." Arcolin's face was closed. "We are to keep order here, in case of rioting — but we don't expect any." In fact, nothing happened in their quarter. The men and women went about their work without looking at the soldiers, and the children scampered in and out of the water freely. But the noise from across the city did not quiet down, and in the evening Cracolnya's cohort was pulled out to join the Halverics in calming the disturbance. They returned in the morning, tired and grim; Paks did not hear the details until much later. But the Duke's Company marched out of Immerdzan the following day, and the bodies hung on the wall were eloquent enough.

In Ka-Immer, rumor had arrived before they did. The gates were closed. With no trained troops for defense, and only the same low walls, the assault lasted only a few hours. This time the entire population was herded into the market square next to the seawall. While the Halverics and Phelani guarded them, Alured's men searched the streets, house by house, bringing more and more to stand with the others. When they were done, Alured himself rode to the edge of the square. He pointed at a man among the others. His soldiers seized him, and dragged him out of the mob. Then two more, and another. Someone yelled, from across the square, and a squad of Alured's men shoved into the crowd, flailing them aside, to seize him as well. The first man had thrown himself down before Alured, sobbing. Alured shook his head, pointed. All of them were dragged to a rough framework of spars which Alured's troops had lashed together.

A ripple of sound ran through the crowd; the people crammed back against each other, the rear ranks backing almost into Paks's squad. She and the others linked shields, holding firm. She could hardly see over the crowd. Then the first of the men lifted into sight, stretched on ropes slung over the framework. Paks stiffened; her belly clenched. Another. Another. Soon they hung in a row, one by the feet and the others by their arms. Alured's men pelted them with mud, stones, fish from the market. One of them hung limp, another screamed thinly. Paks looked away, gulping back nausea. When her eyes slid sideways, they met Keri's, equally miserable. She did not see the end, when Alured himself ran a spear into each man.

She felt, through the movement of the crowd, that an end had come, and looked up to see the bodies being lowered.

But it was not the end. Alured spoke, in that strange language, gesturing fiercely. The crowd was still, unmoving; Paks could smell the fear and hatred of those nearest her. He finished with a question: Paks recognized the tone of voice, the outflung arm, the pause, waiting for an answer. It came as a dead fish, flung from somewhere in the crowd, that came near to its mark. His face darkened. Paks could not hear what he said, but his own soldiers fanned out again, coming at the crowd.

Before they reached it, the crowd erupted into sound and action. Jammed as they were against a thin line of Phelani and Halverics holding the three landward sides of the market, they somehow managed to turn and move at once. Paks's squad was forced back, by that immense pressure. They could hear nothing but the screams and bellows of the crowd; they had been ordered to guard, not attack. But they were being overwhelmed. Most of the people had no weapons; their weapon was simply numbers. Like Paks, they were reluctant to strike unarmed men and women — but equally, they did not want to be overrun.

Behind, in the streets that led to the market, Paks could hear other troops coming, and shouted commands that were but pebbles of noise against the stone wall around them. She tried to stay in contact with the others, tried to fend off the crowd with the flat of her sword, but the pressure was against them all. A man grabbed at her weapon, screaming at her; she raised it, and he hit her, hard, under the arm. Almost in reflex, Paks thrust, running the sword into his body. He fell under a storm of feet that kept coming at her. She fended them off as best she could, pressing close to the rest of the squad as they tried to keep together and keep on their feet.

A gap opened between them and the next squad; the crowd poured through, still bellowing. Paks was slammed back into the building behind her; she could feel something — a window ledge, she supposed — sticking into her back. Faces heaved in front of her, all screaming; hands waved, grabbed at her weapon. She fought them off, panting. She had no time to look for Stammel or Arcolin; she could hear nothing but the crowd. They had broken through the ring in many places, now, and streamed away from the market, lurching and falling in their panic. A child stumbled into her and fell, grabbing at her tunic as he went down, screaming shrilly. Paks had no hand to spare for him, and he disappeared under the hurrying feet.

By the time she could move again, most of the crowd had fled. She could see Alured riding behind his soldiers as they tried to stop those in the rear. She finally saw Arcolin, and then Stammel, beyond the tossing heads. Then she could hear them. The cohort reformed, joined the others, and was sent in pursuit of the fugitives. But by sundown, barely a fifth had been retaken, mostly women and children too weak to run far, or too frightened. Paks, still shaken by the morning's events, was sickened by the treatment of those she helped recapture. Alured was determined that none of Siniava's sympathizers would survive, and that all would acknowledge his rank and rule.

To this end, he intended, as he explained to Phelan in front of the troops, to frighten the citizens into submission.

Paks expected the Duke to argue, but he said nothing. He had hardly seemed to smile since Siniava's death, and since reaching the coast had spent hours looking seaward. She did not know — none of them knew — what was troubling him. But more and more Paks felt that she could not live with what was troubling her. The looks of fear and loathing turned on them — the muttered insults, clear enough even in a foreign tongue — the contempt of Alured's troops, when the Phelani would not join them in "play," which to them meant tormenting some helpless civilian — all this curdled her belly until she could hardly eat and slept but little, waking often from troubled dreams.

Paks tried to hide her feelings, tried to argue herself into calm. She had spoken out once — that was enough for any private. As long as she wore the Duke's colors, she owed him obedience. He was a good man; had always been honorable . . . she thought of the High Marshal and wished she had never met him. He had raised questions she didn't want to answer. Surely the Duke's service was worth a little discomfort, even this unease.

When they marched out of Ka-Immer, leaving a garrison of Alured's men behind, Paks tried to tell herself the worst was over. But it wasn't. In town after town, along the Immerhoft coast, Alured suspected Siniava's agents, or found someone who expressed doubt that a pirate could legally inherit a dukedom. The mercenaries did not participate in the executions and tortures, but they all knew that without them Alured lacked the troops to force so many towns.

None of them knew how long it would last — where the Duke was planning to stop. Surely he would. Any day he would turn back, would march to Valdaire. But he said nothing, staring south across the blue, endless water. Uneasiness ran through the Company like mice through a winter attic.

Paks thought no one had noticed her in particular until Stammel came to her guardpost one night. He stood near her, unspeaking, for a few minutes. Paks wondered what he wanted. Then he sighed, and took off his helmet, rumpling up his hair.

"I don't need to ask what's wrong with you," he began. "But something has to be done."

Paks could think of nothing to say, any more than she had been able to think of anything to do.

"You aren't eating enough for someone half your size. You'll be no good to any of us if you fall sick — "

"I'm fine — " began Paks, but he interrupted.

"No, you're not fine; neither am I. But I'm keeping my food down, and sleeping nights, which is more than you're doing. I don't want to lose a good veteran this way. We don't have that many. All those new people we've picked up here and there. They aren't the same." Stammel paused again. He put his helmet back on, and rubbed his nose. "I don't know if they ever will be — if we ever will be — what we were." His voice trailed away.

"I keep — keep seeing — " Paks could not go on.

"Paks, you — " Stammel cleared his throat and spat. "You shouldn't be in this."

She was startled enough to make a choked sound, as if she'd been hit. "What — why — "

"You don't." His voice gathered firmness as he went on. "By Tir, I can't stand by and see you fall apart. Not for this. You've served the Duke as well as anyone could. D'you think he doesn't know it? Or I?" Now he sounded almost angry. "You don't belong here, in this kind of fighting. That High Marshal was right; even the Duke said you might be meant for better things." He stopped again, and his voice was calmer when he resumed. "I think you should leave, Paks — "

"Leave the Company?" Despite the shock, she felt a sudden wash of relief at the thought of being out of it, then a stab of panic. She had already made this decision; she couldn't make it again.

"Yes. That's what I came to say. Tir knows this is hard enough on me — and I'm older, and — But you leave, Paks. Go back north. Go home, maybe, or see if you can take knight's training somewhere. Don't stay in this until you can't stand yourself, or the Duke either."

"But I — how can I ask — I can't go to him — " The memory of his expression, that night when she had opposed his will, haunted her still. Even though he had seemed to hold no grudge, she did not want to risk another such look.

Stammel nodded forcefully. "Yes, you can. Tell Arcolin. The captain'll understand — he knows you. He'll tell the Duke — or you can. They'll recommend you somewhere, I'm sure of it."

That wasn't what was bothering her. "But to leave the Duke — "

"Paks, I've got nothing to say against him. You know that. He's been my lord since I started; I will follow him anywhere. But — you stopped him once, when he — he might have made a mistake. Maybe — if you leave, maybe he'll look again — "

Paks was speechless, faced again with the decision she thought she'd settled in Cortes Immer. How could she leave the Company? It was closer to her now than family, more familiar than the rooms of the house where she'd been born.

"Paks, I'm serious. You can't go on the way you have been. Others have noticed already; more will. Get out of this while you still can."

"I — I'll have to think — "

"Tonight. We'll be in Sord tomorrow — more of the same, I don't doubt."

Paks found that her eyes were full of tears. She choked down a sob. Stammel gripped her shoulder. "That's what I mean, Paks. You can't keep fighting yourself, as well as an enemy. Tir knows I know you're brave — but no one can fight inside and outside both at once."

"I gave my word," she whispered.

"Yes. You did. And you've already served your term, and more. You've seen Siniava die, which ends that oath, to my mind. I don't think you're running out — and I don't think Arcolin or the Duke will, either. Will you talk to them?"

Paks stared up at a dark sky spangled with stars. Torre's Necklace was just rising out of the distant sea. She thought of the distant past, when she had dreamed of being a soldier and seeing far places, and of the last town they had been through. "I — can't — go into another — "

"No. I agree."

"But it's too late." Surely the captains were all in bed; she could not wake them, or the Duke, for such an errand. Relief washed over her; she didn't have to decide *now*.

His voice was gentle. "Would you if it weren't so late?"

That gentleness and the certainty that it *was* too late relaxed her guard. She was so tired. "Oh, I — I don't know. Yes. If the Duke would let me — "

"He will," said Stammel. "Or I don't know Duke Phelan, and I think I do." Before she could answer, he called back toward the lines for someone to take her place on guard. "Come on. If I know you, you'll convince yourself by morning that you owe it to the Duke to work yourself blind, deaf, and crazy."

She followed him to Arcolin's tent, sick and trembling again, but the following hour was not as difficult as she feared. The other captains who had been talking with Arcolin melted away when Stammel asked Arcolin for a few minutes of conference. Arcolin himself looked at Paks steadily, but without anger or disappointment.

"You are overdue for leave," he said. "You've served faithfully; if you want either leave, or to quit the Company entirely, you have the right. I would hate to see you leave us for good; you've done well, and I know Duke Phelan is pleased with you. Would you consider a year's leave, with the right to return?"

Paks nodded. "Whatever you say, Captain." She could not really think; her mind spun dizzily from fear to elation to sorrow.

"Then we'll speak to the Duke about it." Arcolin pushed himself up from his table. "You should come too. He may wish to speak to you about your service."

The Duke also had not gone to bed. His gaze sharpened when he saw Paks behind Arcolin, but he waved them into his tent. Arcolin explained what Paks wanted, and the Duke gave her a long look.

"Are you displeased with my command, Paksenarrion?"

"No, my lord." She was able to say that honestly. It was not his command, but his alliances, that bothered her.

"I'm glad for that. You have been an honest and trustworthy soldier. I would hate to think I had lost your respect."

"No, my lord."

"I can see that you might well wish to leave for awhile. A northern girl — a different way — but do you wish to leave the Company forever, or only for a time?"

"I don't know — I can't imagine anything else, but — "

"How could you? I see." He gave a short nod, as if he had decided some issue she hadn't noticed. "You know that High Marshal suggested you might need to leave this Company; he told me that as early as Sibili, after you'd been wounded." Paks noticed that he did not use the High Marshal's name. Nor did he mention her earlier insistence that she would stay. "Perhaps this is the right time. You would benefit from advanced training, I think. If you decide to enter another service, I will be glad to recommend you. My own advice is that you seek squire's training somewhere. You're already good with single weapons — learn horsemanship as well, and you might qualify for knight's training." He stopped, and looked at Arcolin. "She'll need maps for the journey north; I suppose you've already arranged about pay and settlements — "

"Not yet, my lord. She came just this evening."

"Well, then. You might stay with the Company, Paksenarrion, until you have decided how you will travel. The state Aarenis is in, going alone would not be wise. I'll be sending someone back to Valdaire a little later, if you wanted to wait — " The Duke had more advice, but none of the condemnation Paks had feared. He seemed more tired than anything else, a little distracted, though kind. She shook his hand, and returned to the cohort area with Arcolin, a little let down at how easy it had been.

Stammel was waiting. "You go on to bed. Tomorrow — "

"But tomorrow is Sord — "

"No. That's the day after. And you won't march with us. I'll have something for you to do — "

"But — "

"Don't argue with me! I'm still your sergeant! By the time *you* get into Sord, you'll be free of all this. Now get over there and go to sleep."

That night Paks slept through to daylight without waking.

Chapter Two

"From Duke Phelan's Company, eh?" Paksenarrion nodded. The guard captain was a burly dark man of middle height. "Leaving the Company?"

Paks shrugged. "Going home for awhile."

"Hmm. Wagonmaster says you want to leave the caravan halfway — ?"

"It's shorter — "

"Mmm. Wagonmaster talked to your sergeant, didn't he?"

"Yes, sir."

"It'll do, then, I suppose. Do you handle a crossbow?"

"Not well, sir. I have used a longbow, but I'm no expert."

The guard captain sighed. "Can't have everything, I suppose. Now listen to me — the caravan starts making up day after tomorrow, and we'll leave the day after that or the next, depending on how many merchants join up. I'll want you here by high noon day after tomorrow, ready to work. You come in drunk, and I'll dock your pay. We have to watch the wagons as close in the city as on the trail. Don't plan on sleeping that night. Be sure to get some armor; the caravan doesn't supply it. I'd recommend chainmail. The brigands we'll run into along the coast use powerful bows. That leather you're used to won't stop arrows. You can buy mail from us, if you want." He cocked his head at her. "Clear so far?"

"Yes, sir. Be here at noon day after tomorrow, with armor."

"And not drunk."

Paks flushed. "I don't get drunk."

"Everyone gets drunk. Some know when. And by the way, no bedding with the merchants; it's bad for discipline."

Paks bit back an angry retort. "No, sir."

"Very well. See you day after tomorrow." He waved her off. As she left the room, she passed two armed men in the hall outside; one of them carried a crossbow.

"I can't believe you're going." Paks had hoped to slip out quietly, but Arñe, Vik, and other friends had found her. "What'll you do by yourself?"

"I won't be alone," she said. "I'm doing caravan work — "

"Caravan work! Tir's gut, Paks, that's — "

"Some years the Duke does some. You know that."

"Yes, but that's with us — with the Company. To go out there with strangers — "

"Arñe, think. How many strangers are in the Company this year?"

"You're right about that. But still — we're — we're your friends, Paks. Since I came in, you've been my friend."

"Yes, but I can't — "

"Is it that Gird's Marshal? Are you going to join the Girdsmen?"

"I don't know. No, I don't think so. I'm just — " Paks stared past them, trying to say it. "I'm taking leave — we're all owed leave — and I might come back or I might not."

"It's not like you." Vik scowled. "If it was Barra, leaving in a temper, I could understand it, but you — "

"I'm leaving." Paks glared at him. "I am leaving. I have talked to Stammel and Arcolin and the Duke himself, and I'm leaving."

"You'll come back," said Arñe. "You have to. It won't be right." Paks shook her head and walked quickly away.

As she was leaving the camp, one of the Duke's squires caught her. "The Duke wants to see you before you go," he said. She followed him to the Duke's tent. Inside, the Duke and Aliam Halveric were talking.

" — and I think that will — Oh, Paksenarrion. The Halveric has a request to make of you."

"My lord?"

"Since you are going north — I understand you are planning to cut across the mountains?"

"Yes, my lord."

"If you'd be willing to delay your journey home long enough to carry this scroll to my steading in southern Lyonya, I will pay you well. It won't be much out of your way if you take the eastern pass."

"I would be honored, sir." Paks took the scroll, in its protective leather case, and tucked it into her belt pouch.

"Come look at this map. You should come out of the mountains near here — if you go north, you'll come to an east-west trail that runs from southern Fintha all the way to Prealith. You'll find Lyonyan rangers, if you're in Lyonya, or traders on it in Tsaia, and any of them can tell you how to find it." He pointed it out on the map. "Tell them Aliam Halveric's, or they'll send you north to my brother or uncles. You don't want to go that far out of your way. When you come there, be sure you give it to my lady: Estil, her name is, and she's several hands higher than I am. Your word will come to her sooner than a courier going back up the Immer, I think."

"Yes, sir."

"And I can trust you, I'm sure, to tell no one of this. There are those who would be glad to steal that scroll, and cause trouble with it."

"No, sir, I will tell no one."

"I thank you. Will you trust my lady to pay you, or would you take it now?"

"Of course I will trust you — your lady, sir. I have not delivered it yet, though I swear I will."

329

"Phelan says you may seek work in the north; is that so?" Paks nodded. "Well, then, Estil may be able to help. She will do what she can, I promise you."

"Paksenarrion," said the Duke, extending his hand. "Remember that you are welcome in my hall, and in my Company, at any time. May the gods be with you."

"Ward of Falk," said the Halveric. Paks left the tent half-unwillingly. It was hard to think that she had no right here anymore. If anyone had stopped her then, and asked her to stay, she might have changed her mind. But she saw none of her friends, and passed through the sentries without challenge. As she neared the city gates, the thought of the journey ahead drew her on.

She moved quickly through the crowded streets of Sord. Now that she was out of the Duke's colors, in rough brown pants and shirt with a pack on her back and a longsword at her side, she heard no more of the catcalls that bothered her so. It felt very strange, being in trousers again after so long. Her legs were hot and prickly. The longsword, too, rode uneasily at her hip. She pushed it farther to the back, impatient. The pack was heavy . . . she had thought it was too hot to wear the chainmail shirt, and warm woollen clothes as well were folded into the pack. She cocked an eye at the sun, and strode on.

At the inn, the caravan master bustled about the court; three wagons were already loaded. He grunted as he saw her, and jerked his head toward the inn door. Paks looked and saw the guard captain there.

"Ha," he said. "You're on time." He looked her up and down critically. "Where's your mail?"

"In my pack, sir," said Paks.

"Best wear it," he said. "With all the confusion around here, I wouldn't trust leaving it anywhere. Then you can put your gear in that wagon — " He pointed. "For now, just patrol around the packed wagons. As soon as some of the others arrive, I'll organize guard shifts."

By the time they had been on the road a few days, Paks felt more comfortable with the other guards. She still did not feel like trusting them in a bad fight, but she found them much like other soldiers she had known. A few outcasts of this company and that militia, but most were reliable and hard-working. Some had never been anything but caravan guards, and had no skills beyond aiming a crossbow. Others were well-trained, and had left respectable military units for all sorts of unimportant reasons. Drinking, fighting, and gambling topped that list.

Days passed. It was hotter on the Copper Hills track than any place Paks had yet been; the others told her this was the hottest part of the year.

"The smart ones take the spring caravans," said one, hunkered in the shade of a wagon one noon.

"When there is a spring caravan," said another.

"Yes, well, what can you expect of merchants?"

330

"High prices." A general laugh followed this. Paks sweltered in her chainmail, and looked east, toward the distant line of ocean. On some of the higher ground, when the heat haze didn't blur it, she could see sand and water form long, intricate curves. It looked cool out there. Finally she asked someone why they didn't travel closer to the ocean.

"Where are you from?"

"The north," she said. "Northwest of Vérella."

"Oh. That's inland, isn't it? You don't know much about the sea. Well, if we went closer to the sea, we'd get down in the worst country you can imagine. Sand — have you ever tried walking through sand?"

"I walked on a little bit of beach, between Immerdzan and —"

"No, not a beach. Dry sand — loose sand. It's — oh, blast. It's — it's worse than a dry plowed field." That Paks could understand, and she nodded. He went on. "So think about these wagons — the wheels sink in, and the mules labor. We labor. And then it's swamp. Sticky, wet, salt marsh. And more sand. And it's not cool — it's beastly hot, and the water is salt, and everything stinks. Ycch."

"And don't forget the pirates," put in another of the guards.

"I was coming to that. Pirates — they call it the robber's coast, you know."

"But how do pirates live there?"

"Some people like eating crabs and clams and things. There's plenty of that shellfish. There are fresh-water springs here and there, so they say. A few miserable shacky villages. And the pirates have ships, and can sail away."

Despite the ominous name of robber's coast, and the caravan master's precautions — or because of them — no bandits showed their faces, and the caravan crawled steadily northward without trouble. Paks practiced the crossbow, and impressed the other guards with her fencing. She, in turn, spent plenty of time spitting out dirt after trying unarmed combat with the others. They had tricks she had never seen in the Company.

Finally she saw a smudge on the horizon ahead, where the Dwarfmounts crossed the line of the Copper Hills. As they came closer, she could see that the mountains ran east of the present coast line, and saw the angle of shore change from sand and mud to rock again.

"That's the Eastbight," said a merchant, when he saw her looking. "If you sail, you have to get well out for the best currents.

"And where you don't ever want to go," added one of the guards, "is over there — " He pointed to a wide bay that lay in the angle. "That's Slaver's Bay. If there's a robber on the coast, there's ten in Slaver's Bay. It'd take a Company the size of your Duke's to keep you safe in that place."

"I've traded there," objected another merchant. The guard looked at him.

"Well," he said finally, "They must not have liked your face — or your fortune."

The caravan had reached the crossroads, and turned west for the pass

331

through the Copper Hills into the Eastmarches of Aarenis. Paks began to look at her map again, hoping she could find the trail that led to the eastern pass of the Dwarfwatch. The other guards kept suggesting that she find a companion, but she was reluctant to ask anyone; she didn't want everyone on the caravan to know where she was going. Finally they took it on them-selves to look.

"If you want a traveling companion, there's another that's leaving us at the Silver Pass." Jori, some years older than Paks, had been one of the most insistent that she find a companion.

"Oh?" Paks kept working at the crossbow mechanism. "Who is it?"

"That elf." She looked up, startled. She hadn't known there was an elf with the caravan. Jori grinned wickedly. "Proud as elves are, you won't have to worry about 'im bothering you."

Paks ignored that. "What's he leaving for?"

Jori's smile faded. "Oh — says he's going to the Ladysforest. You know, the elf kingdom. But he'd be going part of the way with you."

"Huh." Paks set the crossbow down and stood up, stretching. "Where is he?"

"Over there." Jori cocked his chin at the group around the big fire. "I'll introduce you, eh?"

"Not yet. I want to see him first."

"In the gray cloak, then," said Jori.

He looked to be a fingersbreadth shorter than she was, Paks thought, and he didn't look like the elves she had seen, but for something a little alien in the set of his green-gray eyes, and his graceful way of moving. His voice held some of the elven timbre and music.

"No, I have business in my own kingdom," he was saying to a merchant of spice.

"But don't you fear the high trails alone?" asked another.

"Fear?" His voice mocked them and his hand dropped lightly to the golden hilt of a slender sword. The merchants nodded and murmured. Paks looked closely at the sword. Very slender — a dueller's blade, she thought. If he had not been elvish, she would have suspected bravado rather than confidence in that word. He was slender and moved lightly. She could not tell, for the strange billowing style of his tunic, whether his shoulders were broad enough for a practiced warrior. His hands were sinewy, but she saw no training scars or calluses. Was it the firelight, or did elves not callus? One of the merchants looked up then and noticed her.

"Ho, a guard! It's that tall wench — come to the fire, girl, and be warm." He waved an expansive arm. Paks grinned and stayed where she was.

" 'Tis warm enough here, by your leave. But I heard talk of the high trails, and came near to listen."

"What do you want with that? Are you planning to skip the caravan and go north?"

"I'd heard of several trails," said Paks. She didn't want to say exactly how

332

much she knew. "And I knew someone who'd been over Dwarfwatch. But if there's a shorter way — "

"Oh, shorter," said another merchant. "That's with where you're going in the north — " He looked closely at Paks, but she didn't say anything. After a moment he shrugged and went on. "If you go straight across at Silver Pass, you come out between Prealith and Lyonya, but there's a good trail on the north side that will bring you west again and out near the southeast corner of Tsaia." Paks nodded. She felt rather than saw the elf watching her. "That trail meets the one crossing from Dwarfwatch; there's a cairn at the crossing, and a rock shelter. If you're headed for Tsaia, the distance isn't less, but you can travel faster alone, and the passes themselves are easier than the Dwarfwatch route. That high one — " he broke off and shook his head.

Paks followed this with interest. "I thank you, sir," she said. "I have no great knowledge of mountaincraft; I had heard only that the pass was short."

The merchant laughed. "Aye — it's short enough. If you get over it. Ice in midsummer, and blizzards — dangerous always, and for one alone — well, were I you, I'd take the eastern passes, the ones we spoke of. You'll be in mountainous country longer, but none of it as high or as cold. Does the Wagonmaster know you're leaving?"

"Of course, sir!" Paks was angry, but she saw by the reactions of the others that no insult was meant.

"I would ask him to free you for the eastern pass," said the merchant seriously. "Especially since you're traveling alone."

Paks nodded and said no more. The merchants returned to their usual topics: what product they had found in this or that port, and how well they sold; who ruled what cities, and what the recent war would do to the markets.

"What I worry about," said one enormous man in a heavy yellow cloak, "is what it will do to the tolls. They say the Guild League spent and spent for this last year's fighting — they'll have to get it back somehow, and what easier than by raising the tolls?"

"They need us too much," said another. "And they were founded to give trade a chance. The Guild League won't rob us, take my word for it."

"If they do, there's the river," suggested another. "Now Alured's settled down to play Duke, he'll be letting us use the river again — "

"Ha! That old wolf! By Simyits, you can't believe a pirate's changed by gaining a title — can you? And what have we ever got, come to that, from the noble lords and their kind? They want our gold, right enough, when a war's brewing, but after that it's — oh, those merchanters: no honor, no loyalty — tax 'em down, they're getting too proud." Paks found herself laughing along with the rest, though she, too, thought of merchanters as having no honor — like the militia of Vonja. It had never occurred to her before to wonder what the merchanters thought.

When she came off watch that night, and stopped by the guards' fire for a mug of sib, a cloaked figure rose across the circle of light to greet her. She caught a flash of green from wide-set eyes.

"Ah. Paksenarrion, is it not?"

Paks stood stiffly, uncertain. "Yes — it is. And you, sir?"

He bowed, gracefully, but with a curious mocking style. "Macenion, you may call me. An elf, as you see." Paks nodded, and reached for the pot of sib. "Allow me — " he said softly, and a tin mug rose from the stack beside the pot, dipped into the liquid, and rose to Paks's hand. She froze, her breath caught in her throat. "Go on," he said. "Take it." She looked at the mug, then her hand, then folded her fingers gingerly around the mug's handle. She nearly dropped it when it sank into her grip. She let her breath out, slowly, and sipped. It tasted like sib — she wondered if he had put anything into it. She froze again as another mug rose from the pile, filled itself, and sailed across the fire to Macenion. He plucked it from the air, bowed again to her, and took a sip himself. "I apologize," he said lightly, "if I frightened you. I had heard you were a warrior of some experience."

Paks drank her sib, wondering what to make of this. She certainly did not want to admit being frightened of a little magic, but he had seen her reaction. She set the mug down firmly, when she finished, and sat down slowly. "I had not seen that before," she said finally.

"Evidently," he replied. He brought his own mug back to the stack and sat near her. "When I asked," he began again, "everyone assured me that you had an excellent reputation." Paks felt a tingle of irritation: what gave him the right to ask about her? "You were in Phelan's Company, I understand." He looked at her and she nodded. "Yes. One of the other guards had heard about you. Not the usual sort of mercenary, he said." Again Paks felt a flickering anger. "And this evening past, you said you were going north over the mountains before we reached Valdaire. Alone, I assumed — ?" Paks nodded again. "I might," he said, looking down at his hands clasped in his lap, "I might be able to help you. I know those trails — difficult for one with no mountain experience, but safe enough."

"Oh?" Paks reached out and refilled her mug.

"Unless you prefer to travel alone. Few humans do."

Paks shrugged. "I have no one to travel with. I'd appreciate your advice on the trail." She was remembering Stammel's warning about those who might seek to travel with her.

The elf moved restlessly. "If you are willing, I thought we might travel together — as far as the borders of the Ladysforest, at least. I could tell you about the trails from there." He sat back, and looked at her from under dark brows. "It would be far safer for you, Paksenarrion, and a convenience to me. While the trails are not as dangerous as these caravan roads, all trails have their hazards, and it is as well to have someone who can draw steel at your back."

Paks nodded. "I see. It is well thought of. But — forgive me, sir — you seem to know more of me than I of you."

He drew himself up. "I'm an elf — surely you know what that is."

"Yes, but —"

His voice sharpened. "I fear I have no relatives or friends nearby that you can question. You will have to trust my word, or go alone. I am an elf, a warrior and mage — as you have seen — and I am returning to my own kingdom of the Ladysforest."

"I'm sorry to have angered you, sir, but —"

"Have you been told bad tales of elves? Is that it?"

Paks thought back to Bosk. "Yes — some."

His voice eased. "Well, then, it's not your fault. You must know that elves are an elder race, older far than men. Some humans are jealous of our knowledge and our skills. They understand little of our ways, and we cannot explain to those who will not listen. But elves, Paksenarrion, were created by the Maker himself to be the enemy of all evil beings. It is elves that orcs hate most, for they know their destiny is on the end of our blades: the dark powers of the earth come never near the elven kingdoms."

Paks said nothing, but wondered. She had heard that the elves were indeed far older than men, and that elves never died of age alone. But she had not heard that elves were either good or evil, as orcs and demons were clearly evil, and saints like Gird and Falk were clearly good.

In the next few days, she found out what she could of elves in general and Macenion in particular. It was not much. But as the higher slopes closed in on the caravan track, she saw how easy it would be to miss her trail. Traveling with someone who had been there before seemed much wiser.

Paks saw the last of the caravan winding away to the west, higher into Silver Pass, with great relief. She had not felt at home with the other caravan guards; she had not been able to give them her trust, as she had her old companions. But now she was free — free to go north toward home, to adventure as she would. She imagined herself, as she had so often, riding up the track from Three Firs to her home, with gifts for everyone and money to spend at a fair. She could almost hear her mother's gasp of delight, the squeals of her younger brothers and sisters. She imagined her father struck silent, awed at her wealth and the sword she bore. She turned to grin at Macenion beside her, whose longsighted gaze lingered on the caravan's dust.

"Well, they're all gone but the smell. Let's get moving."

He turned his gray-green eyes away from the pass and glared at her. "Must you be in such hurry? I want to be sure no thief drops out to trail us."

Paks loosened her sword in its sheath. "Unlikely now. And with your magic arts, and this sword, we shouldn't have much to fear. I wanted to find a good camping spot before dark."

"Very well. Come along, then, and keep a good watch. Move as quietly as a human can."

Paks bit back an angry retort. It wouldn't do to quarrel with her only companion for the trip across the mountains; she had no other guide, and

335

elves made dangerous enemies. She turned to the sturdy pack pony she'd bought from the Wagonmaster, and checked the pack a last time, then stroked Star's neck, and started up the narrow trail that forked away from the caravan route. She hoped Macenion would mellow as they traveled. So far he had been scornful, sarcastic, and critical. It seemed obvious that he knew a great deal about the mountains and the various trails across them, but he made his superior knowledge as painful as possible for anyone else. Now he walked ahead, leading his elven-bred horse whose narrow arched neck expressed disdain for the pack on its back.

But at the campfire that night, Macenion seemed to have walked out part of his bad temper, and regained his original charm. He lit the fire with one spell, and seasoned their plain boiled porridge with another. He set a spell to keep the horse and pony from wandering. Paks wanted to ask if he could not set one to guard the camp, so that they could both sleep through the night, but thought better of it, and offered to take the first watch instead.

Hot as it had been in the afternoon, it was cold that night, with that feeling of great spaces in movement that comes only on the flanks of mountains. Nothing threatened them that Paks could see or hear, but twice the hair on her arms and neck stood straight, and fear caught the breath in her throat. Macenion, when she woke him at the change of watch, and told him, simply laughed lightly. "Wild lands care not for humans, Paksenarrion — neither to hunt nor hide. That is what you feel, that indifference." She surprised herself by sleeping easily and at once.

For two days they climbed between the flanks of the mountain. Midway of the second, they were high enough to see once more the caravan route below and behind them, and the twist where it crossed the spine of the Copper Hills. Paks could barely discern the pale scar of the route itself, but Macenion declared that he could see another caravan moving on it, this time from west to east. Paks squinted across the leagues of sunlit air, wavering in light and wind, and grunted. She could not see any movement at all, and the brilliant light hurt her eyes. She turned to look up their trail. It crawled over a hump of grass-grown rock — what she would have called a mountain, if the higher slopes had not been there — and disappeared. In a few moments, Macenion too turned to the trail.

To her surprise, the other side of the hump was forested; all that afternoon they climbed through thick pinewoods smelling of resin and bark. Paks added dry branches to Star's pack. They camped at the upper end of that wood, looking out over its dark patchwork to the east, where even Paks could see the land fall steeply into the eastern ocean. Macenion gazed at it a long time.

"What do you see?" Paks finally asked, but he shook his head and did not answer. She went back to stirring their porridge. Later that night he began to talk of the elves and their ways — the language and history — but most of it meant little to Paks. She thought he seemed pleased that she knew so little.

"My name's elven," she said proudly, when Macenion seemed to be running down. "I know that much: Paksenarrion means tower of the mountains."

"And I suppose you think you were named that for your size, eh?" Macenion sneered. "Don't be foolish; it's not elvish at all."

"It is, too!" Paks stiffened angrily. She had always been a proud of her name and its meaning.

"Nonsense! It's from old Aare, not from elves. Pakse-enerion, royal tower, or royal treasure, since they used towers for their treasuries."

"That's the same —" Paks had not clearly heard the difference in sounds.

"No. Look. The elven is —" Macenion began scratching lines in the dust. "It has another sign, one that you don't use. Almost, but not quite, the same as your 'ks' sound — and the first part means peak or high place. The elven word enarrion means mountain; the gnomes corrupted it to enarn, and the dwarves to enarsk, which is why these mountains are the dwarfenarsk — or in their tongue, the hakkenarsk. If your name were really elven, it would mean peak or high place in the mountains. But it doesn't. It's human, Aaren, and it means royal treasure."

Paks frowned. "But I was always told —"

"I don't care what you were told by some ignorant old crone, Paksenarrion, neither you nor your name is elven, and that's all." Macenion smirked at her, then pointedly lifted the kettle without touching it and poured himself another mug of sib.

Paks glared at him, furious again. "My grandmother was not an ignorant old crone!"

"Orphin, grant me patience!" Macenion's voice was almost as sharp as hers. "Do you really think, Paks, that you or your grandmother — however worthy a matron she may have been — know as much about the elven language as an elf does? Be reasonable."

Paks subsided, still angry. Put that way she could find no answer, but she didn't have to like it.

Relations were still strained the next day when they came to the first fork of the trail. Macenion slowed to a halt. Paks was tempted to ask him sharply if he knew where he was going, but a quick look at the wilderness around her kept her quiet. Whether he knew or not, she certainly didn't. Macenion turned to look at her. "I think we'll go this way," he said, gesturing.

"Think?" Paks could not resist that much.

His face darkened. "I have my reasons, Paksenarrion. Either path will get us where we wish to go; this one might provide other benefits."

"Such as?"

"Oh —" He seemed unwilling to answer directly. "There are ruins on some of the trails around here. We might find treasure —"

"Or trouble," said Paks.

His eyebrows went up. "I thought you claimed great skill with that sword."

"Skill, yes — but I don't go looking for trouble." But as she spoke, she felt a tingle of anticipation. Trouble she didn't want, but adventure was something else. Macenion must have seen this in her face, for he grinned.

"After these peaceful days, I daresay you wouldn't mind a little excitement. I don't expect any, to be sure, but unless you're hiding a fortune in that pack, you wouldn't mind a few gold coins or extra weapons any more than I would."

"Honestly — no, I wouldn't." Paks found herself smiling. Ruins in the wilderness, and stray treasure, were just the sort of things she'd dreamed of as a girl.

Macenion's chosen path led them back west, by winding ways, and finally through a narrow gap into a rising valley, steep-sided, where the trail led between many tall gray stones. These stood about like tall soldiers on guard.

"What are those?" asked Paksenarrion, as they began to near the first ranks of them. The stones, roughly shaped into rectangles, gave her an odd feeling, as if they were alive.

"Wardstones," said Macenion. "Haven't you ever seen wardstones before?"

Paks gave him a sharp look. "No. I wouldn't have asked, if I had." She didn't want to ask, now, what wardstones warded or whom. But Macenion went on without her question.

"They're set as guardians, by the elder peoples," he said. "Humans don't use them, that I know of. Can't handle the power, I suppose."

Paks clamped her lips on the questions that filled her mind. How did they guard? And what?

"It's the patterns they make," Macenion went on. "Patterns have power; even you should know that — " He looked at her, and Paks nodded. "If intruders come, then, it will trouble the pattern, and that troubling can be sensed by those who set the stones."

"Are we intruders?" asked Paks.

Macenion laughed, a little too loudly. "Oh my, no. These are old, Paksenarrion, very old. Whatever set them is long gone from here."

"But are they still in those — those patterns you spoke of?" Paks felt something, an itch along her bones.

Macenion looked around. "Yes, but it doesn't matter — "

"Why not?" asked Paks stubbornly. "If it's the patterns that have the power, and they're still in the patterns, then — "

"Really, Paksenarrion," said Macenion loftily. "You must realize that I haven't time to explain everything to you. But I do know more about this sort of thing than any human, let alone a very young soldier. You must simply take my word for it that we are in no danger from these stones. The power is long past. And even if it weren't — " he fixed her with a glance from his brilliant eyes, then tapped his wallet suggestively. "I have spells here to protect us from such as these."

Paks found nothing to say to this. She could not tell whether Macenion

338

really knew about such magic, or whether it was all idle boasting, but her bones tingled as they passed between the wardstones, rank after rank. Did Macenion not feel it because of his greater powers? Or perhaps because of his duller perceptions? She did not care to find out. For the next hour, as they climbed between the stones, she thought as little as possible, and resisted the temptation to draw her sword.

They were nearly free of the stone ranks when Paks heard a sharp cry from behind. Before she thought, she whirled, snatching her sword free of the scabbard. Macenion was down, sprawled on the rocky trail, his face contorted with pain. When he saw her standing with naked sword in hand, he gave another cry.

"No! No weapons!" He was pale as milk, now. Paks felt, rather than heard, a resonant thrum from around them. She spared a quick look around the valley, and saw nothing but the shimmer of the sun on many stones. She moved lightly toward Macenion.

"Don't worry," she said, grinning at him. "It's not drawn for you. What happened?"

"Sheathe it," he said. "Hurry!"

Paks was in no mood to listen to him. She felt much better with her sword in hand. "Why?" she asked. "Here, let me help you up." But Macenion had scrambled away from her, and now staggered to his feet, breathing hard. She noticed that he put little weight on his left foot. "Are you hurt?"

"Paksenarrion, listen to me. Sheathe that sword. At once." He was staring behind her, over her shoulder.

"Nonsense," said Paks briskly. "It's you that's being silly now." She still felt a weight of menace, but it was bearable as long as she had her weapons ready. "Come — let's be going. Or shall I bring Star, and let you ride?"

"We must — hurry, Paksenarrion. Maybe there will be time — " He lurched toward her, and she offered her left arm. He flinched from it, and started to circle her. Paks turned, scanning the valley again. Still nothing. Sun glittered off the wardstones, seemed to shimmer as thick as mist between them. She shook her head to clear her vision. Macenion was already a few yards ahead of her.

"Wait, now — " she called. "Let me lead, where I can guard you." But at her call Macenion stumbled on even faster. He reached the horses, and clung to Windfoot's saddle as he clapped Star on the rump. Paks lengthened her stride, angry now, and muttering curses at cowardly elves. The quality of light altered, as if to match her mood, rippling across the stones. Paks was too angry to be frightened, but she moved faster. For an instant Macenion turned a white face back toward her; she saw his eyes widen. Then he screamed and flailed forward. Paks did not look back; she broke into a run as Macenion and the animals took off up the trail. She felt a building menace behind her, rising swiftly to a peak that demanded action.

As they passed the last pair of stones, the light seemed to fail for an instant, as if someone had filled the valley with thick blue smoke. Then a blaze of white light, brighter than sunlight, flashed over them. Paks saw her shadow, black as night, thrown far ahead on the trail. A powerful blow in the back sent her sprawling face-down on the trail; she had no time to see what had happened to Macenion or the horses. Choking dust rose in clouds, and heavy thunder rumbled through her body. Then it was gone, and silence returned. From very far away, she heard the scream of a hawk.

When Paks caught her breath and managed to rise to her feet, she saw nothing behind or before her on the trail. Afternoon shadows had begun to stripe the narrow valley; shadows of the stones latticed the trail itself. Ahead, upslope, the trail was scuffed and torn where Macenion and the horses had fled. Paks scowled at the place the trail disappeared behind a fold of mountain. Alone, in unknown wilderness, without supplies or her pony. . . . She looked back at the valley and shook her head. She knew without thinking about it that she had no escape that way. And perhaps she could catch up to Macenion — he had been limping, she remembered.

In fact, by the time she reached the turn that left the valley safely behind, she could hear him, coaxing the horses to come. When she trudged around the last rocks, she saw him, limping heavily, trying to grab Windfoot's rein. The horse edged sideways, nervous, keeping just out of reach. Paks eyed the situation for a moment before speaking.

"Would you like some help, Macenion?"

He whipped around, nearly falling, his mouth open. Then he glared at her. "You fool!" he said. Paks had not expected that; she felt her ears burning. He went on. "What did I tell you — and you had to keep waving that sword!"

"You told me there wasn't any danger," snapped Paks, furious.

"There wasn't, until you drew your sword," he said. "If you had only — "

"What did you think I'd do, when you let out a yell?"

"You?" He sniffed, twitching his cape on his shoulders. "I should have realized the first thing a fighter would do would be draw steel — "

"Of course," said Paks, struggling to keep calm. "You hadn't said a word about not drawing, either."

"I didn't think it was necessary," muttered Macenion. "I never dreamed you would, for no reason like that — " Paks snorted, and he went on hurriedly. "If we went through quietly, nothing would happen — "

"You told me nothing *could* happen." Paks felt the length of her blade, lightly, to see that it was unharmed, then slid it into the scabbard. "If you'd warned me, I wouldn't have drawn. I don't like liars, Macenion." She looked hard at him. "Or cowards. Did you even look to see if I was still alive?"

"I'm no liar. I just didn't think you needed to know." He looked aside a moment. "And I was coming back as soon as I caught Windfoot or Star, to find you — or bury you."

Paks was not at all sure she believed that. "Thanks," she said drily. "Why did you choose this path — the real reason, this time."

"I told you: it's shorter. And there are ruins — "

"And?"

"And I'd heard of this place."

Paks snorted again. "I'll warrant you had. So you wandered in to see what it looked like, eh?"

"I knew what it looked like." He glared at her. "Don't look at me like that, human. You nearly got us both killed — "

"Because you didn't tell me the truth."

"Because all you thought of was fighting — weapons. I knew what it looked like because I'd spoken to someone who was here — "

"It wasn't you, I suppose, two lifetimes ago, or something?"

"No. It was — a cousin of mine. She said it was quite safe for peaceful folk." He emphasized peaceful. Paks had nothing more to say for the moment. She looked at Windfoot, and spotted Star behind a screen of trees. She clucked softly, holding out her hand. Windfoot looked from her to Macenion, and took a few steps back down the trail. Paks stepped into the middle of it, and clucked again. Windfoot's ears came up; the horse looked at her. Paks walked forward, and took the dangling rein in her hand. The other rein was broken near the bit ring. Macenion was staring at her strangely; she handed him the rein without comment, and called Star. The pony nickered, pushing through the undergrowth. Once out of the trees, she came to Paks at once, pushing her head into Paks's chest.

"All right, all right." Paks untied one side of the pack, and pulled out an apple. They were going soft anyway. "Here." The pony wrapped her lip around the apple and crunched it, dribbling pungent bits of apple from her mouth. Windfoot whuffled, watching Star, and Paks dug out another apple for the horse. "How's your foot?" she asked Macenion, who had watched this silently. "I saw you were limping."

"Not bad," he said. "I can walk." Paks started to say he could run, but decided not to. She turned back to Star, checking her legs and hooves for injuries, and the packsaddle for balance. Everything seemed to be in place. Macenion, meanwhile, mended the broken rein. They traveled until nearly dark, hardly speaking.

Chapter Three

More than ever Paks realized how she had depended on the plain honesty of her friends in the Duke's Company. Perhaps they were not magicians or elves with mysterious powers — but they did not pretend to powers they did not have. What they promised, they performed. And in a fight of any kind, they would never leave her behind, possibly injured or dead. Now, wandering in the mountain wilderness with Macenion for a guide, she wondered if he even knew where they were. He had said nothing more about the wardstones — nor had she. He seemed as confident as ever. But she felt almost as trapped as if she were in a dungeon.

Their way — or the way Macenion led them — continued upward, day by day. The distant sea was hidden behind the shoulders of mountains now. Paks had asked if that meant they were across the pass, but Macenion had laughed. He tried to show her, on the map, how far they had come. But to Paks, the intricate folds of the mountains and the flat map had little to do with each other. Most of the time the trail ran through open forest, broken with small meadows. Paks thought it might be good sheep country. Macenion said no one farmed so far away from any market.

Wild animals had been scarce. Macenion told her of the wild sheep, the black-fleeced korylin, that spent the summers just above timberline. He had pointed out an occasional red deer in the trees, but Paks lacked the experience to spot them. They had seen plenty of rock-rabbits and other small furry beasts, but nothing dangerous. Nor did Macenion seem especially worried. Wolves, he'd said, were scarce in this region. The wild cats were too small to attack them, at least until they were high above timberline. If they saw a snowcat, he said — but Paks had never heard of snowcats.

"I'm not surprised," said Macenion, with his usual tone of superiority. "They are large — very large. I suppose you've seen the short-tailed forest cats?" Paks had not, but hated to admit it. "Hmph. Well, snowcats are about three times that size, with long tails. They're called snowcats because they live high in the mountains, among the icepacks and snow; they're white and gray."

"What do they live on, up there?"

Macenion frowned. Paks saw his shoulders twitch. Finally he answered. "Souls," he said.

"Souls?"

"And anything else they can find, of course. Wild sheep, for meat. But — I don't think we'll have much trouble, at this season, Paksenarrion. The pass should not be snowed in. But if we do see one, remember that they're the most dangerous wild creature in the mountains. I don't except men — a snowcat is more dangerous than a band of brigands."

"But how? Are they — ?"

"I'm telling you. The snowcat is a magical beast, like the dragon and the eryx. It lives on both sides of the world, and feeds on both sides. For meat it eats wild sheep, or horses, or men. For delight it eats souls, particularly elven and human, though I understand it takes dwarven souls often enough that the dwarves fear it."

"I thought elves didn't have souls — "

Macenion suddenly looked embarrassed. "I didn't know you knew so much about elves — "

"I don't, but that's what I heard — they don't have souls because they don't need them — they live forever anyway."

"That's not the reason — but in fact, you're right. Elves don't have souls — not full-blooded elves. But — " he gave her a rueful smile. "I don't like to admit it, Paks, but in fact I am not pure elven."

"But you said — "

"Well, I'm more elven than human — I do take after my elven ancestors much more. You yourself wouldn't call me human — "

Paks had to agree with that, but she still felt affronted. "Well, if you're not elven — "

"I am. I am — well — you could say — half-elven. Human-elven. If you must know, that's how I gained my mastery of human wizardry as well as elven magic." He drew himself up, and took on the expression she found most annoying.

"Oh." Paks left this topic, and returned to the other. "But the snowcat — can't we fight it off? We have a bow, and — "

"No. It is truly magical, Paksenarrion. It can spell your soul out of you before you could strike a blow. I am a mage and part elf; it will desire mine even more."

Paks thought about it. It seemed to her that this meant nothing more than death. She started to ask Macenion, and he turned, startled.

"No! By the First Tree, you humans know nothing, even of your own condition! It is not the same thing as being killed. When you die, your soul goes — well, I don't know your background, and I'd hate to upset your beliefs —" Paks glared at him, and he went on. "You have a soul, and it goes somewhere — depending on how you've lived. Is that plain enough? But if a snowcat eats your soul, it never gets where it should go. It's trapped there, in the snowcat, forever."

"Oh. But then — what does it want with a soul?"

"Paksenarrion, it's magical. It does magic with souls. I don't know how it started, or why; I only know it does. Somehow the souls it eats feed its magic powers. If we see a snowcat, we'll flee at once — try to outrun it. Whatever you do, don't look into its eyes." He walked on quietly some hundred paces. Then: "Paksenarrion, how did you make Windfoot come to you?"

She had not thought about his surprise since that day. "I don't know. I suppose — he knows me now. He knows I have apples. Horses have always liked me."

Macenion shook his head. "No. It must be something more. He's elfbred; our horses wouldn't go to humans unless — do you have any kind of magical tools? A — a bracelet, or ring, or — "

Paks thought of Canna's medallion; surely that wouldn't have moved an elfbred horse. "No," she said. "Not that I know of."

"Mmph. Would you mind if I checked that?"

"What?"

"I could — um — look for it."

"For what?"

Macenion turned on her, eyes blazing. "For whatever you used, human, to control my horse!"

"But I didn't! I don't have anything — "

"You must. Windfoot would never come to a human — "

"Macenion, any horse will come to anyone kind. Look at Star — "

"Star is a — a miserable, shaggy-coated, cow-hocked excuse of a pack pony, and — "

Paks felt the blood rush to her face. "Star is beautiful! She's — "

Macenion sneered. "You! What do you know about — "

"Windfoot came to me. I must know something." Paks realized that her hand had found her sword-hilt. She saw Macenion glance at it. He sighed, and looked patient.

"Paksenarrion, I'm sorry I abused Star. For a pony, she's nice — even beautiful. But she is a pony, and human-bred; she is not an elfbred horse. There's a difference. Just look at Windfoot." They both looked. Windfoot cocked an ear back and whuffled, whether at Star or Paks was uncertain. Paks could not sustain her anger, with Windfoot's elegant form before her. Macenion seemed to recognize the moment her anger failed, because he went on. "If you're carrying a magical item, without knowing it perhaps, it could be dangerous — or very helpful. Magical items in the hands of the unskilled — "

Paks bristled again. "I'm not giving you anything — "

"I didn't mean that." But Paks thought he had meant exactly that. "If you have such an item, I can show you how to use it. Think, Paksenarrion. Perhaps it's something that would call danger to us — wolves, say — or — "

"All right." Paks was tired of the argument. "All right; look for it. But Macenion, what I have is mine; I'm not giving it up. If it calls danger, we'll just fight the danger."

"I understand." He looked pleased. "We can camp here — I know it's early, but I'll need time. And the horses could use the rest. They can graze in this meadow."

Shortly they had the camp set up, and both animals had been watered and fed. Macenion withdrew to one side of the fire, and brought out his pouch. Paks watched with interest as he fished inside it. He looked up at her and glared.

"Don't watch."

"Why not? I've never seen a mage — "

"And you won't. By Orphin, do you want to get your ears singed? Or your eyes burnt out? Can't I convince you that magic is dangerous?" Paks did not move. She was tired of being sneered at. Macenion muttered in what she supposed was elven, and turned his back. She thought of circling the fire to see what he was doing, but decided against it. Instead, she lay back, staring up at the afternoon sky bright overhead. So far they had had good travel weather; she hoped it would continue. She shifted her hips off a sharp fragment of rock, and let her eyes sag shut. She could hear the horses tearing grass across nearby; to her amusement, she could distinguish Star and Windfoot by sound alone. Star took three or four quick bites of grass, followed by prolonged chewing; Windfoot chewed each bite separately. She opened her eyes to check on them, and glanced at Macenion. His back still faced her. She closed her eyes again, and dozed off.

"I found it." Paks opened her eyes to see Macenion's excited face. She rubbed her face and sat up.

"You found what?"

"The magic ring you're wearing." Macenion sounded as smug as he looked.

"What? I don't have any magic ring!"

"You certainly do. That one." He pointed to the intricate twist of gold wires that Duke Phelan had given her in Dwarfwatch.

"That's not magic," said Paks, but with less assurance. The Duke had said nothing about magic, and surely he would have known.

"It is. Its power is over animals; that's why you could use it on Windfoot."

"I didn't use it on Windfoot. I just called him and held out my hand . . . "

"That's all it would take. You touched it — perhaps accidentally, since you say you didn't know about it."

"I didn't — and I don't believe it." But Paks was already half-convinced.

"Where did you get it?"

"It was — my commander gave it to me, after a battle."

"As a reward?"

"Yes."

"Was it part of the loot?"

"I think so."

"Siniava's army?"

"Yes."

"Well, then. He and his captains used magic devices often, so I heard. Perhaps your commander didn't know. It is magic and it is how you controlled Windfoot. You can prove it — call him now, with the ring. Don't say anything, or move, but touch the ring and think that you want him to come."

Paks looked across the meadow to see Windfoot and Star grazing side-by-side. She clenched her hand around the ring, and thought of Windfoot. She didn't like the idea that a ring — a ring she had received from the Duke — could have such power. She had always liked horses; horses had always liked her. She thought of Windfoot: his speed, his elegance. A quick thudding of hooves made her look up. Windfoot came at a long swinging trot, breaking to a canter. Star followed, her shorter stride syncopating the beats. Windfoot stopped a few feet away, and came forward, ears pricked.

"All right," said Paks quietly, holding up her hand for Windfoot to sniff. Star pushed in and shoved her head in Windfoot's way. "But I didn't call Star — "

"No, she came for company, I think. But that is definitely a magic ring, with the power to summon animals. See if you can make Windfoot go away."

Paks wrinkled her brow. It did not seem fair to control Windfoot this way. She flipped her hand, and the horse threw up his head and backed.

"Not that way," said Macenion, annoyed.

"Yes." Paks pushed Star's head away. "Go on, horses! Go eat your own dinners." She stood up. "I believe you; it's magic. But I don't like the idea."

"You'd rather have the power in yourself?"

"Yes. No — I don't know. It just doesn't feel right, to be able to call and send them like that."

"Humans!" snorted the elf. Paks glared at him, and he modified it. "Non-magicians don't understand magicians, that's all. Why involve right and wrong in it? The ring is magic, it's useful magic, and you should use it."

Paks had had no idea what a mountain pass would be like. Macenion told her that the pass at Valdaire wasn't really a mountain pass at all. "It's just high ground," he said. Now, as they climbed past the forested slopes to open turf and broken rock, she wondered how, in this jumble of stone, anyone could find the way. It was a gray morning, and she felt the cold even through her travel cloak. Macenion pointed out marking cairns.

"But it's just another pile of rock."

"No, it's not just a pile of rock. It's a particular pile of rock. Look — do you see anything else like that?"

Paks looked. Rocks everywhere, but nothing that tall and narrow. "No."

"Now, look here." He pointed to a smaller pile on one side. "This is the direction."

"What is?"

"This — Paksenarrion, pay attention. The big pile tells you that this is the trail, and the little pile tells you which way is downhill."

"But are we across the pass? Aren't we going uphill?" Then she realized the simple answer, and felt her face burning. "I see," she said quickly, before Macenion could tell her. "I know. We go the other way."

"Yes. And we know it's the right trail because of the runes."

"Runes?"

"Look at this." He lifted the top rock of the small pile and turned it over. On the under face were angular marks goudged in the rock. "That's the rune for silver, which means that this is the way to Silver Pass."

"Oh." Paks looked around again. "But that only says what's downhill. Can we tell where this will come out?"

"Easily." Macenion's smile was as smug as ever. He turned over the top rock of the big pile and showed her another rune. "This means gnomes, and means that this trail ends at the rock shelter on the border of Gnarrinfulk, the gnome kingdom south of Tsaia."

"I didn't know there was one."

"Gods, yes. And you don't want to wander in there without leave." Macenion replaced the stones carefully. "It's simple, really. The big pile points uphill and has the uphill trailend rune, and the small one points downhill and has the downhill trailend rune. Can you remember that?"

"Yes," said Paks shortly.

"Good. Let's hurry. I don't like the smell of this weather." Macenion looked at the sky above the peaks, which was, as they had often seen from below, thickened into cloud. As if his words had been a signal, a cold rain began to leak down, thin at first. They started upward.

As they climbed, forty paces at a time, Paks watched the stones near the trail darken in the rain. Instead of the rustle of rain on leaves, the water tinkled, as if a thousand thousand tiny bells rang in the stillness. The slopes around them closed in, and the trail steepened. It was more like a stairway than a trail. When they stopped for rest, Paks looked up. The clouds seemed lower. She looked back down the trail. The cairn had disappeared into a hollow behind and below them. She was surprised at how far they had climbed.

Macenion shivered beside her. "It's getting colder — we'd better keep climbing. There's no good place to stop until we're over the top."

"You mean, this is the actual pass?"

"Yes — didn't you know? What I'm afraid of is snow — it can snow all year up here. We've been lucky with weather so far, but this rain — and if it gets colder — "

"What if it does?"

"Then we keep going. There are some undercut ledges near the top, but they aren't good shelter. We won't stop if we can possibly make it through."

But as mountain weather changes from minute to minute, so it thickened around them. Rain changed to sleet which coated their cloaks and the horses' packs, and made the trail treacherous. Paks did not even suggest stopping to eat. She fumbled a strip of meat from under her cloak and chewed it as they climbed. Wind funneled the sleet, now mixed with snow, down the trail. Macenion showed Paks how to wrap a cloth around her face to keep it from freezing.

All too soon the rocky slopes around them whitened as snow flurried past. They climbed higher, leaving clear tracks that filled quickly behind them. Rocks disappeared under the snow. Macenion had to shout in Paks's ear that he thought the snow had been falling at this height for more than a day. As they came around a shoulder of mountain on their right, the pitch flattened. Paks expected a change to a downhill slope, but instead met a blast of wind that nearly took her off her feet. Macenion, ahead of her, disappeared in a white fog of snow. She stumbled, and forced her way on, dragging Star behind her.

Paks finally found Macenion by stumbling into him. Windfoot was sideways to the wind, trying to turn. Macenion grabbed her arm and yelled into her ear.

"Paks! We can't go any farther this way. Drifts! Go back!"

"Where?"

"Back!" He pushed her a little, and Paks turned carefully, bracing against the wind. Star had already turned, and Paks followed her back the way they had come. At least, she hoped it was the way, for nothing remained of their tracks. With the wind at her back, shoving her along like a giant hand, she could see a little way. A dark smudge to one side caught her eye; before she could ask, Macenion's arm on her shoulder pushed her that direction. "It's one of those overhangs," he yelled in her ear.

Star and Windfoot shouldered their way to the back of the shelter and stood, heads down and together, their breath making a cloud in the gloom. Paks swiped the snow off Star's pack and rump, and wiped the pony's face clear. Ice furred her eyelashes and muzzle. Both animals trembled with cold and exhaustion. Macenion, meanwhile, was doing what he could for Windfoot. When he had the saddle off, he turned to Paks.

"We need to block the ends of this completely," he said. "Snowdrift will help, but we'll have to work hard before we dare rest."

Paks groaned inwardly; she wanted nothing but to fall on the ground and sleep. She looked where he pointed. Snow blocked most of the uphill end of the overhang, but some blew in above the drift. Wind roared through the gap, swinging the horses' tails wildly and freezing their sweat.

"We'll use the cover off your pack," Macenion went on. "Anchor it with rocks — " He was picking rocks off the floor of the shelter as he spoke. "If we're lucky, we won't have to compress the snow much — that's the hardest work." Paks struggled with the cover on Star's pack. The knots were frozen, and the rope stiff as iron, but she dared not cut it. She took off her gloves to fight with it, and muttered a curse as the rope scraped her fingers raw.

"Here — " said Macenion suddenly. "Let me help with that. Get your gloves on; you don't need frozen hands." Paks sat back. Macenion glared at her and she backed farther away. He moved his body between her and the pack, and said a few words she did not know. When he stepped back, the knots were untied, and the ropes were supple again. Paks shook out the pack cover, and Macenion reached for it.

By the time Macenion was satisfied that their campsite was safe, Paks felt she could not move another inch. They had managed to secure the pack cover in the upwind gap. Snow drifted against it quickly, and now — so Macenion said; Paks had not gone back out in the wind to see — covered it several feet deep. The other end of the shelter was still open; they had nothing large or strong enough to block it. Macenion wanted to form blocks of snow, but finally gave up when Paks simply stared at him, exhausted. He managed to light a small fire of the wood they had packed along, despite the wind that still gusted in and out of their overhang. Paks helped steady their smallest pot above it. She thought longingly of hot food, hot mugs of sib. But the snow that finally melted and boiled was hardly hot enough to warm her hands.

"It's the cold demons," explained Macenion. "They're jealous of their territory; they hate the warm-bloods who come up from the plains. So they steal the heat from fire, up on these heights."

Paks drank the lukewarm sib, and decided she might never be warm again. Marching in a cold rain now seemed like a pleasant excursion. Only a few feet away, the wind whirled veils of snow past their shelter. She huddled in every scrap of clothing and blanket she could find. But as the afternoon wore away, she regained both strength and warmth. The horses, too, seemed to recover. Paks gave them some of the warm water, and dampened Star's grain. Macenion claimed that elven horses didn't need such coddling, but Paks noticed that Windfoot tried to push Star away from hers. She poured warm water on the pile of grain Windfoot had been ignoring, and the horse ate eagerly. Macenion glared, but said nothing more. He ventured outside several times, trying to judge the weather. As the light faded, he reported that both snow and wind were lessening.

"We might get through tomorrow, if the drifts downhill on the other side aren't too bad. It'd be easier without the beasts — "

"You wouldn't leave them!" said Paks, horrified.

"No, of course not. We need the supplies. But we can walk over drifts they'll stick in. Anyway, get what sleep you can. If we can get out tomorrow, it will be early — as soon as it's light. I'll watch tonight — I'm more used to the cold and the height."

Paks resented his usual tone, but was too tired to resist. She fell quickly into a light doze, waking as Macenion replenished the fire. She squinted around the shelter. The horses stood head-to-tail near the rock wall; she could see firelight reflecting from Star's eyes. Hardly man-high, the ledge of rock overhanging them glittered as if it were full of tiny stars. Paks blinked several times, and decided the rock itself had shiny fragments to catch the light. Firelight turned the snowdrifts into glittering gold and orange — pretty, she thought, when you didn't have to be out in it. She snuggled deeper into her blankets, took a long breath, and slid back into sleep.

Macenion's choked cry brought her halfway out of her blankets with sword in hand before her eyes were open. He stood rigid beside the fire, mouth open. Paks tried to see beyond him, to the outside. Nothing but a wavering dark. She glanced back at the horses. Both of them were alert, heads high, nostrils flared. Star's ears were back; Windfoot's tail was clamped tight. Paks began to untangle herself from the blankets as unobtrusively as possible: she felt they were both easy targets, in the firelight.

It was then she saw the pale blue glow of eyes.

"Paksenarrion!" Macenion's whisper was hoarse and desperate.

"I'm awake," she said softly. What, she wondered, had eyes like that? Farther apart than human eyes, that was all she could tell. Big eyes.

"Paks, it's a — " he choked, and then recovered. "It's a snowcat."

"Holy Gird," said Paks without thinking. When she realized what she had said, she wished she'd kept quiet.

"What?" asked Macenion.

Paks felt herself blushing in the dark. "Nothing," she said. "Now what?"

"Can't you see it? "

"No — nothing but eyes."

"I don't know what we can — " Macenion's voice suddenly sharpened. "Paks! Your ring!"

"What?" For a moment Paks had no idea what he meant. Macenion spared a glance at her, furious.

"Your *ring*, human! Your *special* ring," he went on. Paks nodded, then, stripping off her glove to touch it.

"But are you sure it will work? Maybe the thing — the snowcat — will just go away if we let it alone."

As if in answer to that suggestion, the glowing eyes moved closer. Now Paks could see a suggestion of the body's outline, a long, powerful catlike form, crouching as if to spring.

"You fool!" cried Macenion. "It knows we're here! It's about to jump. Stop it! Hold it!"

Paks thought she could see a twitch in that long tail, like the twitch she had seen in the mousers at the barn, the last instant before they sprang on a rat. She pressed her thumb hard on the ring and thought "Hold still, cat." She wondered if those words would work.

"Are you?" asked Macenion hoarsely.

"Yes," said Paks. "How long does it — "

"As long as you concentrate. Keep holding it."

Paks tried to concentrate. She wished she could see the snowcat better. Macenion turned to rummage among his things. She was afraid to look sideways at him, lest the cat jump. She forced her eyes back to the shadowy cat-form. Suddenly light flared around her, and she jumped.

"Don't look," said Macenion harshly. The light was clear and white, brilliant enough to show true colors. Now she could see the snowcat clearly. Its body was man-long; its shoulder would almost reach her waist. As Macenion had said, its fur was white and blue-gray, patterned with dapples that reminded Paks of snowflakes enlarged. The ears bore long tufts of white, and it had a white beard and short ruff. The eyes, despite the blue glow they'd had before, shone amber in Macenion's spell-light.

"Macenion, it's beautiful. It's the most beautiful — "

"It's spelling you," he said firmly. "It seems beautiful because it's trying to use magic on you."

"But it can't be. It's — " She stopped as Macenion came forward into her field of view. "Macenion, what are you doing?"

"Don't be silly, Paks. I'm going to kill it."

"Kill it? But it's helpless — it can't move while I — "

"That's right. Just keep holding it still. It's the only way I have a chance — "

"But that's not fair — it's helpless — " Paks let her concentration waver, and at once the snowcat moved, shifting in a kind of constricted hop, as she caught her control back. She was distracted again by this evidence of her power and its limitations, and the cat managed to rear, swiping at Macenion's head with one massive paw. He ducked, and Paks forced the cat to stillness again.

"Damn you, human! Hold that beast, or we're both dead. Worse than dead — you remember what I told you!" Macenion glared back at her, then turned, raising his sword.

Paks felt a wave of fear and pain sweep through her mind. It was wrong, terribly wrong — but what else could she do? "Macenion — " she tried again, staring into the snowcat's huge amber eyes. "It's not right — "

"It's not right for us to end up soul-bound to a snowcat, no," he said roughly. "It's easy enough, though, if you forget yourself one more time. If that's what you want, go ahead."

Paks looked down, biting her lip. She could not watch, and then she thought she must. The snowcat made no resistance — could make no resistance — but it could cry out, in fury and pain, and so it did. That wailing cry, ending in an almost birdlike whistle, brought tears to her eyes. She blinked them back, and watched stonily as Macenion wiped his sword on the dead snowcat's fur. He came back to the fire almost jauntily.

"A snowcat. That's quite a kill, even if you don't think it was fair. I'll just take the pelt before it freezes — "

"No." Paks glared at him.

"What d'you mean, no? Snowcat pelts are nearly priceless, it's so rare to take one — you noticed how careful I was not to damage it when I killed — "

Paks erupted in fury. "By the gods, Macenion, I wonder if you ever tell the truth! You dare pride yourself on killing a helpless animal? It might as well have been a sheep trussed up, for all the courage and skill it took — "

"I didn't notice you out there — "

"You told me to stay here — "

"I told you to hold it still. You could have helped me, if you were able to hold more than one thought in mind at a time. As it was you nearly killed me — "

"I!" Paks flourished her own sword. She noticed with some satisfaction that Macenion backed up a step. "I but tried to save your honor and mine — not that I would have thought an elf would care so little for it — "

351

"You know nothing about elven honor, human!" Macenion seemed to swell with rage. "You are my travel companion, oath-bound to defend me — as I defended you just now — against all dangers. As for the snowcat having no defense, it was trying to spell you the entire time."

Paks felt her anger leak away into the cold. Had she been half-spelled? Had she nearly failed her oath because of it? Macenion took quick advantage of her hesitation. "I don't blame you," he said more quietly. "You are human, unused to magicks of any kind, and this may be the first magical beast you've seen." She nodded unwillingly. "It would have killed all of us, and feasted many days while our souls were enslaved to it, if we had not managed to kill it. Or send it away." He cocked his head and gave her a sly grin. "If you'd been able to think of it, o lover of animals, you might simply have sent it away."

"Sent it — it would have gone?"

"Oh, yes. I'm surprised it didn't occur to you, Paksenarrion. Just as you sent Windfoot — oh, that's right. You didn't. But you could have."

"Then you didn't have to kill it," Paks cried, angry again. "You told me —"

"I told you what seemed best to me. Kill it and it's gone forever. Send it away and it might come back — though you could have laid a compulsion on it to avoid us. Besides, this way we have a valuable pelt." Macenion turned again to his pack, and pulled out a short, wide skinning blade. Paks moved between him and the snowcat; when he rose and saw her, he frowned.

"I won't let you," said Paks, fighting back tears. "You told me I had to hold it, or it'd kill both of us — and you lied about that. It isn't the first lie, either. You're not going to profit by it, Macenion — I was wrong to hold it that way, and that's the worst thing I've done. I won't let you do more."

"You mean you'd waste a perfectly good pelt — already back in winter coat — just because you didn't think of sending it away?"

"No — because you lied to me." Paks had backed slowly and carefully across the ledge outside their shelter, until she bumped her heels into the snowcat's corpse. Now she turned, and with a powerful heave pushed the snowcat over the edge.

"You're a stubborn fool," said Macenion, but without the anger she had feared. "That's enough gold for both of us to live on for a month, that you threw away. But —" He shrugged. "I suppose it meant something to you. Now don't stand there and freeze, Paksenarrion — we still have to cross the pass tomorrow."

It was not the next morning, but the one after that, when they finally ventured from their shelter. Dawn that day rose clear, the wind hardly moving, and nothing in the white drifts below looked like the remains of a snowcat. They had said little to each other in the storm-whitened hours between — only what must be said about the fire, the care of the animals, and packing up their campsite. Now they moved through a pale rose and blue world, leaving blue-shadowed tracks behind. Once through the pass, Paks could see — not the rolling forests of the Eight Kingdoms she had hoped for — but more ridges and steep valleys. Far below and ahead, forests clothed the slopes. Somewhere beyond, the mountains ended. She hoped to make it there.

Chapter Four

Paks had not slept well since the killing of the snowcat. Despite Macenion's sarcastic reassurance, she knew that she had dishonored her sword, and the ring she had used. She had stayed with him only because she had no other guide out of the mountains. Now, as they came through a gap in the trees into yet another narrow valley, she wondered whether she should refuse to accompany him any farther. Surely here, with the bulk of the mountains behind her, she could find her own way north.

"Well, indeed — " said Macenion, in a tone that meant he wished to be asked what he meant.

"Well, what?" Paksenarrion turned half away from him, and bent to check her pony's hooves.

"It's what I hoped to find — the right valley."

Paksenarrion looked at the valley, this time, and saw, in its widest span, a group of stone piles. "More of your ruins?" she asked sourly.

"Much more important," said Macenion. He was grinning again, and when he caught her eye he winked. "Didn't I say there was treasure to be won in these mountains?"

"You've said a lot." Paks had turned back to Star, and was adjusting the ropes on her pack.

Macenion sighed. "Come now, don't be tiresome. You're carrying a new sword, for one thing, and — "

Paks knew Macenion had parted with the elf-wrought blade, if it was one, only because he wanted to soothe her after the snowcat's murder. The sword felt well enough — it was better than the one she'd bought — but she resented the whole incident. And she wasn't about to be grateful.

"And you say there's more. And, as usual, you want me to bodyguard you while we get it — right?"

"I will need your help." Macenion sighed again. "Paks, I'm sorry about the snowcat. I didn't know you'd feel that way — "

"I'd have thought an elf would — "

"So my human parentage betrayed me. It's not the first time. But listen, at least, before you stalk off in outrage."

Paks looked around at the tree-clad slopes. She thought she saw a faint trail across from them, leading south, but she knew the ways of apparent trails that appeared and disappeared and tangled together. She shrugged and stared down at the ruins while Macenion talked.

"This valley," he said, "is forbidden to elves. My mother's cousin told me that, and also told me how to find it. He meant the directions to keep me away. But here is a great treasure — the stories are clear on that — and much of it is magical. Something happened here that the elves don't want to talk about, and so they went away and never came back."

"Elves lived here?" Paksenarrion frowned. "I thought they lived in forests, not stone buildings."

"It's true that elven cities are surrounded by trees and water, but they're constructed, nonetheless."

Despite herself, Paksenarrion was interested. "What happened, then? Why did the elves leave?"

"I don't know." The answer had come so fast that Paks disbelieved it and gave Macenion a sharp look. He spread his hands. "It's true — I don't know. I suspect, but I don't know. They say they haven't come back because the valley is haunted by evil, but I'm fairly sure that they just don't like to admit mistakes."

"You were more than fairly sure that the wardstones wouldn't work any longer," Paks reminded him. Macenion scowled.

"This is different," said Macenion loftily. "Those were human artifacts. This is elven. My elven blood will sense the truth — and my magic will enable us to pass safely what might be perilous for others." He patted the pouch that held his magical apparatus. Paksenarrion said nothing. "And the treasures here are worth a risk. Elf-made weapons, Paks, and magic scrolls and wands: I've heard about them. They were all abandoned when the elves fled. My relatives — well, I hate to say anything bad about the elves, but they haven't been any too generous with their goods. I feel I have a right to whatever I can find in there." He nodded toward the ruins.

"But what about the evil whatever-it-is?"

"That's why I've waited this long. First, my power as a mage is much greater now; I've spent years in study and practice, and I have some power-ful new spells." He showed her the polished end of a scroll case. "And, as well, I'm traveling with a very experienced and able warrior — you."

"I see."

"I'm quite sure that whatever is there — if anything — will be no match for the two of us."

"What do you think is there?"

"Oh — if the underground passages are still open, some animals may have moved in. Perhaps even an orc or two. As for an evil power — " Macenion tilted his hand back and forth. "If it were very strong, I'd be aware of it here. And I'm not."

Paksenarrion looked around again. She felt nothing. After the wardstones, she thought she might, if anything like that were going on. She touched her sword hilt for comfort. "Well, then, I suppose we could take a look."

Macenion smiled, and turned to lead the way down.

It took longer than she expected. The path they had followed from the slopes above disappeared in a tangle of undergrowth that cloaked tumbled rocks as big as cattle. The sun had long disappeared behind the western peaks when they hacked their way free of the thorny stuff and found themselves on short rough turf still several hours away from the ruins. In fact, these were no longer visible; the floor of the valley was uneven.

"Let's make camp," said Paksenarrion. "It'd be full dark by the time we came to the ruins. The horses could use a rest, too." Star had a long bleeding scratch down one leg, and Windfoot was streaked with sweat.

"I suppose so." Macenion was staring toward the ruins. "I wish we could go right on, but — "

"Not in the dark," said Paks firmly. He seemed to shake himself.

"You're right." Still he sat, facing west, silent, while Paks gathered wood from the brushy edge for a fire. She touched his arm when it was ready to light, and he jumped.

"The fire's ready," she said, pointing.

Macenion looked around at the gathering darkness, and threw back his cloak. He glanced up at Paks. "Perhaps tonight we should use the tinderbox."

"You? The great magician?" Paksenarrion turned to the horses. "I thought you were sure it was safe."

"There's no sense making it obvious we're here — just in case."

"Then we shouldn't have a fire at all." Paks pulled her own pack near the stacked wood. "That's fine with me; I know fires draw trouble."

"Yes. Well — let's not, then." Macenion pulled his cloak around him again, and began to unload his horse. Paks eyed the hollow they were in. It was not particularly defensible, if Macenion thought they might be attacked. But when she asked, he was disinclined to move. Paks shrugged, and pulled her sword from its sheath. As the darkness closed in, the rasp of her whetstone on the blade seemed louder and louder. When she tested the blade, and found it well enough, she noticed how still the night was.

Paks woke in the first light of dawn; the peaks behind were just showing light instead of dark against the sky. For a moment or so she was not sure where she was. The visions of her dream were still brilliant before her eyes. She shook her head vigorously and rolled on her side, hardly surprised to find that she held her sword hilt in her hand. She looked toward Macenion, a dark shape in darkness. Was he stirring? She spoke his name softly.

"I'm coming!" His answer was a shout, and he sprang to his feet. "Begone, you foul — " She heard a gasp, and then, in a different voice, "By all the gods of elf and man, what was that?"

"I don't know. I thought you were waking, and called, and you jumped up — "

"A dream." Paks heard Macenion's feet on the grass. "It must have been a dream."

"What dream?" Paks wondered if this were a haunted place, a place that gave dreams. Hers had been vivid enough.

"It was — it's hard to say. I felt something — almost as if — " He paused for a long moment. Paks tried to see his face in the dimness, but could not.

"I dreamed too," she said finally. "A — I don't know what to call it — a spirit of some sort, I suppose — was imprisoned, and calling for help — "

"Yes — and was there a yellow cloud that stank of evil?" Macenion's voice sounded alert and eager.

"I saw no cloud," replied Paks. "But something tall, in a yellow robe, with a staff. I wondered if it was an elf."

"That was no elf, whatever it was. I must have seen the aura of power, and you saw the physical form. But it was evil, and the — " Macenion paused again as if searching for a word. "I can't think," he said finally. "I should know what it was, that was calling. Something to do with elves, and the places they've lived for long. It needs our help."

"So that was a sent dream," said Paks. "Not something we dreamed on our own."

"It was sent, certainly," said Macenion. "The question now is — "

"Who sent it."

"No, I wasn't worried about that. The question is, what do we do? I know what we should do, but — "

"I still want to know who sent it."

"One of the gods, of course. Sertig or Adyan, probably. Who else would?"

"The — the thing itself? The one that needs our help? It might want us to come, and cause the dream."

"Nonsense. If it's strong enough to do that, it wouldn't need our help against a mere sorcerer or wizard."

"I don't know — " Somehow Paksenarrion could not believe Macenion's explanation. He had been wrong about so many things. She wished, not for the first time, that she knew more about the world beyond the Duke's Company. She had not realized, until she left it, how little she had learned in three years of soldiering. For all she knew, Macenion himself could have caused the dream, to ensure that she would be willing to enter the ruins. She pushed that thought aside. Until they were clear of the mountains, she had no real choice; Macenion was the only available guide. Her hand found its way to the pouch that held Canna's medallion. She stopped herself from taking it out, and squatted down to reroll her blankets.

"In your dream — did you — did it offer you any treasure?" Macenion, too was packing up.

Paks nodded, realized it was still too dark for him to see that gesture, and spoke instead. "Yes. I didn't know what all of it was, but the weapons and armor were beautiful."

"It can't hurt, Paksenarrion, to take a look — " His voice was almost pleading.

Paks laughed despite her worries. "No, I suppose not. Don't worry, Macenion, your hired blade is still here and won't leave you. I've got more loyalty than that. But I hope you really do have the skill to handle whatever magic comes up."

"I think so. I'm sure of it." But his voice carried no certainty.

It took them most of the morning to reach the ruins. As they came nearer, Paks recognized that the grassy mound before them had been a defensive wall. They entered through a gap that had once been a gateway, still framed by tall upright stones. Although they were scarred as if they had been scorched, much of the decorative carving was still visible. Paks stood bemused, enjoying the intricacy of the interlacing designs, until Macenion touched her arm.

"It's meant to do that," he said, grinning. "Elves use patterns for control. In fact, elves taught men how to set the patterns for the wardstones. You'd better not let yourself look at any of the decoration that remains, just in case."

Paks felt herself flush with embarrassment. She said nothing, but followed Macenion deeper into the complex of ruins, her hand on her sword.

Little remained but irregular mounds overgrown with grass and weeds. Here and there a bit of stone showed through, and a few doorways still stood wreathed in ivy. Although Paks could hear birdsong in the distance, the ruins themselves were quiet. No lizards sunned themselves on the mounds, to scuttle away as they passed. No rabbits found shelter in the occasional briar. Macenion moved almost as carefully as Paks could have wished, pausing beside each mound before crossing the next open space. As they went deeper into the complex, the silence grew more intense. The horses' hooves made no noise on the turf. Paks could not bring herself to speak. The breath caught in her throat, but she could not cough. At last Macenion raised his hand for a halt. When he turned to look at her, his face looked pale. He swallowed visibly, then spoke, his voice soft.

"We'll leave the horses here. They won't stray. They have grass, and there's a fountain ahead. I'll put a spell on them, as well."

Now that the silence had been broken, Paks found she could speak, though it was still an effort. "Have you found the way to what we're looking for?"

"Yes. I think so. Look there — " Macenion pointed out one of the mounds ahead, and Paks saw that under an overgrowth of ivy and flowering briar (flowering? at this season?) it was almost intact: a curious round structure with columns on the outside and a bulbous roof. She could see, as well, the fountain that lay before it, a clear pool whose surface rippled as if in a breeze. "I've heard that such a building lay in the center of this place," Macenion went on. "From it, passages lead to the vaults below and to other buildings. I'm sure that the being we are to help is trapped somewhere below; this is the surest way down."

Paks frowned. "If so, it's known to others, as well. To the enemy of that being, for instance. I'd rather not go in by such a public entrance."

"Scared?" Macenion's face twisted in a sneer. He glanced at her sword, then back at her face.

Paks fought back an angry retort. "No," she said quietly. "Not any more

357

scared than you, with your pale face. But you brought a soldier along for a soldier's skills, and I learned in my first campaign that you don't go in the door that the enemy expects. Not if you want to live to have your share of the loot."

Macenion flushed in his turn, and scowled. "Well, that's the only way down that I know how to find. Besides, in my dream, this was shown as the way."

"Did your dream show both of us going in that way?"

"How else?"

"You hadn't thought we might need a rear guard?"

"What for?"

"What for?" Paks glared at Macenion. "Haven't you any experience? Suppose that whatever-it-is, that evil thing, has its own way to the surface. It could come after us, and attack from the rear, or trap us underground."

"Oh, I'm sure it wouldn't — couldn't — "

"Like you were sure about the other things? No, Macenion, I'm not going down there without knowing a little more about it. Surely your magic can show you something, or guard the way behind us."

Macenion looked thoughtful. "If you insist, I suppose I can think of something. It might be better, after all — " He burrowed into his tunic, then gave Paks a sharp look. "You can walk around a bit — look for another entrance — "

"I wish you'd quit worrying. I'm not another magician, and I couldn't use anything I might see."

Macenion drew himself up. "It's a matter of principle."

Paks snorted, but moved away. She decided to take the pack off Star and see if there was anything she might want to take underground. Macenion, she noticed, hadn't thought of that. As she went through their gear, she wondered again what she was doing following such a person. She did not like the thought of going underground, in an unknown place against unknown dangers, at all. Especially with someone like Macenion. Perhaps with a squad of the Duke's Company, but a single half-elf? But a scene from her dream recurred: after victorious combat, she was receiving the homage of those who had asked her help — she was given a new weapon, of exquisite workmanship, and a suit of magical armor. Honor — glory — her reputation made, as a fighter. She shook her head, driving the vision away. A chance for glory, Stammel had always said, was a chance to be killed unpleasantly. Still — she had left the Company to seek adventure and fame and a chance to fight for such causes as now lay before her. Could she miss the chance? She piled on one side the things she thought would be useful, and made the rest into a small bundle.

"We'll need something to light the way," said Macenion suddenly. "Whatever the elves used may not be working, and I don't want to use magical light until it's needed." He was going through his own pack. "This should do. This oil — these candles — and yes, I can set a spell at our backs that will keep out any trouble — at least give us warning. We probably won't be that long, but I suppose we should take water and some food."

"How about the fountain? Is it safe?"

"I should think so. Try it." Macenion held out his water bottle to Paks. She frowned.

"If it's elvish, you try it first."

"What a brave warrior! Very well, then." Macenion dipped his bottle in the fountain pool. Nothing happened. "You see? Just water."

"Good." Paks, too, filled her water bottle from the fountain pool, then bent to drink directly from it. The water was cold and had a faint mineral tang. Although the water seemed perfectly clear, she could not see the bottom of the pool. Somehow, after drinking, she no longer considered not following Macenion under the ruins.

Macenion led the way through a tangle of ivy into the building. From within, Paks could see that the original domed roof had been pierced by a number of skylights, each with an ornamental molding around it. The interior walls had been inlaid with many-colored stones that formed a dazzling array of designs. The floor was a mosaic of cool grays and soft greens, rounded pebbles that looked like those in any mountain stream, but chosen carefully to match in size and shape.

"Here it is," said Macenion, pointing to a circle of darker stones laid in the center of the room.

"What?"

Macenion looked smug. "The door — the way in."

"That?"

"Yes." He drew out a short black rod; Paks looked down, more frightened than she cared to admit. Something sizzled, and she looked quickly at the circle: it was gone. A hole in the floor revealed a spiral stair. Dust lay thick on the stone steps.

Paks took a deep breath. "Do you think we're the first to come this way? The first to be asked for help?"

"I don't know. Probably not. Only a magician could find this way down, you know. Perhaps others couldn't find a way to help and went away. You stay here a moment, while I take a quick look down." Macenion set a careful foot on the first step. Nothing happened. He went down several more, bending to look beneath the floor. Paks looked out the way they had come in, half expecting some monster to appear on their trail, but saw only Macenion's horse moving past the opening to drink at the fountain; she heard it sucking the water up. When she looked back at the hole in the floor, Macenion was coming back up. "Just below, the ceiling's much higher; we won't have any problem. And I don't see that anything's disturbed the dust. The only thing is, the stair is only one person wide — "

Paks suppressed a last shudder of doubt about the wisdom of this whole project, and grinned at him. "I suppose you'd like the fighter to go in front, eh? Well, I can't see behind myself; I'd just as soon know who's at my back." She drew her sword as she spoke. "But I'll have this out, just in case. What about light? Must I carry a candle or torch?"

359

"No-o — " said Macenion, climbing out of her way onto the floor. "There's light."

"What sort of light?"

"I'm not sure. It may be the same the elves used. But it's easily light enough to see."

"What if it goes out? You'd best keep some sort of flame alight, Macenion."

"Why should it go out if it's lasted this long? Oh, all right — " he answered her look of disgust. "But you're so suspicious."

"I'm alive," said Paks, "and I intend to stay that way."

"As a fighter, an adventurer?"

"Some do," said Paks, starting down the stairs. "And from what I hear, those that do stay suspicious. Magicians, too."

The stair dropped steeply, and curved to the right, back under the floor. Paks found that she did not have to duck at all; when she thought about it, she remembered that elves were, in general, taller than humans. Light filled the stairwell as far as she could see, a gentle, white light with no apparent source. She looked back once, to see the deep scuffing footprints she had made in the dust. Macenion was just in sight, several steps higher. After what she judged was the first half-turn, the steps were not so steep. She could move more easily now, and, of course, anything coming up could do so as well. She glanced back again, for Macenion, and thought of the spell he had promised to put at their backs.

"What did you do up there?" she asked softly, nodding upward.

"It's open," he said. "If I'd closed it, and anything happened to me, you couldn't get out that way. But I put a spell on the opening that should repel anything from outside trying to get in. And just in case, I put another spell on it to give us an alarm if something does go through."

All that sounded impressive to Paksenarrion. She hoped it would work. "Do you know how far down this goes?"

"No. It should open into a wide hall at the bottom, though."

Paks went on. The mysterious light bothered her. The silence bothered her. She felt her hand grow sweaty on her sword hilt, and that bothered her. Nothing had happened; no danger appeared, and yet her breath came short, just as if she were a recruit in her first battle. She concentrated on the construction of the stair: pale gray stone underfoot, and slightly darker gray stone on the walls and vaulted ceiling. The stair treads were ribbed, under the dust, and when she touched the walls, she found them lightly incised with an intricate design. Remembering Macenion's warning, she took her fingers off the wall. She looked back over her shoulder again. Macenion, too, had one hand on the wall; when he met her eyes he smiled at her.

"It's decoration and information both," he said. "I can read some of it, though I'd have to stand here a long time to figure it out. But for those who lived here, it would be a way of telling how far they had come, though that's not what it says, exactly." He moved his hand along the section of wall nearest him. "This, for example, is part of an old song: 'The Long Ride of Torre.' Do you know it?"

Paks nodded. "If that's the same Torre as Torre's Necklace."

"Of course. Do you know the story?"

"Yes." Paks turned again and kept stepping down. The dust seemed no thicker, and with no changes in light or silence, she had a hard time judging how far they had come. At last she saw an opening ahead, rather than a curving wall. As she came to the last step, and waited for Macenion to close in behind her, she could see a space of dusty stone paving, and nothing else. Although it was light beyond the opening, any walls were too far away to show.

"Now this, I believe, was the winterhall," said Macenion, peering past her. "Go on, Paksenarrion."

"And have whatever's waiting beside the door take my head off? Let's be careful." Paks unslung her small shield and reached for Macenion's walking staff.

He jerked it away. "What?"

Paks sighed. "Remember what I just said about doorways? Better a piece of wood than my neck."

"Oh, all right." Macenion handed over his staff grumpily. Paks tied the shield quickly to one end, and stuck it through the door. Nothing happened. She pulled it back, handed Macenion his staff, tightened the shield on her arm, and slipped quickly through the doorway, putting her back to the wall beside it.

She stood in a large bare hall, lit by the same mysterious means as the stair. It stretched away on either side on the doorway she'd come through for twice the distance of its width. No furniture remained, and dust covered the broad floor. Macenion came through after her, and looked up. Paks followed his gaze. Far overhead the arched ceiling was formed into intricate branches and vaults, a tracery of stone such as Paks had never seen. Between ribs of dark stone, patterns of smaller colored ones gave almost the effect of a forest overhead.

"That's — beautiful — " she whispered, hardly aware of speaking.

For once, Macenion did not take a superior tone. "It's — I've never seen the like myself. I knew this was once the seat of the High King, but I never imagined — " He took a few steps out into the hall, and looked at his footprints. "Certainly this has not been disturbed for many years — perhaps not since they left."

Paks had noticed, at the right end of the hall, a darker alcove. "What's that?"

"That should lead to other passages. But I can't understand why there are no signs at all." Macenion stopped and shook his head. "We won't find out anything by standing here. Let me think — "

Paks scanned the walls again. At the left end of the hall was a dais, four steps up from the main level, and at the back of it an arched doorway. Two heavily patterned bronze doors closed the opening. Across from her, on the

361

other long wall, were four doorways, also closed with heavy doors. At the right end, no doors showed save the alcove, if that was, as Macenion said, an opening.

"Do you know where any of these doors leads?" she asked.

"The door on the dais leads to the royal apartments. The others — no, blast it, I can't remember. We'll have to look and see."

"Would the doors be locked?"

"I doubt it. They may be spelled, though. Luckily I have ways of handling that. Perhaps we should start with the royal apartments. We might find something worthwhile there."

Paks felt a twinge. "We're here to help that trapped thing, first. I don't think treasure hunters would be lucky here."

"I was thinking we might find something that would help us free the spirit, Paksenarrion. It wasn't just greed."

Paks was not convinced. She turned from one side to the other, trying to feel which way to go. Was that a pull toward the right end? Or the door directly across from her? And if it was, did it come from the one they wanted to help or from the enemy? She shook her head, as if to clear it, and watched Macenion approach the royal doors. A feeling of wrongness grew stronger. He reached the foot of the dais.

"Macenion! No!" She surprised herself as much as him with her shout.

He whirled to face her. "What?"

"Don't go that way." She was utterly certain of danger. She moved quickly to his side, and lowered her voice. "That's wrong; I'm sure of it. If you go up there, we'll — "

"Paksenarrion, you're no seer. I assure you that we may very well find, in the royal apartments, clues to what sort of spirit may be locked here. We'll certainly find information about the layout of the underground passages."

"That may be, but if you open that door, Macenion, you'll wish you hadn't."

He looked at her closely. "Have you had some sort of message? From a — a god, or something like that?"

"I don't know. But I know you shouldn't go that way. And I may not be a seer, Macenion, but I have had warning feelings before, and they've been true."

"A fighter?" He arched his brows.

"Yes, a fighter! By the gods, Macenion, carrying a sword in my hand doesn't mean I don't carry sense between my ears. If a warning comes, I heed it."

"I wish you'd told me before about your extra abilities. It comes hard to believe in them now, when I've never seen them." He gave her a superior smile. "Very well, then . . . since you're so sure. We'll wander about down here with no other guidance than your intuition. Perhaps you're turning into a paladin or something."

Paks glared at him, angry enough to strike, but relieved that he had turned away from the dais. Macenion looked around the hall.

"Which door would you suggest, since you don't like my choice?"

"What about that alcove?" asked Paks. "Or the center doors on the long side there?"

Macenion shrugged. "It doesn't matter to me. Why not the alcove? It's as far as possible from those you fear." Paks flushed but held her peace as they walked the length of the hall.

The alcove was deeper than it looked; the light was deceptive. Within it were two doors, both bronze. One had a design on it that reminded Paks of a tree; the other was covered with interlacement bands that enclosed many-pointed stars. Macenion looked at her. "Do you have any feelings about either of these? My own preference would be for the stars; stars are sacred to elves."

Paks felt, in fact, a stubborn desire to use the door with the tree, but she felt no special menace from the other one. With Macenion grinning at her in such a smug way, she didn't want to press a mere preference. "That will do. I don't have anything against it, anyway." When Macenion simply stood there, she asked sharply, "Aren't you going to open it?"

"As soon as I figure out how. It's locked, spell-locked — if you laid a hand on it, you'd be flat on your back. I'm surprised your intuition didn't tell you that."

Paks wondered herself, and thought that if her intuition worked on bigger things, they'd better pay attention to it. She said nothing, however, and as Macenion stood in apparent thought, she turned to keep watch on the rest of the room.

When she looked the length of the room toward the dais, she thought she saw a faint glow around the doors there. She looked at the other doors in the hall. They looked the same. When she looked back at the dais, the glow was more definite. It had an irregular shape, and seemed to be coming from the joint between the doors — as if it were seeping through.

"Macenion!"

"What now?!" He turned to her angrily. Paks pointed toward the dais. "I don't see — by the gods! What's that?"

"I don't know. I don't like it. Did you step up on the dais?"

"No. You yelled, and I — I may just have touched the lower step with my foot —"

"I hope not. It's brighter, now."

"So I see. I wonder if it's — by Orphin, I'd better get this spell correct."

"What is it?"

"Not now! Just watch. Tell me if it gets more than halfway down the hall."

"But what can I do to hold it back?"

"If it's what I think, nothing. Now let me work."

Paks turned to stare at the mysterious glowing shape, which grew slowly as she watched. It seemed to spread, widening itself to the width of the dais, and slowing its forward movement as it did so. At first she had been able to see through it clearly, but as it grew and thickened, she could no longer see the doors behind it. She felt sweat crawling through her hair. Her intuition had been right, but what was this thing? Surely there was a way to fight it.

Now it reached the forward edge of the dais. Paks could hear Macenion muttering behind her. She heard a faint sizzle, then a little pop. Macenion cursed softly and went back to muttering. The glowing shape extended along the front edge of the dais, and began to grow taller. Slowly it filled the space above the dais, from the doors behind to the lowest step in front, rising higher and higher to the canopy that hung between the dais and the ceiling. When this space was full, the glow intensified again. It seemed more and more solid, as if it were a definite shape settling there. As it solidified, it contracted a little, no longer so regular. Just as Macenion's triumphant "Got it!" broke her concentration, Paks thought she could see the shape it was condensing toward.

"Come on, Paks. Quickly!" Macenion grabbed her arm to hurry her through the now-open door, and looked back. "Great Orphin, protect us, it is a — Come on!"

Paks tore her eyes from the glowing shape, and darted through the door after Macenion. He waited on the other side and threw his weight against the heavy panel. As it swung closed, a curious hissing noise came from the hall they had left.

"Help me — close it!" Macenion looked as frightened as Paks had ever seen him. She, too leaned on the door, as Macenion fumbled for something in his pouch with one hand. It seemed reluctant to stay closed, as if pressure were on it from the other side. "Don't let it come open," warned Macenion. "If that gets out, we're dead."

"What is it?"

"Not now! I'm trying to — " Macenion grunted suddenly, and began to mutter in a language Paks didn't know. Suddenly Paks felt a great shove from the other side of the door. "Blast! Wrong one." Macenion began muttering again, as Paks held the door with all her strength. She heard an abrupt click, and found that she needed no strength to hold the door. Macenion sighed. "That should do it," he said. "I expect it will. You can let go now, Paks."

"What was that?" Paks noticed that Macenion still looked worried.

"I don't know how to explain it to you."

"Try."

"A sort of evil spirit, then, that can take solid form, and attack any intruder, elves preferred. It has many ways of attacking, all of them unpleasant."

"And a sword would be no use against it?"

Macenion laughed. "No."

"Is it the thing we came to find? What's holding the other thing prisoner?"

"No. Unlikely. I fear, though, that it may be in league with it. This may prove harder than I thought. And we certainly can't risk returning this way to the surface."

"Unless we've destroyed that thing." Paks felt better. Her intuition had been right after all, and, as always, the joining of the fight roused her spirits. Macenion looked at her curiously.

"Don't you understand? We can't destroy that — and we don't know any other way out. If what we're looking for is as bad or worse, we may never get out."

Paks grinned. "I understand. We took the bait, and we're in the trap: and we don't even know the size of the trap. But they, Macenion, don't know the size of their catch." She drew her sword and looked along the blade for a moment. "You managed to shut the door against that thing. I can deal with more fleshly dangers. And — I've been in traps before."

"Yes, but — Well, there's no help for it. We'd better keep moving. We want to be well away from that door if it breaks through."

They were in a short corridor, lit as the stairwell and hall had been, and ahead of them an archway gave into a larger room. Here, too, the floor was thick with dust. Paks led the way forward, sword out and ready. Macenion followed.

The room had obviously been a kitchen. Not a stick of furniture remained, but two great hearths, blocked up with hasty stonework, told the tale of many feastings. On the left, a narrower archway led to another corridor. On their right, a short passage led to another room, just visible beyond it.

"That should have been the cellar," said Macenion. "I wonder if any of the wine is left."

Paks chuckled. "After so long? It wouldn't be worth trying."

"I suppose not. We'll go this way, then." He gestured to the left. As they crossed the kitchen, Paks looked around for any sign of recent disturbance but saw nothing.

"Was that thing back there what drove the elves out?" asked Paks.

"No. I don't think so. Enough high elves together would be able to drive it away. It's — well, you humans know of gods, don't you? Good and evil gods?"

"Of course." Paks glared back at him for an instant.

"Do you know of the Court of Gods? Their rankings, and all that?"

Paks shook her head. "Gods are gods."

"No, Paksenarrion, they are not. Some are far more powerful than others. You should have learned that in Aarenis, even as a soldier. You fought in Sibili, didn't you? Yes — and didn't you see the temple of the Master of Torments there? I heard it was sacked."

Paks shivered as she remembered the assault on Sibili. "I was knocked out," she said. "I didn't see it."

"Well, you've heard of the Webmistress — "

"Of course. But what — "

"Liart — the Master of Torments — and that other, they're both fairly low in the court of evil. Between the least of the gods and the common evils of the world, there are still beings — they have more power than any human or elf, but not nearly so much as a god."

Paks was suddenly curious. "What about the heroes and saints like Gird and Pargun?"

"Who knows? They were humans once; I don't know what, if anything, they are now. But that creature, Paks, is more powerful than any elf, and yet is far below the gods. Our gods — the gods of elves."

The corridor they traveled curved slightly to the left. Paks glanced back and saw that the kitchen entrance was now out of sight. Ahead was a doorway blocked by a closed door, this one of carved wood. As they neared it, Paks noticed that the dust on the floor was not nearly so deep; their footsteps began to ring on the stone and echo off the stone walls. She wondered what had moved the dust. Macenion, when she pointed it out, looked around and shook his head.

"I don't know. Draft under that door, possibly — "

"Underground?" Paks remembered that she didn't know much about underground construction, and put that thought aside. She moved as quietly as possible toward the door. In the cool white light of the corridor, its rich red and black grain and intricate carving seemed warm and alive. She reached out to touch it gently. It felt slightly warm under her hand. "That's odd. It's — "

The door heaved under her hand; Paks jumped backward just in time to avoid a blow as it swung wide. Facing them were several armed humans in rough leather and woolen clothes; the leader grinned.

"'Ere's our bonus, lads!" he said. "The ears off these'll give us something to show the lord — "

Paks had her sword in motion before he finished; his boast ended in a howl of pain. She took a hard blow on her shield, and dodged a thrust meant for her throat. Behind her, she heard Macenion draw, then the ring of his blade on one of the others. The noise brought two more fighters skidding around the corner ahead to throw themselves into the fight. Paks and Macenion fought almost silently; they had no need for words. Paks pressed ahead, finding the attackers to be good but not exceptional fighters. She had the reach of most of them, and she was as strong as any. Macenion yelped suddenly, breaking her concentration; as she glanced for him, a hard blow caught her in the side. She grunted, grateful for the chain shirt she wore, and pushed off from the wall to skewer her opponent. Macenion's arm was bleeding, but he fought on. Paks shifted her ground to give him some respite. She took a glancing blow on her helmet that gashed her forehead as it passed. She could feel the blood trickling down toward her eye. Macenion lunged forward, flipping the sword away from one of their attackers; Paks downed the man with a blow to the face. They advanced again; the other attackers seemed less eager. Finally only two were still fighting. The others, dead or wounded too badly to fight, lay scattered on the corridor floor. Paks expected them to break away and flee, but they didn't; instead, they fought doggedly on, until she and Macenion managed to kill them.

Chapter Five

Paks leaned against the wall breathing heavily. Her side ached, and she could feel a trickle of blood running down the side of her face. Her shield had broken; she pulled the straps free and dropped the pieces. Macenion had ripped a length of cloth from his tunic, and was wrapping the wound on his arm. As he moved, she caught a glimpse of the bright mail under his outer clothing.

"If I'd known you wore mail," she said finally, "I wouldn't have worried so much. I was sure you were being skewered."

Macenion glanced up. "I nearly was. By Orphin, you're a good fighter in trouble. I wouldn't have made it alone, even with mail." He looked at her more closely. "You're bleeding — is it bad?"

"I don't think so. Just a cut on the head, and they always bleed — a mess." Paks swiped at her face with her free hand, and found the cut itself, a shallow gash near the edge of her helmet.

"Here — " Macenion sheathed his sword and came over. "Let me clean that out." Paks looked at the bodies on the floor as he wiped out the cut with something from a jar in his pack. It burned, but the bleeding stopped. The bodies did not move, this time. When Macenion finished, she pushed herself off the wall, grunting at the pain in her side, and wiped her sword clean on the dirty cloak of the nearest enemy. She wished they could stop and rest, but she distrusted the flavor of the air down here.

"I suppose we ought to keep going," she said, half hoping that Macenion would insist on rest and food.

"Definitely. Whatever set these guards will know, soon enough, that we've passed them. If we're to have any surprise at all, we'll have to go on. Why? Are you hurt?"

"No." Paks sighed. "Bruised, but no more. I wish we were out of here."

"As do I." Macenion gave a short laugh. "I begin to think that my elven relatives have more wit than I gave them credit for — they may have been right to tell me that I would find more trouble here than treasure."

But along with her fear and loathing of the underground maze in which they were wandering, Paks felt a pull of excitement. In a corner of her mind, she saw herself telling this tale to Vik and Arñe in an inn somewhere. She checked her sword for damage, finding none, and turned to Macenion. He nodded his readiness, and she set off carefully, sword ready.

They passed an open door into an empty room on their right, and another like it a few feet down on the left. Ahead of them, the corridor turned again. Paks looked at Macenion and he shrugged. She flattened against the wall and edged forward to the turn. She could hear nothing. She widened her nostrils, hoping for a clue to what lay ahead. Her own smell, and Macenion's, overwhelmed her nose. Finally, with a mental shrug, she peeked around the corner. An empty corridor, its dusty floor scuffed and disturbed. Four doorways that she could see in the one quick look she allowed herself. A crossing corridor a short run ahead.

"Do you have any of your feelings about any of this?" asked Macenion when she described what she'd seen.

"No. Not really. The whole things feels bad, but nothing in particular."

"Nor can I detect anything. I wish our friend who wants our help would give us some guidance."

Paks felt around in her mind to see if anything stirred. Nothing but a faint desire to get moving. She sighed. "Let's go, then."

The doors that opened off the corridor were all of wood; all bore the scars of some sort of fire. One gaped open, and they could see into a small room with stone shelves built into the walls. At the cross corridor, Paks took one corner, and Macenion the other. To the right, her way, the corridor ended in a blank stone wall perhaps fifty paces away. To the left, it opened after perhaps thirty paces into a chamber whose size they could not guess. Macenion cocked his head that way, and Paks began to edge along the wall of the cross corridor toward the chamber door. Macenion stayed where he was.

As she neared the opening, Paks felt a wave of confidence. Surely they were going the right direction. Macenion was being too cautious, as usual. She hesitated only a moment before putting her head around to see what the chamber was like.

Here, for the first time, she saw something not desolate and ruined. The floor, laid of pale green and gold stone blocks, had been swept clean of dust so that the pattern was clearly visible. At the far end of the chamber, a great ring of candles seemed to hover in midair. After a moment, Paks realized that they were attached to a metal framework suspended from a chain that ran to a ringbolt in the high ceiling. Candlelight warmed the cool white light of the corridors to a friendlier hue. In that warm glow, on a brilliantly colored carpet, stood a tall figure robed in midnight blue. Its face was subtly like Macenion's, and yet different; Paks knew at once that she stood in the presence of an elf of high rank. Along the far wall of the chamber stood several motionless figures clad in rough garments of gray and brown like poor servants.

Paks looked at the elf's face. Its bones showed clearly under the skin, yet with no sign of age or decay. The eyes were a clear pale green. She felt no fear, though she was fully aware of the elf's power, so much greater than Macenion's. The elf's wide mouth curved in a smile.

"Welcome, fair warrior. Was your companion too frightened to come so far with you?"

Paks shook her head, uncertain how to answer. She had the vague thought that no elves should be here. But perhaps this was the person they had come to help? She could not seem to think clearly. The elf was not frightened of her, and did not seem angry — and elves were, if uncanny, at least not evil. As she thought this, she realized that she was walking forward, moving out into the chamber.

"Excellent," the elf continued. "I shall be glad to receive you both into my service." He gestured to the line of servants. "You see how few I have, and you have just killed some of my best fighters. It is only fair that you take their place."

Paks found her voice at last. "But, sir, I have a deed to perform, before I can take service with another." She tried to stand still; her feet crept forward despite her efforts. She knew she should be afraid but she could feel nothing.

"Oh?" The silvery elven voice was amused. "And what is that?"

Paks found it difficult to say, or even think. A confusion of images filled her mind: the Halveric's face as he handed her a sealed packet, the Duke's parting words, the images of victory and glory that had come in the dream of the night before. She had advanced to the edge of the carpet. This close to the elf, she noticed a distinct, slightly unpleasant odor. Even as her nose wrinkled in distaste, the odor changed, becoming spicy and attractive. She drew a deep breath.

"Now — " the elf began, but at that moment, Macenion cried out from the far end of the chamber.

"Paks! What are you — "

Only for a moment those green eyes shifted from Paks; then the elf chuckled. "Well, so your companion finally gathered his courage. Stand near me, fair warrior, and show him your allegiance." And Paks stepped onto the soft carpet and stood silent beside the elf, unable to move or speak. She could just see Macenion from the corner of her eye. The elf went on. "You think yourself a mage, I understand — you have scarcely the powers to match me, crossbred runt."

Macenion reddened. "You don't know what I might have — " he began.

"If you had any abilities I need worry about, you'd not have walked into this trap. You sensed nothing, at the last turn — you said so."

Macenion glared, and slid his hand stealthily under his cloak.

The elf nodded. "Go ahead — try your little spells if you wish. It won't do any good. Nor will that wand. But try it, if you like — " He laughed. "Do you not even wish to know who it is that you face, little mage? Are you in the habit of loosing spells on chance-met strangers?"

"We are not chance-met, I fear," said Macenion. He came forward a short distance, then stopped. "And if I cannot put a name to you, still I have a good idea what you are."

"What and not who? What erudition! And what makes you think I cannot charm you to obedience, as I did your — delightful — companion, here?"

Macenion smiled in his turn. "Charm a mage? You well know what that would get you. If you would use me as a mage, you need my mind unclouded — "

"But not unbroken, little one. Remember that."

Macenion bowed, as arrogantly as Paks had ever seen him. "Yet a pebble," he said, "may be harder to break than a pine, though insignificant beside it."

"Are you to quote dwarvish proverbs to me?" The elf sounded slightly less amused than before. Paks, listening to all this, could scarcely pay attention to it; her mind seemed to float at a slight distance.

Macenion bowed again, even more elaborately; as he rose, he made a complicated movement of his right hand, and said a few words Paks did not understand. But she heard the hiss of breath indrawn beside her as the elf gasped. Before he could move, she felt a wave of nausea and fear. She whirled, sword at ready, before she even knew she *could* move. Where she had seen elven beauty, she now saw the ruin of it, and the stench stung her nose.

"Paks!" shouted Macenion. He was cut off by a great shout from the elf. A blast of energy poured down the chamber. Paks thrust at the elf, but her sword met another in his hand.

"Cross blades with me, will you?" The green eyes blazed. Paks tore her gaze from them to watch the sword hand. "No human has skill to match an elf — and I am no common elf." Indeed, the first ringing strokes revealed his ability. Paks fought on a rising wave of anger. Elves were never evil, ha! She avoided a quick trapping ploy, and thrust again. The tip of her blade seemed to hesitate an instant — an instant that let the enemy escape. She pressed on, furiously. Macenion had probably been killed by the blast, or disabled, but he had won her freedom from whatever spell had bound her. She would fight to the end, and show this creature what human skill could do.

Again and again she managed to slip aside from a deadly blow, and just as often her own attacks fell short. Sweat rolled down her ribs, and she heard herself grunting with every stroke. The elf did not seem to tire. The same smile curved his lips; the same arrogance arched his brows. Now her wrist began to ache, as he used every advantage of height and reach. She was usually taller that those she drilled with; she was not accustomed to adjusting to a longer reach. One of his blows fell true; the force of it drove her to one knee. She felt the links of mail sink into her flesh; she barely ducked the next blow and staggered back. She wanted to look for Macenion, but dared not. The elf's smile widened.

"You are outclassed, human fighter," he said lightly. "You are quite good, for a human, but not good enough. But look at my eyes, and acknowledge me your lord, and this can end."

Paks shook her head, as much to clear it as to refuse. Was that a movement behind the elf? She lunged again; her blade struck, but she narrowly avoided his. He seemed not to notice her blow. Suddenly a bit of hot wax fell

370

on her face. As quick as the thought that followed, almost before she knew what she meant to do, Paks leaped high, grabbing the framework the candles were set on with one hand, and jerking her legs away from the elf's astonished stroke. The frame swung wildly, spattering them both with wax. With one arm over the ring, Paks swung at the elf from above. He grabbed at her leg and missed as she kicked out. She heard a squeal from above and glanced up to see the ringbolt slipping from the ceiling. She threw herself to one side, trying to clear the frame as it fell. The elf, pursuing, was struck. Before he could free himself from the ring, Paks attacked. Hampered by the framework and the candles, which caught his robe afire, he parried her blows weakly.

And then Macenion came up, panting and pale, and threw the whole of their oil supply on the elf. Paks jumped back as the candle flames flared on this fuel. A foul stench filled the chamber, and a black cloud swirled up from the fire, denser than smoke. Paks felt a wave of cold enmity that sent her staggering to her knees. The flames roared, now more blue than any fire of oil could be. Air rushed into the chamber, whistling round the corners. Paks realized that Macenion was tugging at her arms, pulling her away. She could hardly move. She managed to look around, and saw that the others in the room, the servants, were shuffling out a door in one corner as fast as they could.

When the flames died down, Paks still crouched helplessly where Macenion had dragged her. The elf's body had not been consumed in the fire, though it was horribly blackened, and all the clothing was gone. Macenion stood by it, frowning.

Paks tried several times before she could speak. "What's — wrong? He's dead, isn't he?"

"I wish I knew. That kind of power — it was some spirit of evil, Paks, that took over the body of an elf. Of an elf lord. And the body is here still. I wonder if he is dead — truly. I've heard tales of such — "

Paks didn't want to move. Every muscle hurt. She managed to flex her hand, and found she still held her sword. She took a deep breath, which also hurt, and forced herself to her feet. She felt as if her legs and body were only loosely connected. Another deep breath. It was hard to believe that she and Macenion were still alive, and the elf was dead. Or dead in some way. She walked over to see.

"Your magic has done well so far, Macenion. We wouldn't be here without it. Can't you do something to make sure he stays dead?"

For once Macenion did not seem complacent. "No," he said soberly. "That's beyond my abilities. I wish my old master were here. We are fortunate that he chose a simple spell to bind you. Perhaps he wanted to have plenty left for me, or perhaps he had more in use than we know. But now — "

"Couldn't we put a stake through his heart?"

"What do you think he is, a kuerin-witch? Are you thinking of dragging his corpse to a crossroads, too?"

371

Paks flushed. "I don't know. I just remembered some old stories . . . "

"That won't work for him. Whatever took him over won't be withheld by any simple measures."

"We could — " Paks swallowed hard, then went on. "We could cut — dismember him."

"You? I? I know what you would think of such. As for me, I tell you, Paksenarrion, I don't even wish to touch that corpse, if corpse it is. Nor should you. That power may still dwell in it, and could reach out to us. You see that the body was not consumed by the fire as it should have been; the skin is blackened but unblistered."

"Well, then? Do we wait to see what comes of it, or what?"

Macenion shook his head. "I don't know. I wish I knew a spell to free this body from whatever power holds it so."

"But since elves are immortal, do their bodies burn or decay?"

"Elves do not die of age alone, but they can, as you saw, be killed. And yes, their bodies can burn or decay or return to earth in many ways."

Paks shifted her shoulders, easing the stiffness. Suddenly she was hungry — and thirsty. She put up her sword and fumbled to unhook her water flask. After a couple of swallows, she felt much better. "It's too bad," she said, "that you don't know what's in that fancy scroll you're so proud of."

Macenion scowled and opened his mouth for a quick retort, then paused. "I never thought of that," he said. "I wonder if — " and he rummaged around inside his tunic until he came out with the tooled scroll case Paks had commented on. "It's difficult — " he went on, as he flicked off the lid and slid the scroll out. "You remember I told you how expensive it was?" Paks nodded. "Thing is, a magical scroll — one that has on it a workable spell — can be written only by a magician who can cast the spell without it. I don't know why; it seems a silly rule, and it certainly gives far too much power to men who do nothing but study, but there it is. Usually a scroll belongs to the man who wrote it, or to someone he trusts: his journeyman, say, or a brother mage. He knows which scroll is which — or he sets his private mark on each — and all's well. But for someone who comes across one of these scrolls — far away from the person who wrote it — it's difficult to tell what it is without reading it."

"Then read it," said Paks, gnawing on a slab of dried meat. It was delicious. "You can read — ?"

"Of course, I can read! That's not the point. That's how it's used — by reading it. If I read it, whatever it is happens."

"Oh. So there's no way to — to peek?"

Macenion allowed himself to look amused. "No. Not that I ever heard of. There are a lot of teaching tales for young apprentice magicians that tell of attempts to peek and what happened afterwards. No, I must decide, by examining all the marks on the outside of the scroll and by my own abilities, whether it's worth chancing that the spell or spells on it will do us any good." He peered at the scroll itself, then at the case, and then back at the scroll.

"I might just take a look into the corridors," said Paks casually. "In case someone is coming — "

"Good idea. Then you'll be out of range if something does happen." Paks had not realized that Macenion would find her motive so obvious. She said nothing, but looked into the corridor diagonally opposite that from which she'd entered the chamber. This was the way the "servants" had left. She could see no one before the corridor turned, some twenty paces away. She looked back at Macenion. He was still examining the scroll, but he looked up at her and nodded. "Go on — not too far. I think I'll try one of these; for what I paid for them, they should be fairly powerful." Paks went on as far as the turn.

It seemed a long time before he called, a high excited yell. Paks swept out her sword and ran back to the chamber. She was just in time to see a blue flare lance to the ceiling from the elf's body. A dry clatter brought her eyes back to the floor; bones lay scattered there, and as she watched, they crumbled to dust. A draft scattered the dust. She looked up to meet Macenion's eyes. He was pale and trembling.

"It worked," she said unnecessarily.

"Yes. It — by Orphin, I'm tired. That — even reading it — that was beyond my powers — " He reeled, and Paks moved quickly to catch him before he fell. He lay some time unmoving. She could feel a pulse beating in his neck, so she folded her cloak under his head and let him rest. Some time later he opened his eyes and blinked. "What — ? Oh yes. That." Silently Paks offered him water and food. He took a long drink, and shook his head at the food. After another swallow, he rolled up to a sitting position and shook his head sharply.

"Do you think, Macenion, that that creature was what we came here to fight?" Paks had been worrying about this; if it were the servant of some greater evil, she had little hope of escape.

"I think so. That — was a considerable power. If it had chosen a better spell for you, or been more practiced at swordplay — we wouldn't be here."

"Then what were we to free? The elf's body? That couldn't have called us. What else is there?"

Macenion rubbed his face with both hands. "No. You're right. We haven't been greeted with cries of joy and armfuls of reward, have we? Something still to be done — by Orphin, I don't know if I can manage any more spells today."

"Maybe you won't need to. If whatever it was is trapped somewhere, all we need to do now is find it."

"I hope it's that easy." Macenion stood up, swaying slightly at first. "I just had a thought. I hope whatever it is wasn't trapped in a jewel or something worn by the elf. Some magicians do that sort of thing. If so, we're out of luck."

"If only we get out of this," said Paks, "we'll be *in* luck."

"True. Did you see anything down that corridor?"

"No. Nothing."

* * *

Paks was never afterwards sure what had guided their choice, with so many ways to go, and no knowledge. At first, as they walked the bare stone corridor, Macenion continued to eat, reaching out now and again to touch the walls as if for balance. Then the corridor sloped down, and he paused.

"Wait — " Macenion's face, when Paks turned, was grim. He pulled out his own sword, and tested the balance. "I sense something — "

"Not that thing in the Winter Hall!"

Macenion shook his head. "No. Not so dire as that. But it's as if my blood tingled — some enemy is below, and coming nearer."

Paks looked around for a good place to fight. The corridor was slightly too wide for two to hold. "We'd better go on, then, and hope for something we can use."

Macenion nodded, and came up beside her as they started off again.

"Don't you want to stay back and prepare your spells?"

"I told you — I can't do that again today. I'd never be able to cast a simple fire spell, let alone anything useful."

The corridor turned right, and continued downward. Paks felt edgy; she was increasingly aware of the weight of stone and earth above her. She found herself whispering words from a Phelani marching song. Macenion looked at her curiously, and she blushed and fell silent.

Suddenly Paks caught a foul whiff that stopped her short. "What's that?"

Macenion looked eager. "Ah. I might have known. Orcs, that's what. They would move in when the elves were driven away."

"Orcs?" Paks had heard of orcs; they had raided Three Firs in her great-grandfather's day, but she had not expected to meet any.

"Ugly but cowardly," said Macenion briskly. "If that was their master, they'll want nothing better than escape. They won't be looking for experienced fighters like us — "

"If they want to escape, we can let them," suggested Paks.

"Let orcs loose? Are you crazy? They're disgusting. Vermin, killers, filthy — "

"How many are likely to be in a group?" Paks didn't care how disgusting they were; enough orcs could kill them.

"Oh — not more than seven or eight. We can handle that many. I killed three by myself one time."

"But, Macenion — "

"Paksenarrion, I've seen you fight, remember? We have nothing to worry about. If we can handle that thing up there — " he jerked his head back where they'd been, " — we can handle a few orcs. Trust me. Haven't I been right on this so far?"

"I still think we should wait until we know how many there are. What if there's twenty? Let's find a hiding place, and — "

"Where?"

Paks looked around. Ahead, the corridor turned again twenty paces away, still going down. They had passed no doors for the last two hundred paces. She shrugged, and went on.

Around that corner the stench was stronger. Trash littered the floor. Paks looked for someplace to hide. Halfway to the next turn a doorway shadowed one wall. They had nearly reached it when they heard a harsh voice from somewhere ahead. Paks darted forward. The doorway was an empty gap opening into a tiny bare room. She grabbed Macenion's arm and pulled him in.

He glared at her, but said nothing as the voice came nearer in the corridor.

The first orcs were uglier than Paks had imagined. Greasy leather armor covered their hunched torsos; long arms banded with spiked leather hung nearly to the floor. The first carried a curved blade, badly nicked along the inner curve, and the second dragged a spear short enough to use in the corridor. Paks noted the spare knives in sheaths on both hips, and helmets that came low over the nose. Behind the first pair came another, whose voice they had heard. It wore a filthy fur cloak over its armor, and carried a spiked whip as well as a sword. Whatever it was saying to the others must have been unpleasant, for the spear carrier turned suddenly and growled back at it. Paks flattened herself into the angle of wall away from the door, and hoped the orcs would quit arguing and go on. Macenion, however, leaned toward the door. She realized suddenly that he was about to go out and attack. He looked back at her and cocked his head at the door.

If he attacked them and was killed, they'd be sure to look in the room. Paks cursed the stupidity of all magicians, and moved to the other side of the door, sword ready.

"It's only three," hissed Macenion. "We can take them easily."

Paks hoped so. The argument outside grew even louder. At least they could surprise the orcs. She took a deep breath and crouched. Now!

Her first blow caught the third orc low, in the thigh. His leg was harder than she'd expected, but she got her sword back, and he went down, bellowing. Macenion had gone for the spear carrier, and missed; the other sword bearer took one wild swipe at Macenion's head, then turned to Paks. The orc she had wounded flung its whip at her sword, and she dropped the tip just in time. The orcs moved faster than she'd expected. She parried the curved blade on one side, and danced back from the wounded orc's whip. Macenion was trying to get past the guard of the spear carrier. She didn't envy him.

Once out of reach of the wounded orc, she found fencing with the other one strange but not as hard as she'd feared. Its reach was almost as long as hers, but low; it couldn't match her height. She had little trouble defending herself. Attack was harder. Her overhead blows fell on heavy armor. Paks abandoned that tactic, and tested its quickness. Perhaps she could get behind it. She heard a yelp from Macenion, then a guttural command from the fallen orc. When she looked, Macenion was fencing left-handed, shak-

375

ing blood from his right hand. That was the second wound to that arm. She attacked her own orc with sudden ferocity, and made a lucky stab under the right shoulder. The orc fell, snarling, and stabbed at her legs. Paks skipped back and ran to Macenion's opponent. He could not use a spear in two directions at once. Paks ran him through when he thrust at Macenion. But before they could do anything about the first orc she had wounded, it was bellowing even louder.

"Gods above!" gasped Macenion. "There's more of them!"

Paks heard the clamor almost as he spoke. "Which way?"

"I don't know! I — " He stared wildly around.

"Here!" Paks ripped a length of cloth from his cloak, and wrapped it around his arm. "If we've got more to fight, you don't need to be dripping like that." She still could not tell where the sound came from; the corridor echoed confusingly.

"We'll go down," said Macenion suddenly.

"Down! But — "

"Come on!" He whirled away from her and strode down the corridor; the noise was much louder. Paks looked after him an instant, and ran to catch up.

"How do you know they're not — " But Macenion wasn't listening. He hurried ahead, and again she had to stretch her legs to catch him. "Macenion!" She caught at his arm as he neared the next turn.

It was too late. From around the turn erupted a wild band of orcs, stinking and dressed in filthy leather armor. Before she could guess how many they faced, she was engulfed in a deadly lacework of iron: swords, knives, and axes swung around her. The harsh clamor of their voices and the ring of blades filled her ears; all she could see was weapons and armor. Then she realized that Macenion was nearby, fencing with skill she had not suspected. That slender blade he bore had more strength than she'd thought.

"This way, Paks!" he yelled. He seemed to be edging ahead, still, and downward. Paks grunted and lunged toward him, taking a solid blow in one side as she came away from the wall. She felt the rings of her chainmail shirt dig in to the same place she's been hit earlier, but it held whatever blade that was. She caught one orc under the chin, and dodged another. The place swarmed — she saw a doorway, now, and another doorway, and orcs in both. She slipped on something underfoot, and staggered. Luckily they couldn't all reach her at once, and she hacked on, grimly determined to kill as many as she could before they killed her. She couldn't see Macenion.

Suddenly the orcs gave way in front of her, and she plunged through them to find herself in a circular chamber. In front of her, Macenion lay face down as he had fallen, an axe standing out of his back. Beyond his body was a focus of light that changed color as she looked. She whirled to face the orcs. They blocked the doorway, grinning and muttering. One at the rear of the mass yelled out, and they started toward her. She gave one quick glance to the chamber — no other door. And entirely too many orcs: no hope of winning through them all. She took a deep breath and laughed, at peace with her fate.

Afterwards she was never sure how she came to move into the light. As the orcs came forward, she ran to fight them over Macenion's body. They were too many, and pressed her back, and back again. Someone or something was calling her — wanted her to do something — but she had no time, no hands, for anything but the fight. As in a dream she felt one ragged blade catch her arm, and another stabbed deep into her leg. Orc stench choked her nose; she gasped for breath, with a sudden memory of the young soldier in her first battle, a wry grin for the girl who would never get home. Back, and back again, a step at a time. She kept expecting a blow from behind, but it never came. Her arm felt heavy and clumsy; her sword slid off an orc helmet as the dagger in her left hand parried another blade. She took a deep breath — her last, she thought — and lunged hard at the orc in front of her.

She could not reach him. He stood as close as her own arm, but his sword, thrusting at her, jabbing wildly, touched her not at all, nor hers, him. And a pressure filled her head, as if a river poured itself in one side and found no outlet. She felt herself falling under that pressure, her hand loosening, losing its grip on the dagger.

— Take — It was more picture than word: a hand, grasping.

Paks stared at her own hand, open as if it were reaching for something.

— Take . . . this . . . *thing* — The pressure moved her eyes; she looked as it directed, and saw a blue egg-shaped object. She could not tell how far away it was, or how big, or even what it was. She tried to frame a question. Instead, the command returned, and filled her whole head; she felt it would burst — TAKE IT —

She reached toward the object, and felt an unpleasant oily sensation on the insides of her fingers, as if they were sinking slightly into it. But her hand closed around the object firmly. It felt disgusting, in ways she could not describe, and had never imagined. She would have dropped it, thrown it far away, but it clung to her hand. When she tried to open her fingers, they wouldn't move. All at once she felt the pain of all her wounds, the exhaustion of all the fighting, a great heaving wave of sickness that seemed to cut her legs from under her. She tried to raise her sword for one last blow.

And the pressure within suddenly burst out in a vast roar, a vibration so deep she felt it in her bones and hardly at all in her ears. The light was gone — darkness churned around her — she caught a last confused glimpse of orcs screaming, falling stones, Macenion's body glowing blue as fire — then a deafening, whirling confusion.

And silence.

Chapter Six

When she managed to lift her head, she was lying on the turf near the well. The building they had entered had collapsed in a heap of stones. It was broad daylight, with the sun's warmth filtered through high clouds. Paks took a breath, and sneezed. She felt stiff and sore, and it was hard to think what had happened. Her head felt empty; her ears rang like a bucket. She looked at her hands — the one still cramped around the hilt of her sword, and the other empty, but with the feel of something filthy on it. She scrubbed it in the grass. Her eyes watered, and she swiped at them clumsily, with her sword hand.

She knew she should get up, but she wished she could lie there and rest forever. After a moment, sighing, she forced herself up: elbows, knees — she rested there for a bit. Her legs felt shaky and uncertain. She looked at her sword; blood and dirt were caked on it. She shuffled on her knees to the well, and took a handful of water to clean it. After a mouthful or two of that clear water, she began to feel more alert. The sword slid back in its scabbard sweetly — it feared nothing near. She looked around for the horses. Macenion's had disappeared; that seemed right. Star grazed unconcernedly across the well from her. There were the packs, lying open outside the ruins of the little building. Whatever had happened, there below, was over. She could do nothing for Macenion now. She must go on.

Even so she might have sat beside the well for the rest of the day if something had not moved her. The pressure she had felt before seeped back into her mind. This time it was more delicate: she was aware of it as a separate being. There were thanks, for her and Macenion. There were directions, specific and detailed. Slowly she rose to her feet, and slowly she gathered up her belongings. She wondered what to do with Macenion's things, and the being told her. This to the well, and that under a stone, and those to lie open on the grass, for the wind and sun to play with. Star came to her quietly, and she tied her pack to the frame.

Before she left, the being demanded one thing more. She was tired and found it hard to think, but the pressure gave her no ease until she obeyed. In that mound, through that gap — and take those things. She packed, vaguely aware that much of it was treasure: weapons decorated with gold and jewels, coins, rings and baubles. But why the scrolls? She didn't understand, but she obeyed, picking up what she was bid, and stowing it away in

Star's pack. As she worked, the clouds thickened overhead, and a chill wind rolled down from the mountains. She didn't notice. She felt no triumph, only a great tiredness.

As she stumbled away on the narrow track she had been nudged to follow, the first dancing flakes of snow fell from the thickening clouds behind her. Soon a light dusting whitened the tops of the mounds in the valley, outlined the limbs of trees and clung to the cedars in little furry clumps. The clouds reached out, northwards, and gathered in the trail Paks had taken. Snow hung in the air around her, filling her lungs with its damp clean smell. She hardly noticed. It was harder and harder to walk. Every step seemed to take the last of her strength, as if she were pulling her legs out of the ground. Her left hand still felt dirty, and she rubbed it on her trousers as she walked, without realizing it. Uphill — it was all uphill, trying to clear the ridge on the far side of the valley. Paks caught at Star's pack, clung to it, and the sturdy pony plowed on, through the deepening snow, ears flat and tail clamped down. Her left side caught the blast of wind off the mountains. Soon it was numb, and she stumbled, lurching into Star, and then back, to fall face-down in the snow. A wave of nausea swept over her, but she had nothing to heave. Her stomach cramped. She couldn't push herself up; she felt the snow on the back of her neck, and then nothing.

In the darkness the first elf mistook her snow-covered body for a drift of snow, and stumbled over it. His muffled curse disturbed the pony, huddled in a thicket nearby, and she snorted.

Quickly the next elves found the pony and soothed her, whisking the snow from her back, and running deft hands over the pack straps. Meanwhile the first elf felt what was under the drift, and called for more light. Torches flared in the windy darkness.

"A human." Contempt laced the silver voice.

"A robber by the look of it — her," said another, holding out the patched cloak.

"Robber indeed," said one of the elves near Star. "This little one is loaded with such treasure that she can hardly walk. And more than that, it comes from the banast taig."

"Mother of Trees! I had not thought even the humans bold enough to rob there. Or skilled enough to escape." The leader of the group looked at a dagger and sheath from the pack and shook his head. "With such to carry, it must not be escape, but something worse."

"She is alive," said the first elf, after finding a pulse.

"Not for long," said the leader. "We may not be able to challenge *that* evil, but we can deal with its minions. We can leave — "

"Look at this," said one of those going through the pack. He held out to the leader the sealed message from the Halveric. "Is this stolen as well?"

"We must know what we have here, before we decide what to do," added the one at Paks's side. "I feel no great evil in her." He had brushed the snow off her, and now caught his breath as he saw the rings on her hand. He worked off the one with the Duke's seal, and read the inscription inside. "This is no common robber, cousins. Here is a ring given for honor to a soldier of the Duke Phelan — Halveric's friend, and — "

"And we all know of Kieri Phelan. Yes. If she did not steal that as well. We shall wake her, then, and see what she says. I doubt that any fair tale can be told resulting in such as this bringing treasure out of the banast taig. But we shall see."

Paks was vaguely aware of voices talking over her head before she woke fully. They were strange-sounding voices, musical and light but carrying power nonetheless. Light glowed through her eyelids. She struggled toward it, and finally managed to raise her heavy lids.

"You waken at last," said one of the strange beings before her. He turned to speak to another, and Paks saw torchlight play over the planes of his face. It was clearly unhuman, and in it she saw full strength the strangeness that Macenion had shared. These must be elves. He looked back at her, his expression unreadable. "You were very cold. Can you speak now?"

Paks worked her jaw around, and finally managed to say yes, weakly.

"Very well. We have many questions for you, human warrior. It would be well for you to answer truthfully. Do you understand?"

"Who — are you?" Paks had no idea of elven politics, if any.

"Do you not know elves, human, when you see them?"

"I thought — elves — but who?"

Arched eyebrows rose up his forehead. "Do humans now concern themselves with the genealogy of elves, having so little themselves? If you would know, then, I am of the family of Sialinn — do you know what that means?" Paks shook her head. "Then you need know no more of my family. Who are you, and what lineage gives you the right to question elves?"

Paks remembered now Macenion's pride, and how Bosk had always said elves were haughty and difficult.

"I am Paksenarrion Dorthansdotter," she began. "Of Three Firs, far to the north and west — "

"Far indeed," said one of the other elves. "I have seen that place, though not for many years. Is there a birch wood, a day's ride west of it, in the side of a hill?"

"I don't know, sir; I never traveled so far before leaving to join the Duke's Company. Since then, I have never been home, or near it."

"Whose company was this you joined?"

"Duke Phelan's. He has a stronghold in northern Tsaia, and fights in Aarenis."

"A red-haired man?" Paks nodded, and the elf went on. "This packet sealed by the Halveric, in your baggage: how came you by that?"

"I was given it, by the Halveric, to take to his home." Even as she spoke, Paks felt the cold darkness rolling over her again. One of the elves exclaimed, and she felt an arm under her shoulders. A cold rim touched her lips, and fiery liquid trickled into her mouth. She swallowed. Warmth edged its way along her bones.

380

"Not too much of that," said the first elf who had spoken to her. "In case we must — " He broke off and looked at her again. "You have come to a strange place, soldier of Duke Phelan and messenger of the Halveric. You have come to a strange place, and you seem — forgive me — weaker than I would expect such a soldier to be. Give us now an account of how you came here, and what you were doing in the valley of the banast taig."

Paks found it difficult to tell a coherent story. Events and places were tangled in her memory, so that she was hard put to distinguish the encounters of the last day or so from those in the Valley of Souls. Still she managed to convey the call she and Macenion had received, and the outline of their adventures underground. The elves listened attentively, interrupting only to ask for clarification. When she finished, they looked at each other in silence. Then a burst of elven; it sounded to her like an argument. The leader turned to her again.

"Well, Paksenarrion Dorthansdotter, you have told an unlikely tale, to be sure. Yet on the chance that it is true, I am sending one of my party into the banast taig to find out. Should he not return, or return in jeopardy, it will go hard with you."

In the snowy darkness, Paks could not tell how long the elf was gone. She lapsed into a doze, hardly aware of her surroundings. She was roused by a hand on her shoulder.

"Awake, warrior. You will need this — " and a hot mug pressed against her lips. She swallowed, still half asleep, and found the taste strange but pleasant. Slowly her drifting mind came back to her. She tried to sit up on her own, but was still too weak. The elves had pitched a shelter over her, and a tiny fire flickered in one corner, under a pot.

"You still need healing," said the elf leader. "I admit surprise, Paksenarrion. I would not have believed such a thing without proof. The banast taig freed to be the elfane taig again, and the pollution gone from its heart! We rejoice to know that. But you have taken more damage from that combat than you know; humans cannot fight evil of that power unscathed. Without healing, you would die before daylight."

Paks could not think what to say. She felt weak, and a little sick, but no worse than that. She had no idea what "banast taig" and "elfane taig" were; the being that had summoned them had never named itself to her. As the elf seemed waiting for something, she finally asked, "Was — did you find out about Macenion?"

"Macenion!" It was very nearly a snort. "That one! The elfane taig buried him cleanly with his orcish murderers; he is well enough."

"But he was an elf — half-elf, I meant. I thought you would — "

"Macenion a half-elf? Did he tell you that?" Paks nodded, and the elf leader frowned. "No, little one, he was not half-elven — not a quarter elven, either. He had so much elven as might your pack pony have of racing blood."

"But he said — " Paks broke off. It was hard to talk, and she realized that

381

Macenion's behavior made more sense the less elven he was.

"He lied. What did he tell you, Paksenarrion, to get you into that valley?"

"That — his elven cousins — denied him his rights to elven things. That he knew of — treasure there — that should be his."

"Did he not warn you of evil at all?"

"Yes — but he said his magical talents could fight that; he needed a warrior for protection against — physical things. Like the orcs."

"I see that you speak truly. I apologize, Paksenarrion, for the untruth of this distant cousin; it shames me that any elven blood could lie so."

"That's — all right." Paks felt as if she were slipping down a long dark slope.

"No! By the gods of men and elves, we shall redeem the word of our cousin." And the elf shook her again, lifting her up until she could drink from a cup one of the others held. The darkness crept back. The elven faces came back into focus. Then one of them laid his hand on her head, and began to sing. She had never heard anything like that, and in trying to follow the song she forgot what was happening. Suddenly she felt a wave of strength and health surge through her. The elf removed his hand, and smiled at her.

"Is that better now?"

"Yes — much better." Paks sat up, and stretched. She felt well and rested, better than she'd felt in days.

"Good. It will be day, soon, and we must be going. We have much to say to you in the few hours left us."

The snow had stopped before dawn. A light wind tore the last clouds to shreds and let the first sunlight glitter on the snow. In daylight the elves bade her farewell, and Paks saw their beauty clearly. She felt ashamed to have thought Macenion elvish-looking. One of them caught her thought, and laughed, the sound chiming down the long slope.

"No — don't be sorry, fair warrior. Your eyes saw truly, to find what was there in so little. Remember what we have told you, and fare well."

And as she turned to climb the slope upward to the ridge and the trail the elves had spoken of, she felt far distant from the self of yesterday. She felt a surge of the same spirit that had sent her away from home in the first place, a sense of adventure and excitement. Anything might happen — anything had happened. She still found it difficult to think clearly what it was — what nature of thing she and Macenion had fought against, and what had helped her at the end. The words elfane taig meant nothing to her. The elves' explanation meant very little more.

But she was on a trail once more, alive and eager to be going. Star moved slowly, burdened heavily by the gifts of the elfane taig. Paks had transferred some of that to her own back. The pony snorted a little with each heave of her hindquarters. Paks grinned to herself. No more mountains, they had told her. These, that would have been mountains anywhere else, counted as foothills, and in another two days she would be in the gentler lowland slopes.

On the far side of the ridge, only a few patches of snow whitened the trail, and by noon these had melted. Now other trees mingled with the pointed evergreens — duller greens, more rounded shapes. Paks did not need her cloak for warmth. She was alert for danger, but the elves had told her that they sensed nothing dire moving in the area. She hoped they were right. As far as she could see, the forested slopes wove into each other endlessly, the trail angling down one and up another, always edging west and north.

Her solitary camp that night was almost too silent. She had resented Macenion's lectures — yet to sit alone, in the middle of a vast wilderness, was worse than anything he had ever said to her. She doused her tiny fire early, and sat awake a long time, staring at the stars. The night was half gone when she realized that she was missing more than Macenion. She had never, in her life, spent an entire night alone like this. Not even once had she slept outside, out of hearing or sight of others. The thought itself made her shiver, and she got up to check on Star. The pony's warm rough mane reassured her. She looked at the stars again, her hands still tangled in Star's mane. The night sky seemed to go on forever, up and up without ending, as if the stars were sewn on veils that lay one behind another. She looked for Torre's Necklace; it was still behind the mountains. Of the other stars she knew nothing.

A breeze slid lightly along the ground, chilling her. Star moved away from her hand, and lowered her head to graze. Paks went back to the blankets she'd laid out. A wild animal cried out in the distance; she stiffened, but no sound followed. Paks felt an urge to take out Canna's medallion; her hand found her pouch before she thought. Her fingers touched it, smoothed the crescent shape. When she pulled it out, Saben's little horse came along; the thongs were tangled. She woke stiff and cold in the morning, with Star nosing her face, and the horse and crescent still clutched in her hand.

That day warmed quickly. Paks looked over the whole treasure she had been given, and made her first estimate of its value. She had not realized what she'd taken — it was too much — it shouldn't be hers. But she could not return to the elfane taig with it, that was certain. She thought the elves must have examined it as well, and if they said nothing about it. . . . Sunlight glittered on the items she'd laid in the grass — the ruby-decorated dagger and sheath, the gold and jewel inlaid battleaxe, gold and silver coins, both familiar in stamp and strange, a set of chainmail that felt oddly light when she lifted it, and looked as if it would fit. She thought about that, looked around, and tried it on. It did fit — perfectly — which made her scowl, thinking. Where had she heard of enchanted mail, evil stuff — ? But when she reached for Canna's medallion, nothing happened; it felt easy in her hand. Was it dress mail, then, good for nothing? She tried her own dagger on the sleeve, notching the dagger. Lightweight, the right size — she scowled again, but kept it on. Over it she put on the best clothes she had — not that any of them looked like much, she thought ruefully, remembering the money she'd spent in Sord to outfit herself.

It was late when she started moving again, and she traveled slowly, as much for her own benefit as the pony's. She was beginning to wonder what she would find when she came out of the wilderness into settled lands again. The elves had been quite specific in their directions — go to Brewersbridge, they had said, by this trail, and tell the Master Oakhallow and Marshal Deordtya about the elfane taig. But they would say no more about either Master Oakhallow or the Marshal, or why these would want to know about events so far away.

As Paksenarrion came around the slope of the hill, she could see cleared fields and orchards some miles ahead, their straight edges easily visible against the broken forest and meadowland. The track's gradient lessened as she descended; sheep grazed on the slopes to her right, a barelegged child with a crook watching them from a rock. Gradually the track changed from rock to dirt. Star stepped out more easily. Paks lengthened her own stride to keep up. She saw smoke rising from the center of the cleared area; perhaps it was the village the elves had spoken of. She wondered if the people were friendly. At least it was the north again: home.

Soon she was among the fields and orchards. She had passed two farmsteads set back from the road. The farms looked prosperous; she noted tight barns, well-made stone walls, sleek livestock. A boy picking early apples from a tree near the track told her the village ahead was Brewersbridge; when she'd passed she looked back and saw him running for the farmhouse. Now the track joined a lane, bordered on either side by a wall, wide enough for wagon traffic. She noted wheelruts grooving the surface. On the right, a wedge of forest met the road; she could not tell how large it was. Ahead were a cluster of buildings and another road coming in from the right.

Two cottages now on the left, one opening directly on the road. Beyond them was a large two-story building with a walled courtyard to one side. A bright green and yellow sign hung over the road, and a paved area fronted it. Paks squinted at the sign: *The Jolly Potboy*. It must be an inn; it was too big for a tavern. She looked around.

The inn sat at the crossroad, facing north. The road Paks had come on continued generally west, wandering among houses and shops. The north road was straighter, with buildings along its west side, and forest on the east. The ground floor of the inn had a row of tall windows facing the road; these were open, and Paks heard the murmur of many voices from inside. She wondered if she had enough money to stay there. The treasure — but she didn't know what it was worth, or if they would accept the old coin.

As she hesitated, a stout man in a big apron came out and spoke to her.

"Just arrived?"

"Yes, sir."

"Will you be wanting a room?"

"I don't know, sir. How much are they?"

"A silver in the common loft; that includes bread and beer for breakfast. A gold crown for a private room; two for the suite. A silver a day for stabling, including grain, hay, grooming, and safe storage for your tack."

Paks thought a moment. It seemed high, but she had enough southern money for a night or two. She could always find a cheaper place the next day. Star could use a good bait of grain. "I'd like a private room," she said. "And stabling for Star."

"That'll be in advance, please," said the man. "I'm Jos Hebbinford, the landlord."

Paks wrapped Star's lead around her arm and dug into her belt pouch. "Here — " she handed over the money. "I'm Paksenarrion Dorthansdotter, from Three Firs."

The landlord looked closely at the coins she had given him. "Hmm. From Aarenis — that your home?"

"No, sir. Three Firs is north and west of here. I was with Duke Phelan's Company in the south, and I'm headed home."

"I see. A fighter, are you?" Paks nodded. "Are you a Girdsman too?"

"No. I've known those who were."

"Hmmm. We don't think much of brawling, here."

Paks flushed. "I'm not a brawler, sir."

"Good. Just a moment — Sevri! Sevrienna!" At his call, a short stocky redheaded girl came out of the courtyard and ran up. "My daughter, Sevrienna," said the landlord. "Sevri, this is Paksenarrion, who will be staying this night. This is her horse — " He glanced at Paks.

"Her name's Star," said Paks. "She's gentle."

"Sevri will take her to the stable," said Hebbinford. "If you'd like to see your room — ?"

"If you don't mind, sir," said Paks, "I'll just give Star a rubdown first, and check her hooves. She's come a long way over rocks."

"Very well. Sevri will help you. When you come in, I'll take you to your room."

"Come on — this way," said Sevri. Paks followed. The walled courtyard was large, paved in flat slabs of gray stone. A flock of red and black hens scratched and pecked in the entrance of the stable that ran along one side; a black cock with gold on his throat and a green tail stood atop the dungheap. Along other sides of the courtyard were barns full of hay and an open shed with two wagons and a cart beneath it.

Sevri led Paks to a box stall big enough for a warhorse; all the stalls were big. "I can rub her down," Sevri offered. "You're paying for grooming."

Paks smiled at the child. "I want to check her and make sure she hasn't hurt her hooves on the rocks. If you want to rub her down — "

Sevri nodded. "Surely. She'll be easier than the big horses, and I do them. Do you want her to have grain, or would a mash be better?"

"A mash would be good for her, if it's not too much trouble."

"I'll put one on, then come back and start on her. If you want water to work on her feet, here's a bucket, and the well is out there." Sevri jerked her head toward the courtyard.

When Sevri had gone, Paks untied the bundles from the saddle, and lifted them down. Star sighed. "Poor pony," said Paks. "That was a load. Here now —" She uncinched the pack saddle and lifted it from Star's back. Underneath, Star's coat was matted and damp. Paks moved the bundles to one side of the stall, and bent to feel Star's legs. Then she took the bucket Sevri had pointed out, and filled it at the well. Back in the stall, she lifted Star's feet, one at a time. They were dry and hot. Paks found a rag in her pack that she'd used for a headcloth and dipped it in the water. She washed out each hoof and dampened the coronary band. The pony reached down and mumbled Paks's hair. "No, Star; stop that." Paks shoved the pony's head away. She found a cut on the off hind pastern, and cleaned it carefully.

"You must like her a lot," said Sevri. Paks jumped.

"I didn't hear you come."

"That's because I'm barefooted," said Sevri. "Are her feet all right?"

"Yes, but for one little cut. Just dry from the rocks."

"She is wet. You want me to start rubbing her now?"

"Yes. Just let me get these things out of the stall." Paks grunted as she hoisted the bundles. She dumped them in the aisle. Sevri was watching her.

"That must be awfully heavy."

"It is," said Paks shortly.

Sevri had brought two lengths of coarse woolen cloth and a brush. When she picked up one cloth and started work on Star's sweaty back, Paks took the other and began the other side.

"You don't have to help me," said Sevri. "I can do it by myself."

"Do you mind, though? I'm used to doing her."

"No-o. But I am strong enough."

"I don't doubt that," said Paks, though she did. Star turned her head and nudged Sevri with her soft nose. Sevri stopped and stroked Star's head.

"She's gentle," said Sevri. "Have you had her long?"

"Not very. She is a good pony, though — seems to like everyone. Only don't come near her with apples unless you want to lose a few."

Sevri laughed. "I'll bring her one. Is she greedy about other things?"

Paks shrugged. "She's a pony. I've never known a pony that wouldn't eat anything it could find, have you?"

"That's true." Sevri looked across Star's back at Paks. "Are you a fighter?"

Paks paused before answering. "It depends on what you mean by fighter. Your father seems to think a fighter is the same as a brawler, a troublemaker. That's not what I am. I was a mercenary, a soldier in the Duke's Company."

"But you can use that sword?"

"Oh, yes. I can use a sword. That's how I've earned my keep since I left home. But that doesn't mean I go picking fights everywhere."

"I see." Paks thought by the tone of Sevri's answer that she didn't see. She decided to change the subject.

"Sevri, I have a message for two people here: can you tell me where to find them?"

"Surely."

"One is a Master Oakhallow — " She stopped as Sevri gasped audibly.

"You — you know Master Oakhallow?"

"No, I don't know him; I've never been here before. But someone I met a few days ago gave me a message for him. What's wrong?"

"Nothing. He's the Kuakgan, that's all."

Paks felt a chill. "Kuakgan? I didn't know that."

Sevri nodded. "He's a good man, it's just — he's very powerful, Master Oakhallow. My father's told me about him; he helped in the troubles."

Paks said, "Well, I must speak to him, at least. Where is he?"

"In his grove, of course. I'll show you, when we're through. Which way did you come in?"

"From the southeast." Paks pointed.

"Well, then, you saw part of the grove on your right, as you came into town."

"I remember. I was surprised to see uncleared forest so near the town."

"Don't go in except by the entrance," said Sevri. "It's dangerous. Now: who else was it you wanted to find?"

"There's a grange of Gird here, isn't there?" Sevri nodded. "I must speak to a — a Marshal, I think it was, by the name of Deordtya."

Sevri stared. "She isn't here any more. We have a new Marshal now, called Cedfer, and a yeoman-marshal called Ambros. But what kind of message can you have for the Kuakgan and the Marshal?"

"I'm sorry, Sevri, but I must speak with them first."

"Oh. Of course, I shouldn't have asked."

"That's all right. Now, where can I put the packsaddle, and where's a safe place for these bundles?"

"Here — " Sevri ducked around Star and led Paks down the aisle. "Put your things here — and I'll be around watching, if you'll trust me. You can leave your bundles here too."

Paks looked at the freckled face and wondered.

"They'll be safer here than in your room," said Sevri frankly. "The rooms have locks, but father's fairly sure we have a thief staying with us. Nothing's happened yet, but — I can watch your things, out here."

Paks sighed. "All right, Sevri. I'll be back when I've made my visits."

"Don't miss supper," said Sevri, grinning. "We have good food."

Paks smiled back at her. "I won't miss dinner, not after my journey." She left the stable and entered the inn. The landlord saw her at once and came forward.

"Sevri taking care of you?"

"Yes, sir. She's most helpful."

"Come this way — upstairs — to your room." He turned and led the way

387

across the main room to a broad stone stair. Paks followed, glancing about. The main room evidently served as both tavern and dining room; it was furnished with tables and benches. Half a dozen men were scattered about the tables drinking; two were men-at-arms in blue livery, one was dressed all in black, with a black cloak over trousers and tunic, two looked like merchants, in long gowns, and one was a huge burly fellow in a patched leather tunic over russet hose. Two women sat near the fireplace: the gray-haired one drew out yarn on a hand spindle, while the dark one marked something in a book. Paks went on up the stairs.

A landing at the top of the stairs opened onto a passage on one side and a fair-sized room with pallets in it on the other. The landlord led the way down the passage, past two doors on the left, and three on the right, to stop at the third on the left. He took a ring of keys from his belt and fitted one to the lock. The door swung open silently.

The room was compact but not cramped. A sturdy wooden bedstead with a thick straw pallet on it stood against the left-hand wall. Linen sheets were stretched over the pallet, and two thick wool blankets were folded at the foot. A three-legged stool stood at the foot of the bed, and a low chair of leather stretched on a wood frame stood under the window. A row of pegs ran down both walls of the room, and a narrow clothespress stood beside the door. The walls were whitewashed, the wooden floor scrubbed, and the room smelled as clean as it looked. Paks looked out and saw the the window overlooked the crossroads.

"Will this do?" asked the landlord.

"Oh, yes. It's very nice," said Paks.

"Good." He worked the key to the room off his ring and handed it to her. "Return this, please, before you leave. Is there anything more?" Paks shook her head, and he turned away. Paks shut the door, then took down her hair and combed it. If she was to see a Kuakgan and a Gird's Marshal, she would be neat, at least. She brushed her cloak as well as she could, rebraided her hair, and left the room, locking it carefully behind her.

Chapter Seven

Paks left the inn, wishing she didn't have to go. She felt eyes watching her from the inn's wide windows; her shoulders twitched. Evening light glowed in the changing foliage of the trees on her right; a few shrubs were already brilliant crimson. She saw two men-at-arms in the local livery coming toward her. They stared, and she returned the stare coolly, hand near the hilt of her sword. One opened his mouth, but his companion nudged him in the ribs and they passed by in silence.

Ahead on the right she saw a break in the wall of trees and leaves. As she came closer, she saw that it was an arch of sorts: vines binding branches, with a narrow path winding away toward the wood. Paks paused before the opening. She could wait until morning, she thought, and started to turn away — but there on the road were more men-at-arms, and these moved toward her. She stepped under the arch and went in.

She had taken only a few steps when she became aware of the silence. Voices from the road did not penetrate the grove. Her own breathing seemed loud. She slowed, and looked around. Trees, irregularly spaced. More light than she would have expected under the trees, but — she looked up and saw leaves worn and frayed with autumn. Golden light spilled through. The path, though narrow, was easy to see, picked out in rounded white stones that looked like river cobbles. She moved on, alert and watchful. Sevrienna had not had to warn her about Kuakkganni and their groves. Everything she had ever heard about them told of their peril.

A gust of wind stirred the dry leaves around her. As that rustling faded away, she heard somewhere ahead the gentle laughter of falling water. The path twisted once, then again. The trees framed more light: a glade, open to the sky. Almost in its center, she saw a simple fountain, water welling up in a stone basin and trickling over the edge to fall into another, and then another. The last formed a small pool from which Paks could see no outlet. Beside the fountain stood a rough block of stone with a wide bronze basin on top. Paks moved toward it, alert and watchful. Now she could see a low gray house, close under the trees on the far side of the clearing; it looked rough as a fallen tree trunk. Paks made out a door and windows, shuttered, but nothing else. The clearing was otherwise empty.

Still nervous, Paks neared the fountain. Its water lay perfectly clear, a silken skin that rippled with every breath of air; the falling drops from one

389

level to the next sparkled like jewels in the long, slanting rays of the sun. She tore her gaze from the water and approached the bronze basin on its pedestal of stone. An offering basin, she was sure: but what offerings were acceptable to Kuakkganni? Childhood memories of the dark tales her grandfather had told clouded her mind. Blood, he'd said. Kuakkganni follow the oldest gods, and blood they demand.

"It is customary to place one's offering in the basin." The voice rang deep and resonant, complex. Paks jerked her head up and found herself face to face with a tall, dark-faced man in a hooded robe of greens and browns. Her heart leaped against her ribs; she felt sweat spring out on her back. She had heard nothing.

"Sir, I — " she swallowed, as her voice failed, and tried again. "Sir, I know not what offerings would be acceptable — to a Kuakgan."

The heavy brows arched. "Oh? And why would one with no knowledge of Kuakkganni come seeking one?"

Paks found it hard to meet those dark eyes. "Sir, I was told to."

"By whom?"

"By the elves, sir." Paks did not miss the sudden shift of shoulders, the movement of brows and eyelids.

"Go on, then. What elves, and why?"

"Sir, the elves of the Ladysforest. The one who sent me said that he was of the family of Sialinn."

"And his message?"

"That the elfane taig was once more awake, and lost elf freed."

"Ahh. That is news indeed. And did he chance on you, to be his messenger, or had he other reasons?"

"I had been there — " Paks began to shiver, remembering as if it were happening the final conflict in the round chamber.

"Hmmm. So there is more reason than chance. Well, then, I'll have your name, wanderer, and you shall indeed offer something to the peace of the grove which you displace."

"My name is Paksenarrion Dorthansdotter — "

"From the northwest, by your patronymic. And for an offering, what have you?"

Paks pulled the little pouch out of her tunic. "Sir, as I said, I do not know what would please — but I have these — " She poured out on her palm the largest jewels from the treasure.

"Any would be acceptable," said the Kuakgan. "Place your offering in the basin." Paks wondered why he did not simply take one, but chose a green stone from them and set it carefully at the base of the bowl. The others she returned to the pouch.

"And I," said the Kuakgan as if continuing a sentence, "am Master Oakhallow. As you knew, a Kuakgan. But I think you must have strange ideas, child, of what Kuakkganni are — what, then?"

To her surprise, Paks found herself telling her grandfather's lore. "And he said, sir, that — that Kuakkganni ate babies — sir — at the dark of midwinter."

"Babies!" The Kuakgan sounded more amused than angry. "That old tale still! No, child, we don't eat babies. We don't even kill babies. In fact, if you use that sword you're wearing for anything but decoration, I daresay you've spilled more blood than I have."

Paks stared at him. Despite the undertone of amusement in his voice, he still radiated power. She wondered if he could tell what she was thinking. Macenion had said that wizards could — were Kuakkganni the same?

"Are you a warrior?" he pursued, when she said nothing.

"Yes, sir."

"Hmm. And involved somehow in the wakening of the elfane taig. Well, then, tell this tale: where are you from that you came to that dread valley, and what happened?"

Paks looked again at his face, trying to gauge his mood. She could have done as well with a stone, she thought, or a tree. His dark eyes seemed to compel her to go on. She began, haltingly enough, to explain that she had left a mercenary company in Aarenis to return to the north. When she came to tell of her companion, the Kuakgan stopped her abruptly.

"Who did you say? Macenion? He said he was an elf?"

"Yes, sir." Paks wondered at his expression. "Later he said he was but half-elven — "

"Half-elf! Hmmph! No wonder the elves sent you here." He motioned for her to continue. She went on to tell of the early part of their journey, at first slowly, but warming up to it when describing Macenion's behavior among the wardstones. Her resentment flared again: he had lied to her, he had pretended to knowledge he didn't have, he might have gone on and left her. . . . She stopped abruptly, at the look on the Kuakgan's face. Suddenly that quarrel seemed silly, like the attempt of a half-drunken private to explain to Stammel that a drinking companion was really to blame. She rushed on, skimping the rest. This was no time to bring up the snowcat. Then she came to Macenion's decision to enter the valley of the elfane taig.

"He said whatever was there wouldn't hurt me, because I was human, and the power was elvish. He said that the elves had tried to keep him away out of jealousy, but he knew he could control whatever evil was there, and regain his inheritance."

"And what did you think, human warrior?" Paks could not tell if his deep voice was scornful or merely interested. She felt the same confusion at his questions as at the elves' persistent interrogation. Why would anyone expect her to have an opinion about something like the elfane taig? She explained about the dreams, and Macenion's confidence in his own wizardry.

"Did you trust him?" asked the Kuakgan, in the same tone.

Paks remembered too well the sinking feeling she'd had as they entered the outer wards. But he had died well; if he had lived, she would have trusted him more. "Yes," she said slowly. "He could be good with a sword. And he could make light, and windshift, and that."

The Kuakgan looked at her closely. "Don't lie to me, child. Did you truly trust him, as you would have trusted a member of your old company?"

"No, sir." Paks stared down at the grass blades between her feet.

"And yet you went with him, knowing that powers a human should not face lay below?" Put that way, her decision sounded worse than foolish.

"Not *knowing*, sir." She took another breath, and tried to explain. "I felt danger, and was worried, but I didn't know what we faced. And we had traveled together for weeks. Besides, he knew more than I — "

The Kuakgan frowned. "You said that before. You seem to be convinced of it. And so you followed this so-called half-elf, whom you did not trust, into unknown dangers. Followed him, it seems, even to the depths of that ruin?"

"Yes, sir." She went on with her story, not quite sure how much detail to put in. When she came to her first sight of the old elf-lord, she stopped short, trembling and sweating. She could scarcely get her breath, and her vision blurred.

"No," came a firm voice, like a command, and a sharp scent tickled her nose. She took a long breath, and saw the Kuakgan's brown hand beneath her face, tough fingers twisting some aromatic gray herb. "You must tell this tale," he said, "but I will make it easier. Sit there, on the pool's edge." Paks sank down, her sword banging against her leg. The Kuakgan scattered more leaves on the pool, and their scent seemed to clear her head. "Now," he said above her. "Now go on."

She was able to continue by clenching her mind to the task, forcing out the words phrase by phrase. Since her wakening to the elves' care, she had carefully avoided those memories, and they lay bright and sharp as shards of glass, still painful. She could see the elf-lord's ravaged face, the strange blue flames, the very chips and notches on the orcs' weapons. Their stench sickened her; their hoarse cries rasped her ears. Macenion's body lay once more dead at her feet.

"We couldn't stay together," said Paks bleakly, unaware of the tears that ran from her closed eyes. "I tried to stay near him, but — "

"Enough." A strong hand gripped her shoulder. "And what of the elfane taig?"

"The elfane taig?"

"That which you freed."

She had never understood what happened at the end; describing it clearly was impossible. But again the disgusting touch of whatever she had had to take shriveled her mind. And then, with relief, she told of the escape, of the journey from the valley, and the falling snow.

"When did the elves find you?" asked the Kuakgan.

"That night, I think. I don't remember. I woke, and it was cold, and snowing, and dark. I couldn't move. The elves were there; at first they seemed angry, and then suddenly they were kind."

"Hmmm." The Kuakgan sat, suddenly, in front of her. "Paksenarrion Dorthansdotter, you give your name freely — look at me." Paks looked, and could not look away. She could not say afterwards how long she met the Kuakgan's gaze. He broke it at last, rose, and offered a hand up. "Well," he said briskly, "you're an honest warrior, at least. Kuakkganni rarely have to do with warriors, but I've been known to make exceptions." Paks stood, once more aware of the glade's silence. "Are you planning to be here long?" he asked.

"I don't know, sir. I might be, if someone hired me; otherwise I'll be going on when Star has rested from the mountains."

"You're looking for work? As a fighter?"

"Yes, sir. At least — I want to send my father what he paid on my dowry before I left."

The Kuakgan's eyes shifted to look at the jewel winking in the offering basin. "Hmmm. If you've many of that quality, I'd think they would cover most dowries. Was your father a wealthy man?"

"No, sir. A sheepfarmer, near Three Firs. He had his own land and flocks, but he wasn't rich. Not the way people are in cities."

"I see. You should have those things valued, then. I think you have enough for repayment of any likely sum. But tell me, what sort of employment were you hoping for, after the mercenaries?"

Paks flushed at the tone of his question. "It was an honorable company, sir," she said firmly. "I wasn't sure — I thought a guard company perhaps. The Duke suggested that."

"Duke? What Duke?"

"Duke Phelan, of Tsaia — "

"Ah," he broke in. "The Halveric's friend? A redhead?" When Paks nodded, the Kuakgan went on. "So that's the company you've been in. Why did the Duke suggest you leave, young warrior?"

Paks did not want to get into that question, least of all to a Kuakgan. Her confusion and reluctance must have shown, because the Kuakgan shook his head. "Never mind, then. I have no right to ask that, unless the answer poses a danger for those under my care, and I judge it does not. But tell me, did the elves give you any other message here?"

"Not to you, sir. They did say I should speak to Marshal Deordtya, but the innkeeper's daughter said that she was no longer here: she said a Marshal Cedfer had taken her place."

"The elves sent you to Girdsmen?" The Kuakgan seemed surprised at this.

Paks didn't want to answer any more questions. "Yes, sir, and I'd better be going now — "

"You just arrived this afternoon. Are you in such a hurry?"

Paks sensed more behind the simple question and took refuge in stubborn adherence to duty. "Yes, sir. They told me to come to you, and to the Marshal. I should do that as soon as I can."

"Well, then, Paksenarrion, I expect I'll see you again. You may come here, if you want to, and you need not bring such an offering each time. One of Jos Hebbinford's oatcakes will do."

"Yes, sir. Thank you." Paks was not sure why she was thanking the Kuakgan, but she felt much less afraid of him, though she didn't doubt his power. When he nodded dismissal, Paks turned and went back along the path to the north road. As she stepped through the arch of vines and trees, the village noises returned. A boy and a small herd of goats were jogging toward the crossroads; the goats baaing loudly. Somewhere nearby a smith was at work; the cadenced ring of steel on anvil made Paks think of Star's worn hooves. She wondered if it was a farrier or a weaponsmith. She looked about, but the sound came from behind the first row of buildings, and she decided not to look for it right away. At the crossroad, she turned right, as Sevri had told her, toward the Gird's grange, and followed a curving lane past one small shop after another. Faces glanced out at her, curious; those she passed in the street looked sideways: she felt the looks.

The lane angled around a larger building, set back in a fenced yard, and dipped toward a small river. Over the river rose a stone bridge, unexpectedly large, with handsome carved endposts on the parapets. Upstream a millwheel turned slowly; downstream on the near bank was a large building and yard. At first Paks thought it was another inn, for a group of men sat on its wide veranda drinking ale, but the sign over the gate said "Ceddrin and Sons: Brewmasters" with a picture of a tapped barrel. Across the river from the brewery, and a little downstream, was a yard full of hides hung on frames, and stinking tubs: the tanner's. Paks crossed the bridge, and saw a great barnlike building looming over the cottages between. According to Sevri, that was the grange.

As Paks came nearer, she noted the construction of the Girdsmen's meeting place. It looked very much like the barns she'd seen in grain-growing regions, stone-walled to twice a man's height, with closely fitted boards above that. Tall narrow windows began in the top course of stones and rose to the eaves of a steeply pitched roof. On the end nearest the road, wagon-wide doors of heavy dark wood were barred shut. Above them was a square hay-door with the hoist in place. Paks wondered what they could possibly use that for. Along one side of the grange a stone wall half again as tall as Paks enclosed a space as wide as the building. Through a narrow gate of iron palings she could see that it was nothing but a bare yard, beaten hard by heavy traffic. Across from the outer gate was another, of wood. She wondered what was behind it.

"It's not the time for meeting," said a voice close behind her. Paks whirled, her hand dropping to her sword hilt. The man who had spoken led a donkey, its back piled high with sticks. He wore no weapon, but his brawny shoulders and muscular arms were no stranger to fighting: he had training scars on both arms, and a long scar on his leg that had come from a spear.

"How would I find the Marshal?" asked Paks. She had noticed that he had not flinched when she reached for her sword; his eyes met hers easily.

"Oh. You're a traveler, aren't you? Well, the Marshal — " He cocked his head at the sky. "This time of day he'll be just finishing his drill with the young'un, I don't doubt. Go round the side there, past the barton, and ask at the door you'll come to. Gird ward you, traveler." He nodded and stepped away before Paks could answer.

394

The walled yard, or barton, was not quite as long as the grange itself. Despite what she knew of Girdsmen, Paks felt uneasy about losing sight of the lane and its traffic as she picked her way around the outside of the barton wall, and up to the door in its angle between the wall and the grange. That door too was shut, but she gathered her nerve and knocked.

Nothing happened for a few moments, then the door was swept open and she found herself facing a red-faced young man in a sweaty homespun tunic. The red lumps of fresh bruises marked his arms; he had a rapidly blackening eye. For an instant they stared at each other, silent, until a voice called from within.

"Well? Who is it, Ambros?"

"Who are you?" asked the young man quietly. "Did you want to see the Marshal?"

"I'm Paksenarrion Dorthansdotter," began Paks. "I have a message for the Marshal."

"Wait." The young man turned and called her name to the interior. In a moment an older man, a hand shorter than Paks, came into the room. He had brown hair, streaked with gray and matted with sweat, and a short brown beard. The younger man stepped back to let him come to the door.

"Paksenarrion, eh? A fighter, I see. Yeoman, are you, or yeoman-marshal?"

"Not either, sir," said Paks. He grunted and looked her up and down.

"Should be, with your build. Well, let's have your message. Come on in, don't stand dithering in the door." He turned abruptly and strode into the room, leaving Paks to follow. "You got those boots in Aarenis, I'll warrant," he said over his shoulder. "I hear it's been lively over the mountains this year." Paks did not answer, but followed him into a narrow passage, and then a small room fitted with desk and shelves on one side, and two heavy chairs on the other. The man dropped into the chair nearest the desk. "Have a seat. So — you're not a Girdsman at all?"

"No, sir."

"Who sent you?"

"The elves, sir, that I met — "

"Elves!" He looked at her sharply. "You run with elves? Dangerous company you keep, young warrior. So: what message did they have for the Marshal of Gird in this grange?"

"To tell you, sir, that in a high valley east and south of here the elfane taig had been wakened, and the lost elf-lord had been freed."

The Marshal sat straight up. "Indeed! That old evil gone, eh? And they had done this, the elves? I thought they claimed they could not."

"Sir, they hadn't done it. They — we — it happened, sir, while I and another were there — "

"Happened! Such things do not happen, they are caused. Are you the cause? Did you fight in that valley and live to return?"

"I fought there, yes. But they did not say the evil was gone, only that the elf-lord was freed."

"I understand. But the evil has lost its body; it will have some trouble to find a new one that will serve so well. And the elfane taig awake. Hmmph. That will please none but elves and Kuakkganni. But tell me more. You were there; you are a fighter. What was your part in this?"

For the second time that afternoon, Paks found herself telling over what had happened. It was not so hard, talking to the Marshal: almost like telling Stammel or Arcolin back in the Company. When she finished, the Marshal looked grave, his lips pursed.

"Well," he said finally. "You have been blessed by the gods — and I would think by Gird himself as well — to come through that alive and free of soul. I'd not dare call it luck that a party of elves found you, and knew what to do. For all I've just finished drill, we'll go into the grange and give you a chance to show your appreciation. Unless your allegiance forbids — ?" Paks had no idea what he meant, but saw no harm in entering the grange. She had been curious about them since talking to the High Marshal near Sibili, curious and reluctant at once.

Marshal Cedfer led the way into the grange, first along a passage, past the door to the outer room, and through another door set at an angle. Inside, the vast room was already dim in the fading light. Paks could see the glint of weaponry here and there along the walls. The Marshal struck a spark and lit a candle, then lifted the candle toward a torch set in a bracket above him. Paks saw that most of the floor was stone paving blocks, worn smooth. But at the near end of the room a platform of wood rose knee-high, floored with broad planks. It was six or eight spans long and the same wide, easily large enough for many men to stand on. The Marshal, meanwhile, had lit several more torches. Paks wondered what the platform was for, and then noticed Ambros's face in the doorway. So did the Marshal.

"Come on in, Ambros. Good news! Paksenarrion, here, brings word that the elf-lord possessed by the demon is freed. She's a little travel-weary, but I just finished drill, so that will be fair." He went over to a rack on the wall and took down a sword. "This should do. Now, Paksenarrion, since you are not a Girdsman, I suppose I should explain. You know that Gird is the patron of fighters?" Paks nodded. "Good. Well, for thanks and praise we honor him with our skill, such as it is, in fighting. You have escaped not only death, but great evil: you owe the High Lord and Gird great thanks. We shall cross blades, therefore, and by the joyous clash of them the gods will hear our thanks. Unless — " He paused suddenly. "Do you have a wound that would pain you? I should have asked before."

"No," said Paks. "I have none. But what is the purpose to which we fight? Am I to wound you, or — ?"

"Oh no. It's like weaponsdrill. We are not enemies that I know of, to draw blood. Gird is no blooddrinker, like some gods. This will not take long; just spar with me."

Paks drew her sword and stepped up onto the platform with the Marshal, who had thrown off his robe to reveal a tunic as drab and worn as

Ambros's. He eyed her thoughtfully. "Are you sure you won't take off your cloak? You might find it troublesome." At that, Paks realized that she was still wearing her chainmail shirt; she hardly thought of it these days.

"Sir, it will not trouble me, but is it right that I wear mail? If I must change — " She wondered as she said it why she was so willing to please him by this exercise.

"Oh no. Oh no, that's no problem. I'm a Marshal, after all; if I can't face mail without it, I'm a poor follower of Gird, who fought in an old shirt and a leather apron, or less than that. Now, Ambros, turn the quarterglass, and we'll begin."

And with a quick tap of greeting, the Marshal began testing Paks's control of her weapon. When she proved strong, he tried quickness. When she proved quick — and he smiled broadly when his lunges failed — he tried movement. Paks met his attacks firmly, but concentrated on defense: she did not want to know what would happen should she injure a Marshal of Gird in his own grange.

He was skilled indeed, perhaps as skilled as any human she had faced but for old Siger. Still, he did not penetrate her defenses, though she had to shift ground more than once. She sensed the sand passing through the quarterglass, and changed her tactics slightly, pressing the Marshal a bit. Was he just a little slower to the right? Were his returns to position sluggish there? She felt the impact of the blades through her wrist. It had been long since she had such good practice.

Suddenly the Marshal quickened his pace, surprising her; she'd thought he was slowing. She gave back, turning, her rhythm broken, fending him off as much by reach as stroke. She took a breath, and stepped back again to gain room for her own attack, but her foot found nothing to step on: she had come to the edge of the platform.

Instantly she threw herself sideways and tucked, hitting the stone floor on her left side, and rolling up to a fighting position. But the Marshal had not followed up her fall.

"Forgive me!" he cried when her saw her up. "I had forgotten, Paksenarrion, in the fighting, that you were not one of us, and did not know the platform well. It was ill-done of me to press you so close to the edge." He racked his sword and came to her side. "Were you hurt in the fall?"

Paks took a breath. Her side hurt, but that was as much the old bruises as the new ones. "No, sir. It's all right, truly it is. I've had harder falls."

"Oh, aye, I'm sure you have. But you're not a yeoman here for training. I should have warned you — glad you're not hurt." As Paks sheathed her blade, he picked up his robe. "It's customary," he said, "to make an offering toward the armory, too. Though as you're not a Girdsman, it isn't strictly required — " Paks found that Ambros had come to her side with a slot-lidded box. She fished out the pouch from her tunic again, thinking to herself that it seemed hard to be dumped on the floor and then asked for money. She took the first jewel at random and dropped it into the box. The Marshal did not appear to be watching.

397

"You're very good with that longsword," he commented. "Don't most mercenary companies use a short one?"

"Yes, sir, we do, but we had the chance to learn other weapons. And out of formation a longsword has great advantage."

"Yes, of course. With your height, too. I was surprised to see that you moved so freely with it, though. Most who come from formation fighting are used to depending on the formation, and are static. Though you're not a Girdsman, you're certainly welcome to drill with us here at the grange, as long as you're in Brewersbridge. We have open drill three nights a week, in the barton usually. You'll find most of the local yeomen fairly good at basic things, though few of them are up to your standard. And I'd be honored to partner you for advanced swordsmanship — or Ambros, here: he's certainly up to a bout with you. Have you had any training at unarmed combat?"

"Yes, some. And some with polearms," added Paks, hoping to forestall further questions.

"Excellent! I certainly hope you'll come; you'll be most welcome. Tonight's a beginner's class in marching drill — I hardly think it would interest you — but tomorrow?"

"Perhaps, sir. I thank you for your invitation." Despite herself, Paks was curious to see the sort of drill a Marshal of Gird would conduct. And she needed to keep her own skills honed; it couldn't hurt to come once or twice.

Outside the grange night had fallen; stars shone overhead to the east. She made her way quickly back to the inn, where the great open windows laid bars of yellow lamplight across the crossroad. As she entered, Jos Hebbinford caught her eye.

"I thought you weren't going to make it back for the meal," he said, half-laughing.

"Mmm. My errands took longer than I thought." Paks looked around the common room, now crowded with men-at-arms and other guests of the inn. "Where — ?"

"I've no single tables left. How about over here?" He led her to a round table where two men were already halfway through a substantial meal. "Master Feddith is a stonemason, a local here, and that's his senior journeyman." Feddith, a burly man in a velvet tunic, looked up and nodded briefly as the innkeeper introduced Paks, then went back to his conversation with the journeyman. Paks ordered roast and steamed barley and looked around the room while waiting for her meal. Nothing Feddith was saying made much sense — it had to do, she assumed, with stonework — she had never heard of coigns or coddy granite or buckstone.

Few other women were in the common room besides serving wenches. One, the same white-haired woman Paks had seen in the afternoon, sat knitting by the fire with a glass of wine beside her. At another table, two women in rough woollen dresses sat with men dressed like farm laborers. And a group of youths, drinking a bit too much ale together, included a sulky-faced girl whose dress was tight across the shoulders and loose everywhere else. Paks watched Hebbinford go to their table in response to

398

another shout for ale, shaking his head. One of the youths started to argue, and a hefty man with a short billet appeared beside the innkeeper. They all subsided, and after a moment threw coins on the table and left. The girl looked quickly at Paks before she went out the door.

"Here, miss," said a serving wench at Paks's shoulder. She turned to find a platter piled high with roast mutton and a mound of barley swimming in savory gravy. With it came a loaf of crusty bread and a bowl of honey. "And will you take ale, miss, or wine?"

"Ale," said Paks. She drew her dagger to slice the bread and found the master mason watching her.

"You're not from around here," he challenged.

"No, sir."

"Are you a Girdsman?"

"No, sir."

"Ummph. A free blade, then: that's not any livery I know."

"Yes, sir."

"Humph. Were I you, young woman, I'd keep my blade sheathed here. We're not partial to troublemakers."

Paks flushed. "I've no wish to make trouble, sir, wherever I am."

"Maybe not, but free blades are trouble as often as not. What gods do you serve?"

Paks put both hands on her thighs and looked him steadily in the eyes. "The High Lord, sir, and the gods my father served, back where I came from."

His gaze flickered. "Well enough. But if you're planning to stay here long, you'd best find a master can vouch for you." Before Paks could think of anything to say, he had pushed back his stool and gone, his cloak swirling. Her stomach clenched with anger. Why did they all think she was a brigand, trying to cause trouble? Then she thought of the wandering fighters in Aarenis — perhaps they had had trouble here, though she had not heard of such in the north. She took a deep breath to calm herself and settled to her meal.

Hebbinford, as he came back past her table, had a smile for her. "Did I hear Master Feddith growling at you? Don't take offense; he's on the Council here, and we've had some trouble. I hear you visited our Master Oakhallow and Marshal Cedfer this afternoon — no wonder you were late. They say Marshal Cedfer alone can take up half a day, with his drills and lectures."

"Does everyone here think fighters are bad?" asked Paks.

"Well — no. Not all fighters. But we've had those come through that were: got drunk, broke things, started fights with local boys, even robbed. You've known some like that, surely."

Paks nodded.

"So, you see, we've got careful. As long as nothing happens, you're welcome, but we don't want the street full of idle blades looking for mischief."

"I can see that."

"Now, Sevri tells me you're quiet-spoken even to servants, and Master Oakhallow had nothing against you, so — " He broke off as someone yelled across the room, smiled again, and left. Paks finished eating. It had been too long since she'd eaten well-cooked food. She finished with a slice of bread drenched in honey. Most of the men-at-arms were gone, and the rest were leaving, throwing down coppers and silvers as their boots scraped on the stone. Paks decided to check on Star before going up to bed; she found the pony dozing, wisps of hay dangling from her mouth. She went up the stairs to her room, tired, full, and determined to put off tomorrow's worries until tomorrow.

The bed was so soft that at first she could not sleep. Her room was far enough from the common loft that she heard nothing from it, but boots rang on the stone outside the inn from time to time. Even with the window open to the cold night air, it seemed strange to be sleeping inside again.

Chapter Eight

She woke at first light, to the clatter of small hooves in the road below. Looking out, she saw a herd of goats skittering along the north road. She looked east, at a clear dawn lightening over the hills, and shivered in the cold. Minutes later she was downstairs. The innkeeper was poking in the fireplace, and she could smell fresh bread from the kitchen.

"You're an early one," he said, surprised. "Did you want breakfast now?"

Paks grinned. "Not yet. I want to check on Star."

"Sevri'll feed her —"

"Yes, but she's used to me. And I'm used to being up early." Paks went out the side door of the common room into the stable yard. The green tailed rooster was racing after a hen, and a clutter of cats crouched near the cowbyre. Paks watched as a stream of milk shot out the door, neatly fielded by one of the cats. She went into the stable, and found Star looking over the top of the stall door. The pony looked well-rested, and Paks rubbed her behind the ears and under the jaw. When she checked her tack, the packbags were intact.

"Is it all right?" asked Sevri, who had come into the passage.

"Yes, fine. I didn't realize I'd gotten up too early for you."

"It's not. Most of the travelers sleep late, that's all. Some of them sleep through breakfast. Star doesn't get much grain, does she?"

"Not when she's not working. Let's see your measure — oh, half of that, and tell me where your hay is — I'll bring it."

"Over there — " Sevri nodded toward a ladder that rose to the loft. "You can just throw it down, if you want."

Paks was already up the ladder. "Why don't I throw down what you need for all of them?"

"You don't have to — but if you wish — " Sevri looked up as Paks tossed down an armload for Star.

"It's no trouble; I'm already up here."

Sevri peered up at her. "I didn't think soldiers knew how to care for animals."

"I grew up on a farm," said Paks shortly. "How much more hay?"

"Just pitch it down, and I'll tell you." Sevri disappeared from the hold, and Paks threw down several armloads. "That should do it. We have just the two big horses in." Paks climbed down, brushing off the hay.

401

"Who does your milking?" she asked, wondering if Sevri did everything but the inside work.

"My brother, Cal," said Sevri. "He's got bigger hands; it takes me too long, and Brindle is a crabby cow." Paks laughed.

"We milked our sheep," she said.

"Sheep?"

"Yes. I've never milked a cow, but I've milked my last sheep. I hope." Paks watched as the girl dumped hay into each feeder. She noticed a blaze-faced black horse that laid its ears back when Sevri neared the stall: obviously one of the "big horses" she'd mentioned. "When can I ask for breakfast, without being rude?"

"There won't be anything cooked, yet," said Sevri doubtfully. "The bread's out, and you could have eggs and cold roast and bread, if that's enough."

"It's plenty." Her stomach churned in anticipation.

"Just tell father, then."

"Thanks." Paks returned to the common room to find the innkeeper waiting.

By the time she had finished breakfast, other guests were stirring. First down was a man in dark tunic and trousers over soft boots. He gave Paks a look up and down that lingered on her sword-hilt, and sat down to his meal with no comment. Then came two heavily built men that Paks classified as merchants, followed by a tall man in a stained leather tunic over patched trousers. He had a longsword at his hip, a dagger at his belt, and the hilts of two more daggers sprouted from his boot tops. Paks noticed that he chose a seat against a wall, far from the others.

After breakfast, she managed a private word with Hebbinford. He willingly told her about the moneychangers in town.

"Well," he began slowly, "as you ask me, I'd say Master Senneth. He's a Guild member, but the northern guild's not the same as that in Aarenis, if that means anything to you."

"Which guild?" asked Paks.

"The moneylender's, of course. I've heard that down south they were mixed up in a lot of — well — all sorts of trouble, let's say. But Master Senneth is as honest as any of that sort, say what you will. He's given me honest weight, at least. Or there's Master Venion — some prefer him. He's not a Guild member, but some say his commission's less. But for myself, I'd see Senneth."

Paks did not know what he meant by commission, and asked.

"Well, if he takes your raw gold and gives coin, say, or changes southern coin for local, he's got to make something on the trade. Or if he arranges a transfer far away — you said you wanted your dowry to go home. If you don't want to take it yourself, he could arrange it for you. But it would cost you. Now Venion might charge you less, but — how would you know it got there? The Guild, now, it'll see things are done right. It's whether you want to pay for it, that's all."

Paks nodded. "Where is Master Senneth?"

"Just across from the Hall." Paks looked blank, and he explained. "When you went to the grange last night, before you crossed the bridge: did you see the large building on your left with a fenced yard?"

"Yes."

"Well, that's the Hall. Master Senneth is right across from it. It's easy to find. He's got a guard at the door." Paks raised her eyebrows. "And you won't be able to take your weapons in, either. The guard stacks them for you."

Master Senneth was a brisk, trim man in a tight-sleeved gown of black wool. He smiled at Paks as she came through the door. "Yes? What may I do for you?"

Paks explained her needs.

"Hmmm. Valuation, yes. It would be better for you, actually, to take anything really valuable to a larger town, or to Vérella. For one thing, you can get several appraisals, and for another, they can offer more who have a market to hand. I'll tell you frankly that I probably can't give you the best price you could get, except for southern coin. That's because we trade coin across the mountains each year. Some items I may not be able to take at all; those, of course, I'll note as we go along. Now transfer — if it's money alone, that's the easiest. If it's specific items, that can be quite expensive. Have you brought it all along?"

"Yes," said Paks. "But most of it's outside; your guard said he would watch the packs." She had tied Star to the railing outside.

"Well, let's bring it in and take a look, if you wish." Paks nodded and he came from behind his counter to the door. "Arvid, bring this lady's packs in, please." The guard unloaded Star, staggering a bit at the weight, and carried the packs inside. As he left, Master Senneth called after him. "And see that we're not disturbed until we're through, Arvid." Then to Paks. "I suppose you don't want half the town wandering in as we're counting, and knowing just what you have."

"I hadn't thought of that," admitted Paks.

"Ah, they would," he said darkly. "They saw you come in yesterday, and watched you come here with a loaded pony. If they could look through walls — " He made a warding sign. "But they can't. Now, what's first?"

Paks began unstrapping the packs. "I don't know what — some of this is weapons, but fancier ones than I'd use." She pulled out the pair of jewelled daggers sheathed in silver. Senneth caught his breath.

"My — those are lovely. *Where* did you say — no. No matter. Only — " he looked at her sharply. "Were these stolen, somewhere in Aarenis?"

"No." Paks shook her head. "I didn't steal them. You can ask Marshal Cedfer or Master Oakhallow, if you like."

"You're not a Girdsman nor a kuakgannir." He said that with certainty; she wondered how he knew.

"No, I'm not. But they know where these are from, and how."

403

"I see." He returned to the daggers. "What lovely tracings. And these gems are valuable in themselves, not just in this design."

Paks pulled out the small battle-axe. She had forgotten the gold inlay tracing runes along the blade.

"That's dwarf-work!" Senneth shook his head. "A rare piece, though I don't know where I'd find a buyer. That's the sort of thing you'd get a better price for in Vérella." Looking at it again, Paks wished she could keep it. But she knew she had no use for a battleaxe, one weapon she'd never handled. She pulled out the ivory-handled dagger with a red stone set in the pommel, and the matching sheath with the dragon carved around it, and two red stones for eyes. Laying these aside, she pulled out one of the sacks of coins.

Master Senneth looked at the treasure, then at Paks, with dawning respect. "Young lady, that's a remarkable amount of wealth you have there. Are you sure you're not an elf princess in disguise, checking to see if humans are still greedy? I assure you, my honest commission for handling all this will well repay my time."

Paks sat back on her heels, grinning. "No, Master Senneth, I'm no princess, elf or human. A very lucky young warrior, yes. And my old sergeant said, if ever we got a chance to set some aside, to do it. If there's enough, after sending my dowry home, that's what I'll do."

"Not spend it all on new clothes and wine, eh? Wise head on young shoulders — and a fighter, at that. You're a new one on me. What was your name again?"

"Paksenarrion."

"Lady Paksenarrion, what other surprises have you?" He smiled over the coins, sorting them quickly into heaps of like kind, while Paks pulled out everything else. When all the coins had been counted, he turned to the jewels, rolling them out on a square of black velvet on his counter, and angling a mirror to catch sunlight from the window. His fingers moved among them deftly, turning them this way and that. At last he looked up.

"Unless your father was a very wealthy man, I'd say you have ample to repay any dowry, and my commission for the transfer, and enough over to live well for a long time. Let me start making notes. If you don't accept my value for anything, just retrieve it: as I said, you can get more for many of these things in a city. Now — " He opened a tall book, fetched a pen and a soft piece of chalk to mark the slate that topped one end of his counter. "Let me start with the coins. You realize that those are all quite old. I don't even know the issue on the ones where the imprint is visible. They have value only for the metal content; they'll have to be melted and re-struck. So I use the weight to determine the value — " He pulled out a set of scales.

As Paks walked back toward the inn, leading Star, she tried to think how much money she actually had. She was hungry; by the sun it was long past time for lunch. How many hours, then, had she been closeted with the moneychanger? She had seen the spiky columns of figures climb up the pages of his account book, as he added the value of coins, jewels, the small pieces of weaponry. But she couldn't make sense of it in terms of her salary in the Duke's Company. He spoke of gold crowns and silver coronets and halflings instead of the natas and nitis she was used to. But it seemed she could send home twice what she thought her dowry had been and have plenty left. She could buy a riding saddle for Star — perhaps even a full-sized horse. She need not take the first guard job that came along. She had left most of her money on deposit with Master Senneth, but she had enough with her to order a few new clothes, and eat the best *The Jolly Potboy* offered for that night's dinner.

On the way back, she remembered Sevri's directions to the smithy, where Master Doggal shod all the horses for miles around. Now she turned from the main road, and led Star between two small stone buildings down an alley that led to the forge. In the paved courtyard before the blacksmith's shop, the tall, rough-looking man from the inn was haggling with the smith over the cost of shoes; his black warhorse, its ears twitching nervously, stamped and shifted, the shoes in question ringing on the stones. Paks recognized it by the blazed face; it had tall white stockings on all four legs.

"I charges fair," the smith rumbled. "Nobody says but what I charges fair. That beast of yours has feet so big, and stands so bad — aye, he come near tearing loose, that he did, and kicked me as near as maybe. It's not the shoes being set wrong has him tittupy like that: he's a wrong 'un, and too handy with them white socks." The smith was a head shorter than the other, but his massive arms and shoulders made his hammer look small.

The tall man put his hand to the hilt of his sword, but the smith hefted his hammer.

"You just pay me, now," the smith went on. "Pay as you ought, and we'll have no trouble."

"And if I don't?" The black horse shied at that harsh voice; the tall man jerked the bridle viciously. Neither man had noticed Paks, but the horse winded Star and stood still, head high and ears pricked, snuffing.

"Well, if ye don't, I'll have the law on ye — "

"The law, is it!" The tall man laughed contemptuously. "In this town? What law here could touch me?"

"This," said the smith, and quick as a snake's tongue his hammer tapped the man's shoulder.

With an angry snarl, the big man dropped the reins, drew his sword, and swung at the smith. The black horse walked over to Star as Paks dropped the lead and whipped out her own blade. Only then did the smith see her.

"Another one of ye, eh?" He blocked one swipe of the big sword with his hammer; she noted that he handled it as if it were weightless. "Well, I can take two of ye, no doubt, but still — Aieeeh! By the Maker!" His bellow split the early afternoon stillness. Paks heard a startled outcry in the distance, as she ran forward.

"Not against you, Master Smith," she said as her sword rang against the other. "But you, you coward. I can see that horse has new shoes — and you owe the smith — and you've no business attacking an unarmed man with a sword!" The swordsman had turned, furious, with her first blow, and now concentrated on her.

"Unarmed, is it?" cried the smith. "And you a woman? Is any smith unarmed that has his hammer and the strength of the forge in his arm?" Paks made no answer; the tall man had more skill than she'd expected from a bully, and she saved her breath for the fight. The smith threw his hammer on the ground and bellowed at them both. "Is it a barton of Gird you think I have here, and not a smithy? By the Maker, is a smith to be reft of his fight by any wandering female? I can collect my own debts, you silly girl, without your help. I was just teaching this fellow a lesson — " Paks quit listening. The tall man had the reach of her, and a heavier blade. She missed her helmet and shield; he had a round iron pot on his head, and heavy bracers on both arms. His black eyes gleamed from under the helmet.

"Eh — the girl from over the mountains! A wild one, I see. I like wild ones." He grunted as her sword pricked his shoulder. "I'll tame you, little mountain-cat, and then I'll see to him — " He jerked his head at the smith, without giving Paks an opening.

"You will, will you?" yelled the smith. "By the Maker, you're a fine one, if you think you can!" And before Paks realized what he was about, he darted behind the tall man and brought the hammer down on his head with a resounding clang. The tall man sagged to his knees and fell over in a heap. The smith glared at Paks over the crumpled body. "A sword," he said severely, "is a pitiful weapon, young woman, and only fit for those that don't have the strength for a hammer. It was by the hammer that Sertig the Maker forged the world on the Anvil of Time. The hammer will always win, with the strength of the faithful behind it."

Paks had dropped the tip of her sword and stood panting. "Uhm — yes — "

"Don't forget that."

"No — " She took a deep breath and wiped her sword on her leg before sheathing it.

"Not that yours isn't a fine bit of work," the smith went on. "It's just that swords are inferior weapons." Paks did not feel like arguing with him. She was, however, a bit disgruntled. She'd only tried to help someone.

"Doggal!" A shout from the alley. "Need help?" Paks could see two hefty men, armed with clubs.

"Nay, nay. 'Twas a bit of trouble with a fellow from outside, that's all." The smith sounded smug. "He'll have a headache, if he wakes at all."

"Will you need someone to take him away?"

"He's not dead yet. He's still snorting. If this lady will lead his horse back to the inn, I can throw him over — " He turned to Paks. "If you're going that way, that is." The men waved and turned back up the alley.

"I was coming here," said Paks. "To get my pony shod. But if — "

The smith suddenly grinned, and looked like a different man. "Oh?

That's no problem. He'll keep a bit, just there. I did wonder what you were doing up my alley, to be sure, but if it was on business, then — " He looked around. "That your pony, with the star?"

"Yes. Just a moment." Paks started toward Star, who stood stiffly, nose-to-nose, with the black horse. Both shifted away from her, eyes wide.

"Come on, Star," said Paks crossly. She felt the smith was laughing at her. "Come on, pony." She rubbed her thumb on the gold ring. The wildness left Star's eyes, and the pony minced toward her. The black horse, too, lowered his head and stretched his neck.

"Catch up that fancy-socks, if you can," called the smith. "Be careful: he's a mean one, but he'll do no good running loose." Paks caught Star's lead, and rubbed the ring again, talking softly to the black.

"Come on, then, big one. Come on. I'd like to have one like you some-day." The black horse came forward step by slow step until she could reach the reins. She talked on as she led them toward the smithy itself. She could feel the horse's fear trembling in the reins as they neared the building.

"Well!" The smith sounded surprised. "You've a rare way with a horse, that you have. I'll take the pony, then, if you'll hold that one. What sort of shoes? Are you going into the mountains again?"

Paks shook her head. "No. And she won't be carrying as much weight. I'll be going toward Vérella, I think."

"Umph." He had one of Star's feet up, then another. "I'd still say low caulks in front. It'll frost before these wear out."

By the time Star was shod and the shoes paid for, the tall man had grunted and groaned and shifted around on the stones. His eyes were still closed, though, and he had said nothing coherent.

"You wanted to help," said the smith with a bit of his earlier belligerence. "Suppose you take him back to the inn for me. I'll tell the watch about it, and Jos can ask me, if he wants. And look — " The smith bent down with a grunt and opened the man's belt pouch. "You know he owes me for the shoeing of that devil there: see, I'm taking just what he owes." Paks nodded, and the smith heaved the man upright and slung him over one broad shoulder. "Now, I think your pony would carry him better than his horse. Can you lead both?"

"Yes — " Paks was reluctant, nonetheless, to go out on the streets leading another man's horse, with the man himself slung unconscious over her pony. "But don't you think that — I mean, since *you* hit him, shouldn't — ?"

"A warrior like you doesn't want credit for defeating him?" The smith's voice was scornful, and his look more so. Paks reddened. Nothing and no one in this town had been what she expected. "I'd have thought," the smith continued, "that such as you were quite used to hauling bodies around. Or did you just leave them?"

Paks opened her mouth and shut it again. There seemed nothing to say to that. But as the smith folded the man over Star's back, the Gird's Marshal walked into the courtyard. His glance rested on Paks, then on the smith and his burden.

407

"I heard, Master Doggal, that you had had a disturbance."

The smith stopped, with a hand on the tall man's back where he lay across the pony. "If you heard that, Marshal, you heard I needed no help."

The Marshal glanced at Paks again. The smith caught the look and raised his voice. "No, and I didn't need her, either. Is that it, is she one of your precious yeomen?"

"No. I merely wondered."

The smith began tying the man to Star's pack pad with the thongs. "Took you long enough. If I had needed help, I'd have been dead long since." He turned to Paks. "Now, lady, just you work whatever magic you used on that horse, and take him and this fellow back to the inn for me." Paks saw the Marshal give her a sharp look at the word magic, but he turned back to the smith as that individual kept talking. Paks started to move away, but the Marshal raised his hand to stop her.

"You seem to think, Marshal, that we'd have no order here without you Girdsmen. I'm not denying you're a brave bunch, and useful when we have trouble too big for one man or two. But I can hold my own with any single man, and most two or three. As I was telling this lady — " Paks wondered why she had been promoted from "girl" and "female" to "lady." "As I said to her, the Maker's hammer wielded by a faithful arm will stand over a sword any time."

"Yet the Maker is said to have made many a blade, in the old tales," said the Marshal, with a kindling eye. "And you, I know, have made most of the blades in this village — "

"Oh, aye, that's true. When I have time. And it's a test of the art, that it is, to make a fine-balanced blade that will hold an edge and withstand a hard fight. I won't say against that. But I will say — "

"That you can hold your own in a fight. And I'll agree to that, Master Doggal. But the captain did ask me to keep an eye on things, after that last trouble, and the Council as well — "

The smith had calmed down a lot, and the discussion seemed, to Paks, to be working over well-plowed ground. "That's so. If it's for the Council, then I might as well tell you all that happened. Saves seeing the watch. This fellow came to have his horse shod — that black one there — and quarreled with my price, after. The horse is vicious: doesn't look it now, I'll admit, but just you try and put a shoe on it. I charged more for it. Always do, as you know. If I'm to risk my head, I must have gain for it." He paused and the Marshal nodded. "Well, then, he said as much as that I'd no way to make him pay. I tapped his arm to show I meant my words, and he drew on me. Then this lady — I'd not seen her come — she drew as well. I thought they were together, and raised a yell. Then it seemed she thought to aid me — but, you see, I'd already raised a cry — so I thought I'd let her fight, was she so eager to. They were well-matched. He'd the reach of her, and was heavier, but she was quicker and her blade had more quality. Then — well — it's hard to stay out of a fight, so I broke his head with the hammer, after all."

"Mmm." The Marshal looked at Paks. "I'd have told you our smith can handle himself in a fight. It's not well for newcomers to brawl in the streets."

Before Paks could answer, the smith was defending her. "'Tis not her fault, Marshal. I'd think you'd be pleased, even if she's not one of yours. She thought she saw an old man — " he rumpled his thin gray hair, " — beset by an armed bully. She did well."

"Hmm. Well, I suppose — if you have no complaint against her — " The Marshal was frowning.

"Not at all. Not at all. Suppose I had slipped and fallen? She was trying to help. And, you might notice, on the side of that law and order you praise so highly. I've no complaint. In fact — but go on, now, and get that lummox out of my yard." He turned abruptly and dove back into the forge.

"I'll walk with you to the inn," said the Marshal to Paks in a neutral tone. Paks followed him down the alley, leading both animals. She kept her thumb firmly on the ring.

They were almost to the crossroad when the Marshal spoke again. "If I'd defended you," he said without preamble, "old Doggal would be lodging a complaint to the Council somehow. He won't agree with me on anything but smithing itself if he can help it."

"Then — you aren't angry with me for this?"

"For going to his aid? Of course not. You might wait, another time, to see whether your aid is needed, or someday you'll be killed over some little thing, and nothing gained. I'll just have a word with Hebbinford," he said as they came to the inn door. "You take that horse around back."

Paks found herself leading the tall black warhorse to the stable before she quite realized the Marshal had taken Star's lead. She heard, behind her, the innkeeper's voice and the Marshal's, and the exclamations of the serving wenches.

Chapter Nine

When she came in to supper that night, the common room stilled. Someone dropped a dish, and it clattered on the floor. She could hear the rustle of cloth as someone bent to pick it up. Paks carefully did not meet any of the eyes in the room, but picked her way to an empty table. As she sat down, a muted hum resumed. She heard a phrase here and there, but tried to ignore the voices. They all knew, as she did, that the tall man lay unconscious in his room upstairs. She didn't know what stories were going around, but obviously she was in them. She ordered the special dinner: roast beef, mushrooms, hot bread and pastry. She was halfway through it before she remembered that she'd thought of going to weapons-practice at the Girdmen's that evening. If she ate all that — she sighed and pushed the dishes away.

"Is something wrong with your meal?" asked Hebbinford, pausing by her table.

"No, not at all. I thought I'd go to the grange this evening, though, and drill — and not on a full stomach."

"I see. Well, we can put that by for you, for when you get back, if you like."

"Thank you." Paks had not thought of that. "I'd like that — this food is too good to waste. If it's not too much trouble — ?"

"Not at all. Marshal Cedfer mentioned that you might be visiting this evening. I suppose, a warrior must always practice, eh?"

"Yes, if we want to stay good. And it's been too long since I had a proper drill."

"Fights don't count?" No mistaking the ironic tone. She wanted to answer sharply, but knew better.

"No. Not really. A fight may not last long enough, or call out what you need to practice. I should drill every day — we did in the Duke's Company. But no one can practice well on a full belly." Paks leaned back and fished into her pouch for the correct silver piece. As she stood and turned to leave, she noticed several of the diners watching her.

Although it was full dark, she had no trouble making her way along the street. Uncurtained windows open to the cool evening air spilled light into the lane, and torches burned at either end of the bridge. Ahead, the grange

410

was ablaze with light: torches flared atop the barton wall as well. As Paks came nearer, she could see that the gate to the barton and door to the grange both had sentries before them. She saw two dark shapes enter the barton ahead of her, pausing to exchange greetings with the sentries.

Up close, she realized that the sentries were very young. They carried long billets of wood, and struggled to maintain the dignity of their posts. Paks wondered which entrance to use. She heard the mutter of voices through both. Finally she decided on the barton gate. The youth there stared up at her, eyes wide.

"I'm Paksenarrion Dorthansdotter," she said. "The Marshal invited me to come to weapons-practice."

"Oh — eh — you're the lady as has come over the mountains, eh?"

"Yes," said Paks. "May I pass?"

"Oh — well — if the Marshal said — yes, lady, go on in. Are — are you really a fighter, like they say?" This last, as she was nearly past.

Paks turned back to him, hand on the hilt of her sword. "Yes. Did you doubt it?"

"Oh, no, lady. I — I just wondered, like."

Paks turned back to the barton itself and looked about her. The bare little yard was ringed with torches set high on the wall. One man was stretching, arching his thick back with a grunt. Two more were looking over a pair of pikes, smoothing the shafts with pumice. Out of the side door of the grange came Ambros with an armful of short clubs that reminded Paks of hauks. She heard more men coming in the gate behind her, and a confused sort of clatter and mumble from the grange itself. She watched, uncertain, as Ambros dumped the clubs in a heap near the wall. When he straightened, he saw her.

"Ah, Paksenarrion. Welcome. Marshal Cedfer will be glad to see you. Will you come in? Or he'll be out here in a few moments."

"I'll wait," said Paks. "I can warm up out here." She unbuckled her sword and laid it by the wall, then began limbering exercises. Others were busy with the same. One man belched repeatedly; a cloud of onion followed him.

"Eh, Gan," said another. "If you've ate as much as I smell, you won't last the night."

"Air and onion won't slow any man," retorted Gan, grinning. "Might just set off my opponent — "

Paks ignored them. It reminded her of drill in the Company — the familiar mixture of joking and criticism. She finished her exercises and went to buckle on her sword. The barton was half-full of men — she saw no other women — and they were all mature and well-muscled. Most had picked up one of the short clubs; four had pikes, and one had a sword of medium length.

A bell rang, a single mellow stroke. Everyone stilled, and Marshal Cedfer came into the barton, followed by five other men.

"Are you ready, yeomen of Gird?" he asked.

411

"We are ready, Sir Marshal," they answered in unison. Paks was silent.

"Then may Gird strengthen your arms and your hearts, and keep them strong for the safety of our land."

"In the name of St. Gird, protector of the innocent," came the response.

"We have a guest here tonight," said the Marshal less formally. "Paksenarrion, come forward. I want all our yeomen to know you." Paks edged past the others to stand near the Marshal under the torches. "Though she is not a Girdsman, Paksenarrion is an experienced warrior. She has accepted my invitation to drill with us. Those of you who drill with swords will have a chance to cross blades with her if you wish. Now, bring your weapons and let me see — " The Marshal began to look over the weapons, commenting on their condition. He was as thorough as any of the Duke's armsmasters. Ambros explained that some of the weapons belonged to the men, and the rest were stored in the grange. Then the Marshal began assigning drills: some to one-on-one, others to two-on-one, and others to more basic exercises. When they were all occupied, he led Paks to a corner of the barton where Ambros waited with two short swords.

"If you don't mind," said the Marshal, "I'd like to work with these short swords. I suspect you are far more skilled with a short blade than I am. It would be best for the yeomen, I think, to learn the short. Of course, you'll want a chance to work with your own, but — "

"That's fine," said Paks. "But I haven't drilled with a short sword since leaving Aarenis. I may be clumsy with it."

"Not as clumsy as I am," said the Marshal. "I haven't been able to teach the men to fight in lines with it."

Paks unbuckled her long sword, racked it, and took one of the short ones from Ambros. "We used a small shield with these, in formation," she said. "Do you have shields?"

"Yes, but we rarely practice with them. As I said, most of our men are not at all skilled with swords. Once they learn that, then we'll try adding the shields." The Marshal, too, had taken a short blade; he gestured at another man to come over. He looked closely at Paks. "You aren't wearing your mail."

"No. I didn't think all of you would have mail." Paks wished she had a banda, but was not about to ask for one.

"Mmm. I always say, the stripes you take in training reinforce the lesson." The Marshal looked pleased, and the other two grinned. "Now — we'll warm up in pairs, then go two-against-two. Is that all right?"

"Surely." Paks moved the sword around, feeling its balance. It felt subtly different from the one in the Duke's Company. Lighter, she finally decided.

As she had expected, the Marshal was not nearly as inexperienced as he'd claimed. They tested each other's ability and strokes, without either making a touch, for a few minutes. Then the Marshal gestured a pause.

"Yes, indeed," he said. "I see you have much to teach us. Now, Ambros, you stand with her, and Mattis, you take my right."

Paks shot a look at the young man who came to stand beside her. She felt

412

queer, standing in formation with a stranger against strangers. But if she joined a guard company somewhere, this is what it would be like. Again the blades came up in salute, and the drill began.

Ambros, she saw at once, wanted to move around too much. He shifted from side to side with each stroke, alternately crowding and leaving her flank uncovered. The Marshal's partner, Mattis, looked as if he couldn't shift at all, but at least he kept some sort of line. Paks managed to cover Ambros's lapses at first, but finally the Marshal's blade leaped in and rapped his side sharply. Paks had managed two touches on Mattis, but none on the Marshal. He signalled another halt.

"I think I see our problem," he said. "Ambros, you aren't holding your position. Isn't that it, Paksenarrion?"

She was not sure how critical she could be without angering them. "Well — yes, part of it. A line works only if it holds together. But I think those who learn a long blade first have more trouble. It seems to me that you, sir, and Ambros both are trying strokes more suited to a long blade. More wrist, and less elbow and shoulder."

"Ah. I see. Suppose you stand out, and watch us, and give corrections." The Marshal lined up with Ambros this time, and a nervous Mattis braced himself to meet both of them. Paks shook her head.

"No, sir, by your leave. Let all of you line up, and go slowly — do you ever count the cadence for a slow drill? Yes? Good. If those of your men with the short clubs use much the same strokes, they can partner you, and the line can be long enough to work. I can anchor the center of the opposing line." The Marshal agreed, and soon they had a line of four swords (for another man took up a blade, a little uncertainly) against Paks and three men with clubs. At first the drill was very ragged, but in a few strokes they all caught on, and Paks was able to talk them through it.

"You see," she said, as the blades met clubs with light taps, "if you are in close formation you'll hurt your partners if you shift too much. And leave yourself open, as well. There is a rhythm — and a trust — that your partner will be there. Not so much turn to the side — yes — and if you have a shield as well, you may foul your partner's blade if you turn." As practice went on, they grew used to the limited sideways movement, and Paks encouraged them to increase the tempo. After some minutes, the Marshal called a halt.

"Very good!" he exclaimed. "Very good indeed. Anything else?"

"I didn't notice it in the others, sir," said Paks, "but you and Ambros still seem to have too much flex in the wrist. You are trying to do more with the point than a short sword allows — it's the quick thrust you want, not fencing about." She expected him to be angry, but he was not.

"So. Each craft has its masters, and a knight's training ill-suits an infantry soldier. I'll try to remember that. Perhaps you'll give us the benefit of your training again. And now, since you carry a long blade by choice, you should have the chance to practice with it, if you will. He handed Ambros his short blade and gestured to Paks. She handed over the short sword and went to pick up her own blade. When she had settled it to her satisfaction, the Marshal had also armed himself, and awaited her.

"I suggest we go into the grange itself," he said. "The light is better."

Paks followed him in. So, she noticed, did many of the other men.

"I don't suggest the platform, since you aren't used to it. But here —" his glance cleared a space in the crowd, and he drew.

"Now," said Paks, smiling, "I expect you will have plenty to teach me."

The Marshal grinned. "I should hope so. You have some good strokes; I noticed that yesterday, but —" He moved to attack.

For the next few minutes they circled first one way then the other, blades ringing with stroke after stroke. Paks had to use everything she knew, and all her size, to keep from being pricked again and again. Sweat poured down her back and stung her eyes. The Marshal met every thrust with a firm repulse, and she found herself more often defending than attacking. She found no weakness she could exploit, and wondered what old Siger would do against him. That thought almost made her laugh — she'd still back Siger against anyone, even a Marshal of Gird.

"Very good," the Marshal said finally, still hard at work. "You certainly have a thorough grounding in long blades. I have a few tricks, but as far as plain fighting goes, you do very well." Paks said nothing, needing all her concentration. Despite her best efforts, he made a touch the next moment, ripping her left sleeve from shoulder to elbow. "There, now," he said. "I have regained the respect of our yeomen. Would you rest a bit?" He stepped back, and Paks lowered her weapon.

"I could stand to," she said ruefully, wiping her face. "I see I still have a lot to learn — just as I thought."

"The willing student learns quickly," he said. "You need naught but experience to master this weapon as well as the other. Common swordsmen you could defeat now, quite easily I imagine."

"Ah, but I like learning weaponcraft," said Paks. She thought of Saben's teasing with a pang. "I always have."

"Good, then. You're welcome here, any time. I'll be glad to drill with you; you're good enough to give me practice. Ambros, too. And mind —" he said briskly, fixing her with a sharp glance, "Mind, I intend to have you a Girdsman before long. Such skill as yours should be dedicated to a good cause. We need such fighters on the side of right, not running loose after idle gain." Paks felt a flicker of anger at that, and her chin came up. "No —" He stopped and rubbed his head. "I shouldn't say that of you, when I don't know your allegiance, but Gird knows we've trouble enough coming, and few to meet it." He grinned at her suddenly. "I still think you'll make a fine Girdsman someday — even a Marshal, who knows?"

The others milled about, replacing weapons in racks on the grange walls, and taking their leave. Paks sheathed her sword, and turned to go. The Marshal was talking seriously to two men, low-voiced.

A hand touched her arm. It was Ambros. "If — if you'd come again, I'd like to drill with you —"

414

"Oh, I'll come again, while I'm here. It's good practice. But — don't you have any women drilling with you?"

Ambros shook his head. "No. Not at this level. We'd had some in the beginners' class — in fact, we have two there now. But those who want to go on, the Marshal sends elsewhere for more training."

"I see." She wondered why, but felt it would be impolite to ask.

"Were there many women in your company?"

"Maybe a quarter of us. One of the cohort captains."

"I've heard of Duke Phelan. Isn't his title from the court of Tsaia?"

"Yes. He has lands in the north of the kingdom, on the border." Paks sighed. "I might — I might be going back there."

"But you left his company, didn't you? We thought you were a free sword."

"Well — I was due leave, and — and the Duke thought perhaps I should try another company — another service — for a time. But I miss it; I've thought of going back."

"Oh." Paks could hear the unasked questions. Ambros stopped at the door, started to say something and stopped, and finally said, "Well — Gird go with you. We'll be glad to see you again."

It was late; few torches burned along the lanes. Paks made her way down the dark streets with care, following some distance behind several others from the grange. Cold night air, damp from the river, soothed her hot face. She caught a whiff from the tanner's crossing the bridge. As she neared the crossroad, she saw light spilling from the inn's windows. She slipped in the door, ignoring the few who sat late in the common-room, and went up the stairs to her own room. Her shoulder ached pleasantly. She pulled off her tunic and washed the sweat off, then remembered her unfinished dinner. She put on her other shirt and went back downstairs. Hebbinford rose from his place near the fire.

"Do you want the rest of your dinner?"

"Yes, if it's not too much trouble." Paks settled at an empty table. Hebbinford brought a candle; a serving wench came with a tray. They had heated the leftovers by the kitchen fire, and the gravy was bubbling hot. She cut a slice of bread and began eating.

Several of those who had been at the drill clustered at one table over mugs of ale, chatting. One caught her eye and grinned and waved. The man in black that Paks had seen the previous night sat across the room, a flagon of wine at his elbow. Two men in merchants' gowns diced idly nearby. One of them, looking around the room, saw her and nudged the other. They both rose and came to her table.

"I'm Gar Travennin," said the older. "A merchant, as you see, from Chaya. Could we talk with you?"

Paks nodded; her mouth was full. They sat across from her. Travennin was balding, with a gray fringe. The younger man was blond.

"We hear you came over the mountains, from Aarenis." Paks nodded again. "I heard there was more fighting than usual down there, and no trade this year. Is that so?"

Paks took a sip of her ale. "Yes. That's so. Had you heard of Lord Siniava?" The man nodded. "Well, he tried open war against the Guild League cities and the northern mercenaries all at once. He lost."

"Ah . . . so. Do you think, then, that trade will be back to normal by next spring? I held off this year, but I've a caravan of fine wool that needs a buyer."

Paks thought back to the turmoil in Aarenis. She spread her hands. "I can't say, sir, for certain. I came north with a late caravan, as far as the Silver Pass, but whether they made it safe to Valdaire I don't know."

"Were you with a regular company?" Travennin asked as if he had heard already.

"Yes. Duke Phelan's Company. The Duke was — much involved." Paks was not sure how much to say; the old habit of silence held her still.

"Mmm. And why did you leave?"

Paks felt irritated; it was none of his affair. "Why, sir, I enlisted for two years. My time was up."

"I see. You had had no trouble — ?"

Merchants! she thought disgustedly. No honor at all. "No, sir. No trouble." She went on eating.

"I heard the Duke and Aliam Halveric were much in each other's pockets," said Travennin, his eyes roaming around the room.

Paks gave him a hard look and returned to her meal. "Oh? I couldn't say."

"After some kind of trouble last year — over the pass? Some border fort, I forget the name — "

She thought of Dwarfwatch at once, and said nothing. The smell of that mountain wind came to her, and her last sight of Saben and Canna in the rain, and Captain Ferrault's dying face.

" — do you know it?" the merchant persisted.

Paks stopped eating and slowly put both hands flat on the table. He glanced at her and froze as she glared at him. "Sir," she said finally, in a voice she hardly recognized. "I have nothing to say about our — the Duke's — Company. Nothing. And by your leave, sir, I'll finish my supper in peace." She stared at him until he reddened and pushed back his stool. She had lost her appetite. All those deaths, that grief and rage — The merchants she had traveled with had not been so crass. But of course, they had been in Aarenis during the war. They knew. Her breathing slowed; she took another sip of ale. The merchants were back at their own table, heads together. The man in black was watching her. As he met her eyes, he lifted his glass in salute and grinned. She looked away. All at once she wished she were anywhere but here. No, not anywhere, but back with the Company, laughing with Vik and Arñe, talking with Stammel or Seli or Dev. Tears stung her eyes and she blinked them back angrily. She drew a long breath and drank more ale.

416

She had thought she'd feel at home in the north; she was northern. But Brewersbridge was far from home. Maybe that was it. She thought of Vérella, thought of going straight on to Three Firs. She had money enough; she could make more show than even her cousin. She imagined her mother's smile, her father's scowl — but he might not be angry, with the dowry repaid. She wondered what she would tell them, and what they would ask. Her musings ended there. She could not tell them anything they would understand. They would see her as these folk did: dangerous, wild, a stranger. She started to pour more ale, and found the tankard dry. She was still thirsty. She beckoned to Hebbinford, but when he came she doubted the steadiness of her voice and asked for water. His expression approved that choice. The merchants left the room and went upstairs.

Paks drank the water and thought of what she would do the next day. She needed new clothes, at least a new shirt. A saddle for Star. She knew where the tailor's shop was, and the leatherworker's — if he made saddles. She would order a shirt or two, and then think about how long to stay. Suddenly she remembered the tall man the smith had felled. How was he? She was unwilling to ask the innkeeper. She picked up the pastry from a dish she had pushed aside and bit into it absently. It had been a long day.

Chapter Ten

Next morning she woke again at dawn. This time Hebbinford seemed to expect her when she padded down the stairs and out to the stableyard. There she stretched and twisted, working the stiffness out of her shoulder. When Sevri came out, they fed the horses together. Paks stopped to watch the black horse eat. She wondered what would happen to it if its master died. She imagined herself riding away on it — then wondered if she could even mount it.

The tailor, she found after breakfast, was away on a trip. "Buying cloth up at the Count's fair," said his wife. "He's got a commission to make cloaks for the new council members, and has gone to buy cloth. He won't be home for a sennight or more. But what did you need, lady? Perhaps I could serve?"

"Well — some shirts, at least. I'd wanted a cloak, a heavy traveling cloak for winter."

"Fur? I couldn't do fur, nor does he, without it being paid in advance."

"No, not fur. Just good warm wool, weatherproofed — "

"Plain shirts, or fancy ones?"

Paks thought of her money. "Plain. Maybe one fancy one."

"The plain shirts I can do. And here — here's our silks, from the south. They say you've been there; you'll know these are good."

Paks looked at the goods. The silk slid across her hands like water — she decided on a silk shirt, green, with gold embroidery on the yoke. For that, the woman said, she'd have to await the tailor's return. In the meantime, a linen shirt — Paks explained the cut she wanted, to free her arms for swordplay. The tailor's wife took her measurements.

"You're as big as a man," she said, a little nervously. "Even in the neck — "

Paks laughed. "It comes of the fighting," she said. "Wearing a helmet every day would thicken anyone's neck. Makes it harder to cut through." But the woman didn't take the joke, and only looked frightened. Paks sighed, and ordered trousers as well, of the local wool, thicker and softer than she'd found in Aarenis. The tailor's wife knew someone who knitted for sale, and by noon Paks had ordered new socks and gloves for the coming winter.

As she came back to the inn, well satisfied with her morning's work, she noticed a crowd round the door. She slowed. A group of men came out, car-

418

rying something on a plank. Boots, scuffed and worn, poked out from under a blanket. The tall man. Paks shivered. Marshal Cedfer, walking with the carriers, nodded shortly to Paks as he led the group toward the grange. Paks went on to the door, staring after them.

Just inside the inn door, Hebbinford was talking to Master Oakhallow.

" — doesn't do the inn any good," he was saying. "And besides — Oh. Paksenarrion. Master Oakhallow was looking for you."

Paksenarrion felt a tremor in her gut. The Kuakgan was looking at her without expression. She opened her mouth to say something about lunch, and thought better of it.

"For a simple warrior," said the Kuakgan, "you certainly have managed to make a stir in our quiet village." Hebbinford moved away, into the common room. Paks thought of several things to say, and decided against all of them. "You were about to eat?" Oakhallow went on.

"Yes, sir." Paks tried to judge his expression. "But if you needed — "

"No. I think I'll join you for lunch, if that's acceptable."

Paks wondered what he would say if she said no. Instead she nodded, and followed him into the common room. He murmured something to Hebbinford, and the innkeeper waved them on into the kitchen. The serving wenches were wide-eyed. The Kuakgan moved to a table at the kitchen window, overseeing the courtyard, and sat down. Paks hesitated, then sat opposite him. Hebbinford brought a platter of sliced meat, a loaf of bread, and a round of cheese to the table. One of the girls brought a pitcher of water and two mugs.

"You might as well know," the Kuakgan began, as he pulled out a dagger and sliced the round of cheese, "that you're causing a stir. I don't mean that dead bully, necessarily, though that's part of it. Not your fault, I agree with the Marshal, but you were involved. Then Master Senneth, after you left his place, has had a — how shall I put it? — a complacent look. And he called you 'lady,' I hear. In his vocabulary, that means rich. Folk here know the Halveric Company, and most have heard of your duke. After your comments last night, to the Chaya merchants, no one has much doubt that he's still your lord. You gave both to me and to the grange a jewel worth a knight's ransom — apparently without knowing their worth. You walked off with a horse that the smith claimed was an outlaw." He paused to eat a slice of cheese.

Paks was still staring at her food; she shook herself and speared a slice of meat. Put that way, it almost seemed that she'd tried to show off. She finished that slice, and tore off a hunk of bread. She had no idea what was coming, or what to do.

"Marshal Cedfer says," the Kuakgan went on, after pouring himself some water, "that you're uncommonly good with that sword, and also good with the short-sword — which I'd expect, where you've been — and also good at instructing in weapons. We didn't expect that of one so young, a mere private. Sevri tells me you're good with all the animals, and helpful as well. Fighters aren't, as a rule. In fact — " Paks looked up and was caught by his dark gaze. "In fact, Paksenarrion Dorthansdotter, you are very different from the usual ex-mercenary. Now Kuakkganni — " He gave a slow smile that changed his whole face. "Kuakkganni have their own ways of learning things. From what I know, I judge that you're as honest as most youngsters are, and mean no harm — not that no harm comes of it. You have some secrets rankling in your heart which must come out — and soon, I judge — if they're not to hurt you later. But unless you choose to confide in me, it's not my business." Paks thought of the snow-cat with a mental wince, and looked down. "Marshal Cedfer thinks you need only join the grange to be a fine addition to our town: that's a compliment; he's hard to please. But you've come to the notice of our local Guard, and the Council, and it's best you know the eyes you have on you."

Paks stirred restlessly. "But, sir — Master Oakhallow — why should they be so interested? I won't be here long — "

"No? Are you sure? The simple answer, child, is that they can't fit you into a known pattern. You aren't one of the Count's Guard at the new Keep. You aren't an ordinary soldier on leave. You aren't a Girdsman, which would put you under command of Marshal Cedfer, or a kuakgannir, which would put you under mine. You have no skill but war, isn't that so?" Paks nodded. "And you come from war, from Aarenis, where I hear the whole land is one great bubbling stew of fighting. Where an army might come over the pass, the short way, and be on us before we could send for aid. Can you imagine a southern army up here?" Paks thought of it and nodded. "And you come with treasure — how much, only you and Master Senneth know, but I can guess. Agents carry such treasure, Paksenarrion. Agents hiring troops, or buying loyalty ahead of invasion."

Paks stared at him, shocked. She couldn't speak. Finally she choked out: "Agent? But — but I never thought — "

"No," said the Kuakgan grimly. "You didn't think. That much is obvious. An agent would think, would have acted very differently. But the Council can't know what I know. They are concerned. So they should be. Your tale of the elfane taig, and elves' aid, and having to see me and Marshal Cedfer, and treasure — well, it would be stupider men than our Council that could see where that might come from." He went back to his meal. Paks sat frozen, her appetite gone, the food she had already eaten a cold lump in her belly. She watched him eat. Finally he pushed his plate away. "And on top of all," he said, "a green shirt. With gold embroidery. I suppose you don't know what that means?" She shook her head. "Hmmph. You must have gone straight from your sheepfarm into the Company, and straight into Aarenis from there."

"Yes, sir."

"Well, child, Brewersbridge is near the border of Tsaia and Lyonya. Our local Count, such as he is, is a vassal of Tsaia. His colors are blue and rose. Green and gold are the colors of the royal house of Lyonya."

"Oh." Paks thought suddenly of the Halveric colors: dark green and gold. She did not even consider asking.

"I told them you didn't mean anything by it. I assume you just like the colors? Yes. They'll be asking you anyway. There's a Council meeting tonight, and you're summoned. I'll be there, and Marshal Cedfer. You met our Master Mason the other night. Captain Sir Felis Trevlyn, the Count's military representative, and commander at the new Keep. Probably his mage, Master Zinthys. Jos Hebbinford you know, and Master Senneth. Our mayor is Master Ceddrin, the Brewmaster. You'll be asked for a clear account of yourself, and for news of what's happened this past year in Aarenis." He stopped again. Paks nodded, and he went on.

"I thought you might give a clearer account, if you had the afternoon to think about it. If there's anything you haven't told the truth about, you'd better be prepared to, tonight. You'll probably be asked to submit to an Examination of Truth — "

"What's that?" asked Paks.

"A spell. Under its influence, you cannot lie. You can refuse to answer questions, however, should you wish. The Council consented to my telling you this, because of my judgment of you. I think you have nothing to fear from the Examination or the Council, but you must expect sharp questioning: don't get angry. If you are unwilling to come before the Council, you must leave Brewersbridge at once. You can't go north, deeper into the Count's lands, without Sir Felis's permission, which you won't get. You could go west, if you went swiftly, and were beyond the bounds by sundown. East, as you know, has its own hazards, and south is back up the mountains. And if you go, they'll assume you've lied. I advise you to stay."

"I wouldn't have run away," said Paks.

"Good. Jos Hebbinford will tell you what time to come. After supper. You might want to dress for it, if you can." He stood, and Paks scrambled to her feet. "You are, you know, as welcome at the grove as at the grange." He turned away. Paks thought of the snowcat again. Should she tell him? She wondered what he would say; she was half-afraid she knew.

By midafternoon, Paks had bathed and washed her hair. Her good shirt, mended, dripped from a line in the stableyard; she wore the ragged one in her room. She had oiled her boots, and was working on her sword belt while her hair dried in the breeze from the window. She heard boots coming down the passage, stopping before her door. She froze, and reached for the sword, where she'd laid it on the bed. Someone knocked, and called her name softly.

Paks glanced around the room, then at the door, conscious of her loose hair, the mail shirt hanging on a peg. She shrugged, and answered.

"Yes?"

"I'm Arvid Semminson, lady, a traveler also staying here. You've see me in the common room, in black tunic and trousers. I heard you were staying in this afternoon, and I've been wanting to speak with you. May I come in, or could we meet downstairs shortly?"

Paks thought of the man in dark clothes. She had no idea what his profession was, which itself made thief most likely. She thought of the

Council meeting that night, and decided that she didn't want to meet anyone privately. "I'll be downstairs a little later, if that will suit."

"Very good," came the voice through the door, a mellow and pleasant voice. "I shall be honored to buy you a tankard of Hebbinford's best ale, or wine, whichever you prefer." The footsteps went away, back toward the stairs. Paks ran her hands through her hair, which was almost dry, and began to comb it. Somehow she did not feel like a fighter with hair down her back and wisping into her face. She braided it tightly, then finished her work on the sword belt. Her sword was clean and sharp, as always. She took off her trousers and looked them over. The previous mending still held. She could do nothing more for the shirt she had on. She had patched the worst rents, but the other holes and scorches remained. She had brushed and aired her cloak, but it, too, was stained and worn. The leather tunic, though bloodmarked, looked better over her shirt than nothing. She slipped it over her head, decided against the mail, and felt her boots. Still damp and oily. It would be another hour or so before they were dry. She pulled out the thin leather liners she'd worn in the high mountains, and put them on. More respectable than socks or bare feet. She strapped her sword belt on over the tunic, made sure she could get her dagger easily, and went downstairs.

Arvid Semminson had chosen a table with a good view of the stairs. He smiled as he saw her, and waved. Paks came to his table. Only one other person was in the common room, a great cheerful youth she had seen before, happily downing a tankard of ale at a swallow. He leaned on the wall behind his table, and looked half asleep.

Semminson's clothes, Paks noticed as she came closer, were, if not new, at least unpatched and whole. By the drape of the shoulder and sleeve, the cloth was of fine quality. The belt at his waist was polished black leather, new enough that the edges had not curled; his dagger's sheath was well-oiled and unscarred. He himself had neatly trimmed dark hair, a smooth-shaven face, and bright black eyes. His mouth quirked in amusement.

"Do I pass your inspection, lady?" he asked pleasantly.

Paks thought of her own ragged shirt and patched trousers, and reddened. "I've no right to inspect," she muttered.

"No, but you were. Everyone does. I expect that. See here, lady, I'll be straight with you — no secrets. I'm no merchant, nor mercenary fighter. Our esteemed innkeeper thinks I'm a thief, though I haven't robbed him. That's neither here nor there. But you, either you're — how shall I say? — in a related business to mine, or you're simply unaware of the situation. Either way, I can't let such an attractive young woman wander into a trap without warning. Do you follow me?"

Paks shook her head. She felt a certain distaste for his attempt at flattery. After the tailor's wife's comments, she had no illusions about being "an attractive young woman" by local standards.

"Well — " he looked her up and down. "It might be that our interests

422

would lie together. Or if not, a favor done might earn a favor later, who knows? But you know there's a Council meeting set for tonight?"

"Yes, but —"

"And you've agreed to go."

"Yes." She wondered how he knew that. She could not imagine Master Oakhallow telling him.

He snorted. "Then either you're a great deal more knowing that you act, or you know nothing at all." He leaned closer to her. "You can't hope to come out of that easily, you know. They'll get you one way or the other."

"What do you mean?"

He ticked off the points on his fingers. "A stranger in town, with plenty of money, and no liege to worry about angering, and under no protection that they know of? Don't be silly. They'll find some excuse, and then pfft! You're in trouble."

"But I haven't —"

" — done anything," he finished for her, and laughed again. "And just what do you think that has to do with it, eh? No, let me give you some advice. It's too late to escape, if you would. But be very careful. After they back you in a corner, they'll probably offer you some sort of deal, if they can't find anything to imprison you for at once. Consider it very carefully, whatever it is. Very carefully. Make no promises you can avoid. Beware of that wizard, if he's there: he'll try to bind you with some sort of spell, if you aren't careful."

"But why are you telling me all this?" asked Paks, thinking hard.

"As I told you. A favor. I may need one from you someday. You can't do me any good if you're in a cell, or dead. And if they do offer you a deal, I'd like to know about it. Before I came here, I'd heard the Council had hired outsiders for some kind of interesting work. Since I arrived, no one will tell me anything. Maybe they'll tell you, if they think they have a hold on you. And if you end up taking a job — well, you might want someone with you who wasn't one of theirs, if you know what I mean."

Paks was both fascinated and repelled. What he said almost made sense, almost fit with the Kuakgan's words. She still could not understand what sort of hold anyone could have on her, or why they would want to find her guilty of something. In Aarenis, they might have wanted an excuse to seize her for the slave market, but not in Tsaia. She wondered if Semminson was the kind of agent that the Kuakgan had been talking about. Would anyone, ever, try to help a southern army invade the north? She was sure not, until she remembered that Sofi Ganarrion was planning to come north to fight for his throne. She said nothing, rubbing her toe against the top of the other foot. Semminson was watching her.

"Well," she said finally. "Whatever comes, I'll be meeting with the Council tonight."

"Just keep what I said in mind," he urged.

"Mmm. I will." She noticed Hebbinford watching her from the kitchen door. She looked away and stood.

"Good luck to you," said Semminson softly. "I fear you'll need it." Paks went on out to the stableyard to gather her clean clothes from the line.

All in all, she had little appetite for supper that night. Her clean shirt had only the one tear, which she had mended, and everything was as neat as she could make it, but she still felt shabby. She wondered whether to wear her mail. If Semminson was a thief, she hated to leave it behind, but she didn't want them to think she was looking for trouble, either. She thought it over, and finally cornered Hebbinford to ask him.

"It doesn't matter," he said. "It's valuable, and you're a fighter — wear it if you wish. You can't carry a sword into Council, but the guards will keep it for you. Whatever you're comfortable with."

She wasn't comfortable at all, but decided to go upstairs and put on the mail. Semminson was coming out of a room farther along the hall, and he gave her a knowing look. She put on the heavy jingling shirt, buffed her helmet on the blanket, and put that on as well. With a captain of soldiers coming, she might as well look like a soldier.

Hebbinford sent one of the girls to her room to call her; she came down the stairs with a sort of muddled determination to do the right thing and not be trapped. He was waiting at the door, dressed in a long blue gown under a fur-collared cloak, instead of his usual tunic and apron. He smiled and they set off for the Hall together. Paks heard horses behind them, and moved to the edge of the street automatically. Hebbinford turned to look, and waved to the lead rider.

"Ah, Sir Felis. You haven't been in town these past few days."

"No. There's enough to do at the keep." Paks looked up at the mounted figure, his face lit by his escorts' torches. He wore chainmail and helmet, and she could tell nothing about him except that he sat his horse like a soldier. He looked down at her and spoke to Hebbinford. "Is this the person I've heard of?"

"Yes, Sir Felis. This is Paksenarrion Dorthansdotter."

"Hmmph." She saw the glitter of his eyes as they scanned her. "You look more like a soldier than a free blade, young woman. You were with Duke Phelan's company?"

"Yes, sir."

"What rank?"

"As a private, sir. File leader, my last year."

"I see. What — ? No, I'll wait until we're in session." He gave a causal wave of the hand to Hebbinford, and rode on past them.

The Hall, when they reached it, was lighted by torches in brackets along the front, as well as inside. Two of the captain's escort stood guard at the door. Paks felt sweat spring cold on her forehead; she wanted to yawn for no reason. Semminson's veiled warnings seemed suddenly appropriate. She heard voices inside. Hebbinford nudged her, and she surrendered her sword to the guard on the right, and went on through the door.

At the far end of a large room, much larger than the common room at

424

the inn, a knot of people clustered around the one table. Paks recognized Marshal Cedfer, now in mail, and looking much more like the Marshal she'd seen in Aarenis. His surcoat bore the crescent of Gird on a dark blue field. Master Oakhallow, in the same long robe he had worn in the afternoon, was already seated, and talking to one of the other men. Another man in mail — Paks assumed it was Sir Felis — stood at the end of the table, lips folded tightly as he listened.

Paks heard someone come in behind her, and turned to see the stonemason, Master Feddith. He gave her a cold look and stumped over to the table at once. Hebbinford, too, moved to that side of the room, and Paks followed slowly. A man she had not seen in town before, tall, with a generous belly, sat behind the table and looked up as the master mason and Hebbinford approached.

"Ah," he said. "We're all here, then. Have a seat, Councillors, have a seat. Let's get on with this." He looked at Paks. "So you're the young woman I've heard so much about? Paks — " He looked down at a sheet before him. "Paksenarrion Dorthansdotter? Of Three Firs?"

"Yes, sir." said Paks. The others were all taking seats around the far side and ends of the table.

"Good. Let me introduce you to the Council. I'm the mayor, Brewmaster Ceddrin. You saw my place on your way to the grange. You know Marshal Cedfer, and Master Oakhallow, and Master Hebbinford already. Captain Sir Felis Trevlyn, our count's military representative — " Sir Felis nodded shortly; in this light Paks could tell that he was a lean, weather-beaten man somewhat shorter than Duke Phelan. His beard was carefully trimmed. " — and Master Zinthys, the mage — " Paks looked at the slender, handsome young man in a long velvet robe lavishly banded with braid. He had rings on both hands, and a great polished crystal hanging by a silver chain on his chest. Master Zinthys smiled. The mayor went on. "This is Master Feddith, the stonemason, and I believe you also know Master Senneth, the moneychanger." He looked up and Paks nodded. "Also with us tonight are past Councillors: Master Hostin, our miller, Trader Garin Garinsson, and Master Doggal, the smith. Eris Arvidsdotter is here representing the farmholders." Trader Garin wore merchants' robes, and Eris Arvidsdotter wore a wool gown and cloak. She was as tall as Paks, and broad-shouldered; her gray hair was in a braided coil. The mayor paused until Paks had nodded at each of these. Then he picked up a heavy gavel lying on the table and rapped three times; the table boomed.

"The Council of Brewersbridge is in session," he said loudly. "I ask the protection of all the gods, and the guidance of all good spirits, to be over us in this meetintg. May wisdom and truth prevail. In the name of the High Lord, and all the powers of light." It sounded stilted, as if he didn't open the Council formally that often.

"May it be," responded the others.

"We are met," he said in a lower tone, "to learn what we can of a traveler here, one Paksenarrion Dorthansdotter. We have heard disturbing things all this year of trouble in Aarenis. We will examine this person to see what her business is here, and how it may be bound in with what has happened there." He waited, and Paks noticed that both the mage and the Marshal were taking notes. "Does anyone object to my asking the questions?" asked the mayor. Heads were shaken around the table. "Very well, then. If you have other questions, when I'm through, just say so. Now — is Paksenarrion Dorthansdotter your true name?"

"Yes, sir, but I'm called Paks, since I left home."

"I see. And you come from Three Firs? Where is that? In Tsaia?"

"I — I'm not sure. The closest larger town was Rocky Ford; that's where I joined Duke Phelan's company — "

The Marshal cleared his throat. "Excuse me, Mayor, but Rocky Ford is just within Tsaia, near the Finthan border in the north."

"I see. Three Firs was small, then?"

"Yes, sir. Much smaller than Brewersbridge. My father's land was a half-day's sheep drive out on the moors. We went to Three Firs rarely."

"And Rocky Ford?"

"I'd never been there before I — I ran away to join the company."

"So you went directly from home to Duke Phelan's company — hmm. And what was your father?"

"A sheepfarmer," said Paks. Then, anticipating the next question, she added, "I learned about mercenary companies from my cousin Jornoth; he'd left several years before, and came back with a horse, and gold, and said he was in the guard."

"Where? In Tsaia?"

"He didn't say, sir. But he said I couldn't go directly to a job that good. He said I'd have to start somewhere else, and he told me what to do."

"Hmm. Not common, for a girl from a remote farm to join an army."

"No, sir. But I'd always wanted to be a warrior — "

"As a mercenary?" put in the Marshal.

Paks blushed. "Not — exactly, sir. But Jornoth said that was the way to start."

The mayor took control again. "You say you were trained at Duke Phelan's stronghold, and went from there to the wars in Aarenis?"

"Yes, sir."

"How long were you in Aarenis?"

"I was there for three campaign seasons, and in winter quarters in Valdaire."

"You must have had a short season this year," he said, looking at her sharply. "Why did you leave your Company?"

Paks hesitated. "The war — Siniava had been killed, and my two years were up."

"You have told Marshal Cedfer and Master Oakhallow what happened to you; we also would like to know, from your own lips."

"Yes, sir." Paks gathered her wits. She hurried over the first part of the trip with Macenion, merely mentioning his half-elf ancestry and the

426

knowledge he claimed of the mountains. Then she described the valley of the elfane taig as they had first seen it, and the dream that came to both of them. The Councillors listened without interrupting as she described the underground passages, and the chamber where they'd found the elf lord. Through the battle with him, the burning, and the running fight with the orcs, and the last struggle that ended, beyond her comprehension, with her alone on the surface, no one spoke or stirred. "Some sickness came on me," she said finally. "I couldn't go far along the trail; a snowstorm came down off the mountains, and I fell. Then it was that the elves came. They healed me, and entered the valley to see whether I had told them the truth. When they returned, they told me how to find my way here, and gave me messages to Master Oakhallow and Marshal Deordtya. I was to say that the elfane taig had awaked, and the elf lord was freed." Paks stopped, and looked up and down the table. The faces were intent, but no longer hostile.

After a moment's silence, Sir Felis turned to the mayor. "If you don't mind, I'd like to ask a few questions."

"Go ahead."

"Paksenarrion, you say you served three campaign seasons. How soon after you joined the regular company were you made private from recruit?"

"The first battle, sir."

"What was your file position?"

"File second, the first year, sir, and the second. This past year we moved around a lot, but at the end I was file leader."

"I'm not clear on something. You've spoken both of leaving the company, and of being on some sort of long leave. Are you still the Duke's soldier, or not?"

Paks sighed. "Sir, the Duke had reason to give me a long leave. He and others had suggested that I might leave the company for a year or so. For other training, or experience, they said. But the Duke said I would be welcome back any time. I hadn't decided yet, sir, how soon to return."

"But you have no complaints against Duke Phelan, or he against you?"

"I have none against him, sir, and as far as I know he has none against me. And the Company is all I've known. I miss them."

"Have you any sort of token or pass from your duke, that might prove what you say of his opinion?"

Paks remembered the ring he had given the survivors of Dwarfwatch, and reached into her pouch for it. "Here is a ring —" She handed it to the mayor, who peered at it, and passed it along the table. When they had all looked at it, the mayor passed it back.

"Dwarfwatch," the mayor said. "Isn't that the name of that Sorellin fort on the south end of Hakkenarsk Pass?"

"So the traders say," said Master Senneth.

"So. Those rumors, last spring, of a major battle there —" mused Hebbinford. "You must have been there. Why were you so angry with the merchants, Paksenarrion, for mentioning it?"

Paks glanced quickly at Sir Felis and the Marshal, then back to Hebbinford. "Sir, it is the Duke's business. I don't talk of it with merchants. But — by treachery, most of my — of a — cohort was lost at Dwarfwatch, to Lord Siniava. Most of a cohort of Halverics, too. For those of us who lived, the Duke had these rings made."

"So he's fought understrength this past year," commented Sir Felis. "And the Halveric too, I presume."

The Marshal was not deflected from the original story. "What was it, a siege, or what?"

"If she considers it her duke's business, Cedfer — " began the Kuakgan.

"Nonsense. Anything that's happened almost a year ago is public knowledge in Aarenis, and we'll know the details here sooner or later."

Paks took a deep breath and tried to shove her private memories back into hiding. All the mercenary companies in the south knew the story; Cedfer was right. She gathered her wits and began. "One cohort of the Duke's company was detached from the siege of Rotengre — the Guild League cities had joined in that — and garrisoned Dwarfwatch while the Sorellin militia, who had been there, helped with the grain harvest." She paused, and they all nodded. They listened intently as she described Halveric Company's approach, the surrender, the departure of all but a guard cohort of Halveric's and Siniava's attack, the fate of the prisoners marched away toward Rotengre, and the desperate defense of the few who held the fort.

"And you were in that. I see." Marshal Cedfer glanced at the Kuakgan and back to Paks. "Were you one of those sieged in the fort, or were you taken prisoner?"

"Neither, sir. Three of us were not taken — by chance, we were gathering berries in the brambles and they didn't see us. We took word to the Duke." Paks stopped there and looked at them. Sir Felis was leaning forward, alert and eager; the Marshal's eyebrows were up; the Kuakgan was frowning slightly. The rest merely looked interested.

"How far did you go?" asked Sir Felis. "Where was the Duke?"

"Outside Rotengre, with the rest of the company," said Paks. She wished they would go on to something else. She didn't want to think about that journey, about Saben and Canna.

"I can see," said the Marshal, "why you would be trusted by Duke Phelan. Remarkable. Well, then — so the Duke relieved his force at the fort. And where was the Halveric? I should think he'd have been there too."

"He had taken most of his Company toward Merinath," said Paks. "They arrived the next day, too late to fight there: but they came to Rotengre."

"And how many troops did Siniava have?"

"We thought about eight hundred, altogether — "

"But Phelan's force is what — three cohorts altogether?"

"Yes, sir. He had help from the Clarts and Count Vladi — "

428

"And Gird, no doubt," said the Marshal firmly. "Well, indeed. That's quite a tale, but straight enough. Now, what's happened this last year? We've heard of widespread fighting, open war from the mountains to the sea, armies marched clear from the Westmounts to the Copper Hills. What about it?" The mayor was watching the Marshal closely, but did not interfere.

Paks wondered where to start. "Sir, after the year before, the Duke and the Halveric were certain that Siniava meant to conquer all of Aarenis. The Guild League cities blamed him for the piracy of Rotengre, and other things as well. My lord Duke pledged to spend himself on a campaign against Siniava, for what he had done to us. He gathered most of the northern mercenaries to his aid. And the Guild League cities fought on their own lands, and sometimes marched abroad as well."

"Aha!" Master Senneth was rubbing his hands together. "I always suspected the like, sirs, I did indeed. Too many caravans were robbed on the trade roads between Merinath and Sorellin, and none of the goods ever showed up here. They must have been taken on south. And I'd heard through — well, I'd heard that Siniava had bought into some of the guilds."

Paks nodded. "We heard the same, sir, after Cortes Cilwan fell."

"Cilwan fell?" asked Sir Felis sharply. "What happened to the Count?"

"He was killed," said Paks. "But Vladi's men got his heir out, the boy, and he's safe in Andressat, the last I heard."

"Succession wars," muttered the Marshal. "They'll have succession wars, as well as everything else."

"Go on," said the mayor, with a gesture that silenced the others. "What then?"

Paks shrugged. "I don't know it all, sir; I was only a private, after all." She described the campaign as best she could. Sir Felis and the Marshal listened intently, their fingers moving as if on maps. The others reacted more to descriptions of cities fallen, battles fought, factions implicated in this plot or that. Finally, dry-throated with the length of the tale, she came to that last few days, when Siniava's remaining soldiers were neatly trapped with the help of Alured the Black. "We caught up with the last of them," Paks explained, "in an old ruin where the Immer and Imefal meet."

"Cortes Immer," said the Kuakgan softly. "No one's held that since the old duke's line died."

Paks looked at him. "Is that what it is? It's still a great citadel, built into the living rock like Cortes Andres. Anyway, Siniava was killed, trying to escape secretly from the citadel, and after that his army surrendered to the militia."

"I can hardly believe Siniava is truly dead," mused the mayor. "How many years have we worried that he might gain control of Aarenis and come over the mountains? I remember the first word we had of him, don't you, Master Oakhallow?"

"Indeed yes."

"And now he's gone. And no more agents of his will come through, trying to spy out defenses, such as they are."

Chapter Eleven

"*If* she's telling the truth," said Feddith harshly. "If. 'Twould be months before we could check her tale. She might be an agent herself."

Paks tensed, but Sir Felis answered. "I don't think so," he said. "She carries the Duke's ring, and showed it willingly. I know that crest."

"It could have been stolen," said Feddith stubbornly.

"She fights like a soldier trained in Phelan's Company," commented the Marshal.

"And as well," said the mayor, with a look at the mage, "we have a way to tell if she lied. If Master Zinthys is willing — "

The mage looked at Paks, and smiled disarmingly. "I should say, if the lady is willing. Without any special arts, sirs, I see no liar there. An honest soldier, it seems to me, and I daresay to Captain Sir Felis." He caught Felis's eye, and the captain nodded. "I would not wish to cast a spell on her if she's opposed, sirs; I would not indeed."

The tradesmen of the Council looked taken aback. Master Oakhallow smiled faintly. Marshal Cedfer spoke up, brisk as always.

"I'm sure she'll have no objection; it's an honorable request. Isn't that right, Paksenarrion?"

Paks felt the tensions in the room, and wondered what to do. She wished they'd agreed with the mage to let her alone. What was this truth spell like? Even with the Kuakgan's assurance, in the afternoon, she feared to be involved in more magic.

"Sirs," she began cautiously, "the only time I've been spelled, it was by that elf lord. Could I ask what the spell is, that Master Zinthys would use? I have no wish to put myself in another's power for anything but the truth alone."

"Well said," murmured the Kuakgan. The others nodded, and Master Zinthys smiled at her.

"It's not like that at all — or rather, it may be a bit like that, but this spell is quite limited. You're absolutely right, not to let yourself be spelled without safeguards. I'll explain it to you. The power of this spell is that you cannot lie while it is active. Nor, for that matter, can anyone standing very close to you. I could, of course, cast it so that no one in the room could lie, but that takes a great deal of power. The limit of the spell is that while you cannot lie, you are not compelled to say anything at all. Nor does it affect

430

acts other than speech — either compulsion or prevention. And when the spell wears off, you can lie at will. As a practical matter, the spell will wear off fairly soon; I see no reason to expend the power for a longer duration. Is all that clear?" He seemed quite proud of his explanation.

"Yes," said Paks slowly. "But — " she looked around at them all. All strangers. "Forgive me, sirs and lady," she said, trying to be very polite, but aware that no one could say what she intended politely, "but I know none of you well, and at most have known you for a few days only. How do I know that you — ?" Her voice trailed off as they reacted. Some of the faces went red at once. The mason began to sputter, but the smith laughed out loud.

"She's got you there," he chuckled. "Ah, lady, you have hit on it. I should have known that anyone who could lead that black devil away would think in the end. You don't trust us to say truth, and no wonder."

"That's right," said Master Zinthys quickly. "I hold no rancor, lady, for your doubts. Nonetheless, the Council has a reason to make sure of you, and your tale."

"Is it that thief, Paks?" asked Hebbinford. "I saw him talking to you this afternoon."

"Sir, I don't know. I didn't believe much that he said, no. But — Master Oakhallow said I had caused so much talk — I've been foolish, it seems. It may be late in the day, but I think I should be careful now, however I've acted. I never traveled alone before, as I told you. I never thought how it would seem, coming alone from the mountains with a load of treasure. I can understand your suspicions. But still — I don't want to be magicked into anything."

The mayor, still red-faced, nodded. "I see. You don't know me at all; no use to tell you how my family founded this town, generations back. You've no call to trust me. Are there any here you could trust? Did you know any Girdsmen before? Or were you kuakgannir?"

Paks thought about it. "Sir, I didn't mean to insult you, but I did, didn't I? Yes, I have known Girdsmen, and the elves sent me to both the Marshal and the Kuakgan. If they say it is all right, I am willing."

The mayor looked at her shrewdly. "You may simply be as inexperienced as you seem. We'll see. Well, Master Oakhallow? Marshal Cedfer?"

"To my knowledge," said the Kuakgan, "Master Zinthys is an honest mage, and the spell he speaks of works just as he said it did. Certainly I pledge that we are not planning any other magic on you."

"And I the same," said the Marshal. "I assure you that Master Oakhallow and I are quite competent to prevent anything else, too."

"Yes, sir," said Paks miserably. "I just wanted to ask." She looked at Master Zinthys, fighting a hollow feeling in her belly. "Whenever you're ready, sir."

"You'd best sit down," said the mage. He rose and dragged a chair over for her. "It might make you dizzy for a moment. Now, try to relax." Paks had the feeling that he enjoyed showing his skill before the others, as he gestured fluidly with his long graceful hands.

Once she was seated, the mage took from his robe a small pouch and from that a pinch of colored dust, which he tossed at Paks. It spread in the air, and seemed to hang a long time before settling. Then he took four wands from up one sleeve, and set them on the floor around her chair. Finally he stood back and began to chant in a language Paks had never heard before, while gesturing with one hand in front of her face. Behind him, the faces of the others at the Council table were intent. Only the Kuakgan's showed amusement in the quirk of his mouth. She wondered why. At last the mage finished, and said in the common tongue: "Speak truth, or be silent, until the spell is done." Paks was surprised to feel nothing. No tingles, no pain, nothing at all different from before. She did not plan to lie, but what would happen if she did? Had the spell worked?

The mayor began the questioning, asking much the same things as before: her name, background, reasons for leaving the Duke, reasons for coming to Brewersbridge. He asked little about the conflicts she'd described, and no details she had not already given. She answered, as before, honestly. It went more quickly, since no one interrupted. When he was done, the mayor sat back and looked at the others.

"She's not lied. Her story's unusual, but true."

"Then why did she resist being spelled?" asked the mason, still hostile. "And how do we know the spell is working?"

The mage flushed and sat up straight, but Master Oakhallow's deep voice forestalled what he might have said. "Master Mason, Zinthys is a competent wizard. The spell is good."

"If you say so," muttered the mason.

"I wonder myself," said the Marshal, "that a soldier of her experience would show fear of a simple spell. But if the sorcery she suffered before were severe enough — "

The Kuakgan looked at him sharply. "Come, Marshal, you know as well as I the power in that place. Only a witless fool would want to risk that again."

"True — true."

"How long, Master Zinthys, will the spell last?" the Kuakgan asked.

"Not long. Another quarter-glass, perhaps, though I can counteract it now, if you wish."

"It would be more courteous," he murmured, and the rest of the Council nodded.

Paks watched as the mage came near. He picked up the wands and stowed them up his sleeve, then began another incantation. When he finished, he grinned at her.

"There. That wasn't so bad, was it?"

"No, sir." Paks still felt nothing. Foolish, maybe. She wished she'd agreed at once to the spell, since it had done her no harm. The mayor cleared his throat.

"We've been here for some time, and there's more to come." Paks tensed again. "Let's take a short break now, and ease our throats with a bit of ale. Is that all right with you, Paksenarrion?"

"Yes, sir." Paks wondered what was coming next, and thought of Semminson's warnings. What might they want her to do? Meanwhile, she stood when the others did, and followed them out to the yard before the building. The mayor spoke to a man in servants' clothes standing there, and told him to fetch ale. It was quite dark out, and cool; Paks shivered. Sir Felis came up to her.

"I'm more than glad to know Siniava's dead," he began. "One reason the count had me down here is in case an army came over the pass. It will be a year or more before the keep is finished. But you haven't seen that, have you?"

"No, sir."

"That's my command. When it's finished, we'll have a place to fight from, if it's necessary. The last time there was a battle near here, we had no fortified position. No place to store arms, or haven for those who couldn't fight — nothing."

"We've built the grange since then," put in the Marshal.

"Oh, yes. But then, it's not designed as a keep, though it is stone. You couldn't hold it against assault."

"No, you're right. Not against a trained force. It would hold against bandits, though — we've used it for that."

"Before my time, Marshal — and wasn't it before yours?"

"Oh, yes. That was Deordtya's doing, not mine, years back. I suppose I shouldn't say 'we' when I mean Gird's grange; it's just habit."

The servant appeared at their side with a tray of tankards; each took one.

"This will be Ceddrin's private brew," commented the Marshal. "I doubt you've tasted as good, Paksenarrion."

Paks blew away the foam and sipped. It was rich and hearty. "It's very good," she said.

"Just what sort of training did Duke Phelan suggest you look for?" asked Sir Felis. "I'd have thought he could offer anything you or he might need."

"He thought, sir, that I might learn mounted warfare, and something of fortifications and defense — "

"Huh. Sounds as if he were planning the education of a squire, not a man-at-arms. Had he suggested you work toward a knighthood, or something like that?" His voice hinted at the unlikeliness of this.

Paks nodded. "He said, sir, that nothing was certain, but that I might have the ability to become a cohort captain, or some such, years from now."

Sir Felis frowned. "The land's full of captains; I wonder that he'd risk losing a good soldier. Had he ever given you any command?"

"I was temporary corporal for awhile, sir, when one of ours was injured. And at the end of the campaign, when Siniava was trapped in — Cortes Immer, was it? — I led those who watched the bolthole."

"Did Siniava come that way?"

"Yes, sir." Paks offered no details.

"I see. Phelan obviously thought well of you. I must tell you that there's

433

not much chance my count would hire you, if you were hoping for that. He's done no recruiting this past year. You could, of course, go and ask him directly."

"I hadn't thought of it, sir. I know little of this country, or who holds which keep."

"Mmmm. I'll show you a map — can you read maps? Good. I've one of the kingdom, showing the principal fiefs. It may give you some idea where you could hope to hire on. Marshal Cedfer can tell you of opportunities of the grange and Hall. The Fellowship of Gird, you know, maintains several training centers for fighting men at every level. For that matter, they have fighting orders, as do followers of Falk and Camwyn."

"Is that where paladins come from?" asked Paks. "We saw a paladin in Aarenis."

Sir Felis choked on his ale. "Is that what you —!? Sorry. No, not exactly. The Marshal can tell you more than I, if you're interested in that. There's an order of knights, the Knights of Gird, just as there are Knights of the Dragon's Breath, followers of Camwyn Dragonmaster."

Paks was confused. "I thought knights were all the same. Noblemen born, or those knighted for service."

Sir Felis stared. "Oh, no. Whatever gave you that idea? Oh dear, no. Where did you say you were from? A small border village, wasn't it? Now let me try to explain." His explanation hardly enlightened Paks, since she knew few of the places and none of the rulers he mentioned. He finished his lecture with a gesture to the small gold device on his collar, shaped like a peal of bells. "For instance, I was knighted in the Order of the Bells, one of the three orders created by the royal house of Tsaia. The oldest, I might add." He paused for a swallow of ale; his glance expected a reaction. Paks was acutely aware of how little she knew, and how important he thought it.

"Now," he went on, after wiping his mustache, "members of my order may be followers of any honorable god or hero. I myself am a Girdsman, but my father's brother is Falkian, and so are my cousins. Our loyalty is to the crown of Tsaia — or, more accurately, to the heir of the House of Mahierian. But Knights of Gird swear their loyalty to the Marshal-General of Gird, through their Knight Commander. The — er — rules governing admission to each order depend — er — on the order, and the circumstances." He looked her up and down, doubtfully, as if she were an unpedigreed horse at a sale.

"I see," said Paks, more to stop him than because she did. She was still confused. She was actually relieved when the mayor tapped her arm.

"Let's get back; we have yet a good bit of business to talk over."

This time they asked her to sit down at the beginning of the session, and the rest spread themselves around the table on all sides. Only the master mason still seemed hostile.

"We appreciate your cooperation," began the mayor. "Now that we know something of your background, let me explain how things stand in Brewersbridge. We're on a major trade route from the west to the sea. We

434

have a lot of traffic through, and want it — we depend on it. Nonetheless, I hope you won't be insulted when I say that the Council is opposed to having free blades around town. Some of them, like you, are honorable folk, and cause no trouble intentionally. Others, like the fellow who died, pick quarrels everywhere. We've learned it's best to insist that soldiers and warriors either find a local lord or commander, to be responsible for their behavior, or move on." He smiled, as he said this. Paks wondered what was coming next.

"Now you," he said, "are perhaps a special case. While Master Senneth, even for the Council's peace of mind, won't divulge how much treasure you desposited with him, he has assured us that you will not need to rob anyone for the price of a meal before Midwinter Feast." A chuckle went around the table. Even the mason smiled. "So, since you've given honest account of yourself, we have less to worry about. Nonetheless, our tradition is clear: since Sir Felis has no employment for you, we would not willingly have you stay too long idling about. That would mean more than a few weeks, in your case: I understand that you've ordered goods from some of our local tradesmen. Certainly you may stay until they're completed, as long as nothing happens. On the other hand, we are prepared to offer you certain employment — the Council is, I mean. If you took it, we would not consider you in the same class as an adventurer."

Paks remembered Semminson's warning. "What sort of employment, sir, did you have in mind?"

"Work suitable for your abilities and training, I believe. And so says Marshal Cedfer. I think Sir Felis would now concur, would you not?" Sir Felis nodded. "We have been plagued, hereabouts, with brigands preying on caravans in the region. You can understand why that is critical for us; we depend on their trade. Sir Felis has swept the area several times, finding nothing. He has direct orders from the count to concentrate his time and men on the building of the keep north of town. We need someone to search out the brigands' hiding place, and lead a force against them. None of us have the training — or, to be frank, the time to take away from our trades. Would you be willing to take this commission?"

Paks could not suppress a grin. It sounded like fun, at least the part about finding the brigands' camp. But as for killing or catching them — "Sir, it is an interesting proposal. But, whatever Marshal Cedfer may think, I am hardly able to defeat a band of brigands on my own."

"Not at all," said the mayor. "Of course not. We would expect you to *lead* a force, including some of the local militia. And you could confer, perhaps, with the Marshal or Sir Felis, on the best method for defeating them, once you had found their camp."

Put that way, it sounded even more attractive. Whenever Paks thought of brigands, she thought of those who had killed Saben and Canna. She nodded at the mayor. "I have no love for brigands," she said. "I'll be glad to hunt them for you."

"Good. What we propose is this: we will authorize you to call on members of the local militia who have free time, and they — or the town — will supply their weapons. We will not pay you, but we will grant you a share of any recovered goods, and a head-price for each robber killed or captured. If you need extraordinary aid, come to Marshal Cedfer, and he will arrange it as he sees fit. Is that satisfactory?"

Paks had no idea what such contracts were usually like, but it seemed reasonable. If many caravans had been robbed, surely the plunder would make a fair return. "Yes," she said. "That will do. But do you have any idea where they might be?"

The mayor leaned forward. "An idea, yes, but we aren't sure. Caravans have been attacked on all the roads around. But Eris — " he nodded to the farm woman, who nodded to Paks, " — Eris tells us that farms have been robbed, too — and one or two wiped out — west of here. None close in, but those farther out have lost livestock. There are several ruins out that way which might be useful to brigands, though Sir Felis found no one there — "

"That's not to say they might not use them," Sir Felis broke in. "We've had no time for more than a fast sweep — they could have been hiding nearby, if they were clever."

"We think," the mayor went on, "that they must have some spy in town. More caravans are robbed on their way out — especially those that have come on a market day, and sold things in our market. I won't conceal the fact that these men — if it's humans — are dangerous. Typically they kill all the caravaners, merchants and guards alike. That's ten to twenty guards, maybe five merchants or so, and the drivers. They've killed two farm families we know of — I suppose they surprised them robbing — "

"But," Sir Felis interrupted again, "it may be that some farmer out there is in league with them." Eris Arvidsdotter shook her head angrily, but Paks remembered the setup at "uncle's" in Aarenis. It would make sense. "Northwest of here," Sir Felis continued, "was Baron Anseg's land, but he died without a close heir years ago, and the title of that land is still being argued in Vérella. Once you're away from the river, and well into the woods beyond Brewersbridge, there's no lord for two days' travel, until Baron Velis's outside Bingham."

"The merchants' guilds," put in the mayor, "naturally have an interest in the safety of the roads. We have no Guild League, as in Aarenis, with real authority, but the guilds will support any effort to keep the roads safe where no lord has the responsibility."

"I see," said Paks. She was becoming confused again, and clung to what she did understand. "So you want me to hunt around and find where the brigands are hiding, and lead a small force to drive them out? Do you want them driven away, or killed, or captured, or what?"

"Killed or captured, definitely," said Marshal Cedfer. "Drive them out, and they'll return as soon as you're gone."

"I say kill them," put in the mason. "What good are brigands anyway?"

Paks wondered if he'd ever killed anyone. Himself.

"And if you find out who is — I mean, who *may* be giving information here in Brewersbridge — " added the mayor.

Paks grinned. "You expect a stranger to find out what's going on when you, who know everyone, can't? I might be able to find the brigands, sir, and I know I can fight, but I've no experience in finding out secrets like that."

"Well, but if you should happen to learn — "

"I would tell — Marshal Cedfer, you wished me to report to? Is that right?"

"Yes, that's right. Or me. But Marshal Cedfer is best."

Paks looked around the table. Everyone was watching her. The mage gave her a bright smile, as if to encourage her. The Marshal and Sir Felis looked impatient, as if she were a slightly stupid recruit. Master Oakhallow's level gaze held a challenge. She felt, suddenly, very tired. To fight brigands was well enough, and she'd be glad of an honest, above-ground battle again, but she had the feeling that they all expected something else. Something more.

"Yes," she said finally. "I'll do that — or try to. I suppose the first thing is to look for the places they might be. Do you have a map, perhaps, of the local — "

But at that they all began to talk.

"How good of you — "

"No need for that tonight, now that you've — "

"Perhaps tomorrow you can meet with Marshal Cedfer — "

" — out to the keep, and I'll introduce you to my sergeants — "

The mayor banged his gavel once, and everyone quieted. "One last thing. The town, as I said, will supply the militia, their food and weapons. But do you have what you need for yourself? I see you have armor — " He waited for her answer. Paks thought about her gear. To move about the countryside, as far as he had mentioned — a day's ride away? — she would need a horse of some kind.

"I could use a horse or mule," she said. "My pony's not the right animal for prowling around."

Sir Felis frowned. "I haven't any spares, right now. We've thrush in the stable, and horses lame."

The mayor shook his head. "It's so late in the season. The horses in town now are work horses — and in use every day. Marshal Cedfer?"

"No. Sorry. My own mount, and Ambros's, that's all I've got. If you wanted to buy one, perhaps Sir Felis could send to the count's stable — "

"There's one spare horse," said Hebbinford. "In my stable — that black horse."

Paks felt a surge of excitement. She had not thought of the black, but that was the sort of horse she had dreamed of in the past. A true warrior's horse. She looked at the mayor, and Hebbinford, and back again. "What about that one, then? No one else is using it."

"I suppose that's all right," said the mayor slowly. "I can see you need a horse, to go looking all over the country. If the rest of you agree — "

"What of the man's heirs?" asked Master Feddith. "He looked a friendless man, but if he had heirs, they'd have some right to the beast."

"What of the fines he'd have owed, for trying to rob our Master Smith, if he'd lived?" asked Senneth sharply. "I say the Council can claim his horse for damages, and sell it to Paksenarrion if we choose."

"Perhaps, sirs," said Paks, uncertain if she should speak. "I could but have the use of the horse at first — paying Master Hebbinford for his keep, of course. It may be that I have not the skill to master such an animal — " She paused as the smith snorted loudly, and all eyes went to him. "Even if I do, I will not need it after this, I think."

"That's well spoke," said the smith abruptly. "'Twould do that beast good to be worked, that it would, and the trying of him out would be a reason for her to ride about the countryside. But as for skill — " He looked hard at Paks. "You've either skill of a horse-breaker, girl, or magic in your fingers, and that's a fact." Paks saw both the Kuakgan and the Marshal give her hands a quick glance. She was glad they were clasped to cover the ring.

"Well, then," said the mayor, "how think you? I see no harm in that, and it saves Master Hebbinford risking his own neck to keep the beast exercised, for I doubt you'd let Sevri try it, would you Jos?"

"Never," said Hebbinford, with a ghost of a grin. "Nor is my lass that crazy. I'm for it."

"And I," said the other Council members.

"And I hope you'll decide to buy that horse," said Senneth, as they rose. "If you go, and leave it here, the Council will be left with the care of it all winter until the spring fairs. We'll give you a good price, I swear."

"We can do better than that, Senneth," said the mayor, clapping him on the shoulder. "Should she succeed in routing all the brigands, we might call it a reward. Then she could not refuse, and we need not worry about the feed."

The others laughed, and gathered around Paks for a few words each before leaving. When she had retrieved her sword from the guard at the door, she found Hebbinford and the Kuakgan waiting to walk with her. The night had turned even colder, and she looked forward to the new cloak the tailor would make.

Chapter Twelve

After so late a night, Paks would have been glad to sleep later than usual, but anticipation of the black horse woke her at dawn. Could she ride it? She felt sure of the power of the ring, but once mounted she could not concentrate on her ring finger. She knew she should be thinking of the brigands, and less of the horse, but the black horse fit her old dream of adventure so perfectly . . . she could almost see herself riding through admiring crowds.

She had hoped to work with it in privacy first, but early as it was everyone in the inn seemed to have business in the stableyard. She began with grooming; the beast had nearly caught Sevri with a massive hoof, and after that his owner had done it. Paks kept her thumb firmly on the ring as she picked up a brush and eased into the stall by its head. The ears were alert but not flattened, and the great dark eye watched her calmly as the horse worked on its ration of grain.

"There now," crooned Paks, setting the brush to that massive shoulder. "There, quiet, stay calm, black one." She began to brush, more gently than would do for a thorough grooming, and with a wary eye on the ears. The horse stood taller and more heavily built than the Duke's warhorses, as tall as Arcolin's favorite. She worked her way along the ribs, the croup, the rump. Dust and scurf flew; the horse had not been well-groomed for some time. She brushed down the haunches, saw them tense, and concentrated on the ring for a moment. "Nothing's wrong, horse. I won't hurt you. Quiet, now, easy — " Bunched muscles relaxed; she saw the fetlock sink deeper in the straw. "You'd like to be out of here, wouldn't you? Go for a ride? Out in the open air — along the roads — good horse — " Soon she had brushed both sides, the belly (another pause for the ring's action there), brushed out the heavy tangled mane. She looked up and saw Sevri's awed face over the stall wall.

"I didn't think you could really do it," said Sevri.

Paks grinned at her, thumb firm on the ring. "I wasn't sure I could myself. Can you bring me a pick?"

"You're going to touch his *feet*?"

Paks shrugged. "What if he has a stone? If he's taken this much, he should take that."

Sevri handed over a hoofpick. "I just finished Star. Here."

Paks leaned down beside the near fore, impressed again by the size of those platter-like hooves. "Come on, black one — let's have a hoof." She could feel the tension above her, and glanced up to see the horse watching, ears stiffly turned back. "No — come on, now — " She pinched the tendons as she'd been taught, wondering briefly if she should have done this outside a stall, just in case. But the hoof came up, at last, and she cleaned around the frog with her pick. The other front hoof went as well, but as she bent to touch the near hind, the horse squealed and slammed a kick into the stall wall, narrowly missing her. Paks thought a loud NO through the ring, and the horse froze, trembling. She could see the cracked board where the hoof struck, and heard a murmur of voices at the stable door. Sevri urged the watchers away.

Slowly, concentrating on the ring, Paks slid her hand down the hind leg, over slick black hide to the white feather below the hock, and through that heavy hair felt along to the fetlock. The scar was hidden by the thick hair above it — a deep scar, and still sensitive, for the horse blew a rattling breath, despite the ring's compulsion, as she touched it. Paks straightened. "Easy — I'd warrant you have another on the off side as well. No wonder you don't like having your legs handled. I wonder what did that? Nothing good. Well, perhaps we can leave that a day, until you trust me more." She came back to the horse's head, and scratched under his jaw until the strained look left his eyes. "Surely the smith didn't do that, holding you to shoe you?" The horse relaxed enough to stretch its neck. Paks slipped out of the stall, shaking a little with the strain of using the ring for so long.

"Will you ride today?" asked Sevri, who was waiting by the door.

"He needs exercise," said Paks. "But he's got some injury to his back legs — that's why he's so touchy, I think. I hate to ride him out until I can handle those legs, but he's had as much as he can take, for now. Maybe later."

Paks went in to breakfast, trying to ignore the curious looks of the others. If she was going to lead a group out against brigands, and train a horse, she needed several things from the shops. She made a list during breakfast, and asked Hebbinford where she could find some of the items. When she returned, everyone seemed to be out of the way but Sevri.

"If you want me to leave, as well — " she said shyly.

"No, but don't get too close. I don't know what he'll do. Tir's bones, I don't even know how to rig that saddle." She went into the stable. The black horse nosed over the stall wall; she had not yet touched the ring. Perhaps it was not a true outlaw. Sevri brought the bridle, red leather decorated with copper rings tarnished green. The reins were broad and heavy, and the bit — Paks shook her head.

"I can't use that! Look at those spikes, Sevri."

"The warhorses we see here all have bits like that," said Sevri. "Are you sure?"

"I'm sure of this — I won't use that bit. The Duke didn't use anything like that. Where can I buy another one?"

440

"You can use my father's old one, if it'll do. He had a hauling team once, before he sold it to a caravaner that was short. Try this — " Sevri brought out an old, rusty-linked bit like those Paks had seen on cart horses. While Sevri shook it in a sandbag to get the rust off, Paks worked at the stiff lacings of the bridle. At last she had the old bit off, and the smooth one in place.

"If he's used to that mess in his mouth, he won't take the bit easily," said Paks. "Let's see — " And as she walked up with the bridle, the black horse threw up its head, snorting. Again she thumbed the ring, which quieted the noise. Sevri darted off for an apple.

"Will this work?"

"It might." Paks was glad of anything that would conceal the action of the ring. She offered it, concentrating on the ring, and in a moment slid the bit in place, and the crownpiece over the horse's ears as its teeth crunched the apple. She waited to fasten the noseband and throatlatch until the apple was finished, and the last lumps passed down the black throat.

"I hope you can hold him with that," said Sevri doubtfully.

"With what?" came a brisk voice from the door, and they all jumped. Paks clenched her left hand on the ring and turned. Marshal Cedfer stood there, with Ambros just behind him.

"She changed bits," said Sevri, before Paks could think what to say. "She wouldn't use that old one — " She nudged it with her toe, where it lay in the aisle.

"That's a mouthful indeed," said the Marshal, picking it up. "But what are you using instead, Paksenarrion? That 'magic' Doggal mentioned?"

"No," said Sevri again. "It's one of my father's old bits, a smooth one that he used when he had a team. But I thought warhorses had to have spiked bits."

The Marshal's face relaxed. "Good, Paksenarrion, very good. No, Sevri, a horse can be trained to any bit, but the smooth ones are better. Hasty warriors try to use rough bits instead of training to get their horses' attention. A good horseman uses as smooth a bit as he may." He took a step forward to look at the horse more closely. "As I recall, Duke Phelan's troops use horses for transport only. I'm sure you ride — perhaps well — but I thought I could help you with the commands peculiar to warhorses."

"Thank you, Marshal," said Paks. "I realized this morning that even the saddles we used are not like this one — " she gestured at the heavy saddle with its tangle of rigging, on a peg nearby.

"You haven't cleaned it yet," said the Marshal, frowning.

"No, sir." Paks flushed as if Stammel had found her with dirty equipment.

"Hmm. Clean tack, Paksenarrion, is very important. Sevri, bring us a fresh pad, at least. Lead him out to the yard, Paksenarrion."

With her hand clenched around the ring, Paks led the black horse out. He followed as calmly as Star, for which she was grateful. Her neck prickled as she placed the sheepskin pad. The Marshal handed her the saddle.

"I see you know how to work with a bridled horse — see, Ambros. She's

441

got her arm in the rein, just as I keep telling you. Now, Paksenarrion, let me explain all those extra straps." Paks needed the help, but wished it were someone else. "That — yes, that one — is the foregirth. Fasten it first. Good. Now the breastband — see those hooks on the saddle? Yes. Not tight — just lying smoothly. That's so the saddle cannot slip back under any strain. Now the rest of that — by Gird himself! That fellow didn't know how to stow his gear. Roll that mess slowly out over his rump — be careful, girl! Yes. Now see that loop on top? The tail goes through that. Wait, though — " The Marshal moved to the horse's rump and felt of the loop. "Heh. I might have known. Feel this. It's too stiff; it's probably rubbed him raw already. We'll take all this off — " and he began to work at fastenings on the back of the saddle as he talked. "You don't really need it yet. Oil and clean it — get it all soft — and I'll show you how to put it back on. In a fight, or traveling in rough country, it keeps the saddle from slipping forward, just like the breeching strap on a pack animal." He went to the other side, and finished there. "Here, Sevri, take these away." He watched as Paks checked the stirrup length; she left it unchanged. "Do you want me to hold him while you mount?"

Paks looked at the horse, which suddenly seemed much taller. Yet she had ridden Arcolin's horse, that once. Her mouth was dry. If the Marshal had not been there, she could have led the horse to a field, where she could hope to land soft. Instead, she sighed inwardly, and thanked him. "I must admit, sir, that this is the biggest horse — "

"You've ridden," he finished. "Yes, I thought it might be." He took the rein, and the horse stiffened. Paks got her foot in the stirrup, and tried to swing up, but the horse shifted suddenly with her weight. She fell into the saddle with an ungraceful scramble. It was built high and close to her body; she had almost landed on, and not in, it.

"With a horse like this," said the Marshal, "you need to be quicker. Or else train him to stand." He stepped back, releasing the rein, as Paks straightened.

The saddle felt strange, as if it were hovering over the horse's back, and the ground looked very far away. Paks nudged the horse lightly with her heels, and it lunged forward. She thumbed the ring, thinking "Easy!" and it settled again, ears flicking. Paks saw eyes at the inn door, and cursed silently. She could feel the horse tensing under her, the hump in its back that kept the saddle too high. "Settle down, horse," she said softly. "Settle down, and we'll go for a walk somewhere." It took one stiff step, then another. She laid the rein against its neck, to turn it around the dungheap, and it whirled on its hind legs, almost unseating her. "*Easy!*" she said. Arcolin's horse had been nothing like this! For a moment she longed for gentle little Star, but she was conscious of the Marshal and Ambros watching. She was a warrior, and this was a warrior's horse. If she was ever to be a knight — She talked the horse forward, hardly daring to touch it with her heels. Nearly to the cowbyre: she had to turn. Again the light touch of rein, and the lightning spin, but this time she was ready for it.

442

"You might see what happens if you pull one rein lightly," called the Marshal. "Those that are trained to spin on one cue usually turn slowly on the other."

Paks tried a gentle pull, and the horse veered left. It walked more freely now, and she finally managed a circle around the stable yard.

"Now the other way," commanded the Marshal. This, too, went well, though Paks could still feel a knot of tension in the horse's back. They walked around the yard once, then twice. She pulled back for a halt, feeling more confident, and the horse reared. Paks lurched backward and grabbed for mane. Someone in the inn door laughed, and cut it off. The horse stayed up — and stayed up — she felt like a fool. How could she get him down? She closed her legs, and the horse leaped forward, snapping her head back. It landed charging, whirling about the stableyard as Paks fought to stay on. The saddle, so uncomfortable before, seemed to grip her. She could hear frantic yells, and the clatter of shod hooves on stone. At last she remembered the ring, and thought "Whoa!" The horse skidded to a stop and stood rigid. Paks was breathless; pain stabbed her side, and her hands were shaking. She had been sure she'd fall. It was hard to believe anything so ponderous had moved so fast. It had seemed easy when she'd seen others riding — she grinned at the memory.

"You can stay on, at least." The Marshal's voice broke into her thoughts. "But that beast may still be too much for you. Best not ride through town until you have better control."

"I — I won't, sir. I had — no idea — "

"Not well-trained, either." The Marshal was walking around the horse. "He's got the makings of a fine animal, Paksenarrion, but he's been ill-trained, and I would judge ill-used. If you can retrain him, you'll have a formidable mount."

"I'm not sure," said Paks ruefully, "that I'll be able to figure out how to ride down the road, let alone fight on him."

"You're a long way from that, but — a stableyard is not the best place to learn. If you can get him as far as the grange, you can ride in the drillfields behind, and I'll be glad to instruct you. If you go behind the inn, and ride south of town, there's a ford upstream of the bridge."

"Thank you," said Paks. "I'll try. But how will I stop him? If a pull on the reins doesn't work, what will?"

"May I try?"

"Of course, sir." Paks slid off, finding it harder than she'd thought to clear the unfamiliar saddle. She held the rein for the Marshal, who mounted in one smooth motion.

As she stepped back, the black horse exploded in a fit of bucking. Paks flattened herself beside Ambros, near the stable door, appalled at the unleashed power.

"Don't worry," said Ambros. "The Marshal's good with horses." And indeed, after scattering a good part of the dunghill over the yard, the horse trotted stiffly around, neck bowed, obedient to the Marshal's rein and legs. Paks could not see what the Marshal had done when the horse stopped, but he told her.

"To halt, you'll need to stiffen your back and sit back slightly. That's all. Right now I wouldn't use the rein at all; we can retrain him later. Think you can manage?"

Paks wasn't at all sure, but she nodded. She would try, at least. The Marshal swung off as easily as he'd mounted, and handed her the rein. He grinned after a look around the stableyard, and spoke to Ambros.

"Well, I made a considerable mess, didn't I? We'd best get at it, Ambros, if we want to keep our welcome —"

"No, Marshal, that's all right —" Sevri looked dismayed, nonetheless.

"No, it isn't. Ambros and I will take care of it." And to Paks's surprise, and the obvious surprise of other watchers, the Marshal took the shovel from Sevri, and Ambros found another. They began shoveling the scattered dung back into a heap. Paks led the black horse to his stall, and returned with another shovel to help. The Marshal smiled, but said nothing as he worked. Soon the yard was tidy once more. "There now." The Marshal wiped sweat from his forehead, and handed Sevri the shovel. "Paksenarrion, early morning is a good time to train horses. Bring him along after feeding tomorrow."

"Yes, sir." Paks hoped she wouldn't be thrown before she got to the grange. The Marshal waved and left. Only after he was gone did she realize that she now had a perfect excuse to ride around the countryside and spend hours with the Marshal. No one would wonder, after hearing about the black horse's performance, why she rode alone, or why she went to the grange every day.

By that afternoon, the tailor's wife had one shirt ready for her to try on. Paks would gladly have taken it then, but the woman insisted that she must do more work. "See on the inside, lady? The edges there? I'll turn those down, and they'll not ravel or be rough —"

"But —"

"Nay, we're proud of our work, my husband and me — we won't let such as this leave our hands. But I'll have it tomorrow, by lunchtime, and the other plain shirts in two days — unless you'd rather have the trousers first?"

Paks thought of all the riding she'd be doing, and asked for the trousers next. Outside the shop, she headed for the saddler's, and bought a jug of the heavy oil he used on his leathers. In Doggal's yard, she found the smith forging heavy wagon fittings, and waited outside until he paused.

The next morning she was able to bridle and saddle the black horse without help — but with constant support from the ring. Sevri offered to hold the rein, but Paks feared the horse might hurt her. Instead, she faced him into a corner. Her attempt at a quick mount felt as rough as the day before, but she had gained the saddle before he moved out from under her. She pulled the left rein gently, and he turned toward the gate. Once out from between the walls, the horse seemed slightly calmer. Paks turned him along a path between the back of the inn yard and a cottage garden, and then through the fields behind the village. She found the ford the Marshal had spoken of by following a cow path, and the black horse pranced gingerly through the swift shallows, rocks rolling under his hooves. Now she had reached the lower end of the grange drill field; she could see the Marshal standing near the grange. Ambros, mounted on a rangy bay, rode around the barton wall from the street as she came up.

"You made it safely, I see," said the Marshal. "Ambros rides three times a week, and this will give both of you practice in riding with others."

Paks said nothing. The black horse had laid his ears back flat at the sight of the other horse.

In the next few days, Paks acquired a whole new set of bruises. The Marshal was as hard a riding master as Siger had been in weapons training. Like all occasional riders, Paks hated to trot — but the Marshal insisted that they trot most of the time. He was particular about the placement of her feet, the way she held the rein, the angle of her head. But the black horse no longer jumped out from under her. She could control his pace, and stop him, turn and return, without difficulty. Much of the time she did not need the action of the ring, except for grooming and mounting.

She could ride along the roads, now, and spent several hours a day learning where they led. The Marshal had told her that such quiet slow work was excellent for a high-strung mount.

But at night she dreamed of the snowcat, and woke, sweaty and trembling. Once it was the black horse's neck that Macenion hacked at, instead of the cat. Another time a shadowy spotted creature followed her along the trails she'd ridden that day, disappearing when she tried to turn on it. Every time she used the ring on the horse, she felt a pang of remorse. At last she decided to talk to the Kuakgan about it.

This time, as she came in sight of the clearing, she saw the Kuakgan talking to another near the fountain. Uncertain, she paused. She could hear nothing from where she stood, and wondered whether to intrude or go back. She turned to look the way she had come, and froze. No path lay behind her. The white stones that should have marked one had disappeared, and a tree rose inches from her back. She shuddered, sweat springing out on her neck and back, crawling down her ribs. She looked forward, and the clearing was open before her. Master Oakhallow beckoned. She saw no one else. Paks took a deep breath and stepped out of the trees. As she came nearer the fountain, she felt the quiet deepen. She laid the oatcake Hebbinford had given her in the basin.

"It is well," said Master Oakhallow in his deep voice, "that you did not try to leave again. The unsteady of purpose find my grove unsettling."

"Sir, it is not that," said Paks. "But you were speaking to another. I would not intrude."

He smiled. "Your courtesy is appreciated. But you could not have come nearer than I wished. Enough: you came with a purpose. What troubles you?"

Paks did not want to meet his eyes. "Sir, I did not take the time to tell you all that happened on our way across the mountains — "

"You had no need to tell me all, or anything you would not," he inter-

445

rupted. "But you shied from some part of your tale, and it speaks in your eyes yet. Is it this you came for?"

Paks felt her heart begin to hammer against her ribs. She wished she had gone to Marshal Cedfer. She wished she had done nothing at all. From everything she had heard of the Kuakkganni — their deep love of wild things, their distaste for men's arts, their contempt for war and soldiery — she was in danger now, danger against which her sword was no protection. She ducked her head lower yet.

"Yes, sir. It is. I — did something, sir, and I — I can't — I don't know what to do."

"Are you sure," he asked, "that I am the one you wish to talk to? You have spent much time lately with Marshal Cedfer. You are not kuakgannir; I have no claim on your actions."

"I'm sure," said Paks, fighting the tremor in her voice. "It — has to do with — with the elf, and wild things, and he — Marshal Cedfer — he would think it silly. I think."

"Hmm. By elf, I presume you mean Macenion? Yes. And wild things. I doubt, Paksenarrion, that he would think it silly, but I am more used to dealing with those than he. Now — " His voice sharpened a little, and Paks flinched at the tone. "If you can spit out your tale, child, and let us see what it is, perhaps I can be of some use."

Paks took a deep breath, and began, haltingly, to tell of the night in the pass. The Kuakgan did not interrupt, or prompt her. When she told of the coming of the snowcat, she felt through the bones of her head the sharpening of his gaze and struggled on.

"Then he — Macenion — told me to use the ring — "

"The ring?" His voice might have been stone, from the weight of it.

Paks held out her hand, and withdrew it. "This ring, sir. He said it was made to control animals." She explained how she had caught Macenion's horse, and how that had upset him, how he had cast a spell to identify any magic item, and had found her ring.

"You did not know that before?"

"No, sir. I thought the horse came because — well — I like horses. Star always came to me."

"Mmmm. So, you had a ring made to control animals, and you used it on a horse without knowing its power. Where did you get it?"

"From the Duke, sir. He — he gave it to me, at Dwarfwatch last year, for bringing the word to him." Suddenly tears ran from her eyes as she thought of the honor of that ring, and how she'd used it.

"Did he know what it was, do you think?"

"No, sir. It was part of the plunder from Siniava's army that we'd beaten. He said he chose it for the form — the three strands for the three of us that went — "

"The others?"

"Died, sir." She expected him to ask about that, but he did not. Instead, he returned to her original story.

"So then you were faced with the snowcat. Had you heard of one before?

446

No? And Macenion told you to use the ring. How?"

"He said, sir, to make — make the cat hold still. Not jump at us or the horses. And it worked — " Paks could feel, in memory, the surprise of that. She had really believed her ring was magic until the great beast crouched motionless on the trail before them, the snowflake dapples on its coat blending with the falling snow. "And then he — told me how dangerous it was — "

"You didn't see that for yourself?" The Kuakgan's voice was edged with sarcasm.

"Sir, I could see that it was a hunting creature, and big — but it was so beautiful. I didn't know about the magic it had, until Macenion told me. He said we had no chance — and — " Paks faltered again.

"Go on." The Kuakgan was implacable.

"He told me to — to hold it still — and — " Paks squeezed her eyes shut against the memory. "And he took his sword — and killed it."

There was a long silence. Paks dared not move or speak. Her skin prickled all over.

"You held it still, by magic, while Macenion killed it? Helpless?"

"Yes, sir," said Paks faintly. "I — I knew it was wrong. I asked him — "

"What!" The word shook the ground with power.

"I asked him not to," whispered Paks. "But he said — he said it was the only way — then — and I — I shouldn't have, sir, I know that, but what can I do now?"

Another long silence. "And men wonder," the Kuakgan said finally, in a quiet voice worse than a shout, "why evil roams the land. I should hope you knew it was wrong. Wrong, yes: bitterly wrong. And I assure you, Paksenarrion, that Marshal Cedfer would not think light of this. It was an evil deed, and whatever else they may be, the Marshals of Gird abhor evil. Do you claim, as your defense, that it was Macenion's fault, because he told you to do so?"

"No, sir," said Paks. "I should have thought — he told me, later, when I spoke of it, that I could have used the power to send the beast away — "

"Macenion said that? After telling you to do it in the first place?"

"Yes, sir. I know it was my doing. I know it was wrong. But — what now? I thought you would know what to do."

"To make amends?"

Paks nodded. "I thought — even — I had dishonored my sword. I should — give it up, if you said so: not be a warrior." She had come to that, after dreaming that the victim had been the black horse.

"Look at me." Paks could not resist the command, and met the Kuakgan's dark eyes, her own blurred with tears. He looked every bit as angry as she had expected. "You would give that up? Your own craft in the world? You take the injury so seriously?"

"Yes." Paks fought again for control of her voice. "Sir, it was *wrong*. I have not slept well since. How can I be — what I want, if I could do that?"

"But you are a soldier," he mused. "I judge you are a good one, as soldiers go. Have you any other skill?"

"No, sir."

"I think, then, that you must stay so. Kuakkganni do not hate soldiers, but the necessity of war. If you have dishonored your sword, you must cleanse it with honorable battles. As for amends — the snowcat is dead, and by now the eagles have feasted. Nothing can change that." He looked closely at her, and Paks nodded. "As I said, I have no responsibility for your actions. But if you will be bound by me, I will take a blood payment from you. Give me the ring, with which you bound the snowcat, so that you cannot misuse such power again."

Paks froze. Give up this ring? Her hand closed on it. She could hear the Duke's voice as he gave it, feel the throb in her injured leg.

"I will not compel," said the Kuakgan. She could feel, however, the withdrawal behind his words. She unclenched her hand, staring at the ring's twisted strands that meant so much more than power over animals. Then she pulled it from her finger, feeling the tiny ridges for the last time, and laid it in the Kuakgan's waiting palm. His hand closed over it. She felt a cold wave sweep through her heart: that ring she had never meant to lose, save with her life.

"Child, look at my face." She looked again; he was smiling gravely. "You did well, Paksenarrion. I think the evil was not rooted too deeply in you, and this may have it out. Choose your companions with more care, another time, and trust your own honor more. No one can preserve it but you."

"Yes, sir."

"Go now. You have much to do, if you would accomplish what the Council set you — and train that black horse you've been busy with."

Paks started. She had forgotten, until then, that she had been using the ring on the black horse.

The Kuakgan gave her an open grin. "We will see whether Macenion was right, and all your skill with horses mere ring-magic. I think myself you have a way with animals, ring or no. And you can trust yourself, now. Is it not so?"

"Yes, sir." Suddenly Paks felt much better. She had not known how much it bothered her to control the horse with the ring.

"You may take a few extra bruises, but — I heard from Sevri the care you gave your pack pony when you arrived. Such care, Paksenarrion, and not magic, will accomplish what you hope for." He took her shoulders and turned her away from the fountain. "And there's your path out. Don't stray from it — and don't look back."

"Thank you, sir," said Paks. She walked toward the white stones, and along them to the lane.

Lighter in heart, Paks headed for the inn, thinking of what had passed. Her finger felt sore and empty without her ring. She would not have bartered it for food if she had been starving. But the Duke, she felt, would rather have had her give it up than keep it in dishonor. She turned aside from the inn door, and went around by the stableyard. Sevri was currying a trader's heavy cart horse outside. Paks went into the stable. Star pushed her head up over the stall side,

448

and Paks scratched her absently, watching the black. He seemed more relaxed; he stood at ease, nose resting on the stall door, tail switching at intervals. Paks fed Star half an apple and took the rest to him.

He stiffened as she neared the stall, then caught the scent of apple. Paks held it on the flat of her hand. His nostrils quivered; his lip twitched. Slowly he reached out and lifted it from her palm. She reached up and scratched him, just as she would Star. Still crunching, he leaned into the caress. Paks murmured to him, the meaningless, friendly talk that soothes, and watched his eyes slide shut. She heard Sevri behind her in the aisle, leading the cart horse to its stall.

All at once Paks decided what to do. "Sevri?"

"Yes? Do you need something?"

"Only to tell you something." Paks paused. It wasn't going to be easy. She liked the girl. "Sevri, I — haven't been fair with you." The girl's face was puzzled. "The smith was right, Sevri, about this horse. I was using magic on him. To quiet him."

"What kind of magic?" She seemed more interested than surprised.

"A ring. It worked to quiet animals — to control them. That's why I could work with him at all."

"Oh. Are you using it now? Which ring is it?"

Paks spread her hand. "I don't have it any more. It was the gold one. I'm sorry, Sevri, I should have told you — "

"Why? All horse trainers have their secrets. And you weren't using it to hurt him. What happened to your ring? Was it stolen?"

"No. I gave it to Master Oakhallow." Paks was surprised at the girl's reaction. "But Sevri — your family are kuakgannir, aren't they? I thought you would think it wrong."

Sevri shrugged. "I don't think you needed it. Master Oakhallow says the heart shows in all things. You were always kind to Star and the black, and that's what works with horses. If you used the ring to quiet him until he could trust you — it shortened your work, that's all."

Paks felt a wave of relief. She had feared the girl's disapproval more than she knew. "I — I thought you should know, that's all."

"I'm glad you trust me," said Sevri seriously, older than her years. "But I wouldn't tell those others. Let them think what they will. If they knew you'd had one magic ring, they might come looking for others. I learned that working here in the inn."

"I hadn't thought of that," said Paks. "Thank you. But now I suppose we might as well see how the training has gone, and bring him out."

To her surprise, the black horse was no worse than any other morning. Paks had just finished grooming him and turned to reach for the saddle, when she saw the Kuakgan beside her.

"You are doing well with him," said the Kuakgan. Paks could find nothing in his voice but polite interest. "Have you been able to cure the injuries he received earlier?"

Paks laid a hand on the horse's shoulder to steady herself. She had not

449

thought to see the Kuakgan again so soon; her breath came short. "Sir, his mouth healed quickly, but — there's one thing. He has deep scars on his hind legs, and I don't know what can be done for them."

"I'll take a look." At the Kuakgan's touch, the horse relaxed even more, and did not flinch even when the Kuakgan ran his strong hands down the hind legs. He paused when he came to the scar on the near leg. "A rope or wire cut him deeply here; it's a wonder he was not crippled by it. The wound healed cleanly, but the scar has grown to hamper the action of the joint a little. Do you find he sometimes seemed to drag his hoof there?"

Paks shook her head. "I've never seen it myself. But Marshal Cedfer says he does so, when I'm training with him."

"Hmmm. Perhaps I can ease that for him." Paks did not see him do anything, but he laid his hand over the scar a long moment, and then on the other leg. "Now," he said, as he straightened up, "I would see you ride, young woman."

Paks felt her belly clench. Would he make the horse rear and buck? Run away? She was sure he could do that. Or would he criticize what Marshal Cedfer had taught her? Her fingers felt huge and clumsy as she set the saddle on the horse's back, arranged the crupper and breastband, girthed up, and bridled. The Kuakgan inspected the tack, running the leather through his hands, touching the bit with his fingers. At last there was nothing to do but mount. The horse had picked up Paks's tension, and stiffened his ears, but he stood still while she gained the saddle.

Once up, habit reasserted itself, and she gave to the horse's movement. She rode around the stableyard twice, then made a few circles and other figures around the dungheap. She looked at the Kuakgan; he gestured for her to ride outside. Paks sighed, nodded, and guided the black through the gate.

The Kuakgan led her out of town, eastward. Paks followed, the black horse stepping along lightly. He turned as she caught up with him.

"I think you have done well so far," he said. "Ride ahead, now, and turn back when you come to the edge of the grove."

Paks nudged the horse into a slow trot, halted and turned where she was bid, and rode back.

"He should have no more trouble with those scars," said the Kuakgan. "He's moving easier. Could you feel it?"

"It seems springier, somehow."

"Yes, and he will be able to do some of those fancy things the Marshal would like to teach you. Too bad they're used for fighting only. If it did not risk his death or yours, I'd be happier about it." He smiled up at her. "But you and he were meant to be so, perhaps. I wish you well, Paksenarrion. You may come again to the grove, if you wish; you have a definite talent with animals. That is, in part, what hurt you so when you misused it." He waved and turned away. Paks sat still, and watched him cross the road and enter the grove by leaping the wall. She almost called a warning, then realized that it would hold no perils for him. He had disappeared among the trees when she lifted the reins and rode to the grange along the street for the first time.

Chapter Thirteen

In the next few days, Paks rode along most of the roads near town, and began to explore the small lanes and paths that led to outlying farmsteads. She found nothing; she was not even sure what she was looking for. But at least, she thought, she had a better idea of the surrounding land. It was richer than the land around Three Firs. Most farm folk had an orchard of apples and pears; for grain they grew wheat as well as northern barley and oats. Redroots, onions, and other vegetables grew in every kitchen garden. Paks saw the local hogs, hefty red beasts with yellow eyes, rooting in the roadside woods and hedges. Sleek dun-colored cattle with dark horns grazed the pastures.

Then, returning to Brewersbridge on the west road one afternoon, she got her first clue. Low sun behind her threw her shadow far ahead. In that slanting light, she saw something glint on a treetrunk beside the road. She rode toward it, suddenly alert.

As she came nearer, she saw that it was nothing but the tree itself — instead of dark furrowed bark, pale underbark lay open to the sun from a narrow gash. Paks halted the black horse, her brow furrowed in thought. She'd heard of such signs — the scouts in the Duke's Company had had a system of marks on trees and wayside rocks. But she had no idea what this one meant — if indeed it were anything but an accident.

She turned the black horse off the road, and made a half-circle in the woods around the marked tree. Nothing but a game trail, that ended a few yards from the road. She came out to the road again, and thought about it. Game trail? Why would a game trail stop suddenly? She had seen others that crossed the road. Her neck prickled, and she looked around at the silent trees. Nothing. She thought of returning to the mysterious trail, but decided to ride on as if she had found nothing. As she jogged on toward town, she heard a distant call off to her right — a herdsman, perhaps, or perhaps someone else.

That night was drill night again. Paks drank a quick bowl of soup in the crowded common room, then went upstairs to change. When she came downstairs, the tall young man she'd noticed the first day in the common room called to her.

"Lady Paks! Going to drill? Walk with us, why don't you?" His grin was nearly as wide as his shoulders. Two other men, that Paks remembered but

451

vaguely from the first night's drill smiled at her.

Paks nodded at them. She wondered who they were.

"I'm Mal Argonist," said the one who had called her. "I'm the forester here, since my brother went away. I saw you the day you came in."

"Amisi," said the dark one at his side. "I'm a farmer, just east there — beyond the grove, those grain fields."

"Adgan," said the redhead. "I work for Amisi, right now."

"He's my senior herdsman."

"They're just learning sword drill," said Mal. "I told 'em they should use an axe, but — "

"Mal, for Gird's sake don't start on that — "

"What?" asked Paks.

"Axes. Mal thinks everyone should fight with an axe. It's all right for him, as big as he is, and using an axe every day. But — "

"In formation?" Paks tried to imagine it. She knew that some knights fought with small axes, but she'd never heard of a foot soldier using one.

"Nah — not formation exactly." Mal laughed loudly. "It's a right Girdish weapon, that's all, being taken from our tools, you see. And I've killed wolf with it — "

"With an axe?" Paks stared at him.

"Oh, aye. Just you swing it from side to side, see — like the Master Smith does his hammer, that's all. It's the very thing. Won't break like a sword will." He laughed again, and Paks eyed him narrowly. If she had seen him in a tavern in Aarenis, she'd have thought him a stupid lout. He was two fingers taller than she, and built like an ale barrel. She'd seen him drain a tankard at one swallow. Yet he didn't move like a drunkard, and his great arms showed solid muscle.

Several more yeomen had joined them, hurrying out of side lanes. For a few moments, Paks felt almost at home, almost as if she were going somewhere with Stammel and other friends. Then one of them nudged another and spoke.

"Is it true, lady, that the Council has hired you?"

Paks was too surprised to make a good pretence of ignorance. "Why do you ask?" she said finally.

"Well — you've got money enough, that's obvious, and you make no sign of leaving. Could be you bribed them, or could be they hired you."

"Doryan!" Mal's bellow startled Paks as much as the statement.

"Don't yell at me, Mal. I've a right to ask, as much as anyone." Doryan shifted away from Mal, nonetheless, and winked at Paks. He was middle-aged, slightly stooped, and she had no idea what his trade was. "If you don't want to say, that's all right. Just asking."

Paks thought what she could say. The Council had not told her to keep her mission quiet, but she had planned to say nothing. How else could she find the spy they thought lived in Brewersbridge? "The Council decided," she said, "that I was no threat to the peace here. I had ordered goods, and they gave me leave to stay until these were made up. They did say you'd had trouble with brigands attacking caravans. Since I have been a soldier, they asked me to consider leading some volunteers against them."

"Huh!" Mal grunted and rubbed his neck as he walked. "Have to find them first, don't you? We all know they're out there, but no one's seen them."

"But who would go with you?" asked Doryan. He had an irritating whine in his voice. "We don't know you — the militia don't — and they don't think you could fight all those brigands alone, do they?"

Paks answered Mal first. "You're right, no one can say where they are. I don't even know where to start looking. If I ever get that black horse tamed down —"

"I've seen you riding out," said Adgan. "One time I saw him shy, and you nearly went over his ears."

Paks blushed, grateful for the evening gloom. "Yes — the Marshal's teaching me, but I still fall off now and then. Anyway, I thought I could ride around and look for the brigands that way, but not until I can look at something besides his ears."

"You rode through town today," said Doryan. Paks began to dislike him very much.

"Yes," she said shortly.

"You don't want to go looking for brigands alone," said Mal, more quietly than she'd heard him speak. "What if you found them?"

"I'd ride away," said Paks. "Very quickly."

"That's right; you're not a Girdsman." Doryan managed a sneer. Before Paks could react, Amisi and Adyan took him up on it.

"Doryan, that's stupid —"

"What's she to do, be hogstuck by a dozen brigands? That's not Gird's way; you know the Marshal says Girdsmen have to think as well as fight."

"I still think —" began Doryan. Mal punched his shoulder hard enough to make him gasp.

"Doryan, you don't think. You just talk. The lady Paks is our guest in the grange, and if you treat her like this she never will join the Fellowship. We've all seen her drill; we know she'd be a good Girdsman. Marshal hopes she'll join the grange, and so do I. Leave her be, man. You haven't caught any brigands yourself."

By this time they were approaching the barton gate. This time the boy on guard recognized Paks and grinned at her as she entered. Drill went much as before, with most of her time spent teaching the few swordsmen to use short blades in formation. Ambros and the Marshal did much better; Paks decided they must have been practicing in private. As he was dismissing them from drill, the Marshal asked Paks to carry a message to Sir Felis.

"Cal or Doryan could take it," he said, as some of the men turned to listen. "But even though they live on that side of town, it's an extra couple of miles for either of them — and they start work early in the morning. It wouldn't take you long, to ride out there —"

"I'll be glad to," said Paks honestly. She had been looking for a good reason to talk to Sir Felis in privacy.

"And I can't work with you for a couple of days," the Marshal went on. "That's why the message must go tonight. I'm leaving for barton court rounds immediately. Ambros here will handle matters at the grange. Drill as usual — " he said to the others. "I expect I'll be back in a few days, but Ambros will take drill if I'm not. Paksenarrion, I suggest that you and Ambros ride together an hour or more a day — but don't try mounted drill until I return. And if you can give him a couple of hours of swordplay, it'll be good for both of you."

The other men left at last, and the Marshal ushered Paks back to his study. On his desk was a leather tube; Paks could see the paper rolled inside. He nodded at it. "That's for Sir Felis; it explains what I'm doing. Now — you seemed uneasy tonight. What have you found?"

Paks told him about the blazed tree, and the "game" trail that ended a few yards from it and the road. The Marshal nodded. "I think you've found something important. If you'll take my advice, don't ride that way tomorrow. If you were seen pausing there — well, it could be very dangerous. Right now a single arrow could end your campaign. Anything else?"

Paks hesitated. She glanced at Ambros, leaning against the door. He shrugged and moved back into the passage. "I — I'm not sure. One of the yeomen said something — "

"Asked or said?"

"Asked, at first, about my business with the Council. He asked if I'd been hired or if I'd — I'd bribed them."

The Marshal's face stiffened. "Who?"

"Sir, I don't think he meant insult — "

"I didn't ask that. I asked who it was."

"I think his name is Doryan."

The Marshal nodded. "That doesn't surprise me. Doryan is — difficult, sometimes. He became a Girdsman after he moved here. Anything more?"

Paks thought of Doryan's words and decided none of them were important. "Not really, no."

He looked thoughtfully at her before going on. "Paksenarrion, it's my business to defend my yeomen, if they need it. Don't be afraid to tell me what they say."

"But I don't want to be — " she couldn't think how to say what she meant, that no soldier held another to close account for every word, or told even a sergeant what a friend had said.

"You are not of our fellowship yet," said the Marshal with a smile. "Now — I meant what I said about you and Ambros riding out together. Race the horses, if you will — anyone will understand that. Ride north and east for a day or so. Wear your mail, and keep alert. If you find where the brigands are hiding out, talk to Sir Felis before you do anything. Don't wait for my return, if you need to take action, but don't rush things, either. Ambros will not be able to go with you on an attack; until I return, his primary responsibility must be the grange."

A little later, Paks rode north out of town toward the keep. Most of the houses were dark; the black horse's hoofbeats echoed in the quiet streets. She had put on her mail shirt, and kept one hand close to her dagger.

At the keep, torches burned at the perimeter fence and on the building itself. An alert sentry challenged her; she waited while he took her name in, and returned to escort her to the entrance. There another soldier led her upstairs to Sir Felis's workroom, a long room with two tables littered with papers and maps. Sir Felis and Master Zinthys, standing together near one table, looked up as she entered.

"You have an urgent message from the Marshal?"

"Yes, sir." Paks pulled the leather tube from her tunic and passed it over. Zinthys smiled at her, as Sir Felis, frowning, worked the paper out of the tube and unrolled it. Zinthys wore a different, but equally rich-looking velvet robe, trimmed in white fur around the shoulders. Paks noticed, once again, the graceful movements of his hands.

"Why don't you sit down, Paksenarrion? We have spiced wine ready on the fire — would you care for some?"

Paks shook her head, not certain what courtesy demanded, but sat in the chair Zinthys pointed out. He moved to the one next to her, and sat down with a sigh, stretching his legs.

"I'll have some then, if you permit." He hooked a potlift in the handle of a can on the hearth, and poured the wine into his mug. "Ah. These chill autumn nights make the best of wine. You should try it." He slid his eyes sideways at her. "Or perhaps you drink only ale?"

"I — most soldiers drink ale," said Paks. "Wine — we had that with an herb in it, if we were wounded."

"Numbwine. Yes. Not as good as a potion, but good enough. But you're hardly a common soldier now, lady, and you might find you liked spiced wine." Zinthys poured another mug full and passed it to her. Paks took it, and sipped. Zinthys watched her, his eyebrows raised. "Well?"

"It's — very good." She looked down, and sipped again. It was good, a red wine flavored with her favorite spices.

"Have you found any trace of our brigands?" asked Zinthys.

"No, sir, unless something I saw today — " She told him about the blazed tree, and answered his questions. She started to add what the Marshal had explained about the possible uses of such a blaze in setting an ambush, but remembered in time that Sir Felis probably already knew that. He nodded.

"Fresh blazes. There's that merchant from Chaya in town now — wasn't he planning to leave tomorrow, Zinthys?"

"That's right. Master merchant Cobai Trav-something, and his gnome partners — "

"Gnomes?" asked Paks, sitting up.

"Yes. What is it, haven't you seen gnomes before?"

"No. I've heard of them — " she remembered Bosk talking about gnomes, elves, and dwarves on her first trip south.

"Well, around here you'll see gnomes fairly often. I'm surprised you

455

didn't see these at the inn today. Two of the gnome kingdoms are less than a three days' ride from here. If you meet them, remember that they're very strict."

"Strict?"

Zinthys laughed. "They make a court judge look like a juggler, Paksenarrion. They are full of dignity, and pride, and the right way to do everything — Ashto help you if you laugh at a gnome, or fail to complete a contract."

"They don't like wizards," said Sir Felis drily. Paks glanced at him, and he grinned slightly, cocking his head at Zinthys. Zinthys flushed.

"It's not that, Sir Felis — it's that they're so — so — " He waved his hands in the air. "Sober," he finished. "Dead serious all the time, that's gnomes."

"Anyway," Sir Felis went on, "there's a west-bound caravan in town now — headed for the gnome kingdoms next, and then Vérella. And if that blaze is fresh, it could mean that the brigands are planning to attack."

"It won't do any good to tell gnomes," said Zinthys.

"No, perhaps not. But I will send word to the caravan master. Not you, Paks — " he said, as she opened her mouth. "I don't want you to ride with this caravan — you weren't hired as a guard. If the brigands do strike, they should leave some trace you can follow to find their lair."

Sir Felis agreed with the Marshal's advice to ride out in other directions for the next day or so. Paks took this chance to look at his maps one more time, and fix in her mind the location of the ruined buildings he thought might harbor brigands.

The next morning when Paks went out to care for the black horse, she found the inn yard noisy and crowded. The day before she had been so excited about the blaze that she hardly noticed the new arrivals. Now teamsters were hitching teams of heavy mules to wagons. Paks realized that the short fellows she'd dismissed as someone's boys were actually not human — gnomes, she assumed. They were not so stout as the dwarves she'd seen; they wore plain clothes of gray and brown. Sevri merely nodded to her, darting quickly from one stall to another as she finished her morning's work. Paks decided to eat breakfast at the inn, after feeding the horses, so that she could watch the caravan leave.

It was not nearly so large as the one she had been with in Aarenis: seven wagons loaded with barrels and bales, with two guards besides the driver on each. The merchants — a blond human and two gnomes in sober colors but richer cloth than the gnome teamsters — rode saddle mules. Paks noticed that none of the gnomes smiled, though the human merchant grinned a farewell to Hebbinford, and promised to bring a barrel of "Marrakai red" on the way back. She went on with her breakfast, and was just washing down the last crumbs of it when Ambros appeared outside. She leaned out the window and called to him.

"I thought I'd come here," he said, dismounting. "If we're riding east today — "

"Just a moment —" Paks gestured to Hebbinford, who came to take her coins. "I know I'm late, but I thought I'd have time to breakfast before work today."

"Don't rush." Ambros did not seem in any hurry. "Shall I saddle your horse for you?"

"No. I don't know how he'd behave." Paks hurried up to her room, remembering the Marshal's injunction to wear mail every day. She was startled to see the black-clad man lounging in the upper passage. Had he been trying her door? But he smiled and nodded, as if glad to see her. Paks unlocked her door thoughtfully and latched it behind her. Everything seemed to be in place. She donned the lightweight mail the elfane taig had given her, pulled her shirt back over it, and caught up her old cloak. With that rolled into a bundle under her arm, she came back into the passage, and found it empty. She had heard no footsteps passing.

By the time she was back downstairs, Ambros had led his horse into the inn yard. He was munching a hot pastry, and grinned at her as she went into the stable. Sevri was busily cleaning out stalls; Paks thought of telling her about the black-clad man, but decided against it. She saddled the black horse without trouble, led it into the yard, and mounted. Ambros swung into his own saddle and they rode out, turning right onto the east road.

"How far out this way have you ridden?" he asked.

"Not very. I came in this way — on a trail that joins the road from the south."

"I know the one."

"I've ridden that far — no more."

"Let's go to the border, then," said Ambros. Paks looked at him. He seemed happy and younger, like a child at a fair. She wondered what the life of a yeoman marshal was like.

"How far is that?"

"Oh — if we keep moving, we can be there and back by tonight. Late tonight."

"Should we?"

Ambros grinned at her. "Probably not. But it would be fun. I grew up near the border; I know the country. We won't get lost, and I don't think anything this way will bother us."

"Well, the Marshal said —"

"The Marshal said ride other ways than west. This is other. By Gird, Paks, I haven't had a day to myself since —" he stopped suddenly, and ran his hand through his hair. Paks remembered suddenly that she had not brought her helmet, and felt stupid. What good was mail, when a head-blow could kill so easily? "Anyway," he went on, more calmly, "I don't see that it will hurt to ride all day. If we don't make it that far by noon, then we'll turn back. Why not?"

Paks wondered if he really wanted to visit his home. She did not want to ask. She wondered what Ambros would say if she turned back for her helmet. Would he think she was a coward? Was he even wearing mail himself?

She tried to see, and could not tell. The mail from the elfane taig, she had found, did not jingle as her other mail shirt had; she thought perhaps good mail did not. In the end she said nothing, and they jogged on together, into the morning sun.

When nothing happened for some time, Paks quit thinking so much about an arrow in the head, and instead enjoyed the ride. A thin haze covered the sun, thickening to a gray ceiling as they rode. Ambros frowned at the sky.

"If that keeps up, we'd better turn back."

"Why?"

"From that direction, it means rain, or even an early snow." He sighed. "I might have known that Gird himself would shorten my leash, with the Marshal gone."

Paks stared at him; he looked both unhappy and slightly worried. "Ambros, what is it?"

"I — I'll tell you, Paks, but please don't tell everyone. I'd hoped to — to go as far as my father's farm. It's been over a year, now, and it less than a day's ride away. And I wonder if I'll ever see them again."

"But if it's that close, why haven't you — ?"

"Because the Marshal hasn't allowed it," said Ambros shortly, reining his bay around to the west. "It's been one thing after another — chores, drills, whatever. My father's been in to Brewersbridge, of course, to the markets. My mother came once, last spring. But it'll be spring before either of them come again. I just wanted to see them one more time before winter." He sighed again. "It was a foolish idea."

"But why? I mean, just because it's going to rain — I don't melt in the rain, Ambros — not even in snow. How far is it?"

He shook his head. "No. Paks, you're not a Girdsman; I can't explain. But I tried to go on my own, and it's not what I should do. With Marshal Cedfer gone, the grange is my responsibility. The clouds are another warning; the first was in my own heart. We'll go back. I pray Gird that no more will be required."

Puzzled, and a little put out, Paks followed Ambros back toward Brewersbridge. The clouds thickened, and soon a fine drizzle wet her face. It was not enough to penetrate her cloak. She nudged the black horse and rode up beside Ambros.

"Ambros, do you really think Gird made it rain because you wanted to see your family?" She thought even less of Gird if that was his sort of action.

"No, not exactly." Ambros spoke slowly, as if more lay behind his words than he wanted to say. "I don't know, to be honest, where the clouds came from — the High Lord may grant the wind's keys to any he wishes, I daresay. But Marshal Cedfer did say the grange was my responsibility — even if you find the brigands, he said, I cannot fight them with you."

"But did he tell you not to visit your family?" Paks persisted.

"No. I think — I think he knew I would want to go, but did not insult me by telling me my duty." Ambros gave a short laugh. "He should have."

458

"But you —"

"Paks," said Ambros, with a look that stopped the words in her mouth. "Paks, you have been a soldier in many battles — have you ever had a dream of death?"

She stared at him, surprised into long silence. "Not — exactly," she said finally. "Some of my friends have — I have had disturbing dreams, though, if that's what you mean."

"Have you — did you ever know someone to have a true dream like that?"

"Once." Paks swallowed with difficulty. She wondered what dream had come to Ambros. When she glanced at him, he was staring at his horse's mane, fists clenched on the reins.

"I — I saw myself," he said softly. She could barely hear him. "I saw myself fighting — and struck — and dying. And then nothing. I know — " he said, turning to meet her eyes. "I know that all Girdsmen train for this, to fight evil to the death. But — but Paks, it was so soon. You know this cut — " He pushed back his sleeve to show a cut she had dealt him in practice the night before. "It wasn't healed yet; I could see it, under the other marks."

Paks shivered violently. Ambros's face seemed to waver, changing from the ruddy living countenance before her to the pale fixed expression she had seen on so many dead. "It was a dream," she managed to say. "And not all dreams are true."

"I know." He nodded, seeming more at ease. "I know that. But I thought — I thought I'd like to see my father and mother again." He looked sideways at her. "Do you think less of me for that?"

"No. Of course not." But she felt older than a boy who had seen his parents within the past half-year, who had been home a year ago.

"I wondered — you being a soldier, and all. You've seen more fighting than I have. To be honest, I've never faced an actual enemy."

Paks did not know what to say. She did not feel like boasting of her experience. She thought, as she often did these days, of her own home, and wondered for the first time if she would see her own family again. But she had had no troubling dreams, and had no fears. She smiled at Ambros, hoping to reassure him. "You fight well, Ambros, in practice; I expect you'll fight well when need comes. I hope it is not as soon as you fear. Will you tell the Marshal of this dream?"

"I would have, if he had not left already. Yes, he must know, in case it is an evil sending. I thank you, Paks, for not laughing at me."

They were back at the inn in time for a late lunch; Paks persuaded Ambros to eat with her. She had decided to show him the scrolls from the elfane taig; if she had not laughed at his bad dreams, perhaps he would not laugh at her slow reading. But they ate slowly, and it was near midafternoon when she started upstairs to get the scrolls. She had them in her hand when a disturbance in the street below brought her to the window.

A yelling crowd surrounded a blood-stained man bareback on a fat

459

mule. As Paks watched, Ambros erupted from the inn door, followed by Hebbinford. The crowd spotted him, ran to him.

"Robbers!" she heard. "Robbers! The caravan!" The man on the mule slid off sideways; two men caught him, half-carried him toward the inn. Paks saw Sevri's red head move through the crowd and take the mule by the bridle. She waited to see no more, but turned away and ran quickly downstairs.

Hebbinford and Ambros bent over the man, who half-lay in a chair near the fireplace, his clothes torn and bloody. Paks saw the black-clad man leaning quietly against the wall behind several others, who were chattering loudly. He caught her eye and smiled; Paks felt herself blushing. Ambros glanced up and saw her.

"Paks, good. Come here, will you?" Paks moved through the group, aware of curious glances. She had seen, from above, that Ambros commanded more of their respect than she'd thought — at least when the Marshal was away.

"What is it?" she asked.

"This man says he was a teamster on the caravan that left this morning. They were attacked by brigands on the west road, and all the guards were killed."

Paks looked at the man — a stocky, darkly tanned man of medium height — and wondered just where on the west road. Ambros was asking more questions; she could not hear the soft answers. Hebbinford began clearing the others out of the room. Over his shoulder he said, "I'll tell the mayor." Paks wondered who would be sent to Sir Felis.

With the room empty and quiet, Paks could hear the man's replies to Ambros's questions — hundreds of bandits, he said shakily. Hundreds and hundreds, with horses and bows and swords. They took the whole caravan, every animal and wagon, and killed all the guards, and —

"How did you escape?" asked Ambros. "Isn't that one of the caravan mules?"

Paks would not have thought the dark face could darken, but it did. "I was the last wagon, sir. I heard a noise — that stretch of road has an evil name, you know — and so I cut the lead offside mule free, and — "

"Ran for it," finished Ambros, with the same tone Paks thought the Marshal would have used.

"Well, I tried." Paks watched the man's face as he took a long difficult breath. "But that Simyits-damned son of a Pargunese jackass bucked me off, that he did. And ran away, after dumping me flat in the midst of it all. So I lay there too stunned to run or fight, and I reckon that was best, in the end. One of 'em poked me a little, but I made shift to lie still and be quiet. I heard 'em talking, telling each other to be sure all the guards were dead. Then they tried to catch my mule, but they couldn't lay a finger on him, so they went off. I waited a bit — and I was some sore, too, sir — and then when I did sit up there was that damned mule not a length away, heehawing at the blood smell. Then he came to me, and thank the luck for that. I counted all the guards' bodies, sir, and so I know — "

460

"What about the merchants, and the other teamsters?"

"The teamsters are all dead, gnome and man alike. I didn't see the merchants' bodies, but I doubt they live."

"Hmm." Ambros sounded, again, very like the Marshal. "Where was this? It seems to me you're back soon and luckily with such a tale."

The man paled a little. "Sir, please! I swear it's the truth. We left early this dawn, the landlord can tell you. And the road was dry; we made good time. Old Cobai — that's the master — he didn't want to stop for nooning in that stretch of woods, so we pressed on, eating on the seat as we drove. I had just finished my pickle when I heard the noise. Coming back, sir, I fair beat that mule to a lather."

Ambros gave Paks a quick look; she could not tell his meaning. But something made her speak up. "How badly are you hurt, can you tell?"

The man looked at her gratefully. "They poked me some, lady, and I fell hard before that. I wrapped my own shirt on it — this is off a guard — " He indicated his blood-stained shirt.

"Well, you'd best let us see. Yeoman-marshal, is there a surgeon in town?" She hoped she was right to use his title.

"Yes," said Ambros. "At the keep, with Sir Felis." He looked aside. "We'll need clean cloths, and water — it's too bad the Marshal is gone."

"That's what they counted on, no doubt," said the driver. Paks, meanwhile, had unwrapped the rag he had bound to his head; underneath was an ugly gash. She thought it looked bone-deep.

"It's no wonder they thought you dead with that head wound," she commented. "What's your name?"

"Jeris, lady. Jeris Angarn, of Dapplevale in Lyonya. Do you know it?"

"No. Be steady, now." Paks helped Ambros uncover the man's other injuries — mostly bruises but for two shallow gashes in side and back. "You're lucky, Jeris. They could easily have killed you."

"I know it." He shifted uneasily as they began to clean the wounds. "It — ouch! — sorry. If that mule hadn't bucked, they might have got me sure; they had horses. I don't deserve it, that's the truth, but that's luck. It comes as Simyits pleases — "

"You think Simyits has more power than the High Lord?" asked Ambros. "Is that what you learned in Lyonya?"

"Oh, sir — in Lyonya, I was a boy, and had a boy's faith. But I've been on the roads near twenty years, now, and I've seen good luck and bad come to all. As for the High Lord, he made the whole world, so I hear, if it wasn't Sertig instead, but what does he have to do with a mule driver? The good men, you might say, died today — they that was brave, and tried to fight. And here I am, alive a bit longer, and able to give you word, because a mule bucked me off on my hard head. Does the High Lord extend his power to make a mule buck?"

Paks stifled a laugh. She had heard of Simyits only as the thieves' god, and the gambler's patron, but the muleteer seemed honest if not brave. Ambros, however, was sober, and crouched down to meet the man's eyes.

"If the High Lord wanted your mule to buck, Jeris, be sure he could do it. But there is one more near us than that — Gird Strongarm, a man once, like you. He had a hard head himself, and it's said he knows how to convince another. I would not call it luck alone, if I found myself alive, when my companions were all dead — and a mule nearby to ride on, despite the blood-smell. Does your mule love you so, to buck you off, escape capture, and then return for you?"

Jeris's face furrowed as he tried to think. "Well — now — I see what you mean. To be honest, I wouldn't have thought that donkey-spawn would stay near new dead like that. But why would Gird, if he wanted me alive, dump me on my head first? Why not save the whole caravan and set fire to the brigands?"

"Why is there winter? Why does water flow downhill only?" Ambros sounded even more like a Marshal. "The High Lord lets men deal with men, as often as not. As for you, perhaps Gird knew your mule could not outrun their horses — or perhaps he was seeking an entrance into your hard head, and tried knocking first."

"Peace, Ambros," said Sir Felis from the doorway. "You can convert the man later, but for now I'd like to know what happened." Behind him a surgeon carried a cloth bag of gear; Master Zinthys, in still another robe, followed him, and smiled at Paks.

When the man had told his tale again, and the surgeon had settled him in one of the inn's rooms, Sir Felis, Zinthys, Ambros, and Paks conferred in a small room opening off the kitchen.

"Hundreds of brigands I simply do not believe," said Sir Felis. "They haven't stolen enough food and forage for anything like that number. In this case they killed twenty, and captured several — we aren't sure how many. But out of ambush, that wouldn't take more than a score of well-armed, disciplined troops. Perhaps fewer. Certainly I don't think they can have more than — " he paused, looked up at the lamp, and thought a moment. "Thirty, I'd say. And fewer horses than that. Most of the caravans they've hit have been carrying dry goods, weapons, that sort of thing — not food."

"Yes, but now what?" asked Ambros. "You know Marshal Cedfer said I couldn't go — what do we do now?"

Sir Felis looked at Paks. "It's your choice, since you accepted the task — but if you want advice — "

"Yes, sir."

"Then I would say let me take a troop out there, as everyone expects, and pick up the bodies. Contrive some reason for riding that way yourself tomorrow — not just riding, something else — and see if you can find a trace of the wagons' movement. I won't even look; it'll be dark by the time I get out there with my men. If you find it, don't be in too much hurry to follow it up. They'll be watching the road pretty closely for a day or so, I expect. Give them time to relax. Then — if it's where we think — go after them."

Paks shook her head. "By your leave, sir, I have another thought. An assault on a keep — even a ruined keep — is no easy matter. We tried that once in Aarenis. Why not try to frighten them out — catch them at their bolthole?"

"The game trail you're thinking of?"

"Yes, but close by the keep. If a show of frontal assault — "

"With what?" asked Sir Felis. "I can't give you a troop."

"No, but Master Zinthys might have some magical means." She glanced at him. "Macenion — the part-elf I was traveling with — had some illusions. I thought perhaps — "

Zinthys looked pleased, though Ambros frowned. "In fact, Lady Paksenarrion, illusions are a specialty of mine. Far less dangerous to the onlooker than, say, *real* firebolts."

"And easier to do," muttered Ambros softly. Zinthys glared at him.

"Young sir, if you think it is easy to produce even illusory fire, I suggest you try. My old master, who is well-known in the arts, always said that a fine, convincing illusion was far *more* difficult — because reality carries its own conviction, and saves its own appearances. If you make a flame, it is a real flame, and you don't have to worry, once you've got it. But an illusory flame can go wrong in many subtle ways — even such a thing as forgetting which way the wind is blowing, so that it flickers the wrong direction."

"Sorry," said Ambros, staring at the table. Paks thought he didn't sound sorry at all. She smiled at Zinthys.

"I don't know anything about it," she said, "But could you make something to scare them out — something to make them think a large force was coming at them?"

"I might do," said Zinthys, still obviously ruffled. He twitched his shoulders and glanced at Sir Felis. "It would be easier if I had a small matrix to work on, as a pattern."

"A what?"

"A form — a framework — or, in plain terms, if I had a few real men-at-arms, that I could simply multiply in illusion, rather than creating the whole thing out of my head. It's easier to keep them in step, you see."

Paks didn't see, but nodded anyway. Sir Felis made a steeple of his hands. "How many, Zinthys?"

The mage looked at him, considering. "Oh — a half dozen, say?"

"Four." Sir Felis set down his mug. "Four is plenty to save your hide if it doesn't work, and I can't waste the time of more."

"Four," repeated Zinthys cheerfully. "You'll see, Lady Paksenarrion — I'll do you an illusion that'll have them running out the back door for cover — by the way, how do you know there *is* a back door?"

"Never saw a keep without one," said Paks cheerfully, thinking of Siniava's many tricks. "Gods grant we choose the right place."

"That," said Zinthys with satisfaction, "is up to you soldiers. Just tell me when and where you want them frightened — I'll take care of that."

Chapter Fourteen

Mal, when Ambros explained the plan, seemed shrewder than Paks had expected. He spoke quietly enough, with a rumbling chuckle when amused. Paks began to think he might be an asset after all.

"So we're to find the place first, and find sign — then she'll lead a troop?" He gave Paks a sharp look. "Have you led troops before, lady? I don't mean to be like Doryan, but — "

"I was acting corporal in one of the cohorts," said Paks.

"That means yes, I take it." He turned back to Ambros. "And what if their place is fortified? Do we try to take it?"

"No. There's a plan to get them out — if it's the place we think it might be, or one like it. Have you been out near the old Seriyan ruins lately?"

"Gird, no! I told the Marshal a few years ago that was a bad place — unlucky, that is. Is that where you think they are?"

"It could well be — considering the sign Paks saw a few days ago."

"Then they're a brave bunch, that's all I can say. I wouldn't stay there for a silver a day. Not even for a cask of ale."

"And for you, that's saying a lot. All right, Mal — I know you don't like it. But if they're wicked enough, it might not bother them."

"What is it?" asked Paks. "Why are the ruins so bad?"

Mal and Ambros looked at each other. Ambros broke the silence. "It's from before my time — I was just a boy, living over near the Lyonyan border. But there was a wizard who settled in there — built a stronghold all in one year, by magic, some said. Like most wizards, didn't care more for bad and good than a deaf man cares for music."

"I don't know as that's fair," Mal broke in. "Master Zinthys is a nice enough fellow."

"Who buys you ale every quarterday. But would you trust him, Mal, at your back in a fight?"

Mal considered. "Well — yes. If Sir Felis or the Marshal were there, at least."

"I like him myself," said Ambros. "I think he's as honest as any wizard, but they care more for magic and money than anything else — it's their nature. But this other wizard, Seriyan, wasn't much like Zinthys. No. He came here, so I was told, because he wanted to rule. That's not what he said; he said he had come to study. But he had a small horde of magical

464

creatures that he let loose, and then he threatened worse if people didn't pay "taxes" for protection from them. Brewersbridge had no keep then, just the grange."

"It wasn't Marshal Cedfer here then," Mal put in, grinning at Paks. "Nor yet Deordtya, but the one before her. I don't recall his name."

"It doesn't matter," said Ambros shortly. "He made the mistake of believing the wizard harmless when he came, and it ended with a lot of lives lost when the yeomen had to storm the place. He blew himself up, at the end, rather than be taken."

"I hope he blew himself up," said Mal darkly. "The way that place feels, I'm not so sure."

"He may have left spells," said Ambros. Paks found herself hoping that the brigands were hiding somewhere else. She did not want to meet a wizard who had only pretended to blow himself up. But she had to agree that Seriyan's old keep was the closest of the known ruins to the blaze she'd found, and Mal agreed to go out with her the next day to take a look at the trail sign.

Mal arrived at the inn driving a sturdy two-wheeled cart with a large shaggy pony between the shafts. His big axe stood head-down in the corner beside him. Two more wheels filled the bed of the cart.

"This way," he said quietly, downing the tankard of ale which Hebbinford brought him without being told. "This way I'm just hunting a good straight bole of limber pine for the Town Hall extension. With these extra wheels, I can haul anything we find." Paks wondered how; she had never seen foresters at work. Mal saw her confusion and laughed loudly. Paks noticed others watching and listening. "See, lady, you don't know everything yet." Now his voice was louder, and more accented. "What I do is cut a short heavy piece for the axle, to bind these wheels together, and then tie them near the end of the bole. With the front end resting in the cart, and the other held by the wheels — now do you see?" Paks nodded. She started to ask why the second set of wheels didn't fall out from under the tree trunk, and then realized that he could tie it securely to the wood that held the wheels together.

"Ride along with me," said Mal, as if she had planned something else, "and I'll show you some more things you don't know about."

"I should find Ambros — " she said doubtfully, as they had arranged. Mal laughed again.

"Oh, Ambros! By Gird, you don't want to spend every day with him, do you? He's a yeoman-marshal, after all. Come on, now — " He gave her an enormous wink, and swaggered back to his cart after handing one of the serving wenches his tankard. Someone laughed. Paks grinned.

"You go on ahead; I'll catch up when I've got my horse ready. Which way are you going?"

"Oh, west again. I remember a few years ago, out that way, there was a straight, tall, limbless bole right near the road. Not so hard, you see, if the trees I want are next to the road."

465

"Good," said Paks. "That way I can tell Ambros I won't be riding with him this morning." Mal waved and went on, and she ducked into the stable to saddle the black horse. She hoped their act had gone off well. She hated to think of a spy in the village, but the evidence for such was persuasive.

She caught up with Mal before he was well into the forest on the far side of Brewersbridge; he had stopped to chat with the woman at the last roadside farm. He waved her to a stop.

"Paks, do you know Eris here?" It was the same woman Paks had met in Council. Paks began to think Mal was even smarter than she'd thought.

"Yes, I remember you," said Paks, swinging down from the saddle. She was no longer afraid to mount and dismount in front of witnesses; the black was learning manners. "I didn't know this was your farm."

"It wasn't, a few years ago," said Eris, with a slow smile. "We used to be out there — " She pointed southwest. "But raiders — bandits — something — kept breaking our fences, and running off stock. Finally after my husband died, and the boys married, I bought this farm from a cousin, just to be closer to town."

"It looks good," said Paks. The small farmhouse looked in good repair, and the orchard next to it was obviously flourishing.

"Oh, it's a good farm," said Eris. "I miss the spring we had before — the best water I ever had, and only a few steps from the door. But when you find dead animals in it, day after day — "

"Ugh — " Paks shuddered.

"Do you like apples?" she went on. "The good ones are coming ripe now — I'd be glad for you to have some."

"Between me and the horses," said Paks, "we'd eat half your orchard full. I'll buy a measure of good ones for me, and a double measure of bruised ones for the horses."

"I would have given — "

"Eris," said Paks, wondering as she said it whether she should have given her the Council title, "I grew up on a farm myself. Right now I have the money, and you have apples to sell."

"Very well," said Eris. "When you come back by this evening — or whenever — I'll have them near the gate, under the hedge."

"And you know I want some, Eris," said Mal.

"You! I thought you lived on ale, Mal!" But she was laughing as she said it.

They continued down the road, chatting freely. Paks continued to lead the black horse, since Mal was walking beside the cart. He pointed out different trees, but Paks quickly grew confused with it: colors and patterns of bark, and shapes of leaves, and the form of the tree meant little to her. She could tell a star-shaped leaf from a lance-shaped one, and both those from the ferny-looking compounds, but that was her limit. Mal teased her gently. In the meantime, they both watched the road for the signs of the caravan — the fresh wheel ruts and narrow mule hoofmarks. These they did not mention.

466

Paks wondered what would be left at the ambush site, since Sir Felis had sent a troop of his soldiers out to retrieve the bodies. Would she even notice it? As the sun neared its height, she began to worry that they'd missed it. But it was clear, when they came to it. Deeper tracks, round-hoofed, of ridden horses, and the mules' tracks veering from side to side. Bloodstains on the fallen leaves, and on the rocks that edged the road. A few spent arrows, mostly broken. Mal pointed out the traces she missed, chatting the while about trees. In the end, Paks found the way the wagons had been taken. Freshly cut boughs, the leaves hardly withered, disguised the wagons' track into the woods; the brigands had chosen a stony outcrop for the turn off the road. It led, or so Paks thought, the wrong direction — north — but Mal looked grim when he saw it.

"There's a farm to the northwest," he said. "Or was, until it burned. If they're using it, they may be using the old farm lane to bring the wagons back, and cross this road farther along. As I remember, that other farm lane hits this road in about the same place."

"Well, do we follow this?" asked Paks.

"No. Not with horses. We'd make a noise like an army in there, with a third of the leaves down as they are. If you'll take my advice, we'll go along the road and look for that other place, where the lane comes in."

Paks could just see the lane coming in ahead when Mal stopped abruptly. "Ha," he said loudly. "There's the tree I come for." She stared at him, surprised, and he winked. "You'd best go on up the road a ways," he went on. "I want to drop it right here in the road. Tell you what. You take these two wheels along with you, eh? Go on — yes — right along up there, at least as far as that lane. This'un'll fall long, I tell you." Paks finally caught on, and wandered slowly up the road as he bade her. Behind her, the axe rang on the tree. She wondered if it really was a "limber pine" or whatever.

It was hard to roll the wheels along with one hand and lead the black horse with the other. Several times a wheel got loose, and she had to bend to pick it back up. When she got both wheels as far as the lane crossing, she dropped them with a grunt and wiped her hands on the fallen leaves. The black horse nudged her, and she scratched his chin idly. She could just see Mal bending to his work.

"How long will you be?" she called back to him. The rhythmic axe blows stopped, and he stood up.

"Eh?"

"How long will you be?" She made it loud and distinct. "I thought I'd ride on and find water for my horse."

"Oh — say — a finger or two of sun. Not longer. There's a spring up that lane — used to be a farm there, some years back. You could bring me some — my can's back here; this fellow won't fall till I drop him."

Paks mounted and rode back, to another of Mal's winks, and he handed her a tall can with a wire bail. "It's good water, or used to be," he said. "Look out for wild animals, though. I've heard of wolves using it."

"I'll be careful," said Paks, and drew along the black horse's neck the

467

tracks she'd seen: wagons and teams both. Mal nodded and waved her away.

Paks made no attempt at silence as she rode along the lane that led south. She found a thread of water beside the lane, and then a cobble-walled springhouse. Beyond was a half-overgrown clearing with the ruins of a farmhouse and outbuildings. She didn't look at it, but dipped the can in the spring, and let the black horse drink afterwards. It was not really thirsty, and wanted to sniff at fresh droppings a few feet away. Paks reined it around slowly, and rode back, glad of her helmet and mail shirt.

Mal had the tree down by the time she got back, and loudly directed her in placing the wheels under one end of it. He had trimmed the ends of the axle log into rough rounds, and once the wheels were in place split the ends and placed cross-wedges in them.

"Thing is," he said, "the wheels have to turn on the axle, not with it — else it'd walk right off the end of the tree." Paks hadn't thought of that problem. Nor had she noticed the can of grease he'd brought to put on the axle. She did wonder how he'd gotten the large end of the tree into the cart. Surely he wasn't that strong. She glanced overhead for something he might have slung a line from.

"Don't look up," he warned quietly. Paks froze. "If you want to know how I lifted that monster," he said more loudly, "I used its own limbs for levers. Trimmed 'em after, that's how I do it. Some men use lines, but then they have to have a taller tree nearby. Not always handy. By Gird, I'm thirsty!" He drained the can at one swallow.

The journey back was slower; Mal's pony moved the tree at an easy footpace. The black horse fretted. Paks got off again and walked alongside. When they reached Eris's, they picked up the apples; Mal told Paks what the current price was, and she left it wrapped in the cloth Eris had put over the baskets. From there into town they talked softly of what Paks had seen. Mal said he had spotted a watcher in the trees. They agreed it would be too dangerous to scout the game trail if the brigands were still so alert.

It was nearly dark when they passed the grange; Ambros and several other yeomen were talking in the barton gateway, and called greetings.

"You can come help me on the bridge," Mal yelled back. "Paks here isn't much of a teamster."

"That's not a team," Paks retorted, sure by now that such joking was acceptable.

"I'd be glad to hitch your black up and let him do some work," said Mal.

"I doubt that." Ambros came up to them. "You weren't there the first time she saddled him. He'd be impossible in harness. Come on Jori, give us a hand here." Ambros and the other yeoman helped Mal get the wheels aligned on the bridge. Still talking, they followed along. Mal untied the log beside the Council Hall, and drove it off the back wheels. Then he let the weight drag it out of the cart. His pony gave a heavy sigh as the log fell, and the men laughed.

"Come on to the inn," said Mal. "I'll buy a mug for you."

They nodded and walked along; Jori and Ambros returned to some grange matter; Paks did not know what grange-set was, or what it had to do with a farm's sale. She hardly listened, intent instead on figuring out just what Mal Argonist really was — not a simple forester, that was clear. She was beginning to wonder if anyone was actually a simple anything. Until Brewersbridge, she had not considered that an innkeeper might be a council member as well — that many people had more than one role, and considered them all important.

The common room was moderately busy, but quiet. News of the attack made solemn faces. Paks stabled the black horse, and went back in to find that the others expected her at their table. She shook her head at Mal's offer of ale, and asked Hebbinford for supper instead.

"I eat before I drink," she said in answer to Mal's question. "I don't have your — " She paused and looked at him with narrowed eyes, as the others laughed. " — capacity," she said finally. Mal shook the table with his laughter.

"You didn't start young enough," he said. "When I was scarce knee high, my old dad had me down tankards at a time."

"Of ale?" asked Ambros.

"No — ale costs too much. Water. But it's the habit, Ambros, of an open throat. The feel of it sliding down — "

"Then why didn't you stick with water?"

"Oh, that was my brother." His face grew solemn, but Paks thought she could sense the laughter underneath. "He said a yeoman of Gird must learn to drink like a man. So I did."

"If that's your reason," said Ambros, "you should be a kuakgannir — you don't drink like a man, you drink like a tree."

They all laughed. Hebbinford brought Paks her platter of sliced meat and gravy. Mal grabbed a slice and stuffed it in his mouth. She looked at him.

"It's luck," he said. "It's your good luck if someone else eats the first bite."

Paks shook her head, and began eating. By the time she was through, the room had almost emptied. Ambros and Mal had gone out together. Sir Felis, Paks knew, would be coming in later for her report. She asked Hebbinford for another of the apple tarts, and settled back comfortably. The black-clad man was still in the room, and met her eyes. She had not talked to him since the afternoon before the Council's summons; now he came to her table.

"May I sit?"

Paks nodded, her mouth full of apple tart. She reached for her mug to wash it down.

"I don't mean to pry," he said. "You seem in good favor now; I hope for your sake that is true. But if anything is going to be done about that attack on the caravan — and if you are going to be part of it — I wish you'd consider my offer to come along. You might well want someone who was not — let's say — from here."

Paks looked at him a moment before answering. "Sir — Arvid, didn't you say? — " He nodded, smiling slightly. "You seem to be telling me that these people can't be trusted. Is that so?"

"I don't think I'd put it like that. I do think that those who live in small villages are more trustworthy to others of the village than to strangers. Haven't you found that to be true, in your travels? That these village folk stick together?"

"I suppose." Paks took another swallow from her mug, and prodded the remains of the tart. "It might be a reason not to trust them fully, but — pardon me — why should I trust you?"

He gave her a suggestion of a wink. "Ah — I knew you knew more than you showed at first. That mountain traveling is enough to scramble anyone's wits. Now I don't have anything to say about their character — everyone knows how honest the Girdsmen are — at least to Girdsmen." When Paks didn't rise to this, he smiled a little and went on. "But you aren't Girdish. Or of this village. I don't think they'd lie, exactly, but they might shade the truth. And if it came to your skin or theirs — ?"

"I see your point," said Paks quietly. "But you have still to answer mine."

"My dear," he began, as he drew his dagger and carefully trimmed his fingernails with it. "You should trust me only because it is in your interest, as well as mine. I am neither Girdish nor a native here — therefore I am unlikely to sacrifice you for a brother's reputation or a friend's life. I don't expect you to trust me as you trusted your companions in Duke Phelan's company — of course not. But I have no good reason to kill you — and several to keep you alive."

"And they are?" asked Paks curiously. She picked up the rest of her tart and ate it, waiting for his answer. His eyes narrowed. He resheathed his dagger.

"I told you before that our interests might march together. I think they do. I wish the brigands no luck; I would be glad to see them dead. You need not know why. Obviously, no one official is going to encourage me to go after them — I'm not an experienced soldier, and that's what it takes. But if that is the charge they gave you, then I would be glad to assist. Perhaps to make sure it is done thoroughly."

"Have you a grudge against them?" asked Paks, honestly curious now. "Have they done you or your family an injury?"

"I will not tell you that at this time." Arvid turned a little, and signalled Hebbinford, who came over with a sharp glance for both of them. "Wine, sir, if you please." Paks shook her head, and the innkeeper moved away. "I perceive, lady, that you are of sufficient experience to have caution — but insufficient to recognize an honest offer. Nonetheless it stands. My word you would have no reason to trust — but I will tell you honestly that I will not kill you, and I will defend you within reason, if you accept me as one of your company. If you were wise enough to know what I am, you would know what that is worth."

Paks frowned, not liking the bantering tone or the subtle insults. It reminded her too much of Macenion. She looked up at him again. "If such a command is offered me, and if I accept you — what other suggestions would you have?"

His brows arched. "You ask much, with nothing given."

"I do? What of you — you ask my trust, with no evidence of your character. I have had such chances, sir, as make me distrust most strangers."

"But Girdsmen." His tone was sour.

"Most soldiers have found Girdsmen to be honest, at the least, and usually brave as well. I don't know your allegiance, either to gods or lords."

Arvid sighed. "I am a guild member in good standing. As such I obey my guildmaster, in Vérella. It is an old guild, long established there — "

"What craft?" asked Paks.

He laughed. "What — do you think the Master Moneychanger here tells everyone when he travels what his guild affiliation is? Don't you know that some guilds bind their traveling members to secrecy? Do you want to bring down on me that very plague of thieves you think I represent?"

"No — " Paks flushed, confused.

"I'm sorry," he said quickly. "I shouldn't have laughed. I understand your suspicion — and it does you credit. Any experienced adventurer is suspicious. But I cannot tell you my guild — at least not without asking — at this time. I cannot tell anyone here. I can only tell you what I have told you. In my judgment — and I am not without experience in the world myself — it is in both our interests to cooperate. I have an interest in those brigands — I want to see them removed. Does that sound like a thief or worse? You, I believe, have the Council's permission to mount an attack on them. And you could use someone at your back who has no reason to wish an honest witness dead. Suppose they are actually living in town — related to one of the Council members. Do you honestly think they'll thank you for capturing such as that? Let you take the risk, yes. Let you kill and capture them, yes — perhaps. But let you live to take the credit, when it's their own? I doubt that much. If the brigands really are strangers, then you have no problem. But otherwise — "

Paks nodded slowly. She was not truly convinced, but she had worried that the spy the Council wanted her to find might turn out to be someone they liked. And, as well, they had asked her to involve the other adventurers in town if she could. Surely this Arvid Semminson was an adventurer.

From the hill west of the keep, the crooked path down the moat was clearly visible, as were the signs of age and decay: stones from the outer wall tumbled into the moat, leaving ragged gaps in the wall through which the battered interior could be seen. Paks, concealed behind a thick-leaved but prickly shrub, stared down at the broken walls and waited for the diversion Sir Felis had promised. She had a motley group: Mal and several other yeomen of Gird, including Doryan, the two traders she'd met some days before, who said they wanted to avenge the attack on the caravan, a servant of theirs whom they said was a good bowman, one of Eris's sons (a Falkian, Mal had reported sadly, but a good man), and Arvid. The sun rose higher, burning off the last of the mist from the moat and swamp around. Paks insisted that her group stay well back in cover, and refused to let them talk or light pipes. A subdued grumble followed these commands.

"Stands to reason," muttered the heavy-set bowman, "that if they could see us, we could see them. We can't see a thing, through these leaves. We could smoke, at least."

Paks shook her head fiercely. "Sun's in our eyes. They've got the better light. Think: how far can you see a shepherd's breakfast firesmoke? There could be a dozen eyes looking out of that gap, from the shadow, and we'd never know it. Be still."

Someone cursed, but softly, and they rested as best they could in the positions Paks had chosen for them. The sun rose higher. Paks had to force herself to stay still. She wanted to walk back and forth, from post to post. Was this why the captains had so often walked the line before battle? She could hardly believe that she, the same old Paks, was commanding a group like this — a group of strangers.

She looked again at the keep, which seemed a different shape as the shadows shifted with the sun, and wondered if the magician who built it had, indeed, left a curse. A light wind sifted through the trees, shuffling the leaves and making the shadows dance. She wondered if the militia had left Brewersbridge on time. They were supposed to have left just enough time for her to get her group into position. It had been too long. She squinted at the sun, feeling the sweat spring out on her neck, chill as it was. She swallowed against the fear, and glared around at the others. Someone had shifted carelessly, and a rock clattered. She turned back to the keep. Nothing moved there but a cloud of midges over the moat, a shimmer in the sun.

At last she heard the rhythmic noise of marching men and horses. She eased forward to the edge of the wood, trying to see the north side of the keep, where the forest left a wider opening. The sound came louder, eddying in the uncertain wind. Now she could hear it distinctly. A movement in the distance caught her eye. A horn call swam through the air, mellow and long. She looked back at the keep. There: a flicker, quick as a lizard's tail, on the highest part of the ruin. The horn call came again, louder. She could hear a bellowed command from the oncoming force. She looked back at her group; they were all alert. Mal grinned at her, shifting his broad shoulders. She realized that he had moved forward, coming between her and the others. But she had no time to think of that.

The front of the captain's "show of force" was out of the trees now. She could not tell from this distance how many of them were illusion. Nor could she tell which was Zinthys. None of them wore the kind of robes she had seen on him so far.

"There's one," said Mal, so softly she almost missed hearing it. Then she, too, saw the brown-clad man peering from a low gap in the keep wall. He passed through, carrying a plank, and laid it on the edge of the moat. It extended to one of the fallen blocks farther out. He moved out onto the plank, and at once another came, this one in a heavy mailed shirt, dragging another plank. The second plank bridged the moat from the stone to the near shore. A third man appeared, carrying bows, and the three slipped across the bridge and spread to cover it. After a glance upslope, they concentrated on the corners of the keep.

Noise from the north side increased. Paks could not tell if it was a fight, or just noise. Suddenly a gout of flame rose up, and a thunderous boom echoed across the woods. Birds flew up screaming. The bowmen below did not flee, though one of them half-stood, to be pulled back by the others. Another gout of flame, and another, followed. The noise was appalling, even though Zinthys had warned them. A deer broke cover and bounded through the woods, crashing and snorting. A hurrying file of men slipped from the gap and teetered across the bridge. Paks saw the glint of mail on most of them; they had their swords out, and bows slung to their backs. She counted as they came, hoping that Sir Felis's estimate was right.

She knew the last had come when the bowmen moved. The entire group — just over a score — started up the hill, as she had expected. The archers stayed in the rear, and two swordsmen took the lead, several strides ahead of the rest. Paks frowned. With that spread, some of them could escape, if they were quick. She thought they would be quick.

She turned to the stocky bowman. "Shoot low. Just in front of 'em."

"Why?" But he complied. Two arrows thudded into the ground, and the two brigands in front slowed and peered up the slope.

"So they'll bunch up," said Paks. "As they are now."

He gave her a quick look. "Hunh. That's quite a trick. Where'd you learn — ?" But they were all together now, and Paks called for another volley, from this man and the Girdish archers as well. Four of the brigands fell; Paks saw one of them struggle up and begin to crawl away along the slope. The others, furious and frightened, charged up the slope.

The bowmen shot as fast as they could, hitting seven more of the brigands before Paks led the rest of her group to break the charge. Some of those fell; others turned aside, limping, or jerked the arrows free and kept with the main group. She hardly noticed; in the lead, full of the old excitement, she met the first brigand with a sweeping blow that broke his sword at the hilt. He jerked out his dagger and thrust, but she was past him, the sword carving into another man's side. A blade she didn't see caught her in the ribs; she felt the blow, but rolled off it to take another brigand in the neck. She heard the yeomen of Gird call on their patron as they followed her. But compared to the battles she'd been in with the Duke's Company, this was short and easy. Almost before she knew it, the clash of weapons ceased.

She looked around. Arvid Semminson was wiping the blade of his narrow sword; it was stained to the hilt. One of the merchants nursed an wounded arm; his bowman stood guard over him, dagger drawn. Mal had one brigand down, and was tying his arms; two of the other yeomen were guarding the few who could stand. Ten of the brigands were down, dead or dying of serious wounds. In the distance, Paks thought she saw two or three huddled forms limping away. None of her own force seemed badly hurt, barring the merchant. Paks walked over to look. He had a long, deep gash on the arm, not a killing wound, though he seemed dazed. She hadn't expected much from him anyway.

"What now, Paks?" asked Mal. "Do we kill them, or take them back, or what?"

Paks glared at him, before she remembered the agreement. For an instant she had thought he might seriously mean to kill the prisoners. In that moment, the other merchant spoke.

"We ought to kill them."

"No." Paks shook her head for emphasis. "We'll take them to Sir Felis. He's the Count's representative."

"But they killed — "

"We've killed enough. How many do you want?" Paks turned away, and squatted beside Mal's prisoner. She recognized the man who had led the others up the hill. He was bleeding from a cut on his head that had split the leather helm, and from a deep gash in one leg. "Better bandage that," she said to Mal, who nodded. She wiped the blood off her own sword and sheathed it. The prisoner watched her, dark eyes alert. He flinched when Mal touched his leg, then held still as it was bandaged. Paks said nothing, looking around at the others as she caught her breath. Then she met the prisoner's eyes.

"Your name?" she asked.

"Why should I tell you? We're just going to be killed — "

"Probably," said Paks. "Any reason why not?"

"Reasons!" His mouth worked and he spat blood. "Being poor's reason enough — that and going looking for work. That'll get you killed, that will — going along, trying to find a place, and nothing — nothing." He twisted his neck, wincing, to look around.

Paks felt an obscure sympathy she had not expected with this weather-worn robber. He did not look as if he'd enjoyed his life. For that matter, he didn't look as if he'd profited by it. "How many of you were there?"

"They're the lucky ones," he said sourly. "Dead and over with. Gods above, what chance did we have — "

"Chance?" rumbled Mal, coming back to confront him. "About the chance you gave Eris at her farm, I suppose. Poor, eh? You think we're all rich?"

The prisoner closed his eyes briefly. "I don't — dammit, man, I never thought to be a robber. Not back when I — I had land once myself. A few cattle, enough. If I hadn't come here — "

"What about 'here'?" asked Arvid, who had come up softly behind Paks. "What's so special here?"

"I — " The man seemed to choke, shook his head, and said no more. Paks pushed herself up. All of her group could travel as they were; of the

474

brigands, four that might live could not walk. Those whose wounds were mortal she despatched herself, not trusting the others to give a clean deathstroke. But she told the others to gather the weaponry, such as it was: she had always hated stripping bodies, and had avoided it most of the time. She had the yeomen supervise the prisoners in making litters for those who could not walk.

"Paks, what about those that got away?" Mal swung his bloody axe slowly in his hand.

"We'll have to track them. They're all wounded." Paks sighed. "I don't know how many —"

"I thought four or five. There's a couple down there still —" He jerked his head toward the slope.

"I'd better go —"

"No. You stay here — I'll take Doryan. You don't need him here." Paks started to protest, but thought better of it. She was sure Mal was trustworthy.

He had just started down the hill when five horsemen broke from the woods on the south side of the keep. Paks saw a flurry of motion in the bushes near them, and then four of the horsemen charged, driving out the remnant of the robbers. That was over in a few seconds. Zinthys rode across the slope to greet her.

"Well done, Lady Paksenarrion," he said cheerfully. "Sir Felis will be pleased."

"You too. That was a real show, that —" Paks stopped short, wondering if she should reveal his work as illusion. Zinthys grinned at her confusion, and spoke up.

"Most people find a fireblast alarming," he said casually. "I sent the rest of the troops back when we found the main keep empty — you seemed to have everything well in hand back here."

Paks wondered what he would have said if she'd blurted out the truth, but merely smiled. "I'm glad you thought to send a few around back for the stragglers."

"Oh, of course. I see you have quite a few prisoners — how about transport?"

"If you could have someone send a cart or wagon out from town — and Master Travannen is wounded. It would be better for him to ride —"

"Certainly. Why don't I see to moving your mounts back along the road — then you can come out the way we came in. It's easier traveling."

"Fine." Paks looked around. The prisoners had rough litters ready, covered with their cloaks. They loaded the wounded, and prepared to march out. Zinthys rode off with a wave of his hand; the soldiers from Sir Felis's command joined her, flanking the party. One of them offered his horse.

"No, thank you," said Paks. "I'll walk to the road." He shrugged and moved back into position. She wondered if she should have taken his offer.

"I wonder," said Arvid quietly at her side, "that you are unhurt. Didn't you know that a sword broke on your armor?"

Paks thought back to the fight — it hardly deserved the name of battle. "I don't — oh — I remember a blow in the side — "

"Yes. I was just behind you then. It was a fair blow, and the man was as heavy as you, or more. I thought you'd get a broken rib out of it, at the least."

Paks took a deep breath, feeling nothing. "No," she said. "It must have caught at an angle."

Arvid shook his head. "I saw it. Either you're a good bit tougher than I thought — which is unlikely — or your armor has great virtue. Where did you get it?"

Paks gave him a straight look. "I found it," she said. "In a ruin."

"Hmm. That's a good sword, too."

"Yes." Paks looked around. Everything seemed to be secure. Mal was moving up beside her. He had wiped the axe blade on something; it was clean.

"The others are dead," he said. "Too bad hurt to make it; the riders trampled some of 'em. I did it quick." He looked past Paks at Arvid. "You fight good, for a city man."

Arvid laughed easily. "Do you think all soldiers begin in a farmyard?"

Mal's forehead creased. "Nay, not that, sir. But the ones I know all did, and the city men I know are mostly merchants. This lady, now, says she comes from a farm. Isn't that so?"

Paks nodded.

"Many good things come from cities," said Arvid.

"Oh, I didn't mean any different. I know that. Fine clothes, and jewels, and that. But there's more thieves in cities, too. My brother always said that wealth draws thieves like honey draws bees."

"I suppose." Arvid didn't sound interested; he turned to Paks. "What are you going to do now?"

Paks shrugged. "First things first. Get the prisoners to Sir Felis. Then he can find out how they've been operating, and if they've had contacts in town."

Chapter Fifteen

Sir Felis met the party coming into town. Ambros was with him, as were several other yeomen. Some of the townspeople cheered; Paks felt her face redden. She was glad she had the black horse; at least she didn't have to look up at Sir Felis.

"You've done well," he said, after a quick look at the group. "None of your men killed — or even badly hurt — "

"My arm — " began the merchant. Sir Felis gave Paks a quick look of amusement, soldier to soldier, before speaking to the man.

"I'm sorry, sir; I didn't see. The surgeon has been alerted; he's at the inn."

"Good. It was a terrible fight — "

Paks saw one of Sir Felis's men roll his eyes. She choked down a laugh. Her knees felt shaky. In the stir around them, the black horse began to fidget. She met Ambros's gaze.

"How was it?" he asked.

"Went well." She worked the black horse over to the side of the road near him. "They all came out the bolthole, just as we thought. Your yeomen are good fighters — steady."

Ambros smiled. "I know. The Marshal's trained them well. I'm glad they were willing to go with you."

"What now?"

"Well — Sir Felis will take them to the keep. I suppose he'll ask you along. The Council's heard; of course they're happy about it. Do you think you got them all?"

"Twenty-one came out; we left eleven dead and have ten prisoners. Unless some stayed in the keep — and I wouldn't have, with what Zinthys did." Mindful of spies, Paks did not elaborate on that.

"They don't — they don't look so bad," said Ambros thoughtfully.

"Who, the brigands?"

"Yes. I thought — "

Paks glanced at him. "They'd all look like orcs?"

He flushed. "I know I don't have your experience — "

"Don't be silly. I didn't mean that." Paks found herself annoyed with his sensitivity. "I was surprised myself, if you want to know. The only brigands I'd seen, in Aarenis, looked as vicious as they were. These men look like any poor farmer or soldier. The leader — that one in the litter there — he said something about not wanting to be a robber — "

"Eh, once he's caught, what'd you expect him to say?" The uninjured merchant had pressed close to Paks's side. "He's not likely to admit he's been a thief from birth."

"He hasn't been," said Arvid, with a certainty that made Paks wonder.

"How do you know?"

"Lady, I, like Master Zinthys, prefer not to reveal all the sources of my knowledge. But I will tell you that had he been a thief from birth, he would not have been in that keep."

"But how do you know?" Both Paks and Ambros stared at Arvid. He smiled, bowed, and passed on toward the inn.

"That one," muttered the merchant, idly putting his hand on the black horse's neck. It jerked aside; by the time Paks had it calm again, the merchant and most of the group had passed. Sir Felis beckoned; Paks moved the black horse beside his at the tail of the procession.

"Come on out with me to the keep, will you?" he asked. "I'd like to hear what happened. My cook should have something ready, too."

Paks nodded. She realized that Sir Felis might want her to be present when he questioned the prisoners. She wondered what the customs were.

"And you too, yeoman marshal, if your duties permit," said Sir Felis smoothly. "Since the Marshal is not here, I would like a representative from the grange to be present."

"The grange's honor, Sir Felis," said Ambros. "May I ask how long this might take? It is customary for the yeomen of Gird to give thanks in the grange for the success of such a mission; I would like to tell them when — "

Sir Felis pursed his lips. "I am not certain, yeoman-marshal, but surely by dark. These men do not look so desperate as I thought."

Paks had feared that Sir Felis might, like Alured the Black of Aarenis, torture his prisoners; he did not need to. By the time Sir Felis, trailed by Paks and Ambros, came down the stairs to question them, the brigand leader had decided to tell what he knew.

"We was all honest men once, sir," he said weakly. "I was a farmer, myself. Some of the others was trade or craft, but most was farmers. But that bad drought three years ago, in Verrakai lands — that's what drove me out. The taxes — and then no grass, and the cows dying — so my lord Verrakai put me out, and I went wandering. No one had honest work, sir, and that's the truth of it." He closed his eyes a moment; Paks looked around at the other brigands. The wounded lay quietly; the rest squatted against the dungeon wall, heads down. "I suppose Elam and I were the first," the man went on after a long pause. "He and I'd known each other back home — we traveled together. We come on this place in a storm — went in to get dry — and then — seems we couldn't leave."

"What stopped you?" asked Ambros.

"I don't know. Something. It — it called, like. We stayed there a couple of

478

days — shot a bird for food, Elam was a good bowman. I stuck one of those things in the moat, but we couldn't eat that."

"What thing?" asked Sir Felis.

"You know. One of them — big things, like a frog only near man-sized. Smell rotten. They have teeth, too. Anyway we stayed there. Took a goose from a farm nearby — I'd asked for work, and they drove us off. Called us robbers, they did, and we hadn't robbed before that. Made me mad." He stopped again, and rubbed his nose. "Elam wanted to go on somewheres else, but when we got an hour or so away, we both got the cramps bad. Had to come back. Then the others came." He nodded toward the other men. "One or two at a time, every week or so. Soon we'd hunted out all the woods around. If we took from the farms — well, most of us had farmed. We didn't want to."

"So then he said take caravans," put in one of the others, leaning back against the wall and tilting his head up to look at Sir Felis. "He says what's a caravan to you — them merchants are all rich, and what has rich done for you? That's what he says. Steal from caravans, and get rich yourself." The man spat. "Rich! Heh! All we ever see's enough to eat, and that not all the time. A few coppers now and then — a new cloak — that's all."

"You shouldn't talk about *him*," said the first robber, pushing himself up. "It's bad luck. He'll — "

"He can't do much here," said the other. "Teriam, think! It's listening to him has got us here — in jail, when we were born honest men. Robbers, we are, and it's him as profits by it."

"But you know what he said. He can reach us anywheres — that's why we couldn't leave. He could touch us here — right now — and — "

"And what? Kill us deader than they will, when they're through talking?" The man gave Sir Felis a bitter grin. "Tell you the truth, sir, if you can kill that devil, you'll do yourself more good than killing us. And I'll be glad of it."

Paks saw that some of the other brigands seemed very frightened, but they said nothing. The leader had fallen back, and now lay silent with eyes closed and jaw clenched.

"Who is this man that ordered you to rob?" asked Sir Felis. "Was he captured or killed?"

"Not him," said the spokesman angrily. "Not him. He's got his own place, safe and deep, and all we know's his orders. I don't know his name, sir, or who or what he is — and I'm not sure he's a man, even. Teriam knows, I think — " He glanced at the leader.

"I don't." It came out as a harsh whisper. "I swear I don't know — I never seen him but the one time, and after that I couldn't — I couldn't — " He gripped his head, rocking back and forth. "He — he had black robes, that's all, and some kind of — of thing on a chain — it — like a hand spread out, only it had too many fingers — "

Paks felt, rather than saw, Ambros stiffen beside her. "Gird's arm!" he said softly. Then more loudly, "Like a spider, maybe?"

479

The man's head turned towards him. "It — it might be — if — NO!" He began to flail about on the straw. "No! Don't let him — not here — !"

Sir Felis swore, a soldier's curse Paks had heard many times. She could see nothing but the frightened man, waving his hands at nothing and trying to flee something no one could see. Ambros moved forward before the others shook off their surprise, and caught his arm.

"Be still, man — Teriam's your name? Be still; Gird will ward you from that evil."

"No one can — he said he could — "

"Gird's grace on you, Teriam. Gird Strongarm *will* ward you; give him a chance."

"You-you're a Marshal? Of Gird?"

"I'm the yeoman-marshal of this grange," said Ambros. "I am sworn to Gird's service, and known to him. I give you my word that I place your name before Gird."

"Please — " The man's eyes were open now, and fastened on Ambros. "Please, sir — I'm not afraid to die — just not that filth, please, sir — "

Ambros freed one hand and held out his medallion. Teriam touched it with the tips of his fingers. "You have been spelled by some evil, is that not so?" asked Ambros. "You fear that it will take your soul?"

Teriam nodded. "He said — he said he could do that. Wherever we tried to run, whatever we did — he would find us, and see us in — " He stopped, and lowered his voice. Paks could not hear what he said to Ambros, but she saw the sudden twitch of Ambros's shoulders.

"Well, and do you believe that the High Lord and Gird are stronger than *that* one?"

"I — I know I should, sir, but I'm feared — I'm feared they won't be for me — "

Ambros looked around at the other robbers. "And you? What do you think of the power of that evil one, when you are here? Do you think the High Lord is weaker?"

Some shook their heads; some simply stared. The man who had spoken so boldly before pushed himself to his feet. "Sir — yeoman-marshal — I was a yeoman of Gird once. Not a good one, you'll say, and I won't argue that. I never thought to find myself bound by such evil — just a drover like me. I don't know what that black-cape can do, but I will say the High Lord is right, if he kills me for it."

Ambros gave him a bleak smile. "Yeoman of Gird, you must face the Count's judgment, but the High Lord knows his own servants."

The man's face lighted. "I swear, yeoman-marshal, that it was not fear of the Count's court that kept me there. Whatever the grange-court demands — "

"Gird will have somewhat to say in that, yeoman."

"Aye, yeoman-marshal." He turned to Sir Felis. "Sir, if you will, if the court demands my life, permit the grange to report the death of a yeoman."

Sir Felis looked at Ambros, brows raised. Ambros nodded.

"The Marshal would say the same, Sir Felis. A yeoman may be spelled into evil deeds; I judge it was so with him, and perhaps with some others. The punishment must fall, but their names remain on the grange rolls. Only those who willingly serve evil, and refuse to repent, are cast out."

"He won't tell you," said Teriam softly, "but I will. He tried to get away more than once — we kept him until the curse softened him."

"I pray the High Lord's mercy on you, Teriam, for your deeds and your confessions."

Back upstairs, in Sir Felis's conference room, Ambros reddened under their gaze. Zinthys studiously ignored the others, setting wine to heat on the hearth. Sir Felis simply watched Ambros, his weathered face fixed in a neutral expression. Paks tried to see, behind that youth and inexperience, the power he had seemed to have with the prisoners.

"Well," said Sir Felis suddenly, as if he'd made a decision. He looked at Paks. "I say again, Paksenarrion, that you did very well. Very well indeed. I am not now surprised that your Duke recommended you for advanced training. I do not think many novice commanders could have taken over a score with a dozen, and had no casualties."

"I could not, without Master Zinthys's help," said Paks. "And your soldiers caught the stragglers."

"Even so," said Sir Felis. He looked her up and down. "And you, yourself, have no injury? I see your tunic is slashed."

"No, sir," said Paks. "I wear mail, of course."

"Hmmph. Yes. Well, then, I think we'd better have a formal report to the Council — you know the sort of thing — I'll speak to the mayor, and I expect we'll meet tonight. You'll be summoned. Yeoman-marshal — " Sir Felis turned to Ambros.

"Yes, Sir Felis?"

"Since some of the prisoners claim to be yeomen, I will delay trial until the Marshal returns."

"Thank you, Sir Felis."

"I will not promise that it will make any difference — "

"Of course not, Sir Felis. The grange understands that."

"Good. I'll see you later, then — will you be at Council in the Marshal's place?"

"Yes, Sir Felis."

"Good. Paksenarrion, do you wish to make your own reckoning of the arms recovered?"

"No, sir." Paks saw no reason to distrust Sir Felis's count.

"Then I'll see you later. If you'll excuse me — " He shrugged into his heavy cloak.

"Certainly, sir." Paks and Ambros followed Sir Felis down the winding stairs and out to a sunny afternoon. A soldier brought their horses forward; Sir Felis had already mounted ridden off.

They were almost back to *The Jolly Potboy* when Ambros turned to Paks. "Can I have a talk with you?"

"Me?" Paks had been thinking about the report she would have to give to the Council; she dreaded it. "Of course — but what about?"

"Come on to the grange; I don't want to talk about it here."

Paks sighed. She had been up since long before dawn, and she had looked forward to a hot bath. She had not had time for more than a brief handwash before the simple lunch Sir Felis had served. But Ambros looked so concerned that she nodded finally and turned the black horse away from the inn.

"I should have thought — " Ambros said quietly, nodding to a child in the street. "You're tired, aren't you?"

"I'm dirty and stiff as much as tired. And don't you still have to do whatever ceremony you were talking about?"

"Oh — yes. I'd forgotten, Gird forgive my thick head. Blast. But you'll want to see that, even you aren't Girdish. The Marshal would want you to be there."

"All right." Paks wished he'd get to the point. She saw Sir Felis's horse and escort outside the Brewmaster's gate as they passed.

Once at the grange, Ambros took charge quickly. "I'll rub down the black, and put him up — with the Marshal away, we have plenty of space. You can wash up if you want — there's plenty of water in the scullery — and if you need any bandages or anything — "

"No," said Paks, abandoning the idea of a good soaking bath. "Just to get this dust off — " She took off her helmet and sluiced her head as Ambros led horses away. The cold water revived her; she wiped her neck with a wet cloth and had most of the grime off her hands and arms before Ambros returned.

"Now," he said, leading the way into the grange proper. "I expect the other yeomen will be here soon — they saw us ride by. What I want to know is whether you'll come with me when I go to seek that blackweb priest."

"What?" Paks was completely confused.

"Didn't you hear him? There's a blackweb — a priest of Achrya — somewhere in that keep. I've got to go and — "

"Wait — Ambros, didn't the Marshal tell you *not* to go after the brigands?"

"The brigands, yes. And I didn't. This is different. A true evil, Paks — something like this — I can't let it alone."

"But Ambros, you're not a Marshal. *Can* you fight such a thing? Wouldn't it be better to wait for the Marshal to come back? He said to stay with the grange."

Ambros shook his head. "What if he moves? Now we know where he is — the center of evil for this whole area — and it's my responsibility."

"What about your dream?"

"That's just it." Ambros looked sober but determined. "Paks, such a dream could be an evil sending — to keep me from doing what I should. If I don't try — for fear of dying — what kind of Girdsman am I?"

482

"It could be a warning from Gird, couldn't it?"

"Yes — but I can't tell."

"Then I think you should wait." Paks stuck her hands in her sword belt. "Ambros, you don't know anything about what's there except what a robber said. How do you know he's telling the truth? Even if he is, you don't know enough. A priest of Achrya — very good so far. But alone? With other troops? Human or other?"

Ambros had been pacing back and forth; he stopped. "I — see. I hadn't thought of that. It's your experience, I suppose."

"Not just that. I would go with you — but you said, the other day, that you had to obey the Marshal."

"I have to obey Gird. Ordinarily that means the Marshal, but — " He stopped as the yeomen who had been with Paks that morning came into the grange. Paks noticed that none of them had changed from their blood-stained clothing; she wondered why. Mal winked at her, as they all came to the platform. Ambros climbed onto it.

What followed seemed strange to Paks. He called on each one to give an account for his own actions. After each recital, Ambros crossed his blade with the man's weapon. When it came to Mal, the big man grinned as Ambros's sword tapped his axe blade. Then Ambros inspected all the weapons, and supervised their return to the grange racks — for only Mal had carried his own. After that, they all repaired to the inn for a round of ale.

Here the others who had been involved joined them. Paks slipped upstairs for a bath and change of clothes. She put on her new clothes, enjoying the feel of good cloth. It was hard to believe that she'd been in a battle that morning — she thought back to the Duke's Company, and laughed to herself. Very different indeed. No company chores, no guard duty at night. And the others had fought well. Perhaps she could get used to having strange companions at her side — or none. Even so, she slipped the mail shirt back on and pulled her best leather tunic over it.

She opened the door to find a girl leaning on the wall opposite. Paks recognized her as one of the junior yeomen. The girl stood away from the wall as Paks came out.

"Please — lady — could I speak to you?"

"Yes," said Paks. "What is it?"

"You're a fighter, aren't you? I mean — I know you are, but isn't that — I mean, don't you make your living that way?" All this in a rush.

"Yes," said Paks, trying not to laugh. "Why?"

"Well — " The girl looked down, then back at Paks. She was as tall, Paks realized, and nearly as broad-shouldered. "I want to be a fighter too," she said finally. "I — they laugh at me here, the people in town. I want to show them — the Marshal says I'm good — "

"Umm." Paks looked at her wrists. They were strong, already marked with training scars. "Well, I can tell you it's possible. I did it. But — "

"I know — I know. They say — those who saw you fight today — they say you're good. The senior yeomen told us, too, after they'd drilled with you. I know I can do it too. But will you let me?"

"Let you? How do you mean?"

"I want to — to train with you. Like a — a squire, or something."

"But I'm not a knight." Paks stared at her, bewildered. "I don't need a squire — "

"I'll earn my way," the girl went on, heedless. "I swear I will. I'm a hard worker, and I'll do anything you say, if you'll let me fight beside you."

"Listen — " began Paks, then stopped. She remembered too well how much she had wanted what she now had. What could someone have said to her, at that age? "I don't even know your name."

"Suli — "

"Suli, it's not that easy — I don't know what I'll be doing next — "

"You're not going to quit fighting!"

"No. But I don't know when — or what — yet. I don't even know what training you've got. What if you can't — "

"You could talk to the Marshal — or even Ambros. They know me. Please, Lady Paks — I'll do exactly what you say. I can groom your horse, and take care of things — "

"If you want to learn to fight, Suli, why don't you join a mercenary company? The Halverics recruit around here, don't they?"

Suli shook her head. "I've heard about that — all marching and drill, and the same old thing day after day. I could do that here — just drilling with the yeomen. I want — " She looked down the passage as if across a field. "I want excitement. Battles. Travel. Like you've had."

Paks grinned. "Suli, I started as a mercenary. Gods above, I had as much travel and excitement as I could take. It's the best training — I swear it."

Suli shook her head again. "And you left. Why should I do it at all, when it's not what I want in the end? Please, please let me fight with you. If you don't like me, after awhile, then you can send me away. But give me a chance." Her eyes held a look that Paks could not name — she was flattered and disturbed at once.

"I'll think about it." Paks started down the passage; Suli was at her shoulder. She started to speak, but Paks held up her hand. "No, I didn't say yes. What does your family think about this?" She could hardly believe she had asked that. She, who knew only too well what families thought.

Suli scowled. "My family — they don't get along here. My dad's a trapper. He does a bit of day work in the tannery sometimes. He's gone mostly, expects me to take care of everything. But my brothers — they're old enough to work, and all that. I don't care what he thinks."

"Mmm." Paks turned to the stairs. "My father didn't want me to leave either."

"You see? I said we were alike. Please — "

"Enough, Suli. I said I'd think about it." Paks could see the others still clustered around two tables pulled together. Arvid and one of the yeomen were arm wrestling. Mal looked up and waved to her; she came to the table, aware of Suli watching her back.

"We were wondering if you'd decided to leave us for good," said Mal.

"No. Suli wanted to talk to me."

"Oh." Mal and several of the others exchanged glances. "Is she bothering you?"

"Bothering me? No. She has an exalted idea of my achievements." Paks snatched the top of a pile of fried cakes a serving girl put in front of Mal. "Good luck for you," she reminded him; the others roared.

"By Gird's arm, you're quick," said Mal, slightly redder than usual. "I never had anyone turn that trick back on me."

Paks smiled with her mouth full. A tankard appeared in front of her. She picked it up and took a sip.

"Seriously," began Ambros, "if Suli pesters you too much, I'll speak to her."

"I should speak to you, rather. She wants to train with me — and work with me. As a squire, she said — but you know I'm not a knight, what would I do with a squire?"

"As for that, you know much more than she does. She fights well, for the little training she's had — but she's got no more experience in actual fights than I have."

"Not exactly," said Mal. "She's been in some rows."

"Brawls," said Ambros. "That's not the same."

"No, I know that. She's an interesting girl, though." Mal took a long pull at his tankard; one of the other men shook his head. "Seriously — she's one of the best of the junior yeomen."

"As far as fighting goes — but fighting's not all of it," said Ambros.

"Well, it's the most important part, isn't it? For Girdsmen, anyway. You know she's not happy here, Ambros — not since Deordtya left. She wants — "

"She wants excitement and glory," said Ambros tartly. "She's more apt to get a broken head. Or don't you agree, Paks?"

Paks nodded slowly. "I told her she should join a mercenary company for more training. I haven't seen her fight; I don't know what she can do. Still, I can understand — I couldn't wait to get away from home. If someone like me had come through Three Firs, I'd have walked on fire to talk to her."

"I can't recommend her exactly," said Ambros, looking at his hands, "but I think she'd be honest and loyal. If you want someone — "

"I hadn't thought about it." Paks took another fried cake off Mal's platter. She wondered what it would be like to have a squire. The Duke had squires — she tried to imagine herself coming down that trail from the ruined wall, and someone like Suli throwing herself between an enemy and her own shield. It didn't seem right. She was not a knight; she had never been a squire herself; she didn't know what a squire should do, or how to teach it.

"Many free swords travel in pairs or trios," said Mal. "Then they have

485

someone they can trust." He leaned back to let the other yeomen past — they nodded to Paks and Ambros, and went out.

"Sometimes." Ambros shook his head. "Not always. But if you wanted to hire her, Paks, go ahead. I don't think you'd do her any harm, and though she's a little wild, she'll serve you honestly."

"Is she a Girdsman?"

"Well — not exactly. She's not old enough for the final oaths, and her family isn't Girdish. She's sworn to the local grange only. Of course I'd rather she found a Girdish patron — "

"I wondered about that."

"But you seem honest enough yourself. Master Cedfer hopes you'll end up a yeoman of Gird."

"I might," said Paks thoughtfully.

"If it's permitted to answer," broke in Arvid, "I'd like to know if you found how those robbers were fencing their spoils."

"Fencing — ?" Paks didn't know the term. Ambros did, and looked sharply at Arvid.

"He means, Paks, selling stolen goods somewhere — thieves call that fencing them."

Arvid smiled. "So do others, young sir — I see that you know the term."

Ambros scowled. "Indeed — honest men must learn thieves' speech or lose by it. But to answer your question, as much as I may — no, we didn't find out where the goods are being sent, or how."

"I told Paks, yeoman-marshal, that I did not believe those men had been thieves for long." Arvid sipped his ale, and went on. "I know you are suspicious of me — but that is the truth. And if I'm right, then someone else is running them — taking the stolen goods, fencing them — and that person, not those poor men, is the dangerous one. Until that person is caught, these attacks will continue." Paks saw a gleam of interest in Mal's eyes, but he was apparently relaxed and half-asleep, leaning on the wall.

Ambros leaned forward. "How, if Paks has killed or captured all the active robbers?"

Arvid snorted. "How hard is it to fool poor men? How were those men trapped into thievery? As long as the world holds men whose arms are stronger than their wits or will, just so long will subtle men find simple ones to risk and die for them." Paks thought that could have more application than Arvid intended; she glanced at him and met a sardonic glint that set her mind on edge. Ambros missed it.

"I think, sir," he said quietly, "that you and I — and Paks, perhaps — should have a quiet word together."

"I think that indeed, young sir. Yet I would not have it noticed — for I am convinced that someone in this town is telling dangerous tales."

"You may be right — "

"I am," said Arvid with calm authority. "We must meet — and we must meet quietly."

Mal sat forward. "Isn't that the way to be noticed, sir, in this town?"

486

Arvid glanced at him. "You would know, I expect."

Mal grinned broadly. "Oh yes . . . I would know. And if you're speaking to our yeoman-marshal, I guess I'd like to be there."

"Mal!"

"No offense, yeoman-marshal, but I've seen his sword-work, remember? You know I can keep quiet."

Arvid smiled the same charming smile at Mal. Paks noticed that Mal simply absorbed it, without changing expression — he looked very much like a stupid country lout. "That's fine with me, sir. I am not intending assassination of your yeoman-marshal — or corruption, either — and you are welcome to watch me as closely as you wish."

The Council meeting that evening was straightforward. Paks, seconded by Mal, gave her account of the attack. Sir Felis reported his interview with the captured robbers, and turned over a list of the captured arms and other valuables. Paks was asked why she had not entered and explored the keep, but the Council accepted her explanation without surprise or comment. Even the Master Stonemason seemed content. They argued a bit over the arms, and finally awarded her a third of their value. Hebbinford recommended that the black horse be given to her outright, and after some discussion it was done. No one mentioned the master-thief that Ambros, Arvid, and even Sir Felis believed to be still lurking in the ruins.

Afterwards, Ambros, Paks, Mal, Sir Felis, and Arvid all gathered at the grange. Arvid lagged behind them, and when they were all sitting down in the chairs Ambros fetched from the Marshal's study, he lounged against the door.

"I have endured quite a bit of your suspicion," he said calmly. "I think perhaps I should tell you precisely what I'm doing here — though I should prefer that you don't tell everyone else."

"Why not?" asked Sir Felis, looking grim.

"Because I can be a great help to you," said Arvid. "If you choose to spread my fame too widely, I'll simply leave."

"Well, then?"

Arvid looked pointedly at Ambros. "The yeoman-marshal is the one I'd like to speak to. Will you, young sir, swear to say nothing of my guild or mission?"

"I — I don't know." His hand was on his medallion. "If you're evil — "

"Evil!" Arvid laughed. "Sir, I am not what you would call good, but I serve no evil deity — that I will swear, and on your Relic, if you demand it." He looked at Paks. "I am no more evil than this warrior — she is not Girdish, nor am I, but we have both spilled robbers' blood today alongside your yeomen."

Ambros flushed. "I will keep your secrets, sir, as long as they do not dishonor Gird. But as to that, I will be the judge."

"Fair enough. I trust the honor of the Fellowship of Gird." Arvid glanced around, gathering all their eyes on him. "Now: some of you — and many others — have thought I was a thief. I am not. I am, however, acquainted with the Thieves Guild." He paused, and the silence thickened. "I am, in fact, on a mission for them at this time."

"And you ask me, a yeoman-marshal of Gird, to keep silence?" Ambros jumped up. Arvid's hand rested on his sword.

"Wait, sir. Hear me out. Your own yeoman will tell you I was happy enough to attack robbers this morning; I am no thief myself. The situation is more complicated than that." He waited until Ambros was seated again, and then pulled a chair near the door for himself. "Now, be attentive. The Thieves Guild, however little you like its craft, is like any guild designed to keep the craftsmen in order. As far as its power runs, and that is far, it controls not merely the theft but also the sale of stolen goods. Some time ago, the Guild Headquarters in Vérella realized that caravans were being robbed near here — and their goods appeared distantly, sold without Guild authority. Or taxation." He looked around to be sure they were all listening. "You see the problem. It could not be permitted to continue. A renegade thief is a danger not only to you, but to other thieves. The Guild Council determined to find out who was responsible. They sent — investigators, I suppose you could call them. Your amiable Marshal, young sir, being a most diligent worker for good, caught one and scared another two out of town. Yet another disappeared entirely. So at last," he smiled at them all, "they sent me."

"And you are?" asked Sir Felis in a low growl.

"I am, as I said, Arvid Semminson. A man hired to find the false thief in charge of this operation, and either force him into the Guild, with full payment of dues and fines owed, or kill him."

"But you're not a thief."

"Oh, no. Never. Or at least, let's say that I am not presently in need of anything which it would be worth my while to steal. And I have no joy in theft, as some of our weaker members have. I have stolen a few items in my time — I suppose most people have — but does it make this lady a thief that she stole a ham in Aarenis while in flight from Siniava?"

Paks was amazed that he knew about that — then remembered that she had mentioned "uncle's" establishment to the Marshal and Ambros. The others looked at her for a moment, a little confused by the change of emphasis.

"Of course not," barked Sir Felis. "But — "

"What I am saying, Sir Felis, is that I want this ringleader dead as much, if not more, than you do. It was obvious at once to me that the robbers we captured were not in charge. They had not been fencing caravans of goods anywhere — they were poorly dressed and dull of wit. Whoever has been running this operation is not stupid. So we all have an enemy still at large — an enemy, moreover, who knows that we know where he's hiding — and who is responsible for his defeat. I think he's powerful, and probably either a magician or something worse — he probably spelled those poor men to keep them in his power."

"How would you know about that?"

"Please — I am a man of experience in the world. All kinds of experience. Why should I not know of wizardry, and the greed of those who live by it? And, for that matter, something of the evil ones, as well. I judge we must move quickly against the ringleader, before he can gather new forces. I can help you — I am a skilled fighter, and I have other skills that you will find helpful. Underground in that old keep, for instance, you would find me a good tracker, and wary of traps. If you choose to let him go, you will shortly find that he is more powerful and dangerous — even deadly — to this whole community."

"I thought of that," said Ambros suddenly. "I was telling Paks — if it's a priest of Achrya, say, then we must move quickly. Every day may be important."

"Well, we can't do anything until the Marshal comes back," said Sir Felis. "You can't hope to go against anything like that by yourself, Ambros."

"I don't know when he'll be back, Sir Felis. He said I wasn't to go chasing robbers, that's true — but this is different."

"I don't see that. Orders are orders."

Ambros sat up straight. "Sir Felis, with all respect, my orders come from Gird, as well as Marshal Cedfer."

Paks saw a gleam of satisfaction in Arvid's eyes. Sir Felis shook his head stubbornly.

"It wouldn't be the first time a junior officer thought he had divine guidance when he was simply aching for an adventure. I tell you, Ambros, that you're a fool if you tackle Achrya with a thief and a mercenary for aid." He gave Paks a hard look. "Assuming you're thinking of going with him. I think you're honest, but — "

Paks felt a burst of anger. "Sir Felis, if you have cause for that — "

"No. All right, I'll admit you've done well so far — I said it earlier. But you're all young, and like any young fighters, you've got the sense of a clatter of colts. Wait for the Marshal, Ambros. Don't drag others into your romantic dream." Sir Felis pushed himself up and made for the door, pausing beside Arvid. "And you, master thief-not-a-thief, if you push that boy into rash action, I'll not forget who started it."

"Sir Felis," said Arvid coolly, "I'll not forget who was unwilling to root out the deepest evil." He moved aside from the door, as Sir Felis spat where his feet had been and went out.

Chapter Sixteen

Arvid's black-clothed form seemed to melt into the shadows as they moved farther away from the stairway, where dim light came from above. Paks felt a tightness in her chest. She did not like dark underground places, and wondered for a moment why she had agreed to come. Ambros nudged her in the back. She waved a hand at him, and took another careful step. Another. Surely it was ridiculous to come on something like this with only six, one of them an untried junior yeoman, an eager girl who would be all too likely to do something silly trying to prove herself. Arvid signalled, a wave of his arm, and Paks moved lightly toward him. He was the scout, accustomed, he said, to noticing traps. Paks, the most experienced sword fighter, came second.

After her, Suli and Ambros together. Paks hoped the yeoman-marshal would be steadied by steadying the junior yeoman. Mal brought up the rear with Jori, a friend of his.

"Door," said Arvid quietly in her ear. "I'll try it. Hinges right. Swings out." Paks flattened herself to the left of the door; she saw a gleam of teeth as Arvid smiled. He ran his hands over the door for a moment, then did something Paks could not see to the lock. A nod of satisfaction; he drew his own blade and slowly pulled the door open. Paks waited, ready to strike. Nothing happened. She craned her neck and looked. Even deeper blackness. A sour smell wafted out, a stench like old rotting leaves and bones. Arvid put his sword through the door. Nothing. With a shrug, he leaned around the frame, poking at the darkness as if it were a pillow.

"Light?" asked Ambros softly. He had come quite close.

"Not yet. It makes a target of us."

"Yes, but we aren't cats — "

"Quiet. Wait." Arvid had told them their main danger would be haste. Make a noise, he had said, clatter around like a horse fair, and our quarry will be ready for us. Paks waited, trying to see into the darkness by force of will. Spots danced before her eyes. Gradually she found she could see a little better. The room ahead was clearly a room — all shades of darkness, but smaller than the banquet hall above them. She tried to see if anything lurked in it. It seemed as if something — a pile of something — obscured the floor, but without light she could not tell.

"Go now," said Arvid, in Paks's ear. Together they moved under the lin-

490

tel, separating at once on the inside to flatten against the inner wall. The others waited outside.

In here the smell was stronger. Paks wrinkled her nose, trying to decide what it was. It smelled — meatier, she decided. Rotting straw, bones, meat, and something like the inside of a dirty boot. She shook her head, trying to clear it, but the smell seemed stronger every second. Arvid sniffed, a tiny sound she could hear clearly.

"That smell — " she heard from outside. She thought it was Mal.

"Quiet," said Ambros. Paks stood still, trying to hear anything past the pulse in her ears.

"We'll go forward five paces," said Arvid quietly, "and then if nothing happens, we'll try a light."

Paks heard the scrape of his boot on the stone flags as he took the first step, and moved with him. One step. Two, three — and she stumbled over something, staggering on soft, springy, uneven footing. A yelp got out before she closed her throat; Ambros behind her scraped flint on steel at once. As the spark caught, that little light showed that she'd caught her foot on the edge of a pile of garbage. Dirty straw, old clothes, bones chewed not-quite-clean, a broken pot — she started to laugh with relief. Ambros's candle seemed brighter than she'd expected. She turned to Arvid; his eyes were wide with surprise.

"Just trash," she said, waving her sword at the heap. It was half her height, and easily three times her length. "They must have — "

Part of the pile heaved up — and up — a vast hairy shoulder topped by an equally vast hairy face. A rheumy eye glared at her from under shaggy brows. Then the mouth opened on a double row of very sharp teeth. By reflex, Paks struck at the arm that swiped down from the darkness. Her sword bit into it, slicing deep, but the arm's strength nearly cost her the grip. A deep bellow split the air, and the entire pile shuddered. Paks nearly lost her footing as the creature trampled its bed and attacked.

She had no time to wonder what it was. Taller, broader, than any human, it had a roughly human shape. Heavy pelt over thick skin — it turned Ambros's first stroke — long arms ending in clawed hands, and a surpassingly ugly face — Paks noticed these without trying to classify them. Its deep-voiced bellows shook the air around them.

"Get back, Ambros!" cried Arvid. "Keep the light — this thing can see in the dark."

Ambros made a noise, but moved back. Suli had come up beside Paks, and was doing a creditable job with her sword — except that she couldn't penetrate the thick hide. Paks had wounded the creature several times, while dodging raking blows from its claws, but it was still strong. Arvid, she saw in a quick glance, was trying to attack its flank, but it moved too fast — he couldn't seem to get a killing blow in. Paks had just begun to wonder where Mal and his friend were, when she saw him working his way around the creature to its back. Once there, he swung his big axe in a mighty arc and sank it into the creature's back. It screamed, a hoarse, high-pitched sound, deafening in that space.

"The axe does it," he yelled. "It's got — " But the creature heaved backwards; Paks heard the axe-haft smack into something, and Mal grunted. She jumped forward, unsteady on the piled trash, and sank her sword deep in its belly. Now it lurched forward, bending. She dodged. Arvid got a stroke in on its left arm. Mal pulled the axe out of its back and swung again, this time higher. It went to its knees, moaning. Paks aimed a blow at the neck, and blood spurted out, drenching her arm. Still writhing, it sank to a heap, its eyes filming.

"So much for silence and caution," said Arvid tartly, when they had caught their breath. Mal and Suli had lit candles now as well, and they all took a close look at what they had killed. Half again as tall as Paks, and heavily built, it was like nothing she had ever seen.

"What is it?" she asked, wiping the blood off her hands and face. The blood had an odd smell, and tasted terrible. Ambros shook his head. Arvid looked at her.

"I'm not sure, Paks, but it might be a hool. I've never seen one myself, but I've heard."

"A hool?"

"Big, tough, stupid, dirty, likes to lair underground. If you can imagine a solitary giant orc — "

"I thought hools were water giants," said Ambros.

Arvid shrugged. "Maybe I'm wrong. Whatever it is, it's dead. And we have just announced ourselves to the entire underground."

"I never did think trying to sneak in was a good idea," said Ambros. "Gird is not subtle."

Arvid raised one brow, and smiled. "No. That's why I'm not a Girdsman. But don't worry — now you'll have every chance for a suicidal frontal assault."

Paks had been poking gingerly through the trash heap that the creature had laired on. A copper armband gleamed; she picked it up. "Look. This is human-size."

"Hmm. Not worth much," said Arvid.

"No, but — I wouldn't have thought the robbers would throw it away."

"That's true. I — " Suddenly he stopped. They had all heard the sound: a rhythmic pounding, not loud, but distinct. Paks looked around. In flickering candlelight, she could just see a doorway across from the way they'd come in, and another door, closed and barred, centered the right-hand wall. Otherwise the room seemed empty.

"It's that door — the closed one," said Mal. He wrenched his axe free of the creature's backbone and started for it. Paks got there first, sword drawn. Arvid and Mal levered the heavy bars up and threw them aside. Then they pulled the door open.

Candlelight showed a small room, hardly more than a cell. A gnome, one shoe off, stood poised by the door; his shoe was in his hand, where he'd been pounding the door. Another gnome lay on the bare stone floor, covered in cloaks.

The standing gnome nodded stiffly and put his shoe back on. Then he addressed Paks in gnomish. She shook her head, and he frowned, then spoke in clipped accented Common.

"It is that you lead this rescue? Or do you claim us prisoners?"

"I — " Paks looked sideways at Arvid. He spoke.

"Lady Paksenarrion commanded us for the capture of the robbers, and now we have come to see what else hides in this keep."

The gnome bowed from the waist, and met Paks's eyes as he stood upright. "It shall be that you have the reward of the Aldonfulk, lady. For this indeed shall value be given. It is that our partner of Lyonya is eaten by that monster, true?"

"We haven't seen him," said Paks, thinking of the arm-ring with a shudder. "Is that what you think happened?"

"It took him. It seemed hungry. We heard cries. We could see nothing; I will not say what happened when I have not knowledge, but that is logical."

"Is your friend hurt?" The gnome on the floor had not moved.

"Only slightly — he was hit by arrow of robbers. He sleeps to gain strength."

Paks was surprised by the gnome's composure. Despite days of imprisonment in a dark cell, the death of one companion and the wounds of another, the gnome showed no distress. He turned to the other gnome, and spoke loudly in gnomish. Paks could not understand a word of it. She looked around to see if the others did, but they looked as blank as she felt. The gnome on the floor stirred, and opened his eyes.

"Surely you are hungry or thirsty," said Paks, counting how many days they'd been imprisoned. "We have water and food."

The response was less than she'd expected; the unwounded gnome nodded and came forward. "It is not so bad as you thought. The robbers brought food the first day or so. They fed the creature something too. Then they were gone. Then we had nothing. You will take us back to Brewersbridge?"

Paks handed him her water flask; the gnome uncapped it carefully and carried it to the other, who drank a few swallows. Then the first gnome drank. "We need not so much food as you," he said, returning the flask. "If you take us now — "

"But we haven't found the priest," said Ambros.

"Priest?" asked the gnome, with no change of expression.

"We believe that a servant of Achrya is nearby — perhaps deep in this place — and directed the robbers."

"Oh." The gnomes looked at each other. "It is a matter for humans. We are not daskdusky, to search after the webspinner's lair. If return to Brewersbridge, the return of your favor will be granted."

"We might as well," said Arvid. "We've lost all chance of surprise."

"And we can't leave these behind us," said Paks. "They can't defend themselves, with one of them wounded, and weakened as they are. We should get them to safety."

"I agree," said Mal. He had a large swelling bruise across his forehead. Paks realized that the axe-haft must have hit him on the face. "I don't know as I can fight as good as most days." Ambros looked at him in surprise, then concern. His voice seemed slurred.

"Will your friend need to be carried?" asked Paks.

The gnome bowed again, and gave Paks a small tight smile. "It is generous of the lady to think of that. If it is possible, he should not walk so far."

In the end, they came back to Brewersbridge that same evening, with the two gnomes alive and well, and clear evidence of the human trader's death. Ambros and Mal hacked off the creature's right hand and an ear as proof of what they'd found. The gnomes took rooms at *The Jolly Potboy* — they were well known enough that Hebbinford trusted their credit. Paks, her clothes still stained with blood, found Suli dogging her every step.

"Did I — I mean, I couldn't get through the hide, but did I do all right otherwise? I didn't scream, or anything —"

Paks felt tired. "No. You did fine, Suli — I said that —"

"Yes, but — you are going back, aren't you? You'll let me come? And I can take your clothes, now, and get Sevri to wash them —"

"No!" It came out harsher than she meant it, and Suli looked worried. Not frightened, Paks noticed, but worried.

"But —"

"Sevri has her own duties — she's not a washing maid. I'll do it; any soldier learns to keep her own gear clean." Paks could see that this was not pleasant news to Suli. She nodded, remembering her own feelings during training. "I told you before, Suli — being a warrior's not what you thought. Most of it is like this — cleaning gear, and keeping weapons in trim, and practice. If you don't do it yourself, you can't be sure it's done right."

The girl nodded, and leaned against the wall, evidently planning to stay until she was tossed out.

"Your own sword, for instance," said Paks severely. "Have you inspected it yet? Is it clean? Have you taken care of any nicks or dents? It's the grange's sword — you should return it in perfect condition."

Suli reddened, and pulled it from the scabbard — sticky with drying blood and hair.

"Go clean that," said Paks. "When you've got all the blood off, then polish it, and clean the scabbard. If you leave all that muck in the scabbard, then —"

"But how?" asked Suli. "It's inside, and —"

Paks took the scabbard and looked. Unlike hers, this was a simple wood casing, pegged in several places and glued along the edges. The upper end was notched for attachment to a belt.

"You're lucky. This is all wood. Take some wet grass or sedge — sedges are better — and tie them to a limber switch, and scrub inside with that. Then run clean water in and out of it. That should do. Set it in a cool place to dry — don't put the sword back inside, or it'll rust. If it smells clean tomorrow, you're done. Otherwise you may have to take it apart."

"Seems a lot of trouble, just to get a bloodstain off," grumbled Suli. Paks glared at her, sure now of her ground.

"Trouble! You don't know what trouble is, until you leave something to rot in your scabbard, and then nick yourself with dirty steel." She remembered the surgeons talking about wound fever, and poisoned weapons. "It's the way some tribes of orcs poison weapons, Suli. Store 'em in rotting flesh and blood." She was glad to see the girl turn green and turn to go without further argument. "Check with Ambros at the grange later this evening — you'll need to pick up another scabbard, and he can tell you where and when to meet us."

"Yes, Paks," said Suli, subdued.

Paks had just finished cleaning up, with her wet clothes hanging behind the kitchen, and her wet hair still chilly on her head, when Hebbinford came to tell her the gnomes wanted a word with her.

"Why?" she asked.

"Gird knows," he said. "Being as it's gnomes, it's some trading matter, I'd say. Remember that they're as full of pride as bees of sting — and as quick with it, too. They don't like jokes, and they don't like someone misjudging them on their size. Gnomes see everything as exchange — good for good, and blow for blow. They don't do favors, but they're perishing fair, if you can understand their idea of fair. And they never forget anything, to the ends of the world."

"Oh." Paks hoped they would understand ordinary courtesy as courtesy.

Both gnomes were seated before the fire in one of Hebbinford's private rooms when Hebbinford announced her. One jumped up and bowed. Paks made a sketchy bow in return. She thought she could see a gleam of satisfaction in that flat dark eye.

"Master Hebbinford if you would bring ale." The gnome gestured to a chair, and Paks sat; he returned to his own seat. His speech lacked the pauses and music of human language; Paks found it hard to follow, even though the words were pronounced correctly. "Is it that you were hired for our rescue?"

"No," said Paks, "not exactly."

"Then this rescue was in hope of reward?"

"No — what is it?"

"That is what I try to find out. For what service were you hired, if not for our rescue?"

Paks wondered how much she should say of the Brewersbridge Council's affairs. "Sir — pardon, if I do not know the correct address — " He took her up at once.

"Lady, it is our mistake. We thought you would not care to be precise. I am Master-trader Addo Verkinson Aldonfulk, sixth son of my father's house: the polite address in Common would be Master-trader Addo Aldonfulk, or Master Addo if in haste. This my companion is journeyman-trader

Ebo Gnaddison Gnarrinfulk, the fourth son of my father's third sister: he should be styled Journeyman Ebo. And thine own naming?"

"Master-trader Addo — " Paks got that far before losing track. The gnome nodded anyway.

"That will do."

" — I am Paksenarrion Dorthansdotter, of Three Firs — "

"Three Firs is thy clan?"

"No, Master-trader Addo; it is the place of my father's dwelling." Paks found her own speech becoming both stilted and formal.

"Ah. We know that some humans have no clans." He paused as Hebbinford himself returned with a large flagon of ale and three tankards. "Be welcome to ale as the guest of Aldonfulk, Paksenarrion Dorthansdotter; no obligation is thine for partaking of this gift."

Paks stared, then caught her wits back. "I thank you, Master-trader Addo." She took the tankard he offered, and sipped cautiously. "You asked of my employment, sir. The Council of Brewersbridge has, as you may know, a policy against idle swordsmen in the town."

The gnome nodded. "An excellent policy. Human towns are too lawless as it is and human vagabonds cause trouble. We allow no masterless humans in the gnome kingdoms."

Paks reddened, but went on. "Master-trader Addo, the Council examined me, and decided that I might stay some time, but they asked a favor."

"Favor! What is a favor?"

She remembered Hebbinford's warning. "Sir, my — my vows are to another; I am traveling from Aarenis to the far north." That seemed safe enough. The gnome relaxed in his chair. "But they asked my aid in finding the hiding place of a band of robbers — the same who attacked you — and asked that I lead a force against them if I could find them."

"And what pay did they offer for this?"

"Well — that I could stay longer than they would otherwise allow, and the use of a horse, and a share of goods recovered from the hideout, if there were any."

"Hmmph." The gnome chattered in gnomish with his companion. Paks could not tell how old they were, or if the journeyman were younger than the master. They had earth-brown, unwrinkled faces, and thick dark hair. Addo turned back to Paks. "It seems little payment for an uncertain task. How many days were you bound to stay and work at it?"

"No time was set. But I had money enough, and reason to dislike brigands."

"Hmm. And after our caravan was taken did they say aught about rescue?"

"No, Master-trader Addo. It was thought you had been killed with the others. One man escaped to tell of the attack. Many bodies were found."

"I see. Why then were you in the keep? To look for goods?"

"No. The robbers we captured said that someone else took over the

496

goods. Ambros, the yeoman-marshal, thinks it is a priest of Achrya. Arvid Semminson says the goods are being sold at a distance."

"And you did not expect to find us."

"No, sir. But we were glad to find any that had survived."

Another conversation in gnomish. Paks finished the ale in her tankard, and thought about pouring another. But she felt constrained to wait until it was offered. Finally Addo turned to her again.

"If you did not come and search the keep would anyone else have come?"

"No, Master-trader Addo. Most people around here think it is bad luck."

"Superstition. Luck is a fallacy of humans; things either are or are not. That creature who ate our companion — was it dangerous to armed men?"

"Yes, sir. It was very large, and fought well; it took several of us to kill it."

"It is true you command this force?"

Paks frowned. "I would not want to mislead you, sir. I was asked to command, and did command, the force which killed and captured the robbers themselves. Today's foray was not entirely my idea — yeoman-marshal Ambros insisted that it must be made at once. But because I have experience, I was at the head of the party."

Addo shook his head. "Even among humans, one must take command, and be responsible for all — I ask again if that was you or another. If another who would it be?"

"I — in that way, sir, you could say I commanded." Paks thought it was not too great a boast — they had followed her orders, such as they were.

"You are not boastful as many human fighters are," he commented; she wondered if he could read her thoughts. "It is important to know who commands. It is this person the clans owe thanks to." He took a ring off his finger, and reached out to her. "At this time we have been robbed; we have nothing. But this is in earnest of your just claim on Aldonfulk and Gnarrinfulk; it shall be redeemed fairly, on my word as Master-trader." Paks took the ring; it was black, like iron, and heavy. She nodded, wondering what to say.

"I thank you, Master-trader Addo Aldonfulk — and Journeyman Ebo."

"It is but right. You had no obligation; you had not been hired for this task. I ask your trust that this will be redeemed."

"Master-trader Addo, you have that trust. But I would free anyone from such captivity — "

"Oh?"

"It is right — "

"You have an obligation to a god? Are you sworn to such deeds, then?" He looked almost as if he might ask for the ring back.

"No, sir," said Paks. "But I serve the gods of my father's house, and they oppose evil."

"Umph. That is well, to stand with tradition. And such belief does not interfere with our owing. Keep the ring, Paksenarrion Dorthansdotter. You returned our lives."

"It was my pleasure to do so." Paks sat a moment; the gnomes were silent. "Would you," she ventured, "be my guest for another flagon of ale? With — with no obligation?" Both gnomes nodded.

"We would not willingly owe thee more," said Addo, "but it is mannerly of thee to offer. We will be thy guests."

Their brush with death had not discouraged Ambros at all. He insisted that they go again the next day. Mal grunted; he was purple from hairline to jaw where the axe-haft had caught him, and he breathed noisily.

"I wouldn't have said it before, yeoman-marshal, but I'm still head-thick from this, and I don't trust my speed. A thick eye's bad enough in daylight."

"Then you can stay," said Ambros tartly. "I've other yeomen."

Mal sighed loudly. "By Gird's arm, Ambros, I'm willing enough, but — "

"Mal, I can't wait. I can't. Something bad is going on here — I have to deal with it."

"Ambros, we did well by scouting around before attacking the robbers," said Paks. "Why not look for the place where the goods are moving out? That might be a better way in." She was thinking of the tunnel at Rotengre.

"No." Ambros shook his head stubbornly. "It takes too long — let the priest think we were frightened back by that monster. It's a door-guard, I imagine — "

"Certainly so," said Arvid.

"Then, when he knows we've killed it but have gone away, he may be careless for a space. A short space, in which we must strike."

Arvid looked at him curiously. "Are you angry, yeoman-marshal, that I bade you stay back with the light?"

"I was," said Ambros frankly. "Then I realized that you had to have light to fight. This time we'll let another carry the flint — and another be prepared to light candle or torch for us as it's needed. Now — to plans."

This time, the stench from the open door nearly turned Paks's stomach. The dead creature already swarmed with vermin — in the light of the candles, a flurry of rats scuttered away, squeaking. Beyond, the open doorway gaped. Again, Paks and Arvid were in the lead. Ambros had found six yeomen to come with them, including Mal. Two of them carried lighted candles. Suli followed Paks closely.

Beyond the empty doorway, a passage sloped downhill, its rough stone floor heavy with dust churned by many feet. Paks could see and hear nothing. She glanced at Arvid.

"Let me lead," he said quietly. "Stay close, but don't pass me, and be ready to stop on my signal. It's the very place for some trap." He stepped forward. Paks waited until he was three paces ahead, and then followed. The passage went on for twenty paces — twenty more — then Arvid stopped. Paks caught his hand signal and froze in her tracks. Suli bumped her from behind. The others' footsteps seemed loud. Then silence, as they all stood still. Arvid was touching the side walls lightly. He looked back at

Paks, and gestured her forward — one step. She took it. He pointed at the floor. She could see nothing, until he pointed again. A slight ridge in the dust, a ripple she would never have noticed. Where the feet had passed it, she could see an edge of stone.

"It's the trigger," he said softly. "If someone steps on that, then — " he pointed up. "That will fall." In the dimness overhead, Paks could make out a dark slit, and shining points. "A portcullis. It probably makes a noise, as well. There should be a safety block on one side, though, if they carry heavy goods through here. Ah-h." Paks could not see what he did, but a small block of stone suddenly slid out of the wall a handsbreadth. "That should do it. We might want to come out this way in a hurry. Meanwhile, make sure no one steps on the trigger stone."

Paks passed this information along, and everyone stepped carefully over the ridge. Arvid had gone on. He disarmed another such trap thirty paces farther on. "I expect," he said quietly to Paks, "that both would close together, and open arrow-slits in the walls as well. But we shall hope not to find out." After that, Paks kept her eyes roving on all sides, trying to spot traps — but she missed the next, after the passage turned and dipped steeply. Arvid halted at the top of the steepening ramp.

"Now this," he said, "may be a chute trap."

"What?"

"If you step on the trigger of a chute trap," he said, "it tips up and dumps you in someone's pot — or prison cell. It's the same. We're meant to go on — but you don't see footprints in that dust, do you?"

"No — but it's been disturbed — "

"Umm. More like something's been dragged on it. They may use it for the caravan goods — saves carrying. I'd rather arrive on my feet. We need another door."

Paks could see nothing but stone-walled passage. Arvid went over every stone with his long fingertips. The others fidgeted; Paks shushed them. Finally he tapped one section of wall and smiled. "This is the entrance. The trouble is that I don't know what's on the other side. They may have a guard right there — in which case, we're in trouble. It may be trapped to sound an alarm — I can't tell. But I judge it's a safer way down than that — " He nodded at the chute.

"Well — we have to try something," said Paks. "Can you tell which way it opens?"

"No. I don't think it will rotate, like an ordinary door. It should either come forward or sink in, and then slide sideways. I can't tell which." He looked at her, challenging. Paks was determined to figure it out for herself.

"Well, then — you're the one who can open it. I'll cover you, on your left side. The rest of you move three paces back and stay flat against this wall — you won't be hit by arrows, if there's an archer, and you can see how it works. Shield the candles with your hands, in case of a strong draft. Anything else?" She looked at Arvid. He shook his head.

"You've a feel for this, lady," he said.

She heard a click as he worked the mechanism. The stone before him sank back; faint light came through the gap. Soundlessly the stone slid to the left. Behind it was a landing; stairs went down to the left, where the light brightened, and up to the right. Across the landing was an alcove; four cross-bows hung from pegs. Paks moved quickly through the opening, and looked both ways. Nothing. She signed to Arvid, who nodded and motioned the others in. He did something to the touchstone lock, and murmured that he hoped he'd jammed it open. His eyes slid to the crossbows. Paks quickly cut their strings. The two quivers of bolts she simply took and tied to her belt.

Down toward the light they crept, stair by stair. Halfway down, Paks could see that a passage led away ahead and another to the right. She motioned those behind her to the right-hand wall of the stair. Now she could see a door, closed, at the foot of the stairs to the left. Arvid stayed in the lead, one stair before her. At the foot, he stopped a long moment to scan the passage ahead and the foot of the stair itself. The forward passage ended in another closed door not twenty paces away, heavy wood bound with iron. Neither hinges nor bars showed on this side. The light they had seen came from torches in brackets on both sides of the passage: four ahead, and obviously more to the right. The flame-tips bent toward the left-hand door, and even on the stairs Paks could feel the draft that kept the air fresh.

Arvid put the tip of his sword past the corner. Nothing happened. Very slowly he eased his face to the corner. Paks waited, feeling her heart race. He drew back, and motioned her back a step. Then he spoke softly in her ear. "It goes twenty-thirty paces, then turns left. Wide enough for four fighters. Torch every four paces. Mark on floor, good for bow."

"Run it," suggested Paks.

"Only way," he agreed. "Got to be quiet and fast." Paks did not see how they could all be fast and silent, but she told the others. Ambros and another yeoman moved up beside her; she told Suli to stay in the second rank.

They started off at a quick jog, as quietly as possible. Paks saw the pale stripes on the floor, four of them, and stepped over the first. Then she heard a noise from somewhere ahead, and leaped into full speed, the others with her. Four crossbowmen appeared at the far end of the passage; the first flight of crossbow bolts whirred by. Paks heard a yelp from behind; something clicked on her helmet. Behind them four more, shooting even as the first four dropped their bows and leaped forward with shortswords in hand. Paks did not hesitate; it would be suicide to stop in that bare passage. She reached the first swordsmen before they were set in position; Arvid and Ambros were hardly behind her, and they forced the line back into the others. Now all eight defenders had dropped their bows.

Paks had never faced a shortsword formation with a longsword. She found herself fighting as if she had her Company weapon. At least they didn't have shields — she smiled as her sword went home in one of them. He folded over, to lie curled on the floor. The man behind thrust at her, and

500

she raked his arm. She noticed that Arvid, beside her, had downed another. The first man down tried to stab at her legs; Paks edged by, and Suli got him in the throat. Paks and Arvid were one step ahead of Ambros and the yeoman. Paks was beginning to think they might get through without too much trouble when four more men appeared.

"Blast!" said Arvid. "I'd hoped this was the first wave."

Paks said nothing, fighting her way forward a step at a time. She was beginning to use the longsword more freely, with effect. Another man went down before her, and those behind seemed less eager to engage. But the noise in the passage was considerable. Ambros was yelling Girdish slogans, as was the yeoman; each had now defeated his man, and they were back in line. The clash of steel rang from the walls.

Then the torches went out as if they'd been dipped in water. Paks felt something rake across her torso; the mail held. She thrust hard ahead of her, and heard someone grunt, then sigh. She shook the weight off her blade and thrust again. Nothing.

"Arvid?" she asked.

"Here." His voice beside her was calm. She wasn't. Ambros cursed, off to Arvid's right. Paks could hear heavy breathing in front of them somewhere. She moved forward a step, and her boot landed on something soft and moving. She kicked, hard, and stepped back.

"Light," said Ambros testily. She could hear the scrape of flint and steel, but saw no spark.

"You want light, servant of Gird?" came a silky voice out of the dark ahead. "I thought you Girdsmen claimed the knowledge of lightspells."

Paks tried again to move toward the voice, but Arvid grabbed her arm. She froze in place. She could sense that he was fumbling in his cloak. As her eyes adjusted to the darkness, she could tell that somewhere around the bend torches were still burning — vague shapes stood out against that dim glow. She could not tell how many. If they were reloading crossbows — if they had spears — we're crazy to stand here, she thought, like sheep in a chute. With a wild yell, she jumped forward, a standing leap that took her to the first of the dark shapes. She heard Arvid's curse, the others jumping after her. Her sword clashed against another, suddenly glowing blue. She heard other weapons striking, and pressed her own opponent hard by instinct, since she could scarcely see. She felt a blow on her shoulder, and another on the ribs. Her own blade flickered, a dancing blue gleam that lit only its target. Something raked her free hand, burning like fire or ice. She shook it, still fencing.

Their surprise attack brought them around the turn of the passage, over bodies now crumpled beneath the fighters. Ahead was a short hall with a door to the right. Against the golden glow from that door stood a tall, slender robed figure. They were within four paces of it, when that same smooth voice spoke, a word Paks had not heard before. Her muscles slackened, as if she had been hit in the head; she nearly dropped her sword. Arvid fell back a pace. Even Ambros stopped where he was, and dropped the tip of his blade. The defenders leaped forward.

501

"Gird!" cried Ambros, in that instant. Paks felt her body come alive again; she covered Arvid's side with a desperate lunge, and took a glancing blow on her helmet. Suli pushed past Arvid, throwing a quick glance at Paks, and lunged at the man before her. Paks had time to notice that she was indeed quick, and quite good. Then the defenders retreated past the door, and turned to run. Paks faced the doorway. It was empty.

Within, the steady glow of lamplight revealed a chamber hung with rich tapestries in brilliant colors. In the center of the chamber stood a handsome young man in long black velvet robes edged with black fur. He smiled at them, and held out empty hands.

"Don't you think you're being discourteous?" he asked. His voice was mellow as old ale. "It is friendlier to announce oneself, don't you think?"

"You — !" began Ambros. Paks noticed Suli edging forward and plucked at her sleeve. Suli turned, frowning, but obeyed when Paks gestured her back. "Spawn of Achrya," Ambros went on. The man laughed easily.

"Alas, young sir yeoman-marshal of Gird, I am not Achrya's spawn — if I were, you might have found another welcome. 'Tis true I have done her some service, but — what is that to thee?"

"I am the yeoman-marshal — "

"Yes, of Brewersbridge. This is not Brewersbridge. This is my keep, and you have broken in, attacking and killing my men — and you are not even the Marshal. It's not your grange."

"It is. It was left in my care. And you — corrupting men, robbing caravans, killing and looting — Gird's teeth, it's my business!" Ambros took a step forward, toward the doorway.

"So you really think a yeoman-marshal of Gird is a match for me? Or are you relying on your muscle-bound women for protection?" Suli lunged forward, and Paks caught her in the midriff with a stiff elbow. Suli gasped, and Paks spoke over her shoulder.

"Don't be a fool, he's trying to anger us. Stay back."

The man looked directly at her. Something about his gaze warned her, and she dropped her eyes to his neck. "My," he said sweetly, "a wise head rules that magic sword. Perhaps you are not what you seem, eh? I had heard of a strange lady swordfighter in Brewersbridge — a veteran of Phelan's company, they said, who left because she would not see evil done. Is that you, then?" Paks fought back a surge of rage that roared in her ears and threatened to haze her vision. "Defeated that elven mage, and freed the elfane taig, that's what I heard. Near enough a paladin, I should think — not a Girdsman yet, what a shame — if, that is, you defeat me. Do you think to defeat me, pretty one?"

This too Paks ignored, keeping her attention on his neck. She thought how she would like to sink her sword in it. But she heard what he said. Near enough a paladin? The thought beckoned, like a finger in the mist. But Arvid spoke up, having regained his position beside her.

"You, sir, seem to have some power of enchantment, or why do we stand here speaking to you? For me, I would see your blood on that handsome

502

rug, and put an end to such delay." He moved forward a handsbreadth and stopped, as if he'd hit a wall.

"Enchantments? Yes, indeed. And, since you've robbed me of robbers and guards alike, I'm in need of servants. You, I believe, will do nicely. And the women; Achrya will be pleased if I interfere in the growth of a paladin of Gird. I hope, indeed, to convert all of you. How pleasant it will be to have spies in the grange of Brewersbridge."

"No! By Gird!" Ambros leaped forward, sword high. Paks shook herself, suddenly alert to her musings, and followed him. She was not surprised to see a sword appear in the man's hand, a dagger in the other. Ambros met the sword with his own, narrowly missing a dagger thrust. Paks came in on the Achryan's sword side. She turned his blade and thrust. Her blade seemed to stick in his robes; she jerked it free with an effort. Meanwhile his blade had raked her shoulder. She could feel the links of mail along that track.

No one else came to join them. As the priest of Achrya turned, Paks had time for a quick glance back. The others stood motionless, clearly unable to break free. Meanwhile the priest fought superbly, sweeping away their blades again and again. It seemed impossible to wound him. Every thrust that Paks thought went home caught in his robes, and he fought on unhindered. She did not notice that he worked them toward a corner of the room where dark blue velvet rose behind a carved black chair. He backed, backed again, turned, and grabbed for the chair arm. Paks, hearing a rustle above, jerked back and looked upward. A tangled mass of black webbing fell down, catching her off-balance. Where it touched her clothes, they turned black, charring. She slashed at the cords, her sword hissing as it sliced them. But they were tough and sticky; she could not free herself quickly.

Ambros had jumped forward, a long lunge at the priest, and the web caught only one foot. Before the priest could strike, he had cut himself free. Now they fought behind the chair, great sweeps of sword parting the air and ringing together.

"You might as well quit," the priest said. "You can't win now — two of you couldn't defeat me."

"Gird's grace," said Ambros between clenched teeth. "I won't quit — I will kill you."

"I think not, boy," said the priest with a smile. He made a gesture toward Ambros's face, and a length of something gray flicked at him. Ambros blinked but kept fighting. "You're a stubborn fool, boy — are you hunting your death?" Paks struggled with the web, hardly aware of the Company curses she shouted. She could see blisters rising on Ambros's face, like the mark of a fiery whip. The priest spared her a look. "You won't get clear of that in a hurry, sweetling. 'Tis made of Achrya's own webs. As is this —" He lashed once more at Ambros's face. The yeoman-marshal screamed, one hand clawing at his face. "You see, boy, what you drive me to? Why will you not submit?"

Paks could see that the blow had caught his eye, but somehow Ambros had kept hold of his sword. He fought on, with less skill now, his movements jerky. Paks sawed frantically at the web, cursing again when it touched her bare skin; it burned like fire. The priest said something, a string of words she did not know, and the web moved, shifting around her, so that the cut strands were out of reach. Ambros called to her.

"Paks — call on Gird! With me — " he gave a sharp cry of pain as the priest's gray whip touched him again.

Paks opened her mouth to say something else, and found herself yelling, "By the power of Gird Strongarm, and the High Lord, and all the gods of right — " Ambros, too, was yelling, holding his Girdish medallion now with one hand, as he flung himself on the priest. Light flared around them; Paks could hardly see, in the flurry of movement, what happened. Then the web lay still around her, and nothing moved in the heap of robes behind the chair. And the rest of the party, suddenly freed, ran forward full of questions and noise.

Chapter Seventeen

Suli grabbed the web strands that bound Paks, then yanked her hand back as welts rose on her palm. Arvid ran past Paks to look at Ambros and the priest.

"He's dead," he said shortly.

"Both?" asked Mal.

"Yes. Both." Arvid sighed, then turned back to help Paks and Suli hack the web apart. "Lady, that's a dire trap you're caught in."

"I know." Paks could hardly speak for mingled anger and shame — Ambros was dead, and she had not been able to fight. She kept cutting grimly, until finally she could step out of the web. Her clothes were charred to rags, and Arvid looked at her mail with respect.

"That's . . . very good mail you're wearing."

"Yes —" Paks touched one of the burns on her face gingerly, and went to look at Ambros's body. The priest's gray lash had laced blistered welts across his face. Together, she and Mal straightened his body, wrapping his cloak around it. Arvid and the other yeoman stood watch at the door, but no sound came from the corridor. Paks suspected that with their master dead, and his control broken, the men they'd fought had fled, either to the surface, or to deeper hiding places. Suli roamed the room idly, staring at the tapestries, then stooped over the dead priest's body.

"Look at this," she said, lifting a silver chain around the dead priest's neck. "It's got —"

"Drop that!" Paks remembered the Achryan's medallion in Rotengre. "It's magic."

Suli looked startled, and dropped it less quickly than Paks intended. But nothing happened.

Paks could not define what she felt. She had not wanted to go back underground; she had not wanted to meet another evil mage. But she liked Ambros, had gotten used to his cheerful face. When he told her his dream, she felt his trust in her — and as always, gave trust for trust in return. In a vague way she had hoped — and made herself believe — that what they might face under the keep was not nearly so bad as the possessed elf-lord had been. She had thought Ambros's dream was the dream of an untried soldier, a recruit thinking too much of the coming battle.

Now he was dead. She had failed him. She, the seasoned soldier, had not

505

been able to fight. The untried recruit, the boy (as she thought of him), had fought on, alone, and died without her aid. He was as dead as Macenion, as Saben, two others she had not saved. As she took the precautions she knew to take — setting a watch, planning their return to the surface — her mind roiled.

Only after they had started back did she begin to realize what her position might be. What Sir Felis would think. What the Marshal would think. What everyone would think, when their yeoman-marshal lay dead and the experienced fighter let herself be trapped in a net. She did not know how grim her expression was until Arvid spoke.

"Lady? Do you foresee some trouble I do not? Your sorrow for the yeoman-marshal, yes, but — what else?"

Paks shook her head. "I did it all wrong."

"All wrong?" Arvid looked at her with obvious surprise. "We went against a larger force, on their ground, and have only one dead and a few wounded, and you think you did it all wrong? By Simyits's eyebrow, lady, we could all be dead."

"No thanks to me that we aren't."

"Nonsense. You forget that you fought that priest too. Quite well, I might add — and you were right to jump ahead in the dark when you did. I only thought afterward that if flint and steel wouldn't spark, then my oil flask probably wouldn't burn anyway. That young man died bravely, but not because you failed. Though I expect you won't miss an overhead net trap again."

Paks shook her head, but felt a little better. The others said nothing, but smiled at her shyly when she looked at them. They were at ground level again when Arvid beckoned her aside.

"I'll be saying farewell," he said with a smile. "Good luck to you, Lady Paksenarrion — you have the makings of a great warrior. You're already a good one. Keep thinking on all sides of a question — "

"But what do you mean, are you going?"

"Yes."

"But why?"

"My work is done," he said with a shrug. "I was hired, as I said, to kill or convince the fellow to join the Guild. In my judgment, he would have made a poor member, even if he had been willing to join. I have seen him dead, and I have taken enough value to repay the Guild some of what it lost by his unlicensed theft." Paks had not seen him take anything; while she was still sorting that out, he dipped into a pocket and handed something to her. "Here — a gift for you. Unlike your gnomish friends, I prefer to pay my debts at once." Paks felt a something like a handful of pebbles through the thin leather of her glove. "No — don't look now. Gratitude bores me. You see, I don't think I'd like to explain everything to the Marshal — or have another talk with Sir Felis. You have enough witnesses to your actions; I need none for mine, if I go now." He lifted her hand, still clenched around his gift, to his lips; Paks had never seen or imagined such a gesture. Before

506

she could say anything, he had dropped it and moved lightly away, not looking back. She stuffed the handful, still unseen, into a pocket in her tunic, and turned to the others.

"And if I say it's the most preposterous thing I've ever heard? Ambros, at his age, to go haring off after a priest of Achrya! You, to let him — !" The Marshal, brows bristling in fury, strode back and forth in the grange, hands thrust into his belt. Paks, Mal, and the other yeomen stood against the wall; Ambros's body lay on the platform, still wrapped in his cloak.

"Marshal, if I may — " Sir Felis looked almost as angry as the Marshal. The Marshal stopped in midstride, balanced himself, and nodded shortly. Sir Felis looked at all their faces before he spoke. "Marshal, when he told me what he planned, I thought as you. A fool's plan, I told him. I think — I think I was wrong."

"Wrong! With him dead, and — "

"Wait, Marshal. I told him he had no experience. I told him that orders were orders. I insulted her — " he nodded at Paks, " — and told him he was a fool to go anywhere with a thief and a mercenary. And then he told me, Marshal, that his orders came not only from you but from Gird."

The Marshal's face contracted, showing wrinkles it would not bear for many years. "It wasn't — "

"I didn't think it was Gird. I told him that, too — that too many youngsters thought the gods blessed their folly. But Marshal — I think I said too much. Gird graces the hard head, as well as the strong arm. He was angry, at me, and that made him — "

"Maybe not." The Marshal sighed. "If it was Gird, if it wasn't just a childish stunt — " He looked at the others. "What do you know about this? Were you all in it with him — did he think it up — or what?" For a moment no one answered. Then Mal, his voice still distorted by the bruises on his face, spoke up.

"Sir Marshal, Ambros was determined to find the priest as soon as he came back from talking to the robbers. He told me then that Paks thought he should wait for you — but he was sure that he couldn't."

"Is that true, Paksenarrion? Did you try to dissuade him?"

Paks nodded. "Yes, sir. When he first told me, on the way back from the keep, I thought he was crazy." She felt the blood rush to her face, and glanced down. "I — he had told me, sir, of a dream, a few days before. He dreamed he was killed, in some battle. It was the day after you left."

"Did he think it was a true dream?"

"He wasn't sure. He asked me — I didn't know. He thought it might be an evil sending to frighten him from doing what he should. That's what finally made him do this, sir, I'm sure. I tried — I tried to tell him it could be a warning from Gird — or something like that — but he thought he had to find out."

"But why couldn't he wait? At least a few days — " The Marshal looked toward Ambros's body.

"He — he thought it must be soon, sir." Paks felt the tears burning in her eyes. She hoped Ambros would not mind her telling the dream now. "He could see — in the dream — the marks I gave him that last night at drill. The cut hadn't healed." The Marshal nodded, silent. Then he looked at the others.

"Did he tell any of you this dream?"

"No, sir." They answered in a ragged chorus. Mal went on. "I knew something was wrong, sir — he didn't say about the dream, but when I said something about not being in best shape to fight, he took me up on it and said I should stay behind."

The discussion dragged on for hours. Finally the Marshal dismissed them, having, as it seemed, worn out his anger. Paks was so tired she could hardly walk, but her mind kept buzzing at her. She made it to the inn, and up the stairs, without a word to anyone. Stretched on her bed, still wearing her armor, she wondered what she'd done with her horse, and was too tired to get up and find out. She thought she would never go to sleep. Cold air rolled over her from the window. At last she managed to pull a blanket over her and slept.

Dawn came gray and foggy. She had left the shutters open; the floor near her window was wet and cold. Paks looked at the beads of moisture with narrowed eyes; she didn't want to move. She heard noises from the rest of the inn, footsteps and voices. Her legs hurt. Her shoulder ached. Something was poking a hole in her side. That finally moved her — that hard lumpy something which seemed to be underneath a rib no matter how she squirmed. In one rush she threw back the blanket and staggered to her feet. Her boots skidded on the wet floor as she reached for the shutters.

The remains of her clothes hung on the fine chainmail like dead leaves on a shapely branch. Only her leather tunic was whole, though scarred by the net as if it had been touched by flame. She ripped the rags free, glad she had worn her old clothes for that trip, rather than the new ones. She slid out of the mail, noticing as she did a lumpy pocket in her tunic. Arvid's present. She reached into it and pulled out a handful of fire.

After a moment, she could see what it really was. A string — several strings, interconnected — of fiery jewels, some white and some blue. It poured through her hand like sunlit waterdrops. The clasp was gold. She stared, openmouthed, then tucked it quickly away. When she opened the door, she nearly fell over Suli, who was curled up asleep outside.

"It won't work," said Paks firmly. She avoided Suli's eyes, tracing a design on the table with one finger. "It won't work because I'm not what you hoped for — and it's not as easy as you think."

"I know it's not," said Suli. "I know — I saw Ambros die — it was terrible!" Paks shot a glance at her; the girl's face was solemn. "I still want it — even though I know — and I don't see why you won't — "

"You *don't* know!" Paks lowered her voice after that. "Suli, if you think that was bad — one man dead, and quickly dead — you don't know anything." She thought of Effa's broken back, of Captain Ferrault at Dwarfwatch. "You think because you've survived a couple of fights — difficult fights, yes, I'll grant you — that you're ready — "

"Just to be your squire," pleaded Suli. "I know I couldn't earn my way yet, as a soldier. But you could teach me — "

"I don't know enough myself. No, don't argue. I know what a private in the Duke's Company knows, and a little more. You think it's a lot — that's because you don't know — " Paks broke off, shaking her head. Would this have convinced her, the year she left home? Would anything convince Suli, now glaring at the table? She could feel that stubborn resolution as if it were a flame. She tried again. "Suli, I do think you can be a good soldier. You are strong, fast, and fairly skilled. More skilled than I was when I left home. I'm not trying to keep you from becoming a fighter. If you don't want to join a mercenary company, try one of the guards' units. Or ask Marshal Cedfer about training in the Fellowship. But all I can teach is fighting skills, and I'm finding out how much more I need. Why, when I first came, I'd never stayed in an inn before — "

"That's why I don't want to join a company," said Suli. "Staying all together, never on my own. I already know how to live on my own — and I can help you with that."

"You fight too much," Paks said. She had heard that from Mal and the others. Suli blushed. Paks went on. "My old sergeant said soldiers were fools to get in brawls. Most folk don't like soldiers anyway, and you get a reputation for causing trouble, they're glad enough to see you in the lockup or sold to slavers."

"We don't have any slavers here," muttered Suli.

"No, but you've got a lockup." Paks drained her mug. "Look, Suli, that's beside the point. It's not you. It's me. I'm not ready to take on someone to train. I was looking for more training for myself. If I were just adventuring, it'd be different, but I'm not. I want — "

"But I'll never have another chance," Suli burst out. "Nobody pays any attention — I'm just a crazy girl, that's what they think. I thought you would help — you're a woman, after all — and I'll never get out of this place if you don't — "

Paks slapped the table. "That's just what I've been telling you, Suli. How to get out and get the training you need. But you don't want to do it the right way. You want it to come all at once. I can see it in your eyes — you look at my sword, and my mail, and that big horse, and see yourself. What you don't see is the years in between, the years it took me to get all that. And there's no other way. Yes, I was lucky — I got some of it by a lucky chance. But the experience, the fighting skill, no. That came from years of just what you say you don't want — daily drill, daily work, battles that *you* call dull. That's what gave me the skill to take a chance when it came. You can't just leap from being a village girl with a knack for swordplay to — " she paused, uncertain how she would describe herself honestly.

509

"It could happen," said Suli. "It could. If you had found someone before you joined the company, she could have taught you everything you needed. You might have been rich and famous before now."

"I might have been dead before now, too. And Suli, knowing what I know now, I wouldn't have hired myself back then. It took the Duke's recruit company months to train any of us."

"But I've been training, with the Marshal. You've seen me — I'm not a beginner."

Paks sighed. She wondered if she had seemed so — so young, when she'd joined the Company. All that eagerness. At least she had taken Jornoth's advice, had not just run away to search for adventure on her own. She was trying to frame an answer, aware of Suli's intense gaze, when a shadow fell on her. She looked around. One of the senior yeomen nodded to her.

"Lady Paksenarrion? Marshal Cedfer would like to speak with you in the grange." He smiled at Suli, who reddened. "They say, Suli, that you fought well with this lady."

"She did," said Paks.

"We'll have to see about transferring you to the senior rolls," said the man to Suli. "Might make a yeoman-marshal, might she?" he asked of Paks.

"I — don't know how you choose yeoman-marshals, but Suli is a good swordsman." Paks stood up. "If you'll excuse me, I'll get my cloak — " The yeoman sat down and began talking to Suli; Paks was relieved.

The Marshal's office was slightly cold; Paks wondered why he had lit no fire in the small fireplace. Then she saw that the Kuakgan stood leaning in the corner, quiet as a shadow.

"Come in, Paksenarrion," said the Marshal. "We've been talking about you." She glanced quickly at the Kuakgan, who said nothing. What had they said? The last talks with the Marshal had been painful enough; she knew he no longer blamed her for Ambros's death, but she still blamed herself. She sat down when he gestured at a chair; the Kuakgan moved forward to take another.

"You will be wondering why," the Marshal went on. "I, as you know, would like to see you join the Fellowship of Gird. As a Marshal of Gird, I am interested in all soldiers, as well as the cause of right. In your case, something more moves me. It is for this that I contacted the Kuakgan, and talked with him about you."

"Yes, sir," said Paks, when he paused as if for some comment. She didn't know what else to say.

"Before we go on, would you mind telling me whether you have accepted Suli's service? I know she wants to be your squire, or some such — she's been wanting a way out of Brewersbridge for the last three years."

"Marshal Cedfer, I was talking to her when your yeoman asked me to come here. I don't — I know I'm not a knight, and have no way to use a squire. I'm not a wandering free sword — which she seems to think — and I don't need a companion. I told her that."

"Have you any complaint of her?"

"No. None at all. She fought bravely against the hool, as I told you, and did well against the priest's guards. But, sir — she's not ready to be a soldier, I don't think. And I'm not the one to train her. I need more training myself, to be what — what I'd like."

"Do you know yet what that is, Paksenarrion?" asked the Kuakgan.

"No — not exactly." Every time she tried to imagine herself in some noble's troops — even the Tsaian Royal Guard — the picture blurred and blew away. "Not a mercenary — what people think of as a mercenary. Not a caravan guard the rest of my life."

"A knight?" asked Marshal Cedfer. "A captain, perhaps?"

"Maybe." Paks looked at her hands. "I am a soldier, I enjoy swordplay, I want that kind of life. But not just for — for fighting anything, or for show. I want to fight — "

"What needs fighting?" suggested the Kuakgan.

Paks looked at him and nodded. "I think that's what I mean. Bad things. Like the robbers in Aarenis that killed my friends, or Siniava — he was evil. Or that — whatever that held the elf lord. Only I don't think I have the powers for that. But I want to fight where I'm sure it's right — not just to show that I'm big and strong. It's the same as tavern brawling, it seems to me — even if it's armies and lords — "

The Kuakgan nodded. "You've learned a lot, Paksenarrion, besides what most soldiers know. I thought so before, but now I'm sure. Do you know anything of the rangers in Lyonya?"

"No." Paks frowned. "Why?"

"You have fought with the elfane taig. It may be that you can sense the taigin, and if so you would be able to work with them."

"Master Oakhallow — " the Marshal began. The Kuakgan waved him to silence.

"Marshal, I don't question the sincerity of Girdsmen. You know that. We honor the same gods. But some fighters have abilities Gird does not use. She may be one of them." He turned back to Paks. "Paksenarrion, we agree that you have shown ability to fight evil. You have shown a desire to know more of good, and to fight for it. We both think you have been touched by the evil you've fought — not to contaminate you, but in such wise that you should not go back to ordinary soldiering. Do you agree?"

Paks was too bewildered to answer. Marshal Cedfer spoke up.

"Paksenarrion, when you came you said your Duke had recommended additional training — even toward a captaincy. We are prepared to guide you toward such training, but you must choose. I can give you a letter to the Marshal-General at Fin Panir; she will probably take my recommendation and let you study with the training order there. From that you can become a knight in either of the two Girdish orders — or even a paladin, if Gird's grace touches you."

"And I can give you introduction to the rangers of Lyonya," said the Kuakgan. "If you satisfied them, they might recommend you to the Knight-Commander of the Knights of Falk. That would be a few years away, however. But in either case, you would use your skills only in causes of good. If that way of fighting did not appeal, you could always leave."

"You could not take Suli with you, either way," said the Marshal. "That's why I asked. If you had contracted with her, the gnome merchants have told me that they can get you a contract from the gnome prince of Gnarrinfulk. Something in the way of soldiering, I don't know what. But if you aren't taking Suli, then — " He stopped and cocked his head, waiting for her answer.

"But I'm not Girdish," she managed to say. Nothing else came out.

"No. But I daresay that in Fin Panir, at the High Lord's Hall, after training with others of the faith, that Gird would make plain his interest in you." The Marshal leaned back a little in his chair. "I think he has already, Paksenarrion. When I think of the things you have come through — " Paks thought to herself that he didn't know the half of it. She had not told him all about Aarenis. She remembered what the priest of Achrya had said: "near enough a paladin. . . . Achrya will be pleased if I interfere in the growth of a paladin of Gird . . . " And the training at Fin Panir was famous throughout the north. She might become a knight — or even a paladin — she pushed the thought away. It was for the gods to think of such things, not a soldier. But the other way. Rangers — she knew nothing of them. The thought of more powers like the elfane taig daunted her, though she hated to admit it. And years of service, before she might think of the Knights of Falk.

She looked at the Kuakgan again, meeting his dark eyes squarely. "Sir — Master Oakhallow — I honor you — "

"I know that, child," he said, smiling.

"If you have a — " she stopped, knowing what she meant, but not how to say it. If he demanded it, in return for releasing her from guilt for the snowcat's murder, she would go. She saw understanding in his eyes.

"I have no commands for you, Paksenarrion," he said softly. "You have served Brewersbridge well; you have fulfilled my trust in you, and my hope for you. Go with my blessings, whichever way you go."

"Then — " She looked back at the Marshal. Was it for Ambros, who had trusted her with his fears and died beyond her help? Was it for Canna, who had left her the medallion? Or for something else, something she felt dimly and could not define? "I would be glad, sir, of your recommendation," she said formally. The Marshal shot a triumphant glance at the Kuakgan; Paks nearly took her words back. But the Kuakgan's smile was open and friendly. He spoke to her alone.

"Paksenarrion, the Kuakkganni treasure all life created in the first song. We study, we learn, but we do not order a creature from its own way. And the creature itself knows its own way best, unless it is sorely hurt. If the other way had been best for you, you would have known." He turned back to the Marshal. "Marshal Cedfer, we are no more rivals than two men who

512

plant a seed neither of them knows, and argue until it sprouts whether it will be fireoak or yellowwood. The seed knows itself; it will grow as its nature demands, and when the first leaves open, all arguments are over."

To Paks's surprise, the Marshal looked shamefaced. "You're right, Master Oakhallow. I have no right — but I was hoping so, for some good to come of Ambros's death."

The Kuakgan nodded gravely. "And yet you know that good has come of it. The webspinner's priest is gone, and you will clean that filthy place from end to end. Ambros has shown that your training prepares untried lads for the worst of wars, and the best of ends. You live in constant combat, Marshal, and it makes you alert to each advantage — but the gods move in longer cycles, as well. Be at peace, honest warrior." He rose and left the room. For a long silent time, Paks and Marshal Cedfer sat in quiet, contented. Then the Marshal shook himself like a wet puppy and snorted.

"Gird's grace, that fellow could cast a spell on stone. He may have time enough, but I live a normal span, like any man. Paksenarrion, I will write my letter this afternoon. When will you be fit for travel?"

"In a day or so. I'd like to get everything cleaned up."

"Good. I think you should not linger; winter will close some roads soon, and it makes bitter traveling to the northwest. About Suli — do you want me to talk to her?"

"I told her she should talk to you, but she — "

"She doesn't want it; she knows what I'll say. I've said it before. All right. I'll say it again. I can send her to another grange — a larger one — with more women training. Let her know what she can work toward — yeoman-marshal, or something like that. Tell her to come, if you see her." Paks wondered if it would help, but said she would.

Chapter Eighteen

As autumn darkened into winter, Paks rode north and west, into Vérella of the Bells, and west along the Honnorgat, through one town after another, as the river narrowed. She passed from grange to grange, enjoying the hospitality of each, as the Marshal's letter opened the doors. She thought of turning aside at Whitemeadow, and following a branch of the river north to Rocky Ford, and then on to Three Firs. But had her dowry arrived yet? Would she be welcome? She decided to wait until she had her knighthood, and ride home with Gird's crescent on her arm. As she neared Fintha, she tried to think of a more elegant name for the black horse, something suitable for a warhorse, but she had thought of him as Socks from the first, and it stuck in her mind.

Frost whitened the ground the morning she first caught sight of Fin Panir. She had been on the road before dawn, the saddle cold as iron beneath her, and her breath pluming out before. When the sun rose into a clear cold sky, the ground sparkled in rose and gold; the tree branches interlacing overhead glittered with frost. It was like riding inside a pearl. A little wind blew the sparkling frost in swirls before her. Paks found herself grinning, and nudged the black horse into a trot. He squealed and kicked out before settling down. She laughed aloud.

Then the forest broke apart, and she saw across a bend of the river the spires of the High Lord's Hall, gleaming in silver and gold against the blue sky. Beneath lay a tangle of roofs and walls, multi-colored stone, tiles, sliced into fantastic shapes by the sharp shadows of a winter sun. She rode toward it, yearning.

Within an hour she could pick out the gates. Between her and the walls, a small company of horsemen rode, armor glittering and banners dancing above. When she was near enough, they hailed her.

"Ho! Traveler! Where are you bound?" The leader was deep-voiced, a man of middle height in chain mail with a blue mantle bearing Gird's crescent.

"To the Hall in Fin Panir," said Paks. "I have a letter from Marshal Cedfer of Brewersbridge."

"For the Marshal-General?" he seemed surprised.

"Yes, sir. Can you direct me?"

"Yes, of course. But you might ask at the gates; she may be abroad this morning. You will have left Tor's Crossing early — or did you camp out last night?"

"I left early, sir."

"Well, the Marshal-General's quarters are in the Hall Courts. Take the first left, after the gate, and then a right — go straight past two turns, and then left again under the arch. Someone will take your horse there, and guide you. But, as I said, ask at the city gates if your message is urgent; they will know if she's ridden out somewhere."

"Thank you, sir." Paks lifted her reins and started forward. One of the other riders spoke to the leader, and he lifted a hand.

"Wait a moment — " He looked closely at her. "Are you a Girdsman?"

"No, sir." He looked puzzled. "You are carrying something of great worth — is it a gift from the Marshal?"

"Gift? No, sir." Paks thought of the jewels she still had, and wondered if that was what he meant. Somehow she didn't think so.

At the city gates, a neatly uniformed guard waved her through after she explained her errand. When she asked, he said that the Marshal-General had gone to the practice fields west of the city, but that she might wait at the Hall if she chose. Paks followed the directions through stone-paved streets of middle width, and arrived at an arched entrance through a wall. Far above she could see the towers of the Lord's Hall. A grizzled older man stepped out of an alcove in the arch and asked her business.

"Marshal-General, eh? She'll be out until noon; can you wait?" At her nod, he stepped forward. "Good, then. I'll get someone to take your horse — "

"I can take him," Paks interrupted. "If you'll tell me where."

His bushy eyebrows rose. "A guest take her own horse to stable? What do you think we are, ruffians?" He turned and bellowed through the archway. "Seli! Seliam!" Paks heard the clatter of running feet, and a boy raced up, panting. "Take this horse to the guest stables, Seli. Have the stableboys see to him." The boy laid his hand on the rein, and Paks dismounted. She rummaged in her saddlebags for Cedfer's letter to the Marshal-General. "Seli will take your saddlebags to the guest house in a few minutes," the man said. "Would you prefer to wait there, or in the Marshal-General's study?"

"Could I — " Paks suddenly felt shy. "I — I haven't been in Fin Panir before," she began again. "Could I see the High Lord's Hall? Is it permitted?"

His face split in a grin. "Permitted! Of course it's permitted. Let me find someone for the entrance, and I'll take you in myself. Haven't been here before, eh? I daresay you've heard tales, though, haven't you?" He turned away without waiting for an answer, and yelled again through the arch. This time another older man answered the summons.

"What is it, Argalt? An invasion of orcs?"

"No. A newcomer, who wants to see the Hall while waiting for the Marshal-General."

515

"And you want to show him — her, excuse me." The man smiled at Paks. "Gird's grace, lady, you've made Argalt's day. He loves to show off the Hall. And you've bright sun for it, too." He waved them away, and Paks followed the man through the arch and across a cobbled courtyard to the entrance of the High Lord's Hall of Fin Panir.

Broad steps led up to a pair of tall bronze doors, cast in intricate designs. Paks stopped to look at them, and her guide began to explain.

"These doors are not the original — those burned, hundreds of years back, the year the Black Lady fought to the steps here. But these were designed and cast by the half-elven craftsman Madegar. The middle of each door bears the High Lord's Seal — it's inlaid in gold, as you see. All around are the seals of the saints, and a little picture of each one doing something famous. There's Gird, with the cudgel, and Falk with a sword and the tyrant of Celias, and Camwyn riding a dragon, and Dort shearing the golden sheep, do you see all that?"

"Yes." Paks traced the designs with her finger, as far as she could reach. She found Torre and her magical steed, Sertig with his anvil. She stared, fascinated, until the man tapped her on the shoulder.

"Come along in, now, and see the rest."

From the great doors, the Hall stretched away, longer than any grange Paks had seen. The grange at Brewersbridge, she thought, would have fit in sideways, and three more with it. The soaring arches that held the roof were lifted from stone columns like treetrunks springing from the floor. It reminded her, in that way, of the elves' winterhall underground. At the far end, a double platform with a low railing took the place of the usual training platform in granges. On either side a railed gallery with stepped seating offered a clear view of the floor.

But all this she saw later. First she was aware of the great wash of brilliant light, broken into dazzling chips of color, that poured through the great round window in the far end. All along both sides, high windows of colored glass spread fanciful patterns of light on the floor. She turned to the guide, who was chuckling at her reaction.

"How?" was all she could say.

"You had seen glass in windows before?" he asked.

"Yes, but — " she waved a hand at the magnificence.

"It's colored glass, laid in a pattern, and bound in strips of lead. And I'll have you know, it wasn't an elf designed that." Now that the first dazzle had passed, Paks could see that the colored glass made designs — even pictures, in some of the windows. The round window held a many-pointed star in shades of blue with accents of gold. Along the sunny south side of the Hall, she saw Gird with his cudgel striking a richly dressed knight, Camwyn riding a dragon whose breath seemed literal flame, a harper (she could not remember the name of the harper's patron saint) playing to a tree that seemed to be turning into a girl, and Torre partway through her Ride, with half the stones of the necklace turned to stars. The longer she looked at each window, the more she saw. Each had smaller scenes inset in medal-

516

lions around the main picture. Paks walked over to Torre's window. There was her home, with its six towers, and that must be her sorrowing father with the wicked king threatening him. Here was the stable, with the strange horse standing loose between the stalls, the ring of coals around its neck. A white flower stood for the first trial of her Ride, and three snowflakes for the next. A fat dwarf held the blue ring, and an elf in green held out the branch of yellowwood in flower, complete with two bees. The wicked king's red banner blew from a tower on a cliff. A sleeping baby in a basket floated on a river. At the very top of the window, the stars of Torre's Necklace blazed out of blue glass just as they did in the sky.

Paks tore her eyes away and looked around again. The shadowed, northern side windows were pictures as well. Sertig pounding on his anvil, and Adyan writing the true names of everything in his book. Alyanya, the Lady of Peace, wreathed in flowers, with fruitful vines trailing around her. Some pictures she did not recognize at all. One seemed to be all animals, fitted into every available niche, all mixed together, large and small. One was simply a tree, whose gnarled roots and branches filled up the space above and below, curling and recurling until Paks could not tell how many little rootlets filled even one small section.

When she finally left the windows to look at the rest of the building, it was equally engrossing. The floor was paved with flat slabs of stone in a subtle pattern. Many of the slabs were engraved with names and dates that meant nothing to Paks — but much to her guide, when she asked.

"That there's Lolyin's marker — he was Marshal-General over a hundred years ago, and converted the King of Tsaia to the fellowship of Gird. That was the great-grandfather of the present crown prince. Under his name is the paladin Brealt. You might have heard of him, since I can see you've been in Aarenis. He freed the captives of Pliuni, and fought two priests of Liart by himself to do it." Paks had not heard of him, but she nodded. The old man went on. "Marshal-Generals and paladins of Gird — and a few others — they have their names and dates put here. Some say their deeds should be added, but the rule is that those who want to know should look them up in the archives. There's not one of them but is worth remembering. Take this — " he led her up near the platform. "This is Gird's own marker, put here by Luap — the oldest we have." The stone was worn in a hollow, and the letters were faint. "In the old way, all that joined the knights of the fellowship, or became paladins of Gird, would spend part of a vigil washing that stone, to keep Gird's name pure. But then they realized they were wearing it down, and only the Marshal-General does it now."

Paks could think of nothing to say. She had never imagined that anything built by men would be as beautiful as the Hall. That soaring space seemed to liberate something inside her, as if it called for wings within. When they came out at last, she blinked in the sunlight, her head still full of what she'd seen.

* * *

She had no idea what to expect of a Marshal-General. The Marshals she had met had been matter-of-fact, much like the Duke's captains. But what she'd seen of feudal commanders, and the splendor of the Hall, led her to think that the Marshal-General might be more — she tried to think of a word — impressive? magnificent? As the servant led her through the passages and up a broad stair to the Marshal-General's office, she felt her stomach flutter.

The door was open. Paks looked across a fairly large room to a table set under one of the south windows. Behind it stood two people, a woman and a man, both in blue tunics over gray trousers. Both had Gird's crescents on chains around their neck. They were looking at something on the table as the servant knocked; the woman looked up.

"Yes?"

"A messenger, Marshal-General, from Marshal Cedfer of Brewersbridge." He gestured at Paks.

"Ah yes. Argalt mentioned you — your name?"

"Paksenarrion Dorthansdotter," said Paks, uncertain of the correct address.

"You're not a Girdsman?"

"No — my lady." Paks thought that was safest.

"Then you may not know I'm Marshal-General Arianya. But you're a warrior — that's clear enough." Paks nodded. "Well, then, let me see your message."

Paks walked into the room and handed over the Marshal's letter. The Marshal-General was a tall woman of middle age, her graying curly hair cropped short. She wore no sword, but her tunic was marked by sword belt and scabbard. Her right hand bore a wide scar; Paks wondered how it had missed severing some tendons. The Marshal-General looked up from what she was reading.

"Do you know what Cedfer's written?"

Paks felt the blood rush to her face. "Some of it, my lady. He said he — that you — that I might take some training here."

"He's recommended that you be admitted to a probationers' class in the Company of Gird. And he's said why — " She paused and looked at Paks closely. "It's most unusual, you know, for anyone not of the fellowship to be admitted here."

Paks felt her heart sink. She had only begun to realize, during the trip to Fin Panir, the power wielded by the granges of Gird. When the Marshal had suggested a half-year in the training program, it had seemed like fun, certainly more to her taste than wandering the woods as a ranger in Lyonya. She had always been quick to learn warrior's skills. But now it seemed a more serious commitment. She said nothing, and met the Marshal-General's eyes steadily.

"What has he said, Marshal-General?" asked the man. Paks glanced at him. He was a little taller than the Marshal-General, and had a short gray beard.

"He recommends her highly — " The Marshal-General paused again, and looked once more at Paks. "You fought with Duke Phelan of Tsaia, is that right?" Paks nodded. "Cedfer was surprised to find you so good with a longsword; he implies that the Duke himself suggested you seek advanced training. That's so?"

"Yes, my lady." Paks felt very uncomfortable. She knew what was coming next; she still did not want to talk about those last weeks in the Duke's Company. But the Marshal-General's next question surprised her.

"Do you think he would be pleased to have you here?"

Paks knew her face showed her astonishment. "Why — why of course, my lady. Why wouldn't he? It would be an honor — "

The Marshal-General looked away. "Duke Phelan, Paksenarrion Dorthansdotter, is not without his quarrels with Gird and Gird's granges."

Paks thought of the subtle tension between the Duke and the Marshal in Aarenis. His words to the paladin at Cortes Immer came back to her. She shook her head, driving them away. "No — I'm sure he would be glad. He is not a Girdsman himself, but he is a good man — a good fighter — and he would be glad for any honor that came to me. And training here would be an honor."

"Why would you think it so, when you are not of our fellowship?" asked the man quietly. Paks turned to him.

"Sir, it is widely known. The Knights of Gird, the paladins of Gird — all of them train here, and many others beside, who serve honorably in the royal guards of several kingdoms."

"I see." He glanced at the Marshal-General, but she was looking at Marshal Cedfer's letter. After a moment she looked up at him.

"Kory, if you'll excuse us, I'd like to talk to Paksenarrion. Cedfer almost persuades me, but I must see for myself what she is."

"Of course, Marshal-General."

"Paksenarrion, have you had anything to eat?"

"No, my lady. Not since breakfast."

"Then we'll eat together here. Kory, ask them to send something up, will you?"

"Certainly." He bowed, and left the room. Paks met the Marshal-General's gaze.

"Well, Paksenarrion, have a seat — there — and let's find out more about you. Cedfer sent word at once about the elfane taig, but few details. Where are you from, and how did you come to join the Duke's Company?"

"I'm from Three Firs, my lady. My father is a sheepfarmer."

"Three Firs! I know that country — far from the Honnorgat, or any city, isn't it?"

"Yes — "

"So you left to join the Duke's Company? Or for another reason?"

"I wanted to be a warrior." Paks thought back to the mood of what now seemed her childhood, when Jornoth had come visiting with a bright sword and his purse full of silver. "My father didn't — so I ran away." The

Marshal-General nodded. "I joined the Duke's Company at Rocky Ford, and then — " She shrugged. "I was a recruit, and then a private in the Company."

"You fought in the north, or in Aarenis?"

"In Aarenis. For three seasons." Paks stopped, uncertain how much to say about those years.

"Cedfer says the Duke evidently favored you — had given you some important missions. Can you tell me about them, or would that violate a secret of the Duke's?"

Paks shook her head. "No. Nothing secret — I don't know how much to say. The last year, I was acting corporal for awhile, when Seli was hurt. And I helped capture Siniava."

"Siniava. Then — wait — " The Marshal-General's face furrowed for a moment. "Did you meet a paladin in Aarenis? Fenith?"

"Yes, my lady." Paks didn't want to talk about that, either: the one time the Duke had not lived up to her image of him.

"You're *that* Paksenarrion!" The Marshal-General stared at her. "Fenith wrote about you — you took on a priest of Liart, and lived! Gird's grace, child, I hadn't heard of such a thing. Neither had he. He sent the High Marshal to your Duke to find out about you, and the Duke nearly took his head off for suggesting you might not be what you seemed."

"He did?" Paks didn't remember any such thing.

"I suppose your Duke didn't tell you. Fenith also said you were the one to spot Siniava in shapechange. He thought it had something to do with a Gird's medallion you carried — a gift of a friend, he said — "

"Yes." Paks did not want to discuss Canna's gift, which she had not worn since the night Siniava died.

"You told him, I understand, that you would stay with the Duke's Company — yet here you are on our doorstep. What happened?" The Marshal-General's eyes were as shrewd as the Kuakgan's; Paks realized that there was no way out of this but the long one — the whole truth. Haltingly, at first, she began to tell of the last year in Aarenis. The Marshal-General did not interrupt, and the pressure of her attention kept the tale flowing. When a servant carried in a tray of food, bowls of stew and a couple of loaves of dark bread, Paks stopped. The Marshal-General spread the food on the table, and waved the servant out.

"Gird's grace be with you, Paksenarrion, and with me, and may we gain strength to serve the High Lord's will. Go on, now, and eat." She took up her spoon and began. Paks did the same. After the stew was mostly gone, the Marshal-General looked up. "I can understand why you left, and why you were reluctant to leave. But I am still not sure why you quit wearing Canna's medallion. Do you know?"

Paks laid down the hunk of bread she'd picked up. "I thought — it seemed that it — it led me into things. Trouble. I never knew if it — if I — how they happened."

"It led you into trouble? And you a mercenary?" The Marshal-General's voice had an edge of scorn. "You had not chosen the most peaceful life."

"No, my lady. But I don't know what it did, or didn't do. I don't know if it healed Canna, or didn't, or if it really saved me from the man in Rotengre — "

"Wait. You haven't told me about that yet. Canna is your friend who died and left it to you, isn't that so? What's this about healing?"

Paks felt the sweat cold on her neck as she began to tell the Marshal-General about their flight from Dwarfwatch. Knowing that she would insist on hearing those parts of the journey that made Paks the most nervous didn't help. She had not mentioned the prayers over Canna's wound to anyone but Stammel; it came no easier now. The Marshal-General seemed to grow more remote and august as she listened.

"You, no follower of Gird, suggested praying to Gird for healing? Don't you think that was presumptuous? Had you planned to join the fellowship afterwards?" Paks had not thought of it like that at all.

"My lady, we had need — I didn't know much of Gird, then, and — "

"Your friend had not told you? And she a yeoman?"

Paks shook her head. "We didn't talk about it much; she was our friend. We knew she was a Girdsman, and she knew we had our own gods."

"You know more of Gird now, I'll warrant — what do you think now, of such a thing?" Paks thought a moment.

"I don't think Gird would mind — I can't see why he would. If he had been a nobleman, perhaps, but — why would it be wrong to try? Healing is good, and Canna was one of his yeomen."

The Marshal-General shook her head slowly, but more in doubt than disagreement. "I'm not sure, child. What happened?"

"That's what I don't know." Paks remembered clearly Canna's yelp of pain, and then the seeming improvement in her condition. "It didn't go away at once," she went on, carefully telling the Marshal-General everything. "But she had been getting weaker, and feverish, and she was stronger afterwards. It looked cleaner and drier the next time we changed the bandage. But you see, we'd found some ointment in that farmstead, and used that too. I don't know which worked, or why."

"You didn't tell this to Marshal Berran or Fenith," said the Marshal-General.

"No — I wasn't sure — "

"Go on, then. What happened with the man in Rotengre?" That, too, Paks told, even Captain Dorrin's remarks afterwards. The Marshal-General nodded.

"Your captain had the sense to see what lay before her. Is she Girdish?"

"No, my lady. Falkian — or that's what one of the sergeants said."

"I see. What did you think then, when two times the medallion had acted for you?"

"I didn't — I was frightened of it, lady. I didn't know what to do."

"Did you not think of speaking to a Marshal?"

521

Paks shook her head vigorously. "Oh no. I —"

"You were with Duke Phelan. I suppose you had no chance."

"I didn't want to, not then. I — I suppose I wished that it would just — just be over. I kept thinking about them —"

"Canna?"

"And — and Saben. He was my — our friend, that was with us."

"Your lover?"

"No." The old grief and longing choked her again. When she looked up again, the Marshal-General was stacking the bowls on the tray.

"Taking those events with the later ones, Paksenarrion — with surviving the blow of Liart's priest in Sibili, the warning of ambush, and withstanding the enchantments when Siniava tried to escape — don't you think that there's clear evidence of Gird's action in your behalf?"

"I don't — I can't be sure —"

"Gird's teeth, girl, what do you want, a pillar of fire?" The Marshal-General glared at her. "D'you expect the gods to carry you up to the clouds and explain everything in words a sheepfarmer's daughter can understand?"

"No, my lady." Paks stared at her hands, near tears again. It wasn't fair; she only wanted to be sure . . . if the gods had a message, surely they'd make it clear. She heard a gusty sigh.

"How old are you, Paksenarrion?"

Paks counted it out aloud. "I was eighteen winters when I left home — and then nineteen was in the stronghold, and twenty — twenty-one after Dwarfwatch — near twenty-two, my lady."

"I see. Are you set against the fellowship of Gird?"

"Oh no, my lady! The more I know, the more — but you see, my family was not Girdish. And I still think it's better to abide the gods you know —"

The Marshal-General sighed again. Paks looked up to find her gazing out one of the narrow windows, her face stern. After a long moment she turned back to Paks. "We are not," she said firmly, "a training camp for those who want fancy skills to show off." Paks felt her face reddening again. "If what you want is an accomplishment to display — like someone stringing another pearl on a necklace — you don't belong here, and I won't lend Gird's name to it. Those we train must go out as Gird's warriors, to serve the lands and defend them against the powers of evil. They must care, Paksenarrion, for this cause more than their own fame. Those sworn to the fellowship of Gird I have ways of testing. If you persist in remaining aloof, I must assume that your dedication is unproven. I will not — absolutely not — let you take advantage of this company, and go off boasting that you trained with the Company of Gird at Fin Panir, unless you can show me what you will pay. Not in money, young warrior, but in your life."

Paks managed to meet her eyes steadily, though she felt as frightened and helpless as she had when a new recruit. She said nothing for some time, wondering what if anything she could say. At last she looked away and shook her head ruefully.

"I don't know, my lady, what I could say to convince you. For me, I have been trained as a warrior, not to argue. I think perhaps you feel what I felt in Brewersbridge — there was a young girl there, who wanted to join me, and be a squire to me. I knew I didn't know enough to be her — her commander, or whatever, but also — I used to think she only wanted the glory she could see. To wear a sword like mine, to have a scar to show, perhaps — but she didn't know what it cost, what lay behind it. I tried to tell her, tried to get her to join a regular company, as I had — "

"And did she?" The Marshal-General's voice was still remote.

Paks shook her head. "Not as far as I know. I tried — but she wanted adventure, she said. It would be too dull, she didn't like people yelling at her; she said she could get enough of that in Brewersbridge." Paks stopped before saying, "She had a very bad father, my lady."

"You ran away from yours."

"Oh, well . . . he wasn't like that. But I see what you mean — you think I want to — to make a name for myself, from the fame of your Company. That would be wrong. You're right. But — I can't swear to follow Gird until I know — until I'm sure of myself — that I can do it."

"That's coming out differently than what you said before. Then you didn't seem to trust Gird — "

Paks floundered, unable to define what she meant. "I don't — I mean, you all say Gird is a saint, and I won't argue. But *I* don't know Gird — I have known good Girdsmen, but also good warriors following other gods and saints. How do I know Gird is the one I should follow?"

The Marshal-General's eyebrows went up. "You would not believe the evidence of the medallion?"

Paks set her jaw stubbornly. "I'm not sure. And I won't swear to something I'm not sure of."

To her surprise, the Marshal-General laughed. "Gird be praised, you are at least willing to be honest against the Marshal-General. Child, such stubbornness as yours is nearly proof that Gird claims your destiny — but it may take Gird's cudgel to break a hole in your head to let his light in. The gods grant you are this stubborn about other things that matter." She sat forward, leaning her forearms on the table between them. "Now, what sort of training did you look for?"

Paks could hardly believe her ears. "You mean — you'll let me stay?"

"Let you! By Gird, I'm not likely to let someone like you wander the world unconvinced without giving my best chance to convert you. Of course you'll stay."

"But if I don't — "

"Paksenarrion, you will stay until either you wish to leave, or you give me cause to send you away. When — notice that I do not say if, being granted almost as much stubbornness as you, by Gird's grace — *when* you find that you can swear your honor to Gird's fellowship, it will be my pleasure to give and receive your strokes. Is that satisfactory, or have you more conditions for a Marshal-General of Gird, and Captain-Temporal of the High Lord?"

Paks blushed. "No, my lady. I'm sorry, I — "

"Enough. Tell me what you thought to learn."

"Well — everything about war — "

The Marshal-General whooped. "Everything? About war? Gird's grace, Paksenarrion, no one knows that but the High Lord, who sees all beginnings and endings at once."

"I meant," muttered Paks, ears flaming, "weapons-skills, and things about forts — things the Duke's captains knew about, like tunnels — "

"All right," said the Marshal-General, wiping her eyes on her sleeve. "I see what you mean. Things about forts. Honestly! No, sorry, I see you're serious. Well, then. I'll assign you to the training company. Many of them are younger than you — nobles' youngsters, from Fintha and Tsaia, mostly. They've been someone's squires, and now they're preparing for knighthood. Some have come up through the granges, and have been yeoman-marshal somewhere for three years. You may not know, but all our marshals are trained here, along with the knights. You'll be assigned space in the courts — we don't have open barracks, for you'll need to study alone. You do read, don't you?" At Paks's nod, she went on, now writing swiftly on a loose sheet of paper. "Weapons practice daily — the senior instructor will assign the drills once he's examined you. Riding — do you ride? Yes, because Argalt mentioned putting up your horse. You're a few weeks behind one group; they arrived just after harvest. That's when we start the new cycles. But we'll see if you can catch up to them." She looked up from her writing. Although she was smiling, it seemed to Paks that she was even more formidable. "What weapons do you have?" she asked.

"This sword," said Paks, laying her hand on the hilt. "Another one, not so good — "

"That one's magical," said the Marshal-General. "Did you know?"

"Yes, my lady. And a dagger, and a short battle-axe."

"Do you use all of them?"

"No, my lady. Just sword and dagger, and I can use a long-bow, though not well."

"And I see you have mail as well. For the first weeks, though, you will not use your own weapons. The weaponsmaster will assign you weapons for training; yours may be stored in your quarters or in the armory, as you prefer."

"Yes, my lady."

"Your clothes — " She glanced at Paks's traveling clothes. "We have training uniforms, but we are not strict, except during drill and classes. We discourage display of jewels and such, but you don't look the type to show up in laces and ribbons."

"No, my lady."

"Very well." She signed the end of her note, and handed it to Paks. "Take this down, and ask Argalt to direct you to the Master of Training. He'll assign your quarters, and see that you're set up with the instructors. You will take your meals in the Lower Hall — by the way, you have no difficulties with the elder races, have you?"

"Elder races — you mean elves and dwarves?"

"Among others. We have quite a few here — you'll be meeting them. Don't get in fights with them."

"Oh no."

"Good. You may go, Paksenarrion. May Gird's grace be on you, and the High Lord's light guide your way." She rose, and Paks stood quickly, knocking her hand on the table edge.

"Thank you, my lady — "

"Thank the gods, Paksenarrion, for their bounty. I have done nothing yet to deserve your thanks."

Chapter Nineteen

Argalt, when she finally located him again, after losing herself in a maze of passages on the ground floor, looked her up and down. "Training Master, eh? So you're going to become a Knight of Holy Gird, are you? Or a Marshal? Or is it paladin you're thinking of?"

Paks felt her ears burning again. "I — don't know, sir."

Argalt snorted. "I'm no *sir*, not even to the newest member of the training company. Argalt: that's my name, and that's what you'll call me, young woman."

"Yes, si — Argalt."

"That's better. You're no hothouse flower of a noble house — where are you from?" Paks told him. He looked at her with surprising respect. "Sheepfarmer's daughter? That's like Gird's daughter herself — barring he raised cattle and grain, so the story goes. But still it means you know what work is, I'll say, and a few blisters on the hands. Where'd you learn to wear a sword like you could use it?" When she mentioned the Duke's name, he stared. "You were in the Fox's company? And came *here*? I'll believe anything after that!" He shook his head as he led her across the courtyard, past the Lord's Hall. "I was in the Guards at Vérella when I was young; what I don't know about that Duke — " But Paks asked nothing, and did not expect that he would have answered if she had. He gave her a long look outside the Training Master's office. "If you need someone to talk to, sometime, sheepfarmer's daughter — I'll share a tankard of ale with you."

"Thank you," said Paks, still not sure of his reasons. He nodded and turned away.

The Training Master was a hand taller than Paks herself, a hard muscular man in dark blue tunic and trousers, with Gird's crescent embroidered on the breast. He read the Marshal-General's note, and Cedfer's letter, in tight-lipped silence. When he looked up, his ice-blue eyes were hard.

"If you're to catch up with the others, you'll have to work — and work hard. You'd best not loll about."

Paks repressed a surge of anger. She'd never been lazy. "No, sir," she said stiffly.

"It means extra work for the instructors as well. I shall take you myself for tactics in the evenings after supper. I hope Cedfer's right about your weapons-skills. That would let us chop a glass or so off there, and give you more time in supply — though why the Marshal-General bothers with that, for you, is beyond me." Paks felt her shoulders tighten, and forced herself to be still. He sighed, heavily. "Very well, then. How much gear do you have?"

"Only what was in my saddlebags, sir," said Paks. "I suppose it's — "

"They'll have it brought to your quarters." He glanced for a moment at a chart on his wall. "Let me think. There's a room on the third floor, next to the end of the corridor. You can have that, for now. It's small, but it won't mean moving anyone else tonight. If it's too small, we can change things in a week or so." If you stay that long, his tone clearly said. "You'll need clothes; I'll have the steward send something up. Come along." He pushed past her to the corridor, and led the way upstairs.

The room he opened seemed amply large to Paks — larger than her room at *The Jolly Potboy*, with two windows looking out over a lower roof to a walled field. Besides a bed and chest, and a curtained alcove with hooks, it had a table, stool, and low chair. A narrow shelf ran along the wall over the table. Several blankets were folded neatly on the foot of the bed. Paks had hardly taken all this in when he began speaking again.

"Students do not wear weapons except at practice," he said, with a pointed glance at her sword. "We prefer that personal weapons be stored in the armory, but the Marshal-General has given permission for you to keep yours with you." Paks did not want to let the magic sword out of her control; she said nothing. Just then a servant came in with her saddlebags; behind him was the steward, with an armful of clothing, all dark gray but for the blue cloak. The steward eyed her.

"You said tall, Master Chanis; this should fit near enough for now. What name do you use — Paksenarrion, or Dorthansdotter?"

"Paks is all."

"Paksenarrion," said the steward cheerfully. "I need something long enough it can't be mistaken in anyone's handwriting. Come by for measurements, or if you have something that fits well — "

Paks unstrapped her saddlebags, and pulled out her green shirt. "Will this do?"

"Good — good material, too. From Lyonya, is it?"

"No, but near there. Brewersbridge."

The steward shook her head. "I don't know it. Trousers, too, if you've an extra pair." Paks pulled out the patched ones, which the steward took without comment, and handed over a pair of socks as well. The steward checked the number of blankets, and left the room.

"If you're ready," said the Training Master, "there is time to see the weapons instructors before supper. No need to change now; in the morning is soon enough."

Paks set her swords neatly on the shelf, and the saddlebags behind the curtain, before following him out of the room.

"You have fought mostly in a mercenary company, I understand."

"Yes, sir."

527

"Short-sword or polearm?"

"Short-sword."

"But you carry a longsword."

"Yes, sir."

"Have you used a bow?"

"In training, yes — it's not my best weapon."

"Polearms?"

"Only in training."

"Mace? Axe? Crossbow? Siege weaponry?" At each shake of her head, his lips seemed to tighten. Paks wondered if he really thought all of those important. She had trouble keeping up with his long sweeping strides, and noticed little of the building around them — only rows of doors, open and shut, and the stone flags of the hallway. They came out into a small court surrounded on three sides by stables; a pile of dung centered the court, and two youths were shoveling it into a cart. Past a row of box stalls, each holding a massive warhorse, the Training Master ducked through a narrow archway into another passage. This time they emerged on the edge of the walled field Paks had seen from her windows. On their right, the stone building sprouted a long finger; the Training Master turned toward this.

It was a single room, and resembled a small grange except that it had no platform and no doors at the far end, only the one on either side. It was empty at the moment, but Paks could hear grunts and the clash of weapons from the far side. The Training Master led her through it, and out the other door.

Here were perhaps a score of fighters, all in training gray, practicing with swords and — Paks was surprised to see — hawks. To one side a burly man in blue watched them closely. He glanced over at the Training Master, and waved. Paks followed as they walked around the training area to meet him.

"This is Paksenarrion Dorthansdotter," said the Training Master abruptly. "The Marshal-General has assigned her to this class."

Sharp black eyes met hers. "Ha. She's no novice."

"So I understand. If you can spare her for more time in other studies, Cieri, do so."

"Am I to hood hawks so they may learn music?" Paks thought by the tone that this was an old argument begun again. The Training Master's face relaxed.

"There are other skills of war, Cieri — "

"Oh, and so there are, but none of them any good if you can't keep a blade from your guts." He shook his head. "Never mind, Chanis, I know what you mean, and the Marshal-General too. If she can spare the time, I'll see to it. But only if, understand that." He cocked his head at Paks, and looked her over.

"See that she knows where to go, when you're through," said the Training Master. He turned to Paks. "Gird be with you, Paksenarrion. If you have any need, come to my office at any time."

528

"Thank you, sir," said Paks, still ruffled.

"Well, now." Cieri, the weaponsmaster, was walking around her. She turned to watch him. "Where have you fought? What weapons? I see marks of a longsword on your clothes." For the third time that day, Paks outlined her training. Cieri, at least, showed no doubt. "That's good. Three fighting seasons with Phelan — that means you know your way with short-sword and formation fighting. And you've used a longsword since — very good. Many who come to us with your background cannot fight without the others in formation. Not until I've trained them, that is." He grinned broadly. For all that he was younger and heavier, he reminded Paks of Siger. "What about unarmed combat?"

"I've done it," said Paks cautiously. She knew that Siger himself had mastered only a few of the many styles.

"Can you fight mounted? I know Phelan has infantry."

"I have, some. Marshal Cedfer in Brewersbridge was teaching me, and I fought a little with a sword."

"Without cutting up the horse? Good. I see you're wearing mail — Chanis didn't give you time to change, eh? But we don't wear mail in prac-tice sessions — you must not come to count on it. Today I'll test you, but tomorrow you show up in training uniform, right?"

"Yes, sir." Paks noticed that the others were watching covertly, slowing their own practice to see what she was doing. Cieri noticed that too, and bellowed at them.

"Gird's gut, may the ale hold out, you dolts keep gaping like that and I'll run you all around the field ten times before supper. D'you think an enemy'd let you gaze all around like a bunch of calves in pasture? Get to your work, or — " But the tempo had speeded back up at once. Cieri picked up two swords from a stack near the edge of the practice area. "Here — we'll start with what you're comfortable with."

Paks took a sword, and moved it, testing its balance. It was heavier than her own, and broader across the blade. Cieri stood casually, touched her blade with the tip of his, and leaped in so fast that she almost missed her own stroke.

"Aha!" he said. "If you were that slow with enemies, you would have more scars than you do. Don't hold back, girl — I'm better than Cedfer, if you want the truth of it." Indeed he was, and Paks found herself working hard to keep his blade from clashing on her mail. She had gotten used to the delicate balance of the magic sword — that responsive light spring — and she felt, at first, that she was fencing with a length of iron firewood. Several minutes later, sweating freely, she found her balance, and tried of-fensive strokes as well as defensive. Cieri countered them easily, but grinned even more widely. "You're learning," he said. "You've got a reach on you, too. And reasonable speed." He tried one of the tricks she knew about, and she thrust it aside, lunging quickly to mark his tunic. "And you know something. Very good. You haven't wasted your time." But in a flash he shifted his blade to the other hand. Paks, confused, missed her parry,

529

and felt the sharp blow along her side. Another, in the same place, and then she countered with a blow that drove him back a step.

She had forgotten that he wore no mail, until after a fast exchange of heavy blows she caught his arm and blood darkened the tunic. "Hold," he said, but she had already lowered her blade. He glanced at his arm, and then at her with new respect. "You do know something. By Gird, we may have a swordsman in this class after all."

"I'm sorry — " she started to say.

"No matter. In a Hall full of Marshals, little wounds like these are no problem. Look here — " He pulled aside the ripped sleeve to show a narrow jagged wound already closing. "You must all learn to fight, and strongly, and therefore I take a lot of healing."

Paks was startled. "But I thought — "

He looked closely at her. "Oh. You're not Girdish, are you? Most are. With an arm like that, you should be. It's nothing, here — Marshals can heal themselves as well as others, and Gird does not begrudge healing to weaponsmasters."

"Then you're — "

"A Marshal, yes. You didn't know? Most of your instructors here are Marshals."

"Oh."

"Now put away that sword you obviously know how to use — not that you can't learn more — and let's see what you do with staves." Paks had never fought with staves before, and collected a quantity of bruises proving her incompetence. Cieri then tried her in archery; her form, he said, was passable, but her ability to judge windage was abysmal. She could not throw a javelin at all, and when he saw her grip on a battleaxe, he told her to put it down at once. "And I won't have you try unarmed combat in mail just yet — tomorrow will do for that." By this time Paks was sweaty, tired, and sore enough to be glad of a rest. "You're beyond most of the class in sword handling," he said, after thinking a few moments. "Some of them have had lessons for years, but no actual fighting. That's what makes the difference. You'll need regular practice with the sword, but instead of new tricks with it, I want to improve your other weapons skills. When you finish, you should be able to instruct with at least five weapons. More if you're interested. Tomorrow morning, come with the others for mounted drill — do you have your own horse?"

"Yes, sir."

"Well, you can ride your own horse tomorrow. If it's trained enough, you'll bring it to every session, but we switch around. Marshal Doggal takes most of the mounted classes. Mounted work first thing in the morning, then your other studies, before and after lunch, then drill here. Is that clear?"

"Yes, sir. But — what about my horse? Where is he, and what about grooming — "

"You've been caring for your own? Good, good. You won't do that, for

530

awhile — this autumn session, we keep the class busy enough without, but in the spring each student is assigned a mount to care for. Just show up at the right time in the mornings, and saddle up."

"Oh." Paks thought of explaining Socks's character, but decided not to.

"Now — " He looked at her closely. "I don't mean to insult you, but the order provides adequate clothing. Leave your soiled things near the door each morning, and they'll be cleaned." Paks nodded. "You look to be in fair condition, but you'll be sore and stiff with the schedule you've got. Hot baths are available each night. Many students prefer to bathe and change before supper — if they have time." He looked around at the rest of the students, and shook his head. "Nearly time to quit, and they know it. As you've come in from traveling, and are wearing mail, I won't send you — but we end with a run most days." He turned to the others, and raised his voice. "Rufen!" A young man with dark brown hair stepped back from his partner, and came forward. "This is Paksenarrion; she's a new member. Take her back to the House, and show her where things are. She's got a horse for tomorrow, but doesn't know where it's stabled."

Rufen bowed, giving Paks a quick glance. She thought he was several years younger than she, half a hand shorter, and more slender. As he led her away, back through the empty armory, he looked at her again. "You're not a Girdsman?" he asked. Paks could not place his accent, which seemed slightly melodic.

"No," she said. She was not going to explain everything all over again. Not then.

"You fence well," he said, with another sidelong glance. "I've never seen Cieri move so fast, except against the knights. What kind of horse have you?"

Paks answered stiffly, suspecting a joke. "Just a — a black horse. Warhorse."

They were in the stable courtyard by then, and he asked one of the workers. "That black with the stockings? And a wide blaze? He's in the new court stables."

"That's where guest horses are housed," explained Rufen. "I expect they'll move him in here, if they've got a free stall." He led the way through a tack room full of racked saddles into another, larger, stable complex. Before he could find someone to ask, Paks heard Socks, and saw his wide head peering out over a half-door. Rufen looked startled when she pointed him out. "That's yours? If he's not Pargunese-bred, I'll take up the harp. Look at the bone of him." By this time they were at the stall, and Socks had shoved his nose hard into Paks's tunic.

"I don't have any," she said sharply. He seemed in good shape, and had obviously been groomed carefully; no saddle marks showed on him. Rufen hung over the door, still talking.

"Great gods, what a shoulder. How's he trained? Did you train him? Do you have a pedigree? No speed, I'd say, but a lot of bottom." Paks had no chance to answer; the questions came too fast, and Rufen wasn't paying attention to her anyway. A groom came up.

"This horse yours?"

"Yes."

"He don't like his hind legs messed with, do he?"

"No — did he kick?"

"Kick! Look there at that board — " the man pointed. It had split along its length.

"He was hurt before I got him," said Paks. The groom eyed her sourly.

"That's what they all say," he said. "Hurt before I got him, pah! Could have trained him out of it, couldn't you?"

"I did," said Paks, suddenly angry again. "Look." She jumped up on the stall door. Socks threw his head up and snorted. "Be still," she said firmly, and slipped onto his broad back, then down to stand beside him. She ran her hand over his massive rump, down the hind leg, and chirped. He lifted his hoof obediently into her hand, and she tapped the sole, then put it down. "There, you see?" The groom nodded.

"All right. Now tell that beast to let someone else do it."

"Come on in." The groom opened the stall door. Socks stiffened his ears, and clamped his tail. Paks soothed him with a hand, and the man followed her gesture and picked up the other hind hoof. "I suppose, come to think of it, that no one's handled his legs but me since I got him," she said.

"I hope he'll remember this," said the groom.

"Try apples," said Paks.

"Bribe a horse?"

"That's what I did."

"It works," put in Rufen. "They're such greedy-guts, horses are. We use apples in our training."

"Yes, my lord," said the groom, with a slight bow. Rufen colored, glancing at Paks. When the man had left, and they were walking back across the stable court, he sighed.

"I suppose you know we use only one name here?"

"No — " Paks hadn't thought about it.

"Well, the — the servants and all, they know our full names. But don't worry about it. Just call me Rufen."

"And I'm Paks," she said. He nodded, and led her back into the maze of buildings.

"It's simple, really," he said a few minutes later, after taking her to the Low Hall where they would eat, and then to the bath house and past some of the classrooms. "The High Lord's Hall opens into the Forecourt, and directly across from it is the Marshal-General's Hall. Her quarters are upstairs, but they hold large meetings downstairs. And several other Marshals live there as well. Where you came in — that archway — that's all quarters for the gate guards and some of the servants. The other side of the Forecourt is the Training College — where we live and meet for classes. It used to be quarters for the Knights of Gird, but when the order grew too big for it, they converted it for us. The ground floor is much larger — rooms on the back side look over the roofs. That's because it doesn't have cellars; all the storerooms are above ground."

"Why?"

Rufen shrugged. "I don't know. I never wondered; they just told us when we came. Anyway, the Low Hall is more-or-less behind the Marshal-General's quarters; you saw where the kitchens were, between the steward's office and the Hall. The stables are really confusing, and I hear they're thinking of redoing them. Most of our horses — those assigned to training — are stabled in that little court just back of us. But the only way from there to the guest stables is through the tackroom — so you'll have to ride out the back of the guest stables, and around the smithy. Then the Knights' horses are stabled on the other side, south of the training armory."

Paks was still confused, but hated to admit it. "There are other armories, then?"

"Gird's teeth, yes. Each order of knights has its own, of course, and the paladins have theirs — and by the way, don't even think of trying to see what magical things they've got. Elis of Harway tried that, a year ago, and was knocked senseless for two days by the guard power they've set."

"Oh."

"And the Marshal-General chewed her out when she came to, and had her assigned to be Suliya's servant for a week." When Paks looked blank at that, he explained. "Suliya's a paladin — she — well, she stays here now." Paks said nothing, since he seemed uneasy. Finally he went on. "Sometimes, they say, even a paladin is defeated. You think of them dying, but sometimes — " He shook his head. "Of course, I've never seen her. Elis said it was — well, she said she'd fight any of us if *we* tried violating paladin secrecy. You don't know Elis, of course."

Paks began to think she'd like to know Elis. She was about to ask which of the students was Elis, when Rufen went on. "You won't, anyway, unless she comes back before you leave."

"Was she dismissed?"

"Elis? No, but her father died, and she was the oldest. She had to take his place. As soon as one of the others is old enough, she wants to come back. And she will. In the long run, if Elis wants it, she gets it."

They were now in the passage outside Paks's room. A neatly lettered card fitted into a slot she had not noticed before, so that anyone would know it was her room.

"I'm down four doors, across the passage," said Rufen. Paks finally found words for something that had puzzled her.

"How did you know about Elis? I thought the Marshal-General said the new class had been here only a few weeks."

"Oh, them." Rufen laughed. "There are — oh — a dozen of them. They're all younger than you. I've been here a year and some."

"Were all those in practice with you?" Paks did not want to reveal how unskilled they had seemed to her.

"No — we train in groups according to skill. That's the most basic group, in sword-work. My father, you see, planned for me to be a scholar. I had a badly broken arm, as a boy, and he thought it would never hold up to fighting. I thought differently."

533

"Oh." Paks found his composure as interesting as his story. He did not sound angry, or defensive — he might have been talking about the training of a horse.

"You won't do your sword-work with us, I'm sure. But then Aris and Seli won't do staves with you. By Gird, I've never seen anything so clumsy as your grip on a staff." Paks flushed, but he obviously meant no insult. "It gives me hope for my swordwork, for I was just as clumsy to start — perhaps you were so with a sword, and yet you've learned great skill."

"Well — I'll work hard," said Paks, trying to copy his calm.

"Oh, you'll learn. Cieri could teach a cow grace, if he wanted to. And he likes you somewhat — not that that will take the sting out of his blows. But if we want baths before supper, we'd best get going. The rest of them'll be crowding in soon enough." He went in his own room, and Paks turned to hers. Already two complete sets of gray tunics and trousers were folded neatly on her bed. She took off her mail, and her sweaty clothes, and put on the loose bath-gown of heavy gray wool. A knock on her door. Rufen called from outside. "I forgot to tell you — lots of us don't wear the uniform to supper. It's up to you, but don't wear mail, or weapons but the dagger."

"Thanks," she called back. She rummaged among her things, and decided finally to wear her second-best shirt from Brewersbridge. Perhaps they would think it strange if she showed up in students' gray at once. Then she thought of the Training Master, and wondered. It seemed that she could be wrong either way. Why hadn't they told her exactly what to do? She was willing to do what she was told. She looked from one stack of clothes to the other, biting her lip nervously, trying to remember exactly what the Training Master had said. At last she took up her own shirt and trousers, and headed for the bath house.

Bathed and dressed once more, Paks returned to her own room, wondering now how she would know when it was time to eat. No one had mentioned a gong or other signal. Rufen's door was shut; she was too shy to knock. She heard voices in the passage, but could not distinguish the words. Suddenly a commotion began — shouts, thuds — Paks leaped for her sword, then stopped short. No weapons. She snatched at her door, and looked out.

A black-haired boy in red velvet lay flat on the floor, blinking up at two who had their backs to Paks. She saw Rufen's door open, and his narrow good-humored face peering out.

"And if you come up here again, Aris — " said one of those standing.

"What are you doing now, Con?" asked Rufen.

"Don't bother yourself, Rufen. Just reminding the juniors that they've no right to come up here — "

"I do!" began the boy in red, but the second of the standing pair laughed shortly.

"You do, eh? Then we've a right to dump you on your tail." He took a step forward, but Rufen came out of his room.

534

"No one has a right to brawl, Jori, and you and Con know it. I don't know where you got the idea that this is your passage — "

"You'd dispute that?" asked Con scornfully. "You? By Gird's toe, Rufen, I can throw you with one arm alone."

"I doubt that," said Rufen. The boy had started to roll to his feet, but Con aimed a kick in his direction.

"Stay there, little boy."

Paks had been growing angrier. Jori sneered at Rufen, and said, "We have to do something — the Master's put one of 'em on our floor!"

Rufen cocked his head. "So?"

"So, we'll have to teach them all a lesson — I don't suppose a peasant girl can be much trouble."

Paks felt her anger like a leaping flame. "You don't?" she asked, trying for a pleasant tone. The two whirled; she saw the shock in their faces as they saw her size and condition. Behind them, Rufen helped the boy in red to his feet. "What kind of lesson," she asked, rocking slightly from heel to toe, "did you think to teach me?" She hoped they would jump her; she wished she had gone for them at once.

"Who in Gird's name are you?" asked Con, glancing sideways at Jori for support.

"Paksenarrion Dorthansdotter," said Paks quietly, still ready to jump. "A — peasant girl, I believe you said, wasn't it?"

"You're the new — ?" Con seemed unable to believe it.

"Yes." Paks waited, suddenly finding it funny.

"Paksenarrion," said Rufen pleasantly from behind them, "is a veteran of the wars in Aarenis. I believe she is known to Sir Fenith, as well as Marshal Cedfer of Brewersbridge and others." Paks glanced at him quickly, still balanced to fight. The boy Aris was grinning openly.

Con shook his head. "I'm sorry for what I said, then. You're no novice, barely trained as a squire. I had heard you were a sheepfarmer's daughter, but obviously — "

"I am a sheepfarmer's daughter," said Paks, dangerously quiet. "Does that change your opinion?"

He looked confused. "But you're not Girdish. Where did a — a girl like you learn warfare, outside the granges?"

"In Duke Phelan's Company," said Paks, glad to see the surprise return. "I began there, as a recruit."

"Phelan!" That was Jori. "But he's — " He looked quickly at Con.

"Yes?" Paks let her hand slip to her dagger hilt.

"I didn't say a thing — " began Jori. He held out his hands, palm up.

"Look, Pak-Paksenarrion — I don't know Duke Phelan, I only know what I've heard. Don't — "

"And what is this?" The Training Master had turned into the passage from the stairs. Paks, facing them all, saw their faces stiffen at his voice. She stood silent, waiting to see what would happen. No one spoke for a long moment. Then — "Well? Have you set a gauntlet for our new student to run? Aris, I thought you were to escort her to supper, and now I find you all standing about up here as if you had all night to chat."

Even Rufen seemed to have no quick answer to this. Paks moved forward, passing Con and Jori without looking at them. "Pardon, sir," she said. "I did not know the usual signal for supper, and delayed them talking about your customs. You did say, did you not, that I need not change to the student uniform for tonight?"

"Yes — I did." The Training Master looked taken aback. "But — "

"Is it permitted to wear one's own dagger to the table?"

"Yes, of course, but — "

"Then," she said, with a glance back to the others, who were watching in some kind of shock, "I apologize again for making everyone late. Aris, will you show me the way?"

The boy in red seemed the least dazed of them all, and came quickly to her side, nodding respectfully to the Training Master, who looked down at him thoughtfully. "Someone downstairs reported a disturbance up here," he said at last.

"Oh, sir?" Aris managed to look doubtful.

"Yells," said the Training Master.

Paks intervened. "They were expecting a peasant girl," she said, carefully not looking at Con and Jori. "I think I surprised them."

"I see." The Training Master looked them all over carefully. "I will see you after supper, Paksenarrion; we must be sure you understand the rules of the house."

"Certainly, sir. Where shall I come?"

"Aris can show you." Aris colored at this, and Paks surmised that he had been called often to the Training Master's study. With a last nod, the Training Master turned away; they all descended the stairs behind him, silently. When he turned away, and they were alone in the passage between the kitchens and the Lower Hall, Rufen spoke.

"Paks, thank you for not going into all that with him — "

"I thought we were in for it," added Con. Paks looked at him with distaste.

"Soldiers don't complain to commanders about every trifle."

Con reddened. "That's not what I meant — "

"It's what I meant." She turned pointedly to Aris, who had not spoken to her yet. "Where are you from, Aris?"

"From Marrakai's House, in Tsaia — do you know it?"

Paks laughed. "No — but I've heard of Duke Marrakai."

"My father," said the boy proudly. "I'm the fourth son."

"And knows it, too," muttered Jori, from behind them. Aris whipped around.

"At least *my* father is a duke!" he said. "And I have three estates already to my name — "

"Oh Gird's grace," muttered Con to Jori, "did you have to start him off again?" Even Paks was tempted to smile at the boy's intensity. But they

536

were at the doors of the Lower Hall, and looking for a place to sit at the crowded tables. Obviously more than students ate here: it seemed to Paks that a whole village was in the room, and the noise confirmed it. She followed the others between the tables, to a serving hatch. There her platter was stacked with sliced meat, a dipper of redroots in gravy, a small loaf of bread, and a slice of something that looked like nutbread dipped in honey. On a table beside the hatch were mugs; she had seen that each table had two pitchers.

The Hall was so crowded that they could not sit together; Aris found a space for the two of them, and the other three wandered away. Paks was hungry and began eating at once. When she slowed down enough to look around, the crowd was thinning out a little. Aris was chatting with another fairly young boy across the table — he was straw-blond, with gray eyes, and slightly crooked teeth. The person next to Paks had left without her noticing. She mopped up the rest of her gravy with the bread, and looked around the table. Next to Aris was a heavy-set redheaded man in a blue tunic, munching away steadily. Next to him, on the end, was a tall, slender — Paks stopped, and stared.

The elf looked up, and smiled at her. "I did not hear your name, lady — will you share it?" The voice held that strange music that all elves voices shared, a hint of harpstrings or bells.

Paks choked down the last bit of bread. "Paksenarrion Dorthansdotter, sir."

The cool gray eyes sharpened. "Would you be that Paksenarrion who traveled with one Macenion?"

"Yes, sir."

"Indeed. It is my pleasure, then, to welcome you — you are welcome to us, as to the Girdsmen. I am one of the embassy from the Westforest elves to Fin Panir; my elven name would be difficult for you to say, but you can call me Ardhiel."

Paks realized that Aris was staring at her, open-mouthed. He hissed at her. "Paksenarrion! The elf spoke to you? He's never said anything to me!"

Silvery laughter fell around them; the elf's eyes sparkled. "I do not know your name, young sir — and what would I speak with you about?"

Now the man beside Aris was also alert, listening.

Aris changed color. "I — sir, I — I only meant that — that I thought elves didn't talk to — "

"To students, rarely. We fear it might distract you from your own affairs — and your affairs, young sir, are not mine."

"But I — but she — but my father is Duke Marrakai!"

"Oh — you are the Kirgan?"

"No, sir. I'm the fourth son; the Kirgan is my brother Juris." The elf waved his hand, dismissing.

"Whatever, young Marrakai — your father's affairs might march with mine, but yours — no. I mean you no discourtesy, but — "

"I'm not a child!" insisted the boy. Paks had to admit he seemed childish

537

even to her; the elf's face expressed nothing, but she could feel his withdrawal.

"No? For me, young Marrakai, all in this room are but a summer's memory. If you would be comfortable with elves, you must admit this. I have known your family for more generations than you have lived in your House." Aris flushed, and set his jaw stubbornly. When his friend across the table whispered, he rose to go, looking pointedly at Paks.

"The Training Master said I was to show you where to go."

"Yes — thank you, Aris, I'll be right there." She looked back at the elf, whose eyes seemed for a moment sad. "Sir, I thank you."

"Lady Paksenarrion, it is nothing. I hope to see more of you hereafter."

Chapter Twenty

In the next few days, Paks felt that her mind and body both were battered and confused. Her instructors were forthright with both praise and criticism; other students accepted her presence without comment, but tested her skills relentlessly. Yet they tested each other just as freely, and seemingly held no rancor. She found it somewhat like being a recruit at the Duke's Stronghold, with the many hours of required drill. Yet out of class and drill there was no regimentation, no barracks chores. Clean clothes appeared in her room each day, and the room itself was cleaned while she was out. Someone else maintained the jacks and the bath house; someone else groomed the horses and polished tack. She began to wonder if this was the way the nobles lived, playing at war with weapons drill, but with someone else doing the dirty work. She had to admit she liked it.

Once she knew where everything was, and which place to go when, she began to enjoy it as she had never enjoyed anything else. Most of the students cared as much about weaponry and tactics as she did. They sat up late, arguing problems assigned by the instructors: where should a cohort of archers be set, or which order of march was best in heavy forest. At first Paks was shy of speaking up to Marshals and High Marshals, but silence was no protection: they would ask her. For Marshals in Aarenis had brought reports of the last season's fighting to Fin Panir, and the problems set were those she had fought through.

It started with an analysis, in a discussion of supply, of the march from Foss Council territory to Andressat. "Assuming a march of five days," Marshal Tigran said, "what would you need to supply a cohort of a hundred soldiers?" Paks tried to remember if it had indeed been five days. When the others had answered, and she was called on, she simply remembered how many mules they'd used, and blessed Stammel for insisting that she learn how to divide everything by three.

"Mules?" asked Tigran, and someone laughed. He frowned at them. Paks shook her head.

"To carry the supplies, Marshal."

"Aha! That was going to be my next question — how to transport it." Somehow Paks was getting credit for a right answer she had never actually given. But the next one she earned on her own. "Then," he went on, "how do you figure the extra transport for the supply taken up by transport?"

Paks knew that, from Stammel's many tirades on the subject. One Tir-damned mule in four, he'd muttered, just to make sure the beasts have enough for themselves. Tigran looked at her with respect, as did the rest of the class. When he found she knew how long fresh mutton or beef could travel in different seasons, and how long it took to grind the grain for a cohort's bread ration, he grinned, and turned to the other students. "This is the value of practical knowledge," he said. "Some of you know in theory, and the rest of you are learning, but here's a soldier who has been in the field, and knows what the ration tastes like."

"Can you tell us if it's true what Marshal Tigran says, about not being able to fight without supply even for one day? I still think brave troops could do without — not for long, maybe, but for a day or so." That was Con, more interested than aggressive. Tigran nodded to Paks, and she thought back to the various campaigns, and the day of the ambush in the forest near the Immer.

Paks described the enemy's apparent retreat, her Company's forced march trying to catch them, and the ambush in the forest. No one inter-rupted with questions; even Con was quiet. She told them of the damp cold that night, when the wounded had no shelter, and no one had food, when the smell of the enemy's food drifting across the locked squares made their hunger worse. And the next morning's attack, their allies' arrival. And finally the sudden weakness that toppled more than one of them, that long march and heavy fighting without food or rest.

"It's not a matter of bravery," she said. "You can live long without food, and stand and fight for a time, but not march and fight."

Tigran nodded at her. "Most of you have never been hungry for long — and since you aren't seasoned warriors, never when fighting."

"I wonder why you came to study, Paks," said Con after that class. "You already know as much as the Marshals — "

"No. No, I don't." She wondered how to explain what she didn't know. "I know what a private knows — the soldier in the cohort — "

"It seems plenty — "

"No, listen. I always wanted to learn, and so I paid attention to the ser-geants, and the captains when they talked in my hearing. But I only know it from the bottom. I don't know how to plan — how to think of more than one cohort at a time. You know how to reckon amounts for any number — right?" He nodded. "Well, I don't. My sergeant taught me to divide by three, to find our cohort's share of the Company's supplies. And I can add that three times, to go from a cohort's share to the whole Company. But that's all. He told me one time that Marrakai, when he goes to war, has five cohorts. I can't reckon in fives at all."

"You can't? But it's not hard — "

"No, maybe not. But you know how, and I don't. And in tactics, I know some things not to do, but I don't always know why. I can write well enough, and read — but I can't write a description of a battle, as Marshal Drafin showed us, or read one and make sense out of it. The sand table is one thing, but those books — "

540

"Huh. I thought after the first night that you knew everything — or thought you did."

Paks shook her head again. "I won't ever know anything — there's not time enough to learn all I want to know — "

"Now that's an interesting sentiment." The Training Master had appeared, as usual, without warning. Paks had begun to wonder if he had magical powers. "Are you serious in what you say?"

Paks was, as always, wary around him. "Yes . . . sir."

"You feel you have much more to learn — even with your practical experience?"

Paks felt an edge of sarcasm in his voice. She stiffened. "Yes. I said that."

"Don't bristle at me." To her surprise, he was smiling. "One thing that worried the Marshal-General was the possibility that you might find these things too boring — "

"Boring!"

"Don't interrupt, either. We have had a few other veterans who found them so — who were so intent on what they had done already that they could not learn new things." He looked intently at Con, who colored. Paks wondered what that was about, but was glad enough he wasn't after her. "How are you coming with your reading?" He was after her. She wondered if he'd heard what she had said to Con. She hated having to admit her weaknesses.

"Not — very fast, sir."

"I thought so." It did not sound too sarcastic. "Paksenarrion, the only way to learn to read faster and better is to read — just like swordplay. You can't learn swordplay from a book, or reading from your sword."

"But if I can listen to someone who knows — "

He shook his head. "Paksenarrion, no one knows everything — you're not alone in that. Writing stores knowledge, for others to use who may never know the writer. You know how tales told change in the telling — " She nodded, and he went on. "That's why writing is so important. Suppose you are in a battle; if you can write well enough to describe it accurately, then others can learn from your experience many years from now."

"It's too late." Paks looked down. She had hated turning in her scrawls when the others wrote neat, legible hands. "The ones who can write started earlier."

"And when did you start with staves? And you're already out of the novice class, into intermediate. Work at it. As for you, Con," the Training Master turned to him. "You quit worrying about your standing with the juniors, and start spending your evenings on tactics. And supply. Perhaps if you'll explain reckoning in all numbers to Paks, she'll explain why you can't march a cohort for two days on sixteen measures of barley and a barrel of apples."

"Apples? I meant to write salt beef."

"Your writing is not much better than Paks's — neither Tigran nor I

541

could decide what you really meant, so we called it apples. So might your supply sergeant, someday."

She could not remember when she had felt so at home. Not even in the Company, that last year. Instead of Saben and Canna, she had Rufen, Con, and Peli. They spent hours with pebbles and beans, teaching her reckoning. She taught them all one of her favorite sword tricks, so that Cieri, bested three times in one day, glared at them all, and accused Paks of trying to get his job as weaponsmaster. She began to read faster, and understand more complicated books and scrolls. They began to realize, as Rufen explained one night, that the soldiers they might command one day were real people.

"I knew they were," he said thoughtfully, "and yet I didn't. Here we talk about supplying a cohort, or positioning a squad of archers over here, and a couple of cohorts of pikes there. They're just — just bodies. Soldiers. Gird forgive me, being a Girdsman, but I looked like that at my father's guardsmen . . . they all wore a uniform, they all wore the same weapons. But after knowing you — and you were, as you say 'just a private' — I know they're real people."

Paks looked down, suddenly moved almost to tears. She felt, for the first time, that these were real friends. She could talk to them about the Company — about the people in it — with no betrayal of trust. Little by little she opened up, a few words at a time about Stammel and Devlin, Vik and Arñe — even Saben and Canna.

She had special status with the juniors — for Aris Marrakai had told his friends about her protecting him from Con's bullying. They did not venture to intrude on the upper floors very often, but she was conscious of shy smiles and friendly greetings from the whole group that Con despised.

Then there were the other races, seen close-to for the first time. The elf who had spoken to her the first night often ate at her table. When he saw her interest, he taught her a few words of elventongue — polite greetings and other courtesies. Some evenings he played the hand harp and sang; Paks and the others listened, entranced. Paks might have thought him a mere harper and wordsmith, but he came to weaponsdrill from time to time, and only the most advanced students fenced with him. Paks lost her sword twice in one session.

The dwarves kept more to themselves, and Paks might not have met them but for an accident with an axe. She had asked to learn axe-fighting, remembering Mal's effectiveness, and Cieri shook his head.

"I can teach axe-work, but to be honest, Paks, I don't know as I've ever seen a good swordfighter take to the axe. You're likelier to make a good spearman than be good with it. But whatever you want — as long as you keep improving with staves."

"I still don't understand why that's so important."

Cieri grinned. "You don't, eh? Well, keep in mind that the rest of us are Girdsmen. Gird was a farmer, not a lord's son to have a sword at his side. He

542

won the freedom of the yeomen with weapons they could find or make: clubs, staves, cudgels — and an occasional axe. Every Girdsman learns to use those first; every Knight of Gird can not only use, but teach the use of, the weapons you can find anywhere. Then no yeoman of Gird is helpless, so long as a stick is within his reach."

Paks thought about it a moment. "You mean — ordinary farmers — fighting regular soldiers?"

"Yes, exactly. Surely you've heard that?"

"Well, yes — but — "

"But you still don't believe it?" He shook his head. "You were a farmer's daughter — and you wanted to fight — so in your mind you built up what a soldier's weapon can do. When you become a Girdsman, Paksenarrion, I'll show you, wood against steel, how Gird won."

"Why not now?"

Cieri gave her a long look. "Because you are not under Gird's law yet, and I just might lose my temper."

"Oh." Paks was not sure what he meant, and didn't think she should ask more.

"But as for axes, that's a Girdish weapon. Have you ever used one much for chopping?"

"No — we didn't have forest where I grew up."

"And in Phelan's company?"

"The sergeants said they didn't have time to teach us axe-work."

"Wise. Well, go get one from the armory, and we'll start."

For a few days things went well; the basic drills were not hard, and Paks soon adjusted to the heavy axe-head hanging on the end of her arm. Or so she thought. Then Cieri set up a roughly carved log for her to "fight." It had a couple of branches for "arms." Paks looked at it disdainfully. She had seen the amusement on the others' faces.

"Isn't this just like chopping a tree?"

"Yes, but you haven't chopped any trees, and we don't happen to need any trees chopped. This will be fuel for the main kitchens later, if you'll get busy and do what I tell you." He took the axe from her, motioned her back, and with two smooth swings took a four-finger deep chunk out of the log. "Like that," he said. "And remember what I told you about backswing and bounce. Wood is harder than flesh, but softer than armor — at least this wood is."

Paks took the axe, which now felt comfortable in her grip. The basic stroke, he had explained, was much like the sideswing in longsword — but for using two hands. Paks had not used a two-handed sword; she did not think that mattered. She swung the axe back over her shoulder, and brought it around smoothly. Harder than flesh — softer than armor: she put what she thought was the right force into it. Whack! She felt the blow in both shoulders, and the axe-head recoiled, dragging her off balance, and missing her knee by a fingersbreadth.

"You have to hit harder than that, Paks," said Cieri. "A two-handed blow is a twisting blow; get your back into it."

543

The next stroke caught the axe-blade in the wood. She struggled to wrench it free, while Cieri described what happened to fighters whose weapons caught in an enemy. She felt the back of her neck getting hot; yet she knew he was right. That didn't help. When she began again, she managed a series of effective strokes, knocking off chips much smaller than Cieri's, but not making any serious mistakes. He called a halt, and nodded.

"You're doing well for a beginner. Now see if you can hit a certain target." He brought out his pot of paint, and daubed red on both of the "arms," as well as two spots on the "body." "Let's see you get the left arm first, then the upper body, then the lower body, then the right arm. Make your strokes work; use as few as you can. Remember, he's got a spear he's poking at you in the meantime."

Paks looked at the targets. "Axe fighters don't carry shields, do they?"

"Not using this kind of axe. There's a light battleaxe for riders that you can use one-handed — you could carry a shield with that. But here it's your quickness."

"I could break the spear with the axe, couldn't I?"

"You'd better. But that's a smaller target than you're ready for. And it moves. You've something to learn before you face a live spearman with an axe."

Paks nodded, and turned to the enemy tree. She had just gotten in position for a stroke at the left-hand branch when Cieri stopped her.

"Now look, Paks — you've got more sense than this. Look where you are."

She was sideways to the "enemy," in easy reach of the right "arm."

"You can't face him directly with that axe — think! Where can you strike, and be out of range."

Paks was annoyed at herself. She moved around the side of the tree, and swung at the left branch from there. She heard the wood creak as the axe sank deep, and was halfway into the next stroke when Cieri yelled again.

"Gird's blood! Do you think he'll stand still while you chop him up? Move, girl!"

Paks felt the blood rush to her face. She jumped, whirling the axe high, and swung again at the branch. It split before taking the full force of her blow, and the axe swung on to lay a deep gash in her leg as she landed from the jump. Furious, she ignored the pain and aimed a vicious slash at the main trunk, straight at Cieri's mark. The axe stopped in midstroke, wrenching her shoulders, and hung in the air.

"Let go," said Cieri mildly. Paks looked at the axe, down at her leg, and then unwrapped her hands from the axe handle. The axe fell with a clang. "If the blade's damaged," Cieri went on, "you can grind it down yourself. I'd thought you too seasoned a fighter to lose your temper for a little thing like that."

Paks said nothing, still angry. Pain from her leg began to demand attention. He came forward, and picked up the axe, running his fingers over the head and blade edge. Then he looked at her.

544

"You're damned lucky, Paks. Now will you believe me about axes?"

"I can learn." She was surprised at her own voice, furry with anger.

His eyebrows rose. "Oh? How? By cutting off your limbs one at a time? The way you're going, you'll be an axe-fighter about the time you're holding the axe in your teeth."

"I could — if you weren't badgering me." Paks glared at him, saw the flash of his dark eyes.

"Me! You — not even a yeoman — you're telling me, the weaponsmaster, that I shouldn't heckle you? I thought you had more sense — and here you stand flatfooted like a novice yeoman, then lose your temper just because I tell you so, and then this! I suppose I should be glad you aren't a Girdsman."

"I — " Paks was suddenly conscious of all the other listening ears. "I'm sorry," she muttered.

"So you should be," he said crisply. "You'll miss days of work with that leg, and I don't think you'll find yourself in the same class when you come back. If you do."

Paks looked up, startled, to meet a grim cold Cieri she had never seen. "Sir?"

"It might pass in a novice, Paksenarrion, but not in someone who claims to be a veteran. Was all that just an act?"

"What?" Now she was completely bewildered. It must have shown, for Cieri's face softened a trifle.

"That even disposition you showed until today. That smile, that willingness. Which is the real you, Paksenarrion? Do you know yourself? Or are you acting a part all the time, inside and out?"

"I — I thought you — liked me," she said. She knew at once it was the wrong thing to have said.

"Liked you? Gird's arm, what do you mean by that? Listen, Paksenarrion, you come here on trial, not even a Girdsman — you come in full of life as a yearling colt, showing off, taking every trick I know, everything the other Marshals can teach you — and teaching your own tricks to the others — and you expect us to like it? Well, any teacher likes a willing student — but that's not enough for us. We're training Knights of Gird, Paksenarrion, and paladins, who will go and and die for the justice Gird brought. You — you're playing with us, enjoying a safe, exciting time doing what you like to do. Then you'll go where you please, using what you've learned for your own ends. The rest of us aren't playing a game." He shook his head. "I've let you play; after all, you're a good practice partner for the others. I thought, from the way you seemed to be, that you might join the Fellowship and justify the time I've spent. But I won't waste my time on games any more. We'll see what the Marshal-General says, before you return." Paks could hardly believe her ears. He was turning away when he glanced at her leg. "Better wrap that; you've bled a lot."

Paks watched him walk without a backward glance toward the other students, who were staring in the same shock she felt. He had them back to their drill in seconds, and did not look her way again. Paks forced herself to think, to move. She took off the scarf she had wrapped around her head against the cold, and bound it tightly around her leg. The bleeding had slowed, but she had left a sizeable stain on the ground. She could do nothing about that, but she did take a few seconds to stack the hacked limb neatly near the rest of the tree before limping back to the armory. Cieri still had the axe.

She looked back from inside the armory. Cieri was fencing with Con; no one looked her way. She felt cold, inside as well as out. She had been stupid — even rude — but was it really that bad? And had they all been resenting her since she came? She tried to think what to do. She took a roll of bandage material from its box beside the armory door, and retreated toward the stableyard, which had a well. It was midmorning; a stable worker trundled a barrow full of dung out the far archway as she came into the yard. No one else was in sight. Paks pulled the scarf away from her leg, wincing, and washed the wound out until the bleeding stopped before wrapping it with clean bandages.

The Training Master, she was thinking dully. I must see the Training Master — and then the Marshal-General. Her leg was hurting in earnest now, throbbing in time with her pulse. She rinsed the scarf in a bucket of water, and wrung it out, her fingers stiff from the cold water. When she looked up, two dwarves were watching her.

"Your pardon is it?" said the darker one. "Is it that you can say what way to the training field for the knights?"

Paks worked the meaning out of this. "Did you want Marshal Cieri?" she asked.

They nodded gravely. They hardly topped her head, the way she was leaning over the bucket, and she didn't think it would be polite to stand. The darker one carried a double-bladed axe thrust into his belt; the yellow-bearded one carried his in his hand. "It is that we were asked to show something of this skill with the axe," he said. "It is Marshal Cieri who teaches this, is it not so?"

"It is." Paks felt her ears redden. She felt even worse than before. If he had asked dwarves to come and teach her — "It is through that arch," she said, nodding toward it, "and then right, and through the building there." She could not explain; besides, it might be something else.

"What is it that you do here?" asked the darker dwarf, peering into the bucket. "It looks blood."

Paks blushed deeper. "It is — I cut myself, and this wrapped it at first."

The dwarf nodded. "Cut — are you then not a student of the weaponsmaster?"

"I — am," Paks hesitated, wondering if she should claim that now.

"But he is Marshal, yes? It is that he heals those injured in training?"

"Not this time," said Paks, hoping they would go.

Four shrewd eyes bored into her. She could not read their expressions. Then the darker dwarf emitted a rough gabble of words that Paks had never heard before: dwarvish, she thought. The yellow-bearded one spoke to her. "I am Balkis, son of Baltis, son of Tork, son of Kertik, the sister-son of Ketinvik Axemaster, the first nephew of Axemaster. It is that you are not Gird's?"

Paks had never met a dwarf, and did not know that this introduction was normal. She was trying to remember it all when the question came, and for a moment did not answer. The dwarves waited patiently. "I am not of the Fellowship of Gird," she said finally.

"But you are here," said the darker dwarf. "How is it that you are here?"

"I was offered a time of training here," said Paks carefully, "because of something I had done."

"Ah." Another pause. Finally the yellow-bearded dwarf, Balkis, asked, "Is it that we might know your clan?"

Paks realized, belatedly, that she had not responded to his introduction with her name. "I'm Paksenarrion Dorthansdotter, of Three Firs."

An exchange of dwarvish followed this. Balkis spoke in Common again. "Please — is it that Three Firs is a clan? We do not know this name."

"No, Three Firs is the village nearest my father's home. It is far from here, to the north."

"Ah. And your father is Dorthan, but of what clan?"

Paks wondered how to explain. "Sir, my father's father was Kanas Joris-son, but I do not think we have the same kind of clans you do — "

Both dwarves laughed loudly. "Indeed, you would not! No — no, you would not. But some men *think* they have clans as we do, and give themselves names for them, and if you were such then we wished no insult by failing to acknowledge that name." Then Balkis leaned back on his heels, watching her. "What is it that you did, to make a hurt the weaponsmaster would not heal?"

Paks looked down. "I — cut myself."

"Yes, but — " He stopped, and leaned close to place his face before her. "I would not have you to think that it is our nature to be inquisitive."

Abruptly, Paks found herself grinning. "Oh, no," she said. "I wouldn't think that."

"Good. But we have to study men, who come into our rocks and want things of us. So it is that you will tell us what is that cut?"

"I was trying to use an axe," said Paks slowly. "And I became angry, and struck too hard, and cut my leg."

"Ah. Angry with an axe is dangerous."

"So I found," said Paks ruefully.

"And this the weaponsmaster found badly done, is it so?"

"Yes. And I was rude." She wondered why she was telling them, but their interest seemed to pull it out of her.

"Rude — to a Marshal." Suddenly the darker one loosed a volley of dwarvish, and both of them began to quiver. Paks looked up to see their eyes sparkling with mischief. "You fear not Marshals?"

"I — " Paks shook her head. "I *should* fear them more. I was here as a guest, and my rudeness will cost my place."

"Ha!" Balkis nodded. "They are as a clan of adoption, and you are not adopted. So it is they can be unjust."

"It wasn't unjust," said Paks. "It — they think I have been unjust, to take their hospitality without giving in return."

Now they frowned. "You haven't?"

"No." Paks poured the stained water out on the cobbles and watched it drain away between them. "I thought — but I haven't."

"Hmph." The snort was eloquent. "But it is you that are the fighter interested in axes?"

"Less than I used to be," said Paks.

"Would you try again?" asked Balkis. His voice held a challenge.

"I might — if I have the chance."

"If it happens that your weaponsmaster refuses you, I will show something," he offered. "It is not every human that will be rude to Marshals of Gird, and be willing to work with axes past the first blood drawn."

"But I was wrong," said Paks, thinking ahead to what the Training Master would say. The dwarves both shrugged, an impressive act with shoulders like theirs.

"It is the boldness of the fighter," said Balkis. "We dwarves, we will not take lessons from Marshals, despite their skill, for they are always insulting us. Did you know any dwarves, where you came from?"

"No," said Paks. "You are the first I have ever met, though I saw dwarves in Tsaia and Valdaire."

"Ah. Then you know not our ways. It involves no clan-rights, but perhaps you would sit at our table some night?"

"If I'm here," said Paks.

They shrugged again, and passed out of the stableyard toward the training fields. Paks gathered up the damp scarf, pushed herself upright, and limped back toward her room. On the way, she saw the Training Master turn into the corridor ahead of her and called to him. He stopped, looking back, and came forward, looking concerned.

"Paksenarrion — what's happened? You're hurt?"

"Yes, sir. I — " Suddenly she felt close to tears. She pulled herself upright. "It's not that, sir, but I must speak with you."

"Something's happened?"

"Yes, sir."

"Well, come along, then." He led the way to his study, and waved her to a seat. "What is it?"

Chapter Twenty-one

Paks took a long breath, clutching the sodden scarf in her hands. "Sir, I — I lost my temper, and was rude to Marshal Cieri, and he doesn't want me in his class."

"I see." His face looked almost as cold as the first day. "And you come to me about it — why?"

"I thought I should." She swallowed painfully the lump that had been growing in her throat for the past half-hour. "Sir."

"You want me to plead for you? Without hearing his story?"

"No, sir." Why was everyone misunderstanding what she meant? Paks plunged on. "It isn't that — I thought I was supposed to tell you — "

"He told you to?" That was with raised brows.

"No, sir," said Paks miserably. "I mean — you're the Training Master — if this were the Company, I'd have to tell the sergeant — "

His voice gained a hint of warmth. "You're saying that you are doing what you would have done in Duke Phelan's Company? Reporting something you did wrong?"

"Yes, sir."

"I see." His fingers drummed on the desk. "You agree that whatever happened was your fault?"

Paks nodded. Thinking back, she knew that Siger or Stammel would have reacted just as Cieri had — if not worse.

"Well, suppose you tell me about it. And by the way, how did you get hurt?"

"You knew I'd asked to learn axe fighting?" Paks waited for his nod, then went on. "I'd been doing drills with the axe — not hitting anything, and today Marshal Cieri set up a target. A log, with limbs." Paks stopped. It seemed even worse as she tried to think how to say what had happened.

"Yes?"

"Well — sir — I had trouble with it — he'd said I would — "

"And you lost your temper over that?"

"No, sir. Not then. After awhile I made some chips of it, and then he wanted me to hit specific targets. Only when I started, he — he got after me for not thinking of it as live, for giving it a chance to hit back." She looked up to see the Training Master's lips folded tightly. As bad as that, then. She went on. "Then I hit a limb — he said to think of it as an arm — and when I went to hit again, he

549

was angry that I hadn't allowed for it to move. So I jumped at it, and hit it really hard, and the limb broke and the axe hit my leg."

"How badly?"

"Just a cut. But then I was angry, and I was about to — to swing as hard as I could, and he stopped the axe." Paks looked up again. "I didn't know he could do that."

"It's not something we demonstrate very often," said the Training Master, in a neutral voice. "Go on."

Paks ducked her head. "Then he said he thought I knew better than to lose my temper, and that I wouldn't be any good at axe-work, like he'd said. And that's when — "

"What did you say, Paksenarrion?"

"I said — " she paused to remember the words. "I said I could learn, if he wouldn't harrass me. It — I was wrong, sir, and I know it. I knew it as soon as I said it — "

"Did you apologize?"

"Yes, sir; I told him I was sorry — "

"Did you mean it?"

Paks looked up, startled.

"Were you sorry for being rude, or sorry he was angry with you, or sorry you'd lost your temper in the first place?"

"I — I don't know, sir. I suppose — I was just sorry about everything."

"Hmph. So then what happened?"

Paks told the rest as well as she could, and on being prompted added the conversation with the dwarves. When she had finished, the Training Master sighed.

"So you came to me, because you thought you should, and you expect me to do — what? What do you think will happen now?"

Paks met his gaze squarely. "I think you'll send me away," she said. "If that's what all of you think — that it's unfair to spend the time when I'm not a Girdsman. And even if I were — he said it would be bad — you might still."

"Do you think we should send you away?"

Paks didn't know what to say to this. For a moment she looked away, but when her eyes returned to his face it held the same quiet expectancy. She thought the question over. "Sir, I — I don't know what your rules are — what your limits are. If I do what you don't want, then of course you have the right to send me away. But I can't think what is best for you — for the Fellowship. If it is best to, then you will. Otherwise — I don't know."

"Well, if you are convinced we will send you away, why come to me? Why not simply go pack your things and leave? Or tell us you're leaving, and not wait to be dismissed?"

"But — I couldn't do that. It would be — " She could not think of the right words; she knew it would be wrong, and somehow worse than wrong. "Discourteous," she finally said. "Ungrateful. It's my fault, and you have the right; I don't."

550

He shook his head slowly. "I'm not sure I follow your reasoning, Paksenarrion. You agree that we have the right to dismiss you, if you displease us — but you think you have no right to withdraw?"

"If I didn't want to stay — or if something happened, perhaps to my family or something — then I could, but it wouldn't be fair to — to walk out when it was my fault."

He pounced on that. "Fair. You're trying to be what you think is fair?"

"Yes, sir."

"And you said 'if I didn't want to stay' — does that mean you do want to stay?"

"Of course I do," said Paks, louder than she'd meant to.

"There's no 'of course' to it," he replied crisply. "Many who come here to train don't like it, and don't want to stay. Are you saying that even after Cieri's thrown you out of his class — in front of everyone — you'd still prefer to stay here?"

"Yes, sir."

"Why?"

Her hands twitched. "It's — it's what I always wanted to learn. These weeks have been the best of my life."

"Until today."

"Yes, sir." Then she looked at him again. "If I could stay — today is not much, really — "

"Oh?" His brows went up again; Paks's heart sank. "You call an axe wound, and having the senior weaponsmaster refuse to have you in his class 'not much'? We have different views, Paksenarrion."

"I'm — "

"You're sorry. I'm sure." He sighed again. "Paksenarrion, we accept occasional outsiders — non-Girdsmen — because we know that good hearts and good fighters may choose another patron. You have an unusual background; it may be that you have seen that which makes today seem minor to you. But to us it is important. We have all watched you, for these weeks, and been puzzled. You are capable, intelligent, hardworking, physically superior to most of the others. You have gotten along with the others, juniors and seniors both. You don't brawl, get into arguments, get drunk, or try to seduce the Marshals. If you were a Girdsman, we would be more than pleased with your progress. Yet you have reserves, you harbor mysteries, which we cannot fathom. All our skills say these are not evil — yet great evil has been known to masquerade as good, just as a beautiful cloak can cover an evil man. This — today — is the first chink in your behavior. Is it characteristic? Is this the true Paksenarrion coming out? And why have you refused to make any commitment? Marshal Cieri does, in this way, speak for all of us. We would welcome you gladly as a knight-candidate — perhaps more — if you were of the Fellowship of Gird. But until you show us some willingness to give in return for what you are given — more than that surface pleasantness you have shown, I must concur with him."

Paks sat still, unable to move or speak. She had never really believed that

551

anyone could think she was evil. She longed to be back with the Duke's Company, where Stammel, she was sure, would defend her against any such accusation. Why had she ever left that safe haven? Into that shock, her leg intruded, throbbing more insistently. She blinked a few times, and lifted her head.

"Yes, sir," she said, through stiff lips. "I — I will go pack."

"Gird's right arm!" The Training Master's voice must have echoed through the entire first floor. "That's not what I said, girl!" Paks stared at him. "You have the choice — make it!"

"Choice?" Paks could not think.

"You can become a Girdsman," said the Training Master crisply. "Has that not occurred to you?"

"No," said Paks with more honesty than tact.

"Then it should have. By the gods, girl, you think better than that in tactics class. You recognize what the problem is: you want to stay for more training, and we are unwilling to give more training without some return. How much do you want to stay? What are you willing to give? And what did you want the training for, if not to follow Gird?"

Paks felt her heart pounding so that she could scarcely draw breath. "You mean I could join — but if you think I'm bad, why would you — "

The Training Master gave a disgusted snort. "I didn't say I thought you were evil. I said it was a possibility. Do you *want* to join the Fellowship of Gird? Will you pay that price?"

"I — " Paks choked a moment and went on. "Sir, I want to stay. If that is what — but will Gird accept it?"

"We can talk of Gird himself later, Paksenarrion. What we, the Marshals, are looking for is something less than what Gird may ask. Is it something your Duke told you, that makes you dislike Gird so? Or have you another patron you haven't told us about?"

Paks shook her head. "No, sir. It's nothing like that; all I have been told of Gird I admire, and here you teach that Gird is a servant of the High Lord, not a god to worship instead of him. But — " She could not explain the obscure reserve and resentment she felt, and worked her way toward it haltingly. "When I was in the Duke's Company, I knew Girdsmen. Effa was killed in her first battle — but that doesn't matter. I think it was when Canna was captured and killed. She was a Girdsman, but it didn't help. She died, and not in clean battle, even though we were trying to reach the Duke, and tell him about Siniava's capture of the fort. If Gird saved anyone, why not Canna, his own yeoman? Why me?"

"You don't like the notion that great deeds reward the hero with a quick death?"

Paks shook her head more vigorously. "No, sir. And hers wasn't quick, by what I was told. Capture, and a bad wound — that's no reward for faithful service. And she was the one hit at the fort itself, by a stray arrow. Why didn't Gird protect her then? She kept us together, led the way — it should have been her chance, that last day, not mine." She felt the old anger smouldering still, and fought it down. "And more than that — the captain said it was probably Canna's medallion that saved me from death in Rotengre — but I'm a soldier. Why didn't Gird save the slave, or the baby? Why did they have to die?" Now more scenes from Aarenis recurred: the child in Cha, the frightened rabble in Sibili, Cal Halveric's drawn face, old Harek dying after torture. And worse things, from the coastal campaign. She set her jaw, feeling once more that old sickness and revulsion, that helpless rage at injustice, that had driven her from the Duke's Company to travel alone.

The Training Master nodded slowly; she could see nothing mocking in his face. "Indeed, Paksenarrion, you ask hard questions. Let me answer the easiest one first. You ask why Gird did not save his own yeoman, and the answer to that is that Girdsmen are called to save others, not be saved." He held up his hand to stop the questions that leaped into her mouth. "No — listen a moment. Of this I am sure, both from the archives and from my own knowledge. Gird led unarmed farmers into battle with trained soldiers — do you think they won their freedom without loss? Of course not. Even the yeomen of Gird — even the novice members of the Fellowship — have to accept a soldier's risks. Above that level, as yeoman-marshal, Marshal, High Marshal, and so on — and as paladin — Girdsmen know that their lives are forfeit in need. Gird protects others through the Fellowship — he does not protect the Fellowship as a shepherd protects sheep. We are all his shepherds, you might say."

Paks thought about that. "But Canna — "

"Was your friend, and you mourn her. That is good. But as a yeoman of Gird, she risked and gave her life to save others — or that's what it sounds like you're saying."

"It's true."

"Now — about those innocents who are not Girdsmen, and are killed. This is why the Fellowship of Gird trains every yeoman — to prevent just that. But in many lands we are few — our influence is small — "

"But why can't Gird do it himself, if he's — "

"Paksenarrion, you might as well ask why it snows in winter. I did not make the world, or men, or elves, or the sounds the harp makes when you pluck the strings. All I know is that the High Lord expects all his creatures to choose good over evil; he has given us heroes to show the way, and Gird is one of these. Gird has shown men how to fight and work for justice in the face of oppression: that was his genius. It is not the only genius, nor dare I say it is the best; only the High Lord can judge rightly. But as followers of Gird, we try to act as he did. Sometimes we receive additional aid. Why it comes one time and not another, or why it comes to one Marshal and not another, I cannot say. Nor can you. Nor will you ever know, Paksenarrion, until you pass beyond death to the High Lord's table, if that happens." He gave her a long look. "And I think that you blame Gird because you are still blaming yourself for these deaths. Is that not so?"

Paks looked down. She could still hear Canna's voice, that last yell:

"Run, Paks!" And she had run. She could still hear the others. "It might be," she said finally.

"Paksenarrion, Gird does not kill the helpless — someone alive, with a sword or club or stone, does that. If you still think, after the time you have been here, that the followers of Gird act that way — "

"No, sir!"

" — then you should leave at once. But if you see us trying to teach men and women how to live justly together, and defend their friends and families against the misuse of force, then consider if that is not your aim as well. Gird may ask your life, someday, but Gird will never ask you to betray a friend, or injure a helpless child. Consider the acts of your Girdish friend, and not her death, and ask yourself if these were good or bad."

"Good," said Paks at once. "Canna was always generous."

"And so you are rejecting Gird because he has not acted as you would — is that it?"

Paks had not thought that clearly about it. Put that way it seemed arrogant, to say the least. "Well — I suppose I was."

"You are not rejecting his principles, it seems, but the fact that they aren't carried out?"

Paks nodded slowly, still thinking.

"Then it seems, Paksenarrion, that you ought to be willing to try to carry them out." His mouth quirked in a smile. "If the rest of us are doing so badly."

"I didn't say that!"

"I thought you just did. However — " He leaned forward, elbows on the desk. "If you don't think we are too corrupt, perhaps you will give us the benefit of your judgment — "

"Sir!" Paks felt her eyes sting; her head was whirling already.

"I'm sorry." He actually sounded sorry. "I went too far, perhaps — I forgot your leg. We'll talk again later — we must get you upstairs and let the surgeon see that."

"See what?" A voice in the doorway interrupted. Paks tried to turn her head, but felt too dizzy. Her ears roared.

"She's got a small wound, Arianya," said the Training Master.

"Not that small," said the voice. "It's bled all over your floor, Chanis. Better take a look."

Paks tried to focus on the Training Master as he came back around the desk to kneel beside her chair. Her eyes blurred. She heard the two Marshals talking, and then another excited voice, and then felt a wave of nausea that nearly emptied her stomach. She clamped her jaw against that, and roused enough to know that they were carrying her along the passage. Finally the motion stopped, and her stomach quieted. When she got her eyes working again, she was lying flat on a bed, staring at the ceiling. Her mouth was dry, and tasted bad. She rolled her head to one side. That was a mistake. Her stomach heaved, and she hardly noticed the pail someone pushed under her mouth until she was through.

From a distance, someone said, "If she had the sense to match her guts,

554

she'd be fine — "

"I don't call fainting from a simple cut like that guts, Chanis."

"She didn't, and you know it. We all pushed as hard as — "

"Well, however you say it. I still think — "

Closer, someone called her name. "Paksenarrion? Come on now, quit scaring us." She felt a cup at her lips, and drank a swallow of cold water. Her stomach churned, but accepted it. She opened her eyes again to see the Marshal-General's flint-gray eyes watching her. Before anyone else could speak, Paks managed to force out her own message.

"I want to join — the Fellowship — even if you send me away."

Silence followed this. The Marshal-General stared at her. Finally she spoke.

"Why now?"

"Because I was wrong about him — Gird. And so — and so I want to join, and do better."

"Even if I send you away? Even if you never go beyond yeoman?"

"Yes." Paks felt as stubborn now on this ground as she had before on others.

"I hope you feel the same when you've remade a couple of skins of blood." The Marshal-General sat back, and grinned. "Gird's ten fingers! Did you have to lose half the blood in your body to learn sense?"

"I didn't," said Paks. She had the curious feeling that her body was floating just above the bed. She knew she understood more than the others, only it was hard to speak. "It isn't lost — it's not in the same place, is all."

"And you're wound-witless. All right. If you still want to make your vows when you're strong enough, I daresay Gird will accept them. But that will be some time, Paksenarrion. For now you must rest, and obey the surgeons."

Not until some days later did Paks hear the full story of that day. She had had no visitors at first but the surgeons, the Training Master, and the Marshal-General. Finally the surgeons agreed that she could move back to her own room. She was surprised at how shaky she felt after climbing the stairs — from one simple cut, she thought. She sat down hard on her bed, head whirling, and leaned back against the pillows. Rufen and Con woke her some time later when they discovered her door open and looked in to see why.

"Paks?"

She woke with a start; the last sunlight came through her window. "Oh — I forgot to shut the door."

"Are you all right? You look pale as cheese," said Con. Paks gave him a long stare.

"I'm fine. I just — dozed off."

"The Training Master said you were back. He said not to bother you, but your door was open — "

"That's all right." Paks pushed herself up. She wondered what they were thinking about, and felt her ears going hot.

"I've never been so mad in my life," said Con, moving into the room to sit at her desk. "I'd have taken Cieri apart if I could have — "

"Instead of which, he dumped you — how many times?" Rufen leaned against the doorframe, smiling.

"That doesn't matter. Listen, Paks, if they'd thrown you out, I'd have — have — "

Paks shook her head. "Con — it's all right."

"No, it's not. It wasn't fair — we could all see that. I couldn't believe it, the way he hounded you — and you the best of us. Gird's flat feet, but I'd have blown up at him days before."

Paks stared at him in surprise. "But I thought you'd be on their side — I thought you'd agree that it wasn't fair for me to be here as an outsider."

Con shrugged. "That! What difference does that make? I've been a Girdsman all my life, and I never will be as good a fighter as you are. It's not as if you were bad: you don't quarrel even as much as I do. No one's ever found you doing something underhand or cowardly. They ought to be glad you're willing to come here at all. And that's what I told him."

"And then what?" Paks could not imagine that scene at all.

"And then he told me I didn't know what I was talking about, and until I did I should kindly keep to my own business, and I told him my friends were my business. And he said I should choose my friends with care, and I said I'd learned more from you since you'd come than from him since I'd been here — " Con stopped, blushing scarlet.

"And then," Rufen put in with a wide grin, "then Cieri said maybe he should have long yellow hair to catch Con's attention, and Con swung on him, and ended up flat on his back. Cieri asked the others what they thought, and apparently everyone was on your side. I wish I'd been there — I knew I'd regret being in that lower class after you got here. I don't know if I could have done any more, but — "

"But you shouldn't have," said Paks, looking at Con. "He's — he's the weaponsmaster, you shouldn't argue with him."

"But he was wrong," said Con stubbornly, his eyes glinting. "Paks, if you've got a fault it's that you're too willing to be ruled. I know what you'll say — you'll say that's how a good soldier is. Maybe so, for a mercenary company. But we're Girdsmen; Gird himself said that every yeoman must think for himself. I don't care if Cieri is the weaponsmaster, or the Training Master, or the Marshal-General, if he's wrong, he's wrong, and if I think he's wrong I should say so."

"Just because you think he is wrong doesn't make him wrong," argued Paks. "How do you know you're right?"

"I can tell unfairness when I see it," growled Con.

"How do you *know*?" Paks persisted. "Sometimes things seem unfair when they happen, but later you can tell they weren't — so how do you know when something is truly unfair?"

"Well, when it's — I mean — by Gird, Paks, it's easier to know than to say. I know Cieri was unfair to you; he kept picking at you, trying to make you mad, and then when you got mad he blamed you for it. And you were hurt, dripping blood all over, and he didn't even offer to heal it for you."

Paks shrugged. "If he thought I was wrong, he wouldn't."

"But it was his fault. And so it wasn't fair. Don't you know anything? Didn't you ever have brothers or someone in your Company that kept trying to put things on you — surely you know what I mean."

Paks shrugged again. "Con, I know enough to know that looking for the final fault, who's really to blame, just keeps trouble alive longer. I shouldn't have lost my temper, no matter what. If he was wrong to push me that far, it was still my fault. And the Marshal-General told me when I came that they were reluctant to train someone who had given no vows of service."

"But now you're joining the Fellowship, is that right?" asked Rufen.

"Yes. The surgeon says I should be up to a bout at Midwinter Feast."

"How bad is your leg?"

"Not bad. They stitched it up; it's healing clean. It's mostly blood loss; I should have tied it up tighter to begin with." Then she thought of something else. "Con — did some dwarves show up at the field after I left?"

Con looked startled. "How did you know about them?" Then he grinned broadly. "That was something, let me tell you. Two of 'em came marching up, right into the class, in the middle of the row we were — anyway, came into the class, and interrupted us. I can't talk like they do — all that 'it is that' and 'is it that it is' — but the long and short of it was that Cieri had asked them to come and demonstrate axe fighting, and they were ready. Cieri told them he'd dismissed his student, and they grumped about being called out for nothing. So he said they could show the rest of us, and they glared around and said they wouldn't show anyone who didn't have the guts to learn. One of them challenged Cieri himself. Well, we saw some axe-fighting, let me tell you, and that axe you were using won't ever be the same."

Paks felt a guilty twinge of satisfaction. She tried to conceal it; Con needed no encouragement. "Is Master Cieri all right?"

"Oh, yes. He got a scratch or two, but you know he can heal that — it's nothing to him. Anyway, now that you're joining the Fellowship, you'll be coming back to class, won't you?"

"I suppose. I haven't seen Master Cieri." Paks wondered if he would hold a grudge against her.

"You are staying, aren't you?"

"Yes."

"Then you'll be back with us. That'll be good. And listen, Paks, you keep in mind what I said. As a yeoman, you have a right to think for yourself. You're supposed to — "

"I do," said Paks. "You — "

"You do, and then you don't. I know what you're thinking, about me and the juniors, and you were right, there. You stand against us — the others in the class — when you think differently. But you don't stand against anyone over you — I'll bet you never argued with your sergeant, or captain, or the Duke — "

Paks found herself smiling. She could not imagine Con arguing with Stammel more than once, let alone with Arcolin. But she defended herself.

"I did argue with the Duke once — well, not exactly argue — "

"Once!" Con snorted. "And he was wrong only once in three years? That's a record."

She shook her head at him; it was useless to try to explain. She tried anyway. "Con — privates don't argue with commanders. Not unless it's very important, and usually not then. And we don't see everything, we can't know when the commander is wrong."

"So what did you argue — not exactly — about?"

Paks froze. She had never meant to get close to that night in Aarenis again. "I — you don't need to know," she said lamely.

"Come on, Paks. I can't imagine you arguing with anyone like that — it must have been something special. What was it? Was he going to start worshipping Liart, or something?"

Paks closed her eyes a moment, seeing Siniava stretched on the ground, the Halverics at his side, the angry paladin confronting her Duke. She heard again the taut silence that followed the Duke's outburst, and felt the weight of his eyes on her. "I can't tell you," she said hoarsely. "Don't ask me, Con; I can't tell you."

"Paks," said Rufen quietly. "You don't look ready for supper in the hall; we'll bring something up for you." His gentle understanding touched her; she opened her eyes to see them both looking worried.

"I'm all right," she said firmly.

"You're all right, but you're not well. If you're to make your vows at the Midwinter Feast, you don't need to be scurrying up and down stairs again today. It's no trouble — " he went on, waving her to silence. "If we go now, we can all eat up here in peace. Come on, Con." And the two of them went out, closing her door softly and leaving her to her thoughts.

Chapter Twenty-two

Marshal-General Arianya headed the table; three High Marshals, two paladins, and five Marshals (three attached to granges, and two from the college itself) completed the conference.

"Will that new yeoman be ready to test for the Midwinter Feast, Arianya?" asked the oldest of the group, Marshal Juris of Mooredge grange.

"I think so. She says she's well enough now, but the surgeons don't want her fighting for another few days."

"That would look good," muttered High Marshal Connaught, Knight-Marshal of the Order of Gird. "Nothing like a candidate fainting in the ceremony."

"She won't faint," said the Marshal-General firmly. Someone chuckled softly, thinking of it, and she frowned around the table.

"It's not that often we bring new yeomen in here," she reminded them. "It's serious to her — "

"I know that," said Marshal Kory, the Archivist. "It just slipped out, Marshal-General."

"Very well. And while we're on the subject, I would like to suggest something else."

"What you and Amberion were chatting about yesterday?" asked Marshal Juris. "If it's what I think, I'm against it."

The Marshal-General glared at him. "You might at least give me a chance to present the idea, Juris." He waved his hand. She glanced around the table. "You know we're desperately short of paladins — " They nodded. "I have word from Marshal Calith down in Horngard that Fenith was killed a few months ago."

A stir ran around the table. Several of the Marshals glanced at the two paladins, who stared ahead and met no eyes. Fenith had been Amberion's close friend, and Saer was his great-niece.

"We need to select a large class of candidates, if we can: the paladins in residence here agree that they can each take on two candidates — "

"Is that necessary?" Juris broke in, looking from face to face.

"I think so." The Marshal-General spread a short parchment in front of her, and ran her hand down the page. "Juris, for the past two hundred years or so, the Fellowship of Gird has had from twenty to thirty paladins

559

recorded at a time. Those on quest vary from fifteen to twenty-five at any one time. We now have on quest only five — " She waited for the murmurs to cease, nodded, and went on. "You see? And here in Fin Panir we have only seven who can take on candidates for training. As you know, any of these may be called away at any time. If we can find fourteen candidates — two for each training paladin — it will still be well over a year before any of those are ready to go. And in the meantime, we have no one to train a back-up class — "

"I think we should feather that," said Marshal Kory. "If we chose seven now, then they might progress faster, having more of the paladins' time. In a half-year or so, choose more. Then we'd get a few out faster, and have more coming along."

The Marshal-General nodded. "That's a good idea — Amberion, what do you think?"

"I like that better than taking on two novices at once," said Amberion. "But I don't know if that will shorten the time any. Remember that each candidate has had, by tradition, all the time a single paladin-sponsor can give. We dare not test these candidates any less because times are desperate. It is in desperate times that we need most to be sure of them."

"What list do we have?" asked High Marshal Connaught.

"A short one." The Marshal-General rubbed her nose. "I sent word to all the granges last spring, when Fenith wrote that Aarenis would be at war by summer. We talked of this last year, remember? But we've lost eight paladins in the past year — "

"Eight!"

She nodded gravely. "Yes. We all know that great evil has been moving in Aarenis and the Westmounts. Nearer home, we have seen outbreaks again in eastern Tsaia. Some reports indicate serious trouble in Lyonya. Marshal Cedfer, of Brewersbridge, reported that a priest of Achrya had been laired between his grange and the gnome kingdom nearby. Apparently he had preyed on nearby farms and caravans using spellbound robbers."

"They'd say they were spellbound," muttered Juris.

"That may be, of course. I have only his report to go by. But Brewersbridge has been a healthy community for years — since Long Stones, at least. If Achrya can have a priest there, where else may we not expect trouble?"

"What happened to the paladins, Amberion?" asked Marshal Kory.

"We are still finishing the reports for the archives, Marshal," said Amberion slowly. "Chenin Hoka — he was from Horngard originally; he hadn't been north of the mountains for years — was killed by Liart's command, in Sibili, during the assault on that city — "

"I thought that's where Fenith was."

"He was there, yes. Chenin was taken some time earlier, while helping a grange near Pliuni defend itself; a witness thought he was dead. But Siniava's troops got him to Sibili, to the temple — and he was killed, finally, after long torments." Amberion said nothing more, and silence filled the room. Then he sighed, and began again. "I knew him, when I was a candidate; that was the last time he was north. He knocked me flat, I remember, and I lay there wondering why I'd ever wanted to be a paladin. Anyway. Doggal of Vérella was lost at sea; he was sailing east along the Immerhoft coast. He'd told a Girdsman at Sul that he had a call to come north. The ship was seen going onto reefs near Whiteskull, and his body was recovered some days later. We have no reason to doubt the identification. Garin Garrisson was killed in battle at Sibili; Fenith saw that. The two of them were holding light against a darkness cast by Liart's ranking priest. A crossbow bolt got him in the eye. Arianya Perrisdotter held a daskdraudigs away from a caravan in one of the mountain passes in the Dwarfwatch, but it fell on her in the end. Tekki Hakinier was apparently killed by a band of forest sprites — whatever they call them in Dzordanya. The only word we have is from a witness that says he was 'stuffed with pine needles like a pinpig,' which I suppose is what they call a hedgehog."

"No." Marshal Kory shook his head. "No, a pin-pig is bigger and lives in trees. They call it that because its flesh is sweet like pork. It sounds like those mikki-kekki — they come in waves, hundreds at a time. But what was he doing up there?"

Amberion shrugged. "I didn't know he was there until we got the word he'd been killed. The witness said something about a varkingla of the long houses of Stokki, whatever that means."

Kory nodded. "It means Stokki's clan thought they had to move somewhere, the whole bunch. That's not common. Tekki was Dzordanyan, wasn't he?"

"Yes."

"I would guess that they asked his protection, to move the clan through the forest, and the mikki-kekki didn't cooperate. They usually don't."

"Have you ever seen one?" asked the Marshal-General.

"Oh yes. When I was a rash boy, my three cousins and I sailed across the Honnorgat to visit Dzordanya. That was the plan, at least. My uncle had told us we couldn't sail across the river like that; of course we thought he was just trying to spoil our fun."

"Why can't you?" asked Saer, speaking for the first time.

"You're from the mountains, aren't you, Saer? Yes. Well, any time you sail across the river, you've got its current to consider, just like rowing. But at the mouth of the Honnorgat, it's that and the tide and the sea current, all together. The short of it is that we ended up a long way up the coast. We couldn't even see Prealith any more. The way the current set, we couldn't sail back without going far out to sea. We may have been rash, but we had more sense that that, to sail a skin boat out of all sight of land. We thought we'd walk back along the shore, carrying the boat, until we got to the Honnorgat."

"Carrying a boat?" Saer was clearly skeptical.

"Skin boat. Not as heavy as you'd think. Hard work, though, with the sail and lines and all. Anyway, the forest in Dzordanya comes right down to the sea — and I mean all the way. You can walk with one foot in the waves, and slam into limbs. With a boat, we had to weave in and out as we could. Not easy. Halory, my oldest cousin, thought we should climb onto level ground, back in the forest, and go that way. Seemed a good idea to me. I'd nearly had my eye poked out by too many twigs already, trying to watch my footing.

"For a time everything went well. Not too much undergrowth, just tall dark firs and spruce, spaced so we could make it between them with the boat. Then we heard the first voices."

"The sprites?"

"Mikki-kekki. Nasty whispers, that you couldn't quite identify. Squeaks, little cries like someone sitting on a hot tack. I started to feel my neck sweat, and so did the others. Halory tried to hurry us, and we fell right into one of their traps. A sort of cone-shaped pit, lined with pine needles, and slippery as grease. We'd hardly caught our breath when they were all around it, chittering at us. They're much less than dwarf-tall, with greenish fur all over, and very long arms with long-fingered hands. It was the boat that saved us. When they started with their darts, we got under it and shook."

"What do they use, bows?"

"No. A sort of tube. They blow into it, and the dart flies out. They throw them by hand, too. The darts are poisoned, usually. Inory, my middle cousin, was hit by one and though he lived he was sick for weeks. That night we thought he'd die. If it hadn't been for some clan's longhouse near-by — their sentries heard the mikki-kekki laughing and taunting us — I wouldn't be here. They drove them off, and pulled us out. It was two days before we got home, and my uncle — well, you can imagine." Kory shook his head.

"Well," said Amberion, "now we know about mikki-kekki. He went on with his list. "Sarin Inerith went into Kostandan, as you know, because we had word that Girdsmen were held in slavery there. Her head returned to Piery grange: we have no idea what happened, where, or how. Jori of Westbells finally died of the lungfever that's plagued him these four years. And Fenith, as you heard, died in Horngard."

"What of the current candidates? Don't we have any who will finish this year?" That was High Marshal Suriest, Knight-Marshal of the Order of the Cudgel.

"At best we may have five this year, Amberion tells me. Kosta has withdrawn his candidacy, and transferred to the Marshal Hall. Dort withdrew. Pelis may withdraw. And of course we don't know what will happen in the Trials. Because we had so few paladins here to train, we don't have any scheduled for the following year; we would have had Elis, but she had to leave, as you remember. She may be back, but not soon enough."

"Which leave us with the new list — what have we got?"

The Marshal-General shifted the papers in front of her, and glanced at another one. "We've talked over most of these before. Are you still opposed to the Verrakai squire, Amberion?"

He nodded. "Marshal-General, we cannot define the problem, but we would not be happy with him."

"Nor I," said High Marshal Connaught. "Look at the time we put in on Pelo Verrakai, and what came of that!"

"Well, then, as I see it we've got five good candidates. Four in the knight's classes, and Seddith, the Marshal we spoke of last time."

"And we need seven."

"And we need as many as we can find," said the Marshal-General. "Now —"

"I know what you're leading up to," interrupted Juris. "You want to include that new yeoman."

"What!" High Marshal Suriest turned his head; Connaught snorted. The Marshal-General held up her hand, and they all quieted.

"Juris, you could have let me say it — but yes, I do. Before you say anything, consider. She's a veteran of the Aarenis wars —"

"That's a recommendation?" But Kory subsided when the Marshal-General looked at him.

"We had a report from Fenith about her; he thought she should be considered a possibility if she ever joined the Fellowship. Marshal or paladin, he said. Cedfer reports that she freed the elfane taig, in the mountains southeast of Brewersbridge. He checked that report with full elves — and so have I, here. Also she cleared out that nest of robbers, and was able to fight the Achyran priest alongside Cedfer's yeoman-marshal. As far as weapons-skills, she heads the list. Since she's been here, Chanis reports that she has worked hard on everything we've thrown at her. She's even shown skill in teaching; Cedfer reported that from Brewersbridge, and I've seen how the other students follow her here."

"It's too soon, Marshal-General," said Juris, and several other heads nodded. "I grant she may be what you say, but what do we know of her as a Girdsman? Nothing. She's not even a member of the Fellowship yet. How can you think of giving this honor to an outsider?"

"But she won't be an outsider after she takes her vows," said the Marshal-General.

"No, but —" Juris squirmed in his seat. "I know we need candidates. But we need the best candidates. We need to be sure they're strong Girdsmen first, and then —"

"Watch them get spitted by better fighters?" The Marshal-General's voice sharpened. "Right now this outsider, as you call her, can outfight most of the Marshals here, unless they use their powers. I've seen her — Amberion has seen her — ask Cieri."

"Why isn't he here?" asked Juris.

"He will be — he had a problem." The Marshal-General folded her hands on the table. "Juris, I know it's not usual. But we haven't found anything wrong with her. Gird knows we've tested, prodded, tried — Cieri had to set her up for days to make her lose her temper even once. And then she agreed she was wrong. Of course she's not perfect — no one is. Of course

563

we wish she'd been Girdish all along, come up through the grange training. But allowing for that, she's the best candidate on the list. And if anything is amiss, it will come out in the stress of training, or in the trials. It's not that we're choosing her over someone else — we haven't *got* anyone else."

Juris shook his head. "Arianya, you're wrong — and I don't think I can convince you. Suppose she is a potential paladin, that Gird will approve and call. But right now what she is, is a good soldier and a novice Girdsman. I don't care if she knows all the answers, can recite the Ten Fingers backwards and forwards: she hasn't experienced a grange. If she's so good, send her to me — or to another grange — for a half-year. Let's see how she does as a yeoman among yeomen. We've had unpleasant surprises before."

"Gird's gut, may the ale hold out! If I had a half-year, Juris, I'd send her. But we don't have it."

The argument went on some time, but the shortage of paladins won over caution. "We must have the candidates," said the Marshal-General finally. "We must. She will be with the others here, under our protection. Unless you can suggest a better, Juris, I must insist — "

"All right." He frowned, sucking his cheeks, but finally nodded. "All right, then. But be sure you do ward her, Marshal-General. Don't rush that one through the training. She's not a knight yet, remember, and she's never had that sort of training."

Paks, called to the Marshal-General's office, knew nothing of the argument. She expected to be told more details of the ceremony that would make her a Girdsman. She found the Marshal-General, the Knights-Marshal of both orders, and a stranger waiting for her.

"Paksenarrion, there are High Marshal Connaught, High Marshal Suriest, and Sir Amberion, a paladin of Gird presently attached to the Training Order. Please sit here."

Paks sat where she was told, her heart pounding. What now? Was she suspected of something so bad that it would take two High Marshals and a paladin to deal with it?

"You have not changed your mind about joining the Fellowship?" asked the Marshal-General.

"No, Marshal-General."

"You are ready to accept Gird as your patron, as you now accept the High Lord's dominion?"

"Yes, Marshal-General."

"Do you feel any particular — um — call, such as we have talked about in the past days?"

Paks frowned. "Marshal-General, I have felt something, something I could not define, for some time. It began in Aarenis, when I was still in Duke Phelan's Company. I felt the need for a different kind of fighting — but I'm not good with words, Marshal-General. I don't know how to say what I feel, but that here it seems right. I feel that it's right for me to join the Fellowship of Gird; I feel that here I will find the right way to be the fighter I always wanted to be."

"You told Marshal Cedfer in Brewersbridge that you didn't want to fight for gold alone — you wanted to fight against 'bad things.' Is that still true?"

Paks nodded. "Yes, Marshal-General."

"Paksenarrion, I have talked to Marshal Chanis and Marshal Cieri about your progress, and with these High Marshals and Sir Amberion about that and your past. They needed to hear what you have said from your own mouth." She looked at the others. "Well?"

One by one they nodded. Paks watched their faces, confused. What could she have said that was wrong? The Marshal-General tapped her fingers on her desk. Paks looked back to her.

"Paksenarrion, you must know — there's no way you couldn't know — that you are one of the best young fighters in the training company. Cedfer was right to send you. You can qualify easily for either of the knightly orders, if that's what you want." She paused, and Paks held her breath. The Marshal-General resumed. "Or — there is another possibility. Ordinarily I would not make this offer to someone who is not yet a Girdsman — in fact, ordinarily it comes only to those of proven service to Gird. But from the reports I've received, Gird has accepted as service several of your deeds in the past. The Training Council has agreed to it. So — would you accept an appointment as a paladin candidate?"

Paks felt her mouth open. She could not speak or move for an instant of incredulous joy. She saw amusement on their faces, felt her ears flaming again. "Me?" she finally squeaked, in a voice very unlike her own. She swallowed and tried again. "You mean — me? A — a paladin candidate?"

"You," said the Marshal-General, now smiling. "Now — this is not an order; if you don't feel you can say yes, then refuse. We will not hold it against you — indeed, there are those who think you need more experience."

"But — but I'm so young!" Paks could feel the tears stinging her eyes. Her heart was moving again, bounding, and she felt she could float out of her chair. "I — "

"You are young, yes; and you will be a novice yeoman, which is worse. But if we didn't think you could be a paladin, Paksenarrion, we would not suggest this." The Marshal-General turned to Amberion. "Sir Amberion, you might just tell her what the training is like, while she considers this."

Paks turned to the paladin, a tall, dark-haired man somewhat younger than the Marshal-General by his looks. His open smile was infectious. "Paksenarrion, paladin-candidates receive training simultaneously as knights and as Gird's warriors. Each candidate is attached to one of the knightly orders, but spends much of his or her time with a paladin sponsor. The training is lengthy and intensive; the candidate must be tested in many ways, for any weakness could open a passage for evil. And even then, the candidate may fail, for the final Trials require proof that the gods have bestowed on the new paladin those powers which paladins must have. Of the few who begin this training, more than half never become paladins."

"It means, as well," said the Marshal-General, "giving up all thought of an independent life. Paladins are sworn to Gird's service; they own nothing but their own gear, and must go wherever Gird commands, on whatever quest Gird requires. For many, these restrictions are too onerous; even we Marshals have more freedom. So we do not expect that all to whom we offer candidacy will take it — or complete the training — and we respect those who withdraw no less than those who go on."

Paks tried to control her excitement, but she could not think of anything but her oldest dreams. Paladin. It meant shining armor, and magic swords, and marvelous horses that appeared from nowhere on the day of the Trials. It meant old songs of great battles, bright pictures in her mind like that of the paladin under the walls of Sibili, all brightness and grace and courage. Another picture moved in her mind, herself on a shining horse, riding up the lane from Three Firs to her father's farm, with children laughing and cheering alongside. Her mother smiled and wept; her brothers gaped; her father, astonished, finally admitted he had been wrong, and asked her pardon. She blinked at that unlikely vision, and returned to hear the Marshal-General saying something about opportunities to change her mind later. But her mind would never change, she vowed. When the Marshal-General paused, she spoke.

"I am honored, Marshal-General; please let me try."

The others looked at each other, then back to her.

"You are sure, Paksenarrion?"

"Yes, Marshal-General — if you are. I can't believe it — " She fought back a delighted laugh, and saw by their faces that they knew it. "Me — a sheepfarmer's daughter — a paladin-candidate!"

Now they laughed, gently. "Paksenarrion," said the Marshal-General, "we are pleased that you accept the challenge. Now let me explain why we are taking a chance on hurrying you." Quickly she outlined the situation: the shortage of paladins, the growing assaults of evil power in several areas. "You see, we must replenish the ranks — as fast as we can — or risk having no paladins to train new ones."

"How long does the training take?" asked Paks.

"It depends in part on the candidate's previous status. For you, it means becoming a knight first, and then a paladin — more than a year, likely two years. It means some isolation — paladin candidates withdraw from the main training order, sometimes for months at a time, for meditation and individual instruction. Not all the candidates progress at the same rate. Do not be surprised if someone finishes before or after you who begins the same night."

"We will be taking the vows of the new candidates the same night you become a Girdsman," said the Marshal-General. "This is unusual — as I said — but I feel that it is even more important for your vows to be public. Then — if anything happens — " But Paks was determined that nothing

566

would happen — everthing would go well. At that moment, she would have done anything they asked, for the sheer joy of having a chance to prove herself a worthy paladin-candidate.

She hardly felt the stairs under her feet as she went down. As she came through the arch to head for her quarters, she nearly ran into Argalt. She had spent a couple of evenings with him and his friends at a nearby tavern. He grinned at her.

"Well — so you haven't been sent away, eh?"

"No." Paks felt like bouncing up and down. She wasn't sure if she should tell him; they had said nothing about keeping her selection secret.

"It must be good news. How about sharing a pitcher later?"

"I can't." Paks couldn't contain it any longer. "I have so much to do — you won't believe it, Argalt!"

"What — did they select you for paladin-candidate, now you're joining the Fellowship?"

Paks felt her jaw drop. "Did you know?"

He laughed. "No — but it's what I would do. Well, now, sheepfarmer's daughter, I'm glad for you. And you so stiff when you came — remember what I said?"

"Yes — yes, I do." Paks threw back her head in glee. "I have to go — I have things — "

"To do, yes. I heard. I'll be watching you, now. You'd better show us something."

Paks had never imagined Midwinter Feast in Fin Panir. Back home, it had meant a huge roast of mutton, sweet cakes, and the elders telling tales around the fire. In the Duke's Company, plenty of food and drink, speeches from the captains and the Duke, and a day of games and music. Here, the outer court erupted at first light with all the juniors starting a snow battle. Paks took one look at the fortifications, and decided that they must have stayed out half the night building them. When the Training Master came out to quell the riot, he was captured, rolled in the snow, and rescued only when Paks led the seniors in an assault on the largest snow-fort. But by then he had agreed (as, she found later, was the custom) that the juniors had the right to demand toll of everyone — of any rank — crossing the court. Those who refused to pay were pelted with snowballs; some were even caught and held for ransom. The day was clear, after several days of snow, and no one could possibly sneak across the yard undetected.

The feasting started with breakfast. In place of porridge and cold meat, the cooks offered sweet cakes dipped in honey, gingerbread squares, hot sausages wrapped in dough and fried, and "fried snow," a lacy-looking confection Paks had never seen. All day long the tables were heaped with food, replenished as it was eaten. And all day long the feasters came and went, from one wild winter game to another.

Paks had been told that she was free until midafternoon. With that, she joined a group that rode bareback out onto the snowy practice fields, where they jousted with blunt poles until only one remained mounted. Paks lost her pole early, but managed to stay on the black horse for most of the game, winning her bouts by clever dodges, and a quick straight-arm. She did not recognize the woman who finally shoved her off into a snowdrift; she floundered there, laughing so hard she could not work her way out for several minutes. After this, they tried to ride in a long line, all holding hands and guiding the horses with their legs. Soon they were all in the snow again, and after another few tricks they came back for more food.

Now the tables held roasts and breads as well as sweets. Paks piled her plate with roast pork and mutton, a half-loaf of bread yellow with eggs. Four juniors staggered in, their faces bright red with cold. Behind them came the dwarves she had met, eyes gleaming. They saw her, waved, and came to sit across from her.

"Is it that you have recovered, Paksenarrion Dorthansdotter of Three Firs?" asked Balkis.

"Yes, indeed," said Paks. "But the surgeons didn't want me fighting until after today."

"Ah, we have heard that you make adoption into the Fellowship," said Balkis, stuffing a leg of chicken into his mouth. "This will make it that you are blood-bound to the others, is it not?"

Before Paks could answer, the woman who had dumped her in the snow slipped into a chair beside her, and answered the dwarves. "No — it is not that, rockbrothers. Ask not the child of the father's business." To Paks's surprise, both dwarves blushed. She looked at the woman in surprise.

"You're the one who — "

"Yes." The woman grinned as she took a sweet cake from a tray. "I'm the one who dumped you. I'm Cami, by the way — that's what everyone calls me, but my real name is Rahel, if you need it." She said something in dwarvish to the dwarves; Balkis looked startled, but the darker dwarf burst into laughter. Paks eyed her. Cami (or Rahel) was small and dark, a quick-moving woman who reminded Paks a little of Canna.

"Why are you called Cami if your name is Rahel?" asked Paks.

"Oh that. Well, it started when I came here. They used to tease me that I should have been Camwyn's paladin instead of Gird's — "

"You're a paladin?" Paks had not thought of any paladin being so light-hearted; Cami seemed almost frivolous.

"Yes." Cami stuffed the rest of the cake into her mouth, and then spoke through it. "It was what I did when I was young and wild. I won't tell you; you don't need ideas like that. But they started calling me Camwynya, only that was too long, and then Cami. You're a candidate, right?"

"After tonight," said Paks.

"I thought so. It's good that you know these rockbrothers already — "

"I don't, really — " began Paks, but Cami shushed her.

"Better than many do, I can tell. Balkis Baltisson, I will speak no more

568

dwarvish, for this lady knows it not, but it is not the blood-bond of brethren that she joins this night."

"Not? How so? It is the Fellowship of Gird."

"Yes. The Fellowship is the blood-bond of Gird with each yeoman, sir dwarf; not each with the other."

"But it is that brother of brother is brother," insisted the dwarf. "It is that makes the clan-bond, the blood-bond."

"It is that for dwarves," said Cami. "For man it is other. The bond is like that of the Axemaster for each member of the clan, not between members."

"It is not possible to have one without the other," said Balkis, his eyes flashing. "If the Axemaster accepts adoption from any outlander, the outlander is blood-bound to the clan. All of it."

Cami shot Paks a quick look. "Paks, no one has ever convinced dwarves of this — and I won't — but I'll keep trying." But now the second dwarf spoke for the first time.

"Lady Cami, you know me, Balkon son of Tekis son of Kadas, mother-son of Fedrin Harasdotter, sister-son he of the Goldenaxe, but to this lady I have not spoken in my own name." His voice was higher than Paks expected when speaking Common, midrange for a man, but much higher than Balkis's.

Cami nodded politely, and Paks copied her, wondering if she should state her own name again.

"You say this lady is to be paladin as you are?"

"Yes," said Cami, with another quick look to Paks.

"Last time we saw Paksenarrion Dorthansdotter, she had hurt of an axe, and no healing of Marshal. That I thought was disgrace, or punishment. To be candidate must be honor, is it not? Why this then?"

Now it was Paks's turn to blush. She did not know how much Cami knew of the whole situation. But someone had to explain.

"Sir — sir dwarf," she began, copying Cami's style of address, "I said then it was not unfairness of the Marshal — "

"But we thought it so. It might be you did not know, being nedross." At that word, Cami choked on her food, and shook a finger at the dwarves. Paks, confused, waited for a moment, then went on.

"It was not unfairness. I told you they thought I had taken value from them in training, and had not returned value." Now they nodded, and she hurried on. "So they said if I wished to stay I must make a commitment; I was willing to make it, even if they did not let me stay, for the truth I felt of it."

"Truth." Balkon looked at her sharply. "It is that you have that power to see truth itself?"

"She might," interrupted Cami. "And not even know it. Nedross, indeed!"

"What is that?" asked Paks.

"I hope," said Cami severely, "that they're using it in the gnome sense, unwilling or unable to see insult, and not in the dwarf sense of cowardly."

Both dwarves burst into speech, protesting.

"It is not that we — "

"That is not what we — "

Balkon shushed his friend, and continued. "Lady Cami, Lady Paksenarrion, we did not think that this lady, this lady who would use an axe, would be cowardly. No — only that it is not always the same for man and dwarf when words be said, that some should be taken and others not. If it is that we make mistakes, and think someone unfair to this fine lady, who would use an axe, Sertig's first tool, then we ask pardon of the lady, but we are glad to see that she has honor now in this house, and is blood-bound to a clan we honor."

Paks was thoroughly confused. Cami turned to her with an exaggerated sigh. "I'd advise you to accept their good wishes, and apologies, and be glad you have found dwarven friends. They truly did not mean to say you were cowardly."

Paks smiled at them. "Sirs, I know not your words, but I thank you for your good wishes."

They both grinned back. "That is very good," said Balkon. "And if you wish to learn, we still will teach you what we know of axes."

Paks nodded. "If I am permitted, in my training, I will ask it of you."

"Paks!" Aris Marrakai had come up behind her, with several of his friends. He shuffled from one foot to another when she turned. "I — I brought you something."

"Aris — you shouldn't have — " Paks took from his hand a carefully worked leather pouch, fringed and decorated with tiny shells. "It must have cost — "

He shrugged. "Not that much. And anyway, Rufen told me that paladins never have any money and can't buy things, and so I thought maybe you'd keep it and — and remember us."

"I'd remember you anyway, Aris," said Paks. "But thank you — I will treasure this." She knew already what would go in it: Saben's little red stone horse, and Canna's medallion. Aris darted away; Paks met Cami's eyes.

"It isn't quite that bad," said Cami. "We don't get rich, but we can buy a fruit pie occasionally."

"That's good," said Paks. "I like mushrooms, myself."

"Then pray you aren't assigned to the granges west of here for your grange duty," said Cami, laughing. "Dry and high — not a mushroom for days and days."

"When do we have grange duty?" asked Paks.

"Just before the Trials," said Cami. "You may find it strange; you've never been in a normal grange, have you? No — then it's even more important for you. We all must know what limits Marshals face, and granges, and not think because we are gifted with powers that it's so easy for others."

"Cami!" The hall was filling now, as more and more cold revellers came in for warmth and food. Paks was startled to see the Training Master grab

Cami by both shoulders and hug her. "Gird's right arm, I thought you were still in achael!"

"Through Midwinter Feast? Master Chanis, even the High Lord wouldn't keep me in achael through the best day in the year!"

"I suppose not. Are you out, or just on leave?"

"Out. Gird's grace for it, too; if I had missed Midwinter's Feast, and the installation, I'd have burst something."

"And are you fit to sing, Cami?" asked Sir Amberion, who had followed the Training Master into the hall. Cami looked at Paks.

"Ask Paksenarrion — I only dumped her a couple of times this morning."

Paks could not help grinning. "Only once — "

"Ah, but who stuck her foot in your black's ribs, in the line, to make him crowhop? And you flew off then, too."

"Was that you?" Paks joined the roar of laughter.

"It was," said Cami, "and I could do it again. Fit to sing? By the dragonstongue, I could sing and blow the lo-pipe at the same time." Again laughter, and Paks saw someone scurry away, yelling that a lo-pipe was coming up. But as she watched Cami move a tray out of her way and settle onto the table, the Training Master touched her shoulder, and beckoned. Paks followed him away from the hall.

The rest of the day she spent in preparation for the night's ceremonies. She had to change into the plain gray of the training company, but the steward handed her, as well, the white surcoat of a paladin-candidate. She would have to change hurriedly between ceremonies. Paks had lines to learn, and, like the Finthan youngsters who were making their final vows that night, she spent some time in the High Lord's Hall in meditation. When spectators began arriving, the group was led away to a small bare room off one end. Paks felt her stomach tightening. Her mouth was dry. The others in this room were not the paladin candidates, but junior yeomen making their vows as senior yeomen — the honor of taking these vows at Midwinter Feast in the High Hall came to those whose grange Marshals had recommended them. Most were about the age Paks had been when she left home — eighteen or nineteen winters. They eyed her as nervously as she watched them.

The summons came with an ear-shattering blast of trumpets, as High Marshals Connaught and Suriest opened the door and called them out. The High Lord's Hall was brilliantly lit by hundreds of candles. The spectators sat and stood on either side of the wide central aisle. With the others, Paks stood just below the platform. The trumpet music ended, followed by an interlude of harps. Then another trumpet fanfare introduced the Marshal-General, resplendent in a white surcoat over her armor, with Gird's crescent embroidered in silver on the breast. Following her were the other High Marshals presently at Fin Panir, all in Gird's blue and white. Behind them came those visitors who would be honored during the ceremonies:

two Marshals of Falk, in long robes of ruby-red, with gold-decorated helms set in the crooks of their arms. A Swordmaster of Tir, in black and silver; Paks remembered the device on his arms from Aarenis. Last of all came the seven paladins resident and whole of limb in Fin Panir, each in full armor, carrying Gird's pennant.

Paks watched them come up the aisle, her heart pounding with excitement and joy. This was exactly what she had thought about in Three Firs — the music, the brilliant colors — she tried to take a long breath and calm down. She recognized Sir Amberion and Lady Cami, but none of the other paladins. They mounted the platform behind her, and she heard the footsteps move away to its far side. Then the trumpets were still, and the Marshal-General's clear voice called out the ancient greeting:

"In darkness, in cold, in the midst of winter
where nothing walks the world but death and fear
let the brave rejoice: I call the light."

"I call the light!" came the response from every voice. It seemed to shake the air.

"Out of darkness, light.
Out of silence, song.
Out of the sun's death, the birth of each year." Paks half-listened, knowing the words better than any other she'd heard from the Marshal-General. Just so had her grandfather said them, when she was small, and just so her father had said them, the last Midwinter Feast she was at home.

"Out of cold, fire.
Out of death, life.
Out of fear, courage to see the day." With the others, she gave the response. And together they all completed the ritual, raising first one hand then the other, and finally both, to defy sundeath and greet the sun.

"In darker night, brighter stars.
In greater fear, greater courage.
In the midst of winter, the world's birth.
Praise to the High Lord." This would be repeated between every segment of the ceremonies, until sunrise the next dawn. Paks remembered falling asleep, year after year — and the first year that she had managed to stay awake, the last year of her grandfather's life, to light the first morning fire with new wood. For with sundown, all fires were destroyed — to show respect, her grandfather had said, and to prove their courage to endure. Here, too, the fires went out when the sun fell, to be kindled at daybreak. Only those desperately ill were allowed a fire on Midwinter Night.

"Yeomen of Gird," said the High Marshal then, and Paks pulled her mind back to the ceremony. "We have with us those who seek to join the Fellowship of Gird; by our ancient customs we will test them in their steadfastness, and you will witness their vows."

"By Gird's grace," came the response. Paks felt her neck prickle. She was suddenly cold, and wanted to rub her arms.

"Stand forth, you who would swear fealty to the Fellowship of Gird," said

572

the Marshal-General. With those on her side of the aisle, Paks faced toward the center of the Hall. One at a time they would mount those steps and face a Marshal for the ritual exchange of blows. Paks suspected that in her case it might be something more than a ritual. Her leg itched; she resisted the urge to rub it on her other leg.

Before she had time to worry, she heard her name. All at once she felt eager, and went up the steps quickly. To the questions she made response firmly: she acknowledged Gird as the High Lord's servant, the patron of fighters, the protector of the helpless. She swore to keep the Code of Gird, and obey "all Marshals and lawful authority over you." And then the questioner stepped back, and she faced the Marshal-General, who held out two identical staves.

Paks took one, with an internal prayer that she wouldn't look too foolish. The Marshal-General smiled, feinted, and aimed a smashing blow at her. Paks rolled aside, countering as best she could. The power of the Marshal-General's blows carried all the way up her arms. Ritual exchange of blows indeed, thought Paks. The staves rattled. She took a blow on the thigh, and managed to touch the Marshal-General's arm with a leftover move that carried little sting. Then her staff seemed to twitch in her hands and go flying through the air; the Marshal-General's staff tapped her head firmly before she could dodge. And the Marshal-General stepped back, bowed, and greeted her.

"Welcome, yeoman of Gird, to Gird's grange." As she spoke, she placed a Gird's medallion over Paks's head.

Paks bowed as she had been instructed. "I am honored, Marshal-General, to be accepted in Gird's Fellowship." Then, dismissed, she left the platform and moved to a space behind it, where the Training Master waited to help her on with the candidate's surcoat and her new Gird's medallion.

The paladin candidates were presented just before dawn, after ceremonies honoring Marshals and paladins killed in the past year. It seemed to Paks a very plain affair: the candidates were simply named and shown to the spectators, and assigned to one of the knightly orders and a sponsoring paladin. After the events of the day before, Paks had hoped to get Cami as her sponsor, but instead Amberion led her before the crowd. Cami was sponsoring a yeoman-marshal from somewhere in the Westmounts, she heard later. Paks knew none of the candidates well, and only four of them at all; the others had been sent from distant granges after earlier selection.

She had one more day of freedom — for the second day of Midwinter Feast was as lively as the first — and fell into bed that night completely exhausted and as happy as she could ever remember being.

Chapter Twenty-three

Paks's first experience as a paladin candidate was a familiar one — moving into new quarters. These were south of the main complex, in an annex to the Paladin's Hall. She was surprised to find that she would still have a room to herself, but Amberion explained.

"You will spend time in solitary exercises; you will need the privacy. Later, you will learn the skills of meditation even when surrounded by noise and upheaval, but for novices it's easier to learn in solitude."

Paks nodded silently. She was still shy of her paladin sponsor; it was hard to believe that he and Cami were in the same order. He seemed more sombre, far less approachable. She unpacked her things quickly, wondering a little at the requirement that her sponsor must see everything she owned. But for that, too, he had a reason. Paladins must be willing to go anywhere, anytime — able to endure hardship, not just discipline. Those who clung to treasured possessions, favorite foods, even friends, might make fine Marshals or knights, but not paladins. So in the early days of training, they must do without accustomed possessions. Those who withdrew would have theirs restored, but those continuing had to face the possible loss of items deemed too luxurious. Paks understood the reasoning, but could not imagine anyone preferring fancy clothes or jewelry to being a paladin. She said so, and Amberion grinned at her.

"I've seen it myself. And there is always something hard to give up. If not material things, habits and ways of thought. This may be a trivial test for you, but there are others. No one passes through this training without struggle." He looked over her gear as he spoke, and told her to keep Saben's red horse and Canna's medallion. Aris's gift, her weapons, the shining mail the elfane taig had given her — all these went into storage. Then he said, "What about money? Do you have any gold or silver?"

Paks handed over the heavy leather sack she'd brought from Brewersbridge. "This, and some on account with the Guild in Tsaia."

His eyebrows went up. "Did Marshal Cedfer know how much gold you had?"

"I don't know." Paks thought back to Brewersbridge, already distant to her mind. "I told him the elfane taig had gifted me; he saw the jewel I gave the grange, and knew I had money for food, lodging, and clothes."

Amberion frowned, and Paks wondered what she'd done wrong. "Did you know that most orders of knights charge a fee for their training, which is waived for poor applicants?" he asked. Paks shook her head. She had assumed that the training company was maintained by the Fellowship of Gird, through contributions from the granges. "Perhaps Cedfer expected you'd become a Girdsman, as you have, and didn't bother to mention it," Amberion went on. "As a paladin, you may not hold wealth. We are bound to keep this for you, and restore it if you fail, but if you *are* called as a paladin . . . well . . . "

"You mean I owe the Training College?" asked Paks.

"Not precisely owe. Cedfer sponsored you here, at first, and you accepted this chance freely, as a gift. It would be ill grace on our part to ask alms of you now. On the other hand, while we would ask nothing of a farmer's daughter who had nothing, we would ordinarily ask a fee of someone who could pay. And that gold, that fee, would not be returned, whatever happened." He shifted the bag from hand to hand. "What had you planned with this?"

"Well — " Paks had trouble remembering the clutter of plans and dreams with which she'd ridden from Brewersbridge. "I had sent money to my family, to repay my dowry, but I'd planned to send more if I became a knight, for then I could always earn my own way. And I'd thought of a new saddle for Socks — my black horse."

He nodded slowly. "You thought of warriors' needs ahead, and your family. Are they poor, Paksenarrion?"

"Not really poor, like some I've seen. We had food enough, if not too much; we always had clothes and fire in winter. But there's no money, most times. It took me years to save up the copper bits I left home with. And all the other children to be raised and wed — " Paks shook her head suddenly. "But now I'm here — and if I'm a paladin, I won't need a saddle, will I? Someone else will take Socks. And I won't be looking for work. Tell me what the fee is, sir, and I can send the rest to them and be done with it."

Amberion smiled at her with real warmth. "You choose well. Would you agree to give this bagful to the Fellowship, and send whatever is on account to your family?"

"There's more on account," said Paks.

"No matter. We are not here to fatten ourselves at the expense of farmers. Now — what's this — ?" He pushed at the little bundle of scuffed and tattered old scrolls left in her saddlebags. "I thought you weren't a scholar."

"I don't know," said Paks. "I found them in my things after the elfane taig. I was going to ask Ambros about them, but that's when the caravan was attacked, and after that I forgot. I couldn't read them then — maybe now — " She started to unroll one of them; the parchment crackled.

"Here — wait — " Amberion took it from her. "These are old, Paksenarrion — we must be careful with them, or they'll go to pieces." He peered at the faded script. "Gird's arm, I can't — what do you think that is?" He pushed it back to Paks, who leaned close.

"I'm not sure. 'For on this day — something — Gird came to this village where was the — the — ' is that word knight?"

"I think so," said Amberion. "I think it's 'knight of the prince's cohort, and there they — ' something where that's rubbed out, and then 'and as he said to me, that he did, and called the High Lord's blessing on it' — " Amberion looked up at her for a moment. "Where did you say you found these?"

"I didn't find them, exactly," said Paks. "After the fight underground, the elfane taig got me back to the surface — somehow — and then had me pack up a whole load of things. I was too sick to notice much, but the elfane taig insisted. A day or so later, when I looked through the packs, the scrolls were there. I tried to read them, but — " Paks flushed. "I didn't read that well — and the script is odd."

"Yes — it is." Amberion seemed abstracted. "Paks — this has nothing to do with your training, but I believe these scrolls may be valuable. They're old — very old — and I've read something like this in the archives. Would you let the Archivist see them?"

"Of course," said Paks. "I'd be glad to know what they are and why the elfane taig gave them. I almost threw them away, but — "

"I'm glad you didn't," said Amberion. "If they're really an old copy of Luap's writings — "

"Luap? Is that Gird's friend?"

"Yes. Most of what we know about Gird comes from the Chronicles of Luap. This — " he nodded toward the scroll he held, "seems to be part of that — it's talking, I think, about the battle at Seameadow." He put the scroll down and looked around the room. "That's all, then? Good. Now about your horse — what do you call him?"

Paks felt herself blushing again. "Socks," she mumbled. She had had enough comments to know that it should have been something grander. But Amberion did not laugh.

"Better, to my mind, than some long name you can't shout at need. You know that if you pass the trials you'll have a mount?" She nodded. She had heard more than once of the paladins' mounts that appeared after their Trials, waiting fully equipped in the courtyard outside the High Lord's Hall. No one knew whence they came; no one saw them come. "But in the meantime you can use Socks for training. Doggal says he's good enough. In fact, the Training Order would take him when you pass the trials, unless you want to sell him elsewhere."

"Yes, sir."

"Take the things you won't need back to the steward, and then come back here; you'll meet the other paladins and candidates."

For some days after that, Paks heard nothing more about the scrolls. Her schedule kept her too busy to ask. It was unlike any training she'd had before. Instead of weapons drill or military theory, she found herself immersed in history and geography: which men had come to which area, and when, and why. She learned of their laws and their beliefs; she had to memorize article after article of the Code of Gird. Gradually she built in her mind a picture of the whole land about, and the beliefs of the people. She could see, as in a drawing, her father's family perched on the side of a moor north of most trade routes. They had believed in the High Lord, and the Lady of Peace, but also in the horse nomad deity Guthlac, and the Windsteed. Their boundary stones, and the rituals for keeping them, came from Aarenis; the well-sprite for whom she had plucked flowers every spring was called the same — Piri — from Brewersbridge to Three Firs, and south to Valdaire. But in Aarenis proper, the well-spirits were multiple, and called *caoulin*: they had no personal names.

She learned that elves claimed no lands: the elvenhome kingdoms cannot be reached by unguided humans anyway. In Lyonya, where elves and humans ruled together a mortal kingdom, human land-rights were held provisionally, and any change of use had to be approved by the crown. Dwarves claimed daskgeft, a stonemass, but cared little who traveled the surface. Gnomes held all property by intricate law, and to step one footlength on gnomish land without legal right could bring the whole kingdom down on the criminal. Even in human lands, the laws of property differed. In Tsaia, where land was granted by the crown in return for military service, those who actually farmed rarely owned the land they worked — but in Fintha nearly all farms were owned by the farmer.

High Marshal Garris taught them the lore of the gods — all that was known of the great powers of good and evil. Paks learned that Achrya, the Webmistress, had not been known in Aare — proof, according to Marshal Garris, that Achrya was a minor god, for the great gods had power everywhere in the known world. Liart, on the other hand, had been known in old Aare, but not to the northern nomads or the Seafolk until they met the men from Aarenis. She learned that her fear of the Kuakkgani came from mistaking them for kuaknom, a race related to elves but devoted to evil; the Kuakkgani, Garris insisted, were never wholly evil, and often good. Of the greatest evils, Marshal Garris taught only their names and general attacks: Nayda, the Unnamer, who threatened forgetfulness, and Gitres, the Unmaker.

"They are one in destruction," he said firmly. "They try to enforce despair, and convince you that nothing matters, for they will wipe out all. Never believe it. The elves call them A-Iynisi, the Unsinger who unravels the Song of the Singer, but they know as well as we that the Singer lives, and living must create."

"But are they really one, or two?" asked Harbin, the yeoman-marshal sponsored by Cami.

High Marshal Garris shrugged. "No man knows, Harbin; no man needs to know. I think — but it is only my thought — that it is only one, but one who appears in the guise you most fear. One fears the loss of fame, of being unknown and forgotten, and another fears having all his works unmade. All mortals have some form of this fear, and in search of immortality among men may do great evil without intention. It is hard to trust that the High Lord's court will remember and reward a good life, hard to risk fame or lifework when those are at stake."

Along with this, all the candidates were encouraged to learn languages.

Paks had already found, in her travels, that she was quick to pick up new phrases. Since she had made friends among the elves and dwarves in Fin Panir, Amberion urged her to spend her evenings with them, speaking elven and dwarvish in turn. At first this went quickly: she could ask for food and drink, and greet her friends politely, after only a few lessons. But the more she wanted to say, the harder it got. A simple question, like "where are you from?" would bring on a flurry of discussion. Paks found the dwarves more willing to explain than the elves, but she could not follow their explanations.

"It is simple," said Balkon one night, the third time of trying to explain dwarf clan rankings. "Let us begin with the Goldenaxe." They had begun with the Goldenaxe before, but Paks nodded. "The Goldenaxe has two sons and a daughter."

"Yes, but — " Paks knew that something difficult was coming.

"Wait. The Goldenaxe that was, before this, had a sister who had a son, and so this Goldenaxe is the sister-son of the Goldenaxe that was."

"His nephew?" ventured Paks.

Balkon scowled. "No — not. In Common that is son of either brother or sister, yes? And this is only for sister-son. Brother-son is mother's clan."

Paks started to ask why, and thought better of it.

"Now — this Goldenaxe has no sister, only brother, and brother has no sons. But a daughter. It is clear?"

Paks nodded. She still had a thread to follow. The current Goldenaxe had a brother, with a daughter, and two sons and a daughter of his own.

"So will inherit to the title either the son of his brother's daughter, or his oldest son, or the son of his daughter."

"But why not just his son?" asked Paks.

"Because that is not his blood," said Balkon. "His son's son is not his clan, you see that — only his daughter's son — "

"Then why not his daughter?" asked Paks again.

"What? She be the Goldenaxe? No — that would rive the rock indeed. No dwarfmaid wields coldmetal — "

"They don't fight?"

"I did not say that. They wield not the coldmetal, the weaponsteel, once it is forged. You, lady, would not stand long against a dwarven warrior-maid in her own hall."

Paks went back to asking the names of common objects after that. With elves the trouble was different but equally impenetrable. Some questions were simply ignored, others answered in a spate of elven that drowned her mind in lovely sound. Ardhiel gladly taught her songs, and encouraged her to learn the elaborate elven courtesies, but as for learning more about elves themselves, it was "Lady, the trees learn water by drinking rain, and stars learn night by shining." Paks found individual words easy to speak and remember, but her best efforts at stringing them together sounded nothing like Ardhiel's speech, though he praised her.

She had also much to learn of paladins, as did the other candidates. Most of them had thought, like Paks, that being Gird's holy warrior meant gaining vast arcane powers — they would be nearly invincible against any foe. Their paladin sponsors quickly set them straight. Although paladins must be skilled at fighting, that, their sponsors insisted, was the least of their abilities. A quest might involve no fighting at all, or a battle against beings no steel could pierce.

"Paladins show that courage is possible," Cami said to them one day. "It is easy enough to find reasons to give in to evil. War is ugly, as Paks knows well," she nodded toward Paks, who suddenly remembered the worst of Aarenis, the dead baby in Rotengre, the murdered farmfolk, Ferrault dying, Alured's tortures. "We do not argue that war is better than peace; we are not so stupid as that. But it is not peace when cruelty reigns, when stronger men steal from farmers and craftworkers, when the child can be enslaved or the old thrown out to starve, and no one lifts a hand. That is not peace: that is conquest, and evil. We start no quarrels in peaceful lands; we never display our weaponskills to earn applause. But we are Gird's cudgel, defending the helpless, and teaching by our example that one person *can* dare greater force to break evil's grasp on the innocent. Sometimes we can do that without fighting, without killing, and that's best."

"But we're warriors first," said Paks before she thought. She wished she'd kept still. She had already noticed that the others, with their years in the Fellowship and service in the granges, had different views. Now they all looked at her, and she fixed her gaze on Cami.

"Yes," said Cami slowly. "Some evils need that direct attack, and we must be able to do it, and to lead others in battle. Did you ever wonder why paladins are so likeable?" It seemed an odd remark, and threw Paks off-balance. Apparently others were confused as well, by the stirring in the room. "It's important," said Cami, now with that grin that pulled them all together. "We come to a town, perhaps, where nothing has gone right for a dozen years. Perhaps there's a grange of Gird, perhaps not. But the people are frightened, and they've lost trust in each other, in themselves. We may lead them into danger; some will be killed or wounded. Why should they trust us?" No one answered, and she went on. "Because we are likeable, and other people will follow us willingly. And that's why we are more likely to choose a popular yeoman-marshal as a candidate than the best fighter in the grange."

Paks dared a sideways glance. From the thoughtful and even puzzled faces around her, the others had never considered this. She herself, remembering the paladin in Aarenis, realized that she had trusted him at once, without reservation, although the Marshal with him had annoyed her.

"But you see how dangerous that could be, if someone wanted to do evil," said Cami, breaking into her thoughts. "We choose from those with a gift for leadership, those people will follow happily. Therefore we must be sure that you will never use that gift wrongly. Another thing: because we come and go, we make demands on those we help for only a short time. It's easier for them to follow us quickly, and then go home. Never scorn Marshals: when we have left, they must maintain their yeomen's faith. Perhaps we showed them what was possible — but we left them with years of work."

As for the powers legend had grafted onto paladins, in reality there were four.

"We all have powers, but not all of us have them equally," said Amberion one day. "Any paladin can call light — " A glow lit the end of his finger. "It is not fire, which gives light by burning, but true light, the essence of seeing. There are greater lights — " At his nod, Cami suddenly seemed to catch fire, wreathed in a white radiance too bright to watch. Then it was gone; all the candidates blinked. "More than that," Amberion went on, "some paladins — but not all — can call light that will spread across a whole battlefield." Paks remembered the light in Sibili. "It is the duty and power of a paladin," said Amberion, "to show the truth of good and evil — to make clear — and that is what our light is for. It is a tool. Sometimes we use it to prove our call, but it must never be used for the paladin's own convenience or pride."

"But how do you make the light?" asked Clevis, one of the other candidates.

"We do not make it. We call it — ask it, in Gird's name. Later in your training we will graft this power onto you, for awhile, so that you can learn to use it — but it will not be your power until you are invested as a paladin, in the Trials, and the gods give or withhold your gifts."

"You mean we won't know until then?" asked Harbin.

"You knew that, surely?"

"Well, yes, but — " He shook his head. "It seems a long time wasted, if we don't become paladins. Can't you tell earlier?"

"We can tell if you are doing badly," said Amberion. "But we have no power over the gods' decisions, Harbin. We prepare the best candidates we can find as well as we can, and then present them. Then they choose — why, we do not know. That's one reason the failing candidates are honored: it does not mean they are not worthy; they are the best we could find. Even those who withdraw from training are honored for having been chosen to attempt it. Any one of you — " he looked around the small group. "Any one of you would make a fine knight in any order. Most of you would make a fine Marshal — one or two, perhaps, are too independent of mind — but you would all do. But to be a paladin requires more than weaponskills, a gift for leadership, the willingness to risk all for good, the deep love of good and hatred of evil. Many good men and women share these with you. Beyond that, you must have the High Lord's blessing on that way for you, as shown by the gifts you receive in the Trials." They thought that over for some minutes in silence.

Saer, a black-haired woman with merry blue eyes, explained the gift of healing, second of the paladin's special abilities. This too was a gift, to be prayed for; the gift might be withheld at times. As well, it required knowledge of wounds and illness, the structure of the body and its functions. Paks would like to have asked her about Canna's wound — had she healed it, and was that any proof of Gird's favor? — but she was shy in front of the others. After a short discussion, in which she took no part, they passed on to other matters.

Sarek, who reminded Paks of Cracolnya in the Duke's Company, with his stocky body and slightly bowed legs, explained about the detection of good and evil. "A paladin can sense good and evil directly," he began. "Now you might think that makes everything simple: on one side are the bad people, and you kill them, and over here are the good people, and they cheer for you." Everyone laughed, including the other paladins. "It would be nice," he went on, "but that's not how it works. Normally you will experience people much as you do now — liking some, and not liking others. Most people — and that includes us, candidates — are mixtures, neither wholly evil nor wholly good. But if you are close to someone intent on evil — an assassin, Achrya's agent, whatever — you will know that evil is near and be able to locate it.

"That's not the same as doing anything about it," he said, again waiting for the laughter that followed. "You must learn to think. Suppose you are trying to decide whom to trust in a troubled town. An evil person may lie, but he might tell the truth, if truth serves his plan. A good person may lead you wrong, being good and stupid. You, young candidates, are supposed to be good — and smart." Again they laughed. "But more of this later. Only realize that like any gift, it is a tool — and you must learn to use it carefully, or it can slip in your hand." He gave them a final grin, and waved Cami up.

"Most important of the gifts," said Cami, now more serious than Paks had ever seen her, "is the High Lord's protection from evil attack. Of course you can be killed — we are human, after all. But as long as you are Gird's paladin, your soul cannot be forced into evil by any power whatever. All magical spells that assault the heart and mind directly will fail. No fear or disgust, no despair, can prevent you from following the High Lord's call if you want to follow it. Moreover, you can protect those with you from such attacks. This is one reason our training is so long and so intense — for this, of course, we cannot test in training. We must be sure you *do* want this with a whole heart, that you are indeed under that protection, before you go out to battle the dark powers of the Earth."

For that reason, they were told, their every act and word would be scrutinized; even small faults could reveal flaws too dangerous to be granted such power.

"But would the High Lord grant the powers to someone unfit to bear them?" asked one of the candidates.

"No. But evil powers might grant a semblance of such. It is hard to explain — though you will understand if you succeed — but during your training you are more open to evil influence than before. We must so harrow your minds, and as in a harrowed field both sun and frost strike deeper, so in your minds both good and evil can strike a firmer root. That is why you are kept apart from the others, once you begin the final training, and why you are always in the company of your sponsor, who can sense any threat and protect you from it."

"But we're supposed to be more resistant anyway," grumbled Harbin. Paks agreed, but said nothing. It almost sounded as if they were weaklings.

581

"You are — you were — and you will be," said Cami. "But right now, and for the time of your training, we are looking for weakness — searching for any crevice through which evil can assail your hearts. And we will find things, for none of us is perfect, or utterly invincible, except in the High Lord's protection." Paks wondered uneasily what weakness they would find in her, and what they would do about it.

"And," added Sarek, closing that session with a laugh, "remember that while a demon can't eat your soul, once you're a paladin, any village idiot can crack your skull with a rock. By accident."

Other such discussions followed. They learned that paladins never married unless — and this was rare — they retired from that service to another. Yet although celibate on quest — Paks saw someone frown, across the room, and wondered if he would drop out — they might have lovers in Fin Panir or elsewhere, as time allowed. "But those you love most are in the most danger," pointed out Amberion. "Choose your loves from those who can defend themselves, should Achrya's agents be seeking a weapon against you. We are here to defend the children of others — not to protect our own. And if we had children, and were good parents, we would have no time for Gird's work."

Soon Paks knew the paladins as people. She knew the room would bubble with excitement when Cami arrived, that Saer brought with her an intensity and mysticism almost eerie to experience, that Sarek's jokes always had a lasting sting of sense, that Amberion was the group's steady anchor. She, like the others, opened up under Kevis's warm and loving regard; and like the others she found her determination hardened by Teriam's stern logic. Garin, last of the seven, left on quest shortly after his sponsored candidate withdrew — the first of their group to fail. Paks had not known Amis well, and did not know why he had left. She knew less of the candidates than she'd expected, for when not in classes together, they were each with a sponsor or learning to meditate alone.

But even so she was conscious of a difference between these young Girdsmen, long committed to their patron, and herself. Matters that she thought trivial were cause for hours of discussion, and the simple solution she always thought she saw never satisfied them. They picked away at the motives they claimed lay behind all acts, creating, Paks thought, an incredible tangle of unlikely possibilities. She had imagined herself committed to the defense of good . . . but was good this complicated? If so, why was Gird the patron of soldiers? No one had time to think of definitions and logic in the midst of a battle. The way Sarek had said it first made the most sense to her: here are the bad people, and you kill them; there are the good ones, and they cheer for you. Surely it was only a matter of learning to recognize all the evil. She prayed, as Amberion was teaching her to do, and said nothing. She was there to learn, and in time she might understand that other way of thinking. She had time.

Busy as she was, Paks had almost forgotten the mysterious scrolls when she received a summons to the Master Archivist, Marshal Kory. She found him at a broad table set before a window, with the scrolls all open before him.

"Paksenarrion — come and see the treasure." He waved his hand at the array. "Amberion tells me you had no idea what you brought?"

"No, sir."

"Well, if it were all you ever brought here, Paksenarrion, the Fellowship of Gird could count itself well repaid. We have all examined these — all those of us in Fin Panir with an interest in such things. I believe — and so do many others — that these scrolls were penned by Luap himself, Gird's own friend. How they got where you found them I doubt we will ever know for certain."

"But how can you know what they are?"

Marshal Kory grinned. "That's scholar's work, young warrior. But you would know a sword made in Andressat, I daresay, from one made in Vérella — "

"Yes, sir."

"So we have ways to know that the scrolls are old. We have copies of Luap's chronicles and letters; we compared them, and found some differences — but just what might have come from careless copying. And these scrolls contain far more than we have: letters to Luap's friends, little sermons — a wealth of material. We think the writing is Luap's own hand, because we have preserved a couple of lists said to be his — and one of the letters here mentions making that list of those who fell in the first days of the rebellion."

Paks began to feel the awesome age of the scrolls. "Then — Luap really touched those — I mean, he was alive, and could — "

"He was a real person, yes — not a legend — and because he writes so, we know that Gird was real, too. Not that I charge you with having doubted it, but it's easy to forget that our heroes were actual men and women, who got blisters when they marched, and liked a pot of ale at day's end. Luap now — " His eyes stared into the distance. "That isn't even his name. In those days, *luap* was a kinship term, for someone not in the line of inheritance. The military used it too. A *luap*-captain had that rank, for respect and pay, but had no troops under his own command: could not give independent orders. According to the old stories, this man gave up his own name when he joined the rebellion. There are several versions with different reasons for that. Anyway, he became Gird's assistant, high-ranked because he could write — which few besides lords could do in those days — and he was called Gird's luap. Soon everyone called him 'the luap,' and finally 'Luap.' Because of him, no one used luap for a kinship term after that; in Fintha the same relationship now is called 'nik,' and in Tsaia it's 'niga' or 'nigan.'" The Archivist seemed ready to explain the origin of that and every other term, and Paks broke in quickly, sticking to what she understood.

"And he speaks of Gird?"

"As a friend. Listen to this." Marshal Kory picked up one of the scrolls,

583

and began to read. " ' — and in fact, Ansuli, I had to tell the great oaf to quit swinging his staff around overhead like a young demon. I feared he would hit me, but soon that great laugh burst out and he thanked me for stopping him. If he has a fault, it is that liking for ale, which makes him fight sometimes whether we have need or no.' And that's Luap talking of Gird at a tavern in eastern Fintha. I'm not sure where; he doesn't name the town."

Paks was startled. "Gird — drunk?"

"It was after their first big victory. I've always suspected that the reason several of the articles in the Code of Gird dealt with drunkenness is that Gird had personal knowledge of it." He laid that scroll down and touched another with his fingertip. "We have had the copyists working on these every day. It is the greatest treasure of the age — you cannot know, Paksenarrion, how it lifts our hearts to find something so close to Gird himself. Even when it's things like that letter — that just makes him more human, more real to us. And to have in Luap's own words the last battle — incredible! Besides that, we now have a way to prove whether or not these scrolls are genuine. Have you ever heard of Luap's Stronghold?"

Paks shook her head. "I had not heard of Luap until I came here, sir."

"There's been a legend for a long time that Luap left the Honnorgat Valley and traveled west, to take Gird's Code to distant lands. For a time, it was believed, he had established a stronghold, a fortress, in the far mountains, and some reports had Girdsmen traveling back and forth. But no one has come from the west with any reports of him for hundreds of years, so most scholars now think it was just a legend. But in one of these scrolls, sent back, he says, at the request of the Marshal-General of that day, he gives the location of that stronghold. If someone were to go there, and see it, that would prove that these are, indeed, the scrolls of Luap."

Paks thought of it, suddenly excited. "What are the western lands like?"

"All we have are caravan reports. Dry grassland for some days travel, then rock and sand, then deep gouges in the rocks, with swift-running rivers in the depths. Then mountains — but they don't go that way, skirting them on the south, to come to a crossways. North along that route is a kingdom called Kaelifet; I know nothing about it. Southward is more desert, and finally a sea."

Paks tried to imagine those strange lands, and failed. "Will you go, then, Marshal Kory?"

"Me!" He laughed. "No, I'm the Archivist — I can't go. Perhaps no one will. Some think it is an idle fancy, and the trip too long and dangerous to risk with evil nearer to hand. But I hope the Marshal-General sends someone. I'd like to know what happened to Luap — and his followers — and why they left Fintha. Perhaps there are more scrolls there — who knows?" He looked at her. "Would you go, if you could, or does this seem a scholar's question to you?"

"I would go," said Paks. "A long journey — unknown lands — mountain fortress — what could be more exciting?"

Chapter Twenty-four

Early spring flowers were just fading when Paks rode west up the first long slopes above Fin Panir. She still thought nothing could be more exciting. With the caravan, the year's first, rode Amberion, High Marshals Connaught and Fallis, and four knights: Joris, Adan, and Pir, from the Order of the Cudgel, and Marek from the Order of Gird. A troop of men-at-arms marched with them, and a number of yeomen had signed on as drovers and camp workers. Most of the caravan was commercial, headed for Kaelifet, but Ardhiel and Balkon rode with the Girdish contingent as ambassadors and witnesses for their people.

Paks continued her training under the direction of the paladin and High Marshals. If she had thought the trip would provide a respite from study, she quickly learned otherwise. By the time they reached the Rim, a rough outcrop of stone that loomed across their path, visible a day's journey away, Paks had passed their examinations on the Code of Gird and grange organization. She began learning the grange history of the oldest granges, the reasons for locating granges and bartons in certain places, the way that the Code of Gird was administered in grange courts and market courts in Fintha. Now she knew how the judicar was appointed in Rocky Ford, and why the required number of witnesses to a contract varied with the kind of contract.

Their encounter with the horse nomads was a welcome break. She had been marching along muttering to herself the names of the Marshal-Generals who had made changes in the Code when one of the Wagonmaster's sons came pelting along the line, crying a warning. As he neared the Girdsmen, he yelled "Sir paladin! Sir paladin! Raiders!"

"Where, lad?" Amberion was already swinging onto his golden chestnut warhorse.

"North, sir! The scouts say it's a big party."

Paks felt her stomach clench as she hurried to untie Socks from the wagon. Socks was tossing his head, and she scrambled up, uncomfortably aware of her awkwardness. At least she had her own armor and sword for the journey. She swung Socks away from the wagons, and unhooked her helmet from its straps. Amberion was already helmeted, shield on arm.

"Paksenarrion!" he called. "Bring spears." Paks unfastened her shield from the saddle and slid it on her arm. At the supply wagon, she called for two spears, and a young yeoman slid them out the rear. Paks locked them under her elbow, whirled Socks, and rode off to find Amberion. To the north she could see a smudge of dust. The caravan itself suddenly swarmed with armed troops. Their score of men-at-arms marched as a rear guard; the regular caravan guards rode atop each wagon, crossbows loaded and cocked. High Marshal Connaught carried a bow; he, Sir Marek, and Ardhiel rode toward the head of the caravan. The other three knights waited on High Marshal Fallis, whose bald-faced horse was throwing its usual tantrum. Paks grinned to herself. She'd had to ride that horse a few times herself; she could imagine the struggle to get helm and shield in place while staying aboard.

Then a bellow from the Wagonmaster brought Amberion back. He shrugged at Paks, and she followed him to the cluster of mounted fighters. High Marshal Connaught was glaring, but the Wagonmaster never looked up.

"You can't do it, I say, and you agreed when I took you on that you'd be bound by my orders."

"Thieves and outlaws — " began Connaught. The Wagonmaster interrupted.

"Horse nomads. Horse nomads I've met before, and will every year, whether you ride with me or not. Maybe you could hold them off — if it's one of the half-decent clans like Stormwind or Wintersun. But what about next year? We skirmish a little for honor's sake, pay our toll, same as a caravan would on the long route through Tsaia, and that's it. None of your Girdish sermonizing here, Marshal: it'll get me killed."

"And if they attack?" said Amberion. Paks noticed that the Wagonmaster's fixed glare softened a little.

"We fight, of course: that's why I have guards. But they won't, with you in sight. I'm glad enough to have the extra blades and bows, and that's truth, but for the rest of it, I'll pay toll." Connaught started to speak, but Amberion caught his eye, and he closed his mouth. Amberion smiled at the Wagonmaster. "Sir, we agreed to follow your command while we traveled with you; forgive us for our eagerness to defend you."

Soon they could see the advancing warriors clearly: a mass of riders on shaggy small horses, armed with lances. Paks watched the war party ride closer — and closer. Now she could see the shaggy manes, the glitter of bridle ornaments, the colors of the riders' cloaks. On tall poles long streamers of cloth fluttered in the wind: blue, gray, and white. She could hear the drumming of those many hooves.

The Wagonmaster had insisted that all but the parley group he led stay near the wagons, but he had invited Amberion to ride out with him. Paks followed, at his nod. As they moved toward the nomads, the Wagonmaster gave them his instructions. Finally they faced their enemy only a bowshot away. Amberion waved his spear slowly, left to right. The nomads halted. Several of their horses whickered.

A single figure in the front of the group waved one of the streamered poles and yelled something in a language Paks didn't know.

"Parley in Common!" yelled Amberion.

The figure rode forward ten yards or so. "Why we halt?" he called. "Yer on our pasture, city folk. On the sea of grass, only the strong survive. Can ye stop us taking all you have, and feeding ye to the grass?" His speech was thickly accented, a mixture of several dialects.

"Aye, easily enough." The Wagonmaster sounded confident.

"Ha! Five against fifty? Are ye demons, then, like that black one that walks north?"

"We are servants of Gird and the High Lord," said Amberion. The Wagonmaster shot him a glance, but said nothing.

"Well met here, *servant* of whoever. Go tell yer master that those who travel our lands must pay our tolls — unless ye'd rather fight."

Amberion turned to the Wagonmaster, brows raised. The Wagonmaster nodded. "Oh, these aren't bad. These are Stormwinds — that's old Carga out there; he don't torture prisoners at all. Keeps slaves, of course, they all do, but if there's a good horse nomad, it's Carga. He'll take our tribute and leave us alone. You notice he changed his demand, that second time?"

The Wagonmaster had assembled a bale of striped cloth, a small keg of Marrakai red wine, several skeins of red and blue yarn, a sack of river-clam shells, and a bundle of mixed wooden staves of a length for arrowshafts. Now he waved, and some of the drovers carried the goods toward them.

The nomad leader rode forward slowly, alone, close enough that Paks could see the curl of hoof on its thong around his neck, the spirals tattooed on his cheeks, the clear gray eyes under dark brows. He rode without stirrups, in knee-high boots whose embroidered soles had surely never been used for walking, clear as the colors were.

"Ye ride with strange powers, cityborn trader," he said. "Yer men I know, but him — " He pointed at Amberion. "Wizard, is it?"

"A paladin of Gird," said Amberion. The nomad shrugged and spat.

"Never heerd of him, nor paladins neither. But ye stink of power." He watched closely as the goods were displayed before him, and finally nodded. "Go yer way, scarfeet riders — " It took Paks awhile to understand this reference to their stirrups, and the marks those left on boots.

She hardly had time to enjoy the memory of the nomads before High Marshal Connaught had her hard at work again. Spring passed quickly into summer, the hot windy summer of the grasslands. At times it seemed they rode in the center of a bowl of grass, and Paks wondered if the world might be turning under them, so that they would never be free. Then the green turned grayer; the grass hardly reached their horses' knees. The dry air rasped in her nose, chapped her lips. Paks could see the ground's color showing through, as if the grass were a threadbare rug over the land, and then the grass failed. The trail went on, a deep-bitten groove of dust and stone.

They moved from water to water. Paks learned to ride with a cloth over her face, and keep her mouth closed against the dryness. The horses lost flesh, despite their care. The caravaners showed the Girdsmen how to turn over every rock before sitting down: Paks loathed the many-legged creatures that lurked in that cool shade, and carried poison in their tails.

It took days to cross the first deep canyon: first to ease the wagons down that steep trail without losing control of any of them, then to warp them across the roaring river, red with ground rock, then to drag them back up, foot by foot. And when they came out on top again, Paks could see little of where they had been. After another such canyon, the caravaners pointed out a line of purple against the northern sky. Mountains, they said. Elves, they said also, with sidelong looks at Ardhiel.

Paks asked him, and Ardhiel answered that those mountains were home to elves, but not of his family. He seemed troubled by something, but Paks knew better than to ask. Balkon, looking north, muttered eagerly about stone. He had confided to Paks that his family, the Goldenaxe clan, was looking for more daskgeft, more stonemass for the increase of the family. He hoped to find some; the descriptions Luap had written of the land made him think the stone there might be "dross," or suitable. Paks wondered again how dross could have so many meanings in dwarvish: courage, wit, strength — almost anything good, it seemed to her, was dross.

Day by day the mountains seemed to march nearer their flank. Ahead was only the rolling level of the desert, broken by watercourses. Paks began to feel a pressure from those mountains; she understood why the caravaners would go around rather than through them, for that alone. Then one morning an edge of red rock showed ahead. As they marched toward it, it rose higher and higher. By the next afternoon, they could see the lighter rock below, great sweeping curves of white and yellow — the same color, Paks thought, as the walls of Cortes Andres. And two days later, marching under those great stone ramparts, the Girdsmen turned aside.

Here a river emptied itself from those stone walls into the sand and rubble outside. The caravaners muttered and made gestures, but finally moved on, while High Marshal Connaught examined the map again. When the caravan was gone, he mounted his bay horse and led them up the watercourse, the horses lunging through the dry sand. Ahead, Paks could see towering white walls closing in. She wondered how they could ride in such a narrow space if the water came up.

"Bad place for an ambush," said Amberion beside her.

"Yes, sir."

"By the map, we'll be leaving this soon, and climbing into another stream's valley. I hope the route can be climbed by horses."

Paks had not thought of that, but looking at the sheer walls of stone, she realized what they might face. "If they can't — "

"Then we'll leave them. Build a stout camp, leave the novice yeomen and most of the men-at-arms."

Before the canyon walls closed completely, High Marshal Connaught turned left away from the river, leading them onto a rough slope of broken rock. He seemed to find a trail; Paks, far back in the group, could not see anything ahead to guide them. Socks heaved upward, stride by stride. They stopped often to rest the animals; the warhorses were curded with sweat. Amberion's horse, alone of all the animals, never showed the marks of hard riding, always slick-coated and fresh. Paks had noticed that about all the paladin's mounts in Fin Panir. Far back she could see the mules, head down, picking their way delicately and almost without effort over the rocks. Below, the canyon they had come from disappeared into a jumble of shadow and light. Now she could see far to the right, more swooping curves of stone, patterned by dark cracks. Far up on the heights, she thought she saw trees.

By late afternoon, she could see a strange shape against the sky: a dark cone with a scoop out of the point. Amberion pointed to it.

"That's marked on the map. Blackash cone, it said: we must bear left of it." As they came nearer, always climbing, the rock changed abruptly from white to red. The trail led through a break in that vertical red wall. Suddenly the black cone was close; it looked like a loose pile of dark rock sitting on the red stone around it. Paks stared. Had someone — some giant, surely — built a cairn? Long shadows streaked the land, making weird shapes of the wind-blown rocks around them. Now they could see that the canyon they had climbed from was only a small section of something much larger that extended far to the east, ending at last in a higher rampart of white topped with forest. South, the land dropped abruptly into that hole. It was hard to believe they had climbed anything so sudden. Westward the land dipped to a rumpled plain of sand, and that again dropped sharply: Paks could just see against the setting sun distant mountains beyond that drop. Northward, their view was blocked by the black cone and the higher land behind it. Red cliffs, these, with fortress-size blocks lying at their feet. Paks wondered if the others felt as small as she did.

That night they camped on the sandy plain just southwest of the black cone. A cold wind brushed the camp; stars blazed brighter than Paks had ever seen them. She woke several times to hear Ardhiel singing. Dawn came early on that high place. Paks saw the white stone below begin to glow even before she was aware of light in the sky. Then the high wall to the east stood clear against a green dawn. First light turned the red peaks north of them to fiery orange; then the light crept down to meet them, throwing blue shadows below.

They had some trouble to find the trail from there. Just to the left of the black cone, layers of stone like those that peel from a boiled egg curved downward, but the horses skidded and slipped. High Marshal Connaught sent Thelon ahead; he reported that the stony way ended in a drop four or five men high. Then they searched for a way around. Paks decided that walking in deep dry sand was harder than any marching she had ever done. The wind rose, blowing sand into their eyes. The horses flattened ears against it. The first three trails they tried led to sheer cliffs, and it was early afternoon before the scout found a safe route.

It began in a narrow grove of pines, where broad low boles rose from drifted sand, old trees bent by strong winds into a tangled thatch of branches. Below the trees, the trail followed a twisting ravine, its bed choked with boulders of garish red and black on a bed of sand; they radiated heat like coals. Across the ravine, as they went down, they could see outcrops of red rock. Suddenly the cleft they traveled angled back to the left, then crooked right again. They stood on a narrow platform above a small valley that led straight away toward a tangle of cliffs and canyons. On either side, sheer cliffs rose hundreds of feet, rose-red and orange, striped with black. To the right, an arm of the valley angled back away from them. Down the valley a stream reflected the sky; it looked wider than Paks had expected.

As they rode down into the valley, Paks heard conflicting opinions.

"What a farm that'd make," she heard from one of the yeomen with the mules. "Wind-shelter from those cliffs — water — must be good soil with all that grass."

"A long way to market," said another. "Unless you founded a grange out here, Tamar."

"Marry me, and we might," said the woman, laughing.

"Marry — I'd have married you in Fin Panir, but you wouldn't have it."

"And miss this? Come on, Dort, you weren't any more ready to settle down than I was. But couldn't we make a farm here?"

"I'll tell you that when I find the nearest market." Paks heard them laughing for some moments after.

"It is not good," muttered Balkon, who had turned his pony aside from the others to look closely at the rock wall nearest them. "See — " He poked at it with his axe-haft and a chunk came away; sand sifted after it. "It is soft here. Good rock there — " he pointed at the east wall of the valley, and at great cliffs beyond it. "But something is wrong here. With those cliffs, it must be deeper."

"Strange," murmured Ardhiel as Paks rode by. "It has an odd feel — very strange."

But most of the company liked its looks — green grass and water, walls far enough apart to allow maneuvering, yet close enough for protection. Then they rode out of the last rock-strewn mouth of the ravine, and found themselves once more in deep sand — this time damp.

"Ah," said the dwarf, eyes gleaming. "It is that this valley is choked with sand — something blocks it there — " he pointed at the far end. "The side rock goes down, very far below this; I feel it meet under our feet."

"Find us firm ground," said High Marshal Connaught to the scout. "These horses can't handle boggy — " He threw himself off as his horse sank hock-deep by one leg. They all dismounted. Close up the valley was smaller than they had thought; its hills were low dunes rising above the level, its stream only a trickle across the sand surface. "But plenty if we dig," the High Marshal assured the others. "It's like those waterholes in the low desert."

590

While the scout and several men-at-arms searched for a firm path to the north end of the valley, the Marshals and knights looked at the angled canyon that wound away to the right. That way the ground seemed firmer, and the little stream, though narrower, gurgled ankle deep over fine gravel.

"It's too bad we aren't going this way," said High Marshal Fallis. "I suppose it's blocked at the far end by another cliff."

"Let's look at it," said Marek, one of the knights, and the only member of the Order of Gird. "We ought to learn the shape of the land, in case of trouble."

"In case of trouble," said Joris drily, "nothing in this land offers comfort. We should have been born with wings."

"I agree with Marek, though," said Connaught. "We should know, and mark the map."

They set off on foot, the High Marshals, Amberion and Paks, the knights, and Ardfiel and Balkon. In a few minutes an angle of rock cut them off from sight of the others. On either hand the cliffs rose straight out of the sand, as if carved by a knife. Paks noticed a great arch set into the northeast wall. Under it a dark shadowed space looked large enough for a building. She looked from cliff to cliff, uneasy. In several places the stone seemed to have broken away leaving an overhanging arch, some much smaller than others. She nudged Balkon.

"Why does the rock do that? Is it natural? Did something shape it?"

"What — oh, it is the arch you mean? That is stone itself. I have not seen before, but I have heard. It is good stone that can take an arch; the arch is the drossen shape — " He saw her puzzled look, sighed, and tried in Common. "The shape that stone holds when it is sound — strong — healthy. Not nedross, like that stone that we came by, where the wall broke to let us in. Look in the High Lord's Hall — you see that even human masons know the right shape, the good shape, for stone holding stone. The longer the arch, the better the stone."

"Oh." Paks shivered. She did not like this valley; it was hard to judge how high the cliffs were, how far they had come from their friends. She looked back, to see someone leading a horse across the stream, heading down the valley. She could not see the other men-at-arms or horses at all; cliffs cut off her view of the main valley. She craned her neck to look at the large arch again. Surely the whole party could shelter there — if you could get horses up the cliff. She started to laugh at that idea, and suddenly stopped. Something had moved in its shadow. For an instant she could not speak, but then she called to Amberion.

"What is it?" he asked, turning. Before Paks could answer, Ardhiel cried out in elven, swinging his bow from his shoulder and snatching arrows. Paks pointed upward, then staggered as an arrow slammed into her helmet.

"Keep your faces down!" bellowed High Marshal Fallis. "Eyes — " But Paks knew that, and had already dashed for a leaning rock. Pir and Adan

591

huddled there too. More arrows clattered on the rocks around them. She heard a high-pitched cry from above, and then the terrible smack of a body on rocks. Another scream from across the canyon. Then silence.

"That won't be all," said High Marshal Fallis. Paks looked around. Ardhiel was close to the cliff on the far side; she saw Fallis near him. Connaught, Amberion, and Joris had taken shelter behind another rock near her, and Marek and Balkon behind yet another. She risked a quick glance upward, but could see nothing for the overhang.

"Beware!" Ardhiel's voice rose again, and he yelled something in elven. Paks saw a swarm of black-clad figures leap from cracks in the rock, turned just in time to meet more of them attacking on her side. She and the two knights leaped to their feet.

At first it seemed they might be cut down in their separate groups. The attackers were skilled with their narrow blades, and had numbers and height on their side. Adan staggered; a blade had gone deep in his leg. Paks covered his side; together she and Pir managed to fight their way back to High Marshal Connaught, half-carrying Adan between them. Fallis and Ardhiel dashed across to join them, and the group locked into a unit, back to back with Adan in the center. From her position, Paks could not see if any of the others, far back down the valley, had noticed any disturbance. She was fighting too hard to have breath to yell. She did not even recognize what she was fighting until the tip of Pir's sword flicked back one of the hoods.

"Elves!" she cried; the fine-boned face, the long graceful body now seeming the same as Ardhiel's. But the elf called to them.

"No — not elves. Iynisin — unsingers — once of our blood — "

"And we are still the true heirs," called one of the enemy, in elven. Paks could just follow the words. The voice held the same music as Ardhiel's, but was colder. "We have not changed; you have fallen, cousin, making alliance with mortals and rockfolk, to the insult of your blood."

"Daskdusky scum," muttered Balkon, swinging his axe wide from his corner position.

Though outnumbered, the little group was able to shift slowly back toward the main valley. High Marshal Fallis, facing that way, told them he saw the men-at-arms coming. Paks, Pir, and Amberion, holding the rear, stepped back cautiously, keeping the enemy blades at bay. Then Marek called a warning. Paks glanced up at the nearest cliff. There, moving swiftly on the sheer wall as if it were level, a great many-legged thing dropped down on them. At the overhanging ledge it stepped into the air and fell, swinging on a shining line behind it, leaping from its first touch on the ground to arc high above their heads. Pir swung and missed; Paks twisted, trying to strike behind her; her sword clashed on Fallis's, and the thing leaped out to whirl and attack again.

While they were still shaken by this creature, from high overhead a loud voice cried a single word. Paks stopped short, hardly able to breathe. She felt as if she'd been dipped in ice. Her eyes roved, following the great monster. Now she could see it had almost the form of a spider, many legs around a bulbous body. She felt her hand loosening on her sword.

But with a ringing tone like that of a great bell, white light glowed around them. Paks could move again; she felt her heart beating wildly, but her hand clenched on the sword. As the monster leaped, she hacked at its head. Her sword skidded off the hard surface, but Pir's severed a leg. Paks thrust again, for the eyes. It reared back, aiming small tubes along its belly at her. Amberion shoved her aside. A gout of grayish fluid missed her; she heard Adan cry out behind. But by then Amberion's sword had severed the head, and the thing lay twitching on the ground.

"Stay close," said Amberion. "It is a spell of fear laid on us." Paks felt no fear, now, and fought on.

In the space of the monster's attack, more enemy fighters had come from the cliffs to cut them off from the rest of the party. These were bowmen, close enough that their arrows could wound even through armor. Between them and the bowmen were two ranks of swords. Paks took a deep breath. She had not expected to have such a short career as paladin — not even paladin yet, she reminded herself — but she thought she would as soon die in this company as any other. She saw Balkon bend to kiss his axe. High Marshal Fallis had done something for Adan; he was standing more steadily. Connaught frowned at the enemy, lips folded. Amberion touched Paks on the arm.

"It's only five to one," he said, smiling. "Your Duke has faced worse than that."

Paks grinned. "Oh well — we'll win through easily, then."

"You stay close, though. You have no protection of your own against that fear." Paks thought she had, but wasn't going to argue the point. She saw Connaught draw breath to send them forward; she wondered why the archers hadn't shot yet. Then Ardhiel moved, taking from his side the old battered hunting horn he had carried from Fin Panir. He set it to his lips.

Paks had expected nothing like the sound of that horn. It began sweet and tender, swelling louder and louder to a triumphant blast that nearly shattered her bones. Wind swirled into the canyon, a great column of whirling air funneling into and from the horn's throat. A roiling mass of pink and gold-lit cloud blotted out the hard clear blue of a desert sky. Paks could not see the cliffs — the enemy — or Ardhiel himself. The cloud shimmered, steadied, became a piled and rumpled staircase of gold. Down it came a brilliant shining creature, winged with rainbow colors, so bright she could hardly stand to see it, and so beautiful she could not look away. On its back was Someone in mail brighter than polished silver, wearing a blinding white cloak. He spoke: the language was elven, the voice rang with authority and troubled the heart like elven harps. And Paks saw Ardhiel bow, and move to his side, and saw him mount that fabulous beast, and saw them rise once more into the clouds.

When the clouds blew away, in the last throbbing notes of that horn-call, the enemy was gone, though the rattle of their flight through the rocks echoed from wall to wall. Ardhiel lay unconscious on the ground, smiling, and the horn in his hand showed its true nature: the finest horn Paks had ever seen, jeweled with rubies and emeralds, shining gold.

With no delay, Connaught had them carry Ardhiel back to the others.

"It's an elfhorn, it must be," he said over his shoulder. "I'd heard of them, but Gird knows I never expected to see one. Let alone hear one. By the gods, this is a bad place. You were right, Balkon. Bad for an ambush, and I walked right into it. I hope it doesn't kill Lord Ardhiel. That'll take some explaining. 'Old hunting horn,' indeed. No wonder he wouldn't play on it for our dancing that night. It makes my skin itch to think of it."

"It's Gird's grace he brought it," said Amberion. "I wonder why they didn't shoot at once? They could have gotten us — "

"Or thought they could." Fallis grunted as his foot turned on a rock. "Damned treacherous ground. Probably a damned kuaknom behind every stone."

"Kuaknom?" asked Paks.

"That's what we call them — kuaknom, tree-haters — as elves are tree-lovers. The elves call them iynisin, the unsingers. Remember, it's the kuaknom that used to be confused with Kuakkgani."

Paks wondered how anyone could confuse those horrible parodies of elves with a Kuakgan. Confuse with elves themselves, yes — for her mind held the memory of the same beauty, the same grace. "Were they the same as other elves once?"

"Aye," answered Balkon, before anyone else could. "And some say they are still, the blackheart rockfilth. The elves like to pretend all the kuaknom failed away many years ago. But here we see the truth of that! By Sertig's Hammer, all the fair-spoken ones would rather have a tongue of silver, though it lied, than tell iron truth at need."

Amberion shook his head. "Your pardon, sir dwarf, but in this I judge you wrong. The kuaknom parted long ago from the true elves, in a quarrel that began before men — "

"Not long before," muttered Balkon. "The Kuakkgani — "

"If they are truly men, then it was not before — but it was before other men. And the cause of that quarrel — "

"Was the Tree. Aye, I've heard that. But it seems a foolish quarrel to me. Would a dwarf enact rage because iron bends to any smith, or stone to any chisel?" He shook his head, and challenged them all with his look. "No, I deem not, and you know the truth of it. But I call no harsh name on Ardhiel's head, for his call saved us, and he has paid for that. The best of elves are fair indeed — aye, though we grumble, being made rough and ugly as rock and iron, we honor them for their grace. Well they name their lord the Singer of Songs; the best of them are true songs, well-sung; but we are other, hammered on Sertig's anvil to bear the blows of the world. Our songs are the ring of steel on stone." Paks was astonished; she had never heard any dwarf speak so. He bowed stiffly, and was silent thereafter until they reached the men-at-arms, now coming forward in battle order.

The High Marshals led them swiftly out to the trail the others had found, and the whole company moved down the main valley while it was still light. Here the walls were nearly a bowshot apart. Thelon, sent ahead once more, had found a trail leading out: not where the valley seemed to end, for that was a jumble of house-size stones ending in a twenty-foot cliff, but climbing again over a shoulder of the western wall.

"But it is no trail you could take in the dark, Marshal Fallis," he reported. "Even the near part will tax the horses; after that it is easier, but the first of the trail going into the canyon beyond is worse. I could not go far enough to be sure they can get down. We may have trailwork to do; I judge you will not want to leave them here."

"By no means," said Marshal Fallis. "We had thought of that, when we saw this fertile valley, but we can leave no one behind to suffer attack of the kuaknom. And it is by no means so fertile as it seemed." For they had found all the valley floor to be sand, dry or wet or boggy; the green growth was sedge, not grass, and only a few trees dared that sandy expanse.

They made their camp near the foot of the trail, watering the beasts in a hole dug downstream. Paks helped with that, for it took two to dig away the sand that slithered into the hole while the horses and mules drank. The High Marshals ordered a line of fires between the camp and the eastern wall, the one they expected the kuaknom to use. Paks wondered briefly if the kuaknom might infest the western cliff as well, but she could see no holes or caves for access. By this time the valley lay in shadow, lit by the sky. Gradually it faded. Paks had the late watch, and she rolled herself in a blanket against the surprising chill. The sand made a comfortable bed. She slept soundly almost at once.

Thelon, the scout, woke her for her turn at watch. Paks stretched, stiff from sleeping in armor and took off her helmet to scratch her head. When she replaced the helmet, she let it sit loosely on her braid as she came to the main fire for a mug of sib.

"Nothing so far," reported Thelon. "I wandered across the stream — if you can call it a stream — far enough from the fires to see better, but I saw nothing. But it feels strange, and I don't like it."

Paks yawned. She took a long swallow of sib, aware of sand sifting through her clothes, itching. "I don't mind it feeling strange, as long as those kuaknom, or iynisin, or whatever they are, let us alone."

"Iynisin is the better word," said Thelon seriously. "Elves are the sinyi, the singers of the First Singer's songs, and these scum are those who not only refuse to sing, but who unsing the songs, going against the Singer's will in everything. So, being created as the sinyi are to love trees and flowing water, these hate them, and burrow in stone, fouling bright water with their filth, or choking it — like this one — with stone dust. For the daskin race, the dwarves, it is right to live in stone; they are the dasksinyi, the stone-singers, whose song is stone and its metals. They honor the stone. But these iynisin defile it. So Balkon will tell you."

"Yes, but he calls them something else —"

"In dwarvish, yes — but dwarftongue is not truesong; for the right names, the truenames of things, ask an elf. The Singer is known by some as Adyan, the Namer of Names — "

"I thought that was different," said Paks.

Thelon laughed lightly, in the elven way. "Some also say that the god of men should be called the Sorter of Beads, for men worry more of such division, and not right and wrong." Paks scowled at him, but he held up his hand. "Indeed, you call your god the High Lord, and speak of his Hall as a seat of justice. What is justice, then, but judging and choosing — sorting fact from fact, and laying on one side the true, and on the other side the false? Now I, being but half-elven, have less pride of race than elves: my own thought is that the great king is one only: He Named the first Names, and Sang the first Song, and He rightly judges all things as true or false, good or evil. I would even say that Sertig the Maker is but another name for him — for surely one only came first, and did these things. Now we spend one time singing, and another time fighting, and another time learning or praying — but we are mortal — and even the immortal elves live mostly in one line — we divide, therefore, like a man who says that this mountain is gnomeland on one side, and his land on the other. But it is all one mountain."

Much of this Paks did not understand, but she liked the idea that the High Lord might be the same as Adyan and Sertig. She finished her sib, and went to her post, on the south end of the camp.

The nearest watchfires burned low, scarcely more than a heap of coals, for they had found little wood to burn. High Marshal Connaught had told them to keep wood back, in case of trouble. A chill wind drifted down from the higher land; Paks heard a distant moan where it poured over the lip of the valley into the lower canyons beyond. One of the other watchers coughed; a horse stamped. She thought of Socks, tethered with the others at the north end of the camp, just under the bluff they would climb in the morning. Against the bright starry sky, the eastern cliff loomed, a black presence. It was strange to camp so near a stream and hear no water sounds, but the sand-choked flow moved silently. Something hissed along the sand near her; Paks jumped and looked around. Nothing. Her scalp itched; she pushed her helmet back again to scratch.

All at once the night was full of dark fighters, striking at every post. Paks yelled, with the other sentries, and the camp crashed into wakefulness. Someone threw wood on the nearest fire; by that light she saw the iynisin eyes gleaming under their hoods. She could not tell how many attackers they fought. Blades swept toward her out of the dark; she felt the force of their blows stinging along her arm as she countered them. Something struck her head. Her helmet, still loosely set on her head, bounced off, and her long braid thumped on her back. She had no hand free to find the helmet; several swords faced her. The iynisin cried aloud in their beautiful voices, words she should know — but she was fighting too hard to translate. She was forced back — and back again. Then her foot came down on some-

596

thing that rolled beneath it, and she fell, trying desperately to tuck and come up, but the heavy sand caught her. A great weight fell on her, forcing her face into the sand. Before she choked, she felt a blow to her head, and nothing.

The attackers fled as swiftly as they had come. When High Marshal Connaught called the roll, four failed to answer. Sir Joris was dead, with an arrow through his eye. Two of the men-at-arms had suffered mortal wounds. And Paksenarrion had disappeared. They found her helmet, and her sword, but no trace of her.

Chapter Twenty-five

At first Paks was hardly aware that she was aware. It was dark and cold and the stone beneath her was hard and slightly gritty. She wondered vaguely if she was dreaming about the cells under the Duke's Stronghold. She tried to move, and a savage pain shot through her head. Not a dream. It was hard to think. Dark. Cold. Stone. She felt about with one hand. It met a wall rising from the surface she lay on. Fighting nausea from the pain in her head, she struggled to sit up and feel about her. Wall — another wall — yet another. All were stone; she could not feel any joints. Solid stone? She could not remember what might have happened — where she might be.

As she moved, she realized that her skin itched and stung as if she had rolled in nettles. She reached up to see what she had on — a tunic of some kind. It felt scratchy. She grew aware of something uncomfortable around her throat — something heavy, and slightly tight. And cold uncomfortable bands around her wrists and ankles. She reached to feel the thing at her throat. Pain stabbed her fingers, and she jerked them back with a gasp. Her throat tingled; it was hard to swallow.

For a few moments she held very still, fighting a rising panic. She tried to remember anything at all that would give her a clue to where she was. She thought again of the Duke's Stronghold. That wasn't right. A caravan. A caravan where she was riding, not walking. A tall black horse with white stockings and a blaze. My horse, she thought. All right . . . what next? She thought of gold, and at once remembered Amberion on his chestnut, remembered his name and the nature of the quest. She pushed at the cloud across her memory. They had been — coming into a canyon. No, they were in it. A day later — smoke from the cliffs, arrows — but nothing more. She remembered Ardhiel saying something about the black cousins, the iynisi the elves did not like to remember.

Suddenly she thought where she must be. Underground, taken by the iynisin. She felt around frantically for her weapons. They were gone. Of course, she thought. No sword, no battle axe, no armor — and no medallion of Gird. All gone.

She found herself breathing rapidly, almost gasping, and tried to regain control of herself. Think about it, she told herself. No, think about the others. Do they know? Will they come? *Can* they come? They will come,

598

she thought hopefully. They won't leave me here; they will come. She tried to picture them, fighting their way down tunnels to find her. What if they fail? her mind asked suddenly. What if we all die under these rocks, and no one ever knows what happened? She tried to call on Gird, but something about the place — the quality of the silence, perhaps — stopped the words at her lips, and she could not say Gird's name aloud.

Yet thinking about Gird and Amberion helped. Whatever happens, she thought — and forced back the imagination of what might happen — I am a warrior of Gird. Whether I can fight my way free or not, I can fight to the end. She remembered Ambros falling as he gave the death-stroke to Achrya's priest. That would not be so bad. Any soldier expected to die someday. She had heard tales enough, in Fin Panir, of paladins and knights fighting against impossible odds, for the glory of Gird. For a moment she saw herself, fighting alone against — what? — she imagined many black-cloaked swordsmen — in a blaze of light.

Paks leaned on the wall and pushed herself up, dizzy as she was. Much better standing. The darkness was more than absence of light; it had a malign and bitter flavor. She edged around the walls, feeling her way along the stone. Wall. Wall — and something other than stone, colder than stone, and smooth. She felt along its edge. A door? Yes. Iron, she thought. She could find nothing but a smooth surface: no bars, no grill, nothing but the smooth metal itself until it met stone. Panic rose again. Suppose they just left her there forever?

You're not a silly recruit any more, she told herself firmly. Don't think of that. And if it happens, it happens. She moved past the door, feeling for hinges, but found none. Without that clue, she could not tell which way the door would open — could not even try to surprise someone coming in. She went on around to the next corner, and the next — which would be opposite the door, she thought — and leaned into it. It was hard to keep her eyes open in the dark. She felt herself slipping down the wall, and straightened with a jerk. Whenever they come, she vowed, they will find me on my feet.

Despite that vow, she woke on the floor of the cell when she heard scraping outside the door. She made it up before the door swung open, but her heart was racing, shaking her body, and her mouth was dry. She squinted against the light that poured in — a lurid yellow-green blaze. Something stank. Facing her was a tall slender figure, caped and cowled in black, face hidden by the shadow of its cowl. Evil radiated from it as it entered the cell. On its chest was a silver carved spider, a handspan across, hanging from a silver chain. Paks moved her hand in the warding sign she had learned as a child. The figure laughed, a liquid sound that would have been beautiful but for the evil aura.

"That won't help you," said the silvery voice, lovely as all elves' voices are, but utterly cold. "Surely they are not sending children, now, with children's little superstitions?" Paks said nothing. She glanced past the first figure to see two torchbearers; the green-flared torches smelled like rotting flesh — the stench rolled from them in heavy waves. A third attendant, also black-hooded, carried a wooden box hinged and strapped with leather. "We were informed," the first one went on, "that you were a warrior of some importance — even a candidate for the order of paladins, or some such nonsense. I find that hard to believe, as easy as you were to capture, but we shall see." It came closer yet. Paks braced herself, whether to take a blow or give one she could not have said. "No, mighty warrior," it said. "You cannot touch me if you try." Suddenly it threw back its cowl to reveal a face entirely elven but the reverse of Ardhiel's: the same fine bone structure, but expressing only evil, its nature cruelty and lust. She was instantly convinced that it was male.

Despite herself, Paks shivered as he reached out a slender long-fingered hand and touched the band around her throat. She could not move back; the band tightened just slightly.

"You see," the iynisi continued, "you wear already the symbol of our lady, and while you wear it you cannot harm any of her servants. Nor can your puny saint — whatever his name is — aid you. You have only yourself, your own abilities — if you have any — to help you here. If you amuse us, and learn to serve us, you may yet live to see the sky again. But, of course, if you prefer to starve alone in this cell —" He looked at her, waiting for an answer.

Paks tore her gaze from his eyes, and looked around the cell, in the green light. It was stone, cut out of living rock: just long enough to lie down in. Nothing else. Her glance flicked down her own body. The tunic she wore was black, and slightly fuzzy. The bands on her wrists were black, with hasps for chains. There were no chains in the cell. Yet. She tried to think of Gird, of Amberion, but her mind froze, clouded.

"Perhaps you need to partake of our sport before you can choose," said the iynisi. "You are already familiar with this cell. Since we want no foolish uproar —" He beckoned to the attendant with the case, who opened it. The first iynisi took out what appeared to be a hank of gray yarn. He unwound the stuff, which seemed slightly sticky, and reached for Paks's wrists. "One of our lady's arts," he said. "Not so cumbersome as chains, and no use to you as a weapon. But you'll find it strong enough; it will bind dwarves, let alone humans. I advise you not to fight it. For now I am using the wristlets, but if you are troublesome, I'll wrap your bare flesh with it, and this —" he laid a strand against Paks's arm; it burned like a coal, like the strands of the net in the Achryan priest's stronghold, "— is what that feels like."

Paks shivered again, but made no sound. The iynisi nodded. "So there is something warrior-like in you after all. That is well. We should lose our amusement were you entirely craven. Come along, now." The iynisi turned to leave; Paks felt a tug at her wrists, now bound closely together. For an instant she thought of resistance to the pull, but the other attendants showed the long knives in their hands, and she knew it would be futile.

"Excellent," said the iynisi, as she took the first step to follow. "We had heard you were capable of thought and planning. It is so important for a warrior to know when fighting is hopeless."

No, thought Paks; it is never hopeless. You can always die. But she was already walking down a stone passage as she thought this, between the first iynisi and a torchbearer in front, and the other torchbearer and attendant behind. She thought of lunging at the one in front, tried to gather herself for it, but her body ignored the thought and kept walking. They passed a branching passage, then another. She tried to look around her, tried to pick out directions and openings, and orient herself, but the speed at which she was led, and the peculiar green light, made this impossible.

They turned into a wider corridor, dimly lit by a greenish blur along the angle of wall and ceiling. Paks could not see what it was, but it gave off a sour smell different from the rank stench of the green torches. Here were other iynisin, that hissed as they saw her. All wore black, but not the cape and hood of her escort, or the great spider emblem. They melted from her path — or from the iynisi with her. As they went on, she thought she heard more and more following behind.

Her escort turned into a narrow passage that sloped downward to the right, falling away from the roof. Ahead of the iynisi, Paks could see a wider opening, and brighter light. She was led through it into a wide flat area, slightly oval. Surrounding it were tiers of stone seats, already half-full, and filling with more iynisin. On one side, a dark gaping maw replaced the first two tiers. As the torchbearers of her escort moved around the oval lighting torches set on brackets, she realized that the dark space was not empty. Eight eyes as big as fists reflected chips of green light. A vast bloated body hung in the web that stretched across the opening. Each of the eight legs, Paks saw, was as long as she was tall.

Paks was hardly aware of the chill that spread over her as she stared at the great spider in horror. Was this Achrya herself? Beside her the iynisi chuckled. "I see you have noticed our ally. No, that is not our lady — merely one of her representatives, you might say. But do not let fear of her make you less nimble. While you wear her symbol, she will not pursue you." By this time the torchbearers had finished lighting the whole circuit; now more green light flared from above. Paks looked up to see a great hanging framework, also made in the likeness of a spider with legs outspread on a web, holding more torches. By this light she could see that the seats were almost filled, and not alone with iynisin. Hunchbacked orcs clustered in one section; groteque dog-faced beings in another. All stared down at her, eyes glittering in the flickering light.

"Your reputation has preceded you, Paksenarrion," said the iynisi, with a mocking smile. "You were involved in the loss of our friend and ally Jamarrin, in Brewersbridge." His voice rang out, now, and the rest of the chamber was silent but for the sputtering torches. "We would see for ourselves what skill in arms, what brilliance of strategy, defeated so fair a servant of our lady." Paks did not answer. She tried to think what this was leading up to, besides a miserable and public execution.

"We could, of course, simply kill you here," he said, echoing her thought. "Our lady would be pleased to see the — inventiveness — of our methods, and the torment of one who destroyed her servant Jamarrin. But such sport lasts briefly, with you human folk. Perhaps, also, you have been used by those you think your friends. Certainly the elves have not treated you fairly, stealing from you and clouding your memory." He reached out quickly and laid a cold, dry hand along her brow. As suddenly as light springs into a dark closet, she remembered the Halveric's scroll that she had sworn to take to his wife in Lyonya — and remembered the elves who had sent her instead to Brewersbridge, to take their messages, while they took the scroll. The iynisi smiled and nodded.

"They 'healed' you, as you thought — indeed, yes, and cast their glamour on you, to turn an honest soldier into their errand-girl, made oathbreaker and faithless by their enchantment. Was that well done? I see you have doubts of it now, and so you should. How much of what you said and did was their bidding? Perhaps you have never acted of your own will yet. We shall give you a chance, therefore, to earn your next day of life." Despite herself, Paks felt a leap of hope. If they would let her fight, even outnumbered — even unarmed — that would be a better death. Surely if she fought, Gird would come and help her, would protect her from the worst. She pushed the thought of the elves away: later she could worry about that, if later came. No doubt they had merely meant to save her trouble. But a faint doubt lingered, souring her memory of them.

"There are many here who would be glad to prove your reputation unfounded," the iynisi continued. "I myself think you do have some skill. We shall see. For your first trial you will face but a single opponent. Hardly a test of your ability, but he will be armed, and you not. If you dispute the fairness of it, you may always forbear to fight, and be cut down without resistance." The other attendants had gone away while he was speaking; Paks looked around as the iynisi stepped back. With a swift stroke of his knife, he cut the strands that tethered her wrists, and stepped farther back, bowing. Then he turned to the surrounding seats, one arm upraised. "Let the sport begin!" he cried. The spectators rose in their ranks and cheered. The caped iynisi ran lightly to the web across the arena, bowed to the huge spider, and swarmed up the web to the seats above.

Paks, alone now on the floor of the arena, looked about for her opponent. She tried again to call on Gird or the High Lord, but could feel nothing when the words passed through her mind. It was like calling in an empty room. For the first time she wondered whether Gird would even listen. Surely if he could hear, he would help — in something like this — but the words she'd been taught echoed in her head, unanswered. She heard the scrape of boots from the passage by which she had come, and turned to see an orc stride into the lighted space. He wore leather body-armor and helmet, as well as the boots, and carried a short-thonged whip in one hand, and a curved knife in the other. Paks took a deep steadying breath and rocked from heel to toe, loosening her muscles. With her own weapons, such an opponent would have been no problem at all; without even a dagger, she was at a severe disadvantage. Still, she could fight — she reached for the spark of battle anger, and welcomed it.

602

The orc came to her slowly, with a low, smooth gait unexpected in such a bent shape. Paks crouched slightly, up on her toes, ready to shift any direction as chance offered. The orc grinned at her, and screeched something which the watching iynisin understood, for they laughed. She supposed it was a challenge of some sort. She felt a rising excitement, hot and joyous. Perhaps this was Gird's gift, instead of his presence?

"Come on, then," she said to the orc in Common. "Many of your kind have I killed; come join them."

Closing abruptly, the orc swung the whip at her head; Paks ducked to save her eyes, watching its knife hand. Sure enough, as the knotted thongs bit into her neck and shoulders, the knife thrust toward her belly. She pivoted away from the thrust and caught the orc's wrist with one hand, jerking him forward. He went to his knees, and she tried to make it to his back. But he rolled as he fell, and she met another slash of the whip. This time the thongs wrapped her legs, and she fell heavily, narrowly missing another thrust of the knife as she twisted away from his hand. He was on his feet an instant before her, aiming another blow of the whip. She scrambled away from it; the iynisin above her tittered.

"Sso . . . we . . . teach . . . to . . . humnss . . . what . . . iss . . . mannerss," said the orc in barely understandable Common. He grinned again. "For thiss one . . . no sswordss . . . jusst whipss enough." He swung the whip around his head; the thongs hummed. Paks kept her eye on the knife blade. He edged toward her again. Paks took a deep breath, from the belly, summoned up all the anger she could rouse, and charged an instant before he did. The whip was still in backstroke; she threw all her weight on him, both hands on the wrist of his knife hand. To her delight he sprawled backwards. She tucked as they hit the stone floor and rolled on, still digging her thumbs into his wrist. The knife clattered to the stone. He had already recognized the danger, and dropped the whip to grab for it with his free hand. Paks kicked it away; it skittered across the arena. The orc squealed and grabbed her leg, then sank its teeth in her ankle. Paks let go of the wrist, and reached for the whip. Again the orc anticipated her, and snatched it up an instant before she reached it. She rolled away, taking another hard lash of the whip before she was scrambling for the fallen knife.

This time she reached the prize first; she turned to face the orc with a weapon in her hand. She scarcely felt the whip welts or the bite. She grinned back at the orc as he came. Even now it would not be easy — the blade was short, and the orc's armor tough — but she, at least, was sure of the outcome. The orc paused, and screeched again in its unknown tongue. The iynisin were silent, except for one voice that by its tone denied a request.

"Did you wish to quit, orc?" asked Paks. "Have I endangered your soft hide too much?" It was the worst insult she knew, for Ardhiel had told her that the orcs' name for themselves meant iron-skins.

The orc glared at her, baring its fangs and running a tongue around its mouth which was stained with her own blood. Paks spared a quick glance to see where she was. Nearly in front of the spider's web — not where she wanted to be at all. She slid sideways in a crouching glide. The orc turned to follow her, more slowly this time. She led it around the arena until its back was to the spider. By then the orc was beginning to grin again. She watched how it moved, decided where to strike.

Suddenly she stood at full height and stretched her arms upward, like someone just arising from a comfortable sleep. As she expected, the orc darted in and aimed a vicious slash at her exposed torso. She sidestepped left, taking the force of the blow without pausing, and rammed her suddenly lowered right arm into the orc's neck. She had shifted the knife blade in that instant to a side-hold, and it slashed his throat from side to side, catching edge-on in the neckbone. The orc fell, blood pouring over her arm as she tried to free the blade. Above her the silvery voices clamored for an instant and were still. Paks rolled the dead orc on his back, and levered the knife free. It had a notch, where the bone had chipped it. She crouched, looking up at the circle of faces, as she tried to catch her breath.

"Well enough," called the caped iynisi from above the spider's lair. "It might have been done with more artistry, but the final stroke was admirable. Continue to amuse us so, and you may yet survive. For your next trial, you may keep the knife you have earned. For now, stand against the wall — " he gestured to the wall behind her.

Already the entrance to the arena was filled with heavily armed iynisin. They fanned out around her and forced her back with their pikes. She could not have touched them with the knife, and did not resist. She watched as two of them dragged the orc's body across the the spider's web, and bowed as they placed it just beneath the lowest strands. With horrible quickness the vast bloated body came down and grasped the corpse, the huge abdomen bending around it so that Paks could see cords of silk from the spinnerets twisting around and around. Soon the orc was a neatly cased packet hanging in the web. Paks swallowed against a surge of nausea. So that's what would happen if she failed — she thrust that thought aside hurriedly. Holy Gird, she thought, just help me fight.

As the battle anger left her, she began to tremble. She was terribly thirsty; the orc-bite on her leg throbbed; the whip welts spread a cloak of pain about her. She wondered again how long she had been underground. Surely they knew she was gone — surely Amberion would come looking for her. Her vision blurred, and she leaned on the wall behind her. She had not noticed that the pike-bearing iynisin were gone until the caped one spoke again.

"I hope that is not weakness we see," came the silvery voice. "Surely such a champion does not think the trial is over after a trifling skirmish like that? No, no . . . we must see more of your far-famed skills. Even now your opponents approach; do not disappoint us."

Paks ran her tongue around her dry mouth. How could she fight again without water or rest? She forced herself to straighten, to look toward the entrance tunnel. Get out in the open, she told herself. You've got to have room. She had stiffened, even with that brief respite, and now she limped on the bitten leg. I have to keep fighting, she thought. I have to.

Out of the dark entrance came two orcs, this time armed with short swords and shields. Holy Gird, she repeated to herself. I can't fight two of them, two swords, with only a notched knife! But Siger's words, spoken long ago in Aarenis, trickled into her memory: the enemy's weapon is your weapon if you can take it. Two swords — if I can get one, then it's one to one. Even a shield will help —

As the orcs came forward, she edged back to the wall. Until she got one of them down or disarmed, she wanted something at her back. She noticed that these two did not seem as eager as the first. One of them held its sword awkwardly. A trick? She waited, and let them come to her, heedless of the iynisin catcalls.

The taller, more skillful orc came in on her right hand, her knife hand. The other edged to her left. Again she noticed that this one held the sword like a stick. The tall one thrust at her. She parried the thrust with the knife, thankful for her long arms. From the corner of her eye, she saw the small orc rush, sword extended stiffly. Paks leaped back to the wall, slamming against it, and grabbed the awkward one's wrist. The orc fell forward as Paks jerked, and she caught a glimpse of a terrified face under the helmet. This one's no fighter, she thought. She dug her thumb into the pressure point, and the orc's sword hand opened. Paks reached for the sword as the taller orc aimed a slash at her over the struggling body of its partner. She ducked. The orc she was fighting tried to slam the edge of its shield into her arm, but she had the sword hilt, as well as her knife, in her right fist. She kicked the orc, hard, and danced back to the wall, switching the knife to her left hand. A surge of triumph gave her momentary strength — that would show them!

The tall orc howled at her and charged, trying to force her sideways into the other one. The shorter orc tried to move in, staying low. Paks slid sideways along the wall, countering the furious thrusts and slashes as well as she could. She felt herself slowing; exhaustion clouded her vision. Only the reflexes developed under hours of Siger's instruction kept her blade between the orc's sword and her body. She had the reach of him, but she could not get past his shield. She tried to force him back, with quick thrusts of her own, but failed. The other orc closed in again, this time grabbing at her knife hand. Paks aimed a kick at the orc's knee, but it snatched at her foot and threw her off balance.

Paks fell heavily on her side, trapped close under the wall. Just over her, the taller orc's blade clanged into the wall. She stabbed at his feet with her knife, rolling toward him to get inside his stroke. Again he missed her. This time his blade landed on the shoulder of the smaller orc, who was trying to grapple with Paks's legs. The little orc screeched and sat back. Paks jerked her legs into a curl and launched herself straight up at the tall orc. She had both blades inside his shield; the sword rammed through his body armor into his belly, and the knife slid into his neck.

Before Paks could free the blades, she felt a weight hit her back, and a strong arm wrapped around her neck. Then the smaller orc's teeth met in her shoulder. Paks threw herself backwards. The orc grunted as it hit the ground, but did not lose its grip with hand or teeth. Paks saw its other hand groping toward the sword the tall orc had dropped. She swiveled, pushing hard with her legs, to get the orc out of reach of that blade. Her own knife was free, but the sword stuck fast in the dead orc's belly. She felt herself weakening, her left arm useless with that grip on her shoulder. The orc began to heave up from underneath; if it once got on top, she would have no chance.

Paks shifted her grip on the knife and struck back over her shoulder, feeling for the orc's eyes. She felt its jaws loosen even before the screams, and stabbed again. Then she raked the knife along the arm around her throat, feeling for the tendons. The grip softened. Paks worked the knife deep into the orc's elbow and twisted. The grip was gone. She rolled quickly and thrust into the orc's throat, trying not to look at its face.

She tried to push herself up from the dead orc. I must get that sword, she thought. I must be ready. But her breath came in great gasps, and she could not see. She felt herself slipping into nothingness, and fell back across the orc's body. With her last scrap of consciousness, she tried to call on Gird, but the name rang in her head, empty of meaning.

She woke in a cell, whether the first or another like it she could not have said. A torch burned in a corner bracket; by its light she saw a pitcher, mug, and platter near her. Her wounds smarted as if they'd been salted, but the bleeding had stopped, and she felt much stronger. She reached for the pitcher, then paused. Someone had said something about the danger of taking any food or drink from the iynisin — or was that something from a child's tale she'd heard long ago? She tried to lick her dry lips, but her tongue was swollen and sore. If she had to fight again, she would have to drink something. And if they poisoned her, she would not have to worry. She shook her head, and winced at the pain. Was she thinking straight? But she had to be able to fight. Gird honored fighters. She was going to die here, almost certainly, but she had to fight.

She took the pitcher and looked into it, but in that green light she could not tell what the liquid was. She poured it out, her hands shaking. Whatever it was, she thought, it was still liquid. She raised the mug to her lips, sniffing, but the torch stank so much she could smell nothing else. She took a swallow. It burned her throat all the way down, but she wanted more of it. She drained the mug. On the platter was a slab of some dried meat and a hunk of bread. Her stomach knotted, reminding her of the hours since she'd eaten. The bread was hard, and tasted salty and sour. The meat was salty too; not until she'd eaten most of it did she think what the salt would do. Thirst swamped all other sensation; she drained the pitcher at one draught, only to find that it gave strength without easing her thirst. She felt the burning liquid work its way along her body, stinging it awake. She was afire all over, with thirst and the wounds and that terrible itching she had felt since the first.

She found herself growling softly. Fight, she thought. Oh, I will fight —
by holy Gird, I will fight exceedingly. She thought of the combat past, the
unfairness of it, the knotted whip, the orc's teeth in her leg, her strokes, the
orcs' strokes. For a moment she grimaced at the thought of the last encounter, when she had stabbed the orc's eyes, but she forced the revulsion
down. I had to, she thought. It wasn't fair; I was outnumbered, I had to do
— whatever. She drew grimness around her like a cloak. Gird of the
Cudgel, she thought. If that's what you want, putting me in a place like this,
that's what I'll do — I'll fight. Protector of the helpless, strong arm of the
High Lord: I will be true. I will fight.

But a moment of doubt had her frowning. Gird was not for fighting only
— she thought she remembered that. Fairness — truth — she shook her
head, trying to think. She seemed to see Stammel's face, telling the recruits
not to brawl, then the look he had given her in the cell when Sejek had
banned her. Something was wrong; she should know something better. But
of course something's wrong, she thought irritably. I've been taken by
iynisin; I had to fight three orcs unarmed; the stuff they gave me was
poisoned —

When she heard scraping outside the door, she sprang to her feet, a little
surprised at her body's quick response. She felt ready — even eager — for
what was to come. They wanted to see fights, did they? She would show
them fighting such as they had never seen.

"I see you have recovered from your shameful collapse." The caped
iynisi entered the cell. It flicked a glance down at the pitcher and platter.
"Ah — refreshed yourself, have you? I fear you may find our ale a bit thirst-
provoking, don't you? But it is strengthening. And if you are successful this
next trial, we might give you water as a reward. What do you think, eh?"

Paks felt her lips draw back in an involuntary snarl. The iynisi laughed.
"I suppose we must not expect to find fighters courteous," he said. "But
how you humans do reveal your needs. It is a weakness of yours, which the
elder races have learned to control." The iynisi snapped his fingers and an
attendant brought forward the box from which he took another hank of
the gray stuff. "'Tis a pity this is necessary," he said. "If we had your word
that you would cause no trouble — no? Discourteous. Perhaps we shall
have to teach you manners as well. Hold out your hands, and pray that I
remember to cut the bond before your combat begins." Paks found that she
had extended her hands without thinking about it, nor could she jerk them
back when she tried. She wondered if the iynisi used a spell — a ring? —
surely *something* to control her.

As before, she was led into the small arena; this time the seats were full
when she came in. A sword, dagger, shield, and helmet were stacked in the
center. "You earned these last time," said the iynisi. "Possibly the body
armor as well, but we differed on that. Convince us, if you can."

The combat that followed was a whirling confusion that was never after
clear in Paks's memory. How many she fought, in that bout or another, or
what arms they had, she could not say — only that she fought at the limit of

607

her strength and skill again and again. She had no memory of individual strokes, how she won, or what wounds she took. When she won, she was rewarded with a dipper of water, a short rest, a weapon to replace one that had shattered. When she collapsed, of wounds and exhaustion — and she did not know how many times, or how often, that happened — she would awake in a cell, her wounds no longer bleeding, but afire with whatever had been used to treat them. She was given food and drink that did nothing to ease her hunger and thirst, but gave her strength to fight once again.

Soon she could think of nothing but the opponent at hand, the weapon that menaced her, the hands that wielded it. For a long time she tried to call on Gird before each onset, but she could never bring the name out aloud. At last it drifted from her mind while she lay unconscious between encounters. She fought grimly, then, to the shrill squeals of the watching iynisin and their allies, and never knew what she fought, or how. There was only pain, and danger, and the bitter anger that kept fear at bay.

That anger grew after every bout: it spread to include all she thought of. The High Lord should never have made the world to include iynisin, she thought bitterly, and if elves could turn so to evil, he should not have made elves. Now the distrust of true elves the iynisin had sown flowered in bitterness. She remembered the elf lord laired deep under stone, bound to some power of evil, and drawing her to his side with irresistible enchantments. Macenion's lies, his greed and cowardice with the snowcat, his arrogance. Even at their best, elves toyed with humans, clouded human memory for their convenience, sent them into dangers they could not assess, with that glamour upon them. Were a few tinkling songs and flowery compliments in a sweet voice a fair exchange for all this disdain of human lives and needs? Hardly. In a world where such evil existed, it ill-behooved elves to sit aside and cast human lives like dice for their pleasure.

It was monstrous that such evil existed — that innocents were tormented in dark places — that she was alone and helpless and frightened. But she wasn't frightened, she reminded herself. Death was the end of all things, and darkness surrounded all light, but she was no child to be frightened of what must come. If Gird wouldn't help — or didn't exist — she would get along without him. She would fight until the end, and then grapple death itself. That would show them.

When she thought at all of her friends, in bits and scraps of memory, she saw them standing idly in the sunlight while she was fighting against impossible odds underground. She had an image of Arñe and Vik, chatting peacefully in Duke Phelan's barracks — of the other paladin candidates, safe in Fin Panir, looking forward to their own tests — of the rest of the expedition, feasting around a fire, leaving her behind with a shrug. For awhile she knew this was untrue; she reminded herself that her friends were better than that. But in the end that truth slipped away as well. They would find out, she thought grimly, and enjoyed imagining their grief and their pride in her deeds. And if they never knew — that might even be better. She was no longer angry with them; they could not understand, it was not their fault. It was their weakness, all those silly thoughts of right and wrong, the rules made for gentler combats: if they had been where she was, they would know that only the fight itself mattered, the enemy's death, the anger sated by blood.

She awoke, once more in a narrow cell, to find the caped iynisi standing over her. She blinked, still under the influence of the healing methods they used. He beckoned one of his henchmen, who quickly raised her head and held a mug to her lips. She swallowed: the same burning liquid. As always, she wanted more. With every swallow, strength flowed back into her. She gulped down two mugs full before he moved away, then she rolled easily to her feet.

"You have given us good sport, Paksenarrion," said the iynisi. "Such sport that we are minded to reward you greatly. You remember your friends, don't you? Your friends outside?"

Paks felt her forehead wrinkle, as she tried to remember. Friends. Yes, she had friends somewhere — she could not remember their names, but she had friends. She nodded.

"Your good friends," he coaxed. "Such good friends." Paks felt a surge of anger. Why was he being so tedious? "Your friends are worried about you; they have come to find you. To free you."

Paks growled, then stumbled over the words. "Can free myself. Can fight."

The iynisi smiled. "Yes, that's right. You can fight. You can free yourself. We will let you fight, Paksenarrion. Just one more fight, and you will be free. You will be with your friends."

Suddenly Paks's mind cleared for an instant; she seemed to see Amberion, Ardhiel, and the Marshals before her. Those were her friends. Were they here? Mingled worry and hope rose in her. She glared at the iynisi: what did he mean, fight herself free?

"Ah — some memory coming back. That is well. Now listen to me. You must fight once more, fight your way through some of our lesser servants, to reach your friends. If you can do this, you may go free. Otherwise, you will die, and so will they. We will arm you in what you have won."

Before she could reply, he waved into the cell several iynisin carrying a suit of black plate armor, a black helmet crested in black horsehair, and a handsome longsword with a curious design at the crosshilts. Paks had no time to examine it. The iynisin began to fit the armor on her; she found, as always, that she could not move when the caped one commanded her to stand still. The armor had a strange feel; it made her uneasy. The helmet was even worse. As it neared her head, she felt a sudden loathing for it, and tried to duck aside. The effort was hopeless. Down over her head came the helmet, close-fitting around her ears and cheeks. She felt breathless. Someone pulled the visor down. She squinted through the eyeslit, but found that everything wavered as if seen through a blowing mist.

"I can't see!" she said.

"That's all right," the iynisi answered. His voice echoed unpleasantly in the helmet. "All down here are your enemies, yes? All are enemies. Here — take the sword." She felt the sword hilt pressed into her right hand. She hefted the blade. It felt good. "All enemies — " said the iynisi's voice, now behind her. "Go — fight — fight for your rights, Paksenarrion. Fight your enemies. Fight — "

She hardly needed that encouragement. She was walking down the corridor, away from the cell, walking alone and unguarded for the first time. At first she could barely see well enough to stay away from the walls, but then her vision cleared a little. She saw iynisin ahead of her, all running somewhere. Those who looked at her screamed, and ran faster. Behind the visor, she smiled. Soon. Soon she would show them. She was no longer helpless; now she had the power she had longed for all those dark hours. She wondered which way to go, heard a confused clangor from a wide cross passage, and turned to see what it was. A fight. A big fight. She saw the passage choked with armed figures: iynisin, orcs, others. She drew breath and stalked forward, sword ready.

She struck the back of a confused mass, hating the black-clad iynisin who had laughed at her. Wide sweeps of her sword parted heads from shoulders, and cleared a space around her. Those in front turned to face her; she leveled the great blade and swiped from side to side, laughing. The black cloaks melted away. Beyond them were greater ones, huge to her eyes. Hatred and anger flared together in her mind. You too, she thought. I will fight. I will fight through all of you, whatever you are. Fight through to my friends. By Gird — the name leapt into her mind, and she opened her mouth to yell it out loud. This time, at last, the sound passed her lips: not as a yell, little louder than a whisper: "In the name of Gird."

A vast space opened in her mind, and out of it a voice like stone said, "Stop!" She froze. One arm held the sword up for another swing, one foot had nearly left the ground. At once she was bereft of vision and hearing, and plunged into darkness.

610

Chapter Twenty-six

Paks woke to darkness. She lay a moment, feeling cool air — living air — wash over her face. She lay wrapped in something soft, on something more yielding than stone. She blinked. She could see something glittering overhead. Stars. The current of air quickened; it smelled of pine and horses and woodsmoke. She could not think where she was. Her mouth was dry. She tried to clear her throat, but made a strange croaking noise. At once a voice — a human voice — spoke out of the darkness.

"Paks? Do you want something?"

Tears filled her eyes, and ran down her face. She could not speak. She heard a rustle of clothing, then a hand came out of darkness and touched her face.

"Paks? Are you crying? Here — " The hand withdrew, and after a sharp scratching noise, a light flared near her and steadied. She thought: lamp. Her tears blurred everything to wavering points of light and blackness. The hand returned, a gentle touch, stroking her head. "There, Paks, it's all right. You're safe now; you're free."

She could not stop the tears that kept flowing. She began to tremble with the effort, and the person beside her called softly to someone else. Another person loomed beside her. "The spell's going, I think," said the first voice.

"About time, too. Can she speak yet?"

"No. But she's aware. I hope we can get her to drink; she's as dry as old bone."

"I'll lift her." The second person slipped an arm under her shoulders; Paks felt herself shift as she was lifted to lean against a leather tunic. "There now. Paks? You need to drink something. Here — " She felt a cool rim at her lips, and sipped. It was water, cold and clean. She swallowed again and again. "Good," said the voice. "That's what you need."

"I'll get more," said the first voice, and she heard the rasp of footsteps. She drank another flask full. Tears still ran from her eyes. She did not know who these people were, or where she was, or what had happened. Only that it was better now. At last she slipped back into sleep, still crying.

She woke in daylight: light blue sky overhead, red rocks against the sky. She turned her head. She lay on a sandbank above a stream. She could see horses across the stream, and men in chainmail grooming them. Nearer was the pale flickering light of a campfire. Around it were three men, a woman, and a dwarf. One of the men and the woman left the campfire and came toward her. They were smiling. She wondered why.

"Paks, are you feeling better this morning?" That was the woman. Paks felt her way along the words, trying to understand. This morning. Did that mean that it was last night, the voices and the crying? Better? She tried to roll up on one elbow, but found she could hardly move. She felt utterly weak, as if she were hollow from the bones out.

"Can you speak at all, Paks?" asked the man. She looked at him. Dark hair with a few silver threads, short dark beard. Chainmail under a yellow tunic. They wanted her to say something. She had nothing to say. They were smiling at her, both of them. She looked from face to face. The man's smile faded as she watched. "Paks, do you know who I am?" She shook her head. "Mmm. Do you know where you are?" Again the headshake. "Do you know who you are?"

"Paks?" she answered softly, tentatively.

"Do you know your full name?"

Paks thought a long moment. Something seeped into her mind. "Paks. Paks — Paksenarrion, I think."

The man and woman looked at each other and sighed. "Well," said the woman, "that's something. How about breakfast, Paks?"

"Breakfast — " she repeated slowly.

"Are you hungry?"

Again Paks thought her way to the meaning of the words. Hungry? Her stomach rumbled, answering for her. "Food," she murmured.

"Fine," said the woman. "I'll bring it." She strode off.

Paks looked at the man. "Who is that?" she asked.

"The woman? Pir. She's a knight." His voice held slight coolness.

"Should — should I know her?"

"Yes. But don't worry about that. Do you remember anything of what happened?"

Paks shook her head before answering. "No. I don't remember anything much. Did I — did I do something bad?"

"Not that I know of. What makes you ask that?"

"I don't know." Paks turned her head to look the other way. She was looking up a narrow valley or canyon walled with red rock on both sides. Nothing looked familiar.

The woman returned, carrying a deep bowl that steamed, a mug, and a waterskin slung from one wrist. "Here — stew, bread, and plenty of water. Can you sit up?" Paks tried, but again was too weak. The man propped her against a pack he dragged from a few feet away. The women set the bowl on the sand, poured water into the mug, and offered it. Paks tried to wiggle a hand free from the blanket around her, but the woman had to help her even with that. When she took the mug, her hand shook so that much of the water slopped onto her face and neck; it was icy cold. But what she managed to drink refreshed her.

"I'll help you with the stew," said the woman. "You're too shaky to manage it." She offered it spoonful by spoonful. Paks ate, at first without much interest, but with increasing relish. She began to feel more alert. A thread of memory returned, though she could not tell if it was recent or remote.

She looked at the man. "Is this Duke Phelan's camp?"

His face seemed to harden. "No. Do you remember Duke Phelan?"

"I think so. He was — not so tall as you. Red hair. Yes — I thought I was still in his Company. But I'm not. I don't think so — am I?"

"Not any more, no. But if you remember that, then your memory is coming back. That's good."

"But where — ? I should — I should know you, shouldn't I? You asked me that. And I can't — I don't know you — any of you — or this — " Her voice began to shake.

"Take it easy, Paks. It will come back to you. You're safe here." The man turned away for a moment, and waved to someone Paks could not see.

"But if I — when I was with the Duke, I was a soldier. I must have been. And you're wearing mail. What happened?" Paks tried again to push herself up; this time she got both arms out of the blanket around her. She had on a loose linen shirt; below its sleeves her arms were seamed with the swollen purple lines of healing wounds. Her wrists were bandaged with strips of linen. She stared at them, and then at the man. "What is this place? Did you — "

He reached out and took her hand; his grip was firm but gentle. "No, Paks, I did not deal those injuries. We brought you out of the place where that happened." He turned to another man who had just walked up to them. "She's awake, and making sense, but her memory hasn't returned. Paks, do you know this man?"

Paks stared at the lean face framed in iron-gray hair and beard. He looked stern and even grim, but honest. She wanted to trust him. She could not remember him at all. "No, sir," she said slowly. "I don't. I'm sorry."

"Don't apologize," said the second man. "I wonder," he said to the first, "whether we should try to tell her what we know."

"Names, at least," said the dark man. "Or she'll be completely confused. Paks, my name is Amberion; I'm a paladin of Gird. And this is Marshal Fallis, of the Order of the Cudgel."

The names meant nothing to Paks, and the men looked no more familiar with strange names attached. She looked from one to the other. "Amberion. Marshal Fallis." They looked at her, glanced at each other, then back at her.

"Do you remember who Gird is, Paks?" asked Marshal Fallis.

Paks wrinkled her brow, trying to think. The name woke a distant uneasiness. "Gird. I — I know I should. Something — it's — what to do — to call — when — " she stopped, breathing hard, and tried again. "When you start to fight — only — I couldn't say it aloud! I tried — and it wouldn't —

613

something on my neck, choking — No!" Paks shouted this last loud enough to startle the entire camp. She had shut her eyes tightly, shaking her head, her body rigid. "No," she said more softly. "No. By — by Holy Gird, I will fight. I will — not — stop. I will *fight*!"

She felt both men's hands on her shoulders, steadying her. Amberion spoke. "Paks. Listen to me. You're out of that. You're safe." Then, more quietly, to Fallis. "And what do you suppose that was about. Surely she wasn't free to fight them?"

"I don't know," was Fallis's grim reply. "But I suspect we'd better find out. Considering how we found her — "

"I won't believe it," said Amberion, but his voice had thinned.

Paks opened her eyes. For a moment she stared blankly at the sky, then shifted her eyes to look at Amberion. She could feel patches of memory coming back, unconnected still, but broadening. "Amberion? What — "

"You were injured, Paks. You don't remember much."

"I feel — strange. Will you tell me what happened?"

"We don't know all that happened. And it might be better to let you remember it for yourself."

Paks looked around. "I don't recognize this place. But the color of the rocks — something — is familiar."

"We moved the camp after you — after the fight."

"Are we in Kolobia yet?" Paks saw Amberion's face relax a little.

"Good. You are remembering. Yes, we're in Kolobia. How much do you remember of the trip here?"

"Some of it — we were in a caravan, for a long way. We saw the horse nomads, didn't we?" Amberion nodded. "And I remember a bald-faced red horse, bucking — "

"That's my warhorse," said Fallis. "Do you remember why we were coming to Kolobia?"

Paks shook her head. "No. I wish I didn't feel so peculiar. Did something hit my head? Was it a battle?"

Fallis smiled at her. "You've been in several battles. Both on the caravan, and here as well. I think you'll remember them on your own when you've rested more. Your wounds are healing well. Do you need anything more?"

"Water, if there's enough."

"Certainly." The Marshal walked away and returned with a full waterskin. He set it beside Paks, then he and Amberion walked upstream, looking at the cliffs on the far side. Paks managed to get the waterskin to her mouth. She took a long drink, then looked around again. The dwarf was looking her way, talking to the woman. When he caught her eye, he rose and came toward her. She tried to think of his name.

"Good morning, Lady Paksenarrion," said the dwarf. His voice was higher and sweeter than she'd expected. She wondered how she knew what to expect. "How fare you this day?"

"I'm all right. A little — confused."

"That is no wonder. Perhaps even names have escaped you. I am Balkon of the House of Goldenaxe."

The name fit; Paks could almost think she remembered it. As she looked at the dwarf, the distant silent scraps of memory came nearer and seemed to fuse in his face. "Yes," she said slowly. "Master Balkon. You came with us from Fin Panir. You know about rock, where it will be solid or weak. You are a cousin of the Goldenaxe himself, aren't you?"

"Eighth cousin twice removed," said the dwarf with a smile. "I think you must be recovering very swiftly. We are glad it should be so, who saw you in such dismay."

"Dismay?" Paks felt a twinge of fear.

The dwarf's face constricted into a mass of furrows and then relaxed. "Is that not the correct term? You must excuse me, Lady Paks. I have not the skill in wordcraft as were I an elf. Dismay? Distress? Dis — oh, I cannot find the word, plague take it! But you were much hurt by those blackhearts, and that your friends sorrowed to see. And you are now much better, and we are glad."

"Thank you, Master Balkon," said Paks. She did not understand what he was talking about, exactly, but his kindness was welcome.

"I wanted to ask you — if it will not be too great a sorrow to speak of it — what those rockfilth used on your injuries."

Paks stared at him. "Rockfilth?"

"They corrupt the very stone, good stone, by living in its heart. Those blackheart elf cousins, I mean, who took you."

"Took me?" Paks shook her head, as a sudden chill ran over her. "I have no memory of such a thing, Master Balkon."

"Ah. Magics, then." The dwarf muttered rapidly in dwarvish; Paks caught only one or two words. He stopped abruptly and looked sharply at her. "You remember none of it at all?"

"None of *what*?" Paks began to feel a prickling irritation. Everyone else knew something about her, but wouldn't tell what it was. It was unfair. She glared at the dwarf.

"Tcch! Be still. That Lord Amberion, your paladin, and the Marshal Fallis, they will not have you told too much, for seeing what you shall remember in time. Do you make noise, they will come to see what we speak."

"Will you tell me?" asked Paks with rising excitement.

The dwarf smiled, a sly sideways smile. "And should I say what such men of power want not to be said? I am no prince or lord to rank myself above them. But they did not say to *me* what not to say — it is a point on which it is possible to differ. So — " He looked at her again. "I will say what I think should be said, as it would be done in the House of Goldenaxe."

Paks forced herself to lie still, remembering this much about dwarves, that they cannot be hurried in the telling of anything. The dwarf pulled out his curved pipe, packed it, lit it, and drew a long breath. He blew three smoke rings.

"Very well, then," he said, as if he had not paused. "You were taken by those blackheart worshippers of Achrya," he spat after saying that name, "such as elves like Ardhiel do not like to admit exist and are of elvish origin — despite having their own word for them. That was when they attacked our camp, the second night in this canyon, and they carried you away down their lairs, under that cliff yonder — " he jerked his head to indicate the cliff across the stream. "And there they held you, some days. We know not what befell you in that dark place, save the marks you carry. Dire wounds enough, they must have been, to deal such marks. We had some trouble to follow your path and find you — do you truly remember nothing of this?"

Paks had been listening in rising horror. She stared at the cliff, the rust-red and orange rocks streaked with black, and shook her head. "I don't — don't remember. Yet — as you talk — something comes back. Like — like seeing a valley from a hill, faraway and hazy."

"That will be the magics, I don't doubt, or the knocks on your head that left such lumps. Well, then, when we found you, that was a strange thing too. We had fought several times in the dark ways, and came to another band of the enemy. None of us knew what was that black warrior so tall behind the others, all in black armor. You — but we did not know then it was you — were killing them, the ones we faced, and when they parted seemed like to kill us too. Then — " he paused to puff on his pipe and blow more rings. Paks waited impatiently, a feeling of pressure swelling her head. "Then, Lady Paksenarrion, you were still, all at once, sword arm so above your head. Very strange. Very strange indeed. Lord Amberion and Marshal Fallis went to look — being careful, too, for any treachery. Then they lifted the visor of the helmet — and a nasty, evil thing that was, that I could sense from where I stood — and there was your face behind it, pale as cheese, and your eyes seeing nothing. All that bad armor was magics — enchanted — your paladin and Marshal had their way with Gird. It split, finally, lying around you like a beetle's wingcases, then it shrivelled and was gone. But that wasn't all. Around your neck — "

"Master Balkon!" Neither Paks nor Balkon had noticed Amberion's approach. He looked more than a little displeased. "Is this well done, to tax her beyond her knowledge?"

"Tax her? I but tell her what things are lost to her."

"But you knew we thought it wise to tell her nothing."

"That you thought it wise, yes — but you never forbade such telling to me. And of the ill-doing of elves and their kindred we dwarves have more knowledge than those the elves would make their allies. To my wisdom it seems right that she should not be left to anxious wondering."

Paks felt a wave of irritation that they would talk over and about her as if she were not there. "I asked him, Sir Amberion, as I asked you. And he chose to think me whole-witted enough to answer me as one fighter to another, not as if I were a witless child." She surprised even herself with the bitterness in her voice.

Amberion looked at her, brows raised. "Surely, Paks, you realize that we

616

do not think you a child — you, of all people. We were concerned that if we told you what we knew, you might never regain your own memories, which must include much that we cannot know. Have you so forgotten the fellowship of Gird, that you mistrust a paladin this way? It must be your wounds that make you so irritable."

Paks felt herself flush at the mild reproof. "I'm sorry," she muttered, still angry. "I — I was worried." Her voice trailed away, and she looked beyond Amberion to the cliffs beyond.

"Are you in much pain?" Amberion went on.

Paks realized that she did, in fact, ache all over as if with a fever; her head throbbed. "Sir, I do ache some."

He felt her forehead, and frowned. "It may be fever — and no wonder with your wounds — yet you feel cold. Let me see what I can do." He placed a hand on either side of her head, and began to speak. Paks felt she should know the words, anticipate the phrases, yet she could hardly concentrate enough to hear them. Her vision hazed. For a few moments the throbbing in her head merged with her aching body in one vast rhythmic pain, then it eased. As it disappeared, she knew how much pain she had felt, and wondered for an instant why she had not known it — had it been even worse, that she could accept it as normal? Her vision cleared. She felt Amberion's warm palms leave her head.

"Does that ease the pain?" he asked.

Paks nodded. "Yes, sir. Thank you. I had not realized how much it was." Now her outburst of a few moments before seemed unreasonable to her; she could not understand why she had said such a thing to Amberion.

"Good." Amberion sighed, and sat beside her, across from the dwarf. He looked tired. "Master Balkon, I heard but the last of what you told her. Was it just the tale of her capture and our pursuit?"

"Aye, it was, and scantly told, at that. I did not speak of the capture itself, since none of us saw it, only that she was taken. Nor did I speak of the debate when she was found missing, or — "

"Well enough," Amberion interrupted. The dwarf scowled at him. "Paks has any of that come back to you as he was telling it?"

"It seemed, sir, almost as if something were trying to break into my head. Something I should know. But as I told Master Balkon, what I do recall seems faraway, dreamlike."

"That's not unusual. By Gird, I wish that elf would wake!"

"By his face," said the dwarf sourly, "that one is enjoying some rare dream such as elves delight in, too rare a dream to wake for our need."

"Elf?" asked Paks.

"Ardhiel," said Amberion. "From the embassy to Fintha — "

"Oh!" A live memory flashed into Paks's mind. "I remember him. In Fin Panir, when we — " she looked at Amberion, then went on more slowly, with dawning comprehension. "When we planned this expedition — I remember that now. I was there. I was taking training, and then — " In her excitement, Paks tried to sit up, but could not.

"I'll get another pack for you," said Amberion. He brought a fat blanket roll, and propped her higher on it. For an instant she was dizzy, but recovered.

"I do remember," she said eagerly. "On the caravan, and when we turned off — those canyons with the white stone high above. A black hill with a dip in the top. Is this farther down the canyon we went into, the one Master Balkon said was not as deep as it was meant to be?"

"Yes, Lady," said the dwarf. "This is the canyon choked with sand. I have not yet had the time to look, but I expect something — some rock fall, perchance — has blocked the downward end."

"And at the high end — that's where the cliffs were that the smoke came from?"

"Yes, in a branch canyon to this one. Do you remember the fight?"

"Something of it. One of those black fighters called out, and it was hard to move after that."

Amberion nodded. "It affected most of our party, save Master Balkon and me."

"Then you did something, and it eased; they were shooting arrows down. Ardhiel and Thelon were shooting back — "

"Yes," said Balkon. "And then that black scum who called down the fear on us came down the cliff in the shape of his lady — " the dwarf spat again. "That one."

"Like a spider," said Paks. "I remember. It was horrible — he just came down the rocks, straight down, and then more and more of them swarmed out of holes in the walls, and Ardhiel blew that old hunting horn he carries, only it didn't sound like a hunting horn."

"No," said Amberion. "And after he blew it, its own shape returned. It was under some enchantment. It's an elven horn, the only one I've ever seen, and a rare treasure. Whatever or whoever it was who appeared when the horn sang, I know not, but great goodness and power were allied in him."

Paks shook her head. "I don't remember anything but the sound of it."

"Pretty enough," grumbled Balkon, "but I'd like to know what it means."

Amberion stretched and sighed. "It meant trouble for our enemies that day, and a long sleep for Ardhiel. Paks, I think your memory will come back; as it does, I'd like to know about it." She nodded. "Master Balkon, we still think it would be best to let her recall these things on her own."

"I worry about those wounds," said the dwarf frankly. "The elves have some means of speeding and slowing growth. Something like that must have been used by those rockfilth — she'd still be bleeding, else. It's dangerous. I would know what was used on her, and would wish you to think what may be done." He grinned at Paks for an instant and went on. "Besides that, it is this talk which has brought her memory so far. Surely more would be better."

"It is that," said another voice, "which distinguishes dwarves from more

618

temperate folk — they always think more is better." Paks looked over to see a dark man in stained leather clothes; she remembered that this was Thelon, their half-elven scout. Master Balkon bristled at his words, but Thelon laughed gently, and lifted his hand. "My pardon, Master Balkon, but I could not resist. It has been long in this camp since anything seemed funny."

"I don't see — " began Balkon; Thelon shook his head, then, and bowed. "Sir dwarf, I am sorry. I had no intention of insult; I'll say so before all, and confess a loose tongue."

Balkon shook his head, and finally smiled at Thelon. "You are but half-elven, and a ranger — which is another word for hardy, as we dwarves know. And I confess I am as fond of plenty as you are of enough. Let it pass, Thelon; I will not bear anger to you."

Thelon bowed again. "I thank you for your courtesy. I came to ask Amberion to attend the Marshals. Ardhiel may be rousing from his sleep, and they asked for you."

Amberion looked sternly at the dwarf as he rose. "Master Balkon, we are as concerned as you, but if Paks doesn't remember, she can't tell you what they used. It would be better to let it be."

Balkon nodded. "If the elf is wakening, he might know far more than I — only he should be told at once, if he can listen."

"Then — ?"

"Then I will but bear her company, and no tales tell, until you bring word of Ardhiel," said the dwarf. And with that Amberion had to be content, and he turned away. Paks watched the dwarf, hoping he would resume his talk, but he did not meet her eyes. He poked and puffed at his pipe, until the smoke rose steadily. Then he looked at her. "I am not one to break my word," he said fiercely, "even so little of it as that. Bide still; the time will come, and you will hear it all."

Paks slept again while waiting for Amberion to return, and woke hungry. She was able to feed herself this time. With help, she managed to stand and stagger a short way to the shallow sand pit that served the camp for jacks. But that exhausted her, and she fell into sleep again as soon as she came back to her place. It was evening when she woke, with sun striking the very highest line of the opposite canyon wall.

No one was beside her at the moment. She saw the dwarf, hunching over the campfire. Pir stood at a little distance, staring up at the sunlit rock far overhead. Off on her right, Amberion and the Marshals stood talking to another taller figure. Paks recognized this as Ardhiel, the elf. She stretched, slowly. She felt a vague ache again, not so strong as before, and wondered at it. The only other time she had experienced a paladin's healing, the wound and pain had disappeared at once and forever. Perhaps she'd been lying awry.

She pushed up her sleeves to look at the marks on her arms. Ordinarily she'd have said the wounds were several weeks old; the scar tissue was raised and dark. But the others had said she'd been missing only a few days. She tried to remember what had happened. What Balkon had told her seemed to fit, yet her memories gave no life to his words. Captive — underground — that almost made sense. But what about the wounds? Had she actually fought? And who had she fought, and how? The marks gave her no clues — they looked like any healing cuts, could have been given by knife or sword or pike. The only unusual thing about them was the number — more scars than she had collected in three seasons of fighting with Duke Phelan. She could not understand how she had fought at all — how she had survived — with so many wounds, all given at once. Yet something about them seemed to convey that they'd been given in combat, rather than inflicted on a bound and helpless prisoner.

Amberion's voice interrupted her thoughts. "Paks, I'm glad you're awake again. Ardhiel is with us now, and he examined you this afternoon." Paks was suddenly angry. What right had they to stare at her while she lay helpless? She remembered what the iynisin had told her about the elves who took the Halveric's scroll. She fought the anger down, surprised at its strength, and tried to conceal it. She knew they would not understand. Amberion went on. "He would like to talk with you, if you feel well enough."

"Yes, of course. I'm just — " she decided not to mention the aching to Amberion; he would think it weakness. "I'm still confused," she said finally. Ardhiel sat beside her; he seemed thinner than she remembered, but his face was alight with some joy.

"Lady Paksenarrion, I sorrow that I was not here to defend you. I did not know that when I blew the elven horn I would be carried away — "

"Carried away?"

"In spirit. I had always been taught that elves have no souls, that we are wholly one with our bodies; I had no idea that I could be plucked out, like a hazelnut from its shell, and be gone so long. It did not seem long to me — only a day at the High King's Court — but when I returned, I find that you have spent many dark hours with the iynisin."

"So they say." Paks looked away, frowning. "I can't remember."

"Not at all?"

"Only vaguely. Balkon told me some, and it seemed to make sense — I had the feeling that he was right, as far as he knew. But I don't remember it, clearly, on my own."

"Ah." Ardhiel leaned back on the sand, staring skyward at the glowing blue that deepened as the sun lowered behind distant mountains. "I wish I knew more. We elves prefer to ignore the iynisin — even to pretend they do not exist, or are not distant kin. But at such times as these, that way is proved dangerous, for us and for our allies. I do know that they have the same magical abilities that we have, and share in the powers of those they worship: Achrya and Nayda, Gitres and Liart."

Paks shuddered as the four evil names seemed to foul the air. A face swam before her: elven, but evil. Frightening. "I — don't remember," she said.

620

"If it is truly wiped from your mind, by a blow on your head, for example, that is one thing. But if the memory has been blurred by the iynisin or their deity, then we must do what we can to bring it back. I could not tell, this afternoon — I was still half-enchanted by my own experience." Ardhiel sat up, stretching. "Amberion. Did you want to do this before or after eating?"

"Do what?" asked Paks, alarmed. Amberion turned from watching the distant line of mountains, and smiled at her. She thought his face looked flat and featureless in the dimming light. He sat on her other side, and reached for her hand.

"We need to find out what magic the iynisin used on you, Paks. Surely you realize that. Ardhiel and I will each try what we know — "

"But — " Paks tried to think of some argument. "Isn't it — didn't you tell me that — that paladin candidates must not submit to spells?"

Amberion frowned. "Usually, that's so. But this is a special case — you have already been spelled, we think, by the iynisin. And you were assigned to my care. Gird knows, Paksenarrion, what I feel that I did not save you from that capture. But now — we must do what we can for you."

Paks nodded, meeting Amberion's eyes with difficulty. She could tell that he was concerned — even worried. For herself, she felt more annoyance than anything else. In time she would heal, as she always had, and be strong again; the memories would come, or not come. She wanted to hear what they knew — wanted them to trust her enough to tell her, as Keri and Volya had told her about the sack of Sibili.

"Amberion tells me that these wounds were already so healed when they found you, Paksenarrion." Ardhiel laid his longfingered elven hand on her wrist. Paks tried not to flinch. "You were missing so short a time — either the wounds were never what they look like — that is, they were not real wounds, but created in this halfhealed state — or they were magically healed."

Paks looked at her arms again. "Could they be made that way? I never heard of such — "

"No. It's not widely known that it can be done, and it would only be done by evil intent. But the other is bad, too. To force flesh to such healing, out of time — that has its own hazards. I have known an elf, long ago in your time, and far from here, who could speed growth and healing. He used the gift on plants only, but animals too could be treated so. What we will do now, Paksenarrion, is try to lift the cloud from your memory. If it is what I think it may be, a cloud the iynisin placed there, you can then remember what you need."

As much as Paks had wanted to know what happened, she still shrank from this. Now that she knew her memories could be made or unmade at elven will, as the iynisin had shown her, she wanted no more of that. But some doubt of them kept her from mentioning the Halveric's scroll. The elf's glowing eyes seemed dangerous as coals. She looked at Amberion. He nodded. "Ardhiel has convinced me that this is best, Paksenarrion. The iynisin powers should be countered as soon as possible."

621

"Then Balkon was right — " she murmured.

"Right in his way," said Ardhiel. "You do need to remember, but you need to remember for yourself. It is this I will try."

"Well, then — go ahead." Paks looked from one to the other of them. "What should I do?"

"Think on Gird and the High Lord," said Amberion. "They will guide your thoughts — and your memories, we hope — while we free them."

Paks closed her eyes and lay still. She could not keep from pushing at the dark curtains in her mind, and felt more and more breathless and trapped as she lay there. She was hardly aware of Ardhiel's hand when it moved to her brow, or Amberion's firm grip. Ardhiel began chanting something in elven — she did not even try to follow the meaning.

Shadows moved in her mind. Some were darker — some moved away from her, and others menaced her. She saw again an elven face, pale against a dark hood. She felt a burning pain at her throat, and tried to raise her hand, struggling. The shadows seemed to harden, thickening into reality. Sounds came, faintly at first, then louder. Shrill cries, mocking laughter, the clatter of weapons. Bitter fluid stung her throat, the stench of it wrinkled her nose. The faces came clearer out of the darkness: orcs, their fangs bared, their taloned hands holding swords, knives, whips. Other fighters, whose kind she did not know, in armor of leather and plate. The light was green, a sickly shade that turned spilled blood black.

Gradually she was able to remember the bargain the iynisin had made: she had had to fight, fight for their amusement against opponents of their choosing, fight with whatever weapons they gave her, for the chance to live a little longer. As it had happened, so in the memory Ardhiel's treatment roused: she could not remember how long these fights had gone on, or the intervals between them. But she could remember, as if reliving them, the pain of her wounds, the hunger and thirst and exhaustion, the fear that she would never see daylight again, the grim and bitter anger she had summoned against that fear. When Ardhiel took his hands away from her brow, she was aware. And the memories she had lost lay in a cold heap in her mind. She hated the thought of them, of stirring through them, but she had no choice. That, too, she resented: she had had no choice with the iynisin, and no choice here.

Chapter Twenty-seven

For of course Amberion insisted on knowing what, if anything, she remembered. She replied as quickly as possible, surprised at her own distaste, with an outline of the iynisin bargain and her fighting. She remembered even the black armor, and her reluctance to wear it.

"And you called on Gird before each encounter?" asked High Marshal Fallis, who had come up to listen.

"I tried. I couldn't — couldn't say it out loud." Paks hoped he would say nothing more about it.

"But you tried — you intended to?" Amberion's eyes held hers.

"Yes — sir." Paks looked away with an effort. "I tried. At least, all the times I remember — "

"That should be enough — " But his tone lacked conviction, and he looked across her to Ardhiel.

"I don't understand. What's the matter?" Even Paks could not be sure whether irritation or fear edged her voice.

Fallis sighed. "Paksenarrion, you had no way to tell — but if you handled cursed weapons, and in a cursed cause — "

"And that black armor was definitely cursed — "

"But I killed orcs — some iynisin — and they're all evil — "

"Yes. I know. That's why we think it may work out." Amberion shook his head, nonetheless. "I wish you hadn't touched those things — "

"But — " Paks felt ready to burst with the unfairness of it. She had been trapped, alone, captive, far underground — she had fought against many enemies and her own fear, to survive — and now they said she should never have touched a weapon. I'm a fighter, after all, she told herself. What should I have done — let them kill me without lifting a hand? Bitterness sharpened her voice. "I thought Gird would approve — fighting against odds like that."

"Gird does not care for odds, but for right and wrong." Fallis sounded almost angry. "That's what we're trying to — "

"Then should I have stood there like a trussed sheep and let them cut my throat?" Paks interrupted, angry enough now to say what she felt. "Would you have been happier to find my corpse? By — by the gods, I thought Gird was a warrior's patron, in any fight against evil, and I did my best to fight. It's easy for you to say what I should and shouldn't have done, but you were safe in the sunlight, while I — "

623

"Paks!" Amberion's voice, and his hand on her arm, stopped her. "Paks, please listen. We know you had little choice; we are not condemning you. You are not a paladin. We do not expect such wisdom from you. And now you are still weak and recovering from your injuries. We shouldn't have told you our worries, I suppose, but we did. I think myself that you will be all right when your wounds heal, and you have rested. Eat well tonight, and sleep; tomorrow we need to move camp again, and be on our way."

Paks stared at him, still a little angry, but appalled at her own words when she remembered them. Had she really spoken that way to a paladin and a High Marshal? "I'm sorry," she said quietly. "I — I don't know what — "

"Anyone," said Amberion firmly, "anyone, coming from such an ordeal, would be irritable. Can you walk as far as the fire to eat, or shall we bring food here?"

"I'll try." Paks was able to stand with Amberion's help, and made it to the fire, walking stiffly but alone. She said little to the others, concentrating on her own bowl of food. Master Balkon eyed her from across the fire, but said nothing. She wondered how much the others knew. She felt empty and sore inside, as if she had been crying for a long time.

After the meal, High Marshal Fallis asked Ardhiel to tell the company about his experience. The elf smiled, sketched a gesture on the air, and began. Paks, listening, recovered a little of her first enchantment with elves. The intonations of his voice, even in the common tongue, gave it a lyrical quality. His graceful hands, gesturing fluidly, reminded her of tall grass blowing in the wind. He caught her eye, and smiled; she felt her own face relax in response. The story he told, of being taken away on the flying steed they'd seen, and feasting in the High King's Hall, was strange enough. Paks was not sure whether Ardhiel thought the High King was the same as their High Lord — or whether that was someone else entirely — but she did not ask.

When he had finished, full darkness had fallen, and the stars glittered brightly out of a cloudless sky. Paks began to wonder if she could make it back to her place; she did not feel like moving again. Someone else began to talk with Ardhiel she was too sleepy to notice who it was. Then she was asleep, hardly rousing when someone draped a blanket over her.

She roused again before dawn. One cheek was stiff with a cold wind that flowed down the canyon; the sky was pale green, like a bruise. She could see both rock walls clear against the sky, but down in the canyon shadows hid all detail. She rolled her face inside the blanket, and warmed the cold side of it with her breath. She felt stiff and sore, but much stronger than the day before. A horse whinnied; the sound echoed from the walls. Another one answered, louder. Now several of them called. Paks thought she could pick out Socks's whinny from the rest. She pushed herself up. Cold air swirled under the blanket and she knew she'd have to get up to get warm. A dark shape crouched over the fire, muttering. This morning she recognized one of the men-at-arms.

624

When she came to the fire, he handed her a mug of sib, grinning.

"'Tis cold, these early mornings," he said. "It must be the mountains; I've always heard it's cold all year round in mountains."

"That's true of the Dwarfmounts," agreed Paks. She shivered, and spread her hands to the flames. She had on a linen shirt over her trousers; the wind seemed to go through it as if it weren't there. Where were her clothes? Which pack?

As if he had heard her thought, Amberion dumped a pack beside the fire. "Your pack," he said, and reached for a mug of sib. "Glad you're up. We'll be riding today."

Paks found a wool shirt to cover the linen one, then paused. "Should I wear mail?"

"Yes — better not take a chance. Oh. That's right — yours is gone. We'll have to find you some." He finished his sib and stood up. Paks donned the wool shirt, and unrolled her cloak. She was still cold. She moved around near the fire, trying to warm up. Gradually the stiffness eased, though she still felt a deep aching pain along her bones. It was much lighter. Someone had started a pot of porridge for breakfast; when she looked for the horses, she saw several men at work, tacking them up. Socks was still bare, tied to a scrubby tree. Paks walked toward him.

"Will you be riding him today?" asked one of the men.

"I suppose so." She had no idea what sort of trail they would take, but if they had to fight, she wanted Socks. He stretched his neck when she neared him, and bumped her with his massive nose. She rubbed his head and neck absently, scratching automatically those itchy spots he favored. The man reappeared with her saddle and gear. Paks thanked him, and took her brush from the saddlebags. When she tried to lift the saddle to the horse's back, she was surprised to find she could barely get it in place. Every muscle in her back protested. She took a deep breath, and fastened the rigging. Foregirth, breastband, crupper, rear girth. Saddlebags. She was panting when she finished. Socks nosed at her. She fitted the bridle on his head, and untied him.

By the time they had ridden out of the canyon, onto a shoulder of the heights to one side, Paks felt she had been riding all day. Socks and the other horses toiled upward. Paks tried to take an interest in the country once more rising into view — the great cliffs of raw red stone, the fringe of forest on the plateaus above. Far to the north an angular gray mountain, dark against all the red, caught Balkon's attention.

"There! See that dark one? Not the same rock at all — that one comes from hot rocks, rocks flowing like a river, all fire-bright. It will be sharp to the feet if we come there."

"We shouldn't," said Amberion. "The map gives us a cross-canyon next, deeper than the last, and Luap's stronghold is somewhere nearby."

"Nearby, eh," grumbled the dwarf. "Nearby in this country can be out of reach." They were riding now through a little meadow of sand, carpeted with tall lupines in shades of cream and gold. Ahead the trail led up toward a curious spire of rock that looked, to Paks, as if it were made of candle-drippings that had been tilted one way and another while still soft.

"Is that some of your rock that flowed like a river?"

"No." Balkon grinned at her. "Rock that flows doesn't look like it after-wards — this is all sand-rock. Like that below, in the canyon.

All this time, the distant cliffs that Amberion and Fallis were sure lay beyond the cross canyon drew closer. Paks could not believe that much of a canyon lay between them and the cliffs — until they reached the spire, and the rock fell away beneath their feet. A thin thread of trail angled back and forth down the rocks.

"Gird's breath, Fallis — we can't get the horses down there." Amberion took a few steps down the trail, stumbling on loose ledges of rock. "It's as steep as a stair. Mules, mayhap, but the warhorses — "

"We can't leave them here." Fallis looked around, frowning. "Those kuaknom, or iynisin, or whatever could come back — and you know the scroll mentioned dragons, as well."

"Yes, but — " Amberion slipped again, and the dislodged rock rattled down the trail several lengths before stopping.

"I'll scout ahead," said Thelon, pushing his way forward. "This may not be the best way down — "

"By the map it's the only way down."

"Still — "

"You're right. Take someone with you — " He glanced at Paks, and she thought herself she should go — but her legs felt soft as custard. Amberion's gaze slid past her to one of the men-at-arms. "Seliam — you're hill-bred, aren't you?"

"Yes, sir." The man slipped by Paks and together he and Thelon disap-peared down the trail, quickly out of sight. Meanwhile everyone dismounted, and moved the sure-footed mules to the front of the line.

"Though I'm not sure that's best," said Connaught. "This way the horses can fall on the mules. Of course, they're as like to fall completely off the trail as down it."

In the end it took the rest of that day to get everyone down to the bot-tom. They had only the one trail; Ardhiel and Thelon might have been able to take another way, but no one else. They took everything that could be carried down by hand, climbing back up for load after load, and then led the mules down one at a time. The horses were last and worse; Paks was ready to curse their huge feet and thick heads by the time she had Socks down beside the stream that flowed swiftly and noisily in the canyon.

Here at least they had good water and plenty of wood. That night's camp, on an almost level bank some feet above the water, brought no surprises — Amberion and Ardhiel both thought the iynisin had been left behind. Paks said little. She could not understand why she was so tired, when Amberion and the High Marshals had done their best to heal her. She had found the strength to work with the others, but it had taken all her will to do it — nothing was easy, not even pulling the saddle off Socks.

The next day dawned clear again, and the two High Marshals began looking for the clues in Luap's notes. Paks forced herself to rise when they did, managed to smile in greeting, and almost convinced herself that nothing was wrong. Others were groaning good-humoredly about their stiff joints; she had nothing worse than that. She brought deadwood for the fires, and thought of washing her hair and bathing. Thelon reported a bath-size pool, only a few minutes' walk downstream, already sunlit.

But when she stripped and stepped into the pool, the cold water on her scars seemed to strike to the bone. She shuddered, seeing the scars darken almost to blue against her pale skin; she felt suddenly weak. The current shoved her against the downstream rocks; they rasped her nerves as if she had no skin at all. She crawled out, gasping and furious. What would the others think, if she couldn't take a cleansing dip like anyone else. Her vision blurred, and she fought her way into her clothes. Let them think what they liked — she shook her head. No one had said anything. Maybe they wouldn't. She felt an obscure threat in her anger, in everything. By the time she climbed back to the camp, she could hardly breathe; her chest hurt.

But Amberion had gone with the High Marshals, and no one spoke to her. Paks crouched by the fire, worried but determined not to call attention to herself. They had enough other problems. When the scouting party came back, jubilant, having found the mysterious "needle's eye of rock" through which the detailed map of the stronghold could be seen, she was much better. She ate with the rest of them, and that afternoon they all prepared for the next day's journey. That night Paks slept better, and woke convinced that nothing but fatigue was wrong. She was even able to saddle Socks without great effort. They started on their way soon after daybreak.

Very shortly they came to a side canyon, emptying into the main one at almost right angles. They turned up this, clambering over and around great boulders until the horses could go no further. Here there was a glade, and a deep pool of water. Connaught left Sir Malek in command of half the men-at-arms, the other two knights, and the other yeomen, and told them to keep the animals out of the main canyon.

"The scrolls mention a dragon — and I've never seen country that looks more like it should have a dragon in it. But in this narrow cleft, you should be safe. Gird's grace on you. If we are successful, we can open a closer entrance from inside. Wait for us at least ten days before giving up."

The rest of them made their way around the pool, and began climbing the rock on the far side. It seemed to Paks like a great stair, each step perhaps ankle high and an arm deep, but with the treads tilted downward. She looked up and gasped, forgetting her pain and exhaustion.

There, far overhead, a great red stone arch hung in the air, spanning the distance from one massive stone buttress to another. Behind her, she heard Balkon mutter in dwarvish. Everyone stopped for a moment in amazement. Connaught called back to the yeomen below, and Paks saw them come around the pool and look up.

"I see it," shouted one. "By the High Lord, that's a wonder indeed."

They kept climbing. The stone slope, roughly shaped into tilted stairs, curved below and under the arch. Connaught led them toward the nearer, southern end of it. As they neared the vertical buttress walls, it was clear that someone had shaped the natural stone, flattening the increasing tilt of the treads. They reached the vertical cliff, and moved along it. Now the stairs were hewn clean, like any stone stair — except for the crescent of Gird chipped into the rise of every other one, alternating with an ornate L. The stairs steepened. Paks fought for breath; her chest burned and her eyes seemed darkened. She nearly bumped into Amberion, in front of her, when he stopped.

"Now we'll see if we have understood the message," said Connaught. "This should be a door — if I can open it — "

Paks could not see, from her position many steps down, what he did. But suddenly those in front of her moved, and she climbed wearily to a last small platform before an opening in the rock.

Inside she saw with a pang of dismay that the steps continued — even steeper, they spiralled up into darkness. Light flared above her; it must be Amberion lighting the way. Paks bit her lip and started up. When she reached a level again, her legs were quivering. The stairs had come out in daylight, on top of the cliffs. Amberion touched her shoulder.

"Are you all right, Paks?"

"I'm tired," she admitted, hating that weakness. "I shouldn't be, but — "

"It's all right," he said. "Let me try to help." Paks did not miss the looks the men-at-arms shot her, as Amberion's hand touched her head, but the warmth of that touch and the strength she felt dimmed her embarrassment for a time.

They had come out on the clifftops; from below, Paks would have thought that the top of the mountain, but now she could see another lower row of cliffs and a rounded summit, heavily forested. A trail led south, along the edge of the cliffs; Thelon reported that it ended at a small outpost, a simple rock shelter carved into the stone. Another led west, toward the forested heights, but the main trail led north — out onto the rock bridge that they had seen from below. Paks felt her stomach heave at the thought. Others, she saw, had faces as pale as hers felt.

"Are we goin' out on that?" asked one of the men-at-arms.

"We must," said Connaught. "It is the only way to Luap's stronghold."

"And where is the stronghold?" asked the man, looking around that wilderness of great rocks in confusion.

"There." Connaught pointed to the opposite buttress. "Inside that mountain."

"I give them praise," said Balkon suddenly. Paks looked back to see his eyes gleaming. "That is a worthy stone; such a place would suit our tribe."

Despite her fears, when they walked out on the stone arch it was not bad. Wind was the worst problem, whipping past their ears from the southern

628

desert and moaning in the great pines below. But once on the bridge they could not see below; it was too wide for that. It seemed, in fact, wide enough to drive a team on. They were almost at the far side when they were faced with a huge man in shining mail, who held a mace across his body. They stopped short.

"Declare yourselves," said a strong voice. "In whose name do you invade this place?"

"In the name of Gird and the High Lord," answered Connaught. The figure bowed, and stepped aside. As Connaught's foot touched the stone beyond the arch, it vanished as suddenly as it had come. Paks felt a cold shiver all the way down her back.

On the far side, the trail was clear, a nearly level groove in the stone leading east along the buttress to its eastern end. From here they could see far to the north, to distant red rock walls, and that irregular gray mountain that Balkon insisted was fire-born. Eastward a still higher plateau broke suddenly into the maze of canyons they had wandered. On the very point of the buttress, another guardpost carved into the rock gave a clear view.

The way into Luap's stronghold was a circle carved in the rock, with Gird's crescent and Luap's *L* intertwined in its center. When High Marshal Connaught stood there, and called on Gird, the stone seemed to melt into mist, revealing a stone stair. They clambered down, with sunlight pouring in the well. Paks could not tell how far the steps went down. They seemed to spiral slowly, after the first straight flight, around an open core where the light fell. Finally they ended in a square hall with four arched entrances leading from it. Over each was a symbol, lit by its own fire: Gird's crescent, the High Lord's circle, a hammer, and a harp. Through each a passage could be seen, but nothing else. In the center of the hall a circular well opened to the depths.

They stood a moment, bemused by the designs, then without a word moved slowly toward one or another of the arches. Paks saw Balkon strut through the one under the hammer, and Ardhiel stepped under the harp. She and most of the others stepped under Gird's crescent.

They entered a Hall, as large as the High Lord's Hall at Fin Panir, its great stone columns carved on the living rock. Gentle light lay over it without a source that Paks could see. The floor was bare polished stone, the same red as the rest, except for a wide aisle where some polished white and black slabs had been set in, forming a pattern that Paks found compelling but confusing. Far up at the other end, rows of kneeling figures, robed in blue, faced a shallow platform. Paks looked around at the others, and met Balkon's surprised gaze. Beyond him was Ardhiel.

"I did not come with you," murmured Balkon. "I went under the Hammer, and saw — and saw great wonders of stone, and yet am here. This has the Maker of worlds shaped well."

Paks nodded, speechless. She had not thought she would like being so far underground, with the whole mountain's weight above her, but she could feel no fear. The Hall seemed to cherish them, protect them — Paks could not even feel the ache along her bones that was becoming familiar.

The two High Marshals walked slowly up the aisle; the rest of the party followed. As they neared the rows of kneeling figures, Paks was suddenly seized by fear: would they turn and attack? But they did not move. She could not see even the gentle movement of breath, and then feared they were dead. Ahead, High Marshal Connaught turned to look into the faces of the rearmost row. He said nothing, and passed on. The silence pressed on them; it reminded Paks of the silence of the elfane taig, but it had a different flavor, at once more familiar and more majestic.

When she reached the platform with the others, and turned to look, she saw rows of faces — perhaps a hundred in all — that seemed to be in peaceful sleep. Each held a weapon — most of them swords — point down, with hands resting on the hilts. Paks shivered. She saw the men-at-arms eyeing the figures, and then one another.

"Gird's grace, and the High Lord's power, rest on this place of peace," said Connaught softly. The words sank into the silence. And then as if a drop of dye had fallen into clear water, the silence took on another flavor, and *shifted*, pulling away from them to drape itself around the sleepers, protecting their rest, while leaving the company free to talk. It was as if a king's attention had passed to someone else, setting the pages free to whisper along the walls of the chamber.

"Well," said High Marshal Fallis, with a little shake of his shoulders. "I never expected to find *this* sort of thing."

"Mmm. No." Connaught had stepped onto the platform. "Look at this, Fallis." The platform was itself stone, apparently all one great slab of white stone, and into the upper surface a brilliant mosaic was set, unlike anything Paks had seen. "I wonder where he found someone to do this — " He turned to Paks. "You were at Sibili, weren't you? Didn't they have work like this?"

Paks shook her head. "Sir Marshal, I don't remember — I had a knock on the head and don't remember anything. But — let me think — someone in our Company mentioned pictures made of chips of stone."

"Yes. I thought so. Along the coast of Aarenis they do this work; I've heard that it was used a lot in old Aare."

"It could have come from Kaelifet," said Amberion. "I've seen bronze and copper ware from there ornamented with bits of colored stone; perhaps they do stone mosaics as well."

"It might be." Connaught walked slowly from one end of the platform to the other, looking at the design. It spread from a many-pointed star in shades of blue and green to an intricate interlacement of curves and angles in reds and golds. "I would like to know what it is."

"It is a place of power," said Ardhiel suddenly. They all looked at him.

"I feel power in all this," said Amberion. "But what do you mean?"

Ardhiel nodded toward the pattern. "That is a pattern of power. This place is made of many such. That — " he pointed to the black and white of the aisle, "is another of them."

"What do they do?" asked Fallis.

Ardhiel smiled, a quick flash of delight. "Ah — you men! You hear that I am saying more than elves are wont to say, and you hope to learn great secrets. So — listen closely, and I will say what I can in Common. And in elven, for those who can hear." He threw Paks a smile at that. "This place is sustained by patterns of power, else those sleepers would have died long since, and the dust of time half-filled this chamber. How was it we each saw and followed the symbol of our lord — Master Balkon, I daresay, saw and followed the dwarf's secret symbols, and was met and welcomed as a dwarf, just as I saw and followed the Singer's sign, and was met and welcomed as an elf. Is it not so?"

"It happened," said Balkon.

"Yes. Then together we found ourselves in this Hall. A pattern of great power. I think more than men had the shaping of it."

"But — " began Fallis, and the elf waved his hand for silence.

"I will be as brief as the matter allows, Sir Marshal. In haste is great danger; the right use of power requires full knowledge. This pattern, on the platform, is much like one placed in every elfane taig, in the center of every elvenhome kingdom. I do not know if I can explain how — and I know to you that means much. We elves — we think that as the Singer sang, and we are both songs and singers ourselves, we both are and make the Singer's patterns. So our powers grow from the patterns of our song. We do not enjoy putting these aside — outside us." Paks could tell he was having a hard time saying what he meant in Common; for once an elf's speech seemed halting and out of rhythm.

"You mean, as men do in machines?" asked Amberion.

Ardhiel nodded. "Exactly. We have — we are — the power — as you paladins are: and I know what you will say, that it is the High Lord's, and he but lends it. That is also so of us, though we are given more — more — " he faltered, waving his hand. "We can choose more for ourselves, how to use it," he said finally. "But on occasion we have used built things — patterns of stone or wood, or growing things, to make patterns of power that any elf can use, even if he lacks a certain gift."

"At the elfane taig — " Paks spoke without intention, and Ardhiel looked at her sharply. "The stone's carving — if I looked at it — it held me — "

"Yes. Instead of having some always on guard, elves have used such to bemuse and slow an enemy. This pattern, though, is used for other things." He seemed reluctant to go on, but finally sighed and continued. "I might as well tell you, since it is clear that men used it before. With such a pattern, it is possible for a small group to travel a great distance all at once."

"What!"

Ardhiel nodded again. "Look here — and here — you will see that each of the high gods and patrons is included by symbol. This pattern draws on all their power, and can be used by a worshipper of any of these: elf, dwarf, gnome, those who follow the High Lord, Alyanya, or Gird, Falk, Camwyn, and so on."

"But how do you know where you'll go?" asked Fallis.

"I am not sure. If it were exactly the same as the elven pattern, you would go where you willed to go. You would picture that in your mind, and that you would see, and that is where you would go. It would be possible, however, to set such a pattern for a single destination."

"And to set it off?"

"An invocation of some kind — I do not know. Perhaps you will find guidance somewhere else in this place." Ardhiel was reverting to the more usual enigmatic elven reticence.

"In that case, I think we can wait. Perhaps we will find some guidance elsewhere." Fallis gestured to a narrow archway leading out of the Hall behind the platform. "Perhaps we should take a look?"

The group followed the High Marshals across the platform — Paks noticed that they skirted the pattern gingerly — and through the arch into another stone passage, well-lit by the same sourceless light. At intervals they passed arched doorways into rooms hollowed from the stone; most were empty. But one chamber, when they came to it, was very different. A desk and two tables were littered with scraps of parchment and scrolls. Shelves along the walls held neatly racked scroll-cases as well as sewn books; a brilliantly colored carpet on the floor showed the wear of feet, but no touch of moth. A hooded blue robe hung from a hook. And a pair of worn slippers, the fleece lining worn into little lumps, lay under a carved wooden chair, just where the wearer must have slipped them off to put on boots. Connaught touched them with a respectful finger.

"These — must be his. Luap's or his successor's — Gird's grace, I can hardly believe it — "

"He might have stepped out only moments ago," said Fallis softly. "There's no dust — no disarray — " He glanced at the loose sheets on the work-table. "Look, Connaught. Supply lists — names — and here's a watch-schedule of some king: south outpost, east outpost, north — "

"I wonder what happened," murmured Amberion. "I feel no evil here at all, only great peace and good, but — some sleep, and others are gone — "

Connaught sighed. "Amberion, we wouldn't know if Falk himself slept out there with the others. Who knows what he looked like? The legends say he was thinner than Gird — and none of us ever saw Gird. I don't suppose," he said, turning to Ardhiel, "that you happen to be of an age to know what Falk looked like — "

Ardhiel shook his head. "Sir Marshal, I am sorry that this is not a mystery I can solve for you. Only I agree with Sir Amberion, that this is not a place of evil. Whatever happened here, happened for good."

"So — now what?" asked Fallis. "I feel strange, rooting around in these things that seem untouched. If it were a ruin, and everything half-destroyed — but here, I feel like a — a robber, almost."

"We asked Gird's grace, and the High Lord's power, Fallis. They know our need, and the needs of this place. We will be warned, I daresay, if we trespass where they do not wish us to go."

Fallis nodded. Connaught turned to the others. "Amberion, if you don't mind, you might lead a group looking for a lower entrance. They must have had a way to get animals in and out, and heavy loads."

"With all the magic this place holds," said Amberion drily, "perhaps they simply wished them inside." Connaught chuckled, then sobered abruptly. "By Gird, Amberion, I hope you're wrong."

Before Amberion got out of hearing, however, Fallis had found a map of the complex, in the wide desk drawer. They called Amberion back.

"Look — this is the main Hall — "

"And this is Luap's office, as we thought. So that corridor, if we'd gone on, would lead to the kitchens — "

"I wonder what they do for firedraught, so far down," said Fallis. "Master Balkon, do dwarves have any trouble with that?"

"Firebreath? No, it is important to make a hole for it, that is all."

"Look at these red lines, Amberion — could that be shafts?"

"It could be anything until we go and look. Let me — ah. Look here. Is there another sheet?"

"Yes. Two more; I put them on the table there."

"Good. Let me see — yes, look at this. I thought so. This keys to the other sheet, and this must be the ground level — if his mapmaker followed Finthan tradition, then this sign means a spring."

"But we saw springs coming out of the rock very high," said Connaught.

"Yes, but look — isn't that a trail sign? And it's twisting here, as in natural land, not straight or gently curved like these corridors."

Paks, looking over their shoulders, could make little of the brown, red, and black lines on the maps. She had found the Hall easily enough, and Luap's study, but the maze of corridors, and the strange marks that Amberion insisted meant ramps or stairs, confused her.

"I only hope," Fallis was saying, "that your trail isn't like that rockclimb we had."

Amberion laughed. "No — I'm sure it's not. We'll go down that way and see. How many would you like left with you?"

"Who has a good writing hand?" asked Connaught. "We should make copies of what we find." Paks and one of the men-at-arms, who was known to write clearly, stayed with the High Marshals.

Paks heard later that day how Amberion had led the little group through echoing passages of stone, ever deeper, down gentle ramps. They had found a stone stable, clean but for a few ancient bits of straw, and the deep-grooved ruts of the carts that had carried in fodder and carried out dung. They had found great kitchens, three of them, and Balkon had told them why — that whatever way the wind blew, one of the hearths would draw perfectly. They had found storerooms still full of casks and bales — but across the doors lay a line of silvery light that Amberion would not try to pass. And finally, when the last wide corridor ended in a blank face of stone, Amberion had touched it with one glowing finger, and the stone vanished in a colored mist. The cold, pine-scented air of the canyon blew in, swirling a little dust around their feet. Some of the men were reluctant to go out, fearing the passage would close again, but it stayed open like a great grange door behind them.

Paks spent that time copying what seemed to her a very dull list of names. She supposed that the High Marshals had some reason to need a complete list of Luap's followers, with the years of their coming, but she could not understand it. Behind her she could hear them at the shelves, gently taking down one scroll or book after another, and murmuring to each other. She used up the small amount of ink that Fallis had had, and asked him for his inkstick. He reached over to Luap's desk, where a bowl of ink sat waiting, as it seemed, and handed it to her.

"Use *this*?" Paks asked.

"Why not?" He hardly looked at her, face deep in a large volume bound in cedarwood.

"But it's — it might be — "

"It's just ink, Paksenarrion. What else could it be?" Paks felt her shoulders tighten at the sneer she thought she heard in his voice, and ducked her head. How did he know it was just ink. Ink doesn't stay wet for years — all the years this place had been — whatever it had been. She stabbed at the ink with the pen, and felt vindicated when it clicked on the surface.

"It won't write," she said. "It's dried up."

"Oh?" Fallis put the book down, picked up the bowl, and tilted it. "That's odd. It looked wet, and I'd have sworn it shifted. Hmm. Well, here's the inkstick and — yes — here's a bowl for it."

Silently, Paks mixed a measure of ink with water from her flask. She pushed it over so that Elam could use it too.

Amberion reappeared to say that he had found the lower entrance, and had started moving the animals and others toward it.

"It's nearly dark, though, so I thought it better to camp for the night — that trail is barely passable in daylight. Will you come out, or shall I have food sent in?"

"We'll come out," said Connaught. "Everyone needs to hear all about this, and we should be together."

"I thought you might want to set sentries on the old guardposts."

Connaught shook his head. "Until we know more about how this place works, that would simply call attention to us. Paks — Elam — that will do for today. Let's go have some supper."

And Paks, rising from her seat, realized how stiff and hungry she was. She followed the others out without a word.

In the next two days, some of the party explored as much of the old fortress as the light would allow. One rash yeoman tried to pass a doorway barred with silver light, and fell without a cry. Amberion touched his head, and did nothing more.

"He'll wake with a headache, and more respect for these things. Someone stay with him, until he wakes."

Paks spent her time copying records. She wished she could roam around, seeing the things others spoke of in the evenings; it didn't seem fair that she had to act as scribe all the time. But no one had asked her what she wanted to do, and she refused to bring it up. Surely they could tell, if they thought about it, she thought bitterly. Finally, when one of the yeomen was describing a long climb up a narrow corridor to an outlook on the very top of the mountain, among the trees, Paks exploded.

" — and you could see so far," the man said, gesturing. "North of here, and west — what a view. Of course it was cold up there, and after climbing all that way my legs quivered like jelly." He grinned at Paks. "You're lucky, lady, that you get to sit all day in the warm, just wiggling your fingers with a pen."

"Lucky!" Heads turned at the bite in her voice. "Lucky to sit all day? I'd give anything to be where I could see something besides another stinking scroll! How would you like to travel all the way out here and then be stuck in a windowless room? I've already been underground as much as I care to — " She stopped short, seeing the worry in Amberion's face, the High Marshals' stern expressions.

"You could have asked, Paks," said Fallis mildly. "We thought it would be easier for you, with your wounds still healing, than climbing all over."

"I'm sorry," she muttered. Now that she'd said it, she felt ashamed, and still somehow resentful. She shouldn't have protested — she shouldn't have felt that way. Yet she did, and it was unfair.

"Take some time tomorrow," Amberion said. "I'll show you some things if you wish." But Paks felt that he was humoring her, as if she were still sick.

When she tried to follow Amberion around the stronghold the next day, she found that in one thing the High Marshals were right. She was too weak to climb far. She pushed herself, determined not to show what she felt, but when Amberion turned back toward the lower levels, near midday, she was glad. That afternoon she copied lists without complaint, and that evening the High Marshals announced their decision to try to use the pattern on the Hall's platform.

"We won't take everyone; enough must stay here to go back, as planned. The maps show another way out this canyon, down through the western cliffs, and a clear trail to the trade route from Kaelifet. We suggest that instead of the trail that would take you past the kuaknom again. But if the transfer works, we will return and the rest of you can travel easily that way. Wait ten days for us to return before you leave; Ardhiel assures me that if we can use the pattern at all, we can return in that time."

Paks was elated to find that they wanted her to try the pattern with them. High Marshal Connaught, commander of the expedition, was staying behind; those returning were Amberion, High Marshal Fallis, Ardhiel, Balkon, and herself. With Connaught watching, they mounted the platform, standing as near the center as they could. Paks watched Balkon; he had confided to her that if he was to travel like this, he might as well go home if he could. Then the High Marshals together lifted their voices, calling on Gird and the High Lord. Ardhiel's silvery elven song joined them, then Balkon's chant in dwarvish. Paks thought she heard a faint and distant call of trumpets.

Chapter Twenty-eight

As the Hall of Luap's stronghold faded around them, the sound of trumpets seemed to come nearer. Abruptly they were standing on the lower dais of the High Lord's Hall at Fin Panir, facing the Marshal-General as she came forward between the ranks of knights: the fanfare had just ended. The Marshal-General stopped in midstride, her face a stiff mask. Behind her, the knights drew sword; others burst into shouts, questions, even one scream, chopped off short. The Marshal-General's arm came up, paused . . . the hubbub stilled, no one moved. Then Amberion spoke, a formal greeting that Paks hardly noticed because she'd realized that Balkon was not with them, and grinned to herself. She had no doubt that he had chosen to return to the Goldenaxe, and hoped his magic worked.

In moments, the Marshal-General had reached the dais, touching each of them, eyes bright. And again the Hall was full of sound: greetings, whispers, comments, the scrape of feet, the rasp of weapons returned to scabbard and rack. To Paks, it seemed noisy as a windstorm after the calm of Luap's Stronghold. She felt at once submerged in it and remote, a solitary stone washed by contending waves. Eventually the noise receded, the crowds dispersed, and she went to her quarters, hardly noticing the shy greetings and questions of those few students who spoke to her.

A few hours later, the Marshal-General summoned her. When she arrived in the study, she found the Marshal-General and Amberion waiting.

"I have been telling the Marshal-General," began Amberion, "about your capture and ordeal with the iynisin — the kuaknom — " he said quickly, after a glance at the Marshal-General.

Paks nodded, at once alarmed and defensive.

"I wondered what your plans were, Paksenarrion," said the Marshal-General. "From what Amberion says, and the way you look, it seems that you may need a rest. Such wounds would slow anyone. Have you thought of it?"

"No, Marshal-General. I did not know if— I mean, I am tired, yes, but I don't know about rest. Do you mean you want me to leave?"

"No, not that. Amberion thinks you are not fit for a full schedule of training; he thought several weeks of rest would help. There are many things you could do here, without much strain, or — "

"I know what I would like," said Paks suddenly, interrupting. "I could

636

go home — visit my family in Three Firs. It's been four years and more." As she spoke, the longing to go home intensified, as if she had wanted this all along.

Amberion frowned. "I don't think that's a good idea," he said slowly.

"Why not?" Paks turned to him, annoyed. "It's not that far, by the maps. I'm surely strong enough to ride that far — and there's no war — and —"

"Paksenarrion, no. It's too dangerous, as things are with you, and —"

Paks felt a wave of rage swamp her mind. She was not weak, just tired from the fighting and the trip. They kept trying to make her believe something was wrong — "There's nothing wrong with me!" she snapped. "By Gird, just because I'm tired — and you said anyone might be — you think I can't ride a few days to see my family. I traveled safely alone on foot, with no training at all, four years ago. Why do you think I can't do it now? You keep trying to convince me something's wrong — and whatever it is, it's not wrong with me!" She glared at them, breathing hard.

"It's not?" The Marshal-General's voice was quiet, but hard as stone. "Nothing wrong, when a paladin candidate feels and shows such anger to the Marshal-General of Gird? Nothing wrong, when you have not thought what such a visit could do to your family?"

"My family — what about them?" Paks was still angry. She could not seem to fight it back.

"Paksenarrion, you have attracted the notice of great evil — of Achrya herself. Do you think you can travel in the world — anywhere in the world — without evil knowing? Do you think your family will be safe, if you show Achrya where they live, and that you still care for them? Gird's grace, Paksenarrion, be on your mind, that you think clearly."

Paks sat back, stunned. She had not thought. She shook her head. "I — all I thought was —"

"All you thought was what you wanted to do."

"Yes —"

"And you resented any balk — any balk at all —"

"Yes." Paks stared at the tabletop; it blurred as her eyes filled. "I — I thought it was over!"

"What?"

"The — the anger — Amberion can tell you. I thought it was past — that I had — had beaten it —" Paks heard the rustle of clothing as the Marshal-General moved in her seat. She heard Amberion clear his throat before beginning.

"Immediately after we got her out, she had a — I don't quite know how to describe it. Fallis and I thought we should let her memories return naturally — at least until Ardhiel awoke. But Balkon — the dwarf, you recall — he disagreed, and began telling her some of it. Anyway, I stepped in and interrupted, and Paksenarrion became angry. Very angry. I thought at the time it was the pain of her wounds, and attempted a healing —"

"It did help," said Paks softly, trying not to cry. "It eased them — and then I could see I was wrong —"

637

"But whatever it was recurred. A couple of times, in the next days — nothing bad, if it had been someone else, someone more irritable to start with. But it was not like Paksenarrion — not the Paksenarrion we knew. We spoke to her of it, and made allowances for the wounds — which Ardhiel said had been healed so far by some kuaknom magic — and she seemed to have recovered, but for the weakness and exhaustion I spoke of to you."

"I see." The Marshal-General was silent a long moment, and Paks waited, as for a blow. "Paksenarrion, what do you, yourself, think of this anger? Is it just the wounds? It's not uncommon for people to be irritable when recovering from illness or wounds."

"I — don't know. I don't feel different — except for being tired. But if Amberion says I am, then — " She shook her head. "I don't know. In the Duke's Company, I didn't get in trouble for fighting, or anything like that, but I did get angry. I can't tell that it's any more now than it was then."

"Our fear," said Amberion, "was that the type of fighting she did, with the iynisin — the kuaknom — would open a channel for Achrya's evil — "

"I would hate to think so," said the Marshal-General. "I would hate that indeed. Paksenarrion?"

"I don't feel that, Marshal-General. Truly, I don't — and I care for Gird, and for his cause, as much as ever I did. The anger is wrong — to be angry at you, I mean, but I can control it another time."

"Hmm. Amberion, had you any other concern?"

"No." He smiled at Paks. "She has not begun beating horses, or cursing people, or telling lies — it's just an uneasiness. Ardhiel feels the same."

"Paksenarrion, I hope you agree now that you should not travel to Three Firs — " Despite herself, Paks felt a twinge of irritation at this; she masked it with a nod and smile. "Good. Take a few days to rest; let our surgeons look you over. It may be that rest and good food will bring you back quickly. Don't start drill again until I've talked with you. We may want you to help instruct a beginner's class."

Paks left the Marshal-General's office with mixed feelings. The thought of instructing was exciting — she could easily imagine herself with younger students, as she had worked with recruits in the Duke's Company — but the prescribed days of rest were less attractive. Though tired and jaded, she was restless, and could not relax.

"I'm about to do a dangerous thing," said the Marshal-General, pulling out a blank message scroll.

"What?" Amberion watched her closely.

"I'm going to write Duke Phelan of Tsaia." Arianya trimmed her pen, dipped it, and began.

"Phelan? Why?"

"I think you're right. I think this child is in serious trouble. And I think we don't know her well enough. Phelan commanded her for three years; he will know which way she's turned."

"Then you sensed something too?"

"Yes. Not much, as you said. But deep, and so rooted that it will grow, day by day, and consume her. By the cudgel of Gird, Amberion, this is a sad thing to see. She had so much promise!"

"Has still."

"Maybe. Right now — we must keep her from leaving, and from hurting anyone else. If she leaves us — " She shook her head. "The only thing standing between Achrya and her soul is the Fellowship of Gird. Ward her, Amberion."

"I do, and I shall."

It was some days later that Paks came into the forecourt to find familiar colors there: three horses with saddlecloths of the familiar maroon and white, with a tiny foxhead on the corners, and a pennant held by someone she had never seen before. She lingered, wondering if the Duke himself had come to Fin Panir, and what for, but she had urgent business with the Training Master, and had to go. Upstairs, in the Marshal-General's office, she herself was the topic of conversation — if such it could be called.

Duke Phelan faced the Marshal-General across her polished desk, his eyes as cold as winter seawater. "And you want me to help you? You, who could not protect, for even a year, a warrior of such promise?"

Arianya sighed. "We erred, my lord Duke."

"Tir's guts, you did, lady! Not for the first time, either! I thought I'd never be so wroth with you again, as when my lady died from your foolishness, but this — !" He turned away, and paced back and forth by the window, his cloak rustling, then came to lean on the desk again. "Lady, that child had such promise as I've rarely seen in thirty years of fighting. Your own paladin saw that in Aarenis. You could not ask better will, better courage, than hers. Oh, she made mistakes, aye — beginner's mistakes, and rarely twice. But generous in all ways, willing — we hated to lose her, but I thought she'd be better off in some noble service. She had a gentle heart, for a fighter. I was glad to hear that she'd come here for training. She'll make a knight, and well-deserved, I thought. And then — !" He glared at her.

"My lord, we thought — " began Amberion.

"You thought!" The Duke leaped into speech. "You never thought at all. Make her a paladin, you thought, and then you dragged her into such peril as even you, sir paladin, would fear, and without your powers to help her. You think me stained, Girdsmen, compared to your white company, but I know better than to put untrained raw recruits into hot battle. 'Tis a wonder you have any paladins at all, if you throw them away so."

"We don't, Duke Phelan," said Marshal Fallis. "They do not go out untrained. But in her case — "

"She did. Do you even know how young she is? What years you have wasted?"

"Duke — " began Fallis angrily.

639

"Be still!" roared the Duke. "I'll have my say; you asked me here for help and you'll hear me out. I have no love for you these fourteen years, Girdsmen, though I honor Gird himself. Protector of the innocent and helpless, you say — but where were you and where was he when my lady met her death alone and far from aid?" He turned away for a moment, then back. "But no matter. If I can help this girl, I will. She has deserved better of us all." He looked around for a chair, and sat. "Now. You say she was captured, and is now alive but in some trouble. What is it?"

"My lord Duke, a paladin candidate can be assaulted in spirit by evil powers; that's why we normally keep them sequestered. We think that in defending herself during captivity she became vulnerable to Achrya's direct influence. This is the thought of Amberion and Fallis, who observed her at the time they brought her out, and also of Ardhiel the elf, who knows how kuaknom enchantments might work."

"I see. Then you think she is now an agent of Achrya?"

"No. Not yet." Arianya met his eyes squarely. "My lord, all we have noticed so far is irritability — unusual for her, for we have known her to be always goodnatured, willing, and patient. It would hardly be noticed in another warrior — indeed, many expect all fighters to be touchy of temper."

The Duke grinned suddenly. "I am myself."

"I noticed. But she has not been so since we've known her. You have known her longer; we thought you could tell us if she has changed."

"You want me to tell you if she has become evil?"

"No. She has not become evil, not largely. That I could certainly sense for myself. I want you, if you will, to speak to her — observe her — and tell us if she is changing in the wrong way. Becoming more violent, less control-led — that is a sign of contamination."

"And if she is? What then will you do?"

The Marshal-General paused long. "I am not sure. She is a member of our fellowship, and a paladin candidate — as such, she is under my command. As she is, she cannot be a paladin — "

"You're sure."

"Yes. I'm sorry, but so it is. What is of no account in another may be a serious flaw in a paladin. If she had gone over to Achrya, it would be my duty to kill her — "

"No!" The Duke jumped to his feet.

"Please. Sit down. She has not — I am not saying she has — I am saying *if* that were true, which is not true. Yet. But if she is changing in that way — if the evil is growing — then, my lord Duke, we cannot tolerate an agent of evil among us. We *cannot*. Somehow, before that happens, we must prevent it."

"What can you do? Can you heal her, as you heal wounds?"

"Unfortunately not. Her wounds, indeed, have not yielded to our heal-ing. The elf, as I said, says that this is because of some kuaknom magic used on them. As for her mind. . . . I think that we might be able to destroy the

640

focus of evil — if, indeed, I am not misnaming it — but like any surgery it would leave scars of its own."

"You speak of magic?"

"If you consider the gods' powers and magic in the same light, my lord, which I do not. The High Lord has given us — Marshals and paladins both — certain powers. With them I might try to enter her mind and cleanse it."

The Duke shifted in his seat. "I don't like it. I don't like it at all, Marshal-General, and that's without any rancor for the past. It's bad enough that she had to bear such captivity, and such wounds as you describe. That she had to have that filth trying to corrupt her mind. But then to let someone else in, to stir the mess further — "

"Believe me, I don't like the idea either. But what else is there? If we are right, and the evil is rooted there, and we do nothing, she will come to be such as even you, my lord, would admit must be destroyed. Could anything — even death now — be worse than that dishonor?"

"No, but — I dislike being the means of it. She is — she was, I should say — my soldier, under my command and protection. She has a right to expect more from me — "

"Now?" asked Fallis.

"Yes, now. By the gods, Marshal, I don't forget my soldiers when they leave. She served me well; I will not serve her ill."

"My lord, one reason I wrote you was that she had so often spoken of her respect for you. We are not looking for an accuser, my lord, but a friend who knew her in the past — "

"And do you think I will condemn her to you, having known her?"

"I trust you for that. You have always been, by all repute, an honest man — and so she thinks of you."

"I will not persuade her to your opinions — "

"We don't ask that. Go, talk to her, see for yourself. If you come and tell me I'm a fool, I will be best pleased by that. I don't think you will — but do your best for her."

The Duke ran his hand through his hair. "I'll tell you what, Marshal-General, you have set me a problem indeed. But you have one yourself. All right. I'll see her. But I think perhaps I'll have a new captain for my Company out of it, and you'll be a paladin the less."

"That may be so."

Paks came from the Training Master's office in the black mood that had begun to seem familiar. She was not to ride out with the others to hunt the following day, and she was not to plan on taking part in the fall competitions. She lengthened her stride, hardly noticing when several students flattened themselves out of her way. At least, she was thinking, I can take Socks out to the practice field. She turned hard right into the stable courtyard, and nearly bumped into a tall man in a maroon cloak. Before he turned, she knew who it was.

"My lord Duke!" She fell back a step, suddenly happier.

"Well, Paks, you've come far in the world." He looked much the same, but he spoke now as if she were more his equal.

"Well, my lord, I — "

"They tell me that's your horse, the black."

"Yes, my lord — "

"Will you ride with me? I'd like to see how the training grounds are laid out."

"Certainly, my lord." Paks turned toward the tack room, but a groom was already leading Socks out, ready to ride. The horse had recovered his flesh, and showed no ill effects of the expedition. The Duke's own mount waited, and after they mounted, he rode beside her.

"We were glad to hear," he began, "that you'd been accepted here. I had two years with the Knights of Falk, and I understand that the training here is as good if not better."

"It's thorough, my lord," said Paks. He laughed.

"Fortification? Supply? Field surgery?"

"Yes, my lord, and more."

"Good. And you enjoyed it?"

"Oh yes. Last winter was the happiest time of my life — " she stopped suddenly and looked at him. "I mean, my lord, after leaving the Company."

"Don't be silly, Paks — you weren't happy with us, that last year. Few were. Of course you'd like this better. Now — what's that?" For some minutes they rode in the training grounds, the Duke commenting and questioning on the equipment and methods of training that they observed. Then he turned to her again. "Did they teach you such riding here?"

"No, my lord. That was Marshal Cedfer in Brewersbridge, where I got my horse."

"Brewersbridge — that's in southeast Tsaia, isn't it?"

"Yes, my lord." Paks wondered if he would ask her about the details of her journey across the Dwarfmounts, but he said nothing for a bit. Then — "What's this journey you've been on, that they talk of so? And they said you were captured by some kind of elf — is that so?"

Paks shivered, unwilling as always to remember that too clearly. "Yes, my lord. It goes back, sir, to when I left your Company: in the journey over the mountains, a traveling companion and I were enchanted by the elfane taig, and had to fight a demon-possessed elf underground."

"By Tir! And you lived?"

"Yes, my lord. And the elfane taig rewarded me with great riches, and gave me also a scroll. It seems that the scroll was written by Luap — it's very old — and contains much about Gird and his times that was not known, for the scroll had been lost. It was in this scroll that the stronghold of Luap was mentioned, and map besides. So the Council of Marshals, and the Marshal-General, declared a quest that search should be made for this stronghold, and the rumors of lost powers."

"But why did you go? You were a paladin candidate, isn't that so?"

"Yes — but they asked if I wanted to. Because I'd brought the scrolls, you see: it was a reward, an honor."

"I see."

"They didn't know, my lord, that I would have such trouble."

"No, but they might have thought." He shook his head. "Well, enough of that. How did you come to be captured?"

Paks told the tale as best she might, and the Duke looked grave, but listened without comment. When she finished with Ardhiel's treatment, he sighed.

"Are you well, then?"

"I think so. They — " Paks looked aside, but no one was near. "My lord, they seem to think not, but I don't know why. I have lost my temper once or twice — even spoke sharply to the Marshal-General — "

"That's nothing," said the Duke quickly. "I've done as much."

Paks grinned, thinking of it. Then she sobered. "My lord, I don't want to be bad; you know I never did." He nodded. "I don't think I am, yet they don't trust me any more. Just today the Training Master told me not to ride out hunting tomorrow — and not to join in the autumn competitions, either. Is that fair? I haven't done anything — I've been careful — I do all they ask me — I don't know what more I can do!" Her voice had risen; she took a deep breath and tried to continue more calmly. "They — they say that evil begins as a little thing — too little for me to sense. That it will grow, and consume me, until I become one of Achrya's minions. But, sir, you know me — you've known me all along. Am I so bad?"

Phelan looked at her, a piercing gaze that she found it hard to meet. Then he shook his head slowly. "Paks, I see you much as you were: a good soldier, loyal and courageous. You bear scars that I would not care to have, and you have suffered under both enchantments and blows. I do not see evil." Paks relaxed, but he went on. "But Paks, I am no Marshal or paladin, to discern evil directly. The gods know I have no great love for the granges of Gird, but they are not evil. I think perhaps you should submit yourself to their judgment."

"My lord!"

"And if it is not fair, or if you do not agree, leave them. I will not forsake you; as you were my soldier, so you can be again. As I recall, you held the right to return when you left."

Paks said nothing, and after awhile they rode back silently. She suspected that the Duke had come to Fin Panir because of her — and this was confirmed when she answered a summons late that afternoon to the Marshal-General's quarters. She was shown to a study she had not been in before, a level higher, with windows on three sides. Amberion, Fallis, Ardhiel and Duke Phelan, as well as the Marshal-General, were all in the room. The Marshal-General began by explaining what they thought was wrong, and what she thought could be done about it, a sort of surgery of the mind.

Paks nodded gravely, trying to pay attention through a numb haze that

643

fogged her mind. Arianya paused, for that nod, then went on.

"So much we think we can do. But that is not the whole story; I want to be fair with you. We are sure that if you live the evil will be destroyed, but some good may be destroyed as well."

"What sort of good?" asked Paks, her mouth drying with fear.

Amberion looked away, at a tapestry on the outer wall. Arianya glanced down, then met Paks's eyes squarely. "Paksenarrion, the worst evils come from the degradation of good: in your case, those qualities you've worked so long to strengthen. You may not be a fighter afterwards — "

"Not a fighter!" Paks felt the blood leave her face.

"No. I will not lie to you. You may be weak, clumsy, uncertain. You may lose your will to fight — your courage."

"No!" Paks clenched her fists, anguish twisting her face. "I cannot! You cannot want me to be so!"

"Lady Paksenarrion," said Ardhiel "what we want is that you be healed and whole, and free of any taint of evil. But our powers are limited, and it is better to be free of the dark one's web than be a prince under her control."

"But — " Paks shook her head. "But you ask that I give up the only gifts I have — chance them — and if I survive a weakling or a coward, what good is that? To you or anyone? My lady," she said to Arianya, "the granges would not let me in, if I were a coward. I would be better dead, indeed. You say I am not so bad, yet. If I cannot be a paladin, I can still fight your enemies. Then if — if I go wrong, then perform your treatment, or kill me."

Arianya started to speak, but Duke Phelan interrupted. "Paks, when you were in my Company, you learned that wounds must be treated at once, lest corruption begin. And if the surgeon cuts away good muscle, it's better than leaving the least infection to spread and engulf the whole body."

"Yes, my lord, but — "

"Paksenarrion, the Duke speaks truly. If we thought the evil would not spread, or would spread but slowly, we would not try such a drastic cure. But it is the nature of such to spread with awesome speed. You yourself, being damaged already by this poison, cannot perceive how far it has gone already."

"But my lady — to lose all — and think how long I might live — what could I do? So long in disgrace — "

"It will not be disgrace, Paksenarrion, however it turns out. You have already won honors beyond your years. Nor will any grange of Gird be closed to you: that I promise. And if you have these troubles — and you might not — we will help you find another way to live."

Paks thrust back her chair and rose abruptly, striding to the window to stand braced against the embrasure, looking out at evening sunlight yellow on the cobbled court and the roof of the High Lord's Hall across the way.

"I always dreamed of being a warrior," she said softly. "Silly, childish dreams at first, of being the hero in old songs, with a silver sword. Then Jornoth told me about soldiering, and I was going to be a mercenary, a good one, and earn my living with my sword, and see strange lands, and win honor serving my lord. So I joined Duke Phelan's Company, and prospered as well, I think, as any recruit. You've heard they thought well of me." She glanced at the Duke, who nodded gravely, then turned back to the outside view.

"I stayed three seasons, but — no fault of my lord Duke, who's as fine a leader as I ever hope to fight under — I saw things I didn't want to be part of. So I left, thinking I'd go north and home, and join some castle guard. You know what happened with the elfane taig, and near Brewersbridge. Marshal Cedfer . . . Master Oakhallow . . . they showed me fighting, but for cause, not for a person. My dreams grew — more than being a guard captain instead of a sergeant, I dreamed of fighting as Gird fought — for right, for the protection of the helpless. And you encouraged me: you, Marshal-General, and you, Marshal Fallis, and you, Sir Amberion. You said learn: learn languages, art of weaponry, supply and surgery, fortification — you said all these things were right." Paks's voice broke, and her shoulders shook. The listeners were silent, each with his own memories, his own visions. Paks took a deep breath, then another, and turned to face them, tears filling her eyes.

"And then you honored me, sheepfarmer's daughter, poor commoner and ex-mercenary, beyond all dreams I'd dared. You, my lady, offered me the chance to become a paladin. A paladin! Do you — can you — have any idea what a paladin means to a child on a sheep farm at the far edge of the kingdom? It is a tale of wonder, all stars and dreams. A — a fantasy too good to be true. I had met paladins! And you said 'Come, be one of them. That is your destiny.' " She stopped for breath again, then went on, looking from one to another as she spoke.

"I could not argue, my lady. I felt *you* must know; you wouldn't say it if it weren't true. I wondered, and rejoiced, and then — to go on quest, with Amberion and the others! I was glad to chance all dangers in such company. And all of you were most courteous to so young a warrior. You remember, Amberion, that first attack? You said I did well, then."

"Paks — " he said, but she went on heedlessly.

"And — then I was taken. No, my lords!" She said as both Amberion and Ardhiel started to speak. "I blame you not, I said so before. The evil ones wanted me; it was my weakness or flaw that drew them to me. How could I blame you, who followed into the rocky heart of their lair to free me, outnumbered as you were? No. And while I was thus, in their hands, I tried to pray to Gird and the High Lord for aid, but I had to fight against their servants lest they kill me. I was alone — in the dark — I thought that to fight so — Gird would approve. I thought that was right."

She looked down, suddenly, and shuddered. "It wasn't — wasn't easy." Then she faced them again. "Now you say that because I fought them, because I didn't just die, I have opened a passage for great evil. I can't feel this myself; I don't know . . . But to chance all I can do, to chance losing all I've learned, all I am — that you helped make me — and to think how long I must live if it goes badly . . . Could such a one as I be a — a potter, or a weaver? Oh, better to kill me, my lady, and quickly."

Silence followed her words; Paks turned again and stared blindly out the window. Then Arianya took breath to speak, but Ardhiel forestalled her. "Lady Paksenarrion, elf-friend, may I tell you a true tale?"

Paks gazed at him, white-faced and desperate. "Yes, Ardhiel; I will listen."

"We elves, milady, know not death from age, and thus our memories are long, and we see slow processes in the world as easily as you might see the start and finish of a meal. Once, long ago, before ever this Hall was built or men had found their way over the mountains from the south, I walked the green forests with an elf known for the beauty of his voice and the delight of his songs. From him I learned that very air I taught you, milady, when we first met. It was his craft to shape his instruments of living wood — a delicate business, to urge the growth of linden or walnut or mahogany so that it grew fitly shaped for harp or lute or lo-pipe. And to shape it so that in time the complete instrument could be separated from the tree without harm to it or to the creature it grew from. Long years of growth and shaping were required for a single instrument, but long years we elves have in plenty, and delight in filling them with such work.

"In that time, he was growing a harp: not a lap-harp, as might be grown from any angle of applewood or pear, but a great harp, on which he hoped to play before the throne of our king. If you think of the shape of a great harp, you will realize how difficult this would be, for if the harp frame were strong enough to withstand the tension of the strings, removing it would cause severe damage to its tree. I cannot tell you how it was done — it is not my craft — but he caused a part of the tree, the part between the instrument and the main plant, to withdraw, as it were. This process must be complete when the instrument was grown, else it became gross and unmusical, and required shaping with tools, which he abhorred. But if it was begun too soon, the withdrawal weakened either instrument or tree, and could allow woodrot and other decay to attack both.

"It happened that he had just begun shaping his harp-tree when our king determined to wed. Not immediately, for that is not our way; but the courtship and preparation began, and in twenty years or so, as humans would measure time, the wedding day was announced to all elf-kind. It would be another forty years, for the beauty of elf-maidens does not fade or wither, and the king's subjects would have time to prepare all good gifts for the festival.

"When he heard this, my friend determined that his wedding gift would be the great harp he was then shaping, a kingly gift indeed. He brought me to see it growing, though little I could see: he had to point out which twig would grow to take the fret, and which root-sprout would form the shorter leg. The frame, you see, was to be grown all in one piece: trunk, branch, root, and sprout top-grafted to the branch. In twenty years, I happened by again, and the shape was far clearer. But my friend was dissatisfied. By his craft, he knew that as it grew, it would grow too slowly — it would not be ready for the king's wedding. I laughed, I recall, and reminded him that elves have no need of hurry. For such a royal gift, the king would be well content to wait. He laughed with me, and seemed reassured.

646

"But though elves are not by nature hasty folk, we are proud of our crafts, and love ceremony. And ceremony means things done fitly, and in time, and by that love and desire that his gift might be the means of great pleasure at the wedding feast, he was betrayed into haste.

"I know not when he did it, or exactly what he did; he had ways of speeding and slowing the growth of all plants he worked with. Indeed, I've seen him grow a lo-pipe in but one season. If it cracked in ten years, what matter, if it served the need to gift a dying man? But somehow he tried to speed the growing of his harp, and the withdrawal of the parent tree, and out of this haste a flaw came into the wood. A part of the withdrawal moved into the harpwood, and weakened it, and the great post that would have to bear the greater strain of the stringing grew awry.

"I well remember the day he showed me, sorrowing, what had gone wrong. Fifty years and more of work, and a little space where the rot crept in had ruined it. To heal that, and reshape the post, would not only take time — years of time — but would also require that the weak part be burned out, regrafted with live wood, and supported while new growth took over. And, he said, 'twas more than likely that it would never grow true in shape, but be clumsy and crooked even if strong enough. Yet to ignore the woodrot would doom the harp and the tree that bore it. I asked him what he would do. He looked at the tree awhile, and said 'It is not the fault of the wood, which grew true to its nature. I will amend what I can, and tune it as it will bear.'

"Lady Paksenarrion, it is not through your failure that this trouble has come, but we who should have been wiser tried to rush your growth into that beauty we saw possible. Yet now we cannot leave you to perish by our mistake; we must try to mend, though mending is not sure."

Paks had watched his face as he told the tale, but found it as mysterious as all elven faces; it held surmise but no answers. "Sir — you have always been kind to me," she faltered. "But need it be now? Could I not go to the green fields, just once, to be a — a memory?"

"Lady, I have known you — I, an elf, who will not die except in battle. You are in my memory and the memory of my people, and there you will not fade in all the years to come when men may forget. We will make songs of you, lady, whatever happens."

"That's not what I meant," said Paks miserably.

"Paksenarrion, we cannot force you to this," said Arianya. "It would be better to do it quickly, but we cannot — and would not — force you. But you cannot wander alone, with this peril on you. Nor, I think, should you be much abroad with others. Whatever you decide, and whatever happens, it need not become common gossip."

Paks looked from one to another of those in the room, meeting troubled eyes everywhere, doubt and wariness where once she had seen delight and encouragement. Cold despair assailed her heart, more bitter than she'd felt in captivity. Then she had only enemies against her; these were friends. At last she looked at Duke Phelan, leaning against the wall in one corner, arms folded. He gazed back at her, holding her with the intensity of his gray eyes. After a moment, he came to her, still holding her glance at rest.

"Paksenarrion Dorthansdotter," he said. "I will trust you. I will trust you with my Company, the one thing I have built in my whole life, if you desire it. You may come with me, in spite of them, and take command as a captain, and I will trust you, who never failed my trust before, to decide if you can do so in good honor. By my faith, Paksenarrion, you are a good soldier and a good person, and worthy of the trust you have had, and the trust I offer you. You will not fail in this. You have never failed me, and here's my hand on it." And Paks felt her hand swallowed in the Duke's as her face flushed scarlet in relief and joy.

"Tir's gut, you fools!" the Duke went on to the stunned group. "You'd think you were dealing with a weak, witless chit of a girl who couldn't do the right thing without being led in strings. Whatever she decides, whatever she is when you wise folk get through with her, she's got courage enough now, and wit enough now, for the lot of you. If you didn't think she could be trusted, you shouldn't have been trusting her." He turned to Paks. "Don't cry, captain. My captains don't cry before outsiders."

Paks, her hand still clasped in the Duke's, struggled against a wild mixture of emotions. Joy in the Duke's trust — that someone still trusted — came to her as a flash of light that let her see what lay within. Her arguments of minutes before showed false as tinsel, though she had believed herself true as she spoke. In a few moments she had mastered that turmoil, and the sudden change of her expression brought silence and attention to the chamber.

"My lord Duke," she said. "You have given me more than you offered, for by the light of your trust I can see what honor requires. I may never come to serve you again, my lord, as I should to thank you for this gift, but you will live in my memory, however short it may be."

"Paks — "

"No, my lord. You know what it must be; I would not forfeit your trust. Sir — I would ask your blessing — " Even as she spoke, a prickle of anger stung her; she fought it away.

The Duke wrapped his arms around her and held her close for a moment. "My child — may all good be with you, wherever, however, whenever — may all evil begone from you forever. And if ever you come to me, Paksenarrion, in whatever state you are, I will help you as I can."

"Thank you, my lord."

"And," he added with a growl, "I will stay until I see how you fare with these — "

"Thank you, my lord. Marshal-General — ?"

"You are ready, then?" Arianya's eyes were wet, but she rose steadily, and waited the answer.

Paks stepped away from the Duke. She was trembling, but kept her voice firm. "Yes, my lady. It must be done; and, as you say, will be no better done for waiting."

Chapter Twenty-nine

A circle of light centered the world. Paks watched it change color: first golden yellow, then glowing orange like coals, then red, deepening to violet, then bursting into blue and white, then back to yellow. After some time, she wondered where and why and similar things. She was sure, looking at a circle of red, that it would darken to violet and blue, then burst into brilliant white. Distant sound disturbed her: ringing, as of bit chains, chain mail, herdbells. The crash of stone on stone, or steel on steel. Voices, speaking words she didn't know.

She opened her eyes at last to find a finger of sunlight across them, and blinked. She felt as light and empty as an eggshell. She had no wish to move, fearing pain or loss. A shadow crossed her vision: a shape she should know. A person. She felt the shifting of what she lay on, a draft of cooler air and easing of pressure. Something damp and cold touched her skin, then warm hands, then warmth returned. She blinked again, seeing, now, a Marshal she had met casually the previous winter, but did not know well. The face was remote, quiet, contained. Paks stared at it without intent. It was a puzzle she had to solve.

The face turned to hers; she saw the surprise on it, and wondered vaguely. "Paksenarrion! You're awake?"

Paks tried to nod. It was too hard; she blinked instead.

"How do you feel?" The Marshal leaned closer. Paks could not answer, closing her eyes against the strain. But a hand touched her forehead, shook her head with what she felt as immense force. "Paks! Answer — "

"Wait." Another voice. "We don't know yet — " Paks opened her eyes again. The Marshal-General, robed in white, stood by the bed. She smiled. "Paksenarrion, Gird's grace be on you. The power of Achrya is broken; she cannot control you. You are free of that evil."

Paks felt nothing at these words, neither joy nor fear. She tried to speak, but made only a weak sound. The other Marshal glanced at the Marshal-General, and at her nod fetched a mug from a table.

"Here," she said. "Try to drink this." She lifted Paks against her shoulder, and pressed the mug to her lips. Paks drank. Water, cold and sharp-tasting, cleaned her mouth.

"Can you speak now, Paksenarrion?" The Marshal-General pulled a stool near the bed and sat.

649

"I — think — yes, my lady."

"Very good. You have been unconscious some days, now. We were just in time, Paksenarrion, for the kuaknomi evil had invaded deeply, spreading throughout your mind." The Marshal-General touched her head; Paks shivered at the touch, then quieted. She watched those eyes, wondering what the Marshal-General was seeing. Finally the Marshal-General pulled back her hand and sat up with a sigh. "Well," she said to the other Marshal, "we've done that much at least. It's gone." She looked back at Paks. "How do you feel?"

Paks was beginning to remember what she'd been told before; she tried to feel around inside herself, and found nothing. Nothing strange, nothing bad, nothing at all. "I don't feel bad," she said cautiously.

"You aren't." The Marshal-General sighed again. "You weren't bad anyway, Paksenarrion, any more than someone with an infected wound is bad. Evil had invaded you, as decay invades a rotting limb. We have destroyed it, all of it, but I cannot yet tell what else we may have destroyed. Remember that we are your friends, and your companions in the Fellowship of Gird. Whatever happens, we will take care of you." She rose, and arched her back. "Gird's grace, I'm tired! Haran, get Paksenarrion whatever she wants to eat, and keep watch until Belfan comes. If she feels strong enough, Duke Phelan would like to see her."

"Yes, Marshal-General." Marshal Haran glanced back at Paks, and followed the Marshal-General to the door. Paks could not hear the low-voiced question, but heard the answer. "No. By no means. An honored guest, Haran."

When she had gone, Haran came back to the bed. Paks tried to focus on her face, tried to understand what was going on. They had done something to her: the Marshal-General, Amberion, the elf Ardhiel, others. She felt no pain, only great weakness, and wondered what, after all, it had been.

"Are you hungry?" asked Haran abruptly.

Paks flinched at the tone. Why was Haran angry with her? She nodded, without speaking.

"Well, what do you want? There's roast mutton — "

"Good." Paks looked around the room. "It's not — my room — "

"You didn't think you were with the other candidates, did you? After that — " Haran looked at her, another look Paks could not interpret. "You're in the Marshal-General's quarters, in a guest room. When she's sure — " her voice trailed away.

"Sure of what?" Worry returned, a faint icy chill on her back.

"Sure that you're well. I'll be back shortly with food." Haran left the room, and Paks looked around it. The bed she lay on was plain but larger than the one in her quarters. A window to her right let in daylight sky, a smooth gray. Several chairs clumped around a small fireplace opposite the bed.

Haran returned with a covered tray. "Have you tried to get up? If you can sit at the table — " But Paks could not manage this. Haran packed pillows behind her shoulders with a briskness that conveyed disapproval, put

650

the tray on her lap, and went out again. Paks struggled with the food and utensils. She could not grasp the fork properly; it turned in her hand. By the time Haran returned, with a tray for herself, Paks was both annoyed and worried.

"Marshal, I'm sorry, but I can't — " as she spoke, the fork slipped from her grasp entirely and clattered on the floor. Haran stared at her.

"What is it? Can't you even feed yourself?"

"I — can't — make it work." Panting, Paks fought with the knife and a slice of mutton. She felt as clumsy as an infant just learning to reach and grab.

"You're holding that like a baby," said Haran, with exasperation. "All right. Here — " She put down her own tray and came to the bed. "I don't see why you can't — " And with a few quick motions, she cut Paks's meat into small bites and retrieved the fork from the floor. "Now can you do it?"

Paks stared at her. She could not understand Haran's hostility. "I — I hope so."

"I, too." Haran strode back across the room, shoulders stiff, and began eating her own meal without another word. Paks tried again with the fork. Her hands felt as big as pillows, and it was hard to get the food to her mouth. After a few more bites, she stopped, and lay watching Haran eat. When the Marshal finished her own meal, she came to take Paks's tray.

"Is that all you'll eat? I thought you were hungry."

"I was. I just — "

"Well, don't decide you want more in an hour or so. Finish your water; you need it." She stood over Paks until the mug was empty, then snatched it away. In a moment she had left the room, carrying both trays. Paks sank back on the pillows, still confused. What could she have done while unconscious to anger someone she'd only met once before? A knock on the door interrupted her musings. She spoke, and recognized the Duke's voice.

"Come in, my lord."

He opened the door and entered quietly. "Where's your watchdog?" Paks could not think what to say, and he went on. "That Marshal who keeps your door. Haran, I think she's called."

"She's taking trays back." Paks felt, as she had when a recruit, the menace of the Duke, the sheer power of the man. He prowled around the room like a snowcat, tail twitching.

"I've been wanting to see you, and they keep saying wait." He turned to her. "Are you well? How are they treating you?"

"I don't know. I just woke a little while ago. I can't feel much of anything . . . "

"That's for the best, I'd think, after what they — I tell you, Paks, I came near to killing the lot of them."

"What?"

"To see you like that, with all of them working over you. I feared for you."

"My lord, they had to — " Now she remembered more, and fear grew in her.

651

"Hmmph. Have you been up yet?"

"No, my lord. I couldn't get up to eat."

He shrugged. "It's been some days; the weakness is normal after so long asleep."

"I wish I knew —" In his presence, still more of the warnings came clear, and the emptiness inside was no comfort at all.

He looked sideways at her. "What?"

"If I will be all right again. I don't know how I'll know. And now that I remember what they did, I can't think of anything else."

He sat near the bed, and laid a hand on her arm. "Don't fret about it. You remember that worries before a battle don't help. When it's time, when you're stronger, then you'll find out."

"But what do you think, my lord. Do you think it's gone?"

He sighed, and did not ask what she meant. "Paks, from what I saw, they stirred the very roots of your mind with powerful magicks. From such stirring nothing would be safe. You don't look different, bar being pale from days in bed, but I can't tell by looking. The test of a sword is not its polish, but its temper."

"I want to be . . . myself." Paks whispered the last, thinking.

"You are yourself, Paks, and always will be. Yet people change with time, with age —"

"Not like that. I can't stand it, my lord, if I can't — if I become —"

"Paks." His grip on her arm tightened. "Look at me." His face, when she looked, was as grim as ever she'd seen it, his eyes hard. She feared him suddenly. "Paks, you are yourself, and you can stand whatever comes. I swear to you. I was not always a duke, I had —"

"But you were always brave, always a warrior!"

"No." His gaze slipped past her into an immeasurable distance. "I will not tell you that tale now, but no: I was not always brave. And you do not yet know you have lost anything. Take heart, Paks, until the time comes."

"But why does Haran dislike me so?"

"Haran?" His face relaxed, puzzled. "I don't know. The Marshal-General assigned her here; perhaps she'd rather be elsewhere. Has she been unkind?"

"No. But she seemed not to like me, or something I'd done."

"My lord Duke!" Haran's voice, from the doorway, was indignant. The Duke turned slowly. Paks saw the muscles bunch in his jaw.

"Marshal Haran." His tone would have warned anyone in his Company.

"What are you doing with her?"

"I? I came to see how she was, and found her awake and willing for company. Have you an objection?"

"No. I would have sent, later, to tell you she was awake —"

"Thank you. As you see, I found out for myself."

"I had to take the trays back —" Paks realized Haran was defensive.

"No matter." The Duke waved, as if a squire were apologizing for an

652

overdone loaf of bread. "Tell me, if you can — is the Marshal-General satisfied with her recovery?"

Haran bristled visibly. "I can't speak for the Marshal-General. She knows best. But she did say — " a sharp glance at Paks, "that the evil was safely destroyed."

"And at what cost?"

"That she did not say." Marshal Haran sat down near the fireplace. "Whatever the cost, it would be worth it."

"Whatever?" The Duke turned to her, his hand still on Paks's arm.

"Duke Phelan, I am a Girdsman. A Marshal. The most important thing is that evil be defeated — destroyed. Nothing else matters. Whatever stands in the way — "

"A life?" asked Phelan softly.

"Yes." Haran looked stubborn, her brow furrowed. "I have risked mine. Any Girdsman knows the risk: we are to serve good, and only good."

"Ah, yes. Good. Are you sure you know good?"

"Of course." Her chin was up; she met his look boldly.

"Yes. Of course. You are sure, Marshal, that you know what is good, but I am not so sure." He paused, as if waiting for her comment, but she said nothing. "I have not been sure, for some years, that you Gird's Marshals really do know good from evil, and as yet nothing I've seen here has convinced me." His hand left Paks's arm; she could feel the taut control of that movement. "You do not, perhaps, think I have any such standards myself. But I assure you, Marshal, that a professional soldier, as I am, has had more combat experience than you. I have seen men and women under great stress, repeated stress. And I know those soldiers more thoroughly than you ever will." He paused again. Haran looked furious, but still said nothing. "Paks is one of them."

Paks stirred, and said, "My lord — "

"Paks, this is not your argument; you but furnish the opportunity. What I am saying, Marshal, is that you have known her but a short time; I have known her for years. You have seen her in one trouble; I have seen her in many. I know her as someone trustworthy in battle, in long campaigns, day after day. You see some flaw — some little speck on a shining ring — and condemn the whole. But I see the whole — the years of service, the duties faithfully performed — and *that* is good, Marshal. Is there one of us with no flaws? Are you perfect, that you indict her?"

"I don't — I never said — "

"Not you personally, but the Girdsmen here. You're one of them; you said so."

"Well — I — " Haran looked at Paks, then back at the Duke, clearly gathering herself for an attack. "She's supposed to be so special — "

"What!" Paks flinched at the Duke's tone even though he spoke to Haran.

"She came only last fall; she was paladin candidate after Midwinter Feast. That's different, if you like! Promising, they all said. Remarkable.

653

Chosen to go on quest, when she's not even past her Trials. And then she gets herself captured, like any half-wit yeoman without battle experience, and rather than die honorably, as most yeomen would have done, she cooperates with the kuaknom and is contaminated by Achrya." Haran slapped the table and drew another breath. "And now they make this fuss over her — I can understand it from you, who aren't even Girdish, but the others! It makes me sick!"

"Haran!" None of them had noticed the Marshal-General's arrival. She looked almost as angry as the Duke. Haran paused, then shook her head.

"Marshal-General, I'm sorry, but I don't care. It's true. Paksenarrion should never have been accepted as a candidate; she wasn't fit, she hadn't served long enough. Of course the evil had to be rooted out; if something was lost, she'll just have to live with that. It's nonsense anyway: if she had had sufficient courage, there would be no danger of losing it. I don't see all this pussyfooting. It's not that she's special, it's that she's had special treatment. And far too much of it!" Haran turned on her heel and stalked out. The Duke moved to follow, but the Marshal-General held up her hand.

"Please, my lord Duke! Hear my apology first, and allow me to discipline my own."

"I'm listening," he said grimly.

"I am sorry — I did not know Haran felt that way, or I would never have had her here. I wanted Paks to have Marshals, whose oath of secrecy I could trust, caring for her. I knew Haran was a bit prickly — she always has been; it's why she has no grange — but she has always been fair before."

"Well, then. And what of Paks?"

The Marshal-General came past him to Paks. "To you, as well, I apologize for Marshal Haran's words. May I ask if she has done you any harm?"

"No, my lady." Paks still felt numb from the force of Haran's attack.

"No harm but to bully and insult her," put in the Duke.

"My lord, I understand that."

"Good. Marshal-General, I came hoping you would be here as well as Paks. Can you tell yet what has happened to her?"

Paks watched the Marshal-General's face, hoping for reprieve from imagined dooms, but it was still and unreadable. "No, my lord," she said to Phelan. "I cannot tell. It is early yet, and she is still recovering." She turned to Paks again, her expression softening. "Paksenarrion, you must have realized, from what Haran said, that some fear you have been badly damaged. I would not lie to you: as I warned you before, great loss is possible. But I think we will not know until you have regained your strength. We worried because you lay senseless so long, but that may mean nothing. Please tell me if you feel anything different in yourself at any time."

"I — I couldn't eat — " Paks said softly.

"Couldn't eat? What was wrong?"

"I couldn't — couldn't hold the — " Suddenly she began to cry, and tried to smother it. " — the fork — I couldn't cut — I dropped — "

654

"Oh, Paks!" The Marshal-General took her hands. "Don't — It will get better. It will. You are weak, it's too soon —"

"But she said — like a baby —" Paks turned into the pillows, ashamed.

"No. Don't say that. She was wrong. It will come back, faster than you think." The Marshal-General looked aside; Paks watched the line of her jaw and cheek. "If you keep trying, Paks, it will come back."

"All of it?" asked the Duke softly, echoing Paks's thought.

The Marshal-General's lips thinned. "My lord Duke, please! We cannot know yet. It will do her — or you — no good to worry about that now."

"But she cannot help it, Marshal-General. Nor could you, if you were in that bed, and she beside it. I, too, tried to tell her not to worry about the future, but that's empty wisdom no one can follow. What can she think about, save this? Nothing but knowledge will ease her."

"I have no knowledge," said the Marshal-General. She shook her head, and met Paks's eyes again. "But believe this: I do not think as Haran does, nor do your other friends. And Haran will not think that way long. Only someone of great courage and strength could have held off that evil so long, once it entered."

A knock on the door interrupted them again. Marshal Belfan, whom Paks had known before the journey to Kolobia, put in his head. "Now or later?" he asked.

"Come on in, Belfan." The Marshal-General got up. "Paksenarrion is awake, but weak."

"So Haran said. Gird's grace to you, Paksenarrion, my lord Duke. Old Artagh says first snow by morning, Marshal-General."

"Winter starts earlier every year," grumbled the Marshal-General; Belfan laughed. He had an easy way with him, and hardly seemed a Marshal most of the time.

"You said that last year," he said. "It comes," he said to Paks and the Duke, "of having a Marshal-General who grew up in the south."

"In Aarenis?" asked the Duke, clearly surprised.

"No. Southern Tsaia." The Marshal-General was smiling now. "Around here they call any place where it doesn't frost the Summereve flowers the south. Gird knows I like hunting weather as well as anyone, but —"

"You're getting older, Marshal-General, that's what it is." Belfan stuck his hands in his belt, chuckling. She gave him a hard look.

"Is it indeed, my young Marshal! Perhaps you'd like to trade a few buffets in Hall and find out just how old I am?"

"Perhaps I'll throw myself down the steps on my own, and not wait for you."

They all laughed, even Paks. Belfan came over to her. "You look enough better that I expect you'll be throwing the Marshal-General down the steps in a few days yourself. What a time we've had! The long faces around here looked more like a horse farm than Fin Panir's grange and Hall."

"What about something to eat?" asked the Marshal-General. "I can have something sent up for all of us."

"Good idea." The Duke smiled down at Paks. "If we stuff her with food, she'll soon feel more herself."

And when faced with a bowl of thick soup, Paks was able to spoon it up with few spills. No one commented on the mess; the Marshal-General wiped it up matter-of-factly, while talking of other things. When they had all finished, she helped Paks sit up on the bed: she could not lift herself, but could balance alone.

The next time she woke, the Marshal-General and Belfan helped her stand, wavering, between them. She walked lopsided and staggering, but with their aid could make it across the room. Several days later she could walk alone, slowly but more steadily. Her improvement continued. When she could manage stairs, she went outside, to the Marshal-General's walled garden. After that came her first walk across the forecourt, to the High Lord's Hall. The glances of the others pricked her like nettles; she looked down, watching the stones under her feet. Haran had claimed that others felt as she did: some of them saw cowardice on her face, with her scars. But she hoped, while fearing her hope was false, that with the return of physical strength she had nothing else to fear.

She had grown strong enough to fret at the confinement of the Marshal-General's quarters, and had begun taking walks on the training fields, usually with the Duke, or one of the Marshals. She did not question their company, noticing that they rarely left her alone, but not wanting to know why. One crisp cold day, she was with Belfan when a thunder of hooves came from behind. They turned, to see several students galloping up, carrying lances. Paks felt a wave of weakness and fear that took the strength from her knees. Sunlight glittered from the lance-tips, ominous as dragons' teeth; the horses seemed twice as large as normal, their great hooves digging at the ground. She clutched Belfan's arm, breathless.

"Paks! We thought you were going to be shut up forever!" It was the young Marrakai boy, waving his lance in his excitement. "I wanted to tell you: I've been put in the higher class! I can drill with you now — " As his horse pranced, Paks tried not to flinch from the sudden movements. Another of the students peered at her.

"You've got new scars. They said — "

"Enough. Begone, now." Marshal Belfan spoke firmly.

"But Marshal — "

"Paks, what's wrong? You're shaking — " The Marrakai boy's sharp eyes glittered; she could see the curiosity and worry on all their faces.

"Go on, now." The Marshal took a step forward. "This is nothing for you."

"But she's — "

"Now!" Paks had never heard Belfan bellow like that, and she jumped as the students did. They rode away, looking back over their shoulders. He looked down at her. Only then did she realize that her legs had failed her, and she had collapsed in a heap. "Here — let me help you up." His hand, hard and callused, suddenly seemed threatening in its strength; Paks had to force herself to take it. She felt the blood rushing to her face. What would the students think? She knew. She knew what she thought. She had never felt such fear, never been mastered by fear like that. Her eyes burned with unshed tears. She heard Belfan sigh heavily. When he spoke again, his voice was still cheerful, though Paks thought she heard the effort behind it.

"Paks, don't think one time means anything. Some days back you couldn't take a single step alone. Now you can walk around the wall. This is the same; this weakness can pass, just as the weakness of your legs passed. What frightened you most?"

But this she could not say. Noise, movement, speed, the sharpness of the lances, the memory of old wounds and what that speed and sharpness could mean, in her own flesh — all these jumbled in her mind, and left her speechless. She shook her head.

"Well, it came suddenly, all at once. Like a cavalry charge, and here you were unarmed: no wonder." But to Paks his voice carried no conviction. "I daresay it will be better, when you begin training with one weapon at a time. Your skills will be slow to return, perhaps, as you were slow to walk, but they'll come back, and so will your confidence."

"And if it doesn't?" She spoke very low, but Belfan heard her.

"If not, then — something will come for you. Most of the world is not fighters, after all. If you'd lost an arm or leg, you'd have to learn something else. This is not different. Besides, it hasn't come to that yet."

Paks returned to hauk drill, in a beginning class: clumsy, as she now expected, in the first days. When someone lost the grip, and a hauk flew through the air, she flinched, and tried to hide it. Afraid of a hauk! She forced herself on, exercising early and late, and the strength and coordination came back. But that only hastened sword drill.

When she first gripped a sword again, it felt odd in her hand. Marshal Cieri looked curiously at her, and adjusted her grip. "Like this," he said. It felt no better. She looked down the length of dangerous metal — for he had seen no reason to try her with a wooden practice blade — and tried not to show her fear. The edges, the point, stood out in her eyes; she was afraid to move it lest she cut her own leg. He faced her, and lifted his own sword. Paks stared at it, eyes widening. It seemed to catch the sunlight and throw it at her in angled flashes that hurt her eyes. She blinked. "Ready?" he asked.

Her mouth was dry; her reply came as a hoarse croak. He nodded and moved forward, lifting the tip for the first drill movement. Paks froze, her eyes following the sword. She tried to force her own arm to move, to interpose her own blade, but she could not. She saw the surprise on his face, the change to annoyance, and then some other emotion she could not read, that terrified her with its withdrawal.

"Paks. Position one."

She struggled, managed to move her arm awkwardly. His blade touched hers, a light tap. She gasped, whirled away, tried to face him again, and dropped her sword. As it clanged on the ground, she was already shaking, eyes shut.

The next time, and the next, were no better. If anything, they were worse. Soon she feared anyone bearing arms, even the Duke when he came to her room with his sword on his belt. As she felt herself weaker and more fearful, she saw the Marshals and paladins and other students as stronger, braver, more vigorous. Despite the Marshal-General's protection, she had heard enough to know that many agreed with Haran. Their scorn sharpened her own.

At last even the Marshal-General admitted that she was not improving. "But as long as you want to try, Paksenarrion — " she said, eyes clouded with worry.

"I can't." Paks could not meet her gaze.

"Enough, then. We hoped the contact would help, but it hasn't. We'll see what else can be done for you — "

"Nothing." Paks turned her head away, and stared at the pattern of the rug. Blue stars on red, white stars on blue. "I don't want anything — "

"Paksenarrion, we are not abandoning you. It's not your fault, and we'll — "

"I can't stay here." The words and tears burst from her both at once. "I can't stay! If I can't be one of you, let me go!"

The Marshal-General shook her head. "I don't want you to leave until you have some way of living, some trade or craft. You're not well yet — "

"I'll never be well." Paks hated the tremor in her voice. "I can't stay here, my lady, not with real fighters." She would not, she told herself, tell the Marshal-General about the taunts she'd heard, the mocking whispers just loud enough to carry to her ears.

"Through the winter, then. Leave in spring, when the weather's better. You can study in the archives — "

Paks shook her head stubbornly. "No. Please. Let me go now. To sit and read all day, read of others fighting — I can't do that."

"But — Paks — what can you do? How will you live?"

Nor would she admit she didn't much care whether she lived. And she had thought of a reasonable plan. "I came from a sheep farm; I can herd."

"Are you sure? Herding's hard work, and — "

Paks drove the thought of wolves away — she would not be alone, on a winter range — and steadied her voice. "I'm sure."

The Marshal-General sighed. "Well. I'll see. If we can find a place — "

Before she left, she had a last talk with the Duke. He showed none of the anger she had feared, and no scorn; his voice was gentle.

"Take this ring," he said, tugging a black signet ring from his finger. "If ever you need help — any kind of help — show this ring to anyone in the Company, or anyone who knows me, or send it. I will come, Paksenarrion, wherever you are, whatever you need."

"My lord, I'm not worthy — "

658

"Child, you did not throw your gifts away. They were taken from you. For your service to me — for that alone — you are worthy of my respect. Now put that ring on — yes. You must not fail to call, Paks, if you need me. I will be thinking of you." He hugged her again, and turned to go. Then he swung back. "To my thinking, Paks, you have shown great courage in consenting to risk its loss, and in trying so hard to regain your skills. Whatever others call you, remember that Phelan of Tsaia never called you coward." Then he was gone, and Paks turned the ring nervously on her finger. It was loose, and she took it off and stuffed it in her belt pouch.

Two days later, the Marshal-General walked with her to the archway. "Remember, Paksenarrion: you will be welcome in any grange, at any time. I have already sent word. Gird's grace is on you, and our good will follows you. If my parting gift is not enough, you can ask more, freely." But Paks was determined not to spend that roll of coins, wound in a sock in the midst of her pack. "Right now you are unhappy, and reasonably so, with the Fellowship of Gird — "

Paks shook her head. "Not so, my lady. Not with you. I think Marshal Haran had the right of it, in part. My error let Achrya's evil in, and my weakness could not withstand what you had to do — "

The Marshal-General stopped and looked at her. "That's not true, and I've told you before. By Gird's cudgel, I hate to let you go, thinking that. All paladin-candidates are vulnerable, and anyone with less strength than you would have been taken over completely far sooner. You must believe in yourself." She paused, rocking from heel to toe, arms crossed. "Paks, please. Promise me that if things get worse, you will come for help."

Paks looked away. She did not want to say what she thought, that more of such help as she'd had would leave her bedbound as well as craven.

"My lady, I'd best go, to be in the market on time." Paks kept her eyes stubbornly on the ground. The Marshal-General's sigh was gusty.

"Very well, Paks. You are sworn to Gird's Fellowship, and Gird the protector will guard your way. All our prayers are with you." She turned back through the gate, and Paks walked on, determined not to glance back.

Chapter Thirty

With that walk down to the market in Fin Panir, where she was to meet the shepherd who would hire her, a pattern was set that continued all that hard winter.

"Eh, you took your time," grumbled Selim Habensson, when she found him talking with several other sheepmen. "Hated to leave the Lord's Hall, I suppose. Let's see — " He looked her over as if she were a ewe up for sale. "The Marshal-General says you're fit, and you've handled sheep — is that so?"

"Yes, sir. My father raised sheep."

"Good enough. Get in there and find me th' three-tit ewe w'the scarred hock and a double down-nick offside ear." As Paks paused to look over the pen of sheep, trying to see a likely earmark, he barked, "Get on, there — get in — I want to see you in with 'em."

Paks swung over the low railing, among the crowded sheep. She had not feared sheep since she had been able to see over their backs, but the shoving of woolly backs and sides made her feel strange. She saw one offside earmark, but it was a single notch. Most of this pen was nearside marked. There — on the far side — was a double down-nick, offside. She pushed her way slowly through the sheep, careful not to startle or disturb them. A quick look told her this was a normal ewe, not hock-scarred; she looked again for the right earmark, and found it in a corner. A ewe, a three-tit, and scarred on the near hock. She looked up to see the shepherd just outside the rail.

"Very well — you do know somewhat about sheep. But you haven't worked 'em lately, I'll warrant."

"No, sir."

"I thought not. Those clothes belong in a shop, not on drive." He spat on the cobbles outside the pen. "I hope to Gird you don't mind getting dirty."

"No, sir."

"All right. When market's over — another glass, say — we'll be moving this pen and those two — " he pointed, " — out to a meadow for tonight. Tomorrow we start for the south. Follow us out — make sure none of 'em stray in the city — and you'll be watching tonight."

Although bothered by the noise and bustle of the market, Paks had no trouble with the sheep on the way out — to her own and the shepherd's surprise. The sheep settled well in their temporary grazing ground, and Paks took up her assigned post on the far side while the other shepherds made camp and cooked supper. She had not thought to bring anything for lunch, planning to buy it in the market, so by evening she was hungry. When the first group had eaten, Selim called in the others to eat. Paks was given a bowl of porridge and a hunk of bread. She ate quickly, hardly noticing the others until she finished. Then she looked up to find them watching her.

"You eat like you thought there was more coming," commented Selim. She had, indeed, assumed there was more. He turned to the others. "Been living in a city for awhile, she has. Fine clothes. Eating well. Listen, now: we're sheepfarmers, not rich merchants or fancy warriors. We work hard for what we get; you'll get your fair share, but not a drop more. Understand?"

"Yes, sir." Paks nodded, and cleaned her bowl. She was remembering that when she first joined the Duke's Company, the food had seemed rich and plenty — she had forgotten, in the years since, how her family had lived, and how she had longed for bakers' treats on market days.

"Good. You'll take first watch. Jenits, you relieve her at change. We'll start out at dawn."

In the next few days Paks became acquainted with hunger again. She felt cold and hunger as a force that dragged on her legs, making her labor to keep up with the flock. When a sheep broke free, and ran, she struggled to chase it, fighting a stitch in her side and leaden legs that would not hurry. Selim scolded her about it.

"By Gird's cudgel, this is the last time I'll hire on the Marshal-General's word! I've a half-grown lass that could do better!" Paks forebore to say that she herself, as a half-grown girl, had done better. She saw clearly that excuses would only make things worse. She ducked her head and promised to work harder. And she tried. But Selim and the others never came to trust her, always saw her as an outsider who had been forced on them by the Marshal-General. In addition, the wounds she'd received from the iynisin began to swell and redden again. They had never faded much, but now they looked and felt much as they had when she first came out in Kolobia. The shepherds looked at the marks they could see and muttered.

So it was that when the flocks were safe in the winter pastures of southern Fintha, Selim turned her away, and refused to hire her through the winter.

"I'm not saying as I think it, mind. The Marshal-General, I expect she'd know the truth of it, and she said as how you was not to blame for any. But they all think you're cursed, somehow. Never saw the like of those marks on your face turning dark like that; it's not natural. We've plenty of young ones in the village that need work can look after the sheep well enough. Here's your pay — " It was not much; Paks did not count it. "And I'll wish you well."

It was a bitter morning, gray with a sharp wind. Paks shivered; she was, as always, hungry. "Is there an inn, here, where —"

"No, not here." His voice was sharp. "We're not some rich town. On that way —" he pointed to a side lane. "You could make Shaleford by tonight, if you get a foot on it, or back the way we came." Paks looked from one to the other, irresolute. "You won't make it shorter by thinking on it," he said, and turned back into his own house, shutting the door.

Paks put the coins he'd given her into her belt pouch, biting her lip. The way they had come was north, into the wind, and the nearest town more than a day's travel. She took the lane to Shaleford.

The lane dwindled to a track, and the track to a hardly visible trail that led up over a rise open to the wind. All that day Paks fought the wind, leaning on its shaking shoulder. She had nothing to eat, and nothing in the bare countryside offered shelter or sustenance. When she topped the rise, she looked into a country already softened by coming night; behind her the sun fell behind heavier cloud to a dull ending. She saw nothing that looked like a town, and wondered if the shepherd had lied. But the miserable trail wound on, and she saw sheep droppings nearby. Sheep meant people, she hoped, and kept on. At least it was downhill.

She was stumbling in the gathering darkness when she saw the first light ahead. Thinking of warmth, food, being out of the everlasting wind, she missed her footing again, and fell flat, jarring every bone. She lay sprawled, listening to the wind's howl, and wondering how far the light was.

Shaleford had an inn, if a three-room hut with a lean-to kitchen could be called an inn. Paks handed over most of her earnings for a pile of straw at one end of the common loft and a bowl of soup. The other customers drank ale, heavily, and eyed her sideways. She paid another of her coppers for a second helping of soup and some bread. She was tempted to spend one of the Marshal-General's coins for a decent meal, but was afraid to show the others that she had anything worth stealing.

The next day she found that no one in Shaleford had need for an extra hand over the winter. By the time she'd asked for work every place she could think of, it was too late to make the next town by nightfall. She could not stay another night at the inn without using some of her reserve. But Shaleford had a grange — she'd seen it, first thing in the morning. She decided to see if they would let her stay there.

The Marshal, said the stocky yeoman-marshal, was out. He'd been to Highfallow barton for their drill, and wouldn't be back until the next day. Yes, there'd been a recent message from Fin Panir, but that was the Marshal's business, and he couldn't say what it was. If she had something from the Marshal-General herself — Paks pulled out the safe-conduct, and the yeoman-marshal pored over the seal. She realized suddenly that he could not read.

"A message for our Marshal? Is it urgent?"

"It's to any Marshal — about me." Paks felt herself redden under his gaze. His glance flicked to her visible scars.

"You're a yeoman?"

"Yes — well — not precisely — "

"Well, then, what?"

"I was at Fin Panir — "

"The training company?"

"Yes."

"And they sent you on a mission?"

Paks was torn between honesty and the likelihood that he would not understand what she really was. "I don't think I can explain it to you," she said finally. "I need to speak to the Marshal, but since he's not here — "

"Even if I went, he couldn't get back before tomorrow."

"No, I understand that. Can I wait for him here?"

"In the grange?" The yeoman-marshal's frown deepened. "Well — I suppose. Come along." He led her through the main room to a tiny sleeping chamber off a narrow back passage. "You can leave your pack there, and come back in for the exchange."

Paks had forgotten that custom. In Fin Panir itself, the exchange of buffets whenever a visitor came to the grange had been abandoned because of the number of visitors. But in outlying granges, it was still usual, and the test of someone who claimed membership in the Fellowship of Gird. She froze.

"I can't." Her voice was thin.

"What!"

"I can't. I — it's in this — " She waved the Marshal-General's letter.

"Hmph." His snort was clearly one of disbelief and scorn. "I see you've been wounded recently — is that it?"

Paks nodded, taking the easy way out, as she thought.

"I'd think if you could travel at all you could exchange a few blows — but — " He shook his head. "You hear all sorts of things from Fin Panir. All right, then. I'll just go put more meal in the pot."

Paks sank down on the narrow bed, frightened and discouraged. Was this the sort of welcome the Marshal-General intended? But of course the Marshal was away. She could not take it to heart. She got up with an effort and looked around for the jacks and the washroom. At least she could be clean.

Her spare shirt smelled of sheep and smoke, but was, she thought, somewhat cleaner. The yeoman-marshal gave her a pail of water and soap for the dirty clothes, and she came to supper feeling more respectable than before. She had oiled her boots and belt, and the sheathe of her dagger. The yeoman-marshal was obviously making an effort to be friendly.

"So tell me — what's new in Fin Panir? Is the quest back from the far west yet? Did they really try to find Luap's lost stronghold, as we heard?"

"Yes. And found it, too." Paks told a little of the quest, hoping to stave off questions. Luckily, the yeoman-marshal was tired, and when she had told what she thought would interest him, he was yawning.

The next day, when the Marshal returned, he nodded when he heard

663

her name. "Yes — Paksenarrion. I've heard of you; the Marshal-General mentioned that you might come this way in her last letter. Where are you bound next?"

"I — I'm not sure, sir."

"You could take a letter to Highgate, if you would. And I know there's traffic there — you might find work on the roads."

"I'd be glad to." Paks found herself almost eager to go. This Marshal, at least, had no scorn for her.

"If you stay a day, you'll be here for drill — oh, I know you can't bear arms, not at this time, but surely you can tell the yeomen about Kolobia, can't you? They like to hear a good tale, and finding Luap's stronghold would interest any of them."

Paks didn't want to face a crowd of strange yeomen, but she felt she couldn't refuse. She nodded slowly. The rest of that day passed easily: she was warm and well-fed for the first time in days, and she dozed most of the afternoon. The Marshal offered a mug of herb tea which he said might ease the ache of her wounds, and it helped. But the next night, facing the assembled yeomen, was difficult. She had told them about the trip west, the fight with the nomads, the brigand attacks in the canyons they crossed, but the closer she came to describing the iynisin attack, the worse it got. The Marshal had said she ought not to mention her own capture — not that she wanted to — but she could hardly talk of any of it. Finally she raced through it, skimping most of the action, and went on to Luap's stronghold. When she finished, they stamped their feet appreciatively. Then one of them, a big man she'd seen in the inn, spoke up.

"If you're one of that kind, what are you doing here?"

"Any Girdsman is welcome in our grange," said the Marshal sharply.

"Aye, I know that. But I saw her come in two days ago, cold as dead fish and smelling of sheep. Hadn't eaten in days, the way she started on her food over there — " He jerked his head toward the inn. "You know's well as I do, Marshal, that knights and paladins and such don't travel like that. The way she talks, she wasn't walking the wagons out to Kolobia — she talks like she fought alongside that Amberion and that elf. So I just wonder why she's — " His voice trailed away, but his look was eloquent. Paks saw others glance at him and nod.

"Yeomen of Gird," said the Marshal with emphasis. "It is not my tale to tell. I can tell you that the Marshal-General has commended her to every grange — every grange, do you hear? — and to all the Fellowship of Gird. I daresay she travels where she does, and as she does, by the will of the High Lord and Gird his servant. I will not ask more — and you would be wise to heed me."

"Well," said the big man, undeflated, "if you ask me, she looks more like a runaway apprentice than a warrior of Gird. No offense meant — " he said with a glance at Paks. "If so be I'm wrong, then — well — you know how to take satisfaction." With that he flexed his massive arms, and grinned.

"You're wrong indeed, Arbad," said the Marshal. "And I'll take the satisfaction for your discourtesy to a guest of the grange, on next drill night, or hear your apology now."

Evidently the Marshal's right arm was well respected, for Arbad rose and muttered an apology to Paks. The meeting broke up shortly after that. A few had come to speak to Paks, but most huddled together in the corners, looking at her and speaking quietly to each other. The Marshal stayed near her, stern and quiet.

At Highgate Paks delivered the Marshal's letter to the Highgate Marshal, and shared a hot meal at the grange. He introduced her to a trader, in town on his way south and east, and Paks hired on as common labor. The rest of that day she unloaded and loaded wagons, and harnessed the stolid draft-oxen. With the other laborers, she slept under one of the wagons, and the next day they started on the road.

Keris Sabensson, the trader, rode a round-bellied horse at the head of the wagons; he had a drover for each wagon, five guards, and two common laborers. Paks was expected to do most of the camp-work, load and unload the wagons at each stop, and help care for the animals. She found the work within her strength, but was terrified of the guards, who tried to joke with her.

"Come on, Paks," said one of them one night when she jumped back from a playful thrust of his sword. "With those scars you've got, you've been closer than this to a sword. You know I'm not serious. Here — let's see what you can do." He tossed the sword to her. Paks threw out her hand, and knocked it away; it fell to the ground. "Hey! Stupid, don't do that! You'll nick it!" He glared at her.

"You can't tell me you haven't fought — what happened, lose your nerve?" Another one had her by the arm.

"Let her alone, Cam — suppose you ended up — "

"Like her? Never. I'll be a captain someday, with my own troop. Who'd you fight with, Paks — tell us."

"Phelan," she muttered. She could not break free, and was afraid to try.

"What? I don't believe it." Cam dropped her arm. "You were in the Red Duke's Company? When?"

"A — a couple of years ago." They were all watching now, eyes bright in the firelight. She swallowed, looking for a way out of their circle.

"What happened? Get thrown out?" Cam's grin faded as he watched her.

"No, I — " She looked into the fire.

"Tir's gut, Paks, you make a short tale long by breathing on it. What happened?"

"I left." She said that much, and her throat closed.

"You left." The senior, a lean dark man who claimed to have fought with the Tsaian royal guard, confronted her. He looked her up and down. "Hmm. You don't get scars like that from not fighting, and you're too old to

665

have been thrown out as a recruit, and not old enough to be a veteran. But you're scared, aren't you?"

Paks nodded, unable to speak.

"Is that why you left Phelan?" She shook her head. "When did you — no, those scars are too new. Something happened — by the look of it, within the past few weeks." She closed her eyes to avoid his gaze, but felt it through her skin. No one spoke; she could hear the flames sputtering against a sleety wind, and the hiss of sleet on the wagons.

"All right," he said finally. She opened her eyes; he had turned, and faced the others. "I think she's told the truth; no one lies about serving with Phelan and lives long to tell it. She's got the marks of a warrior; something's broken her. I wouldn't want to carry that collection myself. Let her alone."

"But Jori —"

"Let her alone, Cam. She has enough to live with. Don't add to it." With that he led them away to one side of the fire. Paks went on with her work, but spent most of that night awake. She began to realize that she could not pass as a laborer; her scars would always betray her past. People she met would expect things — things she no longer had — and each meeting would be like this.

Two days later, a band of brigands struck the wagons. They were deep in a belt of forest, where the guards could not see far, and they had dragged Keris Sabensson from his horse and cut the traces of the first team before the guards got into action. The drovers reacted quickly, defending their teams and wagons with the long staves they carried; the other laborer ran forward and caught Sabensson's horse. Paks froze where she was, terrified. She could not move, could not help or run. And when the fight was over, and the trader, head bandaged, was settled in the first wagon, he fired her.

"I'm not having any damned fools here," he said angrily. "Stupid, cowardly — by all the gods I'd rather have a drunken swineherd to depend on. Get out! Take your pay — not that you've earned it!" He threw a few coins out of the wagon; one hit Paks in the face. "Go on — move!" He poked the drover, who prodded the oxen into motion. Paks stepped back, ignoring the coins at her feet. On the second wagon Cam smirked at her, but she hardly noticed. She stared blankly ahead as one wagon after another passed her, and the oxen blew clouds of steam.

At the last, Jori, now riding the trader's horse, stopped. "Paks, here." He handed her a small leather bag. "It isn't much — what we — I mean — " He touched her head. "I know what kind of soldiers Phelan has. You be careful, hear?"

She stood a long time in the track, holding the bag, until she finally thought to tuck it into her belt and start walking.

At the next town, they had heard of her from the trader, still angry. She trudged past the grange without looking at it, and went on, going the way that the trader had not gone. She had not dared enter an inn, but had bought bread from a baker. At the town beyond that, after a night spent in a ruined barn, she found work in a large inn.

666

"Not inside," said the innkeeper after a look at her face. "No. You won't do inside. But if you're not afraid of work, I can use someone in the yard. Haul dung, feed, clean stalls — you can do that?" Paks nodded. "Sleep in the shed — in the barn if it's not full. You get board and a copper crown a week." Paks thought dully that she must be back in Tsaia — Finthan coins were crescents and bits, not crowns. "Can you work with big horses?" She shook her head, remembering the disaster in Fin Panir when she had been unable to groom Socks, let alone ride him. Somehow her fear transmitted itself to horses, and made them skittish. "Too bad; it's a chance for tips. Well, then, stay out of the way. The grooms'll be glad to have the dirty work taken off them."

So they were. Paks hauled dung from the barns twice a day, pitched straw, bedded stalls, carried feed. Work began before daylight, and continued as late as the last person came to the inn. The shed she slept in was by the kitchen door, and half-full of firewood; it backed on the great fireplace, and she thought she could feel a little warmth in the stones, but that was all. She had no place to wash, and no reason to — the innkeeper was clearly surprised when she asked. She did not mention it again. As for board, the innkeeper was more generous than many: bread, soup and porridge, and a chance at the scraps. Not that much was left after the kitchen help, indoor help, and the rest of the stable help took their share. She hid her own pack behind the firewood, and half-forgot it was there or what was in it.

She noticed that her scars from Kolobia had begun to fade again, as mysteriously as they darkened. This time, however, the pain did not fade with the color. It continued as a bitter bone-deep ache that sapped her strength. She did not think about it; she didn't think of anything much, but whether she could lift another shovel-full. Winter's grip strengthened; even within the courtyard there were days when the wind blew snow into a white mass that made it hard to breathe. She wore all her clothes, and still woke stiff in the mornings. Trade slowed, in the bitter cold, and the innkeeper told her she could sleep in the barn, now half-empty. It was warmer there, burrowing in straw, with animals heating the air.

She hoped to stay there all winter, but one night two drunken thieves drove her away. It began when they arrived, and handed their mule's lead-rope to one of the grooms. The tall one caught sight of Paks and nudged the other. She saw this, and ducked behind a partition, but heard their comments. Late that night, they came out to the barn, "to look at our mule," as they said. The grooms were gone; one to the kitchen, where he had a lover, and one to a tavern down the street. Paks had gone to sleep in a far stall, carefully away from the mule. They found her.

"Well, well — here's a pretty lass. Hello, yellow-hair — like a little present?" She woke to find them standing over her. The tall one whirled something shiny on a ribbon; the other one carried a branched candlestick with two candles. She looked around wildly. She was trapped in a corner stall; they stood in the door, chuckling. She scrambled up, backing away from them.

"By Simyits, I think she's scared. Surely you aren't a virgin, sweetling —
why so frightened?" The shorter man came nearer. "Kevis, are you sure of
her? It's easy to tell she works in the stables."

"Oh, I think so. It's the ugly ones and poor ones that appreciate presents.
See this, sweetheart? It's a nice shiny ring. All for you, if you just —"

Paks jumped for the gap that had opened between them, trying to scream.
As in a dream, little sound came out; the tall man grunted as she bumped into
him, and grabbed her. His hand clamped over her mouth. "Now that's not
nice, pretty lass — behave yourself." She struggled wildly, but the other man
had set the candlestick on the stall partition grabbed her as well. "Quiet down,
girl; you're not going anywh — Damn you, you stinking — " Paks had
managed to get a finger between her teeth, but his other hand gripped her
throat. She choked; the shorter man twisted her arms behind her.

"What, Cal?"

"She bit me, the stupid slut." Paks heard this through the roaring of her
ears as he kept the pressure on her throat. "If we didn't need her, I'd —"

"Let up, Cal. I've got her." The tall man gave a final squeeze, and loosed
her throat. Paks gasped for air; it seemed to scrape her throat as it went in.
She could not stand upright with the pressure on her arms. The shorter
man increased it, and forced her to her knees. The tall man bent near her;
she could smell the ale on his breath.

"Listen to me, sweetheart — you're going to help us, and you're going to
give us a good time. If you do it right, you'll get a little reward out of it —
maybe this ring. If you act stupid, like you just did, you'll die hurting. Now
— do you understand?"

Paks could not speak for terror and pain. She was shaking all over, and
tears sprang from her eyes.

"I asked you a question." A knife had appeared in the tall man's hand; it
pricked her throat. Paks heard herself moan, a terrible sound that she did
not know she could make.

"Simyits save us all," muttered the shorter man, behind her. "It's no
wonder they have this one in the stable. No wits at all."

"No wits, the better lay."

"Kevis — "

"Well, Cal, you know the saying. It tames wild mares and witches. Why
not a stable hand?"

"What about time?"

"So how long does it take?"

"You may be right." Paks heard the grin in the voice behind her, and saw
the man in front fumble with his trousers.

"I'll go first."

"Greedy — you always go first." The man behind her let go her arms,
and Paks fell face-down in the straw. She rolled away, trying again to escape, but they caught her. The tall man backhanded her across the face,
knocking her into the back of the stall.

"That's for the bite, slut. Now don't cause trouble." He grabbed her

668

shirt, and ripped it open. "What a beauty!" His voice was cold. "Where'd you get those scars — somebody whip you once?"

"More than once," said the other one. "By the dark goddess, I never saw anything like that outside of Liart's temples in Aarenis. Kevis — "

"Don't bother me, Cal." The tall man tugged at her belt. "I'm busy."

"Kevis, wait. If this is Liart's bait — "

"Cal, I don't care if it's the crown princess of Tsaia — "

"But Kevis — " The shorter man pulled at his companion's arm. "Listen to me. I know what I mean — Liart won't like it if that's one of his."

"Liart can go — " He had broken the belt, and forced his hands between her thighs. Paks tried to struggle, but he had her wedged against the wall where she could not move.

"Don't say that!" The shorter man used enough force to pull the other's arm away. "Kevis, it's serious. Liart is a jealous god; he'll kill — and I know how he kills — "

"Don't bother me!" The taller man turned away from Paks and pulled his knife. "Hells blast you, Cal, you're as craven as she is. Get back — "

"No! I'm not having any part of this if she's Liart's — "

"Then go away. Don't — I don't care — but don't — " He swayed a little on his feet, and the shorter man took his chance to pull him away from Paks. She watched through a fog of fear as they began to fight. They stumbled into her and away; she took stray blows and kicks, feeling each of them as a shattering force that left her still less will to move, to escape. Finally they staggered into the partition, and knocked over the candlestick. Light flared up from the neighboring stall; the men stopped short, staring.

"Hells below! See what you've done?" The shorter man, breathing heavily, glowered at the other.

"Me! It was you, pighead! Come on — run for it!"

"What about her?"

"Leave the stupid slut." Paks heard their feet on the passage floor, heard the crackling flames in the next stall. She could not move, she felt; her body was a mass of pain. She heard more yelling, and more, in the distance, but was hardly aware when someone grabbed her legs and dragged her out of the burning barn. By the time she had realized what had happened, she was already being blamed for it.

"I let you sleep there, out of the kindness of my heart, and what do you do? You not only whore around in the stalls, but you take candles — candles, open flames, Gird blast you! — into the stable and start a fire! If it hadn't been for Arvid coming back in, we'd have lost five horses. We did lose all that hay. He should have left you there."

"It wasn't — I didn't — " Paks could hardly speak, with her bruised throat, but she tried to defend herself. "They — they tried to rape me."

The innkeeper snorted. "I don't believe that! No one would pick you — gods above, I have comely girls in the house they'd likelier try. You've been using my barn — my barn! — for your tricks. Now get out! Where do you think you're going?"

"My pack — " said Paks faintly.

"I ought to take it for the damage you've done. All right, take the damn thing — it's probably full of lice anyway, dirty as you are." He hit her hard as she tried to leave, and drove her out of the gates with another blow and a kick. She fell heavily into the street, but managed to clamber up as he came toward her, and limped away.

It was dark and bitter cold. She followed the street by touching the walls along it, stumbling into them, choking down sobs. She felt as if a great vise were squeezing her body, twisting it to shapes of pain she had never imagined. When she thought of the past — of last winter — it seemed to recede, racing away into a distance she could never span. A last little bright image of herself at Fin Panir, happy and secure, gleamed for a moment in her mind and disappeared. She stopped, confused. She had no wall to touch, and all around was a howling dark, cold and windy. It was one with the void inside.

Chapter Thirty-one

Marshal-General Arianya
High Lord's Hall
Fin Panir
To all Marshals of Gird, Greetings:

In the matter of Paksenarrion Dorthansdotter, recently a member of Gird's Company here, I request the courtesy and charity of your grange. Paksenarrion was a member of Gird's quest to the stronghold of Luap; without her defense the quest would have failed more than once. Through the malice of Achrya, she has been left unfit for battle, and has chosen to work her own way in the world rather than accept grange gift, which she was offered freely. Marshals, this is not weakness; she was assailed with such power as even you or I might fall before. Give her any aid she needs; report any contact to me in Fin Panir for reimbursement; defend her as you can against malice and evil, for she can no longer defend herself. On my honor as commander of the Fellowship of Gird, she has no taint of evil herself, and Gird's grace is on her.

She is tall, yellow-haired and gray-eyed, and has many fighter's scars, including some that look recent, still inflamed. She carries a safe-conduct from me, but I fear she may be too shy to present it. Look for her. She is under our protection.

Marshal Keris
Shaleford Grange
To Marshal-General Arianya, Greetings:

As you requested, I am writing to report that Paksenarrion Dorthansdotter has been here. I was away when she came, but yeoman-marshal Edsen took her in overnight. She seemed in good health; she seems to me a pleasant young woman, very willing to please, though not steady of nerve. She spoke to our yeomen about the quest to Kolobia, which they had not heard. I sent her with a message to old Leward at Highgate Grange; I know there is much traffic along the way there, even in winter, and thought she might find work. No one is hiring here.

I must say that with the little you wrote, it's hard to explain her to the yeomen here. Even Edsen wondered about her. Perhaps in more traveled areas, they'll be more understanding. If I understood you correctly, she has had her mind damaged by a demon — right?

It looks like another hard winter; I'm having trouble getting all the grange-gift without cutting the farmers too short. I'm sending the rolls; note that Sim Simisson died, and his widow has remarried into Hangman's barton. Their farm was split between the three boys, but Jori and Ansuli have moved away, and young Sim is farming it all. Gird's grace to you.

Marshal Leward
Highgate Grange
To Marshal-General Arianya
Greetings, Arñe!

Did you hear that old Adgan finally died? Kori Jenitson told me a few weeks ago, when he rode by this way. I told him to write you, or send word from Vérella.

Keris sent that Paksenarrion Dorthansdotter to me. What is the Fellowship coming to, after all? I know, I know. You had your reasons. But such things should happen to those of us with years enough to know better. She's nought but a young sprout, I don't care how many years she fought with Phelan. By the way, someone told me he'd been to Fin Panir. Is that true? Is he coming back to the Fellowship?

Anyway, I found the girl a place with a trader I know. She looks strong enough, though much disfigured with those scars. Loading wagons should put a little muscle on her — then maybe she won't find swords so frightening. Keris, the trader, promised to keep her on all the way to the south if she earns her keep. Can't see any reason why she won't. She's certainly polite and better-educated than most. If she weren't scarred as she is, I'd be tempted to find a husband for her.

Remember me at Midwinter Feast. I will roast a pig in the honor of Luap's Stronghold.

Sulinarrion
Marshal of Seameadow Grange
To Marshal-General Arianya, Greetings:

Arñe, I have sad news about your stray. Keris, a small trader, came storming in to complain of her. Leward of Highgate had placed her with him as a laborer, and according to Keris, she ran away, or fainted or something when bandits attacked his wagons. I know Keris of old; we see him in grange-court every few years when he either complains of short weight or gives it. He's a hasty, hot-tempered man who will cling to a mistaken idea until the nomads build walls. Anyway, he says he fired her on the spot — somewhere in the woods west of Lowfallow, if I can tell by his tirade — and left her there. According to him, she was unwounded, and the bandits were all dead, so perhaps she has made it somewhere else. I asked to talk to his guards, and the senior, a Falkian named Jori, from Marrakai's domain, told me that she had simply frozen, neither attacking the bandits nor defending

672

herself. He said some of the guards made up a small sum for her, and he gave it to her. He felt bad about it, he said, but he couldn't leave the wagons. I think it's the best we could hope for.

I've told my yeoman-marshals and my yeomen to keep looking for her, but no one has turned up yet (though they did find a tall blonde thief we've seen before; she's enjoying our hospitality in a different way, awaiting the Duke's Court.) I told Keris what I thought of him, but it didn't do much good. He's so used to covering fear with bluster that he doesn't want to admit anyone can't.

I'm sorry I have no better news. On the bright side, we have had an un-usually good year in all the eastern bartons, and the grange-lands themselves, and can help those west of us who are short. I've heard that some granges can't make their Hall share; you can see from our rolls that we can help out. I hope to come in sometime next spring — do you still have that dappled gray? I'll make an offer you can't refuse.

Sulinarrion
Marshal of Seameadow Grange
To Leward of Highgate Grange
Greetings:

Leward, why on earth did you place Paksenarrion with Keris? You must know what sort of rough clod he is! He came ramping in here complaining of her cowardice, and the dishonesty of Girdsmen, until I nearly hit him on the head to shut him up. Didn't you warn him that she couldn't fight? He fired her after a bandit group attacked the wagons and she didn't defend them. Of course she didn't defend them. I know plenty of men — some of them, unfortunately, yeomen — who would run like rabbits in an unex-pected attack. When I finally got the whole story out of one of his guards, it turns out Keris himself simply fell off his horse and bellowed the whole time. Now she's disappeared, and Gird alone knows what's happened to her. Next time you need something handled with delicacy, don't go to Keris.

Sim Arisson,
Marshal of Lowfallow Grange
To the Marshal-General of Gird
Greetings:

In accordance with your request for information about the whereabouts and welfare of Paksenarrion Dorthansdotter, I am writing you a full report of recent events in this area.

Several weeks ago, I was touring the bartons and was not in Lowfallow for some days. When I returned, the innkeeper of the largest inn called me to attend one of his grooms, who had been badly burned in a barn fire. The short of it is that the innkeeper blamed one of the stablehands for the fire, and claimed she had been in league with two thieves, who had robbed the inn on the night of the fire. I think this person was Paksenarrion, from the description and name given by the innkeeper. Apparently she sought work there a few weeks before the fire, giving her name but no reference to the grange. She worked well, according to Jessim (the innkeeper), and slept in a shed near the kitchen. A few days before the fire he had said she and another stablehand might sleep in the barn, trade being slow. When the fire broke out, the groom discovered her in the barn, with her clothes as much off as on. He could see a candlestick in the midst of the fire. Jessim assumed she'd been whoring, and either set the fire as a distraction for the thieves or made it carelessly. Jessim drove her out that night, being angry, as he said. No one saw her leave town; it was bitter cold and windy, and most were fighting the fire. The next day he reported her description (but not her name, which he had forgotten until I questioned him) to the Duke's militia, as an accomplice of the thieves.

After I spoke to him, he withdrew the charge, and I have cleared her name with the militia, though I have asked them to look for her, and let me know if they find her. I asked the grange here, and none of the yeomen knew her, or remembered having seen her. I swear to you, Marshal-General, that she did not come to my grange for aid; I would have given it gladly. We found no sign of her in Lowfallow or in the farmland around. You will understand that it took some time to look, for I was afraid she might have been hurt in the fire and unable to travel. I had my yeomen look in every ditch and bramble. We were heartened to find no body, but we did not find her.

I delayed writing you because I hoped to have more certain news. Jessim promised to ask any travelers that came in, and I have spread the word to the distant bartons of my grange. Two days ago, one of my yeomen from Fox Barton reported a stranger living with an old widow in an outlying cottage. By the time we rode there, she was gone, but I am sure it was Paksenarrion.

The old woman is not a Girdsman, but has a name for honesty and hard work. She is a widow (her husband died of fever; he was a woodsman) and supports herself and a crippled daughter with weaving and spinning. At first she did not want to talk about it, but after we convinced her we meant Paksenarrion no harm, she told her tale. It seems that Paksenarrion appeared one morning (she could not be sure of the date, but that it was a clear day after a cloudy one) in her shed. She described her as nearly frozen, half-naked, and hurt. Apparently one leg was injured, for the woman told us she limped for most of the time she stayed there. Anyway, the old woman took her in, mended her clothes, and fed her, though that was hard — which I could well believe, looking around. They found Paksenarrion to be, in their words "gentle — she never said a rough word — " and she seems to have helped them by fetching water, finding wood and breaking it up, and so on. They said she offered to pay for her keep, but the old woman could not use her Finthan coins without walking into Lowfallow to change them — which was too far, she said, in winter. I suppose that means she still has the money you gave her in Fin Panir.

They had hoped she would stay, as she seemed strong to them, but she was unable to spin or weave, though apparently she tried to learn. Without extra help, they could not earn enough to keep three. Paksenarrion decided to leave, although they protested, and she insisted they keep a few Finthan coins. The old woman asked me if I could change one for her in Lowfallow. I told her to keep it; that the grange would aid to those who helped Girdsmen. I find that Fox Barton was already providing meat from time to time, but have put these women on the grange rolls. They need someone young and strong to board with them, and learn care of the daughter, who will never walk; we are working on that. In the meantime, I have sent supplies, and an order from the grange for two rugs a year. With your permission, I will name them on the Year Roll. They are not Girdish, but we owe them that.

Anyway, that's all I could find of Paksenarrion. Before I could extend the search, we had a thaw which left every road a quagmire. I have written neighboring granges, but it seems clear that she is avoiding granges. From the descriptions given by the women and by the innkeeper, I doubt that she will be recognized as anything but a vagrant. However, we will keep watch, and report anything we find.

I know you will be disappointed in this report. I think it hopeful that she is clearly still able to serve others weaker than herself. Perhaps some day Gird and the High Lord can restore her trust in the Fellowship and in herself.

Seklis, High Marshal
Marshal-General Arianya
Greetings:

While traveling from Valdaire to Vérella, I met a party on the road who spoke of an ex-Girdish warrior named Paksenarrion. When I reached Vérella, your waiting letter mentioned such a one. My news is meager indeed. At the time I was with the traders, I did not know of your interest, and did not question them as I might have. They said something about meeting an unusual sight — a Girdsman afraid of her own shadow, of barking dogs and horses. One of them said she'd been cursed that way, and gave it as proof that she was lapsed from the Fellowship. I do not recall where they said they had seen her, or where she was going — if they even said — but I report this because of your interest.

More important, I believe, is the continued conflict in Aarenis between the Guild League cities and the old nobility; trade is completely disrupted, and famine this year has been widespread. . . .

End Book II

Oath of Gold

Oath of blood is Liart's bane
Oath of death is for the slain
Oath of stone the rockfolk swear
Oath of iron is Tir's domain
Oath of silver liars dare
Oath of gold will yet remain . . .

—from *The Oathsong of Mikeli*

Chapter One

The village seemed faintly familiar, but most villages were much alike. Not until she came to the crossroads with its inn did she realize she had been here before. There was the paved inn court, and the wide door, and the bright sign — *The Jolly Potboy* — hanging over it. Her breath seemed to freeze in her chest. The crossroads was busier than she remembered; there was much bustling in and out of the inn. The windows to the common bar were wide open, and clear across the road she heard a roar of laughter she recognized. She flinched. They might recognize her, even in the clothes she wore now. She thought of the coins in her purse, and the meal she'd hoped to buy — but she could not go there, of all places, and order a meal of Jos Hebbinford. Nor was there any other place to go: she was known in Brewersbridge, and dared not beg a scrap from some housewife lest she be recognized.

Paks shook her head, fighting back tears. Once she had ridden these streets — stayed at that inn — had friends in every gathering.

"Here now, why so glum?" Paks started and looked up to see a man-at-arms in the Count's livery watching her. He smiled when she met his eyes; his face was vaguely familiar. "We can't have pretty girls down in the mouth in our town, sweetling — let me buy you a mug of ale and cheer you up."

Paks felt her heart begin to pound; fear clouded her eyes. "No — no thank you, sir. I'm fine — I just thought of something — "

The man's eyes narrowed. "You're frightened. Is someone after you? This town's safe enough — that's my job. You look like you need some kind of help; let me know what's wrong — "

Paks tried to edge around him, toward the north road. "No — please, sir, I'm all right."

He reached out and caught her arm. "I don't think so. You remind me of something — someone. I think perhaps the captain needs to see you — unless you can account better for yourself. Do you know anyone here, anyone who can vouch for you? Where were you going to stay? Are you here for the fair?"

For an instant Paks's mind went totally blank, and then the names and faces of those she remembered — Marshal Cedfer, Hebbinford, Captain Sir Felis, Master Senneth — began to race past her eyes. But she couldn't call on them to vouch for her. They had known her as a warrior, Phelan's

679

veteran, the fighter who cleaned out a den of robbers. She had left here to go to Fin Panir; they had expected her to return as a Marshal or knight. Even if they recognized her — and she doubted they would — they would still despise or pity her. She trembled in the man's grasp like a snared rabbit, and he was already pushing her along the north road toward the keep when another memory came to her: a memory of quiet trees and a clear pool and the dark wise face of the Kuakgan.

"I — I was going to the grove," she gasped. "To — to see the Kuakgan."

The man stopped, still gripping her arm. "Were you, now? And do you know the Kuakgan's name?"

"Master Oakhallow," said Paks.

"And you were to stay there?"

"I — I think so, sir. I had a question to ask him, that's why I came." Paks realized as she said this that it was true.

"Hmm. Well — if it's kuakgannir business — you say you were going to the grove: can you show me where it is?"

The entrance to the grove lay a hundred paces or so along the road; Paks nodded toward it.

"You know that much at least. Well, I'll just see you safely there. And remember, girl: I don't expect to see you dodging around town this evening. If I do, it's to the captain with you. And I'll have the watch keep a lookout, too." He urged her along until they came to the grove entrance, marked by white stones on the ground between two trees. "You're sure this is where you're going?"

Paks nodded. "Yes, sir — thank you." She turned away, ducking into the trees to follow the winding path picked out in white stones.

In the grove was silence. Sunlight filtered through green leaves. As before, she could hear nothing of the village, close as it was. A bird sang nearby, three rising notes, over and over. Paks stopped to listen; her trembling stilled. Something rustled in the bushes off to her left, and panic rose in her throat. When a brown rabbit hopped onto the path, she almost sobbed in relief.

She went on. Far over her head leaves rustled in a light wind, but it was quiet below. Under one tree she heard a throbbing hum, and looked up to see a haze of bees busy at the tiny yellow flowers. At last she heard the remembered chuckling of the Kuakgan's fountain, and came into the sunny glade before his dwelling. It was the same as on her first visit. The low gray bark-roofed house lay shuttered and still. Nothing moved but the water, leaping and laughing in sunlight over a stone basin.

Paks stood a moment in the sunlight, watching that water. She thought of what she'd told the soldier, and how the lie had felt like truth when she told it. But there was no help for her, not this time. The Kuakgan had nothing to do with what she had lost. Kuakkgani didn't like warriors anyway. Still — she had to stay, at least until night. She could not go back to the village. Maybe she could sneak through the grove and escape to the open country beyond. Paks sighed. She was so tired of running, tired of hiding from those who'd known her. Yet she could not face them. Make an end, she thought.

She slid out of the pack straps, and dug into the pack for her pouch of coins, the reserve the Marshal-General had given her. To it she added the coppers and two silvers from her belt-pouch. A tidy pile. Enough to live on for a month, if she were frugal; enough for one good feast, otherwise. Her mouth twisted. She scooped up the whole pile and dumped it in the offering basin; the clash and ring of it was loud and discordant. She looked in her pack for anything else of value. Nothing but her winter cloak, an extra shirt, spare boot-thongs — no — there was the ring Duke Phelan had given her the day he left Fin Panir. "Send this, or bring it, if you need me," he'd said. Paks stared at it. She didn't want it found on her when she — She pushed the thought aside and tossed the ring onto the heap of coins. She looked at her pack and decided to leave that too. The Kuakgan would find someone who needed a cloak and shirt. She piled the pack on top of the money, and turned away, wondering where she could hide until nightfall. Perhaps she should start through the grove now.

Across the clearing, at one end of the gray house, the Kuakgan stood watching her, his face shadowed by the hood of his robe. Paks froze; her heart began to race. His voice came clear across the sound of the fountain, and yet it was not loud. "You wished to speak to the Kuakgan?"

Paks felt cold, but sweat trickled down her ribs. "Sir, I — I came only to make an offering."

The Kuakgan came closer. His robe, as she remembered, was dark green, patterned in shades of green and brown with the shapes of leaves and branches. "I see. Most who make offerings here wish a favor in return. Advice, a potion, a healing — and you want nothing?" His voice, too, was as she remembered, deep and resonant, full of overtones. As if, she thought suddenly, he had spent much time with elves. His eyes, now visible as he came closer, seemed to pierce her with their keen glance.

"No. No, sir, I want nothing." Paks dropped her gaze, stared at the ground, hoping he would not recognize her, would let her go.

"Is it, then, an offering of thanks? Have you received some gift, that you share your bounty? Not share, I see, for you have given everything — even your last copper. Can you say why?"

"No, sir." Paks sensed that he had come nearer yet, to the offering basin, still watching her.

"Hmm. And yet I heard someone very like you tell a soldier that she wished to speak with me, to ask me a question. Then I find you in my grove, filling the basin with your last coin, and even your spare shirt — and you have no question." He paused. Paks watched as the shadow of his robe came closer. She shivered. "But I have questions, if you do not. Look at me!" At his command, Paks's head seemed to rise of its own accord. Her eyes filled with tears. "Mmm, yes. You came to me once before for advice, if I recall. Was my counsel so bad that you refuse it now — Paksenarrion?"

Paks could not speak for the lump in her throat; tears ran down her face.

681

She tried to turn away, but his strong hand caught her chin and held her facing him.

"Much, I see, has happened to you since I last saw you. But I think you are not a liar, whatever you've become. So you will ask your question, Paksenarrion, and take counsel with me once again."

Paks fought the tightness in her throat and managed to speak. "Sir, I — I can't. There's nothing you can do — just let me go — "

"Nothing I can do? Best let me judge of that, child. As for going — where would you go, without money or pack?"

"Anywhere. East, or south to the hills . . . it doesn't matter — "

"There's enough dead bones in those hills already. No, you won't go until you've told me what your trouble is. Come now."

Paks found herself walking behind the Kuakgan to his house, her mind numb. She saw without amazement the door open before he reached it; he ducked slightly to clear the low lintel. Paks ducked too, and stepped down onto the cool earthen floor of a large, long room. Across from her, windows opened on the grove which came almost to the Kuakgan's house. The ceiling beams were hung with bunches of pungent herbs. At the far end of the room gaped a vast fireplace, its hearth swept and empty. Under the windows were two tables, one covered with scrolls, and the other bare, with a bench near it.

"Come," said the Kuakgan. "Sit here and have something to drink."

Paks sank onto the bench and watched as he poured her a mug of clear liquid from an earthenware jug. She sipped. It was water, but the water had a spicy tang.

"Mint leaves," he said. "And a half-stick of cinnamon. Here — " He reached down a round cheese from a net hanging overhead. He sliced off a good-sized hunk. "Eat something before we talk."

Paks was sure she could not eat, but the creamy cheese eased past her tight throat and settled her stomach. She finished the cheese and the second mug of water he poured her. By then he had sliced a half-loaf of dark bread and put it in front of her. She took a slice; it was nutty and rich.

Master Oakhallow sat at the end of the table, his hood pushed back, eating a slice of bread spread with cheese. Paks glanced at him: the same brown weather-beaten face, heavy dark eyebrows, thick hair tied off his face with a twisted cord the color of bark. He was gazing out the window beside him, frowning slightly. She followed his gaze. A black and white spotted bird clung to the trunk of the nearest tree; as she watched, it began to hammer on the bark. The strokes were loud and quick, almost like a drum rattle. Paks wondered why its head didn't split. She'd never seen anything like it, though she had heard that sound before without knowing its source. Bark chips flew from the tree.

"It's a woodpecker," he said, answering her thought. "It seeks out insects under the bark, and eats them. A forest without woodpeckers would be eaten by the little ones devouring the trees."

Paks felt her muscles unclenching, one by one. "Is it — are there more than one kind?"

The Kuakgan smiled. "Oh, yes. Most of them are speckled and spotted, but some are brown and white or gray and white, instead of black and white. There are little ones and big ones — bigger than this — and many of them have bright color at the head. This one has a yellow stripe, but it's hard to see so far away."

"How can they pound the tree like that without hurting themselves.?"

He shrugged. "They are made for it; it is their nature. Creatures are not harmed by following their natures. How else can horses run over rocky ground on those tiny hooves? Tiny for their weight, I mean." He reached to the jug and poured another mug of water for Paks, and one for himself.

Paks took another slice of bread. "I heard a bird when I came in; it sang three notes — " she tried to whistle them.

"Yes, I know the one. A shy bird. You'll never see it; it's brown on top, and speckled gray and brown below. It eats gnats and flies, and its eggs are green patterned with brown."

"I thought most birds — except the hawks and carrion-crows — ate seeds."

"Some do. Most sparrows are seed-eaters. There's one bird that eats the nuts out of pine cones. Watch, now — " He took a slice of bread and crumbled it on the broad windowsill, then took a slender wooden cylinder from his robe and blew into it. A soft trill of notes came out. Paks saw the flickering of wings between the trees, and five birds landed on the sill. She sat still. Three of the birds were alike, green with yellow breasts. One was brown, and one was fire-orange with black wings. Their tiny eyes glittered as they pecked the crumbs and watched her. When the bread was gone, the Kuakgan moved his hand and the birds flew away.

Paks breathed again. "They're so beautiful. I never saw anything so beautiful — that orange and black one — "

"So. You will admit that you haven't seen everything in this world you were so eager to leave?"

She hunched her shoulders, silent. She heard a gusty sigh, then the scrape of his stool as he rose.

"Stay here," he said, "until I return."

She did not look up, but heard his feet on the floor as he crossed the room, and the soft thud of the door as he closed it behind him. She thought briefly of going out the window, but the grove was thick and dark there as the sun lowered. The spotted bird was gone, the hammering coming now from a distance. She put down the rest of her slice of bread, her appetite gone. The room darkened. She wondered if he would be gone all night; she looked around but saw no place to sleep but the floor. From the grove came a strange cry, and she shivered, remembering the rumor that the Kuakgan walked at night as a great bear.

She did not hear the door open, but he was suddenly in the room with her. "Come help me bring in some wood," he said, and she got up and went out to find a pile of deadwood by the door. The last sunglow flared to the west. They broke the wood into lengths and brought it in. He lit candles and placed them in sconces along the walls, then laid a fire in the fireplace, but did not light it. He went out again and came back with a bundle that turned out to be a hot kettle wrapped in cloth. Inside, a few coals kept several pannikins warm. As he unwrapped the cloth, a delicious smell of onions and mushrooms and meat gravy rose from the kettle. Paks found her mouth watering, and swallowed.

"Hebbinford's best stew," he said, setting the dishes out on the tables. "And you were always one for fried mushrooms, weren't you? Sit down, go on — don't let it get cold. You're too thin, you know."

"I'm not hungry," said Paks miserably.

"Nonsense. I saw your look when you smelled those mushrooms. Your body's got sense, if you haven't."

Paks took a bite of mushrooms: succulent, hot, flavored with onions and meat. Before she realized what she was doing, she saw that the mushrooms were gone, and so was the stew. She was polishing the bowl with another slice of the dark bread. Her belly gurgled its contentment; she could not remember when she'd eaten so much. Not for a long time, not since — she looked up. Master Oakhallow was watching her.

"Dessert," he said firmly. "Plum tart or apple?"

"Apple," said Paks, and he pushed the tart across. She bit into the flaky crust; sweet apple juice ran down her chin. When the tart was gone, the Kuakgan was still eating his. Paks cleaned her chin with a corner of the cloth that had been around the kettle. She found herself holding another slice of bread, and ate that. She felt full and a little sleepy. He finished his tart and looked at her.

"That's better," he said. "Now. You'll want to wash up a bit, and use the jacks, I expect. Let me show you — " He touched a panel beside the fireplace, and it slid aside to reveal a narrow passage. On one side was a door, through which Paks caught a glimpse of a bunk. On the other, a door opened on three steps down to a stone-flagged room with a channel along one side. Paks heard the gurgle of moving water, and the candlelight sparkled on its surface. "Cold water only," said Master Oakhallow. "There's the soaproot, and a towel — " He lit other candles in the chamber as he spoke. "If you're tired of those clothes, you can wear this robe." He pointed to a brown robe hanging from a peg. "Now, I'll be out for awhile. When you're through, go on back to the other room. Whatever you do, don't go outside the house. Is that clear?"

"Yes, sir," said Paks. "I won't."

"Good." He turned and went back up the stairs; Paks saw the light of his candle dwindle down the passage.

The little room was chilly and damp, but smelled clean and earthy. Paks started to wash her hands, gingerly, but the cold water merely tingled instead of biting. She splashed it on her face, started to dry it, then glanced warily at the door. Surely he was really gone. She went up the steps and looked. Nothing. She came back down and looked at the water for a moment, then grunted and stripped off her clothes: she felt caked in dirt and sweat. She wet the soaproot and scrubbed herself, then stood in the channel and scooped water over her soapy body. By the time she had finished, she was shivering, but vigorous towelling warmed her again. She looked at her clothes and wished she had not put her spare shirt in the offering basin. Her clothes were as dirty as she had been. She looked at the brown robe, then took it off the peg. It felt soft and warm. When she came from the jacks, she looked at her clothes again. She wondered if she could wash them in the channel, but decided against it: she needed hot water and a pot. She shook them hard, brushed them with her hand, and folded them into a bundle. She slipped her bare feet back into her worn boots and went up the steps, down the passage, and into the main room.

The Kuakgan had lit more candles before he left, and the room had a warm glow. He had drawn shutters across the windows; she was glad of that. She sat down at the table to wait, wondering how long he would be. She thought of where she'd expected to be this night — alone in the hills, perhaps to see no dawn — and shivered, looking around her quickly. This was pleasant: the soft robe on her shoulders, the good meal. Why didn't I ever — ? I could have bought mushrooms at least once — She pushed these thoughts away. She wondered where the Kuakgan was, and if he'd bought the meal with her offering. And most of all — what was he going to do? She thought she should be afraid, but she wasn't.

She eased into sleep without knowing it, leaning on the table; she never knew when he came in. When she woke again, she was wrapped in a green blanket and lying on the floor against the wall. The windows were unshuttered and sunlight struck the tree trunks outside. She felt completely relaxed and wide awake at the same time. Her stomach rumbled. She was just unwrapping the blanket when the door opened, letting in a shaft of sunlight.

"Time for breakfast," said the Kuakgan as he came in. He carried a dripping honeycomb over a bowl. Paks felt her mouth water. She climbed out of the blanket, folded it, and came to the table where he was laying out cheese, bread, and the honeycomb. "You won't have had this honey before," he said. "It's yellowwood honey, an early spring honey, and they never make much of it." He glanced at her and smiled. "You slept well."

Paks found herself smiling in return. "Yes . . . yes, sir, I did." She sat down.

"Here," he said, pouring from the jug. "It's goat's milk. Put some honey in your mug with it."

Paks broke off a piece of comb and floated it in the milk. He sliced the cheese and pushed some towards her. She sipped the milk; it was delicious. The honey had a tang to it as well as sweetness. The Kuakgan dripped some on his cheese; Paks did the same, and had soon eaten half a cheese, each slice dripping honey. Bees flew in the window and settled on the remains of the comb.

"No, little sisters," said the Kuakgan. "We have need of this." He hummed briefly, and the bees flew away. Paks stared at him; he smiled.

"Do you really talk to bees?" she asked.

"Not talk, exactly. It's more like singing; they're a musical folk. They dance, too; did you know that?" Paks shook her head, wondering if he was teasing. "It's quite true; I'll show you someday."

"Can you speak with all the animals? Those birds yesterday, and bees—"

"It's a Kuakgan's craft to learn the nature of all creatures: trees and grass as well as birds, beasts, and bees. When you know what something is — what its nature is — how it fits into the web of life — you can then begin to speak its language. It's a slow craft; living things are various, and each one is different."

"Some mages speak to animals," said Paks.

The Kuakgan snorted. "Mages! That's different. That's like the ring you had. A mage, now, wants power for himself. If he speaks to an animal, it's for his own purposes. Kuakkgani — we learn their languages because we love them: the creatures. Love them as they are, and for what they were made. When I speak to the owl that nests in that ash" — he nodded to the window — "it is not to make use of him, but to greet him. Of course, I must admit we do get some power from it. We can ask them things, we know their nature. But we are the ones who serve all created things without wanting to change them. That's why the Marshal in the grange is never quite sure I'm good enough for an ally."

Paks watched him, feeling that she should be able to find some other meaning in what he said, something that would apply to her. She could not think of anything. She wondered when he would start to question her.

He sat back from the table and looked at her. "Well, now. Your clothes are drying on the bushes out there, but they'd be clammy yet. You'll be more comfortable outside in something other than that robe, I daresay." He rose and went to a chest near the wall. "This will fit close enough." He held out homespun trousers with a drawstring waist, and a linen shirt. "Come outside when you're ready; I want to show you something." He went out the door and shut it behind him.

Paks looked at the clothes. They were creased as if they'd been in the chest a long time. She fingered the cloth, looking nervously at the windows. She looked for the passage beside the fireplace, but the panel was closed, and she couldn't find the touchlock. At last she sat on the floor beside the table, breathing fast, and changed from the robe to the pants and shirt. She put on her belt over the shirt and looked for her dagger; it was on the table.

When she pushed on the door, it opened silently. Outside, the sunny glade seemed empty, until she saw the Kuakgan standing motionless by the end of the stone-marked path. He gestured to her, and she walked across the glade.

"You must stay near me," he said. "The grove is not safe for wanderers; experienced pathfinders cannot be sure of its ways. If we are separated, be still. I will find you. Nothing will harm you as long as you are still, or with me. It may be that I have to leave you suddenly. . . . I hope not, but it might happen. Just stay where I left you. You will find enough beauty to watch until I come back." He began to move through the trees, as silent as a current of air; Paks followed closely. From time to time he stopped, and touched a tree or herb lightly, but he said nothing, and Paks was silent as well. As the morning warmed, more birds sang around them, and the rich scents of leafmold and growing things rose from the ground. Paks found herself breathing slowly, deeply. She had no idea where they were in the grove, but it didn't matter. She began to look with more attention to the trees and bushes they walked past. The Kuakgan touched a tree trunk: Paks saw a tiny lichen, bright as flame, glowing against dark furrowed bark. She saw for herself a clump of tiny mushrooms, capped in shiny red — a strawberry in flower — a fern-frond uncurling out of dry leaves. She realized that the Kuakgan was standing still, watching her. When she met his eyes, he nodded.

Chapter Two

So passed the rest of that day, with the warm spring sun and the silence unknotting the muscles of back and neck that had been tight so long. They came on a tiny trickle of clear water, and drank; for awhile in the early afternoon they sat near a mound of stone, and Paks fell asleep. When she woke, the Kuakgan was gone, but before she had stretched more than twice, she saw him coming through the trees. From time to time her mind would reach for the memory of yesterday's pain, but she could not touch it: it was as if a pane of heavy glass lay between that reality and this. She could not think what she might do next, or where to go, and at last she quit trying to think of it.

They came back to the Kuakgan's house in the last of the sunlight. Paks took her clothes, now dry, from the bushes, and folded them in her arms. She felt pleasantly tired, and slightly hungry. The Kuakgan smiled.

"Sit here in the warmth, while I bring supper," he said. "Or will you come with me?"

Paks thought of the inn, and the misery returned full strength. This time she felt the tension knotting her brow and hunching her shoulders, and tried to stand upright. But before she could frame an answer, the Kuakgan shook his head.

"No. Not yet. Stay. As I feared, it will take more than one day of healing." And he was gone, across the glade and along the path to the village.

She sat trembling, hating herself for the fear that had slammed back into her mind. She could not even go to an inn — even here, where she had had friends, and no enemies. She stared at her hands, broad and scarred with the years of war. If she could not hold a sword or bow, what could she do? Not stay forever with the kuakgan, that wouldn't do. Her hand felt for her belt pouch, and she remembered that she'd put it in the offering basin. Everything was gone; everything from those years had gone as if it had never been. Warriors can't keep much, but that little they prize; the loss of the last of her treasures to the kuaknom still hurt: Saben's little red horse, Canna's medallion. Now she had not even the Duke's ring left (the third ring, she thought ruefully, that he's given me and I've lost somehow.)

As before, she wasn't sure how long the Kuakgan had been gone when he returned. He was simply there, in the evening dimness, carrying another kettle. She forced herself up as he came toward her. He nodded, and they went into the house together. This time she helped unpack the kettle, and made no protest at eating. He had brought slices of roast mutton swimming in gravy, redroots mashed with butter, and mushrooms. Again. She looked up, to say something about the cost, met his eyes, and thought better of it. She ate steadily, enjoying the food more than she expected to, but fearing the questions he would surely ask after supper.

But he said nothing, as long as she ate, and when she finished, and stacked her pans for return, he seemed to be staring through the opposite wall. His own dishes were empty; she reached for them, wiped them, and put them in the kettle. He looked at her suddenly, and smiled briefly.

"You're wondering when I will start to question you."

Paks looked down, then forced herself to meet his eyes. "Yes."

"I had thought tonight. But I changed my mind." A long silence. Paks looked away, around the room, back to his face. It was unreadable.

"Why?" she asked finally.

He sighed, and shook his head. "I'm not sure how — or how much — to tell you. Healing is a Kuakganni craft, as you know." Paks nodded. "Well, then, one part of the healing craft is knowing when. When to act, and when to wait. In the case of humans, one must also know when to ask, and when to keep silent. You are not ready to speak of it, whatever it is."

Paks moved restlessly. "You — I would have thought you'd have heard something. . . . "

"Hmmm." It became as resonant as his comments to the bees. Paks looked at his face again. "I hear many things. Most of them false, as far as talk goes. Brewersbridge is a little out of the way for reliable news." He looked at her squarely. "And whatever I might have heard, what is important is you, yourself. Just as you, yourself, will heal when you are ready."

Paks looked away. She could feel the tears stinging her eyes again.

"There. You are not ready, yet. Don't worry; it will come. Let your body gain strength for a few days. You are already better, though you don't feel it."

"But I couldn't go — " Her voice broke, and she covered her face with her hands.

"But that will pass. That will pass." She felt a wave of warmth and peace roll over her mind, and the pain eased again.

But several nights later, the dream returned. Once more she was fighting for her life far underground, tormented by thirst and hunger and the pain of her wounds. She smelled the rank stench of the green torches, and felt the blows of knife and whip that striped her sides. She gasped for breath, choked, scrabbled at the fingers knotted in her throat — and woke to find the Kuakgan beside her, holding her hands in his.

Soft candlelight lit the room. She stared wildly for a moment, lost in the dream, trembling with the effort of the fight.

"Be still," he said softly. "Don't try to talk. Do you know me yet?"

After a minute or two she nodded. Her tongue felt too big for her mouth, and she worked it around. "Master Oakhallow." Her voice sounded odd.

"Yes. You are safe. Lie still, now; I'll get you something to drink."

The mint-flavored water cleaned remembered horrors out of her mouth. She tried to sit up, but the Kuakgan pushed her down gently. A tremor shook her body; as she tried to fight it off, the pain of those wounds returned, sapping her strength.

"You still have pain?" he asked.

Paks nodded.

"How long ago were those wounds dealt?"

She tried to count back. Her mind blurred, then steadied. "From — it would have been last summer. Late in the summer."

"So long?" His eyebrows rose. "Hmm. What magic bound them?"

Paks shook her head. "I don't know. The paladin and Marshal both tried healing. It helped, but the — the kuaknom had done something to them —"

"Kuaknom! What were you doing with them?"

Paks looked down, shivering. "They captured me. In Kolobia."

"So. I don't wonder that you have grave difficulties. And they dealt these wounds that pain you now?"

"Not . . . exactly. It — " As the memory swept over her, Paks could not speak. She shook her head, violently. The Kuakgan caught it, and held her still.

"No more, then, tonight. Sleep." He answered the fear in her eyes before she could say it. "You won't dream again. That I can still, and you will rest as you did the first night, and wake at peace. Sleep." She fell into his voice, into the silence beyond it, and slept.

In the morning she woke rested, as he had promised. Still the shame of her breakdown was on her, and she came to the breakfast table silently and did not smile.

"You will not have those dreams again," he said quietly, as she ate. "When I release your dreams again, those will be healed. This much I promise. I have waited as long as I could for your body's healing, Paksenarrion; it is now time to begin on the mind. Whatever ill you have suffered has clearly injured both."

She nodded, silent and intent on her bread.

"I will need to see these wounds you spoke of." He reached for her arm. Paks froze an instant, then stretched her hand out. He pushed up her sleeve. The red-purple welts were still swollen. "You have more of these?"

"Yes."

"Many?"

"Yes." Despite herself, she was shivering again.

"And they are all over a half-year old?" Paks nodded.

"Powerful magic, then, and dangerous. Have they faded at all? How long did it take for them to heal this far?"

"They . . . fade sometimes," Paks said softly. "For a week or so, as if they were healing. Then they swell and redden again. At first — I don't know how long it was. I think only a day or so, but I lost track of time."

"I see. Have any true elves seen this?"

"Yes. One that came with us. He thought they had used something like the true elves use to speed and slow the growth of plants."

"Ah. It might be so, indeed. Perverted, as they would have it — to heal quickly partway and then stay so. But why that far?"

Paks fought a desire to roll into a ball like a hedgehog. It was harder to speak than she had expected; that was hard enough. "So — so I could fight."

"Fight?" The Kuakgan paused. When she said nothing, he went on. "You said they did not deal these wounds themselves. They wanted you able to fight, but hindered. And now you cannot fight. Was that their doing, too?"

"No." She could not say more. She heard the Kuakgan's sigh.

"I need to try something on one of the wounds. This will probably hurt." He took her arm, and held it lightly. Paks paid no attention. She felt the fingers of his other hand running along the scars. After a moment she felt a trickle of cold in one, then heat in another. The feelings ebbed. She glanced at his face; it was closed and remote. A savage ache ran up her arm from the wrist, and was gone instantly. A pain as sharp as the original blow brought a gasp from her; she glanced at her arm; the scar was darker than ever. Then it passed, and the Kuakgan's eyes came to focus on her again.

"The true elf was correct in his surmise. These will heal no better without intervention. Did he try?"

"He said he had not the skill. He had known one who had, but — "

"I see. Paksenarrion, this will take time and patience. It will not be easy for you; it is a matter of purifying the wounds of the poison they used. If you can bear the pain a short while longer, you should be strong enough in body for the healing. Can you?"

Paks forced a smile. "After these months? Of course."

His face relaxed briefly. "Good. And now we must come to the other — it's not for this pain that you were ready to throw away your life. What else did they do to you?"

"Do I have to — ? Now?"

"I think so. Healing those — getting that poison out — will take strength from us both. I must know what else is wrong, what reserves you have, before I start that." He started to gather up the remains of breakfast, though, as if it were any other morning. Paks sat where she was, unspeaking. After brushing crumbs onto the windowsill for the birds, he turned back to her. "It might be easier outside. Sunlight cleanses more than dirty linen. Come walk with me."

They had wandered an hour in the grove before Paks began to speak, starting with her first days in the training barracks at Fin Panir, and the sun was high overhead when she came to the kuaknomi lair. Even in the bright sunlight (for they had come again to the glade) she felt the darkness and the foulness of that place. Her words came short, and halted, but the Kuakgan did not prompt her. The fountain's chuckling filled the silence until she spoke again.

691

"I could not say his name," she said finally. "I couldn't call on Gird. I tried, at first. I remember that. But after awhile . . . I couldn't say it. And I had to fight: whenever I woke again, they were there, and I had to fight." She told what she could remember of the battles in the arena, of her horror at seeing the great bloated spider that devoured those she defeated. "After awhile, I don't remember more. They said — those who came and found me — that I was wearing enchanted armor, and wore Achrya's symbol around my neck."

"Who found you?"

"Others in the expedition: Amberion, Marshal Lord Fallis, those. I don't remember that at all. They told me that after a day I was awake and talking to them clearly, but the next I remember is walking along a trail in another canyon, and finding the way to Luap's stronghold."

"So it was real — you found it?"

"Oh yes, it's real. A great citadel, deep in the rock, full of all kinds of magic." In her mind's eye the dark lairs were replaced by that soaring red rock arch between the outpost and the main stronghold. "We'd hardly be back to Fin Panir by now had it not had magic. That's how we came."

"Magic, then, but no healing?"

Paks stopped short. "No. Not for me, anyway." She went on to tell him what had happened when she returned to Fin Panir. How the Marshal-General had said she was deeply tainted with kuaknomi evil, and how she had come at last to agree. She shivered as she spoke, and the Kuakgan interrupted.

"Let's go back for supper. It's late." Already the sun was far behind the trees. When they came to the house, Paks feared to stay alone, and could not say it. But instead of leaving her, the Kuakgan came in and brought out bread and cheese. They ate in silence, and he seemed abstracted. After supper, for the first time, he lit a fire on the large hearth, and they sat before it.

"Now go on," he said. "But don't hurry yourself. What did your Marshal-General propose to do? Why did she think Gird had not protected you?"

"She didn't say why," said Paks, answering the last question first. "But I think they believe I was too new a Girdsman, and too vulnerable as a paladin candidate. They'd said we were more open to evil, in our training. She said that fighting under iynisin command had opened a passage for their evil into my mind. It could be taken out, but — " Paks broke off, steadied her voice, and went on, staring into the flames. "She said the evil was so close to the — to what made me a fighter, that to destroy it might destroy that too."

"And what did she say that was?"

"My courage." She barely breathed the words, but the pain in them rang through the room.

The Kuakgan hummed briefly. Paks sat rigid as a pike staff, waiting for his reaction. He reached a poker to the fire, and stirred it. Another pause, while sparks snapped up the chimney. "And now you are not a fighter. You think that is why?"

"I know it. Sir." Paks sat hunched, looking now at her hands locked in her lap.

"Because you know fear? Did you never fear before? I thought you were afraid of me, the first time I saw you. You were afraid of Master Zinthys's truth spell — you said so."

"Before I could always face it. I could still fight. And usually I wasn't afraid. Very."

"And now you can't." His voice expressed nothing she could take hold of, neither approval nor disapproval.

"That's right. As soon as I could get out of bed again, afterwards, I tried. But my own armor frightened me. Weapons, noise, the look on their faces, all of it. It was some little time before I could walk well, and I was clumsy with things at first. The Marshal-General had said that might happen, so when I picked up my sword and it felt strange, I wasn't upset. At first. But then — " She shook her head, remembering her first attempt at arms practice. "It was just drill," she said slowly. "They knew I'd been hurt; they wouldn't have injured me. But I couldn't face them. When that blade came toward me, I froze. They told me later that I fainted. It didn't even touch me. The next day it was worse. I started shaking before I got into the practice ring. I couldn't even ride. You know how I loved horses — " she looked up, and the Kuakgan nodded. "My own horse — the black I got here — I couldn't mount him. Could not. He sensed my fear, and fretted, and all I could think of was the size of his feet. They all thought it would help somehow, so they lifted me onto a gentle little palfrey. I sat there stiff, and shaking, and as soon as she broke into a trot I fell off."

"And so you left them. Or did they throw you out?"

Paks shook her head. "No. They were generous. The Marshal-General offered to have me stay there, or train me to any trade I wished. But you know, sir, that Gird is a fighter's saint. How can they understand? It's not right, and Girdsmen know it. And the Duke — " Her voice broke again.

"Was he there?"

Paks fought for control. "Yes. He came when he — when they told him I — what they might do. He said he would take me then, as a captain or whatever. But — I knew — they were right. Something was wrong. It had to be done. I still think so. And he was there after, when we knew it had gone badly. He gave me — "

"That ring you left in the basin." Paks nodded. The Kuakgan sighed. "Your Duke is a remarkable man. He has no love for the Girdsmen in general, and the Marshal-General in particular. He must think a lot of you."

"Not now," said Paks miserably.

"He gave you the ring afterwards, did he not? After he knew what had happened? Don't underestimate your Duke, Paksenarrion." He stirred the fire again. "I saw him once, long ago. I wondered then what sort of man he would be. I have heard of him, of course, in the years since, but only what anyone might hear. For the most part."

693

"Why does he dislike the Girdsmen so?" asked Paks.

The Kuakgan shook his head. "That's not my story to tell. I have it only by hearsay, and may have it wrong. Perhaps he will tell you someday."

"I . . . don't think so."

"Because you think you'll never go back? Nonsense. In courtesy you must see him again, and ease his concern."

"But — "

"You must. Whether you draw sword for him again or not, Paksenarrion, you cannot leave him wondering whether you are alive or dead. Not tonight, no, nor tomorrow — but you must go. And when you go, you will agree with me on that."

Paks said nothing. She could not imagine going to the Duke's hold with her fear still unconquered. Unless she regained her courage, and could fight, she could not face the Duke and her old companions.

"One thing more, tonight, and then you will sleep. What was it like, when you first thought your courage gone? How did you know it?"

Paks thought how to describe it. "When I first trained, with the Duke," she began, "I could feel something — an eagerness — in the drill. When Siger — the armsmaster — threatened with his blade, I felt it rising in me. Excitement, eagerness — I don't know how to say it, but I wanted to fight, wanted to — to strike, to take chances. When he hit me, the pain was just pain, like falling. Nothing to be afraid of, or worried about. And after that, in the battles — I was scared, the first year, but even then that feeling was inside, to draw on. As soon as the fight started, it seemed to lift me up, and carry me along. It never failed me. Even in the worst times, when we were ambushed, or when Macenion and I faced the old elf lord, I might think that I was likely to be killed, but it didn't affect my fighting. Unless, perhaps, I fought all the better for it. That's how we all were; those that feared wounds or death left the Company. That danger was our life. Some, indeed, loved the fighting so much that they were kept from constant brawling only by the rules. I had had one trouble with brawling; I didn't want more. I liked my fights for a reason." Paks stopped again; she was breathing faster, and her mouth was dry. The Kuakgan rose and brought the jug of water. They each had a mug of it, then she went on.

"At Fin Panir it was like a dream. Everything I'd ever thought about, when I was a girl: the knights, the paladins, the songs and music, training every day with warriors known all over the Eight Kingdoms. There were none of the — the things that bothered me, in the south. We would fight only against true evil. And I met real elves, and dwarves. I could learn any weapon, learn as much as I could. They said I did well; they wanted me to join the Fellowship of Gird, they asked me to become a paladin-candidate. For me, for all that I'd dreamed of, that was — " She stopped, poured another mug of water, and took a sip. "I never dared dream so high, before. It came like a burst of light. All the strange things that had happened in Aarenis seemed to make sense. Of course, I agreed. I felt I was coming to my true home, the heart of my life."

694

"And now?"

"It was the happiest time of my life." Paks drank the rest of her water. "It will seem silly to you, Master Oakhallow, I don't doubt. A sheepfarmer's daughter with silly daydreams of wielding a magic sword against monsters, a runaway girl joining the mercenaries, still holding that dream somewhere inside. I couldn't make them understand, in Fin Panir; maybe it's so silly it doesn't matter. But I had tried to learn my craft of fighting well enough to be of use, and there, where all were dedicated to honor and war — there I was happy indeed."

"I don't think it was silly," said the Kuakgan. "Such a dream is most difficult to fulfill, but it is not silly. But tell me, now, what it was that changed, after the Marshal-General did whatever she did."

"It was gone, that's all. That feeling or whatever that came when I was fighting. It was gone, and left emptiness — as if the ground suddenly disappeared under one foot, and left me with nothing to stand on. I had no skill and no courage to cover the lack. I thought at first it would come back; I kept trying. After awhile I could move better, and control my sword, but as soon as I tried to fence with someone the emptiness seemed to spread and spread until all was gone. Sometimes I fainted, as I said, and sometimes — once I ran away, and once or twice just stood, unable to do anything. Now when I try to face something, when something frightens me, I have nothing inside to do it with."

"So you left Fin Panir and — did you plan to come here?"

"No! Never! I wandered along the roads, looking for work. I thought I could do unskilled work, at least: farm labor, and that. But so many things frightened me — things that frighten no one but a little child — " She wondered whether to tell him about the trader's caravan, the robbers at the inn, and decided not to. What difference did it make, after all? "I wandered, mostly. I didn't know this was Brewersbridge until I came to the inn. I would have fled, but a guard thought I was acting strangely and wanted to take me to the keep."

"Wouldn't Marshal Cedfer have vouched for you? You said the Marshal-General promised safe-conduct in all the granges of Gird."

"I suppose he would have, sir, but I couldn't ask him. I asked, once, in Fintha — they don't understand. If I had lost an arm or leg, something they could see, they might. But as it is — cowardice — they think of that as shameful weakness, or punishment for great evil. With soldiers it's even simpler. Cowardice is cowardice, and nothing else. I suppose they're right, sir, but I can't — " Her voice broke, and tears burst from her eyes. "I can't — live with that — with their scorn. The Marshal knew me before — he'd say I wasn't a criminal — but he'd despise — "

"Enough. I know the Marshal better than that. He is fair, if sometimes narrow-minded. And you are not being fair to yourself. But it is late, and you need rest. We will talk more of this tomorrow. Don't fear to sleep; your dreams are withheld for the present."

Paks thought she could not face the morning, but when she woke, she

695

felt more at peace than she had for a long time. She awaited the Kuakgan's questions. But he said nothing during breakfast, and afterwards called her to walk with him in the grove as usual. The first hour or so passed in silence. As always, Paks found something new to look at every few paces. She had never lived near a forest before, and it had not occurred to her how full a forest could be. Finally he turned to her, and spoke.

"Sit down, child, and we'll talk some." Paks sat against the trunk of a tree, and he stretched on the ground nearby. "You are stronger of body than when you came, Paksenarrion; are you aware of it?"

"Yes, sir." Paks felt herself flushing. "I've been eating too much."

"No, not too much. You were far too thin; you need more weight even now. But the day you came, you could not have endured what you did yesternight without collapse."

"But that was my mind—"

He made a disgusted noise. "Paksenarrion, your body and mind are as close as the snail-shell and the snail. If you poke holes in the snail-shell, will the snail live?"

"No, but—"

"By the Tree, you must be better, to argue with me!" He chuckled a moment, then turned serious again. "You did not say, when I first saw you, how you planned to die — if you'd thought about it — but it was clear that you were near death for some reason. Some trouble I could see at a glance: your thinness, your weakness. Some seemed clear, more was certain. I began with what was easily cured; good food and rest heal many wounds of body and mind both. Then you were frightened even by that rabbit on the path as you came in. Is that true now?"

"No . . . not here, with you. I don't know what it would be like outside." Paks tried to imagine it, tried to see herself walking down a street somewhere. The panic fear she had felt before did not return. "I can think of being somewhere else, at least."

"Very well. Your body is beginning to heal, and with it the mind heals also."

"But I thought you said the wounds would need more?"

"Yes. They will. But that will sap your strength again, for a little, and I wanted to build it first. It is a delicate thing, Paksenarrion, to choose the best time. First to gain your trust, so that even the pain I must cause you will not awake the panic. Then to let food and rest do what they may with the parts of your body that were not wounded, so that the strength there offsets — Do you understand any of this?"

"Not really. I would think if the food and rest could heal—"

"It should heal all? Ordinarily it might. But the kuaknomi have difficult magic, and their poisons outlast normal human lifespans. The poison takes the strength from you, and will, until we get it out. And until your body is clean of it, your mind shares the poison."

"Oh."

"And you fear what I might do to heal you," he added shrewdly.

"Yes. Sir, I — I went through that once. They were saying it was in my mind, but the same thing. Evil. Something to be ripped out. And now you — "

"Hmmm. Yes. But I can show you what I will do. Look at that scar on your arm — the one that hurt you so that night." Paks shoved up her sleeve and looked. It had been redder the following morning, but now had faded to a dull pink. When she prodded it with a finger, it held no underlying soreness.

"Is it truly healing?" she asked.

"Yes. In a few weeks it should be pale as your old scars. I could not use quicker methods, after what they had done."

"But the others?"

"You remember the pain of that one? It was almost like the original wound, wasn't it?" Paks nodded. "And you have many others. To work on them all at once will be very painful for you. I could force you into a sleep, but then we are faced with the trouble in your mind. If you still wish to die, you could go then, while I was busy with your wounds. I cannot care for both, alone. I would prefer to have your cooperation, mind and body, before I begin." He seemed to look past her, over her head, into some distance. "I might have called on another Kuakgan for aid, or on the elves — or even Marshal Cedfer — but until I knew where your trouble lay, and from what cause, I had no right to do so."

"But you can heal the wounds," said Paks, confidently.

"Yes."

"Will that heal the — the other? Is that what caused it, truly?"

"I don't know. I think you were already weakened so by the wounds, by the poison in them, that even without the Marshal-General's intervention your mind would have been affected in time. Without probing deeply into it, I am not sure what she did. But anything that would remove a deep-seated evil would be likely to affect other things; evil spreads like ink in water, staining everything it touches. Your body was damaged again, by that: you said when you woke from her treatment you could not walk at first. What I hope is that thorough healing of the body will allow your mind to heal, too. Whether what you have lost will regenerate or not, I cannot tell. But you are already better, in both, and that gives me hope."

Paks stared at the ground before her. "I'm still scared. Not the pain, so much — that comes anyway — but the other."

"I know. I can treat one at a time, but that will take months. And I must warn you that the poison itself will resist, given time for it. The last ones will be much harder to cure than the first. Yet to do this, without your free consent, is likely to widen the rift in your mind. It is for this that I waited, hoping that you would be able to trust me."

"How long would it take?"

"All at once? A day of preparation for me; you would have to keep quiet within doors, and let me meditate. I have most of the materials I need; I could gather the rest today. Then a day or two for the healing itself: I cannot tell, until I have seen and tested each wound, exactly how long. You would be very weak for the first day afterwards, but your strength would come quickly."

"And I would sleep through it?"

"The healing itself, yes. I would recommend it. Even if you were willing to endure all the pain awake, your reaction could break my attention to the healing."

"I wish — " she began, and then stopped. She took a deep breath and went on. "I wish it could be done, and over, and I didn't have to decide."

His voice was gentle. "No. It is not the way of the Kuakkganni to force a good on someone if there is time for choice. Each creature has its own way to travel; we learn much of them, but we do not change the way. And for humans, the way involves choice."

"You forced me to eat, that first day."

"Then there was no time. I had to buy that time, to find out what was wrong. Now you are beginning to heal, and I judge you well enough to make a choice for yourself. I will give you advice, and have, but you are free to follow it or not, as you are free to take what time you need for the decision."

Paks had taken a twig from the ground, and was digging little holes in the dirt at her feet. She made a row of them, then another row. For a moment she saw them as positions in a formation, then scraped the twig across the design.

"You think I should let you do it now?"

"I think you should ask yourself if you can trust me. I think you should ask yourself if you can trust your own mind to hold on until your body has a chance to heal. If when you are well again you still wish to waste your bones on the hills, I've no doubt some orc or wolf will be glad to assist."

"I don't, now," she said very softly.

"Good."

"I think — I know I want to be well again. If it can happen. If what is wrong is that poison, then — I must let you do it. Whatever it is."

For the rest of the afternoon, they gathered herbs and other materials from the grove. Most of it was unfamiliar to Paks; the Kuakgan explained little, merely pointing out the plants to take. That evening he went to the inn for food, after telling her to stay inside. When he came back, one of the potboys from the inn was with him; Paks heard his voice outside. The Kuakgan had him leave his burden on the step, and when he had left, called Paks outside to carry it in.

"We'll need food for several days," he explained. "You must eat well tomorrow, while I meditate, and I must eat something during the healing." He unpacked loaves of bread, a small ham, sliced mutton in pans, eggs, and other rich foods.

It seemed to Paks that the next day lasted forever. She had become used to wandering outside; she was restless in the house. The Kuakgan had left the hidden panel open, and she spent some time taking a bath and washing her hair, but that left hours of idleness. She forgot to eat at noon. Sometime in the afternoon her belly reminded her, and she ate several slices of ham, then some cheese. As the daylight faded outside, she wondered if the Kuakgan would appear for supper. The door to his private room had been closed all day; she dared not knock. But she felt it would be discourteous to eat without him.

The last light had disappeared, and she had lit candles in the main room, when he came to the door of the passage. Without a word, he nodded to her, and went to close the shutters. Paks started to speak, but he forestalled her with a fluent gesture of one hand. He laid a fire on the hearth, and lit it. Paks stood, wondering what to do. He pointed to the ham, and then to her. When she offered him a slice, he shook his head, but sat at the table to watch her eat. Her appetite had vanished; the ham lay in her stomach like a huge stone, and her mouth was dry. She looked over at him; he was watching her, his dark eyes warm. That gaze soothed her, and she was able to eat a bit more, and drink a mug of water. At last he reached and touched her hand, and gestured toward her pallet against the wall. She looked toward it, and at once the panic she thought had gone rose in her mind like a fountain, bursting her control. She choked on the breath in her throat, shut her eyes on the tears that came unbidden, and sat with her hands clamped on the table. He said nothing. Time passed. At last she could breathe, could see again her white-knuckled hands, could unclench those hands finger by finger. She did not try to meet his eyes again, but forced her stiff unwilling body to rise from the table and cross the room.

His hands on the sides of her head were dry and cool, impersonal as the bark of a tree. She lay with her eyes shut, rigid and waiting. When the first touch of power came, it was nothing like she expected. It seemed more a memory of recent mornings, of spring itself, of gold sunlight filtering through young leaves. She felt no pain, only peace and quietness, and let herself drift into that light like a leaf in the fountain. She did not know when the dream of light faded.

Return from that beauty and peace was more difficult. A call she could not answer, struggle, confusion, the return of fear. She woke with no knowledge of time or place — for a few moments, she thought she was back in the Duke's Company, trying to reach the Duke after the Siniava's attack on Dwarfwatch. "The Duke," she managed to say. "Saben — " Then she remembered enough to know that Saben was dead, and the Duke far away. The Kuakgan's face was strange to her, and only slowly did she come to know where she was.

"You wandered a long way," he said at last. His face was lined and drawn. "A long way indeed. I was not sure you would return." He reached for her wrist, and felt her pulse. "Much stronger. How do you feel?"

"I — just weak, I think. I don't want to move."

"No wonder. You need not, for a time." He sighed, then stretched. "I wonder that your Marshal-General did not see how bad those were. It may be they've gotten worse. But, Paksenarrion, you were almost beyond my healing powers. One of the wounds still had a bit of the weapon in it — a stone blade of some sort — and that one I had to open completely." He reached for a jug and poured out a mug of liquid. "You must try to drink all of this." He raised her shoulders and held the mug to her lips. Paks sipped slowly, and finally drained it completely. She was desperately tired. Later she could never remember if that first waking had been in daylight or night.

She slept, and woke again, and slept. Finally she woke to firelight, hungry for the first time, and able to move a little by herself. The Kuakgan was beside her, as always. When she stirred, and spoke to him by name, he smiled.

"You are certainly better. Hungry? I should hope so. Let me help you to the jacks first."

She wavered when she stood, dizzy and weak, but by the time they had gone down the passage and the stairs, she could support herself along the wall to the jacks. She came back alone, and slowly, still touching the wall. She tried to think, but had no idea how much time had passed. In the meantime, the Kuakgan had set food on the table: stew and bread. She half-fell onto the bench, and propped herself on the table. But she ate the last bite of her food, and was able to walk more steadily back to her pallet.

The next morning she woke normally, no more weak than if she had worked too hard the day before, or fought too long. Her mind seemed curiously empty of all feelings, but her body obeyed her, if a little sluggishly.

Chapter Three

"You will not regain your full strength for some time," Master Oakhallow said, as he sat with her at breakfast. "But we need to consider your other problem now." He paused for a long swallow of sweetened goat's milk. "If you still have one. Can you tell?"

Paks shook her head. "I don't feel much at all right now. When I think of fighting, it's very far away."

"Hmm. Maybe that's for the best. Perhaps you will be able to think more clearly." He cut another slice of bread, and bit into it. Paks swallowed her own milk. She was discovering that nothing hurt; she had not known how that constant pain had weighed on her. For a little while she did not care whether she could fight or not; it was pleasant enough to sit eating breakfast without pain. She felt the Kuakgan's gaze and raised her eyes to meet it. His face relaxed as he watched her. "At least the poison's out. Your face shows it. Well — are you ready?"

"For what, sir?"

"To talk about courage."

Paks felt herself tensing, and tried to relax. "Yes."

"Very well. It seems to me that two mistakes have clouded your mind. First is the notion that having as little courage as an ordinary person is somehow shameful, that you must have more than your share. That's nothing but pride, Paksenarrion. So it is you felt you couldn't live with the meager amount of courage most folk have: it was too shameful. And that's ridiculous. Here you are, young, strong, whole-bodied now, with wit enough — with gifts above average — and you feel you cannot go on with still more bounty of the gods."

Paks blushed. Put that way . . .

"Paksenarrion, I want you to think of those common folk awhile. They live their lives out, day by day, in danger of fever, robbers, fire, storm, wolves, thieves, assassins, evil creatures and powers — and war. They most of them have neither weapons nor skill at arms, nor any way to get them. You've lived among them, this past winter: you know, you *feel*, how helpless is a farmwife against an armed man, or a craftsman against a band of thieves. You are right, they are afraid — full of fear from moment to moment, as full of fear as you have been. And yet they go on. They plow the fields and tend flocks, Paksenarrion, and weave cloth for you to wear, and

701

make pots, and cheese, and beer, and boots, and wagons: everything we use, these frightened people make. You think you don't want to be like them. But you *must* be like them, first. You must have their courage before you get more."

"But — sir, you said they had none."

"No. I said they were frightened. Here's the second mistake. Courage is not something you have, like a sum of money, more or less in a pouch — it cannot be lost, like money spilling out. Courage is inherent in all creatures; it is the quality that keeps them alive, because they endure. It is courage, Paksenarrion, that splits the acorn and sends the rootlet down into soil to search for sustenance. You can damage the creature, yes, and it may die of it, but as long as it lives and endures, each living part has as much courage as it can hold."

Paks felt confused. "That seems strange to me — "

"Yes, because you've been a warrior among warriors. You think of courage as an eagerness for danger, isn't that so?"

"I suppose so. At least being able to go on, and fight, and not be mastered by fear."

"Right. But the essence is the going on. A liking for excitement and danger is like a taste for walnuts or mushrooms or the color yellow. Most people have a little — you may have noticed how small children like to scare themselves climbing trees and such — but the gift varies in amount. It adds to the warrior's ability by masking fear. But it's not essential, Paksenarrion, even to a warrior. The going on, the enduring, is. Even for the mightiest warrior, a danger may be so great, a foe so overwhelming, that the excitement, the enjoyment, is gone. What then? Is a warrior to quit and abandon those who depend on his courage because it isn't fun?" Paks shook her head. "No, and put that way it's obvious. You may remember such times yourself. It's true that one who had no delight in facing and overcoming danger would not likely choose to be a warrior, except in great need. But consider your own patron Gird. According to legend, he was no fighter until need — his own and his neighbors' — drove him to it. Suppose he never enjoyed battle, but did his best anyway: does that make him unworthy of veneration?"

"No, sir. But if what you say is so, will I always be like this? And can I fight again?"

Master Oakhallow gave her a long considering look. "And how do you define *this*? Do you feel yourself the same as when you came here?"

Paks thought a moment. "No. I don't. I feel I can go on, but I still wish I were the way I used to be."

"It was more pleasant, doubtless, to feel no fear and be admired."

Paks ducked her head. "Yes, sir, but — I could do things. Help — "

"I know. You did many good things. But if we consider whether you will stay as you are now, we must consider what you are now, and what you wish to be. We must see clearly. We must have done with daydreams, and see whether this sapling — " he touched her arm, " — be oak, holly, ash or cherry. We can grow no cherries on an oak, nor acorns on a holly. And however your life goes, Paksenarrion, it cannot return to past times: you will never be just as you were. What has hurt you will leave scars. But as a tree that is hacked and torn, if it lives, will be the same tree — will be an oak if an oak it was before — so you are still Paksenarrion. All your past is within you, good and bad alike."

"I can't feel that, any more. All that happened before Kolobia . . . I can't reach it."

"That we will change. It's there, and it is you. Come, you are strong enough to walk today; the sun will do you good."

As they wandered the grove's quiet trails, he led her to talk about her life, bit by bit. She found herself remembering little things from her childhood: watching her father help a lamb at birth, rubbing it dry, carrying her younger brother on her shoulders from the fields to the house, listening for wolves' wild singing on winter nights when they ventured near the barns. It seemed that she was there again — where she could never go — clinging to the hames on the shaggy pony as her father plowed their one good field, or catching her fingers in the loom as her mother wove the striped blankets they slept under. Seen so, her father was not the wrathful figure of those last days at home, but a strong, loving man who made a hard land prosper for his family.

"He cared for me," she admitted at last, staring into the fire that night. "I thought he hated me, but he wanted me to be safe. That's why — "

The Kuakgan nodded. "He saw danger ahead for you as a fighter. Any father would. To think of his child — his daughter — exposed to sword and spear, wounded, dying among strangers — "

"Yes. I didn't think of it like that. I wanted danger."

"And danger you had. No, don't flinch. You'd have made a very bad pig farmer's wife, wanting to be a warrior. Even now, you'd make a bad pig farmer's wife."

"Not for the same reason."

"No. But your pig farmer — what was his name? — is better off with whoever he has."

Paks had not thought of Fersin Amboisson in years. She had never wondered whom he married instead. Now his pleasant, rugged face came back to her. He had looked, but for being a redhead, like Saben.

"I hope he found somebody good," she said soberly.

"The world's full of good wives," said Master Oakhallow, and turned to something else.

Day by day the talk covered more and more of the years. Her first days in the Duke's Company, her friends there, the trouble with Korryn and Stephi (which seemed to interest the Kuakgan far more than Paks could understand — he kept asking her more and more details of that day — things that seemed to have nothing to do with the incident itself.)

And as she talked, her life seemed to gain solidity — to become real again. She felt connected once more to the eager, adventurous girl tagging after older brothers and cousins, to the determined young woman running

703

away from home, to the young soldier fighting beside trusted companions in the Duke's Company. This, it seemed, was her real self — bold, self-willed, impetuous, hot-tempered, intensely loyal once trust was given. She began to see how these same traits could be strengths or weaknesses in different circumstances. Trust given the Duke would lead to one thing; given to Macenion, to a far different outcome.

"I never thought, before," she said, as they sat one day in a sunny spot. "I never thought that I should choose. I thought others were either good or bad, and nothing in between. Vik warned me about that, once, with Barranyi, but I didn't understand. It's still me, isn't it? I have to decide who is worthy of trust, and even then I have to decide each time if something is right or wrong."

The Kuakgan nodded. "It's hardest for fighters, Paksenarrion. Fighters must learn to obey, and often must obey without question: there's no time. That's why many of us — the Kuakkganni, I mean, now — will have nothing to do with fighters. So many cannot do both, cannot give loyalty and yet retain their own choice of right and wrong. They follow chaos, whether they know it or not. For one like you, who has chosen, or been chosen for, a part in the greater battle, it is always necessary to think as well as fight."

Paks nodded. "I see. And I didn't, did I? I did what I was told, and assumed that those I followed were right. If I liked them, I assumed they were good, and forgot about it." She paused, thinking back. "Even when I did worry — when I wanted the Duke to kill Siniava quickly — I couldn't think about it afterwards."

"Yes. You pushed it out of your mind and went back to being a plain soldier. You were challenged again and again, Paksenarrion, to go beyond that, and think for yourself: those incidents with Gird's symbol you told me about, but — "

"I refused. I went back. I see." Paks sighed, and stretched suddenly, reaching toward the trees with her locked fists. "Hunh. I thought I'd never refused a challenge, but I didn't even see it. Was that cowardice, too?"

"Have we defined cowardice? Why did you refuse? If you refused simply because you were certain that you should be a follower, that's one thing. But if you were afraid to risk choosing, risk being wrong — "

"Then it was. Then while I thought — while everyone else thought — I was brave, maybe I — "

"Maybe you were afraid of something, like everyone else. Don't be ridiculous, child! You're not perfect; no one is. What we're trying to do is find out what you are, and what you can be, and that does not include wallowing in guilt."

Paks stared at him, startled out of her gloom. "But I thought you were saying — "

"I was saying that you consistently refused to make some choices. That is something you need to recognize, not something to worry about in the past, where you can't change it. If you want to, you can decide to accept that challenge from now on."

"I can?"

"Certainly. I'm not speaking, now, of returning to soldiering. As a fighter, you're tempted to see all challenges in physical terms. But you can certainly decide that you, yourself, will consider and act on what you see as right and wrong. Whatever that may be."

Paks thought about that in silence. When she turned her head to speak, the Kuakgan was gone. She thought about it some more as she waited for him to return.

When he came, he was accompanied by another, clearly of elven blood. Paks scrambled to her feet awkwardly; she had seen no one but the Kuakgan all this time.

"This is Paksenarrion," he said to the elf. "She was gravely wounded by the dark cousins — " The elf murmured something softly, and the Kuakgan frowned. "You know the truth, Haleron; they are no myth. Paksenarrion, this is Haleron, an elf from Lyonya. He tells me that the rangers in the southern hills there are looking for new members. I think that would suit you; the outdoor work would restore your strength, and they will hire you on my recommendation."

Paks was so surprised that she could not speak. The elf frowned at her, and turned to the Kuakgan.

"We have no need of the weak," he said in elven. "Let her find another place to regain her strength. And is she not the one I heard of, from Fin Panir, who — "

Paks felt a wave of anger, the first in months. "May it please you, sir," she said in her best elven, "but I would not have you think me an eavesdropper later."

He stared at her. "My pardon, lady, for the discourtesy. I didn't know you were learned in our language."

"She knows more than that," said the Kuakgan. "And I assure you that she is quite strong enough for your woods work." He and the elf stared at each other; Paks could feel the battle of wills. The elf seemed to glow with his intensity; the Kuakgan grew more and more solid, like a tree. At last the elf shook his head.

"The power of the Kuakkganni is from the roots of the world." It sounded like a quote. The elf turned to Paks. "Lady, the rangers are in need of aid. If indeed you seek such employment, and have the skills of warfare, we would be glad to have your assistance."

Paks looked at the Kuakgan. His face was closed; she felt shut out of his warmth into darkness. She thought of the things he'd said, and sighed. If he turned her out. . . .

"I would be glad to aid the true elves," she said carefully, "in any good enterprise." She shot a quick glance at the Kuakgan; his eyes were alight, though his face showed no expression.

The elf nodded. "Very well. I leave at dusk — unless you require more rest — if you are weak — ?"

Paks felt fine. "No. I'd like to eat first."

"Of course. And pack your things, no doubt."

"I have none." She thought of her pack, cloak, and clothes, but did not even glance toward the Kuakgan. The elf raised his eyebrows. She stared back at him in silence.

"And where, Master Oakhallow, shall we eat?" the elf asked.

"Oh, at the inn, I think." He was watching Paks; she could feel the weight of his eyes. She swallowed, and braced herself for that ordeal.

But, in fact, it was no ordeal. No one seemed to notice her on the street, though several people glanced sideways at the elf. At *The Jolly Potboy*, the elf and the Kuakgan argued briefly and quietly over who would pay, and the elf finally won. She kept her eyes on the table at first, concentrating on the good food, but finally looked around.

The inn was not crowded, as it would be later, but she saw one or two familiar faces. Mal leaned on the wall, as usual, with a tankard at his elbow. Hebbinford's mother, in the corner, knitted on another scarf. Sevri darted through on her way outside; she had grown two fingers, at least, since Paks had seen her. But no one seemed to recognize Paks, and she relaxed. She listened to the talk, the clatter of dishes — so loud, after the Kuakgan's grove — but it didn't frighten her as it had. She almost wished someone would call her by name. Almost. The Kuakgan ordered tarts for dessert. The elf leaned back in his seat, and glanced around the room. Paks watched him covertly. He was a half head taller than she, with dark hair and sea-green eyes. The leather tunic he wore over shirt and trousers had dark wear-marks at shoulder and waist: Paks decided these were from sword-belt and bow. He caught her looking at him and smiled.

"May I ask, lady, where you learned our language?"

"I was honored with the instruction of a true elf from the southern mountains." If he knew she came from Fin Panir, he would know that already.

"You speak it well for a human. Most are too hasty to take time for it."

"Paksenarrion, though a human warrior, knows the folly of haste," said the Kuakgan. Paks looked at him, and he smiled at her, lifting his mug of ale.

"That is a wonder," said the elf. "Are the younger races finally learning patience of the elder?" He was watching the Kuakgan.

"From experience," said the Kuakgan. "Where all who know it learned it. Surely elves have not forgotten their own early days?"

"Alas, no. However remote, the memory remains." He turned to Paks. "I beg pardon again, lady, for any discourtesy."

"I took no offense," said Paks carefully. She wondered if the Kuakgan and the elf were old enemies. Surely the Kuakgan wouldn't send her to someone evil. She thought of their last conversation and wondered.

As they came out of the inn, the sun dropped behind the high hills to the southwest. A group of soldiers from the keep was coming down the north road toward the crossing; despite herself, Paks shivered.

"Are you cold?" asked the elf.

706

"No. Just a thought." She looked at the Kuakgan. He smiled.

"If you come this way again, Paksenarrion, you will be welcome in the grove."

"I thank you, sir. I — " But he was already moving away, nodding to the approaching soldiers, waving to a child in a doorway.

"We'd best be going," said the elf quietly. "I mean no discourtesy, but we have far to go, and if you have been unwell you may find it difficult to travel at my pace."

Paks tore her gaze away from the Kuakgan. She had not thought to part so soon. "I — yes, that's fine. I'm ready."

"You have nothing to take with you? Nothing at all?"

"No. What I have, I'm wearing."

"Hmmph. Those boots won't last the trip."

Paks looked at her feet. "I've worn worse for longer."

The elf laughed, that silvery sound she remembered so well. "Very well, then. Come along; we go this way first." She started a pace behind him, then caught up. They were walking east out of Brewersbridge, on the road she had come in on a year and a half before. The Kuakgan's grove was on her left, dark and alarming in the evening light. On the right were cottages: she tried to remember who the people were. The woman in the second one had knitted socks for her, socks that had lasted until this last winter.

Past the last plowed field, with the young grain like green plush, the elf turned aside from the road.

"This way is the shortest for us, and we will meet no other travelers. Follow in my footsteps, and they will guide your way."

Paks did not like that instruction, but she did not want to start an argument, either. She wanted to think about the Kuakgan, and what he had done, and why. She dropped behind the elf as he started across a sheep pasture. The sky was still pale, and she could see her way well enough. As the evening haze darkened, though, she saw that the elf's footsteps were marked in a pale glow. When she stepped there, she found a firm flat foothold.

By dawn she was heavily tired, stumbling even as she followed his tracks. She had no idea how far they had come, or which direction: she had not been able to check that by the stars and see his steps at the same time. But she had smelled woods, then grassland, then woods again.

"We will rest here awhile," the elf was saying.

Paks looked around. They were in open woodland; clumps of trees left irregular meadows between. The elf had found a spreading oak near a brook, and was spreading his cloak on the ground. Paks stretched her arms overhead and arched her back. Those casual strolls around the grove had not prepared her for such a long march. Her legs ached, and she knew they would be stiff after a rest.

"Here," he said. "Lie down and sleep for awhile. I will watch."

Paks looked to see if he mocked her, but his smile was almost friendly. "You have walked as far," she said.

707

"I have my own way of resting. If you know elves, you know we rarely sleep soundly. And you are recovering, the Kuakgan said, from serious wounds. Go on, now, and sleep. We have a long way to go."

Paks stretched out on the cloak after removing her boots. Her feet were hot and swollen; she took her socks off and rubbed the soreness out of her calves and feet. When she looked up, the elf was looking at her scars.

"Were those truly given by the dark cousins?" he asked.

"Not by them," said Paks. "At their command, by orcs." The elf tensed, frowning, and looked away.

"We had heard that they dealt with the thriband, but I had never believed it. I would think even iynisin would call them enemy."

Paks shook her head, surprised that she was able to talk about it without distress. "Where I was, the kuaknom — iynisin, I mean — commanded orcs as their servants and common warriors. When I was captured, in a night raid on our camp, the iynisin made their orcs and other captives fight with me. Unarmed. I mean, I was unarmed, at first."

The elf looked at her with a strange expression. "You fought unarmed against the thriband?"

"At first. Then they gave me the weapon of one I killed, to fight the next battle with. Only then there were more of them. And the next — "

"How many times?" he interrupted. "How many battles did you fight?"

"I don't know. I can't remember that. If you count by scars, it must have been many."

"And you lived." The elf sat down abruptly, and met her gaze. "I would not have thought any human could live through their captivity, and such injuries, and still be sane. Perhaps I should admit I have more to learn of humans. Who cleansed the poison from your wounds?"

"The Kuakgan. Others had tried healing spells, but though that eased the pain for awhile, the wounds never fully healed. He knew another way."

"Hmm. Well, take your rest. I think you will do well enough in Lyonya."

Paks lay for a few minutes watching the leaves overhead take shape and color as the dawnlight brightened, then she slept. When she woke, it was warm afternoon, and sunlight had slanted under the tree to strike her face. The elf had disappeared. She looked around, shrugged, and made her way to the brook to drink and wash her face and feet. She felt stiff and unwieldy, but after stretching and drinking again she could think of the night's march without dismay. When she came up from the brook, the elf was standing under the tree, watching the way they had come.

"Trouble?" asked Paks. She could see nothing but trees and grass, and the flicker of wings as a bird passed from tree to tree.

"No. I merely look to see. It is beautiful here, where no building mars the shapes. We will not be disturbed on this journey. I have — I don't think you will understand this — I have cast a glamour on us. No mortal eye could see us, although other elves might."

"Oh." Paks looked around for some revealing sign — flickering light, or something odd. But everything looked normal.

708

"Are you hungry? We should leave in a few hours. It's easier to blur our passage when we cast no sharp shadows."

Paks was hungry indeed; her stomach seemed to be clenched to her backbone. She nodded, and the elf rummaged in the small pack he wore. He pulled out a flat packet and unwrapped it.

"It's our waybread. Try it."

Paks took a piece; it looked much like the flat hard bread the Duke's Company carried on long marches. She bit into it, expected that toughness, and her teeth clashed: this bread was crisp and light. It tasted like nothing else she had eaten, but was good. One piece filled her, and she could feel its virtue in her body.

That night they crossed into Lyonya. The trees loomed taller as they went on, and by dawn they were walking through deep forest, following a narrow trail through heavy undergrowth. When they stopped, the elf pointed out berries she could eat. "It's a good time for travelers in the forest," the elf said. "From now until late summer it would be hard to starve in the deepest wood, did you know one plant from another."

"I know little of forests," said Paks. "Where I grew up we had few trees. They called the town Three Firs because it had them."

"Ah, yes, the northwest marches. I was near Three Firs once, but that was long ago for you. I had been to the Kingsforest, far west of there, and coming back found an incursion of thriband — orcs as you call them. The farmers there had fought them off, but with heavy losses."

"There were orcs in my grandfather's time. Or maybe it was my great-grandfather."

"And no war since, that I've heard of. What made you think of becoming a soldier?"

"Oh — tales and songs, I suppose. I had a cousin who ran away and joined a mercenary company. When he came home and told us all about it, I knew I had to go."

"And did you like it?"

Paks found herself grinning. "Yes. Even as a recruit, though we none of us liked some of the work. But the day I first held a sword — I can remember the joy of it. Of course there were things, later — I didn't like the wars in the south — "

"Were you in the campaign against Siniava?" Paks nodded. The elf sighed. "Bitter trouble returned to a bitter land. When we lived in the south — "

"Elves lived there?" Paks remembered being told that elves lived only in the north.

"Long ago, yes. Some of the southern humans think that the humans from Aare drove us out. They have their dates wrong; we had left long before."

Paks wanted to ask why, but didn't. After they had walked another long while, and the sun was well up, he went on.

"Elves are not always wise, or always good. We made mistakes there, in

709

Aarenis as you call it, and brought great evil into the land. Many were killed, and the rest fled." He began to sing in a form of elvish that Paks could not follow, long rhythmic lines that expressed doom and sorrow. At last the music changed, and lightened, and he finished with a phrase Paks had heard Ardhiel sing. "It is time to rest again," he said quietly after that. "You have said nothing, but your feet have lost their rhythm." They had come without Paks noticing it to a little clearing in the undergrowth; a spring gurgled out of the rocks to one side.

"Tell me about Lyonya," said Paks after drinking deeply from the cold spring. "All I know of it is that Aliam Halveric has a steading in it some- where. And the King is half-elven, isn't he?"

His voice shifted again to the rhythms of song and legend, his eyes fixed on something far away. "In days long past the elves moved north, long before humans came to Aarenis, when the towers of Aare still overlooked the deserts of the south. All was forest from the mountains to the Honnor- gat, and beyond, to the edge of the great seas of grass, the land of horses. In Dzordanya the forest goes all the way north to the Cold Lands, where noth- ing grows but moss on the ground. We settled the forests between the mountains and the great river, rarely venturing north of it. The forest was different, over there, alien to us." He paused, looked at her, and looked away. "Are you by any chance that Paksenarrion who was involved with the elfane taig?"

"Yes."

"Mmm. You may know that elves do not live, for the most part, in build- ings of stone. We have ceremonial places. That — where you were — was one such, a very great one. It centered a whole region of elves; the elfane taig was both powerful and beautiful. But old trouble out of Aarenis came there, and the most powerful of our mages could only delay it long enough for the rest to escape. He paid the price for that delay with the centuries of his enslavement."

"That was the one we saw? The same?"

The elf nodded. "Yes. He risked that, to save the rest, but he could not save himself. We have no worse to fear than such slavery. A human can al- ways hope for death; you will not live even a hundred years, but for an elf to endure the touch of that filth forever — " He stopped abruptly and stood up, facing away from her.

Paks could not think of anything to say. She had finished her piece of the waybread, and she went to the spring for another drink of water. When she returned, the elf had seated himself again, and seemed calmer. "Do we travel again tonight?" she asked.

"No. We will meet the rangers here, at this spring. If you are not ready to sleep, I could tell you more of Lyonya — "

Paks nodded, and he spread his cloak and reclined on it.

"I told you how the elves came here," he began. "The land was not empty even before. The rockfolk, both dwarf and gnome, quarried the mountains and hills. Orcs harried the forests, in great tribes; we drove

710

them out, foot by foot. Other, smaller people lived here; they all vanished, quite soon, and we never knew them. For long we had the forest to ourselves, and for long we planted and shaped the growing of it, flower and tree and moss. Then men came." He stopped, frowning, and paused long before going on. "The first to come was a shipload of Seafolk, fleeing enemies up the broad Honnorgat. They cut a clearing on the shore, and planted their grain. We watched from afar. A colony began along the coast, where Bannerlith is now, and another across the river's mouth. More ships came. We held council, and decided to meet with them."

"What happened?"

"They were hasty men, used to war. I think they thought they could drive us all away. But one sea-captain's son, and his crew, befriended an elf trapped by wolves along the shore, and as one note suggests a harmony, one honorable deed suggests the possibility of friendship. After awhile those who wanted to live with us settled on the south shore, and the rest took the north. Elves are not much welcome in Pargun and Kostandan. Then men began coming from the south. These were different, and they moved into Fintha and Tsaia. When we met them, they had friendly words, not blows, for us. Many of them had met elves in the mountains west of the south marches. Here, in Lyonya itself, we made pacts with the humans, and agreed on lands and forests. We had begun to intermarry, very slowly, and when Lyonya grew to become a kingdom, elven blood ran in the royal family, though little enough in the present King."

"And it's now shared by elves and men?"

"Yes — as much as immortal and mortal can share anything. Those that will meet us here are both elven and human — most of mixed blood."

"Aren't you one of them?"

"I?" He laughed softly. "No. I wander too much. Master Oakhallow knew of the need, and used me for a messenger and guide. He is, as all the Kuakkganni are, one to make use of any chance that comes."

"Don't you like him?"

"Like him? What has that to do? The Kuakkganni are alien to elves, though they know us as well as any, and we are alien to them. They took our place with the First Tree; some of us have never forgiven that, and none of us have forgotten it. I neither like nor dislike a Kuakgan. I respect him."

Paks stretched her legs, then her arms. She was glad they would not have to travel that night.

"You had best sleep," the elf said. "I will watch."

Chapter Four

Paks did not see the rangers before they stepped into the clearing; their soft green and tawny cloaks and tunics, patterned in muted shades of the same colors, hid them well in the woods. Haleron greeted them.

"Here I am back, friends, from Tsaia, with a recruit for you for the summer. This is Paksenarrion, a proven warrior."

"Greetings to you, lady," said the tallest of the rangers. "Do you know our tongue?"

"Yes, by the kindness of Ardhiel of the Kierin Vale," replied Paks, as formally as she could. He nodded to her, with a brief smile, and turned back to Haleron.

"We thank you, Haleron, for your help, though we had hoped for more than one."

Haleron frowned, and shot a quick glance at Paks. She had the feeling he wished she didn't speak the language. She started to speak, but could think of nothing to say. The tall one noticed her discomfort, and gave her another smile.

"It is not that we think you are unable, Paksenarrion, but we lost so many to the fever that were you a demigod you might find more than you could do. May I ask what experience you have had? Haleron's word is enough for your character, but each sword has its own virtue."

Paks had expected some such question; she hoped her hesitation would be laid to the unfamiliar language. "Sir —"

"My pardon!" he interrupted. "You have not had the courtesy of our names yet. I am Giron, of mixed elf and human parentage, as are most of us. And these are Phaer, Clevis, Ansuli, and Tamar." The others nodded to Paks, and she nodded back. "Now, if you will?"

The pause had restored her calm. "Yes, sir. I was in Duke Phelan's Company for three campaign seasons, as an infantry soldier. Then — for a few months — on my own — " She was reluctant to bring up the elfane taig.

Haleron was not. "Do not be modest, Paksenarrion. Giron, she freed our brother and the elfane taig — you know that tale."

"Indeed! You are that Paksenarrion, then. I had heard that you went from that to the Girdsmen at Fin Panir."

Paks nodded. "I did. I trained with them for half a year, and then rode with the expedition to Kolobia."

"And was Luap's stronghold found?" Giron seemed genuinely interested.

"Yes." Paks felt her throat tighten; she did not want to tell these strangers all that had happened. Again Haleron broke into the conversation.

"Paksenarrion was staying with the Kuakgan of Brewersbridge when I came there. She had recovered from old wounds under his healing; he recommended her to me."

"Ah." Giron looked hard at Paks. "You left the Girdsmen, then. Why?" From his tone and look, she thought he must have heard something, and wondered which tale it had been, and whether false or true.

"I could not fight, for a long time. They — I — thought I might never be able to again. So I left."

"The Kuakgan healed what the Girdsmen could not?" Paks nodded. "Mmm. You have left a lot unsaid, Paksenarrion. Can you fight now? We need no ailing rangers; we have enough of those."

"I think so, sir."

"We have come from Brewersbridge as fast as I would have cared to come alone," said Haleron.

"That may be, but — " He shook his head, and smiled ruefully. "We need help, yet I must not accept someone who cannot serve our need. People change, as swords weaken and break. I judge that you do not fully trust yourself; how then can I trust you?"

"The Kuakgan — " murmured Haleron softly.

"The Kuakgan! You yourself have no love for the Kuakkganni; shall I let an old man in a distant grove choose my sword-companion? Whose blood will run to the tree-roots if he is wrong? Not his, I daresay!"

For an instant everyone was still as Giron's anger roiled the glade; the sun seemed to fade slightly. Paks wished desperately for the leap of anger she knew she would have felt a year ago — for the courage to confront him and demand a chance. It did not come. She was aware of the others staring at her, aware of their scorn, only barely withheld. She could almost see herself through their eyes: rumpled, dirty, threadbare clothes, boots worn thin, no weapons at all. Not much of a warrior, to look at. Suddenly she found it almost funny. How was it that *nothing* of her past had stuck to her — that nothing remained of the armor and weapons she had used, nothing of the skills she had learned?

She found herself smiling at Giron. "Sir, while each warrior wishes to choose a weapon for his hand, it is foolish to choose one by looks alone. The blade with 'I am a champion' inscribed down the rib may be a piece of fancy-work done for a prince's court. Gird himself found that a length of hearth-wood could fell a knight, were it applied to his skull. Perhaps all that's left to me is to be a rough club: but if you have the skill to use the skills I have left, that would be better than no one at all. However, please yourself. I can walk back to Brewersbridge, even without Haleron's guidance."

The others were smiling now; Tamar, the only other woman, grinned widely. Giron shook his head again, but relaxed. "I see you have wit

713

enough, at least. And you are brave, if you would walk back alone. How would you eat?"

Paks grinned. "Well, sir — if I could not forage something, I must go hungry, but that's nothing new."

"Hmmph. Can you use a longbow?"

"I have used one. I would not claim to be an expert in it."

"You were a swordfighter, I heard."

"Yes."

"How long since you last fought?"

"Something more than half a year."

"Tamar, lend her your blade; it's the lightest we have here." Tamar came forward, and drew her sword for Paks to take. She offered it over her wrist, in the elven way.

Paks felt her heart pounding. Could she? She wrapped her hand around the hilt, and sent a mental cry to Gird: Protector of warriors, help me now, or never. After so long, the sword felt strange as she hefted it. She turned her hand minutely, and felt it settle into her palm. There. At least she would not drop it. She heard the soft ringing of steel as Giron drew his own blade. When she looked up, he was eyeing her.

"I would see your skill, before deciding," he said. "I will not speak of rumor, but I must know what you are." He took a step forward. For an instant, Paks was sure she would bolt. Her vision wavered, and her breath stuck in her throat. She clamped her hand on the sword, and tried to think of Gird. The Kuakgan's voice came instead: courage is going on. She nodded abruptly, and came to meet Giron.

With the clash of the blades her mind seemed to clear a little. Her arm moved of itself, countering his first slow strokes. She could tell they were slow, could tell that he intended to probe no more than he had to. He moved a little faster. She watched the play of his wrist, remembering slowly what it meant. If this, then that. The elbow bent *so* allows the angle here — she met each stroke squarely. It felt as if she were learning all over again: she had to think about almost every move. More came back to her; she tried a thrust past his guard. Blocked: but he looked surprised. So was she. Her body moved less stiffly, the sword began to feel natural in her hand again. He circled; she turned to meet him. Her feet shifted without her thought. Again he circled, and speeded his attack. She was frightened now, but pushed the panic down, and blocked each thrust with a grunt of effort. Only think of the strokes, she told herself. Only that. Her left foot came down on a stone, and she lost her rhythm momentarily. His blade raked her arm, leaving a narrow line of blood. She caught his next thrust on her blade and blocked it. He stepped back.

"Enough." He looked at her with new respect. "You need practice, but you have plenty of skill to draw on. We use the sword little; bows are more use in the woods. But you are welcome to stay with us."

Paks heard, but did not answer at once. She felt dizzy with relief: she had not dropped the sword, had not run away, had not fainted. The slash on her arm stung, but did not bother her; it was not pain she had feared.

714

"Are you all right?" he asked. She looked up.

"Oh yes. Well enough. It has been a long time, that's all." She looked for Tamar, and held out the sword. "I thank you for the use of it; it's a fine blade, indeed."

"A family weapon," said Tamar, smiling. "It was my aunt's before me, and her mother's before that." Paks thought of old Kanas's sword that hung over her father's mantle. "Here — " She took out of her pouch a little jar and a roll of cloth. "Clean that scratch and put some of this on it." Paks thanked her and rolled up her torn sleeve to wipe the blood away.

"You have scars enough," commented Giron. Paks nodded without speaking, and spread ointment from the jar along the line of the cut. "You'll need more clothes, too," he said. "We should make the nearest karrest by nightfall; plenty of stores there. You haven't asked what pay you'll get."

Paks looked up, then handed the jar back to Tamar. "No. I haven't. Whatever I earn, I expect."

He laughed, for the first time a natural laugh. "Well enough. It won't be as much as it might, since we must outfit you with clothes and weapons. But the crown of Lyonya has its honor."

Within a week, Paks felt at home with the rangers, almost as comfortable as with the Duke's Company. She wore their green and russet with leaves and crown woven into the pattern, and she was getting the same calluses on her fingers from the great blackwood bow she'd been given. So far she had seen no fighting; she had wandered the woods with the same small band, uncertain just what they were doing or where they were.

"I still don't understand," she said one day as they were stretched in the sun resting. "Are we guarding a border, or hunting robbers, or what?"

"Lyonya is not like other kingdoms," said Giron. Paks had heard that so many times that she was tired of it; it wasn't the explanation he seemed to think it.

"I know that, but — "

"Impatience!" Tamar laughed gently at her. "You are all human, aren't you?"

"All but my name. Go on."

"In Lyonya, we have not only the borders to worry about — the clear borders — but the taig of the forest itself. You met the elfane taig, in the valley, and that was but one taig. Each place has its own, some greater and some lesser. Here the forest is unbroken enough to have a taig — I should rather say, to be a taig."

"Does it have a name?"

"If it does, I am not the one to know it. The taig of a forest would not speak to me, not directly. It is too mighty for that. Even the kuakgannir would not claim to speak to a taig so vast."

"I still don't know just what a taig is."

They all laughed, but it was friendly laughter. "No. And I don't know how to explain it. If you live long enough, Paksenarrion, perhaps this

715

understanding will come to you. But you can feel a taig, as you know, even when it does not speak to you: you felt the lure of Ereisbrit." Ereisbrit, they had told her, was the name of a tiny waterfall only two spans high, that poured itself into a moss-edged slash of blue-gray rock. When she first saw it, she had stood frozen in delighted awe.

"Yes. I remember that."

"We are to feel the taig of the forest, and tell the King if anything goes amiss in it. We can wander far, listening and feeling for anything wrong. As for robbers, there are few in Lyonya, and the lords have their own guards to hunt them. They may ask our help, and if we have time we give it. Borders — yes, we guard those. But surely you are aware that we have more than mortal borders here." He looked at Paks sharply. She glanced around the sunny glade where they lay.

"I'm not sure — "

"Lyonya is human and elven. Elves are immortal. Does that tell you nothing?"

Paks thought hard. Haleron had said something about elven magic, about other levels. "Magical borders?" she guessed finally.

He grunted. "Magical — yes. Elves — the true elves, not we mixbreeds — are not wholly in the world humans know. In the elven kingdoms, the borders are so other that unescorted humans never pass them: never know they are there. Here, in a mixed kingdom, we have both kinds of borders. We rangers worry less about the obvious ones. With loyal lords holding close to Tsaia — and Tsaia itself an ally, for the most part — we need not look for armies of that sort. Brigands — if we see them, we deal with them, but the lords of steadings rarely need help. To the south, though, in the high mountains, are remnants of old troubles: these sometimes come down and try to invade. And through both borders. Thus the thriband — what you call orcs, or urchii — and sometimes far worse."

"Like that — whatever it was that held the elf lord?"

He nodded. "That and others. Some are very subtle. Not all evil desires immediate dominion. The foul weaver of webs — I will not name her — " he glanced at Paks. She shuddered and nodded vigorously. She did not want to hear that name aloud. "Her minions have tried our borders again and again. They insinuate themselves — hiding, perhaps, or feigning to be merchants or farm folk. For years they will bide without action, weaving slow coils of evil about them, plotting in many ways. A little gossip, a little rooting of secrets they can sell. No ordinary guard can detect them. But we are to sense, in the taig of forest and field, that slight unease. The fern knows when it has been trodden by a cruel foot; the sly levets — "

"Levets?" Paks had never heard the word.

"Swift running, long but low. Hunters of mice and such. Dark bright eyes, sharp claws and many teeth. Farmers call them bad, for they will take eggs, and the large ones even hens on the nest. But like all such little creatures they are not truly good or bad but only levets. The levets, though, are much prized by the web-worshippers, and their bodies may be used in evil rites. Also they can be spelled, and forced to serve as messengers. This we can detect, by their behavior and that of their prey."

"I see. But if you have that ability because of your elven blood, how can I help? Except to fight, if that is necessary."

"You do feel the taig," said Tamar quickly. "We saw that at once. And you had contact with the elfane taig before."

"Besides," said Giron, "the Kuakgan of Brewersbridge sent you. He would not send someone wholly blind to the taig."

"You didn't accept — "

"I didn't accept his judgment of your ability to fight, Paksenarrion. I had listened to rumors, to my shame. But I knew you would be able to sense evil in the taig."

A few days later, threading along another forest trail between Tamar and Phaer, Paks felt a strange pressure in her head. She stumbled, suddenly dizzy; Phaer caught her arm before she fell. Tamar whirled, alert.

"What happened?" Phaer looked closely at her face. Paks could feel the sweat springing cold on her neck.

"I — don't know. Something inside — in my head. It all whirled — " She knew she wasn't making sense. Her stomach roiled. Pressure crushed her chest; she fought for breath. Out of her past came the image of Siniava's ambush in the forest, the day of the storm. "Danger — " she managed to gasp.

"Where?" Giron, now, stood before her. Paks felt, rather than saw, his concern. She leaned against Phaer, unable to speak, sick and shaking with fear and the unbearable touch of some evil. She heard Giron say "Stay with her, Phaer. The rest of you — "

She was huddled on the ground; beneath her nose the soil had a faint sour tang. At last she managed to draw a full breath, then another. Whatever it was had not disappeared — she could still feel that loathesome pressure — but it seemed to be concentrating elsewhere. Paks pushed herself up on hands and knees. Above her, Phaer's voice: "Are you better?"

She nodded. She didn't trust her voice. Slowly, feeling at every moment that she might fall into separate pieces, she sat back on her heels, managed to rise to her feet. Deliberately she took the great bow from her shoulder, and braced her leg to string it. With the bow strung, she pulled an arrow from her quiver, checked the fletching, then took another, to hold as she had been taught. She looked around. The others had disappeared into the trees; only Phaer was visible, standing beside her now, his own bow strung and ready.

"Can you speak? Are you spelled?" She knew instantly that one of his arrows would be for her, if she were.

"No." Her voice surprised her; clear and low, it held none of the unease she felt. "No, it's looking elsewhere. It is very close, but I can't tell where — too close."

Phaer nodded. "After you fell, we all could feel something wrong. Did it attack you, or — "

Paks shook her head. "I don't think it did. Somehow I must be sensitive to it — whatever it is — as night creatures are to a flash of light."

"It is rare for a human to be more sensitive to anything than an elf or part-elf." Phaer sounded faintly affronted. "Do you have a god, perhaps, enlightening your mind?"

Paks did not want to discuss it. The sense of wrong and danger was as strong as ever, though it didn't center on her. Now that the sickness was past, she tried to feel her way toward its location. She turned her head from side to side, eyes half shut. A slight tingle, there. She could see nothing openly. Phaer was watching her, still alert.

"I think — that way — " Paks nodded to the uphill side of the trail.

"I still don't feel any direction." He looked worried. "Perhaps we should wait until Giron comes."

"No. If we move, we have a chance of surprising it, whatever it is. If we wait here — " Paks took a cautious step off the trail. The tingle intensified: a sort of mental itch. She shivered, and moved on. She looked at each tree and stone as the rangers had taught her: she knew the names, now, of nearly all the trees and herbs. When she glanced back at Phaer, he was following in her tracks, his bow already drawn.

A fir, another fir, a spruce. A massive stone ledge, high enough to break the forest roof and let in more light, lay just uphill. Paks went forward, one slow step after another. She felt a wave of vileness roll down from above.

"Now I can tell," murmured Phaer from behind her. "Don't move, Paks; I'll call — "

But the ledge itself heaved and shuddered, lifting in stinking coils. Without thought, Paks flipped her first arrow into position, drew, and saw it fly across that short sunlit space to shatter on rock-hard scales. She had the second arrow already nocked to the string.

"Daskdraudigs!" yelled Phaer. This meant nothing to Paks. The menace, too large to conceive, reared above them, tree tall, and yet the ledge still shifted, as if the stone itself were moulting into a serpent. Paks breathed a quick prayer to Gird, and loosed her second arrow at the underside of a lifted coil. It seemed to catch between two scales, but did not penetrate. She hardly noticed. Great waves of hatred and disgust rolled over her mind. She struggled to keep her eyes fixed on the thing, tried to fumble another arrow out of her quiver. Suddenly something slammed into her back and knocked her flat. "Daskdraudigs, I told you!" Phaer growled in her ear. "Stay down, human; this is elf work." Through the noise in her head she yet managed to hear the other rangers: Giron shouting in elvish; Tamar's higher voice rising like a stormwind's howl. She turned her head where she lay and saw Phaer fitting an arrow to his bowstring.

"Why can't I — "

"Special arrow. You don't have these." Paks noticed now that the fletching looked like stone; the arrowhead certainly was a single piece of chipped crystal. Phaer stood, drawing the bow. Above them more and more coils

718

had risen, and the front of the creature was moving downslope to their left. He stepped forward, looking along the monster's length (she could not tell for what purpose), then shot quickly and threw himself down.

The arrow flew true, and sank into the monster's scales as if they were cheese. As Paks watched, that coil seemed to stiffen, to return to the stone she had first seen. Already Phaer had pulled out another of the special arrows. This time he aimed for the next coil ahead of his first target. Again his aim was true. But the unbound coils of the monster's trailing end whipped and writhed, rolling down upon them. Before Paks could leap up to run, the trees they sheltered in were crushed, broken off like straws. Coils as heavy and hard as stone rolled over them.

Chapter Five

Paks was aware of something cold and hard touching her skin before she could think what had happened. It was dark. She began to shiver from the cold. A pungent, resinous odor prickled her nose. When she tried to rub it, she found she couldn't move her arms. Sudden panic soured her mouth: dark, cold, trapped. She tried to squirm free. Now she could feel pressure along most of her body. Nothing moved. She heaved frantically, heedless of roughness that scraped her. She stirred only dust that clogged her nose and made her sneeze. The sneeze stirred more dust; she sneezed again.

A ghost of reason returned: if she could sneeze, she was not being crushed utterly. She tried to think. Her head hurt. Her arms — she tried to feel, to wiggle her fingers. One was cramped under her; she worked those fingers back and forth. The other moved only slightly as she tried it. It felt as if it were under a sack of meal — something heavy, but yielding. When she tried to lift her head from the dust, it bumped something hard above her: bumped on the very place that hurt so. Paks muttered a Company curse at that, and let her head back down. Her legs — she tried again, without success, to move them. They were trapped under the same heavy weight as the rest of her body. She rested her cheek on the dust beneath it and wandered back into sleep.

When she heard the voices, she thought at first she was dreaming. Silvery elven voices, much like Ardhiel's, wove an intricate pattern of sound. She lay, blinking in the darkness, and listened. After a moment, she realized that the darkness was no longer complete. She could see, dimly, a gnarled root a few inches from her nose. Remembering the hard barrier above her head, she turned cautiously to the side, and tried to look up. Tiny flickers of dim light seeped through whatever held her down. The voices kept talking or singing. It might not be a dream. She listened.

" — somewhere about here, if I heard the call rightly. Mother of Trees! The daskdraudigs must have fallen on them."

"So it must. Look how the trees are torn."

"But the firs would try to hold — "

"No tree could hold against that." Paks suddenly recognized a voice she knew. Giron. Rangers. A dim memory began to return.

"They must be dead." A woman's voice. Tamar? Yes, that was the name.

"I fear so." Giron again. "I fear so, indeed. Yet we must search as we can.

I would not leave their bones under these foul stones."

"If we can move them." Another man. Clevis, or Ansuli — Paks could not think which. He sounded weary, or injured; his voice had no depth to it.

"Not you, Ansuli. You but watch, while Tamar and I search and move."

It occurred to Paks, as slowly as in a dream, that she should say something. She tried to call, and as in dreams could make no sound: her mouth was dry and caked with dust. She tried again, and emitted a faint croak. She could hear the bootsteps on nearby stone; that sounded louder than her attempt. Once again — a louder croak, but no human sound. Then the dust caught her nose again and she sneezed. Boots scraped on rock.

"Phaer! Are you alive? Paksenarrion?" The sounds came nearer.

Paks tried again. "Ennh! 'Ere. Down here." It was not loud, but the rangers' hearing was keen.

She heard a scraping and swishing sound very close; more light scattered down from above. "Under this tree?" asked Giron, overhead somewhere. "Who is there?"

"Paks," she managed. "Down here."

"Where's Phaer? Is he alive?"

"I don't know." But as she said it, she realized what the "sack of meal" weighing down her right arm must be. She tried to sense, from that arm, whether he breathed, but could not; the arm was numb. "I — think he's under this too."

"Can you move, Paksenarrion?" That was Tamar, now also overhead.

"No — not much. I can turn my head." She tried to unfold the arm cramped under her, without success.

"Wait, then, and don't fear. We'll free you."

"What is it that's holding me down?" There was a brief silence, then:

"Don't worry about it. We'll free you. It will take some time."

In fact, it seemed to take forever. The sky was darkening again when Tamar was able to clamber down cautiously and touch Paks, passing a flask of water to her lips. Then she planted one foot in front of Paks's nose and went back to work. By the sound of saw and knife, Paks knew that much of the weight and pressure came from a tree — or many trees. Gradually a wider space cleared before her. She could look down her body now, and see Tamar trimming limbs away from her hips. Directly above was the main trunk of the tree; she still could not raise her head more than an inch or so from the dust. She worked her left arm out from under her body. It felt heavy and lifeless; she could not unclench her fist. She turned her head carefully to look the other way.

Phaer's face was as close to her as a lover's. Cold and pale, stern, and clearly dead. Paks froze, horrified. She had not known he was so close — and being so close, how had he been killed while she was safe? She crooked her neck to look over her right shoulder. Phaer lay on her arm; tree limbs laced across him, and on the limbs a tumble of great boulders that ran back up the slope to the base of the ledge she had seen. Paks tried again to pull her arm free, but she couldn't move it.

721

"Tamar!"

"We're working, Paks. We can't hurry; the tree could turn and crush you completely."

"I know. But I can turn a little, and I saw Phaer — "

"We know." Giron's voice came from the other side of the rock pile. "Tamar was able to see past you."

"But he — " Paks found her eyes full of tears suddenly.

"He died well. He shot the daskin arrows, didn't he?"

"Daskin? Those with the crystal?"

"Yes."

"Yes — he did. They both went in. But then the tail end whipped over — "

"I know." Giron sighed; he was close enough for her to hear it. "Yet we must call ourselves lucky, Paksenarrion, to lose only two to a daskdraudigs. We might all have been killed, and the foul thing loose to desecrate the very rock. I honor your perception; none of us sensed it before you did, and none of us could find it. That is its skill, to spread its essence through the very stone so that it cannot be found."

"Paksenarrion," said Tamar, now back at her head. "Can you tell how much of your body is trapped under Phaer's?"

"No — at least my right arm — maybe a leg — "

"We cannot hurry this, but you are weakening. Here — drink this, and let me feed you."

Tamar sat in the space she had made, and held the flask to Paks's lips. She drained it slowly; she could not take more than small sips. Tamar massaged her left arm, and slowly sensation came back, first as prickling, then as a fiery wave. Paks flexed her fingers, wincing at the pain, but was able to take a bit of waybread from Tamar and get it into her own mouth. Meanwhile, Tamar had taken off her own cloak, and she spread it along as much of Paks's body as she could reach. "Don't lose heart," she said. "We will certainly free you, and Phaer's body."

"What *is* a daskdraudigs?" asked Paks. "Phaer kept yelling that, and I didn't know."

"Hmmmm — " It was almost as long as the Kuakgan's hum. Finally Tamar said, "If you truly don't know, I would rather not speak of it here. Time enough when we are far from this place, and at peace."

"But it's dead — isn't it?"

"Do you sense any life in it?"

Paks shivered; she didn't want to feel for that foulness again. But nothing stirred in her mind — no warnings, and no revulsion. "No," she said finally.

"Good. Then we needn't worry, for now." Tamar stood, after laying her hand lightly on Paks's brow. "Trust us, and lie still. Be ready to answer us when the load begins to lift. We do not wish to cause you more injury."

But darkness rose from among the trees of the forest as they worked. The stones in the pile were large and heavy, and awkward to lift or move.

722

Twice they shifted suddenly under Giron's feet. He and Tamar both came near being crushed by the stones they tried to move. Ansuli came and tried to help; Paks heard the pain in his grunts of effort. Finally Giron stopped them.

"We cannot work this pile in the dark; we could all be crippled by a misstep here. We must make a light, or use other means, or — Tamar, do you think Paksenarrion can last the night?"

Hearing that question, Paks wanted to cry out. She could not — could *not* — stay under that tree, motionless, another night. She clenched her jaw. She could not make them do anything: if they decided to leave her there, there she would stay.

"Giron, she has withstood more than I would expect of any human. But another night, in this cold — with no way to ease her limbs — no. We must keep working somehow."

"We agreed we would not use the elfane hier before her — "

"She is one of us now. We owe that to our own."

"I think so too," said Ansuli. "She has seen the elfane taig, she has been in the hands of the daskdusky cousins — and were we not told that the Lord Ardhiel blew that elfhorn, of which it is said that the High Prince of the Lord's Inner Court will hear the call, and bring aid. She has seen as much elfane hier as many elves, already."

Paks tried to make sense of this. The elfane taig she knew — but what was the elfane hier? The blowing of the elfhorn — she could never forget that, and the beauty of the winged steed that bore an unearthly warrior. Before she could think further, she saw a soft white light, as if all the stars' lights were mingled together in one place. She could not see where it came from; it seemed to spread, like sunlight in mist, without shadows.

"Have you the strength for the lifting?" asked Ansuli.

"More than you," said Giron. "Maintain the light, if you would. Tamar?"

"I am ready."

Again Paks heard the rasp and scrape of stone on stone, then distant thuds as stones were dropped. She could not see, past Phaer's shoulder, the size of the pile remaining. Cold edged into her, from the ground and the stones she touched. She tried to stay calm, and save her strength; at last she slept, exhausted.

Sharp pain woke her. Her right arm, her back, her legs: all were afire. Someone was pulling at her, dragging her, and she had no skin left — She opened her mouth to scream, and saw Tamar's face before her.

"Paksenarrion. Be still. You are free. You feel the blood returning, that's all. By some miracle of the gods, you have not even a single broken bone."

Paks could not have told that from the feel. Everything ached, stabbed, throbbed. She tried to take a deep breath, and found herself coughing convulsively. Tamar held her, offered a flask of water. Paks managed to swallow some between coughs, and the spasms eased. Gradually the pains settled down to recognizable bruises and scrapes. Cramped muscles relaxed, fibre by fibre. She looked around. Giron had kindled a small fire; she could feel the warmth along one side. She did not know where they were. She could see a lump of blankets beyond the fire: Ansuli, resting at last.

"Phaer's body is laid straight in the forest," said Tamar, as if answering a question. "Tomorrow we will lay the boughs upon him; for tonight, Giron has set a warding spell to guard. Clevis, who was killed when the forward end of the monster came upon us, has been laid straight as well. You and Ansuli will mend, though you will be weak some days, I expect." She moved her arms out from under Paks's head. "I'll get you something hot from the fire; you're still chilled."

The hot drink began to ease the rest of Paks's pains. She tried to move her feet, and felt them drag slowly against the ground. Her right arm still seemed numb and unresponsive. Tamar began to move it for her, bending and straightening the elbow and wrist. At last the feeling seeped back. She had been able to move all her limbs on her own, and was thinking of sleep again, when she noticed the first lifting of dawnlight in the sky. Giron, who had been standing guard outside the firelight, came back to cook a hot meal. Tamar went for water. Ansuli rolled partway over, groaned, and pushed himself up on one elbow.

"How is she?"

"I'm fine," said Paks. She still felt heavy and stiff, but knew that would pass.

"Well," said Giron, looking from Ansuli to Paks and back, "if she's not fine, she's better than we would have expected." He stirred the cookpot again. "Tamar says you don't know what that was. Is that so, Paksenarrion?"

"Yes, I had never heard the name."

"Daskdraudigs. Rockterror. Some call it rockserpent, though it is not a serpent. It has only a similar form, being long with a writhing body and coils. Some say, too, that the dasksinyi, the dwarves, breed such creatures to guard their treasure vaults. I think that is a lie: dwarves and elves seldom agree, but dwarves are not evil. Most of them, anyway. As you saw, it seems rock until it is aroused: most often a ledge, but sometimes in the form of ruined walls or buildings." Paks thought of all the ruins she and Macenion had ventured near — what if one had been such a creature? "Even when it rouses," Giron went on, "it has the strength and weight of rock. Ordinary weapons blunt or break against its scales. The daskin arrows, dwarfwrought, will pierce its substance and fix the stone in place. Their virtue passes but slowly along its length, though — so the daskdraudigs has time to avenge itself. And worse, in after times it can renew itself and regain its mobility."

"But why did it attack my mind?"

"I know not, Paksenarrion, why you were so sensitive to it. The revulsion you felt is what all who can sense the taig feel, when they come within range. The creature terrifies and confuses. Those who cannot sense a taig may wander near enough to be consumed. We do not understand why a creature of stone would desire kyth-blood, but so it seems. Certainly it is an evil thing, and the gods of light designed the races of the kyth for good. Perhaps that is enough."

Hot food restored a sense of solidity, but Paksenarrion was still stiff and weak. She looked along her arms; dark bruises mottled them, and she was sure the rest of her body looked as bad. Ansuli had been hit by flying stones; he had a couple of broken ribs and a bad gash on his leg. Tamar had only a scrape across her forehead — from the tree limbs, she explained — and Giron limped slightly from a bruised foot. They all rested around the fire after breakfast. Then Giron sighed and stood.

"We must see to the bodies of our friends," he said. "Ansuli, can you walk if I help you?"

"For that, of course." Ansuli pushed himself up, grunting with the effort, and Giron steadied him.

"Paksenarrion, I doubt you can stand — but if you would try, Tamar will help." Paks felt as stiff as stone herself, but with Tamar's aid was able to stand at last. She tried to take a step and nearly fell. Giron shook his head. "You can't go so far. Lie down again — "

"No." Paks shook her head, waking the pain in her skull. "I don't want to stay here alone — "

Giron raised his brows. "You would face a daskdraudigs and fear this peaceful site? But perhaps you sense something again?"

"No. I meant — Phaer was with me. He — we — we fell together, and if he had not pushed me ahead, I too — "

"Ah. You wish to join us in honoring him."

"Yes. With Tamar's help, I can walk." She took another step to prove this, and stayed upright, though with difficulty.

"Very well. We will go slowly." They had spent the night, Paks saw, on the edge of the band of trees splintered and torn by the falling daskdraudigs. She wondered again how she had escaped being crushed by either tree or stone. Giron led them downslope, back to the trail they had been on and beyond. In a small glade surrounded by silver poplars, Phaer and Clevis were laid side by side, their bows beside them.

"Stay here and watch," said Giron, "while Tamar and I seek the sacred boughs." Paks and Ansuli sank down, one on either side of the clearing, to watch and wait. For some time they said nothing. Sunlight glittered on the leaves of the silver poplars; Paks smelled the rich mold of leaves decaying under them. She looked at the fallen leaves: each one a delicate tracery of veins, each one different. Her eyes kept straying to the two bodies laid bare in the sun; she glanced quickly away each time. It seemed indecent to leave the faces uncovered — she had heard the elves' ways were different, but had not seen them. In the sun that poured into the clearing as if into a well, the elven bone structure of brow and jaw seemed more alien than when they were alive. Paks shivered. She was sure Ansuli wondered how she had survived, when an old comrade, a half-elf, had been killed. She was sure he was watching her. She looked across and met his gaze.

"You have no elven blood; you do not understand our way?"

"I — we bury our dead —"

"And wonder why we leave ours prey to the winds and animals?" Paks nodded. "You humans fear harm, do you not, to the spirits of the dead from harm done even to their dry bones? Yes? Elves, and those of the part-elven who adopt elven ways, need have no such fear. Humans are of the earth, and like all earth-beings share in the taigin." Paks stared at him; she had never heard anyone speak of men and the taigin together. He smiled, and nodded. "Yes, indeed. Some of you are more — are granted more by the high gods — but all humans are to their bodies as the taig to its place. But elves, when they are killed, have no longer any relation to the bodies they used, and harm or injury done the body cannot affect them. An elf may be possessed, but only while alive. Death frees elves from all enchantments. Thus we return the bodies to the earth, which nourished them, without care except for the mourners. It is for ourselves that we lay straight, and bring the sacred boughs."

Paks nodded, but still had trouble looking at the bodies. Ansuli went on. "You surely lost comrades before, when you fought with the Halveric's friend?"

"Yes. But —" She looked at Ansuli, trying to think how to say it. "But if Phaer —"

"Be at rest, human. Some god gave you the gift to sense evil, and to trace it. Phaer placed two daskin arrows in a daskdraudigs, by what you said, and that's enough to make a song for him. He did what he could, and the fir tree moved as its heartwood willed, and by these acts your gift was not wasted. Would you quarrel with the gods' gifts?"

"No. But —"

He laughed shortly, as if his ribs hurt him. "But humans would quarrel with anything. No, I'm not angry. Paksenarrion, do you think we regret that you lived? We mourn our friends, yes, but you did not kill Phaer or Clevis." Paks said nothing. She still felt an outsider, the only one who had no elven blood. And she had not fought the daskdraudigs. Ansuli coughed a little. "I was wondering about this gift of yours," he said then. "How long have you had it?"

"Please?"

"The gift to sense evil. How long have you had this? All your life?"

"I don't know," said Paks. "In Fin Panir they said that paladins could sense good and evil — that it was a gift given by Gird when they were chosen and trained. They had some magics, as well, so that we candidates could feel what it was like, but —"

"I don't mean humans in general. I mean you."

"Oh. Not — not long. Not before yesterday —" but as she spoke, Paks thought back to those mysterious events in the Duke's Company. She told Ansuli of them, but finished: "But that must have been Canna's medallion, not my own gift, for the Marshal-General said that the gift was found only in paladins of Gird —"

"She denied the power to paladins of Camwyn and Falk?" His voice was scornful.

726

"No, but — "

"However wise and powerful your Marshal-General of Gird, Paksenarrion, she is not as old or wise or powerful as the gods themselves. Nor as old as elves. Did you know that there are elves in the Ladysforest who knew Gird — knew him as Ardhiel knew you?"

"No — " Paks had not thought before of the implications of elven longevity. She looked curiously at Ansuli. "Did you?"

"I? No. I am not so old, being of the half-blood only. But I have spoken to one who knew him. Your Marshal-General — and I grant her all respect — did not. She is not one to bind or loose the gods' gifts. I think she would say that herself, did you ask her. In her time, perhaps, in Fin Panir, the gods give the gift to sense evil to those chosen from among paladin candidates. But in old times and other places, the gods have done otherwise — as they have with you. Your friend's medallion might focus the power for one unknowing and unskilled in its use, as you were, but the gift was yours."

Paks felt a strange rush of emotions she could not define — she felt like crying and laughing all at once. And deep within, the certainty of that gift rooted and grew. Still she protested: "But — the way I am now — ?"

"Ah, you will speak of it, eh? Giron is not the only one who had heard rumors. Yet you mastered the sickness, did you not? Arrows are missing from your quiver; I suspect you, too, shot at the daskdraudigs — "

"The arrows broke," whispered Paks, staring at the ground.

"So would any but daskin arrows, on such a beast. Get you better weapons next time, warrior; it was not your skill that failed." He laughed again, softly. "I wonder what other gifts you have hidden, that you have not seen or used. Are you a lightbringer or a healer? Can you call water from rocks, or set the wind in a ship's sails?"

"I — no, I am no such — I can't be such. It would mean — "

"It would mean you had some great work to do, which the gods gave you aid for. It would mean you should learn your gifts, and use them, and waste no words denying what is clear to — " He broke off as they heard Giron and Tamar returning, singing softly one of the evening songs.

Giron led the way into the clearing, not pausing in his song as he moved to help Ansuli stand. Tamar helped Paks to her feet, and together they moved to the center of the clearing and laid the boughs of holly, cedar, rowan, and fireoak on the bodies. Paks followed the pattern Tamar set, not knowing then or for many years why they were laid as they were.

When they were done, Tamar helped Paks back to their camp, and she slept the rest of that day and night. The next morning she was able to rise by herself, though still sore and stiff. Ansuli lay heavily asleep, his narrow face flushed with fever. When Paks had eaten breakfast, Giron and Tamar came to sit near her.

"Can you heal?" asked Giron, as calmly as if he asked whether she could eat mutton. She answered as calmly.

"I tried to, once, using a medallion of Gird belonging to a friend. I don't know whether it worked — "

"Wound or sickness?"

"An arrow wound."

"And did it heal?"

"Yes, but not at once. It might have been — we found surgeon's salve, and used that as well."

"Did it leave a scar?"

"My — my friend died, a few days later." Paks looked down. "I don't know if it worked or not."

"Hmm. I see. And you never tried again?" She shook her head.

"Why not?"

Paks shrugged. "It never seemed right — necessary. We had surgeons — a mage — "

"Healing gifts require careful teaching," murmured Tamar. "Or so I have been told. Without instruction, you might never know — "

"We must see, then. You have experienced such healing at the hands of others, haven't you?"

"Yes." Paks thought of the paladin in Aarenis, and of Amberion in Fin Panir. And of the Kuakgan, so different and yet alike.

"Then you must try." When she looked at him, surprised despite his earlier words, he smiled. "You must try sometime, Paksenarrion, and you might as well begin here. Ansuli has painful injuries, as have you yourself. Try to heal them, and see what happens."

"But — " She looked at Tamar, who merely smiled.

"We shall tell no tales of it," said Giron. "If you have no such gift, it is no shame to you; few do. If you come to be a paladin later, it will no doubt be added to you. But here and now you may try, with no prying eyes to see: no god *we* worship would despise an attempt to heal. And if you succeed, you will know something you need to know, and Ansuli will be able to take the trail again."

"But I have not called on Gird these several months," said Paks in a whisper. "It seems greedy to ask now — "

"And whence his power? You told us he served the High Lord. Call on him, if you will."

Paks shivered. She feared to have such power, yet she feared to know herself without it. She looked up and met Giron's eyes. "I will try." Giron picked her up, and laid her next to Ansuli. This close, Paks could feel the heat of his fever. She rested her hand on his side, where she thought the ribs might be broken. She did not know what to expect.

At first nothing happened. Paks did not know what to do, and her thoughts were too busy to concentrate on Gird or the High Lord. She found them wandering back to the Kuakgan, to the Duke, to Saben and Canna. Had she really healed Canna with the High Lord's power? She tried to remember what she had done: she had held the medallion — but now she had no medallion. She looked at Ansuli's face, flushed with fever. She knew nothing of fevers, but that they followed some wounds. We're short of men, she thought, and wondered that Giron had said nothing of it.

They had needed her, and more, and now two were dead and another sick. She tried to imagine her way into Ansuli's wound, past the dusky bruises.

All at once the bruise beneath her hand began to fade. She heard Giron's indrawn breath, and tried to ignore it. She could feel nothing, in hand or arm, to guide her, to tell her what was occurring. . . . only the fading stain. She looked quickly at Ansuli's face. Sweat beaded his forehead. Under her hand his breath came longer and easier. Paks felt sweat cold on her own neck. She did not know what she had done, or when to stop. She remembered the Kuakgan talking about healing — his kind of healing — and feared to do more. What if she hurt something? She pulled back her hand.

Chapter Six

Dressed in the russet and green of Lyonya's rangers, Paks moved through the open woodland toward the border almost as quietly as the elves. They had given her the long black bow she'd used all summer, and offered a sword if she would stay with them until Midwinter Feast, but Paks felt she must return to the Duke as quickly as she could.

Now she was near Brewersbridge again. I know this town better than my own, she thought ruefully. She could scarcely remember where in Three Firs the baker was. Ahead she could see the dark mass of the Kuakgan's grove. She turned toward the road: she would not risk that grove despite her new woods learning.

A caravan clogged the way; she had seen its dust rising over the trees without thinking about it. It was headed east, into Lyonya. As she came across the fields, she saw the guards watching her. So close to Brewersbridge they would think her a shepherd or messenger, not a brigand. She neared the road.

"Ho, there! Seen any trouble toward the border?" That was a guard in chainmail, with his crossbow cocked, seated on the lead wagon.

"No — but I've not been on the road. Headed for Chaya, or the forest way to Prealith?"

He scowled. "Chaya, if it matters to you."

"I can't help you then. I was in the southern forest three days ago; it's quiet there."

"You're a ranger?" He was clearly suspicious. Paks turned up the flap of her tunic to show the badge. His face relaxed. "Huh. Don't see Lyonyan rangers this far into Tsaia, usually. You don't — pardon me — look elven."

"I'm not." Paks grinned. "I hired on for the summer. If you see a band near the spring they call Kiessillin, you might mention me — tell them I was safe in Brewersbridge."

"Tell them who — a long lass with yellow hair?"

"Paksenarrion," she called, as the wagon rolled on. He looked startled, but subsided.

She had not been in Brewersbridge in the summer. At *The Jolly Potboy*, horses and mules crammed the stableyard; five wagons blocked the way outside. Paks threaded her way between the crowds of people. She heard Hebbinford turning a party away as she passed the door. Down the north

730

road came another group of wagons; these were ox-drawn, and the drovers looked as heavy as their beasts. At last she understood how the town had grown so big. Clearly she could not find room at the inn; the fallow fields near town were full of campsites already. Probably every spare room had its tenant. That left Gird's grange or the Kuakgan. She must speak to Marshal Cedfer, certainly, but — she turned up the north road to the entrance of the grove.

A party of soldier hailed her. "You! Ranger!"

After the first twinge of fear, she could stand and talk to them. "Yes?"

"What are you doing in Tsaia? Is the border secure?"

"As far as I know. I've left the rangers; I'm headed north."

"North? Where? And who are you?" None of the group looked familiar.

"To Duke Phelan's stronghold; I'm Paksenarrion Dorthansdotter — "

"Oh!" said one sharply. "You're the Paksenarrion who — ?"

"Quiet, Kevil!" A heavy-set man with red hair peered at her. "Paksenarrion, eh? Known to anyone here?"

"Yes." Paks was surprised herself at how calm she felt. "Marshal Cedfer knows me, and Master Oakhallow — I daresay Master Hebbinford will remember me."

"Well, then." He sucked his teeth. "D'you know our commander?"

"Sir Felis?" He nodded, and Paks went on. "I knew Sir Felis, yes."

"Hmph. We've had a bit of trouble lately — have to watch strangers — "

Paks looked at the crowded streets and grinned at him. "Keeps you busy, does it?"

He did not grin in return. "Aye, it keeps us busy. It's not funny, neither. I'd heard you were a swordfighter, not an archer."

"The rangers use bows," said Paks. "I spent the summer with them."

"Ah. Well, where are you staying?"

"I don't know yet. The inn's packed. I wanted to see Master Oakhallow — "

"Thought you were a Gird's paladin or some such," said one of the other soldiers, with an edge to his voice.

"No," said Paks quietly. "I am a Girdsman, but not a paladin."

"Quiet," said the red-haired man again. "You've been here before, from what I hear — if you are the same Paksenarrion. But we've had trouble, you see — we don't want more — "

"I don't intend — "

"That's all I mean. If you stay with the Gird's Marshal, or the Kuakgan, or some friend, well, that's fine. Or if not, come out to the keep, and I daresay Sir Felis will speak for you. Only I'm supposed to keep order — "

"I understand," said Paks. He nodded abruptly and led the group away. Paks could hear them talking, and the redhead shushing them, before they had gone ten yards.

As she came to the grove entrance, she suddenly wondered how many times she would come there. It seemed for a moment that she was constantly entering and leaving the grove. She shook her head and went on. As suddenly as always, the street noise dropped away, leaving only the sound of leaves and wind and small creatures rustling in the growth. This time she knew the different trees, knew the names and flowers and berries of the little plants that fringed the path, knew the names of the birds that flitted overhead. She knew enough to be surprised that incense cedar and yellow-wood grew side by side, that a strawberry was still in flower.

Again, that empty glade with the fountain murmuring in its midst. Paks had been thinking what she might put in the basin. When it came to it, she laid a seed she had found, from a tall flowering tree she had not seen anywhere but in one part of Lyonya. No one appeared; she stood beside the fountain, listening to the water, for some time. Was the Kuakgan gone? She had never imagined the grove without him. What kind of trouble had the local soldiers so upset? Her feet hurt; she folded her legs and sat beside the lower pool to wait.

Then he was there, not three yards away, smiling at her. Paks started to stand, but he motioned her back down.

"So," he said. "You carry a bow now. You are well?"

"Yes." Paks felt she could say that much honestly. Not as she had been, but well.

"Good. You look better. Where are you bound?"

"To Duke Phelan's. I felt it was time."

He nodded soberly. "It is, and more than time. Did you fight, Paksenarrion?"

"Yes. I didn't — I couldn't feel the same. But I can fight. Well enough, though I can't tell if it's as well. The rangers have different training."

"True. But you are a warrior again? In your mind as well?"

She hesitated. In her own mind a warrior longed for war — but she knew what he meant. "Yes — yes, I think so."

"Did you want to stay here a night or so?"

"I thought to stay at the inn, but it's full. If I could, sir — "

"Certainly. I told you when you left you were welcome to return. Besides — " he stopped suddenly and turned to something else. "Have you eaten?"

"No, sir. Not since morning."

"That's not what I taught you." His voice was severe, but she caught the undertone of laughter. "What did I say about food?"

Paks grinned, suddenly unafraid. "Well, sir, the rangers fed me well enough — as you can see — and I just didn't stop at noon. I wanted to get here well before dark — "

"We'll eat at the inn, if that's agreeable." He stood, and she clambered up. "You might want to leave your bow here; the local militia have become nervous of weapons — "

"I noticed. What about the Girdsmen?"

"They don't bother the Marshal, of course. The others — well, they don't carry weapons much, anyway. It's the rumors, mostly — that Lyonya is in trouble, that the king is dying — " He led the way to his house.

"There's a fear of invasion, from Lyonya — stupid, really, since if they've got trouble, they'll be fighting at home. But our count worries." Paks followed him indoors, and stood her bow in the corner of the front room, laying her quiver of arrows carefully beside it. "Did you want to wash?"

"Yes. Thank you." Paks had bathed in a creek that morning, but morning was many dusty hours back. When she came from the bathing room, she felt almost rested. The Kuakgan was looking at her bow.

"Blackwood," he commented. "I'm surprised they sold you one of these."

"They didn't," said Paks. "It was a gift."

He raised his eyebrows. "Indeed. You did well, then, in Lyonya."

"I tried to." Paks finished tying up the end of her braid. "Now that you've mentioned food — "

He smiled, and they left the house for the inn.

Hebbinford knew her at once. "Paks! I never thought — I mean, I'm glad to see you again." His eyes were shrewd. "You've heard about not wearing weapons or armor, I see — "

"Yes, thank you."

"I'm sorry we're full — I haven't a room, not even a loft — "

"No matter. I have a place."

Hebbinford looked at the Kuakgan, and back at Paks. "I'm glad indeed to see you. You will eat here?"

"If you have enough room for that," said the Kuakgan. "And enough food. Paks tells me she is truly hungry — "

"And you know my appetite," said Paks, grinning. Hebbinford waved them in.

"Of course. Of course. Fried mushrooms — I don't forget. I'll call Sevri, too — she's asked many times — " He moved away.

"You have many friends," said the Kuakgan. "Only a village innkeeper, perhaps, but — "

"Hebbinford?" Paks looked at him. "You know better than to call him *only* a village innkeeper."

"Good. You might like to know that Sevri has defended you — to the extent of a black eye or so — when the subject of your — uhm — problems came up."

"I'm sorry she got into fights for that."

"Loyalty isn't trivial, even if the insult was."

"Paks!" It could only be Mal, whose delighted bellow would carry across any intervening noise. "Paks! You're back! Where's your big sword? Where's that black horse of yours?"

The Kuakgan's eyes were dancing with mischief. Paks sighed and braced herself for Mal's hug.

"I can't carry a sword here — remember?"

"Oh, that. Well, it shouldn't apply to you, Paks. Talk to the Marshal, or Sir Felis, and — "

"I've been in Lyonya," said Paks, heading him off. "I've been using a longbow."

"You?" Mal looked at her critically. "My brother Con used a bow."

"You said so before, so I thought I'd try it."

"I still like an axe." Mal had settled at their table, and the serving girls were already bringing a pot of ale. "I told you before, Paks, an axe is better than any of 'em. It'll break a sword, and a mace, and — "

"Yes. I tried an axe myself."

"You did? Where? Isn't it better?"

"Not for me," said Paks. "I nearly cut my own leg off."

"Well, it's not for some," conceded Mal. "My brother Con, that uses the bow, he says that. But if I had to have a sword, and then I was out working in the forest, and I was chopping a tree, and something came along — then I'd have to drop the axe, and find the sword. I say, give me an axe." He took a long pull at his mug of ale, and refilled it from the pot. "Listen, Paks, is it true what I heard?"

Paks felt her stomach lurch. "Is what true?"

"Some man came along and said you got in trouble in Fin Panir — stole something from the Hall — and the Girdsmen threw you out and that's why you aren't a paladin. That's not so, is it?"

"No," said Paks with relief. "That's not so."

"I didn't think so." Mal settled back in his seat, and glared around the room. "He came saying that, and I said it was a lie, and he laughed at me." He looked sideways at her to catch her reaction, then looked at the Kuakgan. Paks said nothing. "So I broke his arms for him," Mal went on, with relish. "Liar like that. Thinks we don't know anything down here, being a little town. You wouldn't steal nothing, I told him, and if you had you wouldn't get caught. I remember you sneaking around in those tunnels, quiet as a vole."

Paks shook her head. She wanted to laugh, but she didn't want to start any more questions, either.

"Is that the fellow that complained to Sir Felis?" asked the Kuakgan. "I remember some sort of trouble."

"Oh, aye. Said I'd attacked him for no reason. Wanted me up to the Count's court. Couldn't have gone, anyway. I had all those trees to trim up for the new work on the town hall. Anyway, he told Sir Felis what I did — and I told Sir Felis what he'd said — and Sir Felis told me to go home, and sent him away."

"I heard he told you to go home and stay there and not break any more arms." The Kuakgan's voice was quiet.

"Oh . . . he might have. Something like that. But you know, sir, I don't go breaking arms for no good reason. Not like some. But a liar like that. And Paks. Well, even if it was true, he shouldn't be saying it. Not around here, anywhere, where folks know her." Mal stared at the tabletop. "No, the one who got mad was the Marshal. You'd think I was a yeoman, the way he gets after me. I said the man was a liar, and he said even so, and I said he needed more than his arms broke, and he said — "

"I said, Mal, that if anyone needed to defend Paksenarrion's name, it would be the Fellowship of Gird." The Marshal stood beside the table, his eyes challenging.

"And I said you hadn't broke his arms yet, and I was glad to." Mal sat back and grinned, the wide gap-toothed grin that Paks remembered so well, then pushed himself to his feet and wandered away.

"Paksenarrion. I'm pleased to see you again." The Marshal's unasked question *What are you doing with the Kuakgan?* hung between them.

"And I you, Marshal Cedfer," said Paks. "Will you eat with us? I just arrived in town."

"So I heard from Sergeant Cannis. I'll sit with you; it's a drill night." He paused, then asked. "Will you be coming to drill?"

"Not tonight, I think, Marshal." Paks did not elaborate.

"Ah. You've journeyed long today, I imagine." He looked at her, then around the room. "You've found our busiest season, this time. You're — " he looked sharply at the Kuakgan. "There's a place for you at the grange, any time," he said formally. "Even without any notice from the Marshal-General — "

"Marshal, I thank you. I will be traveling on tomorrow; I'm heading north, to the Duke's stronghold. And tonight — "

"You're staying in the grove." He sighed. "Perhaps it's best. But I hope you will come by the grange before you leave. We still count you in our fellowship — here in Brewersbridge, perhaps, more than elsewhere."

Paks was moved. She had still feared Marshal Cedfer's reaction. "Sir, I will do so. I have been with the rangers in Lyonya this summer — "

His face lightened. "Indeed! Very good. And did you — " He stopped, and she wondered if he had been about to ask about fighting. "I mean," he amended, "if it's not breaching some vow of your service, I wondered how things stand in Lyonya. You may have heard rumors here — "

"Yes." Paks was glad the conversation turned this way. "I cannot say much, since I spent my time in the southern forest. But my companions were concerned about some threat to the realm as a whole. They even mentioned trouble coming from Tsaia."

"Tsaia! From us? Surely not. These kingdoms have been at peace for generations. We have no designs — "

"Nor they, I assure you," said Paks. "They mentioned only rumor, as you have had here. They didn't understand it, but feared the work of — " she paused and looked around the busy room. "Achrya," she said softly.

The Marshal's face tightened, and the Kuakgan frowned.

"That one," said the Marshal. "*Her.* Well, it might be so. That was her agent near here. Yes, and her doing with the other moneychanger, as I recall. Well. If she's active again . . . "

"Is she ever inactive?" asked the Kuakgan. "And would anything please her better than trouble between friends?"

"You're right," said the Marshal. "Gird's cudgel, this will be a mess if that

735

happens." He looked at Paks. "Well, if you've been with the rangers, I expect you've learned some archery."

"Yes." Paks wondered if he would ask her to demonstrate, but he shook his head, and got up.

"I have drill, as I said, and must get ready. If you change your mind, Paksenarrion, you'll be welcome." He waved as he went out.

The Kuakgan raised his mug in salute. "I told you once the Marshal would surprise you. You have come far, Paksenarrion, since last spring."

"Yes." She looked into her own mug, drained it, and refilled it.

"Yes, but? Not all the way, eh?" She did not answer, but shook her head briefly. "Does it bother you so much, now?" he went on.

"No. Not really. I wish for it, but I can do without it." She traced a design on the table with one finger. "I wonder, though, what would happen in serious trouble — "

"You don't consider a daskdraudigs serious?"

Paks looked up, startled. "You knew about that?"

"Mother of Trees, did you think I'd send you off like that and not pay attention? Yes, I know about it. I know you didn't kill it yourself, and I know you did face danger steadily." He paused to drain his own mug. "Ah . . . here comes the food." Neither of them spoke while a serving girl laid the trays on their table: roast meat, gravy, mushrooms, bread, and cheese. A dish of onions, and one of redroots, and one of stewed pears. Finally she left, taking the empty jug, and promising to bring another. "I know you didn't panic, Paksenarrion, when you might have. And they tell me you were able to sense the daskdraudigs before anyone else."

"Yes." Paks was piling meat on a slab of bread. "I was still frightened, you know. But I kept thinking of what you'd said, and then what I'd been taught of fighting — this arm here, and that step there — and I was able to keep on." She bit into the food. "I threw up afterwards," she said around a mouthful of bread and meat. "The first time, at least."

"Yes. But you were able to keep on. Good." They ate in silence awhile. Paks was just about to say something, when Sevri came to the table. She had grown even more over the summer.

"Paks? Dad says you aren't staying with us — I could've found room — you could've slept with me."

"Sevri. Are you tired of everyone saying how you've grown? Are you still working mostly in the stable?"

"No, and yes. I do some in the inn, too, but I like the stable work better." She had the same friendly smile as before. "Are you all right, Paks? You look different without your sword."

"I'm fine. When did they start telling everyone not to wear a sword?"

"Over the summer. It's helped a little, with the caravaners. We've had fewer fights." She glanced at the Kuakgan. "I'm sorry, Master Oakhallow, that I didn't greet you — "

"No matter."

"Do you still have the black horse, Paks? Or did you get another?"

736

"I'm traveling on foot right now," said Paks carefully. "I left Socks in Fin Panir — they said they'd keep him until I came for him."

She could see the thoughts passing through Sevri's eyes, but Sevri finally said, "I hope he's all right. I remember how scared I was of him at first, and by the time you left I could feed him from my hand." She looked at Paks's clothes curiously. "Are you a ranger now? Or shouldn't I ask?"

"I spent the summer as a ranger. Now I'm going to see Duke Phelan." Paks tried to think of something comforting to say, and couldn't. Sevri sat in silence a moment, and then got up.

"I'd better get back to work. We're feeding one of the caravans, too, and they'll be sending in for it any minute." She started away, then turned back for a moment. "I'm glad you're here, Paks. I hope you come back."

"Sevri's talked of joining the grange," said Master Oakhallow. "She's said she would like to be like you."

Paks shivered. "She shouldn't. She's too —"

"She's tougher than you think. She'd make a good fighter — in some ways like you — though I think she shouldn't plan to make her living at it. But if trouble comes here — she could fight, I think, and well."

Though it was nearly dark when they left the inn, the streets were just as crowded. Paks felt sleepy and full: the meal she'd eaten, on top of the long day's march, had her longing for a bed — any bed. But the Kuakgan, when they came to his house, laid a fire and lit it. He seemed wide awake and ready for a long talk.

"The seed you brought me is indeed rare," he said. "I have no arissa in the grove, and I am glad to have the chance to sprout one. Did you see it in bloom?"

"Yes." Paks yawned. "Like — like great lights, high in the forest. Not the sort of flowers most trees have."

"Tell me something of the forest you traveled." Paks wanted to sleep; she yawned again, but began to talk of her summer's work, remembering as best she could the trees, flowers, vines, birds, and animals. The Kuakgan interrupted now and then with questions. Then he asked about the daskdraudigs.

"It felt — bad. Sick." Paks felt itchy talking about it. "I felt it, inside my head — I fell down, at first."

"And then?"

"And then I could tell which direction. Not very well." She described the search for the daskdraudigs, and the fight when it was found. She was wide awake again. The Kuakgan sat crosslegged in front of the fire, staring into it as she talked. When she was done, he turned to her.

"Paksenarrion, do you have yet any hope of being made a paladin?"

Paks stopped short. "I — haven't thought of it." That was not quite true, for the rangers had prodded her to acknowledge and use her gifts. She could not quite believe their hints; she could not wholly disbelieve, when she looked at Ansuli, obviously healed and free of pain. She thought of it then, thought of the dream she had had, of the pain when it died. Had it

737

died? Once, yes, and then it had sprouted again, as a dead seed revives in spring. But was it the same dream, or another?

"You said you considered yourself once more a warrior. A warrior for what, or with whom?"

"I—" She stopped. "I have to say? Yes. A warrior for — for good."

"Still that."

"Yes."

"Which means a paladin, to you? Or a knight of Gird, or Falk, or Camwyn or some such?"

"It means — just what I said. To fight, but only for what I think is good."

"What *you* think is good? Not at the direction of others?"

Paks thought hard. "Well — no. Not really. Not any more. But if the gods — if I knew that the gods said — "

"Ah. But no man or woman."

"No." As she said it, she felt herself cut off from all the warriors she'd known — for she was forswearing allegiance to any lord, any captain, any king, even. Could she consider herself in the fellowship of Gird, if she would not take the orders of the Marshal-General? She shivered a little. Did she mean it? Yes.

He sat back, as if satisfied, and turned again to the fire. "Did the elves tell you, Paksenarrion, of the origin of paladins?"

"No, sir." Hints, yes, but nothing clearer for her questions; she had finally quit asking.

"Hmmmm. Once the gods themselves chose paladins, chose them from among those mortals who desired good and would risk all danger to gain it. The gifts which all expect paladins to have were given by the gods, some to one, and some to another, as they grew into their powers. The heroes whose cults have grown up over the world — some of them now called saints — were chosen and aided the same way. Or so it is said. But after awhile, the cults themselves began to choose candidates, and prepare them, and — so it is said — began to intervene between the gods and the paladins. Although, once chosen, the paladins were supposed to take their direction from the saints or gods — " Paks thought of Amberion. Had Gird truly told him to take her to Kolobia? Or the Marshal-General?

"I'm not attacking the Girdsmen," the Kuakgan said slowly. "Though it must sound like it. The fellowship of Gird has done much for these kingdoms, and the fighters it trains have at least some care for the helpless. But what was once a grace bestowed freely by the gods — flowers wild in the field and woods — has become a custom controlled by the clerics: flowers planted in safe pots along a path. The flowers have their virtue, either place, but — " He stopped and looked at her.

"It may be, Paksenarrion, that once in a while the gods decide to do things *their* way once more. If you are, as you declare, no longer depending on man or woman for your guidance of good and evil — and yet you have, as you've shown, some of the gifts found in paladins — " She wondered how he knew that, but if they'd told him about the daskdraudigs . . .

Paks ducked her head. "I — don't know. I don't know how I would know."

"There's that. A paladin unbound to some knightly order or cult is rare these days. And a Kuakgan is hardly one to know much of these things." Paks found that hard to believe, at least of this Kuakgan. "When you were here last," he went on, "you left everything you came with in the basin. Willingly, at that time."

"Yes." Paks did not like to think of that mood, even now.

"Hmmm. But you gave a gift you had no right to give."

"Sir?"

"This." He held out to her the Duke's ring, the foxhead graved on the black stone. "This was not yours to give, Paksenarrion, and I cannot accept it."

Paks stared at it a moment, then at him. "But, sir — "

"Take it. You are going to him; you can take it back." He held it until she reached out, then dropped it in her hand. "Put it on." Paks slipped it onto a finger. She had not expected to see that ring again. She turned it with her thumb until the seal was inside, invisible, the way she had worn it before.

"You have been well enough to fight," the Kuakgan went on. "You seem to be wholly well in body, and you are well enough in mind to sense evil and good — a gift that cannot work when the mind is clouded. Do you still desire that joy of fighting you had before, or can you see it as a danger — as a temptation to fight without cause?"

"Sir, I have had enough experience to know what comes of fighting for the joy of it alone. It is not that. But I still wish I could feel the joy when it's needed. Or perhaps I should not say needed, since I can do without it, but — I heard a woodworker, sir, say how much he liked the feel of his plane slipping along the grain of the wood, and the smell of the shavings. My father liked being out with his sheep — I can remember him standing on the moor, drawing in great breaths of that wind and smiling. Isn't that natural, in a craftsman, to enjoy his work as well? And I wish for that, to enjoy it sometimes. To pick up a sword with pleasure in its balance, not always overcoming fear of it."

"Is the fear any less?"

"I think so. Or else I am getting used to it."

"Yet you haven't asked me, Paksenarrion, if I have any healing magic to restore this to you."

"No, sir. You have done much for me already, and — I thought — if you wished to do more you would say so."

"Yes. I don't know. What I can do has been done." Paks felt the certainty of this, and braced herself to carry her fear forever. "But," he went on, "there may be more you can do. You have spent a summer with elves and part-elves and the powers of the forest. I think you have spent it well — not thinking only of fighting, but learning, as you could, of the natural world. I cannot promise success — but if you have the courage to try a desperate chance, it may return your joy in your craft."

"I will try," said Paks at once.

"I have not told you what it is."

She shook her head. "No matter. I will try."

"Very well." He stood up and moved to the woodbox. "I have saved these from the spring; they'll be dry by now." He began to stack short lengths of wood by the fireside. "This is eart'oak — to look at, much like any red oak. The elves call it fireoak. And here are two lengths of blackwood — don't worry, not long enough for a bow, even for a child. I wouldn't burn bowwood. And — let me think. Yellowwood, shall it be, or rowan? What do you remember best, Paksenarrion, about your visit here this spring?"

She tried to think; the bees that had come in to the honeycomb came to mind. "Bees," she said. "You sang them away."

"From yellowwood honey. Very well." He pushed most of the existing fire to one side of the wide hearth, and quickly piled the sticks he'd selected in its place. Then he lit them with a brand from the fire. Paks flinched: flames roared up from the tiny pile as if it had oil on it. They were bright, brighter than the yellow flames on the other wood. The room came alive in that dancing light. "It won't last long," said the Kuakgan, turning to her. "You must name your gods, to yourself, at least, and place your hands in that flame. The heartwood of fireoak, for courage, and blackwood for resilience and endurance, and yellowwood for steadfast loyalty to good. Quickly!"

Paks could not move for an instant — the magical flames were too bright and hot. She could feel the sweat break out on her face, feel the clenching of her stomach, the roiling wave of fear about to sweep over her. She spread her hands in front of her and leaned to the fire.

The flames leaped up joyously to engulf her. She would have jerked back, but it seemed too late — the fire was too big. If I'm going to burn, she thought, I might as well do it all. She had forgotten to ask what would happen — if the flames would really burn — if they would kill her — and it was too late. Gird, she called silently, Gird, protector of the helpless. And it seemed to her that a stocky powerful man held his hand between her and the flames. And her memory brought her another vision, and other names: The High Lord — and the first man stepped back, and trumpets blew a fanfare, and in the fire itself a cup of pure silver, mirroring the fire — Take it — said a voice, and she reached into the flames to find herself holding a cool cup full of icy liquid — Drink — said the voice, and she drank. Flames roared around her, hot and cold together — she could feel them running along her arms and legs. A wild wind shook the flames, drums thundered in her feet: she thought of horses, of Saben, of the Windsteed, father of many foals. She rode the flames, leaping into darkness, into nowhere, and then across endless fields of flowers, and the flowers at last wrapping the flames in coolness, in sweet scents and breaths of mint and cinnamon and spring water. Alyanya, she thought at the end. The Lady of Peace — strange patron for a warrior. And kind laughter followed, and the touch of healing from the Lady's herbs. Then she thought of them all together, or tried to, and the flames rose again like petals of crystal, many-colored, closing her off from that vision as the Hall's colored windows from the sky. Higher they rose, and higher, and she walked through them, wondering, until she saw in the distance an end.

And recovered herself sitting on the cold hearth of the Kuakgan's house, with every bit of wood consumed to ash. The Kuakgan sat beside her, as she could feel, in the darkness. She drew a long breath.

"Paksenarrion?" He must have heard the breath, and been waiting for it. She had never heard him sound so tentative.

"Yes." It was hard to speak. It was hard to think. She was not at all sure what had happened, or how long it had been.

He sighed, deeply. "I was beginning to worry. I feared you might be lost, when you did not return at once."

"I — don't know where I was."

"I do not propose to suggest where you were. How are you?"

Paks tried to feel herself out. "Well — not burned up — "

The Kuakgan laughed. "And not burned witless, either. That's something, I suppose. Let me get a light — "

Without thinking, Paks lifted her hand: light blossomed on her fingertip.

"Mother of Trees!" The Kuakgan sounded amazed. "Is that what happened?"

Paks herself stared at the light in confusion. "I don't know what I did! I don't know — what is it?

"It's light — it's a light spell. Some paladins can do that — haven't you seen it?"

When she thought of it, Paksenarrion remembered the paladins making light. "Yes, but then — "

"Then what? Oh, I see. Well, as I half-suspected, you are a paladin outside the law, so to speak. Human law, that is."

"But it can't — I mean I can't — and anyway, how do I do it? Or stop it?" She was still staring at the light; she was afraid to look away or move her hand.

"Just a moment." The Kuakgan rose and took a candle from the mantle, and touched it to her hand. Nothing happened. "Ah."

"What?"

"It's true spell-light, not witchlight. Witchlight lights candles, but not spell-light." She could hear him rasping with his flint and steel. The candle flared, a yellow glow pale beside her hand. "Now you don't need it. Ask for darkness."

"Ask who?" Paks felt stupid.

"Whom did you name? Whom were you with? You're a paladin, remember, not a mage: you don't command, you ask."

— Please — thought Paks, still in confusion. The light vanished. A bubble of laughter ran through her mind. "But do you mean it?" she asked the Kuakgan, turning to watch him as he lit more candles. "Do you mean I really am a paladin, after all that's — " Her voice broke.

741

"I am no expert on paladins," he said again. "But something certainly happened. I know you aren't a Kuakgan. We both know you aren't a Marshal of Gird. You aren't a wizard. Nor an elf. That leaves few explanations for your gifts and abilities. Paladin is the name that fits best."

"But I was — " She didn't want to say it, but knew he would understand.

"Hmmm. I used to wonder how the paladins of Gird could be considered protectors of the helpless when they had never been helpless. Rather like asking the hawk to feel empathy for the grouse, or the wolf for the sheep. Even if a tamed wolf makes a good sheepdog, he will never understand how the sheep feel. You, Paksenarrion: you are most fortunate. For having been, as you thought, a coward, and helpless to fight — you know what that is like. You know what bitterness that feeling breeds — you know in your own heart what kind of evil it brings. And so you are most fit to fight it where it occurs. Or so I believe."

Paks stared at the finger that had held light. She wanted to argue that it could not be true — she had been too badly hurt — she had too much to overcome. But far inside she felt a tremulous power, a ripple of laughter and joy, that she had not felt before. It was much like the joy she remembered, yet greater, as the light of her finger had been greater than candlelight.

Chapter Seven

The road north from Vérella seemed vaguely familiar, even after three years. Paks stayed most nights in village inns; the fall nights were cold. She made good speed during the days, but did not hurry.

As she came over the last hill before Duke's East, a cold thin rain began to sift down through the trees, dulling the brilliance of their changing leaves. Paks grinned to herself: so much for her imagination. She'd hoped to arrive at Kolya's looking fairly respectable. She unslung her bow, and put the bowstring in her belt pouch to keep it dry. At least she wouldn't have to stay on the road if it got muddy, as she had in the Company. She pulled the hood of her cloak well over her face and trudged on. It grew colder. She had to blink the rain off her eyelashes every few minutes. At least it was downhill, she told herself. The rain came down harder. The slope levelled out, and Paks began to look for the village ahead. There. There on the right was the stone cottage with apple trees around it, Kolya's place, and there ahead was the bridge, with the mill upstream.

Paks looked at her muddy boots and wet cloak, and decided to go on to the inn. Kolya wasn't expecting her — might not recognize her — Paks turned away from the gate and went on. Under the bridge the water ran rough and brown. They must have had rain up in the hills, she thought. The stones of the bridge were bluer than she remembered.

Although it was still daylight, few people were in the street. Light glowed behind curtained windows. Paks turned left out of the market square, toward the inn. It loomed ahead, and she hurried toward it, thinking of warm fires and a hot meal. The inn door was closed tight against the wind and rain, but swung easily when she pushed it. Paks slipped through and closed it behind her. The common room was bright with lamps and the fire on the hearth. Her wet cloak steamed. She blinked the rain out of her eyes as she pushed back her hood.

"Well, traveler, may I help you?" The wiry innkeeper looked just as he had the year she left. Then she had been an awed recruit, wondering if she would ever go there casually, as the veterans did.

"Yes," said Paks. "I'd like a meal and a bath — "

"A room for tonight, as well?"

"I'm not sure." Paks shrugged out of her pack and cloak.

"It's late to be starting out again in this weather — " He stopped suddenly, and Paks saw he was looking at the black signet ring on her right hand. He looked up, frowning. "You're one of the Duke's — ?"

Paks nodded. "I was with the Company. The Duke gave me this, the last time I saw him, and said to come if — when I had — finished something."

The innkeeper's eyes were shrewd. "I see. And you were planning to make his stronghold by tonight, eh?"

"No. Actually, I planned to visit a friend here in town first. Kolya Ministiera."

"Kolya! A friend of yours — might I ask your name?"

"Of course. Paksenarrion." She could not interpret the look on his face, and did not care to try. They would all have heard some story or other. She busied herself with the fastening of her pack. "I was in Arcolin's cohort."

"Yes. I've — heard somewhat — " He looked hard at her a moment. When he spoke again, his voice was brisker. "Well, then. Food and a bath — which would you first?"

"Bath," said Paks. "I've clean clothes in here, but I'm mud to the knees. And do you have anyone I could send with a message to Kolya?"

"My grandson will go. Do you wish writing materials?"

"No. Just ask him to tell her that I'm here, and would be glad to see her again."

"Very well. Come this way, and I'll arrange your bath."

A short time later, Paksenarrion was scrubbing the trail grime off with a linen towel, hot water, and the scrap end of scented soap she'd bought in Vérella. When she was done, she poured the rest of the hot water over herself, then dried in front of the little fire in the bathing chamber. She'd hung her clean clothes near the fire to take the chill from them. They felt soft and warm when she put them on. She counted the coins in her purse and decided that she could afford a good dinner. When she came back down the passage to the common room, she felt ready to face anyone. The big room was empty, but for a serving girl. Paks chose a table near the fire, leaning her bow against the wall. The girl came to her at once.

"Master said would you want a private room to eat in?"

"No," said Paks. "This will be fine. What do you have?"

"Roast mutton or beef, redroots, white cheese or yellow, mushrooms with gravy, barley pudding, meat pasties, pies — "

"Enough," said Paks, laughing. "Let's see — how about roast mutton and gravy, barley, mushrooms, and — do you have soup?"

The girl nodded. "We always have soup. If you're cold, I can bring mulled cider, too."

"Good. I'd like that." The girl left the room, and Paks pushed the bench closer to the wall so that she could lean against it. She stretched out her legs to the fire. The fire murmured to itself, occasionally snapping a retort to some hissed comment. She could hear the rain fingering the shutters, and the red curtains on the windows moved uneasily, but by the fire she was warm and felt no draft. She wondered what Kolya would say to her message. What had Kolya heard? Her eyes sagged shut, and she slipped a bit on

744

the wall. She jerked awake and yawned. This was no time to go to sleep. She ought to be thinking what to say to Kolya, and to the Duke.

The door opened, letting in a gust of cold wet air and a tall figure in a long wet cloak. Paks thought at first it might be Kolya, but as the woman came into the light, Paks saw that she was younger, and certainly had both arms. A man came in behind her. The woman threw back the hood of her cloak to reveal red-gold hair, stylishly dressed. Under her cloak she wore a simply cut gown of dark green velvet, and when she drew off her gloves, she wore rings on both hands. Her companion, who seemed vaguely familiar to Paks, wore black tunic and trousers, and tall riding boots. Paks wondered who they were — they belonged in some city like Vérella, not up here. Before she thought about it, she had turned the Duke's ring round on her finger so that only the band was visible. The serving girl had appeared as the door closed, and led the pair at once down a passage toward the interior of the inn. They must be known, then, thought Paks. She felt uneasy as they crossed the common room to the passage, but they did not seem to look at her.

"Here you are," said the innkeeper, breaking into her thoughts. The platter of food steamed, and smelled good. "And Councilor Ministiera sent you a message — she's in a meeting right now, but would be pleased to have you stay with her. She'll come here when she's through with the meeting." Paks thought that Kolya's invitation impressed him. "This room is often crowded from suppertime on, and noisy — if you'd prefer a quieter place to wait, I have several rooms." Paks thought about it, and decided she would rather not see Stammel just yet.

"Yes — thank you. I think I will. But I'll finish supper first — no need to move this." She gestured at the platter and bowls. He smiled and left her. The mutton was tender and tasty; the soup warmed her to the toes. By the time she had finished, several townsmen had come in and ordered meals, staring at her curiously. She signalled the serving girl, and asked directions to the jacks and the private rooms.

"Right along here," said the girl. "And master said you were to have this room — " she pointed to a door, "when you were ready." Paks opened the door to find a pleasant little room with a fire already burning on the small hearth. Three chairs and a small round table furnished it, with a bench along one wall. The girl lighted the candles that stood in sconces on either side of the mantel. "Will you be wanting something from the kitchen?"

"No, not now. Probably when Kolya comes." Paks tried to compute the probable cost of the meal, bath, and private room. But she wouldn't be paying for a room tonight, and she had enough.

When she came back from the jacks, she settled into one of the chairs by the fire, and took her bow across her knees. She inspected it as she'd been taught, and rubbed it lightly with oil until it gleamed. She took the bowstring from her pouch and slipped it on, then bent the bow to string it. It was as supple and responsive as ever in her hands. She unstrung it and set it against the wall.

Her hand found her dagger, and then she was standing, staring at the door. She shook her head and sat down. Silly. Here, of all places, alone in a room in the Duke's realm, nothing could menace her. She turned his ring again, looking at the seal in the black stone. It must be simple nervousness — fear of what Kolya had heard, or what she might say. Paks realized her dagger lay unsheathed in her hand. She stared at the blade, and felt the edge with her thumb. Sharp enough, and smooth. She slid it back in its sheath and stood again, pacing the length of the little room.

At the far end, away from the fire, she could just hear the murmur of other voices. It could not be coming from the common room, she recalled — it must be from another private room on this passage. She stared at the wall, her sense of something wrong growing, then turned back to the fire. She pulled her chair to face it, and found she could not turn her back on the far wall. She could not sit still; her earlier sleepiness was gone. Nothing like this had happened on the journey north, and she was still fighting with herself, a little angry, when a knock came on her own door.

"Yes?" The door opened, and the innkeeper glanced in.

"Councilor Ministiera," he said, and stepped aside. Kolya appeared in the door as Paks stood up. The gray streak in her hair had widened, but otherwise she seemed the same. Her strong dark face was split with a broad grin.

"Paks! You brought more rain with you." She gave Paks a long, considering look.

"Come on in. Don't you want some ale? Or cider?"

"Ale," said Kolya. "I get all the apples I want at home." She entered and sat in one of the chairs, while Paks spoke to the innkeeper about ale. She cocked her head up at Paks. "You will stay with me tonight, won't you?" Paks nodded. "Good. You're looking well. The Duke will be pleased to see you. We heard several things — " She paused, and gave Paks another long look.

But Paks had been ready for this reaction. She smiled. "No doubt. There have been several things to hear. I have a message for you, Kolya, from Master Oakhallow — " She turned and rummaged in her pack until she found the scroll in its oilskin wrapping, and the little oiled pouch that she had never opened.

"Thank you." Kolya started to speak, but paused as the innkeeper brought their ale, and left. "He sends me seeds and cuttings — did you know he helped me start my orchard, after I lost the arm?"

"No." Paks was surprised; she knew only that Kolya was kuakgannir. She had not known even that until the Kuakgan gave her his message to take.

"Yes. He knew me, before I joined the Company."

"Are you from Brewersbridge?"

"No." Kolya did not explain. She was looking at the scroll, which she'd unwrapped. She looked up. "Well, I see that some of the tales we've heard cannot be true."

"Ummm." Paks poured the ale into both mugs. "I don't know what you've heard, Kolya. Some things are true that I wish were not. But now—"

"Now you're a warrior again — aren't you?" Kolya picked up one mug and sipped. "As the Duke said you would have been without the Girdsmen's interference."

"I am a warrior, yes." Paks wondered how much to tell her, and how soon. Seeing Kolya again, she realized how much older the other woman was, how young she might appear. "What happened was not the fault of the Girdsmen," she began.

Kolya snorted. "The Duke thinks so. You're not going to tell me you—" She stopped, obviously looking for a tactful way to say it.

"I am telling you that they did what they knew how to do. The Kuakgan knew more — of some things."

"Are you kuakgannir now?"

"No." Paks did not know how to explain.

"Still of Gird's fellowship?" Doubt lay behind that.

"No — well, in a way — it's difficult to explain—"

"But how do you feel, now? You can fight again?"

"Yes. I feel fine. I spent the summer with the rangers in Lyonya; we saw some fighting there."

"You're not wearing a sword," said Kolya.

"No, that's true. I used a borrowed one there; I haven't the money to buy my own. But they said they'd keep my arms in Fin Panir. Even if they haven't, I expect they'd give me a sword when they got over the shock."

"Shock?"

"Well — they didn't expect me to recover like this."

"Oh. But the Duke said they gave you money . . . what happened?"

"It's a long tale — the short end is it's gone."

Kolya nodded. "When are you going back to Fin Panir?"

"I don't know." Paks felt the uneasy restlessness she'd struggled with before Kolya came. "I wanted to come here first; to see you, to thank the Duke for all his help. I thought perhaps I could do something for him — I don't know."

Kolya drained her mug. "You could join the Company again, if that's what you want. I know he'd take you. Or are you still set on being a paladin?"

Paks shifted the mug in her hands. "I have no choice, Kolya — or you could say I've already made it." She finished her ale, and set the mug down. "I — don't want to talk about it here. Can we go?"

Kolya stared at her in surprise. "Paks, it's safe here. Piter's the Duke's man as much as I am. He tells no tales."

Paks stood up. "I don't doubt you, or him, but something — Kolya, I cannot explain this here and now, but I must not ignore these warnings." She stepped to the door, opened it, and glanced into the passage. Nothing. "I'll go pay the reckoning."

"I'll come." Kolya stood, and Paks collected her bow and pack. She slipped the bowstring off the bow again and rolled it in her pouch. Then she led the way down the passage to the common room.

It was noisy and crowded there now, and it took a moment to catch the innkeeper's eye. He came to them, and greeted Kolya, then asked Paks what more she needed.

"Just the reckoning," said Paks. "Your hospitality has been more than generous."

He looked at her, then at Kolya. "There's — there's naught to pay, this time."

Paks turned to Kolya, whose face was blank. "What? You can't mean that, sir. I've had a fine meal, good cider and ale, bath, a private room — "

The innkeeper looked stubborn. "No. You carry the Duke's seal. One time for each of the Company — I've been a soldier; I know what need is."

Paks felt herself blushing. "Sir, I thank you. But another time, I might have need. This time I have the means to pay."

"You aren't carrying a sword. No, if you come back someday, with all your gear, and want to pay, that's fine. But not a copper will I take this night, and that's final." He glared at her.

"Well — my thanks, then. And I hope to enjoy your brew many a cold evening." Paks and Kolya went out into the cold windy night. The rain had stopped, though the wind smelled wet. They said nothing for some distance, but as they turned into the market square, Paks asked, "What was that about?"

"What?"

"Not paying. Does he really give a free meal to each of the Duke's men? I wouldn't think he could make a living that way."

"Paks — wait until we reach the house." In a few minutes they had crossed the bridge, and neared Kolya's gate. Kolya led the way up the flagged walk to the cottage, and pushed open the heavy door. Inside, a fire on the hearth lit the front room dimly. Kolya poked a splinter into the fire until the end flared, and lit candles in sconces around the room.

"If you need to dry anything, here's a rack," she said, pulling a wooden frame from one corner. Paks dug into her pack for her wet clothes, and spread them on it, glancing around the room. It served as both kitchen and living room, with cooking hooks in the fireplace, a dresser holding plates, mugs, and two blue glasses, a net of cheeses, one of onions, and a ham hanging from beams, a sturdy table and several chairs near the fireplace. The other end of the room held a desk and stool, and more chairs around a striped rug on the floor. Under the front windows was a long bench covered with bright weavings. Kolya disappeared through a door beside the fireplace, and returned with a deep bowl of apples and a small one of nuts.

"You may be tired of apples, but these look good," said Paks.

"They are. This is the first year I've gotten much from these two trees. The green and red striped ones are from Lyonya: Master Oakhallow sent the seedlings years ago. The dark ones are a new strain, according to the

748

traders — at least it was new when I bought some. These trees are — oh — about nine years old by now. What I sent you, in the south, were Royalgarths — what they grow in the king's groves in Pargun. They travel well, and are sweet, but these are better — thinner skinned." It was clear that Kolya was glad to talk of something harmless. Paks fell in with this.

"How many kinds of apples do you grow?"

"As many as I can acquire. Apples do better if you mix varieties, and some tend to skip years in bearing. Right now I've got seven that are bearing well: these two, the Royalgarths, the Westnuts from Fintha, Big Ciders and Little Ciders, and Westland Greens. I've got two kinds that just started bearing this year, but not heavily: another summer apple, but yellow instead of green, and a big red and yellow stripe that does well in the markets south of here. And the pears have come in since you left. Over twenty bushels of pears this year."

Paks had taken a bite out of the green and red apple. Juice flooded her mouth. "This one is good," she said, swallowing. Kolya had cracked two nuts against each other in her strong hand; she began picking the meats out of the broken bits of shell.

"Yes. Paks — you are welcome to stay here; I hope you do. But — what did you come here for? Was it just to thank the Duke for his help? Or — ?"

Paks took another bite of apple. "I'm not sure I can tell you. I don't know how much you know of what actually happened to me — "

"The Duke told us — the Council — some of it. Nothing to blame you for — "

"He didn't know all." Paks could feel Kolya's look as if it were a hand on her face.

"He said it was the Marshal-General's fault," said Kolya. "He's never blamed you for it — "

"It was not her fault. Not in the way he means. Did he tell you about Kolobia? What happened there?"

"Not really." Kolya shifted uneasily. "Something about capture, and evil powers."

"Yes." Paks struggled for calmness. Surely she should be able to tell this tale calmly by now. "I was taken by the kuaknomi, who serve Achrya." Kolya nodded, eyes intent on her bowl of nuts. "They offered the chance to fight — to fight for a chance at escape. Or that's what I thought they offered. Fighting against orcs, for the most part, in a sort of arena they had underground."

"Most part? How many times — ?"

"I don't know." Paks set the apple down carefully, as if it were alive. "I don't remember. Many times, to judge by the marks they left. At the end, I was forced into charmed armor — "

"Mother of Trees!" said Kolya, staring now. She had brought up her hand in the warding sign. Then she looked at her hand, and shook her head. "Sorry. Go on."

Paks took another apple out of the bowl, and looked it over. "In the fighting great evil entered my mind. It grew beyond my control. This is what the Marshal-General saw, in Fin Panir. She was not the only one to see it, Kolya. Even I, when they — " She stopped to take a long breath. "Anyway. They saw but one possible cure. And the Marshal-General, two paladins, and an elf tried to cut that evil from within. Which they did."

"And left you, the Duke said, as crippled as if they'd cut off your legs."

Paks shook her head. "Not so. You — forgive me, Kolya, but you have truly lost an arm. Nothing, now, will make it grow back. I had my limbs — legs and arms both — but not the use of them for awhile."

"And within? The Duke said they did more damage within, that they had ripped the very heart out of your self, the courage — "

"So I thought, and they thought, but the Kuakgan showed me that this was not so."

"Are you certain?" Kolya peered closely at her. "We had heard that you were to be a paladin yourself — and here you are without money enough, you say, to buy a sword — "

"Do riches make a paladin? Or do I look so scared, to you?" Paks smiled at her.

"Well — no. You don't. But you wouldn't be scared of me, anyway."

"I would have been. I was. Kolya, I cannot hide this: I was, for those months, as craven as you can imagine. I don't know what the Duke told you, but he saw me unable to lift a sword even in practice. He saw me afraid to mount a horse — even a gentle one. He saw me — a veteran of his Company — faint in terror because an armsmaster came toward me with his sword raised."

"You'd been hurt — "

Paks snorted. "You know better than that. Kolya, I have been where very few soldiers ever come — to the fear and helplessness that the common folk have. And I've come back from that, with help. Why I'm here — well, that's a long tale. Tell me, would you think me crazy if I told you — " she faltered, and Kolya looked at her curiously.

"What?"

"Kolya, things have happened to me — since I was first in the Company — which seemed strange to me. In Aarenis — especially the third year — others noticed, too — " It was remarkably hard to say, flat out, that she thought she was a paladin.

"Stammel said something to me." Kolya cracked another pair of nuts. "He said it had to do with a Gird's medallion you'd been given by a friend — you could sense things the others couldn't, he said."

"Yes. That was part of it. That was why I thought they were right, when they said I could be a paladin."

"They weren't?"

"Well — yes. In a way." Paks found that she was sweating. "The fact is — I — do have some gifts. They are somewhat like those paladins have, but I never finished the training and took vows. Master Oakhallow thinks they were given directly by the gods. And if so — " She stopped again.

"If so, then you are a paladin of sorts, is that what you mean?" Kolya glanced sideways at her. "A remarkable claim. Not that I doubt your word — " She went on quickly. "It's only that — I never heard of such a thing. When I think of a paladin, I think of those I saw, when I was in the Company. They were not as you are now."

"I know." Paks leaned forward, elbows on knees. "And I trained with them: I know what you're remembering. Shining mail, on a shining horse, so bright that anyone would follow. I don't claim to be that sort of paladin yet, Kolya. I do say that something — and I believe it to be the High Lord, or Gird his servant — has called me here for a purpose. I sensed, in the inn, some evil thing — and felt in myself the answering call: this is what I came for. I cannot see how this will harm the Duke or his realm, unless he has turned to evil, past all belief."

"Will you tell him this openly?"

Paks shook her head. "No. As you say, I don't look like a paladin. I have no clear message for him. I can but be here, and ready to serve his need, when it comes. I think it will be soon."

Kolya stirred in her chair. "I cannot believe you lie. Master Oakhallow bids me trust you — I have reason to trust him. And what I know of your past — by the Tree, Paks, I wish I understood."

"So do I," said Paks.

"And you are not a Girdsman?" asked Kolya again.

"I cannot say. I am not — I cannot be, any longer — under the command of the Marshal-General. But I swore to follow Gird's way of service: that oath I would not break." Could not, after what had happened in the magical fire.

"The Duke will not be pleased with that." Kolya's voice held some emotion Paks could not identify. Satisfaction? Envy? Paks followed a vague hunch.

"Can you tell me what he has against the Girdsmen, Kolya? I know it is something more than happened to me, but I don't know what. Master Oakhallow wouldn't say."

Kolya's lips tightened; then she sighed. "What do you know about the Duke's lady?"

"Not much. Only that he was married, and she died ten or twelve years ago. He blames the Girdsmen, somehow. Did you know her?"

"Yes. We were in the Company at the same time. Before she married the Duke." Kolya sighed again, and stared at the fire. "Paks, we don't speak of her much — he doesn't like it — but I think you should know the story. It might help you understand." She took a deep breath, and her hand clenched and unclenched as she began.

"Her name was Tammarrion Mistiannyi; we all called her Tamar. She was a fighter, one of the very best. Tall, strong, and — " Kolya shot Paks a glance. "Much like you, though her eyes were bluer. She had the same way of moving. She was a Girdsman when she came — most of the Company were, in those days. She tried to convert me, but gently. The whole Company liked her. She was always cheerful, didn't quarrel, worked hard, and — by all the gods, to have her beside you in a fight! She had a temper, and that's when it showed. Her eyes would go very blue, and she'd laugh just a little, and I never knew anyone to lay a blade on her. Not by the time I came, though she had scars to show.

"The Duke was only a few years older than the rest of us. I think any of the men would have bedded her gladly, but she didn't care about it, or about women, either. But the Duke — He fought with the ranks back then: the Company was just the one cohort, a few over a hundred, and they fought side by side often. And he married her, at the end of my first campaign season." Kolya shifted in her chair again, and picked up one of the striped apples. Paks did not interrupt, and finally Kolya went on.

"Things were very different then. The Company so small, and the stronghold more than half earth walls and wooden huts. Tamar never played the lady with us, but worked as hard as ever, the Duke's other self. Together they planned the buildings there, and in the villages, and together they went over the contracts for each season. Not so much in Aarenis, then — the Duke had to garrison the stronghold by the terms of his grant. Those were good years. I'm no Girdsman, but it was a good Company then, and the contracts meant fighting where you had no doubts. They had a Marshal living in the stronghold. He pestered those of us who weren't Girdsmen, but we liked it anyway. You could trust your companions, and do your work without worrying about what kind of work, if you understand what I mean." Paks, remembering the last campaign in Aarenis, understood very well, and nodded.

"Well, then," Kolya went on, "when the children were born — "

"Children? I never knew the Duke had children."

"No one mentions them. They died with her. The elder was a girl, maybe eight when she died — she would have been about your age had she lived. The boy was just three. When they were born, the Duke wanted Tamar to go somewhere safer, but she never would. Of course she didn't fight for awhile each time, but I remember her riding and working out when she was this big — " Kolya gestured to indicate advanced pregnancy. "And as soon as she could get back in armor, she started training again. She began to stay here, with part of the Company, when he took contracts far away, but she was no fine lady sitting at a loom." Something more than respect warmed Kolya's voice.

"Then one year the Marshal-General — not this one, the one before — wanted the Duke to take the entire Company to some war in Aarenis. It had been cleared with the court of Tsaia. The Duke wanted to leave a force with Tamar, or have her come, but she wanted him to take them all, for the glory of Gird. She said the children were too young for a southern campaign, and she'd be safe with the Tsaian militia that were supposed to come for the summer. She said a member of the Duke's household should be on his land, in case something happened to the king. We all knew, by their way with us, that they were fighting — and we knew they were both high-tempered, not that they didn't — " Kolya faltered a moment. "They were as close, Paks, as any man and wife I've ever seen, close as comrades and lovers both. But if anything, she was bolder. Certainly where Gird was concerned. She finally convinced him to take both cohorts. He started south, leaving her with the children and perhaps ten men-at-arms until the miltia came. And the craftsmen, of course, and the steward and servants, and the Marshal. He was no mean fighter himself. Not that it did any good." Kolya got up and moved restlessly around the room for a moment. "Do you want anything to drink?"

Paks was not thirsty, but thought it would ease Kolya to stop for awhile. "Water — that ale was strong."

"Yes. Just a minute." She disappeared to the back again, and returned with a jug. She took two mugs from the dresser and poured into them. "Here."

"Thanks." Paks took a swallow, and shifted in her chair. She wondered if she should say something. Finally Kolya settled back in her seat, after poking the fire up.

"Nobody knows what happened. We think she went out for a ride with the children — maybe hunting. The steward and the Marshal were with her, and a couple of soldiers to help with the children's ponies. They didn't come back at lunch. No one worried, then. After all — five warriors, all mounted — and there hadn't been any trouble for over a year. But they didn't come back by dark. She would have sent a messenger if they'd intended to stay out.

"The sergeant started searching an hour or so before full dark, and didn't find anything. He took torches, and dogs, and they tried to trail through the night, but something got the dogs off scent, and they didn't find anything until the next day. Back up on the moors, north of the stronghold, they found the first body. That was the old steward: he'd been shot full of arrows, and slashed with a knife or sword. Then they found the rest of them. They must have tried to take Tamar alive, because there was a stack of bodies around her and the children. Young Estil had tried to fight, too — she'd already been training with a little practice sword, and Tamar let her carry a dagger. It was bloody to the hilts. She had fallen across her little brother. We don't think they bothered the children's bodies, but Tamar and the Marshal had been stripped and hacked at. Their armor and weapons were still there, in a heap."

Paks had felt her eyes fill as Kolya talked. She could see in her mind the five adults, desperately trying to protect the children, and the little girl — she thought of herself at eight, wrestling with her brothers — defending the boy with her dagger.

"What were they, Kolya, that attacked? Pargunese? Orcs?"

"Orcs and half-orcs, by the bodies. We found twelve dead, and bloodtrails of others. Two more bodies, about a mile away."

"Were you here, then?"

"Yes. I — Estil, the girl, liked to play with me. Tamar had asked me to

753

stay, until the militia came. That day I had gone into the mill — we had no village here then, only the mill — to bring back a load of flour. When I got back that afternoon, the sergeant was just getting worried. We never knew why they had gone north — of all directions, the most dangerous — or why such a large party of orcs had come out in daylight. Something must have drawn them, but we never could find out what." She cleared her throat and took another swallow of water.

"Well, we brought the bodies back, and sent a courier to the Duke. All of us were terrified. You've seen him, when he's really angry — not something you want aimed at you. And then we felt we should have done something — anything — to prevent it. I must have cried every day for a week; I think everyone did. Then the Duke came. Just about what we'd expected: I thought the very ground would smoke where he stepped on it. He asked each of us, of course, where we'd been, and why we hadn't been with her, but it was all very straightforward. When we had talked to him, he said nothing to condemn us. But all that anger went toward the Girdsmen: he blamed the Marshal-General for taking him away with all his troops, and for Tamar's encouragement. It was very . . . difficult." Paks thought it must have been more than that. "He went storming off to Fin Panir, and Vérella. We were afraid he might disband the Company, but he didn't.

"He did start enlarging it, though, and took a contract in Aarenis every year. He wouldn't have a Marshal around, though he never interfered with Girdsmen, and still recruited them. He began to hire mages for healing. He wasn't as choosy with recruits — not taking riffraff, exactly, but not as careful as they had been. In most things he himself didn't change. Had I still both arms, I'd fight for him, and gladly. He is as brave as ever, as fair and just a leader. But — I heard some things about that last year in Aarenis, Paks, that would never have happened if Tamar had been alive. He wouldn't have wanted to do them."

Paks thought of the death of Siniava, and stared at the fire a long time after Kolya stopped speaking. Finally she looked over to see that Kolya's eyes were closed and tears glistened on her cheeks. "Thank you for telling me. It must be hard to speak of, to one who never knew her — "

"But you are so like her!" Kolya interrupted in a hoarse whisper. "When you joined the Company, Stammel saw it at once. He told me, when I came as a witness that time. When you were well, I could see it myself. And he told me what you did, in Aarenis — when you stopped the Duke. Paks, it must have been like hearing Tamar's voice from the Afterworld — that's what Stammel said. No one else could have stopped him. I think that's why the Duke was so furious when the message came from Fin Panir about you. It was like having it happen all over again — "

"But he never said anything — "

"No. Of course not. You're his daughter's age, after all. He wouldn't tell you. But what did he say when he gave you his ring?"

"That if I ever needed or wanted his help, to bring or send it."

"That's what I thought. When he came back, he told us — his officers,

754

the Councils of Duke's East and West — that if you showed up, or the ring showed up, we were to do anything to help you. Anything. Without question. Spend our last copper, if we had to, or kill if you were in danger, and he would make it good. Whatever. That's why Piter wouldn't take your money. He'd give any Duke's man a meal once, but tonight was the ring, and what the Duke said."

Paks blushed. "But Kolya, I'm all right now. I don't need — "

"He couldn't be sure. You aren't carrying a sword. The Duke said you might look like anything: beggar, thief, slave, common laborer, guard — but unless you showed up mounted, in full armor, we were to assume that you needed our help. And that you'd not admit you needed it." Kolya paused, and sighed. "You are going out there after what I've told you?"

"Yes. Tomorrow, unless you have a reason to wait."

"No. Go on. It will bother him that you don't have a sword."

"You said he would hire me — perhaps I'll earn one from him."

"Oh, he'll have you. He's had fever in the stronghold this year."

"Where did he campaign this season?"

"He didn't tell you? No, I suppose he wouldn't. About the time you left the Company, he heard from the Regency Council in Vérella. They'd found out that he had taken the whole garrison south, and they were furious."

Paks was confused, and must have shown it, because Kolya explained.

"He holds this steading under a grant from the crown of Tsaia. He's supposed to strengthen the stronghold — which he's done — and maintain a garrison against any invader. It was a Tsaian outpost before he got it, you see. Anyway, he always had at least fifty fighters here, usually more. But that last year in Aarenis, he pulled everyone out: active or retired, anyone who could swing a sword. So the Regents claimed he'd broken his oath to the crown, and they would have forfeited the grant. Only no one else wanted to come up and fight the orcs, and cross our Duke in the process.

"Arcolin heard part of it — the Duke said his oath to his men came first, and that he'd had no reason to expect trouble. It was the only time in twenty years he'd failed in the slightest part of his oath to the crown. Then before they could forbid him to go south again, he said he was staying in the north. He'd gotten profit enough, and was short of men. So that winter — winter before last — he routed out the orcs nearby, and recruited replacements for the losses in Aarenis, and that summer recruited some more. He had to get rid of many who'd joined in the south. By this spring he was nearly up to strength. He sent one cohort east to Pargun to help man border forts, but he stayed here."

"So he's been here over a year."

"Yes, except for those weeks with you in Fin Panir. It's the longest he's been here since Tamar was killed."

"How is he?"

Kolya looked away. "Oh — well, I suppose. He's kept busy. He hasn't been sick; he trains all the time."

"But what — ?"

"I don't know what. That trouble with the Regents — with the Marshal-General — and I daresay he worries about an heir. We've wondered if he thinks of marrying again." She rolled the apple around the table under her hand. "There's nothing I can name — only the sense of great anger underneath. We worry — the veterans, the old ones — what will happen when he — if he — "

Paks nodded. "I felt some of that anger, the last season in Aarenis — and when he came to Fin Panir. But he won't do anything bad, Kolya, I'm sure of it."

"You! And I have known him how many years? No, I'm sorry. You may know better than I, indeed."

Chapter Eight

In the morning, a weak sun struggled through low scudding clouds. Paks came over the rise south of the stronghold, and saw its massive walls. She noticed a group drilling to the west and wondered if it was recruits, or regulars. As she came nearer, she could see no changes in the stronghold itself. The Duke's colors swirled in the wind. The main gates stood open, as usual in daylight. Paks kept up her steady pace. Her stomach began to clench. Would the gate guards know her? Who would be in the courtyard?

She thought of her first march toward these gates, and how she'd blushed as Stammel marched them in. It was odd to be so nervous still, after all that had happened. Her thumb felt for the Duke's signet, turning it on her finger.

"Ho there! Traveler!" She looked up to see sentries on the wall. She halted. A man appeared in the gate opening. "Come forward and speak for yourself. What's your business here?"

Paks walked forward. She didn't recognize the dark bearded face. "I'm Paksenarrion Dorthansdotter," she said. "I was a member of this Company. I would like an audience with the Duke."

He scowled; Paks decided that he was quite young — perhaps just beyond recruit. "With Duke Phelan? What makes you think you — *who* did you say you were? With this Company?"

"Paksenarrion Dorthansdotter. I was a member of Arcolin's cohort for three years."

His eyes widened. "Paksenarrion — yes — " His glance fell to her hands, and she held out the signet. "Of course. Come with me; the Duke is in council, but I'll send word in at once. Have you eaten?"

"Yes, thank you." She followed him through the gates into the familiar courtyard with the mess hall and infirmary beyond. Someone led a tall horse across the courtyard. Armed men and women in familiar uniforms walked briskly about on their errands. She tried not to gape, and followed her guide to the Duke's Gate. But they ran into Stammel almost at once.

"Paks! By Tir, I'd hardly hoped it was really you!" He grabbed her in a hard hug. "You're coming back to us, I hope."

Paks found herself grinning widely. "I must see the Duke — "

"Of course. Of course. But stay, Paks — don't be going back to Fin Panir — "

757

"Not for awhile, anyway." She pulled away; the young sentry was watching wide-eyed. Stammel grinned at the boy.

"Go on, then — take her in. You won't find another the Duke would rather see." And to Paks, "I'll see you when you come out." She turned to follow the sentry. She could see unasked questions hanging on his tongue. They were halfway across the courtyard when she heard other voices she knew.

"It looks like — "

"By the gods, it is Paks! Paks! Gods blast it — " Paks turned to find Arñe and Vik almost on her. She was buried for an instant in sound and arms; tears rushed from her eyes.

"I knew you'd come. I knew it." Arñe, who rarely got excited, was laughing and crying together. "No matter what they said, I knew — "

More people crowded around. "Wait until Barra hears — " she heard someone say. Volya and Jenits, her old recruits, joined Arñe in another hug. Paks had not expected this, had not realized how much she missed these particular people. She held up her hands, finally, as the questions and comments rained on her. They quieted, as if she were an officer.

"I — I must see the Duke," she said. "First, and then — "

"You'll be back," said Arñe. "You will, won't you?"

"For awhile, yes. It depends on the Duke."

"He'll have you. He always would." Arñe threw back her head and laughed for a moment. "Ah — what a time we'll have. You beginners — you don't know what you've missed. Just wait."

"Arñe — " Paks began, embarrassed.

"Never mind," said Arñe. "Go on. See the Duke. Then we'll hunt orcs together. You haven't forgotten how, I'll wager."

Paks shook her head, and followed the now-bemused sentry through the Duke's Gate.

She had never been in this part of the stronghold before. The inner court was separated from the main one by the back walls of the mess hall, infirmary and one barracks. The other sides were composed of the Duke's own quarters (where the cohort captains also lived, as well as the Duke's servants), the armory, and the storehouses. In the center of the small courtyard a stone bench surrounded a well; a small tree grew out of the pavement nearby. The Duke's residence took up the north and west sides.

At the door another sentry took over from the first one. Paks did not recognize him, either. But as he started to lead her into the hall, Arcolin came down a passage and spoke to her.

"Paks! Is it really you? The Duke will be pleased — "

"Yes, Captain." Paks found herself reverting, in her mind, to the Company private she had been.

"You look well — are you?"

"Yes. Very well."

"Good. Follow me — " He waved the sentry back and led the way upstairs himself, and along a passage on the north wing. "The Duke's in his office — you haven't been up here before, have you?"

"No, sir."

"It's the third door on the right." But he led her all the way. The door stood open; Paks could see, as they neared it, a large room full of light from windows that opened on the court. He stepped in; Paks paused on the threshold.

"My lord, it is Paksenarrion." Paks could see the Duke, sitting at a desk littered with papers. His head came up; his face had hardly changed, but for looking tired. He looked for her, and his grim expression eased as he met her eyes.

"Come in, Paks. Or do you use your full name, now?"

"Thank you, my lord. Either will do." She stepped into the room, and Arcolin went out quietly. The Duke looked her over.

"You look better than the last time I saw you."

"Yes, my lord. I am."

"Come, sit down." He gestured to a chair near the desk and she took it. "You wear no sword," he said. "Have things stayed, then, as they were?"

"No, my lord. I spent the summer in Lyonya, with the rangers. They use bows, mostly. I hadn't money enough for a sword."

"With the rangers?" His face seemed to come alive, then freeze. "Then you could — " He stopped, and she knew what he would not ask.

"My lord, I can fight again, and did. I came to thank you for your help — and for your trust." As she spoke, he stood, and came to her. He stopped a few feet away and looked her up and down.

"It is repaid by seeing you whole again. What can I do for you — besides give you a sword?"

"My lord, I didn't come to beg a sword of you, but a place. If you have need of another soldier, I have need of work."

"You aren't going back to Fin Panir, then?" He looked pleased.

"If I do, I'd like to have my own weapons," said Paks.

"Ha!" He grinned suddenly. "You are better. But I promised you a captaincy, remember."

Paks laughed. "My lord, you are generous beyond measure. But to be honest, I don't think I can stay with the Company forever."

"What then? Fin Panir and the Girdsmen, or something else?"

"I'm not sure. But I will stay a half year with you — perhaps more — if you'll have me. Not as a captain, though. It would not be fitting for me to take high rank from you; there are those here who have earned it."

"None more than you." The Duke glanced down. "No. I see what you mean. And of course I'll be glad to have you. We've had too much fever this past summer. Let's see. Suppose you go back in Arcolin's cohort. Veteran's pay: that should get you a sword by next spring, without question. You are still thinking of paladin, aren't you?" He looked at her shrewdly. Paks nodded. He asked no more about it but went on. "Then you'll need experience leading — but we've plenty of trouble with orcs: you can take squads this winter. And another thing — "

"Yes?"

"Most paladins are drawn from the knightly orders. They've had the chance to learn manners of court and hall. From what I saw last year, you aren't really easy with that yet. True?"

Paks blushed. "Yes, my lord. I've tried to learn — "

"And done well for a sheepfarmer's daughter. I didn't start in a palace either, Paks; now I can dine with kings without worrying about my elbows. That's something we can teach you, too, if you're willing." He paused briefly, scanning her face. "It won't cause trouble with your companions in the Company; it's going to be obvious that you are not an ordinary soldier. If you agree, you'll spend some of your free time in my library, learning history and other things, and with me and the captains discussing politics and strategy. Well?"

Paks was stunned by the offer. "My lord, I — yes. I would like that. I know very little."

"Very well, then: take this order to the quartermaster, and this to Arcolin, and get yourself settled in. Arcolin will arrange your schedule. I want you to dine with us as often as you can, whenever it doesn't interfere with your duties."

"Yes, my lord."

An hour later, Paks had a sword at her side and the maroon tunic of Phelan's Company on her back. Her legs felt cold and exposed again; she knew they looked chalk-white next to the others. Armsmaster Siger, after an admiring look at her longbow, asked for a demonstration.

"Not now, Siger," said Stammel. "We've still got to get her on the rolls."

"This afternoon, then," said Siger. "Fine bow: I hope you've learned to shoot to equal it. And I want to see what fancy strokes they taught you in Fin Panir."

Paks laughed. "Nothing for a short sword, and I haven't handled a blade that much lately. But when I've practiced — "

"Good. Good. I know they teach knight's work, but I always like a new trick."

Before lunch, Paks had a longer interview with Arcolin. He urged her to accept a corporal's position, both because he needed one, and because she would then have more time and opportunity for the extra study the Duke recommended. Paks agreed, wondering meanwhile if her old friends would resent the promotion. They had been glad to see her, but how would they react to all that had happened, and to her being placed over them? She said nothing of this to Arcolin, who was telling her that she already had a reputation with the newer ones — by his tone, a good reputation.

Through the noon meal, Paks talked with Stammel and Devlin about her new duties and the changes in routine from what she remembered. With all three senior cohorts and the recruits in the stronghold together, there were many changes. Then Stammel called the cohort out for weapons practice, and they went to the field together. Siger was already there with her bow, and had set up the targets.

"Now let me see," he said eagerly. Paks strung the bow and chose an arrow. The wind had dropped a little, but she knew her first shaft might miss. She bent the bow smoothly, and released it. She was lucky: Siger grinned delightedly. "Do it again," he said. She placed three more arrows in a pattern one hand could cover, as fast as she could draw the bow. She heard murmurs from those watching. "May I try?" asked Siger.

"Of course," she said. "It is sized for me, though."

"De, it's a strong pull." Siger eased it back from a half-draw. "You're right, it's very long for someone my height. I'll leave it to you. But let's see your bladework."

"Certainly." Paks unstrung her bow and started toward the targets to retrieve the arrows.

"Don't bother," said Siger. "Ho! Sim! Go fetch those arrows." A lanky youth in recruit brown jogged toward the targets. "Put your bow over here — " He nodded to a bowrack.

Paks set her bow in the rack and returned to the area Siger had cleared for them. He was ready, sword in hand. "Do you want a banda?" he asked.

"Against you? Always." Paks spotted the pile of bandas and shrugged her way into one. She noticed Arcolin standing behind a double row of onlookers. Siger noticed the onlookers.

"By Tir, will you stand around like cows at a fence row? You want to see Paks fight? You'll be facing her yourselves, soon enough. Get on, now, to your own drill, or I'll sore the ribs of the lot of you. Go on!" The others drew away reluctantly, grouping for their own drill. Paks felt a tingle of apprehension. It had been long indeed since she used a short sword, or had drilled as Siger would drill. She drew the sword and stepped forward.

With Siger's first stroke, it all came back. The first stirring of joy she had felt that last night with the Kuakgan woke and surged up her sword arm. She felt she was hardly touching the ground. They stayed with the drill briefly, as Siger increased the pace. Then he shifted to more difficult maneuvers. Paks found that her skill — her instincts — her delight had all returned. Siger got no touches on her for some time. Then with a clever twist he turned her blade and tapped her sharply on the arm. He danced back, grinning.

"I'd almost thought you beyond me, girl." Paks could hear effort in his voice. Was Siger — Siger the tireless — getting tired? She wondered if it were a trick, and pressed her attack carefully.

"You should be beyond me," she said cheerfully. "You started first."

"Ah, but — " He grinned again as he narrowly countered one of her strokes. "But I'm older, now, and slow — " This with a lightning thrust that Paks took on the banda. "You're lucky you wore that," he commented.

"A shield would help, too," said Paks. "Old, indeed. Slow as an adder's tongue, you are." She tried the trick she'd used on him once in Aarenis, but he remembered the counter.

"Your old friend Vik has kept me in practice for that one," he said. Paks tried another, and this time slipped past his guard to rap his shoulder. "Aah!" he cried. "Well enough. Well enough. Let's see what you recall of

761

formation work — we're not all knights, here." He stepped back and lowered his sword. Paks looked around. Despite their attempts to look busy, it was obvious that most of the cohort had been watching.

For some days, Paks was busy and happy, relaxing into the familiar old friendships of her years in the Company. Her duties as corporal kept her scurrying from place to place, and she had forgotten a surprising amount of the formation drills. And in every spare minute, her old friends clustered around asking questions and telling tales. Clearly they did not mind her promotion — in fact, seemed surprised that she was only a corporal. She herself had more questions than tales. She learned that Peska, junior captain to Dorrin in Aarenis that last year, had left the Company as soon as they came north. Instead of an outsider, the Duke's senior squire had taken over as junior captain: first Jori, whom Paks remembered from Aarenis, and now Selfer. Jori had gone for training with the Knights of Falk. Kessim, who had been little more than a boy when Paks knew him, was now the Duke's only squire.

Paks thought about that arrangement and frowned. "That still leaves two cohorts without a backup captain — or the recruits without one."

"Valichi's back with recruits," said Kefer. "You're right, really. Four captains for three cohorts, and Pont is seconding Cracolnya again. But we're staying together, and in one place — we don't really need the others — "

"Gods grant they don't get the fever, any of them. You know, Kef, it would be difficult if Arcolin or Dorrin got sick. Or took an orc arrow." Stammel yawned; it was late.

"But the Duke's never had trouble with fever," she said one morning. "And here, in the north — "

"I know." Vik nodded. "It is odd. The surgeons think it may be that with so many of us — though we clean out the jacks twice a season now — "

"It's not only that," put in Stammel. "We're seeing a lot more trade, now — more people coming in from Vérella and such. They might be bringing it."

"Hmm." Paks thought back to the lectures in Fin Panir on fortifications and water supplies. Surely nothing was wrong in the design — but she thought she'd look for herself.

"Besides, we may be getting something from all the orcs around." Devlin reached across her for another hunk of bread. "Tir knows there's enough of them, the filthy beasts."

"Where are they coming from?"

"Out of the very stone, for all we can tell." Stammel frowned. "You won't know about this, Paks, but off to the northeast is a mess of caves and passages that were full of orcs when the Duke took this grant. The Lairs, it was called, and that's where the trouble started. Thing is, it'd take five Companies the size of this one to find and clear all the caves. And they've been striking west of here — we wonder if they have another complex of caves somewhere west."

"What have you done?"

"Everything the captains can think of. Random patrols? Fine, but some of them are out three days without spotting an orc, and others run into bunches too big to tangle with. Pursuit of each band spotted? The last ones we tried that with took off straight north up onto the moors and kept going. Setting ambushes in likely spots? Again, sometimes a patrol's out for days without any orcs, and another time it's nearly wiped out. Perimeter control? We haven't enough for that, if we're going to hold the two villages, the stronghold, and protect the road at all."

Paks couldn't think of anything else herself.

"So far, they're under control — despite some losses, the crops are still going in and being harvested, and the villages haven't been burned. But they're keeping us busy, day after day. We can't tell exactly what they're after, either. Sometimes it seems they're just asking for a fight. They haven't tried a full-scale assault on the stronghold or the villages — of course that would be stupid of them."

"What I think — " Stammel stopped, and looked around. Most of the others had left, and he glared at Vik until the redhead shrugged and went out. That left Devlin, Paks, and Stammel at that table. "What I think," Stammel began again in a quiet voice, "is the Duke's not keeping his mind on it. That sister of Venner's — "

"I don't believe he'll marry her," said Devlin. "I can't — "

Stammel shook his head. "He's thinking of heirs, now. At his age, if he's to sire his own, it's time he was at it. I don't like her any more than you do, Dev, but she's the only woman around who — "

"I don't understand," said Paks. "You say the Duke is planning to marry? I thought Kolya said he never would, after — " She stopped before saying the name.

"That's what I would have said. But these past two years, staying up here — he's started thinking, you see, what will happen when he's old. I know he's thought of naming one of the Halveric sons his heir. But that might not sit well with the court, they being Lyonyan. He's not one to take a young wife, not now. And this sister of Venner's — she's handsome enough, and knows her way with men — "

"She's a widow," put in Devlin. "So it's said. She came up here to get Venner's help with the estate."

"What does she look like?" asked Paks. "Does she ever come out of his courtyard?"

"She's — well, as I said, handsome. Reddish hair. She rides out with Venner every now and then — "

"Goes to the Red Fox with him," added Devlin. "Piter's told me that. They take a private room and have dinner."

Paks thought back to the woman and man she'd seen the first night. She could not imagine the Duke marrying someone like that.

"It's not our business," said Stammel, but he sounded unconvinced. "If the Duke wants her — "

"It's more whether she wants him. Any woman like that would: he's rich, well-known, with large landholdings — "

763

"I still can't believe it," said Paks.

"Well, we can hope. I only wish he'd either do it or not, and pay more attention to these orcs. I can't believe they're causing all this trouble after years of peace without something else going on."

"If we had a paladin here —" began Devlin, then looked quickly at Paks and flushed. "Sorry, Paks. I didn't think —"

She shook her head. "That's all right." She wasn't ready to claim or demonstrate her gifts. "You're thinking of being able to find a source of evil?"

"Yes. I agree with Stammel that something must have stirred the tribes. What if it's a cover for something else? You had to do with greater evils in Kolobia — what if something like that is out there?"

As the days passed, Paks had her own encounters with orcs, as frustrating and inconclusive as the others had described. What, she wondered to herself, was a paladin supposed to do in a situation like this? It wasn't that the soldiers were unwilling to fight, or were badly commanded. She could think of nothing to do that had not been tried. She knew that Stammel, at least, expected more of her, some miraculous intervention that would solve the mystery of the orcs' interest in the Duke's lands that year, and eliminate them. She prodded her mind, trying to force the vague feeling she assumed came from the gods into something more direct and definite. If she was supposed to be there, why? For what purpose? What sort of danger or evil should she be looking for? But all she found inside was the certainty that she should be where she was, doing what she was doing. And that seemed to accomplish nothing.

Chapter Nine

Paks had hardly seen the Duke in the days since her first interview. Now, preparing to enter the Duke's Court, she had time to wonder what she would find. Would it be like dinner with the Marshal-General? Or the candidates' hall in Fin Panir? She found she had no idea what the Duke and his captains did: what they wore, what they ate, how they talked. Did he have a minstrel? And it seemed even stranger to be coming to his table in her uniform — she shook that feeling away. Simple nervousness, no doubt.

At the door, the sentry nodded. She knew him: a veteran in Cracolnya's cohort. She had another attack of nervousness inside the hall, as she wondered which way to turn.

"Paks? Over here." Dorrin beckoned from the left, a wide passage. Paks turned that way, and came into an oblong room with a large table in the center. "We eat here, and it's also a conference room." Now that Paks knew what to look for, the emblem of Falk that Dorrin wore was plain to see: the tiny ruby glittered in the lamplight. "You're early," Dorrin went on. "Cracolnya's still out on a patrol. Pont won't be here tonight. Arcolin's upstairs with the Duke, and Val's settling the recruits." She looked closely at Paks. "How do you like being back?"

"Very much, Captain." Paks had never had much to do with Dorrin. She was next in seniority after Arcolin; Paks wondered if she had known Tamar. She looked around the room. The table was already set: plates and the two-pronged forks she'd learned to use in Fin Panir were laid before each chair. Goblets of pale blue swirled glass — tall flagons to match — squat mugs for the ale that would follow the meal. Loaves of bread were already on the table, too, as were dishes of salt and the condiments the Duke had grown used to in Aarenis. On one wall were weapons: a gilded battle-ax (Paks wondered at that — she had never seen the Duke use one), a slender sword with a green jewel in the hilt, two curved blades with inlaid runes, in blue sea-stone, on the broad blades, and a notched black blade that made Paks shudder to look at it.

"You should know who else may be at dinner with us. The Duke's surgeons sometimes — you may remember Visanior and Simmitt. Master Vetrifuge, the mage, would be with us, but he's visiting another mage down near Vérella for a few weeks. Kessim, of course. And the Duke's steward: did you know Venneristimon when you were here before?"

"No, Captain."

"Not surprising. He has nothing to do with the recruits. Well, he sits with us, many times. His sister, too, has been visiting here: she's a widow, and he's helping her with her estates. So it's been explained." By a slight chill in this last phrase, Paks guessed that Dorrin didn't like the steward's sister. She wondered if anyone did, remembering Stammel and Devlin.

"Paks. Good, you're here." Arcolin and Valichi came in together. Paks realized suddenly that none of the captains were wearing swords. Arcolin must have noticed her quick look at each hip. "We don't wear swords in the hall," he said quietly. "The Duke sometimes has visitors he would not wish armed at his table."

"But you — " began Paks.

"They cannot object if we do not wear them."

"I see."

"We have nothing to fear from each other," he went on. Paks felt a sudden surge of unease, as if the floor dipped slightly. She almost shook her head to clear it, then looked around. At the door, the Duke stood beside a red-haired woman in a blue gown. She had her hand on his arm, and her body seemed to lean toward him. Paks recognized her at once: the woman she had seen in the inn the first night she returned. Behind them was the slight form of Kessim, the Duke's squire on duty. Arcolin murmured, "That's Venner's sister — Lady Arvys Terrostin."

The Duke led the lady in. She smiled and spoke to all the captains, and to Paks when she was introduced.

"Paksenarrion? What an unusual name, my dear. Kieri has told me so much about you — I could be jealous, if I had any right to be — " She extended a soft hand, and Paks took it, aware of her own rough palm. More than that, she was shaken with revulsion. She fought to conceal it. However much she disliked this woman, she was the Duke's guest. But Dorrin turned the conversation, speaking to Paks.

"Is it a family name, Paks? I remember wondering about that — "

"My great-aunt was named Paksenarrion. I don't know for whom, but I was named for her." Paks wiped her hand on her tunic; she felt dirty.

"Ah. And I was named for my father's grandmother. It was supposed to honor her, but when I turned soldier the family was furious and changed her name in the family records." Dorrin smiled. "They sent me the one letter, to be sure I knew it, and that's all I've ever heard." Paks had never thought of any of the captains starting out.

"Eh, my lord — sorry I'm late — " Cracolnya, in the doorway, unwrapped his swordbelt and tossed it at a servant in the passage outside.

"What did you find?" asked the Duke.

"What we've found so far." Cracolnya stumped over to the table, obviously stiff from the saddle, and poured himself a glass of wine. His mail jingled faintly as he moved. He drank the wine down. "They made for the Lairs again — a band of forty or so. We killed fifteen, and wounded a few, but we couldn't catch them before they went underground."

"I'm sure you tried very hard," put in Lady Arvys. For the barest instant everyone looked at her. Then they all moved to find a seat at the table.

"We're not formal," said Valichi, the recruit captain. "Not unless we have visitors from outside. Just find a place somewhere — " Paks waited until the others had sorted themselves, and took a seat at the far end of the table from the Duke. She noted that Lady Arvys sat on the Duke's left, and Master Simmitt, one of the dark-robed surgeons, was on his right. Cracolnya, Valichi, and Visanior, the other surgeon, took the left side of the table, while Arcolin, Dorrin, and the Duke's steward (who entered at the last minute) took the right side. Kessim sat beside Paks. Servants brought in platters of food, and the meal began. Paks ate quietly, sharply aware of something wrong, but unable to locate it. She remembered feeling like this in the inn; she wondered if it was the red-haired woman. She looked at the faces, trying to pick out the woman's escort that night. Around her the talk was of orcs and their raids.

"After so many quiet years, I simply can't understand it." Valichi gestured with his wine glass. "I must have missed something, staying up here with recruits — somehow I let them build up — but I swear to you, my lord, we had no trouble. No trouble at all."

"I believe you." The Duke's eyes were hooded. "I can only imagine that they are moved by some power — " He paused as Lady Arvys's hand rested lightly on his arm for a moment. She murmured something low into his ear. His face relaxed into a smile, and he shook his head. "Well," he said in a milder tone, "we need not mar our meal with such talk. Tir knows we've covered the same ground before. Has anyone a lighter tale, to sweeten the evening?" Paks saw the others' eyes shift sideways from face to face. She herself had never imagined the Duke being deflected from a serious concern by anyone, let alone someone like Lady Arvys. Meanwhile Simmitt had begun talking of rumors from Lyonya: the king's illness, and turmoil among the heirs. The lady listened eagerly.

"Did you hear anything about Lord Penninalt?" she asked, when Simmitt paused.

"No, lady, not then. Did you know him?"

"Yes, indeed. A fine man. My late husband held his lands from Lord Penninalt, and we went every year to the Firsting Feast." She turned to the Duke. "He is not so tall as you, my lord, or as famous in battle, but a brave man nonetheless."

"You need not flatter me," said the Duke, but he seemed not displeased.

Paks shivered. She looked up to find Venneristimon, diagonally across the table, staring at her.

"Are you quite well, Paks?" he asked. His tone was gentle and concerned, but it rasped on her like a file on bare flesh.

"Yes," she said shortly. Something moved behind his eyes, and he passed a flagon of a different wine down the table.

"Here — try this. Perhaps it will help." Now the others were looking at her, curious. Paks poured the wine — white this time — into her glass. She didn't want it, but did not want to make a fuss, either.

"I'm fine," she said. She passed the flagon back, and speared another sliver of roast mutton. She drenched it in gravy, and stuffed it quickly in her mouth. The others turned back to their own plates. When she glanced up again, Venner was still watching her sideways. His mouth stiffened when she met his eyes. She felt her heart begin to pound; her skin tingled. The lady and Simmitt talked on, idle gossip of court society and politics. Paks looked back at her plate. She had nearly cleaned it, and the dishes on the table were almost empty. She reached for the last redroots on the platter.

"Still hungry, Paks?" The lady's voice, though warm and friendly, had the same effect on Paks as Venner's. "I suppose you work so much harder — "

Paks felt her face go hot. She had not realized the others were through. Her stomach clenched, but Val was answering.

"All soldiers learn to eat when they can, lady." She glanced over to find him cutting himself another slice of mutton. "Paks is not one to talk when she has nothing to say."

"I didn't mean to upset you," said the lady, smiling down the table. "Paks, do say you forgive me. . . . "

Paks's mouth was dry as dust. She took a deliberate sip of the white wine, and said, "It's not for me to forgive, lady; you meant no offense." The wine seemed to go straight to her head; her vision blurred. As if she looked through smoke, she peered up the table and met Lady Arvys's eyes. They changed from green to flat black as she looked. Paks felt the jolt in her head; she looked toward Venner as if someone pulled her head on a string. He was watching her, lips folded under at the corners, like someone satisfied but wary. Her sense of wrong seemed to grab her whole body and shake it. Half-stupified by the wine (how could one swallow be so strong?) she looked from one face to the other. Of course. *Venner* had been her escort. Even so, what was happening?

She might have sat there longer, but Venner spoke. "Ah . . . do you find the wine too strong for you, Paks? Are you still feeling ill?"

A flicker of anger touched her, and with it a warning. The anger, too, was wrong. It felt alien, as if it came from someone else. She reached deep inside for her own sense of self, and found not only that but a call for guidance. Her tongue felt clumsy, but she formed the words: "In the High Lord's name — "

Venner's face contracted; black malice leaped from his eyes. At once the hall was plunged into darkness. Stinking lamp smoke flavored a cold wind that scoured the room. Without thought Paks asked light, and found herself lined with glowing brilliance. She leaped up, looking for Venner. She could hear the scrape of chairs on the floor, the exclamations of the others — and a curse from Venner's sister. The Duke gasped; she knew without looking that he'd been wounded somehow. At Venner's end of the table, nothing could be seen but a whirl of darkness.

"You fool," said his voice out of that darkness. "You merely make yourself a target." Something struck at her, a force like a thrown javelin. She staggered a little, but the light repelled it. She looked at the captains: they sat sprawled in their chairs, eyes glittering in the spell-light, but unmoving. "They won't help you," Venner went on. "They can't. And you are unarmed, but I — " She saw the darkness move to the wall, saw it engulf the terrible notched blade she'd seen there. "While *she* takes care of the Duke, I will kill you with this — as I killed before — and again no one will know. When I let these captains free, it will seem that you went wild — as Stephi did before you — and killed the Duke, while I tried to save his life."

Paks was already moving, clearing herself of the chair. She had picked up a bronze platter — the largest thing on the table — and looked now to the walls for a weapon of her own. She was nearly too late. Venner had taken more than the notched sword: out of the darkness the battleaxe whirled at her. She flung out the platter, and it folded around the axe, slowing it and spoiling the blow. She had her dagger in hand now — far too short against an unseen opponent. The ragged edge of Venner's sword caught the dagger and nearly took it out of her hand. She jumped back.

"You can't escape," his voice said, out of the blackness. "You — "

Paks saw a glow on one wall and leaped for it. The notched blade clattered against the wall just behind her. But she had a sword in her hand — the sword with the green stone. Its blade glowed blue as she took it. Before she could turn, Venner struck again. She felt the black sword open a gash along her side; she tucked and rolled away, and came up ready to fight.

Now she could sense, within the darkness, a core — more like the skeleton of a man than a man entire. One thin arm held the dark blade; the other held a dagger almost half as long. Paks thrust at the dark blade. Her own sword rang along it. Venner countered, stabbing with the dagger. Paks swept it aside, and attacked vigorously, beating him back and back.

"You can't see me!" screamed Venner. "You can't — "

But she could. Dark within dark, his shape grew clearer as they fought. Suddenly the dark was gone, as if Venner had dropped a black cloak. Paks stared, uncertain. He had disappeared; she could see the wall and floor where he should be. A blade came out of nowhere to strike her arm; she felt rather than saw the flicker of movement and managed to counter it. Now she sensed him as a troubling thickness in the air, a nearly transparent glimmer, barely visible in her own brilliant spell-light. She kept after him. The sword she held seemed to move almost of its own will, weightless and perfectly balanced in her hand. Venner retreated again, toward the head of the table. Paks followed. She had not expected the Duke's steward to be much of a swordsman — she hadn't thought of it at all — but he was skillful.

Venner swept the table suddenly with his left arm, sent food and dishes flying between them. Paks slipped on a greasy hunk of mutton. Venner stabbed wildly with the sword. She rolled aside and let the thrust pass. Her sword caught him in the ribs; she heard a rasping gurgle, and he was visible, hand held against his side. Paks lunged at him. He dropped the sword, and dodged. While she was still off balance, he grappled with her, trying to rake her with the dagger. She could see the brown stain along it, surely poison.

"You stinking kellich!" he snarled. "You Girdish slut! You'll die the same as she did, and Achrya will revel in this hall — "

Paks could not use her sword in close; she dropped it and dug her strong fingers into his wrist. Red froth bubbled from his mouth as they wrestled on the floor. He was surprisingly strong.

"Arvys!" he cried suddenly. "Arvys! Help me!" Paks heard noise around the room — chairs and boots scraping on the stone, voices — but she was too busy to listen. Venner had both hands on the dagger hilt, and she had to use both hands to hold it off. "Achrya," he said viciously, glaring at Paks. "You found before you could not stand against her. She will bind you in burning webs forever, you Gird's dog — "

"By the High Lord," said Paks suddenly, "neither you nor Achrya will prosper here, Venner. His is the power, and Gird gave the blessing — "

"You will *die*," repeated Venner. "All in this hall — and she will reward me, as she did before — " But he was weakening, and Paks managed to force him back. She could feel the sinews in his wrist slackening. She closed her own fingers tighter, and all at once his hand sagged open, releasing the dagger. It clattered on the floor. Paks kicked it far aside, and shifted one hand from Venner's left wrist to her own dagger, dropped nearby.

"Now," she said, "we will hear more of this — "

"I spit at you, Gird's dog. I laugh — " But he was choking, and he sagged heavily under her hands.

"Paks! Hold!" Arcolin's voice. She held her dagger to Venner's throat, and waited. "What's — "

"The Duke!" Master Simmitt, this time. "By the gods — "

"He's dead — or dying — " Arvys's voice was savage. "And Achrya will have his soul — and *yours* — " she broke off in a scream.

"Not yet," said Cracolnya. "Don't you know you can't knife a man in mail?" Paks's attention was diverted for an instant. Venner surged up against her hold; without thinking she slammed her hand down. Her dagger ripped his throat, and he died.

She scrambled up to see what else had happened. Shadows fled before her spell-light. Simmitt leaned over the Duke, who was slumped in his seat. On the other side, Cracolnya held Arvys, her arms twisted behind her.

"Light," snapped the surgeon. "Come here, Paks, if that's you making a light." She came around the table. She saw Dorrin working with flint and steel to relight the lamps. The Duke's face was gray; a slow pulse beat in his neck. He seemed to gasp for breath. Visanior too had reached the Duke's seat; the two surgeons maneuvered him from the chair to the tabletop. Simmitt slit his tunic and spread it. There on the left side was a narrow wound — Paks glanced at Arvys and saw the sheath of a small dagger dangling from her wrist.

"That's close — " commented Visanior.

"Poison, or in the heart?" Simmitt bent close to listen to the Duke's heart.

"Poison, and close to it." Visanior turned away. "I've a few drops of potion in my quarters —"

"Too late," hissed Arvys. "You won't save him — or yourselves. Nothing you've got will touch that — and your precious Duke, as you call him, will never take his rightful seat —" Cracolnya tightened his hold, and she gasped.

Paks reached out to touch the Duke's shoulder.

"Get back, Paks — you're no surgeon, and I don't have time —"

"Let her." Dorrin brought a lamp near, its light golden next to the white spell-light. "She alone saw Venner's nature; she alone could free herself to fight him. Perhaps —" She looked at Paks, her own hand going to the tiny Falkian symbol at her throat. "Perhaps you learned more than we knew, is that so?"

Paks felt a pressure in her head, and could not answer. She only knew she had to touch the Duke — had to call what powers she could name. As she laid her hand on his shoulder, the spell-light dimmed except along that arm. She closed her eyes against it: she had no time to study what was happening.

Touching the Duke was like laying her hand on the skin of running water: she felt a faint resistance, a surface tension, and a strong sense of moving power underneath. Without realizing it, she brought her other hand to his other shoulder. She felt within herself the same moving power that she sensed in the Duke, although in her it ran swifter, lighter. She tried to bring the two powers together.

At first it seemed that the surface between them thickened, resisting. The Duke's rhythm slowed and cooled, as if some moving liquid stiffened into stone. But her plea to the High Lord and Gird brought a vision of movement, of sinking through the surface as a hand sinks in water. She let herself drift deeper. In that thicker substance, that cooling stream, she loosed her own fiery essence, the flames that had danced deep within since the night of the Kuakgan's magic fire.

Slowly the Duke responded. Whatever the flow might be, it flowed more swiftly — it moved lightly on its way, with returning joy. Paks followed the flow, to find a source of stagnation — some evil essence. She felt herself touch it, and it dissolved, running away, overtaken by her flame, and then gone. With that, the Duke's body swung back to its own balance. She felt the restored health, and the rejection, at the same instant, and pulled herself back into her own body just ahead of it.

His eyes were open. Blank for a moment, then fully aware: startled and intent all at once. Paks stepped back, shaken by her gift. Simmitt stared at her. They all did. The room's light was golden from lamps; her spell-light had disappeared.

"What — ?" The Duke had his head up now, raking the room with his glance. His hand lay over his ribs, where the dagger had gone in.

"My lord, it was Venner —"

"This so-called lady —"

771

"Paks was the only one who could — "

"Quiet." Arcolin's voice cut through them, and brought order. "Cracolnya, Valichi — guard her: nothing else. My lord Duke, it seems your steward was a traitor of some sort. Paks has killed him. The rest of us were somehow spellbound, unable to move, though we heard enough. Kessim is dead. And that — " he paused and glared at Arvys.

"She stabbed me," said the Duke calmly. "I remember that. Some kind of argument, and then darkness, and then I felt a blade in my side." He sat up on the edge of the table, and looked down at the blood that streaked his skin and clothes. "Heh. No mark now. Who had the healing potion so handy?" He looked at Visanior and Simmitt.

"Not us, my lord. Paksenarrion."

"You heal, as well as fight?" The Duke looked at Paks. She met his eyes.

"With the High Lord's permission, my lord, I have been able to. Sometimes."

He looked at Arvys, and his face hardened. "You," he said, and stopped. "You — will you say why? You were willing, you said, to share my name — why kill, then?"

She said nothing until Cracolnya shifted behind her, then gasped. "You — petty, base-born lout! Duke, you call yourself — that's not the title you *should* bear. I was willing to share your name, as long as it served my Lady's purpose. But you'd have had a blade in your heart someday, as you still shall."

He raised an eyebrow. "Your Lady? And who is that? Is the Queen that angry with me?"

She laughed, a harsh, forced laughter. "Queen! What do you know of queens, who call a mortal human queen? When you see her webs around you, and feel her poison, who has enmeshed those far higher than humans, then you will know a queen. I speak of the webmistress Achrya, whose power no man can withstand."

"And yet I live, and you are captive. Was Venneristimon also her agent?"

"Why should I answer you?"

"Because your mistress is far away, and I am here. You may wish an easy death, though you would deal a hard one."

"Kill as you please," she answered. "Whatever you do, my Lady will avenge me, and him, and give you endless torment."

"I doubt that." The Duke looked among the litter of things swept to the floor and picked up a small narrow-bladed dagger, hardly as long as his hand. "This is yours, is it not? Would you wish to taste your own brew?"

"As you will." She seemed to droop in Cracolnya's arms; Paks and the others stared, surprised at her. Then Paks gasped as her face changed, shifting from the fair-skinned soft curves she had shown to something older and more perilous. Their cries warned Cracolnya, who gripped more tightly as she shriveled in his hold, her red-gold hair turning gray and her rounded limbs wiry and gnarled. She struggled; Valichi moved to help Cracolnya. Paks hunted on the floor for the sword she had dropped, and scooped it up.

772

By the time the transformation was complete, and Cracolnya held a wizened muscular hag instead of an attractive young widow, she had the tip of that sword at the hag's throat.

"Here's something you will like less well," said Paks. "An elf-blade."

"You farm-bred brat!" Her voice, as a hag, chilled the blood. "You saved your precious Duke, eh? Did you? And you will take him to his appointed end, I daresay. Do you think he'll thank you for that? When he dies in the bed *you* make for him?" Her head turned, and more than one in the room flinched from her vicious eyes. "Tell her, Duke Phelan, how you come by your name. Tell her what happened to the last yellow-haired girl to hold that sword." Her voice shrilled higher. "Or shall I? Shall I tell her how the thriband knew where your wife and children would ride that day? And who suggested that trail, where the wildflowers bloomed? He is safe from your wrath, mighty Duke, but your children will never return." She laughed, a hideous laugh. "You, Duke Kieri Phelan — no, let us use it all — Kieri *Artfiel* Phelan — you harbored that woodworm and trusted it as your pet. Your wife it was who suggested he be assistant to the steward — and then — "

Paks pushed the blade gently on the hag's skin. "Be still. You have nothing worth listening to."

"Have I not? You are eager to kill, little peasant girl. Little runaway daughter of a sheepherder — how many times have you run away? Do you guess that I can tell them? The Duke doesn't know the worst, does he? The men in Seameadow? The time you ran from the sheepdog — not even a wolf — in Arnbow?" She stopped, and wheezed a moment. Then: "I know many things that you would be better knowing — and him, too — before he trusts you — " and she stopped and clamped her lips together.

"Ward of Falk," murmured Dorrin, behind them. "Against an evil tongue."

"In the High Lord's name," said Paks. The hag's eyes glittered but she said nothing.

The Duke had come near, and stood looking from one to another. "When one stabs, and another heals," he said, "I know which to trust."

"You! You are no true duke, and she will take you to your end, if you are unfortunate enough not to meet another."

"I'll chance that. Paks, you had scruples before about such things: how should she be killed?"

Paks did not look away from the point of her blade. "Quickly, my lord, as may be."

"I'll save you the trouble," gasped the hag, and she lunged forward, managing to scrape her arm on the dagger the Duke still held. Almost at once she sagged.

"I don't believe it," said Cracolnya. "Paks — or Val — finish her."

Paks ran the sword quickly into her chest, feeling between the ribs for her heart. The limp form in Cracolnya's hold shuddered again, this time shifting from that of a hag to no human shape at all: a great belly swelling below, bursting out of the blue gown Suliya had worn, the upper body falling in to become a hard casing that extended suddenly into more legs. Cracolnya lurched back, loosing his hold. The thing was free, hampered only slightly by the remnants of clothes. The head — no longer human at all — turned a row of emerald eyes on Paks; fangs dripped. Paks alone was able to move; she hardly saw what was happening before her arm went up and a long stroke took off that terrible head. The body twitched; gouts of sticky fluid spurted from the barely formed spinnerets on the belly, but did not reach anyone.

"Gods above," muttered Cracolnya. "What is *that*? A spider demon?"

"A high servant of Achrya," said Paks, watching the body on the floor. "They have that power, to change to her form at will."

"Is *that* what you faced in Kolobia?" asked Arcolin. "Tir's gut, I couldn't — " He stopped, choking.

The Duke himself was white. "Paksenarrion, again — you have gone far beyond our thanks — " He shook himself like a wet dog, and looked around the room. "Captains, we must know what all this means, but for now we must be sure where we are. If I understood any of that — if any of it can be believed — this stronghold is in danger, even with them dead. We'll double the watch. Arcolin, you have been here since we built the place: take some of the older veterans, who know it as well, and start looking for — " He stopped, and rubbed his hand through his hair. "I don't know what, but anything out of ordinary. Dorrin, are there any of the soldiers from Aarenis that still worry you?"

Dorrin thought a moment. "Not in my cohort, my lord. That Kerin fellow, in Arcolin's — "

"Arcolin, turn him out." Arcolin nodded. "Any more, Dorrin?"

"No, my lord."

"See to it, then. About the house servants — "

"And why haven't they come in?" Valichi looked around, worried.

"I don't know. Venner hired them; I don't know if they are innocent or his agents. Bring in a squad — no, two — and we'll go through this end as well. Paks — " he looked at her again, and his eyes dropped to the sword in her hand. "By the — you've got *her* sword!"

"My lord?" Paks looked at the sword in her hand.

"Tammarrion's — my — my wife's — "

"I'm sorry," said Paks. "I didn't know — it was the only one I could reach — "

He shook his head. "You used it well. I do not regret that. But no one has wielded it since she — " He took a long breath and went on. "Paks, you and Val stay with me here — you surgeons, as well. We'll do what we can for Kessim. Cracolnya, take a look in the passage — if we must fight our way out — "

Cracolnya stepped to the door, opened it slightly, and looked out. "Nothing this way, my lord. Let me call the sentry from the door."

"I think not. He's better where he is. Paks — " Arcolin and the Duke leaned over Kessim's slumped form; he had been struck by the battleaxe when Paks deflected the blow from herself. His skull had been crumpled by the blow, and he was clearly dead. The Duke looked up. "Damn and blast that witch! This lad had no chance at all. A fine squire, and would have made a fine man, but for this."

Paks felt a surge of guilt — if she had not thrown that blow aside — she had never thought of Kessim sitting there unable to move — but the Duke forestalled her before she could speak.

"If you hadn't, Paks, we'd all be dead. I certainly would, and you, and I can't imagine the rest would be let live long. Don't think of blaming yourself. Now — "

"My lord, let me check the kitchen entrance." Paks had moved to the other door in the room, from which the servants had brought in the food. She opened the door and looked. This passage was narrower than the front one. She could smell cooked food and smoke from the left; the passage was empty. She shut the door again, and pulled a chair against it. "No one in sight," she reported.

"Good," said the Duke. "Let's arm ourselves, then, captains, and get started. Paks, keep that blade for now — until the Company is roused."

The senior cohort captains left, Cracolnya returning in a few minutes with the Duke's sword and mail. "I told the sentry we'd had a small problem with the steward," he said. "He'll stop any servants from leaving by that door, at least. He heard nothing, by the way. Perhaps Venner's magic kept any of that from getting out, as well as kept us still. Dorrin's squads will be here shortly. What shall we do with the bodies?"

The Duke, struggling into his mail shirt, did not reply until he had settled his sword belt to his satisfaction. "If I knew certainly that Venner was human, I would know — as it is, I don't know whether to burn, bury, or dismember it. Do you, Paks?"

"No, my lord. The shape-changing servants must be beheaded, for they can shift the location of the heart with the change of shape. But Venner — I believe this body is dead, but I don't know what powers he may still have."

She felt within for any warning, and found nothing but distaste. "I feel nothing wrong, my lord, as I felt before — "

"Before?" The Duke's eyebrows went up. "When? Before dinner — no. Not yet. When we're secure, then we'll talk about it. Safe or not, I don't want this mess in my dining hall — we'll take them out — clear outside the stronghold, and just in case we'll behead Venner's corpse as well. Kessim can lie in the other hall, until morning. We'll hold his service tomorrow, and display the others to the troops, so they'll know what's happened." Then a commotion at the door — Dorrin with two squads, eyes wide but disciplined.

"Gather the servants," the Duke told her. "Don't tell them what happened, and don't hurt them — they may well be innocent — but guard them well."

Chapter Ten

By the start of the third watch that night, the stronghold was in a very
different mood. The servants Venner had hired over the years were huddled in one of the third floor storage rooms, guarded by Dorrin's soldiers.
They were clearly confused and frightened. Paks, on the pretext of bringing Dorrin messages from the Duke, had wandered among them. None
triggered her warnings of evil, and the Duke now believed them to be innocent. But he was taking no chances, and they remained under guard for
the next day and a half. Kessim's shrouded body lay in state in one of the
reception rooms, with an honor guard from all three cohorts.

Arcolin and the oldest veterans prowled the stronghold, looking for any
signs of hidden weakness. Some they had already found, in the Duke's
quarters. "I didn't build it this way," muttered an old carpenter, as he pried
a board loose in the back of a closet in the Duke's sleeping room. "Look —
you can see where these boards are newer, and stained dark. 'Tis easy to
open this — like a door — and come through or listen. It'd take a week to
do such a job. Who? Not me, is all I say. But that Venner, now, he'd bring
folks up from Vérella — my wife saw them, time and again, on the road, but
we thought it was your will, my lord — " In the Duke's study, again, a hidden panel swung out giving access to the next room, where files had been
stored.

On the walls, the doubled watch peered through the night. They knew
from their sergeants' faces that this was no night to gossip when they met at
the corners or ask questions at the change of watch. Many had seen the
blanket-wrapped bundles carried out the watch-gate: they didn't know
who, but they knew trouble had already come.

The Duke seemed to be everywhere, with Paks at his side. He walked
the walls himself, midway of the second watch, and strolled through each of
the barracks. In the infirmary, he paused by each bed, until the sick had
seen and recognized him. He paused to speak to sentries and guards at
each post. Gradually the Company settled into watchfulness. The Duke was
alive, and obviously well, and very obviously in command. Some of them
looked sideways at Paks and wondered why she carried a longsword, but
they did not ask.

Midway of the third watch, Arcolin had found nothing amiss in the front
court. "It will take days to search everything, my lord," he reported. "But

776

Siger and I think we've covered the most obvious places for trouble. I'd expect a passage outside, for instance, but there isn't one. We thought of the jacks pit, but the gratings are still locked in. But in here — "

"Yes." The Duke looked tired; he sat heavily in the chair in his study. "We've found so many things already. Mostly ways of spying on me, or on you captains. I daresay we've hardly said a word, these last years, that he did not know. I think I know now how the regency council found out about that last campaign in Aarenis."

"Did you — could you hear what he said as he and Paks fought?"

"No. After the dagger, I heard and saw nothing."

"He did more than that, Kieri. He — "

"Later. I suspect more. But for now — *did* he have a way outside, and are we going to be attacked? And when?"

"More when than if, I think. Has Dorrin checked the lower levels?"

"Not yet. There's so much up here — "

"Did he ask permission for any construction, and changes, in the past year or so?"

"I don't — gods above, Jandelir, he did! The new wine cellar — remember?" Arcolin nodded. "He said he wanted to enlarge, if we were all staying here — and I told him to stay within the walls, but — "

"Let's go." Arcolin stood, and stretched his arms. He yawned widely. "Why that rascal couldn't have started this after I'd had a good night's sleep — "

The Duke was no longer sure which cellar had been extended. He, Paks, Arcolin, and a squad from Dorrin's cohort began the search at the kitchen stairs. A passage ran north, the length of the building. Doors opened off it at intervals. But they found nothing in any of the outside rooms, and no signs of new construction.

"Would one of the servants know?" asked Paks.

"They might." The Duke rubbed his eyes. "Tir's gut, but I'm tired. It must be near dawn. Let's go up and see."

The cooks knew at once which cellar was meant. "Sir, it's the third on the right, the last on that side before the corner. He said 'twas to give room, so's not to run into the well, there in the court. Can you tell us, sir, what's wrong? Is Venner angry with us? We done nothing, sir, I swear it — "

"It's all right. The third on the right?"

"Yes, sir, it — " But they went back out, into a cold dawn, and crossed the courtyard again.

"An inside cellar," said Arcolin. "What was he up to?"

"No good," said the Duke shortly. His shoulders were hunched against the cold. The sentries — four, now — at the door, saluted smartly. One of Dorrin's squad, following, stumbled on the steps. The Duke frowned. Dorrin waited inside.

"My lord, I brought food from the Company kitchens."

"I don't need — " He stopped abruptly, and looked at the others. "Maybe I do, indeed. Thank you. I'd forgotten I have the cooks locked up."

Sometime during the night, Dorrin had cleared away the mess in the dining hall. A steaming pitcher of sib and a kettle of porridge centered the big table. Bowls and mugs were stacked to one side. Paks sat with the others, unconcerned about order and seniority. After a bowl of porridge and several mugs of sib, she felt more awake. The Duke's face was less pinched. Dorrin had had a fresh squad ready inside, and sent the first one off to breakfast with the rest of the Company.

"Well, now," said the Duke, over his third mug of sib. "We'll see about that cellar, and then — barring immediate trouble — we'll get some sleep."

"Agreed." Arcolin stretched and yawned. "Is Pont back, Dorrin?"

"Yes. I sent him on to sleep when he came; he's up again and ready to take the day watches. Nothing's happened outside. Oh yes — my lord, I took the liberty of sending word to the villages — "

"I should have thought of that. Good for you."

"As of this morning, nothing's happened there, either. The Councils will meet with you at your convenience; they've alerted all the veterans. Piter has a list of all the travelers in *The Red Fox*, and they won't be going anywhere today."

"Oh?"

"Something's happened to their horses — or their wagons — and it seems a thief went through last night and stole left shoes."

The Duke laughed, and the others joined in. "That Piter! It's a good thing he's on my side." He pushed his chair back. "Let's get to that cellar, then, and hope to find nothing we need worry about until after rest."

The cellar door in question yielded to none of the keys on the ring. Dorrin had searched Venner's quarters, and had found another ring in a hollow carved into his bedpost. She handed it over. These keys were thinner and newer than the others. One of them slipped into the lock and turned it.

Inside, it looked like any wine cellar: rows of racks with slender green bottles on one side, and barrels, raised off the floor on chocks, on the other. The new extension, clearly visible, made it almost twice as large as before. Along the far wall were more racks for bottles: most of these were empty. They prowled around the cellar, tapping on walls. All seemed solid. Paks stayed near the Duke. It seemed to her that the room could have held many more racks if they had been arranged differently. Racks and barrels both sat well out from the walls. She asked the Duke about it.

"I don't know — " he said, looking surprised. "I suppose — perhaps the air is supposed to move around them — or it's easier to clean."

It was very clean, as if it had been swept recently. Paks bent to look under the racks. Surely there would be dust underneath — they couldn't move all the racks and barrels every time. She saw something dark and heavy. It didn't look like dust. She swiped at it with her hand, and teased it out into view. A dried lump of clay — the same sort of clay that clung to their boots in the field.

"What's that?" asked Dorrin behind her.

"I don't know — clay, I think. But why under there?" As she said it, she thought of mud from boots, falling off, being swept under —

"Hunh. Not exactly like our clay. Grayer."

"Well, it's dry —"

"Even so." Dorrin flattened herself on the floor and looked under the rack. "Is that — can you see that different colored stone, there?"

Paks lay down and looked. One of the square paving blocks that floored the cellar looked a shade darker than the others, but it was under the rack, after all. She reached out to touch it. It was stone. Dorrin had gotten up. The Duke leaned over to look.

"We'll move this rack," he said. Paks and the others laid hands on it and shoved it aside. The stone in question was slightly darker gray. The space between it and the stones around it was filled tightly with earth.

"It can't be a door," said Arcolin. "Look how the crack's filled."

"The others aren't." Dorrin pointed. Between other stones a broom had swept out some of the earth, leaving little grooves. But on this one, the dirt looked unnaturally smooth, filling the crack to the brim. Dorrin drew her dagger and picked at it. It came out in long sections, exactly like dried mud. Beneath that surface of mud the crack was clean and empty.

They all stared at it a moment. "Let's use sense," the Duke said finally. "Without knowing what, who, and how many, we're fools to open that now. Can we block it for a day?"

"We can guard it, certainly. As for blocking it, that depends on what's coming through. But if it's a mage of some kind, the guards could be overcome."

"Two sets," the Duke said. "Clear this room to the walls, and post some inside and some in the passage out there. I don't want to open this until I have some idea what's going on."

While the room was being cleared, and guards set, the Duke went to his quarters for sleep, and ordered the others to do likewise. Paks had thought she would not sleep at all, but she was hardly in her bunk before sleep took her, dreamless and deep.

Stammel woke her in the afternoon; heavy clouds darkened the day, and lamps had been lit already. Paks yawned and shook her head to clear it. Stammel looked around the empty barracks before speaking again.

"The story is that you healed the Duke." He paused, and Paks tried to think how to say what she must say. He went on. "You remember, we talked once, a long time ago, about you maybe being a paladin someday. I never forgot what you said about Canna, that time. I suppose you did heal her. And then the Duke came back — he never said anything to us, but we heard you'd had some trouble in Fin Panir." He stopped again, and looked away, then back at her. "I want you to know that I never did believe all I heard. The Duke, now — I've been in his Company since I left home, and never found a better man to follow. When you left, I had my doubts — but if this is what you came back to do, well — it's good enough." His face relaxed slightly. "But you could have told me, I think, what you could do. We could save the pay of a surgeon, at least."

Paks shook her head, smiling. "I'm still finding out what I can do."

"You mean you didn't know you could heal? What about that other? Glowing light and all?"

"Who told that? No, I knew some of it. It's come slowly. But I still don't know what I can do until I try. That's the second time I've made light; the first time it scared me half to death."

"I suppose it would." Stammel sounded thoughtful. "Was that in Kolobia?"

"No. A month or so ago, in Brewersbridge. With a Kuakgan."

"Kolya's friend?"

"Yes. Anyway, last night — when the darkness came, from Venner, I just — asked for light, I suppose."

"And the healing. You'd healed before — Canna — "

"And one other, in Lyonya. A ranger. But I'm still learning. The elves said healing was a hard art to learn. It isn't power alone, like light, but knowledge, as well. The Duke's wound was a simple stab . . . I'd be afraid to try something like a broken bone."

"Well — we're all glad you did it. I don't suppose you'll be here long, now — ?"

Paks shrugged. "Why not? I don't have any plan to leave. Nothing's called me."

"You had a call to come here, though, didn't you?" She nodded. "I thought so. I thought it was more than bringing the Duke back his ring. Well, then. Are you a paladin, Paks? Gird's paladin?"

She had been waiting for this. "I'm not sure what I am. I have some gifts paladins have. I am a Girdsman. But Gird himself followed the High Lord, and I have had a — " She could not think how to describe her experience at the Kuakgan's that last night. Vision? Miracle? She stopped, paused, and started again. "I have had a call, which I feel bound to follow. It brought me here, with a feeling that the Duke needed me. I will stay until it takes me somewhere else. The Kuakgan and the elves told me that the gods used to call paladins directly. Perhaps I am one, but it's not what I expected."

"A long way from Three Firs," said Stammel soberly. "You were — " He shook his head. "You were such a *young* recruit. I could see the dream in your eyes: songs, magic swords, flying horses I daresay — and yet so practical, too. And the Company wasn't what you expected either, was it?"

Paks laughed. "No. Cleaning, repairing walls, mending uniforms — we all hated that at first."

"But you stuck it out. And now you've saved the Duke's life — again. I don't forget what happened in Aarenis. Well, I've talked long enough. Too long, it may be. The Duke wants you in conference before dinner tonight."

The Duke looked much better; rested and alert, he leaned over the maps spread on the table. The captains were all there but Cracolnya, who had the watch. As Paks came in, they looked up. The Duke smiled and waved her over to the table.

"We're trying to remember, Paks, the details of something that happened when I first took over this stronghold. You've never been to the Lairs, I think. When I first came, we drove the orcs out of there — we hoped for good — and explored some of their tunneling. Unhealthy sport: we lost several men to cave-ins, and I finally forbade any more of it. But Jandelir thinks he remembers one tunnel that led off southwest — toward us — "

"I'm sure of it," said Arcolin. "I remember because it was straighter than the rest, and wider. It wasn't all that long — " He pointed out the spot on the map. "Couldn't have come past here. You know that swampy area where the springs are? It ended there, in a cave-in. Those stupid orcs had tried to burrow mud. We thought they'd intended to get close enough for a surprise attack. Those old rubble walls weren't worth much — "

"The first stronghold," Dorrin put in. "Built by someone from Vérella."

"But now we wonder if that tunnel's been repaired and brought on in," said the Duke. "If it ends, for instance, in that wine cellar — "

"They'll have a surprise," said Dorrin grimly.

"Bad place to fight," said Pont. "Cramped. The way orcs fight, we'll have to count on losing some." He paused for a sip of water. "Better than fighting in their tunnel, though. If they have polearms, that'd be suicide."

"Surely we can trap them." Dorrin rested both elbows on the table. "If we clear the room, we can have archers ready to pop the first ones through. That hole isn't big enough to let more than two out at once."

"If we knew what they're planning — " began Arcolin. The Duke interrupted.

"Exactly. Paksenarrion, you have more experience in this than we have. You recognized the lady as an agent of Achrya, and you have dealt with her agents and clerics before. What can we expect?"

For an instant, as they all watched her, Paks could say nothing. She was the youngest there, the lowest rank — how could she advise them?

"My lord, I am not sure what you already know — "

"Don't worry about that. Start at the beginning."

"Well, then — Achrya, the webmistress, is not high in the citadels of evil, according to my teachers in Fin Panir, but she involves herself directly with men and elves, and is therefore more familiar. She delights in intricate plots, and ensnares men to evil deeds by slow sorceries of years. Where Liart — the Master of Torments — prefers direct assault and torture, Achrya spins web within web, and likes the struggles of the victim as much as the final meal, so they say." Paks paused for a breath. She hated speaking directly of Achrya or Liart either one. "She hates the elves most, it is said, because they see clearly, and her arts cannot fool them — and Girdsmen and Falkians, because they will not compromise with evil for any immediate good. Her plots cannot prosper in peaceful, well-kept lands, so she is always brewing plots and treacheries. Just so might a normal spider encourage clutter in a house, to make its web-spinning easier, if it could keep the housewife from sweeping."

"But what of that shape-changing?"

"I'm coming to that. Some of her clerics have the power to change shape, both from one human form to another, and from human form to that of her icon: the appearance of a giant spider. I saw that in Kolobia, and heard of it at Fin Panir."

"Are all her clerics human, then? I thought you had seen kuaknom in Kolobia — "

"Yes, that's true. The elves that turned from the High Lord — some say when the first of the Kuakkganni sang to the First Tree — worship her."

"But what will she do here?" asked Dorrin. "Will she know her cleric's been killed? And Venner?"

"It depends. I don't know how her clerics contact her. I was taught that Achrya, unlike more powerful deities, does not know all that occurs by her own powers. She depends on her agents for information. If that's true, and Venner and his sister were her only agents here, then she might not. But she might know when her cleric was killed — I can't say. What she will do, when she finds out, depends on what resources she has near here. The orcs, yes — but even for her they are undisciplined and careless fighters. And we still don't know *why* she influenced Venner here — at least I don't. How long had he been steward?"

"Since the old steward was killed — at the same time as Tammarrion," said the Duke. "He had been injured, as a recruit, and became assistant steward. He was so for several years, as I recall, and then after the massacre — well, he knew the job."

"From what he said last night," said Arcolin, "that was his doing as well."

The Duke nodded, his face grim. "I expect so. I wonder if he was her agent from the beginning."

"Surely not. The Marshal wouldn't have missed that."

The Duke looked at Paks, a clear question. She answered. "No, my lord, he wouldn't have missed it if Venner had been committed to her then. But Achrya gains adherents in subtle ways. At first he may not have realized what he was doing — "

The Duke flushed. "Arranging a massacre? How could he not?"

"I didn't mean that, my lord. Earlier. We don't know — perhaps he had cheated someone, or told a minor lie: I have heard that she makes much of that. Or he may have been told lies, about you, that justified him to himself, in the beginning. By the time he realized whose service he had joined, it would have been too late."

"Are you saying it was not his fault?"

"No, my lord. Unless he was spelled the entire time, he was responsible for his decisions. I meant that he may not have intended any evil when he joined the Company . . . may in fact have slipped into evil bit by bit. Perhaps the massacre that killed your wife was the first overt act of evil. The Marshal was killed, too: could it be that the Marshal was beginning to suspect something? That the attack was aimed as much at him as at her?"

"No!" The Duke stiffened, then sat back. "It couldn't be. Yet — "

"She might have noticed, too, my lord," said Dorrin. "Being as she was. And she would be more in the steward's way than the Marshal."

"But we still don't know why Achrya spends her strength here," Paks went on.

"The northern border — it was always important — " But Arcolin did not sound convinced.

"So long a time," the Duke mused. "If Venner was in truth part of a long-laid plan — by Tir, that's more than sixteen years she's been plotting. Against me? Against this holding? We know that she supported Siniava in Aarenis."

Cracolnya shifted in his seat. "If it's to clear this holding for another invasion from the north, why didn't she strike while you were in Aarenis with the whole company?"

"That's when the orc trouble began — "

"Yes, but not enough to wipe us out. Just enough to discredit you. I'd like to know who Venner knew in Vérella. And why you, my lord? I'm not saying you're no threat to evil in this realm, but I'd not have thought you that important, begging your pardon."

"Nor I," said the Duke with a smile. "By the gods, captains, I admit I've been trying to strengthen my position in this kingdom, but I wouldn't have thought I'd succeeded well enough to flurry a demon. Or, for that matter, that my deeds were so good."

"Why didn't Venner simply stab you one night?" Cracolnya went on. "Or is that my nomad heritage showing? It should have been easy enough, with all the hidden passages we've found."

"That's not Achrya's way," said Paks. "She prefers to spoil rather than destroy utterly. Her minions could have killed me in Kolobia, easily enough, but they wanted to make a spoiled paladin, or a useless coward, rather than kill me." She was surprised to find she could speak of this easily. "Whatever her plans here, they will be devious and intricate — the cleric's stab was desperation, not the original intent, I would say."

"Mmph. I wonder. The witch kept me from paying enough attention to the orcs. I should have been thinking why they would come, and why they acted as they do. I've fought orcs before, and they never behaved like this. If she sought to distract me long enough for them to burrow into the stronghold, what then? Death, I expect." He looked around the table. "We need not understand all her motives, I think, to know we are opposed. But how can we foresee what she will do? Will we be attacked by orcs, or by other monsters of her will?"

"My lord, she will not risk herself against a ready foe: Achrya sends others to do her fighting. Orcs we can expect. If she has men or kuaknom nearby, they may attack as well, or she may withdraw, and try to plan other coils. Most importantly, she may have other agents within the stronghold or nearby. Those we must find, and quickly."

783

"You found none among the servants — "

"No, Captain," said Paks to Arcolin. "But I am not sure enough yet that I would. Great evil, yes, but — "

"That brings up another point," said the Duke. "How did you happen to turn up here just when you were needed? And what are you? Can you tell me that you came merely to bring back my ring?"

"No, my lord." Paks looked at him soberly. "While with the rangers in Lyonya, I had a sudden feeling — a call, it seemed — that you had need of me. I did not know why, but I knew I must come."

"And did you know you had these powers? Making light, finding evil, healing?"

"Yes. But I am not sure how to use them all yet, my lord."

"*Are* you a paladin, then, Paks?" asked Dorrin, fingering her Falkian pin.

"Both the rangers I was with and the Kuakgan in Brewersbridge think so," said Paks slowly. "I have no other explanation for the powers. They must come from the gods — from the High Lord, I believe. But the limits of the gifts I do not know. I think, my lord," she said, turning to the Duke, "that you should call a Marshal or paladin from Vérella or Fin Panir — someone who knows how to use these things — and be sure your Company is free of traitors."

"You do not trust your own gifts?"

Paks tried to think how to explain her reserve. "My lord, I trust the gifts, but not yet my mastery of them. You would be wise to make use of another's experience, as well."

"I see." The Duke looked around the table. Arcolin was frowning, rumpling a bit of cloth in his hand. Dorrin sat still, hands out of sight. Pont leaned back in his chair, looking half-asleep. Cracolnya glanced from the Duke to Paks and back. The Duke looked at Paks. "You may not know, but I refused to have a Gird's Marshal in the stronghold after my wife was killed. I have always blamed them for her death — for hiring me and most of the Company away, so that she was left without enough guard, for the Marshal's weakness that day, that he did not save her. It has seemed to me that they claim to protect the weak and helpless, but in fact do not."

"My lord, having lost your wife and children, such bitterness is understandable."

"Mayhap. You do not know all I said to the Marshal-General when I found out about you. For that, too, I blamed them. But you do not, I think?"

"No, my lord. As any Girdsman is the natural enemy of Achrya's plots, I went into that peril knowingly. Certainly Girdsmen — the Marshal-General included — can make mistakes, but those I have known were honorable, if sometimes narrow."

"But they did not heal you. They sent you out alone and helpless — "

Paks laughed. "My lord, you remember they would have sheltered me. I insisted on leaving when I did, despite the Marshal-General's plea. True, they did not heal everything. They did, however, heal the worst of the evil, though it left scars. And — look now. What have I lost? You've watched me fight. If there is wisdom outside the grange as well as within, the Marshals have never claimed differently."

"And you — having suffered under them — would ask me to call them in? Knowing what you do of my past?"

"I know little, my lord, but what you have said here. I cannot imagine them asking you to take the Company elsewhere if they had known of your lady's peril. I cannot imagine the Marshal here doing aught but fighting to the death to save her and your children. Your anger I can understand, and your bitterness — in all honesty, my lord, during those terrible months last winter, I was bitter myself. But it seems now that you — and the Girdsmen — and your family — were all victims of a long-laid plot. A plot so cleverly hidden that not until last night did anyone — even you — recognize the traitor within. I daresay Achrya was pleased when you barred Marshals and paladins from your gates."

The Duke had one hand before his face, and his voice was muffled. "By the gods, I never thought of that. I never thought — but — that she was dead, and I had not been here to ward. And the little ones — "

"And then," mused Dorrin, covering his confusion, "in all the years her influence could act to corrupt the Company. With no one here who could detect evil directly, we could slip, bit by bit, into her ways."

"But that didn't happen," put in Paks. "This Company is honorable — "

"Not as it was," said the Duke, looking up now. His eyes glittered with unshed tears. "Not as it was, Paksenarrion; you never knew it before. When Tammarrion was alive, and a Marshal lived here — " He stopped and drew a long breath. "Well," he said finally. "I have been wrong. I have made as big a mistake in this as any I ever made. It was not the fault of Gird or Gird's followers, and I was blinded by my rage." He looked around the table again. "Do you agree, captains?"

They responded to the new timbre of his voice, straightening in their chairs and nodding. Arcolin spoke first. "My lord Duke, we have followed you in all things — but I confess I was long uneasy with your quarrel with Gird, and I would be pleased to have a Marshal here again."

"I also," said Dorrin quickly, her face alight. "Even as a Falkian."

"I wonder if they'll come," said the Duke. "After what I said to the Marshal-General, she may let us stew awhile — "

"I doubt that," said Cracolnya, grinning. "She'll be too glad to be proved right."

The Duke shook his head. "It will be some while, after these years, before I can learn to think anew. But our enemy now is Achrya, not Gird, and at least we know it. Paksenarrion, you have saved more than one life here. And, with your powers, you must see that you won't do as a corporal. I want you with me — as squire, perhaps? — until this knot is untangled."

"That's right," grumbled Arcolin with a grin. "Just let me get her trained as a good corporal, and then take her away. What am I supposed to do now, conjure one out of thin air?"

"You have plenty of good soldiers. Until a Marshal or paladin comes, she's the only one who might be able to detect another of Achrya's agents." The Duke turned to her. "Paksenarrion, will you accept this?"

"My lord, I came to serve you in whatever need I found. I will do whatever you ask until the gods call me away."

"Good, then. Stay by me. Have you any idea where the nearest Marshal of Gird might be?"

"No, my lord. The nearest grange, as you know, is at Burningmeed, two days south of here. But when I came through, that Marshal had gone on a journey; I don't know when she'd be back. It might be quicker to send a messenger straight to Vérella."

"I dislike such an open move — if Achrya's agents are watching, they'll surely know something has happened."

"I suspect Achrya knows," said Cracolnya. "That one would have spies everywhere, despite our care. 'Tis almost a full day's turn gone, since her cleric was killed. She'll either strike, or vanish to plan again."

Chapter Eleven

An immediate consequence of her new assignment was separation from the rest of the cohort. Stammel was unsurprised when she came to pick up her things from the barracks that night.

"You aren't a common soldier any more," he said bluntly, his composure recovered. "You can't pretend to be. If you need a friend, I'm here, but I'll take your orders the same as I would Arcolin's or the Duke's."

Paks shook her head silently. She could think of nothing to say.

"One thing you've got to be clear on," he went on. "I saw you retreat from this in Aarenis. If you mean to be a paladin — or a commander at all — you must accept being alone, clear through."

Paks found her voice. "The Kuakgan said something like that. I know it's true — I can obey only my own gods, now. But — "

"It takes getting used to. Yes. And you're young. But not as young as all that. Our Duke commanded a cohort at your age — that was all the Company he had then. And Marrakai gave him command — have you heard this?"

"No," said Paks, interested suddenly. She knew very little about the Duke's past.

"You can't stay long, so I'll hurry the tale, but it's worth telling. His first independent contract with the crown of Tsaia was in support of an expedition to Pargun. The crown prince commanded in the field, and the Duke — a captain then — had wangled a direct contract so that he ranked with the other independent commanders, dukes and counts and such. They didn't like that, so I hear. Ask Siger, some time: he was there. They were at the Pargunese border, east of here, when the prince called a conference one night. All the commanders in one tent — and their bodyguards. A force of Pargunese made it through the lines from the rear, and killed nearly all of them. Our Duke was knocked cold; the prince was killed; Marrakai — the most powerful baron, then — was badly wounded.

"Marrakai was widely believed to have ordered the attack — no love lost between him and the crown, so most men thought. The camp fell apart — the prince's commanders quarrelling over command, and the steward threatening to go back to Vérella with his body — and our Duke took command, just by shouting louder than the others, according to Arcolin. Then Marrakai called him in, and gave him command of the Marrakai troops —

787

five fighting cohorts — to attack the Pargunese and avenge the prince. So he did, and routed them, and brought back the head of the Sagon, the Pargunese western commander. That was his first big command, and that's when he got this grant, and the title. The next year, it was, he began recruiting in the north, and I remember seeing him come through my hometown. I was too young, then, but I didn't wait about long."

"I had wondered how he got this land," said Paks.

"You talk to Arcolin, now — he was our Duke's junior, hired away from the Tsaian Guards, when he first came to Tsaia. Siger knew him before that; he was one of Aliam Halveric's sergeants in the old days. That's where our Duke got his first training."

"Do you know where he came from? Before that?"

Stammel shook his head. "No. No one does, unless the Halveric. I tried asking Siger once, and near lost an arm. I wouldn't advise it." He looked at her, smiling now. "You go on now, and do what you came for."

Paks had hardly stowed her few belongings in a cupboard when she heard the Duke's voice in the passage, asking if she was back. She went out quickly, and followed him into his study. Cracolnya and Valichi were there; the other captains were not.

"The more I think about it," the Duke said without preamble, "the more I think Venner was involved in most of what happened here. Val mentioned that trouble you had with the corporal — what was his name? Stephi?" Paks nodded. "It seemed fairly clear he'd been drugged, and at the time that potion was the best source. But if Venner could become invisible, as I understand he did during the fight with you — " He paused, and Paks nodded. "Yes, then he could have drugged the ale as he brought it, and drugged the potion bottle as well."

"I still don't see why, my lord," said Cracolnya, after shooting a hard glance at Paks. "Why would he cause such commotion, and run such a risk, to get Stephi in trouble?"

"It wasn't Stephi, I daresay," said the Duke. "It was Paks — if she was going to become a paladin — "

"Why not just kill her, then?" Cracolnya sounded half-angry. "I'm sorry, my lord, but it seems entirely too roundabout — "

"He had no access to recruits," said Valichi quietly. "He never came out of the Duke's Court, but to visit the villages, and rarely then. He couldn't have marched into barracks without being challenged — "

"But if he could be invisible?"

Paks had said nothing, still uncertain of her status, but now she intervened. "My lord, there's more to it, I'm sure. As with all Achrya's plots, we must look for more than one gain, and for interlacing of design. To discredit any good soldier — Stephi and me both, perhaps — and cause dissension in the Company, between recruits and veterans, between men and women, between Dorrin's cohort and Arcolin's." She paused. Both the captains were nodding slowly; the Duke watched her closely. "Then the other recruits — Korryn and Jens, whom you never knew, my lord — "

"Bad 'uns," put in Valichi.

"Yes, sir. If they had stayed longer, they might have done more harm by influence. Even as it was, the trial and the punishment drove some recruits away — you remember that, sir. And not the worst, either."

"True." Valichi nodded again. "And I daresay Stephi's friends in the Company didn't trust you, Paks, at first."

Paks remembered Donag's early unfairness. "No, sir, they didn't. Stephi did what he could — he was always fair — "

"He was a good man," said the Duke. "If we could have known — " He sighed and quoted a version of the old saying, "*If* never won a battle. We must go from where we stand. I've sent for a Marshal." He looked around at all of them. "Until the Marshal comes, Paksenarrion, we'll hope your gift is enough to warn us. Since you found nothing amiss in the servants, I'm willing to let them go back to their work. We don't need that many, actually, and I'd as soon send some of them away, but it's too near winter for them to find work elsewhere. I know how most places are about hiring in the late fall and winter." His voice sharpened on this last, and Paks wondered how he knew. She had certainly run into that reluctance the previous winter.

"You could board some of them out in the villages," suggested Cracolnya. "That would free your veterans for militia service if it's necessary."

"I could, but I'd want to be very sure they're harmless. We're better equipped to deal with traitors than the villages are. Another thing — are we likely to run into more of those spider-things, Paksenarrion?"

"I don't know." Paks frowned as she thought. "This is only the third one I've seen. The others were in Kolobia. I don't know how common they are. We ought to be ready for another — but I doubt there'd be many of them."

"Are they all shape-changed followers of Achrya?" asked Valichi.

Paks shook her head. "I don't think so. One — larger than the one here — almost seemed to be a pet, or mascot, to the blackwebs in Kolobia. They bowed to it, before the combats, and they said it was Achrya's servant. It — "

"Larger than *that* — ?" Cracolnya seemed to have trouble speaking.

Paks nodded. "Yes, much larger. Each leg as long as I am tall, and the eyes fist-size, at least."

"Great gods! Did it — did it *do* anything?"

"It bound in silk and ate those I defeated."

He looked at her with new respect. "I had not realized — your pardon, my lord, for you told me, but I had doubts I never spoke — that Paksenarrion had faced such peril. In my own land we have many legends of the spider demons, and such a death is the worst we know."

"I don't know how it would fight outside its web," Paks went on. "Those that I know were shapechanged used fangs and spinnerets both, as that one did last night. They move very fast, and can leap higher than a man's head. If they have such, to lead the way through the tunnel, for example, archers might not be able to stop it."

"Did you ever fight against one directly?" asked Cracolnya.

"Not alone. Three of us — the paladin I trained with, a dwarf, and I — fought it together."

"What about the spinnerets?"

"It can't throw the silk ahead while moving; it trails a line, instead. But if balked, it can stand on its rear legs and throw the silk forward. Arrows in the fat back section ruin its aim. The legs are bad too — claws, but a single sword-stroke will sever them."

"Arrows in the eyes should work, shouldn't they?"

"Yes, but it moves fast, and that's a small target. The rest of the head end is hard armored; arrows glance off, as do swords."

"I keep thinking," the Duke said, "that unless Achrya is a very stupid demon, we'll see trouble very shortly. Tonight, I expect. If I were in her place, I'd be moving as soon as I knew of trouble, and she's bound to have had some way of keeping in contact. I wish Master Vetrifuge were here — some of his wizardly fire down there might fry a spider or two."

Paks said nothing, but was just as glad Vetrifuge was elsewhere. Wizards and paladins worked ill together, but she doubted the Duke remembered that.

"We've oil enough in the stores," Cracolnya said. "I daresay one of those wouldn't like fire, wizardry or not. And that cellar is all stone and earth — it wouldn't menace the rest of the building."

The Duke nodded, and turned to Valichi. "Val, has anything moved outside today?"

Valichi shook his head. "Nothing, my lord. No reports of orc sightings from either village or any farmstead."

"That in itself tells me they know something." The Duke looked down at his desk, and shifted the sheets of paper. "Beyond doubling the watch, and keeping a close eye on that tunnel entrance — if that's what it is — I can't think of more for tonight. Can any of you?" Valichi and Cracolnya shook their heads, but Paks spoke up.

"One more thing," she said, and waited for his nod. "Suppose they don't attack here at all, but go past us to attack holdings south of here. Duke's East, or even beyond your lands. If Achrya's purpose is, in part, to discredit you — "

"I had not thought of that. Such a plan could include a small attack here, enough to convince us, with the bulk of them harrying south. Cracolnya — ?"

"They couldn't have moved today, my lord, unless they swung wide of the ridge east of here. We had plenty of men out, and even some miles west on the road. But tonight or tomorrow — "

"To make it work, they'd have to show that they'd come past me," said the Duke. "If they entered from east or west, everyone knows I can't patrol the entire north line alone, and no one holds west of me this far north. Proof — they'd need some proof — "

"Neither of the villages could stand against a large force," said Valichi. "With plunder from there — even prisoners — "

"That's it." The Duke's voice hardened. "By the gods, I think that's it. Paks?"

790

"Yes, my lord. It feels right."

"Now what? Let me think. How many would they commit to an attack on us? In the dark, it wouldn't take much — some fire arrows, an attempt to break into the cellar — maybe fifty against the walls. Cracolnya, how few archers can you hold this place with?"

"Me? Tir's gut! Mmm — most of the cohort — all of it, if you mean hold it very long. There's that tunnel, don't forget."

"I haven't. Even so — I'll leave you a squad of Arcolin's, to back you on the walls, and take two of your archers. Paks, go find Arcolin and Dorrin; tell them to ready their cohorts to march out at once, and then meet me here. You ride to Duke's East — that's where they'll hit, because that's where the Vérella road is. Rouse the militia, and tell them we'll be there as soon as possible. Heribert Fontaine, the mayor, has a great horn — blow it if you see any sign of orcs."

"Yes, my lord." Paks turned to go.

"And even if you are a paladin, don't try to take them on by yourself."

"No, my lord, I wouldn't." Paks grinned at him, and ran out of the room. She had not been able to sense clearly what was wrong before, but this plan felt right.

Dorrin and Arcolin, when she found them, understood at once, and by the time she had saddled a fast horse, the cohorts were arming for the march. Paks led the horse out the postern, and found herself alone in the dark on a cold, windy plain. She mounted, and turned the horse toward Duke's East. The north wind behind her carried the sounds of the Company roused. She legged the horse into a gallop, trusting its night vision over hers. The sounds fell away, as she rode, replaced by the thudding of hooves beneath, and the rush of wind.

She had never ridden in a night so dark. It was like being in a cave: heavy clouds shut out the sky, and she could see nothing, not even the horse's neck in front of her. When they came to the shallow rise a mile out, she knew it only because the horse lunged at the slope, the rhythm of its stride broken. Then down the other side, into the same blackness. She thought of trying to make light, but decided to wait until battle was joined. It would only make her obvious to any watchers to do it now.

At last the watchlights of Duke's East flickered ahead of her. The horse snorted, and lunged ahead. The lights came closer: she could see them now as individual torches, streaming in the wind, on the low bank that had been thrown up on the north side of the village. She pulled the horse down to a long trot, and yelled for the watch.

"Stand and speak," yelled one of the sentries behind the bank.

She hauled at the horse, and it lugged to a halt. "I've word from the Duke for Mayor Fontaine," she yelled back. "I'm Paksenarrion — "

"Come on, then," said the guard. "What is it?"

She rode slowly into the circles of light, and slid off the horse in front of them. "You're to rouse the militia," she said. "The Duke's bringing the Company, as soon as he can — he thinks the orcs will attack here."

"Here? Why?" Paks recognized Piter, the innkeeper.

She shook her head. "It's too long to explain — but he's got reason. Be ready. Where's the mayor?"

"D'you know his house?" asked Piter. Paks nodded. "Go, and I'll call out the rest. Do you know how many?"

"No, but the Duke thinks it will be a large force." Paks started up the lane, leading her horse. Behind her she heard Piter directing the watch, then the clatter of boots as they went to rouse others.

In the mayor's house she found the Council of Duke's East eating a late dinner. Kolya smiled as Paks came in, then sobered quickly as she gave her news.

"When will the Duke come?" asked Fontaine, looking worried.

"The cohorts were forming as I left," said Paks.

"We can't hold a real force," he said. "That bank is just to slow them down and give our watch a chance to fire one flight of arrows. We have fewer than a hundred who can fight — "

"Most of the buildings are defensible," Kolya pointed out. "The Duke's insisted on stone roofs as well as walls, and we can't be burned out. My cottage won't hold, but it's on the south bank anyway."

"We'll move everyone but militia into a few of the strongest houses," the mayor said. "Is there time to bring in any of the farm folk? No, I suppose not. Forget the mill, and the south bank buildings: we'll try to hold around the square."

Paks had not met all the Council before, and did not know who the heavy-set black-haired man was who spoke next. "I'll see to gettin' the south bank folk in, Mayor — "

"Thanks, Tam," said the mayor, and the man went out quickly. The mayor turned to a man whose face was marked with a broad scar. "Vik, be sure the central houses are provisioned; use the winter stores, if you have time to move them. They'll do us no good anyway, if the orcs get them."

"Aye, Mayor — and what about slipping the millstones? If they burn the mill, it might crack the stones."

"Good idea. Tell the miller that. Kolya — "

"I know." She was already near the door, with a last grin for Paks. The mayor clambered up stiffly, and called upstairs to his wife.

"Get out the horn, Arñe, and bring it down here." He looked at Paks. "This house has too many doors; I'll send the family over to the square."

A glass had passed, and part of another. Paks waited at the northernmost angle of the bank around Duke's East, listening, with the others, for any hint of the orcs' attack. They knew it would take the Duke's Company another half-glass at least to march the distance in battle order . . . if the Company met no enemy on the road. Behind, the village was as secure as it could be. All who could not fight crowded into the buildings that bordered the square, all of which had but one door each, and narrow windows easily defended. Those who could draw a bow were by the upstairs windows. Paks raised her head suddenly, and sniffed. She heard nothing, but with a sense of unease came a sour stench on the wind.

"They're coming," she said to the man next to her. He was, as most of them were, one of the Duke's veterans, and limped badly from a wound taken the last year in Aarenis. He'd been a farmer until the orcs burned out his farm. He grunted, passed the word to the man next in line, and drew his sword; she heard it rasp on the scabbard. They had torches ready to light, but until the enemy came, only widely scattered ones were lit.

Paks felt something dire nearby; her skin crawled. Something more than orcs moved in dark. She drew Tammarrion's sword. The blade gleamed blue. Paks squinted into the wind — was that a reflection? With a shout she called on the High Lord, and light swept up from her upraised arm, pure white radiance revealing two of the spider figures only a few lengths away, and a mass of orcs behind them. Paks leaped for the top of the bank. She heard the cries of the watch, and saw the first gouts of flame as torches caught all along the line. The orcs broke into one of their marching chants, fierce and savage, and surged forward. Far back she heard the mayor's deep horn. The spiders had scuttered back at the first of the light, but now bounded forward.

As they came up the bank, effortlessly, Paks slashed at their heads. One sprang sideways, evading her. The one in front reared back, head out of danger, and raked at her with a foreleg. Paks dodged and drove in, striking for the vulnerable neck. Tammarrion's sword swung easily, and parted the black carapace as if it were butter. The head flew off, and the legs jerked. Paks jumped back to the top of the bank, looking for the other spider. It had disappeared: one of the militia waved an arm and Paks saw behind their lines a glossy humped back moving swiftly toward the center of the village.

"Look out!" yelled another man, and Paks whirled to face the first orcs. Swords rang on her blade; beside her the militia had climbed the bank too, and the clash and clatter of swords filled the night air. Paks killed the orc in front of her, and wounded another, but more filled the gaps. The pressure of them forced her back over the top of the bank. Here, for a moment, it was easier — as the orcs came over the top, the defenders could strike from below, where they were more vulnerable. But again, the orc numbers overwhelmed them, and they began to fall back toward the square. They could not even take their dead along, for the orcs poured over the bank in black waves, and they were almost driven out of line as it was.

Then from the left came a harsh blast of sound, and the roar of the Duke's Company's charge. Both cohorts struck the flank of the orcish advance. With the first flurry in the orcs' attack, Paks called the militia around her to fall into double lines. She and the others managed to thrust forward until one end of the line was anchored on the bank again. Beyond her, the line doubled back sharply along a lane, but the defenders had only a short stretch from the bank to the first building with no sort of parapet. While the Duke's charge pulled the orcish interest, they threw up a weak protection of furniture and barrels from that house, and stones from a garden wall.

Beyond this, the orcs were pushed aside to stream past, on through the village.

The orcs had clearly not expected this kind of resistance. Once the line was in place, the militia felt at once the lessening pressure and orcs shifted to the right and beyond. Paks held the point until it was clear that the orcs no longer meant to dispute it. Then she called for reinforcements.

"But where are you — ?"

"That other spider — I must find it." The innkeeper — for he had come at her call — grunted.

"You'd go for that? Go on, then. Gods go with you."

Paks made her way through the remains of the militia toward the square. Even with all the torches lit, it was hard to see clearly; black shadows leaped and twisted everywhere. She looked for the gleam of a hard carapace, or the telltale eyes.

Wagons had been overturned in the gaps between buildings in the square, but this protection had not been enough. Orcs had thrust them aside, and Paks found the square itself full of bodies, orc and human both. Two wagons burned in the middle of the square, lighting it well enough, but she saw no sign of the giant spider.

"Paks!" Kolya's voice came from a high window in one of the houses.

Paks squinted up. "What?"

"Are they gone?"

"Not all — I'm looking for that spider."

"It came over the wagon there — and left that way — " Kolya pointed. Paks waved and started to follow her directions. "Paks! No! Don't go by yourself!"

Paks looked back up at her, and something — a shadowy movement — caught her eye on the roof above the window. She tried to make it out, then realized what it must be. "Kolya! It's on the roof!" As she yelled, the thing dropped suddenly, its anchoring line gleaming. Two legs caught the sill of the window where Kolya had been, and it swung to crawl in. Paks yelled "Someone drop me a bow!"

But Kolya or someone else inside rammed a torch toward the crouching form before it could get through the window, and it retreated, dropping swiftly to the ground. Paks ran to meet it, hoping to strike a blow before the legs found purchase on the cobbles, but the spider pushed off the wall to meet her.

Paks dodged the first leap, swinging at its head, but missed. It leaped again, sideways, and she followed. Quickly it scuttled sideways, turning so that the light of the burning wagon was in her eyes. Paks grinned, and ran wide herself, to snatch a burning length of wood from the fire. It retreated, still poised to leap. Paks moved in slowly, arms wide, ready to strike with torch or sword. She heard an arrow strike the stones, as someone in one of the houses tried to shoot the thing, and missed. The spider leaped at her, forelegs spanning wider than her arms, and tried to clutch. Paks dove toward the belly, thrusting higher with torch and lower with sword. She saw the spinnerets facing her, and the pulsations that would drive out the poisoned silk. Then the spider flipped away from her, the head crisping already from the torch, and the abdomen gaping open. A single gout of grayish fluid struck her hand, burning through the glove; she gasped with the pain of it, but struck again, until the head and body were separated.

By then the Duke's men were coming into the square.

"These midnight conferences," said Arcolin, "are becoming tedious." Paks wondered if he was making a joke of some kind. Arcolin?

"Will the Duke be here?" Heribert Fontaine, back in his mayoral robes, paused as he set out mugs for ale.

"I doubt it." Arcolin rubbed the back of his neck. "Simmitt says he'll be fine, but insists he must rest for a night and a day. The gods know he needs it —"

"But he's sure —"

"He's sure the Duke will recover, yes. Flesh wounds and exhaustion — no more than that, he says, and Simmitt wouldn't lie."

Valichi came in, shutting the door carefully behind him. "Surprisingly little damage across the river, Mayor Fontaine. They broke into Kolya's place, but didn't burn it. Near as we can tell, only two trees were badly torn up. It looks like they panicked and ran on through. We've set up a perimeter for the night, including the south bank cottages, but not the outlying farms."

Paks found the rest as tedious as Arcolin had suggested, for they had to explain the events of the past days in sufficient detail to reassure the Council of Duke's East, no easy task when they kept breaking in with questions, comments, and reminiscences of past campaigns. The revelation that Venner had been closely involved in Tammarrion's death aroused a storm of indignation. But discovering that the Duke had sent for a Marshal silenced them at last. Paks could see relief and satisfaction in some of their faces, dismay in none.

Chapter Twelve

Late fall rain had chilled to sleet; from the parapets the sentries could see only a short distance from the walls. The last bonfires were hard to keep alight. Foul smoke whirled away from the orcs' bodies, but they would hardly burn. Finally the Duke had a barrel of mutton-fat melted and poured on, after all the remains had been dragged to one fire, and the ashes left from that smelled of nothing but ashes.

The next afternoon, a party on horseback came within bowshot of the gates before being seen; fog and sleet together hid them. Paks heard the alarm horn, and met the Duke heading for his stairs. She stayed beside him as he strode across the inner court. By the time they reached the Duke's Gate, the sentries knew who it was: the Marshal, they sent word.

"Name?" asked the Duke irritably. Paks glanced at him. She knew his wounds must be hurting him, though he wouldn't admit it. He had refused to let her "waste," as he put it, a healing attempt on him.

"Connaught, was one, and Amberion, and Arianya — "

"The Marshal-*General*?" The Duke glared at the sentry. "You're sure?"

"That's what they said, my lord, them names. I don't know — "

The Duke silenced him with a gesture and turned to Paks. "Is that likely? And why? Has she come to make mock of me, after all?"

"No, my lord," said Paks firmly. "It would not be that. If this is the Marshal-General, she has come because of the urgency of your message, and because she feels you may need her help. Mockery is not like her."

"No." He rubbed his shoulder, considering. The sentry waited, hunched in the cold. "Blast it! I can't get used to the idea — Go on, man, and let them in. Fanfare, but don't keep them out there waiting while the troops parade: it's too cold." As the sentry jogged back to the gate tower, the Duke strode across the main court, calling his captains. High overhead the fanfare rang out, the trumpeters' numb fingers missing some of the triples. The main gate hinges squealed in the cold, and the gates themselves scraped on blown sleet.

Through the gates, as the gap widened, Paks could see a dark clump of horsemen: sleet whitened the horses' manes, and the riders' cloaks and helms. They rode forward, ducking against the wind that scoured a flurry of sleet off the court and flung it in their faces. Paks could not recognize any of them, until they were less than a length away. The leading rider halted, and threw back the hood of a blue cloak.

796

"My lord Duke?" Arianya's weathered face was pinched with cold.

"Marshal-General, I am honored to receive you in my steading." Duke Phelan took the last few steps, and reached a hand to her. "By your leave, I suggest we continue our greetings in somewhere warmer."

"Indeed yes." But she sat her mount a moment longer, looking around the court as if memorizing the location of every door and window. Then she looked back at him. "Gird's blessing on this place, and all within it, and on you, my lord Duke." The Duke stiffened slightly, but bowed. Then she dismounted, as did the other riders, and one came forward to take her horse. "I hope it will not inconvenience you — we brought some along to care for the gear and horses — "

"Not at all. Arcolin, find room for these, and the animals. If you'll come with me, Marshal-General — "

"To a fire, I hope. By the lost scrolls, this last day's ride seemed straight into the wind, no matter which way the road turned." Then she caught sight of Paks. "Paksenarrion! Is this where you — ?" She broke off in confusion, and looked from the Duke to Paks and back again.

"Is that Paks?" Amberion, now, had come to stand beside her. "Gird's grace, Paksenarrion, I'm glad to see you looking so well." She saw that his glance did not miss the sword at her side. "Are you — ?"

But Paks did not mean to discuss everything standing out in the cold. She knew the Duke was in pain, and needed to get back inside. "Sir Amberion," she said, nodding. "My lord's right, sir; we should get within."

The Duke led the way to the dining hall, and sent a guard to the kitchen for hot food. The visitors stood around the fireplace, their wet clothes already steaming. Within minutes, kettles of sib were on the table, and bowls of soup. Servants had taken away wet cloaks, and brought dry stockings for those whose feet were wet.

"I'm getting old for this," said the Marshal-General frankly. "It's been far too long since I left Fin Panir in wintertime. Ah! Hot soup. I may survive." She smiled at the Duke, then her gaze sharpened. "My lord, you are ill — or wounded. Why did you come out in that cold?"

"I'm not a child!" snapped the Duke. Paks looked at him, worried, but he had already taken a long breath. "I'm sorry, Marshal-General. I was wounded a few days ago — it's painful, but not dangerous. I would be shamed did I not welcome such visitors myself."

"And you want no advice on it. Very well. But, my lord, we came to help, and if you spend your strength on hospitality, we are a burden, not help at all." She took another spoonful of soup. "I would eat cobbles, were they hot like this, but this is good soup. You wonder, you say, why, in asking for a Marshal's aid, you got the Marshal-General. I was in Vérella, having been called to a meeting with the prince and regency council." She drank some more soup, and poured herself a mug of sib. "Then your message came, mentioning Achrya, and traitors, and a possible invasion of orcs. It seemed enough — the council was concerned already about your holdings here. I don't know why." She looked at the Duke, who sipped his own mug of sib and said nothing. "I did not, of course, read them your message, but I thought it would ease their minds to know I was coming."

Arcolin came into the room, followed by the other captains. The Duke looked up. "Marshal-General," Arcolin said, "we have stabled all your mounts, and assigned the rest of your party room in the barracks. Is that satisfactory?"

"Entirely," she said. "Two of them are new with us, and it will be well for them to see barracks life; they're nobles' sons, and convinced we stint them by assigning only single rooms, rather than suites."

Arcolin grinned. "Two of them did try to tell me something about their birth, but I didn't have time to listen."

"Good. Don't. While I'm glad to see the fellowship of Gird expand, and as Marshal-General I can't pass up a single blade, I often wish the nobly born would spend a few years of their youth where no one knew their birth. We do our best to knock some of it out of them, but as Paks knows, we don't entirely succeed."

Paks found herself laughing. She had wondered what it would be like to see the Marshal General again, and had not looked forward to it. Even though she knew she was cured, she anticipated an awkward meeting and difficult explanations. But this was easy. The Marshal-General looked at her, as did the others.

"Paksenarrion, I find it hard to believe what I see, yet by Gird's gift you are more than merely healed. Will you tell us, someday, how this happened?"

"Indeed, I would be glad to," said Paks. "But parts of it I don't clearly understand myself."

"I sense great gifts awakening in you, if not already come," said Amberion. "Are you still a follower of Gird?"

Paks nodded. "I am not forsworn, sir paladin. I gave my oath to Gird in the Hall of Fin Panir, and by that oath I stand. But much has happened that I did not anticipate, or you, I think, foresee."

The Marshal-General's eyes glittered with tears. "Paksenarrion, however you were healed, and by what power of good, matters not to me. We are all glad to see you so; we had all grieved over your loss. Gird witness that if you had turned to Falk or Camwyn and received healing there, I would be as glad, and would not condemn you for changing your allegiance. It was my error — not Gird's — that led you into great peril, and in the end near killed you. I am not mean enough to begrudge any healing."

"But," Paks began delicately, "the powers I have — and some have come — did not come with your dedication at the Hall — "

"We have not all forgotten how paladins began," said Amberion quickly. "The power comes from the High Lord — if he has lent it to the training orders, from time to time, that does not bind it there. If Gird spoke to you directly — " He looked a question at her.

Paks looked from one face to another. "I have not told anyone — not even the Duke — the whole story."

"Nor is this the best time, perhaps," suggested the Marshal-General. "If this stronghold faces peril from Achrya — "

"I think it is past," said the Duke, slowly. "Paksenarrion unmasked the traitors within — when I sent for your aid, they were already dead. We had found a tunnel leading into a cellar from without, and expected an invasion of some sort. It came the next night. We burned the last of the bodies yesterday."

"You have wounded that need healing?"

"Yes — but they are not all Girdsmen."

"We'll try what we can. Are you sure your traitors are all found?"

"I hope so. Paksenarrion wanted me to ask more help; she is not sure she would find them all."

"We can help with that, certainly."

"I had not expected so quick a response — and you come from Vérella — "

"Your messenger, my lord, came to the grange at Burningmeed; the Marshal there, Kerrin — " she nodded at her, "had come to Vérella to meet me. Her yeoman-marshal forwarded the message as fast as he could — which, for us, is very fast."

The Duke nodded. "I remember." He coughed, and Paks watched him, worried again. He took a careful breath, and went on. "My message was short, Marshal-General, as word of peril should be. But you must know that I acknowledge — have already admitted to my captains — that I was wrong, years ago, to blame you for my wife's death — "

"My lord," interrupted Arianya, "in dealing with great evils, as you and I have done, all make mistakes. The High Lord grant I never make a worse — in fact I have made worse." She nodded toward Paks. "There is one, as you rightly said, and the elves said at the time. Certainly neither I nor my predecessor intended harm to your wife and children — or to Paksenarrion. But whether by error or overwhelming evil, harm came. If you can now believe that it was unintentional — that I sorrow for it — that is well enough."

"I make bold to contradict a Marshal-General," said the Duke, with a wry smile. "It is not — quite — enough." He took a long breath, staring into his mug, and none thought to interrupt him. "You may remember that in the years before my wife was killed, this entire Company fought under the protection of Gird."

"I do."

"After that, when I was no longer any way a Girdsman, I thought to keep, nonetheless, the standards of honor, in the Company and in my holdings, that were appropriate."

"So you do," said Marshal Kerrin. "You're known as a fair and just lord, and your Company — "

The Duke waved her to silence. "Compared to some, Marshal, that may be so. But compared to what this Company was — well, you can ask my captains, if you don't believe me." He nodded to Dorrin, Arcolin, and the others. No one responded. The Duke continued. "The last year I campaigned in Aarenis, even I had to admit the changes. We were short of men, through treachery — I expect you've heard the tale of Dwarfwatch — "

The Marshal-General nodded. "Yes. So I called back veterans, and when that wasn't enough, I hired free swords in Aarenis itself. That changed the Company. Worse than that, I used them as I'd never used them before, and when Siniava was caught, I — " He looked up as Paks stirred. The Marshal-General, too, looked at her. Paks wished the Duke would not speak of that time, but he smiled at her and went on. "I was so angry, Marshal-General, at his treachery, at his cruelty to my men and others, that I would have tortured him, had Paks not stopped me. And I was angry with her, at the time."

"But you didn't." The Marshal-General's voice was remote and cool.

"No. I wanted to, though."

"You could have — you, a commander, didn't have to listen to a — what was she then, anyway? Private? Corporal?"

"Private. I did have to — I'd given my word. If you want the whole story, ask her or the paladin who was there."

Amberion stirred. "That would have been Fenith. He died the next year, in the Westmounts."

"So." The Marshal-General took the conversation again. "You chose to honor your word, and by what you say gave up your anger at Paksenarrion — that sounds like little dishonor, my lord Duke."

"Enough," said the Duke soberly. "Enough to change the Company, to risk my people here — for that's what happened, what I left them open to, when I took the veterans that could fight. And then to fall under the spell of Venneristimon's sister — if that was his sister — "

The Marshal-General stood. "My lord, I would hear more of this, if you wish, but if you have wounded, we should see to them."

"As you will. If you'll excuse me, Dorrin can take you to them; if I go over there, the surgeons will scold."

"Perhaps we should begin with you?"

"No. I'm not in danger. Dorrin?"

"Certainly, my lord. Marshal-General, will you come?" Dorrin moved to the door, and the Marshal-General and Amberion followed. Kerrin looked at her, but the Marshal-General waved her back.

"We'll send if we need you, Kerrin; keep warm in the meantime."

When they had gone, Kerrin looked at the Duke. "My lord Duke, I've seen you ride by, but not met you — "

"Nor I you. Yours is the nearest grange?"

"Southward, yes. West you might come to Stilldale a little sooner. It was but a barton until a few years ago." She drained her mug of sib, and poured another. "You won't remember, perhaps, but I had an uncle in your Company: Garin Arcosson, in Arcolin's cohort. He — "

"I remember. He was file-second of the third. Killed by a crossbow bolt in — let me think — the siege of Cortes Cilwan, I think, wasn't it? A lanky fellow, with a white forelock, that turned white early."

Kerrin nodded. "I'm impressed, my lord, that you remember so well. That was years ago—"

The Duke shrugged. "It's important to know one's men. And I have a knack for names."

"Even so. I remember when his sword came home, and his medallion; the Marshal of our grange hung them there for all to see. And my aunt, my lord, lived well enough on his pension." She coughed delicately. "Do I understand, my lord, from what you've said, that you will be placing your Company under Gird once more?"

"That depends. In the years since the last Marshal here died, I have recruited many who were not Girdsmen — indeed, not Falkians, or following any of the martial patrons. Yet most are good men, hard but honorable fighters. I would not have them distressed — I owe it to them — "

"My lord, it would be far from my desire — and I believe I speak for the Marshal-General here — to coerce warriors faithful to another to change faith. I am aware that among your soldiers are those who follow Tir and Sertig as well as the High Lord, Gird, and Falk. And your responsibilities under the crown of Tsaia, I realize, will forbid any venturing of the Company for Gird. But should you desire such protection — even a Marshal resident here — that can be arranged."

"You seem confident." The Duke frowned at her.

"I am." Kerrin turned her mug in her hands. "My lord Duke, it may seem strange to you, who have been at odds with the granges for so long, but Gird himself mistakes no honest heart. We have never shared that quarrel, only watched from afar." The Duke started to speak, but Kerrin went on, heedless. "I swear to you, my lord, that if we had known anything definite — if we had been able to tell who or what was the source of that evil that tainted your lands and gossiped against you at court, we would have told you." The Duke settled back in his chair; Paks noticed that the remaining captains were rigid in theirs. "But," Kerrin went on, "without the right to come here, and investigate, we could do nothing. I don't know if you believe prayer to have any power — but I tell you that at the granges at Burningmeed and Stilldale prayers for you and your Company were offered at every service. We of Gird — and sensible nobles of the Council — well knew that you and you alone stand between Tsaia and the northern wastes, and what comes out of them."

"You could have said something," muttered Cracolnya. The Duke shot him a look, but did not speak. Kerrin cocked her head.

"Could we? Think about it, Captain. How well would you have listened, had I come, or sent my yeoman-marshal, to tell you that something — undefined, but something — was wrong in your cohort or the stronghold? If I had seen the traitor — your steward, Venneristimon, wasn't it?" Cracolnya and the others nodded. "If I had seen him, I might have known. But how to convince you?"

"Prayer," muttered the Duke.

Kerrin gave a tight smile. "Just prayer, my lord. But Gird has more weapons than one in his belt, and he sent a fine sword." She nodded at Paks.

"True enough." The Duke sighed, leaning back in his chair. "With all respect, Kerrin, I would talk to the Marshal-General about this —"

"Indeed."

"Even though I was wrong to be so angry before, still the Girdsmen make mistakes."

Kerrin laughed. "My lord Duke, our legends say that even Gird himself made mistakes. We are but human. The Marshal-General admitted one to you herself. But we all fight, as best we know, against the powers of evil. We all try to strengthen our realm — whether steading or grange — in anything good."

"Yes. Well — " The Duke paused. Paks, watching, noticed a grayer tinge to his face. She glanced at Arcolin, who met her eyes and nodded. He stood and moved behind the Duke's chair.

"My lord, I must remind you of the surgeon's orders."

"Nonsense. We have guests — "

"Marshal Kerrin," Arcolin went on, "the surgeons made me promise to remind the Duke of their opinion. If you will excuse him — "

"Certainly." Kerrin looked concerned. "Should I call the Marshal-General?"

"No. Paks will fetch a surgeon."

"Viniet is upstairs, Captain."

"Good."

The Duke started to protest, then subsided, leaning heavily on the arm of his chair. "Tir's gut, Arcolin — excuse me, Marshal — it's just — "

"A mere cut. I know. I know as well that you were hardly in your bed enough to warm it before going back to work. And if we're truly, as the Marshal says, the one bar to the northern troubles, then we've no desire to lose you, my lord."

Paks did not witness the Duke's meeting with the Marshal-General in his study late that day. They were closeted for several hours; she spent the time talking with Amberion. He had been called to a border fort along the south border of Fintha, and had spent the summer convincing farmers in the area that they could indeed repel the mountain-dwelling robbers.

"Though most of those robbers were poor folk enough," said Amberion thoughtfully. "Some years back they'd left a barony in a mountain valley because of the great cruelty of the baron. There in the heights they could not grow enough food for themselves, and when they lost weapons in hunting, could replace them only by raiding. Some of them would be glad enough to settle in the farmlands, if there were farmland to spare. A few, though — " he shook his head. "It's easy for such demons as Liart to gain worshippers when men must live like wolves or die anyway."

"But why farmers?" asked Paks. "Couldn't the local lord — count or whatever — have held the keep and protected them?"

"No, not in Fintha. In Fintha nearly all farmland is freehold; our lords are those who hold enough that they can't work it all themselves. Even then there are very few with such estates as the Marrakai or Verrakai — or even your Duke — in Tsaia and Lyonya." When she looked puzzled, he went on. "Come now, Paksenarrion, you had more history than that in your months with us. Gird himself was a peasant. Fintha is the center of his cult. By Finthan law, each farmer owns the lands he can plow. Grazing land is usually owned in common, though in the north, where you came from, it may be held by the farmer. But the Hall never makes large grants of land, such as your Duke got, in return for raising a troop. Those who are given a grant must work it themselves, and each man owes service to Gird when it's needed. If someone has more land, it was inherited, perhaps from two families. The nearest lord to that border fort could offer only himself and his older sons to aid. Which he did." Amberion paused. "One of them died there."

By the time Paks had told him about her summer in Lyonya with the rangers, the Duke's conference was over. They were called in, along with the Duke's captains.

"We have settled more than one thing," said the Duke. He was somewhat pale, still, but seemed steadier. "First, it's clear to both of us that the Company cannot go back as it was. It's been fifteen years since my wife was killed, fifteen years during which no effort was made to screen out those who are not Girdsmen. The veterans of those fifteen years have served me well, and I will not change the rules on them now. Yet some of the changes in those years were for the worse, and we will work to reverse them.

"As far as my domain goes, the past fifteen years, again, have seen changes and growth in directions which Tammarrion and I had not planned. My relations with the Regency Council, my duties — these cannot be set aside.

"What we have agreed, then, is this: I will accept, in my domain, the influence of Gird. Granges will be built wherever enough Girdsmen gather; bartons will serve the rest. A Marshal will be stationed either here or on the plain between Duke's East and West, at the discretion of the Marshal-General, and I will grant sufficient land for the support of that grange. Girdsmen among the Company will be encouraged to be active in the grange. As for me — " He looked aside, then around at them all. "Most of you know little of my background. Until I came to live with the Halverics — " a slight stir at this; Paks had not known it until Stammel mentioned it; neither had most of the others. " — until then, I followed no god or patron. I had heard of none I would follow." His face had settled into grim lines. "The Halverics were, as they are, Falkians, and from them and their example I first learned of the High Lord, and of Falk. I had served Aliam Halveric as squire for some years, and he sponsored me as a novice with the Knights of Falk, as a reward. Too great a reward, as I found later; he never told me of the cost of such sponsorship. He hoped, I believe, that I would swear fealty to Falk, and become one of them."

"But then — how did you end up a Girdsman?" Pont's long face was sober.

803

"Well — as to that — I didn't. Precisely." The Duke shuffled a scroll across his desk. "To go back: I was knighted after two years, in the Falkian order, but I had sworn no word to Falk. I'm not sure why, actually, but I never felt a call to do so. Then — again with Aliam Halveric's help — I began on my own as a mercenary captain in Tsaia. Arcolin remembers that. A couple of years here and there garrisoning forts no one else wanted to bother with. Caravan work. That sort of thing. Then my first big contract, as an independent with the crown. We didn't even have a full cohort; Arcolin had to scour the streets to make up our numbers. But out of that came this — " He waved his arm to indicate the domain, "and many more contracts. Then Tammarrion joined the Company, and we married, and she was a Girdsman in full." He stopped, and Arcolin moved quickly to pour him some wine. The Duke sipped, and went on.

"I had hired Girdsmen before because they were honest and hard-working. After her I hired them because she wished it. We married, as you know, in the Hall at Fin Panir — also her desire. But though I lived as a Girdsman, and gave freely to the fellowship of Gird, I never took the vows myself." He took another swallow of wine. "Again, I don't know why. Tammarrion often asked me, and it's one of the few things I failed to do that she wished. I think I felt — " He stopped again, and looked past them all, as if across a field of battle. "I felt sometimes that another vow was waiting somewhere, and that I must be free to take it." He shook his head. "Foolishness, perhaps. Yet Tamar felt, or so she said, that until I made my vow freely and willingly, Gird would not begrudge my waiting. And after she died, I — " His head bowed for an instant. "I would not."

"And now?" asked Dorrin.

"Now is difficult. You, Captain, have argued that I disgraced my former allegiance." For the only time, Paks saw a flush on Dorrin's cheek. "You were right, except that I had none. I agree that I was wrong, and I am willing to amend — but I still feel a reluctance to commit myself to Gird."

"But surely — " Marshal Kerrin looked sideways at the Marshal-General.

"As things stand," she said firmly, "I do not ask Duke Phelan to join the fellowship of Gird."

"But why?"

Her eyebrows arched. "Are you asking what we said to each other? For therein lies the reason. Since you have a nearby grange, I will assure you it is from no lack of trust in him. But I agree with him that the time for making such a pledge has not come to him."

"As for you, my captains," the Duke said, regaining control of the room, "you may choose freely to stay or go, with full honor. I will be trying to do what Tamar and I had once planned, within the limits I've mentioned. I have enough wealth, now, and enough land is in plow, that I need not take the Company to Aarenis again — certainly not for several years. Instead, I will try to make of this domain what our vision was: a fruitful land, governed justly, and serving as a strong ward between the rest of Tsaia and the northern waste. If you are not comfortable with that vision, if you are unhappy with the thought of a Marshal constantly among us, you may come to me at any time, privately, and leave with my thanks and a substantial reward."

"You know I will stay," said Arcolin quickly, and the others nodded.

"That offer stands, nonetheless," said the Duke. "If in the future you change your mind — any of you — you have served me well for many years, and you will not find me ungrateful."

"But when will you tell the Company?" asked Arcolin. "Do you want us — ?"

The Duke shook his head. "No. They should hear it from me, I think. Rumors are flying already, I daresay. Tomorrow — no, for Keri may die tonight. The day after, I think. Plan a formal inspection; the Marshal-General may like to see them up close. And I'll tell them then. The same offer applies — I will be fair to my veterans no matter what their faith."

A sharp wind had scoured all clouds from the sky, and left it pale and clean. Paks, standing now as squire beside the Duke, watched the Company wheel into review formation, after an hour of intricate drill. She glanced sideways at the Marshal-General. Her eyes were alight in that impassive face. Paks looked back at the Company. It had never seemed so impressive. She felt almost like two people — one here beside the Duke, cold from the wind, and another in formation, file first of the second file in Arcolin's cohort, waiting for Stammel's brusque commands.

They halted, lines straight as stretched string. Paks scanned the faces she knew so well. Stammel, his brown eyes watchful. Devlin, somehow conveying grace even while standing still (hard to believe he had five children, one nearly old enough to be a recruit.) Arñe, newly promoted to corporal, trying not to grin. Vik. Barra. Natzlin. Rauf, who would retire to his little farm as soon as they were sure the orcs had gone. The captains pivotted to face the Duke, and bowed. The Duke gestured to the Marshal-General, and they moved to the first cohort, Paks and the others following.

The Duke had a word for most of them. The Marshal-General, beside him, said nothing, but looked into each face. Paks felt very odd, walking along the lines, and knowing so well what it felt like to wait for the inspecting party to pass. When they reached the recruit lines, she was poised between laughter and tears. She knew the strain in the neck, the struggle to look only forward, the trembling hands that stiffened as they went by. One girl forgot to say "my lord," and blushed so that Paks remembered her own lapse as a recruit. A boy's voice cracked on the words, and he broke into a sweat. Another stammered.

At last they were done, and the Duke returned to his place before the Company. He waited a moment, as if for silence, though nothing had made a sound.

"Sword-brethren," he began, and Paks saw as well as felt the response to that old term. "You all remember what I told you after we defeated the orcs attacking Duke's East. You have seen the Marshal-General of Gird, High

805

Marshal Connaught, Marshal Kerrin of Burningmeed, and the Gird's paladin Sir Amberion. Some of you have felt the healing grace of Gird through them. You have sensed, perhaps, that a change has come to me, and through me to the Company. Some of you, I hope very few, may be worried about it." He paused and looked slowly from one cohort to another. "You older veterans, who remember the days when Tammarrion Mistiannyi was my lady here, and our children were growing — " Paks saw the shock ripple across the faces of the older ones. "Yes, I can speak of that now. You will remember how the Company was then, when a Marshal of Gird lived here, in the stronghold, with us. Those days, my friends, are past these fifteen years. Yet good and evil have not changed, and I welcome, from this day on, Girdsmen, yeoman and Marshal, to this domain. I am not myself sworn to that fellowship, but I am sworn, as always, to the crown of Tsaia, and to the cause of good, as the High Lord and his servants Gird and Falk are.

"You have always served me well. You deserve, therefore, this choice: to stay, in spite of these changes, or to go, with my respect and a settlement reflecting your years of service. We will be in the north for a few years — no fat contracts in Aarenis, no chance of plunder. If you prefer such service, I will recommend any of you to any commander you name. Speak to your captains, or to me, and it will be done as you desire." He paused again, but no one moved or spoke. Paks found tears stinging her eyes. "I hope," he went on, "that none of you go. Girdsmen or no, you are all such warriors as anyone would be proud to lead. If you stay, we shall be making, by Gird's grace, a place of justice, a domain fruitful and safe, and a strong defense for the northern border. Whatever you decide, I am proud to have had you — each one of you — in my Company. You may be proud of your deeds." He stepped back, bowed to the captains, and they turned again to their cohorts. The Marshal-General nodded to him.

"You are as generous as just, my lord Duke."

His voice was slightly husky. "They are — they deserve it."

"If they do, I know where they learned it. By Gird's cudgel, my lord, I must say that even after your message I had not hoped for this reception. I thought that at best you would let us help you in the crisis. You are not a Girdsman, and yet you have done as much as if you were — while being more than fair to your soldiers. My predecessor, Enherian, spoke very well of you — told me, when I became Marshal-General, that one of his regrets was the breach between you and the fellowship of Gird. Now I see why."

The Duke moved away, eyes distant. "I have no quarrel with Gird's view of things, as you know."

"No." She walked beside him, and Paks trailed, with the others. "I would like, my lord, to hear Paksenarrion's tale of her healing. Do you mind?"

The Duke looked back to catch Paks's eye. "It's her story, Marshal-General. If she's ready to tell it, I would like to hear it myself. But I will not command it."

"I would be likelier to command a stone to fly, than that. But I confess a professional interest in it — I was wrong, but I'd like to know how I erred so." The Marshal-General turned and grinned at Paks. "Will you tell us, or must we itch with curiosity the rest of our days?"

Paks found herself grinning, even though she had tensed at the question. "I will try, Marshal-General, but it's a tangled tale, and parts of it I do not understand myself."

Chapter Thirteen

The Duke led the way upstairs, past his study door, to his private apartment at the end of the passage. Paks looked around as she came in. A fire burned in the small fireplace at one end of the chamber; several padded chairs were grouped around it and a small footed table. Tapestries hung on the walls. Behind a low divider at the far end of the room, a great bed loomed, but it had neither mattress nor hangings. A narrow bed, made up with a striped blanket, stood along one wall.

"Sit down," urged the Duke, as Paks hesitated. The Marshal-General had already chosen a chair, and propped her feet on a stool near the fire. Paks tried to guess which chair was his, and finally took one to the side of the fire. The arm-rests were carved, beyond the padding, into dragons' heads. The Duke took a seat opposite her, and stretched his legs. "This is how it used to be," he said softly. "When we built this end of the stronghold, this is where we held council. The office I use now was the scribes' room. It's many a night I sat here with Tamar and Marshal Vrelan." He poured out three mugs of sib from the pot on the table, and offered them.

The Marshal-General glanced at him, her eyes bright in the firelight. "If you don't mind my asking, my lord, how old are you?"

"About fifty years. Why?"

"I had thought you younger, when you came to Fin Panir, but remembering that you and your wife had children who would have been, so you say, as old as Paksenarrion, I began to wonder."

The Duke grinned. "I was angry then. Anger makes me younger."

"Not only that. Most men your age are less vigorous, especially after such a life as yours. I have heard you were orphaned, but you must have come from strong stock."

"I don't know." His voice hardened, and the Marshal-General sighed.

"I did not mean to distress you — "

"It is not you who distresses me, Marshal-General, but the thought of it. I have no family — never knew who I was, really. I know nothing of my breeding, nothing of my heritage of strength or weakness, folly or wisdom. My name could come from anywhere in southern Tsaia or the Westlands: I thought when I met another Kieri, my first year in Aarenis, that I'd found a kinsman, but soon learned that Kir and Kieri are common as cobbles there."

"Your family name?"

"Phelan? I found one Phelan in Pliuni, in a wineshop; he said his kin were short and dark. Another in Fossnir, a tailor, and a woolsorter in Ambela. That's all: none like me, and none missing any children. By looks I should be northern; anywhere in the Eight Kingdoms you find tall men with red hair and gray eyes. So take your choice. Unwanted bastard's the easiest, fostered out somewhere and forgotten." Paks could hear the pain in his voice. "And then the family I bred was destroyed. Nothing before me — and like to be nothing after me. Who will I leave this to? I swear to you, it was that thought, and that alone, that let me fall to the spell of Venner's sister. Here I am, in the range of fifty years or so, and I have no heir. I have sworn to go back to building this domain — but for what?"

She nodded. "It is no easy puzzle, my lord. It is hard for any man to work years on such a project, and see nothing ahead — "

"But it falling apart when I die. In what — twenty years perhaps? — I will be too old to lead them, if not before. Indeed, Marshal-General, I wonder that Achrya hurried so. Time alone will do her work here."

"My lord, no!" Paks found herself speaking before she thought. "That isn't so. You will find someone to take over here, I know it. And what you have done so far has been worth doing — "

The Duke smiled, a little sadly. "I'm glad you think so, Paks. I hope the High Lord thinks so, as well. But — forgive me — when I look at you, and think of Estil, my daughter — she would have been so like you — "

"My lord, by your leave, I will think on this, and perhaps be able to make some useful suggestion." The Marshal-General sat forward, hands clasped in her lap. "You have made a settled domain out of wasteland, and the holdings south of you no longer fear invasion every year or so. This in itself is useful, besides the rest. This will not disappear, if the fellowship of Gird can save it."

"Thank you." The Duke sighed, and reached a hand for the poker to stir the fire. "Well, now, Paks, we've set you at ease, no doubt, with this other talk. Tell us, if you will, what befell you after you left Fin Panir."

Paks took a deep breath and set her mug on the table. "You remember," she began slowly, "how it was with me that last week — " They nodded. "I can see now," she went on, "that it was foolish to leave then, in winter, in that mood. It went as badly, Marshal-General, as you had feared."

"I had hoped sending word to the granges would help — "

"It might have, if I had been able to use them." Paks found herself breathing short, and tried to relax. "As it was, I feared the ridicule so that I could not, after the first time."

"Ridicule? I told them — "

"No, lady, not their fault." Paks tried again. "They did not mean to hurt me; the Marshal, where I stopped that time, tried to be kind. But my weakness is the very thing — they would have understood a missing leg," she said hurriedly. "Blindness, something they could see or understand. But Girdsmen are taught that cowardice is shameful, that it comes from within, and cannot be imposed from without."

The Marshal-General nodded slowly. "We ourselves caused you trouble."

Paks shook her head. "I don't blame you. It's the common thought anywhere, not only among Girdsmen. So I thought myself, even knowing how it had happened. I blamed myself for that weakness —"

"Paksenarrion, we told you it was not your weakness, no more than one chooses to lose an arm to a sword."

"So you said, but I could not believe it." Even now, the memory of that misery made the breath catch in her throat. She stared at her right hand, gripping the armrest of the chair. "I — had a difficult winter." They said nothing, and waited. "What Venner's sister said, my lord, about my running away many times — that was true. I did." As quickly and baldly as she could, she told them about it: being run off by the shepherds, being abandoned by the trader when she could not fight against bandits. Her fear of everything, everyone, that reduced her to a shivering wreck.

"How long did this last?" The Duke's voice was gentle.

Paks closed her mouth on the rest of that story. "Until early spring, my lord." She decided to say nothing of the incident in the inn, or the nights she spent shivering in ditches. She glanced at the Duke, and it seemed as if he knew that without her telling; his eyes were bright with tears. "I came back to Brewersbridge," she said flatly, and stopped again. They waited. Finally she went on with the tale. Clearly the Marshal-General wished she had gone to the grange instead of the Kuakgan's grove, but she listened without interruption as Paks told about the initial healing, and the days of quiet talk that had restored some of her spirit. Paks was surprised to see her nodding agreement when she heard the Kuakgan's comments on the nature of courage. Both the Duke and the Marshal-General were fascinated when she told about her service with the rangers in Lyonya. They seemed to know much that Paks had learned only that summer, asking questions about the relations of elves and humans and other matters Paks knew little about. When she told them of the daskdraudigs, and of the rangers' questions afterwards, the Marshal-General choked on her sib and sat bolt upright.

Paks nodded. "That's when I first realized that I had some of those powers given to paladins. They were surprised that I could sense the location of the daskdraudigs. And they asked me to try healing one of them —"

"Gird's grace! I wouldn't have thought —"

"And — it worked. I was as surprised, my lady, as if I'd sprouted wings."

"Mmm." The Marshal-General stared at her. "No wonder."

"Then, toward the end of summer, I began to feel a — a sense of something wrong here, that the Duke needed me. I came back through Brewersbridge." She went on to tell of that last night with the Kuakgan. Both the Duke and the Marshal-General were open-mouthed.

"Gird, certainly," murmured the Marshal-General. "A silver cup — the horse, the flowers — child, you could not have come closer to the gods and still been on this earth."

810

"And then what?" asked the Duke.

"And then, when I was aware of myself again, I found that all the old joy had returned, my lord."

"And you feel no bitterness, Paksenarrion, for that half-year or more of loss?"

Paks shook her head. "No, Marshal-General. The Kuakgan was right. Now I know what Gird himself knew — how those who cannot fight feel when in danger. And I know that the delight in battle, what we soldiers think of as courage, is not essential, even to a soldier. I need not call up anger any more — and the anger I called, in Kolobia, opened the way for Achrya's evil. I know that I can, if I but ask the gods, know what is right, and do it."

The Marshal-General held her gaze for some moments in silence. "Well," she said finally, "You told Amberion you were not yet sworn to Gird — but I can tell, Paksenarrion, that you are no longer my blade to wield. You have gone beyond that. Gird and the High Lord know what they would have you do; I cannot direct you."

Paks smiled. "Yet I respect your wisdom and experience — "

"Don't fence with me, child. I believe you are truly a paladin, called in the old way by the gods directly. And not by one of them, but by several. If you can use any of my experience, you are welcome to it — but I expect you'll use it in ways I cannot foresee."

"If that is so," said the Duke, "then her mission here must have been at their bidding."

The Marshal-General shot him a quick glance. "Certainly. Can you doubt it?"

"But why? What — "

"To maintain the protection you built here. That's one thing. I don't know what else. I don't know if her mission here is finished. Do you, Paksenarrion?"

"I feel no call to go, at this time."

"Then you will stay — if you will."

Paks grinned. "I will stay."

"You have still a horse and armor in Fin Panir. They will be waiting for you when you come. Or ask, and we will send them where you will." The Marshal-General sat back with a sigh. "Duke Phelan, I cannot recall a more surprising few days, and that includes my first half-year as a yeoman-marshal."

"Nor I. Not since — " he said, then stopped, staring into the fire. But when they looked questioningly at him, he shook his head. "One person's tale is enough at one time. Long ago I was saved, suddenly and unexpectedly, from great evil, but I will not speak of that now."

"Do you think many of your soldiers will leave, with the influence of Gird returning?" asked the Marshal-General, in what was obviously an attempt to be tactful.

"I hope not. You and your paladin found none who are truly evil, but some might still find our changes distasteful. Campaigning in the south meant excitement, a chance for riches, the company of other mercenaries — "

Paks herself had sometimes thought that Valdaire, full of mercenaries from a dozen companies or more, was the best place to be. She thought of the times she'd walked in to *The White Dragon* with Vik and Arñe — and before then, with Saben and Canna, for a pleasant evening. They would miss that, with no city nearer than Vérella.

Even so, Paks was surprised when the first list appeared of those leaving. Barranyi, who had joined the same year that she did, headed the list. She realized now that Barra had not been around, those times old friends gathered to talk; she had wondered only briefly, and thought no more of it. Without saying anything to the Duke, Paks went to talk with her. She found her already packing her things, with Natzlin watching, stony-faced.

"You!" Barra said, as Paks came up. "I'm surprised to see you hanging around common soldiers, Paks. But I suppose you remember that I knew you before you became such a famous hero."

"Barra — !" Natzlin's voice shook.

Paks herself was shocked at the venom in Barra's words. "What are you angry about, Barra? I thought we were friends — "

"Friends! If ever we were, it was long ago. Before you started thinking you were the High Lord's special messenger. I saw through you a long time ago, Paksenarrion Dorthansdotter. I knew you'd cause trouble in the end, and so you have!"

"Barra, that's not fair!" Natzlin threw a quick look at Paks, then touched Barra's arm. "She's changed, yes, but so have you."

"We've all changed. She's just — " Barra folded her lips together as she rolled another tunic and stuffed it in her pack. Then she turned to Natzlin. "And you — what's she done to you, that you're staying, eh? Do you think there's room for more than one hero around here? As long as Paks is with the Duke, that's who's going to get the notice. You might as well come, Natzlin; you'll end up a scarred old veteran with nothing to show for it but a few measly apple trees, like Kolya."

"I like apple trees." Natzlin turned toward Paks. "I don't know why she blames you. I know it's not your fault — "

"Tir's gut, it's not!" Barra grabbed Natzlin's arms and swung her around. "Who was it that let herself be banned when it was that man's fault? And who was the 'hero' of Dwarfwatch? And who talked the Duke out of handling Siniava as he should have? Who have we heard about, night and day, this past year? Who, but poor, brave, wonderful Paks! And I thought Effa was a sugar-tit, with her 'Gird this, and Gird that' all the time. And she got killed, and I knew what Gird thought of *her*. But Paks!" Barra flung her pack across the room, startling the junior privates who had been loafing there, and had not heard any of it. She turned to Paks, her face pale under its tan. "You!" she said again. "You were no better when we started. By Tir, I remember giving you plenty of lumps in practice, if you don't. You had no special powers — you said it yourself. But you had all the chances. Everything came to you, praise and plenty all the time — " Paks thought of Saben's death, and Canna's, and the bitter hours she'd spent in combat with dire and dreadful things — the elfane taig, the kuaknom of Kolobia, the daskdraudigs. Praise and plenty? After last winter's starvation and contempt? She said nothing, realizing that the facts meant nothing now to Barra, lost in her own bitterness and anger.

"I could have done better," said Barra harshly, not bothering to lower her voice. "I could have — and I'll tell you this, Paks — I wouldn't have gone craven, as you did, to become the laughingstock of half the north — " So those tales had come this far, Paks realized. At the moment, it seemed less important than Barra's rage. "I'd have died decently," Barra went on, "if I couldn't live decently."

Paks looked at her. Where had the young girl gone, she wondered, who had had the same dreams she had had? Where was the laughing girl, who had snatched the last plum tart from the table one night, and tossed it to Paks across the crowded mess hall? It had disintegrated, Paks remembered, after a dozen or so throws. What had happened, to turn someone who dreamed of being a hero, even a paladin, into this hard and bitter soldier? Had the kernel of evil always been there? An old conversation with Vik trickled out of her memory: " . . . you think she's good because you like her," he had said. "But people aren't like that. . . . " Perhaps it had been there, even then, and her liking for Barra had blinded her. Certainly it was here now, and visible to her senses. She wondered how the Marshal-General and Amberion had missed it, when they walked among the Company searching for just such danger.

"I'm sorry, Barra, that you think this," said Paks quietly. "I expect you might have done better — many might have. But I was the one there."

Barra laughed harshly. "Yes — you were. You always got the chance. Do you remember the night you came into the camp in Rotengre? I wondered, after, why you were the only one to make it through. Did the gods help you, Paks, or was it something you did?"

Her meaning was unmistakable. Natzlin gasped a protest, and Paks was suddenly breathless with rage. Without thought, she was alight, casting a white radiance that dimmed the winter daylight throught the windows. Barra shrank, eyes squinted nearly shut. Paks fought the rage down, and damped her light. She merely looked at Barra, and Barra looked back. Natzlin, tears running down her face, turned her back on Barra and walked out of the room.

"You'll find, someday," Paks found herself saying, "that your own tongue cuts you worse than any blade. I cannot even offer you the satisfaction of a fight, for you could not stand against me — and you know it. Go make your peace with Natzlin before you leave her — she's been a true friend to you all these years."

"A lover isn't always a friend," said Barra, still clenched in her rage.

"Not always. But she is, and you know it. Leave here angry with me, if

813

you will, or with the Duke. But do not leave Natzlin to bear the burden of it." And Paks held her gaze until Barra's rigidity eased, and she looked down.

"Tir's gut," she said crossly, but without the intensity she'd had. "You'd think she was your lover, the way you care about her feelings."

"Good luck, Barra, wherever you go."

"Just don't follow me, Paks!" The intensity was back, the dark eyes snapping with anger. "Just get out of my way, give me a chance."

Outside the door, Paks met Dorrin, who shook her head with a wry smile. They headed across the courtyard to the mess hall. "You won't stop that one," Dorrin said on the way.

"I had to try —"

"You were recruits together, I remember. But she wasn't your friend, was she?"

"I thought so."

Dorrin shook her head again. "Paks, Barra's had as few friends as anyone in the Company. Only Natzlin —"

"Well, she was always prickly —"

"She was always ready to take offense at anything, and she'd hold a grudge until it died of old age. She's a skilled fighter, and honest, and works hard — all good. But I've heard more harsh things about her, from my sergeants, than about the rest of your recruit year put together. She wasn't *bad* — not the way I could complain of — but she hadn't a generous bone in her, and she'd a way of talking that kept everyone miserable. She didn't just love women — that's no problem — but she hated men, as well. And she has the most dangerous of beliefs: that things are unfair for her. The High Lord knows things are unfair. But they're unfair for us all. That's the way the world is." She sighed, and leaned on the mess hall door. "It's Natzlin that will suffer, as usual. I don't know how many times Natz has apologized to others, and smoothed things over. I'm glad she's staying, but I don't know how she'll do."

"I didn't know others had had trouble —"

"No. You haven't been here, or in my cohort."

Paks did not see Barranyi again before she left. Within a week, it seemed the Company had settled into its new routine. The Girdsmen volunteered to work on the grange on their time off. Others joined them, from time to time. Wideflung patrols, riding out on the frosty hills, had not found any concentrations of orcs, and the orc raids on farms had ceased. The last of the damage had been repaired in Duke's East, and the millstones were back in place. The Marshal-General held the first services for Girdsmen, and then declared she had to leave.

"If I don't go now," she said, looking at the sky, "I might end up wintering here. That won't do; I've work in Fin Panir. Thank you, my lord Duke, for your invitation and courtesy, and our prayers will be with you."

"I thank you," he said.

"Paksenarrion," she said, turning to Paks, "you know you are welcome in Fin Panir. You have friends who would be glad to see you. But I know you are under other orders than mine — so if I do not see you again this side of the High Lord's table, you have my prayers and my goodwill."

Paks bowed, and thanked her. It had taken but an hour for the Marshal-General's party to be ready for travel, and now they walked across the Duke's Court before a whipping north wind. Once in the main courtyard, the Marshal-General took a last look around the stronghold.

"Duke Phelan, " she said, "a man who can bring this order out of the chaos that was the north borders need not fear his work will waste. I cannot say what will come, for I have no prophecy, but I feel that your power is only now beginning to come into its strength. Gird's grace, and the High Lord's favor, on all you do." She mounted quickly, and turned her horse to the gate. Again the trumpets rang out. This time, the soldiers in the courtyard raised a cheer, and the Marshal-General and her party rode out onto the windy plain.

Chapter Fourteen

Over the next few weeks, Paks divided her time between attending the Duke and leading scouting parties of archers north and east from the stronghold. No orcs showed, but the Duke took no chances.

"I don't want to take the whole Company into the Lairs," he explained, pulling out the old charts of those tangled burrows and tunnels. "It would take the whole Company, at least — we never did follow these all the way to the end. We'll post a guard closer to the Lairs, and ride patrols, and let that be it in this weather." For hard winter had set in, with a bank of cloud to the north that promised storms of snow.

Although Paks was still uneasy about it, the rest of the Company accepted her unusual status calmly. On patrol, she wore the Duke's uniform and carried a short sword or bow; her friends had gotten over their shyness, and chatted with her easily. But she lived in the Duke's Court, with the captains, and ate at the Duke's table. His armorer was making a set of chainmail for her. She drilled on both sides of the gate: with the captains and the Duke himself at longsword both afoot and ahorse, and with Siger and the others for short sword and bow. She rode in with the Duke to meet with the Councils of Duke's East and West. Here she learned things about farming that she had never learned on her father's farm. She began to see how all the crafts and trades in the Duke's lands fit together, how he could know how much of what supplies to order from Vérella.

In the evenings, she listened as the captains and the Duke discussed not only his realm, but other realms around. She heard the story of his first visit to Kostandan — and why Sofi Ganarrion was willing to help him in Aarenis. Gradually she learned more about the Duke himself — that he had been Aliam Halveric's senior squire once, that he had won his title and domain after taking command of the Tsaian army after the death of the crown prince, and defeating a Pargunese force along the border. Tammarrion's sword, she learned, was a wedding gift from Aliam Halveric; Tammarrion herself had been Finthan, from Blackbone Hill.

With maps and models, the Duke and his captains made clear the relationship of the Eight Kingdoms: the forests and hills, the non-human kingdoms of gnome and dwarf. They reinforced the things she'd learned in Fin Panir, and extended them . . . the correct forms of address for different officers in each kingdom, the insignia of all the knightly orders, the little niceties of etiquette at each court. And they asked for her tales, especially of Fin Panir and Kolobia. At first she was shy of speaking before them, but this soon passed.

Day by day, as the Duke recovered from his wounds, and the threat of orc invasion lessened, the mood of the Company changed. Paks thought it was for the better — more smiles, more laughter in the mess hall, but without any less intensity or eagerness in drill. The Duke himself seemed more relaxed, and at the same time more alert. He gave his whole attention to each problem that came up, from the restocking of orc-burnt farms to the blocking of the tunnel in the wine-cellar. Paks had always thought of Arcolin as stern, and Dorrin as remote and severe, but even these captains thawed, showing her the warmth and humor hidden behind their authority. Part of this was certainly due to the actions of the Gird's Marshal.

Before the midwinter festival, Marshal Kerrin had transferred to the stronghold; her replacement had arrived in Burningmeed. Frost was in the ground before the foundations of the new grange were finished, so she traveled from the stronghold to the villages for services. Paks sometimes rode with her. Although younger than other Marshals she'd known, Kerrin impressed her with her ability. She had served two other granges as yeoman-marshal before training in Fin Panir, and had seen action in western Fintha against the nomads. Her steady, cheerful ways attracted many to the new grange.

The day before Midwinter Feast, Paks rode out with Stammel and a patrol into the hills northwest of the stronghold. As often at midwinter, it was clear, and wind had scoured the snow from the ground. Only a light breeze sifted along the ground, sharp as a sword-edge. Paks kept her face tucked into the hood of her cloak.

A sudden flurry of hoofbeats caught her attention; at the same time the forward scout yelled. She turned to see a red horse gallop out of a gap in the hills.

"A demon horse!" yelled the scout. "It must be! Shoot it!" He yanked his bow from his shoulder.

"No!" Paks twisted to watch as the horse circled the group. "Wait. It's not evil — "

"Are you sure?" asked Stammel, at her side. She nodded, watching the horse, which has slowed to a springy trot.

"I don't feel anything evil in it. I would, if it were a demon."

The others turned their horses to watch. The red horse seemed too slick to have been out in the weather; their own mounts were shaggier. It had white stockings behind, and a white star on the forehead. It pranced around them, blowing long jets of white vapor. Paks noted the size — as tall as her black warhorse, but built more for speed, a little lighter.

"Let's see if we can catch it," suggested Stammel.

"Good idea." Paks waved the others out to form wings, and they tried to pen the horse among them. It flung up its head and bolted, kicking up gouts of snow and frozen earth, and streaking past their horses with a mocking whinny.

"I think it's some kind of enchanted," said Stammel. "No ordinary horse — "

"Oh, it's cold clear weather, and he's playing," said Paks. "Just the same as these would, only he's faster — " She paused as the horse slowed again, out of reach, and looked back at them. "Gird's teeth, he's a beauty. I wonder who's finding that his tether didn't hold."

"If that horse has worn a saddle in the past month, I'd be surprised. Not a mark on him."

"True. And the wild horses north aren't built like that. Hey, there — " Paks spoke to the horse, which stood with pricked ears watching her and the others. "I wonder if he'd let me come on foot."

"Paks, you be careful — "

"He's not evil, I tell you."

"Evil or not, he's not acting like a normal horse. At his size, he could put dents in you if he stepped wrong."

"So could a pack mule." Paks slid from her mount, and handed the reins to Stammel, who heaved a big sigh. She gave him a quick grin before returning her gaze to the horse. "Don't follow me," she said. "Don't spook him."

"Did you ever hear about the demon horses that enchant men to ride on them, and then take them away?" asked Stammel as she walked forward.

"Yes, but he won't."

"Tir's gut, Paks, begging your paladin's pardon, but you're acting half-enchanted now."

"It's all right." Paks felt sure it was all right, and she moved slowly toward the red horse. It stood still now, balanced neatly on all four legs, watching her. Its long mane and tail blew sideways in the breeze, but it did not stir. She came closer, close enough to see the great eyes, purple-brown, with their oblong irises, and the long upper lashes. The white star was perfectly centered. She paused, looking at the straight legs, flat knees, deep chest — the horse whuffled at her. She felt a nudge of urgency. She took another step forward, and another. The soft dark nose reached out, bumped her hand. "Well," she said. The horse nudged her again, more firmly. She put a hand to the side of its neck, and it leaned into the caress.

She moved to its side, and it turned its head to watch. A long neck, well-arched; a sloping shoulder, deep heart-girth, long underline. Although lighter built than the black, those powerful hindquarters did not lack for strength. She laid her hand on its back; it stood poised, waiting. She ran her hands down the near foreleg, and asked for the hoof; it came to her hand without resistance. The unshod hoof showed no chipping or splitting, as if it had just been trimmed. When she stood back, the horse turned to her again, and snorted. It was clearly a challenge. Paks felt a surge of excitement. More than anything else she wanted to be on that horse, moving with that speed and power. Was it enchantment?

She walked around the horse, noting strong hocks, muscled gaskins, everything a well-built horse should have, and nothing it shouldn't. She

818

came again to the head, and started to reach for the lips, to check teeth. The horse threw up its head and gave a snort of clear disgust. Paks chuckled.

"All right. Your age is your business. Gird knows you can't be too old."

"Paks — " Stammel's call carried over the wind. "Don't get on that beast — "

"It's all right." Paks turned to yell back, and the horse blew warm on her neck. She jumped, and glared at it. "Listen, horse — " It whuffled again, and touched her softly. An invitation? A challenge? She raised her hand to its neck again, stroked along it. A real paladin, she told herself, wouldn't be fooled by a demon horse. So either it's not a demon horse, or I'm not a real paladin, and whichever it is or I am, I'm going to have one glorious ride.

With no real fear, she moved to the horse's side and put her hands on its withers. It stood still, merely watching her with one ear cocked back.

"If you buck me off," warned Paks, "and make me look like an idiot, I'll chase you from here to the Cold Waste." The delicate nostrils quivered; the horse did not move. Paks took a deep breath and vaulted up, swinging her right leg wide. The horse stood still as she gained its back and settled herself. She glanced at Stammel, whose face was set in a disapproving scowl. Paks closed her legs gently, and the horse stepped forward. She had not ridden bareback since regaining her powers, and had nearly forgotten the complex shifting of muscles under her. But the horse made no move to bolt, and she adjusted easily. When she nudged with one heel, the horse turned smoothly, angling toward Stammel. Paks stiffened her back, and it halted, perfectly balanced.

"Well," said Stammel grudgingly, "it's not acting like a demon horse. They're supposed to charge off at a run and never stop."

"It's not a demon," said Paks, "but I don't know what it is." The horse threw up its head and whinnied loudly. She laid a hand on its neck. "Sorry — I really don't. Stammel, I'm going to try him out."

His eyebrows went up again. "With no bridle or saddle?"

"So far he responds to legs alone — we'll see. If I break my silly neck, you can tell the Duke I admitted it was my fault beforehand." With that she tapped with her left heel and the horse wheeled to the right. A firmer leg, and it broke to a long swinging trot. Paks took a cautionary handful of mane, and asked for a canter. At this gait, smooth but longer-strided than her other horse's canter, she guided the red horse through circles and figures of eight with legs alone. It did everything she asked, with smooth flying changes of lead when necessary. And as for feeling — it was, she thought gleefully, the best horse she had ever ridden. Perfect balance, perfect rhythm, suppleness . . . she brought it back to halt near the others.

"All right," Stammel said. "I'm convinced. But what will you do with him?"

"I don't know. I — " The horse whinnied again, and Paks ran a soothing hand down the glossy neck. "I suppose I'll ride him back to the stronghold. If he's someone's, they may come by — "

"I don't think it is. Whatever that horse is and wherever he came from, I think he came for you. Not a demon horse, no — but where do paladins get their horses?"

Paks felt her jaw drop. She had forgotten about paladins' horses. In Fin Panir, when paladins were confirmed in the High Lord's Hall, they came out to find their mounts awaiting them in the courtyard. Everyone insisted that the horses appeared — uncalled, but by the gods — and that no one, from the Marshal-General on down, had anything to do with it.

"You're a paladin," Stammel was going on. "Stands to reason you'd have a horse of your own. You can't stay here forever, the way I understand it."

"No — that's true." Paks covered her confusion by smoothing the red horse's mane. "I — hadn't thought about it. Maybe — " She leaned over and met the horse's backturned eye. "Are you a paladin's horse? Are you my horse?" The head tossed, and a forefoot pawed the ground.

Stammel laughed, a release of tension as much as humor. "Gods above, Paks, we never know what will happen with you around. Can we finish this patrol, or does your fancy horse insist on going home?" The horse blew a rattling snort, and Stammel nodded to it. "Begging your pardon, beastie, but some of us have work to do."

"He'll go along," said Paks. "Let's get on with it." And she took the reins of her assigned mount from Stammel, and led the way along their patrol path.

Back at the stronghold that evening, the red horse caused plenty of comment. Paks was hardly through the gates when a crowd gathered to stare. The Marshal, on her way across the courtyard from one barracks to another, stopped short.

"Where did you get that?" she began.

"Came running up to us from far in the hills," said Stammel, before Paks could speak. "He pranced around as showy as a gamecock, then let Paks walk up to him. I feared it was a demon horse, but she said not, and proved it riding him."

The Marshal shook her head. "Not a demon horse — by the High Lord, Paks, you've surprised us again."

"Marshal?" Paks swung down, keeping her hand on the horse's neck.

"I had wondered how you would get your mount — or if you would. You're different enough that I had no idea — But I never thought one would appear here, in midwinter."

"Then you think it is — "

"Your paladin's mount, of course. Of course it is." The Marshal held a hand out to the red horse, who touched it lightly with his nose, then turned to nuzzle Paks. "I only wonder why he didn't come at once."

The horse snorted and stamped. The Marshal looked surprised, then shook her head again. "Paks, paladins' mounts have powers of their own — I don't know if Amberion told you — "

"I've heard somewhat — "

"Good. Not all are the same. I wouldn't venture to say what this one can

820

do — but don't be too surprised." The Marshal nodded briskly to both Paks and the horse, and strode off.

Paks looked around. No one else ventured to say anything, but she caught many intent looks. "I suppose," she said finally, "I'd better find you a place in the stable."

Somewhat to her surprise, the red horse went into a box stall willingly, and began munching hay like any ordinary horse. Paks hurried back to the Duke's Court to tell him about it.

"I suspect," said the Duke, "that it means you haven't much longer to stay here. Your mail is almost finished. . . . "

"Do you feel anything, any call?" asked Dorrin.

"No." Paks looked around the room. "Not yet. But you're probably right, my lord. There's nothing here I'd need a horse like that for."

"Well, you're spending Midwinter here, at least, unless your gods lack sense," said the Duke. "We've planned a feast to remember, this year, and I won't have you miss it."

Paks thought of her last Midwinter, cold and afraid, in hiding from her past and future both, and smiled against that dark memory. "We will celebrate together," she said, and included the captains with a quick glance, "the victory of light over darkness, and courage over fear." The Duke started to speak, but nodded instead.

And when the recruits, freed for the festival days from their usual strict discipline, had the audacity to pelt officers, Marshal, and paladin with sticky fruit pastries, she laughed along with the others. They had been solemn enough when the fires were quenched, and the entire Company stood watch the whole night of Midwinter. On the second day, Paks rode out with the Duke to both villages for the ceremonial exchange of vows. She had not intended to ride the red horse for this, but found him waiting, saddled and bridled, in the forecourt when she came down. The Duke shook his head, then grinned.

"Your gods are pressing you, Paks — best be aware of them."

"I didn't plan to — "

"You keep telling me that paladins don't plan — the gods plan for them. If someone gifted me with a horse like that, I'd never walk."

"Yes, well — " Paks reached out to stroke the red horse's neck; it was a slick as if it had just been groomed. "I'd like to know who saddled him."

"We can ask, but my guess is no one."

"But horses can't saddle themselves — " The red horse snorted, stamped, and bumped Paks hard with the side of its head. "Sorry," said Paks. "I only meant — " The horse snorted again, and the Duke chuckled.

"Come on, Paks; mount the beast before you say something unforgiveable."

Paks swung into the saddle. It felt as if it had been made for her, and the stirrups were exactly the right length. Neither then nor later would anyone admit to having made the saddle (though she suspected the Duke, at first, of having supplied one), or having put it on the horse. Paks followed the Duke out the gate, puzzled but delighted. When they returned that evening, the horse permitted her to remove saddle and bridle, but despite a day's riding no mark marred that satiny coat. Paks hung saddle and bridle on a rack and went back to the Duke's Court, still slightly confused.

Chapter Fifteen

She felt that she had always run away before: from home, from the Company in Aarenis, from Fin Panir. Each time she had tried to escape something, and each time the thing she had refused to face confronted her again. This time, she was not running away — she was sent. She was less embarrassed than she'd expected by the troops in formation to see her off. It might be the last time she'd see them, the old friends who had made her what she was. That fanfare the Duke commanded, ringing through cold sunny air from the gate tower, honored the gods she served. And the Duke — his eyes alight as she had never seen them — they had said all they had to say. She wore Tammarrion's sword at her side, and he had nothing of hers but her prayers. And his life.

Riding through Duke's East, the red horse pranced, snatching his hooves off the cobbles as if they were coals. They all came out, men, women, and children — waving at her, shy to call. She knew the names, the faces, grinned at them and at herself. It was living the old dream, to ride through a town this way, and if it wasn't Three Firs, with her own brothers, sisters, and cousins waving and smiling, it was well enough. She felt the horse's amusement through her legs: he knew; it was why he pranced so, showing her off. He slowed without reining by Kolya's gate. Kolya nodded slowly, squinting up at Paks in the bright sunlight.

"So — it's as I heard. You're going. We'll miss you, Paks. The Duke, too — " She stopped, her eyes fixing on Tammarrion's sword. She looked quickly back at Paks's face. "That, too?"

"Yes. He gave me that — I argued, but — "

"That alone?" Her meaning carried more by look than the words themselves. Paks thought of the talks she'd had, these past weeks, as she waited for the Duke's gift of mail to be finished to his satisfaction. He had insisted on helmet and shield as well, befitting a paladin of Gird. His offer had been as oblique, yet as clear, as Kolya's question.

Paks looked ahead, then back at Kolya. "I am not free, Kolya, to answer all calls. There's better for him." Paks hoped she was right to say that. "Even if I were free — and would marry — I'm not Tammarrion. It's not only age, Kolya."

Kolya sighed. "No. That's so. It's that likeness, though, that keeps the thought in mind. Maybe it's better that you're going, for that as well."

The red horse did not move, but Paks felt his eagerness to be gone, his certainty of which way to go. She glanced around a last time. "Kolya, I must go. I can't linger —"

"I understand. Can you accept the blessing of an old kuakgannir?"

"Of a friend, always."

"Then may the First Tree shade your path, and shed fruit for your hunger, and the wisdom of all wild things be yours."

"And may the High Lord's grace and Gird's protection be on you, Kolya, and the Lady of Peace bring plenty to your orchard." They clasped hands, then Paks straightened, and the red horse moved on. Paks did not look back.

Although Paks had imagined being a paladin, she had never seriously thought what it would be like to travel as one. She had had some vague idea that paladins knew from the beginning exactly where they would go, and what they were to do, that they stayed in granges for the most part. She did not know even yet how other paladins moved around; for her it was different. Besides a feeling that they should go south and east, she had no idea where they were going. The red horse chose his own trails, and these did not lead from grange to grange, or along the roads she knew.

South of Duke's East, they left the now-familiar road that led to Vérella, and struck south-east across wooded country. Paks had already found that the red horse had more speed and endurance than common horses, and she let him choose his own times to rest. That wasn't often. They came to the Honnorgat downstream of Vérella in three days of hard riding. Paks was stiff and cold, and sat staring at the broad gray river while the red horse drew breath.

"Now what?" she asked it. "You aren't planning to swim that, I hope. And the bridges are all upstream, as far as I know." The horse flicked an ear back at her.

Paks stretched and looked around. They were on low water meadows, now covered with frost-dry grass. Along the river itself, a fringe of trees thickened here and there into a grove. Downstream smoke rose from a clutter of huts. Paks thought of that den of thieves in Aarenis and wrinkled her nose. On a low mound still farther downstream a larger building bulked — a keep of some kind, perhaps. Upstream was yet another group of huts, with a stake fence. When the horse pricked his ears, pointing, she could see a herd of dun-colored cattle grazing.

Sound carried well near the river, and she heard the jingle of harness just as the horse threw up his head. A small band of riders jogged her way from the larger building — she had been seen. "I hope you know what you're doing," she said to the red horse. "I hope you haven't crossed the border to Pargun somewhere in those woods." But as the band neared her, she was reassured by their colors, the rose and silver of the Tsaian royal house.

"Ho, stranger!" They were just in hail. Paks sat still and let them come.

The red horse was alert but unalarmed. She recognized the band's uniform now — Tsaian Royal Guard — but wondered what they were doing this far from Vérella. The leader wore Gird's crescent on his chest, and the device of the Order of the Bells. A knight, then, and well-born. Six men-at-arms, trim and fit-looking, rode behind him. When he was within speaking range, he reined in. Paks nodded to him.

"Gird's grace to you, sir knight."

His eyebrows rose. "Gird's grace ... uh ... "

"Paksenarrion Dorthansdotter," said Paks pleasantly.

"You are from — "

"I have just come from Duke Phelan's stronghold," she said. "I am a veteran of his Company, but no longer, as you see, one of them." Her own garb, chainmail under the plain brown cloak she'd bought in Brewersbridge with her Lyonyan coins, gave him no clue.

"Hmm." He rubbed his chin, obviously confused. "On the Duke's business, are you?"

"No. On Gird's business." That got his attention, and that of the others; they all stared. Paks hoped she hadn't stated it too baldly, but she felt a push to do so.

"Are you a — a Marshal?" At his question, her horse snorted, shaking its head. That reaction made her grin, and the knight even more uneasy.

"No, sir knight," she said, trying not to laugh. "I'm no Marshal. Might I ask your name?"

"Oh!" He had clearly forgotten about introducing himself. "I'm Regnal Kostvan, third son of the Kostvan Holding. The Royal Guard has garrisons in all the border keeps right now; that's why I'm here."

"Is there trouble along here with Pargun?"

He frowned. "Not to say trouble. Not more than usual. But the way things are going in Lyonya — " He looked hard to see if she knew what that meant. Paks nodded. He went on. "And so we're to make sure of travelers in this way. Were you planning to cross the river? Because you'd have to have clearance from me to hire a ferry."

"I have reason to cross, yes." Paks did not say more. How could she explain that she didn't know where she was going, or what she was to do when she got there?

"You'd best come back with me to the keep," he said. Paks felt rather than saw an increased alertness in the men-at-arms. They must have had some trouble, to make them to nervous. "My commander will want to speak with you."

"I'd be glad to," she said. "It's a cold day to talk out here." As she eased the red horse forward, she saw the men-at-arms tense and relax.

"I've heard of one Paksenarrion," began the knight tentatively. Paks could feel the ears of the others growing longer as he spoke. She laughed, surprised at how easy it was.

"Sir Regnal, it might have been you heard of me, though I claim no particular fame. But I served with Duke Phelan three seasons in Aarenis, and rode to Kolobia with the Girdsmen from Fin Panir — so if that's what you heard, you heard it of me."

He glanced at her sideways. His horse was enough shorter that she could tell little of his size. "Yes — I had heard of that. And of some other — " he paused, looking away, then back at her. She nodded.

"You may have heard truth and falsehood both, Sir Regnal. And the truth could be the more unpleasant. I do not speak of it much."

"I see." He rode a little way in silence. Then he turned to her again, as they neared a small stone keep whose gate faced the river. "But it is our duty to know what passes here — what manner of man or other being, and with what loyalties. I have heard such things of one Paksenarrion that I would not let that one pass. So these things must be spoken of, and your faiths proved."

The red horse stopped short at Paks's thought. She faced the knight squarely. "Sir knight, my faith has been proved already by such trials as I pray you never face." He reddened, but she went on. "I think you will be convinced, ere I leave, of what 'manner of man or other being' rides such a horse in such a way." She smiled, then, and nudged the horse on. "But it will be quicker to convince you and your commander all in one; let us ride in." And the long-striding red horse caught up and passed the knight's, and led the way into the keep courtyard.

Sir Regnal was stiffly correct in presenting Paks to his commander, a heavy-set older man with the intricate corded knots of a cohort-commander on the shoulders of his velvet winter tunic. Ganarrion Verrakai: Paks recalled from the charts in the Duke's library that this was a second son of the minor branch of that powerful family, second only to Marrakai in influence at court. She bowed, and carefully chose an applicable honorific which recognized his family position as well as his Guards rank.

"Sir nigan-Verrakai."

His eyebrows didn't rise, but he did not miss the wording. "Paksenarrion Dorthansdotter. Duke Phelan's veteran?"

"Yes, my lord. Not presently in his service."

"Ah, yes. On Gird's service, you told Sir Regnal?"

"Yes." She wondered how far they would press.

"Have you any authorization from the granges? From Fin Panir, perhaps?"

"From Gird, my lord," she said.

This time his eyebrows did rise. Not all the Verrakai, she remembered, were Girdsmen. Some were Falkian, some kuakgannir, and some, it was rumored, followed less honored gods. "But you are not a Marshal, you said?"

"No." It was astonishingly hard to say, to actually open her mouth and claim what she was, among strangers. "I am a paladin." At least it sounded all right.

They stared. Finally the commander said, "A paladin." He sounded unconvinced. Paks was not surprised. She was uneasily aware that she was going to have to prove it to them. "Could you tell me," he went on, "why a paladin should come here, where we have no need of one?"

"Because you lie between where I was, and where I must go," she said crisply.

"Oh. And where is that, if you please?"

Paks met his gaze steadily, and his eyes fell first. "I don't think," she said finally, "that that is your concern. If you know anything of paladins, you know we must answer the call at once, and without question. Nor do we answer questions without need."

He nodded. "Yes. I knew that. I just — wondered. But — " He looked her up and down. "I had heard things, last year at court. I mean — no offense meant, but — I heard of a Phelani veteran who went to Fin Panir to become a paladin, and failed. Left Fin Panir. Was wandering around as a — " He paused delicately.

"Coward?" suggested Paks, amazed that she could. He glanced quickly at her, and nodded. "Well," she went on briskly, "you have heard a lot, it seems. Some of it was true. It is also true that wounds heal, and cowards can regain their courage. And it is true that now I am a paladin. When the Marshal-General came to Phelan's stronghold — "

"What?!" The commander looked even more flabbergasted. "The Marshal-General of Gird?"

"Yes. He summoned a Marshal, on my advice, and she came."

"Well. I would never have thought. Phelan hates the Girdsmen."

"He did at one time. No longer. A grange is being built there."

"I can scarcely credit it. And you — you say you are a paladin. Have you any proof?"

Paks smiled, and called light. It lit the room far more brightly than the meager daylight until she damped it, and the commander nodded. The younger knight looked shocked, and blinked warily.

"I have seen such light before," said the commander. His voice had warmed. "Well, then Lady Paksenarrion — you may indeed go on Gird's business. But why do you conceal yourself?"

"I travel as I am bid, my lord; Gird himself was a plain man, and I am a sheepfarmer's daughter. When Gird chooses to have me recognized, I daresay I will be."

"A good answer. A good answer indeed. We are honored by your presence, and will do whatever we can for you. You will cross the river?" She nodded. "Then by your leave I'll send Regnal here to arrange a ferry. Can you wait until morning? I'd be glad to have you at our table this night."

Paks felt no restless urging, and was glad to stay the night. If she had to ride in another boat, she wanted to do it in daylight anyway. The commander set a good table, and Regnal had recovered enough from his surprise to be good company as well. They were full of gossip about the state of affairs in Lyonya.

"I'm not asking, you understand," said Ganarrion Verrakai. "But it will take a paladin, I'm thinking, or a company of them, to save Lyonya from years of chaos — even war. All I've heard for the last half year is how sick the king is. And how muddled the succession will be. And if Lyonya falls apart — our best ally — then it won't take long for Pargun to move, I'm thinking."

"Not long at all." Regnal drained his glass, and stared at the table. "My grandfather was killed by Pargunese — you won't know this, Lady Pak-senarrion, but that was when the Tsaian crown prince was killed as well, and your Duke Phelan captured the Pargunese commander. That was before he got his lands. Pargun has always wanted this territory."

"Yes, but it's worse than that." Verrakai shoved his glass around on the tablecloth. "I remember my grandfather's tales of the old evil, before Tsaia and Fintha joined Lyonya and Prealith to fence it out. With Lyonya in trouble, it could erupt right in the middle of the Eight Kingdoms, instead of hanging about the fringes. It wasn't that long ago, when you think of it, that they fought at Long Stones. I daresay the Master of Torments would like another chance at the inner realms."

"Or *her*," said Regnal. He glanced at Paks. "By what I've heard, you know as much about the webspinner's ways as anyone can, and live."

Paks nodded. "Yes — and I see what you mean."

"By my thinking, *she* probably had something to do with the prince being lost like that," said Verrakai. "No one says so, true, but something evil came to the queen and the prince. If he hadn't been lost — "

"No, I think it was the king dying while the princess was still so young," argued Regnal. "She had the taig-sense, but with no guidance, she never learned to use it fully."

"But that was from grief. If the queen hadn't been killed — "

"When was this?" Paks had heard the story outlined, but was not clear on the earlier details. The rangers had concentrated on more recent problems, including the king's illness.

"Oh, let me think." Verrakai stared at the table. "I was only a boy when it happened. Forty years, it must be, or fifty. Somewhat around there. Do you know the tale at all?"

Paks nodded. "The queen and prince were going somewhere, and at-tacked. She was killed, and he was never found. Is that right?"

"Yes. He was a little child, and the princess only a baby; she had been left behind, being too young to travel."

"The thing is," put in Regnal, "that there's no one else in the line who has enough elven blood. And there's so many that don't want it, because they don't know what it does — " He glanced at Verrakai, who reddened.

"Don't look at me, young Kostvan. I'm no elf-hater; that's my uncle. I've met rangers enough, working for the court, and I know what they mean by taig-sense. I still think Gird's guidance is enough, for human folk at least, but I admit that Lyonya's different. Its a joint kingdom, and the elves have a right to be in the kingship. And where you have elves, you have taigin. But even in Lyonya there are humans who fear more elven influence. And so they don't care, and so they have had two kings, now, with not enough taig-sense to hear thunder before a storm, and no one coming who has any more."

Listening to this, Paks had a curious sensation, a tingling of the mind, which forced her attention more strongly on what was said. For some reason she did not yet understand, it was important to what she was to do. But now Verrakai was smiling at her.

"What they need, maybe, is a paladin ruler instead. That hasn't been tried yet. By Gird, if you can sense good and evil directly, I'd think that would work as well as taig-sense."

Paks knew from her own experiences in Lyonya that it was not the same, but didn't want to explain all that. She merely laughed a little. "Paladins are called to harder seats than thrones, good sir. Granted that rule is not easy; but we are not trained for rule and judgment, but for sharp conflict."

"It might be better the other way. But I am not one to quarrel with the gods' ideas, only I hope something changes for the better in Lyonya, and soon. We have had bands of orcs around here, and worse things seen at a distance. If there's serious trouble ahead, I'd as soon our allies were in shape to help."

In the morning, Paks and the red horse were ferried across the Honnor-gat, its wide surface pewter colored between ice that still clutched each bank. On the far side she mounted, and rode on thoughtfully. She had noticed that her mail shirt was brighter than the day before. No one had polished it, or the rings and buckles of her tack, which were also gleaming. She wondered if her gear were beginning to take on the gleaming cleanliness she had noticed on other paladins.

South of the Honnorgat the land was more settled and richer. She passed through many little villages, and by noon was riding into a larger town. The red horse came to a stop before a handsome grange just as a Marshal stepped out the barton gate.

"Gird's grace, traveler," said the Marshal, eyeing her keenly. "I'm Marshal Pelyan. And you — ?"

"Paksenarrion," she answered. "A paladin of Gird, whose protection lies on all this land."

His eyes opened a little wider, but he merely nodded. "Welcome to our town. Will you take lunch with me?"

"With honor." Paks had already found that a paladin's hunger differed in no way from that of an ordinary soldier. She swung off the red horse, and looped the reins over her arm. "Is there a stable?"

"Around here." He led the way to the back of the grange, and waited while she made the red horse comfortable in a box next to his own brown warhorse. "You have traveled hard," he said, as he preceded her out the stable door.

Paks shrugged. "Not too bad."

"Mmm. Some would consider any travel this time of year hard. But not you, I suppose." They had come to an inn, and he entered, waving his hand at several men who looked up. A landlord came forward, looking at Paks curiously. The Marshal forestalled any questions by asking him for a quiet table. When they were seated, he leaned forward in his chair. "I know I asked for assistance," he said softly, "but I didn't think it required a paladin. Is it really that bad?"

Paks was startled. She had had no feelings about this town at all, and no sense that she was called to do anything here. "Marshal, I'm not here in answer to your call — that I know of. It's true I'm on quest, but somewhere else."

"I see." He looked somewhat relieved. "Do you — would you know if my message was received in Fin Panir?"

"No." Paks shook her head slowly. "I haven't been in Fin Panir for over a year."

"Oh." Now he looked dismayed. "Blast. I wish I knew — " He stopped as the landlord came to take their order, and quickly told the man to bring stew and hot bread. When the landlord moved away, he began again. "Sorry — should have let you order. But I'm that worried, you see. And then you came in, just when I was thinking I'd have to ride at least to Vérella myself." The landlord came with their food, two huge bowls of steaming stew and two loaves of bread. Paks began to eat. The stew was good; she finished it all, and mopped the bowl clean with a hunk of bread.

The Marshal insisted on paying for their meal, and said nothing more about his problems until they were near the grange, and the street empty around them. "I don't mean to delay you," he said, "but if you have a little time, perhaps you could just tell me if I should ride out myself. It's very vexing, is what it is. . . . "

Paks herself was curious what sort of problem could bother him so, and what kind of help he'd asked for. She agreed to take a cup of sib in his office and listen.

"This is solid old Girdish territory," he began. "Has been for generations; we had a grange here before Tsaia claimed it. So we've always had a strong yeomanry. But as we're close to Lyonya — Harway, maybe a half-day's walk east, is on the border — we've had plenty of Falkians, too. I've nothing against them; they're quiet, law-abiding folk, and brave enough in trouble. But this trouble in Lyonya — well, now, folk here are beginning to worry. When the first few Falkians came in wanting to join the grange, I admit I was pleased about it. After all, that's what any Marshal hopes to do, is increase the strength of the yeomanry. The Falkian captain even joked with me about it, wanted to know my secret. But along about last spring, it went beyond any jokes. They've closed their field — that's like our grange — and the captain's left. There's a sergeant now, for the few commons left. And our grange is stuffed with ex-Falkians."

"Why do you think they changed?" asked Paks. It still didn't seem much like a real problem to her.

"Lyonya. I think they wanted to show their loyalty to Tsaia, where the

830

court's Girdish. They don't say so, of course. I wouldn't take 'em if they did. That's a bad reason to change patrons, just for policy like that. And that's part of my problem: all these so-called Girdsmen. I don't have the arms for that many, or the money and time to get arms. Of course the Falkian captain didn't send the arms along with them — very properly, too: I certainly never sent arms with a yeoman who left the grange. But they talk, talk, talk, all the time, worrying themselves — and me — and I have only one yeoman-marshal, and she's been sick. Then there's the visitors."

"Visitors?" Paks asked politely, since he had paused as if waiting for her question.

"Yes." He made a sour face. "Close as we are to the border, you see, families here and families there have intermarried and so on. With all this uncertainty in Lyonya, they've come over here until it settles down — if it ever does. As I said, we're a long-settled area. It's not easy to absorb several hundred more people all at once, and no knowing when they'll leave. Families going short call on the grange for help; we had a good harvest, but most of these people came just after harvest — not during the working season, when they could have made the crop bigger. I wrote Fin Panir back in the spring about getting another yeoman-marshal or Marshal, and maybe starting another grange. They said wait and see what happened. What's happened is that I've got a grange full of people, less than half of them my own, and not enough arms, or time to train, or anyone to work with. I suppose it's not a paladin's concern — " He looked at her sadly.

"Tell me about your yeoman-marshal," said Paks, trying to think what she could do in a short time. "Did you say she was sick?"

"Well, she's not so young any more, and she's had lung fever last winter and this winter both. This last time, she never really got well."

"Why don't I take a look?" said Paks. Then she thought again. "Of course, you've tried a healing — ?"

The Marshal shook his head. "She didn't want one, she said. She's been low in her spirits this last year or so — and that's another thing, but I've had no one to talk to, and been too busy to go anywhere. Something's bothering her — "

"Would she talk to me?"

"I imagine so. A paladin, after all. On a quest. It might interest her."

"Can't you appoint another yeoman-marshal?"

"Well — yes, I could, but — everyone knows Rahel. She's been here since before I came. As long as she's — and it's not as if we were actively fighting — "

"Where is she?" asked Paks.

"Along here." The Marshal rose and led the way along a passage inside the grange. He stopped outside a door, and rapped on it. Paks heard a chair scrape inside, and a heavy cough, then a tired voice responding. "It's the Marshal," he said. "We have a visitor, Rahel — a paladin."

The door opened. Rahel, the yeoman-marshal, was a hand shorter than Paks, with heavy gray braids wrapped around her head; her face was thin, and she stood slightly askew, like someone with a stitch in her side. Paks was aware of a heavy feeling in the air. "Sir Marshal," said Rahel, in a voice without resonance. "Paladin — ?"

"Paksenarrion," said the Marshal, with a gesture. "She is on quest, but stopped here for a meal, and a rest."

"Gird's grace, Lady," said Rahel, with obvious effort. "Will you come in?"

"Gird's strength to you," said Paks in return. "I'd be glad to sit awhile, if it won't tire you."

Rahel smiled without humor. "Nothing tires me, Lady, but living itself." She stepped back, and Paks followed her into a clean spare room with a small fireplace. Two comfortable chairs, a small table, and a narrow bed piled with pillows furnished it. A mail shirt hung from its stand, and several swords hung from pegs on the wall. That was all. Rahel sank into one of the chairs, clearly short of breath.

"How long have you been sick?" asked Paks.

Rahel shook her head. "I am not sure. I have an old wound — every year or so I used to have lung fever in winter or early spring. I can't remember when it was that it first started hanging on too long. But last year — it was near midsummer before I could walk to Harway and back in a day. And just after harvest, I got the lung fever again." She stopped, gasping. Her color was bad, an odd bluish-gray that Paks had seen on men with lung wounds. She coughed again, bending to it. Paks waited, wondering if there were any chance of a healing.

"The Marshal," Rahel went on when she caught her breath, "he thinks I should let him try a healing. But it's too late — too much is gone — I — " She coughed again. "I'm too tired," she said finally. "I fought — years — and I'm tired."

"Would you let me try to ease the pain for you?" asked Paks.

"Ease — ? Not heal?"

"If it can be healed, I will try to heal it. I think you are right, Rahel, that it's gone too far. But I can ease it for you, for awhile."

"I didn't want numbwine," muttered Rahel. "Can't think with that stuff — can't work at all."

"Not numbwine." Paks watched her, recognizing the heaviness for what it was, and wondered why the Marshal had not seen it — or if he had just not wanted to see it.

Rahel nodded. "If you will — I'm sorry, Lady — I can't say the right things — "

"No matter. Would you rather lie down?"

"Yes, if you don't mind. It's hard to — " She pulled herself out of the chair, and went to the bed, piling the pillows at one end. Paks wondered briefly if she should tell the Marshal first, and decided against it. Rahel lay against the pillows, her eyes sagging shut. Paks took a deep calming breath, and called on Gird and the High Lord.

As she touched Rahel's head, she knew at once that no cure would be

832

given. She prayed quietly, hoping to ease the pain, and sensed that Rahel's breathing had quieted. After a few minutes, she felt a clear instruction to stop, and withdrew her hands. Rahel opened her eyes.

"That — is — much better. My thanks, Lady, for this and for Gird's grace."

She looked better, even rested, and Paks fetched her a drink of water from the jug on the table.

"The power is the High Lord's," Paks reminded her. "It is lent me, under Gird's grace; it is not mine."

"True. Oh, it is easier. If it never got worse than this, I could — " she stopped suddenly, with a surprised look, and fell back. Paks knew at once that she was dead, as she had known that death was near. She straightened Rahel's body, and called the Marshal.

Chapter Sixteen

"So it has come." The Marshal did not seem surprised. "I knew it would be soon, but not how soon." Together he and Paks prepared the body for burial. Paks struggled with her own feelings; she was not used to death save by violence. The Marshal spoke softly as they worked. "When death comes in war, quickly, it is easily faced. So also with many illnesses — either life and health, or death. For most who grow old in peace, the weakness of age comes gently, and death is no longer an enemy. But for her — you saw that scar; I think she had pain from it all along. For two years every breath was drawn in pain. She was too strong to die soon, and knew it might last beyond her strength to face it. That fear — that she might not — began to master her. When you took the pain — "

"I knew it might end — " Paks ducked her head. He touched her shoulder.

"You are a young paladin, and so I will be bold to answer what you did not ask. And even to answer what you fear I might ask. Yes, what you did might have caused her death so quickly. Yet I know you intended neither evil nor her death, and I do not think you killed her. For the healing power comes, as you said, from the High Lord — from him comes the end of pain, not pain itself."

"You were listening — you knew — "

"I hoped. She wouldn't let me — and it had gone on long enough. She feared to be weak, and take my help; it had to be someone else."

"Why didn't — why didn't Gird heal that wound in the first place?" Paks was surprised at her own resentment. She knew the danger of that, fought it back. The Marshal finished folding the blanket around the body, laid Rahel's medallion on top of it, and looked at Paks levelly.

"She wasn't a Girdsman then. She — " He looked briefly at the body, and back at Paks. "She was a brigand; Gird knows what gods she followed, if any. The Marshal before me here found her near death, in a cave. The others had left her, after dragging her that far. The wound was too old to heal cleanly, even if she'd been a yeoman. Somehow she lived — he was a good herbalist as well — and, when she was stronger, he converted her. Had to, or the local Council would have hanged her."

"Oh."

"He made her yeoman-marshal not only for her ability, but to protect

834

her from the yeomen and the town. And she served well, the rest of her life."

Riding east the next day, Paks thought about what the Marshal had told her. The land seemed settled enough; she saw none of the disruption that war had brought to Aarenis. Few travelers moved on the road, but it was winter, and cold. She came to Harway before noon. Here she was stopped by men-at-arms in Lyonyan green and gold, but they passed her quickly enough when she gave her name.

"Didn't you serve with the rangers last summer?" asked one of them.

"Yes, with Giron."

"That's what I thought. They send those names all around the border. Go on, then, anywhere you like — but if you go to Chaya, you should give your name at the court, and let the king know you're there."

"I've never seen Chaya," said Paks.

"Stay on this road and you will — it's south and east of here, more east than south. You've worked with elves; you'll like it."

"I'll ride that way if I can. How would I find the Halveric lands?"

"Which Halverics? That's a big family."

"Aliam Halveric — he has a mercenary company — "

"Oh. You were close enough to it last summer — didn't you know?" Paks shook her head. "Well, it's far in the south — I haven't been there myself."

As she rode into Lyonya, the amount of forested land increased. Bit by bit the fields grew smaller, and the blocks of wood between them larger. Near Chaya itself, a wide belt of forest had been left undisturbed; snow whitened the ground on either hand, though the road itself had been churned to frozen mud. Gradually the trees grew larger, and the spaces between them wider. At the inner edge of the forest belt, Paks reined in to look at the city.

Unlike Vérella and Fin Panir, Chaya had not been built for defense: no proud wall encircled it. Instead, it was as if a grove of noble trees had cleared the ground around themselves, and then been invaded by clusters of bright mushrooms. The mushrooms, Paks realized suddenly, were the buildings: of stone and wood both, brightly painted, with colorful tile roofs. The trees — she squinted upward — were immense, each larger of bole than most houses. The lower bark was cinnamon-red, breaking into plates partway up, where the branches began, and showing pale gray and even white above that. Off to one side of the grove a castle faced the widest part of the open ground, now a snowy field. It looked like a model next to the great trees.

"First time you've seen Chaya?" The voice held a little of the elves' song. Paks turned to see a part-elf in hunting leathers behind her.

"Yes — it's — not like anything else — "

"No, indeed. Those are the only such trees outside the elvenhome forests. They are a sign that this kingdom is of both kinships." The part-elf sighed. "As long as it is, they will thrive. But otherwise — "

"Are you one of the rangers?" asked Paks.

"Do you think that is all elven blood has to do in this kingdom?"

Paks did not understand the rancor in his voice. "I don't know," she said. "I was with the rangers in the south last summer, and merely wondered if you knew them."

His face relaxed. "Oh, well, then — I may indeed. I have many friends in the south." But as it happened he knew of them by name only. They moved on toward the city together, both silent for some distance. Then, as they neared the first buildings, he spoke again. "Have you come from them? Few travel so far in midwinter."

"I'm a paladin of Gird," said Paks. "On quest." He stopped short, and Paks stopped in courtesy.

"A paladin? Have you come to heal the king?"

"I am not yet sure why I've been called here."

"It could not be for better cause. Go and see him, at least." He looked about, and hailed a youth in green and gold livery. The boy came near, eyes wide, and bowed. "Here — Belvarin will take you. This lady is a paladin," he explained to the youth. "She must see the king."

Paks followed the youth through the twisting lanes between trees and buildings to a gate in the castle wall. It surprised her with its size, and she realized again that the trees made it look smaller than it was. She dismounted inside the gate, and led the red horse across a wide court. A stableboy came to take her horse, and she warned him not to tie the red horse.

The boy nodded and walked off, the horse following.

Her escort led her into the main part of the castle, along wide passages. She noticed that the many servants bowed as they passed. She felt the slight tingle that indicated she was near to some act of power. She estimated that they had come to the far side of the castle, on an upper level, when they arrived outside double carved doors. Two nobles in rich gowns greeted her escort, and acknowledged the introduction.

"Paksenarrion — a paladin. Welcome, lady, to the court of our king. I am Sier Belvarin; I hope my son has served you well." Paks saw a blush redden the youth's neck. His father was tall and fair, with a red tinge to his hair and beard.

"And I am Sier Halveric. Are you that Paksenarrion who served Phelan of Tsaia?" When Paks nodded, he smiled at her. "Then I daresay you know my nephew Aliam Halveric."

"Indeed yes, my lord." When she looked closely at him, something of the eyes seemed like Aliam, but he was much taller, with red-brown hair going silver.

"Have you come to heal our king, lady?" asked Belvarin, with a sour glance at Halveric which Paks did not miss.

"I would offer my healing if it were welcome," said Paks cautiously. "But the High Lord's power comes at his will, not mine."

"I fear, my lady, that you come too late, if such was the High Lord's purpose in calling you here. Nonetheless, you shall see the king, if you will, and perhaps can ease him." Sier Halveric smiled at her, and turned to the door.

"Not so fast, Jeris. Have you forgotten what the surgeons said? He must rest, the little he can."

"Falk's oath in gold, Tamissin! He's dying anyway — what harm can a paladin do?"

"But the surgeons — "

"The surgeons! Hmph! And is he better for them, these last months?"

Their voices had risen; Paks was not surprised when the doors opened from within, and a man peered out, scowling. "Lords! Lords! Have you no better place to quarrel than before the king's chamber? He but barely sleeps at the best of it — " He caught sight of Paks, and stared. "And who's this? A stranger?"

"A paladin," said the Halveric quickly. "A paladin of Gird, a servant of the High Lord. The king must have this chance — "

"For healing?" The man sounded more than doubtful. Paks intervened.

"Sir, I am here, in Chaya, by the call of the High Lord, to serve his purpose. But as for the king, I can offer only such prayers as I am commanded to offer."

He looked her up and down, and relaxed. "Indeed, lady, it has been long since a paladin came to us. We are honored, and the king would wish to welcome you properly if he could. If you can forgive his inability, perhaps you might consider attending him."

Paks bowed. "By Gird's grace, and the High Lord's power, I will do what I can." She glanced at the other two, who avoided each other's eyes. "Gird's grace be on you," she said quietly, and passed through the opening.

Within, the large chamber was full of light from windows on either side. The king's bed stood on a low dais; besides a fireplace near it, several braziers filled the air with warmth and the scent of light incense. The king lay propped on pillows beneath a spread worked in gold thread; a matching canopy rose from the bedposts. Paks followed the other man closer. A woman sitting by the bed rose and came to meet them. She wore the insignia of a Knight of Falk, but was dressed in robes rather than armor.

"My lady — you are a paladin? You can save him?"

"I don't know. I will do what the gods give me the power to do." Paks looked past her. The king's eyes were closed; he looked much older than she had been told he was, in his middle fifties. She watched closely as the woman went to the king's side and spoke softly. He opened his eyes slowly; they were clouded blue. His gaze shifted around the room and found her; he tried to sit up.

"Be welcome in Lyonya, Lady; we are honored to have you at our court. Pardon my inability to rise — "

"Certainly, sir king. May I approach?" He nodded, and waved a hand. Paks came up beside the bed. "May I ask the nature of your illness?"

"We do not know," said the man behind her. "I am Esceriel, the King's Squire." Paks was surprised; he was of middle age. He read her surprise and smiled. "Lady, the King's Squire is a knight of Falk; so also is Lieth here. But to answer your question, the king's surgeons know not what his illness is."

"What I feel," said the king softly, "is weakness, and pain here — " he touched his chest and shoulder. "My mother had the same thing, and also died of it. The surgeons speak of the heart, and then the lungs — for it seems the air fails me sometimes — and then as well nothing I eat stays with me these days."

Paks stood by the bed, and took his hand. The skin was thin and dry, a little loose on the bones, like that of a very old man. She almost feared to start her prayers, remembering Rahel's sudden death, but the pressure of her call forced her to action. When she released the hand, she had no idea how long she had stood there — but the afternoon had passed into evening. Her knees sagged; Esceriel was quick with a stool behind her. The king lay asleep, peaceful.

Lieth brought her a cup of hot spiced wine. "Lady," she said softly, "I never thought to see such — "

"Nor I," said Esceriel. "Your power was great."

Paks shook her head. It felt heavy as a stone. "Not my power, but the High Lord's. Ah, but I'm tired!"

"No wonder. You'll have a place here. And he's asleep, resting well, for the first time in days."

"But not healed," said Paks. They looked at her.

"But perhaps — " began Lieth.

"No. I'm sorry. I don't know why; I never know why. But he is not healed, only eased for a time."

"It's enough," said Esceriel firmly. "If you're strong enough now, I'll take you to your chamber."

"Are you sure — ?"

He grinned unexpectedly. "You gave us hours to prepare, Lady. You stood there from just after noon until dusk. Can you come?"

Paks pushed herself up from the stool joint by joint. "I can come."

Her chamber was but two doors from the king's, a small room with a fireplace, its walls hung with tapestries. A single window looked out over the inner court and gardens, now white with snow. A high carved bed was piled with down-stuffed coverlets; a fur throw lay folded at its foot. Her pack had been set carefully on top of the carved desk.

"Lady, if you need anything, be sure to ask. Servants are on the way with hot water and bathing things. Would you prefer to eat alone, or in Hall?"

"Alone, if that would not be discourteous here. I am somewhat tired."

"And no wonder," he said again. "With your leave I shall say you wish to rest undisturbed."

Paks nodded. "I thank you, sir. But if the king wakes, and wishes to speak to me, I am always at his service."

"We thank you, Lady, more than you can know. But, Lady — your pardon, but — I did not catch your name — "

"Oh." Paks realized that the quarreling nobles had not introduced her by name. "I am Paksenarrion Dorthansdotter. Once I was a soldier with Duke Phelan of Tsaia, but now I am a paladin of the High Lord and Gird."

He bowed. "Be welcome here, Paksenarrion. The Sier Halveric would no doubt have introduced you properly, or Belvarin would but the two of them have little patience with each other."

"So I noticed." Paks shook her head.

"It is nothing for a paladin's concern, of course, but — " Esceriel broke off as two strong youths carried a deep tub of steaming water into the room. Behind them a wizened man bore a carved box on top of a pile of folded towels. "Ah," he said. "Here's Joriam with your bath things. I'll go now; ask Joriam for whatever you need; he can find me at any time." Esceriel bowed again and withdrew, as did the two youths. Paks met the old man's dark gaze, intent and curious.

"Well, Lady, we hope to please you," he began, setting the towels down on the bed, and opening the box to reveal several balls of scented soap. "Here are andrask, figan, and erris soaps; we judge these best for travelers in cold."

Paks had never heard of andrask and figan; she had once seen erris in a shop, a straggly yellow-flowered herb. The shopkeeper said it was used in soaps and wines both. She watched as Joriam laid the towels and soaps out in a neat row, his every motion precise and ceremonious. He pulled out a tiny drawer in the base of the box, and removed two combs, one of bone and one of horn, which he set above the row of soaps. He glanced at her.

"May I take your cloak, lady?" When Paks nodded and reached for the clasp, he moved behind her to gather it up. Paks unhooked the scabbard of Tammarrion's sword — as she still thought of it — from her swordbelt, and laid it on the bed. She pulled the swordbelt over her head and tossed it on the bed as well, and began to unlace the fur-lined tunic over her mail. She turned to see Joriam staring wide-eyed at the swordhilt.

"What is it?" she asked, when he did not move.

"It's — by the High Lord, Lady, where did you come by that sword?" It was more accusation than question; his eyes blazed with anger.

"It was a gift," she said, watching him closely. "It was given me by Duke Phelan of Tsaia; it was his wife's sword."

"Phelan of Tsaia," he muttered. Then he looked closely at the sword hilt again. "Lady, my pardon — but does this sword have runes on the blade?"

"Yes," said Paks slowly. "What — "

"How old is this Phelan of Tsaia? Is he a very old man, as old as I?"

"By no means. He is of middle age, perhaps fifty."

"And you say this was his wife's sword? How did she come by it?"

Paks began to feel a little annoyance at all these questions, but Joriam's face was honest. "All I know of it, Joriam, is what I was told. It was his wife's sword, and was recovered after her death in battle against orcs. She was killed some fifteen years ago. Those who told me are as honest as anyone I know, and I am a paladin. Now — why do you ask these things? Do you know more of this blade than that?"

Joriam's face contracted to a mass of wrinkles. He shook his head slowly, but answered. "Lady, I can scarce believe my eyes, but — if the runes are the same, this sword comes from this hall — from the queen's hand, I would have said, many years ago."

"What!"

"Yes, Lady. You would not be old enough to remember — you may never have heard. But when I was a young man, in service here, that king ruling was the older half-brother of our present king. He married elven, in the old way, to restore the taig-sense to the ruling line." Joriam looked at her doubtfully. "You are not afraid of elves, are you, Lady? Some Girdsmen are — "

"I am not," said Paks. "I have friends among the true elves, and I spent some time with your rangers in the south. I respect the taig of tree and forest, and the taig of the kingdom."

He nodded, satisfied. "Well, then, perhaps the rangers told you of it. Lyonya is both elf and human, kingdom and holder, root and branch — and in health it is ruled by someone who can sense the shift of taig directly. The old king — Falkieri's father and this king's father too, of course — his first wife was part-elven, and so Falkieri had enough taig-sense, but just enough. He was wise to marry elven, whatever they said afterwards. Their son showed such ability early, and their daughter too, poor lass."

"But what happened to them — the son and daughter — or does the throne go to brothers before children?" Paks wondered if the old man were mixed in his wits, for so far the tale didn't sound like that she'd heard from others.

"No, that's what I'm telling you. This king, and the one before, are from a different mother, half-brothers to Falkieri. The old king's second wife was all human; he didn't think it mattered, with Falkieri healthy and betrothed to a full elf. Anyway, when the first two children were born and weaned, the queen desired to take her son to see her own people. Some kind of elven ceremony; I don't know. I was too young to be told much. So the queen and the prince left Chaya for the Ladysforest, leaving the princess here with the king. And they were attacked, in the forest near the border, and killed."

"Killed?" So it was the same story, but told from a different view.

"Yes. When nothing was heard for too long — for the elves would send word of safe arrival, and besides the eastern taig was troubled — search was made, and the wagons and bodies were found. Most of them, anyway. They never did find the prince's body, but he was small — only four years — and perhaps it was carried off by animals." He paused to see if she had questions; Paks waved him to continue. "Well, then, you can imagine — I suppose — what it was like. The king was frantic. He and his wife had sworn life-marriage; he refused to remarry, even though it left only one heir, his daughter. And though he tried hard, he never mastered his grief; we think it killed him eventually. The princess was then about nine or ten; the king's younger brothers were still too young to rule without a regent, so the king's cousin was named regent for the princess." He paused again, and ran his hands over the towels on the bed. "Pardon, Lady, but your water will cool. This tale can wait until you bathe."

Paks looked at him. He seemed near tears; she would not have thought an old man would be so moved by a tale so old. "Perhaps what you tell me is more important that a hot bath," she suggested.

"Lady, I — I will continue if you wish; I but thought of you cold and tired — " Paks was indeed chilling again, and very tired. Her back felt like a bar of hot metal. She glanced at the tub, still steaming.

"Joriam, I want to hear this, but you're right — I'm tired and cold and I may not pay close enough attention. But until I hear it, I don't want you telling everyone about the sword. It may not be the same — and I'm still not sure whose sword you think it is."

"I will speak to no one, Lady. Only seeing the sword again — it brought back those terrible days — "

"I understand." She didn't, but it seemed the right thing to say. "I won't be long; why don't you bring something hot to eat — soup would be fine — and we'll talk again."

"I'll take your things to be cleaned," he said, nodding. Paks struggled out of her clothes while he pulled one tapestry aside to reveal a niche with clothes pegs and drawers set into one wall. From this he took a long soft robe, and hung it to warm by the fire. She wondered if he would try to snatch the sword and take it as he left, but he did not touch it, or the sword belt.

The hot bath eased her aching body, and she had stretched comfortably on a low seat by the fire when Joriam returned with a tray, followed by the same two servants who removed the water and damp towels. He had brought a deep bowl of soup, a plate of sliced meat in gravy, and two small loaves of hot bread, as well as a tall beaker and mug.

"Sit with me," said Paks, gesturing, "and tell me the rest of this tale."

"Sit?" he sounded almost scandalized. "Lady, I do well enough." He leaned against the wall, and went on. "The king died, as I said, when the princess was about nine or ten. His cousin was an honest man — " Paks could tell that Joriam was struggling to be fair to someone he had not liked. "I believe he did the best he could. But, Lady, you know some humans fear elves — have small liking for them — and he himself had no taig-sense at all. He blamed the queen for the young prince's death — taking that journey — and he disliked the elves at court who would have tutored the princess in taigin."

"But didn't he know that Lyonya must be ruled by someone who can sense the taigin?"

"I think he didn't believe it. Some men are like that — as if blind men could deny sight to others, lacking it themselves. Anyway, our young princess was a fine one, and he did honestly by her, but for that. Only he insisted, since she was the only true heir, that she must marry early. When the elves argued, he sent them away."

Paks thought back to things Ardhiel had told her. "But isn't it true that elves and half-elves — even to quarter elves — come late to such growth, and should not marry too early? Especially the women, I thought, for bearing children too young — "

" — can be fatal," Joriam finished, with some heat. "Yes. And that's what happened to her, poor lass. The regent and Council insisted she marry at the first legal age, and put it to her that such was her duty. She was as brave as could be, that one, and would dare anything for duty. So she married the year she was crowned queen — married the regent's son — "

"Scoundrel — " began Paks angrily, seeing a plot of the regent.

"No. . . . " Joriam was more judicious. "I don't think so. He loved her well, and she had been fond of him from childhood. She need not marry elven, being half-elf herself — all her children would have taig-sense. And he renounced any claim on the crown, should she die. No, I think it was simply fear, fear of the elves — and then they made her marry early, and that killed her. And the child." Joriam looked down. Paks finished the soup she had started, and began on the meat, waiting for him to regain his calm.

"Then things really began to go wrong," he said quietly. "As long as she was coming to rule — even though she had no training, she had a strong gift, to sense the taigin. The regent would listen to her. He was honest, as I said, and did her bidding where he could. But after — the old king's second wife was all human, and from a line with no ability for taigin. With her dead, the Council decided to offer the crown to Falkieri's younger brothers, now of age, even so. They were both good men, please understand me — they were, as our king is now, honest, brave, and faithful to the kingdom. In another kingdom, that might be enough. In Lyonya, no."

"What about this king's heir?"

Joriam snorted. "He has none — not direct. One evil after another, Lady, has stalked this royal house for near fifty years. After him it goes to cousins and second cousins of the old king — half the nobles might have a claim, if it comes to that. War — by the gods, Lady, we have not had war in Lyonya, save along the borders only, since the Compact was made with the elves. Yet now all fear it. It seems nothing will prevent it — and to think of Lyonya at war, the forests fired, maybe . . . and we wonder what the elves will do. It is a joint kingdom, after all."

Paks nodded. "I see. Now — about the sword. Whose was it?"

"The queen's, Lady — not the young queen that died, but Falkieri's elven wife. She carried it; I saw it in her hand, on her wall, when I first came here to serve. That jewel in the hilt — the guards — "

"And runes, you said. What runes?"

"I don't read runes myself. I remember the shape of two of them, because once when I — " he stopped and blushed. Paks watched him, fully alert now. He blinked and went on. "I had broken something, Lady, and was scolded for it. She was nearby, with the sword partly drawn, and I found myself staring at it."

"What were the runes like, that you saw?"

"Like this." With his wetted finger, he drew on the polished wood tray a rude copy of the rune for treasure and something Paks could not read at all.

"Is there anyone else who would know the sword, and could remember all the runes on it?"

Joriam thought. "I'm the oldest servant here, now the elves have gone — "

"Elves gone? Why? How?"

"It was the regent, at first. Later . . . I don't mean there are no elves in Lyonya, of course, but few now come to Chaya, to the king. They are quick to resent a cool welcome."

"So would I be, were I an elf," murmured Paks. Then, louder, "But are there any others?"

"Yes, I think so. The Sier Halveric is older than I, though he doesn't look it — he's part elvish, you see. He was much at court in those days. A few others — old Lord Hammarrin, the Master of Horse — he's near ninety years. Sier Galvary. Tekko, he was Master Huntsman in those days, but he's been retired these fifteen years. All these would know the sword, but Tekko doesn't know runes any better than I do."

Paks had finished her meal; she stretched after pushing the tray farther away. "Well, Joriam, it seems to me that we'd best speak to these others. If I am carrying a treasure of your realm, it must come back to you — isn't that right?"

He stared at her. "But Lady — you're carrying the sword — "

"It's not the first I've carried; I doubt it will be the last. If it belongs here, I will give it willingly — "

"But that's not the point! Lady, please — " His face was troubled. "The sword alone will do us no good. It was her sword, the queen's, before our troubles began. What I meant was — " He shook his head. "I don't know. I'm old; I've never been anything but a servant here. But if we could find what happened to her — if her sword is still here, perhaps she was not killed. Maybe it wasn't her body they found. Perhaps she is prisoned somewhere, and could be freed, to return and rule — "

Paks in turn shook her head. "Joriam, I cannot think what could imprison an elf, a queen, for forty-five to fifty years, leaving no trace for searchers, and still leave her alive and fit to rule when found."

"The — the kuaknom? They say they can take elves — "

Paks felt her face harden, saw the shock on Joriam's at her expression. "I have been among the kuaknom, Joriam. It is a quick return, or none, from their realms."

"Lady, my pardon. I did not know."

"I was captive with the kuaknom for only a few days, and got more scars than in years of fighting in Aarenis. Scars of mind and body both."

"I am sorry, Lady — "

"No matter. But I must talk to these others. I was called here for some reason — your folk hoped it was to heal your king, but perhaps it was to return the sword instead. I ask your silence on this, Joriam, until those you mentioned are gathered together before witnesses. In such a matter all must be done properly."

"Yes, Lady. Will you speak with the Steward first? Or Sier Halveric?"

Paks thought. She did not know the ways of power at this court; the quarrel between Sier Halveric and Sier Belvarin had not escaped her, nor the vigilant authority of the king's squires. And elves were involved, as well.

"I will speak to the king," she said. "It is his right, to know first. After that, if he is able, he will call what witnesses are needed. But I insist that the elves, also, be here. Surely there is one — an ambassador, perhaps?"

Joriam looked worried. "Across Chaya, Lady, in their own Hall — they do not stay here any longer. But why — "

"Because you say the sword was hers. She was an elf. It is their right too, Joriam. She was one of theirs, and this was hers. Perhaps they have a claim to it." Paks moved the tray and table away, and pushed herself up. She was still weary, but the bath and food had refreshed her. And the call that had brought her throbbed in her head.

Chapter Seventeen

By the time Paks had dressed in dry, clean clothes, it was full dark outside. Starlight and torchlight glittered together on the snowy courtyard. Joriam waited outside her door, and escorted her to the king's chamber. Esceriel showed his surprise in raised eyebrows when he opened the door.

"Lady — I thought you were — pardon, you are welcome to enter — " But his voice still held questions.

Paks had put on her shining mail again, and belted on the mysterious sword. "The king?" she asked softly.

"He woke without pain, Lady, and ate with appetite. He has dozed off again — must you wake him?"

Paks met the eyes of both squires. "Let me explain, if you will." They led the way to a window alcove, and stood near. "My call brought me here," Paks began quietly. "I do not know the reason. When I found your king so ill, I hoped the call was for healing. As I found, and told you, it was not." The squires stirred, but said nothing. Paks went on. "While I was setting my things aside to bathe, Joriam noticed what he thought was a treasure of this realm."

"What! Old Joriam?"

Paks nodded. "Yes. If he is right, perhaps my call was to restore this treasure to Lyonya — perhaps it has some power to aid you that neither he nor I know of. Joriam named several others old enough to recognize it — if, in fact, that's what it is. But I thought the king himself should decide how this would be investigated."

Esceriel looked bewildered. "But — Lady — what would you be doing with a royal treasure of Lyonya? Surely Joriam didn't suggest — I mean, you cannot be a thief — "

"No. But I would like to know myself where this thing has been since it left here — if it did — and how it came where I found it. But you have not asked what it is."

"No." Both squires shook their heads. "If you wished to tell us, you would."

"Do you agree, though, that the king should know first?"

They looked at each other. "I suppose." Esceriel looked doubtful. "He has been able to do no work for some weeks. The Council — "

Paks shook her head. "No, if this is what Joriam thinks, it is a relic of the royal house. And it involves elves — high elves — and the king must decide what to do."

"Yes, I see. You're right. But could it not wait until morning? If the king can sleep through the night, even once — "

Again Paks shook her head, and saw that both of them took the meaning of that refusal. Nonetheless she stated it. "I'm sorry — truly sorry. But as I told you, I was not sent to heal him. He may not live that long, and this, I judge, is urgent enough to disturb even the last of his rest. I will do what I can to ease him again later."

They nodded shortly, and left her in the alcove, moving quietly to the bedside to wake the king. Finally Lieth beckoned, and again Paks approached the bed. The king's face showed less strain than before, but his color was no better. His lips quirked in an attempt to smile.

"Lady — I believe you must have some reason for waking me. I am in no pain, but — I feel no strength, either. What is it?"

"Sir king, your old servant Joriam recognized among my gear what he believes is a treasure of your house. If he is right, then the return of this treasure may be my reason here. And since it was elf-made, and belonged to the elven wife of your older brother, who was king many years ago, I believed you should know first, and decide how this is to be handled."

His eyes gleamed. A faint flush of color stained his cheeks. "A treasure? Elf-made, and the elven queen's? That would have to be — " He paused, obviously thinking. "Is it a ring, Lady, or a sword?"

"A sword," said Paks. She did not take it out. He glanced at her side, and she drew her cloak back a little.

He nodded. "It might be — her sword had such a green jewel in the hilt. I remember that much, though I was only a boy when I saw it last. But how did you come by it?"

Paks repeated what she'd told Joriam. The king listened carefully. "I don't see how it could be the same," he said then. "How would such a treasure come to a Tsaian mercenary?"

"If I remember correctly," said Paks, "it was a wedding gift to his wife from Aliam Halveric."

"Halveric!" The king tried to push himself up. Lieth and Esceriel were quick to lift him and pack pillows behind him. "Could it be that the Halverics — no. I won't believe that of them!" But his voice held a measure of doubt. Paks was appalled.

"Sir king, I'm sure it doesn't mean that the Halveric stole it — or had anything to do with the attack. He isn't old enough — "

"Falk's blade! That's right — he's only a few years older than I am. He wasn't even at court. Forget I said any such thing — please. It is my weakness, Lady, and the hour . . . " His voice trailed off. Then it strengthened again. "In fact, now I remember that we were pages together when it happened. Of course it couldn't have been Aliam."

"The Halverics, sir king, have always been loyal supporters of this house," said Esceriel quietly.

846

"Yes, yes — I know. That's why we were fostered as pages to the Halveric estates. I just — for a moment —"

"In such a surprise, sir king," said Paks, "anything may come to mind. But, my lord, I think it is important to identify this sword certainly. I have not taken it from the sheath since Joriam spoke; no one here has seen its blade. Can you describe it?"

"Oh yes." The king nodded. "The hilts — well, I could have seen that, since you've been wearing it. On the blade, as I recall, were runes. I don't remember exactly which. Averrestinil — the queen that was — rarely drew it. And I was just a boy, and seldom at court anyway. The elves would know — if you want to drag them in — and Sier Halveric. Perhaps the old huntsman, if he's still able to see. Averrestinil enjoyed hunting."

"Sir king, the elves *must* be told. They, more than anyone, can confirm whether this sword is the same or another. I know it is of elven make, and magical, but nothing else." Paks looked at the squires, to find both of them staring at her with glowing eyes. She looked back at the king. "I don't know, my lord, what good this sword will do — if it is the one that was lost when the queen and prince were killed —"

"Perhaps it will proclaim the heir — the true heir —" began Lieth. "I have heard of such swords — they take light when drawn by the one who is to rule."

Before she thought, Paks answered quickly, "It can't be that. It lights up when I draw it — " Then she realized how they might take her words. It was too late. Lieth nodded, smiling, and when she looked, the king was smiling too.

"If so, then perhaps your call was to save Lyonya by taking the throne."

"No, my lord!" Paks shrank from the idea. "I am a soldier — a warrior of Gird — not a ruler."

"At any rate, I agree that the sword must be identified and tested. And even by elves." He sighed. "Would that my cousin were still alive — he was regent for my niece before her death — and he was both cautious and wise with elves. I myself have had little to do with them."

"Sir king, do you wish us to gather these people here, in your chamber?" Paks felt the need to push for some definite action that night.

"It must be done openly," mused the king. "A thing of such importance must not be hidden. Yes — bring them here, but give audience to all the Siers, human and part-elven alike."

"But my lord," said Esceriel, with a worried frown. "You are not strong enough — "

The king managed a steadier smile. "Old friend, I will be as strong as I must — this grace the gods have given me so far. If this can leave my kingdom in better state — if it can prevent quarrels and bickering such as I hear through my doors daily — "

"We try, my lord — " said Esceriel.

"I know. I know, and I also know why they come. It will be well worth a day or so less life, Esceriel, to leave my kingdom with hope and peace." He drew a deep breath, that suddenly seemed to hurt, for he stiffened. Paks laid her hand on his, and he smiled again. "No, Lady — I need no more of your strength for the moment. I will save mine for what I must say when they come. Lieth, mix me a warming draught, and call Master Oscarlit. Esceriel, summon these: all the Siers in Chaya, and the kyllan-siers of those who are not here. Also the ranking elf — I don't know who that is, worse luck, but you can find out easily enough."

"I don't know if the elf will come — " said Esceriel.

"They will come if I summon them," said Paks. "May I, sir king?"

"Yes — do. Assemble them, if you will, in the Leaf Hall. If so many come that would be crowded here, you will carry me down."

"My lord — "

"Enough, Esceriel. I know I will die soon; I will die happier if this is behind me. Ward of Falk, Esceriel — be on your way."

"My lord and king." With a deep bow, and a flashing glance at Paks, Esceriel swept from the room. Lieth, having set some drink to warm on the hearth, bowed also and withdrew to find the surgeon. The king beckoned Paks to bend close.

"Esceriel, Lady, loves me too well. He is my son — a bastard, alas, of a human mother with more taig-sense than I — and the only son of mine to reach manhood. This he suspects, but does not know — and has never reached for power for himself. I love him well, Lady, and if you have comfort for him, I pray you give it."

Paks felt tears stinging her eyes. "Sir king, what comfort the High Lord permits, I will give. And now I'd best go, and seek the elves." His eyes sagged shut as she turned away.

Finding the elves in Chaya was not as easy as she had hoped, or as hard as she had feared. No one in the palace seemed to know just where they might be — "They're uncanny, Lady, and wander about — " She had feared they might all be withdrawn into elvenlands, where she had no entry. But after a cold, miserable trek through the streets of Chaya, she heard a few words of elven outside a tavern. She looked up. The sign, lit by a gleam of light from within, was a harp with a wreath of ivy, and beneath it was the elven rune for song. Paks shoved the door open and entered. Light seemed to fail as she came in, shifting in an instant from clear white to the dim reddish glow of a dying fire. Paks felt her bones tingle with magic. She looked around.

"You come late, traveler." The tavernkeeper loomed nearby, tall and stout.

"I am looking for someone," said Paks, in elven. Silence followed. She heard the faint rustle of clothing in one corner, the resumption of breath, where all had stopped for an instant.

"Art thou a true elf?" asked the tavernkeeper in elven. "Art thou of the house of the leaf, or the house of the fountain?"

"I am not," replied Paks, still in the same language. "Yet I have had friends of leaf and fountain, and have been graced by their wisdom and song. I am Paksenarrion Dorthansdotter, named elf-friend by Ardhiel. I have touched the elfane taig, and lain captive of the iynisin longer than I care to tell, and fought a daskdraudigs when my wounds were healed."

"I have heard of such a Paksenarrion," he said. "A servant of Gird Strongarm, so I've heard, and a friend of the Kuakgan of Brewersbridge, and of Kieri Phelan of Tsaia."

"That is true." Paks waited through another silence. Elves, she thought, could be just as slow as dwarves — but then they thought humans were hasty.

"And what do you search for here?" he asked finally. "You carry such magic with you as would satisfy most humans."

Paks laughed easily. "I search for someone, not some thing. For someone who can identify what I carry, and tell me its tale. And not only me. I search, as you must realize, for the elves I thought to find in Chaya, the heart of Lyonya the Fair. For this, I was told, was a kingdom of men and elves together — "

"So it was, once, Paksenarrion," said another voice, from near the dying fire. "Long years ago. But evil betrayed that dream — "

"And good may redeem it," said Paks. She felt a nudge from within, and called light. In that sudden glare the room showed full of elves — many of them high elves, richly dressed. Her light glittered from jewels on fingers and belts and weapons, gleamed on the gold frame of a great-harp, the silver of buckles and mail. Around the walls ran a pattern of interlacement, set in gleaming tiles.

"You are a paladin, then." The tavernkeeper's voice was steady; she had not startled him, at least.

"Yes. And I have come to Chaya on quest, with a call from the gods I serve. This call sent me to find elves — elves who remember the better days, the days when King Falkieri had an elven wife, and two children — "

"Does anyone want those days remembered?" asked the elf in the corner. He sat in a carved chair that resembled a tangle of tree roots formed into a throne; his velvet tunic was embroidered heavily in gold and silver.

"The king does," she answered. "He sent me to ask."

"The king? The *human* king?"

"Yes. He knows he is dying; he wants to leave Lyonya in better hope than now seems likely."

They looked at one another; Paks felt the intensity of those looks. "And on his deathbed he acquires wisdom that might have saved us had he found it earlier." That was a part-elf, squatting on the hearth itself.

"Peace, Challm," said the richly dressed elf. "Wisdom is always worth having, be it never so late. And for a human, whose soul lives after him, it is a priceless gift." He stood. "Paksenarrion, you will not remember, but you have seen me before."

Paks shuffled rapidly through her memories, but to no avail.

He smiled. "You were dying in the snow — you had taken such injuries

849

from an evil power our best efforts were nearly too late and too little. And we did you a discourtesy, in casting a glamour on you that made you forget an errand — though I swear, lady, we took the scroll to Estil Halveric faster than you could have done."

Paks felt her jaw drop. "You! You are one of the elves who found me after — "

"You freed the elfane taig. Yes. Kinsmen, this is an elf-friend indeed. I am glad to see you with such powers, Paksenarrion. From time to time we heard that things went hard with you." She nodded, speechlessly. "You may withdraw your light if you wish; we have our own." He was smiling now, and as Paks damped her light, the elflight, similar but with a more pearly glow, radiated from the air around her. It had no source she could see, and cast no shadows. "You asked my name that night," he went on. "I judged you did not mean any discourtesy, though I was short with you. It went hard to admit that a mere human had done what many elves had tried and failed to do. But now — " He bowed. "Permit me to introduce myself. I am Amrothlin son of Flessinathlin, the lady who holds the heart of the Ladys-forest, and brother of that queen you spoke of."

"The queen who — "

"Who disappeared with her son, the prince. Yes. And if my eyes have not faded — which they have not — you bear at your side the very sword — "

Paks had, in the past few moments, forgotten the sword. Now she laid her hand on its hilt. "It is this, my lord, which — "

He nodded. "I know." His eyes swept the room. "It is time, kindred — time and more than time. We are not hasty, we elves, but the time for mysteries is past, and the time of truth is at hand. I will take six of you: Berris, Gyorlan, Challm, Adreath, Signys, Preliath." He came to Paks. "When does the king wish our presence?"

"As soon as may be, my lord."

"Then we shall come now. He made a gesture, and the elflight died. Paks blinked in the darkness, until her eyes adjusted to the red glow in the hearth. Then she turned, hearing the elves around her, and led the way back toward the palace.

They said nothing during that walk — nothing aloud, at least, though Paks surmised that their thoughts were full. At the palace gates, the guards' eyes went wide when they saw Paks and the others. But clearly they had had their orders, for they swung the gates open and stood at attention. They came to the far side, to the doors of the palace. Lieth stood there, now formal in armor and surcoat of royal green and gold.

"Lady Paksenarrion? It will be in the Leaf Hall; Esceriel called too many lords to fit into the king's own chamber."

Paks introduced the elves with her, and Lieth bowed. "Be welcome, my lords and ladies, in the king's hall. He will be with you shortly." Lieth opened double doors into a long high room with panelled walls, now brightly lit by many candles. Paks estimated that some twenty men and women waited there. Fires blazed in both fireplaces, and at one end a long

850

chair waited for the king. The elves moved into the room; Paks saw some faces light, and others freeze, to see them. She turned to Lieth.

"Will you need help to bring him down?"

"No, Lady. He insisted on donning his formal mail, and Esceriel and I, and two others of his squires, will bear his chair down. He asked that you stay here, until he comes."

"Then I will do so." Paks entered the room. Almost at once, Sier Halveric came to her.

"Well, lady paladin, you have tossed a torch into the oil barrel indeed. What is this, do you know?"

"My lord, I await the king's command to speak of it."

He eyed her shrewdly. "And think I should not ask, eh? Pardon, Lady. I've been on Council so long, and the king's been ill so long, that I am too hasty. The king's business has been our business these many months."

"I hold no anger, Sier Halveric."

He nodded. "I hope I am permitted to thank you for easing him. The word has gone that after your care he slept easily for the first time in months."

"I grieve, my lord, that I was not given healing for him." Paks wondered if she should say even this much; she knew that others were listening.

"I also." He bowed and stepped back. Sier Belvarin stood nearby, frowning, and came forward as Halveric left.

"I wonder, Lady, that you would bring elves to the palace. Perhaps you do not know how we feel — "

"I do not know how you feel, Sier Belvarin," said Paks, with an edge in her voice. "But I know this kingdom is both elven and human, and has been so since humans came here. Elves granted humans land-right here, but the precedence is theirs." Belvarin reddened, and Paks went on. "Besides, I obeyed the king's express command to bring them."

"The king *wanted* elves?"

"Indeed yes," said Paks, now with a smile. "I would bring no one here without his consent, human or other. He told me to find and bring them."

Shaking his head, Belvarin melted back into the crowd. Paks watched him, uncertain. She felt no warning of evil, as she had in Phelan's stronghold, but she knew something was wrong.

"Lords and ladies." At the door, four squires carried the king's chair; he was propped with pillows, gray-faced and gaunt. The speaker was a man in forest green whom Paks had not met. Everyone bowed, while the squires carried the chair forward. In courtesy, no one looked as the squires helped the king from the carrying chair to the one that awaited him. Then they took up their positions on either side of him.

"My lords — ladies — high elves of Lyonya and the elvenlands — " The king's voice was thin but steady. He took a long breath and went on. "This day a paladin of Gird arrived in Chaya — here, in this palace — and because she is here, I called this assembly." He took a sip from a silver goblet that Lieth held ready. "She bears with her what may be — *may* be, I say — a

851

treasure of this house, lost since Falkieri's queen and heir were killed over forty years ago. If it is so, it may have returned to our aid in this time of need. I called you here to witness the examination of this object, and hear what she knows of it."

"In the middle of the *night*?" Paks did not know who that was — a tall dark woman on the far side of the room. But the king smiled.

"Yes, Jonnlith. You all know I have not long to live. The paladin Paksenarrion asked healing for me; it was not granted." He lifted his hand to still the murmurs that ran around the room. "Enough, please. She eased my pain — more ease than I've had since last spring. If the gods have decided that my life is over, who am I — or who is she — to argue? I have no quarrel with her, only great thanks. But in what time is left me, I would learn what I can of this treasure. Paksenarrion, come forward."

Paks moved toward the king's chair, aware of the eyes watching her, and bowed. She felt, rather than saw, that Amrothlin followed her closely.

"Show them the sword in its scabbard," said the king quietly. Paks unbuckled the scabbard from her swordbelt, and held it flat on her arms before her. She saw nothing but interest on most faces, but a few suddenly seemed intent. Sier Halveric. An old man, somewhat stooped, in heavy woolens and a fur-collared cloak. And, of course, all the elves.

"How many think they can name this sword?" asked the king. The Halveric stepped forward.

"Sir king, by the jewel on the pommel, and the shape of the hilts, it is much like the sword that your elder brother Falkieri's elven wife carried. That blade was rune-marked on the the spine; is this?"

"Wait," said the king. "Anyone else?" A thin old man in blue shuffled forward, with a younger one supporting him.

"I saw that sword in her hand," he quavered. "The day she left, sir king, when I led her horse out, and set the lad up behind her, it was belted to her waist. If I can look at the hilts — there was a mark, inside the curve, where the boy had made a scratch with something. She laughed about it, said it was his first mark." He bent over the sword, and poked a bony finger into the place, searching with his fingernail. "Yes — there it is. Can you see it?"

Paks held the sword for the king to see, and he, too, found the scratch. "Thank you, Lord Hammarrin. Anyone else?"

Now the stooped old man came forward. His face was dark and weathered into a nest of deep cracks, but he moved more lightly than the other. He put out one gnarled hand, and touched the scabbard lightly. "I say it is the same, sir king. It — it feels the same, the way it always did. And the stone's the same — " He touched that, too, with a wary finger. "I've seen this sword many a time — at least, this grip and hilts. But it wasn't hers, as I remember, but the boy's — "

"What!" One of the younger lords cried out.

"That's right," said Hammarrin, turning toward them again. "I remember she said something about giving it to him someday. But what does it matter?"

852

"Master Tekko," said the king, "do you know what runes would be on that blade?"

The old huntsman's face creased into a gap-toothed grin. "Me, my lord? Nay, the only runes I know are of track and trail. I can read red deer and wolf well enough. It had something on it, I know that, but not what."

"My pardon, sir king," said Amrothlin quietly. "May I speak?"

The king peered at him. "You are an elf, sir?"

"Yes." The elf's voice held none of the scorn that Paks knew it could convey. "That lady you speak of, the wife of your brother Falkieri, was my sister; this sword and its story are well-known to me."

A scurry of sound like mice ran through the room. The king raised his hand again, and again took a sip of the cup Lieth held. "By your leave, sir elf, we will hear this tale."

Amrothlin turned so that the rest of the room could see his face. "Sir king, in the days when the queen bore her first child she asked her family, in the Ladysforest, to forge him a weapon. She foresaw that his life would be full of danger, and wished him to have the protection of such blades as elves are skilled to make. And so the smiths labored, and after that the singers, to bind into this blade what spells would serve him best."

"But *she* carried it," blurted someone. Paks heard the hushing hisses.

"You're right," said Amrothlin. "So she did. She judged her son would grow to be a tall man, as most half-elven are, and the sword was made full-size. But — " He looked for a moment at the sword Paks held. "It is possible for such a blade, forged to serve one person in particular, to change size and shape somewhat with need. Until he grew to carry it, she kept it in a form she herself could use. It was safer so, she thought, than lying unused. Another thing — although it was made for him, and sealed to him at its making by elven magics, a more formal sealing was planned for that very trip. After that, it could be used by no one else, but until then, anyone might use it. Should evil handle it, it might be corrupted. So she thought to keep it safe for him, and bind her own mother-spells into it as well."

"But how did it get to *her*?" asked Sier Halveric, looking hard at Paks.

"Please, Sier Halveric. Let me finish what I know. The runes on the blade are these: fire, treasure, ward, rejoice, mountain, royal." As he spoke, he traced them on the air in elflight. Paks saw many of the watchers flinch. He turned to Paks. "Are these the runes?"

Paks nodded, and spoke. "Yes, my lord. Those are the runes on this blade." She glanced at the king. "Shall I draw it now, sir king?"

"Wait," he said, looking at the elf. "There is more to this?"

"Yes. The runes can be read several ways, but they were set in the pattern that high elves would read as 'Guard this royal treasure, and the mountains will rejoice.' The royal treasure, of course, being the prince himself. The exact shape and size you see is that chosen by the queen for her own convenience — that's why it looks slender for a grown man's weapon."

"I don't understand," said the king slowly, "how it can have been sealed to the prince, yet not sealed to the prince? And what difference does it make now?"

Amrothlin smiled, but gently. "Sir king, at its making it was spellbound with the prince's name. That meant that no other would ever awake its full powers. As well, the queen had sent, with her request, a bit of cloth with one drop of the prince's blood, and a few hairs of his head. But the final binding, which would make the prince the knowing master of the blade, had to wait until he was old enough to grasp it and speak clearly the words of the ritual. Had their journey been completed, the prince would have been master of the sword. As it was — the prince and queen disappeared, and the sword was lost."

"Yes, but it's here." Belvarin had pushed his way to the front. "It's here now. Where has it been?"

"As for that, Sier Belvarin, I don't know the whole story. For many years it was lost — perhaps stolen by the raiders who attacked the party, or perhaps thrown far into the wood by the queen herself. But I next heard about it when Aliam Halveric sent word to the Ladysforest that he had found an elfblade near three murdered elves, between Chaya and his own lands. His description was exact; it could be no other."

"But you didn't tell him what it was," blurted Paks. "He didn't know, did he?"

"No. Although — " Amrothlin looked away for a moment. "We did not tell him. At the time, sir king, your brother Serrostin had recently come to the throne. We feared that such a relic, at such a time, might stir — might cause unrest. It seemed to us that elves were less and less welcome at court. We feared haste, and the consequences of haste."

"But — " Sier Halveric looked bewildered. "But Aliam never told me about any sword. If he'd told me, I might have remembered — "

The elf sighed. "Sier Halveric, we know that. Aliam had a distaste for talking to you about it."

"You kept him — "

The elf bowed slightly, his eyes glinting. "And if we did, Sier Halveric, it was many years ago, and for reasons we thought wise. We advised Aliam Halveric to give it to the one it was made for — "

"The dead prince?" the king broke in.

"You wanted it sent to his memorial?" asked someone else.

"As you wish," said the elf. Paks felt a curious twist in her mind. The elf's mouth was quirked a little, as if he were secretly amused. But he went on. "Then he told us he was planning to give it to Phelan of Tsaia, as a wedding present, because his betrothed's name was Tammarrion, or 'light of mountains,' two of the runes. We told him that was well enough."

"And when his wife was killed," said Paks in the silence that followed, "the sword was recovered, and hung on his wall until I took it in need."

"Why?" asked the king.

"My lord, Duke Phelan's steward of many years was actually an agent of—" She hesitated to speak that name, and paused for another one. " — the webmistress," she said finally. "He feared my power to detect evil, and tried to kill the Duke and me before I could expose him. No one wore sword to the Duke's Hall; the steward grabbed one from the wall, and I happened to take this one. It was happy to drink his blood."

"I see. And you, not knowing its past, bore it away, and returned it here." The king leaned back, looking even more tired. He drained the goblet Lieth held.

"My lord king, I am sure, now, that I was sent here to return it to its rightful place." The elf stirred beside her, but Paks went on. "I don't know what it can do for you, but such a source of power must be — "

"No." The king shook his head.

"No?"

"No. You were sent here, Lady, that I do not doubt. And I do not doubt that you were sent here with the sword to some purpose. But just the return of it — no. What good will such a sword do, when the one for whom it was made has long died?" He rolled his head sideways to meet the elf's eyes. "Tell me, sir elf — what can such a weapon do, without its master?"

"It is as you see it, sir king. A fine weapon — I've no doubt the lady has found it so — and particularly apt against certain evils."

"Would it be useful to anyone?"

"I think not. It was made in good, for good; it has been used by good, to some purpose. It would not, I think, fight well in a wicked hand."

"How would it be different in its master's hand?"

"My lord king, I know not all its powers. I had no need to know, when it was forged; in fact, I was far away at the time. Like any elf-blade, it gives light when its master draws it: more, if dire evil is near, or if its master's name is in doubt." Paks shifted now, remembering the flare of light from that blade every time she'd drawn it.

"Then if someone drew it," said the king slowly. "If it lit, would that prove anything?"

"It might — I don't know what spells my sister — your queen — put into it."

"I don't remember it lighting up when *she* drew it," said Tekko suddenly. Everyone turned to stare at him. "Many's the time I've seen her with it, too, and I don't recall any light."

"I will tell you all my thought," said the king, raising his voice with an obvious effort. "Here is a paladin come to Chaya, in our deepest need. You know I am dying; I have no heir. Lyonya faces many troubles — between human and elf, between our borders and our allies, with Pargun and Kostandan to the north. This paladin — " he reached out and caught Paks's sleeve, " — has been named elf-friend. She is Gird's warrior, and known to powerful lords in Tsaia and Fintha; this would make our allies happy. The rangers say she can sense the taigin, which I have never done, to my shame and sorrow. And she comes with a treasure of our house, with the sword my eldest brother's wife carried, and which was made, we now know, for her son, who should have been our king. Let her draw the sword — let us see whether it lights for her. If it does — and I believe it will — then I suggest we have found my heir. Can anything be better than a paladin, bearing an elf blade, a friend of elves with taig-sense, to rule in Lyonya?"

Paks turned to him, appalled. "My lord, no!" She heard the rising murmur behind her. "I am no ruler; I am not even noble-born."

"If the gods choose you as a paladin, should I quarrel with your birth?" His voice carried over hers and the hubbub. It stilled as he went on. "Lady Paksenarrion, you have been tested and tried in ways that prove your fitness to wear Gird's crescent — or a crown. I command you now: draw the elf blade made for the heir to this throne, and show us all what it says."

Paks looked around the room, seeing consternation change to anticipation on all the faces. She looked back at the king, soberly. "Sir king, as a paladin, I am bound to honor the gods' commands above all others. But your command does not conflict with theirs. In the name of the High Lord, and Gird his servant — " As she slipped the sword from its scabbard, it flared blue as it had since she first pulled it from the wall. A shout went up.

Chapter Eighteen

"You see?" said the king quietly, beneath it. Paks shook her head, felt the blood rush to her cheeks.

"My lord king," she said, as the noise began to die down. "I fear you have chosen the wrong person even so. I feel no call from my gods to accept this task. Many paladins find their swords give light when drawn."

"Lady, your modesty becomes you." The king's eyes were alight. "Yet see what a solution you are to our problem. A paladin: therefore untainted by evil ambition. A paladin of Gird, which will reassure our neighbors to the west, and warn those to the north. You can sense the taig. You are acceptable, I daresay, to the elves — " He glanced up at Amrothlin. The elf bowed slightly.

"Paksenarrion is, indeed, an elf-friend," he said. "We do not advise on succession, as you know, sir king; but if she held the throne we would not object." Paks gave him a sharp look, seeking for something more behind the words, but his face was smooth and unreadable.

"But I'm not of your House," she insisted. "I'm not Lyonyan at all, or even part-elf — "

"No, but you're honest, brave, and have the power of paladins. These will serve well enough. What has my heritage brought?" The king sounded both tired and bitter. "My Council has not agreed these last two years on a successor. I have found one with more ability than any of their candidates." He looked out at the others in the room. "Would you dispute that, Council members?"

"Not I, my lord," said Sier Halveric quickly. Others murmured agreement, but Sier Belvarin frowned.

"What if she's an agent of Tsaia, my lord? She has been a member of that Phelan's company — he's a Tsaian Duke, after all."

"A paladin?" The king looked shocked. "Belvarin, she's an agent of the gods — that's all." Belvarin looked unconvinced, but nodded. The king turned back to Paksenarrion. "Lady, before the Council and assembled nobles of my realm, and the elves as well, I ask you — I beg you — to take the throne when I die. You can do no worse than I, and I think you must do better, with the gods gracing you as they have. This kingdom — this green land — is the strong heart of the four southern kingdoms. If we — if it falls — then evil is free to ravage Tsaia and Prealith, not to mention the Ladysforest."

857

Paks knelt beside him. "Sir king, I grieve — for you, for this kingdom in distress. But — "

"Someone must, Paksenarrion," the king said more softly. Paks saw his eyes dull with approaching pain. "Please — save it — no one else — " His head sagged. She felt the mingled awe and terror of the others like a cloud.

"Sir king — " Her hand on his conveyed nothing; she had no power to give. She felt the live flesh stiffen, the skin hardening subtly under her fingers like cooling wax. A rustle filled the room. When she looked aside, they were all kneeling, even the elves.

Esceriel moved first. He took a corner of the king's cloak and covered the face. Paks looked up to see tears on his cheeks. He leaned his head against the dead king for an instant, then met her eyes. His gaze carried both challenge and admiration.

"My lords and ladies," said Esceriel slowly. "Our king is dead. He — "

"Our king," interrupted Amrothlin with the slightest emphasis on *our*, "was a brave and great man. We honor his memory."

The squires stood; Paks also rose to her feet. Esceriel finished arranging the king's hands beneath the cloak. He nodded to the group. "Our king has died; he made one last request. I am no longer King's Squire; I am on no Council. I have no right to know, but the king was dear to me, and I would ask whether you will honor it."

"I see nothing else," said Sier Halveric, clambering up from his knees. Others rose as well. "I thought it was a good idea then, and now — Falk rest him well — it's the only thing to do." A low murmur ran around the room, obvious agreement. Even Belvarin shrugged and nodded. Amrothlin gave Paks a keen glance, then a quick bow.

"I have said already that the elves would have no quarrel with such a succession."

"Will you then accept this charge?" asked Sier Halveric, coming forward to confront Paks. "Our land is in need — desperate need — and you have been sent to help us. So much you have said yourself. We offer you the crown for your lifetime, knowing that no harm will come to us on your account."

Paks glanced at the dead king, then looked the Halveric full in the face. "Sier Halveric, I respected your king. I respect your need. But I am bound to obey the calls of my gods. I cannot discuss this here, with your king still — "

"I am sorry you think we have something to discuss," said Sier Halveric. "I had hoped — "

"My lord, if I took the throne, you might find me less biddable than you hoped."

A brief smile lightened his face and made him look more like Aliam. "Lady, if it would persuade you to save our kingdom, I would not mind if you crossed my every whim. Yet I understand; it is not seemly, if you cannot accept without reservations, to discuss it here and now." He turned to the others. "As senior Councillor present, I ask the steward to announce the king's death." The steward bowed low and withdrew. Sier Halveric turned back to the others. "And if the squires would stand guard, as we pay our respects, I will send for the others who should come." He was the first to kneel before the king, and lay his lips a moment on the cloaked face. The others came up, one by one, to do the same. Then they left, and the squires lifted him back to the carrying chair, to take him to his chambers for the formal laying out.

Paks stood until they were out of the room, then faced the group of elves who remained. Their faces were unreadable, even for her. Amrothlin spoke.

"You are very tired, Lady Paksenarrion. Will you council with them, or rest?"

Paks wanted to fall asleep where she stood. She reached in thought for the High Lord and the others. Strength flowed into her, leaching the tiredness away. She smiled at the elves.

"I can sleep when this is settled. The gods give strength when it's needed, as you elves know well, who rarely sleep at all."

"Few are the humans who drink from our springs," said Amrothlin gravely. "But then, few are the humans who have touched an elfane taig directly. Will you say what you have decided?"

"I will say what the gods would have me do, when I know what that is and the Council is assembled," replied Paks.

Outside, Sier Halveric waited for her. "I am sure you are tired, Lady Paksenarrion. If you would rest and pray before meeting with us, we will wait. But the realm's great need requires that we not sit long in uncertainty — may I ask that you speak with us when you can?"

"My lord, if the Council is ready to meet, I will come now. But did you not say that you had messages to send? If some must come from a distance, I would sleep a little."

He nodded. "To assemble the full Council will take some hours more. Those here can make legal decisions, however; we have had to make do so since the king's illness worsened. I have sent to all the Siers who are not present, and to the Knight-Commander of Falk. But in the matter of succession, I fear any delay. I myself resign my claim, to favor yours; at this moment most favor yours, but — "

"What action would be taken by a council of regents, had the king left a minor heir?"

"Oh — the announcement of regents, a proclamation of the terms of regency and that the regents swore their honor to it. Continuance of the alliance, and its terms, and the authority of the courts as presently constituted — "

"Could not the Council act as a regency for awhile?"

"Regent for whom? For you?" He looked confused.

"Let us say, for whomever comes to rule."

"I — hadn't thought of that." He gave her a shrewd look. "Falk's blade in gold, Lady, if you become our queen, as I hope, you promise to be not only good but wise. We could indeed. As well, it would be reasonable, since you are unfamiliar with our laws and customs, to continue as we have until you've time to learn them." He looked past her to the elves who had followed her out. "Would that satisfy you?"

"A temporary regency? That is a matter for the Council to decide, but it seems well enough." Again Paks had the impression of some hidden amusement.

"Then may I see you to your chambers, Lady?" asked Sier Halveric. "Whatever you need —"

Paks nodded, still thinking hard. He led her upstairs and along corridors; Paks realized that they were not returning to the room she'd been given. Before she could ask, he answered.

"The king's chamber is of course where he is being laid out. The room you were given is needed — and would not be quiet, either, in all the bustle. Your things have been moved to the old queen's chambers; servants await you there." He looked over his shoulder to Amrothlin who, with two of the elves, followed them. "Will you grace the palace by staying here for the present? Rooms are available nearby; I can —"

"I will stay near Lady Paksenarrion for the present," said Amrothlin. "Not to speak to her, or impede her rest or prayer, but merely to be present should she have need of any elven lore." Paks shot him a quick glance but nothing showed on his face. The Halveric nodded, as they came to the double doors of another chamber of state.

"The queen's suite has several chambers; I've no doubt you will be comfortable. Lady, if you will come —"

Paks entered. The fair-sized room, bright with firelight and candles, held several tables and comfortable chairs. Old Joriam was there, and two women in the forest green livery of the palace, and Lieth, still in armor. Doors led into other rooms; Paks could see a tall canopied bed in one, book-lined walls in another. A steaming pot sat on the hearth. The Halveric bowed.

"I will leave you now, Lady Paksenarrion. Rest well, and I shall pray that the gods give you leave to grant our king's last request." Then he withdrew. Paks wondered what to do next.

Joriam had no such doubts. "You'll want out of that armor, I daresay," he began, and came to her. "Sela, fetch that robe we've got warming. Sir elf, we've plenty of that good hot punch by the fire. Keris will serve you some, if you will —" The other woman went quickly to a cabinet and fetched out more silver goblets. Amrothlin smiled, and accepted one, as did his companions. By this time Joriam had helped Paks off with the sword, and out of her mail. She had never had such help; he made it easy. Before she knew it, she was wrapped in a warm robe and seated by the fire with a hot drink halfway down. She looked at Lieth.

"Lady," said Lieth carefully, "it was the Council's wish that you be squired as would befit our sovereign. I offered to come this night, having met you. Esceriel mourns."

"I am honored," said Paks. "You know I have given no commitment — "

"I know. But if you do, then it is fitting, and I am glad to serve you even if the time is brief."

"You do not always wear armor," Paks said.

Lieth smiled faintly. "No, Lady. But we are between reigns; you have not yet taken the protection of your crown. And so I thought better to be armed, lest any have secret thoughts."

Amrothlin smiled up at her. "You are a wise squire, Lieth; that was our thought as well."

"You feared for my safety here?" asked Paks, surprised.

"Lady, you are a paladin; you cannot be tainted by evil without your will. But a knife in the ribs will kill you."

"No one would kill her," objected Joriam. "She's — "

"Peace, Joriam. Do you argue that evil has not dogged this realm for many years? Do you think it will give up so easily? If she is, indeed, the hope of this realm, then that could draw the evil powers."

"For that," said Paks, "a paladin exists not to avoid conflict, but to bring it into the open."

Amrothlin nodded. "So I have heard. But here you will be warded by several loyalties: Joriam's lifelong honesty, Lieth's Falkian honor, and the elven sense of the taig. You will have peace for your prayers, and for your rest."

Paks nodded. "Thank you — all of you." A few minutes later, she let Lieth lead her to the bedchamber, and lay for the first time in her life on embroidered sheets beneath a costly canopy figured with flowers and vines. She slept better than she expected, waking in early dawn to a horn call from the palace gates. For a moment she lay still, staring at the pale shape of the window. Everything in the chamber was dark, shade on shade of gray without color. She could just see Lieth's form standing near the window, looking out. She stretched, rustling the covers, and Lieth turned.

"It is early yet, Lady, if you wish more sleep."

Paks felt more awake every instant. "No — I am rested."

"Shall I light a fire here?" Paks remembered that the bedchamber had its own fireplace, but she was not used to that luxury. She shook her head, then, remembering the darkness, spoke.

"No, Lieth. That's all right. Is there a quiet place, where I can be alone to pray?"

"Here — I can guard the door. No one will bother you."

"Very well." Paks pushed aside the covers and swung her legs over the side of the bed. Lieth had already gone out, closing the door softly. Paks padded over the carpets to the window and looked out. There was the courtyard, an eerie uncolored paleness in the dawn. She could see figures by the gate, dark against the dawnlit snow. To the east, the sky was luminous, a band of green beneath the blue.

She pushed the window outward, and craned her head to look up. Winter stars still burned overhead, disappearing as she watched.

She looked at the courtyard again. A puff of smoke came from a chimney across from her window. Then another. She remembered watching for the smoke from the kitchens when she had the night watch at the Duke's. And this was what they would give her: this courtyard, to watch over, to have as her own. This land — the rich farmlands, the great forests full of game. For a few moments, leaning her head on the windowframe, she let herself imagine being queen here. She could be good for them — she knew that. She could sense the forest taig, even here; she could let her mind reach out and sense the taig of the entire kingdom. It lay under her inner eye like a rich tapestry; she could see the places — here, and there, and over there — where something had soiled the fabric, or worn it thin. She thought of having those like Lieth and Esceriel for loyal friends and servants — of hunting in those forests, on a red horse that moved like the north wind. That stopped her. That red horse was no queen's mount, no horse to spend his days in a royal stable champing royal oats. He had not come out of the winter wind for that. She sighed, pushed herself back from the window, and went to sit before the fireplace with its neat pattern of wood waiting for a light.

Her mind emptied of thoughts of thrones and crowns, spilled its images and memories of councils and courts and ceremony. It stilled, gradually, as a forest pool stills when no wind blows. What did she really know? The feel of a sword in the hand. The sickness of fear, and that brother-sickness, rage. She knew the taste of bread to the hungry, the ease of warmth to the cold. One by one, the things she knew of her own experience flicked through her mind. And faces: Saben, Master Oakhallow, Sevri, Stammel, Aliam Halveric, Duke Phelan. These left her. A fire grew in her mind, a fire both warmth and song, and a tree grew in that fire, burning and unconsumed. And a red horse crashed through the flames on a winter wind, taking her somewhere, taking her far away into laughter and flowers.

She came to herself hearing a knocking on the door, and the crackle of flames on the hearth. With a shake of the head, she stood, and opened the door. By then she had seen it was broad day, with sun spearing in the south-facing window.

"We were worried, Lady," said Lieth. Sier Halveric and Sier Belvarin were behind her.

Paks nodded. "My pardon. When the gods speak, it is difficult sometimes to come away." They stared at her, seeing something in her face she did not feel.

"When you're ready," said Sier Belvarin finally, "the Council will be pleased to meet with you."

"I won't be long," said Paks. She could feel her normal wits coming back; she felt strong and rested. The two Siers left the room, and Paks saw that Joriam had bathwater hot by the great hearth. The elves still stood near the outer door; Amrothlin nodded to her.

"I need not ask how you fared, Lady; it is obvious you fared well indeed in the gods' care."

"I have seen your Tree," said Paks. She did not know why she said so, only that it was true and important. Amrothlin stood straighter, if possible.

"Indeed? Then I hope you received the blessing of its leaves, Lady. You are more than welcome to it."

More quickly than Joriam intended, Paks was bathed and dressed; she soothed the old man, while refusing his embellishments.

"Joriam, you are used to serving royalty — and I am a paladin, a warrior of the gods, and not a king or queen. Would you get me used to your luxuries, so that I would miss them on campaign?"

"No — but — "

"You have given me great pleasure already, Joriam. It is all I can take, now."

He grinned at her suddenly. "Now, you say! Very well, then, another time. You'll see — the gods have no hatred for these things, and you are too experienced a warrior to misuse them. I'll wager you like good food well enough, yet can go hungry at need."

"You're right on that, Joriam. Mushrooms — " Paks laughed as Lieth helped her into her mail. "But see here — you save all this for your ruler, eh?"

He nodded. "May it be you, Lady — that's what I say."

"It's the gods' will, Joriam. Your kingdom has great need, and they know best how to fill it."

The Council met in the Leaf Hall. Most of those attending had been at the meeting the night before. Those new to Paks were introduced: the Knight-Commander of Falk, the widower of the half-elven queen, a few nobles. Paks had been ready to dislike the widower, but he was clearly as Joriam had described: a good man, though perhaps narrow-minded, and wholly without ambition. The Knight-Commander was another matter. Half-elven, slightly taller than Paks, he gave her a challenging look when they were introduced.

"Gird's paladin, eh?" he said. His grip was strong, but not painful. "You are not like the others."

"No." Paks said no more.

"I had heard of you," he went on. "Not the most likely candidate for a crown, I would have thought."

"As you will hear," said Paks, "I did not seek one."

"That's what they told me," he said. "If you say you did not, then you did not." He chewed his lip a moment. "I find that hard to believe, but perhaps Falkians emphasize command more than Girdsmen."

Paks thought of the Marshal-General and repressed a chuckle. "I assure you, sir, that ambition for command is found often enough among Girdsmen."

"And to that, as well, you are an exception?"

"It depends on circumstances," said Paks.

"Indeed. And in these circumstances?"

"Sir, when the Council is convened, I will speak to the whole Council of the outcome of my prayers."

"I am well rebuked, Lady," he said, lowering his eyes. Paks did not think he felt rebuked.

By this time everyone was standing behind one of the chairs that had been drawn into a great circle. Sier Halveric looked at Paks; when she nodded, he spoke.

"Sirs and ladies, we are met to discuss our late king's last council and request — and to settle the government of this realm for the time being. I believe you all know what our late king asked — that this lady, a paladin of Gird, who has come to us bearing the sword of Falkieri's heir, take the throne for her life. This she was unwilling to do without consulting the High Lord and Gird her patron. Yet most of us saw her draw that sword in council last night, and saw the sword take light." He turned to Paks. "I ask you now, Lady Paksenarrion, before the Council of Lyonya, acting in regency for the one who will be our ruler, to draw that sword again, and give us your answer."

Paks laid her hand on the sword, but did not draw it. She looked around the circle slowly, meeting each pair of eyes in turn. All were welcoming, as far as she could see, human and elf and those of part-blood alike. When she completed the circle, she nodded once and began.

"Lords and ladies of the realm, elves of the kingdom — I was honored beyond my due by your king's offer. But paladins are bound to the gods they follow. I came here on quest; I am on quest still. After long prayer I believe I now know what that quest is." She paused; the room was utterly silent. Even the fire on the hearth burned without sound.

"It is not to be your queen." At that, an outbreak of sound, rustlings and murmurs. Paks ignored this and went on. "I thought long on this — I would have been glad to take it — but it is not my quest, and I may not turn aside." Now they were quiet again. "But your kingdom's peril, Councillors, is my task, and I believe the gods wish me to find your ruler — the one who should be here, in the place you offered me. I think it was for this that this sword came into my hand. For this that it responds to me — " Now she drew the sword, and its blue glow lit the room. "Not that I rule myself," she said, slipping it back into the scabbard, "but that I find its lawful master."

"But he's dead," said Sier Belvarin. "It was made for Falkieri's son, and he's dead."

"Is he?" asked Paks. Heads turned; she saw the uncertain glances. She looked past them out the tall windows. "I am a stranger here; perhaps I heard things new that you are too familiar with. You think he is dead — but what is the proof of that?"

"They searched — "

"Bodies — "

" — the queen — "

Paks stilled the gabble with a gesture. "They were attacked; the queen was killed. So much is clear. But the prince? His body was never found. What if he lived?"

"If he lived, then why did we never hear of him?" asked one of the others. "And how could a child like that live, alone in the forest?"

"I do not know how he lived, or where he is, or why no one ever heard," said Paks. "But I believe he was not killed. Last night much of this was new to me. So I listened to everyone — and heard what was said, not what I expected to hear." She turned to Amrothlin. "What did you say was the message sent to Aliam Halveric, when he offered to return this elven blade to elves?"

The elf's eyes flashed at her. "He was told to return it to the one for whom it was made."

"But — " Sier Halveric stopped in midsentence, and stared. "You — you knew the prince was alive? *You* knew?"

"The elves would know," said Paks, "if anyone would." She saw the mouths open, the start of an uprising, and spoke quickly. "You all assumed the prince had died in the attack; you all assumed the elves' message meant something or someone else. But if the prince were alive then — and that was how many years ago? — then the elves may have meant exactly what they said."

"*Was* he alive then?" asked Sier Halveric. Amrothlin nodded.

"He was," he said without any emphasis.

"Why didn't you tell us? Why — why it could have saved — "

Amrothlin interrupted. "My lords and ladies, it could not be. At first we too thought he was dead; we could not sense his taig. When at last one of us saw him again, he was — " He stopped, and looked around the room before going on. "He was no longer a prince."

Silence filled the room. Then Sier Belvarin broke it. "What do you mean by that? Born a prince, he would always be — "

"No. He had changed. We judged he might never be fit to rule."

"You judged! How dared you — !"

"You forget, sir, that he was my sister's child!" This time Amrothlin's voice was edged with all the cold fury that elves could show. "My own mother's grandson, a flower of the Ladysforest as much as an heir to your throne — you know, or should remember, how rarely we elves bear children, and how we delight in them. We judged, yes — we, who loved his mother through such ages as you humans call infinite, we judged him. Had you seen him then, sir, you would have judged him too — and perhaps more harshly than we, for you would never have known him for his father's son. Or his mother's."

"What had happened?" asked Paks into the horrified silence.

Amrothlin, still angry, turned to her, speaking with delicate precision. "Lady, we do not know. He bore scars of body and mind, as if he had been enslaved to a cruel master. Far away, I would say, since we had not sensed his taig. Within was fear, but with a core of bitter anger."

Paks turned to the others. "So at one time in the past your prince still lived — years after you thought him dead. Perhaps he lived long enough to father heirs of his own." She looked back at the elf. "Is he still alive, Amrothlin?"

"Do you do well to ask, paladin of Gird?"

"Amrothlin, I ask what I ask by the bidding of the High Lord, if my prayers be true. Not for myself, but for this kingdom."

"As you will, Lady. Then I will say he is alive."

"Do you know where? Do you know his name?"

"I cannot help you," said Amrothlin. "You have not asked yet why he himself never claimed his inheritance. He has no memory of it; it was destroyed. If only — " Amrothlin looked down for an instant, then met Paks's eyes again. "We elves like not that phrase, but in this case, had the attack happened on the way home, the prince could not have been damaged as he was. The wakening of his elven powers would have warded him somewhat. But as it was, he knows not his own name or title. When he returned to the Eight Kingdoms, the man who took him in as a servant eventually guessed who he might be. But he saw no future for him at this court; he concealed what he guessed, and told the boy nothing."

"Who was that?" asked Sier Halveric quickly. "In Lyonya? In Prealith?"

"I cannot help you," said Amrothlin again.

"Cannot, or will not?" asked Paks.

"Lady, I have done what I can. We are not convinced he is fit to rule; he has had the chance to show such ability, and has turned away."

"Why didn't you heal him?" asked Belvarin suddenly. "Couldn't you have done that when you first met him again?"

Amrothlin put up his hand. "We could not heal — or attempt to heal — without risking great harm, both to him and to the kingdom. If we had restored, say, his memory of his name — and not been able to restore the taig of his spirit, would that have been well done? We judged not. Sometimes time itself heals what no magics can, elven or other. We waited. We watched from afar. We did not see the sign of growth we could foster; we did not wish to do more destruction to one who had been so harmed already." He waited until everyone was quiet again, then went on. "As for succession, we do not advise — but we will not help you find someone we think is too flawed to rule. If you find him yourself, against our recommendation, then we will see."

Paks, following all this, began to have a curious feeling that she had already what clues she needed — if only she had the peace and quiet to put them together. But for the next hour no one had peace and quiet. The Council roiled with excitement. They calculated how old the prince must be; they tried to guess who and where, and surprise the elf into an answer. Paks stood aside, listening, trying to think, trying to fix every word that had been said in her memory. Finally, when the same people began to repeat the same words, she raised her hand. They fell silent.

"Lords and ladies, high elves, Councillors: I say again that this is my quest. To find your prince, and restore the rightful king to your throne. I

866

cannot make this quest without your support, for you must agree to accept the king I bring you — " She was surprised to find herself saying this, but went on; the gods surely knew what they did when they took over her tongue. "I will return with your true king, or his heirs. Is this agreeable?"

They argued a while longer; some thought they'd rather have a paladin already there than a mysterious lost prince who, according to the elves, wasn't worth finding anyway. But Paks insisted that she would not take the crown, and finally they agreed. Amrothlin looked long in her eyes before nodding at last.

"If you find him, and if you can show us that his anger will not break the kingdom to bits, we will accept him. And if we can, we will restore his elven powers."

"As the High Lord wills, and Gird gives grace, Amrothlin. I believe the prince will be found, and found able to rule, else this quest would not be laid on me."

"May it be so," said Amrothlin gravely. "May it be so indeed, that the powers of evil find their plots spoiled, and the House of the Fountain break forth in joy."

"I will ask questions," said Paks, "that you would be wise to answer." His eyebrows went up, and a mocking smile touched his mouth.

"You would teach wisdom to elves, paladin? Well, it may come to that, but we shall see. I will answer as I can, for our honor and his."

Chapter Nineteen

"Since you insist your quest is to find our prince," began the Knight-Commander of Falk, "we can only try to help you as we can."

Paks smiled at his expression. "Do you know Marshal-General Arianya, sir?"

His nose twitched. "Yes; I met her in Vérella one time. A remarkable woman."

"She might enlighten you about my past," Paks suggested.

"Oh — " Under direct challenge, he seemed to deflate. "Ward of Falk," he said then. "I've no reason to doubt you're who or what you say — and I know a paladin cannot lie. To be honest, I suppose it galls a bit that the High Lord chose a paladin of Gird for this, when I would have thought a Falkian could do as much."

"Save that someone born and brought up here would have assumed the prince's death, sir. It is that ignorance, perhaps, which makes me suitable."

"I would have expected such reasoning from a kuakgannir, Lady, not a Girdsman. Emptiness calls fulfillment — is that what you mean?"

Paks shook her head. "Not precisely, though as you should know if you do not, the final healing of my wounds came from a Kuakgan. What I meant was that a commander new to a company can see what custom has hidden."

"Oh."

"Where will you begin looking, Paksenarrion? There are many men in the Eight Kingdoms of the right age — and many still when you leave out the black-haired, dark-eyed ones who cannot be the prince." Sier Halveric poured out mugs of sib as he spoke. They had gathered in the queen's chambers, the older lords who remembered the queen and prince, and the Knight-Commander. The elves had withdrawn, to pay their respects to the dead king in their own way, but promised to return if Paks called.

She thought a long moment, trying to feel her way into the gods' will. "I think," she said, "that I must begin with this sword's history. I must talk to your nephew Aliam — see the place where he found it, and hear from him the exact wording of every message the elves sent. They told him once to give it to the one for whom it was made — as if at that time he could have done so, and it would have been right. Surely if he had, the sword would have proclaimed the prince's identity. But he did not know who the prince was — how could he? Nor did he know the power of the sword — or so Amrothlin implied. I must ask him directly. In the meantime, tell me what you remember of the young prince — Joriam, you begin."

"Well, Lady, I was young myself then — I may have forgot — but I remember him as a lively little lad. Going on four or five he was then, a little scrap of a boy. Had reddish golden hair, much like his father's, but lighter, as a child's often is."

"Any marks you'd know him by?"

"No, Lady. I never tended him, ye see. Just saw him about. I remember once he climbed out on a window ledge and knocked off a pot of flowers — "

"I remember that," broke in Sier Hammarrin, chuckling. "By Falk, that little rascal had nerve — always loved to climb things. Down the flowers came, nearly hitting old Fersin, rest his soul, and shattered on the courtyard. He couldn't have been over three at the time."

"They sent you after him, didn't they, Joriam?" asked Sier Halveric. "I remember something — "

Joriam nodded, blushing. "Yes, my lord, they did. I was the closest, and lightweight too — I've always been small — they feared the ledge might go; it was before that section was repointed. And so I started out, and I was feared, Lady, of the height, and he saw it and said 'never mind, Joriam; I'll come in myself' and crawled right to me. Steady as a cat on a limb, he was."

"What else?" asked Paks.

"You mustn't think he was spoiled," said Sier Galvary, a bald old man with gray eyes. "Not more than any prince is. He was loved and wanted by both his parents — the pride of the palace — but his father insisted he be courteous. And he was, for such a little sprite."

"Not so little, really," said Sier Halveric. "For his age he was well-grown. He seemed like to grow into a tall man. But I agree, he was mannerly. Do you remember when his father gave him the gray hound puppy, Galvary?"

Galvary shook his head, but Hammarrin began chuckling again. "I do. I certainly do. That dog was the worst nuisance . . . pick of the litter, indeed! Pick of mischief! He nipped everyone, and must have chewed half the harness in the stables."

"It made your stableboys keep the reins off the floor," said Sier Halveric. "But what I was thinking of was the boy — you know how boys are with dogs; he took a stick to it one day, and I came in on the end of that lecture. Two days later, I found him giving it word for word to some commoner's child outside the walls, who was tormenting a kitten. Word for word, his father's tone of voice, everything: 'It is not the act of a man or a prince to abuse helpless things, nor the justice of kings to give pain when it can be avoided.' It sounded funny enough, from that little mouth — and yet — "

"It sounds as if he would have been a good ruler," put in Paks. "If nothing had happened."

"I believe so." Sier Galvary nodded. "We had no doubts of it. Falkieri and his wife were mature; the boy showed every sign of ability. He did what normal boys do, mischief and all, but there was no meanness in him. And brought up to it, with good examples and good sense, there was no reason for him to go wrong."

"Look at his sister — the young queen — " said Hammarrin. "She did well, even without her mother, with her father dying early, and all that. The same blood: brave, generous, intelligent — "

"I can't believe, whatever has happened, that if Falki lives he is completely unfit to rule." Sier Halveric took another sip of his drink. "The gods know people change, but he had such promise — how could it all be lost, without killing him?"

Paks thought she knew, but hoped it was not true. They had no need to know; she pushed her memories down below the surface. It hurt her to think of a child enduring anything like she had endured, a child living on with the hopelessness she had suffered for less than a year.

"What was his name?" she asked, distracting herself.

"The prince? The same as his father. We called him Falki. His parents had their own pet name for him, of course. His other names — let's see — Amrothlin, I just realized — that's for his mother's brother. Artfielan — for an uncle, wasn't it? Falkieri's mother's brother? And something else — we'll have to look it up. It's too far back for me." Sier Hammarrin shook his head.

"How many names do princes have?" asked Paks.

"Oh, it depends. Usually four or five. You want to please all the families, you know. But the names won't help: every Falkian family has a Falkieri or two, it's one of the commonest names in Lyonya. Artfielan — I've a son named that, a grandson and a nephew. Besides, the elves said he doesn't remember his name, and we don't know what name he's using."

"So," she began again to organize her thoughts. "You say he would be about fifty years old, with red or yellow hair — "

"I expect reddish," said Sier Halveric. "His was still reddish when he disappeared, and his father's had darkened."

"Tall, you think? And what color eyes?"

This began another argument. Paks found it hard to believe that no one had noticed the color of his eyes until she realized that she couldn't name the color of her own brothers' eyes either. Finally they agreed that they weren't green, gold, or dark. Blue or gray or something in between.

But this left almost nothing to go on. A tallish man of late middle age with reddish hair and blue or gray eyes — unless his hair had turned gray already, or he'd gone bald. Paks had trouble imagining a bald prince, but after all, he was old enough to be her father. According to the elves, he had been someone's servant once. She assumed that meant in the Eight Kingdoms, but it might not. He might be a woodchopper somewhere (Paks thought of Mal in Brewersbridge, but of course he was too young) or a farmer. He might be a merchant, a craftsman, almost anything. Paks thought of the number of red-haired men she'd seen in the north and felt depressed. Not only that, he might have gone to Aarenis. Or across the ocean. She found she was making circles on the table with one finger. Everyone had fallen silent; she could tell by the glum faces that they, too, had realized the size of her task.

"Unless the elves change their minds," said Sier Halveric, "I don't see how you can hope to find him in time to do us any good. There are too many —"

"It would help," said Paks, "if they would give me details — what he looked like when they saw him, and so on. But remember, sirs, that the gods have sent me this quest. If the High Lord wants your prince on the throne, can even an elf hide him from me?"

At this they cheered up, and Paks felt herself that somewhere in this she had learned something useful — if only she knew what.

The old king's funeral ceremonies took from sunrise to long after sunset. When it was over, Paks went to her chambers to pick up her gear, packed ready. There she found Esceriel, Lieth, and the other King's Squires waiting.

"You are not the queen," said Esceriel, "but we have no ruler to squire. By your leave, Lady, we will ride with you on this quest. It may be that you will have need of us — or when you find our king, we can serve him well."

Paks looked at him searchingly. She had seen nothing of Esceriel until now; the others had taken their turns in her chambers. But she felt nothing evil in him, and none of them seemed likely to put a knife in her back.

"I do not know how long I will be," she said finally. "Have you leave to be away from court for long?"

"We have no ruler to serve; it was the king who gave or refused leave to his squires, Lady. Other than that, we are all Knights of Falk. Although we have stayed much at court, you will find us hardy travelers and able warriors, should such be needed." He turned aside for a moment, and one of the others handed him a bag, which he held out to Paks. "In addition, Lady, the court of Lyonya will bear any expense of our travels; here is the Council's gift to us, if you permit us to ride with you."

Paks looked each of them in the eye — all steady, all seeming good companions. She nodded. "You are welcome to come with me, as far as you will, as long as your will and the quest I follow travel together. Yet I will not bind you; since I cannot say where and how I go, it would not be right to take your oaths." They all nodded. "If for any reason any or all of you decide to leave me, I will give you no blame for it. But I was planning to ride tonight, squires — or should I call you companions?"

Lieth smiled. "By your leave we will be squires to you, Lady — it will keep us in practice for the king we hope to find. You know Esceriel and me; here are Garris, the oldest of us, but not too old for this, and Suriya, the youngest."

"And we also are ready to ride tonight," said Esceriel. "Our horses are saddled and ready; we have stores packed. We need only our cloaks."

"Very well," said Paks. "Then let us go."

871

They rode out through streets glittering with deathlights, twigs wrapped with salt-soaked wicks that burned green. The sharp smell of the burning twigs carried on the light wind for some time after they left the city. Garris, the eldest of the squires, who had squired for the previous king as well, led the way through the woods southward. They carried torches; light glittered off the crusted snow.

By daybreak, they were far from Chaya, among hills covered with forest. It was a gray morning, with icy mist between the trees, and Garris stopped them.

"We should wait for this to lift," he said. "I know where we are, but I cannot read the taig enough to keep direction in the fog."

"I can," said Paks, "But it will do us no harm to have a hot meal. If we travel today, Garris, can we come to shelter for the night, or must we camp in the snow?"

"If we keep to the way I know, we will come to a steading by midafternoon. But it would be easy to miss — the land is not so settled as that you may be used to in Tsaia."

"We'll see." Two of the squires built a fire; the others brought out pots and began to cook. Paks walked around, stretching her shoulders, and watching their preparations. The night before she had not paid much attention to their gear; now she found that they were prepared for a long march in almost any conditions, with two pack animals along.

"When the king travelled," explained Lieth, "we cared for his things. Had you wanted it, we could have brought the royal tent as well." They had a small one; it would sleep all six of them if they crowded in.

"I shall feel like a rich woman yet," said Paks, as they served out hot porridge and sib. She noticed that they took guard duty in turns, two by two, even though they were in friendly country.

After the break, Paks led the way south, checking with Garris at intervals. She could feel a certain difference in the direction he thought the steading lay, a break in the forest taig. No one suggested stopping long at midday, though they rested the animals, and by midafternoon they had found a large farmstead. A log palisade surrounded a stone house; other houses clustered near it. Dogs ran out barking; a man in furlined leathers came out to look at them, and waved.

Esceriel and Lieth rode ahead. Paks had not realized that they carried pennants until they lifted them: the royal crest on one, and — to her greater surprise — Gird's crescent on the other. By the time she rode up to the man, the squires had explained the quest, and the man bowed.

"Be welcome here, Lady Paksenarrion; luck to your quest. We sorrow for the king's death; the messenger stopped here on the way to Aliam Halveric's and told us of it."

"We thank you for your kindness, sir," said Paks.

"This is Lord Selvis," said Lieth quickly.

"Ride on in," said the man. "There's a barn inside the palisade. We've wild cats in the wood; we stall all the horses at night."

872

All day the red horse had traveled like any other, but when Esceriel reached for his rein, he drew back. Paks grinned. "I'll take him myself, Esceriel."

"He let the stablehands at Chaya —"

"I had asked — and after that perhaps he understood the emergency." They walked to the barn together, the red horse breathing warm on Paks's neck at every step. When she took off saddle and bridle, she found him unmarked as if from a grooming. She picked up a brush anyway, but the horse nudged her hand aside. Esceriel stared.

"I never saw a horse like that."

"Nor I. He came out of the north, one day at the Duke's stronghold, in northern Tsaia. Slickcoated — as he is now — and full of himself."

"How long have you had him?"

"That was this winter — not long." Paks poured a measure of grain in the box, after sniffing it for mold. She pulled an armload of hay down and wedged it in the rack. "I had known that paladins had special horses, but — as you may have heard — I became a paladin in an unusual way. Not at Fin Panir. So I didn't know how — or even if — I would get mine."

"What do you call him?"

"If he has a name, he hasn't shared it with me."

The next day was clear again; they made good time along snowy trails that Garris remembered. That night they camped; the squires did not want to let Paks take a share of the watch.

"I'm not the queen," she reminded them. "And I'm used to night watches — and younger than most of you."

"But we depend on your abilities," said Garris. "You should take what rest you can."

In the end, Paks simply got up when she woke in the midnight hours, and went out to see stars tangled in the bare treelimbs. When she'd used the little trench they'd dug, she spoke to Suriya, the squire on watch.

"I'm wide awake, and I need to think. Go sleep; I'll wake the next in an hour or so." Suriya, the most junior and only a few years older than Paks, nodded and went into the tent.

Paks walked around the camp slowly. It was a windless night, so quiet that she heard every breath each horse took. Her own came to her, crunching the snow, and leaned a warm head along her body. She put her arm across his back and stood for a few moments. Then she pushed away, and went on. Her taig-sense told her that nothing threatened nearby. She caught a flicker of movement between the trees. Another. Some small night animals skittering over the snow. Remembering Siniava, she checked again, but it was nothing — just animals. When the stars had moved several hands across the sky, she shook Esceriel awake and rolled back into her own blankets.

The fifth day a snowstorm caught them between one steading and another. Paks had been uneasy since waking in the night, and had rushed the others through breakfast and farewells. She felt some menace ahead, which it would be well to pass early. But the storm began softly, so that they did not think of turning back until they were more than halfway to the next stopping place. A few flakes — a few more — a gentle curtain of snow that filled the tracks behind them. Then a wind that twirled the falling snow into eerie shapes. And finally the strong wind with miles of snow behind it, that turned their view into a white confusion.

If she had been alone, Paks might have trusted the red horse to fight through the deepening snow and sense dangerous terrain. But with four others, and two pack animals —

"Stop!" she yelled, as Esceriel's horse moved past her, drifting downwind. He reined in; she could just see him. She got the others into a huddle. Slowly they moved into the lee of a large knot of cedars; snow had already drifted head-high on the upwind side. In the struggle of making camp, Paks found herself taking command easily. By the time they were huddled in the tent, which had been cross-braced with limbs against the snow-weight, she felt at ease with the squires for the first time.

"It's too bad we didn't bring lamps," said Esceriel. It was nearly dark inside the tent, and not far from it outside. Paks called light, and they did not flinch from it.

"Handy," commented Suriya. "You never have to eat in the dark, do you?" She dug into one of the packs and pulled out sausage and bread. "I don't suppose you can heat this as well, can you?"

"No," said Paks. "Unfortunately, this light won't even light a candle."

"Oh well. At least it's light." They ate by Paks's light, then rolled up to sleep.

The next morning they had to dig themselves out; it was still snowing, but not as hard. They stamped down a flat area around the horses, fed them, and Lieth climbed a drift to look around. She came down shaking her head.

"It's deep; I can't see the trail at all. And it's still coming down as if it meant to go on all day. We can try to get out, but — "

Paks shook her head. "No. We'll stay here. It'll be hard enough on the horses when we go; they don't need the bad weather as well. If you can't see the trail, you can't see the dropoffs either."

Lieth looked relieved. "I know you're in a hurry."

"Yes, but to find something. Not to fall into a hole in the snow." Garris laughed, and Paks grinned at him. "Gird's grace, companions, paladins are supposed to have sense as well as courage."

Suriya shook her head. "That's not what I've heard."

"You!" said Garris affectionately. "You're hardly old enough to have heard any tales at all. Why, you haven't even heard all of mine."

Suriya groaned, and the others laughed.

"I certainly haven't heard your tales, Garris," said Paks, still laughing. "We'll be here all day — when we've made a fire and have enough wood for awhile, I'll listen if no one else will." But it was some hours before they had time to talk. By then the snow had stopped, and the wind had died away, though the sky was still flat gray, like painted metal. They had trampled down a wide space before the tent, gathered wood, and started a large fire. The horses had been walked about, watered with snow melted over the fire, and fed again. A large pot of stew bubbled merrily; Garris had even set bread twists to bake in a covered kettle.

And then Esceriel, on watch, whistled a warning. Paks reached out in thought, and found nothing evil. The next moment, she heard the familiar trilling whistle of the rangers. Esceriel called out. A few minutes later, two half-elf rangers stepped down into their courtyard of trampled snow.

"We're glad to find you," said one, throwing back his hood. "We knew you were coming, and worried about the storm when you didn't show up at Aula's.

"We should have known that King's Squires and a paladin would be safe," said the other. "But such storms can fool anyone."

"You'll share our meal?" asked Paks.

"Certainly." The first ranger turned to her. "You're Paksenarrion? Giron and Tamar send greetings; we met and passed two days ago. I'm Ansuli — no relation to the one you knew — and this is Derya."

"If you see them again," said Paks, "please tell them I am grateful."

"I will." He warmed his hands at the fire. "As late as it is, you might as well stay here tonight; we would be glad to guide you tomorrow, since the snow is so deep."

"Stew's ready," said Garris. They all ate heartily. After that, in the long dimming hours before they slept, they all told tales of other winter journeys. Paks had no tales she wanted to tell, so she listened. Esceriel told of a wolf-hunt, one year when the Honnorgat froze solid enough to ride over and they nearly found themselves in Pargun. Paks could not imagine anyone riding out on ice over cold black water. Ansuli countered with a tale of winter hunting in the mountains, against "things like orcs, only bigger" that came in tribes and used slings loaded with ice and rock. Lieth told of the time she had tried to go from her father's house to her uncle's in a snowstorm, when she'd been told to bide inside. She claimed her father warmed her so that she forgot all about the cold. Everyone laughed.

"Garris, I thought you had a story to tell," said Paks, turning to the older man.

"A story! Lady, I have stories enough to keep us up all night. But if you want a snow story — though why anyone would, in this cold — did your friend the Duke ever tell you about crossing Hakkenarsk Pass in the winter, with Aliam Halveric and me?"

"You?" Paks was startled. "I didn't know you knew Duke Phelan."

"Falk's blade, I do indeed. I mean, I did. We were squires together at the Halveric's. Until that year, anyway; my father decided it was too hazardous a way to make a man of me, that fighting in Aarenis with Aliam." He chuckled and poked the fire. "Or maybe it was Aliam finally losing patience with my clumsiness; I was a slow lad, in some ways."

"Well, what happened? I don't think you've told this one to me," said Esceriel.

"Or me," added Lieth.

"Maybe not." Garris nodded. "It's been a long time since I even thought of it — when I first came back I suppose I bored everyone in hearing for a couple of years and then forgot it, as boys do. But it was an adventure, all the same." He poked the fire again, and Paks saw determined patience on the other faces around the fire. Perhaps Garris was always this slow to get on with a tale.

"What happened was that Aliam was in a hurry to get home, one fall, and instead of going with his company through Valdaire, he decided to take the short way over the mountains." Garris paused; Lieth handed him a flask, and he took a drink. "Thanks. I was young, then — it was my first year to go into Aarenis with Aliam, though I'd been with him for nearly three. I suppose Kieri was a couple of years older — but then Kieri was always older. We could all tell he'd be Aliam's senior squire in a year or so, and we thought he might become a captain under him."

"Where was the Duke from?" asked Paks.

"Kieri? I don't know. I never asked. I'd never have asked him anything like that — not him. I was a little scared of him. Anyway, Aliam had taken us and four men and gone off north of Sorellin. There's a road partway, and then a sort of trail. And at the foot of the mountains, there's a village — or was. Someone told me it's gone now, and Sorellin has some kind of fort near there."

Paks realized with a shock that he must be talking about Dwarfwatch.

"It was coming on to dark," Garris went on, "and Aliam decided to stay in the village — they had an inn. Kieri and I were supposed to see to the horses, while he ate. It was a mean-looking place; narrow stone buildings and a cold little stream between them. Ugly. Anyway, we had finished with the horses, and were bringing Aliam's things inside, when we saw through the window what they were doing. They had already killed two of the men, and knocked Aliam on the head. Kieri didn't hesitate. He sent me to saddle the horses again, and get them ready. Then he went after Aliam." Garris stopped again to drink.

"I don't know what happened inside. It seemed to take forever before Kieri came out with Aliam — I'd heard plenty of noise, too. Screams like I don't want to hear again. Aliam was dazed; Kieri helped me get him out, and sent me off leading an extra horse for him. He caught up to us some way up the trail, covered with blood. Horse blood, he said."

"Said?" asked Esceriel.

"You'll see. We took off uptrail as fast as the horses could go; that part of the trail is well-traveled, and easy to follow. Aliam could hardly ride; we held him on his horse. When daylight came, I could see the bulge on his head with a crease in the middle — I would have sworn his skull was broken. Kieri coaxed him to eat and drink, and cleaned him up — I didn't know what to do but follow Kieri's instructions. Later that day, Aliam seemed to wake up — he talked sense to us, and told us which way to go when the trail forked. And I realized that Kieri was hurt, too. His saddle had fresh blood on it when he dismounted."

"How about you?" asked Lieth.

"A few bruises from someone who tried to stop us on the way out, nothing else. He had sent me off, you see. Anyway, I tried to help him tie it up; he'd taken a sword gash in the leg, and another in the ribs. That night a troop of dwarves came on us — we were near the top of the first pass, the higher one. Aliam was well enough to tell them what had befallen us; they were not pleased, and said they'd heard ill of that village. Aliam offered that treasure of his which had been left there if the dwarves would avenge his men and bury them; they agreed."

"So then what?" asked Lieth.

"Then it got colder. I swear to you, I have never been so cold in my life — and never hope to be, either. The next morning, Aliam didn't remember the dwarves. We got him on his horse again — he could sit a little better — and I had to help Kieri onto his. Then up, and up, and the snow began. The horses slipped and skidded. We got off and led them; we had to go one by one, and we were afraid Aliam would slip and fall. But he didn't. That night it was colder yet. We had nothing for a fire, and not much food left. The dwarves had said it would be a half day down, after the first pass, then a half day up, and then two or three days down to the nearest settlement. We stopped at the foot of the second pass. Aliam discovered that Kieri was wounded; he'd lost much blood, and had frostbite as well. By the time we got over the second pass, Aliam was better, but Kieri was fevered. Once we got below timberline, we had to stop. He couldn't travel. That's when he cried — it was the fever, of course. Aliam held him." Garris poked the fire again, sending up a fountain of sparks.

"Cried?" asked Ansuli. Garris looked up sharply.

"Oh. Something between him and Aliam, I daresay. I didn't understand, and Aliam didn't explain. But for awhile it worried me — I'd never thought of Aliam as a cruel man — "

"Aliam Halveric? Cruel?" The second ranger, Derya, sounded as shocked as Paks felt.

Garris shook his head. "I shouldn't have said that — he isn't, I know. But Kieri seemed so frightened. It's nothing. Fever — wounds — and anyway it happened long ago. We were only boys. Only I was the younger, you see — I'd always admired Kieri, from the first time I saw him at Aliam's. He was the best with sword or spear, the boldest of any of us. And to see him so frightened — well, it frightened me. And it means nothing. I daresay Lady Paksenarrion can tell us how brave he is."

Paks woke from a kind of reverie to find them all staring at her, waiting for an answer. "I never knew him to be anything but bold," she said finally. "I've seen him both in battles and in hand-to-hand fighting — he's the best in his own company, and one of the best I've seen anywhere."

"You see?" said Garris. "The point is — I shouldn't have gotten off on that other, only it impressed me, being a boy back then — the point is that he got us all over the pass alive. And frankly, when I saw those villains bash Aliam in the head, and a foot of steel sticking out of Rollis's neck, I was sure we were all going to be killed. But he told me — just do what I say, and don't argue, and we'll see our lord alive out of this, gods willing, and so it came out."

By then it was dark, and they all retired to sleep. This time Paks did not argue about being left out of the watch rotation. She had plenty to think about without that.

Chapter Twenty

They arrived at Aliam Halveric's steading just after midday three days later. An escort had met them at the forest border, ten men-at-arms and a boy Paks thought had the family look. He introduced himself as Aliam, son of Caliam, son of Aliam; Paks thought back to Aarenis and realized that Caliam must have had children before that year. She was glad for him. The boy was in his mid-teens, but already wearing mail and sword as if he knew how to use them. Paks was sure he did.

On the way in he said little, only pointing out the steading walls when they came in sight, the location of the mill, the drillfields and exercise lots for horses.

"There's a good ride south, up in the hills," he went on, eyeing the red horse with interest. His own mount Paks classified as good but aged. "If you stay that long — I mean — of course you're welcome to do as you please, but — "

Paks did not wait for his tongue to untangle. "If we are able to stay, perhaps you will show us that ride."

He nodded, not risking words again. Paks smiled to herself, but kept her face grave. As they neared the steading wall, she noticed the other houses scattered near it — only a few clustered together near the walls. She asked the boy about it. He explained that it served to prevent the spread of fire, and also made it easier for defending archers.

"On either side, I should think," said Paks. Near the steading, the forest was cleared back more than a bowshot.

"Yes. He said that's to give those inside a clear shot — the others have to expose themselves."

"Do you really expect trouble from the forest?"

"No." The boy shook his head. "Not for years. But my grandfather says to be ready for anything." He looked sideways at Paks. "Is it true my grandfather knew you before you became a paladin, Lady?"

Paks looked at him. "Yes. In fact, I had to yield my sword to him once." She saw by the boy's face that his grandfather had gained in his eyes.

"A paladin?" he breathed.

Paks laughed. "I wasn't a paladin then. I was a common soldier, a private, in another mercenary company."

"Yes, but — " he looked confused. "I thought paladins were knights before they were paladins."

"Not all of them," said Paks. "I was a common soldier, and then a free sword, and then in the training company at Fin Panir — " She wished suddenly that she had not started this recitation. How could she tell a mere boy what had happened?

"But when my grandfather knew you — " He jumped into the pause. "You were just a common soldier then? Not a squire or knight?"

"No."

"Oh. What company?"

"Duke Phelan's, of Tsaia."

"Oh — I know him. Grandfather doesn't have that chance often, to capture one of Phelan's cohorts. And the last time he did, it all turned out bad — I don't suppose that was when you mean. It was only a few years ago." Now they were near the gates; Paks did not have to answer that. Ahead, in the opening, Aliam Halveric stood to welcome them, flanked by two taller men that Paks assumed were his sons. He was even balder than before, but he seemed as vigorous as when she'd seen him last.

"Well — Paksenarrion." He grinned up at her; Paks threw herself off the red horse and found herself wrapped in a bearhug. He let her go, and shook his head. "My pardon, Lady, if you mind it — but Kieri's told me so much of you, I'd begun thinking of you as our family as well. It's good to see you looking so well."

She had never forgotten the warmth that seemed the essence of Aliam Halveric's character; here on a wintry day it blazed as bright. Now he grinned up at his grandson.

"Get off that horse, you young ruffian, and take our guests' horses. Will you sit there like the king come visiting?" The bantering tone took the sting out of his words. "Come on in, Paksenarrion — may I call you so? And you squires, of course — be welcome here. Paksenarrion, you've never met my Estil — she would have come out, but had something to settle in the Hall."

"My lord," said Paks, "I'd best take my horse to stable myself — he's not always easy to lead."

Aliam looked at the red horse with open admiration. "What a beauty. Paladin's mount, eh? I'm not surprised he won't lead to any hand. Well, come on, then. I'll show you. Cal, if you'll take the squires in and show them the rooms; Hali, see to the baggage." And he strode off, faster than he looked, leading Paks across a large outer court toward an arched opening to the right. She had just time to notice that everything was trim and workmanlike: the court swept bare of snow, the well-cover neatly in place, no loose gear or trash. The stable was equally well-organized. Paks put the red horse into a box stall where water was waiting. As she had found usual, the horse showed no saddle marks. Aliam whistled softly through his teeth.

"Will he let grooms care for him? Or should I warn them off?"

Paks laid a hand on the warm red shoulder. "He hasn't caused any trouble yet — but if he doesn't want to be groomed, he'll push the brush away. Don't argue. And don't let anyone try to tie him."

"No. I'll tell them." Aliam went off to speak to the grooms, who were putting the squires' horses in nearby stalls. Paks looked down the wide aisle, well-lit by windows set high in the inner walls. The red horse nudged her, and she poured the grain Aliam had given her into his box. Then she followed Aliam back across the courtyard into his Hall.

At the door, Estil met them. Paks saw a woman as tall as herself, dark hair streaked with silver, broad shouldered and lithe. She glanced at Aliam, as if for confirmation — he was grinning again, still a head shorter, his hands thrust into his belt.

"It surprises everyone," he said cheerfully. "Estil, this is Paksenarrion. She's a paladin now, you know."

"I know." Estil smiled, and gave Paks her hand. It was a strong hand, hard with work. "Come in to the fire; if you're not cold you should be. We have sib ready."

Paks saw Suriya and Garris already by the great fireplace on one side of the Hall. Garris was talking with one of Aliam's sons; a dozen other people scurried around, bringing food to the tables.

"It's a long way from our first meeting," said Aliam as they came to the fire. "By Falk, I remember you at Dwarfwatch, when you had to give up your sword. Thanks, Cal." He sipped at his mug of sib; Paks found another in her hand. Her eyes followed Cal Halveric as he moved away and joined Garris and the other Halveric son. He looked perfectly at ease, as if he had never been injured. Meanwhile, Aliam looked around at the others, gathering their attention. "She was in her first term of service then, and like all the young hotbloods. I was half afraid that when that sword came out, she'd use it — but Phelan's troops always had discipline. Then when the others dropped theirs, she stooped and laid hers down. Very carefully." He shook his head. "I've seen many things in my years of war, but that — that stuck with me. Damned cocky young idiot — and then I had to coax her into giving parole."

Paks felt herself blushing as she hadn't for some time. "My lord — "

"I'm not taking anything from you — just that you were already headed somewhere else than a sergeant's rank in that company. Or any other." He shook his head again and glanced sideways at her. "I'll wager it'd be a different matter if I tried to take your sword from you now."

In the little silence that followed, Paks pushed back her cloak, and shifted the hilt of Tammarrion's sword forward. Aliam's eyes followed that movement. Paks smiled. "My lord, I will hand you this sword if you can explain how you got it."

His face paled. "Gods above! That's — that's — Tammarrion's — "

"No," said Paks quietly. "This sword was given to her — but it was made for another, for the prince this realm lost many years ago, and the prince we go to seek."

Aliam sat abruptly, paler than before. "It can't be."

"It is. Old men at court recognized it; elves confirmed its forging."

"But it — but they — no one told me." His color had begun to come back; now he sounded annoyed. "I asked the elves, blast them, and they said nothing of a prince — "

"No. So they told us. They told you nothing, and told no one else, either. Until a few days ago, when the king lay dying."

"I don't — Paksenarrion, will you swear to me that this is truth?"

Paks stared at him, surprised. "My lord, I am a paladin; I cannot lie. I swear to you that what I say is what I know, or have been told by those I speak of."

"I must believe you." For an instant, his head sank into his hands, then he looked around for Estil; their eyes met and conveyed something Paks could not read. He looked around at the others, whose interest was clear. "Enough for now. This is a grave word you have brought me; we will take close counsel, Lady Paksenarrion. But first you will eat, and we will speak of other things, less close than this, if you will."

Still a little confused, Paks nodded. "As you wish, my lord — but I may not delay long."

"No. I understand that. When we have eaten together, then — but come to the table now, and let us have this time together."

The meal was what she would have expected from the Halverics — generous, hearty, and far less formal than the Hall implied. A score of soldiers ate at the lower tables — the current watch, Aliam explained. They looked like the Halveric troops Paks remembered: solid, disciplined, experienced fighters. From time to time a glance met hers, and shifted politely away. The King's Squires had insisted, gently but firmly, on serving the high table — the younger lads, banished to the low, watched with relief and envy mixed. Paks, seated between Aliam and Estil, found the pair a fascinating combination. The tall woman kept up an effortless flow of conversation, while directing service and working her way through a plate piled with food.

"You were with the rangers, weren't you?" asked Estil. "Then you use a longbow. I keep telling Aliam what a marvelous weapon it is — "

"For women with long arms, yes," said Aliam a little sourly. "Just because I'm short, she — "

"Nonsense. You shoot well, love, and anyway — "

"I don't want a cohort of bowmen. No. I've said it before. Just because Kieri has one — "

"You see?" Estil smiled at Paks. "He almost started one, years ago, but when he found Kieri had one, he wouldn't."

"Had to let the lad do something I didn't do first." Aliam speared a slice of meat, and went on talking around it. "He'd have burst himself if I'd turned up with the kind of bowmen Estil would train."

"Aliam! I never said I'd train your bowmen." But her eyes were sparkling with delight. Paks eyed her broad shoulders and strong wrists: she *could* be a bowman. Certainly she was strong enough, and tall.

"And who else? Me? Gods forbid. I'm a swordsman who can shoot a bow when my sword breaks in half."

"I hadn't realized that the Duke — that Phelan — was with you so long," said Paks. "Garris was saying — "

Aliam broke into a laugh. "Oh, that brings back tales. Yes, indeed, Garris was a squire here — "

"And always glad to return, my lord," said Garris, passing by with a tankard of ale.

"Garris, you've been calling me Aliam to my face for twenty years, ever since you were knighted — don't start lording me now."

"It's being here like this — "

"Then sit down. We've nearly more squires than eaters — and we're all nearly full anyway. Sit down, all of you — this is no royal banquet. You've all been riding in the cold. Eat." He waited until they had all found a seat, then turned back to Paks. "Garris, Lady, was the most hare-brained, witless, hopeless lad I've ever tried to turn into a warrior."

"My lord!"

"Until you call me Aliam I can't hear you, Garris. I nearly sent the boy home a dozen times, Paksenarrion. He was willing enough — generous — never a bit of meanness to him. But he couldn't keep his mind on anything — he'd fall over a stick in the courtyard, and then stumble on, not even picking it up."

Aliam turned to Garris, who managed to look like a chidden boy despite his gray hair. "Not to say that you haven't turned out a fine man, either — I was young then myself, and had less skill at training boys than I thought. I was so damnably sure I knew what I was doing — of course I *had* to be sure. Any of them — boys or men — would have scented it if I hadn't, and the whole thing would have fallen apart." Aliam paused to pour himself ale, offered it to Paks, and then resumed.

"Anyway, there was Garris, amiable as a young pup and falling over his own feet, and there was Kieri, a few years older and made for war as a sword is." He ate silently for a few moments, then went on. "They made friends, of course. Actually it surprised me. Kieri made friends hardly, in those days; he kept to himself a good deal. Some of the lads I had were court-bred, and full of blood-pride until I sweated it out of them. But Garris followed him around, and followed him around, and in sheer self-defense Kieri began to teach him what I could not." He looked down the table. "I suppose you told her about Hakkenarsk Pass?"

"Yes, my — Aliam. What I could remember."

"Garris, I'd wager you remember every miserable step of that trail. I do, save where the knock on my head shook it loose. That's the trip that changed you, I believe, though you had grown so much that summer already — "

"I had?" Paks was sure Garris hadn't meant to say that aloud, or in such a tone.

"Indeed yes. Boys don't always know when they're changing, Garris, but I saw it. You surprised me all that summer — and so less in the crisis that you might have supposed." Paks noticed that Garris sat a bit straighter, with a curious expression. Aliam went on. "I had planned to ask your father if you could stay with me until you were ready for the Knights of Falk; after Hakkenarsk, of course, your father insisted that you come away at once."

"Sir — I always thought you sent me away — I thought — "

"Good heavens, no! Where did you get that idea? Didn't he tell you?" Aliam shook his head. "I wish I'd known — no, he thought it was too risky, letting you fight in Aarenis any more. I'd have been glad to have you."

"He said that," Garris said. "But I didn't believe him . . . my brothers saw combat as squires, after all. I thought you had finally tired of me . . . " He stopped short, embarrassed, and stuffed meat into his mouth.

"It startled me," said Paks into the silence that followed, "to hear Garris speak of Duke Phelan as your squire. I think I knew it — the Duke mentioned it this winter — but it didn't seem real to me. I never imagined him anywhere but in his own place or in Aarenis with the Company."

"It's always hard," said Aliam, "to realize that older people have had other lives before you met them. I remember an elf I knew once, who told me one rainy afternoon about seeing my grandmother picking flowers as a child. I was never able to relax with him after that." He sipped his ale. "Even though he said she was beautiful."

Paks opened her mouth, and shut it again. Twice she had tried to get Aliam talking about the young Phelan, as a safe topic they both knew, and twice he had evaded it neatly. She looked sideways at Estil, to find a worried look on that lady's face. Estil looked quickly along the table, and called to the kitchen for more sweet pies. Paks ate steadily.

As soon as the meal was over, Aliam and Estil led Paks to Aliam's study. She wondered if he would still hedge about, but as soon as the door was shut, and they were all seated around a table hastily cleared of map scrolls, he began.

"You carry the sword I gave Kieri to give Tammarrion at their wedding, the sword they found on her body after her death. And you tell me now that sword was forged for the prince that disappeared over forty years ago. And that the elves concealed this from me. Is there more?"

Paks told him the story she had pieced together, and ended with the elves' revelation that the prince had not only survived the attack, but was still alive.

"The true heir to Falkieri's throne, if he lives — and the elves say he's alive." Aliam looked down at his locked hands. "Did they say who he was, or where?"

"No, my lord."

"You, too, may call me Aliam. Kieri wrote me some of your story; I've heard more; you are not so young as your years."

"I would prefer — "

"Very well. Why didn't the elves tell me? Why didn't the elves tell anyone about the prince? Did they deign to say even that much?"

"Yes. They say that whatever damaged the prince made him unfit to rule."

"Umph. What do they mean by unfit?"

"They didn't say that."

"I suppose they wouldn't." Aliam got up and moved restlessly around the room. "And you are convinced this is the same sword?"

"My lord, your uncle and several other older men at court recognized it — could describe the runes on the blade without seeing them. Also the elf, Amrothlin, whose sister was the queen, and the prince's mother — "

"I never told Jeris about finding the sword," mused Aliam. "I should have thought of that — but it never occurred to me that he might know anything. He's been at court most of his life, and — "

"The elves said they — desired you not to speak to your uncle about it."

"Blast them," said Aliam, not sounding as angry as Paks would have thought. "They're always so clever. I've said often enough you can be too clever sometimes — clever enough to tie your own bootstrings together. And they are sure the prince lived?"

"So they say. But they will not say where or who. That is what I am to find out."

"You're sure that is your quest?" asked Estil. "How do you know?"

Paks shook her head. "My lady, the king, as he was dying, asked that I take the throne, because I had brought this sword, and was a paladin. Others agreed. But a paladin is not a ruler; I was not called to rule, but to save the realm by returning its rightful king. I am as sure of this as I am of the call I received in the first place, but I cannot tell you how."

Estil opened her mouth, but Aliam spoke first. "How do you hope to find him? And what do you think he will be like, after all these years?"

Paks recited the guesses they had come to in Chaya: age, hair color, eyes, and so on. That he had been a servant, and according to the elves had forgotten his past, even his name. "But so many men could fit that description," she said. "So I thought to trace this sword back, as I could. The elves reported that you had found it, and tried to return it to them."

"That's so," said Aliam, facing her again. "I found it near the bodies of three elves and many orcs. I sent word to the Ladysforest, by the rangers, and got back the message that I should give it to the one for whom it was made."

"And you had no idea who that was."

"No. All I knew of the sword was that it was elven."

"You hadn't seen it at court?"

"No." Aliam answered slowly. "I had not been at court yet, when the queen disappeared. I was a page at my uncle's, along with the king's younger brothers — the old king's, that is: they were kings themselves later."

"Did you know of any such sword?" Aliam shook his head. "Then what did you think, when they told you that?"

Aliam frowned. "I thought it was typical elven arrogance, to be honest. They knew something I didn't, and were having a joke at my expense. I saw nothing on the scabbard, and then I saw the runes on the blade. It looked like a woman's blade, and from the runes I judged her name might have been elven. None of the runes fit Estil, or my daughters, and none of them wanted the sword, with that message hanging over it. I wouldn't sell it, of course, or send it out of my own hall without telling the elves. I daresay they knew that. I thought I'd be left with it until some elven lady walked to claim it. Then Kieri Phelan came to tell me of his wedding — and his wife's name was Tammarrion Mistiannyi. Two of the runes — light or fire, and mountains. I thought of that at once, and offered it to him as a wedding gift. Then I told the elves where I'd bestowed it, and they said it was well enough."

"Yes," said Paks, "but was it? Sir, this is what I've been thinking of. The elves think this sword, once held by its true master, will proclaim him and give him some powers he must have. They told you to give it to him — to the one it was made for. Doesn't that mean that you could have? That you knew the man who was actually the prince?"

She did not miss the sharp glance that sped between Aliam and Estil. "What would you have done, my lord, if you had known what sword it was? Would you have had any idea where to bestow it?"

"I — I am not sure." Aliam sat heavily across the table from her. "Paksenarrion, you have brought what you feel is great hope to our kingdom — the hope of finding our lost prince, our true king. But I believe you have brought great danger as well. What if the elves are right? What if this man — now near fifty years, as you said, and without practice at kingcraft — what if he is indeed unfit to rule?"

"My lord, only a year ago, no one would have thought me fit to be a paladin. Not you — not Duke Phelan — not even myself. Least of all myself." For a moment she moved into those bitter memories, and returned with an effort. "Yet here I am, my lord, a true paladin, healed of all those injuries, and granted powers I had scarcely dreamed of." She called her light for an instant, and saw the last doubts vanish from Aliam's eyes. "The gods have given me this quest, to find your king. I do not think they would send me on a vain search. If he is unfit, the gods can cure him."

Aliam nodded slowly. "You may be right. I pray you are. Do you think the others — the Council and all — will agree to accept him? Assuming you do find him?"

"They have sworn to do so, my lord, and Amrothlin says the elves will at least consider it."

"Was the Knight-Commander of Falk there? What did he say?"

"He?" Paks considered a moment. She had not paid that much attention to him. "I think, my lord, that he was unhappy that the gods had not chosen a paladin of Falk for this quest."

Estil laughed. "That's probably true. But did he give any clues?"

"No — could he?" Neither of them answered, and Paks sighed. "I think, my lord and lady, that you know something you haven't told me yet."

"That's so." Aliam got up yet again. "Let me put it to you like this, Paksenarrion. If I once met someone who awoke in me a suspicion that he might be the missing prince — let's say I did — I had then no proof at all. Only that a boy was the right age, with the right color hair, and a face much the same shape as the old king's. Remember that I had never seen the prince myself; I don't even remember what his name was — "

"Falkieri Amrothlin Artfielan . . . " said Paks, watching him closely.

Aliam's hand dropped to his side. "Whatever," he said and waited a moment. "No evidence," he went on. "None from the boy — who remembered nothing to any purpose — none otherwise. The princess was alive and well then, but an orphan. I could not see — I thought — " He stopped, breathing hard. Paks waited. "Gods above, Paksenarrion, I did what I thought wise at the time — what else can a man do? He might have been — might not — I couldn't tell. He didn't know. I didn't tell him — how could I? I was not ready to back his claim against his sister: she was well-known, secure, growing into rule, loved by her people, capable. . . . She was my princess — would be my queen. When I was granted this steading, I had sworn allegiance to her father. What evidence did I have? He might have been a royal bastard — or a noble's bastard — or nothing at all. On the chance, I did what I could for him, kept him in my service, arranged his training, but — "

At that moment the truth blazed in Paks's mind. "Phelan," she breathed. "You're talking about Kieri Phelan!" Everything came together — his age, his coloring, his —

"Yes," said Aliam heavily. "I am. Kieri Artfiel Phelan, so he said his name when he came. Gods! If I'd only paid attention to Jeris — if I'd even known the lost prince's name — but I was a boy! Just a boy!"

"But he doesn't look half-elven," said Paks. "The others I've met — "

"I know. He looks so much like his father — in fact, that's what I saw first. I thought he was someone's by-blow, possibly royal, certainly well-bred, one way or another. Even when I thought of it, it seemed impossible, and that was part of it: he didn't look elven, or show any such abilities. And I was too young to be sure — "

"I don't know if the name would have convinced us, either," said Estil. "Falki's the common nickname, and we knew Kieri as a name from Tsaia or Aarenis."

Aliam shook his head. "What a mess!" Then he looked at her sharply. "But he can't be king. Tir's bones, I'd give my right arm to make him one, but he can't — "

"Why not?"

"If only I'd known about the sword back then," Aliam went on heedlessly. "Then, with Tammarrion alive — maybe he could have come back. But — and wait a moment! He can't be the one — I gave him the sword. Nothing happened."

"Did he draw it, my lord?"

Aliam thought long and looked at Estil. "I don't remember — no, I don't think so. I drew it, to show him the runes. I don't — now I think of it, I don't believe he touched it at all. I wrapped it for him — "

"I remember," said Estil suddenly. "Tammarrion told me, when her first child was born. When he gave it to her, he vowed never to draw it — "

"That's right; you told me." Aliam touched her hair. "I remember thinking Kieri was as sentimental as I am. He wanted her to feel that he was taking nothing from her as a warrior, Paksenarrion, and so he vowed never to draw her sword — it was hers, and only hers. But he was so close — surely it would do something — "

Paks sat for a long silent time with both of them watching her. Finally she shook her head slightly. "Perhaps not. Amrothlin said that although the sword was made for him, and would recognize him in some way, it was meant to be sealed to him by elven ceremony. That's one of the reasons the prince was being taken to the Ladysforest. Perhaps until that ceremony, it would proclaim him if he drew it himself from the scabbard."

"And he was so close — " Estil's voice was awed. "So close all those years — it's hard to believe he never did — "

"Not with him," said Aliam. "His word's been good, always."

"My lord," said Paks, leaning forward in her chair, "You see that I must know everything you can tell me about him. I must know why you thought he was the prince — and what was against it — and why you think he is unfit to rule — " Estil stirred, but Paks went on. "I must know what you know of his past — all of it — no matter how terrible. If he is the rightful king — "

"It would all fit," said Aliam. "The sword — they were telling me to give it to him — if I could figure out the riddle. They thought it was well enough, as they said, when I gave it to Tammarrion — perhaps they were sure he'd draw it in time."

"Well, my lord?" Paks persisted.

"All right. All right." Aliam sighed heavily. "Estil? What do you have? I know you know things about him he never told me." Estil ran her hands through her hair, and began.

"He came to us, Paksenarrion, near forty years ago. I can look it up in the rolls, but Cal was a baby just starting to walk strongly. That would be — let me think — thirty-eight years last fall."

"One of the woodsmen brought him in," said Aliam. "Found him wandering in the forest. I was butchering that day. Anyway, he said he wanted to work, and it was snowing and all." Aliam rubbed his nose. "He was a skinny, dirty, red-haired rat, to look at. All bones and rags. Said he'd come ashore earlier that year on the coast, at Bannerlith — he couldn't say what ship — and had worked his way inland. But no one wanted him through the winter. That's common enough." Paks did not say that she knew it. She waited for him to go on, but he nodded to Estil.

"It wasn't long," said Estil, "before we had him into the Hall. What I noticed was his neathanded way at the table. Most boys that age — that size — they knock things over, trip on their own feet. He didn't. I thought he'd make a fine page — we were out of the way and young to get fosterlings."

"And he was scared — if we have to have it all out, Estil, you can't deny that. The first night at my table, the lad takes amiss something I said and shrinks back like he thought I'd beat him." Aliam gave her a challenging look. Estil colored. Then she met Paks's eyes.

"He did, Paksenarrion. I don't recall what Aliam said, but Kieri flinched from him. I knew that would make Aliam angry; he's never mistreated servants, and to have the boy act like that before strangers — "

" — from Aarenis," Aliam broke in. "Guildsmen — that turned into my first contract."

"Anyway, I took him out, and spoke to him. That's when I found he'd been in a Hall before, somewhere else. He thought — " She looked at Aliam as if afraid to say it, but he nodded. "He thought," she went on with difficulty, "that Aliam had meant him to sleep with one of the guests. As a — a — "

"I understand," said Paks. Estil nodded.

"I don't know any polite word," she said quietly. "Anyway, I told him no, and that nothing like that happened here, or would happen to him with us, and he — he seemed to come alive inside. Then I saw the scars on his head — and later the others he carried — "

"I knew about that," said Aliam. "He told me much later — that time in Aarenis. Some of it, anyway."

"Well, he came to the house, then, as a page, and we thought he was about fourteen. Old enough to start learning weaponry. At first we thought it wouldn't work — "

"I thought he was a hopeless coward," said Aliam frankly. "Couldn't have been more wrong; he didn't understand at first that he was allowed to hit back. Once he realized, nothing could keep him from it. He had no fear at all, as long as he could fight back."

"And he took in knowledge as a plant drinks water," said Estil. "And grew — keeping that boy in clothes was a loom's work in itself. And loyal — he would do anything for Aliam or me. Mind the children, even, which the other squires hated. Cal loved him — they all did."

"Anything but learn to think. D'you remember, Estil, the trouble we had with that boy? Daring — by all the gods, he had no fear and dared anything, but he wanted to impress everyone. He never broke out in mischief, but he was so certain of himself, so sure he could come out ahead — "

"And the fights," put in Estil. She smiled at Paks. "He wasn't a quarrelsome boy, exactly, but then he wouldn't give in. He didn't bully the weaker boys — but until he made senior squire, he was always pushing the senior ones. Nip, nip, nip. Then they'd get angry and jump him, and he'd fight until he was out cold or on top."

"And then I'd have to settle it." Aliam shifted in his chair. "He took to tactics at once — strategy took longer. It was not in his nature to take the long view. And he wanted power — ached for it. He would never try to take it from me, but gods help the weaker squire — or even cohort captain. That Hakkenarsk Pass thing was typical — he thought out a good plan quickly, carried it out brilliantly, didn't forget anything vital, and then nearly killed himself trying to stay in control when his wounds went bad. Or the time in Aarenis, the next year, when I let him take that patrol out. The sergeant was supposed to be in command. Ha. Next thing I know, Kieri lost half the patrol into captivity, then enlisted some unaligned peasants, rescued the men, and fought a small battle — and as the sergeant said, it was like trying to lead a galloping warhorse on a thread. It did what needed to be done, but the risk!"

Paks smiled. "But why, my lord, do you think he is unfit to rule? Look at him now — he has a domain in Tsaia. It's gone from an orc-ridden, outlaw, uncultivated slab of northern hills to a settled, secure, prosperous land under his wardship. Isn't that some sign of his ability?"

"Yes, but that's not all. You are not Lyonyan; you may not know what we need in a king —"

"Taig-sense?" asked Paks bluntly.

"Yes, partly that. As far as I know, Kieri has no taig-sense. At all. And that impatience, that quick anger. You know that — you were there in Aarenis. If Tammarrion had lived — he was very different after their marriage. I wish you had known him then; she was well-named, for she gave him light without changing what he was. But she died, and he turned darker than before. He banished the Marshals — I know he wrote something about talking to them again, after you unmasked his steward, but —"

"They're back," said Paks.

"What?"

"My lord, I think you do not know all that happened this fall when I returned to the Duke. He invited the Marshals back himself; he and the Marshal-General of Gird conferred in his hall, and they have no differences between them."

"Well." Aliam sat back, pursing his lips. "Well. I would never have thought that. I don't know if it's enough, but —"

"My lord, I would agree with you that the man we both knew and fought with in Aarenis that last year would not make a good king for Lyonya — or any land. But that was over two years ago. Last year I was a homeless vagrant, afraid of everything and everyone — a true coward, my lord, as you thought Phelan was. Now I have been changed; now I know he has been changed, for I saw the change myself. At the time, I had no idea what the change might mean to him or to others — but it may have made him able to be your king."

"And the taig-sense?"

"I don't know. Perhaps the sword can restore it. Perhaps the elves can. If his rashness, his anger, are what they feared, and these have diminished, then maybe they will help."

"Do they know what you know of the changes in him?"

"I don't know."

"Then they should. The question is how best to tell them." Aliam turned to Estil. "What do you think?"

"I don't know. I can't think of anything but Kieri — as we knew him — and the sword, so near, and —"

890

"How far is it to the elven kingdom, my lord?" asked Paks.

Aliam looked startled. "Far? I don't know; I've never been. You can't go there, unless they want you to come."

"I know, but I thought maybe the rangers could guide me — Amrothlin claimed the queen was his sister; his mother is in the Ladysforest. If I convinced her — "

"Convince an elf?" Aliam looked at her. "Well, you might at that. But Paksenarrion, think: the elves love children as dearly as we do, perhaps more. And yet they knew he lived, and did nothing — they had some reason for that, but I doubt they liked it. For all we know they've been arguing that one out for all the years since. It's not like elves to leave one of their blood in trouble."

"Perhaps they did help," said Estil suddenly. "Aliam, remember when Kieri was young here — we had a group of elves come by almost every winter. Sometimes they'd stay for Midwinter Feast. Kieri seemed to like elves as well as any of the squires, and he has said since that elves have done him favors from time to time."

"Maybe. I still think, though, that if he's the prince, and half-elven, they will be sore in mind at not having done him much more than occasional favors. Falk's oath, Estil, the elves of all races honor high birth — "

"When it's not been corrupted. Remember the bits of elven lore we know — about the kuaknom, and such."

"That's not the same thing at all." Aliam's face went red. "Kieri may have a hasty temper, but he's nothing like that. I can't believe that they let a prince of their blood — "

"Could they have done better than you, my lord?" asked Paks. "If they didn't want to interfere directly, they knew that you would take good care of him. By all accounts, you took a frightened helpless boy and made a strong man of him."

"I still — " began Aliam. He was interrupted by a knock on the door. "What is it?" he asked sharply.

Chapter Twenty-one

Cal Halveric looked in; Paks could see that he was trying to control his excitement.

"Pardon, sir, but elves have come —"

"Elves?"

"Yes — I know you didn't want to be interrupted, but —"

Aliam nodded. "At once. Paksenarrion, will you come with me? And Estil, of course."

"Certainly, my lord." Paks and Estil followed Aliam down to the Hall, where a group of elves waited.

Paks recognized none of them. They were all wearing mail and furred cloaks, their faces partly obscured by the hoods.

"I am Aliam Halveric," said Aliam, going forward to meet them. "Be welcome in this Hall."

"My lord Halveric," said one of them, "you may not wish to welcome us; will you hear our errand first?"

Aliam froze where he was. Paks saw a band of color flush his neck. "Indeed, elves have always been welcome here, and all my guests are free to speak their minds."

"Your courtesy becomes you, my lord Halveric. But Amrothlin sent word to the Ladysforest that Paksenarrion of Three Firs, a Girdish paladin, had sworn to seek the lost prince. He feared, he said, that the two of you together might discover the prince's name and place. It is this we come to halt."

Paks stepped forward, sensing anger and unease in the elf, but not evil. "Amrothlin did not interfere in the search," she said. "Why should you?"

The elf's eyes blazed at her. "You are that paladin, are you not?"

"I am."

"I have heard of you." That carried all the scorn an elf could put into Common, a cold serving of contempt. "I would not expect *you* to understand; you have no sinyin blood at all. But many of us have long regretted the alliance of men and sinyin in this realm. It was bad enough that our beloved sister wed that mortal king, and died by mortal hands. To lose her children to men's greed — one for money, and one for power — was far worse. And no human peasant girl, no sheepfarmer's child, is going to set a taig-crippled draudigs on the throne. Is that clear? I have come for that sword, paladin, which is none of yours."

892

Paks saw from the corner of her vision the King's Squires group themselves near her, hands on swords. It seemed colder in the room, and every detail glittered. The elf went on.

"It is neither yours nor any human's. It was made for one of ours, and carried by one of ours, and to us it will return. Return it!" He held out his hand, commanding.

"No," said Paks quietly. "I will not."

"You would force me to fight in the Halveric's hall?" The elf threw back his cloak, his own hand now on the hilt of his sword. Paks kept her hands in her belt.

"No, I do not force you to fight. If you fight, it will be on your own conscience." The elf started to speak, but Paks went on. "I will not return the sword to you; it is not yours. The sword belongs to the one for whom it was made — the lost prince, the true king, the one who shall rule in Lyonya, by the will of the High Lord."

"He is gone," said the elf. "He is no more."

"Amrothlin said he lived."

"Amrothlin lied! The body lives, that is all. The prince, the true spirit — that died in him." Now the voice was as pleading as angry. "We cannot accept that the throne be held by a hollow man — one empty of himself — "

"He is not," said Paks. She caught the slight movement as all the elves reacted to that.

"You *know* who it is?" More than the elves hung on her answer.

"Yes." Paks looked around the room, seeing humans as well as elves taut with suspense. "I know — and I know that he is not hollow, as you would say."

"But in Aarenis — " began the spokesman.

Paks held up her hand. "Sir elf, not all here know the name; I would not choose to publish it abroad at this moment — would you?"

"By the Singer, I hope it is never known!" The elf turned to his companions and spoke rapidly in elven; Paks could not follow his words. Then he swung around again. "You meddle in things you do not understand, paladin. It must not be."

"Sir elf, you also meddle in what you do not understand. Would you question the High Lord's judgment?"

"I question any human's ability to discern that judgment. As for you, I have heard of *you*, paladin. You were nothing but a common soldier, a mercenary, a hired killer, and then even lower — "

Esceriel stepped forward, his sword rasping as he drew it; Paks put out her arm and held him back. "No — put it by, Esceriel. I truly believe it is as I said — this elf meddles in what he does not understand. It is no insult to me, to speak truth, and I think his errors more ignorance than malice."

"By Falk!" Aliam burst out. "You cannot speak like that to a paladin in my Hall, elf, whoever you are. She was never a *common* soldier — "

"Peace, my lord. At one time I thought I was, and it satisfied me. Sir elf, my past is past; it may seem strange to you, for whom it is so brief, but to me

893

a year ago is far away. Whatever I was then, I am now a paladin, chosen by my gods for this quest. If you dispute the truth of that, then I must make what proofs I can — but preferably outside. Even as a common soldier I disliked common brawls."

That got a laugh from the men-at-arms still in the Hall; Paks saw Estil's mouth twitch, and one of the elves, in the rear of the party, grinned openly. The spokesman frowned, then shook his head. "If you will not yield the sword willingly — "

"I will not."

"Then I must try to convince you. I thought paladins were sworn to good — "

"I am sworn to the gods who chose me; as you have doubts that any human can discern the High Lord's will, I have doubts that anyone can know good without guidance."

He thought about that a moment, staring past her. "But you are a Gird's paladin?"

"I am a Girdsman, and a paladin, and Gird was part of my choosing. But the High Lord, the Windsteed, and Alyanya were present."

"Present!" The elf gaped. "You have seen — ?"

Paks bowed. For a long moment no one moved or spoke; Paks could hear faint noises from the kitchens, and the hollow sound of hooves on the courtyard paving.

"Well." The elf looked at his companions for a moment and back at her. "If that is true — or you believe that to be true — then I must inform my Lady."

"The — ?" Aliam began.

"The Lady of the Ladysforest." He eyed Paks doubtfully. "I find it hard to believe — "

"So did I, at the time," said Paks. She smiled at him. "So did the Kuakgan of Brewersbridge, who was also there."

"A Kuakgan! A Gird's paladin with a Kuakgan?"

"Yes." Paks nearly burst into laughter at the look on his face. "I never claimed to be a *common* paladin," she said slyly. Everyone but the elf laughed then, and he finally smiled.

"I fear," he said in a different tone, "that you will be hard to convince. So Amrothlin said, and so said Ardhiel, but — no matter. Will you come to the Ladysforest, then? I will swear no harm, and will guide you."

Paks remembered her first enchantment by elves, when she might have come to the Halveric steading but for their interference, however well-meant. She had heard of men being lost for years in the elvenhomes, spending lifetimes there while seeming to enjoy only a few days of ease and delight. She shook her head. "I fear the turmoil of this realm without a ruler, sir elf. I must not delay."

"But our Lady must speak to you — "

One of the other elves spoke softly in elven; the spokesman stopped and turned to him. Heads were shaken. Paks took this chance to give her squires a reassuring look; Esceriel was still scowling.

"It's all right," she said quietly. "I won't give up the sword, and I think he's decided not to fight."

"He'd better," said Aliam grimly. "Sheepfarmer's child, indeed!"

"Well, I am, my lord."

"But that's not what matters! It's — " But the elf had turned back to them, his face now clean of all expression.

"My lord Halveric, I wished to make this easier on you by withholding my name — permit me to explain that I am Serrothlin, cousin of Amroth- lin whom your paladin met, and the Lady's nephew. My companion has made a suggestion, which might serve all our needs."

"Oh?" Aliam did not sound enthusiastic. "I deem it necessary for our Lady to speak with you and with this paladin. The lost prince, such as he is, is her grandson. It is on her that his acts will reflect the most strongly. It was with her consent that her daughter married your human king. She must know for herself what you think mitigates his behavior."

"I see." Aliam stared full at the elf, unmoving. "And so you propose what?"

"If the paladin Paksenarrion refuses to come to the Ladysforest, it might be possible for the Lady to come here — "

"But I thought she never left the elvenhome!" Estil broke in.

"She does not. But the elvenhome — " He hummed a little tune, that Paks thought she remembered hearing from Ardhiel. "The elvenhome borders are other, as you know. Mortal lands in Lyonya are but clearings, as it were, in the fabric of the elven forests. If you granted your permission, Lord Halveric, she might be persuaded to come — to bring the Ladysforest with her."

"She could do *that*?" Aliam stared.

"Indeed, yes." The elf smiled. "We have not told humans all our powers." He looked around the hall. "But before you agree, my lord — if you agree — I must warn you. If you grant this permission, and if she comes, then for that space of time your steading will be part of the elven- home. No human can enter or leave unguided, and none should wander about in it. For the ways of the elvenhome forests are as perilous as any grove of Kuakgan."

"Hmm." Aliam looked down, then turned to Paks. "What do you think? I can see that the Lady has a claim to know what's going on."

"I agree," said Paks. "My concern is time: I will not imperil the quest to enjoy the delights of elven enchantments."

Serrothlin smiled. "Lady, I understand your fears. Indeed this might happen, but not without our will. Would you accept my word that we will not let it happen here?"

"It happened to Ardhiel without his knowledge — can you prevent it?"

"That was different. Have you never been in a trance of prayer? Even an elf can be enchanted by the gods. If you had not thought of the danger, I might indeed have been tempted to leave you ignorant of it, and solve this problem my own way. But although I dislike humans — as you may have surmised — I will not stoop to dishonesty. I will give my word that you will come from meeting our Lady no later than the time of conference demands."

"Are there many," asked Paks, suddenly curious, "who regret the alliance?"

"That number is growing," said Serrothlin, "as it has for some hundred years, as you measure time. It seems clear to some of us that humans have not abided by their word; others excuse them as too short of life to remember. But I remember when elves were most welcome in every hall, when all the forest was open to our hearts, and the heroes you call saints sat at our feet to learn wisdom. Now to be free in our forest we must draw in and in, leaving more of the realm to humans. And lately we have been unwelcome even at court, at the heart of the realm."

"And what does your Lady say?"

He frowned. "I do not speak for our Lady; no one does. You will hear for yourself."

"If Lord Halveric permits." Paks looked at Aliam. "It is up to you, my lord, whether you will risk your steading this way. I believe his words; but it is your land."

"Not all humans distrust elves, Serrothlin," said Aliam. "Not all humans deserve your distrust. I will tell my people to stay close. Will you ask the Lady if she pleases to come?"

Serrothlin bowed and withdrew. Two of the elves in his party stayed, coming forward to greet Aliam and Paks.

"My lord — lady — I am Esvinal, a friend of Ardhiel's," said one. "It is easier if one of us stays, to form the bridge by which our Lady will shift the borders."

"Do you also dislike humans?" asked Aliam.

"I like them less than Ardhiel does, and more than I did when we arrived, my lord," said the elf smoothly. Aliam snorted.

"I'd best tell my people," he said. "If you'll excuse me — " and he left, taking his soldiers and Cal with him. Estil sent the others to warn those living in the hall to keep their places. The squires stayed by Paks. The elf met Paks's eyes.

"I would not have known you from Ardhiel's last description, Lady Paksenarrion. You are not what he remembers."

"I daresay not." Paks was surprised to find herself so calm about it. "Yet what he remembers is not the worst of it. Will you believe that if I can change so, the prince is not beyond hope?"

"That is a hard saying. I saw him once myself." The elf looked quickly at the squires nearby, and Estil. "I — "

"By your leave, I think we should not discuss his past until the Lady comes," said Paks. "Will it be long? How far is it?"

Both elves laughed lightly. "Far? Far is a human word for distances humans travel. And long is a word for human time. No, Lady Paksenar-

896

rion, it will not be long, for it is not far as we elves can travel within our own lands."

"Yet your friend Ardhiel rode and walked the same miles we did," said Paks.

"Oh — to be courteous, when traveling with humans — I've no doubt he did so. And that was outside the elvenhome forests, where other travel is difficult and perilous."

"As hard for you as travel in the elvenhome forest would be for humans?" countered Paks.

"Perhaps," said one of them. "I had not thought of it that way."

Estil came back to them. "Will the Lady stay for a meal, sirs? And what would be appropriate?"

One shook his head; the other looked thoughtful. "I doubt she will stay longer than to listen to Paksenarrion, my lady. If the household can offer something to drink — "

"What season is it, in the Ladysforest?"

"Ah — you are aware, then. It was late summer when we left, but the stretching may thin it."

"I have a good wine for that," said Estil. Paks looked at her in surprise. She had had no idea that the seasons were any different in the elven lands. Estil grinned at Paks. "Some good comes at last, of the time I listened at my great-aunt's door when she spoke with an elven friend. I thought for years all I'd got from that was a whipping."

Estil was hardly out of the room on her way to the kitchen when Paks felt the change. It was as if the room filled suddenly with water, and yet she could breathe. Her blood tingled. The air smelled of late summer, with the first tang of fall apples still unripe. It wavered, then thickened; common objects on table and hearth took on the aspects of enchanted things of song. It would not have surprised her if the table had begun to dance, or the fire to speak.

Paks looked at the squires; their eyes were bright. Suriya leaned forward slightly, her lips parted as if she saw an old friend. The door to the courtyard flew open. Instead of the gray winter sky they had ridden under, a soft golden light lay over the court. Paks heard birds singing, and the dripping chimes of snowmelt running off the roof. The elves in the room seemed unchanged in any detail. Yet Paks thought they moved with even more grace, and when they spoke the music of their voices pierced her heart.

So beautiful was that music that for a moment she could not follow the meaning of the words, and stood bemused. They waited, then spoke again, and this time she realized what they wanted. The Lady of the Ladysforest waited beyond the gate, and called her out. Paks glanced again at the squires. Esceriel's eyes were almost frightened; she knew he feared that she would give up the quest, release the sword, under elven power. She shook her head silently, and went out into the light.

Patterns of power. Paks remembered what Macenion had said about the elves and patterns — their love of them, the beauty, the strength of binding that they worked into them. Now the strange gold light of a late-summer evening seemed to accentuate the patterns of Aliam's steading. Stonework glowed, the joints making intricate branches up every wall. The arches of the stable cloister seemed ready to speak; Paks thought if they did they would sound like deep-voiced horns. The bare sticks of the kitchen garden, with its lumpy green heads of winter-kale poking from the snow, had sprouted a film of new green, lacy and vulnerable. Even as Paks looked, tendrils of redroot worked up the nearby wall.

Yet the light was not all golden. Through the open gate came the silvery opalescent glow of elflight itself. And in that glow, silver in gold, was the Lady of the Ladysforest, in form so fair that Paks could never after bring that face to mind. She was tall, as all elves are, and graceful; she wore robes that shifted about her like mists around mountains. And she conveyed without gray hair or lined face an age greater than Paks could well imagine, and immense authority.

Aliam Halveric bowed, welcoming, and the Lady inclined her head. She came through the gate, looked around, and crossed glances with Paks. Behind her Serrothlin and Amrothlin, not looking at one another, moved to stand beside Aliam.

"Lord Halveric, we have known you from afar; it is our pleasure to know you in your own steading."

Aliam bowed again. "Lady, you are most welcome here, as your kin have been and will be."

"As for us, we shall hope that your friendship endures, Lord Halveric." She looked around. "You have not walled out the trees entirely," she said, noticing the fruit trees trained against one wall. Under her influence their winter buds had opened into leaves and snowy blossoms. "I will mend them," she said, "when we must leave; it would be ill grace to leave you with frost-killed bloom. May we greet your family?"

"Of course, Lady." Aliam called them forward: Estil, then his children in order, and theirs. The Lady smiled at all, but Paks saw true joy in her face when one of the grandchildren reached out to her unbidden.

"What, child? Would you come to me?" She held out her hand, and the baby, still unsteady, toddled forward and wrapped chubby fingers around it. "Can you say your name, littling?" She looked up at the mother, Hali's wife.

"He doesn't say anything yet, Lady; his name's Kieri, for the Duke, Lord Aliam's friend."

"A good name, a brave name; gods grant he grows into it. He's bold enough now." She laughed softly, for the baby had grabbed her robe, and was trying to stuff it into his mouth. "No, child, that's not food. Best go to your mother; she'll find something better for you." She picked the baby up and handed him over in one graceful move; the child's eyes followed her as his mother turned away.

Then she turned to Paks. "And you must be Paksenarrion, who found the scrolls that Luap wrote long ago, and freed the elfane taig."

"Yes, Lady."

Her glance swept the courtyard, and cleared it without a word. The others moved quickly into the buildings; the two elves reappeared with seats, and she waited until they were placed. Paks felt the immense determination behind her courtesy, the weight of years and authority. With a fluid gesture, she sent her son and nephew away, and seated herself. With no less grace, the Lady set about to make her position clear.

"My son and nephew," she began, "brought troubling word of you, Paksenarrion, and of your quest. I had hoped never to face this hour. My daughter was dearer to me than you can know, mortals with many children; when she died, and her son disappeared, my grief matched my love. Once that grieving eased, I laid their memories to rest, and hoped to find solace in her daughter. When first I heard of the boy again, it was that he had borne such injury as left him with no knowledge of himself, and none of his elven heritage. A lesser grief than his death, you might say, but not for me, nor for any who loved him. Patterns end; patterns mangled are constant pain. By the time we found him again, he was here, alive — " she glanced around the courtyard. "In this safe haven. If he could mend, it would be with such love as you gave. So I was told." Paks noticed that she neither gave Kieri Phelan's name, nor asked if they knew it.

"But why didn't you — ?" began Estil. Aliam squeezed her hand. The Lady frowned slightly.

"The elf who brought word, Lady Estil, had it from a ranger first. Then he came himself: Haleron, a distant kinsman, much given to travel in mortal lands. The boy was badly damaged, he told me, in body and mind both. He found no trace of memory that he could use, only the physical signs that we elves read more easily than you. To be sure, he would have had to invade the boy's mind — a damaged mind — and risk more damage to it. As well as endure the pain of it himself." She turned away; Paks saw her throat move as if she swallowed. "Then it was you, who sent the elves all those times," said Aliam. "And we thought they liked us."

The Lady met his gaze directly. "Lord Halveric, they — we — did. We do. You cared for a lost child, a hurt child, and one of our blood — healed him as well as you could. We are forever in your debt; do you think I would shift the borders of the Ladysforest to visit someone for whom I had no regard?"

Aliam shook his head, speechless.

"You ask, and rightly so, why we told you nothing and did nothing. First, for the boy himself. With such damage as Haleron believed he had suffered, we were as likely to harm as help, if we tried to stir his mind. I hear that Paksenarrion can attest to the truth of that — " She looked at Paks, who nodded. "And we judged it would not help him to know what he had lost if we could not restore it. We waited, watching him for some sign that he was healing in more than the body. If his memory returned, if any of his elven abilities came forth — "

"Could they, without your guidance?" asked Paks.

899

"Yes. Lord Halveric knew his sister, who without our aid came to her full powers. She was our second reason for saying nothing. You will remember: the year he came to you was the year his father died, of grief, we were told, for his dead wife and lost son. Already she had been brought up to bear the rule. Unless the prince showed that he was returned to himself, we would be unfair to her, and unfair as well to the realm, to champion a crippled prince over a princess of great ability. You thought that yourself, Lord Halveric, did you not? When you first suspected who he might be?"

"Yes." Aliam looked down at his clasped hands. "I had no proof — and she was just coming to coronation that next year — But how did you know what I thought? I never told — "

"You told the Knight-Commander of Falk. He is part-elven, one of my great-great grandsons."

"Oh." Aliam looked stunned.

"And of course he told me what he knew — which wasn't much. I wish you would tell me now why you thought Kieri Phelan was the prince."

"He told me, finally, when he was my senior squire in Aarenis. I — don't want to go into all that happened, but he told me what little he remembered. Seeing him like that, looking older as men in pain often do, he had a look of the king . . . and his few memories made sense of it."

"What did he remember? Haleron said there was nothing in his memories but pain and despair."

"Well — " Aliam ran his hands over his bald head. "I'm not sure now I recall all he said. Little things, as a very small child might see them. A bowl he ate from, tall windows, a garden with roses and a puppy. A man who picked him up — I think that may have been the king, Lady; he remembered the green and gold colors, and a fair beard. He remembered riding with his mother, he said, and traveling in the woods — that's what caught me, you see — and being attacked."

"That's more than I thought he had," said the Lady quietly. She smoothed her robe with one graceful hand. "Haleron caught none of that."

"The older lords at court remember the puppy," said Paks.

"Yes, it knocked him down, or some such. He remembered that, and being lectured for hitting it." Aliam cocked his head at the Lady. "Forgive me, but one thing still confuses me. If he is the prince, and half-elven, why doesn't he look like it? All the half-elves I've seen show their blood — it's one thing that made me think he couldn't be the prince after all."

"A good question. Even then, there were humans who feared such strong elven influence, and so my daughter thought it would be easier for her children, if they looked more human. This is a choice we have, when we bear children to humans — how much the sinyi blood shows. As well, part of what you see in us is the practice of our abilities, as a swordsman's exercise with a sword shapes his arm and shoulder. Had the prince grown up with that training, he would show some of it — but he would still look more human than elven, as his mother chose." Aliam nodded, looking thoughtful.

900

The Lady frowned again, and leaned toward Aliam. "Lord Halveric, is it true that you did not know anything of the sword you found?"

"The sword? You mean, where it was from? No — nothing — that's what I wrote."

"Yes, but — " She rolled her robe in her fingers. "It's so hard with humans — you surprise us sometimes, with your gallantry and wit, and yet it seems you *know* nothing. That sword was famous at court; everyone knew it — "

"But I wasn't at court then!" Aliam's eyes snapped. "I was a boy — a page — at my uncle's. I never saw it!"

She shook her head. "I thought you were being courteous — offering to let us decide whether to try the sword or not."

"You were *what*?!"

"I truly did not know that you knew nothing. Amrothlin suggested you might not know, but it seemed impossible you could not. And when you said you were giving it as a wedding present — "

"To his *wife*," said Aliam.

"I thought that was your way of letting the gods decide."

Aliam stared at her a long moment. "Would you have told me," he said, "if you'd known I didn't know?"

"I — don't know. Possibly. At the time, as you said, he seemed as fit to rule as the new king, who had no taig sense and no way to beget any."

"But then when nothing happened, why didn't you — ?"

She sighed, and moved her hands slightly. "Lord Halveric, I thought you had left it to the gods, by gifting his wife. Someday he would draw the sword; someday it would act — or, if the gods willed otherwise, it would not. What was I to do? We do not meddle much in mortal affairs, but we were never far from him. We never saw or felt aught to show that he had come to know who he was, or had found any of his elven abilities." She shook her head until her hair shimmered around her. "We were wrong in that, Lord Halveric — I say it; I, the Lady at the heart of my Forest and home. Wrong to think you knew, when you said you did not, and wrong to think we knew, when we knew only from afar. But believe me if you can, my lord, we intended no wrong."

"I believe you," said Aliam heavily.

"But the wrong was done," said Estil suddenly, out of her silence. "We all did it, and for us — for me, at least — it came from taking the quiet way, the easy way. Forget, I thought. Forget, put it behind, look to the future — as if the future were not built, grain by grain, out of the past."

The Lady looked at her with dawning respect. "Indeed, Estil Halveric, you speak wisely there. We singers of the world, who shrink from disharmony, may choose silence instead of noise, and not always rightly."

"And now will you help us, Lady?" asked Paks.

"I would do much to serve this land, Paksenarrion, and much to serve both you and the Halverics — but I am not yet convinced that my grandson can take the throne in any way that will serve."

901

"Because he has not remembered who he is?"

"Because of that, and because he turned to darkness after his wife's death. Even in the Ladysforest, we heard of that, and of his campaigns in Aarenis. We want no civil wars here, Paksenarrion, no hiring of idle blades to fill out a troop and impose his will where he has no right."

"It may not have been so bad as you thought," said Aliam.

The Lady turned on him. "It was indeed as bad — and worse than I have said. And the only bad I know of you, Aliam Halveric, is that you stayed with him through that and supported him."

"You mean Siniava?"

"I mean after Siniava. Do you think we get no word at all?"

"Lady — I don't know if you can understand — " Aliam's hands knotted together.

"I understand evil well enough," she said crisply, "even in my own family. It stinks the same everywhere."

"I would plead, Lady, that things happened which rubbed the same scars. When Siniava tortured his men and mine at Dwarfwatch — "

"Lord Halveric, there is always an excuse. I know that. Such a man does not do wrong for no reason. But there are always reasons. Are we to set him on a throne — in *this* kingdom, set between Tsaia and Prealith and the Ladysforest — to have him find excuses to turn mercenaries free in the forest, as he turned Alured free? You will pardon my saying this: I know of your son Caliam's loss; I know how that angered you. Had it been only the torturing of Siniava — "

"But they didn't!" Paks burst out. "They didn't — "

"Because you withheld them, isn't that so?"

"Well — yes — but — "

"If you want to talk policy with elves, Paksenarrion, you must be ready to see all the truth and speak it." She turned back to Aliam. "Had it been only that, I would worry little. But you know — all of you here know — that it went farther than that. Much farther. We do not want — *I* do not want — the man who helped Alured reduce the coastal cities to show the same character in Lyonya. We would agree to no one's rule, who had done such things, elf or human. Elf least of all, for in this realm where so many fear us, even hate us, an elf's misrule could finally breach that old agreement between human and sinyi. Should we prove ourselves what so many already say we are? Arrogant, cold, uncaring, quick to anger? Should we risk confusion with the iynisin, to give space to his taste for cruelty?"

"Lady, no!" Again Paks broke in. "Please — let me tell you what I know of my own experience — "

The Lady looked at her without smiling. "Paksenarrion, I will listen. But I realize he is capable of love, and caring, for a few. You remind him of his wife, I daresay, or even his daughter; you have seen the private side of tenderness which all but the worst men have. As a king, it is the other side, the outer, that concerns us here." Paks, immersed in the power that flowed from the Lady as steadily as water from a spring, inexhaustible, nonetheless found herself able to perceive more clearly what indeed the elven nature was, and what its limitations. Firstborn, eldest of the Elder Races, immortal, wise as the years bring wisdom, elves were due reverence for all this . . . and yet not gods or demigods, however powerful. Created a choir of lesser singers by the First Singer, they were so imbued with harmony that they endured conflict only in brief encounters, resolving such discords quickly, in victory or retreat. It was not weakness or cowardice that made them withdraw, again and again, when evil stalked their lands, but that they were made for another purpose. This was their gift, with living things or elements or pattern itself to repattern into beauty, endlessly and with delight. From this came their mastery of healing, of the growing of plants, the shaping of the taigin, for they alone, of all peoples of the world, could grasp the entire interwoven pattern of life the High Lord designed, and play with it, creating new designs without damage to the fabric. So also they enchanted mortal minds, embroidering on reality the delicate patterns of their imaginings.

Yet powerful as they were, as powerful as music that brings heart-piercing pain, tears, laughter, with its enchantments, they were as music, subordinate to their own creator. Humans need not, Paks saw, worship their immortality, their cool wisdom, their knowledge of the taig, their ability to repattern mortal perceptions. In brief mortal lives humans met challenges no elf could meet, learned strategies no elf could master, chose evil or good more direct and dangerous than elf could perceive. Humans were shaped for conflict, as elves for harmony; each needed the other's balance of wisdom, but must cleave to its own nature. It was easy for an immortal to counsel patience, withdrawal until a danger passed. . . .

She took courage, therefore, and felt less the Lady's weight of age and experience. That experience was elven, and not all to her purpose. Kieri Phelan himself was but half-elven; his right to kingship came with his mortal blood. And as she found herself regarding the Lady with less awe, but no less respect, the Lady met her eyes with dawning amazement.

"I will grant your ideas," Paks began slowly. "Others have said I look much like Tammarrion. It may well be that he has turned a kinder face to me than to strangers. But I am not speaking — now — of his treatment of me." The Lady nodded, and Paks described the Duke's generosity to his own, from recruits to veterans, and to others who had served him, however briefly.

"That last year — " Paks took a breath before she said it. "He was wrong, Lady. I will say that, and Lord Halveric knows I bear the Duke no grudge. He was wrong to support Alured as long as he did; I think from what I saw that he was unhappy about it, but had given his word, not knowing what Alured would do. Any man is wrong to be unjust, whenever he is. But did you not say, a little bit ago, that you had been wrong? And the Halverics said they had been wrong."

The Lady stiffened; Paks heard the Halverics gasp. Before the heavens fell, she rushed on.

"He was wrong then; I have been wrong, too. But he has asked the Marshals of Gird back, Lady, and apologized for sending them away. He said before the whole Company that he had erred, that he had been hasty in anger. Does that sound like an arrogant man, a man eager to judge harshly, delighting in cruelty?"

The Lady sat long without answering; twice Paks opened her mouth to speak, and shut it again, fearing she had already said too much. Finally she gave a little shake, like someone waking from a reverie, and turned to Paks with a smile.

"It speaks well of any man to gain the love and respect of a paladin. You are not lying about this, though you may have put the best face on it that you could. I did not know he had called in the Marshals. If he admitted his errors — then — I have less fear, though I am not confident. At least he might not be an evil king."

"Kieri's a Knight of Falk, too," said Aliam. "At least, he was knighted, though he never took the vows and wears no ruby. Good thing, too, or it'd have given him a fit of conscience when he became a Girdsman."

"He's not a Girdsman," said Paks.

"What? Of course he is — or was — and I suppose is again, if he's made his peace with them."

Paks shook her head. "No, my lord. He talked to the Marshal-General in my presence. He supported Tammarrion in the Fellowship, and encouraged it, but he never took the vows. He told the Marshal-General that he had always felt withheld from such vows."

The Lady sat forward, eyes bright. "He said what? Say exactly what you remember, Paksenarrion."

"He said that he had been drawn to both — to Falk and to Gird — but that he felt something about other vows awaiting him, and he could not swear with a free heart. And the Marshal-General told her Marshals that she was content — that she did not seek his vows."

"Ahh."

"But why does that matter?" Paks looked at her curiously.

"I am not sure. If it means what it could mean — " the Lady smiled again, and shook her head. "I speak in riddles, you think, as elves are wont to do. Indeed I do, for I have nothing but surmises. But if — and remember that I said *if* — what has withheld him from these vows is a memory of his true nature, even a slight memory, that can be, perhaps, restored."

"But I thought Lyonyan kings could be Falkians — can't they?"

"It has been so — and true of the last two kings, indeed. They were but human. A king of elven heritage, aware of the taig by that blood, would follow the High Lord, as you call him, directly." She sighed, then moved her shoulders. "You have told me much I did not know. It may be that he can become king. I accept, Paksenarrion, your description of your quest: to find the true king of Lyonya and restore him. I accept your decision to prove my grandson, whom you know as Duke Phelan, by the sword's test. But before I agree to his crowning, I wish to see him myself. If he can become what he

904

was meant to become, my powers will aid him. If not — we shall hope for better things than I fear."

The Lady rose; Paks and the Halverics, trying to stand, found themselves unable to move. The Lady's voice was kindly, now, its silvery music warmer than before.

"It will make your task no easier, that all know the Ladysforest has moved to enclose your steading; as I shift the border in return, you will find that none of your people remember a summer's afternoon in winter. For you, I leave you such memories as you need — and from Paksenarrion I withhold no truth. You will not be troubled by any elves of my Household — "

Paks suddenly thought of the evil plots Achrya had woven for the Duke before now — had all this, for near fifty years, been one — ? She wanted to ask the Lady, wanted to explain — but gentle laughter filled her mind.

"Be at ease, paladin; others, too, can see a web against the light."

A knock came on the door; Paks and the Halverics looked blankly at each other. Between them a bowl of apples and a tiny glass flask with a spray of apple blossoms filled Aliam's study with the mingled odors of spring and fall.

"What is it?" Aliam finally croaked.

Cal Halveric put his head in. "It's getting late, sir — did you wish to dine here? Shall I sit for you in Hall?" Paks looked at the small window; outside it was full dark.

Chapter Twenty-two

The three of them looked at each other, still dazed; Paks saw Caliam look at the apple blossoms with disbelief, and then at her. She inhaled that delicate odor, then shook her head. Aliam took a long breath, then thumped the arms of his chair with both hands.

"No — we'll be down. In a few minutes. Cal — do you — ?" But he stopped himself, and turned to Estil. She smiled, and touched his hand, holding her other out to Paks.

"I thank you, my dear, for a very — interesting — discussion," she said. Paks could see in her eyes the memory of the Lady's visit. "I am sorry you must leave as soon as you say, but in the meantime, enjoy our hospitality."

"With all my heart," said Paks. Estil laughed, in her eyes, and they rose, less stiffly than Paks had expected. The squires looked curiously at them as they entered the Hall, where everyone waited at the tables. Now, at evening, more of the seats were filled. Cal and his brothers and their wives sat at the head table with their parents and Paks; the older children fitted in where they could, and the little ones tumbled around them. The Hall rang with laughter and talk. Paks did not miss the many glances sent her way; she knew when one of the younger children sneaked behind her and boldly touched the hilt of the sword. Estil saw that, and snatched the girl back.

"You! Suli, you rascal — you do that with the wrong person someday, and you'll lose a hand, if not your life. You know better than to touch a warrior's weapon."

"It's pretty, grandmother — I just — "

"You just indeed! If you want to speak to a paladin, go ahead — there she is — speak — " And Suli, both frightened and thrilled, was thrust forward to face Paks, who had turned to watch this.

"I-I'm sorry," she quavered. Paks heard one of the boys giggle from a safe distance. Suli threw a sulky glance that way, and then stared at Paks.

"Your grandmother's right," Paks said, bending down to face the child. "I will not hurt you, but another might. And did you know that some weapons are magical? A sword might hurt you, if you were not its true master. You have a bold heart, and that is good — only learn from your grandmother to let a wise head guide it." The child blushed, and Paks turned to see the other children beyond her. "And for you others — it is easy to laugh when another is in trouble — but another's folly does not

make you wise. In this family I would expect you to defend one another."
To her surprise, a boy about Suli's size came forward at once.

"I only laughed because she is never afraid," he said stoutly. "If that was wrong, I'm sorry. But if you had tried to hurt her, I would have come."

Paks smiled at him. "I'm glad you would help. I said what I did because when I was helpless and in trouble, some laughed at me."

"You? I thought — can a paladin be helpless?"

"I was not born a paladin, lad. Even now, I expect there are things I cannot fight except by faith."

"I will not laugh again," said the boy seriously. "Suli — "

"It's all right." Suli put her arm around him. Paks realized suddenly that they were twins. Both of them grinned at her, and then Suli poked her brother in the ribs. They tumbled back, laughing and sparring.

"Ruffians," said Estil calmly. "Those two are wild as colts."

"'Tis because you spoil them, Mother," said a woman down the table. "Every time I come, you — "

"Well, they're good-hearted ruffians," said Estil. "And the only twins in the family. Gods grant we don't have more, the way they are, but still — "

"At home," their mother went on, looking down the table to Paks, "I keep them in more order — when they aren't running off in the woods. But since we spend half the year here, why — "

"Now that's unfair." The tall man beside her grinned. "Shall I tell them all what you said when we packed this time to come?" The woman started laughing, and he went on. "She was so glad we were coming, because then when the twins did something, she could blame you."

"Yes, but — "

"And, she said, they were better behaved when we left than when we came." He tapped his wife's nose. "So you see what you get?"

She shrugged, grinning, and made a face at Paks and Estil. Paks was amazed. She had never been in such a family — had not, she thought suddenly, been in any family since leaving home. There were at least a dozen children in the hall, and more had been carried off after falling asleep. Three or four generations lived here — happily, as it seemed. She looked at Estil — grandmother certainly, and maybe a great-grandmother — and still tall and broad-shouldered. A formidable bowman, her husband said. How had she done it? Paks could not imagine having all those children (for there sat Caliam, Haliam, and Suli — married to a Tsaian but home for a visit — and she had heard of others), managing such an estate, and still finding time to stay fit in weaponscraft. She shook her head; Estil noticed and turned to her.

"Is it too noisy for you, Paksenarrion? We're a noisy family; always have been. Aliam and I love talk and music as much as life itself."

"No, I just — I never — this is very different," said Paks lamely.

"It's just a family. Bigger than most, I suppose — and when you count in the others — " She looked around. The side tables were still full: Paks saw men and women in working garb.

907

"Does everyone eat here, my lady? Every meal?" She had thought that in rich houses, the master and mistress and family ate alone.

"Oh no. Some live in their own cottages; some prefer to eat somewhere else. But in winter, we keep a good fire here, and anyone is welcome. Evening meals in winter are usually a crowd. My sister from northern Lyonya says it's like a barracks, but we like it." Estil smiled. Paks heard the chime of harpstrings from somewhere, and looked around. Caliam's oldest son had brought a harp to the hall, and now tuned it. The tables began to fall silent. When he was ready, he brought the harp to Aliam, and bowed.

"You first, young man," said Aliam. "I'll let my fingers warm to your music first."

The boy began to play, a jigging dance tune that soon had hands slapping the tables. Someone knew the words, but had a flat voice; others took up the tune with better grace. After that, the boy played a slow song like summer afternoons before haying time; Paks felt her eyelids sag. Then a love song, which half the men sang along with. Then Cal took the harp.

"Get the lo-pipe," he told the boy. "Garris, do you still play?"

"I haven't blown a pipe for over a year," said Garris.

"Well, you need the practice."

Young Aliam carried in the long, polished tube of a lo-pipe, and set it before Garris. Cal plucked a note. Garris took a breath and blew; the sonorous mellow note Paks expected came out sour and cracked as a strangled goose. Everyone burst into a roar of laughter.

"Gods' teeth, Garris, I said play it, not break it."

"I told you — " He tried again, producing a deep, hollow sound that rattled dishes. "Now, if I can find another note — " It began well, a rich sound above the other, but it faded and split as he held it. He stopped and looked up, rubbing his lip. "I'll have a blister," he said. "But if you're willing to laugh over it, I'll try 'Cedars of the Valley.' "

"Hmmph. Child's play," said Cal, fingering the harpstrings. The silver dancing harp-notes began to work a pattern on the slower, lower lo-pipe. Garris had trouble; the notes broke again and again, or slid off-key, but Paks could hear what the music was meant to be. Then Hali took the lo-pipe, and Aliam the harp.

"For the paladin who has come on quest," said Aliam to the rest, and the silence was absolute. "You all know that much; I will tell you this much more — she is on quest to find Lyonya's true king, and when she leaves us will leave with all our goodwill and hope. And so for her, and for the quest, Hali and I will give you this, which we do not sing here often. 'Falk and the Oath of Gold.' "

Paks had never heard it sung, though she knew the story of Falk, bound by oath and chains together, held captive many years then riding into the city of despair to free his kindred.

"Oath of blood is Liart's bane
Oath of death is for the slain

Oath of stone the rockfolk swear
Oath of iron is Tir's domain
Oath of silver liars dare
Oath of gold will yet remain . . ."

The refrain first, set to a different tune, and sounding like part of something else. All of them sang it, but at the first verse, Aliam Halveric and his sons sang alone.

"Far the shadows fall,
far on the distant wall.
Under the weight of stone
the lost prince toils alone.
Far they have gone away;
bound by an oath to stay
the true prince toils alone . . ."

As Aliam and his sons sang it, the music drummed in her veins, and it became the song of Kieri the lost prince. She smiled at him; his eyes acknowledged that meaning. Harp, pipe, and voices together wove the long spell, ending with

"His oath at last fulfilled
his captors' blood is spilled
but nothing can restore
the youth he had before.
Yet gold outlasts white bone,
blood, iron, silver, stone:
his honor is his own . . ." as they sang the final verses, and let the music die away.

"Now," he said. "I do not know how long Paksenarrion can stay — for us, as long as she will — but all of you remember that she is welcome to go or stay as she pleases, and take whatever she needs. If any of you can aid her, do it in my name. Is that clear?"

"Yes, my lord," came the response. Aliam nodded to them, then turned to Paks. "And now you will want to rest, you and your squires. Come and go as you will; I will always be glad to speak with you, but if you must go without my leave, know you have it."

"I thank you," said Paks, bowing. She followed him from the table and Hall. Estil and the squires came with them.

She woke from comfortable sleep — warm, clean, grateful for a good bed — to the awareness of danger. Starlight outlined the window; the room was dark but for the faint glow of a dying fire. She could hear the squires' breathing; all seemed asleep. Slowly, silently, Paks eased out of bed, taking up the sword which lay beneath her hand. She did not draw it; she did not need its warning. Out of the narrow window she could see nothing; its lower half was patterned in frost ferns. Still barefoot, she went to the door, and opened it. A black passageway faced her; she could see nothing at all. But the sense of danger increased, pushing at her mind.

Sighing, she turned back to the room and woke her squires. As they rose, she dressed quickly, arming herself. Her sense of menace deepened. She opened the door again, and, on an impulse, called her light.

The entire passage was filled with webbing, strand after strand looped in an intricate pattern that centered on the door of Paks's room. And a black presence hung in the web, scarcely an arm's length away.

"Well, are you less eager to meet me?" The voice was strangely sweet. Paks could see no detail of the presence, could not tell shape or even size. She drew the sword. Its hilt comforted her hand.

"I am always eager to meet evil," said Paks, "with a blade."

"You will not be eager when you know what you have done," said the voice. "You vermin — I have warned you often enough, and yet you kill and kill. You have torn my webs, you have robbed me of my prey —"

Paks laughed; the shade seemed to contract and grow more solid. But it was large, larger than she had imagined it could be. "I have done no more than any good soldier," she said. "In keeping the barracks clean, the webs are swept away."

"Fool!" The word howled in Paks's ears, echoed in her head. She leaned against the force of it. "You think you can stand against me? Mistress of all webs, the spinner of wise plans —"

"Not I, but Gird and the High Lord."

"Who left you open to me: silly girl, I had you in Aarenis, and in Kolobia. You are tainted with my venom already; when I call, you will answer."

"No." Paks heard the squires behind her, and waved them back with her free hand. "By the power of the High Lord, and the grace of Gird, I am not your creature. And by that power I command you to leave this hall."

"If I leave, where do you think I will go, sheepfarmer's daughter? You are mortal still; you cannot be with all you love. You can save yourself: can you save them?" Paks saw her home in that instant: father, mother, brothers, sisters, and thrust the thought aside. If they were doomed, her failure here would not help them. But the sweet voice went on. "And there are others, wiser than you, who will hearken to counsels of caution . . . who will not welcome a warrior's bloody hands on the crown. Even your squires: dare you trust strangers at your back against the powers you know oppose you? I know their secrets; I can use —"

"You can use nothing here; you cannot even hide your intent." Paks drew that belief around her, palpable as armor, against the doubts and concerns the creature sent. "When you must appear openly, you are weakest," she went on, as much for the squires' benefit as anything. "As light shows traps, the truth will reveal your rumors and plots for what they are." She sensed a movement in the darkness, and braced herself.

The darkness thickened, leaped forward; Paks raised the elf-forged blade to meet it. She felt something tangle her arm, shake it, but with a screech the darkness passed. Only the webs remained, swinging to and fro. Paks looked at her arm; it bore no mark, and the sword still shone clean.

"Thanks and praise," she said quietly.

"What was that?" asked Lieth, who was nearest.

"I think it was a servant of Achrya," said Paks. She feared it had been Achrya herself. Its power echoed in her mind, a wailing certainty of doom, but she fought off that sending.

"Where did all that — those — is that web? Or what?" asked Esceriel.

"It's the web-stuff that Achrya's servants spin. Don't touch it; it burns." Paks touched the sword tip to one of the strands; it shriveled and parted. "I'll have to clean all this out."

She had cleared half the passage when Aliam opened his door suddenly. "What's going — " He stopped, staring at the webs.

"My lord, don't touch them; I'm clearing them. I'll tell you what happened when this is done."

"Will a torch help?" Aliam reached back into his room and brought one to the door.

Paks had forgotten about torches. "It will indeed," she said. "Just be sure not to let it touch you." With his help and Estil's, that passage was quickly cleared of web. But they found it was not the only one. All the passages were trapped with it, though not as heavily.

"How quickly can they spin this?" asked Aliam, as they finished. "That thing must have worked since we went to sleep!"

Paks shook her head. "I don't think so; I wakened knowing evil was near. I believe it was done very quickly indeed."

"And why didn't I waken? Or one of the guards — Falk guard us — the guards!" Aliam darted off to the main doors.

"Wait!" Paks yelled. "Don't call an alarm — if others are trapped, they'll blunder into the webs."

"But I must — "

"Garris, go with him; you know the steading. Go quietly, my lord, along the guard posts — be ready to destroy any web. My lady, take Esceriel, and go through the kitchens and storerooms — be particularly careful of places where a person might hide. I will pray, my lord, and see if any evil stays near us."

They moved off as Paks directed; she could feel no evil as strong as that which had left. But she and the others checked each separate room in the main part of the building, in case web had been left to trap sleepers. Aliam and Garris returned soon; the guards had been asleep but unharmed.

"They were spelled," said Paks, when Aliam would have scolded them. "As we were in Aarenis, when Siniava came out — remember? Thank the gods it was no worse than this. My lord, we bring peril on you — we must go."

"But into that?" Aliam stared. "What will you do, beyond the walls?"

"Go swiftly. It was to keep us here, to threaten you and tempt me to delay, for the care of you and yours, that such evil invaded. My lord, I will

911

not tell you exactly where we go — although you surely know, in the main — and I suggest that you tell no one what you know so. Ward this place well; don't let the children wander —"

His face whitened at that. "Falk, no! Not another —"

"Watch them well. Keep together, keep faith. Ask the rangers — perhaps the elves will help you, since they value your aid in the past. I wish I could stay to guard you, but I think the danger will be less when I am gone."

He nodded; Estil, who had come down the stairs, longbow in hand, came up beside him.

"Paksenarrion, surely you can stay until dawn —"

"By nightfall, my lady, I would be far from here — very far."

"As you wish. Is there anything — ? I have plenty of stores —"

"Thank you. Suriya, Garris — if you'll pack, I have a few words to say to the Halverics." Her squires moved away, toward the kitchens, where Paks heard the stirring of servants and cooks. The Halverics came near, and they stood together at one side of the hall. "If you recall anything else — anything at all — about the Duke's past, please tell me now."

Aliam rubbed his head. "After this? Let me think —"

"Anything that would tell us where he was, those lost years?"

"No — not really. Why? You know where he is now."

Paks sighed. "I know. It's just — I'm not sure how to go from here. If I take the King's Squires into Tsaia —"

Aliam relaxed. "Oh, that. I can help you there." He grinned at her expression. "Diplomacy . . . I've been marching foreign troops through Tsaia for years, haven't I? You're right, you can't take Lyonyan King's Squires through Tsaia on a quest without causing lasting trouble. You'll have to go to Vérella first —"

"But the Duke — if someone realizes, and goes for him —"

"If the gods want Kieri on this throne, they'll watch out for him that much. He's in the midst of his own people, safer there anywhere. After the trouble you've told us about, do you think they'll fail to watch out for him? And not because he's a prince, either." He shook his head. "You go to Vérella. Tell the Regency Council about your quest. You needn't name Kieri, not then. Tell them you must consult him about the sword: that's true, and logical since you found it in his Hall, and his wife used it."

Paks nodded slowly. This felt right, far better than trying to reach the Duke secretly.

"Paksenarrion," said Aliam, touching her arm. "If you are killed, what then? Shall I try to tell Kieri, and hope that good comes?"

"My lord, if I am killed on this quest, then my advice is not worth much. I can tell you nothing you could not think of yourself — and you have the advantage of me in experience. Your land will go ill until an able ruler holds the throne; I believe the Duke is able. In the meantime —" Paks found herself reaching out to both of them; for a few moments they embraced. "Guard yourselves; try to hold the kingdom together until I return with him."

912

"You fear trouble here, as well?"

"My lord Halveric, you saw what tangled in your halls this night. If that one is spinning webs of distrust in the kingdom, how long will that patched-up regency council satisfy everyone? Too many people know something bad about the Duke; it will be easy to convince the fearful that he is grim and terrible. Were I you, I would be ready to aid Sier Halveric and the council at need."

"I will be ready," said Aliam.

Paks looked around and saw that her squires were ready to ride; Lieth and Esceriel had saddled the horses and had them by the door, while Garris and Suriya packed all their gear and food. She bowed; the Halverics bowed in response.

"My lord — my lady. Gird's grace be on this house, and the High Lord's power protect it." At those words, her light came, and blazed through the Hall as she and the squires walked out into a cold night. She did not damp it there, deeming it wise to maintain that protection.

So they rode off, in the turning hours of night. Paks, looking back for an instant at the gate, saw two small heads at one window, and wondered if they would remember, in older years, the night they saw a paladin ride away, light glittering on the snow.

Chapter Twenty-three

Dawn found them far north and west of Aliam Halveric's steading. Paks had chosen the direction, which took them across a low rolling ridge of forest toward the Tsaian border. As they rode, she tried to think which path north would bring them to Vérella with the least interference. She thought of going through Brewersbridge again — the Kuakgan might know more of the Duke than he'd said, might know if he could be healed. But Achrya knew she had been there before, knew where her friends were. She could not bring that danger to Brewersbridge. There would be blood in plenty before this was done; she would not start there. In first light, with the low sun throwing long blue shadows across the snow, she turned north.

"Lady?" Garris turned to her. "Are you sure? Where are we bound?"

She rode on some little time before answering. No one hurried her. Finally she halted; they formed a close group around her. "You all saw what we faced last night," she began. They nodded. "It will have occurred to you that evil powers prefer that the true prince not be found. I had hoped we would be further with the quest before they noticed us; but paladins are not the spies of the gods, but their champions. I do not bring peace with me."

"I understand," said Suriya quickly, then blushed as the others looked at her. Paks smiled.

"Suriya, I believe you. I, too, before this — I would have said the same. Now let me go on. I have not told you all I know — nor will I. Believe that it is not my lack of trust in you, but the command of the gods I serve, that prevents me."

"But — if you're hurt — " Garris looked worried.

"Garris, if need comes, I will tell you. But for now, if you will come with me, you will ride into uncertainty."

"We will come," said Esceriel, looking around at the others. All nodded. "We trust you."

"Trust the gods, rather," said Paks. "You follow Falk; I honor him." She looked at the lightening day. "Now," she said, "the Webspinner is a creature of darkness; she toils in secret to plot the downfall of good. I think we will not have much trouble with her as long as we keep close watch by night, and travel swiftly. She does not much like forests, especially not these, where the elves and rangers have sung the taig so often. It is another I worry about more. How many of you know of Liart, the Master of Torments?"

914

"I do," said Garris, shuddering. "In Aarenis—" Paks looked at each in turn.

"We were told, in the knight's training," said Lieth, "that he was evil, but not much more. No one follows him in Lyonya; I didn't pay much mind."

"I thought he came only where there was slavery," said Suriya.

"No," said Paks. "His followers may be anywhere. Liart sometimes allies with Achrya, in large plots. He's hastier. More active. I fear that we have attracted notice in that direction. Liart's followers practice torture as a ceremony; he delights in the fear of those victims. I say this not to frighten you, but to warn. If through some mischance we are separated and any of you is taken, your only shield is prayer. Do not despair; the High Lord will protect your soul, if only you can keep your mind on him."

Their faces were set; none of them asked how she knew. Paks looked at them for a moment. Then she stretched, feeling the return of strength with the morning sun.

"In the meantime," she said more cheerfully, "we have a clear day and far to ride. Gods grant they miss us after all — it's likely enough. And together — well, they'd have a hard fight. Ride for an hour, companions — then it will be warm enough to stop for a meal." And she legged the red horse into a spurt of speed, the snow flying up in cakes and lumps from his feet. Behind her she heard the other horses whinny and run. In a few minutes they slowed again, but everyone was in a lighter mood. The horses jogged on, snorting. Paks started humming "Cedars of the Valley," and Suriya broke in, singing the words.

> "*Cedars of the valley, oh —*
> *firtrees on the hill*
> *where's the lad I used to love*
> *and does he love me still —* "

The others came in on the chorus: "Cedars of the valley, oh, cedars in the wind."

Paks sang the second verse. "Cedars of the valley, say, if I wander far, will I see my home again, or die in lands afar?" Again the chorus. Garris went next.

"Cedars of the valley, sing — tell us all a tale — "

"That's almost as bad as the lo-pipe, Garris," commented Esceriel, grinning.

"You made me lose my place," said Garris. He started again, where he'd left off, and finished the verse: " — and dressed in shining mail."

Paks listened with one ear to the singing, as the song wound on through its many verses (for it had been a marching song a long time), and with the other to whatever set the red horse's left ear twitching sideways. Finally she held up her hand, and Lieth stopped in the middle of a word. Nothing now but the crunching of snow, the jingle of harness and breathing of the animals. They halted. Paks could still hear nothing, but the red horse stared at the woods to their left as if he could do better. He blew, rattling his breath; Paks felt the tension beneath her. Esceriel raised his brows.

"I don't know." Paks answered the look. "But with such a horse, I don't ignore the warning, either." She drew the elf-blade; its blue flash was a warning in daylight. She heard the scrape of scabbards as the squires drew their own weapons. The red horse snorted. Paks looked around. They were in a wide glade, with a frozen stream to their left and forest beyond it, and on their right. They moved on again, more slowly, the pack horses on short reins.

If the red horse had not kept watching to the left, Paks might have decided that nothing menaced them, for they rode a good distance without any sign of trouble. Then the forest closed in on their right, and the streambed plunged into a rocky hollow. Paks slowed, looking for a safe way down through the drifted snow. Ahead and below seemed rougher country, with the tops of boulders showing above piles of snow. She peered into the forest on their right. It was thick here, heavy with undergrowth even in winter, and she could see little but a tangle of leafless stalks and stems. Still, it looked like the way down was gentler off to the right. She reined the red horse toward the forest edge.

"Paks!" Garris's shout brought her head around. Three huge white wolf-like creatures hurtled across the frozen stream, roaring. They were pony-high at the shoulder, with pale green eyes. The pack horses plunged wildly, and Suriya fought to control them. Lieth charged between the creatures and Suriya, striking at one. Garris and Esceriel too were trying to attack, but the creatures were as fast as they were big.

The red horse wheeled; Paks leaned low from the saddle and plunged the elf-blade into one of them. Its howl turned to a scream; she had severed its spine. Another had hamstrung a pack horse, and was fastened to its throat. The third raced in and out, slashing at the horses with its long teeth. Esceriel forced his horse close to the dying pack animal, and stabbed that one. It turned, with a terrifying howl, and flung itself upward against the sword. Lieth buried her sword in its back, just as the third creature attacked her mount. Her horse bucked wildly, and Lieth flew off, landing in a shower of snow.

Paks legged the red horse into a standing leap; they came down beside Lieth, who was just scrambling up. She caught Paks's hand and swung up behind the saddle. Garris had finished the one that attacked Esceriel, but the third was racing after Lieth's horse. Lieth whistled, but her mount kept going.

"Get down, Lieth — get up with Suriya. I'll try to catch — " As she spoke, Paks sheathed the sword, and pulled her longbow from its case to string it.

"Not alone, Lady," said Garris. "That may be what they want."

"But we need the horse — " said Paks. She closed her legs; the red horse surged forward, back down their trail. Garris and Esceriel followed her. She could see the loose horse running flat-out beside the stream; the beast was hardly a length behind. Paks slid an arrow from its case, sparing a thought of thanks to the gods that she'd brought her bow along. Despite her weight, the red horse gained on the other, racing over the snow as if it were a smooth track. Paks drew and released. Her arrow sank into the beast's hindquarters; she saw it flinch and slow. As she set another arrow to the string, the red horse gained still more. Her next shot was easier; they were nearly abreast of it, and she placed her arrow in its ribs. The beast howled, slowed more, running partly sideways now. Blood spattered the snow. She heard Garris and Esceriel yelling, and looked back.

Cutting her off from them were four riders, all in gray armor, with the spiked helms she remembered from Aarenis. One of the riders faced her, a leashed beast at his side; the others attacked her squires. Paks sent a last arrow at the beast she'd been chasing, and tossed her bow aside into a tree. The elf-blade flashed as she drew it again; she leaned from her saddle to behead the wounded beast, then sent the red horse charging at the gray riders.

The one facing her sent a piercing cry across the distance. It meant nothing to Paks, but she saw her squires wince and stagger. That rider unleashed his beast, and the white wolf-like thing flew toward her. But Paks had expected that; she had already gathered her horse, and when the wolf was a length away, they leaped high over it. By the time the beast reversed to follow them, Paks had attacked the first rider.

This close she could see that the gray armor was black, daubed with white paint or stain. He carried a jagged sword in one hand; Paks met that with the elf-blade, which rang to the blow, but held. Her mount shifted suddenly; she glanced down just long enough to see that the other horse had hooked barbs on its harness. The rider struck again, laughing. Paks laughed too, a different sound, as she met it, then slipped her blade under his, and thrust it into his side, where the armor jointed. Just then the red horse leaped, a sideways jump of some feet, and Paks nearly lost her grip on her sword. The white beast, which had leaped across its master's mount, fell to the snow, off-balance for an instant. In that moment the red horse jumped again, coming down with all four hooves on top of it, then jumped away. Broken, it screamed at them, helpless.

But Paks had no time to kill it. Her squires were driven back, into a knot around the dead pack horse. Lieth fought on foot; Suriya's horse was lame, hobbling on three legs. Esceriel and Garris tried to protect them, but one of the other riders carried a hooked lance, long enough to reach past their guard. She saw blood on all of them, and had no time to worry whether it was theirs or the horses'.

The rider she had wounded could still fight, but Paks went on to the others. She had to get that lance away. Before she could attack, two of them turned, leaving the lance-bearer to immobilize her squires. Both of them howled at her, screams of threat meant to terrify.

"Gird the Protector!" Paks yelled back. "The High Lord's power is with us!" She charged one of the two directly, knowing that opened her quarter to the other, but trusting the red horse to jump when necessary. The one she charged fell back, luring her away from the squires. She knew better

917

than that. She spun the red horse on his hocks, and caught the second a solid blow across the chest as he tried to attack from behind. His armor rang, and he rocked in the saddle. His horse rushed by.

Paks spun again, to meet the first rider blade to blade. Her horse reared, driving onto the other horse's neck with both front hooves. Paks deflected a blow that would have severed tendons, and stabbed for the rider's neck. He flinched and parried wildly. Under the pointed chin of his face-guard was a gap above the body-armor. As the horses squealed and fought, the weight of the red bearing the other down, Paks stabbed again for this gap. The rider tried to lean away, just as his horse staggered, backing away from the red but falling to one side. The rider lost his seat and fell half under his mount.

But as the red horse reared away, Paks felt a heavy blow on her back that nearly unseated her. Her left arm fell from the reins, useless, and she felt the pain tingle in her fingers. Just in time she got her sword in place, and met the first rider. He was a skillful swordsman, and strong; Paks felt every exchange all the way to her shoulder. From the corner of her eye, she saw the rider she had wounded ride up slowly; he sagged to one side, but still held his weapon.

"Ward of Falk!" she heard from one of the squires.

"Gird!" she called in reply. "Gird and Falk, the High Lord's champions!" Her blade rang on the other's, again and again. The red horse shifted; Paks thrust at the wounded rider, opening a gash on his leg. Now the other; she aimed a slash at his neck. He jerked aside, swinging for her face. Suddenly Esceriel was there, swinging hard at the rider's back. When he turned on Esceriel with that voice of fear, Paks thrust deep in his side. He slid from the saddle; his own horse trampled him. Paks slammed into the wounded rider again, blow after blow, until he, too, lay in the blood-stained snow.

Now the lance-bearer was alone. But he did not flee. He backed his horse a few steps, and swung down his lance, facing Esceriel.

"Get back," said Paks urgently. "Pray, and get back." He stared at her.

A bolt of light shot from the lance, catching Esceriel full in the chest; he fell without a cry. Quick as a snake's tongue, the rider turned the lance on the others, standing in shocked stillness. Paks had already sent the red horse forward in great bounds, but she could not intercept the bolt that struck Garris from the saddle. The lance swung toward her; the rider mouthed the same dread words. Paks called out, and a light sprang from her sword to meet the other; the noise of that meeting shook her ears. Then she was close enough to strike directly.

At the first touch of his weapon on hers, Paks knew she faced one whose powers would test her limits. Back and forth they fought, their horses trampling the snow to a stained rag. Again and again Paks narrowly escaped a killing blow; the pole of the lance was spiked, and she could see that the spikes were poisoned. As the fight went on, she could feel through her legs that the red horse began to tire. Sweat broke out on his neck, and then foam rose in white curds. Yet he turned and twisted beneath her, saving her

918

time after time. The sun rose out of their eyes, and glared from the snow. Then the red horse slipped, skidding down onto one hock. Before he could scramble up, the lance caught Paks between arm and body, and flicked her out of the saddle like a bit of nutmeat from the shell. She landed rolling; somehow the barbed hooks had not caught in the mail, and she was free. The rider laughed, and charged. But she was up, with sword in hand, and the days were long past when a horse running at her could make her freeze. She dodged the point of the lance, and jumped, grabbing the rider's arm with one of hers, while her sword arm swung.

Both of them fell from the running horse, Paks on top as she'd hoped, and the rider lost his grip of the lance in that fall. And before he could resist, she had cut his throat from ear to ear.

It was suddenly very quiet. Paks pushed herself up, feeling the blood chill and dry on her. His blood. Her blood. She shook her head, feeling cold and tired. A few lengths away, Lieth and Suriya held Garris in the snow. They were staring at her, white-faced. Esceriel lay where he'd fallen, to one side.

Paks took a long breath. "Thanks be to Gird and Falk, and the High Lord himself." She wiped the elf-blade on her cloak. Then she walked over to the squires. "Is Garris — ?"

"He's alive," said Suriya. "He breathes — " She bowed her head, fighting back tears.

"You did well," said Paks gravely. "All of you. Are you wounded, Suriya?"

"No, Lady." Her voice was muffled. "And I — I didn't fight — as I should — "

Paks stripped off her bloody gloves and laid a hand on Suriya's shoulder. "Suriya, you did well. Believe me. These were such as most fighters never face. Lieth — how about you?"

The older woman nodded. "Not badly, Lady, but a few cuts from that lance, and from one of the swords."

"I must check Esceriel — Suriya, you come with me, while Lieth stays with Garris. Then I will do what I can for your wounds."

Esceriel lay on his back, arms wide, as he had fallen; he was cold to the touch, but Paks thought she could feel a breath when she bent near.

"Come — we'll carry him over there." She lifted his shoulders, and Suriya picked up his feet.

"Do you know what that was — that light?" asked Suriya.

"In a way. It's an attack these evil ones have, that strikes as lightning out of the sky. Sometimes it kills; it always stuns." Paks laid her hands on Esceriel's face, then Garris's. "They are both alive, but I cannot yet say if they will live. We must get them into shelter, out of the cold; even if I can restore them, they will need rest and warmth." She looked up, startled to hear hoofbeats on the snow, and saw her red horse jogging slowly away. For a moment she was terrified — why would he leave? — but a reassuring nudge to her mind calmed her. She saw far along the frozen stream Lieth's horse standing uncertain and nervous; her own had gone to bring it in. She looked back at Suriya, whose face was less pinched, and told her to unpack the dead horse, and ready the tent.

Paks turned to Lieth. "Lieth, your wounds are serious; those weapons are poisoned. I must try to heal you, before the others, so that you can help Suriya with the tent; we'll need shelter and food." Paks took Lieth's hands in hers and prayed. She could sense the poison in the wounds, slow-acting to sap her strength and cause pain, eventually killing days later. But the High Lord's power entered her, and spread from her to Lieth. When she let Lieth's hands fall, Lieth had regained her color. "How is it?" she asked.

"Well — very well, Lady. It — I've not felt like this since before the king's illness." Lieth got up slowly, and stretched. "Thank you — and the gods — "

Paks turned to Esceriel, who was in worse state than Garris. He had taken the full force of a deliberate attack. She laid her hands on either side of his face, trying to feel what damage had been done. His skin was stiff with cold; he made no response. Paks let herself sink deeper into awareness of him, calling again on the High Lord's power.

When she looked up again, Lieth and Suriya had set up the tent some little distance away. All the horses but her red one were tied to a picket line. A fire crackled in the afternoon light, and something savory bubbled in a pot over it. Beneath her hands, Esceriel's face held slightly more color; he lived, but did not waken. Garris was gone. "We took him inside, and wrapped him up," said Lieth quickly, as Paks looked around. "Suriya's with him now."

Paks nodded. "Come help me with Esceriel." Together they carried him into the tent. Suriya looked up from her place beside Garris.

"Is he better?"

"A little. Not enough." Paks shivered, suddenly feeling the aftermath of the fight and her attempts to heal. Suriya unfastened her blood-drenched cloak, and wrapped a dry one around her shoulders.

"Sit, Lady. I'll bring you something hot." Paks sank down on a pile of bedding, glad enough to rest for a moment. Lieth smiled at her.

"Lady, even if Esceriel dies — even if I die — I am glad to have been here — to have been part of this."

"Why them?" asked Suriya, coming in with a mug of hot soup. Paks wrapped her hands around it and savored the heat. "Why did he strike at Esceriel and Garris? Why not me?"

"If you're asking why not you, Suriya," said Paks, "all I can say is that I asked the same question of my sergeant, my first year in Phelan's Company, and never did like the answer I got. But I think that Liart's priests value physical strength so much that they assume big men are a worse threat than women. He struck at Esceriel and Garris for that."

"And you," reminded Lieth.

"And me — but I have certain protections, as you saw. Unfortunately, I don't yet know all my abilities. Perhaps if I had, none of you would have been touched." Paks shook her head. "But we've no time to spare for such guilt. Tell me, how are the horses?" One pack horse was dead, and the other injured. Two of the squires' horses were injured as well. They had caught two of the attackers' mounts, who seemed ordinary enough, and might do to replace their own. Paks took another long swallow of the soup, and felt its virtue warming her to the toes. Her injured shoulder was stiff, but she had recovered the use of her arm sometime in the fighting. Lieth was checking Garris and Esceriel; both were breathing, but unconscious. Paks and Suriya went to care for the horses.

When they were done, Paks looked back toward the site of the battle. "What did you do with the bodies and their gear?"

"Nothing — should we? We took the horses' tack off where we caught them, and left it."

"Good: you shouldn't handle anything of theirs."

"Do you think we'll have *more* trouble?" Suriya's face paled again. Paks smiled at her.

"More? Certainly we'll have more — but not, I hope, tonight. Suriya, think: already you've met and survived as dire a threat as most Marshals of Gird. And we live, and they are freezing out there — " She waved her arm. "By the grace of Gird, and Falk, and the High Lord, you and I have met trouble — and trouble found us too tough to swallow. Don't fear trouble — be ready for it."

"Yes, Lady." Suriya's eyes came alight again.

"And since we're traveling like this, can you relax enough to call me by my name? My fighting companions have called me Paks since I left home."

"Call you — Paks?" Suriya looked shocked, but pleased. Paks thumped her shoulder. "Yes, call me Paks. It's the best way to get my attention — as you saw, when Esceriel yelled. When you say 'Lady,' I look around to see where she is." Paks looked over the trampled snow, shaking her head. "What a mess. I'll just make sure of them — "

"They're all dead — Lieth looked — "

"I'm sure she did. But they can fool you, beasts and men alike. That priest, for example — " Paks walked over to the lance-bearer, sprawled where she had left him. "The armor may be enchanted. If it is, we can't leave it here for someone to stumble over." She extended the sword; its glow intensified. "See that? Some peril remains. Ask Falk's aid, Suriya, and I will ask Gird's." Paks touched the dead man's armor with her sword. Through the smear of white and gray that had disguised it, black lines emerged, angular designs that conveyed terror and menace. Paks called her light; the designs seemed to burn, then die away to white ash. Then the armor and body fell in, collapsing to a shapeless heap.

"What happened?" Suriya's knuckles were white on her sword hilt.

"The gods helped us prevent trouble," said Paks soberly. "Let's see what else." All the helmets reacted to her sword's touch, as did two of the other corselets, but the men's bodies did not disappear. The wolflike beasts, dead, were simply dead beasts. They dragged them into a pile. Wood from the frozen streambed, caught against the rocks of the falls, provided fuel for a pyre.

921

"Now what?" asked Suriya, when it was alight.

"Now I go find my bow, in case we need it, and then we get cleaned up and see what we can do for Garris and Esceriel."

Paks turned and found that the red horse was already mincing toward her. "Give me a leg up, will you?" She waved as she rode off, enjoying Suriya's open mouth.

She found her bow easily, hanging from a branch, and retrieved her arrows from the body of the beast she'd killed. By the time she was back at their little camp, the sun was already low against the hills.

Despite her prayers, Esceriel died that night without opening his eyes or speaking. Garris, however, recovered enough to wake and look blankly at them before sleeping again. Paks turned away from them, too tired to weep.

"I'm sorry," she said, aware of Lieth and Suriya watching. "I was given no healing for him — but he died bravely."

Suriya nodded. Lieth unfolded a blanket across Esceriel's body, looking long at his face before covering it.

"He was always that way," she said. "He would always do things for others — " She turned her head aside, choking back tears.

Paks reached out and touched her shoulder. "Go on and cry for him, Lieth. The King spoke of him to me, his beloved son that he could not acknowledge, who never sought anything for himself, even a name. He has earned more tears than ours, and more reward than this."

Lieth turned back to her, eyes streaming. "You're tired — you need sleep. Yes — I'll watch. I'll take care. Sleep, Paks." And Paks fell asleep almost instantly, to the sound of the others mourning.

It was broad day when she woke, another clear morning, with frost furring the inside of the tent. There was Esceriel's body, covered with a blanket, and his sword laid across his chest. She could hear voices outside. When she turned her head, she saw Garris's eyes, still a little blank, watching her.

"Lady?" He spoke with difficulty, running his tongue over his lips. Paks remembered that feeling.

"Garris. You're doing well." Paks pushed herself up; she was not as stiff as she'd expected, but she could feel the blows she'd taken. "I'll bring you something."

His head rolled from side to side. "I don't remember. Did I fall off my horse?"

"Among other things, yes."

"Hunh. At my age, to be thrown — "

"What do you remember, Garris?"

His brow furrowed. "We — were at Aliam Halveric's weren't we? Then — we had to leave. In the night. Something — " He shook his head, and moved an arm. "I don't know. I can't remember beyond riding out in the torchlight."

Lieth looked into the tent. "Paks, are you — oh. Garris. Can I bring you something?"

"Anything hot and liquid for Garris. And me, too." Paks stumbled upright. "Gird's arm, I slept as heavy as a hill." She yawned, and pushed off the helmet she had not removed the night before. Her braid thumped her back as it fell.

Lieth came in with two mugs; Suriya followed with bowls. The food and sib smelled delicious. Garris reached for his mug, then looked around and saw the blanket-shrouded form across from him. The hot sib sloshed over his wrist.

"Falk's oath! Is that Esceriel?"

"Yes," said Paks. "It is. Garris, we had a fight yesterday — we were attacked on the trail. You and Lieth were wounded and Esceriel was killed —"

"But I don't — but what — " His hand shook; Paks took the mug from him and set it down.

"Garris, you had a serious wound — that's why you don't remember."

"But I'm all right now — I don't feel any pain — "

"The gods sent healing for you, Garris. Not for Esceriel. I'm sorry." Paks watched the pain on his face. When it turned to anger, she spoke again. "I warned you this was dangerous. I told you that you didn't have to come. You chose that — Esceriel chose that. He chose more — he chose to come to me, when I needed him, and he killed one of them. Then he faced the same weapon that struck you down, and it killed him."

Garris nodded, his eyes filling with tears. "And you could do nothing?"

"No." Paks sighed. She felt slightly affronted; he expected too much of her — she had, after all, fought all of the enemy. She mastered that feeling, and went on. "I prayed for him, Garris, as for you. I was taught in Fin Panir that some brave deeds so delight the High Lord that he calls the warrior at once to his service — as a reward. So I think it was for Esceriel."

"I see." Garris pushed himself up on his elbows, rolled to one side, and took his mug of sib. After several swallows, he looked back at her.

"Will you tell us yet where we're going?"

Paks thought about it. She had not told them at Aliam's, where someone less wise than Aliam might overhear, and mention that name carelessly. And in the woods, that day, she had felt unsure, aware that the woods might hide enemies. But now, with those attackers dead, now surely she could tell them. She nodded. "I will tell you all, before we go on." She turned to see Lieth and Suriya both watching from the entrance. "Come in, both of you — you might as well hear it all at once." Suriya stayed where she could watch outside; Lieth squatted near Paks.

"We have a space of safety, I believe: those attackers are dead, and our enemies have nothing else close to us. So now I will tell you the prince's name, and where we must go. But that name must not be mentioned aloud — not even in the deep woods. Such evil as assailed us has the great forest taig under attack as well; it is broken into many taigin, and in places the fabric is threadbare; we cannot count on the forest to ward us. Enemies can get through — have gotten through — and the little creatures, if no other, may spy on us and pass along our words to each other. More than that, we shall not ride in forest forever; we must pass among the towns of men. There the many agents of evil will have their chance. I have some protection — nothing evil can change my mind or master my tongue — and you share that protection when you are with me — but you must not say the name aloud, or leave my protection once you know it. Do you understand?"

"I will stay with you," Lieth said quickly.

"And I," said Suriya. They both looked at Garris.

"Oh, I'll stay." He shook his head, then grinned at Paks. "Falk's arm, I might as well — how could I ride home alone and miss the rest of this tale. But I feel as I did the night Kieri started us over the Hakkenarsk Pass — it's a cold road ahead, and no sure fires, it seems to me."

"It is indeed," said Paks. "I am honored that you choose to come; alone I would not have much chance on this quest, and I think it worthy enough to cost all our lives if that becomes the choice." She took a deep breath, and glanced from one grave face to another. "Now . . . "

They started off again at an easy pace after noon, having built a mound of rocks over Esceriel's body. Paks had found a good way down to the lower ground, and none of the horses had trouble with the snow-covered rocks. Garris, though pale, insisted he could ride, and was able to saddle his own mount. Lieth and Suriya rode the grays, who were unharmed, and the injured animals carried their light packs.

Day after day they traveled the snowy woods, a journey that seemed to Paks later a strange interlude of peace, despite the dangers and discomforts of such travel in winter. Hour after hour they rode unspeaking, only the crunch of the horses' hooves in snow, and the creak of leather breaking the forest silence. Behind and around them cold stillness lay untouched. The patterns of branches and twigs, the colors of snow and ice seemed to sink deep into her mind. The only warmth was the blazing fire that the squires kindled every night; the only warm colors were the things they carried. That small company, closer with each evening's campfire talk — it was a return to the close-knit companionship she had valued so much as a soldier. Yet not quite a return. For where once that campfire would have been all she knew of light and warmth, now she felt that magical flame within, a light still flickering across the landscapes of her mind, no matter how cold or dark the outer night, how uncertain her vision of what lay ahead. As the squires comforted each other, and looked to her for comfort and guidance, she found herself reaching within, more and more aware of that flame, and what it meant to her.

924

Chapter Twenty-four

They traveled to Vérella with far less difficulty than Paks had feared —
though with far more publicity than she'd hoped. Marshal Pelyan, whom
she'd met on the way to Lyonya, had heard of the quest before their arrival.
Travelers, he said, had brought word as soon as it came to Harway. And he
himself had passed the word on through the granges. So their arrival in
any town caused excitement but not curiosity. Paks enjoyed the crowds of
children that followed them, the flurry when they entered an inn, but
hoped the admiration was not premature. As well, she remembered the
winter before, when she had stumbled into such towns as a hungry
vagrant, whom the children tricked and harrassed instead of cheering.

In each town, they spent the night in grange or field, for Paks wished the
King's Squires to have such protection at night. The Marshals each had a
measure of news or advice; she listened to all. She did not tell them the
prince's name, but she told what she could of the quest so far. The nearer
she came to Vérella, the more recent the news became. In Westbells, just
east of Vérella, Marshal Torin told her that the Duke had been summoned
to the Council. She had not asked, but it seemed Phelan's call to court was of
interest even to a neighboring town.

"What I heard," he said between bites of roast chicken, "was that after
the Marshal-General went up there, and whatever passed between them,
his friends on the Council thought he should come speak for himself. You
know, I suppose, that there was a motion to censure him."

Paks nodded. She had heard about this from the Marshal-General.

"I never thought so bad of him myself," Marshal Torin went on, "for it
seemed to me that if over half my yeomen were killed by treachery, I'd take
risks enough to stop that. But they say by his charter he's bound to have a
hundred fighting men on his lands, and the word was that this was not the
first time he'd left the north unguarded." He ate steadily for a minute, then
put down the bones and wiped his hands. "I can't believe that, or there'd
have been more trouble. Kostvan, who holds south and east of him, has
never complained. But then there was word about how he fought in
Aarenis — even rumors from a Marshal down there, so I hear. And last
year, instead of staying quiet at home, he went haring off to Fintha because
of — " He stopped short and turned dark red. Paks smiled.

"Marshal, he went haring off to Fintha on account of me — and that may have been foolish, but showed a warm heart."

"Warm heart or not, it made some on the Council angry. They'd bid him stay on his lands, and —"

"But his men stayed," put in the yeoman-marshal, a young man who reminded Paks of Ambros in Brewersbridge. "His captains, and all the men — they could have handled any trouble —"

"I didn't say they were right, Keri. I said they were angry."

"Some of them would be angry no matter what he did." The young man's face had flushed. Paks wondered why he was defending Phelan.

"Court gossip, Keri. Nothing to do with us. You can clear now." The Marshal waited until Keri had left the room before saying more. Paks used the interval to ask her squires about their readiness to ride the next day — an unnecessary question, but they answered without surprise.

"You're going to the Council," said the Marshal, when she had dismissed them to rest, and did not wait for her answer. "You'll find them in a flutter, I don't doubt," he said, shaking his head. "That's why I mentioned Phelan — you know him, and he's likely there, and that's why. He's got friends and enemies both on the Council, and until they've settled themselves about him, they're likely to be skittish with you. The thought that Lyonya had sent a paladin to search in Tsaia for an unknown prince — well, you can see how that will suit. Will they have to acknowledge someone as sovereign of a neighboring realm who has been thought base-born here? How if he's a slave, or a servant?"

"He's not," said Paks quietly.

"You know who it is?"

"Yes, but I am not at liberty to say, until I have spoken to him."

"I see. That makes sense." He chewed his lip a moment. "Someone highborn? How could that be, unless — no, I should not ask. You have your own guidance from Gird and the High Lord, and I pray their grace and strength for you. I doubt your task will be easy, even knowing for whom you go."

"Could you tell me," asked Paks, "which of the Council is the right person to approach?"

"Hmmph. Right for what, is the question. As you have dealt with me, so must I deal with you. I have no right to tell you all that the Marshals of Gird suspect about some families on the Council; we have not the proof, and we are bound not to illspeak without it. Yet I would not talk freely with anyone, and certainly not with the Verrakai family. Kostvan is utterly loyal, but has less power. Marrakai — Marrakai has the power, and I believe is loyal, but the Marrakaien have long had a name for secret treachery. Yet you know that the name is not the reality: the real traitor may not have the reputation. Clannaeth is flighty — they say it's his health, but I have a cousin down there who says it's his second wife. Destvaorn is bride-bound to the Marrakaien, but none the worse for that, if the Marrakaien be sound. Konhalt — there's another I'd go clear of; I know nothing against them, but that three times the neighboring grange has had to chase evil things from their hills. The rest are small, of little power compared to these, or closely related. I might speak to Kostvan first, or Destvaorn, and then to Marrakai. Phelan wields power, but not at the moment; your past connection would be suspect there."

Paks got from him the descriptions of these various lords, and committed them to memory. Then she chanced to mention the Verrakai captain she'd met north of the Honnorgat — a Girdsman, he'd said. "Oh, that branch is sound," said the Marshal cheerfully. "I don't wonder you thought him well enough. That's the trouble with some families — and the Verrakaien aren't the only one — you can't tell by the name. Take the Marrakaien, now: true or treacherous, they're all of one brew, and that a heady one. There's naught to choose one from another, barring looks. But others — well, you have dreamers, drunks, daring men and dour men all in one heap, like mixed fruit."

"I'll keep that in mind," said Paks.

Their entry into Vérella was far different from the first time she'd seen the city. The guards at the first gate had heard of her quest; they saw her coming and held traffic (light enough at this season) to pass her through. She had long forgotten the way from the south gates to the court, but the guard sent an escort to guide her, an eager young soldier whose bright face reminded her of all the recruits she'd ever seen.

On horseback, she could see over the parapets of the bridge; the Honnorgat here had a skim of ice even in midstream. At the inner gate, on the north bank of the Honnorgat, a guard captain waited, mounted on a horse decked in the rose and silver of Tsaia; he dismissed the escort, and led them to the court himself. For a little they rode alongside the tall bare wall that Paks remembered, then turned left, and left again, and came to open gates that gave on a wide courtyard. Here they dismounted, at the captain's directions, and liveried grooms led the horses away. Paks warned the groom assigned to her horse, and the horse trailed him without a hand on his reins.

"Lady Paksenarrion," said the captain, with a low bow, "I have orders to convey you at once to the Regency Council, if you are not too fatigued with your journey." His voice conveyed the secure belief that they would indeed be too fatigued.

Paks returned the bow. "Not at all. It is in answer to Gird's call that I seek the Regency Council; it cannot be too soon."

To her surprise, the captain reddened slightly. "Well — ah — Lady — the council assumed you would wish to take refreshment, whenever you came, and — in fact — they are in session now. But when they come forth, I am sure — "

Paks followed the pressure she felt. "By your leave, Captain, I would not intrude, but by the gods' commands. If you will, guide us to the Council, and make known to them that I would see them."

"They know you're coming — " he blurted, completely flustered.

927

"Yes, but not when — nor exactly what I have come for. Sir, the matter is urgent — " She felt this intensely, as if every moment now mattered. "I believe they will agree on the necessity for this, when I give my message."

"Well, Lady — " Clearly he did not know how to argue with a paladin on quest. Paks smiled at him.

"Come, Captain; take me to the Council, and let them decide if they have time. We do no good standing here in the cold."

At that he bowed, and led the way across the courtyard. The three squires followed Paks closely. She noticed, even in that rapid walk, how different this court was from that in Chaya. Fluted columns of pinkish stone supported a portico on three sides, and rose to frame a pointed arch opposite the gate. Above were walls ornamented with half-pillars separating pointed windows, several rows of them, up to the fretwork of stone that hid the roofs from those below. A lacework of frost or snow glittered from every roughness of the stone, making the palace shimmer with the rose and silver of Tsaia. Suddenly, from far over their heads, a sweet powerful clamour broke out. For a moment Paks could not think what it might be: then she remembered the Bells. The captain turned to her, speaking through the sound.

"You have heard our Bells before, Lady?"

"No." Paks could not say they were beautiful; she wanted only to listen. In the song they were gold, "the golden bells of Vérella"; she wondered if they truly were. The captain talked on, heedless.

"The elves gave them, when Vérella was founded. To look at they are pure gold, but of course they cannot be all gold, for it would not stand the beating. But the elves had them cast, and their voices are sweet to hear." His last words rang loud; the Bells had ceased.

"How often do they ring?"

"It depends on the Council. Always at true dawn, as the elves have it, and sunfall, and at midday when the Council is sitting. And for any festival, of course: Midwinter, Summereve, Torre's Eve, High Harvest, Gird's Victory — for those."

They had come to steps leading up to tall doors under the arch. Guards in rose and silver nodded to the captain and he led them in. Here the floor was set with polished blocks of silver-gray stone. Paks looked around the wide hall; wide stairs rose ahead of her, where the hall narrowed to a passage still wider than the main room in a cottage. To right and left were tall doors folded back to reveal great empty rooms opening into other rooms. Tapestries hung on the walls; the lamp sconces were polished silver. The captain had paused for a moment, looking around. Paks saw a youth in a green tunic with red piping over red hose — Marrakai colors, if her memory served — come into the room on the left. The captain hailed him.

"Pardon, Kirgan — is the Council still sitting?"

The young man — a squire, Paks was sure, though the title was that of eldest son — nodded. "Yes, Captain. Why?" Paks saw his eyes rake over her and return to the captain's face.

928

"It's this — Lady Paksenarrion, a paladin. She is on quest, and must speak with the Council, she says."

"At once?" The boy's eyebrows rose, and he met Paks's gaze with surprising composure.

"I must ask them to hear me," said Paks quietly. "It is in their power to refuse."

He laughed shortly. "They will hardly refuse to hear a paladin, I daresay. It's better than what they have been hearing — "

"Sir!" The captain's tone chilled.

The boy's face reddened. "I beg your pardon," he said formally. "I spoke as ill befits a squire."

"If you will follow me," said the captain, turning to Paks. She nodded, but watched the boy's face stiffen as the captain snubbed him.

"I took no offense, Kirgan," she said to him.

She and the Lyonyan squires followed the captain through two large rooms and down a wide passage to a deep alcove. Here four guards in rose and silver stood before doors inlaid with silver and enamel. The captain spoke to them softly, in a dialect Paks did not recognize. One of them stood aside, and the captain knocked softly at the doors.

At once they were opened slightly from inside. The captain conferred with someone. Paks was aware of tension in the room beyond: it seeped out the open door like a cold draught. Then a louder voice spoke from within, an order, and the captain turned to Paks, clearly surprised.

"They will hear you now," he said.

"Thank you, Captain, for your guidance and help." Paks walked forward; the guards stood aside from the doors, now opened wide. She felt rather than saw the Lyonyan squires following.

Within was a room smaller than those they had passed, well-lit by high windows on both sides. At the far end an empty throne loomed on a dais; on either side were tiered seats behind a sort of fence, rising up to the base of the windows. These were nearly empty, though a few squires lounged there, and — Paks squinted a moment against the light of the top tier — two elves. Taking up most of the floor space was a massive table of dark wood, heavily carved and inlaid with silver. Around this sat the lords she had come to see: the Regency Council of Tsaia. In the seat below the throne, the crown prince, who would be king by Summereve. Paks thought he looked man-grown already. His brother, younger by almost three years, sat to one side: he had no place on Council, and looked as bored as any youth locked into adult discussions of policy when he had rather be hunting. At the prince's left, a burly man in green and red, who reminded Paks of the boy outside: that was Duke Marrakai. Duke Mahieran, in red and silver. Baron Destvaorn, in blue and red. Kostvan in green and blue. Verrakai — she let her eyes linger a moment on Verrakai — in blue and silver. Sorrestin in blue and rose. Clannaeth in yellow and rose. And alone at the near end of the table, facing her now, Phelan in his formal dress: maroon and white. He smiled at her, then moved to one side so that she could approach the table.

The man who had opened the door, a silver-haired old man in the royal livery, announced her.

"Lady Paksenarrion, Paladin of Gird."

Paks bowed toward the prince.

"Your highness, lords of the Council: I thank you for your courtesy in thus allowing me an audience."

The crown prince spoke quickly. "It is our honor, Lady, to receive any paladin in this Court. Pray tell us how we may aid your quest."

"I will be brief." Despite herself, her eyes slid a little toward Duke Phelan. She almost thought she could feel the sword's desire to come to him. "You already know, I believe, that the king of Lyonya died without an heir of the body." They nodded. "I was called to that court, to Chaya, as paladins are called, but not, alas, to heal the king. Instead I bore unknowing a treasure of that realm: this sword." She pulled back her cloak; they peered at the sword hilt. Duke Phelan, as the others, merely looked puzzled.

"What sword is that?" asked the High Marshal into the brief silence that followed. Paks was sure he had already heard the tale, but she merely answered him.

"According to the testimony of lords in Chaya who remember, and the elves themselves, it was made for the son of King Falkieri — the older brother of this king, whose wife and son were lost while traveling to the Ladysforest. Because I bore the sword, the king — the one who lay dying — thought perhaps the gods meant me to take the throne after him, and so he spoke. But this, too, was not the quest for which I was called."

"He would have given his kingdom to *you*?" That was Verrakai. Paks could feel the scorn from where she stood. "To a — a — commoner? A peasant's child?"

From the corner of her eye, Paks saw Duke Phelan's face whiten with rage; before she could speak, the prince did.

"Peace, Verrakai. Gird chose her paladin; whatever her past, she has been given abilities that would grace any throne. And we will not have any guest insulted at this table." He smiled at Paks. "You will forgive Duke Verrakai's surprise, Lady? Those of us who live in the midst of families graced with every talent may find it difficult to credit such talents elsewhere." Paks thought she caught a bite of sarcasm in that; so did Verrakai, who first paled then reddened.

She bowed. "Your highness, I can take no offense for truth spoken. I am a commoner, a sheepfarmer's daughter, and I found the thought of myself on a throne as outlandish as Duke Verrakai might wish. Indeed, that is not my destiny, nor do I seek it. But the dying king, loving his land much, thought a paladin might bring peace — that I can understand. And his lords, your highness, loving their land and peace more than pride, would have agreed." She waited a moment for that to sink in; some of the Council found it hard to believe, by their expressions.

"Instead of that, I was called to search for the rightful king. By bringing this sword where its true nature could be known — by tracing its history carefully — by searching for the man who was once the prince of Lyonya — by all these means I am to find the rightful heir to that throne and return him to his place. In warrant of this, I am accompanied by these King's Squires of Lyonya, who will witness the identity of the man, when we find him, and escort him to Chaya."

"Only three?" That was the younger prince, now listening alertly.

"Four began the quest with me," said Paks. "One died. We have been beset by evil powers, lords, who do not want the rightful king found."

"How will you know?" asked the High Marshal again.

"By this sword." Paks laid her hand on the pommel; it felt warm to her touch. "It was made for the prince, partially sealed to him in its forging. Had the journey they were on been complete, it would have been completely dedicated to him, and no one else could have drawn it. But that did not happen; the journey was never finished. So I have used it, and so have others — but according to the elves, who made it, it will still acknowledge its true master when he draws it."

"And where did you get it?" asked Verrakai, still sour.

"From Duke Phelan," said Paks.

"That thief — " muttered Verrakai. Paks heard it clearly. She laughed.

"Thief?" she repeated. "Not unless he took it as a babe in arms. It was lost from Lyonya over forty-five years ago. He was given it, Duke Verrakai, by Aliam Halveric of Lyonya, who had found it near a dead elf in the forest."

"So he says." Verrakai's insistent distaste was not mellowing.

"So also the elves themselves say," said Paks. "Aliam Halveric told the elves when he'd found it; they did not ask its return, but told him to give it to the one for whom it was made. They thought he knew what sword it was; alas, the elves have trouble remembering the brevity of human lives, and that he had been too young to see the sword at court."

"But then — " The crown prince's voice topped a sudden burst of talk; it stilled, and he went on. "But then the elves knew — they knew who the prince was? Why didn't they simply say?"

"And how did they know?" asked the High Marshal, with a sharp look at the two elves who sat high in the tiers.

"You will remember that Falkieri's queen was elven; the prince was half-elven. It seems that when the tragedy occurred, everyone assumed the boy had been killed. Instead, he was stolen away — beyond the seas, the elves think, since they could have sensed his presence anywhere in these realms."

"Even in Pargun or Kostandan?" asked Duke Marrakai.

"I am not sure, my lord."

"Yes," came a silvery elven voice from the seats above. "Anywhere in these realms or Aarenis, Duke Marrakai, elves could have found him."

"So you see," Paks went on, "the elves also thought him dead, when they could not sense him. Then some years later, he returned to Lyonya: how, I

931

do not know. But elves found him there, fairly quickly, and — "

"And did nothing? Do you ask me to believe that?" Verrakai led the rush of noise that followed. Paks waited until the room quieted; this time the prince had let them talk themselves out.

"The elves said," Paks went on, "that the prince had been treated so badly that he had no remembrance of his past. He knew nothing of his name, his family, or his elven blood. They found him so damaged that they feared he had none of the taig-sense left; they feared to try any intervention lest they damage him further."

"And so they did nothing." The crown prince's voice was calm.

"Not quite nothing, your highness. They watched. Remember that at that time, the prince's younger sister was alive and well — "

"But now," said the crown prince, "Lyonya has no king, and no clear heir, and the elves want a part-elven ruler. Is that the meat of it?"

"Not quite. They do not want this man to rule unless he's fit for it — and they doubt his fitness." Paks waited for the silence. Then she spoke. "I do not doubt it."

"What!" The crown prince leaned forward; all of them stared. "You know — you *know* who it is?"

"I do."

"Then why haven't you said? Why this nonsense about a quest?" Verrakai again, sneering.

"Because, my lord, I have not been granted leave to speak by the gods — or by the king himself. What, would you have me place an innocent man in danger, by blurting his name out for the world to play with? Already one King's Squire is dead, killed by a priest of Liart, to prevent my finding him. Already the powers of evil in Lyonya are massing to keep him from the throne. Suppose I had said his name openly, from the time I first suspected who it would be — would he be alive this day, to take the sword and test his heritage?"

"Well said," said the High Marshal. "Well said, indeed."

"I came here," said Paks, more quietly, "to tell the Council of Tsaia that my quest leads me into your realm. I must go where the quest leads, but in all courtesy, I ask your leave to travel as I must."

"Is he here?" asked the crown prince. "In Tsaia?"

"He is," said Paks, weighing the danger of that admission.

"Can you tell us now who it is?"

"No. Not at the moment, your highness. I must ask Duke Phelan some questions about the sword's history in his house: who handled it, and how."

"We all have questions for Duke Phelan," said Verrakai. "I hope, Lady Paksenarrion, that his answers to your questions are more to the point than his answers to mine."

The crown prince shot a glance at Verrakai that silenced him. Then he smiled at Paks. "We shall defer our questions until you are through, Lady Paksenarrion. A paladin's quest — and such a quest — is a matter of more moment than the Duke's response to matters of law." He rose, and the others rose with him. With a bow, he led them from the room, through a door Paks had not noticed behind the throne. The squires in the tiers followed, and the two elves climbed down to stand near Paks and Duke Phelan.

"Are you certain, Lady, of the rightness of your judgment?"

"I am certain, sir elf, of the rightness of the gods' commands; my own judgment is not at issue."

"Be joyous in your certainty, paladin of Gird," said one of the elves, eyes flashing.

"I hope you are right, indeed," said the other, "for I would see no fires rage in the forests of Lyonya, as have raged in other lands." He turned to the other elf. "Come cousin — we shall know all soon enough; we might as well leave the paladin to her work." And with a bow, the elves also withdrew.

Meanwhile, Duke Phelan had recognized Garris, and come to grip his arm. "Garris — by the gods, so this is where you ended up. King's Squire — a good place for a good man."

"Well, my lord, I — " Garris struggled with his knowledge and the Duke's ignorance.

"You can't my lord me, Garris. Not when we were boys together. Have you told Paks here about all our scrapes?" Phelan turned to Paks, grinning. "Garris was a year or so younger than I, Paks, at Aliam Halveric's, and I got him in more trouble — "

"That's not what I heard," said Paks.

"It's true enough," said the Duke. "But come — let's sit down. Have you been here long? When did you arrive? I had heard nothing until I came to Vérella, where I found word that the king of Lyonya was dead, and you were coming here on quest."

"We have just come, my lord," said Paks, settling gingerly into the chair Duke Verrakai had vacated. "We rode this morning from Westbells."

"Have you had any refreshment? I can certainly have someone bring — "

"No, my lord. Please. We shall have time enough after."

He gave her a long look. "So. It is that urgent, eh? Well, then, Paks, ask what you will, and as I know, I will answer."

Paks began with what she knew of the sword's history, and the Duke nodded. He affirmed what Aliam Halveric had said of the sword when he took it. Without prompting, he spoke of his vow to Tammarrion.

"You see, she had been — was — a soldier, as I was, and she was not giving that up." The Duke glanced quickly at Lieth and Suriya. "You will understand that. So I felt — in giving her a sword — that it would be but courtesy to promise it would always be hers alone."

"What happened when she first drew it?" asked Paks.

"It showed a blue light, much as any magic sword may. Not as bright as when you draw it, Paks, but Tamar was not a paladin. Though as one who loved and served Gird to her death, she might well have been."

"Did anyone else in your household draw it?"

"No. Not that I know of. Tamar was proud of it, and no wonder. Little Estil — our daughter, that was killed — she wanted to, but I remember Tamar saying she'd have to grow into it."

"And even after her death — "

"No. Someone took it and cleaned it, when they found — found them." His voice shook an instant, then steadied. "By the time I came north again, she was in the ground, and it was back in its scabbard, lying across her armor, for me to see. I hung it on the wall, where you found it, Paks, and there it stayed until you took it. I don't think that it would have suffered Venneristimon to mishandle it."

"No, my lord, I don't think so." Paks sighed. She hardly knew what to do; she could feel the stiffness of the squires, waiting for her to do — what? Tell him? Hand him the sword? What? She looked at his face; it was more peaceful than she'd seen it before. Was that peace a kind of defeat? But no — his eyes still held fire enough, and his hands and voice were firm. Now that she knew, she thought she could see the shape of elven blood — not as much as expected, but there. And for a man of fifty, he was remarkably lithe and young. Beside her, Suriya stirred, her cloak rustling a little.

"My lord," she began again, "What do you remember of your childhood?" The Duke's eyes widened. "What!" An instant later he had shoved his chair back, and was standing, pale of face. "You don't — Paks — no." He put a hand to the chair; color seeped back into his face. "I understand. You want to help me, do something for me, but — "

"My lord, please." Paks forced his attention. "Please answer."

"Nothing good," he said grimly. "And you cannot be right in what you surmise."

"I can't?" Paks surprised herself with the tone of her voice. "My lord, I ask you to listen and think of this: the elves, when they heard from Aliam Halveric that he had the sword, told him to give it to the prince. And when he replied that he was giving it to you, they said it was well enough. They erred in thinking that Aliam knew the sword and its properties. But they knew that he suspected who you were."

"Aliam?" Now the Duke's face was white; he clung to the chair with both fists. "He *knew*? Aliam?"

"He suspected, my lord, and had no proof, nor any way to find some. And your sister was betrothed, soon to be crowned."

He shook his head, breathing hard. "I trusted him — Aliam — he said — "

"He said that he did not think your parentage could be proven, or your place restored; indeed, that's what he thought at the time. He was not sure; he had been too young when it happened, and he dared not ask anyone." Paks had feared his wrath with Aliam more than anything, but he was already nodding his head slowly as she spoke.

"I can understand. A boy with no background — what could he say? And my memories — so few, so far back. But — " He looked at Paks again. "Are you sure, Paks? Are you certain it's not your regard for an old commander?"

"My lord, it is not my thought only. I have talked to Aliam Halveric, and to elves of high degree — "

"And why didn't they — ?" The Duke stopped in mid-sentence, his voice chopped off from a rising cry. His hand dropped again to the chair. "Because I was unfit — am unfit — "

"No, my lord. You are not."

"I am. Paks, you know — you have seen — and Lyonya requires abilities I don't have — if ever I did."

"My lord, you are half-elven, with abilities scarce less than the elves, but constrained by a mortal life. I believe you have them still, buried by what you have endured. Why else would the High Lord and Gird have sent me to find you? Would they choose an unfit king?"

"No — "

"And if they can make a paladin out of me, my lord, after all that happened, they can make a good king out of you."

"Perhaps." The Duke sat again, pulling his chair to the table so suddenly that its legs scraped loudly on the floor. "So — you are sure, and the elves are sure, that I am a prince born, and the rightful heir to Lyonya's throne. Is anyone else convinced?"

"Aliam Halveric."

"And any others?"

"We have not used your name, my lord, for fear that evil would come on you before I could reach you. But the lords of Lyonya, gathered together after the king's death, agreed to accept the sword's evidence. The elves had admitted that the prince lived, and might be found. I think most of the lords, if not all, will accept you." She watched him; his eyes had fallen to the table, where he traced some of the silver inlay with his forefinger.

"It would be a matter for laughter, if I could laugh," said the Duke quietly, "that I am born a prince, and of better birth than those lords who have scorned me as a bastard mercenary. They were so sure of my lack — as was I, most times — and now — " His finger paused; he looked up at Paks. "You assume, Paks, that I *want* to be king."

"No, my lord. I only know that you are the rightful king, and must be."

"Hmmph." His gaze went past her to meet each of the squires. "Garris — Lieth — Suriya — if Paks is right, then I am your king. But I must say this, however it seems to you. Many years have gone by since I was a lost and lonely boy, tramping the fields of Lyonya looking for work. Aliam Halveric took me in, taught me my trade of war, taught me respect for the gods, and what I know of right and wrong. Garris, you knew me then — you know what sort of boy I was. Did you ever think I might be a prince?"

Garris blushed. "My lord — sir — I thought you were special, then — you know I did."

"As a younger boy to an elder, yes. But birth?"

"Well, my lord — you *acted* like a prince — "

The Duke's mouth curled in a smile. "Did I? I was trying to act like Aliam, as I recall. But what I mean is this. I had nothing when I came to

935

Aliam. He gave me my start — as you all know, I'm sure. But from there, I made it myself. That land in the north — my stronghold — that is mine. My money, yes, but more than that. I built some of that wall myself; barked my own knuckles on that stone; left some of my blood on the hills when we fought off the orcs. Years of my life — dreams — Tamar and I, planning things. My children were born there, in that chamber you saw, Paks, the night we talked with the Marshal-General. I fought in Aarenis, yes — for that's where the money was, the contracts that let me improve my own lands. The money for that mill came from Aarenis, the food I bought all those years before the fields were large enough. Stock for farmers, fruit-trees for Kolya. But what I cared for — what I gave my heart to — was that land, and those people. My people — my soldiers." His fist was clenched now, on the table before him. "Now I find I'm a prince, with another land, and other people. But can I leave this, that I have made? Can I leave the hall where Tamar ate, and the courtyard where our children played? Can I leave those who helped me, when they knew nothing of princes or kingdoms, only a young mercenary captain who dreamed of his own lands? Already this year they have endured one upheaval. Those that stayed are *mine*." He looked from face to face. "Can you understand this?"

Paks felt the tears stinging her own eyes. When Garris spoke, she heard the emotion there. "My lord, I understand. You were always that way — even at Aliam's, you would take responsibility. Of course you care for them — "

Suriya had pushed back her chair, and gone around Paks to stand beside the Duke. When he glanced up at her, she spoke. "Sir king, if you were unfit to be our king you could not have spoken so. I am most junior of your squires, but by your leave, I will not leave you until you sit in your own throne."

The Duke's face furrowed. "By the gods, Suriya, were you listening at all? I am not sure I want this!"

"Sir king, on Falk's oath I swear, you will be king, and until that day I will ward you." Paks had never seen Suriya like this, completely calm and certain. She smiled at Paks. "Lady, you told us we would have a king worthy of our service; so I find him. If he cannot find his heart in this yet, it will come, and I will await it."

"Gird's grace rest on your service, Suriya," said Paks. And to the Duke, "My lord — or should I say, sir king — I believe it is the gods' will that you take this crown. Surely if you follow their will, good will come even to your lands in the north."

"Think you so? Think you so indeed? It would not be the first time a man has followed what he thinks is the gods' will, and had things go ill indeed."

"You mean your wife's death," said Paks bluntly. "My lord, that was not the gods' will, but Achrya's; I believe her plan was laid longer than you have yet realized. Do you think you were stolen away by chance? Do you recall the words of her agent that night, when she said you were not born a duke?"

936

"Yes." The Duke sighed heavily. "Damn. All those years I worried because I did not know who my father was, and now — " He looked at his closed fist and opened it deliberately. He sighed again, and looked up at Suriya. "You are right, of course, as is Paksenarrion. If I am Lyonya's king — though to my mind that's not yet proven — then I must *be* the king; I cannot sulk on my own estates, and leave Lyonya to suffer evil." Paks felt the tension ease; Garris and Lieth moved from her side to the Duke's without a word. He smiled at them. "So — you would leave Paks unwarded? I assure you, squires, I am in no peril here."

"Paksenarrion is a paladin, and well fit to guard herself," said Lieth. "Though when she goes out alone, one of us will go with her, by your leave."

"Indeed so," said the Duke, as Paks still thought of him. "Until this is settled, I wish that. But now what?" he asked Paks. "Your test is that sword, is it not? Should I draw it here, or before the Council, or in Chaya? What is your word?"

"I do not know," said Paks. "You know more of statecraft than I: here are three witnesses to speak of what happens. Do we need more? I think you should not travel without testing it; the sword will be a mighty weapon for your defense, once you have held it."

"And will leave you swordless," he said, with a small smile. Paks shrugged. "No," he said, "we must find you another weapon; I will not have a paladin of Gird unweaponed for my sake. Let me think. The prince should know as soon as anyone. His father granted my steading, and was my friend; I would have sworn allegiance to this boy with all my heart. Indeed," he went on, with a broader grin, "it's as well you came when you did, Paks. They were urging me to swear now — before his coronation this summer — as proof of my loyalty. And so I might have done, and been bound by that oath, if you had not come in. For I tell you I had no reason to do otherwise."

"Sir king — " began Garris tentatively.

"Garris, you must not call me that — any of you — until the sword proves me so. Please. Your service I accept, but we must observe the courtesies of this court as well. Paks, it must be before them all, I think: the whole Council. To do otherwise would arouse suspicion. Then if it fails — "

"It won't," said the squires at once.

"If," the Duke repeated firmly, "then all will know, and will also know that I made no secret trials. Paks, if you will speak to the lords yourself, it will be better. The prince has no vote, but the Council defers to his wishes where it can; he will determine the hour."

"As soon as may be," said Paks.

"As he wills," said the Duke. "You will find him certain of mind. As were all of us, at nearly twenty."

"How shall we explain the service of the King's Squires?" asked Paks, thinking how it would look to have the Duke trailed by those green-and-gold tunics.

937

"You asked them to look over some scrolls — old accounts — I had brought with me. I have brought the Company Rolls, at the Council's request. Will that do?"

"Certainly." Paks rose, with the Duke, and preceded him to the door. Outside, the elderly man who had announced her waited. "Sir, might I ask an audience with the prince?"

"With the crown prince, Lady?" he asked.

"Yes."

"Come with me, then. Is Duke Phelan free to meet with the Council?"

"Sir, I have asked him to look up something from his records; the squires go with him to take notes. By the time I have spoken to those other lords I must see, perhaps he will be free."

The man bowed. "I will inform the Council, Lady." He called to a page, and gave that message to be taken to all the lords in turn.

Chapter Twenty-five

The crown prince received her in his private chambers; Paks found herself face to face with a tall, self-assured young man of nearly twenty. He waved her to a seat with grave courtesy, and handed her a delicate rose-colored cup of some hot, aromatic liquid.

"I know you are used to sib," he said as she tasted it. "This is brewed from two of the herbs in sib, and another from the far southwest mountains. I like it better, but there is sib in this pot if you don't. They tell me you did not stop even to take refreshment."

"No, your highness. I could not delay."

"And then you asked Duke Phelan some questions, and now you wish to speak with me. I assure you, Lady, that I am too young to have knowledge you need."

Paks cocked her head. "I think you do know what I need, your highness. May I tell you?" He nodded, and Paks finished the drink before going on. "I think that Lyonya's king is in your court at this time. For his safety and reputation, the sword's test should be conducted openly, before your Council."

"He is *here*? Not merely in Tsaia, but in my court — and you know who it is? Whatever you asked Duke Phelan, then, confirmed your knowledge. Perhaps you asked who had come with him?" Paks had not thought to ask that, but the prince seemed not to notice. "It must be someone he knows — a captain of his, or — " He stopped short. "You are not saying it is — "

"I am not saying anyone, your highness, at this time."

His eyes were bright, watching her. "No — you aren't saying, but I have wits enough to guess, I think. Gird's cudgel, this will stir the Council." He laughed, a boy's clear open laugh, and poured her another cup. His face sobered. "And give us a problem, as well. The north — "

"Your highness, I pray you, do not speak of it until the time."

"Oh, very well. But you want a Council session, and it must be before we resume our previous business. You may not be aware that certain lords have been asked to swear their allegiance directly to me even before the coronation. In this case — " his lips twitched, but he controlled the smile, "it might prove inconvenient to your purpose." He poured another cup for himself. "So. A Council session called on special business. The High Marshal will support me there. You will want it as quickly as possible? Yes.

939

Tomorrow morning, then: it will take several hours to arrange, and tonight, as you no doubt recall, is the feast of Luap. We will all be in the grange hall until late, for the High Marshal is knighting a score of youths."

Paks had forgotten about the feast of Luap. "It could not be put off?" His eyes widened. "Luap's feast? The knighting? Gods, no. Relatives of these boys have traveled days to be here. Not if a dragon sat smoking in the inner court. If you have concern about the — ah — person, I can assign guards, though — "

"No, your highness. Only if anyone asks, could you explain that the King's Squires are looking into the Company Rolls for a name?"

He nodded. "That I can do, and will, right gladly. Now, if you'll excuse me, I will summon the High Marshal on this matter we spoke of."

Paks rose quickly and bowed. "Is there aught I can do, your highness, to help with this?"

"I think not. You will confirm your request, of course, to any lord who asks you — but I think they will not ask." He nodded, and Paks withdrew, to find a page ready to escort her back to the rooms she'd been assigned.

Once there, she found Lieth in attendance; her things had been unpacked, and a hot bath was ready for her.

"I thought — " Paks began, but Lieth smiled and put a finger to her lips. "With Garris to look, and Suriya to keep notes, they didn't need me. Here, Lady, let me take that mail." Lieth set it aside, and helped Paks strip off the last of her clothes and climb into the tub. "And I thought," she said very softly, "that you would want no one else near the sword. I chased two chambermaids out of here when I came."

"Thank you, Lieth," said Paks. The hot scented water was delightful; she felt she could acquire a taste for bathing this way. When she was done, Lieth handed her a robe of heavy rose-colored wool that had been warming by the fire. Paks put it on, wrinkling her nose at the silver clasps. "A rich house, the Mahierian," she commented.

"Yes," said Lieth shortly. She went to the door of the next room, and gestured. Two maids came through. "They've set a meal out in there," said Lieth. "Will you come?" She had already gathered the armor; Paks took the sword, and followed Lieth, leaving the maids to clear away the bath things.

The meal of sliced breads, cold meats, and fruit was spread on a round table beneath a narrow window. In this room as well a fire crackled on a clean stone hearth. Yet another room opened from it, this with a narrow canopied bed. Paks sat down with an appetite.

"Come eat, Lieth, unless you've had something in the meantime," she said.

"Thank you." Lieth sat across from Paks. For awhile they ate silently, each thinking her own thoughts. When Paks finished, and sat back, she found Lieth watching her.

"What's wrong, Lieth?" Paks hoped Lieth had not taken a dislike to the Duke. Her first words fed that fear.

"I came to serve the king," she began slowly. "I knew nothing of him, but that you knew who he was."

"Yes?" prompted Paks, when she said nothing more for a moment.

"I am glad to have seen him. I don't know what I was expecting, but not that — and it's better than I expected." She stopped again; this time Paks merely looked her question. Lieth shook her head, answering something Paks did not ask — perhaps a question in her own mind. "I am a King's Squire," she said finally. "A Lyonyan. A Knight of Falk. Here, in Tsaia, among Girdsmen, with my king unknown and disregarded, I am out of place. Lady, if I heard in Lyonya what I have heard this day, I would know how to answer — " Her hand had crept to her sword. "But I am a stranger. I have no rights at this court."

"Lieth, what is it? What are you angry about?"

"Paks, do you know how many enemies the ki — the Duke has?"

Paks frowned. "No. Some, but not so many, I'd thought."

"Then they must all be here. Verrakai — I had words with one of his squires, and a servant or so — "

"Words?" Paks was startled. Lieth had seemed the most placid of the King's Squires.

"Just words — so far. They had plenty to say about the Duke, and all of it bad. That your coming here today was his doing, to avoid swearing an oath of loyalty to the prince. That you were no true paladin — and that I argued, telling them I'd seen you fight myself — but they would not believe. They think their lord has a witness who will make it obvious that you and the Duke are both liars and traitors."

Paks felt a chill down her spine. "I wonder how, since we're not. Did Garris and Suriya hear any of this?"

"I don't think so. They're with him; I was looking for your rooms."

"Anything from the the royal servants?"

"No, not really. Some think the Duke's wild and uncanny, but none seem to harbor any malice. But the Verrakai weren't all. I ran into the whole group together: Konhalt, Clannaeth, a Sorrestin page, and the Verrakai. They were eager to tell me the worst they knew of the Duke — and of you."

"That could be bad indeed," said Paks placidly. She did not fear Lieth's opinion.

"It was bad to hear," said Lieth grimly. "Girdsmen. I'd have thought even Girdsmen would have more respect for a paladin."

"Even Girdsmen?"

Lieth flushed. "Lady, your pardon. It was unseemly."

Paks shook her head. "Lieth, these may not have been Girdsmen. While you are here, try not to remember all you were told of Girdsmen by the Falkians, eh? I'm a Girdsman."

"Yes — I know. I'm sorry, truly." She looked suddenly worried. "Is he?"

"The Duke? No. But his wife was."

"And she is dead. He must marry again. Will he, do you think?"

Paks thought a moment. "Lieth, if he has given his word, he will do more; he is that kind of man. He has said he will take the kingdom; I daresay he knows what that means, and will do more than his duty. But I am not one to speak of kings' weddings."

"You spoke to the crown prince?"

"Yes."

"And what is he like, may I ask? Will he be an ally of Lyonya?"

"He seemed nice enough." Paks did not know how to explain that she could sense only strong evil and good — not the average mixture most men carried. As well, she had no experience of princes. If he had been a recruit or a squire, she would have been well-pleased with him, but as a prince she had to hope the same qualities would serve.

They were interrupted by a polite knock on the outer door. Lieth rose at once to answer it; Paks waited at the table. Lieth came back with a curious expression on her face.

"It's a boy — he wants to see you. He says he knows you."

"Knows me?" Paks looked down at herself quickly; she couldn't receive anyone in a bathrobe, even with silver clasps. But Lieth was already handing her a clean undershirt.

"Here — says he's a young Marrakai. Aris Marrakai — did you ever meet such a one?"

Paks remembered the boy she'd met her first night in Fin Panir — and often thereafter. "Aris — yes. Fourth son, I think. Thanks." She looked at the mail and decided against it, pulling on her swordbelt over her clothes instead. Then she went through to the front room.

Aris had grown even taller, and looked much older in his squire's livery, the dark green and blue of Kostvan House, piped in the red and green of his father's colors. His black hair was longer, cropped just below his ears, but he had no facial hair. He stood stiffly by the door until Paks was halfway across the room, then grinned as widely as ever.

"Paks! I mean, Lady Paksenarrion — I'm sorry. But they said — and I kept telling them you would come back. You look — " He paused, examining her with his head cocked. "Fine," he finished. "But don't you have mail? Silver mail?"

Paks found herself laughing; even Lieth was smiling. "I have mail, Aris, but even paladins take it off now and then."

"Oh." He looked crestfallen. "I was hoping — when Juris, that's my brother who's Kirgan, said he'd seen you today, I wanted to come — and then I could say I saw it, you see?"

"I see. You wanted to make an impression on the other squires, eh?"

Aris blushed as red as the clothes he had worn that first night. "Well, Paks — Lady Paksenarrion — it's like this — "

"You're the youngest squire," said Paks inexorably, "and they tease you, and when you told them about your three estates someone pounded you, didn't they?"

"Yes, but — "

"And you think this will get you out of some scrape?"

"You didn't used to be like this," said Aris.

"No, and you used to be a little boy. Now you're a young man, not my pet brother. You are the fourth son of a powerful Duke, and you should have better things to think about than impressing other squires by claiming acquaintance with a paladin."

Aris nodded. "I'm sorry."

"I'm not. I'm glad you came to see me, and if the others think it's because you're a vain young boy trying to shine by reflection, perhaps they won't pay too much attention to you."

"What?"

"Aris, listen. I know you've wits enough in that head." With that he stood still again, eyes gleaming. Paks went on. "Yes, indeed. As someone told me recently, Marrakaien are all one brew, and that a heady one. I'll tell you what, young Marrakai — you keep your wits about you and you'll have something to hold up your head about — and I'll see that it's known."

"Can I do something for you? Really? What can I do?"

"I want to know the extent of the division in the Council — who opposes your father on what issues, and why, if you know."

"Oh. Right now?"

"If you have anything to tell. But come into the next room; you can take a look at my mail, and have something to drink."

Once seated at the table, Aris recovered his usual ebullience, and told Paks what he knew of Council business with expressions that had Lieth on the edge of laughter. Paks did not correct him, for she wanted his first impressions, scurrilous though they were.

"Part of it's the Red Duke," he said, coming to what interested Paks without any prompting at all. "They call him the fox, and I can see why. Oh — that's right — you know him. Well, then, you know what I mean. My father says it's not slyness, just intelligence, but some of the others don't trust him at all. They say he got too rich too fast. No one could be so lucky as that. Someone had to be helping him, and of course they think it's Simyits or something. Even worse." He took a swallow of ale from the mug Paks had poured him, and went on. "But Lord Verrakai, the Duke's brother, he told his page that he had proof of Duke Phelan's wrong. Someone who had been with him in Aarenis, and seen it."

Paks managed not to move, merely raising an eyebrow. Aris scurried on through his tale.

"A veteran of his, who left because she didn't want to stay with such a man, or he mistreated her, or something. And she's supposed to prove you aren't really a paladin, too."

"That may prove difficult," murmured Paks.

"Well, of course. You are one." Aris snorted. "I haven't seen her, but Dorthan — that's the page — swears he has. Big and black, he says, and shoulders like an ox. But then Dorthan's so skinny he thinks I have big shoulders."

Paks could not think of anyone matching that description. "Do you have a name for this witness?" she asked.

"No. He didn't know that. Why? Would you know her by name?"

"I might, if she fought in the Company the same years I did. Go on."

943

But that was all Aris knew of the mysterious witness. He told a long involved story going the rounds of the squires concerning a second son of
Clannaeth's younger brother, and Konhalt's heir, and a girl of the
Destvaorn household, which supposedly explained why Konhalt was supporting Marrakai's position on the size of the Royal Guard, but Paks found
she couldn't follow either the positions or the reasons. She was about to
send him away when another knock on the outer door drew Lieth. Aris
looked scared.

"If that's Juris, do you have to tell him I'm here?"

"Would he be angry?"

"That I came? Yes. When I told him today that I knew you, he said to let
you alone."

And then Lieth announced the Kirgan Marrakai. Paks got up and jerked
her thumb at Aris. "Come on, Aris, and see what the protection of paladins
is worth."

In the other room, the Kirgan looked both embarrassed and annoyed.

"My pardon, lady, for disturbing you, but I feared my brother might —
aha!" as he caught sight of Aris behind Paks.

"Kirgan Marrakai, your brother has given me information I greatly
needed, and being unacquainted with the household, I knew not anyone
else to ask."

"You *asked* him here?" The Kirgan's eyebrows lowered. Paks smiled.
"Not precisely, no. But I may say I valued his loyalty in Fin Panir, as I do
here. I should not have kept him so long, perhaps, without asking leave of
Lord Kostvan — "

"I had leave for the afternoon," Aris piped up. Paks and the Kirgan both
stared him down. She looked back at the Kirgan and smiled again.

"And now that he has quite finished," said Paks, emphasizing the words,
"I hope you have a few minutes to give me."

"I?" The Kirgan was clearly astonished.

"You. There are things the pages and junior squires know, and other
things which heirs to titles know. Would you?" She waved a hand to the
other door, and the Kirgan came forward, throwing a last glare at Aris as he
hurried out the door.

"Did you really need him," said the Kirgan, "or were you in league with
the scamp?" Despite the words, Paks could feel a warmth in his voice.

"A paladin in league with a scamp?" She spoke lightly. "No, he was a pes-
tiferous little mischief in Fin Panir, and no doubt still is — but he was always
loyal and honest, even in his worst moments. I asked, Kirgan, for gossip —
because I needed to know it — and he told me what he knew, which I
needed to know, and could not ask."

"And from me?"

Paks looked searchingly at him. Earlier in the day, he had seemed to
have the same arrogant enamel as some of the boys at Fin Panir, but perhaps he had the same warm heart as Aris. "I will ask a few questions," she
said then. "Please remember that I am not of this court, and speak only of

944

what I have heard — not in condemnation or even suspicion. Is your father loyal to the crown? Are you?"

His lips thinned. "I should have expected this — you came from the east, didn't you? Through Verrakai lands. My father's inmost heart is his own, Lady, but to my knowledge he is and has always been loyal to the crown. As for me, I love the prince as a brother. Indeed — but I cannot speak of that. I will serve him, Lady, as his loyal servant, when I become Duke."

"Very well. Then another question. Would you know who the witness against Duke Phelan is, that Aris spoke of?"

"No — not by name. I've heard there is one, that's all. A veteran, which surprised us all; his veterans all love him."

"So I would have thought," said Paks. "Then a final question. What do you think of Phelan?"

"I?" He smiled. "I've always liked him. My father does; he says Phelan has more breeding than any noble in the land, say what they will of him. He has always been courteous to me. You were in his Company; you know more."

"I know what I think," said Paks. "But I needed to know what you thought — what others think. When I came in this afternoon, it seemed almost that he was on trial. While I am on quest, I may not delay — but you can understand that after what he's done for me — "

"You would defend him? Good — I mean, it's none of my business, but I can hardly bear it when Verrakai gets started. Gird's blood! I was about to boil over when father sent me out on an errand."

"Tell your father to take care, Kirgan," said Paks seriously. "I will not always be in a position to help the Duke; he will need all his friends before long."

"I will, Lady," said the Kirgan steadily. "May I go?"

"Yes — you may say I have saved your little brother a scolding."

"More than a scolding, if I get my hands on that scamp," said the Kirgan, laughing. "You don't know what he did to my sister's room."

"Nor want to know," said Paks, waving him off. "That's between you — but remember, Kirgan," she said as he opened the door. She saw two servants not a spear-length away down the passage. "If young Aris wants to visit me, I have granted him leave. He was my friend in Fin Panir, and I don't forget my friends, even the young ones. He must have his lord's leave — but not yours." The Kirgan's face, as he bowed, was remote, as if he'd been scolded, but his eyes danced. Paks shut the door behind him, convinced that the Marrakaien were all a heady brew indeed.

Lieth was watching her, brows raised. "That will explain his visit, to all those listening ears."

"So I thought." Paks sighed, stretching. She would like to have rested, but felt she could not take the time. She wondered if the Duke would be at the grange hall that evening. Yet another tap on the door interrupted her thoughts. Lieth answered, opening to a page in royal livery.

"Please, I am to give this to the Lady Paksenarrion's hand, and await an answer."

"Here." Paks took the single folded sheet, and opened it. The High Marshal Seklis wished a short conference before the evening's ceremonies. He would be at the grange hall until dinner, if she could find the time. Paks handed the message to Lieth, who read it quickly and nodded. Paks turned to the page. "I'll come, of course," she said. "Can you guide us?"

"Yes, Lady."

"You'll want your armor," said Lieth quietly; Paks smiled at her.

"In the Hall?"

"Yes." Lieth could convey firmness very quietly, and she did it. Paks did not argue, and retired to the other room where Lieth helped her into it. "I'm coming with you, too," she said before they rejoined the page.

"As you will," said Paks.

The same High Marshal she had seen in the conference earlier met her at the side door of the grange hall.

"If the circumstances of your quest permit, Lady Paksenarrion, I would be glad of your participation in tonight's ceremony."

Paks frowned. "What participation, Marshal — ?"

"I'm sorry — I forgot that we hadn't met; I'm High Marshal Seklis. I've been attached to the court for about a year. Well, you probably know that the Order of the Bells advances its novices to knighthood at the Feast of Luap. We have a score of them this time. And since it's a Girdish order — with a few exceptions — a trial of arms is part of the ceremony. It would be an honor for the candidates to meet your blade in this trial. Of course, we have other Marshals, and senior knights of the Order also help out, but — "

"I thought only knights could act in the trials," said Paks.

"Well, of course — but paladins are knights first, and so — "

Paks shook her head. "No, Marshal; I'm not a knight."

"You — ! But you must be — I mean I heard that you were different, but — "

"Marshal, let me explain. I was not at Fin Panir long enough to qualify; the Marshal General admitted me to the order of paladin-candidate before I was knighted — as is sometimes done."

"Yes, but — "

"And after the expedition to Kolobia, I was unable to continue the training. I believe all Marshals were informed — ?"

He nodded, reluctantly, it seemed to Paks.

"So I left Fin Panir, without being knighted — indeed, completely unfit for any such honor."

"But — you *are* a paladin?"

"Yes. By Gird's grace, and the gifts of the High Lord, I am a paladin — but not through the candidacy at Fin Panir. Marshal, I do not understand the gods' ways or intent; I know only their commands and gifts."

"I — see." He chewed his lip. "I don't know of another case such as this."

"In the event, I might be an embarrassment to you — "

"No. No, indeed." His voice steadied, and he gave her a sharp glance. "If

946

the gods see fit to make a paladin of you, am I to quarrel with your qualifications? You are their champion — their knight, if you will — and that is enough for me, and for the rest."

"Another problem," said Paks slowly. "I have no blade of my own — this one I carry on quest, as you heard, to test the identity of Lyonya's king. I dare not use it for any other purpose."

"Easily solved," grinned Marshal Seklis. "A grange of Gird holds ample weaponry, I would think. Choose a sword from the armory that suits you. But if your quest forbids, I cannot insist."

"Then I would be honored. Only you will have to tell me how the ceremony goes."

"Like most such — but I forgot. Here, then — " And he led her into the grange hall proper and showed how it would be set up. Although somewhat smaller than the High Lord's Hall in Fin Panir, the grange hall was built to the same basic design. Tiers of seats rose on either side of a broad central aisle in which the trials would take place. Candidates would enter through a door at one end, and prove themselves against at least two of the examiners.

"Ordinarily," said Seklis, "we know that each bout will be short, and we don't expect the examiners to have much trouble. It's like the ritual exchange — merely public proof that the candidates are able to face an armed opponent. Even so, some of them surprise us. Last year we had a lad that outfought two Marshals and cost me a hard struggle before I got the winning touch. He's in Marshal's training now, and he'll be a strong arm for Gird in the future. But this time we may have real trouble. Many of them wanted to be in this ceremony because of the prince's coronation this year — to say they were knighted in the same year. So we have twenty zealous and very capable candidates. Besides the honor alone, that's one reason I asked you — I've scraped up every Marshal around, and the best of the senior knights, just in case, but we still have only fifteen examiners. That's more than two bouts apiece, any way you look at it."

Seklis explained the details of scoring, and introduced Paks to some of the pointers, who would keep track of each bout. Then he took her to the armory, and left her to choose a sword from the racks. They were all of similar design, with Gird's seal deeply graven in the pommel, and well-shaped hilts. They varied only in length and weight. When Paks had chosen two, Seklis told a yeoman-marshal to put them aside for her that evening, then turned back to her.

"Oh — by the way — unless your quest requires it, I would ask that you not wear that mail: for the trials, all wear the training armor, and all examiners are in the colors of their orders. You, of course, are entitled to Gird's colors, and there are surcoats enough, as well as the bandas — "

"I see." Paks thought a moment. She could think of no reason why she should be the only participant in full mail, but was yet reluctant to leave it aside. "I hesitate to question the custom — "

"And I the conditions of your quest." The High Marshal cocked his head slightly. "Lady, you know best what evils you face; I would not have them come on you unawares, yet I think they will not brave the grange hall full of Marshals and knights. The candidates — "

"What about the challengers?" asked Lieth. "Or is not that the custom here?"

The High Marshal frowned. "Challengers? Oh, you mean outsiders? Well — I doubt there will be any — "

"What is that?" asked Paks.

"It is the custom," he said, "that anyone having a grievance against the court or any examiner can present a champion for a trial of arms at this knighting. But when any such is planned, it's usual for me to know ahead of time."

"Would that bout be fought on the same terms?"

"No — as a full trial of arms. Do you suspect anything of that sort?"

"To be honest, Marshal Seklis, I don't know what I suspect — besides trouble. We have been attacked already by Achrya's minions and several priests of Liart with their beasts. Until I see the rightful king of Lyonya safe on his throne, I cannot be easy about anything. I am willing enough to test your candidates without armor, but if it comes to protecting the king — "

"Ah. I see."

"If someone came in, claiming to be an outside challenger, could they challenge anyone there, or just the examiners, or what?"

"Anyone."

"Umm." Paks chewed her lip a moment. "I could keep my armor here — nearby — if Lieth will squire me here — "

Lieth nodded, and Seklis smiled. "That's permissable; we'll all have squires to freshen us between rounds; she can keep your mail in case of need. And on my word as High Marshal, I shall be watching for any trouble, and will ward whomever you say."

948

Chapter Twenty-six

Paks came to the grange hall in the padded training armor and surcoat Seklis had provided. Lieth carried her paladin's mail, and the elven blade. Light blazed from the grange hall windows: candles on frames hung high above the floor, more candles set in brackets along the walls and the railing separating the seats from the open space. Paks peeked into the hall on her way to the High Marshal's study: already the seats were filling.

Seklis grinned when he saw her. "Ah — Lady Paksenarrion. Come, meet your fellow examiners. Here's Marshal Sulinarrion, of Seameadow Grange — and Marshal Aris, of Copswith Grange — and Marshal Doryan — " Someone pulled at his sleeve, and he turned away, leaving Paks with three Marshals: a tall brown-haired woman and two men, both gray-haired and dark-eyed. By the time she had them sorted out (Aris was taller, with a wide scar on his forehead), the High Marshal was back, to complete the introductions. Paks was not sure she had them all straight in her mind, but there was no time to worry about it. The great Bells began to peal, and everyone moved into line, with Seklis rearranging as he saw fit.

"You, Suli — and then Seli here — and Paks, you get behind him. There. Gird's grace on all of us."

"Gird's grace," came the response, and they walked quickly into the hall, ranging themselves across the width of it just below the platform.

The seats were filled. Candlelight glittered on jewels, slid along the folds of satin and silk, caught the flash of an eye that glanced, and shone steadily back from the few motionless hands. From the far end of the Hall, a fanfare of trumpets followed the bells into silence. Then the pointers, who would judge the trials, entered in their spotless white uniforms. They came forward, bowing once to the examiners in line, then withdrew in two files to either side. Another blast of trumpets, and the candidates entered in two files, still wearing gray training clothes and training armor. They faced the examiners, bowed, and waited. High Marshal Seklis stepped forward.

"Who presents these candidates for trial?"

"I do." A heavy-set man in the green, rose, and white of the Order stepped into the hall. "Sir Arinalt Konhalt, Training Master of the Order of the Bells."

"Their names?"

As the Training Master spoke each name, the youth bowed. When he had finished, the Marshal General spoke again.

"Here in the very hall where Luap spoke, and witnessed to the deeds of Gird, Protector of the Innocent and Helpless, we meet to test the fitness of these youths for knighthood. Each shall demonstrate in at least two bouts that he or she is skilled in swordfighting and brave enough to face a naked blade before others. Do you all agree to submit to the judgment of the pointers?" A murmur of agreement came from them all. "Then here is the order of the examiners." Seklis introduced each examiner. "Because we have so many candidates," Seklis went on, "we cannot accommodate all bouts at once. The first five candidates will now choose their examiners." As the candidates moved forward, Paks watched their faces. They seemed very young; she reminded herself that they had had at least two years of knight's training, besides serving as squires. None of the first five chose her; she watched as the examiners and pointers led the candidates back down the hall to the fighting areas. The candidates waiting for their turns began to fidget. They could not turn around and watch; they had to face the remaining examiners and try to feign calmness.

At the sound of trumpets, the first bouts began. Swords rang together, and stone echoed the stamp of booted feet. The nearest bout seemed evenly matched at first. Seklis had said that the examiners began by trying standard stroke combinations. No bout could end (except in emergencies) before fifty strokes, no matter what points were scored; most, he said, took between that and a hundred. Paks tried to keep count, but lost it when someone down the Hall cried out. Heads craned, but the bouts went on. Paks looked back at the pair she'd been watching; now the examiner, a Marshal whose name she'd forgotten, was moving the candidate around the area, gaining points with every stroke. The candidate rallied a moment, lunging again and again. But a final flurry by the Marshal broke that attack, and the pointers called the bout just after another one down the Hall.

As soon as a candidate finished one bout, he had to choose his next opponent. This time Paks was chosen, by the only candidate to win his bout. She followed her challenger halfway down the Hall to their assigned area. For the second bouts, the pointers gave the starting word. Paks grinned at the young man; his look of confidence faded. When he lunged, she caught his blade and shed it quickly from hers, then forced him back with a quick attack. He looked startled, as if he had not expected such a strong attack. Before he could recover his timing and balance, Paks pushed him back again, working him around the edge of their space. But he steadied himself, biting his lip, and managed to hold his ground. Paks tested all quarters of his range, probing but not using her full skill against him yet. She let him move into attack again. He quickened; she matched him, saw his surprise, and finished with a decisive rattle of strokes that got past his guard again and again. He would have bruises under his padding. But he bowed politely, and thanked her.

"Lady, it is my honor to suffer defeat at your hands."

"May it be your only defeat, Sir Joris — " For she had been told his name, the ritual greeting: the first use of their title was by the examiner who passed them.

He grinned. "Lady, if I can learn to fight as you do, it will be. But I thought I had not so much to learn. Are you still learning new things?"

"Joris!" That was his proud father, come from the seats to grip his son's shoulder.

Paks smiled at the older man. "Indeed I am, Sir Joris — and that's a good question. You will learn as long as you know you need to."

"Thank you, Lady Paksenarrion," said the father. "He — "

"Please — " The pointers touched the older man's arm. "Sir — please — not here — we have long to go." Paks returned to the front of the Hall, and the new knight joined his successful comrades in the rear.

Paks lined up behind someone who had not yet been chosen — Seklis's suggestion, so that each examiner would have a short rest between bouts. The second five were already on their first bouts, although one bout from the first five was still going on. She looked around the Hall, trying to spot the Duke, but in that mass of color and movement, she could not find him at first. She tried again. "He's fine," said Lieth in her ear. "I saw them come in."

A few minutes later, another candidate chose her, and she fought her second bout, this one much shorter. At the fiftieth stroke, the spotter named her the victor. This candidate had taken a hard blow to the left shoulder on her first bout, and Paks suspected she had a broken collarbone. Her face was pale and sweaty, but she also managed her bow, and thanked Paks for the honor.

By this time, two of the examiners were out, one with a broken collarbone, and one with a cracked wrist. Paks made her way past three bouts going on, and lined up again. She did not feel particularly tired, and so put herself in line for immediate choice. She had another easy bout, which she drew out to near a hundred strokes for the candidate's benefit, and then watched the last two finish. Now the family sponsor for each new knight carried out the new armor which the knights had earned. While the knights changed into their armor (Paks hoped the woman with the broken collarbone would not have to struggle into a mail shirt), the examiners also changed. Then the crown prince formally greeted each new knight by name and presented the tiny gold symbol of the Order. When he was through, the High Marshal stepped forward once more.

"We welcome these new knights to the Order of the Bells, and ask Gird's grace and the wisdom of Luap to guide them in their service. At this time, any outside challenge may be offered: is it so?"

"Challenge!" A voice called from the far end of the Hall, near the outside door. A startled silence broke into confusion; the High Marshal stilled it with a gesture.

"Name your challenge," he said.

A figure in plate armor with a visored helm stepped into view; at the same time, someone in Verrakai colors stood in the seats.

"High Marshal, I call challenge on Duke Kieri Phelan. My champion is below: a veteran soldier from his Company."

Again the hubbub, stilled only when the High Marshal shouted them down. By then Phelan was on the floor, surrounded by the King's Squires and his own companions. Paks recognized Captain Dorrin and Selfer, the Duke's squire.

"Phelan?" said the High Marshal. "How say you?"

"For what cause do you call challenge, Verrakai?" The Duke's voice was calm.

"For your treachery to the crown of Tsaia," he yelled back.

"I protest," said the crown prince, from his place. "This is not the occasion; the matter has not been settled by the Council."

"It is my right."

"You are not the Duke," said the crown prince. "Where is he?"

"He was indisposed, your highness, and could not attend."

"Do you claim to speak for him?"

"He would agree with my judgment of Phelan," said the other. "As for challenge, and this challenger, that is my own act."

"Then may it rest on you," said the prince. "I will not permit Phelan to take up this challenge."

"Your highness —"

"No, Duke Phelan. As long as you are a vassal of this court —" Paks saw the Duke's reaction to that; he had not missed the prince's emphasis, " — you will obey. You may not take it up. You may, however, name a champion."

Paks was moving before any of the others. "If my lord Duke permits, I will —"

"A paladin?" asked the Verrakai. "You would champion this Duke — but I forget — you also are his veteran, aren't you?"

"And nothing more," said the other fighter. Paks wondered who it was; she did not quite recognize the voice.

The Duke bowed stiffly to the prince, and the challenger. "I would be honored, Lady, by your service in this matter. Yet all know you came on quest; I would not interfere."

The Verrakai and his attendants had also climbed down to the floor, and now stood opposite the Duke. Paks and the mysterious fighter advanced to the space between them. She noted that the other matched her height, but seemed to move a little awkwardly in armor, as if unused to it. The High Marshal raised his arm to signal them. When it fell, Paks and the stranger fell to blows at once.

The stranger was strong: Paks felt the first clash all the way to her shoulder. Paks circled, trying the stranger's balance. It was good. She tested the stranger's defense on one side, then the other. It seemed weaker to the left, where a formation fighter would depend on shield and shield partner. Perhaps the stranger was not as experienced in longsword — Paks tried a favorite trick, and took a hard blow in return. So the stranger had fenced against longsword — and that trick — before. She tried another, as quickly countered. The stranger attacked vigorously, using things Paks knew could have been learned in the Company. Paks countered them easily. She had no advantage of reach, against this opponent, and less weight, for she had chosen a light blade (as the High Marshal requested) to test the candidates.

They circled first one way, then the other, blades crashing together. Paks still fought cautiously, feeling her way with both opponent and the unfamiliar sword in her hand. She could feel its strain, and tried to counter each blow as lightly as possible, reserving its strength for attack. Suddenly the stranger speeded up the attack, raining blow after blow on Paks's blade. Paks got one stroke in past the other's guard, then took a hard strike on the flat of her blade. This time the sound changed, ringing a half-pitch higher. Warned by this, Paks danced backwards, catching the next near the tip, which flew wide in a whirling arc. She parried another blow with the broken blade, and then dropped it as it shattered, and backed again from a sweep that nearly caught her in the waist.

"Wait!" shouted the High Marshal, but the stranger did not stop. Paks knew Lieth had her second blade ready, but she was backed against the far side of the space. Dagger in hand, she deflected a downward sweep that still drove the chainmail into her shoulder.

The stranger laughed. "You are no paladin. You had the chances, that's all — "

This time Paks recognized the voice. "Barra!" At that, another laugh, and the stranger raised her visor to show that familiar angry face.

"Aye. I always said I could take you — " Again the sword came up for a downward blow.

But Paks moved first. As fast as Barra was, she had the edge of initiative, and slipped under the stroke. Her fingers dug into Barra's wrist, and she hooked her shoulder under Barra's arm, flipping her over. Barra landed flat on her back, sprawling and half-stunned. Paks had her own sword's tip at her throat before she could move. For an instant, rage and excitement nearly blinded her; she could have killed Barra then. But her control returned before she did more than prick her throat. When she could hear over the thunder of her own pulse, the High Marshal was speaking.

"Your challenge of arms, Lord Verrakai, is defeated."

With ill grace, the Verrakai bowed. "So I see. My pardon, lord Duke."

Duke Phelan bowed, silent, and waited while the Verrakai turned to go. Then the Verrakai turned back. "I should have known better, " he said, "than to believe one of your veterans. Are they all such liars, lord Duke — and if so, can we believe this paladin of yours?"

Phelan paled, but did not move, and the Verrakai shrugged and walked out. Then Phelan looked at the High Marshal. "Sir Marshal, my defense is proved by arms, but at the cost, it seems, of something I hold more dear — the good opinion of my veterans."

"Or one of them, lord Duke. It is a rare commander who has not one bitter veteran. And you were defended by one."

"Yes." The Duke came to where Paks still held Barra at sword's point. "Lady, if you will, permit her to rise."

Paks bowed, and stood back a pace, still holding Barra's sword. The Duke offered a hand, which Barra refused, scrambling up on her own, instead. She scowled at him.

"Will you say, Barra, why you chose to serve my enemy?"

"I think you're crazy," said Barra loudly. Someone laughed, in the tiers overhead, and she glared upward, then back at the Duke. "You could have been rich — you could have done more, but you let others take the credit. And I was as good as Paks, but you gave her all the praise. She got all the chances — "

"That's not true." Dorrin strode across the floor to her side. She gave a quick glance at the tiers and went on. "You and Paks were recruits together — true. And back then, that first year, you were probably her equal in swordfighting. But in nothing else, Barranyi, and after the first year not in that."

"I was — you just — "

"You were not. Falk's oath, Barra, I'm your captain; I know you inside out. You made trouble every way you could without breaking rules. You quarreled with everyone. Paks didn't — "

"That mealy-mouth — "

"Mealy-mouth!" That was Suriya, across the floor.

Barra turned dark red. "Damned, sniveling, sweet-tongued prig! Everyone on her side! Everyone — "

"Barra." Something in Paks's voice stopped her. "Barra, you do yourself an injustice here."

"I? Do myself an injustice? No, Paks: you did that. Make a fool out of me in front of your fancy friends. Think you're such an example — " Barra jerked off the helmet and threw it at Paks, who dodged easily. "I'll show you yet, Paksenarrion — you sheepfarmer's daughter. I know about you. You're a coward underneath, that's what — or you'd have had the guts to kill me. Why don't you, eh? You've got the sword now. Go on — kill me." She threw her arms out, and laughed. "Gird and Falk together, none of you have any guts. Well, chance changes with the time, yellow-hair, and I'll have my day yet." She turned away; Paks said nothing, and waved the guards away when they would have stopped her.

"Well," said the crown prince into the horrified silence that followed her exit, "if that's the best witness Verrakai can find against you, Duke Phelan, I think your defense in Council is well assured. That's her own heart's poison brewed there, and none of your doing." An approving murmur followed this. Duke Phelan smiled at the prince.

"I thank you, your highness, for your sentiments. Indeed, I hope nothing I have done has provided food for that — but I will think on it." Then he turned to Paks. "And you, again, have served me well. Paksenarrion — "

"Lord Duke, in this I am serving my gods, and not you; I am no longer your soldier, though I will always be your veteran. I pray you, remember that: although you have done me the honor to treat me almost as a daughter, I am not. I am Gird's soldier now."

954

*   *   *

Although the trouble had come, and apparently gone, without actual danger to the Duke, Paks was still uneasy that night. When the Duke finally retired to his chamber, she held a quick conference with the King's Squires. On no account must the Duke go anywhere — anywhere — without their protection. If she was not available, they must all attend him.

"But Paks, what is it you fear?"

"The malice Barra feels, directed with more skill," said Paks, frowning. "Companions, we have not crowned our king yet; until then trust nothing and no one." When she returned to her own chamber, with Lieth, she found it hard to sleep, despite her fatigue.

Yet in the morning she found nothing amiss. After breakfast in the Duke's chambers, they went to the Council meeting together. Paks noticed, as they came in, that Duke Verrakai was present, and his brother absent. The two elves were there, sitting lower down, this time. She wondered what they had thought of last night's events; they would have to agree that the Duke had kept his temper under trying circumstances.

"I asked for this special session," began the crown prince, "at the request of Lady Paksenarrion, whom you met yesterday. You are aware that she is on quest, searching for the true king of Lyonya. She believes she has found him, and asked that you witness the elf-blade's test of his identity."

"And who is it, your highness?" asked Duke Verrakai.

"I will let the paladin speak for herself." The crown prince waved for Paks to begin.

"Lords, I will give you my reasons briefly, and then the prince's name." She repeated her reasoning, now so familiar, from the elves' claim that the prince had forgotten his past, to the meaning of the message they sent Aliam Halveric about the sword. "As well, when Aliam Halveric gave the sword to Kieri Phelan, to give his wife, the elves replied that the gift was satisfactory. That seemed, to me, to mean that the prince was someone with whom Kieri Phelan, as well as Aliam Halveric, came into contact. Then Garris, one of the King's Squires who accompanied me on quest, told me of his own boyhood times with Aliam Halveric, when Kieri Phelan was Halveric's senior squire." She saw comprehension dawn on several faces around the table, and turned to Duke Phelan before anyone else could speak.

"Yesterday, lord Duke, I spoke openly to you of this reasoning, and of your past; now, before the King's Squires of Lyonya, and the Regency Council of Tsaia and heir to the throne, I declare that I believe you are the rightful heir to Lyonya's throne, the only son of King Falkieri, and half-elven by your mother's blood." She turned to Lieth, who had carried in the elven blade, and took the sheathed sword from her. "If it is true, then this blade was forged for you by the elves, and sealed to you with tokens sent by your mother. When you draw it, it will declare your heritage. Is it true that you have never laid hands on this sword to draw it?"

"It is true," said Duke Phelan steadily. "I swore to my wife that I would

955

never draw her blade, when I gave it to her, and until you took it from the wall to kill Achrya's agent, she alone drew it."

"I ask you to draw it now," said Paks, "in the High Lord's name, and for the test of your birth."

Duke Phelan's gray eyes met hers for a long look, then he reached out and took the sword's grip in his hand. His expression changed at once, and at the same time a subtle hum, complex as music, shook the air. In one smooth move, he drew the sword free of the scabbard. Light flared from it, far brighter than Paks had ever seen, more silver than blue. The blade chimed. Outside, the Bells of Vérella burst into a loud clamor, echoing that chime until the very walls rang with it. Phelan gripped it with both hands, raising it high overhead. Light danced around the chamber, liquid as reflection from water. As Paks watched, the blade seemed to lengthen and widen slightly, fitting itself to the Duke's reach. Then the light still blazing from the blade condensed, seeming to sink into the blade without fading, and the runes glowed brilliant silver, like liquid fire. The green jewel in the pommel glowed, full of light. Phelan lowered the sword, resting the blade gently in his left palm. When he met Paks's eyes again, his own were alight with something she had never seen there. When he spoke, his voice held new resonance.

"Lady, you were right. This is my sword, and I daresay no one will dispute it." A ripple of amusement softened his voice there. "Indeed, I had never thought of such a thing. What an irony this is — so many years it hung on my wall, and I did not know of it."

"Sir king." The crown prince had risen; with him, the rest of the Council stood. "This is — " Abruptly his mannered courtesy deserted him, and he looked the boy his years made him. "It's like one of the old songs, sir, like a harper's tale — " The prince's eyes sparkled with delight.

"As yet, your highness, I am not king. But your congratulations are welcome — if it means that you do not object."

"Object! I am hardly likely to quarrel with the gods about this. It is like a story in a song, that you should be a king without knowing it, and have on your wall for years the sword that would prove you."

"But — but — he's just a mercenary — " Clannaeth burst into speech. The High Marshal and the crown prince glared at him.

"Gird's right arm," said the prince crisply, "if you'd been stolen away as an infant, how would you have earned your bread? As a pig farmer?"

"I didn't mean that," began Clannaeth, but no one listened.

Paks, watching the Duke's face, was heartened at the transformation. She had feared his lingering doubt, but he obviously had none. Whatever the sword had done for him, it had given him the certainty of his birth. So he listened calmly to the short clutter of sound that followed Clannaeth's comment, until the High Marshal hushed them. Then he addressed the Council.

"Lords, when our prince's father first gave me the grant I now hold, I told him I had no plans for independent rulership. That was true. But now

I find I have another land, a land which needs me — yet for many years, as you know, I have given my life and work to my steading in Tsaia. I cannot expect that you would allow the king of a neighboring land to hold land from this crown, but I do ask that you let me keep it for a short while, and that you let me have some influence over its bestowing. Your northern border — for so long, *my* northern border — is still a perilous one. It will need a strong hand, and good management, for many years yet if the rest of Tsaia is to be safe. Now I must travel to Chaya, and relieve the fears of my kingdom, but my senior captains can manage well enough in the north, with your permission."

The crown prince and the High Marshal approved this, and the others agreed — Paks thought by surprise as much as anything.

She looked at the elves. Their faces were as always hard to read, but she did not see the scorn or refusal she had feared. One of them caught her eye, and made a small hand signal she had learned from the rangers: approval, the game is in sight.

"Do you remember any more now?" asked the High Marshal. Phelan nodded.

"A little — and better than that, it makes sense. I had memories of my father — a tall, red-haired man with a golden beard, wearing a green velvet shirt embroidered with gold. Now I know that the embroidery was the crest of our house. And the court I remember, planted with roses — that will be at Chaya, and I daresay I can lead the way to it."

"Your name?" asked Verrakai.

"I am not sure. Your highness, your father once asked me of my heritage, and then swore never to speak of it. But now, with my birthright in my hand, I will speak willingly. My earliest memories are those I have just mentioned. Then, as you know, the prince — I — was stolen away while traveling with the queen. After that, for many years, I was held captive far away by a man who called himself Baron Sekkady. He was, your highness, a cruel master; I remember more than I would wish of those years."

"What did he — " began one of the lords. Phelan turned toward him.

"What did he do? What did he not do, that an evil and cruel man could think of! Imagine your small sons, my lords, in the hands of such a man — hungry, tired, beaten daily, and worse than beaten. He would have trained me to the practice of his own cruelties if he could."

"Did he know who you were?"

"I believe so. He used to display me to visitors. After one such banquet, the visitor seemed to recognize me, and the Baron put silence on him."

"Put silence — ?" asked the Marshal.

"He was some sort of wizard, sir Marshal. I know little of that, but he could silence men, and hold them motionless, by his powers . . . though what he enjoyed most was hearing them scream. That visitor, whose name I never knew, had some strange powers himself, for he woke me, while he himself was being tormented in the dungeons. He sent me away."

957

"How?" asked the High Marshal, after a long pause.

"I am not sure. By then I had tried escape — and been so punished for it that I had ceased to hope for anything but death. But this man took my fear, and sent me: 'There is a High Lord above all barons,' he said. 'Go to his courts and be free.' And so I climbed out the baron's window, and down the wall, and ran through the woods until I came out of that land. When I came to the coast, I stowed away on a ship . . . and eventually came to Bannerlith, where they set me ashore with their good wishes. I worked my way inland, to Lyonya, at any work I could find, until I fetched up at Aliam Halveric's on a cold winter day, half-starved and frozen. He took me in — first as a laborer, then as a page in the household, and then — when I showed aptitude for fighting — made me a squire. The rest you know. Anyway, it is from that man — Baron Sekkady — that I got my name as I know it. He told me it was Kieri Artfiel Phelan; he called me Artfiel. I use Kieri. What it really is — "

"Is Falkieri Amrothlin Artfielan," said Paks.

"Falkieri — " he breathed. "So close — like the sword — "

"He must have known," said the High Marshal. "He must have known who you were, and delighted in that knowledge. Some scum of Liart's, no doubt. Would you could remember where that was?"

"If I could remember that, sir Marshal, I would long ago have freed his domain of him."

"Vengeance?" asked one of the elves.

"No — not vengeance alone. He was cruel to many others, not me alone. It would lighten my heart to know the world free of him."

"My lord," said the crown prince, "you do not wish me to use your title yet, but I must call you something — what will you do now? Will you travel at once to Chaya?"

Phelan looked at Paks, who nodded. "I think I must, your highness. Lyonya has been too long without me."

"Will they accept you?" asked Duke Marrakai. "Lady Paksenarrion said something about the elves — "

"Their council swore, the night I left, to accept as their king the man the sword declared," said Paks quickly. "At that time I did not know it was Duke Phelan. As for the elves, the Lady of the Ladysforest wished to see him before the coronation: the elves had their fears, as I said."

"And do you still, cousins?" asked Phelan of the listening elves, slightly stressing the last word.

"Lord Falkieri, what the elves feared in you was not to your blame. We feared the damage done by your wicked master. Will you deny your temper, and what has sometimes come of it?"

"No. But I asked if you still feared it."

One of the elves laughed. "Lord, you are not the furious man I had heard of. Here I have seen you accept insult with dignity, and remain courteous and capable of thought to all. For myself — but I am not the one who will decide — I would trust you to govern humans."

958

"But your realm is not all human," the other elf added. "For too many years Lyonya's ruler has lacked any feel for the taigin. This lack hurts us all. You have shown no such ability."

"You believe this, too, was destroyed by Baron Sekkady's cruelty?"

Both of them nodded. "If the small child is not taught — if instead all such sense becomes painful — then it can be lost, for a time, or forever."

"I see. But being half-elven, will not my children carry this ability by heritance, even if I lack it?"

"I suppose — I had not thought — " The elf looked genuinely surprised. "I had heard you swore never to remarry."

"I said so; I never took formal vows, not being in the habit of breaking my stated word. Clearly I cannot refuse to sire heirs for Lyonya, and old as I am, I daresay — "

"Old!" The elf laughed, then sobered quickly. "My pardon, Lord — and lords of Tsaia. I meant no disdain. But Lord Falkieri, you are not old for half-elven. You are merely well-grown. You have many years yet to found a family, though your people will be glad the sooner you wed."

"But I'm — "

"Fifty years — and what of that? No elf-born comes to full powers much before that. Your sister would yet live had she waited to wed and bear children until fifty. Fear not death from age yet awhile, Falkieri; blade and point can kill you, but not age alone until your sons' sons are come to knighthood."

When the elves said nothing more, the crown prince spoke again. "We would honor you with an escort into Lyonya, my lord. Lady Paksenarrion speaks of peril; our lands are old allies. Will you accept it?"

Phelan nodded; Paks saw that he was near tears from all this. He struggled for a moment and regained control. "I brought with me only a small escort, as your highness knows. I would be honored by a formal one. But when could they be ready to leave?"

The meeting dissolved in a mass of details — which unit of the Tsaian Royal Guard would travel by which route, who would take word to Phelan's steading in the north, how best to plan the march, and on and on. Paks listened, starting as the High Marshal touched her shoulder.

"If you have a few minutes, Lady Paksenarrion, I'd like to see you in the grange hall."

"Certainly. I see we won't be leaving for some hours, if today — "

"Not today," said Phelan, catching her last words. "Tomorrow at best — I'm sorry, Paks, but there's too much to do."

She bowed, and beckoned to Garris, who followed her a few feet away.

"Don't leave him, Garris — any of you — for any reason — for even a few minutes. I cannot name the peril, but we know that evil powers do not want him crowned."

"I swear to you, Paks: we will not leave him."

"I will return shortly." And Paks followed the High Marshal away from the chamber.

High Marshal Seklis ushered Paks into his study, and seated her near a small fire. A yeoman-marshal brought a tray of sweet cakes and a pot of sib, then withdrew.

"I understand your concern, Lady," he began, "but it will take the rest of the day to get a troop of the Royal Guard ready to ride on such a mission. Your things, no doubt, are simpler. And the King's Squires will guard him. Now that you've handed over that sword, you'll need another, and I want a favor in return — the story of your quest so far, to write into the archives for the Marshal-General."

Paks told her tale, from leaving Duke Phelan's stronghold to her arrival in Vérella, as quickly and completely as possible, but the pot of sib was empty when she finished. The High Marshal sat back and sighed, then smiled.

"Now I understand your haste. Come — I have no elf-blades here, but we can find something more your weight than the blade that failed you last night." He led her into the armory, where Paks tried one blade after another until she found one to suit. Then they walked back into the palace, to find the Duke's suite a chaotic jumble of servants, gear, and visitors. Paks saw Kolya and Dorrin across the outer room, and worked her way toward them.

"He's not here at the moment," said Dorrin, "but he'll be back. Before you ask, all the King's Squires went with him, as well as Selfer — don't worry. Falk's oath, Paks, if we'd known what you would do someday, I don't know if we'd ever have risked your hide on the battlefield."

"Oh yes, you would," said Paks. "How else could you test a weapon? Not by hanging it on the wall."

"We'll miss him," said Kolya soberly. "The best master a land ever had, and I'm not the only one who thinks so. I'm not ill-wishing — I just wish I could pick up my trees and move to Lyonya."

"He'd find you a grove."

"It's not the same. Those Westnuts I struggled with, learning to dig one-handed — I can't move that somewhere else."

"And he feels it too," said Paks quietly.

"I know. And I'm glad for him. All those years of hearing the others pick and pick — hedge-lord, they'd say, or base-born moneybags — they'll sing a new song now. He was never less than kingly with us; Lyonya's lucky, and he deserves the best of it."

"Who's going with him? For that matter, who's here?"

Dorrin numbered them on her fingers. "Arcolin's commanding back north; Selfer and I came along, and we'll go on to Lyonya. Kolya, you know, and Donag Kirisson, the miller from Duke's West, and Siger. And Vossik and a half-dozen solid veterans. Plus the usual: carters and muleteers, and that. I expect he'll take his own veterans, and I doubt we could peel Siger away from him with a knife."

"And how many of the Tsaian Guard?"

"A score at least. The crown prince would like to send a cohort, but you know what that means in supplies. The Duke — the king — always said the Tsaian Royal Guard traveled on silk."

The High Marshal nodded. "It's court life — I've argued again and again about it, but to no avail. They're good fighters — well trained and disciplined — but any decent mercenary company can march them into the ground."

"It's too bad the Company can't be here," said Dorrin. "They'd be proud of him."

"What is it — a week's march? I agree with Lady Paksenarrion; he must not wait that long to travel. Although his own Company would be a fitting escort."

"If it didn't frighten the Lyonyans," said Dorrin. "They aren't used to troop movements there."

Paks looked a question at her, and Dorrin blushed.

"I trained there, you know," she said. "But I was born a Verrakai."

"You?"

"Yes. They don't admit it any more." Dorrin grinned, shaking her head. "My cousin is furious. I remember getting in fights with him before I left home."

More messengers and visitors arrived. Someone came to Dorrin with a handful of scrolls and a question; she shrugged helplessly at Paks and moved aside to look at them. Servants carried in trays of food. Paks thought of her own rooms, and wondered if Lieth had packed her things before leaving with Phelan. She wormed her way through a cluster of people to ask Kolya when he'd be back.

"I'm not sure — he said not long, but not to worry if it was a glass or so. Some Company matter. He'd already had to talk to his bankers, and draft messages to Arcolin. Why?"

"I'll go down to my rooms, then, and pack up. It won't take long." Paks worked her way out of the suite, past a row of squires bearing messages, and hurried to her own quarters. Lieth had not packed, but she found two of the palace servants straightening the rooms. In a short time, she had rolled everything neatly into her saddlebags or Lieth's. She went back along the corridors with the bags slung over her shoulder. It was midafternoon, and most of the outer court was in shadow. The bustle in Phelan's suite seemed less. A row of corded packs waited in the outer room. Kolya, Dorrin, High Marshal Seklis, and Donag Kirisson sat around a low table near the fire in the sitting room, eating rapidly. Paks joined them, dumping her saddlebags nearby. She reached for the end of a loaf.

"Where is he? Isn't he back?"

"Not yet," said Kolya. "Are you worried, Paks? He has four good squires with him."

"Did he take the sword?" asked Paks without answering Kolya.

"No," said Dorrin. She pushed back her cloak to show the pommel. "He asked me to keep it here — said he didn't want it on the street."

Paks frowned, her worry sharpening. "I wish he'd taken it. I should have said something."

961

"Why?"

"If nothing else, it's a remarkably good weapon. But more than that, in his hands it has great power, and none of us can use it."

"You can, surely."

"Not now," said Paks. "Not after he drew it — it's sealed to him completely now. I would not dare to draw it."

Dorrin looked at it. "If I'd known that —"

"Excuse me, Lady — I was given a message for your hand." Paks looked up to see a page in the rose and silver house livery holding something out. She put out her hand, and took it. The page bowed, and quickly moved away. It was a small object wrapped in parchment. Paks folded the stiff material back carefully. When she saw what it contained, she felt as cold as if she'd been dipped in the ice-crusted river.

Chapter Twenty-seven

There on her hand lay the Duke's black signet ring, the same ring she had carried from Fin Panir to the Kuakgan's grove in Brewersbridge, the same ring she had taken back to the Duke that fall. The others had leaned to see what it was; Paks held out her hand, and watched the faces whiten. No one spoke. Paks flattened the parchment, and saw thin, angular writing she knew at once for blood. She shivered; she knew it must be *his* blood.

Alone, or Lyonya will have no king.

This too she showed the others, handing it around.

"By the Tree — " Kolya was the first to find speech. "What can you do, Paks?"

"Find him," said Paks grimly.

"But how?"

"They will guide me; they intend it." She was shaken by a storm of rage and grief, and struggled to master it. For what must come she had to be calm. She took the ring from Dorrin, who was staring blankly at it, and slipped it on her own middle left finger. "Kolya — " The one-armed woman met her eyes, blinking back tears. "Find the nearest Kuakgan — is there one near enough Vérella?"

"For what?"

"To aid him when he travels. I want the taigin awakened for him."

"Great lords above!" muttered the High Marshal. Paks shot him a quick glance and went on. "Tell the Kuakgan to ask the taigin of Master Oakhallow: and tell him the three woods are fireoak, blackwood, and yellowwood."

"You want him to raise the highfire for the Duke?"

"For me," said Paks quietly. She turned quickly to Dorrin. "Make sure they are ready to ride at once. Whatever it takes, Captain Dorrin: the High Marshal will help you."

"Indeed I will." The High Marshal's expression was as grim as she felt. "Every Marshal in Vérella — "

"And on the way. Sir Marshal, I must speak to you alone." Dorrin and the others left quickly. Paks took a deep breath but before she could speak, the High Marshal asked:

"Do you foresee your own death, paladin of Gird?"

"I see nothing, sir Marshal, but the direction of my quest. It seems likely that this summons means death. But Girdsmen are hard to kill, as you know — " He nodded, with a tight smile. Paks went on. "Sir Marshal, I ask you these favors. Would you ask the Marshal-General to send a sword to my family at Three Firs when she thinks it safe for them, and such word of me as she thinks it wise for them to have?"

"I will," he said. "You are sure you will never return there?"

"I knew that before now, Sir Marshal. However this ends, I cannot return; I would like the Marshal-General to know my wishes in this."

"I will tell her," said Seklis. "Be sure of that. What else?"

"This time I will not have Gird's symbols defaced," said Paks. "I will arrange to return my arms and medallion. If you will leave these in the grange at Westbells, on your way east — "

"You expect to follow?" The High Marshal's voice was completely neutral.

Paks shook her head. "I expect to follow Gird's directions, Sir Marshal. I hope to follow, but — to be honest — I expect not."

He lowered his voice. "It is not the way of the Fellowship to sacrifice any Girdsman — let alone a paladin — without a fight."

Paks managed a smile. "On my honor, Sir Marshal, they will find they have a fight — though not the one they expected, perhaps. And as well — " she found herself grinning at him, "as well, imagine if one paladin can spoil such a long-laid plot. How many years has that black web-spinner been preening herself on the completeness of her webs? And the Master of Torments must have enjoyed what happened to a helpless child. Yet now the rightful king returns, and their attempt to sever Lyonya and Tsaia will fail."

"If you can find him." The High Marshal held her gaze. "If you can pay the price."

"I can find him," said Paks. "As for the price, what I have is the High Lord's, and I will return it as he asks."

"Gird's grace be with you, paladin," said the High Marshal formally.

"And Gird's power rest in your grange," replied Paks. She bowed and strode quickly from the chamber.

She hardly noticed those who moved out of her way in the passages outside. She was wondering how Phelan had been trapped. Were all the squires dead? Was he himself dead, and this message no more than a trap for her? But she did not believe that — else her quest would lead somewhere else. She would find him easily enough; those who had sent the ring would see to that. She came into the outer court and glanced up to see what light remained. In another glass or so it would be dark. No one questioned her at the outer gate, though the guards greeted her respectfully. She nodded to them and passed into the wide street beyond.

Here she slowed to a stroll, and looked around carefully. The street seemed full enough of hurrying people, hunched against the cold and ducking into one doorway or another. Directly across from the palace gate was a large inn, the Royal Guardsman. On one side was a saddler's, with a carved wooden horse, gaily decked, over the entrance. Beyond that was a cobbler's, then a tailor's shop. On the other side was a scribe-hall, then a narrow alley. Paks walked that way, past the ground floor windows of the inn's common room. She was aware when someone came out the inn door behind her. She felt the back of her neck prickle with another's attention. But she walked on, steadily. The footsteps behind quickened. Paks slowed, edging toward the front of the scribe-hall.

"I think," said a low voice at her shoulder, "that you must be Paksenarrion?"

Paks turned; the follower was a tall redheaded woman, in the garb of a free mercenary. Paks saw the hilt of a dagger in each boot as well as one at her waist.

"Yes," she said quietly. "I am Paksenarrion."

The redhead gave her a scornful look up and down. "You are just as Barra said. Well, and did you get our present?"

Paks raised an eyebrow. "If you mean a certain ring — "

"Don't play games with me, paladin," the woman sneered. "If you want to see him alive, follow me and keep your hands off your sword." She turned away.

"Stop," said Paks, not loudly but with power. The woman froze, then turned back to her, surprise in her eyes. "Before I go one step, I will have your word on this: is he alive? What of his squires?"

"They are all alive, Phelan and the squires, but they will die if you are not quick."

"And I should follow so we can all be killed at once, is that it?" Paks forced humor into her tone, and again the woman's eyes flashed surprise.

"No," she said sulkily. "The Master would be glad to kill all of you — and will — but you can buy your lord some time, if you dare it."

"And where do you go?"

"You would not know if I told you. There are places in Vérella that none but the Guild know, and places known only to few of the Guild." She looked hard at Paks for a moment, and shook her head quickly. "I wonder — perhaps Barra has erred — "

"Is this Barra's plot?" asked Paks. "Or Verrakai's?"

"You ask too much. Come." The woman turned away and walked off quickly. Paks followed, her heart pounding.

To her surprise, they did not enter the alley Paks had seen, but kept to the main streets until they were in the eastern end of Vérella. Then the woman turned into a narrower street, and another. Here was the sort of poverty Paks had seen in every city but Fin Panir and Chaya: crowded narrow houses overhanging filthy cobbles and frozen mud, ragged children huddled together for warmth, stinking effluvium from every doorway. She was aware of the curious glances that estimated her sword's worth and the strength of her arm rather than a paladin's honor. The redhead ducked into a narrow passage between two buildings, scarce wide enough for their shoulders. It angled around a broad chimney, and opened into a tiny court. Across that was a double door, painted black with red hinges. On this, the redhead rapped sharply with her dagger hilt; a shutter in the door scraped open.

Paks looked quickly around the open space. It was already draped in shadow, overlooked only by the blank rear walls of the buildings that ended here. Paks wondered at the windowless walls, then saw that there had been windows once — they were blocked up, some by brick and others by heavy shutters. She could hear the redheaded woman muttering at the door, and something small scuttling among the debris across the way. Aside from that, and the distant rumble of street noises, it was ominously quiet.

One leaf of the double doors opened, squealing on its hinges. "Come on," said the woman sharply. Paks did not move.

"I want to see him."

"Inside."

"No. Here. Alive." Paks called light, and it cast a cool white radiance over the grimy stones, the stinking litter along the walls. Several dark shapes fled squeaking into holes.

The woman turned back to the doorkeeper, and muttered again. Paks waited. The door slammed shut, and the woman turned back to her.

"I told you he was alive. You're only making it worse."

"On the contrary," said Paks. "I do what is necessary."

"Necessary!" The woman spat. "You'll learn necessary soon enough."

"That may be, but I will see him alive and well before then."

"As the Master answers, you will see." They waited in heavy silence for some minutes. When the doors opened, both sides gaping wide, two files of armed men emerged. The first were dressed in dark clothes, and carried short swords. Behind them came two priests of Liart, their hideous snouted helms casting weird shadows in Paks's light. But for one being slightly taller, she could see no difference in them. The redhead bowed deeply. The two faced Paks; one of them raised a spiked club.

"Paladin of Gird, have you come to redeem your master?"

"He is not my master, but the rightful king of Lyonya, as you know."

"But dear to you."

"To bring him to his throne was laid on me for my quest," said Paks. "He is no longer my lord, for I am Gird's paladin."

"But you are here because of him."

"Because of Lyonya's king, yes."

"The Master of Torments desires otherwise."

"The Master of Torments has already found that the High Lord prevails."

A howl of rage answered that, and a bolt of blue light cast from the second priest. Paks laughed, tossing it aside with her hand. "See," she said. "You have said that he lives, and that you have some bargain in mind — but I am not without power. State your terms, slaves of a bad master."

"You will *all* die in torment — " began one, but the other hushed him and stepped forward.

"You killed our Master's servants in Lyonya," he said. "You killed them in Aarenis before that. The Master will have your blood for that blood, or take the blood of Lyonya's king."

"Death for life?" asked Paks.

"No." The priest shook his head slowly. "Torment for it, paladin of Gird. Death is easy — one stroke severs all necks, and our Master knows you paladins expect a long feasting thereafter. You must buy the king of Lyonya's freedom with the space of your own suffering. This night and day one will suffer as our Master demands — either Lyonya's king, or you."

"And then you will continue, and kill in the end." Paks kept her voice steady with an effort.

"It may be so, though there is another who wants your death. Uncertainty is, indeed, an element of torment. But the terms are these: you must consent, and come unresisting to our altar, or Lyonya's king will be maimed before another dawn, and will never take the throne."

"Prove that he and his squires live."

"His squires! What are they to you?"

"You would not know. Prove it."

One of the priests withdrew. In a short time, the priest and more armed men appeared, bringing Phelan and the squires, all bound and disarmed. One man carried their weapons.

They gaped across the tiny yard at Paks's light. Phelan's face hardened as he saw her. Garris sagged between his guards, as if badly hurt. Suriya's right arm was bandaged, and Lieth's helmet sat askew above a scalp wound. Selfer limped.

"Paks. I had hoped you wouldn't come to this trap." Phelan's voice barely carried across the court.

"Your ring worked as we hoped." That was one of the priests.

"A paladin on quest, my lord, has little choice," said Paks, ignoring the priest and meeting Phelan's gaze.

"Now you see that we have what we claimed," said the first priest. "Will you redeem him?"

"All of them," said Paks. "The squires too."

"Why the squires?"

"Why should any be left in your hands?" Paks took a long breath. "I will barter for the king, and these squires, on these grounds: one day and night for each — you to restore their arms, and let them go free for those days."

"Paks, no!" Suriya leaned forward; her guards yanked her back.

"You have no power to bargain," said the priest. "We can kill them now."

"And you are beyond your protection," said Paks, "and I am within mine. If you kill them, Liart's scum, I will kill many of you — and your power here will fail. Perhaps I cannot save them — though you would be foolish to count on that — but I can kill you."

"So." The priests conferred a moment. "We will agree on these terms: one day and night for each — that is five you would redeem?"

"Have you more in your power?"

"No. Not at present. Five, then: five days and nights. We will restore their arms and free them when you are within."

"No." Paks shook her head. "You know the worth of a paladin's word. I

967

know the worth of yours. You will free them now, and on my oath they will not strike a blow against you — "

"Paks — "

"Be silent, Suriya. As it is my choice to redeem you, so you are bound by my oath in this. Take your weapons and return to the palace; guard your lord on his journey and say no more." She looked from face to face. "All of you — do you understand?"

Phelan's eyes glittered. "Paks, you must not. You don't understand — "

"Pardon, my lord, but I do understand — perhaps more than you do. I am not your soldier now. I follow the High Lord, and Gird, the protector of the helpless, into whatever ways they call. Do not, I pray you, make this quest harder than it is."

He bowed as much as he could. "Lady, it shall be as you say. But when I am king — "

"Then speak as the king's honor demands," said Paks, meeting his eyes steadily. She looked back at the priest. "You will not harry them for the days of the bargain."

"We will not."

"Then I take oath, by Gird and the High Lord, that when I see them safely freed and armed I will submit without battle to your mastery for five days and nights."

"Unbind them," said one of the priests.

"Wait," said Paks. They paused. "I have one further demand. They shall carry away my own arms, that Gird's armor be not fouled in your den."

"I have no objection," said the priest curtly. He nodded, and the guards untied the bonds. Garris slumped to the ground; Suriya and Selfer struggled to lift him. "Is he dead?" asked Paks.

"Not quite," said Selfer grimly. Paks prayed, certain the Liartian priests would not let her touch Garris to heal him. She felt a drain on her strength, as the healing often seemed, and Garris managed to stand between the other two. Suriya looked at her, and nodded slowly. When they had all been given their weapons, Paks spoke again.

"Come here — near the entrance — and I will disarm." Lieth and Phelan warded her as best they could while she took off her weapons and mail. She folded everything into a neat stack, covered with her cloak against curious eyes, and tucked her Gird's medallion into it. Then she took off Phelan's signet ring and handed it to him. "My lord, your ring. Take your royal sword, and keep it to your hand after this. Lieth, High Marshal Seklis will take my gear. My lord, you must go at once."

"Paks — "

"Gird's grace on you, sir king." Paks bowed; Phelan nodded, and started up the passage with Lieth guarding the rear. She watched just long enough to see them around the chimney, then turned back to the others. They had not moved.

"It is astonishing," said one priest, "that Girdsmen are so gullible." Paks said nothing. "For all you know, that man may be a convert to our Master's service."

At that, Paks laughed. "You know better than that of paladins: if he were evil, I would know. I can read *your* heart well enough."

"Good," said the priest, his voice chilling. "Read it closely, paladin, and learn fear." He nodded, and the swordsmen came forward on either side. "Remember your oath, fool: you swore to come without a battle."

Paks felt her belly clench; for a moment fear shook her mind and body both. Then she steadied herself and faced them. "As I swore, so I will do; the High Lord and Gird his servant command me."

The priests both laughed. "What a spectacle we can offer! It's rare sport to have a paladin to play with — and one sworn to offer no resistance is rarer yet."

Paks made no answer, and when the swordsmen surrounded her, stood quietly. None of them touched her for a moment, daunted by her light, but when the priests gave a sharp command they prodded her forward, across the yard and into the doorway. Once inside, the priests grabbed her and slammed her roughly against the wall of the passage. Her light had vanished. She felt their assault on her heart at the same time, but trusted that no evil could touch her so. Guards bound her arms behind her and her ankles with heavy thongs, drawing them cruelly tight. Then they dragged her down one passage and another, down steep stairs where every stair left its own bruise, along wide corridors and narrow ones, until she was nearly senseless.

That journey ended in a large chamber, torchlit, half-full of kneeling worshippers. The guards pulled Paks upright, supporting her between them so that she could see the size of the room and the equipment gathered on a platform at the near end. It was grim enough; Paks had seen such things before. She would never come out of here; she would die of it, and worse than that, she would be watched, taunted, ridiculed, as it happened. She tried to think of something else — anything else — and felt a nudge in her back, warm and soft, as if the red horse had pushed against her. When the priests confronted her, she knew her face showed nothing of her fear.

When they introduced her to the waiting crowd, she heard the reaction, the indrawn breath — half fear, half anticipation. A paladin — would the high gods intrude? But the priests reassured them: the fool had consented. Her gods would not interfere. Paks saw the gloating eyes, the moist-lipped mouths half-open. At the back, a dark woman who might have been Barra gave her a mocking grin. As the priests talked on, she saw more and more slip into the hall, drawn by rumor and held by delight. A sour taste came into her mouth; she swallowed against it, praying.

Unlike her ordeal in Kolobia, most of what happened in the next five days and nights remained clear in her mind.

They began predictably, by ripping her clothes off and scattering the pieces as the worshippers laughed and cheered at the priests' urging. Paks stared over their heads at the back wall of the chamber. Then one priest handled her roughly all over, squeezing and pinching as if she were a draft horse up for sale. The second one began, slapping her face with his studded gloves, pinching her breasts sharply.

Now they called the worshippers forward, encouraging them all to feel and pry, slap and pinch. It was petty, but not less disturbing for that. The sheer enmity of it — the number of sneering faces, strangers to whom she had never done harm, who snickered and giggled as they ran their dirty fingers over her face, poked her ribs, felt between her thighs. She could not imagine being such a person, taking such pleasure. What could have made them what they were?

One youth reached up and yanked at her hair; that began a round of such antics. One would take a single hair and pull it out; others took a handful and pulled again and again. They pulled other hair, jeering when she flinched, and looking to the priests for approval. She felt the first blood trickle down her face; someone with a jeweled ring had scraped it deliberately across her forehead. But the priests stopped him.

"Not yet," one of them said. "The Master has plenty of time for this one, slave, and more skill than you know. Draw no blood, slaves, at this time — be obedient, or suffer his punishment." The man in front of Paks paled, trying to hide his bloodstained ring. The priest laughed. "Do you think to hide from the Master, fool? Yet you share our vision: you are only hasty. You will taste her blood later — be obedient." He confronted Paks, pushing the spiked visor of his helm into her face. "And you, little paladin? Do you fear yet? Do you begin to regret your bargain?"

"No." To her surprise, her voice was steadier than her limbs. "I do not regret following the commands of my lord."

"Then we will instruct you," he said, and made a sign to the guards. "You have seen the punishments in Phelan's army. See how you like ours." As he spoke, the guards forced her back over a small waist-high block, looping her wrist bonds through a hook on the floor of the platform. One of them leaned a fist on her chest, and two others pulled her knees down and apart. Paks felt her back muscles straining. The priest who had been speaking slapped her taut belly and laughed again. "It bothered you when our servants pulled your hair? Then we will ease you this far, paladin: you will have no hair to be pulled. You know the term *tinisi turin*?" The crowd laughed obediently and the second priest came toward her with a razor. "It may not be as sharp as you would like," he began, "But it has certain — advantages — for our way — of doing things." As he spoke, he yanked on her braid and sliced roughly at her thick hair. In a moment or two, it fell free; Paks could feel the ragged ends stirring, the cool air on her scalp. He walked away. When he came back, two assistants were bringing with him the little brazier she had seen, and the razor he held was glowing hot. "It cuts well this way," he said, laying it lightly along her ribs. Paks tried not to flinch. But by the time he had shaved her head and the rest of her body hair, leaving raw burned patches that the chill air rasped, she was shaking. The watching crowd talked and laughed, like people watching a juggler at a village fair. The priest watching her nodded.

"You will learn despair, little paladin; even now you are finding what you did not expect. And now we will brand you with Liart's mark, that you feel in your own flesh his Mastery." One of them seized her ears, bracing her head, and the hot iron came down, its horned circle held before her eyes a moment before it pressed her forehead. For an instant it felt cold, as it hissed, then searing pain bored through her head. Tears burst from her eyes; she choked back a scream. The priest laughed. "Now you are Liart's. You may stay there, while we attend to other matters that need the Master's touch."

Paks could see nothing of what happened next; she fought to keep control of her own reactions. She heard a name called, and someone cried out in the crowd. A flurry — a frightened voice, a boy's voice, and another one pleading, a man's voice, older. The priest made some accusation; Paks did not attend to the words, but the tone came through. Then the boy's voice again, frightened and rising to a scream of pain. She heard blows — a whip, she thought — and more screams, then the man's voice sobbing. Then the priest — cold, arrogant, demanding, and the man's voice again, in submission. The priest returned to her, and grabbed her by both ears, holding up her head so that she could see the child who hung from his wrists, bloodstreaked.

"See? If we treat children so, think how much worse it will be for you."

"Gird's grace on that boy," said Paks quietly. "The protector of the helpless grant him peace."

The priest dropped her head abruptly. After that came several torments, repeated careful blows of a slender rod, cuffs and blows with padded sticks and weighted thongs. Then she was untied and thrown to the floor, kicked and prodded and beaten again, not enough to break bones, but until she was dizzy and sick. All the time the crowd watched, jeering at her whenever she cried out. Paks fixed her mind on Gird and the High Lord, on the magical fire the Kuakgan had raised, on the feel of the red horse's nose in her back.

Next she was shoved over to the platform where the boy hung, now stirring again and moaning. Blood spattered the floor, streaked his body. The guards untied him, and tossed him aside. Paks winced at the hollow thud his body made, hitting the floor, and muttered another prayer for him. The priest slapped her. "Pray for yourself, fool! Better yet, beg mercy of our Master, who is the only one who can help you now."

"The High Lord has dominion over all the gods," said Paks, again to her own surprise. The priest signalled the guards, and Paks was jerked off her feet by a rope from her bound wrists over the crossbar. It nearly took her shoulders out of their sockets. The guards untied her ankles, and spread her legs, tying them to either side of the frame, then hauled on the rope until all her weight came on her wrists.

"You," the shorter priest said, "are not a god, and therefore our Master has dominion over you — or would you dispute that?"

Sweat ran into her eyes, stinging. Paks gasped, "I am Gird's paladin — your slavemaster has no dominion over me."

"Gird is not helping you now, paladin," sneered the priest. "Nor will you

971

hold a sword again, if we disjoint both shoulders and leave them so."

"Nor is that the limit of our skill," said the other. "Trussed as you are, we can do anything — and you cannot prevent it."

Paks answered nothing; she could not breathe evenly. Pain wracked her shoulders and back; she hardly felt the burns and welts that had hurt so earlier. How long had it been? How much more?

"I will show you," he said. His gloved hands began to move over her body, gentle at first, in mimicry of lovemaking. The crowd laughed loudly as he exaggerated his movements for their benefit. Then his fingers probed her body, finding points that radiated spikes of pain. She could not stand it — had to writhe — could not, for the pressure on her shoulders. Soon she was panting, gasping for breath, tumbled in a roil of pain that brought back the night she'd been attacked at the inn. He stood back, then, and waited until her breathing quieted. Then he did it again. And again. The third time, she passed out.

When she came to, her arms were tied overhead to corners of the same frame, and the shorter priest was lecturing the crowd.

" — you see, you need not maim or kill — not at first. It is the skill, the knowing where to touch, and how hard. Knowing, for example, which child is a father's favorite." A pause; alert silence from the crowd. "Knowing how much punishment to give." Another long silence. "But some of you would already have killed this paladin of Gird — and spoiled our Master's pleasure by so many hours. Watch and learn — enjoy with us, the power of our Master over *all* mankind. Not even the hero-saints of old can save this paladin in her pain. We can do anything — anything at all — and we come to no harm, as you see. Our Master has the power — the only power. Our Master shares his mastery with his slaves, if they are obedient. You, too, can have power over even a paladin. Watch — learn — do as we say, and you can make a paladin bleed and cry out. And if a paladin falls to us, how much more easily an ordinary man, eh?"

He prowled the front of the hall, menacing, predatory, and Paks saw those in front shrink back slightly. Their eyes followed him, wary.

"What power is it you want? Is it money? We have her gold. Is it blood? We have it all — you will see it fall for our pleasure. Is it lust? You will have your chance. Is it mastery itself? You will see her cringe before us, and before those of you chosen to assist. Our Master has power — real power — and you can share that power. Everyone else is helpless in the end — helpless like this paladin. Would you have feared her once, with her big sword, her fancy armor?" His voice dripped contempt. The crowd shifted, not quite answering. "Yes, admit it! You would have feared her, up there on the street — yes you would, unworthy slaves! You might have cringed from her — but look now. There she hangs, bound and helpless. What she has, she has because we left it to her." He waved an arm back at Paks, and some eyes shifted to meet hers and as quickly shifted away.

"You — *you* there in the third row — you could blind her, couldn't you? And *you* — you could cut off her ears. Who would stop you but our Master?

Who could punish you but our Master? Who is worthy of your service but
— " he paused; the answer came quickly from the crowd:

"Master — Master — *Master*." The faces Paks could see were tight with
fear, not so avid for the spectacle as before. She felt a surge of pity for them.

"Yes. Our Master: Liart the strong. You must never say his name, unworthy slaves, until you come to his altar to swear your souls to him forever.
But you know who he is." He raised his hand, fist clenched.

"The Master," came the response.

The priests noticed her open eyes and came to her again. She met their
gaze evenly.

"And you are still with us, little paladin?" asked the taller.

"The High Lord is still with us all," she said. Someone in the crowd
hooted, and others laughed. The shorter priest reached out and stroked
her sides.

"He hasn't done well by you, with these scars," he said. "I'd almost think
you'd been given to our Master already."

"No," said Paks recklessly, "that was Achrya's work."

He slammed his fist into her belly. "Don't say that name aloud, scum."

Paks gasped for breath. "You — *fear* — her?"

Again a blow that took her breath away, and another to her face. One of
the priests took up the barbed whip they had used on the boy, and showed it
to her. "This will teach you something of our Master; he is bolder than that
webspinner." He slashed it across her body, then her legs, and walked behind her. Five rapid blows split the skin of her back; hot blood sheeted
down, dripping from her legs. Paks clenched her jaw against the fiery pain.
Before it dulled, they had brought the next torment, a heated chain held
carefully in tongs. First around her waist — then each thigh in turn. Paks
could smell the charred skin, *her* charred skin.

Again the crowd was invited up, in groups, to participate. Now the men
were urged to arouse themselves. "Not yet," the priest said, to those fumbling at their trousers. "Wait for that — but go on and enjoy what you can."
They traced her scars and the whip welts with their fingers, poked and
prodded every orifice. She saw one man lick his finger after wiping it in her
blood. The thought of it made her sick. The priests laughed. "Good, eh? It's
blood like any other — taste it." Several others did the same thing. Paks
thought briefly of the many soldiers she had killed — the blood she had
shed — but she had never tasted their blood, never seen soldiers as wanton-
ly cruel. Yet some, she could tell, were more frightened than eager: they
took no pleasure in it, their eyes downcast, their faces tense. It seemed a
long time before the priests ordered the crowd back to their places.

The taller priest held up an iron that had been heating in the brazier,
and flourished it.

"Now that you carry Liart's brand, we must do worse than threaten your
beauty. But if we decorate you with deep burns here — " He touched the inside
of her thigh. Pain flared along her leg. " — you might never ride or walk
again." She could not tell how bad the burn was; her whole leg felt afire.

"There are other ways," said the shorter one, conversationally. "If we show you all of them, I fear you will not be able to appreciate the artistry involved. Perhaps we should demonstrate —" and he signalled to the guards. Paks did not notice where they went. Soon they were back, dragging with them a girl Paks had never seen. She looked to be in her mid-teens, someone's servant by her clothes. She was gagged and bound, her eyes wild; as soon as the tall priest ripped the gag roughly away, she screamed.

"Shut up!" He slapped her face. "If you scream again, I'll —" He did not finish the threat; she choked off her cries, and watched him, eyes streaming with tears. He turned to Paks. "From time to time we find our sacrifices in the streets — this girl loitered in an alley, and as we had need, we — borrowed her." As he spoke, the girl turned her head and saw Paks; her eyes seemed to bulge from her face in panic, and she struggled wildly. One of the guards twisted her arm, and she subsided. "Now, paladin, let me offer another bargain."

Paks said nothing.

"You are bound to endure five days and nights — let us say, five days and four nights, now — of our Master's pleasure, whatever comes. But if you will agree that our Master has dominion over all, then we need not waste this girl's limbs showing you the range of our skill. If, however, you still insist that your gods — whatever you name them — are more powerful, then we must teach you your weakness through her. Did you not name Gird protector of the helpless — and you claim to be his paladin? Yes — but you, a paladin of that so-called protector of the helpless, you cannot save this girl from anything, except by our Master's name."

"Please —" The girl's voice was faint, but she looked straight into Paks's eyes. "Don't let them —"

Paks looked away, scanning the crowd, then the priests, then the guards, and finally looking back at the girl. "No," she said steadily. "I can't."

"So," said the tall priest. "You begin to enjoy our entertainment then? You would like to see more, is that it?" Someone in the crowd tittered.

"No," said Paks again. "I take no pleasure in giving pain, or seeing pain given." The girl's mouth opened again, but Paks spoke first. "I cannot forswear my gods, child. I will pray for you — that Gird and the High Lord protect you, comfort you, and strengthen you, that the Lady of Peace bring you peace in the end — but the Master of these slaves is evil, and I will not praise him."

"Then she will suffer, and it is your doing," said the tall priest.

"No. If you harm her, she will suffer because of you. I am not a torturer: *you* are."

"But you could stop it, and you refuse to help her."

"Could I?" Paks managed a smile that seemed to crack her face. "*Could I* stop it? Have I any reason to trust your word? As long as I am trussed here, you can do as you like — and you like to do evil. Besides, your Master is a paltry fellow; I cannot call him great. Liart the strong, indeed! Liart the coward is more like it!"

974

"Girdish slut!" The tall priest snatched up the barbed whip again, and laid two strokes on her before the other grabbed his arm.

"She is stronger than you thought, brother — she taunts you into just such haste. See — if she faints, she rests."

"She will not faint." The tall priest swiped his hand down the bleeding welts and rubbed it over Paks's face, then licked his hand. "And if she does we will add every hour to the length of her bargain. Your blood tastes sweet, paladin. Before long we will try your flesh as well." He turned back to the girl, and his voice calmed.

"There are several ways to cripple without killing, paladin. Some are more . . . artistic . . . that others. Consider this — " He used tongs to pull from the brazier a fist-sized cobble. "A hot stone. Applied to the inside of a joint — say the knee — and bound there, it will burn deeply, and the scars contract, pulling the limb awry. It works best at knee, crotch, elbow, and armpit, choosing the size of stone to conform, of course — " The guards had forced the girl onto her face, and pulled up her skirts. Now the priest set the hot stone against the back of her knee, and the guards quickly forced her leg back against it, and bound it tight with heavy thongs. Her screams echoed off the stone walls. The guards let her go, cutting the thongs that bound her arms, and she thrashed on the floor, shrieking and clawing at her leg.

Paks fought down nausea. She could do nothing; she closed her eyes, trying to concentrate on Gird, trying to pray. But she heard the crowd shouting, jeering now at the struggling girl. Something tugged at her, sending a wave of pain through her. She opened her eyes to see the girl clutching at her ankle, trying to drag herself upward on Paks's body. "Please!" she begged. "Please — stop them!"

"I can't — " muttered Paks. "But Gird — "

"No! You — !" the girl screamed, clawing now. "You won't help — *curse* you — !" She threw herself upward, shaking Paks back and forth in her bonds. Then she collapsed, still screaming. Paks shook her head; tears burned her eyes. Her heart seemed to falter in her chest. The priests waited until the girl's screams died to sobbing, then the guards pinned her again, cut the thongs, and pulled her leg straight. She gave a final shriek as they knocked the stone loose; it left two charred wounds in her leg as it rolled to the floor; smoking bits of her flesh clung to it.

"Well, paladin — did Gird protect *her*?" The taller priest nudged the sobbing girl with his foot. Paks did not answer. She fought the black despair Liart sent, forcing herself to think of the king riding eastward, his squires around him. She would not have spent someone else's pain for that, but even so she did not repent the bargain. After a long pause, he asked, "Do you think he will protect you? Will you fight well, paladin of Gird, with your leg twisted like this? Or imagine your arm — your sword arm — drawn up with scars." He touched the hollow of her elbow, and her armpit; Paks shivered. "I see you do understand. We need not be in haste to show you, then." He turned to the guards. "Tie that one, and leave her; we will want her later."

"No," said Paks.

"No? You dare give orders here? Or are you agreeing that our Master has dominion?"

"I am not. I am telling you not to hurt her more — she has done you no harm."

"What of that? It amuses us — and teaches you to know your helplessness. You can save her only by accepting our Master as yours."

Paks prayed, trying to convey what healing she could across that space, as she had with Garris. But she had known Garris, touched him with healing before. This girl was a stranger. She felt a comforting touch on her own head, as if a firm but gentle hand cradled it for a moment, but nothing that let her suspect she had healed the girl. She could not see the girl's face, where she lay, but the sobs quieted, and the heaving back was still.

For some time after that, she was left hanging before the crowd; she noticed that it ebbed and flowed, and individuals came and left, to return after an interval. From time to time the priests came to her again, repetitions of the torments already begun. Once they tried to rouse the servant girl, and found her dead; they dragged her body aside. Paks could not be sure of the pass of time. Pain and thirst confused her. Whenever she fell into a doze, they roused her, until she longed for rest more than anything. Then the crowd thickened again.

The guards lit new lamps, and set pungent incense burning in a row of censors. The smoke swirled back and forth. Paks watched it, half-tranced by its intricate patterns that seemed to make pictures in the haze. She had managed not to listen to the priests' words, even reciting to herself the ten fingers of the Code of Gird. But now as they approached her again, her concentration wavered. Her belly knotted; her tongue seemed too large for her mouth. Two guards cut the thongs that held her wrists, and shoved. She fell forward, slamming into the floor with stunning force. She was just aware when they cut the ankle thongs and her feet thudded down.

The relief in her shoulders lasted only a few moments. Guards yanked her up by the arms and dragged her to the rough stone altar that centered the platform. They bound her again by wrist and ankles, with the rough-hewn stone rasping her lacerated back. The taller priest laid a single flat stone on her belly. He stood back, and the second priest laid another similar stone on her chest. Paks waited; the stones were uncomfortable, but not painful, except where they lay on the burns. She was too relieved to have her head supported at last, and the weight off her arms. Then returning blood seemed to dip her hands in fire for a few minutes. The priests called the crowd forward.

"We will show you a torment that lasts long only with strong sacrifices, such as this one," said the first. "We will add weight to those stones, a heavy link of chain at a time, until she can scarcely draw breath. Then time alone becomes the tormenter; in the end her breath will fail. And you will help. As you have given to the Master, so in your name will the links be added."

And each person who came by dropped a coin or so into a pot, naming

976

the number; the guards fed a heavy chain from its coil onto the stones, link by link, one or two or three at a time, as the worshipper gave. One heavy man in a silk robe gave a large silver, and twelve links at once dropped onto Paks's chest.

The weight forced her back into the stone; before half the crowd had passed, she was finding it hard to breath. When she tried to keep her chest expanded, they added links to the lower stone, forcing her to use chest wall as well for breath. Her sight dimmed; she let her eyes shut, concentrating on breath alone. She heard the priests' voices, but could not follow their words. No more links dropped. She struggled, fighting for every breath. Air rasped in and out of her throat. Cold water drenched her face; she choked on it, tried to cough, and could not. Before she quite passed out, they took off a few links. Then they watched as she struggled with that weight. When that, too, exhausted her, they removed a few more links.

She longed for rest, for sleep, but could not sleep with that weight; whenever she dozed, she could not breathe. Again, she had no idea how long this lasted; each painful breath seemed to be an hour away from another. She could hear the voices, hear the clank of metal as they played with her, taking off a link or so, and dropping it back on. She felt other pains, as the priests and worshippers prodded her, spit on her, and tried to provoke some reaction, but all that really mattered was air: the struggle to suck it in, the weight that forced it back out too soon.

As the torment continued, a part of her mind was aware of the differences between this and the earlier captivities she'd endured. That night in the Duke's cells, when she'd been so sunk in her own misery that she had not even imagined worse than Stammel's anger. The pain had been real, the fear overwhelming . . . but as the pain and fear of a child stung by a wasp is real. Lost in the moment, the child cannot imagine that the pain will end, or that any pain could be worse. The adult knows better; she pitied the child she had been, so miserable in the dark, alone and afraid, convinced that her chance to be a hero was lost forever. And how Korryn's punishment had shocked her with its cruelty! She had trembled for days at the thought that she might have been whipped and branded instead. Being stripped publicly had been bad enough.

And from that she had gone to a soldier's endurance, learning to stave off pain and fear with anger and defiance, linking hope to vengeance. That righteous anger served well against Siniava, or seemed to, when she avenged her friends' deaths. Yet in Kolobia, that same anger betrayed her to deep evil. She remembered too well that mood, black rage edged with madness, so much less innocent than the panic of the beaten recruit. Under it had been the same fears the child had, disguised but not controlled, a willingness to deal the pain she suffered.

Again, as so often before, her mind filled with the vision of her childhood dream, the bright figure in shining mail, mounted on a prancing horse and waving a sword. It flickered in and out of her sight, shifting in tides of pain and weakness, as it had flickered in her mind's eye these several years. Now she could see its shadow, the dark nest of fears which had brought it to life. Helplessness, humiliation, pain, a lonely death, and nothing after — she had feared these, and made of that fear a dream of power, of freedom, of untouchable strength and courage. *She* would never suffer that, because she would be the hero, the one with the sword, the one who was above such suffering.

And here she was, bound helpless before enemies who enjoyed her pain, an example, as they said, of Liart's power. An example to teach more fear, more hatred, proof that the dream of glory had been false: no power, no bright sword or prancing horse, no protection, even for herself.

But the image of her dream steadied, and did not fade. No one whole wanted to be hurt, wanted to be the victim of such cruelty as held her now. Her fears were as common as a taste for salt or honey, as healthy as the desire for comfort, for love. So much she had learned from the Kuakgan. Now, at last, she accepted her right to share those fears: she did not have to deny them, only master herself.

And this, she saw, her dream had done. She had built against that fear a vision of power not wholly selfish — power to protect not only herself, but others. And that vision — however partial it had been in those days — was worth following. For it led not away from the fear, as a dream of rule might do, but back into it. The pattern of her life — as she saw it then, clear and far away and painted in bright colors — the pattern of her life was like an intricate song, or the way the Kuakgan talked of the grove's interlacing trees. There below were the dream's roots, tangled in fear and despair, nourished in the death of friends, the bones of the strong, the blood of the living, and there high above were the dream's images, bright in the sun like banners or the flowering trees of spring. And to be that banner, or that flowering branch, meant being nourished by the same fears: meant encompassing them, not rejecting them.

She did not know herself when these thoughts linked at last, forming the final pattern, bringing up into her mind the self she had become. It was then as if several selves were present, mysteriously separate and conjoined. Trapped inside her body was the same child she had been, feeling each new torment as a wave of intolerable pain, each ragged scream as a fresh humiliation. The seasoned soldier watched with pity as her body gave way to exhaustion and pain as any body would, feeling no shame at the sight or sound or smell of it, for this was something that could happen to anyone, and she had never inflicted it on others. And someone else, someone newer, refused the soldier's tactics of defiance, anger, vengeance, and looked into her own fear to find the link to those around her, to find the way to reach those frightened tormentors, the ones not already lost to evil.

In the rare respites, when the priests stopped to harangue the crowd and revive her for more torture, she felt curiously untroubled. Not free of pain, nor free of fear, but free of the need to react to that fear in all the old ways. She had no anger left, no hatred, no desire for vengeance, nothing but pity for those who must find such vile amusements, who had no better

978

hope, or no courage to withdraw. It would all happen to her — all the things she'd feared, every violation of body, everything she'd taken up the sword to prevent — and she consented. Not because it was right: it was never right. Not because she deserved it: no one deserved such violation. But because she *could* consent, being what she was, and by consenting destroy its power over her and others, proving in her own body that fear's power came from fear, that greater power could from the same dark roots find another way to the light.

This quietness, this consent, formed a still pool in the center of that violent place. At first, only the priests noticed, and flung themselves into a frenzy of violence against it. But it was not brittle steel to break, or crystal to shatter, but a strength fluid and yet immovable, unmarred by the broken rhythm of her breath, or even by her screams. The quietness spread, from gray eyes that held no hatred for those who spat at her face or tasted her blood, from a voice that could scream in pain yet mouth no curses after, that spoke, between screams, in a steady confirmation of all good.

Those watching could not deny the wounds: they had seen them being dealt: they had helped deal them. They could not deny the sight of blood, the smell of it, the sticky feel of it, the salt taste on too many tongues. They could not deny the stink of burnt flesh, the sight of scabbed and crusted wounds, the dead servant girl, the boy's back striped and bleeding. This was not the quietness of inviolable protection, for she suffered all that was done to her. They had seen a virgin raped, a soldier's scars mocked and redrawn in fresh blood. They had heard a paladin scream, as the priests promised.

And yet she did not hate, and yet she did not fear, and yet she said, when she had breath to speak, that the High Lord's justice would rule in the end. The priests shouted threats, promised more torments, blustered and postured: the silence spread, as a pool rises silently above a new-broken spring when the dry season ends.

One by one the crowd fell still, or joined the mockery with less eagerness. She was so small, after all, broken like that . . . they could think of sisters, cousins, friends they had known, who might be where she was, if she were not there. They had thought it would be satisfying to see a paladin, one of the proud and powerful, brought low. But they knew her story, from the year that cruel rumor spread the tale of her cowardice. She was only a peasant girl, born into poverty. What did it prove to shame a sheepfarmer's daughter who had known shame already? Some among them had been soldiers, and recognized the scars of a common soldier who has seen hard service. They felt no braver for breaking a soldier's scarred hands. And those who had first laughed to see a virgin raped — and even those who had joined in eagerly — now looked from the dead servant girl to the other, and found something pitiful in both, something shameful in themselves, that they could take pleasure in such pain. She was no threat to them — why had they ever thought she was a threat? Paladins never threatened the helpless. The threat was elsewhere, in those who wore Liart's horned circle, who flourished the barbed whips and the heated chains.

By such small degrees the crowd's mood changed, shifting back in sudden fear when the priests turned their weapons on individuals chosen not quite at random, but slowly, inexorably, turning away from the praise of cruelty to some vague sympathy with suffering. Glass by glass, as the torches burned down and were replaced again and again, as the day passed into night and another day, and another night and day, one and another of those watching came slowly and without intent to a new vision of the world.

Of all this, Paks was hardly aware. At best, she knew what she must do, and why, but those moments seemed few. Pain followed pain in sickening procession; at times even her new insight failed, leaving her adrift in self-disgust or despair. For the most part she concentrated on refusing anger and hatred, accepting the pain as a necessary part of something chosen long before. When they broke her hands, each bone a separate torment, she struggled against her old fear of crippling. She had clung to the hope that if she lived, she would still be whole, able to fight. But she knew better, knew from having lived through it that she was more than a hand to hold a sword. She could live, being Gird's paladin, with no more than breath, or die whole, of old age, and be nothing at all. The difference lay in her, *was* her, was what she had become: no one but she could change it. The rapes, that she had feared before as both violation and torment wholly unknown, were then nothing but physical pain, no worse than others. She lost nothing, for she had had nothing, had never invested herself in that, or hoped for that kind of pleasure. It seemed to her that Alyanya came in a dream, and comforted her, but dream, vision, and reality were by then too nearly mixed for clear memory.

Then they held her up once more for the crowd to see. The chamber was crowded with worshippers who had come to see the end of the spectacle. At the priests' command the guards threw her to the floor.

"Will you admit that our Master commands your obedience?" asked one of the priests, nudging her face with the toe of his boot.

"I am Gird's," said Paks, forcing the words out. Her voice was clearer than she would have thought possible.

"You are meat. You are the sacrifice our Master demanded." The priest's voice was cold. "If you will not acknowledge our Master, the stones are heating for you." Paks said nothing. "Do you want to be a helpless cripple?" he demanded.

"No," she said. "But I do want to be Gird's paladin." Again she felt the lightest touch on her head, and a soothing haze came between her and her pain.

The priest snorted. "Gird's paladin! A bloody rag too stupid to know the truth! Then you will suffer it all, paladin of Gird, just as you wish."

Pain exploded in her legs as the burning stones were dropped in the hollow of both knees, and her legs bound tightly around them. She clenched her fists, forgetting the broken bones until too late. The pain was sickening, impossible; she retched, trying not to scream.

"And now, paladin? Where is your lord's protection now?" The priests hauled her up by both arms, forcing weight on her knees.

"The High Lord has dominion," gasped Paks. "Gird has upheld me here; I have not failed." She felt herself falling, and willed to fall into that darkness.

The guards held a bloody wreck between them. The crowd smelled burnt flesh, and shivered, not hearing the priests' final lecture. What had she meant, "I have not failed"? The paladin's head hung down, slack against her chest, the brand of Liart dark on her forehead. Then the priests gestured, and the guards turned her around. The taller priest cut the cords around her legs, and her feet thumped down. With tongs, the priest yanked the stones from their place, ragged bits of skin clinging to them. The hall stank of it. The paladin did not move, or cry out; she might have been dead. For an instant, no one moved or spoke.

Then those in front saw, and did not believe, but recoiled even in disbelief against those behind. For the burnt bloody holes where the rocks had been disappeared, as a wave swept across lines on sand erases them, gone without mark or scar. At the movement, the priests turned, saw, and gaped in equal disbelief. One by one, other wounds healed, changing in the sight of those watching to unmarked skin. Finger by finger, her misshapen hands regained their natural shape. With a cry, the two guards dropped her, flinging themselves back. One of the priests cursed, and raised his whip, but when he swung, it recoiled from her and snagged his own armor. The other drew a notched dagger, and stabbed, but his blade twisted aside. She lay untouched, unmoving.

Now turmoil filled the hall: those behind wanting to see what had happened, those in front frantic to escape the wrath of Gird they were sure would come. The priests called other guards, who yanked her upright, head still lolling — now all could see that Liart's black brand no longer centered her forehead. Instead, a silver circle gleamed there, as if inset in the bone itself. At that, the priests of Liart shrank away, their masked faces averted from the High Lord's holy symbol. The terrified guards would have dropped her, but the priests screamed obscenities louder even than the crowds' noise, and sent them away with her, out the same entrance through which they'd brought her earlier. And then they drove the crowd away, in a rage that could not disguise their own fear.

Chaos scurried through the warrens of the Thieves Guild, panic and disruption, as those who had seen tried to convince those who had not, and those who would not listen tried to find someone to believe. Some fled to the streets: black night, icy cold with a sweeping wind, and patrols of cold-eyed Royal Guards sent them back into the familiar warrens, even more afraid. Factions clashed; old quarrels erupted in steel and strangling cord. Those who had arranged to take the paladin's body outside the city walls wrapped her in a heavy cloak and carried her gingerly, carefully not looking to see if that healing miracle continued, eager to get this terror out of their domain.

And at every grange of Gird, the vigil continued until dawn.

Chapter Twenty-eight

Kieri Phelan rode away from Vérella that dark night in an internal storm of impotent rage and frustration. He had been captured by a ruse he should have seen through — taken in by the plea of one of his veterans. That was stupidity, and he didn't excuse himself that he was distracted by the day's events. So he was Lyonya's king — that didn't mean he could let his mind wander. And then he'd been rescued — beyond his hopes — by another veteran — by Paksenarrion, now a paladin of Gird. She had freed him, and his squires, but she herself was now a prisoner — for five days, she had agreed to suffer whatever torments the priests of Liart inflicted. And he had agreed to that, because he could do nothing else. She made the bargain with the Liartians, and her oath bound him. He shifted in the saddle, glad of the darkness that covered his expression. What must they all think, of a king that would sacrifice a paladin to save his own life?

And yet — he had to admit she was right. He knew who he was, now: the rightful heir to Lyonya's throne, a half-elf, torn from his birthright by slavers. No one else could do what he must do — restore the frayed taig of Lyonya, and the alliance of elf and human, clean the forests of evil influence. Lyonya needed its king — needed *him* — and he could not deny a paladin's right to follow a quest to its end. But Paksenarrion — dear to him as his own daughter — his heart burned to think of her in their hands. All he had seen in thirty-odd years of war came to him that night, and showed him what she must endure.

He forced his mind to his own plans. If she had bought his life, he must make use of it. Selfer would be far north of Vérella by now, riding hard to meet Dorrin's cohort and bring them down. Dorrin herself, in Vérella, would have fresh mounts ready for them, and a royal pass to follow him. Kostvan had agreed to let Arcolin pass through, if it came to that, and would be alert in case the Pargunese tried to take advantage of his absence. He thought ahead. Surely the enemy would strike before he reached Chaya — but where? Not in the Mahieran lands close to Vérella, nor in the little baronies of Abriss or Dai. East of that, in Verrakai domain? At the border itself? In Lyonya? He thought over what Paks had said about Achrya's influence there — some thought of him as a blood-thirsty mercenary. He had no clear idea of the river road in his mind; he'd always gone south to visit the Halverics, cutting eastward from below Fiveway to go through Brewersbridge and avoid Verrakai altogether.

982

At Westbells, the High Marshal and Phelan both stopped to wake Marshal Torin and hand over Paks's gear. Seklis did not explain much, and Marshal Torin, sleepy-eyed and bewildered, did not ask. Kieri touched that bright armor for the last time, as he thought, and prayed to all the gods that Paks might be spared the worst. The first glimmer of light seeped into the eastern sky as they rode away. Around him the ponderous hooves of the heavy warhorses — twenty of them — shook the earth. Behind were the lighter mounts of the infantry and bowmen, and then the pack train. Kieri's mouth twitched, remembering Dorrin's sulfurous comments on the pack train. He would have minded more, except that their slowness gave Dorrin a better chance to catch up. He thought where Selfer would be, on the road he knew best — changing horses, gulping a hot mug of sib, and starting off again, faced with Crow Ridge to climb.

As the day brightened, Kieri glanced around to see what his escort looked like in the daytime. Twenty massive gray warhorses, twenty plate-armored knights with spears and swords. Already the heavy horses were streaked with sweat; they were meant for power, not distance. Twenty mounted infantry, on gray horses much smaller than the warhorses; these carried short swords, with shields slung to the saddles. Ten mounted bowmen, on the same light horses, with the short, sharply curved bow of the northern nomad, to be used mounted or afoot: an excellent bow in the forest, as well. All these were in rose and silver or gray, the royal colors of Tsaia. His own tensquad, still in Phelani maroon and white, mounted on matched bays (how had Dorrin accomplished that, he wondered?), with Vossik at their head. The King's Squires from Lyonya, whom he hardly knew, but for Garris: they rode close around him, with the royal pennant of Lyonya displayed. And the two Marshals: High Marshal Seklis, and Marshal Sulinarrion, both in Gird's blue and white, with the crescent of Gird on chest and cloak. Behind came the pack train — servants, supplies, more than forty beasts extra, which the Tsaian Royal Guard insisted on.

Kieri looked around for the Royal Guard cohort commander. He had met the man the previous afternoon, before leaving the palace, but could not recognize him among the other knights. But the man caught his eye, reined his horse close, and bowed.

"My lord? You wish to rest?"

Kieri nearly laughed, but managed to hide it. "No, Sir Ammerlin. I'm used to longer rides than this. I wanted to ask, though, what your usual order of march would be."

Ammerlin frowned. "Well — it's rare that we travel far; we're the Royal Guard, after all, and we stay with the prince. We should breathe the horses soon, my lord. If they're to go far — "

"I suppose Lyonya is far," said Kieri. It seemed to him that the pace had been but a crawl — a man could have walked the distance as fast — but he knew better than to push another man's command beyond its limits. Ammerlin bowed in the saddle.

"I thank you, my lord." He returned to the head of the column, spoke to the cohort bugler, and a quick signal rang out. Kieri tossed a hand signal at Vossik that halted his own tensquad in their tracks while the Royal Guard straggled to a halt. High Marshal Seklis grinned at him.

"You did that on purpose."

"Marshal, my company doesn't know their signals."

Seklis laughed. "My lord, your company could probably keep an even interval without any signals at all — couldn't it now?"

"It might," said Kieri. Ammerlin had come back, on foot. "How long will we rest?" asked Kieri.

"A quarter glass or so, my lord. I need to check on the pack animals, and make sure everything is holding up well. And each rider checks his own animal."

"Then I'll walk around a bit." Kieri swung off his horse to find that Lieth was already down and holding his rein. "You're quick," he said, smiling. She looked down.

"My lord king, not quick enough."

He knew what she meant; the afternoon before, when they were all captured. He laid his hand on her arm. "Lieth, I will not ask you not to think of it — I think of it every moment. But I need my squires alert now — here — so I will ask that you think of it in the back of your head. Let you not reproach yourself for the past — for all of us have failed someone somewhere."

She met his eyes, her own full of tears, but nodded. "I will not speak of it again."

"We *will* speak of it again, Lieth — to the whole court of Lyonya — but first we will get there." At that she managed a smile, and he walked off the road to the snowy verge, stamping his feet. Suriya and Garris flanked him on either side; Vossik he found close behind him whenever he turned.

The pause lasted longer than a quarterglass, for some of the pack animals needed their packs reset. Kieri contained his annoyance, to Ammerlin's evident relief. High Marshal Seklis was less restrained. "I've wondered, Ammerlin, how you could possibly get to the field in time for a battle, and now I see you couldn't."

Ammerlin reddened. "We could, close to Vérella, but — "

"Gird's shovel, man, you're not an honest four hour ride from Vérella yet!"

"But we had to pack for a journey — "

"I daresay the expedition to Luap's stronghold had less baggage, and they meant to be gone a year," returned Seklis.

"High Marshal," said Kieri quietly, and shook his head. Seklis subsided; Ammerlin stalked off, still angry. "Don't bait him," said Kieri. "We will need his goodwill, when they attack us."

"You think they will?"

Kieri shrugged. "Why else would they have let me go? Paksenarrion said — and it makes sense — that two powerful evils do not want me on the throne of Lyonya. I'm not sure why they didn't kill me at once — but they must intend to do it, and this journey is the best time."

"Then why didn't you wait in Vérella for your company?"

Kieri looked at him sideways. "Marshal, if I had brought down my whole Company — and the gods know what a comfort that would be to me now — do you think I'd have had leave to march it through Verrakai's lands? And what would the Lyonyans think, when I arrived declaring myself their ruler with my own personal troops around me? And what would have happened in the north, where my Company stands between Tsaia and the northern perils? No — that would never do." Seklis and Sulinarrion nodded. "As you know, I did ask — and get — permission to bring one cohort down; if the Royal Guard is slow enough, Dorrin may catch us up before the border."

"How fast can they travel?" asked Sulinarrion.

"They'll be in Vérella three days after they start," said Kieri, then grinned at their expressions. "Mounted, of course."

"Mounted on what?" asked Seklis when he got his breath back. "Flying horses?"

"No — and not warhorses, either. Good, solid nomad-bred beasts. Ugly as sin, and legs like stone."

"What do you use for supply?" asked Sulinarrion.

"For a cohort? A ten-mule string, usually, for a week's journey. Double that for speed. More if there's a lot of fighting, because I don't like to leave my wounded behind; I'll hire wagons, mule-drawn, if necessary."

"Umph." Sulinarrion seemed impressed. "So some of what I heard from Aarenis could be true."

"That depends on what you heard."

"That your Company marched from the upper Immer to Cortes Andres in less than twelve days, including fighting."

Kieri counted on his fingers. "Ten days, it was, from Ifoss to Cortes Andres. Yes. No wagons, though, until we captured some of Siniava's on the north border of Andressat. But that march wasn't bad — ask Vossik here." He smiled at the sergeant, and the Marshals turned to him. In answer to their questions he shook his head.

"No, Marshals, my lord's right. That was across high ground, mostly, and easy enough. I'd say that march through the forest, or across Cilwan, was worse."

"The weather was," said Kieri, "and we had walking wounded, too. And what about that last stretch in Fallo?"

Vossik grinned. "I was hoping to forget that, my lord. That damned mud — those Fallo roads haven't got no bottom to 'em at all, and the fields was wet as creeks. Seemed like we'd been marching forever by then."

Ammerlin came back and bowed stiffly to Kieri. "My lord, we are ready to ride when you please."

"Thank you, Sir Ammerlin," Kieri replied. "I would like to meet the other knights before we begin — it's easier to recognize those you've met in daylight, I find."

Ammerlin relaxed slightly. "Certainly, my lord." He led Kieri to the group of heavy knights waiting to mount. Kieri shook hands with each, noting their strength and apparent determination.

"It's been so long," he said, "since I have campaigned with heavy cavalry that I have forgotten much. Sir Ammerlin, you must be sure to tell me when the horses should rest, and what must be done. A mounted infantry company moves very differently."

Ammerlin thawed another fraction. "My lord, I am sorry that we cannot move faster; the prince said your journey was urgent, and must brook no delay. I know the Marshals think we are soft, but — " he patted his own horse, "these fellows were never meant for speed or distance. Yet in close combat, they are a powerful defense; we can ride down lighter cavalry without getting far away from you. We cannot, it's true, ride into a heavy polearm company, but — "

"If we run into that," said Kieri, "we'll have to go around. Believe me, I appreciate the prince's care in sending such an escort. But to make the best use of it, you must advise me."

Ammerlin appeared to give up his resentment completely. "Well, my lord, they can work all day — if it's slow — or a short time, if it's fast. That's the choice. I'd choose to go at their walking pace — a little slower than the light horses — and rest them at least every two glasses. And a long break at noon, of course." Kieri, calculating this without moving a muscle, began to be sure that Dorrin would catch them before the border. "If we try to move out faster," Ammerlin went on, "we'll have a third of them lame in two days, and then what?" Leave them behind, Kieri thought, but did not say. He knew he would need them.

"Well," he said finally, "let's see how far we go. I would not ask haste, if it were not needed — I hope you understand that."

"Yes, my lord." Ammerlin looked much happier.

"About the order of march — " began Kieri.

"Yes, my lord?"

"What about sending some of the bowmen forward, as scouts?"

Ammerlin's expression was eloquent. "Well — my lord — if you like. But we're in Mahieran lands now — there's no real need."

"True, but then we'll be used to that — when we come to other lands."

Ammerlin chewed on this thought, and nodded. With a wave, Kieri returned to his own horse, and mounted. He watched as the bowmen got their orders and rode forward.

"That makes more sense," said Garris at his side.

"They're not used to maneuvering in hostile territory," said Kieri.

Where the road was wide enough, the heavy horses went five abreast, the four ranks in front of him and the squires. Then his own tensquad (for he had explained that since they had no officer in charge, he must be near them), then the mounted infantry. Now that the bowmen rode as scouts, the pack animals were directly behind the Guard light horse. Kieri fretted, unable to see over the four ranks of large horses in front of him; he had always led his own Company, or had trusted scouts in advance.

By the time they stopped that night, at Magen, Kieri knew it would take them a full ten days or more to reach Harway on the border. Ammerlin agreed, reminding them that he had escorted the prince's younger brother to the Verrakai hunting lodge, ten days on the road both ways. At the Marshal's invitation, Kieri, the Kings' Squires, and the other Marshals stayed in Magen grange, and after supper they deplored the slow progress.

"My lord, they will have plenty of time to deploy a large force — "

"I know. That's why Paksenarrion wanted me to hurry. But they're going to attack — large force or not — and I need the troops."

"What about using yeomen from any grange nearby?"

Kieri shook his head. "Should I involve the yeomen of Tsaia in a battle to protect the king of Lyonya? No, if they choose to fight, I'll welcome them — but I have no right to call them out."

"Besides," said Marshal Hagin, "not all granges would be much help. Perhaps the High Marshal is not aware that some granges in the east have nearly withered away?"

"No — if I'd known, I'd have done something." Seklis scowled. "What's the problem?"

"I don't know. I hear things, from peddlers on the road, and that sort — and we all know about the troubles near Konhalt — and Verrakai."

"Duke Verrakai has never been one of my supporters," said Kieri mildly. Marshal Hagin snorted.

"I'd have put it somewhat stronger than that, my lord, begging your pardon. But he's not as bad as his brother. That one — !"

"But my point is, crawling around the country like this, on the one good road, they'll have time to set up an army — " Seklis bounced his fist on his chair.

"But not a very good one," said Kieri. "What can they do at most — let's look at the very worst."

"Three cohorts of Verrakaien household troops," said Seklis. "For a start."

"Your pardon, High Marshal, but they won't get more than two in the field this time of year," said Sulinarrion. "I've a cousin who married into a Verrakaien family." She held to that, and they considered what other forces might come: a half-cohort or so of Konhalts, ferried across the river, perhaps some local peasantry, ill-trained but formidable in numbers.

"What about Pargunese?" asked Kieri. They froze, staring at him. He went on. "The Pargunese won't want me as king of Lyonya for several reasons. I defeated the Sagon of the west, many years ago — using someone else's army, but I commanded. They know I will be a strong king, and they'll have no chance to gain ground anywhere. And they hate elves."

"But that would mean war between Pargun and Tsaia," said Hagin. "Would they risk that?"

"If they could raid, and get back — with, perhaps, Verrakai's connivance — perhaps not. And after all, it's not Tsaia's king they're after."

"Umm. You think Verrakai would let them through?"

987

"Yes — and blame the whole thing on them, as well."

"Would the Pargunese be stupid enough to fall for it?" asked Lieth suddenly.

"You mean, what would they gain? Well, they'd not have me to deal with — and they don't like me. And perhaps Verrakai has given or promised something else. A foothold on this side of the border? Gold? I don't know, but just how many Pargunese cohorts could the Sagon move if he wanted to?"

"Could he move through Lyonya?" asked Marshal Sulinarrion of the Kings' Squires.

"Not without starting real trouble," said Garris. "We have garrisons all along the river — they've tried that before."

"The Sagon of the west has eight cohorts, they say," said Suriya. "But half of those are stationed along the northwest — "

Kieri laughed. "Yes — and I'm the reason. That leaves four — no more than two will be close enough to meet us, I daresay. So — a couple of Verrakai cohorts, a couple of Pargunese cohorts — and who will command those, I wonder? — and no more than one of Konhalt. What of Liart, Marshals? How many followers will they bring?"

High Marshal Seklis frowned. "I would have said there were no Liartians in Vérella, my lord. Yet there were. Gird knows how many are hiding in the forests."

Kieri shook his head. "They let the rabbits run, companions, knowing they had hounds. They did not know, perhaps, that these rabbits had teeth." The others laughed. "Indeed, my lord," ventured Marshal Hagin, "you have the name of a fox, not a rabbit."

"Indeed, Marshal, I shall have a name worse than that before we are done." Kieri smiled. "But let's take heart: though they oppose our seventy or so with their four or five cohorts, they may not suspect my own marching behind. Two against four sounds better. Despite the slow progress of our escort, I judge those heavy horses will do their work well when it comes to battle."

"I hope so." High Marshal Seklis let out a long sigh. "If you will excuse me, my lord, I would like to pray in the grange — "

"And I will join my prayers to yours, Marshal, if they are sent as I think." For a moment everyone was silent, thinking of the captive by whom they were free and able to travel. This would be her second night of torment.

She woke cold and aching in a murky featureless light that made her doubt her senses. For some time she was not sure whether she was alive or dead: whatever she had expected was not this dim fog and cold. Fragments from a dream wandered through her mind: someone's hands, warm and kind, easing her cramped muscles. A gruff voice, gentled by time, soothing her fear. But this vanished. She felt space around her, as if she were outside in an open place, but she could not see anything but fog. She blinked several times. Then she tried to move. Strained muscles and joints protested; she caught her breath, then moved again. Something soft and warm cushioned her tender head; she managed to get a hand up and felt stubbly hairs growing back in, the shape of a hood covering them, tender lumps and cuts that made her wince. Her fingers explored, found a bundle supporting her head, the cloak that covered her nakedness. When she passed her hand before her face, she could see it; at least she was not blind.

She moved her legs again. Stiffness, whether from lying on cold ground or the torture, she could not tell. But she could straighten them, and when she ran her hands where the burning stones had been, no wounds remained. Her hands moved without pain, as if the bones had never been broken. She pushed herself up, running a swollen tongue over dry lips. Distant sounds: wagon wheels, a bawling cow. Thin snow patched the frozen ground. She found the bundle that had been under her head. It was clothing — her own, torn off her by the guards. Someone had mended it crudely, sewing wooden buttons in place of the horn ones, patching the torn pieces with bits of strange cloth. Underneath it was a small packet of bread and meat, and a flask. Paks pulled the stopper free, and tasted: water, and pure. She drank it down, wincing as the cold liquid hit her raw throat. Then she threw back the cloak, and struggled into the clothes, shivering, not bothering to look at herself and notice what had and hadn't healed. Wrapped once more in the cloak, she tried to think.

Alive, surely: she could not imagine any afterlife where she would find old clothes mended, some bruises still dark, and bad wounds gone entirely. Alive and free, outside the city by the sounds, and with someone's goodwill by the clothes and food. She chewed a bit of meat slowly, her jaws sore. Alive, free, clothed, fed — what more could she want? She thought of several things. Warm would be nice. Knowing what had happened. Knowing where she was, and what day it was, and where the king was — all that. She staggered to her feet. Her unknown benefactor had not provided shoes or boots — she remembered that her boots had been cut away. Socks she had, but she couldn't walk far in winter with socks alone.

Standing, she realized that she was lower than the surrounding ground, in a broad ditch or depression. The slope showed dimly in the fog. She took a couple of stiff steps toward it, glad to find she could walk at all. Something dark showed on the ground nearby. She stumbled that way, and nearly fell over the corpse.

It lay crumpled on the ground, already cold, the face like gray stone in that uncanny light. Paks stared, shaken out of her uncertain calm. Surely she should know that face. A light wind wandering through the depression, robbing her of the little warmth she'd made and stirring the dead woman's black hair. Barra. The corpse wore red, bright even in that light: a red cloak, red tunic, over black trousers and boots. The hand still held a sword. Gingerly, Paks turned the stiff body over, wincing at her own pain. A dagger hilt stood out in its chest, another in the neck. Frozen blood darkened the tunic. Paks swallowed a rock of ice in her throat. She looked at the ground. All around the snow was scuffed and torn, stained with dirt and blood both.

She touched the dagger hilts, lightly, then the sides of her own cloak. She found the thin leather sheaths where those daggers would fit.

She shuddered. No memory returned to guide her: had she thrown those knives, and killed the one who had come to aid her? But she could not believe that Barra had had that intent. Had she fought Barra? But then where had the cloak come from, and the food? A trick of the wind brought her the sound of footsteps: she froze, crouching beside the corpse. The footsteps came nearer, the steady stride of someone certain of the way and unafraid. Then a soft whistle, decorating a child's tune with little arabesques. Then the quick scramble down the slope, and she could see a shape looming in the fog. It moved to where she had been, and called softly.

"Paks? Hell's wits, she's gone. And she can't have gone far."

Paks tried to speak, but made a harsh croak instead. At that the shape came near: a tall man in black. He carried a couple of sacks.

"There you are. I daresay you don't remember me — Arvid Semminson?"

But Paks had already remembered the debonair swordsman in Brewersbridge who claimed to be on business for the Thieves Guild. She nodded.

He came nearer. "Are you sure you should be walking around?" His voice was less assured than she remembered, almost tentative.

Paks shrugged. "I can stand. I can't lie there forever." It sounded harsh even to her, but she could not think what else to say. If she was alive, she had work to do.

Arvid nodded, but his eyes didn't quite meet hers, traveled down her arms toward her hands. "I am glad, Lady, to see you so well. But — " He held out a sack and jug. "I think you need more food and drink before you travel, if that is your intent."

Paks reached for the jug, and he flinched slightly as her hand touched his, almost dropping it into her hands. She glanced at his face; she felt no evil in him, but he was certainly nervous around her. Again his eyes slid away from hers, flicking from her brow to her hands to her feet in their rumpled gray socks. She uncorked the jug, and sipped: watered wine that eased her throat. Then, seeking a way to relax him, she nodded at Barra's corpse. "Can you tell me what happened?"

"It's a long story, Lady, and you may not wish to hear all of it. But the short is that she bargained for you, to have the right to kill you, and they agreed. She would have done it, too, if I hadn't interfered. As it was, she broke my sword: she was good. So I had to use the daggers."

"You killed her?" Paks said. He nodded.

"I had no choice. She would not leave." He proffered the sack again. "Here's more food, Lady. Surely you should eat — "

Paks moved away from Barra's corpse and lowered herself to the ground carefully. Now she could feel some of the injuries still raw and painful under the clothes — but why not all? What had happened? Arvid stood over her, and when she gestured sat down more than an arm's length away.

She took a few moments to open the sack and take out a lidded pot of something hot, another loaf of bread. Arvid shook his head when she offered it to him, and handed her a spoon from his pocket. Paks ate the hot porridge, and tore off a hunk of bread.

"Arvid — " His head jerked up like a wild animal's, all wariness. Paks sighed, almost laughing to see him so, the man who had been so perfectly in control of himself, so offhand in every danger. "I don't bite, Arvid," she said crisply. "But I do need to know what's happened. Where are we? What happened at the end?" Clearly that was the wrong question; he turned white and his hands tightened on his knees. "Where is the Duke?"

"Lady — " His voice broke, and he started again. "Lady, I was not there. I would not attend such — " He paused, hunting for a word, and finding none went on. "That filth. It was in the Guild, yes, but not all of us. Thieves we may be, or friends of thieves, but not worshippers of that evil."

"I never thought so, Arvid," said Paks quietly. He met her eyes then, and relaxed a fraction.

"And so I do not know exactly what happened. I know what some said. I know — I saw — " Again he stopped short. Paks waited, head cocked. He looked down, then away, then back at her and finally told it. The way he'd heard it, Paks thought, sounded incredible, like something out of a storyteller's spiel, and it could not all be true. If Gird himself had come down and scoured the Thieves Hall, or drops of her blood had turned into smoking acid and eaten holes in the stone, surely she'd have been told about the possibility of such things in Fin Panir. She knew from her time in the Company how tales could grow in the telling, one enemy becoming two, and two, four, in the time between the battle and the alehouse. "I wasn't there," Arvid said again, his voice calmer now that most of the tale was out. "I had arrangements to make." For a moment he sounded like the old Arvid, doubled meanings packed into every phrase. "We — *I* — had no intention of having you murdered in the Thieves Hall, though we couldn't do anything before. So certain persons were ready to carry you out to safety."

"Thank you," said Paks. He went on without acknowledging her words.

"You had a mark on your arm — a burn — when we were wrapping the cloak around you. I know nothing of the rest, Lady, but that — " He stopped, and looked her square in the eyes. "That mark, Lady, I saw change. *I* saw it. From a charred burn to red, then pink, then nothing. Slow enough to watch, and swifter than any mortal healing." His breath came fast, and she saw fear and eagerness both in his face. "Lady — what are you?"

Paks bit into the bread, and through the mouthful said, "A paladin of Gird, Arvid. What did you think?"

"Then *why*? Why did Gird let you be hurt so? Was there no other way to save Phelan; is a paladin worth so much less than a king? It was no fakery: the wounds were real! I saw — " He stopped, blushed red then paled, caught for once in his lies. "I but glanced in, Lady, knowing I could do nothing, and having pity for you."

"I know you are not that sort, Arvid," said Paks, and set the bread down. "Yes, it was real." She grinned, suddenly and without reason lighthearted. "No one who saw it will doubt it was real, and that may be the reason." He looked at her now with less tension, really listening, and she wondered how far to lead him. "Arvid, there may have been another way to save Phelan: I don't know. Paladins don't know everything; we only know where we must go. But think of this: was there any other way to save the Thieves Guild?"

He stared at her, mouth open like any yokel's. "Thieves Guild," he said finally. "What does Gird care about the Thieves Guild?"

"I don't know," said Paks. "But he must care something, to spend a paladin's pain on it, and then scare the wits out of you into the bargain."

"Then is *that* what you — ?"

Paks shrugged. "I don't know the gods' purposes, Arvid: I just do what I'm told. As you once told me, I'm very trusting."

His eyes widened, then he laughed, a slightly nervous laugh, and answered the rest of her questions about what had happened to Phelan while she was captive, and what Barra's bargain with the Liartians had been. Suddenly they heard hoofbeats coming closer. "Damn!" muttered Arvid. "I didn't think anyone would — "

The unseen horse snorted. Paks saw a swirl in the fog, and then a big red horse scrambled down the bank. She stood stiffly, and he came to her, snorting again and bumping her with his nose.

"It's loose," said Arvid, surprised.

"It's not loose," said Paks, her eyes suddenly full of tears. "He's mine."

"Your horse? Are you sure?" Arvid peered at him. "I suppose you are." The horse was sniffing along her arms and legs now, nostrils wide. "I did think of trying to get your horse out of the royal stables, but that's a tall order even for a master thief."

"I can't believe it." Paks wrapped her arms around the red horse's neck and leaned on that warm body. Warmth and strength flowed into her. "He must have gotten away on his own — but he's saddled." The bridle she found neatly looped into the straps for the saddlebags. When she turned back to Arvid, he had wrestled Barra's boots off. He shook his head when he saw her face.

"I know you were in Phelan's company together — but she was going to kill you. Blind jealous, that one. You need boots, and she doesn't. You can try them."

Paks pulled on the boots unhappily; they would fit well enough for riding. Arvid meanwhile had freed the two daggers and sword, and cleaned them.

"I don't suppose you'll take my daggers — no? The sword? You can't travel unarmed — or can you?"

"I can get a sword at any grange," said Paks. "But let me thank you again for all your care. Without this cloak, these clothes, and your defense, I would have died here, of cold or enmity — "

He bowed. "Lady, you have done me a good service before, and in this you have served my companions. I count myself your friend; my friendships are limited, as all are, by the limits of my interest, but I will do you good and not harm as long as I can."

Paks grinned at him, hardly aware of the pain in her face. "Arvid, you have a way of speaking that I can hardly understand, but your deeds I have always understood. If you aren't careful, you'll end up a paladin yourself."

"Simyits forbid! I don't want to end up as you did."

Paks shrugged. "Well — it's over."

"Is anything ever over? Would you be here if you had not still a quest? I am honored to have served you, Lady Paksenarrion. Remember me."

"That I will." Paks let the stirrups down on the saddle, thought about bridling the red horse, and decided not to bother. She hoped she would be able to ride. Arvid offered a hand for mounting, and with his help she managed to gain the saddle. It hurt, but not as bad as she'd feared. That was probably the cold, numbing her still. She wondered suddenly how Cal Halveric had been able to ride out of Siniava's camp with his injuries.

"Good luck to you," said Arvid.

"Gird's grace on you," said Paks. He grinned and shook his head, and the red horse turned to climb the bank.

Chapter Twenty-nine

On the higher ground, Paks could see farther; from time to time the light strengthened as if the sun might break through. The red horse seemed to know the way — Paks had explained, as if he were a human companion, that they needed to find the grange at Westbells. She concentrated on riding. Now that she had time to think, she wondered that she was able to move about at all. Something or someone had worked healing on her: her own gift, Gird, the gods themselves. She was not sure why the healing was incomplete, but told herself to be glad she was whole of limb. Enough pains were left that she was glad when they came to Westbells near midday, with the winter fog still blurring distant vision. When she slid from the red horse's back, she staggered, leaning against him. Her feet felt like two lumps of fire.

Marshal Torin stared at her when he opened the door to her knock. "Is it — "

"Paksenarrion," she said. He caught her shoulder and steadied her.

"Gird's grace! I can't believe — we held a vigil for you. All the granges — " He led her inside. "We didn't really think you'd live, or be strong enough to travel."

Paks sank gratefully into the chair he gave her. "I wasn't sure myself." She felt as if all her strength had run away like water; she didn't want to think about moving again.

"Five days!" She wasn't sure if the emotion in his voice was surprise or elation or both. "This will show those — !" He banged a kettle on the rack, and moved around the room, gathering dishes and food. "I won't ask *what* they did, Liart's bastards, but — I presume you need healing, eh? Rest, food, drink — we can do that — " He set a loaf down on his desk, and a basin of clean water, then came to her, easing the hood back from her head. His breath hissed at what he saw.

"Damn them," he said. His hands were warm and gentle. "Some of this needs cleaning." Paks winced as he worked at one cut and another with a clean rag. "What's this?" He touched a swollen lump on the back of her head.

"I don't remember — the stairs, maybe."

"Let's see the rest of the damage." He helped Paks out of her clothes. By the time the water boiled, he had cleaned all the festering wounds — not many — and she was wrapped in a soft robe.

"There isn't as much as I'd expected," he said, handing her a mug of sib. "Five days and nights — " Paks took a long swallow; the sudden attack of weakness had passed, and she was even hungry again. "There was more." Paks sipped again. She did not want to say how much; the memory sickened her. "Broken bones, more burns. They're — gone — " She waved her hand, unable to explain.

"Your own gift healed some of it, no doubt. Perhaps Gird himself the rest — I've heard of that. And left just enough to witness what you'd suffered. As the Code says: scars prove the battle, as sweat proves effort. But with your permission, I would pray healing for the rest, and restore your strength. I daresay none will question your experience now."

Paks nodded. "Thank you, Marshal. I cannot — "

"No. *You* have done all you can; the gifts bring power but consume the user as well. That mark on your forehead — "

Paks grimaced. "Liart's brand. I know." She remembered too clearly the shape of that brand; they had shown her in a mirror the charred design.

"That's not what I see — have you looked? No, how could you — but here — " he handed her a polished mirror; Paks took it gingerly. Her bald head patched with scrapes and cuts looked as ridiculous as she'd thought — bone-white between the red and purple welts, smeared now with greenish ointment, and bristling with pale stubble where her hair was coming back. Beneath, her tanned face hardly seemed to belong to it. But the mark on her forehead was no longer the black horned circle of Liart. Instead a pale circle gleamed like silver. She nearly dropped the mirror, and stared at Marshal Torin.

"It can't — "

"Whatever happened, Paksenarrion, the High Lord and Gird approved; I have heard of such things. Such honors are not lightly won. It is no wonder you are still worn by your trials." She told him then what Arvid had said: rumor, panic, wild tales told by thieves, and unreliable. But if the brand could change like that, and deep burns disappear, what might the truth be? Marshal Torin nodded, eyes alight.

"Yes!" he said when she stopped. "The gods always have more than one purpose. Certainly you were sent to save more than a king, and from that dark warren Gird will gain many a yeoman, many a one who knows that fear is not the only power. Well done, paladin of Gird: well done."

After eating, Paks managed to stumble down the passage to one of the guest chambers. She was asleep almost before the Marshal covered her with blankets.

When she woke, she knew at once that her injuries were healed. She could breathe without pain. The lump on her head was gone, though she could feel uneven ridges of painless scar where cuts and burns had been. She scratched the bottom of one foot with the other; those burns were gone. She looked: scars to witness her ordeal, but nothing left of the weakness and pain. And a clear call to follow . . . she had not finished this quest yet. As she threw the covers aside and sat up, the Marshal tapped on her door.

"Paksenarrion?"

"Yes — I'm awake."

He looked in. "I would let you sleep longer, but that horse of yours is kicking the door."

"Gird's arm. I forgot him."

"He's all right — I fed him after you fell asleep. But he's decided he needs to see you, I suppose. I told him I don't eat paladins, but — "

"How long did I sleep?"

"It's still dark, but morning."

Paks had followed him along the passage, still in the robe she'd slept in; she could hear the steady thumps of the red horse's hoof. The Marshal opened the door, and the horse poked his head into the room.

"You," said Paks. The horse snorted. "I'm all right. I'm getting up. I'll eat before I ride, though." The horse snorted again. "And so should you," said Paks severely. "You could have let me sleep till daylight." The horse leaned into the room, and Paks held out her hand for a nuzzle. "Go on out, now; it's cold. I won't be long." The horse withdrew, and the Marshal closed the door.

"I thought I bolted the door to the stable," he said.

"I'm sure they bolted the stable door in Vérella," said Paks. "That horse goes where he wills. I'd better get ready to ride."

Paks found that she had been left clean clothes as well as her mail and sword. Even boots that fit. Paks hurried into her clothes, then realized her helmet would not fit without her thick braid of hair coiled into it. Finally the Marshal found her an old knitted scarf that served well enough. Back in her own mail, with a sword at her side once more, she felt completely herself. By the time they finished eating, and she had fastened her saddlebags onto the saddle, the eastern sky was pale green with a flush of yellow near the horizon. She mounted, and turned the red horse toward the road. He stopped short, ears pricked at something west down the road. Paks glanced down at the Marshal, who had walked out with her.

"I don't know," he said. "But he thinks there's something — "

"I'd believe it," said Paks. She drew her sword, and settled herself in the saddle. She heard the Marshal's blade coming free from his scabbard. Now the red horse snorted, blowing rollers in the cold dawn wind. He tossed his head, and loosed a resonant whinny.

"That doesn't sound like trouble," said the Marshal. "And it's not spring yet."

Paks chuckled, thinking of the red horse with a herd of mares. "I don't think that's it." The horse whinnied again, and began prancing sideways. "What's got into you, you crazy horse! Settle down."

"Hush," said the Marshal. "I think I hear something — "

Paks strained her ears. A faint echo of the red horse's whinny? The wind died. Now she could hear it clearly: the drumming clatter of many hooves, the squeak and jingle of harness. She felt the hairs on her neck prickle up. She rode into the center of the road and peered west. Was that a dark mass moving in the distance? And who could it be?

"It might be the Guard," said the Marshal slowly, echoing her thought.

"Liart," said Paks. "They let me go, all right, and now they're after the king in force."

"Six — seven — days late?"

"It must be. What else?"

He shook his head, but said nothing for a moment. The early light, still faint, showed the front of the mass of riders moving steadily toward them.

"You won't try to hold them." It was half question. Paks estimated the size of the troop and shook her head.

"I couldn't, not here. I'll try to reach the king first, and then see what I can do."

"They won't catch you on that horse," said the Marshal. "But I'll see if I can delay them."

Paks nodded, and reined the red horse around. He shook his head, fighting the rein as he never had, and moved out stiffly when she nudged him. In a few lengths he tried to sidle back toward the Marshal. Paks bumped him harder with her heels, and wondered what he thought he was doing. Then a horn signal floated across the air, and she froze. It couldn't be. In a single motion, she reined the horse around yet again, and galloped toward the oncoming riders. She heard the Marshal yell her name as she rode by, but did not stop or reply.

Again the horn call: incredibly, the call she knew so well. She rode on; the red horse slid to a stop just in front of the cohort's commander, who was already braced for an attack.

"You!" Dorrin's voice was hardly recognizable.

"I don't believe it," said Paks, believing it. The horn spoke again, and ninety swords slipped back into their scabbards.

Dorrin reached out to grip her arm. "It is really you? The Duke said — "

"It is. And this is you, and how — "

Dorrin pushed up her visor. "We," she said, "are not the Tsaian Royal Guard. It doesn't take my cohort two days to pack and ride."

"I thought he left that night."

"He did, but I nearly had to pack every Tir-damned mule myself. And a third of their heavy horses needed new shoes, and so on. It's a wonder I have a voice left."

"And?" Paks had turned the red horse, and they were jogging together at the head of the column.

"And as soon as he got back, he sent Selfer north, to pick up my cohort."

"All the way to the stronghold?"

"No-o. Not quite. In case of any difficulty, he'd stationed them along the southern line."

They were riding through Westbells now, and Paks waved to Marshal Torin, who stood watching with an uncertain expression. She pulled the red horse out of line, and went to him.

"It's Dorrin's cohort of Phelan's company," she said quickly. "They've come to help."

"I gathered it was his, from the pennant," he said. "By Gird, they move fast. When did they leave the north?"

"I don't have the whole story yet," said Paks. "Someday — " And she turned again and rode after them, for the column was past already. Again at the head of it, riding into the rising sun, Paks felt at home.

Dorrin reined her horse close to Paks's. "Paks, I never expected to see you again, let alone riding at my side this day. And you look — I have never seen you looking better. How did you get free of them? And that mark — "

"Gird's grace," said Paks. "I can't explain it all, but they kept their bargain, at least to leaving me alive. Then the gods gave healing: that mark began as Liart's brand. I presume," she said with a sidelong glance, "that they had more for me to do. Something is stirring the Thieves Guild; they had a part in it."

Dorrin nodded. "The Duke — the king — blast, I must get that straight in my mind — anyway, he said something about the Thieves Guild. They wouldn't let the Liartians kill him there, he said. But how did that help you?"

"Oh — a couple of years ago, after I left the Company, I met a thief in Brewersbridge." Dorrin grunted, and Paks went on. "A priest of Achrya had set up a band of robbers in a ruined keep near there, and the town hired me to find and take them. This thief — he said he was after the commander, because they hadn't been paying their dues to the Guild."

Dorrin shook her head. "I have a hard time imagining a paladin of Gird with a thief for a friend."

Paks thought of Arvid. "Well — he's not a thief — exactly. Or my friend, exactly, either." Dorrin looked even more dubious; Paks went on. "So he says. Obviously he's high in the Guild, but he's never said exactly what he does do. He's not like any thief I ever heard of. But in this instance, he saved my life. He's the one who arranged to have me taken outside the city, alive or dead, when the time was up. And he killed someone who had bargained to kill me."

Dorrin turned to look at her. "A thief?"

"Yes." Paks wondered whether to tell Dorrin that Gird had as much interest in thieves as kings, but decided against it. A knight of Falk, born into a noble family, had certain limitations of vision, even after a lifelong career as a mercenary captain.

"Hmmph. I may have to change my mind about thieves." From Dorrin's tone, that wasn't likely. Paks laughed.

"You needn't. Arvid's uncommon."

"He's never robbed *your* pocket," said Dorrin shrewdly.

"No. That's true. Just the same, he took no advantage when he might have, in Brewersbridge, and he served me here." She rode a moment in silence, squinting against the level rays of the rising sun. "What does the king expect, that he called your cohort in? And what did the Council think of it?"

Dorrin frowned. "He said they would never have released him if they hadn't thought they could take him before the coronation. That they thought, with you out of the way, to attack somewhere on the road. The crown prince would have given him a larger escort, but he refused it . . . said it might be needed even in Vérella."

"What does he have?"

"I suppose near seventy fighters altogether: a half-cohort of Royal Guards, the ten-squad out of this cohort, those King's Squires, the High Marshal and another Marshal. Plus supply and servants — an incredible amount, the Royal Guard insists on. It's easy to see they don't travel much."

"Umm. I wish we had the whole Company."

"So do I. But he said he couldn't strip the north bare, not after the other troubles this winter. And Pargun might move, knowing him so far away. He did tell Arcolin to move the two veteran cohorts to the east and south limits, just in case. Val's got the recruit cohort at the stronghold. He's afraid that the evil powers will move with all violence."

"And we have one cohort," said Paks quietly. Dorrin smiled at her.

"And a paladin they didn't expect us to have."

"And two Marshals — perhaps more, if we're near a grange. That is, if we can catch up to them."

"We will," said Dorrin. "Those heavy warhorses won't make a third the distance we're making. And I daresay that red horse of yours could go even faster. Will you go ahead, then, or stay with us?"

Paks thought about it. "For now, I'll stay with you. He has the Marshals with him; they will know, as I would know, if great evil is near. For all you are a Knight of Falk, Captain, I might be useful to you."

"You know you are. I tell you, Paks, I was never so surprised — and relieved — as when you rode up. It harrowed all our hearts to go without trying to free you. But he said no one must do anything for five days."

Paks nodded. "That was necessary."

"But when I thought of it — " Dorrin shook her head. "Falk's oath in gold! For anyone to be in their hands five days — and you — "

"It was necessary." Paks looked over to Selfer, who had said nothing during all this. "How's your leg?"

"It's well enough," said Selfer. "The Marshal took care of it, before I rode north."

"How long did that take?"

"I left — let me think — well before midnight, and by dawn the third day I was with the cohort. We marched the next dawn — they were ready, but let me sleep until dark, and the Duke — the king — had said to march by day only, to Vérella."

"He didn't want the cohort too tired to fight," said Dorrin. "We were to march out again at once. Selfer brought them in good shape — remarkable, considering the weather and all."

Selfer grinned and flushed. "At least we didn't get a thaw on that bad stretch," he said. "I was worried, when it turned foggy."

"You see, Selfer," said Dorrin, "all those things you must worry about if you're a captain? Do you still want it?"

999

He nodded, shyly. "Yes, Captain, I do. The more I do, the more I like it."

Dorrin grinned at Paks. "He's been acting as junior captain to Arcolin and me both this past year — and he's good." Selfer turned even redder; Paks remembered when she used to blush like that, and wondered how long it had been. She looked back along the cohort, at faces she knew almost as well as those in Arcolin's cohort. All at once she felt like racing the red horse along the road and singing. They were six days behind the king's party. They asked word at every grange, and at each the news was good: they had passed without trouble. Curious eyes followed them; Phelan's colors had not marched that way before. Paks saw the worried glances. Dorrin carried a royal pass, which she showed in every town, but the local farmers were clearly uncertain. That night the cohort stayed in Blackhedge, sleeping a few hours in safety, but they were on the road again before daybreak. The towns rolled past. Now they said the king had passed only five days before. At Piery, they heard that his party had stayed over a day, because some of the Royal Guard mounts were lame. Dorrin muttered a curse, and Paks laughed, pointing out that they could catch them sooner. They had left three mornings ago.

That night they pressed on, passing the grange at Dorton in the falling dark, and camping in a rough pasture far from any village. Paks would have ridden on after only a few hours sleep, but felt she should stay with the cohort. She had spoken to most of them, uncomfortable only with Natzlin, who did not ask about Barranyi. Paks did not tell her. The next day the red horse pulled away from the road; Paks thought she remembered that the Honnorgat made a wide bend. Paks urged Dorrin to leave the road. The captain's face creased in a frown.

"I'm worried about causing trouble," she said. "My pass is for the road to Harway, on the border — unless we're attacked, I can't justify leaving it."

"We won't be attacked," said Paks. "Not yet — but we can save several hours, at least, by cutting the bend."

"Can you tell if the king is in need?"

Paks shook her head. "I do not know if I could tell — and I feel nothing now but an urge to hurry. It may be that he will be in need."

"Paks — are the gods telling you to leave the road? Is it that sure?"

"If I were riding alone, Captain, I would go across country. If you cannot go that way, perhaps I should leave you now and go on. But I never expected to be here at all — and certainly not with a cohort behind me — so I cannot give you orders."

Dorrin gnawed her lip. Everyone waited a for her decision. Selfer opened his mouth and closed it again, catching Paks's eye. Then she sat back on her horse, easing her back, and sighed. "Well — wars aren't won by coming late to the battle." She grinned at Paks. "I hope, Gird's paladin, that your saint will cover us while we follow you. I would hate to raise new enemies for the king by this."

"Captain, the gods have led me into peril, but not without cause."

"So be it. We'll take your way."

Paks led them over fallow fields and through woods, the red horse moving as quickly on rough ground as on the road. No one challenged them; in fact, the country seemed empty under a cold sun. They met the road again at Swiftin. Here the yeoman-marshal said the the king's party had passed only the day before. They paused to feed and rest the horses before they left. Again they rode most of the night, sleeping beside their horses for a few hours in turn. Dorrin seemed almost as anxious as Paks to catch the king's party. A thin cold drizzle began late in the night; Paks pulled her cloak over her mail when she mounted.

By dawn the drizzle had turned to sleet, and then fine snow. Sometime later, it ceased. The clouds blew away to the east, and the sun blazed on the fresh snowfall. Paks decided to scout ahead of the cohort. The red horse cantered steadily onward, flinging up sprays of glittering snow. She passed through one village too small for a grange, then came to a larger town. She barely remembered passing through it in a hurry on the way to Vérella. The Marshal stared at her when she gave her name, but said the king's party was only an hour or so ahead; they had stopped there overnight. They had had no trouble so far, he said. Paks explained about the cohort following her; his eyebrows shot up his forehead.

"You're bringing Phelan's soldiers through here? Through Verrakai lands?"

Paks had known that the Verrakaien held lands in the east end of Tsaia, but not precisely where. "His captain has a royal pass," she said slowly. "Signed by the crown prince himself — "

The Marshal snorted. "For all the good that'll do. Gird grant they don't notice — though I don't suppose they'll miss a cohort of Phelan's troops. Why did he do something like that?"

Paks controlled her temper. "He expected trouble," she said crisply. "He wanted his own troops — trained as he knew — in case of it."

"Well, he'll get trouble enough, stirring an ant's nest with a stick. Why couldn't he ride peacefully to his kingdom without all this pomp?"

Paks looked at him. She knew that Marshals varied in ability and personality, but she did not like his sour, half-defeated expression.

"Sir Marshal," she said, "surely High Marshal Seklis told you that evil powers had already attacked the king — he had no chance to go peacefully."

"Seklis!" The Marshal spat. "It's easy for him — living in Vérella, at court and all. He won't have to keep a broken grange together out here — who's going to help me, when half my yeomen are taken by something in the forest?"

"Gird," said Paks quietly, but with force enough to change his expression. "Tell me your problem, Marshal, and we'll see what can be done. Your yeomen have been taken?"

He glowered at her, but answered straightly enough. "They disappear. We search, and find nothing. I've told them back at Vérella, again and again. There's something out there, and I can't find it. But they don't listen."

Paks nodded, and he went on.

"Then they tell me to keep watch for Phelan — that he'll be coming through and may need help — that fox! And now I understand he's supposed to be a king, or something. In Lyonya, of all places: just what we need, a mercenary king next door, when it's all I can do to keep things quiet as it is."

"I think, Marshal, that you've kept things too quiet." Paks sat back in her saddle and watched him. He flushed, but still met her eye. "Gird did not value quietness over right."

"Gird is not here," muttered the Marshal. "No — I know they say you're a paladin, but it's not the same as being here, year after year, with the yeomen more frightened, more reluctant — "

"Well," said Paks, "you don't have to stay here. Come along and see what we're talking about." He shook his head. Her voice sharpened. "Marshal, you can't hide forever. I suspect we're about to have as splendid a battle as you've ever seen — don't you think your yeomen will expect their Marshal to be in it?"

"They won't care."

"I do." Paks straightened, and called her light for the first time since Vérella. He stepped back, startled. She saw faces turn toward her, in the town square, and reined the red horse into the middle of it. Children scurried in and out of doorways; faces appeared at windows. "What's this town?" she asked the Marshal, who had followed her slowly into the square.

"Darkon Edge," he said. "What — "

"I'll show you," said Paks. She drew her sword and laid it crossways on the saddle bow. "Yeomen of Gird!" Her yell brought heads around, and drew a flurry of movement. "Yeomen of Gird, hear me!" A few men hurried into the square: an obvious baker, dusting flour from his hands, a forester with his axe, several more. When perhaps a dozen had clustered around her, she pointed at the baker. "Is this all the yeomen in Darkon Edge?"

"No — why — what is it?"

"I am Paksenarrion," she said, "a paladin of Gird, on quest. Do you know of it?" They shook their heads. "You know who stayed here last night?" One nodded; the others merely stared. "The rightful king of Lyonya," said Paks loudly. "The king who was stolen into slavery as a young child, and lost all memory of his family. He was taken, yeomen of Gird, to weaken Lyonya, to open a way for the powers of evil to assail both Lyonya and Tsaia."

"So?" asked one of the men.

"So in the end, the powers of Liart and Achrya failed, and he is going to his throne. If he gains it, peace and freedom will have a chance here. Do you think Liart and Achrya like that?"

"But he's a mercenary," yelled someone from a window across the square. Paks faced it and yelled back.

"He was a mercenary, yes — to earn his way, when he knew nothing of

1002

his birth. But he's more than a mercenary. Gird knows Lyonya needs a soldier on the throne, with those against her."

"It won't do any good," said the same voice. "Nothing does. Gird: that's an old tale. The real power's in the dark woods, where — "

"Come out here and say that," said Paks. "Is this light I carry an old tale? Will you face it and say that Gird has no power?"

"Not against Liart." The face at the window disappeared, and the yeomen muttered.

"Who is that?" asked Paks quickly.

"Joriam. He's an elder here," said the forester. "His son's gone, and his nephew's crippled by that there — " But a powerful gray-haired man had come out the door, and strode angrily across the square to Paks.

"You!" he yelled. "Paladin, are you? You come here and tell us to fight, and then you'll go away, and it will start again. What do you know about that, eh?" He looked her up and down. "Fancy armor, fancy horse, fancy sword. *You* never lay bound on Liart's altar! It's easy for you!"

In one swift gesture, Paks jerked off her helmet. Into the shocked silence that followed, with every eye rivetted on her scarred shaven head, she said quietly, "You're wrong. And this is the proof of it. I carried Liart's brand: look now, and see Gird's power."

The man's mouth opened and shut without a word. One of the foresters blushed, and looked away. Paks scanned the square, noting others who had crept in and peered from doorways. She raised her voice again.

"Yeomen of Gird, I have known what you fear. I have been captive — aye, by Liart's priests, as well as others. I have been unarmed, hungry, frightened, cold, naked — all that you have feared, I have known. If it were not a winter's day — " Her voice warmed to the chuckle she felt, " — you could see all my scars, and judge for yourself. But let this — " she gestured at her head, "be enough proof for you. I know Liart and his altars, and Achrya and her webs, and I know the only cure for them. I call on you, yeomen of Gird. Follow Gird; come with me; together we will destroy the evils you fear, or die cleanly in battle. No more bloody altars of Liart, yeomen. Blood on our own blades now." She raised her sword; a shout followed. The faces watching her came alive.

"But — " The old man raised an arm and the shouts died.

Paks broke in. "No, elder Joriam. The time for 'but' and 'maybe' is long past. You have suffered evil; I am sorry for it. Now the yeomen of Gird must take heart and take weapons, and save themselves from more evil. Come!" The red horse danced sideways, clearing a space which filled with men, suddenly swarming from doorways and side streets. "Is it true?" asked the baker, wiping his hands again. "Is it really true that you can find it, and we can fight?"

Paks grinned at them all. "Yeomen, we shall fight indeed." She watched them run to the Grange, bringing back stored weapons, and form themselves into a ragged square before her. Then she heard the drumming hooves of Dorrin's cohort coming into the village, and turned to meet her.

Chapter Thirty

Dorrin looked at the small group of yeomen with distaste. She managed not to look at Paks's head. The rest of the cohort were not as careful.

"What's this?"

Paks met her eyes steadily. "This is the yeomanry of Darkon Edge; they will march with us to meet the enemy."

Dorrin's eyebrows rose. "This?" She said it quietly, but Paks saw one of the foresters redden. She wrapped the scarf around her head, stuffed the helmet back over it, and nodded.

"We will need them," she said. "Gird has called them."

"I see." Dorrin's eyes dropped to her hand on the reins. "Then I suppose — "

"That it's settled. Yes." Paks turned to the Marshal. "Sir Marshal, will you lead your yeomen, or shall I?"

A spark of interest had returned to his eyes; now it kindled into pride. "I will, paladin of Gird. Do we go by the road?"

"For a time." Paks nodded to Dorrin. "Captain, I would recommend battle order, with forward scouts in sight of the cohort. For now I will ride with the yeomen." Dorrin's quick commands soon had the cohort moving at a brisk trot. Paks waited until the Marshal had brought out his own shaggy mount and they rode together at the head of the yeomen. Before he could say anything, she was asking about the road ahead, and the shape of the land around.

Just out of town, the road entered a section of broken, rough land, more heavily forested than that on either side. Already some of the springs had broken; the road surface was a rough mass of frost-heave and mud. The red horse slowed, picking his way around the soggy places and slippery refrozen ice. The yeomen marched strongly, but in a loose, ungainly formation. Paks wondered how they would fight — but anything would be better than the blank apathy of Darkon Edge. The Marshal began to explain some of what had happened in the past several years. She realized that some powerful force had harried his grange, and the next to the south, picking off the strongest and bravest of the yeomen. Only a few had been found, alive or dead. The old man's nephew had returned a cripple, and half-mad from torture. Another, terribly mutilated, had managed to kill himself. She shook her head as he fell silent.

1004

"Indeed, Marshal, you have had hard times. You say you tried to find the source of this?"

"Of course I did!" Now he was angry again. "Gird's blood, paladin, when I came I was as full of flame as you are now. But year by year — one after another they died, and I could find nothing. How can they trust me, when I can't find a center of evil like that, eh? How can I trust myself?"

"And the other Marshals nearby, they did nothing?"

"Garin tried — until he got the lung fever so bad. His yeoman-marshal was taken, too, and that — well, it was bad to see, paladin. I know Berris, east of me, has had trouble too, but we neither of us had much time to meet — it's more than a day's journey across by the road. I've got six bartons outlying, as well as the grange, and always something gone wrong."

"And you quit hoping — "

"Hoping! Hoping for what? What's left? Half the yeomanry I had when I came — Gird's blood, I don't doubt this day will see the half of that half gone. But as you said, a clean death. I don't fear death itself — Gird knows I've tried these years, but — "

"Marshal, I swear to you, this coming battle will see your grange — and granges around — freed of great evil. Some will die — yes, but die as Gird's yeomen should die. That man you call a mercenary will be Lyonya's king — as honest and just a ruler as any land could have — and if you and I live to see it, we will call it well bought, at whatever cost."

"I hope so." He chewed his lip. Then he lowered his voice and rode close to her. "It isn't what I thought of, when I was a young yeoman-marshal: I thought to be a Marshal whose grange increased, spreading justice all around. Instead — "

"You have fought a hard battle, in hard conditions, and held a position until help came. Think of it like that."

His face changed. "Is it?"

"Well," said Paks, grinning at him, "paladins are usually considered help. So is a cohort of Phelani infantry — you could have a worse broom to sweep your dirty corners."

He flushed, but finally smiled, straightening in his saddle with a new expression on his face. Paks looked back at the yeomen. They were settling to the march, beginning to look more like possible fighters.

They worked their way up and over one ridge, then another. The tracks of the king's party and the cohort were clear: massive broad hooves of the heavy war horses, the neater rounded hooves of the cohort's lighter mounts. Paks even recognized the slightly angled print of the off hind on Lieth's horse. Then she heard the swift clatter of a galloping horse and looked up to see Selfer riding toward her.

He pulled his mount to a halt. "Paks! Dorrin wants you — there's trouble ahead."

Paks looked at the Marshal. "Keep coming, but be careful. How far is it, Selfer?"

He looked at the yeomen. "Oh — a half-glass's walk, I suppose. Just over the far side of this ridge."

"Come up to the rear of Phelan's cohort," said Paks. "I'll have word for you there." The Marshal nodded, and she rode after Selfer, who had already wheeled his horse to ride back.

The red horse caught his in a few lengths; they rode together out of sight of the yeomen. Over the ridge, Paks could see down the slope to a clearing at the bottom. The road angled down the slope into a narrow valley which widened to the left, then forded a broad but shallow stream, and climbed along the flank of the next ridge. Forest pressed on the right margin; to the left, a meadow opened from just above the ford downstream to the width of the valley. Fresh snow whitened the slopes between the trees, but the valley floor was churned to dark mud by hundreds of feet.

The clamor of battle carried clearly through the cold air. There were the rose-and-silver colors of Tsaia, a ring around the green knot of the Lyonyan King's Squires. Kieri Phelan lived and fought; the elf-blade in its master's hand blazed with light that flashed with every stroke. But around them surged a mass of darker figures. A trail of horses and men lay dead on the road: the supply animals and servants, cut off from the others in the ambush. Paks did not recognize any standards, but the group of red-cloaked spike-helmed fighters at the edge of the conflict was obviously Liartian. They were unmounted: Paks suspected that they were using some arcane power that would frighten horses.

Clumped on the road only a few lengths ahead was Dorrin's cohort, still mounted but unmoving. Paks drew her sword and rode quickly to the head of the column, to find Dorrin bent over her saddle.

"Captain — what is it?"

Dorrin turned. Paks could see nothing but her eyes through the visor. "It's — can't you feel it? We can't move, Paks — he's being torn up down there, and we can't move!"

Paks reined the red horse forward; she could feel a pressure like blowing wind in her mind, but nothing worse. She looked back. "What does it feel like, Captain? Fear, or pain, or what?"

"Fear," said Dorrin shortly. "Don't you — ?" Paks threw back her head. "That I can deal with. Dismount them, and stay close behind me. Selfer, bring the yeomen down when they top the ridge — be sure they stay together." She called her light, and rode forward; she could feel the pressure veering away on either hand. She glanced back once, to find that they all followed, watching her with wide eyes.

She heard the yell when their advance was spotted; one block of enemy soldiers broke away and moved toward them in formation. Paks turned to Dorrin. "You know best how to maneuver here, Captain; I have a debt to pay those priests." She closed her legs; the red horse leaped forward, charging the Liartian priests. There were five she could see; her heightened senses told her that more fought elsewhere. She felt the pressure of their attack on the cohort lift; a crackling bolt of light shot past her head. Paks laughed, swinging her sword.

"Gird!" she yelled, as the red horse trampled one of them, breaking the

1006

cluster apart. Paks sliced deep into one neck; the priest crumpled. On the backswing, she caught another in the arm. He screamed, cursing her. The other two were already backing away, weapons ready, to join a mob of their followers. Paks laughed again, and her horse trumpeted. Again she charged, this time against a spear-carrier, who poked at her horse to hold her away. But she caught the barbs of the spear on her sword, and leaned from the saddle to grab the haft with her other hand. She reeled him in; he was too astonished to let go, until her sword sank in his throat. The fifth had escaped into the mob, and screamed curses at her from that safety.

Paks looked around quickly. Loosed from the spell, Dorrin's cohort was advancing steadily against the enemy, edging toward the main combat. The yeomen were starting down the ridge. The defenders around the king, harried as they were, had seen her; she heard the king's cry above them all, and raised her sword in answer.

Then she turned to the road. A ragged band of rabble — peasants or brigands — had broken from the forest to strike the yeomen, who faltered. Paks rode into them, the red horse rearing and trampling, and drove her sword into one neck after another. "Yeomen of Gird!" she yelled. "Follow me!" They cheered, then, and charged through the rest of the band. Their Marshal's eyes blazed, and he gave Paks an incredulous grin.

"They did it!" he cried. "They — "

"They're Girdsmen," said Paks loudly, so they could hear. "They're fighters, as Gird was. Come on, Girdsmen!" And she led them quickly to link with Dorrin's cohort. Together the two groups outnumbered the enemy cohort, and it withdrew and reformed. Paks looked for Dorrin; she had found what she thought was a weak point in the attacker's ring, and was shifting the cohort to strike there.

The attackers, finding themselves struck from behind, wavered and shifted. Dorrin's disciplined swordsmen sliced through the layers of fighters like a knife through an onion. Cheers met them, cheers cut off abruptly by renewed assaults on other flanks. Phelan's tensquad merged with the cohort instantly, as if they had never been apart. Even in the midst of battle, Paks saw that the Marshals noticed this. The yeomen, flanked now on either side by seasoned fighters, looked as solid as the others. The attackers wavered again, drawing back a little. Paks moved the red horse quickly to the king's side. His eyes gleamed through the visor of his helmet. "Well met, paladin of Gird. It lifts my heart to see you here."

"Sir king," Paks bowed in the saddle. "How do you find that blade in battle?"

"Eager," he said. "You schooled it well in your service."

Paks laughed. "Not I, sir king. From its forging it has waited its chance to serve you. What is your command?"

"Advance," he said, looking to be sure Ammerlin and Dorrin could both hear him. "We'll use Dorrin's cohort, and your yeomen, with the heavy horse ready to charge and break them."

"But — my lord — the supplies — " Ammerlin hesitated, looking back.

Paks remembered the king's gesture from her years in his Company, but his voice stayed calm. "Ammerlin, we know they have reserves. All that we had behind us is now with us. Our hopes lie before us — and only there. If we can fight through — "

"But — " Paks saw the indecision in his face, and rode toward him. His face turned to her. "And — and that — "

"Paksenarrion," said the king quietly. "A paladin of Gird."

"Ammerlin," said Paks, "take courage. Gird is with us." Ammerlin nodded, his eyes bright. She turned to the king. "My lord king — "

"To Lyonya," he said. And with a few quick commands to Dorrin and the Marshals, the defenders were ready to move.

At first it seemed they might break through to the higher ground along the east road. The priests of Liart commanded a motley crowd of ill-armed peasantry; these could not stand against disciplined troops. The enemy cohorts — Pargunese by their speech, though they showed no standard — put up more resistance, but gave way step by step. Paks could see something back in the trees — brigands, or perhaps orcs — waiting for a chance, but unwilling to fight in close formation.

The Tsaian heavy horse charged again and again, breaking open the enemy formation and letting the foot soldiers advance a few strides with ease. But once on the slope up the next ridge, they could not break through; the enemy still had the higher ground, and outnumbered the defenders two to one. Paks looked around for more of Liart's priests; she was sure more were nearby, but they kept out of sight, only occasionally showing themselves in the midst of their fighters.

They had gained perhaps half the upward slope, when Paks heard a battle-horn's cry above the clamor. At once the enemy attacked in full force, slamming into the defender's lines and forcing them back down the hill. It was all they could do to keep their formation in this retreat; one after another staggered and fell, to be trampled underfoot. Paks sent the red horse directly at the enemy; those in front of her melted away, but on either side they drove on. She found herself surrounded, fought her way back through to stiffen the defense. When she looked up again, the eastward road was full of men: two full cohorts of heavy infantry, in Verrakai blue and silver that gleamed in the afternoon sun. A half-cohort of archers in rose and dark green halted above them and shot down the hill into the defenders. As the Verrakaien infantry charged downhill, the enemy opened to let them through, the force of their charge undamped.

But the king had seen all this as soon as Paks; in moments Dorrin had swung her cohort and the yeomen off the road just enough that the Verrakaien charge slid along the flank of the defenders rather than hitting it squarely. Now they scrambled downhill to level ground as best they could, losing in seconds ground it had cost hours to gain. By the time they were reorganized in the valley, more than a dozen yeomen, and eight of Dorrin's veterans, lay dead.

Shadow already streaked the little valley. They had been fighting for hours;

1008

Paks herself felt little fatigue, but she saw in the drawn faces around her that they could not keep going without a respite. Meanwhile the Verrakaien, finding stiff resistance, had slowed. As the day turned on toward evening, they eased their attack, and disengaged. Paks could see their supply train coming down the road; Liart's followers were scavenging in the king's, pulling packs off the dead horses and mules. The defenders rested as best they could, locked in a tight square, with the king in the center.

When the attackers pulled back, all three Marshals began healing the wounded they could find. By unspoken agreement, Paks stayed alert for any arcane attack of evil. She knew that the Liartian priests were not finished; they would have something else planned. Enemy campfires began to flicker in the fading light. Soon the smell of cooking would come along the wind, tantalizing the defenders. Dorrin edged over to her.

"Paks, my troops have some food — trail bread — and we still have four of our mules. That's enough for one meal, perhaps."

"What about the yeomen?" Paks remembered seeing them stuff food into pockets and sacks.

"I didn't think they'd have any — I'll ask."

In the end, only the Tsaian Royal Guard had nothing; when the rest was shared out, all had an almost normal ration: cold, but strengthening. Water was a harder problem, but one of the yeomen solved it for them. They had been driven back nearly to the ford, but one unit of enemy troops had cut them off from the water. The yeoman, however, knew this stream, and said that its water came near the surface some distance from the stream itself. So it proved: a hole scarcely knee-deep filled with fresh water. They widened the hole until several could fill their helmets at once; the water sufficed for both men and horses. Before full dark, all had drunk their fill, and had eaten enough to feel refreshed.

Yet they were surrounded now by a force three times or more their size. With the Marshals' healing aid, their losses that afternoon were not as severe as might have been expected, but even so too many defenders lay stiffening on the hill. In the center of the square, Paks urged the king to rest while he could. They had made an inner square of the horses, and knights, leaving an open space where it was possible to lie, out of sight of archers (though not, of course, out of range.)

With dark came new troubles. First was the Verrakai commander, who came forward under a parley flag lit by torches. He accused Phelan of invading Verrakai lands, and refused to accept the royal pass Dorrin carried.

"That princeling has no right to give passes — only the Council can. These are Verrakai lands, and Verrakai's road, and you have no right to invade on behalf of that northern bastard."

"Hold your tongue!" bellowed High Marshal Seklis. "He's the rightful king of Lyonya, and no bastard."

"And who are you?" asked the commander. "High Marshal Seklis, of the court at Tsaia, and you'll have the Fellowship of Gird on you for this cowardly attack, sir."

The commander laughed. "The Fellowship of Gird is far away, Marshal; if you insist on sharing this dukeling's fate, it will never know what happened."

"Share his fate — Gird's blood, sir, I'd rather share his fate than yours."

"Besides," the commander went on, raising his voice, "I've heard he sacrificed a Gird's paladin to save his own skin. What kind of a king is that? What kind of commander, for that matter? If you had any honor at all, you'd turn on him now."

Paks called her light and stood forward. "Sir, you know not what you speak of. This king never sacrificed a paladin — I am the paladin involved, and I know."

In her light, the commander's eyes were wide, white-rimmed. "You! But I heard —"

"You heard lies, commander." She saw a ripple of alarm pass through the commander's escort, and her light extended in response. "Would you risk your life — and more than your life, your soul — against a paladin as well as these Marshals and Lyonya's king?"

"It is my command."

"Indeed. Despite the commands of *your* rightful liege lord, the crown prince —"

"He hasn't been crowned yet — not until Summereve —"

Paks laughed. "Sir, you argue like a judicar, not like a soldier. Unless some treachery falls on him, as this has fallen on the king of Lyonya, he will be your ruler, and acts now as such. You must know that the Council and prince together gave Lyonya's king not only passage but also royal escort — have you never see the Tsaian Royal Guard before?"

"He might have hired them," said the man sulkily. At that even the Royal Guard laughed scornfully.

"He did not — and you know it. You know it is the Council's will that he pass safely into Lyonya and be crowned there; it is the prince's wish as well."

"Not Lord Verrakai's," said the man. "And he's my lord, and gives my orders."

"Then he's rebelling against the House of Mahieran?" asked Paks. Again that uneasy movement. "Forming alliance with Pargun?"

"No — not that — but he takes no orders from a stripling boy —"

"Who is his king. That sounds like rebellion to me," said the High Marshal, "and I shall report it so when I return."

"You are not like to return," answered the commander tartly, "unless you agree to disown this so-called king. We've heard enough of him, we have — a bloody mercenary, that's all he is, whatever lies he tells of his birth."

"And is this a lie?" The king had come close behind Paks and the High Marshal. He drew the elven blade; its brilliant light outshone even Paks's for a moment. "This blade is like none you have seen, and no other hand can hold it. It was made for Lyonya's prince, and lost, and when I first drew it, proclaimed me its master. Could that be a lie, commander?"

The man bit his lip, looking from one to another. But finally he shook his

1010

head. "It doesn't matter. You're Phelan, I suppose. My orders are that you must not pass; you and all your soldiers' lives are forfeit for treason and trespass. As for these others, if they forswear your cause, they will be spared as our prisoners. If they fight on, all will be slain."

Bitter amusement edged the king's voice. "Your terms offer little gain, commander."

"Your situation offers less." The commander's voice sharpened in turn. "You are outnumbered, on bad ground, without food or water or shelter for your wounded — "

"Whom you plan to kill anyway," the king pointed out. "By the gods, commander, if we are to die, we need no supplies, and I think you care little what happens to our wounded. Since you say I and my soldiers must die anyway, we shall see how many of yours we can take with us."

"And you?" asked the commander of the Marshals and Ammerlin.

"It is my pleasure and honor," said Ammerlin stiffly, "to serve the king of Lyonya as I have served my prince. You will find the Royal Guard a worthy opponent, Verrakaien scum."

"And you will find Gird's Marshals a hard mouthful to swallow," said High Marshal Seklis grimly. "Since you claim to have the stomach for it, you may gnaw our steel before our flesh."

The Verrakai commander stared at them a long moment, as if waiting for another answer. Then he made a stiff bow and turned away. They heard a flurry of sound as he returned to his own men, and a rough cry in a strange tongue from another enemy unit.

The king's head turned sharply. "That's Pargunese. Something about the Sagon's orders. As we thought, Verrakai and the Sagon have moved together. I dare say, Marshals, they intend none to tell the tale later."

"So I would judge," said Seklis, still angry.

"I would hope for no mercy from them," added Ammerlin. Then he turned to the king. "My lord, I am sorry — I should have foundered every horse in the troop before landing you in this trap."

The king touched his shoulder. "The trap was planned, Ammerlin, before we left Vérella. Without your knights, this afternoon, we could never have come so close to breaking free — nor would we still be standing here, I think. Don't waste your strength regretting it now."

"You do not blame — "

The king laughed. "Blame? Who should I blame but the Verrakai and Pargunese, and Liart and Achrya, who planned all this? By the gods, Ammerlin, if we come out of this, you will hear such praise of the Guard as will redden your ears for the next fifty years. Do you believe me now?"

"Yes, my lord." Ammerlin's eyes glittered in Paks's light. "We will ward you, my lord, until the end."

"Hmmph. I admit, Ammerlin, I see no easy way out of this, but the end I intend is my own throne in Lyonya, and not death in this valley." The king turned to Paks. "You, I know, have seen worse than this, and come out alive and whole — do you despair?"

"No, sir king." Paks smiled at him. "The wolves must come within reach before the spear can touch them. We are in peril, yes — but if we withstand despair, the gods will aid us."

"As they already have, with your return," said the king. "Ah, Paks — I had feared greatly for you."

Paks smiled. "And I for you, as well. Now — in the hours of darkness, they will try what evil they can, sir king. I feel it near — "

"I also," said Seklis. "We have healed what we can of the wounded, my lord. For this night, we Marshals and Paksenarrion must ward your defenders."

The priests of Liart began their assault with loud jeers from their followers: they had brought the bodies of slain defenders down the hill to mutilate them in front of the rest. It was all Paks and the Marshals could do to keep the yeomen in line when they saw their friends' bodies hacked in pieces; the seasoned troops glared, but knew better than to move. That display was followed by others. These ended when the king authorized a single volley from the Royal Guard archers; Paks extended her light, and the front rank of capering Liartians was abruptly cut down.

After that, and a single thrust of fear from the Liartian priests, the enemy camp settled down as if for sleep. Everything was quiet for a time. Then shouts and bellows rang out in the forest to the east.

"What — ?"

Paks could hear shouts in the enemy's camp; the turmoil of troops roused from sleep.

"Whatever it is, they didn't expect it either."

"Trouble for them — good for us?" Seklis stretched; he'd napped briefly.

"We can hope." The king, too, had rested, but Paks could hear the fatigue in his voice. He pushed himself upright, and made his way across the square. Paks extended her light again. They could see dimly as far as the forest edge. Something moved between the trees.

"Whatever it is, it's *big*," muttered Dorrin. "And not alone." The king sighed. "I was hoping for a cohort of Lyonyans, perhaps — just to make things interesting."

In a sudden flurry, a tumbling mass of creatures burst from the edge of the woods. Paks recognized several of them as the same monster that had lived in the robber's lair near Brewersbridge: huge, hairy, man-like shapes.

"Falk's oath in gold," muttered Garris, "that's a gibba."

"I thought they were hools," said Paks.

"No — hools live in water, and aren't so hairy, nor so broad. These are gibbas. And those others — "

Orcs she had seen before, but not the high-shouldered dark beasts that ran with them, like hounds with a hunting party.

"Folokai," said Lieth quietly. "Fast, strong, and mean."

"I'll believe that," said Paks. "Any weaknesses?"

"Not gibbas. The folokai are night-hunters; they don't like fire or bright light. But they're smart, as smart as wolves at least. The best sword stroke is for the heart, from in front, or the base of the neck."

In moments the dire creatures were charging across the open space. Paks called in her light and rolled onto the red horse's back, where she could see. The enemy ranks seemed as concerned as their own; she heard shouts in Pargunese and Tsaian both, and screeches from the orcs, who hesitated for a moment between the defenders and one of the Verrakai cohorts. A priest of Liart strode into the Verrakai torchlight, and snapped an order to the orcs. Paks saw heads turn toward them, saw one of the folokai crouch for a spring. She urged the red horse forward, to the lines.

The orcs swung their short spears around, and ran at the defenders. The folokai jumped high, soaring over the first rank to fall ravening on the secondary. But Paks was there, the red horse neatly avoiding the defenders. She plunged her sword into a heavy muscled neck; the folokai's head swung up, quick as light, and long fangs raked her mail. The red horse pivotted, catching the beast with one foreleg and tossing it away. It reared, threatening the horse with long claws on its forefeet. Paks swung the horse sideways, and thrust deep between foreleg and breast. For a moment the heavy jaws gnashed around her helmet, then its dead weight almost pulled her from the saddle. She wrestled her sword free. Two gibbas had hit the defending line together, and driven a wedge into it. At the point, Lieth and Marshal Sulinarrion fought almost as one, their swords swinging in long strokes that hardly seemed to slow the gibbas at all. Remembering Mal, Paks looked around for someone with an axe. A hefty yeoman in the secondary stood nearby, bellowing encouragement to the front rank, but otherwise free. She tapped his shoulder with her sword, and he swung round, axe ready.

"Come on! Follow me!" She waited for his nod, then forced the red horse through the fight to a point just behind the gibbas. "Get the backbone!" she yelled at the forester, sinking her own sword into the angle of neck and shoulder — a level stroke, she noted, for a mounted fighter. But this maneuver had put her outside the square, and the yeoman as well. She covered his retreat back into the line, then whirled the red horse in a flat spin, sweeping her sword at the orcs who tried to take advantage of the gibbas' position. Dorrin's cohort snapped back into position, straightening the line, and Paks was back inside with the king.

The king, meanwhile, was fighting another folokai that had jumped the lines. Garris had fallen behind him; High Marshal Seklis tried to flank the beast, but it was too fast, whirling and snapping at him, then returning to the king. The king's sword blazed, its color shifting from blue to white with each change of direction. Before Paks could intervene, the king sank his blade into the folokai's heart, and it fell, still snapping.

More orcs poured out of the forest, this time attacking without hesitation. Now the east flank of the defender's block was fully engaged. In the darkness beyond the Verrakai front ranks, Paks saw torches moving.

"The Pargunese," said the king quietly, beside her. "They'll attack now too."

"In the dark?" asked Ammerlin.

"Yes — they've got torchbearers."

"How long — ?" began Ammerlin.

"Paks," the king interrupted. "Can you sustain your light for long?"

"I don't know," said Paks. "I haven't tried to hold it and fight both."

"We'll fight," he said grimly. "Give us light, and we'll fight."

Even before she asked, her light came, brighter than before. For an instant, she remembered the golden light that hung above Sibili the night they took the wall. Now her own light, unshadowed, lit the narrow valley. The Pargunese cohorts stopped abruptly, then wheeled into position. Verrakaien shaded their eyes, then looked down. She saw the orcs pause at the wood's edge, throw up their shields, and keep coming: a dark wave. Her light flashed from shifting eyes, from the edges of swords and the tips of spears. She saw a folokai's teeth glint, then it turned and loped away to the west and north. The red horse wheeled beneath her as her eyes swept the scene. The enemy pressed close, compressing the square into a tight mass. The remaining cavalry mounts shifted nervously, ears back and tails clamped down.

Then the enemy cohorts attacked. Paks ignored the screams, the arrows that flashed by her head, the clangor of arms. With all her might she prayed, holding light above them.

Chapter Thirty-one

How long she might have sustained the light, Paks never knew. All at once the piercing sweet call of an elvenhorn lifted her heart, the sound she had heard in Kolobia, and never forgotten. She looked east. A wave of silver light rolled down the forested slope, as if the starlight had taken form. Out of the trees rode what none there had ever seen. Tall, fair, mounted on horses as pale as starlit foam, they cried aloud in ringing voices that made music of battle. Rank after rank they came, bringing with them the scent of spring, and the light of elvenhome kingdoms that is neither sun nor star.

The orcs nearest them faltered, looked back, and broke. Before the orcs could run, the first rank of elven knights was on them, trampling them. The flank of the Verrakaien cohort on that side panicked and scattered. One group of elves peeled away, harrying the fugitives; the others advanced in order. At their center rode one not in armor. Paks stared, hardly believing her eyes. She looked away, to see that the Pargunese, deserted by the Verrakaien, were withdrawing in order. Another group of elven knights rode by the far side of the square. The light enclosed the defenders, walling them off from their enemies.

The sounds of flight came clearly through the air — the quick thunder of the elven knights' horses, the cries, the distant skirmishes. But all around the king a pool of silence widened, broken less and less by voices and movement, and coming at last to completion. Without a word, the front ranks of the square, Dorrin's cohort, opened a lane for the elven riders. Without a word, the king came forward to greet them.

With the great elven sword still glowing in his hand, he looked a king out of legend. The Lady on her horse bowed to him. He slipped off his helmet, and handed it to Lieth, who had followed him that far. Then he set the sword point down before him, and bent his knee to her.

"Lady," he said, in a voice Paks had not heard him use. "You honor us."

"Sir king," she said, and Paks had to believe now who she was. "You honor us, both our kindred and our land."

He lifted his head. "You consent to this?"

"Rise, sir king." She gestured to the sword. "I have seen my daughter's son defend his own with his own sword. I have heard and seen how that sword answers his need. We came here to greet you in all joy, and we rejoice to greet you in time."

He had climbed to his feet; now he brought the sword to her side. She leaned from her tall mount to touch his head: one light touch, with a hand that glowed like silver fire. Her voice chimed with amusement.

"Were I minded differently, son of my daughter, the enemies you make would be good witnesses for you. No wicked man could contrive to have all these assault him at once; he would ally with one or another of them."

The king laughed. "Lady, I thank you for your faith. Surely a stupid man might blunder into this?"

"I think not. Stupid men are too cautious. But, sir king, I have drawn you from a battle unfinished. Perhaps you would be free to finish it? My knights are at your disposal."

The king glanced back at the defenders. "With your permission, Lady, we will cleanse this valley of such perils for the future." She bowed, and he returned to them.

Suddenly Paks realized that she was not sustaining her own light. Whether it failed from weakness or surprise she did not know; they stood under the elflight alone. But the king, coming back into the square, commanded her attention. Still bareheaded, his face conveyed a majesty that even Paks had not imagined.

"We will not harry the Pargunese," he said. "I suspect they were lured here, and the Verrakaien intended to blame them for the massacre. But the priests of Liart, the orcs, and the Verrakaien — these must be accounted for."

"And you, my lord?" asked Dorrin.

"I will stay, and speak with the Lady, if she will."

That night the enemy found themselves penned by the forest taig, which would not let them pass, while a line of elven knights swept the valley from side to side. Elflight lay over them, leaving no place to hide. The three Marshals and Paks rode with them, hunting the priests of Liart. By dawn, which added a golden glow to the radiance around, Paks had killed two more of them; the Marshals each had killed one, and the elves found one dead of wounds. A score of gibbas lay dead, and more than a hundred orcs, and a score of folokai. The Pargunese cohorts stood in a sullen lump at the far end of the valley, where trees closed off the escape. The Verrakaien had broken into several groups, all now under guard. The Konhalt archers, having lost more than half their number, huddled together not far from the king's company. As for the followers of Liart, they had fled pell-mell, and most had been ridden down in the last of the fighting.

Paks rode back toward the king's company through the blended light of dawn and elven power, still musing over the Lady's arrival. She joined the Marshals in praying healing for the wounded. When the last one lay resting quietly, she felt a presence and turned.

Behind her stood the Lady, now watching Paks as closely as she had watched the king before.

"Paladin of Gird, I would speak with you. Come." Paks followed her a little way from the line of wounded. New grass carpeted the ground; every blade seemed to glow with its own light. The Lady led her near the stream, now edged with starry yellow flowers. Here the Lady spread her cloak on the bank, and gestured to Paks to sit with her. Gingerly Paks folded her legs and sat. For a moment, as it seemed, they listened to the singing water, now released from winter.

"We did not come for battle," said the Lady finally. "I wished to meet Falkieri myself, first, before he came to Chaya."

"I remember," said Paks.

"I do not mean to injure your honor when I say that it seemed better to attend to that myself. We had heard you were taken, that you had asked a Kuakgan to rouse the taig in his behalf." Her gaze sharpened a moment. "If it is a matter of the taigin, Paksenarrion, it is a matter for elves."

Paks shook her head. "I am sorry, Lady — I only knew it must be aware for him, and the Kuakkganni came to mind."

"We forgive you. After all, you were healed by one; we knew you meant no insult. But even so, it seemed wise to us to come and greet him. It is true that we knew he might find trouble, but it has been so long since I traveled in these lands that I did not know how bad it was. The Tree grieves, paladin, to harbor such in its shade, and the Singer is mute." For a moment she was silent, running her hands over the grass as a man might fondle his dog. "Yet the Singer and the Tree joined together in praise, and we came when the time was accomplished. I am well pleased, Paksenarrion, with my daughter's son; you spoke truly when you said he would be a worthy king."

Paks said nothing; reft of argument, she could do nothing but stare at the Lady.

"And I am well pleased with Gird's paladin," she went on. "We have heard how you entered captivity for the king, in Vérella; we grieved, thinking you surely doomed, and yet you are here, defending him still. Will you tell that tale, paladin of Gird, that it may be sung rightly in our kingdoms?"

Paks looked away, watching the swift water tumble and swirl between smooth rocks. She thought she saw the quick metallic flash of a fish. "Lady," she said, "I would not dwell on those days — they are better forgotten than sung. Nor can any human tell a whole tale: only the gods know all of it."

"Would you truly forget your torments? We owe you much, Paksenarrion, paladin of Gird. If you wish we can fill your mind with joy, and erase every scar that reminds you of that pain."

Paks shook her head, meeting the Lady's eyes once more. "No. I thank you for the thought of that gift. But what I am now — what I can do — comes from that. The things that were so bad, that hurt so. If I forget them, if I forget such things still happen, how can I help others? My scars prove that I know myself what others suffer."

"Wisely said," she replied. "Though an elf need see no scar to know what you are and what you have done. But we must make some song of you, for your service to our king."

"Let it be imagined from what you know of the Master of Torments: it is much the same, I daresay, wherever and whenever men desire power and the use of power on others."

"You can tell at least how you escaped, and how you came to be here."

Paks laughed, suddenly and unaccountably eased. "I could if I knew." She related, briefly, Arvid's confused and incredible tale, adding, "Thieves lie, as everyone knows, and tales of wonder grow quickly: but Liart's brand changed to this — " She touched the circle on her brow.

"But you arrived with a cohort of the king's own mercenaries, and a band of yeomen — how was that?"

Paks explained about meeting Dorrin in Westbells, and the journey east, and finding the apathetic Marshal in Darkon Edge. When she had finished, the Lady nodded.

"So the servants of evil forged in their own fires a weapon to defeat them — that makes a well-rounded song. Falkieri through all his years took whatever came to him of good and used it well, learning kingship without a kingdom. You did the same, learning what good you could of all you met — even a Kuakgan." Her smile took the sting out of that. "Truly, the high gods will be pleased with this day's work, Paksenarrion. The forest taig is clean, from here to Lyonya — "

"What?" asked Paks, startled.

"You saw what happened before we came — all the unclean things that ran from the forest?" Paks thought of the folokai and gibbas, and nodded. "Those cannot abide the touch of our kingdoms, so when I rode there, and brought as I must the elvenhome light with me, they fled."

"They were fleeing you?" Paks asked.

"Even so — but they are dangerous in their fear."

"And beyond, the forest barrier — was that you?"

"No. You asked the Kuakkgani to rouse the taigin for you; the Kuakgan who holds the barrier west of this valley will speak to you when you wish."

Paks could feel the blood leaving her face. "The Kuakgan — who — "

The Lady laughed gently. "And what did you think would happen if you roused the taig?"

Paks fought her muddled head. "I thought — I suppose — that it would — would let him know if evil neared — would protect him."

"And so it has. But you asked a Kuakgan; he has done this in his way. I do not interfere with the Shepherds of Trees." She looked past Paks, toward the western side of the valley. Then she smiled again. "But you, paladin of Gird — what can we do for you? Are you beyond any wish we could grant?"

Paks shook her head. "I don't know, Lady. It's enough that it's over: the king is alive, and you accept him — " She said nothing about Gird's other purposes: they would mean nothing to elves.

"Gird is well served in you, Paksenarrion, as the king was. The Singer of Names has sung well. We will see you again; for now, I must return to Lyonya, and prepare for the king's journey. The knights remain, though I think none will trouble him now. Take off your helmet, will you?" Without thinking, Paks slipped it off, and the knitted scarf slid down, exposing her head; she unwound it slowly. The Lady smiled, and touched her head with one hand. It felt cool and warm at once.

"It is little enough," said the Lady, "But I enjoyed your yellow hair in the sunlight, in Aliam Halveric's garden: I would see it again at court, when my daughter's son takes his throne." And all at once Paks felt the long strands warm and heavy on her head, brushing her neck, slipping past her shoulders, a golden tide that flowed to its former length and lay still, ready for braiding. "The Kuakkganni are not the only ones with healing gifts," said the Lady, her eyes bright.

Before Paks could frame an answer, the Lady withdrew, moving lightly to her horse and drawing in the elflight around her until Paks could see nothing but that brilliance. Then it was gone. Only the springing grass, still green, and the flowered border of the stream, were left to show her power. These did not wither in the sunlight of a late winter morning, for the air was still warmer than it had been. Paks sat motionless for a time that might have been only a moment, or an hour. Then she took the long heavy hair in her hands, and braided it quickly, her eyes burning with unshed tears. When it was done, she wrapped the braid around her head, and put her helmet on, then looked around.

There, a few lengths away, the king stood talking to several of the elven knights, with his squires beside him. High Marshal Seklis stood near, and Ammerlin of the Royal Guard. Beyond, yeomen of Darkon Edge and soldiers of Dorrin's cohort sat around two cookfires; already Paks could smell roasting meat. Others were busy gathering and stacking arms and supplies from the enemy's camps and the supply train. A tall man in a cowled robe bent over one of the Royal Guard horses, running his hands down its leg. Paks walked that way. Closer, she could see the deep gash between stifle and hock. The man hummed, touching the wound gently; it closed over, leaving a dry scar.

"That should do," he said to the knight who held the bridle. "See that he gets extra grain, and fresh greens when you can find them." He turned his head and saw Paks watching. "Ah — Paksenarrion. I had word you could not come to the grove, yet needed me."

"Sir, I — " Paks saw the glint of humor in his eyes. "I could not, at that time," she said at last.

"So — and you are here now. From what I saw last night, you also are healed of all the wounds you once bore. Is that true?"

"Yes," said Paks steadily. "By the High Lord's power, that is true."

"And so the gods declare they will not be bound in human patterns," said the Kuakgan. "Which both we and the elves know, who live apart from men." He smiled at her. "If I thought, Paksenarrion, that you were my creation, I would be proud. But you are like all of us a branch of the tree, or a song of the singer, as the elves prefer. I am glad for you, that you have come to your powers. And as always, you are welcome in my grove."

"Sir, I thank you — and you should know how much I have to thank you for."

He waved his hand. "I but freed the trapped wilding, to grow as it could. Your skill is with steel, and mine with living things."

Paks grinned at him. "Yes — and with frightened ones. I have not forgotten, sir, and will not."

"And when did you eat last?" he asked tartly — but it was teasing. "When I needed it," said Paks, laughing. "Will you come with me now, and share our meal?"

"I think not. I would not strain the patience of the knights — and the forest hereabouts is unsettled, and needs calming."

"Master Oakhallow," said Paks, and he turned back, silently. "If Gird sends me elsewhere than your grove, then take my thanks, and know that I remember. I have nothing this time to give you that is mine to give, but this."

He nodded shortly. "Paladin of Gird, Paksenarrion, you have given all you could give to my grove and the taigin before now. Go free of all gifts and returns, and come as you please and as you may. You are in my heart, and in the forest taig, and in the elfane taig; the First Tree knows what fruit it bears." With that he was gone, walking swiftly into the trees where no path was.

Paks found that the King's Squires had already pitched the king's tent; he was sitting under the flap of it, at a table with an elven knight, Sir Ammerlin, and the three Marshals. An empty place was set opposite him; as soon as he caught sight of Paks, he rose and called her over.

"Lady, we are about to eat — come, join us."

She took her seat at the empty place, and almost at once the squires handed around platters of roast meat and bread. She thought it strange to be eating like this with Pargunese and Verrakai troops under guard down the valley, but said nothing. The king seemed completely at ease. Some old hurt was gone, some bitterness had fled; his face showed his kinship to the elf beside him. Paks ate slowly, watching him. She could not define the difference, except that he seemed, if anything, younger than before.

For some time little was said. Beyond the clinking of knives at their own table, Paks could hear the others eating: Dorrin's cohort squad by squad, in order, the yeomen of Gird in a happy, disorderly crowd. Then the king spoke.

"Well, companions, we have seen another day come to birth: more than we thought last night, eh?"

Sir Ammerlin turned to him. "Sir king, I remember that you did not seem certain of death and defeat."

"Of death I am as certain as any mortal, Ammerlin, but defeat is certain only in despair. And I have been well taught that in the worst of times despair is still the work of evil." He looked at Paks, a look that said a great deal. "But we are alive, this fine morning, by the aid of the elven knights you command, sir," and he turned to the elf beside him. "You have our thanks for your timely arrival."

"And you have our regrets that we sent before us unworthy messengers of our coming," said the elf, laughing lightly. "By all the gods, I would not have landed those foul things on you!"

"The contrast," said the king drily, "was all the greater when you came. I did not quite despair, last night, knowing my companions to be who and what they were, but I little thought to be eating such a meal in such comfort as this, with so many of them spared to enjoy it." High Marshal Seklis laughed with the others, then set his elbows firmly on the table.

"That's all very well, my lord, but what about the Pargunese and the Verrakai troops? The Pargunese won't fight elves, but I doubt they'll march in your procession. As for the Verrakai — rotten root and branch, that family—"

"Not so," said the king quietly. "Captain Dorrin, of my Company, is Verrakai by birth. She has never been less than loyal to me, and just and honest to all. She's even crossed my will, where she thought me less."

"I didn't know—" muttered Seklis.

"No. You wouldn't. High Marshal, I am one to prune — severely, if necessary — and not one to root up the tree. I have known other honest Verrakaien in my life; it's probably kept me from quarreling more with the Duke and his brother."

"But this can't be ignored," Seklis said angrily. "By Gird's arm, they defied the prince's power, attacked a traveler under royal protection, threatened to massacre us all—"

"I don't ignore it. They did all that — and for that they should face justice. But not my justice, High Marshal: this is not my kingdom. Were I to hold court here, and rule on this, I would myself be usurping the prince's powers. To him I am either a vassal or the king of a neighboring realm. I can make complaint in either sense, but in neither sense do I have a right to judge or sentence."

"Hmmph." Seklis settled back, disgruntled. The elf leaned forward.

"Then what do you plan, sir king?"

The king looked around the table. "I plan to let Tsaia rule itself, as it should. The prince must know this — the Council must know this — but they also need to know that the king of Lyonya did not exceed his authority. Seklis, you're the High Marshal in Tsaia — on the Council itself. You can bring what charges need be brought. Ammerlin, you're a commander in the Royal Guard, the prince's direct military representative. His authority flows through you; you can take what military action need be taken to ensure peace here until the Council and prince decide what to do. By Tsaian law, you Marshals have court-right over some things — such as the followers of Liart."

"And what will you do, sir king?"

"I will go to my kingdom," he replied mildly. "I have heard that they have need of me."

"Are you taking your cohort with you?" asked Ammerlin.

"I planned to, yes. I would not expect a single cohort to alarm Lyonya — would you think, sir elf?"

"Not at all," said the elf, smiling.

"Then you could stay here, Ammerlin, with the Royal Guard —"

"But we're your escort —"

"You were, yes. But now I have my cohort, and these elves, and you have no need to come farther."

They were interrupted just then by a shout from Dorrin, who had ridden east up the slope. Her cohort leaped back into formation; Paks found the red horse beside her as she stepped beyond the tent flap, and mounted. Then she saw what was coming down the road from the east, and nearly laughed in relief. Gird's crescent on a pennant, and the rose and silver bells and harp of Tsaia on another, two Gird's Marshals, and several hundred yeomen.

"Late," commented Suriya, after a quick look, "but welcome."

When the Marshals arrived, Paks recognized Marshal Pelyan; he introduced Berris, whose grange was the next to the east. He grinned at Paks, and nodded to the other Marshals.

"One of my yeoman came in the other day," he said, "with word of a strange cohort sneaking through the woods between Berris and me. From what he said, I thought it might be Pargunese; we looked and found boats hidden along the river. So I remembered what Paksenarrion had said, and rousted out my grange —"

"And then came storming into mine," said Berris. "I told him I didn't have many fit to fight, but I came along —"

"And we've come too late, I see," said Pelyan, looking around.

"Not so," said the king. "We cannot stay and deal with the Pargunese —"

"I told you!" Pelyan thumped Berris on the shoulder. "I knew those Tir-damned scum would be in this."

" — or the Verrakai," the king went on. "We must be on the road to Lyonya; your arrival gives High Marshal Seklis and Sir Ammerlin enough troops to take care of this."

Pelyan scratched his ear. "Well, sir — sir king — it's good to know we didn't have this long march for nothing. But I should tell you that some of these are Lyonyans, who left Lyonya for fear of war."

The king smiled. "And so you showed them that trouble follows those who flee it? Well done, Marshal; when you have them schooled to your liking, then send them home if they wish to go."

"You don't want to take them with you?"

The king let his eyes rove along the ranks, then pursed his lips. "No — I don't think so. Those in my party are proven fighters. Those who awaited events in Lyonya have shown steadfastness. These — these I leave to your care; you know best what they need."

For the rest of that day, the king's party rested before traveling. Those who had been killed were laid to rest with due ceremony; the enemy's dead was piled and burned. Under the Marshals' directions, the yeomen took control of the Pargunese and Verrakai prisoners, containing them at a distance from the king's encampment. The horses of Dorrin's cohort were found still waiting at the ridgetop to the east, penned, as Paks explained it, by the taig. Dorrin looked at her oddly, but said nothing more about it.

In the morning, they set out for Lyonya again. Paks rode beside the king, at his request. With no pack train to slow them down, they made good time, and rode into Harway just at dark, where the Lyonyan Guard waited in formation to greet him. Bonfires flared as the king came into his own land; candles burned at every window, and torchbearers lined the streets. Both Marshal and captain came to bow before him. Paks saw distant fires spring to life, carrying the news across the darkness.

The king said little: courteous words for those who greeted him, but nothing more. Paks saw tears glisten on his cheeks in the firelight. They stayed that night in Harway, the king at the royal armory, and Paks at the grange, to ease the Marshal's memory of her earlier visit.

By the time the king's party reached Chaya, the last snow had melted away, filling the rivers with laughing water.

"An early spring," said the king, looking at the first flowering trees glimmering through the wood. "I feel the forest rejoicing."

"Do you?" Amrothlin, who had come to meet him, smiled. "That is well. Both the rejoicing of the forest, and your feeling it. Your elven senses wake: you feel the taig singing you home, and your response calls forth more song. So the season answers your desire."

The king looked across green meadows to the towering trees that made the palace seem small, a child's toy. Tears glittered in his eyes. "So beautiful — they almost break the heart."

"This is the heartknot of the joining of elvenkind and man," said Amrothlin. "We put what we could of our elvenhome kingdom in it. Be welcome, sir king, in your kingdom."

Between them and the city a crowd was gathering, pouring out of the city in bright chips of color like pebbles from a sack. The king's party rode through a broad lane, past those who cheered, and those who stood silently, watching with wide eyes the return of their lost prince. Paks felt her own heart swell almost to bursting when the music began, the harps that elves delight in, horns both bright and mellow in tone, all singing the king home.

That music followed into the palace itself, where the lords of Lyonya, the Siers and their families, waited to welcome the king. One by one they knelt to him, then stepped back. When old Hammarin came forward, he peered into the king's face a moment, as if looking for the boy he had known, then reached to touch his hand.

"Sir king — you do your father justice."

"You knew him?" asked the king gently.

"Aye — and you as a tiny lad. Thank the gods you've returned, Falki — let me call you that just this once, as I used to do." Then he stepped back, nodding, for his old knees were too stiff to kneel. When all had acknowledged him, the king turned to Paksenarrion.

"Lady, your quest brought me to this court: is it discharged?"

"Not yet, sir king." Paks turned to the assembly. "You, in Council here, bid me find your lost prince and bring him. I have brought him now, and his sword proves him. Are you content?"

"We are content," they answered.

And of all the deeds of the paladin Paksenarrion, it is this for which she is best known in the middle lands of the Eight Kingdoms, for restoring the lost king to his throne, and thereby saving Lyonya from the perils of misrule and confusion. Which of her deeds most honored the gods she served, only the High Lord knows, who judges rightly of all deeds, whatever tales men tell or elves sing.

In the chronicles of that court, it is said that the coronation of Falkieri Amrothlin Artfielan Phelan (for he kept the name he had used so long) was outdone in joy and ceremony only by his marriage some time later. Falkieri ruled long and faithfully, and in his time the bond of elf and man was strengthened. Peace and prosperity brought honor to his reign. And after him the crown passed to his eldest, and to her son and her son's sons after.

As for Paksenarrion, she was named King's Friend, with leave to go or stay as she would, and when Gird's call came, she departed for another land.

— The End —